THE PLUM IN THE GOLDEN VASE

PRINCETON LIBRARY OF ASIAN TRANSLATIONS

The Plum in the Golden Vase

or, CHIN P'ING MEI

VOLUME THREE: THE APHRODISIAC

Translated by David Tod Roy

PRINCETON UNIVERSITY PRESS

PRINCETON AND OXFORD

Copyright © 2006 by Princeton University Press
Published by Princeton University Press, 41 William Street,
Princeton, New Jersey 08540
In the United Kingdom: Princeton University Press,
3 Market Place, Woodstock, Oxfordshire OX20 1SY
All Rights Reserved.

Library of Congress Cataloging-in-Publication Data

Hsiao-hsiao-sheng
[Chin P'ing Mei. English]
The plum in the golden vase, or, Chin P'ing Mei /
translated by David Tod Roy.
p. cm. —(Princeton library of Asian translations)
Includes bibliographical references and index.
Contents: v. 1. The gathering. v. 2. The rivals.
ISBN-13: 978-0-691-12534-3
ISBN-10: 0-691-12534-1
1. Roy, David Tod 1933–. II. Title III. Series.
PL2698.H73C4713   1993
895.1′346–dc20   92-45054

This book has been composed in Electra

The paper used in this publication meets the minimum requirements
of ANSI/NISO Z39.48-1992 (R1997) (*Permanence of Paper*)

www.pup.princeton.edu

Printed in the United States of America

10 9 8 7 6 5 4 3 2 1

To all those students, friends, and colleagues
WHO PARTICIPATED WITH ME IN THE EXCITEMENT
OF EXPLORING THE WORLD OF THE *CHIN P'ING MEI*
OVER THE PAST QUARTER CENTURY

CONTENTS

LIST OF ILLUSTRATIONS

ACKNOWLEDGMENTS

OF THOSE who have helped to make the appearance of this volume possible in innumerable ways, I wish particularly to thank James Cahill, Lois Fusek, Philip Gossett, Donald Harper, Pieter Keulemans, Victor Mair, Janel Mueller, my copy editor, Anita O'Brien, David Rolston, Charles Stone, Sophie Volpp, and Yü Chün-fang.

To my wife, Barbara Chew Roy, who urged me to embark on this interminable task, and who has lent me her unwavering support over the years despite the extent to which the work has preoccupied me, I owe a particular debt of gratitude. Without her encouragement I would have had neither the temerity to undertake it nor the stamina to continue it.

For indispensable technical advice and assistance concerning computers, printers, and word-processing programs, I continue to be indebted to Charles Stone.

The research that helped to make this work possible was materially assisted by a Grant for Research on Chinese Civilization from the American Council of Learned Societies in 1976–77, grants from the National Endowment for the Humanities in 1983–86 and 1995–96, a Residential Faculty Fellowship from the Chicago Humanities Institute in 1994–95, and gifts from the Norman and Carol Nie Foundation in 1995 and 2000. The Department of East Asian Languages and Civilizations and the Division of Humanities at the University of Chicago have also been generous in allowing me the time and space to devote to this project. For all of the above assistance, without which this venture could not have been contemplated, I am deeply grateful.

Needless to say, whatever infelicities and errors remain in the translation are solely my own.

CAST OF CHARACTERS

THE FOLLOWING list includes all characters who appear in the novel, listed alphabetically by surname. All characters with dates in parentheses after their names are historical figures from the Sung dynasty. Characters who bear the names of historical figures from the Ming dynasty are identified in the notes.

An Ch'en, winner of first place in the *chin-shih* examinations but displaced in favor of Ts'ai Yün because he is the younger brother of the proscribed figure, An Tun; becomes a protégé of Ts'ai Ching and is patronized by Hsi-men Ch'ing, later rising to the rank of secretary of the Bureau of Irrigation and Transportation in the Ministry of Works; rewarded for his part in facilitating the notorious Flower and Rock Convoys and the construction of the Mount Ken Imperial Park.

An Ch'en's second wife.

An, Consort. See Liu, Consort.

An Tun (1042–1104), elder brother of An Ch'en, a high official whose name has been proscribed for his role in the partisan political conflicts of the late eleventh century.

An-t'ung, page boy of Aunt Yang.

An-t'ung, page boy of Miao T'ien-hsiu who is rescued by a fisherman and does his utmost to see justice done for the murder of his master.

An-t'ung, page boy of Wang Hsüan.

Apricot Hermitage, Layman of. See Wang Hsüan.

Autumn Chrysantheum. See Ch'iu-chü.

Barefaced Adept, Taoist master from the Fire Dragon Monastery in the Obdurate Grotto of the Vacuous Mountains from whom Yang Kuang-yen acquires the art of lying.

Bean curd-selling crone who identifies the home of Commander Yüan in Potter's Alley to Hsi-men Ch'ing.

"Beanpole, The." See Hui-ch'ing.

Black-robed lictor on the staff of Ho Hsin.

Black-robed lictor who announces the arrival of Chang Pang-ch'ang and Ts'ai Yu to congratulate Chu Mien.

Black Whirlwind. See Li K'uei.

Brocade Tiger. See Yen Shun.

Busybody who directs Ch'iao Yün-ko to Dame Wang's teashop when he is looking for Hsi-men Ch'ing.

Cassia. See Li Kuei-chieh.

Chai Ch'ien, majordomo of Ts'ai Ching's household in the Eastern Capital.

Chai Ch'ien's wife.

Chai Ching-erh, Sutra Chai, proprietor of a sutra printing shop in Ch'ing-ho.

Chai, Sutra. See Chai Ching-erh.

Ch'ai Chin, Little Whirlwind, Little Lord Meng-ch'ang, direct descendant of Ch'ai Jung (921–59), emperor Shih-tsung (r. 954–59) of the Later Chou dynasty (951–60).

Ch'ai Huang-ch'eng, paternal uncle of Ch'ai Chin.

Ch'an Master Snow Cave. See P'u-ching.

Chang An, caretaker of Hsi-men Ch'ing's ancestral graveyard outside Ch'ing-ho.

Chang, Auntie, go-between who helps arrange Ch'en Ching-chi's marriage to Ko Ts'ui-p'ing.

Chang Ch'eng, a neighborhood head in Ch'ing-ho.

Chang Ch'ing, a criminal innkeeper with whom Wu Sung seeks refuge after the murder of P'an Chin-lien.

Chang Ch'ing's wife.

Chang Ch'uan-erh, a garrulous chair-bearer in Ch'ing-ho, partner of Wei Ts'ung-erh.

Chang the Fourth. See Chang Ju-i.

Chang the Fourth. See Chang Lung.

Chang Hao-wen, Chang the Importunate, Chang the Second, proprietor of a paper shop in Ch'ing-ho, acquaintance of Han Tao-kuo.

Chang Hsi-ch'un, a ballad singer maintained at one time as a mistress by Hsi-men Ch'ing.

Chang Hsi-ts'un, an acquaintance of Hsi-men Ch'ing's who invites him to his home for a birthday party.

Chang Hsiao-hsien, Hsiao Chang-hsien, Trifler Chang, "ball clubber" in Ch'ing-ho who plays the tout to Wang Ts'ai on his visits to the licensed quarter and upon whom Hsi-men Ch'ing turns the tables by abusing the judicial system at the behest of Lady Lin.

Chang the Importunate. See Chang Hao-wen.

Chang Ju-i, Chang the Fourth, wife of Hsiung Wang, employed in Hsi-men Ch'ing's household as a wet nurse for Kuan-ko and later for Hsiao-ko, sexual partner of Hsi-men Ch'ing after the death of Li P'ing-erh, finally married to Lai-hsing.

Chang Ju-i's mother.

Chang Ko (1068–1113), promoted to the post of vice minister of the Ministry of Works for his part in facilitating the notorious Flower and Rock Convoys and the construction of the Mount Ken Imperial Park.

Chang Kuan, brother-in-law of Ch'en Hung and maternal uncle of Ch'en Ching-chi, militia commander of Ch'ing-ho.

Chang Kuan's sister. See Ch'en Hung's wife, née Chang.

Chang Kuan's wife.

Chang Lung, Chang the Fourth, maternal uncle of Meng Yü-lou's first husband Yang Tsung-hsi who unsuccessfully proposes that she remarry Shang
Hsiao-t'ang and quarrels with Aunt Yang when she decides to marry Hsi-
men Ch'ing instead.

Chang Lung, judicial commissioner of the Liang-Huai region.

Chang Lung's elder sister (Chang the Fourth's elder sister), mother of Yang
Tsung-hsi and Yang Tsung-pao.

Chang Lung's wife (Chang the Fourth's wife).

Chang Mao-te, Chang the Second, nephew of Mr. Chang, the well-to-do
merchant who first seduces P'an Chin-lien; a major rival of Hsi-men Ch'ing
in the social world of Ch'ing-ho who, immediately after Hsi-men Ch'ing's
death, bribes Cheng Chü-chung to intervene with Chu Mien and have him
appointed to Hsi-men Ch'ing's former position as judicial commissioner so
he can take over where Hsi-men Ch'ing left off.

Chang Mao-te's son, marries Eunuch Director Hsü's niece.

Chang Mei, professional actor of Hai-yen style drama.

Chang, Military Director-in-chief, official in Meng-chou.

Chang, Mr., a well-to-do merchant in Ch'ing-ho who first seduces P'an
Chin-lien.

Chang, Mrs., wife of Mr. Chang, née Yü.

Chang, Old Mother, go-between who tries to sell two inexperienced country
girls, Sheng-chin and Huo-pao, to P'ang Ch'un-mei.

Chang, Old Mother, proprietress of an inn next door to Auntie Hsüeh's
residence.

Chang Pang-ch'ang (1081–1127), minister of rites, promoted to the position
of grand guardian of the heir apparent for his part in facilitating the notorious Flower and Rock Convoys and the construction of the Mount Ken
Imperial Park, puppet emperor of the short-lived state of Ch'u for thirty-
two days in 1127.

Chang the Second. See Chang Hao-wen.

Chang the Second. See Chang Mao-te.

Chang Sheng, Street-skulking Rat, "knockabout" who, along with Lu Hua,
shakes down Dr. Chiang Chu-shan at the behest of Hsi-men Ch'ing; later
a servant in the household of Chou Hsiu, brother-in-law of Liu the Second;
murders Ch'en Ching-chi when he overhears him plotting against him and
is beaten to death by Chou Hsiu at the behest of P'ang Ch'un-mei.

Chang Sheng's reincarnation. See Kao family of the Ta-hsing Guard.

Chang Sheng's wife, née Liu, sister of Liu the Second.

Chang Shih-lien, Ch'en Hung's brother-in-law, related to Yang Chien by marriage, an official in the Eastern Capital.

Chang Shih-lien's wife, née Ch'en, Ch'en Hung's elder sister.

Chang Shu-yeh (1065–1127), prefect of Chi-chou in Shantung, later pacification commissioner of Shantung, responsible for the defeat of Sung Chiang and his acceptance of a government amnesty.

Chang Sung, Little. See Shu-t'ung.

Chang Ta (d. 1126), official who dies in the defense of T'ai-yüan against the invading Chin army.

Chang, Trifler. See Chang Hsiao-hsien.

Ch'ang, Cadger. See Ch'ang Shih-chieh.

Ch'ang the Second. See Ch'ang Shih-chieh.

Ch'ang Shih-chieh, Cadger Ch'ang, Ch'ang the Second, crony of Hsi-men Ch'ing, member of the brotherhood of ten.

Ch'ang Shih-chieh's wife.

Ch'ang Shih-chieh's wife's younger brother.

Ch'ang Yü, Commandant, officer rewarded for his part in facilitating the notorious Flower and Rock Convoys and the construction of the Mount Ken Imperial Park.

Chao, Auntie, go-between who sells Chin-erh to Wang Liu-erh.

Chao Chiao-erh, singing girl working out of My Own Tavern in Lin-ch'ing.

Chao, Dr.. See Chao Lung-kang.

Chao Hung-tao, domestic clerk on the staff of Yang Chien.

Chao I (fl. early 12th century), Duke of Chia, twenty-sixth son of Emperor Hui-tsung by Consort Liu.

Chao K'ai (d. c. 1129), Prince of Yün, third son of emperor Hui-tsung by Consort Wang.

Chao, Lama, head priest of the Pao-ch'ing Lamasery outside the west gate of Ch'ing-ho.

Chao Lung-kang, Dr. Chao, Chao the Quack, incompetent specialist in female disorders called in to diagnose Li P'ing-erh's fatal illness.

Chao Lung-kang's grandfather.

Chao Lung-kang's father.

Chao No, investigation commissioner for Shantung.

Chao the Quack. See Chao Lung-kang.

Chao, Tailor, artisan patronized by Hsi-men Ch'ing.

Chao-ti, servant in the household of Han Tao-kuo and Wang Liu-erh.

Chao T'ing (fl. early 12th century), prefect of Hang-chou, promoted to the post of chief minister of the Court of Judicial Review.

Chao, Widow, wealthy landowner from whom Hsi-men Ch'ing buys a country estate adjacent to his ancestral graveyard.

Chao Yu-lan, battalion commander rewarded for his part in facilitating the notorious Flower and Rock Convoys and the construction of the Mount Ken Imperial Park.

Ch'e, Hogwash. See Ch'e Tan.

Ch'e Tan, Hogwash Ch'e, a dissolute young scamp upon whom Hsi-men Ch'ing turns the tables by abusing the judicial system.

Ch'e Tan's father, proprietor of a wineshop in Ch'ing-ho.

Ch'en An, servant in Ch'en Ching-chi's household.

Ch'en, Battalion Commander, resident on Main Street in Ch'ing-ho from whom Hsi-men Ch'ing declines to buy a coffin after the death of Li P'ing-erh.

Ch'en Cheng-hui (fl. early 12th century), son of Ch'en Kuan, surveillance vice-commissioner of education for Shantung.

Ch'en Ching-chi, secondary male protagonist of the novel, son of Ch'en Hung, husband of Hsi-men Ta-chieh, son-in-law of Hsi-men Ch'ing who carries on a running pseudo-incestuous affair with P'an Chin-lien that is consummated after the death of Hsi-men Ch'ing; falls out with Wu Yüeh-niang and is evicted from the household; drives Hsi-men Ta-chieh to suicide; attempts unsuccessfully to shake down Meng Yü-lou in Yen-chou; squanders his patrimony and is reduced to beggary; accepts charity from his father's friend the philanthropist Wang Hsüan, who induces him to become a monk with the Taoist appellation Tsung-mei, the junior disciple of Abbot Jen of the Yen-kung Temple in Lin-ch'ing; is admitted to the household of Chou Hsiu as a pretended cousin of P'ang Ch'un-mei who carries on an affair with him under her husband's nose; also has affairs with Feng Chin-pao and Han Ai-chieh, marries Ko Ts'ui-p'ing, and is murdered by Chang Sheng when he is overheard plotting against him.

Ch'en Ching-chi's grandfather, a salt merchant.

Ch'en Ching-chi's reincarnation. See Wang family of the Eastern Capital.

Ch'en, Dr., resident of Ch'ing-ho.

Ch'en, Dr.'s son, conceived as a result of a fertility potion provided by Nun Hsüeh.

Ch'en, Dr.'s wife, conceives a son in middle age after taking a fertility potion provided by Nun Hsüeh.

Ch'en Hung, wealthy dealer in pine resin, father of Ch'en Ching-chi, related by marriage to Yang Chien.

Ch'en Hung's elder sister, wife of Chang Shih-lien.

Ch'en Hung's wife, née Chang, sister of Chang Kuan, mother of Ch'en Ching-chi.

Ch'en Kuan (1057–1122), a prominent remonstrance official, father of Ch'en Cheng-hui.

Ch'en Liang-huai, national university student, son of Vice Commissioner Ch'en, friend of Ting the Second.

Ch'en, Master, legal scribe who assists Wu Sung in drafting a formal complaint against Hsi-men Ch'ing.

Ch'en, Miss, daughter of the deceased Vice Commissioner Ch'en whose assignation with Juan the Third results in his death.

Ch'en, Miss's maidservant.

Ch'en, Mistress. See Hsi-men Ta-chieh.

Ch'en the Second, proprietor of an inn at Ch'ing-chiang P'u at which Ch'en
Ching-chi puts up on his way to Yen-chou.

Ch'en Ssu-chen, right provincial administration commissioner of Shantung.

Ch'en the Third, "cribber" in the licensed quarter of Lin-ch'ing.

Ch'en the Third, criminal boatman who, along with his partner Weng the
Eighth, murders Miao T'ien-hsiu.

Ch'en Ting, servant in Ch'en Hung's household.

Ch'en Ting's wife.

Ch'en Tsung-mei. See Ch'en Ching-chi.

Ch'en Tsung-shan, ward-inspecting commandant of the Eastern Capital.

Ch'en Tung (1086–1127), national university student who submits a memorial to the throne impeaching the Six Traitors.

Ch'en, Vice-Commissioner, deceased father of Miss Ch'en.

Ch'en, Vice-Commissioner, father of Ch'en Liang-huai.

Ch'en, Vice-Commissioner's wife, née Chang, mother of Miss Ch'en.

Ch'en Wen-chao, prefect of Tung-p'ing.

Cheng Ai-hsiang, Cheng Kuan-yin, Goddess of Mercy Cheng, singing girl
from the Star of Joy Bordello in Ch'ing-ho patronized by Hua Tzu-hsü,
elder sister of Cheng Ai-yüeh.

Cheng Ai-yüeh, singing girl from the Star of Joy Bordello in Ch'ing-ho patronized by Wang Ts'ai and Hsi-men Ch'ing, younger sister of Cheng Ai-hsiang.

Cheng, Auntie, madam of the Star of Joy Bordello in Ch'ing-ho.

Cheng, Battalion Commander's family in the Eastern Capital into which Hua
Tzu-hsü is reincarnated as a son.

Cheng Chi, servant in Hsi-men Ch'ing's household.

Cheng Chiao-erh, singing girl in Ch'ing-ho, niece of Cheng Ai-hsiang and
Cheng Ai-yüeh.

Cheng Chin-pao. See Feng Chin-pao.

Cheng Ch'un, professional actor in Ch'ing-ho, younger brother of Cheng
Feng, Cheng Ai-hsiang, and Cheng Ai-yüeh.

Cheng Chü-chung (1059–1123), military affairs commissioner, cousin of
Consort Cheng, granted the title of grand guardian for his part in facilitating
the notorious Flower and Rock Convoys and the construction of the Mount
Ken Imperial Park, accepts a bribe of a thousand taels of silver from Chang
Mao-te to intervene with Chu Mien and have him appointed to the position
of judicial commissioner left vacant by the death of Hsi-men Ch'ing.

Cheng, Consort, (1081–1132), a consort of Emperor Hui-tsung, niece of Madame Ch'iao.

Cheng Feng, professional actor in Ch'ing-ho, elder brother of Cheng Ai-
Hsiang, Cheng Ai-yüeh, and Cheng Ch'un.

Cheng the Fifth, Auntie, madam of the Cheng Family Brothel in Lin-ch'ing.

Cheng the Fifth, Auntie's husband.

Cheng, Goddess of Mercy. See Cheng Ai-hsiang.

Cheng Kuan-yin. See Cheng Ai-hsiang.

Cheng, Third Sister, niece of Ch'iao Hung's wife, née Cheng, marries Wu K'ai's son Wu Shun-ch'en.

Cheng T'ien-shou, Palefaced Gentleman, third outlaw leader of the Ch'ing-feng Stronghold on Ch'ing-feng Mountain.

Cheng Wang. See Lai-wang.

Ch'eng-erh, younger daughter of Lai-hsing by Hui-hsiu.

Chi K'an, right administration vice commissioner of Shantung.

Chi-nan, old man from, who directs Wu Yüeh-niang to the Ling-pi Stockade in her dream.

Ch'i family brothel in Ch'ing-ho, madam of.

Ch'i Hsiang-erh, singing girl from the Ch'i family brothel in Ch'ing-ho.

Ch'i-t'ung, page boy in Hsi-men Ch'ing's household.

Chia, Duke of. See Chao I.

Chia Hsiang (fl. early 12th century), eunuch rewarded for his part in facilitating the notorious Flower and Rock Convoys and the construction of the Mount Ken Imperial Park.

Chia Hsiang's adopted son, granted the post of battalion vice commander of the Embroidered Uniform Guard by yin privilege as a reward for his father's part in facilitating the notorious Flower and Rock Convoys and the construction of the Mount Ken Imperial Park.

Chia Jen-ch'ing, False Feelings, neighbor of Hsi-men Ch'ing who intercedes unsuccessfully on Lai-wang's behalf.

Chia Lien, name to which Li Pang-yen alters Hsi-men Ch'ing's name on a bill of impeachment in return for a handsome bribe.

Chiang Chu-shan, Chiang Wen-hui, doctor who Li P'ing-erh marries on the rebound only to drive away ignominiously as soon as Hsi-men Ch'ing becomes available again.

Chiang Chu-shan's deceased first wife.

Chiang, Gate God. See Chiang Men-shen.

Chiang, Little, servant of Ch'en Ching-chi.

Chiang Men-shen, Gate God Chiang, elder brother of Chiang Yü-lan, gangster whose struggle with Shih En for control of the Happy Forest Tavern in Meng-chou results in his murder by Wu Sung.

Chiang Ts'ung, Sauce and Scallions, former husband of Sung Hui-lien, a cook in Ch'ing-ho who is stabbed to death in a brawl with a fellow cook over the division of their pay.

Chiang Ts'ung's assailant, convicted of a capital crime and executed as a result of Hsi-men Ch'ing's intervention.

Chiang Wen-hui. See Chiang Chu-shan.

Chiang Yü-lan, younger sister of Chiang Men-shen, concubine of Military Director-in-chief Chang of Meng-chou who assists her husband and brother in framing Wu Sung.

Ch'iao, distaff relative of the imperial family whose garden abuts on the back wall of Li P'ing-erh's house on Lion Street, assumes hereditary title of commander when Ch'iao the Fifth dies without issue.

Ch'iao Chang-chieh, infant daughter of Ch'iao Hung betrothed to Hsi-men Kuan-ko while both of them are still babes in arms.

Ch'iao, Consort, (fl. early 12th century), a consort of Emperor Hui-tsung, related to Ch'iao the Fifth.

Ch'iao the Fifth, deceased distaff relative of the imperial family through Consort Ch'iao whose hereditary title of commander passes to another branch of the family when he dies without issue.

Ch'iao the Fifth's widow. See Ch'iao, Madame.

Ch'iao Hung, uncle of Ts'ui Pen, wealthy neighbor and business partner of Hsi-men Ch'ing whose daughter, Ch'iao Chang-chieh, is betrothed to Hsi-men Ch'ing's son Kuan-ko while they are still babes in arms.

Ch'iao Hung's concubine, mother of Ch'iao Chang-chieh.

Ch'iao Hung's elder sister, Ts'ui Pen's mother.

Ch'iao Hung's wife, née Cheng.

Ch'iao, Madame, Ch'iao the Fifth's widow, née Cheng, aunt of Ch'iao Hung's wife, née Cheng, and of Consort Cheng.

Ch'iao T'ung, servant in Ch'iao Hung's household.

Ch'iao T'ung's wife.

Ch'iao Yün-ko, Little Yün, young fruit peddler in Ch'ing-ho who helps Wu Chih catch Hsi-men Ch'ing and P'an Chin-lien in adultery.

Ch'iao Yün-ko's father, retired soldier dependent on his son.

Ch'ien Ch'eng, vice magistrate of Ch'ing-ho district.

Ch'ien Ch'ing-ch'uan, traveling merchant entertained by Han Tao-kuo in Yang-chou.

Ch'ien Lao, clerk of the office of punishment in Ch'ing-ho.

Ch'ien Lung-yeh, secretary of the Ministry of Revenue in charge of collecting transit duties on shipping at the Lin-ch'ing customs house.

Ch'ien, Phlegm-fire. See Ch'ien T'an-huo.

Ch'ien T'an-huo, Phlegm-fire Ch'ien, Taoist healer called in to treat Hsi-men Kuan-ko.

Chih-yün, Abbot, head priest of Hsiang-kuo Temple in K'ai-feng visited by Hsi-men Ch'ing on his trip to the Eastern Capital.

Chin, Abbot, Taoist head priest of the Temple of the Eastern Peak on Mount T'ai.

Chin Ch'ien-erh, former maidservant in the household of Huang the Fourth's son purchased by P'ang Ch'un-mei as a servant for Ko Ts'ui-p'ing when she marries Ch'en Ching-chi.

Chin-erh, maidservant of Wang Liu-erh.

Chin-erh, singing girl in Longleg Lu's brothel on Butterfly Lane in Ch'ing-ho.

Chin-erh, singing girl working out of My Own Tavern in Lin-ch'ing.

Chin-erh's father, military patrolman whose horse is fatally injured in a fall and, for lack of replacement money, is forced to sell his daughter into domestic service.

Chin-kuei, employed in Chou Hsiu's household as a wet nurse for Chou Chin-ko.

Chin-lien. See P'an Chin-lien.

Chin-lien. See Sung Hui-lien.

Chin Ta-chieh, wife of Auntie Hsüeh's son Hsüeh Chi.

Chin-ts'ai, servant in the household of Han Tao-kuo and Wang Liu-erh.

Chin Tsung-ming, senior disciple of Abbot Jen of the Yen-kung Temple in Lin-ch'ing.

Ch'in-tsung, Emperor of the Sung dynasty (r. 1125–27), son of Emperor Hui-tsung who abdicated in his favor in 1125, taken into captivity together with his father by the Chin dynasty invaders in 1127.

Ch'in-t'ung, junior page boy in the household of Hua Tzu-hsü and Li P'ing-erh, originally named T'ien-fu but renamed when she marries into the household of Hsi-men Ch'ing.

Ch'in-t'ung, page boy of Meng Yü-lou who is seduced by P'an Chin-lien and driven out of the household when the affair is discovered.

Ch'in Yü-chih, singing girl in Ch'ing-ho patronized by Wang Ts'ai.

Ching-chi. See Ch'en Ching-chi.

Ching Chung, commander of the left battalion of the Ch'ing-ho Guard, later promoted to the post of military director-in-chief of Chi-chou, and finally to commander-general of the southeast and concurrently grain transport commander.

Ching Chung's daughter for whom he seeks a marriage alliance with Hsi-men Kuan-ko but is refused by Hsi-men Ch'ing.

Ching Chung's mother.

Ching Chung's wife.

Ch'iu-chü, Autumn Chrysanthemum, much abused junior maidservant of P'an Chin-lien.

Cho the Second. See Cho Tiu-erh.

Cho Tiu-erh, Cho the second, Toss-off Cho, unlicensed prostitute in Ch'ing-ho maintained as a mistress by Hsi-men Ch'ing and subsequently brought into his household as his Third Lady only to sicken and die soon thereafter.

Cho, Toss-off. See Cho Tiu-erh.

Chou, Censor, neighbor of Wu Yüeh-niang's when she was growing up, father of Miss Chou.

Chou Chin-ko, son of Chou Hsiu by P'ang Ch'un-mei the real father of which may have been Ch'en Ching-chi.

Chou Chung, senior servant in the household of Chou Hsiu, father of Chou Jen and Chou I.

Chou, Eunuch Director, resident of Ch'ing-ho whose invitation to a party Hsi-men Ch'ing declines not long before his death.

Chou Hsiao-erh, patron of Li Kuei-ch'ing and probably of Li Kuei-chieh also.

Chou Hsiu, commandant of the Regional Military Command, later appointed to other high military posts, colleague of Hsi-men Ch'ing after whose death he buys P'ang Ch'un-mei as a concubine and later promotes her to the position of principal wife when she bears him a son; commander-general of the Shantung region who leads the forces of Ch'ing-yen against the Chin invaders and dies at Kao-yang Pass of an arrow wound inflicted by the Chin commander Wan-yen Tsung-wang.

Chou Hsiu's first wife, blind in one eye, who dies not long after P'ang Ch'un-mei enters his household as a concubine.

Chou Hsiu's reincarnation. See Shen Shou-shan.

Chou Hsüan, cousin of Chou Hsiu's who looks after his affairs while he is at the front.

Chou I, servant in Chou Hsiu's household, son of Chou Chung and younger brother of Chou Jen, clandestine lover of P'ang Ch'un-mei who dies in the act of intercourse with him.

Chou I's paternal aunt with whom he seeks refuge after the death of P'ang Ch'un-mei.

Chou I's reincarnation. See Kao Liu-chu.

Chou Jen, servant in Chou Hsiu's household, son of Chou Chung and elder brother of Chou I.

Chou, Little, itinerant barber and masseur in Ch'ing-ho patronized by Hsi-men Ch'ing.

Chou, Miss, daughter of Censor Chou, neighbor of Wu Yüeh-niang's when she was growing up who broke her hymen by falling from a standing position onto the seat of a swing.

Chou, Ms., widowed second wife of Sung Te's father-in-law who commits adultery with him after her husband's death, for which Hsi-men Ch'ing sentences them both to death by strangulation.

Chou, Ms.'s maidservant.

Chou, Ms.'s mother.

Chou the Second, friend of Juan the Third.

Chou Shun, professional actor from Su-chou who specializes in playing female lead parts.

Chou Ts'ai, professional boy actor in Ch'ing-ho.

Chou Yü-chieh, daughter of Chou Hsiu by his concubine Sun Erh-niang.

Chu Ai-ai, Love, singing girl from Greenhorn Chu's brothel on Second Street in the licensed quarter of Ch'ing-ho, daughter of Greenhorn Chu.

Chu, Battalion Commander, resident of Ch'ing-ho, father of Miss Chu.

Chu, Battalion Commander's deceased wife, mother of Miss Chu.

Chu, Censor, resident of Ch'ing-ho, neighbor of Ch'iao Hung.

Chu, Censor's wife.

Chu family of the Eastern Capital, family into which Sung Hui-lien is reincarnated as a daughter.

Chu, Greenhorn, proprietor of a brothel on Second Street in the licensed quarter of Ch'ing-ho situated next door to the Verdant Spring Bordello of Auntie Li the Third.

Chu Jih-nien, Sticky Chu, Pockmarked Chu, crony of Hsi-men Ch'ing, member of the brotherhood of ten, plays the tout to Wang Ts'ai on his visits to the licensed quarter.

Chu Mien (1075–1126), defender-in-chief of the Embroidered Uniform Guard, an elite unit of the Imperial Bodyguard that performed secret police functions; relative of Li Ta-t'ien, the district magistrate of Ch'ing-ho; chief mover behind the notorious Flower and Rock Convoys and the construction of the Mount Ken Imperial Park, for which service to the throne he is promoted to a series of high posts; one of the Six Traitors impeached by Ch'en Tung.

Chu Mien's majordomo.

Chu Mien's son, granted the post of battalion commander of the Embroidered Uniform Guard by *yin* privilege as a reward for his father's part in facilitating the notorious Flower and Rock Convoys and the construction of the Mount Ken Imperial Park.

Chu, Miss, daughter of Battalion Commander Chu.

Chu, Pockmarked. See Chu Jih-nien.

Chu, Sticky. See Chu Jih-nien.

Ch'u-yün, daughter of a battalion commander of the Yang-chou Guard purchased by Miao Ch'ing to send as a gift to Hsi-men Ch'ing.

Ch'u-yün's father, battalion commander of the Yang-chou Guard.

Ch'un-hsiang, maidservant in the household of Han Tao-kuo and Wang Liu-erh.

Ch'un-hua, concubine of Ying Po-chüeh and mother of his younger son.

Ch'un-hung, page boy in Hsi-men Ch'ing's household.

Ch'un-mei. See P'ang Ch'un-mei.

Chung-ch'iu, junior maidservant in Hsi-men Ch'ing's household serving at various times Hsi-men Ta-chieh, Sun Hsüeh-o, and Wu Yüeh-niang.

Chung Kuei, policeman from outside the city wall of the Eastern Capital into whose family Hsi-men Ta-chieh is reincarnated as a daughter.

Ch'ung-hsi, maidservant purchased by Ch'en Ching-chi to serve Feng Chin-pao.

Ch'ung Shih-tao (1051–1126), general-in-chief of the Sung armies defending against the Chin invaders.

Ch'ü, Midwife, maternal aunt of Lai-wang in whose house on Polished Rice Lane outside the east gate of Ch'ing-ho Lai-wang and Sun Hsüeh-o seek refuge after absconding from the Hsi-men household.

Ch'ü T'ang, son of Midwife Ch'ü, cousin of Lai-wang.

Coal in the Snow. See P'an Chin-lien's cat.

Died-of-fright, Miss, wife of Yang Kuang-yen.

False Feelings. See Chia Jen-ch'ing.

Fan family of Hsü-chou, peasant family into which Wu Chih is reincarnated as a son.

Fan Hsün, battalion commander in the Ch'ing-ho Guard.

Fan, Hundred Customers. See Fan Pai-chia-nu.

Fan Kang, next-door neighbor of Ch'en Ching-chi in Ch'ing-ho.

Fan, Old Man, neighbor of the Hsieh Family Tavern in Lin-ch'ing.

Fan Pai-chia-nu, Hundred Customers Fan, singing girl from the Fan Family Brothel in Ch'ing-ho.

Fang Chen (fl. early 12th century), erudite of the Court of Imperial Sacrifices who reports that a brick in the Imperial Ancestral Temple is oozing blood.

Fang La (d. 1121), rebel who set up an independent regime in the southeast which was suppressed by government troops in 1121.

Feng Chin-pao, Cheng Chin-pao, singing girl from the Feng Family Brothel in Lin-ch'ing purchased as a concubine by Ch'en Ching-chi, later resold to the brothel of Auntie Cheng the Fifth who changes her name to Cheng Chin-pao.

Feng Chin-pao's mother, madam of the Feng Family Brothel in Lin-ch'ing.

Feng, Consort (fl. mid 11th-early 12th century), Consort Tuan, consort of Emperor Jen-tsung (r. 1022–63) who resided in the palace for five reigns.

Feng Family Brothel's servant.

Feng Huai, son of Feng the Second, son-in-law of Pai the Fifth, dies of injuries sustained in an affray with Sun Wen-hsiang.

Feng, Old Mother, waiting woman in Li P'ing-erh's family since she was a child, continues in her service when she is a concubine of Privy Councilor Liang Shih-chieh, wife of Hua Tzu-hsü, wife of Chiang Chu-shan, and after she marries Hsi-men Ch'ing, supplementing her income by working as a go-between on the side.

Feng the Second, employee of Sun Ch'ing, father of Feng Huai.

Feng T'ing-hu, left assistant administration commissioner of Shantung.

Fifth Lady. See P'an Chin-lien.

First Lady. See Wu Yüeh-niang.

Fisherman who rescues An-t'ung and helps him to locate the boatmen who had murdered his master.

Flying Demon. See Hou Lin.

Fourth Lady. See Sun Hsüeh-o.

Fu-jung, maidservant of Lady Lin.

Fu, Manager. See Fu Ming.

Fu Ming, Fu the Second, Manager Fu, manager of Hsi-men Ch'ing's pharmaceutical shop, pawnshop, and other businesses.

Fu Ming's wife.

Fu the Second. See Fu Ming.

Fu T'ien-tse, battalion commander rewarded for his part in facilitating the notorious Flower and Rock Convoys and the construction of the Mount Ken Imperial Park.

Golden Lotus. See P'an Chin-lien.

Good Deed. See Yin Chih.

Hai-t'ang, concubine of Chou Hsiu much abused by P'ang Ch'un-mei.

Han Ai-chieh, daughter of Han Tao-kuo and Wang Liu-erh, niece of Han the Second, concubine of Chai Ch'ien, mistress of Ch'en Ching-chi to whom she remains faithful after his death, ending her life as a Buddhist nun.

Han, Auntie, wife of Mohammedan Han, mother of Han Hsiao-yü.

Han, Baldy, father of Han Tao-kuo and Han the Second.

Han, Brother-in-law. See Han Ming-ch'uan.

Han Chin-ch'uan, singing girl in Ch'ing-ho, elder sister of Han Yü-ch'uan, younger sister of Han Pi.

Han Hsiao-ch'ou, singing girl in Ch'ing-ho, niece of Han Chin-ch'uan and Han Yü-ch'uan.

Han Hsiao-yü, son of Mohammedan Han and Auntie Han.

Han Lü (fl. early 12th century), vice-minister of the Ministry of Revenue, vice-minister of the Ministry of Personnel, brother-in-law of Ts'ai Ching's youngest son, Ts'ai T'ao, grants Hsi-men Ch'ing favorable treatment for his speculations in the salt trade.

Han, Master, formerly a court painter attached to the Hsüan-ho Academy, called upon by Hsi-men Ch'ing to paint two posthumous portraits of Li P'ing-erh.

Han Ming-ch'uan, Brother-in-law Han, husband of Meng Yü-lou's elder sister who lives outside the city gate of Ch'ing-ho; friend of Dr. Jen Hou-ch'i.

Han Ming-ch'uan's wife, née Meng, Mrs. Han, elder sister of Meng Yü-lou.

Han, Mohammedan, husband of Auntie Han, father of Han Hsiao-yü, renter of a room on the street front of Hsi-men Ch'ing's property next door to that of Pen Ti-ch'uan and his wife, employed on the staff of the eunuch director in charge of the local Imperial Stables.

Han, Mrs. See Han Ming-ch'uan's wife, née Meng.

Han Pang-ch'i, prefect of Hsü-chou.

Han Pi, professional boy actor in Ch'ing-ho, elder brother of Han Chin-ch'uan and Han Yü-ch'uan.

Han, Posturer. See Han Tao-kuo.

Han the Second, Trickster Han, younger brother of Han Tao-kuo, "knockabout" and gambler in Ch'ing-ho who carries on an intermittent affair with his sister-in-law, Wang Liu-erh, whom he marries after the death of Han Tao-kuo.

Han Tao-kuo, Posturer Han, husband of Wang Liu-erh, son of Baldy Han, elder brother of Han the Second, father of Han Ai-chieh, manager of Hsi-men Ch'ing's silk store on Lion Street who absconds with a thousand taels of his property on hearing of his death, content to live off the sexual earnings of his wife and daughter.

Han Tao-kuo's paternal uncle, elder brother of Baldy Han.

Han, Trickster. See Han the Second.

Han Tso, boy actor in Ch'ing-ho.

Han Tsung-jen, domestic clerk on the staff of Yang Chien.

Han Wen-kuang, investigation commissioner for Shantung.

Han Yü-ch'uan, singing girl in Ch'ing-ho, younger sister of Han Chin-ch'uan and Han Pi.

Hao Hsien, Idler Hao, a dissolute young scamp upon whom Hsi-men Ch'ing turns the tables by abusing the judicial system.

Hao, Idler. See Hao Hsien.

Ho Ch'i-kao, left administration vice commissioner of Shantung.

Ho Chin, assistant judicial commissioner of the Ch'ing-ho office of the Provincial Surveillance Commission, promoted to the post of commander of Hsin-p'ing Stockade and later to the post of judicial commissioner in the Huai-an office of the Provincial Surveillance Commission, thereby creating the vacancy filled by Hsi-men Ch'ing in return for the lavishness of his birthday presents to Ts'ai Ching.

Ho Chin-ch'an, singing girl from the Ho Family Bordello on Fourth Street in the licensed quarter of Ch'ing-ho.

Ho Ch'in, son of Ho the Ninth who succeeds to his position as head coroner's assistant of Ch'ing-ho.

Ho Ch'un-ch'üan, Dr. Ho, son of Old Man Ho, physician in Ch'ing-ho.

Ho, Dr. See Ho Ch'un-ch'üan.

Ho, Eunuch Director. See Ho Hsin.

Ho Hsin (fl. early 12th century), Eunuch Director Ho, attendant in the Yenning Palace, residence of Consort Feng, rewarded for his part in facilitating the notorious Flower and Rock Convoys and the construction of the Mount Ken Imperial Park, uncle of Ho Yung-shou, entertains Hsi-men Ch'ing on his visit to the Eastern Capital.

Ho-hua, maidservant of Chou Hsiu's concubine Sun Erh-niang.

Ho Liang-feng, younger brother of Magnate Ho.

Ho, Magnate, wealthy silk merchant from Hu-chou, elder brother of Ho Liang-feng, tries to buy P'an Chin-lien after the death of Hsi-men Ch'ing, patronizes Wang Liu-erh in Lin-ch'ing and takes her and Han Tao-kuo back to Hu-chou where they inherit his property.

Ho, Magnate's daughter.

Ho the Ninth, elder brother of Ho the Tenth, head coroner's assistant of Ch'ing-ho who accepts a bribe from Hsi-men Ch'ing to cover up the murder of Wu Chih.

Ho, Old Man, father of Ho Ch'un-ch'üan, aged physician in Ch'ing-ho.

Ho Pu-wei, clerk on the staff of the district magistrate of Ch'ing-ho, Li Ch'ang-ch'i, who assists his son Li Kung-pi in his courtship of Meng Yü-lou.

Ho the Tenth, younger brother of Ho the Ninth, let off the hook by Hsi-men Ch'ing when he is accused of fencing stolen goods.

Ho Yung-fu, nephew of Ho Hsin, younger brother of Ho Yung-shou.

Ho Yung-shou, nephew of Ho Hsin, elder brother of Ho Yung-fu, appointed to Hsi-men Ch'ing's former post as assistant judicial commissioner in the Ch'ing-ho office of the Provincial Surveillance Commission as a reward for Ho Hsin's part in facilitating the notorious Flower and Rock Convoys and the construction of the Mount Ken Imperial Park.

Ho Yung-shou's wife, née Lan, niece of Lan Ts'ung-hsi.

Hou Lin, Flying Demon, beggar boss in Ch'ing-ho who helps out Ch'en Ching-chi when he is reduced to beggary in return for his sexual favors.

Hou Meng (1054–1121), grand coordinator of Shantung, promoted to the post of chief minister of the Court of Imperial Sacrifices for his part in facilitating the notorious Flower and Rock Convoys and the construction of the Mount Ken Imperial Park.

Hsi-erh, page boy in the household of Chou Hsiu.

Hsi-men An. See Tai-an.

Hsi-men Ching-liang, Hsi-men Ch'ing's grandfather.

Hsi-men Ch'ing, principal male protagonist of the novel, father of Hsi-men Ta-chieh by his deceased first wife, née Ch'en, father of Hsi-men Kuan-ko by Li P'ing-erh, father of Hsi-men Hsiao-ko by Wu Yüeh-niang, decadent scion of a merchant family of some wealth from which he inherits a whole-sale pharmaceutical business on the street in front of the district yamen of Ch'ing-ho, climbs in social status by means of a succession of corrupt sexual, economic, and political conquests only to die of sexual excess at the age of thirty-three.

Hsi-men Ch'ing's daughter. See Hsi-men Ta-chieh.

Hsi-men Ch'ing's first wife, née Ch'en, deceased mother of Hsi-men Ta-chieh.

Hsi-men Ch'ing's father. See Hsi-men Ta.

Hsi-men Ch'ing's grandfather. See Hsi-men Ching-liang.

Hsi-men Ch'ing's grandmother, née Li.

Hsi-men Ch'ing's mother, née Hsia.

Hsi-men Ch'ing's reincarnation. See Hsi-men Hsiao-ko and Shen Yüeh.

Hsi-men Ch'ing's sons. See Hsi-men Kuan-ko and Hsi-men Hsiao-ko.

Hsi-men Hsiao-ko, posthumous son of Hsi-men Ch'ing by Wu Yüeh-niang, born at the very moment of his death, betrothed while still a babe in arms to Yün Li-shou's daughter, claimed by the Buddhist monk P'u-ching to be the reincarnation of Hsi-men Ch'ing and spirited away by him at the end of the novel to become a celibate monk with the religious name Ming-wu.

Hsi-men Kuan-ko, son of Hsi-men Ch'ing by Li P'ing-erh, given the religious name Wu Ying-yüan by the Taoist priest Wu Tsung-che, betrothed while still a babe in arms to Ch'iao Chang-chieh, murdered by P'an Chin-lien out of jealousy of Li P'ing-erh.

Hsi-men Kuan-ko's reincarnation. See Wang family of Cheng-chou.

Hsi-men Ta, deceased father of Hsi-men Ch'ing whose business took him to many parts of China.

Hsi-men Ta-chieh, Mistress Ch'en, Hsi-men Ch'ing's daughter by his deceased first wife, née Ch'en, wife of Ch'en Ching-chi, so neglected and abused by her husband that she commits suicide.

Hsi-men Ta-chieh's reincarnation. See Chung Kuei.

Hsi-t'ung, page boy in the household of Wang Hsüan.

Hsiao-ko. See Hsi-men Hsiao-ko.

Hsia Ch'eng-en, son of Hsia Yen-ling, achieves status of military selectee by hiring a stand-in to take the qualifying examination for him.

Hsia-hua, junior maidservant of Li Chiao-erh who is caught trying to steal a gold bracelet.

Hsia Kung-chi, docket officer on the staff of the district yamen in Ch'ing-ho.

Hsia Shou, servant in the household of Hsia Yen-ling.

Hsia Yen-ling, judicial commissioner in the Ch'ing-ho office of the Provincial Surveillance Commission, colleague, superior, and rival of Hsi-men Ch'ing in his official career.

Hsia Yen-ling's son. See Hsia Ch'eng-en.

Hsia Yen-ling's wife.

Hsiang the Elder, deceased distaff relative of the imperial family through Empress Hsiang, consort of Emperor Shen-tsung (r. 1067–85), elder brother of Hsiang the fifth.

Hsiang, Empress, (1046–1101), consort of Emperor Shen-tsung (r. 1067–85).

Hsiang the Fifth, distaff relative of the imperial family through Empress Hsiang, consort of Emperor Shen-tsung (r. 1067–85), younger brother of Hsiang the Elder, sells part of his country estate outside Ch'ing-ho to Hsi-men Ch'ing.

Hsiao Chang-hsien. See Chang Hsiao-hsein.

Hsiao Ch'eng, resident of Oxhide Street and neighborhood head of the fourth neighborhood of the first subprecinct of Ch'ing-ho.

Hsiao-ko. See Hsi-men Hsiao-ko.

Hsiao-luan, junior maidservant of Meng Yü-lou.

Hsiao-yü, Little Jade, junior maidservant of Wu Yüeh-niang, married to Tai-an after Wu Yüeh-niang discovers them in flagrante delicto.

Hsiao-yüeh, Abbot, head priest of the Water Moon Monastery outside the south gate of Ch'ing-ho.

Hsieh En, assistant judicial commissioner of the Huai-ch'ing office of the Provincial Surveillance Commission.

Hsieh, Fatty. See Hsieh the Third.

Hsieh Hsi-ta, Tagalong Hsieh, crony of Hsi-men Ch'ing, member of the brotherhood of ten.

Hsieh Hsi-ta's father, deceased hereditary battalion commander in the Ch'ing-ho Guard.

Hsieh Hsi-ta's mother.

Hsieh Hsi-ta's wife, née Liu.

Hsieh Ju-huang, What a Whopper, acquaintance of Han Tao-kuo who punctures his balloon when he inflates his own importance.

Hsieh, Tagalong. See Hsieh Hsi-ta.

Hsieh the Third, Fatty Hsieh, manager of the Hsieh Family Tavern in Lin-ch'ing.

Hsin Hsing-tsung (fl. early 12th century), commander-general of the Ho-nan region who leads the forces of Chang-te against the Chin invaders.

Hsiu-ch'un, junior maidservant of Li P'ing-erh and later of Li Chiao-erh, finally becoming a novice nun under the tutelage of Nun Wang.

Hsiung Wang, husband of Chang Ju-i, soldier forced by his lack of means to sell his wife to Hsi-men Ch'ing as a wet nurse for Kuan-ko.

Hsiung Wang's son by Chang Ju-i.

Hsü, Assistant Administration Commissioner, of Yen-chou in Shantung.

Hsü-chou, old woman from, in whose house Han Ai-chieh encounters Han the Second.

Hsü, Eunuch Director, wealthy eunuch speculator and moneylender, resident of Halfside Street in the northern quarter of Ch'ing-ho, landlord of Crooked-head Sun and Aunt Yang, patron of Li Ming, original owner of Hsia Yen-ling's residential compound, major rival of Hsi-men Ch'ing in the social world of Ch'ing-ho whose niece marries Chang Mao-te's son.

Hsü, Eunuch Director's niece, marries Chang Mao-te's son.

Hsü Feng, prefect of Yen-chou in Chekiang who exposes Meng Yü-lou's and Li Kung-pi's attempt to frame Ch'en Ching-chi.

Hsü Feng's trusted henchman who disguises himself as a convict in order to elicit information from Ch'en Ching-chi.

Hsü Feng-hsiang, supervisor of the State Farm Battalion of the Ch'ing-ho Guard, one of the officials who comes to Hsi-men Ch'ing's residence to offer a sacrifice to the soul of Li P'ing-erh after her death.

Hsü the Fourth, shopkeeper outside the city wall of Ch'ing-ho who borrows money from Hsi-men Ch'ing.

Hsü Hsiang, battalion commander rewarded for his part in facilitating the notorious Flower and Rock Convoys and the construction of the Mount Ken Imperial Park.

Hsü, Master, yin-yang master of Ch'ing-ho.

Hsü Nan-ch'i, military officer in Ch'ing-ho promoted to the post of commander of the Hsin-p'ing Stockade.

Hsü, Prefect, prefect of Ch'ing-chou, patron of Shih Po-ts'ai, the corrupt Taoist head priest of the Temple of the Goddess of Iridescent Clouds on the summit of Mout T'ai.

Hsü, Prefect's daughter.

Hsü, Prefect's son.

Hsü, Prefect's wife.

Hsü Pu-yü, Reneger Hsü, moneylender in Ch'ing-ho from whom Wang Ts'ai tries to borrow three hundred taels of silver in order to purchase a position in the Military School.

Hsü, Reneger. See Hsü Pu-yü.

Hsü Shun, professional actor of Hai-yen style drama.

Hsü Sung, prefect of Tung-ch'ang in Shantung.

Hsü Sung's concubine.

Hsü Sung's concubine's father.

Hsü, Tailor, artisan with a shop across the street from Han Tao-kuo's residence on Lion Street in Ch'ing-ho.

Hsü the Third, seller of date cakes in front of the district yamen in Ch'ing-ho.

Hsü Tsung-shun, junior disciple of Abbot Jen of the Yen-kung Temple in Lin-ch'ing.

Hsüeh, Auntie, go-between in Ch'ing-ho who also peddles costume jewelry, mother of Hsüeh Chi, sells P'ang Ch'un-mei into Hsi-men Ch'ing's household, represents Hsi-men Ch'ing in the betrothal of his daughter Hsi-men Ta-chieh to Ch'en Ching-chi, proposes his match with Meng Yü-lou, arranges resale of P'ang Ch'un-mei to Chou Hsiu after she is forced to leave the Hsi-men household by Wu Yüeh-niang, arranges match between Ch'en Ching-chi and Ko Ts'ui-p'ing after Hsi-men Ta-chieh's suicide.

Hsüeh, Auntie's husband.

Hsüeh Chi, son of Auntie Hsüeh, husband of Chin ta-chieh.

Hsüeh Chi's son by Chin Ta-chieh.

Hsüeh, Eunuch Director, supervisor of the imperial estates in the Ch'ing-ho region, despite his castration given to fondling and pinching the singing girls with whom he comes in contact.

Hsüeh Hsien-chung, official rewarded for his part in facilitating the notorious Flower and Rock Convoys and the construction of the Mount Ken Imperial Park.

Hsüeh, Nun, widow of a peddler of steamed wheat cakes living across the street from the Kuang-ch'eng Monastery in Ch'ing-ho who took the tonsure after the death of her husband and became abbess of the Ksitigarbha Nunnery, defrocked for her complicity in the death of Juan the Third, later rector of the Lotus Blossom Nunnery in the southern quarter of Ch'ing-ho who provides first Wu Yüeh-niang and then P'an Chin-lien with fertility potions, frequently invited to recite Buddhist "precious scrolls" to Wu Yüeh-niang and her guests.

Hsüeh, Nun's deceased husband, peddler of steamed wheat cakes living across the street from the Kuang-ch'eng Monastery in Ch'ing-ho.

Hsüeh-o. See Sun Hsüeh-o.

Hsüeh Ts'un-erh, unlicensed prostitute in Longfoot Wu's brothel in the Southern Entertainment Quarter of Ch'ing-ho patronized by P'ing-an after he absconds from the Hsi-men household with jewelry stolen from the pawnshop.

Hu, Dr., Old Man Hu, Hu the Quack, physician who lives in Eunuch Director Liu's house on East Street in Ch'ing-ho in the rear courtyard of which Hsi-men Ch'ing hides in order to evade Wu Sung, treats Hua Tzu-hsü, Li P'ing-erh, and Hsi-men Ch'ing without success, prescribes abortifacient for P'an Chin-lien when she becomes pregnant by Ch'en Ching-chi.

Hu, Dr's maidservant.

Hu the Fourth, impeached as a relative or adherent of Yang Chien.

Hu Hsiu, employee of Han Tao-kuo who spies on Hsi-men Ch'ing's lovemaking with Wang Liu-erh, accompanies his employer on his buying expeditions to the south, and tells him what he thinks about his private life in a drunken tirade in Yang-chou.

Hu, Old Man. See Hu, Dr.

Hu the Quack. See Hu, Dr.

Hu Shih-wen (fl. early 12th century), related to Ts'ai Ching by marriage, corrupt prefect of Tung-p'ing in Shantung who participates with Hsi-men Ch'ing and Hsia Yen-ling in getting Miao Ch'ing off the hook for murdering his master Miao T'ien-hsiu.

Hu Ts'ao, professional actor from Su-chou who specializes in playing young male lead roles.

Hua the Elder. See Hua Tzu-yu.

Hua, Eunuch Director, uncle of Hua Tzu-yu, Hua Tzu-hsü, Hua Tzu-kuang, and Hua Tzu-hua and adoptive father of Hua Tzu-hsü, member of the Imperial Bodyguard and director of the Firewood Office in the Imperial Palace, later promoted to the position of grand defender of Kuang-nan from which post he retires on account of illness to take up residence in his native place, Ch'ing-ho; despite his castration engaged in pseudo-incestuous hanky-panky with his daughter-in-law, Li P'ing-erh.

Hua the Fourth. See Hua Tzu-hua.

Hua Ho-lu, assistant magistrate of Ch'ing-ho.

Hua, Mistress. See Li P'ing-erh.

Hua, Mrs. See Li P'ing-erh.

Hua, Nobody. See Hua Tzu-hsü.

Hua the Second. See Hua Tzu-hsü.

Hua the Third. See Hua Tzu-kuang.

Hua-t'ung, page boy in Hsi-men Ch'ing's household sodomized by Wen Pi-ku.

Hua Tzu-hsü, Hua the Second, Nobody Hua, nephew and adopted son of Eunuch Director Hua, husband of Li P'ing-erh, next door neighbor of Hsi-men Ch'ing and member of the brotherhood of ten, patron of Wu Yin-erh and Cheng Ai-hsiang; cuckolded by Li P'ing-erh, who turns over much of his property to Hsi-men Ch'ing, he loses the rest in a lawsuit and dies of chagrin.

Hua Tzu-hsü's reincarnation. See Cheng, Battalion Commander's family in the Eastern Capital.

Hua Tzu-hua, Hua the Fourth, nephew of Eunuch Director Hua, brother of Hua Tzu-hsü.

Hua Tzu-hua's wife.

Hua Tzu-kuang, Hua the Third, nephew of Eunuch Director Hua, brother of Hua Tzu-hsü.

Hua Tzu-kuang's wife.

Hua Tzu-yu, Hua the Elder, nephew of Eunuch Director Hua, brother of Hua Tzu-hsü.

Hua Tzu-yu's wife.

Huia River region, merchant from, who employs Wang Ch'ao.

Huai Rvier region, merchant from, who patronizes Li Kuei-ch'ing.

Huang An, military commander involved with T'an Chen in defense of the northern frontier against the Chin army.

Huang, Buddhist Superior, monk of the Pao-en Temple in Ch'ing-ho.

Huang Chia, prefect of Teng-chou in Shantung.

Huang Ching-ch'en (d. 1126), defender-in-chief of the Palace Command, eunuch rewarded for his part in facilitating the notorious Flower and Rock Convoys and the construction of the Mount Ken Imperial Park, uncle of Wang Ts'ai's wife, née Huang, lavishly entertained by Hsi-men Ch'ing at the request of Sung Ch'iao-nien.

Huang Ching-ch'en's adopted son, granted the post of battalion commander of the Embroidered Uniform Guard by *yin* privilege as a reward for his father's part in facilitating the notorious Flower and Rock Convoys and the construction of the Mount Ken Imperial Park.

Huang the Fourth, merchant contractor in Ch'ing-ho, partner of Li Chih, ends up in prison for misappropriation of funds.

Huang the Fourth's son.

Huang the Fourth's wife, née Sun, daughter of Sun Ch'ing.

Huang-lung Temple, abbot of, entertains Hsi-men Ch'ing and Ho Yung-shou en route to Ch'ing-ho from the Eastern Capital.

Huang, Master, fortune teller residing outside the Chen-wu Temple in the northern quarter of Ch'ing-ho.

Huang Mei, assistant prefect of K'ai-feng, maternal cousin of Miao T'ien-hsiu who invites him to visit him in the capital and appeals to Tseng Hsiao-hsü on his behalf after his murder.

Huang Ning, page boy in the household of Huang the Fourth.

Huang Pao-kuang (fl. early 12th century), secretary of the Ministry of Works in charge of the Imperial Brickyard in Ch'ing-ho, provincial graduate of the same year as Shang Hsiao-t'ang.

Huang, Perfect Man. See Huang Yüan-pai.

Huang Yü, foreman on the staff of Wang Fu.

Huang Yüan-pai, Perfect Man Huang, Taoist priest sent by the court to officiate at a seven-day rite of cosmic renewal on Mount T'ai, also officiates at a rite of purification for the salvation of the soul of Li P'ing-erh.

Hui-ch'ing, "The Beanpole," wife of Lai-chao, mother of Little Iron Rod.

Hui-hsiang, wife of Lai-pao, née Liu, mother of Seng-pao.

Hui-hsiang's elder sister.

Hui-hsiang's mother.

Hui-hsiang's younger brother. See Liu Ts'ang.

Hui-hsiu, wife of Lai-hsing, mother of Nien-erh and Ch'eng-erh.

Hui-lien. See Sung Hui-lien.

Hui-tsung, Emperor of the Sung dynasty (r. 1100–25), father of Emperor Ch'in-tsung in whose favor he abdicated in 1125, taken into captivity together with his son by the Chin invaders in 1127.

Hui-yüan, wife of Lai-chüeh.

Hung, Auntie, madam of the Hung Family Brothel in Ch'ing-ho.

Hung the Fourth, singing girl from the Hung Family Brothel in Ch'ing-ho.

Hung-hua Temple in Ch'ing-ho, monk from, whom Hsi-men Ch'ing frames and executes in place of Ho the Tenth.

Huo-pao, eleven-year-old country girl offered to P'ang Ch'un-mei as a maid-servant but rejected for wetting her bed.

Huo-pao's parents.

Huo Ta-li, district magistrate of Ch'ing-ho who accepts Ch'en Ching-chi's bribe and lets him off the hook when accused of driving his wife, Hsi-men Ta-chieh, to suicide.

I Mien-tz'u, Ostensibly Benign, neighbor of Hsi-men Ch'ing who intercedes unsuccessfully on Lai-wang's behalf.

Imperial Stables in Ch'ing-ho, eunuch director of, employer of Mohammedan Han.

Indian monk. See Monk, Indian.

Iron Fingernail. See Yang Kuang-yen.

Iron Rod. See Little Iron Rod.

Itinerant acrobat called in by Chou Hsiu to distract P'ang Ch'un-mei from her grief over the death of P'an Chin-lien.

Jade Flute. See Yü-hsiao.

Jade Lotus. See Pai Yü-lien.

Jen, Abbot, Taoist priest of the Yen-kung Temple in Lin-ch'ing to whom Wang Hsüan recommends Ch'en Ching-chi as a disciple; dies of shock when threatened with arrest in connection with the latter's whoremongering.

Jen, Abbot's acolyte.

Jen Hou-ch'i, Dr. Jen, physician in Ch'ing-ho who treats Li P'ing-erh and Hsi-men Ch'ing without success, friend of Han Ming-ch'uan.

Jen T'ing-kuei, assistant magistrate of Ch'ing-ho.

Ju-i. See Chang Ju-i.

Juan the Third, dies of excitement in the act of making love to Miss Ch'en in the Ksitigarbha Nunnery during an assignation arranged by Nun Hsüeh.

Juan the Third's parents.

Jui-yün. See Pen Chang-chieh.

Jung Chiao-erh, singing girl in Ch'ing-ho patronized by Wang Ts'ai.

Jung Hai, employee of Hsi-men Ch'ing who accompanies Ts'ui Pen on a buying trip to Hu-chou.

Kan Jun, resident of Stonebridge Alley in Ch'ing-ho, partner and manager of Hsi-men Ch'ing's silk dry goods store.

Kan Jun's wife.

Kan Lai-hsing. See Lai-hsing.

K'ang, Prince of. See Kao-tsung, Emperor.

Kao An, secondary majordomo of Ts'ai Ching's household in the Eastern Capital through whom Lai-pao gains access to Ts'ai Yu.

Kao Ch'iu (d. 1126), defender-in-chief of the Imperial Bodyguard, granted the title of grand guardian for his part in facilitating the notorious Flower and Rock Convoys and the construction of the Mount Ken Imperial Park; one of the Six Traitors impeached by Ch'en Tung.

Kao family from outside the city wall of the Eastern Capital, family into which Chou I is reincarnated as a son named Kao Liu-chu.

Kao family of the Ta-hsing Guard, family into which Chang Sheng is reincarnated as a son.

Kao Lien, cousin of Kao Ch'iu, prefect of T'ai-an, brother-in-law of Yin T'ien-hsi.

Kao Lien's wife, née Yin, elder sister of Yin T'ien-hsi.

Kao Liu-chu, son of the Kao family from outside the city wall of the Eastern Capital, reincarnation of Chou I.

Kao-tsung, Emperor of the Southern Sung dynasty (r. 1127–1162), ninth son of Emperor Hui-tsung, Prince of K'ang; declares himself emperor in 1127 when the Chin invaders took emperors Hui-tsung and Ch'in-tsung into captivity; abdicates in favor of emperor Hsiao-tsung in 1162.

Ko Ts'ui-p'ing, wife of Ch'en Ching-chi in a marriage arranged by P'ang Ch'un-mei with whom he continues to carry on an intermittent affair; returns to her parents' family after Ch'en Ching-chi's death and the invasion by the Chin armies.

Ko Ts'ui-p'ing's father, wealthy silk dry goods dealer in Ch'ing-ho.

Ko Ts'ui-p'ing's mother.

Kou Tzu-hsiao, professional actor from Su-chou who specializes in playing male lead roles.

Ku, Silversmith, jeweler in Ch'ing-ho patronized by Li P'ing-erh and Hsi-men Ch'ing, employer of Lai-wang after he returns to Ch'ing-ho from exile in Hsü-chou.

Kuan, Busybody. See Kuan Shih-k'uan.

Kuan-ko. See Hsi-men Kuan-ko.

Kuan Shih-k'uan, Busybody Kuan, a dissolute young scamp upon whom Hsi-men Ch'ing turns the tables by abusing the judicial system.

Kuan-yin Nunnery, abbess of, superior of Nun Wang, frequent visitor in the Hsi-men household.

Kuang-yang, Commandery Prince of. See T'ung Kuan.

Kuei-chieh. See Li Kuei-chieh.

Kuei-ch'ing. See Li Kuei-ch'ing.

Kung Kuai (1057–1111), left provincial administration commissioner of Shan-tung.

K'ung, Auntie, go-between in Ch'ing-ho who represents Ch'iao Hung's family in arranging the betrothal of Ch'iao Chang-chieh to Hsi-men Kuan-ko.

K'ung family of the Eastern Capital, family into which P'ang Ch'un-mei is reincarnated as a daughter.

Kuo Shou-ch'ing, senior disciple of Shih Po-ts'ai, the corrupt Taoist head priest of the Temple of the Goddess of Iridescent Clouds on the summit of Mount T'ai.

Kuo Shou-li, junior disciple of Shih Po-ts'ai, the corrupt Taoist head priest of the Temple of the Goddess of Iridescent Clouds on the summit of Mount T'ai.

Kuo Yao-shih (d. after 1126), turncoat who accepts office under the Sung dynasty but goes over to the Chin side at a critical point and is instrumental in their conquest of north China.

La-mei, maidservant employed in the Wu Family Brothel in Ch'ing-ho.

Lai-an, servant in Hsi-men Ch'ing's household.

Lai-chao, Liu Chao, head servant in Hsi-men Ch'ing's household, husband of Hui-ch'ing, father of Little Iron Rod, helps Lai-wang to abscond with Sun Hsüeh-o.

Lai-chao's son. See Little Iron Rod.

Lai-chao's wife. See Hui-ch'ing.

Lai-chüeh, Lai-yu, husband of Hui-yüan, originally servant in the household of a distaff relative of the imperial family named Wang, loses his position on exposure of his wife's affair with her employer, recommended as a servant to Hsi-men Ch'ing by his friend Ying Pao, the son of Ying Po-chüeh.

Lai-chüeh's deceased parents.

Lai-chüeh's wife. See Hui-yüan.

Lai-hsing, Kan Lai-hsing, servant in Hsi-men Ch'ing's household, originally recruited by Hsi-men Ch'ing's father while traveling on business in Kan-chou, husband of Hui-hsiu, father of Nien-erh and Ch'eng-erh, helps to frame Lai-wang for attempted murder, married to Chang Ju-i after the death of Hui-hsiu.

Lai-pao, T'ang Pao, servant in Hsi-men Ch'ing's household often relied upon for important missions to the capital, husband of Hui-hsiang, father of Seng-pao, appointed to the post of commandant on the staff of the Prince of Yün in return for his part in delivering birthday presents from Hsi-men Ch'ing to Ts'ai Ching, embezzles Hsi-men Ch'ing's property after his death and makes unsuccessful sexual advances to Wu Yüeh-niang, ends up in prison for misappropriation of funds.

Lai-pao's son. See Seng-pao.

Lai-pao's wife. See Hui-hsiang.

Lai-ting, page boy in the household of Hua Tzu-yu.

Lai-ting, page boy in the household of Huang the Fourth.

Lai-ting, page boy in the household of Wu K'ai.

Lai-wang, Cheng Wang, native of Hsü-chou, servant in Hsi-men Ch'ing's household, husband of Sung Hui-lien, framed for attempted murder and driven out of the household in order to get him out of the way, carries on a clandestine affair with Sun Hsüeh-o before his exile and absconds with her when he returns to Ch'ing-ho after Hsi-men Ch'ing's death.

Lai-wang's first wife, dies of consumption.

Lai-wang's second wife. See Sung Hui-lien.

Lai-yu. See Lai-chüeh.

Lan-hsiang, senior maidservant of Meng Yü-lou.

Lan-hua, junior maidservant of P'ang Ch'un-mei after she becomes the wife of Chou Hsiu.

Lan-hua, elderly maidservant in the household of Wu K'ai.

Lan Ts'ung-hsi (fl. early 12th century), eunuch rewarded for his part in facili-tating the notorious Flower and Rock Convoys and the construction of the Mount Ken Imperial Park, uncle of Ho Yung-shou's wife, née Lan.

Lan Ts'ung-hsi's adopted son, granted the post of battalion vice commander of the Embroidered Uniform Guard by yin privilege as a reward for his father's part in facilitating the notorious Flower and Rock Convoys and the construction of the Mount Ken Imperial Park.

Lan Ts'ung-hsi's niece. See Ho Yung-shou's wife, née Lan.

Lang, Buddhist Superior, monk of the Pao-en Temple in Ch'ing-ho.

Lei Ch'i-yüan, assistant commissioner of the Shantung Military Defense Cir-cuit.

Li An, retainer in the household of Chou Hsiu who saves P'ang Ch'un-mei's life when she is threatened by Chang Sheng and resists her blandishments when she tries to seduce him.

Li An's father, deceased elder brother of Li Kuei.

Li An's mother, persuades Li An to avoid entanglement with P'ang Ch'un-mei by seeking refuge with his uncle Li Kuei in Ch'ing-chou.

Li, Barestick. See Li Kung-pi.

Li Ch'ang-ch'i, father of Li Kung-pi, district magistrate of Ch'ing-ho and later assistant prefect of Yen-chou in Chekiang.

Li Ch'ang-ch'i's wife, mother of Li Kung-pi.

Li Chiao-erh, Hsi-men Ch'ing's Second Lady, originally a singing girl from the Verdant Spring Bordello in Ch'ing-ho, aunt of Li Kuei-ch'ing and Li Kuei-chieh, enemy of P'an Chin-lien, tight-fisted manager of Hsi-men Ch'ing's household finances, engages in hanky-panky with Wu the Second, begins pilfering Hsi-men Ch'ing's property while his corpse is still warm, ends up as Chang Mao-te's Second Lady.

Li Chih, Li the Third, father of Li Huo, merchant contractor in Ch'ing-ho, partner of Huang the Fourth, ends up dying in prison for misappropriation of funds.

Li Chin, servant in the household of Li Chih.

Li Chung-yu, servant on the domestic staff of Ts'ai Ching.

Li, Eunuch Director. See Li Yen.

Li family of the Eastern Capital, family into which P'an Chin-lien is reincarnated as a daughter.

Li Huo, son of Li Chih.

Li Kang (1083–1140), minister of war under Emperor Ch'in-tsung who directs the defense against the Chin invaders.

Li Kuei, Shantung Yaksha, uncle of Li An, military instructor from Ch'ing-chou patronized by Li Kung-pi.

Li Kuei-chieh, Cassia, daughter of Auntie Li the Third, niece of Li Chiao-erh and Li Ming, younger sister of Li Kuei-ch'ing, singing girl from the Verdant Spring Bordello on Second Street in the licensed quarter of Ch'ing-ho, deflowered by Hsi-men Ch'ing, who maintains her as his mistress for twenty taels a month, adopted daughter of Wu Yüeh-niang, betrays Hsi-men Ch'ing with Ting the Second, Wang Ts'ai, and others.

Li Kuei-chieh's fifth maternal aunt.

Li Kuei-ch'ing, daughter of Auntie Li the Third, niece of Li Chiao-erh and Li Ming, elder sister of Li Kuei-chieh, singing girl from the Verdant Spring Bordello on Second Street in the licensed quarter of Ch'ing-ho.

Li K'uei, Black Whirlwind, bloodthirsty outlaw from Sung Chiang's band who massacres the household of Liang Shih-chieh and kills Yin T'ien-hsi.

Li Kung-pi, Bare Stick Li, only son of Li Ch'ang-ch'i, student at the Superior College of the National University, falls in love with Meng Yü-lou at first sight and arranges to marry her as his second wife, severely beaten by his father for his part in the abortive attempt to frame Ch'en Ching-chi, forced to return with his bride to his native place to resume his studies.

Li Kung-pi's deceased first wife.

Li Kung-pi's servant.

Li, Leaky. See Li Wai-ch'uan.

Li Ming, younger brother of Li Chiao-erh, uncle of Li Kuei-ch'ing and Li Kuei-chieh; actor and musician from the Verdant Spring Bordello on Second Street in the licensed quarter of Ch'ing-ho; employed by Hsi-men Ch'ing to teach Ch'un-mei, Yü-hsiao, Ying-ch'un, and Lan-hsiang to sing and play musical instruments; driven out of the house by Ch'un-mei for having the temerity to squeeze her hand during a lesson but allowed to return on many subsequent occasions; assists Li Chiao-erh, Li Kuei-ch'ing, and Li Kuei-chieh in despoiling Hsi-men Ch'ing's property after his death.

Li Pang-yen (d. 1130), minister of the right, grand academician of the Hall for Aid in Governance, and concurrently minister of rites, alters Hsi-men Ch'ing's name to Chia Lien on a bill of impeachment in return for a bribe of five hundred taels of silver, promoted to the ranks of pillar of state and grand preceptor of the heir apparent for his part in facilitating the notorious Flower and Rock Convoys and the construction of the Mount Ken Imperial Park, one of the Six Traitors impeached by Ch'en Tung.

Li P'ing-erh, Vase, Mrs. Hua, Mistress Hua, one of the three principal female protagonists of the novel, concubine of Liang Shih-chieh, wife of Hua Tzu-hsü, commits adultery with her husband's neighbor and sworn brother Hsi-men Ch'ing, wife of Dr. Chiang Chu-shan, Hsi-men Ch'ing's Sixth Lady, mother of Hsi-men Kuan-ko, dies of chronic hemorrhaging brought on by grief over the death of her son and Hsi-men Ch'ing's insistence on trying out his newly acquired aphrodisiac on her while she is in her menstrual period, commemorated in overly elaborate funeral observances that are prime examples of conspicuous consumption, haunts Hsi-men Ch'ing's dreams.

Li P'ing-erh's former incarnation. See Wang family of Pin-chou.

Li P'ing-erh's deceased parents.

Li P'ing-erh's reincarnation. See Yüan, Commander.

Li Ta-t'ien, district magistrate of Ch'ing-ho, relative of Chu Mien, appoints Wu Sung as police captain and later sends him to the Eastern Capital to stash his ill-gotten gains with his powerful relative, accepts Hsi-men Ch'ing's bribes to abuse the law in the cases of Wu Sung, Lai-wang, Sung Hui-lien, Miao T'ien-hsiu, and others.

Li the Third, seller of won-ton in front of the district yamen in Ch'ing-ho.

Li the Third. See Li Chih.

Li the Third, Auntie, madam of the Verdant Spring Bordello on Second Street in the licensed quarter of Ch'ing-ho, mother of Li Kuei-ch'ing and Li Kuei-chieh, partially paralyzed, prototypical procuress who milks her customers for all she can get.

Li, Vice Minister, employer of Licentiate Shui.

Li Wai-ch'uan, Leaky Li, influence peddling lictor on the staff of the district yamen in Ch'ing-ho who is mistakenly killed by Wu Sung in his abortive attempt to wreak vengeance on Hsi-men Ch'ing for the murder of his elder brother Wu Chih.

Li Yen (d. 1126), Eunuch Director Li, entertains Miao Ch'ing in his residence behind the Forbidden City in the Eastern Capital, rewarded for his part in facilitating the notorious Flower and Rock Convoys and the construction of the Mount Ken Imperial Park, one of the Six Traitors impeached by Ch'en Tung.

Li Yen's adopted son, granted the post of battalion vice commander of the Embroidered Uniform Guard by *yin* privilege as a reward for his father's part in facilitating the notorious Flower and Rock Convoys and the construction of the Mount Ken Imperial Park.

Liang, Privy Councilor. See Liang Shih-chieh.

Liang Shih-chieh, Privy Councilor Liang, regent of the Northern Capital at Ta-ming prefecture in Hopei, son-in-law of Ts'ai Ching, first husband of Li P'ing-erh, forced to flee for his life when his entire household is slaughtered by Li K'uei.

Liang Shih-chieh's wife, née Ts'ai, daughter of Ts'ai Ching, extremely jealous woman who beats numbers of maidservants and concubines of her husband to death and buries them in the rear flower garden, forced to flee for her life when her entire household is slaughtered by Li K'uei.

Liang To, professional boy actor in Ch'ing-ho.

Liang Ying-lung, commandant of security for the Eastern Capital.

Lin Ch'eng-hsün, judicial commissioner in the Huai-ch'ing office of the Provincial Surveillance Commission.

Lin Hsiao-hung, younger sister of Lin Ts'ai-hung, singing girl in Yang-chou patronized by Lai-pao.

Lin, Lady, widow of Imperial Commissioner Wang I-hsüan, mother of Wang Ts'ai, former mistress of P'an Chin-lien who learns to play musical instruments and to sing as a servant in her household, carries on an adulterous affair with Hsi-men Ch'ing under the transparent pretext of asking him to superintend the morals of her profligate son.

Lin Ling-su (d. c. 1125), Perfect Man Lin, Taoist priest who gains an ascendancy over Emperor Hui-tsung for a time and is showered with high-sounding titles, rewarded for his part in facilitating the notorious Flower and Rock Convoys and the construction of the Mount Ken Imperial Park.

Lin, Perfect Man. See Lin Ling-su.

Lin Shu (d. c. 1126), minister of works rewarded with the title grand guardian of the heir apparent for his part in facilitating the notorious Flower and Rock Convoys and the construction of the Mount Ken Imperial Park.

Lin Ts'ai-hung, elder sister of Lin Hsiao-hung, singing girl in Yang-chou.

Ling, Master, fortune teller in Ch'ing-ho who interprets Meng Yü-lou's horoscope when she is about to marry Li Kung-pi.

Ling Yün-i, prefect of Yen-chou in Shantung.

Little Iron Rod, son of Lai-chao and his wife Hui-ch'ing.

Little Jade. See Hsiao-yü.

Little Whirlwind. See Ch'ai Chin.

Liu, Assistant Regional Commander, officer of the Hsi-hsia army who gives a horse to Chai Ch'ien, who in turn presents it to Hsi-men Ch'ing.

Liu Chao. See Lai-chao.

Liu Chü-chai, Dr., physician from Fen-chou in Shansi, friend of Ho Yung-shou who recommends him to Hsi-men Ch'ing when he is in extremis but whose treatment exacerbates his condition.

Liu, Company Commander, younger brother of Eunuch Director Liu, indicted for illicit use of imperial lumber in constructing a villa on a newly purchased estate at Wu-li Tien outside Ch'ing-ho, let off the hook by Hsi-men Ch'ing in response to a bribe proffered by Eunuch Director Liu.

Liu, Consort (1088–1121), Consort An, a favorite consort of Emperor Hui-tsung, mother of Chao I.

Liu, Dame, Stargazer Liu's wife, medical practitioner and shamaness frequently called upon by the women of Hsi-men Ch'ing's household.

Liu, Eunuch Director, elder brother of Company Commander Liu, manager of the Imperial Brickyard in Ch'ing-ho, resides on an estate outside the south gate of the city, intervenes with Hsi-men Ch'ing to get his younger brother off the hook when indicted for misappropriation of imperial lumber but supplies Hsi-men Ch'ing with bricks from the Imperial Brickyard for construction of his country estate.

Liu, Eunuch Director, landlord of Dr. Hu's house on East Street in Ch'ing-ho.

Liu, Eunuch Director, resides near Wine Vinegar Gate on the North Side of Ch'ing-ho, patron of Li Ming.

Liu Hui-hsiang. See Hui-hsiang.

Liu Kao, commander of An-p'ing Stockade, friend of Shih En who gives Wu Sung a hundred taels of silver and a letter of recommendation to him when he is sent there in military exile.

Liu, Mr., official serving in Huai-an who passed the *chin-shih* examinations the same year as Sung Ch'iao-nien.

Liu Pao, servant employed as a cook in Hsi-men Ch'ing's silk dry goods store.

Liu, School Official, native of Hang-chou, educational official in Ch'ing-ho who borrows money from Hsi-men Ch'ing.

Liu the Second, Turf-protecting Tiger, brother-in-law of Chang Sheng, proprietor of My Own Tavern west of the bridge in Lin-ch'ing, pimp and racketeer, boss of unlicensed prostitution in Lin-ch'ing, beaten to death by Chou Hsiu at the behest of P'ang Ch'un-mei after Chang Sheng's murder of Ch'en Ching-chi.

Liu the Second, Little, seller of ready-cooked food in front of the district yamen in Ch'ing-ho.

Liu Sheng, foreman on the domestic staff of Yang Chien.

Liu, Stargazer, husband of Dame Liu, blind fortune teller and necromancer who interprets P'an Chin-lien's horoscope, teaches her a method for working black magic on Hsi-men Ch'ing, and treats Hsi-men Kuan-ko ineffectually.

Liu the Third, servant of Company Commander Liu.

Liu Ts'ang, younger brother of Hui-hsiang, brother-in-law of Lai-pao with whom he cooperates in surreptitiously making off with eight hundred taels worth of Hsi-men Ch'ing's property after his death and using it to open a general store.

Liu Yen-ch'ing (1068–1127), commander-general of the Shensi region who leads the forces of Yen-sui against the Chin invaders.

Lo, Mohammedan, one of the "ball clubbers" patronized by Hsi-men Ch'ing.

Lo Ts'un-erh, singing girl of Ch'ing-ho patronized by Hsiang the Fifth.

Lo Wan-hsiang, prefect of Tung-p'ing.

Love. See Chu Ai-ai.

Lu Ch'ang-t'ui, Longleg Lu, madam of the brothel on Butterfly Lane in Ch'ing-ho where Chin-erh and Sai-erh work.

Lu Ch'ang-t'ui's husband.

Lu, Duke of. See Ts'ai Ching.

Lu Hu, clerical subofficial on the staff of Yang Chien.

Lu Hua, Snake-in-the-grass, "knockabout" who, along with Chang Sheng, shakes down Dr. Chiang Chu-shan at the behest of Hsi-men Ch'ing.

Lu, Longleg. See Lu Ch'ang-t'ui.

Lu Ping-i, Lu the Second, crony of Ch'en Ching-chi who suggests how he can recover his property from Yang Kuang-yen and goes into partnership with him as the manager of the Hsieh Family Tavern in Lin-ch'ing.

Lu the Second. See Lu Ping-i.

Lung-hsi, Duke of. See Wang Wei.

Lü Sai-erh, singing girl in Ch'ing-ho.

Ma Chen, professional boy actor in Ch'ing-ho.

Ma, Mrs., next-door neighbor of Ying Po-chüeh.

Man-t'ang, maidservant in the household of Li Kung-pi.

Mao-te, Princess (fl. early 12th century), fifth daughter of Emperor Hui-tsung, married to Ts'ai Ching's fourth son, Ts'ai T'iao.

Meng Ch'ang-ling (fl. early 12th century), eunuch rewarded for his part in facilitating the notorious Flower and Rock Convoys and the construction of the Mount Ken Imperial Park.

Meng Ch'ang-ling's adopted son, granted the post of battalion vice commander of the Embroidered Uniform Guard by yin privilege as a reward for his father's part in facilitating the notorious Flower and Rock Convoys and the construction of the Mount Ken Imperial Park.

Meng-ch'ang, Little Lord. See Ch'ai Chin.

Meng the Elder, elder brother of Meng Yü-lou.

Meng the Elder's wife, Meng Yü-lou's sister-in-law.

Meng Jui, Meng the Second, younger brother of Meng Yü-lou, a traveling merchant constantly on the road.

Meng Jui's wife, Meng Yü-lou's sister-in-law.

Meng the Second. See Meng Jui.

Meng the Third. See Meng Yü-lou.

Meng Yü-lou, Tower of Jade, Meng the Third, one of the female protagonists of the novel, widow of the textile merchant Yang Tsung-hsi, Hsi-men Ch'ing's Third Lady, confidante of P'an Chin-lien, marries Li Kung-pi after the death of Hsi-men Ch'ing, forced to return with her husband to his native place in Hopei after their abortive attempt to frame Ch'en Ching-chi, bears a son to Li Kung-pi at the age of forty and lives to the age of sixty-seven.

Meng Yü-lou's elder brother. See Meng the Elder.

Meng Yü-lou's elder sister. See Han Ming-ch'uan's wife, née Meng.

Meng Yü-lou's son by Li Kung-pi.

Meng Yü-lou's younger brother. See Meng Jui.

Miao Ch'ing, servant of Miao T'ien-hsiu who conspires with the boatmen Ch'en the Third and Weng the Eighth to murder his master on a trip to the Eastern Capital, bribes Hsi-men Ch'ing to get him off the hook, and returns to Yang-chou where he assumes his former master's position in society and maintains relations with his benefactor Hsi-men Ch'ing.

Miao-ch'ü, teenage disciple of Nun Hsüeh.

Miao-feng, teenage disciple of Nun Hsüeh.

Miao Hsiu, servant in the household of Miao Ch'ing.

Miao Shih, servant in the household of Miao Ch'ing.

Miao T'ien-hsiu, a wealthy merchant of Yang-chou who is murdered by his servant Miao Ch'ing on a trip to the Eastern Capital.

Miao T'ien-hsiu's concubine. See Tiao the Seventh.

Miao T'ien-hsiu's daughter.

Miao T'ien-hsiu's wife, née Li.

Ming-wu. See Hsi-men Hsiao-ko.

Mirror polisher, elderly itinerant artisan in Ch'ing-ho who polishes mirrors for P'an Chin-lien, Meng Yü-lou, and P'ang Ch'un-mei and elicits their sympathy with a sob story.

Mirror polisher's deceased first wife.

Mirror polisher's second wife.

Mirror polisher's son.

Monk, Indian, foreign monk presented as the personification of a penis whom Hsi-men Ch'ing encounters in the Temple of Eternal Felicity and from whom he obtains the aphrodisiac an overdose of which eventually kills him.

Moon Lady. See Wu Yüeh-niang.

Ni, Familiar. See Ni P'eng.

Ni, Licentiate. See Ni P'eng.

Ni P'eng, Familiar Ni, Licentiate Ni, tutor employed in the household of Hsia Yen-ling as a tutor for his son, Hsia Ch'eng-en, who recommends his fellow licentiate Wen Pi-ku to Hsi-men Ch'ing.

Nieh Liang-hu, schoolmate of Shang Hsiao-t'ang employed in his household as a tutor for his son who writes two congratulatory scrolls for Hsi-men Ch'ing.

Nieh, Tiptoe. See Nieh Yüeh.

Nieh Yüeh, Tiptoe Nieh, one of the "cribbers" in the licensed quarter of Ch'ing-ho who plays the tout to Wang Ts'ai on his visits to the licensed quarter and upon whom Hsi-men Ch'ing turns the tables by abusing the judicial system at the behest of Lady Lin.

Nieh Yüeh's wife.

Nien-erh, elder daughter of Lai-hsing by Hui-hsiu.

Nien-mo-ho. See Wan-yen Tsung-han.

Niu, Ms., singing girl in the Great Tavern on Lion Street who witnesses Wu Sung's fatal assault on Li Wai-ch'uan.

Old woman who tells the fortunes of Wu Yüeh-niang, Meng Yü-lou, and Li P'ing-erh with the aid of a turtle.

Opportune Rain. See Sung Chiang.

Ostensibly Benign. See I Mien-tz'u.

Pai, Baldy. See Pai T'u-tzu.

Pai the Fifth, Moneybags Pai, father-in-law of Feng Huai, notorious local tyrant and fence for stolen goods in the area west of the Grand Canal.

Pai the Fourth, silversmith in Ch'ing-ho, acquaintance of Han Tao-kuo.

Pai Lai-ch'iang, Scrounger Pai, crony of Hsi-men Ch'ing, member of the brotherhood of ten.

Pai Lai-ch'iang's wife.

Pai, Mohammendan. See Pai T'u-tzu.

Pai, Moneyboys. See Pai the Fifth.

Pai, Scrounger. See Pai Lai-ch'iang.

Pai Shih-chung (d. 1127), right vice minister of rites rewarded with the title grand guardian of the heir apparent for his part in facilitating the notorious Flower and Rock Convoys and the construction of the Mount Ken Imperial Park.

Pai T'u-tzu, Baldy Pai, Mohammedan Pai, "ball-clubber" in Ch'ing-ho who plays the tout to Wang Ts'ai on his visits to the licensed quarter and upon whom Hsi-men Ch'ing turns the tables by abusing the judicial system at the behest of Lady Lin.

Pai Yü-lien, Jade Lotus, maidservant purchased by Mrs. Chang at the same time as P'an Chin-lien who dies shortly thereafter.

Palace foreman who plays the role of master of ceremonies at the imperial audience in the Hall for the Veneration of Governance.

Palefaced Gentleman. See Cheng T'ien-shou.

Pan-erh, unlicensed prostitute in Longfoot Wu's brothel in the Southern Entertainment Quarter of Ch'ing-ho patronized by P'ing-an after he absconds from the Hsi-men household with jewelry stolen from the pawnshop.

P'an Chi, one of the officials from the Ch'ing-ho Guard who comes to Hsi-men Ch'ing's residence to offer a sacrifice to the soul of Li P'ing-erh after her death.

P'an Chin-lien, Golden Lotus, P'an the Sixth, principal female protagonist of the novel, daughter of Tailor P'an from outside the South Gate of Ch'ing-ho who dies when she is only six years old; studies in a girls' school run by Licentiate Yü for three years where she learns to read and write; sold by her mother at the age of eight into the household of Imperial Commissioner Wang and Lady Lin where she is taught to play musical instruments and to sing; resold in her mid-teens, after the death of her master, into the household of Mr. Chang who deflowers her and then gives her as a bride to his tenant, Wu Sung's elder brother, the dwarf Wu Chih; paramour of Hsi-men Ch'ing who collaborates with her in poisoning her husband and subsequently makes her his Fifth Lady; seduces her husband's page boy Ch'in-t'ung for which he is driven out of the household; carries on a running affair with her son-in-law, Ch'en Ching-chi, which is consummated after the death of Hsi-men Ch'ing; responsible, directly or indirectly, for the suicide of Sung Hui-lien, the death of Hsi-men Kuan-ko, and the demise of Hsi-men Ch'ing; aborts her son by Ch'en Ching-chi; is sold out of the household by Wu Yüeh-niang, purchased by Wu Sung, and disemboweled by the latter in revenge for the death of his elder brother Wu Chih.

P'an Chin-lien's cat, Coal in the Snow, Snow Lion, Snow Bandit, long-haired white cat with a black streak on its forehead that P'an Chin-lien trains to attack Hsi-men Kuan-ko with fatal consequences.

P'an Chin-lien's father. See P'an, Tailor.

P'an Chin-lien's maternal aunt, younger sister of old Mrs. P'an.

P'an Chin-lien's maternal aunt's daughter, adopted by old Mrs. P'an to look after her in her old age.

P'an Chin-lien's mother. See P'an, old Mrs.

P'an Chin-lien's reincarnation. See Li Family of the Eastern Capital.

P'an, Demon-catcher. See P'an, Taoist Master.

P'an family prostitution ring operating out of My Own Tavern in Lin-ch'ing, madam of.

P'an the fifth, white slaver, masquerading as a cotton merchant from Shantung, who operates a prostitution ring out of My Own Tavern in Lin-ch'ing, buys Sun Hsüeh-o from Auntie Hsüeh, and forces her to become a singing girl.

P'an the Fifth's deceased first wife.

P'an the Fifth's mother.

P'an, old Mrs., widow of Tailor P'an, mother of P'an Chin-lien, sends her daughter to Licentiate Yü's girls' school for three years, sells her into the household of Imperial Commissioner Wang and Lady Lin at the age of eight, resells her in her mid-teens into the household of Mr. Chang, frequent visitor in Hsi-men Ch'ing's household where she is maltreated by P'an Chin-lien who is ashamed of her low social status, adopts her younger sister's daughter to look after her in her old age, dies not long after the death of Hsi-men Ch'ing.

P'an the Sixth. See P'an Chin-lien.

P'an, Tailor, father of P'an Chin-lien, artisan from outside the South Gate of Ch'ing-ho who dies when P'an Chin-lien is only six years old.

P'an, Taoist Master, Demon-catcher P'an, Taoist exorcist from the Temple of the Five Peaks outside Ch'ing-ho who performs various rituals on Li P'ing-erh's behalf but concludes that nothing can save her.

P'an, Taoist Master's acolyte.

P'ang Ch'un-mei, Spring Plum Blossom, one of the three principal female protagonists of the novel, originally purchased by Hsi-men Ch'ing from Auntie Hsüeh for sixteen taels of silver as a maidservant for Wu Yüeh-niang, reassigned as senior maidservant to P'an Chin-lien when she enters the household, becomes her chief ally and confidante; from the time that her mistress allows her to share the sexual favors of Hsi-men Ch'ing she remains loyal to her right up to and even after her death; after the demise of Hsi-men Ch'ing she aids and abets P'an Chin-lien's affair with Ch'en Ching-chi the discovery of which leads to her dismissal from the household; purchased as a concubine by Chou Hsiu, she bears him a son and is promoted to the status of principal wife, thereby rising higher in social status than any of the ladies she had formerly served as maidservant; comes to Wu Yüeh-niang's assistance when she is threatened by Wu Tien-en and condescends to pay a visit to her former mistress and to witness at first hand the signs of her relative decline; carries on an intermittent affair with Ch'en Ching-chi under her husband's nose and, after Chou Hsiu's death, dies in the act of sexual intercourse with his servant Chou I.

P'ang Ch'un-mei's deceased father who dies while she is still a child.

P'ang Ch'un-mei's deceased mother who dies a year after her birth.

P'ang Ch'un-mei's reincarnation. See K'ung family of the Eastern Capital.

P'ang Ch'un-mei's son. See Chou Chin-ko.

P'ang Hsüan, clerical subofficial on the staff of Yang Chien.

Pao, Dr., pediatric physician in Ch'ing-ho called in to treat Hsi-men Kuan-ko who declares the case to be hopeless.

Pao-en Temple in the Eastern Capital, monk from, tries unsuccessfully to warn Miao T'ien-hsiu against leaving home before his fatal trip to the Eastern Capital.

Pao, Ms., singing girl in the Great Tavern on Lion Street who witnesses Wu Sung's fatal assault on Li Wai-ch'uan.

Pen Chang-chieh, Jui-yün, daughter of Pen Ti-ch'uan and Yeh the Fifth, concubine of Hsia Yen-ling.

Pen the Fourth. See Pen Ti-ch'uan.

Pen, Scurry-about. See Pen Ti-ch'uan.

Pen Ti-ch'uan, Scurry-about Pen, Pen the Fourth, husband of Yeh the Fifth, father of Pen Chang-chieh, manager employed by Hsi-men Ch'ing in various capacities, member of the brotherhood of ten in which he replaces Hua Tzu-hsü after his death.

Pen Ti-ch'uan's daughter. See Pen Chang-chieh.

Pen Ti-ch'uan's wife. See Yeh the Fifth.

Pin-yang, Commandery Prince of. See Wang Ching-ch'ung.

P'ing-an, page boy in Hsi-men Ch'ing's household, absconds with jewelry stolen from the pawnshop after the death of Hsi-men Ch'ing, is caught, and allows himself to be coerced by the police chief Wu Tien-en into giving false testimony that Wu Yüeh-niang has been engaged in hanky-panky with Tai-an.

P'ing-erh. See Li P'ing-erh.

Prison guard on Chou Hsiu's staff.

Pu Chih-tao, No-account Pu, crony of Hsi-men Ch'ing, member of the brotherhood of ten whose place is taken after his death by Hua Tzu-hsü.

Pu, No-account. See Pu Chih-tao.

P'u-ching, Ch'an Master Snow Cave, mysterious Buddhist monk who provides Wu Yüeh-niang with a refuge in Snow Stream Cave on Mount T'ai when she is escaping attempted rape by Yin T'ien-hsi; at the end of the novel he conjures up a phantasmagoria in which all of the major protagonists describe themselves as being reborn in approximately the same social strata they had occupied in their previous incarnations; convinces Wu Yüeh-niang that her son Hsiao-ko is a reincarnation of Hsi-men Ch'ing, and spirits him away into a life of Buddhist celibacy as his disciple.

Sai-erh, singing girl in Longleg Lu's brothel on Butterfly Lane in Ch'ing-ho.

Sauce and Scallions. See Chiang Ts'ung.

Second Lady. See Li Chiao-erh.

Seng-pao, son of Lai-pao and Hui-hsiang, betrothed to Wang Liu-erh's niece, the daughter of Butcher Wang and Sow Wang.

Servant from the household of Chou Hsiu who is sent to fetch P'ang Ch'un-mei with a lantern.

Servant in the inn at the foot of Mount T'ai where Wu Yüeh-niang and Wu K'ai spend the night on their pilgrimage.

Servant from the Verdant Spring Bordello who runs errands for Li Kuei-chieh.

Sha San, Yokel Sha, one of the "cribbers" and "ball clubbers" in Ch'ing-ho who plays the tout to Wang Ts'ai on his visits to the licensed quarter and upon whom Hsi-men Ch'ing turns the tables by abusing the judicial system at the behest of Lady Lin.

Sha, Yokel. See Sha San.

Shamaness brought to the Hsi-men household by Dame Liu to burn paper money and perform a shamanistic dance on behalf of the sick Hsi-men Kuan-ko.

Shang Hsiao-t'ang, Provincial Graduate Shang, son of Shang Liu-t'ang, widower in Ch'ing-ho whom Chang Lung proposes unsuccessfully as a match for Meng Yü-lou, provincial graduate of the same year as Huang Pao-kuang, assisted by Hsi-men Ch'ing when he sets out for the Eastern Capital to compete in the *chin-shih* examinations.

Shang Hsiao-t'ang's second wife.

Shang Hsiao-t'ang's son.

Shang Liu-t'ang, Prefectural Judge Shang, father of Shang Hsiao-t'ang, formerly served as district magistrate of Huang Pao-kuang's district and prefectural judge of Ch'eng-tu in Szechwan, resident of Main Street in Ch'ing-ho from whom both Li P'ing-erh's and Hsi-men Ch'ing's coffins are purchased.

Shang Liu-t'ang's deceased wife, mother of Shang Hsiao-t'ang.

Shang, Prefectural Judge. See Shang Liu-t'ang.

Shang, Provincial Graduate. See Shang Hsiao-t'ang.

Shantung Yaksha. See Li Kuei.

Shao Ch'ien, boy actor in Ch'ing-ho.

Shen, Brother-in-law, Mr. Shen, husband of Wu Yüeh-niang's elder sister.

Shen Ching, resident of the Eastern Capital, father of Shen Shou-shan.

Shen, Mr. See Shen, Brother-in-law.

Shen, Second Sister, blind professional singer in Ch'ing-ho recommended to Hsi-men Ch'ing by Wang Liu-erh but driven out of his household by P'ang Ch'un-mei when she refuses to sing for her.

Shen Shou-shan, second son of Shen Ching, reincarnation of Chou Hsiu.

Shen Ting, servant in the household of Brother-in-law Shen.

Shen T'ung, wealthy resident of the Eastern Capital, father of Shen Yüeh.

Shen Yüeh, second son of Shen T'ung, reincarnation of Hsi-men Ch'ing.

Sheng-chin, ten-year-old country girl offered to P'ang Ch'un-mei as a maidservant but rejected for befouling her bed.

Sheng-chin's parents.

Shih Cho-kuei, Plastromancer Shih, shaman in Ch'ing-ho who prognosticates about the sick Hsi-men Kuan-ko through interpreting the cracks produced by applying heat to notches on the surface of the plastron of a tortoise shell.

Shih En, son of the warden of the prison camp at Meng-chou who befriends the exiled Wu Sung, obtains his assistance in his struggle with Chiang Men-shen for control of the Happy Forest Tavern, and gives him a hundred taels of silver and a letter of recommendation to Liu Kao when he is transferred to the An-p'ing Stockade.

Shih, Plastromancer. See Shih Cho-kuei.

Shih Po-ts'ai, corrupt Taoist head priest of the Temple of the Goddess of Iridescent Clouds on the summit of Mount T'ai.

Short-legged Tiger. See Wang Ying.

Shu-t'ung, Little Chang Sung, native of Su-chou, page boy catamite and trans-
vestite presented to Hsi-men Ch'ing by Li Ta-t'ien, placed in charge of Hsi-
men Ch'ing's studio where he handles his correspondence and caters to
his polymorphous sexual tastes, becomes intimate with Yü-hsiao and when
discovered in flagrante delicto by P'an Chin-lien purloins enough of Hsi-
men Ch'ing's property to make good his escape to his native place.

Shui, Licentiate, scholar of problematic morals unsuccessfully recommended
to Hsi-men Ch'ing as a social secretary by Ying Po-chüeh; after Hsi-men
Ch'ing's death he is engaged by the remaining members of the brotherhood
of ten to compose a funeral eulogy for Hsi-men Ch'ing in which he compares him to the male genitalia.

Shui, Licentiate's father, friend of Ying Po-chüeh's father.

Shui, Licentiate's grandfather, friend of Ying Po-chüeh's grandfather.

Shui, Licentiate's two sons, die of smallpox.

Shui, Licentiate's wife, elopes to the Eastern Capital with her lover.

Sick beggar whom Ch'en Ching-chi keeps alive with the warmth of his body
when he is working as a night watchman.

Silver. See Wu Yin-erh.

Singing boys, two boy singers sent under escort all the way to Hsi-men
Ch'ing's home in Ch'ing-ho by his host, Miao Ch'ing, after he expresses
admiration for their singing at a banquet in the residence of Li Yen in the
Eastern Capital.

Six Traitors, Ts'ai Ching, T'ung Kuan, Li Pang-yen, Chu Mien, Kao Ch'iu,
and Li Yen.

Sixth Lady. See Li P'ing-erh.

Snake-in-the-grass. See Lu Hua.

Snow Bandit. See P'an Chin-lien's cat.

Snow Cave, Ch'an Master. See P'u-ching.

Snow Lion. See P'an Chin-lien's cat.

Snow Moth. See Sun Hsüeh-o.

Southerner who deflowers Cheng Ai-yüeh.

Spring Plum Blossom. See P'ang Ch'un-mei.

Ssu Feng-i, battalion commander rewarded for his part in facilitating the notorious Flower and Rock Convoys and the construction of the Mount Ken
Imperial Park.

Stand-hard. See Tao-chien.

Star of Joy Bordello in Ch'ing-ho, cook from.

Storehouseman in charge of the local storehouse in Yen-chou Prefecture in
Chekiang.

Street-skulking Rat. See Chang Sheng.

Sun, Blabbermouth. See Sun T'ien-hua.

Sun Chi, next door neighbor of Ch'en Ching-chi.

Sun Ch'ing, father-in-law of Huang the Fourth, father of Sun Wen-hsiang, employer of Feng the Second, merchant in Ch'ing-ho engaged in the cotton trade.

Sun Ch'ing's daughter. See Huang the Fourth's wife, née Sun.

Sun Ch'ing's son. See Sun Wen-hsiang.

Sun, Crooked-head, deceased husband of Aunt Yang.

Sun Erh-niang, concubine of Chou Hsiu, mother of Chou Yü-chieh.

Sun Erh-niang's maidservant.

Sun Erh-niang's maidservant's father.

Sun Hsüeh-o, Snow Moth, originally maidservant of Hsi-men Ch'ing's deceased first wife, née Ch'en, who enters his household as part of her dowry; Hsi-men Ch'ing's Fourth Lady but a second class citizen among his womenfolk whose responsibility is the kitchen; enemy of P'an Chin-lien and P'ang Ch'un-mei; carries on a clandestine affair with Lai-wang with whom she absconds when he returns to Ch'ing-ho after Hsi-men Ch'ing's death; apprehended by the authorities and sold into Chou Hsiu's household at the behest of P'ang Ch'un-mei who abuses her, beats her, and sells her into prostitution in order to get her out of the way when she wishes to pass off Ch'en Ching-chi as her cousin; renamed as the singing girl, Yü-erh, working out of My Own Tavern in Lin-ch'ing, she becomes the kept mistress of Chang Sheng until his death when she commits suicide.

Sun Hsüeh-o's reincarnation. See Yao family from outside the Eastern Capital.

Sun Jung, commandant of justice for the two townships of the Eastern Capital.

Sun Kua-tsui. See Sun T'ien-hua.

Sun T'ien-hua, Sun Kua-tsui, Blabbermouth Sun, crony of Hsi-men Ch'ing, member of the brotherhood of ten, plays the tout to Wang Ts'ai on his visits to the licensed quarter.

Sun T'ien-hua's wife.

Sun Wen-hsiang, son of Sun Ch'ing, brother-in-law of Huang the Fourth, involved in an affray with Feng Huai who dies of his injuries half a month later.

Sung Chiang (fl. 1117–21), Opportune Rain, chivalrous bandit chieftan, leader of a band of thirty-six outlaws in Liang-shan Marsh whose slogan is to "Carry out the Way on Heaven's behalf," slayer of Yen P'o-hsi, rescues Wu Yüeh-niang when she is captured by the bandits of Ch'ing-feng Stronghold and Wang Ying wants to make her his wife, eventually surrenders to Chang Shu-yeh and accepts the offer of a government amnesty.

Sung Ch'iao-nien (1047–1113), father-in-law of Ts'ai Yu, father of Sung Sheng-ch'ung, protégé of Ts'ai Ching, appointed regional investigating censor of Shantung to replace Tseng Hsiao-hsü, entertained by Hsi-men Ch'ing who presents him periodically with lavish bribes in return for which he gets Miao Ch'ing off the hook and does him numerous other illicit favors, rewarded for his part in facilitating the notorious Flower and Rock Convoys and the construction of the Mount Ken Imperial Park.

Sung Hui-lien, Chin-lien, daughter of Sung Jen, formerly maidservant in the household of Assistant Prefect Ts'ai who takes sexual advantage of her; sacked for colluding with her mistress in a case of adultery; marries the cook Chiang Ts'ung who is stabbed to death in a brawl; second wife of Lai-wang; carries on a clandestine affair with Hsi-men Ch'ing that soon becomes public knowledge; after Lai-wang is framed for attempted murder and driven out of the household she suffers from remorse and commits suicide.

Sung Hui-lien's reincarnation. See Chu family of the Eastern Capital.

Sung Hui-lien's maternal aunt.

Sung Jen, father of Sung Hui-lien, coffin seller in Ch'ing-ho who accuses Hsi-men Ch'ing of driving his daughter to suicide but is given such a beating by the corrupt magistrate Li Ta-t'ien that he dies of his wounds.

Sung Sheng-ch'ung (fl. early 12th century), son of Sung Ch'iao-nien, elder brother of Ts'ai Yu's wife, née Sung, regional investigating censor of Shensi suborned into traducing Tseng Hsiao-hsü by Ts'ai Ching.

Sung Te, commits adultery with Ms. Chou, the widowed second wife of his father-in-law, for which Hsi-men Ch'ing sentences them both to death by strangulation.

Sung Te's father-in-law, deceased husband of Ms. Chou.

Sung Te's mother-in-law, deceased mother of Sung Te's wife.

Sung Te's wife.

Sung T'ui, eunuch rewarded for his part in facilitating the notorious Flower and Rock Convoys and the construction of the Mount Ken Imperial Park.

Ta T'ien-tao, prefect of Tung-ch'ang.

Tai-an, Hsi-men An, favorite page boy of Hsi-men Ch'ing and his sedulous understudy in the arts of roguery and dissimulation; manages to stay on the right side of everyone with the exception of Wu Yüeh-niang who periodically berates him for his duplicity; married to Hsiao-yü after the death of Hsi-men Ch'ing when Wu Yüeh-niang discovers them in flagrante delicto; remains with Wu Yüeh-niang and supports her in her old age in return for which he is given the name Hsi-men An and inherits what is left of Hsi-men Ch'ing's property and social position.

T'ai-tsung, emperor of the Chin dynasty (r. 1123–35).

T'an Chen (fl. early 12th century), eunuch military commander with the concurrent rank of censor-in-chief, appointed to replace T'ung Kuan in command of the defense of the northern frontier against the Chin army.

T'ang Pao. See Lai-pao.

Tao-chien, Stand-hard, abbot of the Temple of Eternal Felicity at Wu-li Yüan outside the South Gate of Ch'ing-ho.

T'ao, Crud-crawler, an elderly resident of Ch'ing-ho who is renowned for having sexually molested all three of his daughters-in-law.

T'ao-hua, maidservant in the Star of Joy Bordello in Ch'ing-ho.

T'ao, Old Mother, licensed go-between in Ch'ing-ho who represents Li Kung-pi in his courtship of Meng Yü-lou.

Temple of the Jade Emperor outside the East Gate of Ch'ing-ho, lector of.

Teng, Midwife, called in by Ying Po-chüeh when his concubine, Ch'un-hua, bears him a son.

Third Lady. See Cho Tiu-erh and Meng Yü-lou.

Three-inch Mulberry-bark Manikin. See Wu Chih.

Ti Ssu-pin, Turbid Ti, vice-magistrate of Yang-ku district who locates the corpse of Miao T'ien-hsiu after his murder by Miao Ch'ing.

Ti, Turbid. See Ti Ssu-pin.

Tiao the Seventh, concubine of Miao T'ien-hsiu, formerly a singing girl from a brothel on the Yang-chou docks, carries on an affair with her husband's servant, Miao Ch'ing, the discovery of which leads to the beating of Miao Ch'ing and the murder of Miao T'ien-hsiu in revenge.

T'ien Chiu-kao, battalion commander rewarded for his part in facilitating the notorious Flower and Rock Convoys and the construction of the Mount Ken Imperial Park.

T'ien-fu. See Ch'in-t'ung.

T'ien-hsi, senior page boy in the household of Hua Tzu-hsü and Li P'ing-erh who absconds with five taels of silver when his master takes to his sickbed and vanishes without a trace.

T'ien Hu, bandit chieftan active in the Hopei area.

Ting, Director, Wu K'ai's predecessor as director of the State Farm Battalion in Ch'ing-ho, cashiered for corruption by Hou Meng.

Ting, Mr., father of Ting the Second, silk merchant from Hang-chou.

Ting the Second, Ting Shuang-ch'iao, son of Mr. Ting, friend of Ch'en Liang-huai, a silk merchant from Hang-chou who patronizes Li Kuei-chieh while on a visit to Ch'ing-ho and hides under the bed when Hsi-men Ch'ing discovers their liaison and smashes up the Verdant Spring Bordello.

Ting Shuang-ch'iao. See Ting the Second.

Ting the Southerner, wine merchant in Ch'ing-ho from whom Hsi-men Ch'ing buys forty jugs of Ho-ch'ing wine on credit.

Tou Chien (d. 1127), superintendant of the Capital Training Divisions and capital security commissioner.

Tower of Jade. See Meng Yü-lou.

Ts'ai, Assistant Prefect, resident of Ch'ing-ho from whose household Sung Hui-lien is expelled for colluding with her mistress in a case of adultery.

Ts'ai, Assistant Prefect's wife.

Ts'ai Ching (1046–1126), father of Ts'ai Yu, Ts'ai T'iao, Ts'ai T'ao, and Ts'ai Hsiu, father-in-law of Liang Shih-chieh, left grand councilor, grand academician of the Hall for Veneration of Governance, grand preceptor, minister of personnel, Duke of Lu, most powerful minister at the court of Emperor Hui-tsung, impeached by Yü-wen Hsü-chung, patron and adoptive father of Ts'ai Yün and Hsi-men Ch'ing, first of the Six Traitors impeached by Ch'en Tung.

Ts'ai Ching's mansion in the Eastern Capital, gatekeepers of.

Ts'ai Ching's mansion in the Eastern Capital, page boy in.

Ts'ai Ching's wife.

Ts'ai family of Yen-chou in Shantung, family of which Hsi-men Hsiao-ko is alleged to have been a son in his previous incarnation.

Ts'ai Hsing (fl. early 12th century), son of Ts'ai Yu, appointed director of the Palace Administration as a reward for his father's part in facilitating the notorious Flower and Rock Convoys and the construction of the Mount Ken Imperial Park.

Ts'ai Hsiu, ninth son of Ts'ai Ching, prefect of Chiu-chiang.

Ts'ai, Midwife, presides over the deliveries of Li P'ing-erh's son, Hsi-men Kuan-ko, and Wu Yüeh-niang's son, Hsi-men Hsiao-ko.

Ts'ai T'ao (d. after 1147), fifth son of Ts'ai Ching.

Ts'ai T'iao (d. after 1137), fourth son of Ts'ai Ching, consort of Princess Mao-te.

Ts'ai Yu (1077–1126), eldest son of Ts'ai Ching, son-in-law of Sung Ch'iao-nien, brother-in-law of Sung Sheng-ch'ung, father of Ts'ai Hsing, academi-cian of the Hall of Auspicious Harmony, minister of rites, superintendent of the Temple of Supreme Unity, rewarded with the title grand guardian of the heir apparent for his part in facilitating the notorious Flower and Rock Convoys and the construction of the Mount Ken Imperial Park, executed by order of Emperor Ch'in-tsung after the fall of Ts'ai Ching and his faction.

Ts'ai Yu's son. See Ts'ai Hsing.

Ts'ai Yu's wife, née Sung, daughter of Sung Ch'iao-nien, younger sister of Sung Sheng-ch'ung.

Ts'ai Yün, awarded first place in the *chin-shih* examinations in place of An Ch'en when the latter is displaced for being the younger brother of the proscribed An Tun, becomes a protégé and adopted son of Ts'ai Ching, appointed proofreader in the Palace Library, is patronized by Hsi-men Ch'ing; after being impeached by Ts'ao Ho he is appointed salt-control censor of the Liang-Huai region where his illicit favors to Hsi-men Ch'ing abet his profitable speculations in the salt trade.

Ts'ai Yün's mother.

Tsang Pu-hsi, docket officer on the staff of the district yamen in Ch'ing-ho.

Ts'ao Ho, censor who impeaches Ts'ai Yün and thirteen others from the Histori-ography Institute who had passed the *chin-shih* examinations in the same year.

Tseng Hsiao-hsü (1049–1127), son of Tseng Pu, regional investigating censor of Shantung, reopens the case of Miao T'ien-hsiu's murder at the request of Huang Mei and arrives at the truth only to have his memorial suppressed when Hsi-men Ch'ing and Hsia Yen-ling bribe Ts'ai Ching to intervene; submits a memorial to the throne criticizing the policies of Ts'ai Ching that so enrages the prime minister that he suborns his daughter-in-law's brother, Sung Sheng-ch'ung, into framing him on trumped up charges as a result of which he is deprived of his office and banished to the farthest southern extremity of the country.

Tseng Pu (1036–1107), father of Tseng Hsiao-hsü.

Tso Shun, professional boy actor in Ch'ing-ho.

Ts'ui-erh, maidservant of Sun Hsüeh-o.

Ts'ui-hua, junior maidservant of P'ang Ch'un-mei after she becomes the wife of Chou Hsiu.

Ts'ui Pen, nephew of Ch'iao Hung, husband of Big Sister Tuan, employee, manager, and partner in several of Hsi-men Ch'ing's enterprises.

Ts'ui Pen's mother, Ch'iao Hung's elder sister.

Ts'ui, Privy Councilor. See Ts'ui Shou-yü.

Ts'ui Shou-yü, Privy Councilor Ts'ui, relative of Hsia Yen-ling with whom he stays on his visit to the Eastern Capital.

Tsung-mei. See Ch'en Ching-chi.

Tsung-ming. See Chin Tsung-ming.

Tsung Tse (1059–1128), general-in-chief of the Southern Sung armies who retakes parts of Shantung and Hopei from the Chin invaders on behalf of Emperor Kao-tsung.

Tu the Third, maternal cousin of Ying Po-chüeh.

Tu the Third's page boy.

Tu the Third's wife.

Tu Tzu-ch'un, privy councilor under a previous reign living in retirement in the northern quarter of Ch'ing-ho, engaged by Hsi-men Ch'ing to indite the inscription on Li P'ing-erh's funeral banderole.

Tuan, Big Sister, wife of Ts'ui Pen.

Tuan, Big Sister's father.

Tuan, Consort. See Feng, Consort.

Tuan, Half-baked. See Tuan Mien.

Tuan Mien, Half-baked Tuan, one of the "cribbers" in the licensed quarter of Ch'ing-ho patronized by Hsi-men Ch'ing.

Tuan, Old Mother, waiting woman in Lady Lin's household whose residence in the rear of the compound is used as a rendezvous by her lovers.

Tung the Cat. See Tung Chin-erh.

Tung Chiao-erh, singing girl from the Tung Family Brothel on Second Street in the licensed quarter of Ch'ing-ho who spends the night with Ts'ai Yün at Hsi-men Ch'ing's behest.

Tung Chin-erh, Tung the Cat, singing girl from the Tung Family Brothel on Second Street in the licensed quarter of Ch'ing-ho, patronized by Chang Mao-te.

Tung Sheng, clerical subofficial on the staff of Wang Fu.

Tung Yü-hsien, singing girl from the Tung Family Brothel on Second Street in the licensed quarter of Ch'ing-ho.

T'ung Kuan (1054–1126), eunuch military officer beaten up by Wu Sung in a drunken brawl, uncle of T'ung T'ien-yin, military affairs commissioner, defender-in-chief of the Palace Command, Commandery Prince of Kuang-yang, one of the Six Traitors impeached by Ch'en Tung.

T'ung Kuan's nephew. See T'ung T'ien-yin.

T'ung, Prefectural Judge, prefectural judge of Tung-p'ing who conducts the preliminary hearing in the case of the affray between Feng Huai and Sun Wen-hsiang.

T'ung T'ien-yin, nephew of T'ung Kuan, commander of the guard, director of the Office of Herds in the Inner and Outer Imperial Demesnes of the Court of the Imperial Stud.

Turf-protecting Tiger. See Liu the Second.

Tutor employed in the household of Miao Ch'ing.

Tz'u-hui Temple, abbot of, recovers the corpse of the murdered Miao T'ien-hsiu and buries it on the bank of the river west of Ch'ing-ho where it is discovered by Ti Ssu-pin.

Vase. See Li P'ing-erh.

Waiter in My Own Tavern in Lin-ch'ing.

Wan-yen Tsung-han (1079–1136), Nien-mo-ho, nephew of Emperor T'ai-tsu (r. 1115–23) the founder of the Chin dynasty, commander of the Chin army that occupies K'ai-feng and takes Retired Emperor Hui-tsung and Emperor Ch'in-tsung into captivity.

Wan-yen Tsung-wang (d. 1127), Wo-li-pu, second son of Emperor T'ai-tsu (r. 1115–23) the founder of the Chin dynasty, associate commander of the Chin army that occupies K'ai-feng and takes Retired Emperor Hui-tsung and Emperor Ch'in-tsung into captivity, kills Chou Hsiu with an arrow through the throat.

Wang, Attendant, official on the staff of the Prince of Yün to whom Han Tao-kuo appeals through Hsi-men Ch'ing and Jen Hou-ch'i to be allowed to commute his hereditary corvée labor obligation to payments in money or goods.

Wang, Butcher, elder brother of Wang Liu-erh, husband of Sow Wang whose daughter is betrothed to Seng-pao.

Wang Ch'ao, son of Dame Wang, apprenticed to a merchant from the Huai River region from whom he steals a hundred taels entrusted to him for the purchase of stock, returns to Ch'ing-ho, and uses it as capital to buy two donkeys and set up a flour mill, becomes a casual lover of P'an Chin-lien while she is in Dame Wang's house awaiting purchase as a concubine.

Wang Chen, second son of Wang Hsüan, government student in the prefectural school.

Wang Ch'ien, eldest son of Wang Hsüan, hereditary battalion commander of the local Horse Pasturage Battalion of the Court of the Imperial Stud.

Wang Chin-ch'ing. See Wang Shen.

Wang Ching, younger brother of Wang Liu-erh, page boy employed in the household of Hsi-men Ch'ing as a replacement for Shu-t'ung after he absconds, sodomized by Hsi-men Ch'ing during his visit to the Eastern Capital, expelled from the household by Wu Yüeh-niang after the death of Hsi-men Ch'ing.

Wang Ching-ch'ung (d. 949), military commissioner of T'ai-yüan, Commandery Prince of Pin-yang, ancestor of Wang I-hsüan.

Wang Ch'ing, bandit chieftan active in the Huai-hsi area.

Wang Chu, elder brother of Wang Hsiang, professional boy actor in Ch'ing-ho.

Wang, Consort (d. 1117), a consort of Emperor Hui-tsung, mother of Chao K'ai, the Prince of Yün, related to Wang the Second.

Wang, Dame, mother of Wang Ch'ao, proprietress of a teahouse next door to Wu Chih's house on Amythest Street on the west side of the district yamen in Ch'ing-ho who is also active as a go-between and procuress; go-between who proposes the match between Hsi-men Ch'ing and Wu Yüeh-niang; inventor of the elaborate scheme by which Hsi-men Ch'ing seduces P'an Chin-lien; suggests the poisoning of her next door neighbor Wu Chih and helps P'an Chin-lien carry it out; intervenes on behalf of Ho the Tenth when he is accused of fencing stolen goods with the result that Hsi-men Ch'ing gets him off the hook and executes an innocent monk in his stead; after the death of Hsi-men Ch'ing, when Wu Yüeh-niang discovers P'an Chin-lien's affair with Ch'en Ching-chi, she expels her from the household and consigns her to Dame Wang, who entertains bids from Magnate Ho, Chang Mao-te, Ch'en Ching-chi, and Chou Hsiu before finally selling her to Wu Sung for a hundred taels of silver plus a five tael brokerage fee; that same night she is decapitated by Wu Sung after he has disemboweled P'an Chin-lien.

Wang, Dame's deceased husband, father of Wang Ch'ao, dies when she is thirty-five.

Wang, Dame's son. See Wang Ch'ao.

Wang, distaff relative of the imperial family. See Wang the Second.

Wang family of Cheng-chou, family into which Hsi-men Kuan-ko is reincarnated as a son.

Wang family of the Eastern Capital, family into which Ch'en Ching-chi is reincarnated as a son.

Wang family of Pin-chou, family in which Li P'ing-erh is alleged to have been formerly incarnated as a son.

Wang the First, Auntie, madam of the Wang Family Brothel in Yang-chou.

Wang Fu (1079–1126), minister of war impeached by Yü-wen Hsü-chung.

Wang Fu's wife and children.

Wang Hai-feng. See Wang Ssu-feng.

Wang Han, servant in the household of Han Tao-kuo and Wang Liu-erh.

Wang Hsiang, younger brother of Wang Chu, professional boy actor in Ch'ing-ho.

Wang Hsien, employee of Hsi-men Ch'ing who accompanies Lai-pao on a buying trip to Nan-ching.

Wang Hsüan, Layman of Apricot Hermitage, father of Wang Ch'ien and Wang Chen, friend of Ch'en Hung, retired philanthropist who provides aid to Ch'en Ching-chi three times after he is reduced to beggary and who recommends him to Abbot Jen of the Yen-kung Temple in Lin-ch'ing.

Wang Hsüan's manager, in charge of a pawnshop on the street front of his residence.

Wang Huan (fl. early 12th century), commander-general of the Hopei region who leads the forces of Wei-po against the Chin invaders.

Wang I-hsüan, Imperial Commissioner Wang, descendant of Wang Ching-ch'ung, deceased husband of Lady Lin, father of Wang Ts'ai.

Wang I-hsüan's wife. See Lady Lin.

Wang I-hsüan's son. See Wang Ts'ai.

Wang, Imperial Commissioner. See Wang I-hsüan.

Wang K'uan, head of the mutual security unit for Ch'en Ching-chi's residence in Ch'ing-ho.

Wang Lien, henchman on the domestic staff of Wang Fu.

Wang Liu-erh, Wang the Sixth, one of the female protagonists of the novel, younger sister of Butcher Wang, elder sister of Wang Ching, wife of Han Tao-kuo, mother of Han Ai-chieh; paramour of her brother-in-law, Han the Second, whom she marries after her husband's death, of Hsi-men Ch'ing, to whose death from sexual exhaustion she is a major contributor, and of Magnate Ho, whose property in Hu-chou she inherits.

Wang Liu-erh's niece, daughter of Butcher Wang and Sow Wang, betrothed to Seng-pao, the son of Lai-pao and Hui-hsiang.

Wang Luan, proprietor of the Great Tavern on Lion Street in Ch'ing-ho who witnesses Wu Sung's fatal attack on Li Wai-ch'uan.

Wang, Nun, Buddhist nun from the Kuan-yin Nunnery in Ch'ing-ho which is patronized by Wu Yüeh-niang, frequently invited to recite Buddhist "precious scrolls" to Wu Yüeh-niang and her guests, recommends Nun Hsüeh to Wu Yüeh-niang who takes her fertility potion and conceives Hsi-men Hsiao-ko, later quarrels with Nun Hsüeh over the division of alms from Li P'ing-erh and Wu Yüeh-niang.

Wang, Old Mrs., neighbor of Yün Li-shou in Chi-nan who appears in Wu Yüeh-niang's nightmare.

Wang, Old Sister, singing girl working out of My Own Tavern in Lin-ch'ing.

Wang Ping (d. 1126), commander-general of the Kuan-tung region who leads the forces of Fen-chiang against the Chin invaders.

Wang Po-ju, proprietor of an inn on the docks in Yang-chou recommended to Han Tao-kuo, Lai-pao, and Ts'ui Pen by Hsi-men Ch'ing as a good place to stay.

Wang Po-ju's father, friend of Hsi-men Ch'ing's father, Hsi-men Ta.

Wang Po-yen (1069–1141), right assistant administration commissioner of Shantung.

Wang the Second, distaff relative of the imperial family through Consort Wang, landlord of Wu Chih's residence on the west side of Amythest Street in Ch'ing-ho, purchaser of Eunuch Director Hua's mansion on Main Street in An-ch'ing ward of Ch'ing-ho, maintains a private troupe of twenty actors that he sometimes lends to Hsi-men Ch'ing to entertain his guests.

Wang Shen (c. 1048–c. 1103), Wang Chin-ch'ing, commandant-escort and director of the Court of the Imperial Clan, consort of the second daughter of Emperor Ying-tsung (r. 1063–67).

Wang Shih-ch'i, prefect of Ch'ing-chou in Shantung.

Wang the Sixth. See Wang Liu-erh.

Wang, Sow, wife of Butcher Wang whose daughter is betrothed to Seng-pao.

Wang Ssu-feng, Wang Hai-feng, salt merchant from Yang-chou who is set free from prison in Ts'ang-chou by Hou Meng, the grand coordinator of Shantung, as a result of Hsi-men Ch'ing's intervention with Ts'ai Ching.

Wang the Third. See Wang Ts'ai.

Wang Ts'ai (1078–1118), Wang the Third, feckless and dissolute third son of Wang I-hsüan and Lady Lin, married to the niece of Huang Ching-ch'en, tries unsuccessfully to borrow three hundred taels of silver from Hsü Pu-yü in order to purchase a position in the Military School, pawns his wife's possessions in order to pursue various singing girls in the licensed quarter including those patronized by Hsi-men Ch'ing, tricked into becoming the adopted son of Hsi-men Ch'ing during his intrigue with Lady Lin, continues his affair with Li Kuei-chieh after the death of Hsi-men Ch'ing.

Wang Ts'ai's wife, née Huang, niece of Huang Ching-ch'en.

Wang Tsu-tao (d. 1108), minister of personnel.

Wang Tung-ch'iao, traveling merchant entertained by Han Tao-kuo in Yang-chou.

Wang, Usher, official in the Court of State Ceremonial who offers the sixteen-year-old wife of his runaway retainer for sale as a maidservant through Old Mother Feng.

Wang, Usher's runaway retainer.

Wang, Usher's runaway retainer's wife.

Wang Wei, supreme commander of the Capital Training Divisions, Duke of Lung-hsi, granted the title of grand mentor for his part in facilitating the notorious Flower and Rock Convoys and the construction of the Mount Ken Imperial Park.

Wang Ying, Short-legged Tiger, second outlaw leader of the Ch'ing-feng Stronghold on Ch'ing-feng Mountain who wants to make Wu Yüeh-niang his wife when she is captured by his band but is prevented from doing so by Sung Chiang.

Wang Yu, commander of a training division rewarded for his part in facilitating the notorious Flower and Rock Convoys and the construction of the Mount Ken Imperial Park.

Wang Yü, subofficial functionary on the domestic staff of Ts'ai Ching deputed by Chai Ch'ien to carry a message of condolence to Hsi-men Ch'ing and a personal letter from Han Ai-chieh to Han Tao-kuo and Wang Liu-erh.

Wang Yü-chih, singing girl from the Wang Family Brothel in Yang-chou patronized by Han Tao-kuo.

Wei Ch'eng-hsün, battalion commander rewarded for his part in facilitating the notorious Flower and Rock Convoys and the construction of the Mount Ken Imperial Park.

Wei Ts'ung-erh, a taciturn chair-bearer in Ch'ing-ho, partner of Chang Ch'uan-erh.

Wen, Auntie, mother of Wen T'ang, go-between in Ch'ing-ho who represents Ch'en Ching-chi's family at the time of his betrothal to Hsi-men Ta-chieh, resident of Wang Family Alley on the South Side of town, active in promoting pilgrimages to Mount T'ai, patronized by Lady Lin for whom she acts as a procuress in her adulterous affairs including that with Hsi-men Ch'ing, involved with Auntie Hsüeh in arranging the betrothal between Chang Mao-te's son and Eunuch Director Hsü's niece.

Wen Ch'en, one of the officials from the Ch'ing-ho Guard who comes to Hsi-men Ch'ing's residence to offer a sacrifice to the soul of Li P'ing-erh after her death.

Wen Hsi, military director-in-chief of Yen-chou in Shantung.

Wen, Licentiate. See Wen Pi-ku.

Wen, Pedant. See Wen Pi-ku.

Wen Pi-ku, Warm-buttocks Wen, Pedant Wen, Licentiate Wen, pederast recommended to Hsi-men Ch'ing by his fellow licentiate Ni P'eng to be his social secretary, housed across the street from Hsi-men Ch'ing's residence in the property formerly belonging to Ch'iao Hung, divulges Hsi-men Ch'ing's private correspondence to Ni P'eng who shares it with Hsia Yenling, sodomizes Hua-t'ung against his will and is expelled from the Hsi-men household when his indiscretions are exposed.

Wen Pi-ku's mother-in-law.

Wen Pi-ku's wife.

Wen T'ang, son of Auntie Wen.

Wen T'ang's wife.

Wen, Warm-buttocks. See Wen Pi-ku.

Weng the Eighth, criminal boatman who, along with his partner Ch'en the Third, murders Miao T'ien-hsiu.

What a Whopper. See Hsieh Ju-huang.

Wo-li-pu. See Wan-yen Tsung-wang.

Wu, Abbot. See Wu Tsung-che.

Wu, Battalion Commander, father of Wu K'ai, Wu the Second, Wu Yüeh-niang's elder sister, and Wu Yüeh-niang, hereditary battalion commander of the Ch'ing-ho Left Guard.

Wu, Captain. See Wu Sung.

Wu Ch'ang-chiao, Longfoot Wu, madam of the brothel in the Southern Entertainment Quarter of Ch'ing-ho patronized by P'ing-an after he absconds from the Hsi-men household with jewelry stolen from the pawnshop.

Wu Ch'ang-chiao's husband.

Wu Chih, Wu the Elder, Three-inch Mulberry-bark Manikin, elder brother of Wu Sung, father of Ying-erh by his deceased first wife, husband of P'an Chin-lien, simple-minded dwarf, native of Yang-ku district in Shantung who moves to the district town of Ch'ing-ho because of a famine and makes his living by peddling steamed wheat cakes on the street, cuckolded by P'an Chin-lien with his landlord, Mr. Chang, and then with Hsi-men Ch'ing, catches P'an Chin-lien and Hsi-men Ch'ing in flagrante delicto in Dame Wang's teahouse but suffers a near-fatal injury when Hsi-men Ch'ing kicks him in the solar plexus, poisoned by P'an Chin-lien with arsenic supplied by Hsi-men Ch'ing.

Wu Chih's daughter. See Ying-erh.

Wu Chih's deceased first wife, mother of Ying-erh.

Wu Chih's second wife. See P'an Chin-lien.

Wu the Elder. See Wu Chih.

Wu the Fourth, Auntie, madam of the Wu Family Bordello on the back alley in the licensed quarter of Ch'ing-ho.

Wu, Heartless. See Wu Tien-en.

Wu Hsün, secretary of the Bureau of Irrigation and Transportation in the Ministry of Works, rewarded for his part in facilitating the notorious Flower and Rock Convoys and the construction of the Mount Ken Imperial Park.

Wu Hui, younger brother of Wu Yin-erh, actor and musician from the Wu Family Bordello on the back alley in the licensed quarter of Ch'ing-ho.

Wu, Immortal. See Wu Shih.

Wu K'ai, eldest son of Battalion Commander Wu, elder brother of Wu the Second, Wu Yüeh-niang's elder sister, and Wu Yüeh-niang, father of Wu Shun-ch'en, brother-in-law of Hsi-men Ch'ing, inherits the position of battalion commander of the Ch'ing-ho Left Guard upon the death of his father, deputed to repair the local Charity Granary, promoted to the rank of assistant commander of the Ch'ing-ho Guard in charge of the local State Farm Battalion as a result of Hsi-men Ch'ing's influence with Sung Ch'iao-nien, accompanies Wu Yüeh-niang on her pilgrimage to Mount T'ai after the death of Hsi-men Ch'ing and is instrumental in rescuing her from attempted rape by Yin T'ien-hsi.

Wu K'ai's son. See Wu Shun-ch'en.

Wu K'ai's wife, Sister-in-law Wu, mother of Wu Shun-ch'en, sister-in-law of
Hsi-men Ch'ing and a frequent guest in his household.

Wu, Longfoot. See Wu Ch'ang-chiao.

Wu the Second, second son of Battalion Commander Wu, younger brother
of Wu K'ai, second elder brother of Wu Yüeh-niang, brother-in-law of Hsi-
men Ch'ing and manager of his silk store on Lion Street; engages in hanky-
panky with Li Chiao-erh for which he is denied access to the household by
Wu Yüeh-niang when it is discovered after the death of Hsi-men Ch'ing
although he continues to manage the silk store and later, along with Tai-
an, the wholesale pharmaceutical business; accompanies Wu Yüeh-niang,
Tai-an, Hsiao-yü, and Hsi-men Hsiao-ko when they flee the invading Chin
armies to seek refuge with Yün Li-shou in Chi-nan; ten days after the cli-
mactic encounter with P'u-ching in the Temple of Eternal Felicity and
Wu Yüeh-niang's relinquishment of Hsi-men Hsiao-ko to a life of Buddhist
celibacy he accompanies Wu Yüeh-niang, Tai-an, and Hsiao-yü back to
their now truncated household in Ch'ing-ho.

Wu the Second. See Wu Sung.

Wu the Second's wife, wife of Wu Yüeh-niang's second elder brother.

Wu Shih, Immortal Wu, Taoist physiognomist introduced to Hsi-men Ch'ing
by Chou Hsiu who accurately foretells his fortune and those of his wife and
concubines as well as Hsi-men Ta-chieh and P'ang Ch'un-mei; when Hsi-
men Ch'ing is on his deathbed he is called in again and reports that there
is no hope for him.

Wu Shih's servant boy.

Wu Shun-ch'en, son of Wu K'ai, husband of Third Sister Cheng.

Wu, Sister-in-law. See Wu K'ai's wife.

Wu Sung, Wu the Second, Captain Wu, younger brother of Wu Chih,
brother-in-law of P'an Chin-lien; impulsive and implacable exponent of the
code of honor; becomes a fugitive from the law for beating up T'ung Kuan
in a drunken brawl; slays a tiger in single-handed combat while on his way
to visit his brother and is made police captain in Ch'ing-ho for this feat;
rejects attempted seduction by P'an Chin-lien and tells her off in no uncertain terms; delivers Li Ta-t'ien's illicit gains from his magistracy to the safe
keeping of Chu Mien in the Eastern Capital; returns to Ch'ing-ho and
mistakenly kills Li Wai-ch'uan while seeking to avenge the murder of his
brother; is sentenced to military exile in Meng-chou where he is befriended
by Shih En and helps him in his struggle with Chiang Men-shen for control
of the Happy Forest Tavern; is framed by Military Director-in-chief Chang
with the help of his concubine, Chiang Yü-lan, the younger sister of Chiang
Men-shen, in revenge for which he murders his two guards and the entire
households of Military Director-in-chief Chang and Chiang Men-shen; sets
out for An-p'ing Stockade with a hundred taels of silver and a letter of
recommendation from Shih En but is enabled by a general amnesty to
return to Ch'ing-ho where he buys P'an Chin-lien from Dame Wang for a

hundred taels of silver and disembowels her to avenge the death of his brother; once more a fugitive he disguises himself as a Buddhist ascetic with the help of the criminal innkeepers Chang Ch'ing and his wife and goes to join Sung Chiang's band of outlaws in Liang-shan Marsh.

Wu-t'ai, Mount, monk from, who solicits alms from Wu Yüeh-niang for the repair of his temple.

Wu Tien-en, Heartless Wu, originally a Yin-yang master on the staff of the district yamen in Ch'ing-ho who has been removed from his post for cause; makes his living by hanging around in front of the yamen and acting as a guarantor for loans to local officials and functionaries; crony of Hsi-men Ch'ing; member of the brotherhood of ten; manager employed by Hsi-men Ch'ing in various of his enterprises; misrepresents himself as Hsi-men Ch'ing's brother-in-law and is appointed to the post of station master of the Ch'ing-ho Postal Relay Station in return for his part in delivering birthday presents from Hsi-men Ch'ing to Ts'ai Ching; receives an interest-free loan of one hundred taels from Hsi-men Ch'ing to help cover the expenses of assuming office; promoted to the position of police chief of a suburb of Ch'ing-ho after the death of Hsi-men Ch'ing he apprehends the runaway P'ing-an and coerces him into giving false testimony that Wu Yüeh-niang has been engaged in hanky-panky with Tai-an, but when Wu Yüeh-niang appeals to P'ang Ch'un-mei he is dragged before Chou Hsiu's higher court and thoroughly humiliated.

Wu Tsung-che, Abbot Wu, head priest of the Taoist Temple of the Jade Emperor outside the East Gate of Ch'ing-ho, presides over the elaborate Taoist ceremony at which Hsi-men Kuan-ko is made an infant Taoist priest with the religious name Wu Ying-yüan, later officiates at funeral observances for Li P'ing-erh and Hsi-men Ch'ing.

Wu Yin-erh, Silver, elder sister of Wu Hui, singing girl from the Wu Family Bordello on the back alley of the licensed quarter in Ch'ing-ho, sweetheart of Hua Tzu-hsü, adopted daughter of Li P'ing-erh.

Wu Ying-yüan. See Hsi-men Kuan-ko.

Wu Yüeh-niang, Moon Lady, one of the female protagonists of the novel, daughter of Battalion Commander Wu, younger sister of Wu K'ai, Wu the Second, and an elder sister; second wife and First Lady of Hsi-men Ch'ing who marries her after the death of his first wife, née Ch'en, in a match proposed by Dame Wang; stepmother of Hsi-men Ta-chieh, mother of Hsi-men Hsiao-ko; a pious, credulous, and conventional Buddhist laywoman who constantly invites Nun Wang and Nun Hsüeh to the household to recite "precious scrolls" on the themes of salvation, retribution, and reincarnation, who has good intentions but is generally ineffectual at household management and is not a good judge of character; colludes with Hsi-men Ch'ing in taking secret possession of Li P'ing-erh's ill-gotten property but quarrels with him over admitting her to the household; suffers a miscarriage

but later takes Nun Hsüeh's fertility potion and conceives Hsi-men Hsiao-
ko who is born at the very moment of Hsi-men Ch'ing's death; thoughtlessly
betroths both Kuan-ko and Hsiao-ko to inappropriate partners while they
are still babes in arms; makes a pilgrimage to Mount T'ai after Hsi-men
Ch'ing's death and narrowly escapes an attempted rape by Yin T'ien-hsi
and capture by the bandits on Ch'ing-feng Mountain; expels P'an Chin-
lien, P'ang Ch'un-mei, and Ch'en Ching-chi from the household when
she belatedly discovers their perfidy but is unable to cope effectively with
the declining fortunes of the family; forced to seek the assistance of P'ang
Ch'un-mei when she is threatened by Wu Tien-en she has no alternative
but to accept the condescension of her former maidservant; while fleeing
from the invading Chin armies to seek refuge with Yün Li-shou in Chi-nan
she encounters P'u-ching and spends the night in the Temple of Eternal
Felicity where she dreams that Yün Li-shou threatens her with rape if she
refuses to marry him; still traumatized by this nightmare, she allows P'u-
ching to persuade her that Hsiao-ko is the reincarnation of Hsi-men Ch'ing
and relinquishes her teenage son to a life of Buddhist celibacy without so
much as asking his opinion; on returning safely to Ch'ing-ho she adopts Tai-
an as her husband's heir, renaming him Hsi-men An, and lives in reduced
circumstances, presiding over a truncated household, until dying a natural
death at the age of sixty-nine.

Wu Yüeh-niang's elder sister, wife of Brother-in-law Shen.

Yang, Aunt, widow of Crooked-head Sun, paternal aunt of Yang Tsung-hsi
and Yang Tsung-pao, forceful advocate of Meng Yü-lou's remarriage to Hsi-
men Ch'ing after the latter offers her a hundred taels of silver for her support, quarrels with Chang Lung when he tries to prevent this match.

Yang Chien (d. 1121), Commander Yang, eunuch military officer related to
Ch'en Hung by marriage, commander in chief of the Imperial Guard in
the Eastern Capital, bribed by Hsi-men Ch'ing to intervene on his behalf
against Wu Sung and in favor of Hua Tzu-hsü, impeached by Yü-wen Hsü-
chung, reported in a letter from Chai Ch'ien to Hsi-men Ch'ing to have
died in prison in 1117.

Yang, Commander. See Yang Chien.

Yang the Elder. See Yang Kuang-yen.

Yang Erh-feng, second son of Yang Pu-lai and his wife, née Pai, younger
brother of Yang Kuang-yen, a gambler and tough guy who scares off Ch'en
Ching-chi when he tries to recover the half shipload of property that Yang
Kuang-yen had stolen from him.

Yang Kuang-yen, Yang the Elder, Iron Fingernail, native of Nobottom ward
in Carryoff village of Makebelieve district in Nonesuch subprefecture, son
of Yang Pu-lai and his wife, née Pai, disciple of the Barefaced Adept from
whom he acquires the art of lying, husband of Miss Died-of-fright, con man

employed by Ch'en Ching-chi who absconds with half a shipload of his property while he is in Yen-chou trying to shake down Meng Yü-lou and invests it in the Hsieh Family Tavern in Lin-ch'ing only to lose everything when Ch'en Ching-chi sues him with the backing of Chou Hsiu and takes over ownership of the tavern.

Yang Kuang-yen's father. See Yang Pu-lai.

Yang Kuang-yen's mother, née Pai.

Yang Kuang-yen's page boy.

Yang Kuang-yen's wife. See Died-of-fright, Miss.

Yang, Poor-parent. See Yang Pu-lai.

Yang, Prefect. See Yang Shih.

Yang Pu-lai, Poor-parent Yang, father of Yang Kuang-yen and Yang Erh-feng, brother-in-law of Yao the Second.

Yang Sheng, factotum on the domestic staff of Yang Chien.

Yang Shih (1053–1135), Prefect Yang, prefect of K'ai-feng, protégé of Ts'ai Ching, agrees under pressure from Ts'ai Ching and Yang Chien to treat Hua Tzu-hsü leniently when he is sued over the division of Eunuch Director Hua's property by his brothers Hua Tzu-yu, Hua Tzu-kuang, and Hua Tzu-hua.

Yang T'ing-p'ei, battalion commander rewarded for his part in facilitating the notorious Flower and Rock Convoys and the construction of the Mount Ken Imperial Park.

Yang Tsung-hsi, deceased first husband of Meng Yü-lou, elder brother of Yang Tsung-pao, nephew on his father's side of Aunt Yang and on his mother's side of Chang Lung, textile merchant residing on Stinkwater Lane outside the South Gate of Ch'ing-ho.

Yang Tsung-hsi's maternal uncle. See Chang Lung.

Yang Tsung-hsi's mother. See Chang Lung's elder sister.

Yang Tsung-hsi's paternal aunt. See Yang, Aunt.

Yang Tsung-pao, younger brother of Yang Tsung-hsi, nephew on his father's side of Aunt Yang and on his mother's side of Chang Lung, brother-in-law of Meng Yü-lou.

Yang Wei-chung (1067–1132), commander-general of the Shansi region who leads the forces of Tse-lu against the Chin invaders.

Yao family from outside the Eastern Capital, poor family into which Sun Hsüeh-o is reincarnated as a daughter.

Yao the Second, brother-in-law of Yang Pu-lai, neighbor of Wu Chih to whom Wu Sung entrusts his orphaned niece Ying-erh when he is condemned to military exile in Meng-chou; gives Ying-erh back to Wu Sung when he returns to Ch'ing-ho five years later only to repossess her after the inquest on P'an Chin-lien's murder when Wu Sung once more becomes a fugitive; later arranges for her marriage.

Yeh the Ascetic, one-eyed illiterate Buddhist ascetic employed as a cook by Abbot Hsiao-yüeh of the Water Moon Monastery outside the South Gate of Ch'ing-ho, physiognomizes Ch'en Ching-chi when he is reduced to penury and working nearby as a day laborer.

Yeh Ch'ien, prefect of Lai-chou in Shantung.

Yeh the Fifth, wife of Pen Ti-ch'uan, mother of Pen Chang-chieh, originally a wet nurse who elopes with her fellow employee Pen Ti-ch'uan, carries on an intermittent affair with Tai-an while at the same time complaisantly accepting the sexual favors of Hsi-men Ch'ing.

Yen the Fourth, neighbor of Han Tao-kuo who informs him of Hsi-men Ch'ing's death when their boats pass each other on the Grand Canal at Lin-ch'ing.

Yen P'o-hsi, singing girl slain by Sung Chiang.

Yen Shun, Brocade Tiger, outlaw chieftan of the Ch'ing-feng Stronghold on Ch'ing-feng Mountain who is persuaded by Sung Chiang to let the captured Wu Yüeh-niang go rather than allowing Wang Ying to make her his wife.

Yin Chih, Good Deed, chief clerk in charge of the files in the Ch'ing-ho office of the Provincial Surveillance Commission who recognizes that Lai-wang has been framed by Hsi-men Ch'ing and manages to get his sentence reduced and to have him treated more leniently.

Yin Ching, vice-minister of the Ministry of Personnel.

Yin Ta-liang, regional investigating censor of Liang-che, rewarded for his part in facilitating the notorious Flower and Rock Convoys and the construction of the Mount Ken Imperial Park.

Yin T'ien-hsi, Year Star Yin, younger brother of Kao Lien's wife, née Yin, dissolute wastrel who takes advantage of his official connections to lord it over the Mount T'ai area with a gang of followers at his disposal, colludes with Shih Po-ts'ai, the corrupt head priest of the Temple of the Goddess of Iridescent Clouds on the summit of Mount T'ai, in attempting to rape Wu Yüeh-niang when she visits the temple on a pilgrimage after the death of Hsi-men Ch'ing; later killed at Sung Chiang's behest by the outlaw, Li K'uei.

Yin, Year Star. See Yin T'ien-hsi.

Ying, Beggar. See Ying Po-chüeh.

Ying-ch'un, disciple of Abbot Wu Tsung-che of the Temple of the Jade Emperor outside the East Gate of Ch'ing-ho.

Ying-ch'un, senior maidservant of Li P'ing-erh who after the death of Hsi-men Ch'ing agrees to be sent to the household of Chai Ch'ien in the Eastern Capital and is raped by Lai-pao on the way.

Ying the Elder, eldest son of the deceased silk merchant Master Ying, elder brother of Ying Po-chüeh, continues to operate his father's silk business in Ch'ing-ho.

Ying the Elder's wife.

Ying-erh, daughter of Wu Chih by his deceased first wife, niece of Wu Sung, much abused stepdaughter of P'an Chin-lien who turns her over to Dame Wang when she marries Hsi-men Ch'ing; repossessed by Wu Sung when he returns from the Eastern Capital after the death of her father; consigned to the care of his neighbor Yao the Second when he is condemned to military exile in Meng-chou after his first abortive attempt to avenge the murder of her father; taken back by Wu Sung on his return to Ch'ing-ho five years later and forced to witness his disembowelment of P'an Chin-lien and decapitation of Dame Wang; repossessed by Yao the Second after the inquest and provided by him with a husband.

Ying, Master, father of Ying the Elder and Ying Po-chüeh, deceased silk merchant of Ch'ing-ho.

Ying Pao, eldest son of Ying Po-chüeh, recommends his friend Lai-yu to Hsi-men Ch'ing who employs him as a servant and changes his name to Lai-chüeh.

Ying Po-chüeh, Ying the Second, Sponger Ying, Beggar Ying, son of the deceased silk merchant Master Ying, younger brother of Ying the Elder, father of Ying Pao and two daughters by his wife, née Tu, and a younger son by his concubine Ch'un-hua; having squandered his patrimony and fallen on hard times he has been reduced to squiring wealthy young rakes about the licensed quarters and living by his wits; boon companion and favorite crony of Hsi-men Ch'ing, member of the brotherhood of ten; a clever and amusing sycophant and opportunist he has the art to openly impose on Hsi-men Ch'ing and make him like it while he is alive and the gall to double-cross him without compunction as soon as he is dead.

Ying Po-chüeh's concubine. See Ch'un-hua.

Ying Po-chüeh's elder daughter, married with the financial assistance of Hsi-men Ch'ing.

Ying Po-chüeh's grandfather, friend of Licentiate Shui's grandfather.

Ying Po-chüeh's second daughter, after the death of her father she is proposed by Auntie Hsüeh as a match for Ch'en Ching-chi but turned down by P'ang Ch'un-mei for lack of a dowry.

Ying Po-chüeh's son by his concubine Ch'un-hua.

Ying Po-chüeh's wife, née Tu, mother of Ying Pao and two daughters.

Ying the Second. See Ying Po-chüeh.

Ying, Sponger. See Ying Po-chüeh.

Yu, Loafer. See Yu Shou.

Yu Shou, Loafer Yu, a dissolute young scamp upon whom Hsi-men Ch'ing turns the tables by abusing the judicial system.

Yung-ting, page boy in the household of Wang Ts'ai.

Yü, Big Sister, blind professional singer in Ch'ing-ho frequently invited into Hsi-men Ch'ing's household to entertain his womenfolk and their guests.

Yü Ch'un, Stupid Yü, one of the "cribbers" in the licensed quarter of Ch'ing-ho who plays the tout to Wang Ts'ai on his visits to the licensed quarter and upon whom Hsi-men Ch'ing turns the tables by abusing the judicial system at the behest of Lady Lin.

Yü-erh. See Sun Hsüeh-o.

Yü-hsiao, Jade Flute, senior maidservant of Wu Yüeh-niang, carries on an affair with Shu-t'ung the discovery of which by P'an Chin-lien leads him to abscond and return to his native Su-chou; after the death of Hsi-men Ch'ing agrees to be sent to the household of Chai Ch'ien in the Eastern Capital and is raped by Lai-pao on the way.

Yü, Licentiate, master of a girls' school in his home in Ch'ing-ho where P'an Chin-lien studies for three years as a child.

Yü-lou. See Meng Yü-lou.

Yü Shen (d. 1132), minister of war who suppresses Tseng Hsiao-hsü's memorial impeaching Hsia Yen-ling and Hsi-men Ch'ing for malfeasance in the case of Miao Ch'ing, rewarded with the title grand guardian of the heir apparent for his part in facilitating the notorious Flower and Rock Convoys and the construction of the Mount Ken Imperial Park.

Yü, Stupid. See Yü Ch'un.

Yü-t'ang, employed in Chou Hsiu's household as a wet nurse for Chou Chin-ko.

Yü-tsan, concubine of Li Kung-pi, originally maidservant of his deceased first wife, who enters his household as part of her dowry, reacts jealously to his marriage with Meng Yü-lou and is beaten by him and sold out of the household.

Yü-wen, Censor. See Yü-wen Hsü-chung.

Yü-wen Hsü-chung (1079–1146), Censor Yü-wen, supervising secretary of the Office of Scrutiny for War who submits a memorial to the throne impeaching Ts'ai Ching, Wang Fu, and Yang Chien.

Yüan, Commander, resident of Potter's Alley in the Eastern Capital into whose family Li P'ing-erh is reincarnated as a daughter.

Yüan-hsiao, senior maidservant of Li Chiao-erh who is transferred to the service of Hsi-men Ta-chieh at the request of Ch'en Ching-chi after her former mistress leaves the household, accompanies her new mistress through her many vicissitudes while also putting up with the capricious treatment of Ch'en Ching-chi in whose service she dies after he reduced to penury.

Yüan Yen, professional actor from Su-chou who specializes in playing subsidiary female roles.

Yüeh Ho-an, vice-magistrate of Ch'ing-ho.

Yüeh-kuei, concubine of Chou Hsiu much abused by P'ang Ch'un-mei.

Yüeh-niang. See Wu Yüeh-niang.

Yüeh the Third, next door neighbor of Han Tao-kuo on Lion Street who fences Miao Ch'ing's stolen goods and suggests that he approach Hsi-men Ch'ing through Wang Liu-erh to get him off the hook for the murder of Miao T'ien-hsiu.

Yüeh the Third's wife, close friend of Wang Liu-erh who acts as an intermediary in Miao Ch'ing's approach to Hsi-men Ch'ing.

Yün, Assistant Regional Commander, elder brother of Yün Li-shou, hereditary military officer who dies at his post on the frontier.

Yün-ko. See Ch'iao Yün-ko.

Yün Li-shou, Welsher Yün, Yün the Second, younger brother of Assistant Regional Commander Yün, crony of Hsi-men Ch'ing, member of the brotherhood of ten, manager employed by Hsi-men Ch'ing in various of his enterprises, upon the death of his elder brother succeeds to his rank and the substantive post of vice commander of the Ch'ing-ho Left Guard, later appointed stockade commander of Ling-pi Stockade at Chi-nan where Wu Yüeh-niang seeks refuge with him from the invading Chin armies but dreams that he attempts to rape her.

Yün Li-shou's daughter, betrothed while still a babe in arms to Hsi-men Hsiao-ko.

Yün Li-shou's wife, née Su, proposes a marriage alliance to Wu Yüeh-niang while they are both pregnant and formally betroths her daughter to Hsi-men Hsiao-ko after the death of Hsi-men Ch'ing.

Yün, Little. See Ch'iao Yün-ko.

Yün, Prince of. See Chao K'ai.

Yün the Second. See Yün Li-shou.

Yün, Welsher. See Yün Li-shou.

THE PLUM IN THE GOLDEN VASE

Chapter 41

HSI-MEN CH'ING FORMS A MARRIAGE

ALLIANCE WITH CH'IAO HUNG;

P'AN CHIN-LIEN ENGAGES IN A QUARREL

WITH LI P'ING-ERH

Equally endowed with wealth and distinction,[1]
  his inheritance is ample;
Streams of officials, in crimson and purple,
  congregate at his door.
His office is high and his position important,
  like those of Wang Tao;[2]
His family is prominent and his estate affluent,
  like those of Shih Ch'ung.[3]
Amid painted candles and brocade curtains,
  he whiles away the moonlit night;
Surrounded by silk clothing, rouge, and powder,
  he is drunk in the spring breeze.
As indulgence in pleasure, by day and by night,[4]
  continues year after year;
How can he ever make the effort to remain
  constant from beginning to end?

THE STORY GOES that the clothes for his womenfolk that Hsi-men
Ch'ing had engaged the tailor to come to his home to make were all finished
before two days were over.

On the twelfth, the Ch'iao family sent someone to remind them of the
invitation to their lantern viewing party. That morning Hsi-men Ch'ing had
already sent appropriate presents over to their place. That day Wu Yüeh-niang
and her sister-wives, along with her sister-in-law, the wife of her eldest brother
Wu K'ai, set out together in six sedan chairs, leaving Sun Hsüeh-o behind to
look after the house. They were accompanied in two smaller sedan chairs by
the wet nurse, Ju-i, carrying the infant Kuan-ko, and Lai-hsing's wife, Hui-
hsiu, whose job it was to wait on them and fold their clothes.

Hsi-men Ch'ing remained at home, where he looked on as the fireworks specialist hired by Pen the Fourth prepared the racks of fireworks, and lanterns were hung in the main reception hall and the summerhouse. He also sent a page boy with a calling card to the mansion of Wang the Second, the distaff relative of the imperial family, to engage the services of his troupe of actors, but there is no need to describe this in detail.

That afternoon he paid a visit to P'an Chin-lien's quarters. Chin-lien was not at home, but Ch'un-mei waited upon him, serving him with tea and something to eat, and setting up a table at which he could have some wine.

Hsi-men Ch'ing then said to Ch'un-mei, "On the fourteenth, when we are entertaining the wives of the various officials, it would be a good idea if the four of you senior maidservants would all get dressed up and assist your mistress in serving wine to the guests."

When Ch'un-mei heard this, she leaned nonchalantly on the table and said, "If you call on anyone to do that, call on the other three. As for me, I'm not going to do it."

"Why won't you do it?" asked Hsi-men Ch'ing.

"The ladies of the household have all had new clothes provided for the occasion," said Ch'un-mei, "so they will look good when entertaining the wives from the official families. As for us, each and every one looks just like a scorched pastry roll. Why should we have to put in an appearance for no good reason, only to make laughingstocks of ourselves?"

"Each of you have clothing and jewelry for yourselves," said Hsi-men Ch'ing. "You can come out in full dress, with your cloud-shaped chignons sporting ornamental flowers bedecked with pearls and kingfisher feathers."

"I guess I can make do with my head ornaments," said Ch'un-mei, "but how can I wear that couple of old rags of mine, the only ones that amount to anything? I'd be ashamed to be seen in them."

"I understand you, little oily mouth," laughed Hsi-men Ch'ing. "The ladies of the household have had new clothes made for them, which has put you all in a huff. It doesn't matter. I'll get Tailor Chao to come and make up three articles of clothing for each of the four of you, and my daughter, Hsi-men Ta-chieh, into the bargain. Each of you shall have an outfit consisting of a satin jacket and skirt and a brocade vest."

"I'm not to be compared to them," said Ch'un-mei. "I demand a white satin skirt to wear, along with a vest of scarlet brocade."

"If that's what you want," said Hsi-men Ch'ing, "it doesn't matter. But I'll have to provide one for Hsi-men Ta-chieh as well."

"The young lady already has one, but I don't," said Ch'un-mei. "She's got nothing to complain about."

Hsi-men Ch'ing thereupon procured the key, opened the door to the second floor room, and selected five outfits of satin clothing, two brocade vests, and a bolt of white satin, out of which two white satin jackets that opened down the middle were to be made. Only Hsi-men Ta-chieh and Ch'un-mei were to have vests of scarlet brocade, while those of Ying-ch'un, Yü-hsiao, and Lan-hsiang were all of blue, their outfits consisting of scarlet satin gold lamé jackets that opened down the middle, to be worn over trailing skirts with kingfisher-blue borders. It added up to seventeen items of clothing in all.

Hsi-men Ch'ing sent for Tailor Chao and had them all duly made to order. Ch'un-mei also demanded that a bolt of yellow silk be used to make the linings for the skirt waists, all of which were to be of Hang-chou silk. Only then did Ch'un-mei profess satisfaction and agree to spend the rest of the day drinking wine with Hsi-men Ch'ing. But let us put the situation at home aside for the moment and say no more about it.

To resume our story, Wu Yüeh-niang and her sister-wives duly proceeded on their way to the home of Ch'iao Hung. It so happens that on that day Ch'iao Hung's wife had invited the wife of Provincial Graduate Shang Hsiao-t'ang, the wife of her next-door neighbor Censor Chu, her husband's elder sister Mrs. Ts'ui, her nephew Ts'ui Pen's wife Big Sister Tuan, and her niece Third Sister Cheng, the wife of Wu Shun-ch'en, and had also engaged two singing girls to entertain the gathering.

When she heard that Wu Yüeh-niang and her sister-wives, along with Yüeh-niang's sister-in-law, the wife of her elder brother Wu K'ai, had arrived, she hastened out to the ceremonial gate that led into the second courtyard and ushered them into the reception hall in the rear compound, where the usual amenities were observed. She addressed Yüeh-niang as Aunt, and Li Chiao-erh and the others as Second Aunt, Third Aunt, and so forth, adopting the terms of address she had heard employed in the home of Wu K'ai's wife. When the newcomers had finished exchanging greetings with the wives of Provincial Graduate Shang and Censor Chu, Big Sister Tuan and Third Sister Cheng came forward to pay their respects, and everyone sat down in order of precedence.

When the maidservants had finished serving everyone with tea, Ch'iao Hung himself came out to greet them, and to thank them for their presents, after which his wife invited her guests into the master suite where they could loosen their formal clothing and relax. A table was set up for tea, at which the fare consisted of fancy steamed and deep-fried appetizers, stuffed pastry treats, preserved fruits, sweetmeats, and every kind of delicacy, all set out in a most elegant fashion. The guests were invited to sit down and partake of the repast, while the wet nurse, Ju-i, and Hui-hsiu looked after Kuan-ko in another room, where they were separately entertained.

In a little while, after the guests had finished their tea, they moved into the reception hall, where:

Screens display their peacocks' tails, and
Cushions conceal their hibiscus blossoms.

There were four tables arranged along the upper end of the hall. Yüeh-niang was seated in the place of honor, followed in order of precedence by the wife of Provincial Graduate Shang, Wu K'ai's wife, the wife of Censor Chu, Li Chiao-erh, Meng Yü-lou, P'an Chin-lien, and Li P'ing-erh, while Ch'iao Hung's wife assumed the role of hostess. Another table was set up to one side to accommodate Big Sister Tuan and Third Sister Cheng, making a party of eleven in all.

The two singing girls, situated to one side, played and sang for their entertainment. After soup and rice had been served, the chef came out to present the first course, which was jellied goose, and Yüeh-niang rewarded him with a tip of two mace of silver. The second course was slow-boiled pig's trotters, for which Yüeh-niang rewarded him with a tip of another mace of silver. The third course that he presented was roast duck, for which Yüeh-niang rewarded him with yet another mace of silver. Ch'iao Hung's wife then left her place in order to serve wine to her guests. After serving Yüeh-niang first, she went on to serve Provincial Graduate Shang's wife.

At this point, Yüeh-niang got up and retired to the inner room to change her clothes and redo her makeup. Meng Yü-lou also followed suit. When they arrived in their hostess's bedroom, what should they see but the wet nurse Ju-i who was looking after Kuan-ko. She had put him down on a little sleeping mat that was spread out on the k'ang frame, where he was lying right next to Chang-chieh, the newborn daughter of their host. The two of them were playing happily at:
You hit me a blow and I'll hit you one back,
which tickled Yüeh-niang and Yü-lou no end.

"The two of them are just like a couple," they exclaimed.

On seeing Wu K'ai's wife come in after them, they said to her, "Come and take a look. The two of them are really like a little couple."

"That's true," said Wu K'ai's wife with a smile. "The way the children on the k'ang are:
Reaching out their hands and kicking their feet,
playing at:
You hit me and I'll hit you,
makes them look like a predestined little couple."

When Ch'iao Hung's wife and the other female guests came into the room, Wu K'ai's wife repeated what she had said, thus and so.

"Distinguished kindred, listen to me," responded Ch'iao Hung's wife. "Such mean folk as ourselves would hardly dare aspire to a marriage alliance with the household of such a one as our aunt."

"My dear kinswoman, how can you say such a thing!" Yüeh-niang protested. "What sort of person do you take my elder brother's wife to be? What sort of person is Third Sister Cheng? It is wholly appropriate that you and I should:

The Interplay of Two Infants Leads to a Marriage Alliance

Cement the bonds of affection with the bonds of marriage.
After all, the little boy from my household is unlikely to disgrace the daughter of your house. How can you say such a thing?"

Meng Yü-lou nudged Li P'ing-erh, saying, "Sister Li, what have you got to say?" But Li P'ing-erh only smiled.

"If my kinswoman, Mrs. Ch'iao, does not consent," said Wu K'ai's wife, "I'll be upset."

The wife of Provincial Graduate Shang and the wife of Censor Chu chimed in, saying, "Mrs. Ch'iao, in response to the generous sentiments of your kins-woman, Mrs. Wu, you really ought not to decline."

They then went on to ask, "Your girl Chang-chieh was born in the eleventh month of last year, wasn't she?"

"Our little boy was born on the twenty-third day of the sixth month," said Yüeh-niang, "so he is the older by five months. They truly would make a couple."

Thereupon:
    Without permitting any further explanation,
the whole group insisted on dragging Ch'iao Hung's wife, Wu Yüeh-niang, and Li P'ing-erh to the front reception hall, where the matrons of the two households formalized the betrothal of the children by exchanging cuttings from the lapels of their blouses,[5] while the two singing girls played and sang to entertain them.

Once the situation had been explained to Ch'iao Hung, he brought out boxes of candied fruit, along with the customary three strips of red bunting, and proceeded to serve his guests with wine. Yüeh-niang, for her part, ordered Tai-an and Ch'in-t'ung to return home immediately in order to let Hsi-men Ch'ing know about it, and they subsequently returned bearing two jugs of wine, three bolts of satin, artificial flowers made of stiff velvet and gold thread, with red petals and green leaves, and four boxes, inlaid with mother-of-pearl, containing candied fruit.

The members of the two families then proceeded to hang up the red bun-ting and celebrate the occasion with a drinking party. Within the reception hall:
    Painted candles are elevated on high,
    Decorated lanterns flare resplendently,[6]
    The fragrance of musk is luxuriant,
    The sound of joyous laughter resounds.
In front of the gathering, the two singing girls:
    Opened their ruby lips,
    Exposed their white teeth,
    Lightly plucked their jade mandolas, and
    Casually grasped their balloon guitars,
as they sang the song suite that begins with the tune "Fighting Quails."[7]

Inside kingfisher-hued window gauze,
Underneath mandarin duck azure tiles,
Hidden by peacock-adorned silver screens,[8]
Amid hibiscus-decked embroidered couches,
Curtains of gossamer silk are rolled up,
Incense smolders in duck-shaped censers,[9]
Lamps are suspended above,
Blinds are lowered below.
This is the residence of a Minister of the
    Department of State Affairs,
The son-in-law of the reigning emperor.

To the tune "Prelude to Purple Blossoms"

The soldiers in his entourage are clad in red,
    bearing painted halberds;
The officers of his command wear "Hooks of Wu"
    hanging from brocade belts;[10]
The guest at his feast sports an embroidered cap
    adorned with palace flowers.[11]
The entertainment accords with that of the Music Office,
The extravagance compares with that of the Palace Garden.
The tempo is provided by clappers of red ivory,[12]
The strains of a classic melody are
    about to be performed.
Two rows of beauties as pretty as pictures
    stand to either side.
Powdered faces abut silver psalteries,
Jade fingers pluck at balloon guitars.[13]

To the tune "Golden Plantain Leaves"

All I can see is crimson candles burning brightly
    in silver candlesticks,
As slender fingers raise aloft
    jade goblets.
Noting that his demeanor is both dignified
    and elegant,
I go over under the lamplight so I can
    take a good look at him.

To the tune "Flirtatious Laughter"

This gentleman is surely someone I have
    seen somewhere before.

Can it be that my eyes are deceiving me?
Ah! Putting my hand to my teeth,[14]
   I try to remember.
Once having set eyes on him, I can't help being
   disturbed at heart.
Could he turn out to be my adversary in delight[15]
   from five hundred years ago?[16]
Before whose house has he tethered his horse
   to the green willows?[17]
It must have been no more than a dream vision of
   clouds and rain in Witch's Gorge.[18]

To the tune "Impatiens Blossoms"

Having played through the melody on the jade flute[19]
   under the verdant peach trees,
A single moment was worth a thousand pieces of gold.[20]
Under the lamplight he is looking me over
   out of the corners of his eyes,
In such a way that my face is suffused with
   the glow of sunset clouds.
My master is afraid I am remiss in letting
   your wine cup remain empty.
I am just seventeen, and have not been betrothed,
A budding peony, delicately nurtured[21]
   by my master.

To the tune "The Spectral Triad"

He has uttered but a handful of
   disconsolate words,
Which cause my tears to fall in
   incessant cascades.
I cannot control the monkey of my mind
   and the horse of my will.[22]
I am no more than a delicate
   Lo-yang flower,
In danger of becoming a target
   of romantic gossip.[23]
These words may sound like a joke,
   but they're not a joke;
This allegation may seem to be false,
   but it isn't false.

That one is trying to pull up the trees
    to investigate the roots,
While this one is pointing to a deer
    and calling it a horse.[24]

To the tune "Shaven-Pated Rascal"

My efforts to admonish him are as futile as
    trying to immerse a melon in water;[25]
His staring at me is about as effective as
    gazing at flowers in a mirror.
It is said that young scholars have always been
    frivolous in their affections;
And here he is flirting with a dainty maiden
    from a good family.

To the tune "Sacred Bhaiṣajya-Rāja"

How am I to rescue the situation?
My master is difficult to placate.
As in the receptions of Kung-sun Hung, there is
    a hubbub in the Eastern Vestibule.[26]
The feast on tortoiseshell mats is disrupted.
The parrot-beak-shaped conch goblets are discarded.
The silver candlesticks and crimson silk lamp shades
    have been kicked over.
He has drawn his three-foot sword from its scabbard.

Coda

It has always been true that scholars possess
    lustful daring as big as the sky,[27]
Which frightens this fainthearted Cho Wen-chün
    half to death.[28]
It's a case of a too hot-tempered Cho Wang-sun,
And an overly ardent Ssu-ma Hsiang-ju of the Han.[29]

Thereupon, the assembled guests saw to it that Wu Yüeh-niang, Ch'iao Hung's wife, and Li P'ing-erh stuck the artificial flowers in their hair, while red bunting was hung up, drinks were offered to them, and they formally saluted each other. When this ceremony was completed, the feasting was resumed, and everyone sat down to continue drinking together.

The chef first presented a course consisting of little molded cakes of glutinous rice flour, with a sweet stuffing, and the character for long life embossed on their surfaces, along with a lotus pod soup filled with auspicious ingredients, such as double-headed lotus blossoms, that suggest the beauty of a summer pond, after which he proceeded to carve a dish of roast marbled pork.

Yüeh-niang, who was seated in the place of honor, was utterly delighted by all this and, calling Tai-an over, instructed him to award the chef with a bolt of crimson fabric, and to give one to each of the two singing girls as well, for which gratuities they all kowtowed in gratitude.

Ch'iao Hung's wife was still unwilling to let her guests go, but invited them back to the rear hall to sit down a while longer. A profusion of serving dishes, along with partitioned boxes of assorted delicacies, were laid out for them there. The party continued until the first watch before Yüeh-niang finally said her farewells and prepared to go home.

"Kinswoman," she said to her hostess, "tomorrow, whatever you do:
    Deign to drop in on our humble abode,
and visit with us for a while."

"Kinswoman," replied Ch'iao Hung's wife, "I appreciate your generous hospitality. But my husband has said that it might not be appropriate for me to join you on this occasion. I'll come and visit you another day."

"My dear kinswoman," protested Yüeh-niang, "it's not as though there will be anyone else there. You're just being standoffish."

She then suggested that her sister-in-law, Wu K'ai's wife, should remain overnight, saying, "If you don't go home today, you can accompany Kinswoman Ch'iao to our place tomorrow."

"Kinswoman Ch'iao," said Wu K'ai's wife, "it doesn't matter if you don't go on any other day, but you surely mustn't fail to pay a visit on the fifteenth, which is your new kinswoman's birthday."

"If the fifteenth is my kinswoman's birthday," said Ch'iao Hung's wife, "how could I presume not to go?"

"If my kinswoman fails to come," said Yüeh-niang, "I've turned the responsibility over to you, Sister-in-law, and I'll hold you accountable."

Thereupon, after insisting that Wu K'ai's wife remain behind, Yüeh-niang and her entourage said goodbye and got into their sedan chairs. Two orderlies preceded them, holding large red lanterns, and shouting to clear the way, while two page boys, also holding lanterns, brought up the rear. Wu Yüeh-niang's sedan chair went first, followed by those of Li Chiao-erh, Meng Yü-lou, P'an Chin-lien, and Li P'ing-erh, in single file, while the chairs of Ju-i and Hui-hsiu followed in their wake. Inside her sedan chair, the wet nurse saw to it that Kuan-ko was tightly wrapped in a little red satin coverlet, to protect him from the cold, while she propped her feet on a brass warmer below. With the two page boys following behind, they arrived in due course at the front gate and dismounted from their sedan chairs.

Hsi-men Ch'ing was drinking wine in the master suite when Yüeh-niang and the others came in, exchanged salutations, and sat down, after which the maidservants came in and kowtowed to them. Yüeh-niang wasted no time in telling him all about the betrothal that had been arranged at the feast that day.

When Hsi-men Ch'ing had heard her out, he asked, "Who were the other female guests at the party today?"

"There were the wife of Provincial Graduate Shang," said Yüeh-niang, "along with the wife of Censor Chu, our host's elder sister, Mrs. Ts'ui, as well as her two nieces."

"If you've made a betrothal," said Hsi-men Ch'ing, "I guess that's that. But it's not an entirely appropriate match."

"The fact is, it was all my sister-in-law's doing," said Yüeh-niang. "When she saw their newborn baby daughter and our child reclining on the k'ang frame together, under the same coverlet, and playing at:

You hit me a blow and I'll hit you one back,

she thought they looked just like a little couple and called us over to see. She brought the possibility up, and right at the party:

Without premeditation or forethought,[30]

we agreed to this marriage alliance. It was only then that I sent the page boys over to tell you about it, and to arrange for the delivery of the artificial flowers, red bunting, and boxes of candied fruit."

"Since you've made this betrothal, I guess that's that," said Hsi-men Ch'ing. But it's not an entirely appropriate match. Although the Ch'iao family is wealthy enough at present, he is no more than a well-to-do householder in the district, of commoner status. Whereas, in our case, I currently occupy this official position and manage affairs in the yamen. In the future, at the betrothal celebrations, he will only be entitled to wear the informal skullcap of a commoner. How will he be comfortable associating with an official family such as ours? It really won't look right.

"Just the other day, Military Director-in-chief Ching Chung sought the aid of our relative Chang Kuan of the local garrison, in repeatedly suggesting to me a marriage alliance with his family. He said that their daughter was just five months old, so that she would be the same age as our child. But I was concerned that she didn't have a proper mother, having been born to a concubine, so I refused the offer. I scarcely anticipated that we would end up making such a marriage alliance after all."

P'an Chin-lien, who was standing to one side, picked up on this, saying, "If you object to someone's having been born to a concubine, who among the parties involved was not born to a concubine? This child of the Ch'iao family was also born to a concubine. Truly:

When the Spirit of the Perilous Paths runs into
    the God of Longevity;[31]
If you refrain from commenting about my height,
I'll not complain about that shortness of yours."

When Hsi-men Ch'ing heard these words, he was enraged and cursed at her, saying, "You lousy whore! Mind your own business. While we're talking here, for you to:

Stick your beak in and wag your tongue,
is completely out of place."

Chin-lien's face turned crimson with embarrassment, and she beat a hasty retreat, muttering as she went, "Whoever said I had the right to speak? It's obvious I haven't the standing to say anything."

Gentle reader take note: When Chin-lien observed the way in which Yüeh-niang and Ch'iao Hung's wife agreed to the betrothal at the party that day, with the result that Li P'ing-erh was draped in red fabric and had artificial flowers stuck in her hair, while wine was presented to her, she became very sore at heart. The fact that Hsi-men Ch'ing saw fit to curse at her this way on her return home only made matters worse, and she withdrew to Yüeh-niang's inner chamber to cry.

Hsi-men Ch'ing then asked, "How come your sister-in-law didn't come back with you?"

"Kinswoman Ch'iao," explained Yüeh-niang, "on learning that so many wives of officials would be at our place tomorrow, declined my invitation, and I suggested that my sister-in-law stay on at their place, so she could bring her along with her on the morrow."

"Just as I said," remarked Hsi-men Ch'ing, "the seating plan at the party tomorrow is going to be awkward to arrange. I don't know how we're going to handle it when we get together in the future."

They talked for a while longer, after which Meng Yü-lou came into the inner room and found Chin-lien crying there.

"What are you so upset about?" she asked. "Let him have his say, and forget about it."

"Fortunately you were there to hear it with your own ears," said Chin-lien. "What did I say that was disparaging of him? But I had a point to be made. He said that the other family's child was born to a concubine. I said, 'Was the Ch'iao family's child not born to a concubine? She was also born to a concubine.' Does he think that:

By wrapping it in a paper bag,
He can fool anyone?

You'll come to a bad end, you lousy ruffian! Then he opened his eyes wide and started cursing at me in a way that was so:

Unfeeling and unjustifiable.

Why shouldn't I have the right to say what I think? He's had a change of heart, and, in the days to come, he'll:

Suffer the consequences before my very eyes.[32]

What I didn't say was that that infant relative of the Ch'iao family's at least came into this world with something of Old Man Ch'iao's spunk in her, whereas that child of your's:

Has strayed out of familiar territory.

Who knows whose seed he was sired by? If people want to play the game of seeking marriage alliances in order to enhance their social standing, what right does that give you to take out your annoyance on me? What's my cunt got to do with it that you should start in cursing me? How old is your son, anyway? He's nothing but a puny armload of a bladder's spawn. And you're already putting him on the marriage market for no good reason.

> You've got so much money you don't know
>> what to do with it.
> If you tug on the sheet until it's torn,
>> you'll have no cover.
> The dog who bites the inflated bladder,
>> will find his excitement deflated.

Right now the relationship may be wet enough, given the age of the parties involved, but, in the future, if you don't watch out, it may turn out to be no more than an arid pseudo relationship.

> If you blow out the lamp and close your eyes,
> You can hardly expect to see what is to come.

People may feel well disposed toward each other at the time they make such alliances, but, more often than not, they end up feeling differently three or five years later."

"As disingenuous as people may be nowadays," said Meng Yü-lou, "they seldom go in for this sort of thing. If you stop to consider it, it's early days yet. For children who are hardly out of the womb, what's the point of exchanging cuttings from your lapels? It's no more than playing the game of seeking marriage alliances in order to enhance one's social standing, that's all."

"Even if that wife of yours is so wantonly anxious to play the marriage alliance game," said Chin-lien, "what right does that give the lousy refractory ruffian to start cursing at me for no good reason? It seems that:

> All you get for raising toads is dropsy.

What's the point of it all?"

"Whoever told you to blurt out your thoughts in such an imprudent way?" said Yü-lou.

> "If he doesn't curse you,
> Should he curse the dog instead?"

"It would have been awkward for me to say it right out," said Chin-lien. "Was I supposed to pretend that the child was not born to a concubine, but to the principal wife? Even though the Ch'iao family's child was born to a concubine, at least it came into the world with something of Old Man Ch'iao's spunk in her, whereas that child of your's:

> Has strayed out of familiar territory.

Who knows whose seed he was sired by?"

When Yü-lou heard this, she sat for a while without saying another word, until Chin-lien went back to her quarters.

On noticing that Hsi-men Ch'ing had gone outside, Li P'ing-erh, once again:

Like a sprig of blossoms swaying in the breeze,

kowtowed to Yüeh-niang, saying, "Elder Sister, in this matter of the child today, I thank you for all the trouble you went to."

Yüeh-niang, with a smile, knelt down and returned her salutation, saying, "Congratulations to you."

"And to you, too, Elder Sister," said Li P'ing-erh.

When they had finished kowtowing to each other, Li P'ing-erh got up and sat down to chat with Yüeh-niang and Li Chiao-erh.

What should they see at this juncture but Sun Hsüeh-o and Hsi-men Ta-chieh, who came in to kowtow to Yüeh-niang and greeted Li Chiao-erh and Li P'ing-erh in turn. Hsiao-yü served them with tea.

As they were drinking their tea, what should they see but Hsiu-ch'un, the maidservant from Li P'ing-erh's quarters, who came to fetch her mistress, saying, "The little fellow is looking for you in your room, and Father has sent me to ask you to return there."

"The wet nurse hurried off without anyone's knowing it," said Li P'ing-erh, "and carried him back to the room. It would have done just as well for us to go back together. As it is, there was probably no lantern for the child."

"When we came in the gate just now," said Yüeh-niang, "I told her to take him back to your room. I feared it was getting late."

"Ju-i took him back just a while ago," said Hsiao-yü. "Lai-an carried a lantern and escorted them on the way."

"That's all right then," said Li P'ing-erh, who, thereupon, took her leave of Yüeh-niang and returned to her quarters, where she found Hsi-men Ch'ing and Kuan-ko, who was asleep in the arms of the wet nurse.

"So there you are," she said. "Why didn't you speak to me before carrying him off that way?"

"The First Lady saw that Lai-an was there with a lantern," said Ju-i, "so I took advantage of that fact to bring him home. The little fellow cried for a while, and I only now managed to pat him back to sleep."

"He clamored after you for some time," said Hsi-men Ch'ing, "before finally going to sleep."

When Li P'ing-erh had finished asking about the baby, she turned to him with a simpering smile and said, "Today the child has been betrothed, for which I'd like to express my gratitude to you with a kowtow."

Thereupon:

Just as though inserting a taper in its holder,

she knelt down and made him a kowtow. This pleased Hsi-men Ch'ing so much that his face became wreathed in smiles, and, hastening to help her to her feet, they sat down together, and she told Ying-ch'un to serve them with wine. The two of them then proceeded to drink wine together in her room.

To resume our story, P'an Chin-lien returned to her quarters in a huff and was not in the best of moods, knowing perfectly well that Hsi-men Ch'ing was at Li P'ing-erh's place.

As a consequence, when Ch'iu-chü was slow about opening the gate, no sooner was she inside than she boxed her ears twice and cursed her in a loud voice, saying, "You lousy slave of a whore! How is it that I've had to call all day long before you opened the gate? What have you been up to? I'll not have anything more to say to you today."

Thereupon, she went into her room and sat down.

When Ch'un-mei came in to kowtow to her and serve her with tea, the woman asked her, "That lousy slave! What was she doing in here?"

"She was just sitting in the courtyard," said Ch'un-mei. "When you called for her I urged her to get a move on, but she didn't pay any attention."

"I'm perfectly aware," said Chin-lien, "that when he and I have a falling out, it's just like the way:

Defender-in-chief Tang Chin learned
    to eat steamed dumplings,
By imitating the way other people did it.[33]

She thinks she, too, can take advantage of me."

Chin-lien wanted to give her a beating there and then but was afraid that Hsi-men Ch'ing, who was in the adjacent quarters, would hear her, so she kept her anger to herself. Meanwhile, she took off her fancy attire, had Ch'un-mei lay out her bedding, got into bed, and went to sleep.

The next day, when Hsi-men Ch'ing had gone off to the yamen, the woman made Ch'iu-chü balance a flagstone on her head and kneel down in the courtyard until she had finished combing her hair. She then told Ch'un-mei to pull down her trousers and bring her a heavy bamboo cane with which to flog her.

"What a filthy slave!" complained Ch'un-mei. "If you have me pull down her pants, it will only dirty my hands."

She then went up front and called for the page boy Hua-t'ung to come and pull down Ch'iu-chü's drawers for her.

The woman then proceeded to cane her, cursing as she did so, "You lousy slave of a whore! Since when did you become so uppity? Other people may see fit to favor you, but I'll never favor you. Sister:

You know it and I know it.

You'd do better to slack off a bit. What need is there for you to stick your neck out and put on airs for no good reason? Sister, you'd better give up any such presumptions. From now on, I'm going to keep my eyes peeled where you're concerned."

As she vilified her, she continued to beat her, and as the beating continued, she gave vent to further vilification. The caning continued until Ch'iu-chü:

Howled like a stuck pig.

P'an Chin-lien Punishes Ch'iu-chü to Get at Li P'ing-erh

Li P'ing-erh, in her adjacent quarters, had just gotten up and looked on as the wet nurse suckled Kuan-ko and then put him back to sleep. He was startled back awake, however, by the commotion next door. She overheard perfectly clearly everything that Chin-lien had to say while caning her maidservant, as she blurted things out:

Without any consideration for the consequences.

Rendered quite speechless, in her consternation, she merely covered Kuan-ko's ears and told Hsiu-ch'un, "Go over and say to the Fifth Lady, 'Don't beat Ch'iu-chü any more. The baby has just had some milk and has gone back to sleep.' "

When Chin-lien heard this, she beat Ch'iu-chü all the harder, cursing as she did so, "You lousy slave! You'd think someone were sticking ten thousand knives into you, the way you scream for mercy. Well, it's just my temperament, but the more you scream, the harder I'll beat you. You've already succeeded in arresting the attention of a passerby, who's come to contemplate the sight of a maidservant being beaten. Well, my good Sister, you can always tell your husband about it, and get him to give me a hard time."

Li P'ing-erh, from her vantage point next door, understood perfectly well that Chin-lien's abuse was really directed at her. She was so upset by it that her two hands turned cold, but she chose to:

Swallow her anger and keep her own counsel.

Though she dared to be angry,

She dared not speak.

That morning she didn't even have a drop of tea but clasped Kuan-ko in her arms and went back to sleep on the k'ang.

When Hsi-men Ch'ing returned home from the yamen, he came into her room to see Kuan-ko and found that Li P'ing-erh was lying on the k'ang, and that her eyes were red with weeping.

"How come you still haven't combed your hair or straightened yourself up?" he asked. "The lady in the master suite would like to have a word with you. What have you been rubbing your eyes for, until they're so red?"

Li P'ing-erh made no reference to the way in which Chin-lien had vilified her, but simply said, "I'm not feeling very well."

"Our kinfolk of the Ch'iao family have sent birthday presents for you," said Hsi-men Ch'ing. "A bolt of fabric, two jars of southern wine, a tray of sweetmeats in the shape of birthday peaches, a tray of birthday noodles, and four kinds of savories. They've also sent some holiday gifts for Kuan-ko, consisting of two trays of Lantern Festival dumplings, four trays of candied fruit, four trays of premium grade nuts, two beaded hanging lanterns, two folding-screen-shaped lanterns spangled with gold, two bolts of crimson government-grade satin, a black satin cap with gold pins representing the eight auspicious symbols[34] attached to it, two pairs of boy's shoes, and six pairs of women's shoes. Before we have even paid them a formal visit, they have sent these holiday gifts for our child.

"Right now, the lady in the master suite would like you to go and discuss the situation with her. They have sent the go-between, Auntie K'ung, to represent them, along with their servant, Ch'iao T'ung, who is in charge of delivering the gifts, and our sister-in-law, the wife of Wu K'ai, has come ahead to say that Kinswoman Ch'iao will not be able to come tomorrow but will pay a visit the following day.

"Their family also has a relation, Madame Ch'iao, who is the widow of that distaff relative of the imperial family, Ch'iao the Fifth. When she heard that they were forming a marriage alliance with us, she was pleased as could be, and she would also like to visit us on the fifteenth. We'll have to send her an invitation."

When Li P'ing-erh had heard all this, she finally got up, reluctantly, to comb her hair and set off for the rear compound to pay her respects to Sister-in-law Wu and Auntie K'ung. She found that tea was being served to them in Yüeh-niang's room, and that the presents were on display in the parlor. After looking them all over, she arranged to send back the boxes in which they had come, gave gratuities of two handkerchiefs and five mace of silver apiece to Auntie K'ung and Ch'iao T'ung, wrote a thank-you note, and also sent someone to deliver an invitation to Madame Ch'iao. Truly:

> Only inclined to entertain their favorites
>   with bells and drums,
> Would they have herded with dogs and sheep
>   for the nation's sake?[35]

There is a poem that testifies to this:

> Hsi-men Ch'ing, enjoying his singular wealth,
>   is altogether too complacent;
> Agreeing to a marriage alliance for his son,
>   while he is still in diapers.
> Not only does he squander his property
>   as though it were mere muck;
> But he ought to pay more attention to
>   the fate of his posterity.

> If you want to know the outcome of these events,
> Pray consult the story related in the following chapter.

Chapter 42

A POWERFUL FAMILY BLOCKS ITS GATE
IN ORDER TO ENJOY FIREWORKS;
DISTINGUISHED GUESTS IN A HIGH CHAMBER
APPRECIATE THE LANTERNS

The moon and stars dominate the void
   as a myriad candles blaze;
In the human realm, and in Heaven above,[1]
   there are two Lantern Festivals.
When music is performed in the spring
   it sounds especially good;
As people return from the revels by night
   even their horses are smart.
Do not waste the fullness of your youth,
   so quickly does it pass;[2]
With total impartiality, white hair
   does not let anyone escape.[3]
Since even a thousand pieces of gold buys
   such a little time;
Let the watchman take his time striking
   the watches of the night.

THE STORY GOES that when Hsi-men Ch'ing had seen off the representatives of the Ch'iao family, he came back to the master suite to talk things over with Yüeh-niang, Sister-in-law Wu, and Li P'ing-erh.

"Since their family has anticipated us by sending over holiday gifts for our child," said Yüeh-niang, "we can hardly avoid buying holiday presents of our own to send to their daughter, Chang-chieh. They can be regarded as being temporary equivalents of betrothal gifts. That way we won't be remiss in our social obligations."

"Our side of the family ought to select a go-between," said Sister-in-law Wu. "It would make the negotiations back and forth more convenient."

"They have chosen Auntie K'ung," said Yüeh-niang. "Who should we select for the job?"

"One guest does not trouble two hosts,"
said Hsi-men Ch'ing. "We might as well give the job to Old Mother Feng."

Thereupon, eight invitation cards were hastily written out, and Old Mother
Feng was sent for. She was instructed to take a letter box containing the invitations and deliver them, along with Tai-an, inviting Kinswoman Ch'iao, Madame Ch'iao, the widow of Ch'iao the Fifth, the wife of Provincial Graduate
Shang, the wife of Censor Chu, Kinswoman Ts'ui, Big Sister Tuan, and Third
Sister Cheng, along with Sister-in-law Wu, to a lantern viewing party on the
fifteenth in celebration of Li P'ing-erh's birthday.

At the same time, Lai-hsing was sent off to the confectioner's with the necessary silver to place an order for steamed-shortcake pastries, which were to be
served on large square trays. He ordered four trays of steamed pastries: two of
stuffed moon cakes, and two of rose-flavored Lantern Festival dumplings. He
also bought four trays of fresh fruit: one of prunes, one of walnuts, one of
longans, and one of litchis; and four trays of casseroles: one of roast goose,
one of roast chicken, one of pigeon, and one of dried whitebait. In addition
there were two outfits of brocaded tussore clothing, one little crimson robe, a
miniature fret of crepe and gold filigree, two translucent ramshorn lanterns
from Yunnan, as well as a box of trinkets containing a pair of little gold ban-
gles, and four gold rings set with precious stones.

Ying Po-chüeh happened to show up at this juncture in order to speak to
Hsi-men Ch'ing about the question of when the merchant contractors Li
Chih and Huang the Fourth would receive payment for the consignment of
goods they had undertaken to purvey for the use of the imperial household.
When he saw the flurry of activity, he asked what it was all about.

Hsi-men Ch'ing told him about the marriage alliance he had made with
the household of Ch'iao Hung and went on to say, "On the fifteenth, whatever
happens, I hope that your wife will be able to come and keep company with
our new kinsfolk."

"If my sister-in-law so wishes," said Ying Po-chüeh, "my wife will be sure to
come."

"Today," said Hsi-men Ch'ing, "my wife is entertaining the wives of the
various officials, so we can convene at the house on Lion Street."

That day, the fourteenth, when the presents had been packed, he had his
son-in-law, Ch'en Ching-chi, accompanied by Pen the Fourth, dressed in his
black livery, deliver the gifts. They were duly entertained by the Ch'iao household, who lavishly returned the compliment by sending the gift boxes back
filled with numerous examples of needlework and footwear, but there is no
need to describe this in detail.

To resume our story, that day Wu Yin-erh in the licensed quarter also
brought gifts ahead of time in honor of Li P'ing-erh's birthday. She had purchased a tray of sweetmeats in the shape of birthday peaches, a tray of birthday
noodles, two roast ducks, a set of pig's trotters, two gold lamé handkerchiefs,

and a pair of women's shoes for the occasion, in order to pay obeisance to Li P'ing-erh as her godmother and get herself acknowledged as an adopted daughter. Yüeh-niang accepted the gifts on her behalf and sent the sedan chair back home.

Li Kuei-chieh did not arrive until the following day, and when she saw that Wu Yin-erh was already there, she surreptitiously asked Yüeh-niang, "How long has she been here?"

Yüeh-niang told her, thus and so, "Yesterday she brought gifts and paid obeisance to the Sixth Lady in order to be acknowledged as her adopted daughter."

When Li Kuei-chieh heard this, she hadn't a word to say, but she was huffy with Wu Yin-erh all day long, the two of them refusing to speak to each other.

To resume our story, the troupe of twenty actors that Hsi-men Ch'ing had borrowed from Wang the Second, the distaff relative of the imperial family, arrived in the front reception hall, carrying their trunks. They were under the supervision of two instructors and kowtowed to Hsi-men Ch'ing on their arrival. Hsi-men Ch'ing gave orders that they should use an anteroom on the western side of the front compound as their green room, that they were to be provided with food and drink, and that when the female guests arrived they should welcome them in with a flourish of wind and percussion instruments.

In the main reception hall:

Tortoiseshell mats look spruce
Brocade carpets cover the floor.

The first guests to arrive were the wife of Commandant Chou Hsiu, Director-in-chief Ching Chung's mother, Madame Ching, and the wife of Militia Commander Chang Kuan, all of whom were in large sedan chairs, escorted by orderlies who shouted to clear the way, and attended by the wives of their household retainers. Yüeh-niang and her sister-wives, all dressed in formal gowns, came out from inside to greet them and ushered them into the rear reception hall, where, after the appropriate salutations had been exchanged, they were invited to sit down and have some tea.

They were waiting for the arrival of the wife of Judicial Commissioner Hsia Yen-ling before tea was to be served, but who could have anticipated that although they waited until noon, she had not yet come. Page boys were dispatched to urge her on her way two or three times, but it was not until early afternoon that she finally arrived, with escorts shouting to clear the way, bearers carrying her dressing cases, attended by the wives of her household retainers, and surrounded by a retinue of servants. After she had been escorted to the rear reception hall to the strains of martial music and exchanged amenities with the other female guests, they all sat down in order of precedence.

First tea was served to them in the summerhouse, after which they were invited to take their seats in the main reception hall. Refreshments were served and wine was poured by Ch'un-mei, Yü-hsiao, Ying-ch'un, and Lan-hsiang, all of whom were adorned with cloud-shaped chignons, pearl necklaces, gold lantern earrings, brocade vests, scarlet satin jackets, and kingfisher-blue gold lamé skirts, with the exception of Ch'un-mei, who sported pendant earrings set with precious stones and a scarlet brocade vest.

That day the private troupe of Wang the Second, the distaff relative of the imperial family, performed *Hsi-hsiang chi*, or *The Romance of the Western Chamber*. We will say no more for the moment about how the party progressed:

> Deeply secluded within the decorated hall:[4]
> Amid clustering pearls and kingfisher ornaments,[5]
> Song and dance and wind and string instruments,

but return to the story of Hsi-men Ch'ing.

That day, after he had seen that the female guests in his home were offered tea, he mounted his horse and proceeded to the house on Lion Street, where he had arranged to meet with Ying Po-chüeh and Hsieh Hsi-ta. He directed that one of the four racks of fireworks that he had ordered should be taken there, and that two of them should be set up for the entertainment of the female guests that night. On the second floor of the house on Lion Street standing screens and a table of refreshments were set up, lanterns were hung, a chef was engaged to relight the fire in the stove, two food boxes containing meat and vegetable dishes and two jars of Chin-hua wine were dispatched from home, and two singing girls, Tung Chiao-erh and Han Yü-ch'uan, were engaged for the occasion.

It so happens that Hsi-men Ch'ing had previously sent Tai-an to hire a sedan chair and invite Wang Liu-erh to join him at the house on Lion Street.

On seeing her, he said, "Auntie Han, Father has invited you to the house over there to enjoy the fireworks this evening."

"I'd be too embarrassed," the woman laughed. "How could I do that? Wouldn't your uncle Han be upset if he found out about it?"

"Father has already spoken to Uncle Han about it," said Tai-an. He wants you to get yourself ready as quickly as possible. He would have sent Old Mother Feng for you, but they are entertaining the wives of the various officials today, and the Sixth Lady has told her to help tend Kuan-ko, so she's over there looking out for herself. Father insisted on sending me instead. He has engaged two singing girls, and there is no one to keep them company."

When the woman had heard him out, she was still unwilling to make a move, but before long, who should turn up but Han Tao-kuo himself.

"Well, if it isn't Uncle Han," said Tai-an. "Auntie Han here won't believe what I tell her."

The woman turned to her husband and said, "Do you really want me to go?"

"The master has repeatedly remarked that there is no one to keep the two singing girls company," said Han Tao-kuo. "He has invited you over there to enjoy the fireworks tonight. He's waiting for you. Haven't you gotten yourself ready yet? He also told me, just now, to close up the shop and come visit with him myself this evening. Lai-pao has also gone home for the time being. It's his turn to spend the night at the shop this evening."

"Who knows how late it will be before the party breaks up," the woman said. "When you go over there, stay a little while and then come home. There's no one to look after the place, and you don't have to spend the night at the shop."

When they had finished speaking, she dressed up for the occasion and, accompanied by Tai-an, went straight to the house on Lion Street. Lai-chao's wife, "The Beanpole," had previously straightened up the bedroom and its k'ang frame, put out the ready-made curtains and bedding, lit some benzoin and aloeswood incense which exuded a pungent fragrance, hung up two gauze lanterns in the room, and ignited the charcoal in the brazier on the floor. The woman walked in and sat down on the k'ang. After a while, Lai-chao's wife, "The Beanpole," came in, bowed to her, saying, "Many felicitations," and served her with tea.

Hsi-men Ch'ing and Ying Po-chüeh, after having looked at the lanterns for a while, finally arrived at the house, where they sat down on the second floor to play backgammon together. There were six windows with suspended blinds on the second floor overlooking the Lantern Market below, where:

The merrymaking was at its height.

After they had played backgammon for a while, they put the game away and had something to eat. The two of them then proceeded to look down on the Lantern Market from inside the blinds. Behold:

The people from ten thousand households
    are attired in brocade;
Their perfumed carriages and fine steeds
    rumble like thunder.
Hills of lanterns soar into the heavens
    above the azure clouds;
From whence do revellers not congregate
    to take in the sights?[6]

Ying Po-chüeh happened to ask, "How many people from the Ch'iao household are coming to your place tomorrow?"

"Their relative Madame Ch'iao, the widow of Ch'iao the Fifth, the distaff relative of the imperial family, is coming; but I won't be home tomorrow. In the morning I've got to go to the temple to attend the *chiao* rites of cosmic renewal in celebration of the Festival of the First Prime, and after that, Commandant Chou Hsiu of the Regional Military Command has invited me to a party."

As he was speaking, Hsi-men Ch'ing noticed that, amid the throng of people below, Hsieh Hsi-ta, Chu Jih-nien, and a man wearing a square-cut scholar's cap were standing beneath a lantern stall, looking at the lanterns.

Pointing them out to Ying Po-chüeh, he went on to ask, "Do you happen to recognize that man wearing the square-cut scholar's cap? What is he doing tagging along with them?"

"He has a familiar look about him," replied Ying Po-chüeh, "but I don't recognize him."

Hsi-men Ch'ing then instructed Tai-an, "You go down there and surreptitiously invite Hsieh Hsi-ta to come up here. But don't let Pockmarked Chu, or that other fellow, catch on."

Now the page boy Tai-an was the sort of knave of whom it could be said:
   He doesn't miss a wink.
He went straight downstairs and insinuated himself into the midst of the crowd. Waiting until Chu Jih-nien and the other person had moved along, he stepped out from one side and gave Hsieh Hsi-ta a tug with his hand, which startled him into turning around to see who it was who had accosted him.

Tai-an said to him, "Father and Master Ying the Second are on the upper floor here and would like to have a word with you."

"You go ahead," said Hsieh Hsi-ta. "I understand. Wait until I've accompanied the two of them as far as the place where they're making artificial plum blossoms. I'll come to see your master after that."

Tai-an then disappeared in a puff of smoke.

Who would have thought that, no sooner did they arrive at the place where they were making artificial plum blossoms, than Hsieh Hsi-ta ducked into the crowd, leaving Chu Jih-nien and the other person to look for him in vain, and made his way upstairs to see Hsi-men Ch'ing and Ying Po-chüeh.

Upon seeing the two of them, he said, "Brother, if you were coming here to see the lanterns, why didn't you say something about it this morning to let me know your plans?"

"I didn't feel like mentioning it in front of everyone this morning," said Hsi-men Ch'ing. "I did send Brother Ying the Second to your place to invite you, but you were not at home. By the way, did Pockmarked Chu see that you were coming here just now?"

"And who was that fellow wearing the square-cut scholar's cap?" he went on to ask.

"The person wearing the square-cut scholar's cap," said Hsieh Hsi-ta, "is Wang the Third, the son of Imperial Commissioner Wang. Today he came to my place with Pockmarked Chu to ask for my assistance in arranging a loan of three hundred taels of silver from the moneylender Hsü Pu-yü, or Reneger Hsü. He has asked me, along with Blabbermouth Sun and Pockmarked Chu, to be guarantors for the loan. He wants to pursue a career by purchasing a position in the Military School, but I can't be bothered to take an interest in his private affairs. Just now I was accompanying him for a stroll in the Lantern Market, when your esteemed servant summoned me, so I simply saw them as far as the place where they're making artificial plum blossoms and then, taking advantage of the crowded situation, gave them the slip and came to join you."

Turning to Ying Po-chüeh, he then went on to ask, "How long have you been here?"

"Brother initially sent me to your place, but you weren't at home," said Ying Po-chüeh. "So I came here and have been playing backgammon with him for a while."

"Have you eaten yet?" asked Hsi-men Ch'ing. "I'll have the page boy bring you something to eat."

"You must know," said Hsieh Hsi-ta, "that after leaving your place this morning, I've spent the whole day with those two, so how could I have had anything to eat?"

Hsi-men Ch'ing instructed Tai-an, "Go down to the kitchen and prepare something for Master Hsieh to eat."

Before long, the table was wiped clean, and a platter of assorted cold hors d'oeuvres, two bowls of different kinds of soft-boiled fricassee, a bowl of blanched pork and vermicelli soup, and two bowls of white rice were placed before him. Hsieh Hsi-ta set to and polished it off all by himself, leaving the utensils spick-and-span, within and without; after which he poured the remaining gravy over his rice and gobbled it all up. When Tai-an had cleared the dishes away, Hsieh Hsi-ta sat to one side and looked on as the other two played backgammon.

What should they see at this juncture but the two singing girls who got out of their sedan chairs at the door and came in smiling, while the sedan chair bearers brought in their bundles of clothes.

Ying Po-chüeh, who had already spotted them through the window, said, "So, the two little whores are only now arriving."

He then instructed Tai-an, saying, "Don't let them go into the rear of the house. Have them come upstairs to see me first."

"Which two have been engaged for today?" Hsieh Hsi-ta asked.

"It's Tung Chiao-erh and Han Yü-ch'uan," replied Tai-an.

Then, hastening downstairs, he said to them, "Master Ying the Second wants to have a word with you."

The two of them refused to comply but proceeded straight back to the rear, where they were greeted by "The Beanpole" and ushered into a room where they encountered Wang Liu-erh.

On her head she sported a fashionable fret with a twisted center and a gold-spangled sheepskin headband; on her torso she wore a purple jacket of Lu-chou silk, a jet cloak with a stiff-standing, tilelike collar, over a white drawnwork silk skirt; beneath which appeared the upturned tips of her two golden lotuses, enclosed in black satin, flat-heeled shoes that were chain stitched with sand-green thread. Her temples were adorned with two long spit curls, she had a rosewood complexion, and she did not use much face powder, attempting to emulate the style of a person of middling status. From her ears dangled a pair of clove-shaped pendant earrings.[7]

On coming in the door, they made her an obeisance and then sat down on the edge of the k'ang. Little Iron Rod served them with tea, and Wang Liu-erh joined them in drinking it. The two singing girls could not take their eyes off her, looking her over from top to toe. After staring for a while, the two of them laughed awkwardly, not knowing who they were in the presence of.

Later on, when Tai-an came in, they surreptitiously asked him, "Who is that person in the room?"

Tai-an didn't know what to reply, merely saying, "She's the master's aunt, who's been invited here to see the lanterns."

When the two of them heard this, they returned to the room and began anew, saying, "We didn't realize, just now, that you were an aunt in the family, so we failed to show you proper respect. Please don't take it amiss."

Thereupon, as though inserting a taper in its holder, they kowtowed to her twice, which flustered Wang Liu-erh into hastily returning half a kowtow to them. Later on, refreshments were served, and they ate them together. The two of them then got out their instruments and sang for Wang Liu-erh's entertainment.

When Ying Po-chüeh had finished a game of backgammon, he came downstairs to relieve himself. Hearing the singing in the interior of the house, he beckoned to Tai-an and asked him, "Tell me. Just who are the two singing girls performing for back there?"

Tai-an merely smiled, without making a sound, and said, "You're like:
        The intendant of the Ts'ao-chou Military Defense Circuit:
        The area of your jurisdiction is broad.[8]
What's it to you whether they sing or not?"

"Why you lousy little oily-mouth!" said Ying Po-chüeh. "If you refuse to tell me, you needn't fear that I won't find out."

Tai-an laughed and said, "If you can find out, so be it. What are you asking me for?" After saying which, he headed straight into the rear of the house.

Ying Po-chüeh went back upstairs, where Hsi-men Ch'ing went on to play three more games of backgammon with Hsieh Hsi-ta.

Whom should they see at this juncture but Li Ming and Wu Hui, the two of whom suddenly came upstairs and kowtowed to them.

"Wonderful!" exclaimed Ying Po-chüeh. "The two of you have arrived in the nick of time. Where have you been, and how did you know we were here?"

Li Ming knelt down, deferentially covered his mouth with his hand, and said, "Wu Hui and I initially dropped by His Honor's residence, but the people there said that he was having a party with all of you at the house over here, so we came over to offer our services."

"That's fine," said Hsi-men Ch'ing. "You can stand up and wait in attendance."

Then, turning to Tai-an, he said, "Go quickly across the street and invite your uncle Han to come join us."

Before long, Han Tao-kuo arrived, made a bow, and sat down. A table was then set up, a platter of assorted cold hors d'oeuvres suitable to accompany a drinking party was brought up from the kitchen, and Ch'in-t'ung stood at their side, decanting the wine from a brass warming pan equipped with a wire-mesh strainer. Ying Po-chüeh and Hsieh Hsi-ta occupied the positions of honor, Hsimen Ch'ing played the role of host, and Han Tao-kuo took a seat to one side. As soon as they were seated, wine was poured, and Tai-an was dispatched to the rear of the house to invite the singing girls to join them.

After a brief interval, Han Yü-ch'uan and Tung Chiao-erh, the two of them:

> Just as slow and easy as you please,

came up the stairs, and:

> Neither correctly nor precisely,

kowtowed to the company.

Ying Po-chüeh took them to task, saying, "I wondered who they were, and it turns out to be these two little whores. Just now, you knew I was here, and that I was calling for you, so why didn't you come to pay your respects to me first? What a nerve! In the future, if I don't give you both something to remember me by, you'll get completely out of hand."

"Brother here," said Tung Chiao-erh with a laugh, "has been reduced to:

> Making faces at me over the wall;
> He's scaring me to death!"

"As we all know," chimed in Han Yü-ch'uan:

> "The little darling, in flashing his animal mask
>   over the ramparts;
> Is just a child, displaying his ugliness."

"Brother," said Ying Po-chüeh, "there's a downright redundancy around here today. Since we already have Li Ming and Wu Hui to sing for us, what do we need these two little whores for? You'd better send them packing as soon as possible. On the evening of a major festival like this, they can still pick up a few coins for themselves. If you wait until it's too late, there will be no one around to want them."

"Brother," protested Han Yü-ch'uan, "how shameless can you get? It's His Honor who called for our services. We're not here to cater to you. Brother, how can you bring yourself to vent your spleen so aimlessly?"

"Why you silly little splay-legged whore!" exclaimed Ying Po-chüeh. "You're here right now, and if you don't cater to me, to whom are you going to cater?"

Han Yü-ch'uan responded:

> "When Fatty T'ang fell into the vinegar vat,
> Enough got splashed on you to turn you sour."

"Why you lousy little whore!" said Ying Po-chüeh. "It's turned me sour, has it? Just you wait. When we break up and you're ready to go home, I'll have something to say to you. One way or the other, there are two different things I can do, so you needn't expect to escape."

"And what two things are those?" demanded Tung Chiao-erh. "Tell me about them."

"The first thing I can do," said Ying Po-chüeh, "is to report you to the police and have you arrested for violating the curfew. Then the next day I could send a card to Commandant Chou and have you subjected to a good finger-squeezing. Or, if you were really recalcitrant, it would only require three candareens worth of distilled spirits to get your chair bearers drunk enough to take advantage of you. Then, when you got home late, with no money to show for it, the madam would be sure to give you a beating for your pains, which would be no skin off my back."

"If it gets too late," said Han Yü-ch'uan, "we won't go home, but spend the night in His Honor's house here. Or else, we can get His Honor to send someone to escort us home.

Whether Dame Wang gets her hundred cash or not,
It's not up to you.[9]
What a rot-talking sl/imy kn/ave[10] you are!"

"If I'm a slave," said Ying Po-chüeh, "the world, nowadays, must be topsy-turvy. The time has come to:

Call a spade a spade."

When they had talked and laughed together for a while, the two singing girls stood to one side and sang a song celebrating the beauties of spring. Only after that did the company proceed to devour the refreshments that had been provided for them.

At this juncture, who should appear but Tai-an, who came in to say that Master Chu had shown up; which news failed to elicit any response from the company.

Before long, Chu Jih-nien came up the stairs and, on seeing that Ying Po-chüeh and Hsieh Hsi-ta were there, said, "So, the pair of you are feasting away, are you? What sort of conduct is that?"

"And as for you, Tagalong Hsieh," he went on to say. "If Brother invited you up here, you might have given me the word, instead of slipping off that way without anyone's knowing it, and leaving me to look for you in vain around the area where they make the artificial plum blossoms."

"I just happened to stray out of the way," explained Hsieh Hsi-ta, "and chanced to see Brother up here playing backgammon with Brother Ying the Second. When I came upstairs and saluted them, Brother asked me to stay."

Hsi-men Ch'ing then instructed Tai-an, "Go get a chair for Brother Chu, and give him a seat at the other end of the table."

Thereupon, Tai-an provided a place setting for him at the lower end of the table, and he sat down. Soup and rice were brought up for him from the kitchen, and he joined the others in consuming the refreshments.

When Hsi-men Ch'ing had eaten only a single steamed bun, and swallowed a mouthful of soup, he noticed that Li Ming was standing beside him and gave the remainder of his food to him, to take off and eat by himself. Meanwhile, Ying Po-chüeh, Hsieh Hsi-ta, Chu Jih-nien, and Han Tao-kuo consumed a soup of eight ingredients served in a large, deep porcelain bowl decorated with a blue and white pattern and ate three large steamed buns apiece, as well as four steamed open-topped dumplings, the tops of which were adorned with peach blossoms. Only a single steamed bun was left to anchor the plate. After the servants had cleared away the soup bowls, wine was decanted and they proceeded to drink.

Hsieh Hsi-ta then asked Chu Jih-nien, "How far did you go with him before you managed to get away, and how did you know that I was here?"

Chu Jih-nien, thereupon, told him about it, thus and so, saying, "After looking around for you a while without success, I accompanied Wang the Third to Sun T'ien-hua's house, where we had agreed to meet, and then proceeded to Hsü Pu-yü's place to arrange a loan of three hundred taels of silver. But Blabbermouth Sun, the old oily-mouth, had composed a defective loan contract."

"Leave my name out of the contract," said Hsieh Hsi-ta. "I don't want any part of it. One way or the other, you and Old Sun can act as guarantors, and dun him for a guarantor's fee to spend on yourselves."

"What did he get wrong on the contract, anyway?" he went on to ask.

"I had told him," replied Chu Jih-nien, "to word the contract in somewhat slippery terms, stipulating three preconditions for the repayment of the loan; but he did not follow my suggestion, so I had to rewrite the document from scratch."

"So how did you word the contract?" asked Hsieh Hsi-ta. "Read it aloud for our benefit."

"This is the way I worded it," said Chu Jih-nien.

The contracting party, Wang Ts'ai, scion of the household of Imperial Commissioner Wang, (instead of "because he wants money to spend," amended to) wanting money to spend, has arranged, through the good offices of Sun T'ien-hua and Chu Jih-nien, to borrow the sum of three hundred taels of (instead of "silver," amended to) soft currency, and agrees to remit (instead of "interest," amended to) a "plum" of five hundred cash per month, and commits himself to repay the principal (instead of "next year," amended to) when three preconditions are met. These three preconditions are: firstly:

When the windblown axle of a windlass
knocks a goose out of the sky;

secondly:

> When the fish underneath the surface
>> leap onto the shore;

and thirdly:

> When the rocks submerged underwater
>> dissolve into powder.

Only when these three preconditions are met will repayment of the loan become due. (He had written "In the year when the boundary stones nod their heads repayment of the loan will become due." But I pointed out that the precondition "when the boundary stones nod their heads" might be met if there should be an earthquake some year. Where would that leave you? So I amended it to read) If the borrower should lack the funds to repay the loan, the guarantors will make themselves scarce. Lest questions should arise in the future, this written contract as set down is hereby declared invalid. (At the end I also had him append the words "null and void.")

"If you word it that way," said Hsieh Hsi-ta, "it could hardly be said not to be slippery enough. By the time the rocks submerged underwater have been reduced to powder:

> Who knows whether the monk will still
>> be around or not?"[11]

"That's to put too good a construction on it," said Chu Jih-nien. "If someday there should be a drought and water levels are low, the court would order the dredging of the waterways, and the submerged rocks might be hacked to powder with two or three blows from a workman's mattock. Where would that leave you? In such a case you'd be unable to avoid paying back the loan."

As the group of them talked and laughed together for a while, it gradually became evening, and Hsi-men Ch'ing directed that the lanterns should be lighted. Two translucent ramshorn lanterns of extraordinary intricacy were suspended under the eaves, one on either side.

Who could have anticipated that at this juncture Yüeh-niang, back at home, should have sent Ch'i-t'ung and an orderly to deliver four partitioned boxes of mouth-watering sweetmeats and fancy fruits for their delectation. There were:

> Blazing yellow kumquats,
> Fragrant red pomegranates,
> Delectable bittersweet olives,
> Verdant green apples, and
> Redolently fragrant pears.

And there were also:

> Honeysweet candied persimmons,
> Sugar-soaked giant dates,
> Butterfat pine nut pastries,
> Elephant-eye-shaped sesame candy,
> Domino-like deep-fried sweetmeats, and
> Honey-basted chain-shaped crullers.

In addition there were:
> Willow-leaf candy, and
> Ox-hide taffy.

Truly, they were things:
> Rarely found in this world,
> Seldom seen in the universe.

Hsi-men Ch'ing called for Ch'i-t'ung to come forward and asked him, "Has the conclave of ladies at home broken up yet, or not? Are they still there drinking wine? And who sent you to deliver these treats here?"

"The First Lady sent me to deliver them," replied Ch'i-t'ung, "for you to enjoy here with your wine. The party has not broken up completely yet. After four scenes of the hsi-wen drama had been performed, the First Lady kept them for another round of drinks at the front gate, so they could enjoy the fireworks."

"Are there onlookers there?" asked Hsi-men Ch'ing.

"The people who came to watch filled the street," replied Ch'i-t'ung.

"I told P'ing-an," said Hsi-men Ch'ing, "to retain four black-clad orderlies and station them at the gate, with staves in hand, to hold back the crowd if necessary, and not let any riffraff press too close."

"P'ing-an and I, along with the orderlies, were all there to oversee the fireworks display," said Ch'i-t'ung. "It was only after most of the company had left that the First Lady sent me here. There weren't any riffraff causing trouble."

When Hsi-men Ch'ing heard this, he ordered that the leftovers remaining on the table be cleared away and replaced with the boxes of treats that had just arrived. A serving of stuffed Lantern Festival dumplings was brought up from the kitchen, and the two singing girls poured the wine.

On the one hand, Hsi-men Ch'ing told Ch'i-t'ung to go home and look after things there, while, on the other hand:
> More vintage wine was poured, and
> Another feast of delicacies was spread.

Li Ming and Wu Hui were then asked to entertain the company with a song suite in celebration of the Lantern Festival, to the tune "Fresh Water Song" in the *shuang-tiao* mode:

> On this festive day in the metropolis
>> we enjoy the Lantern Festival.[12]
> Encompassing the hills of lanterns,
>> auspicious clouds gather.
> One gazes at the pure luster of the stars of the milky way,
> And observes the moon's orb, high over the celestial moat.
> The strains of a classic melody are struck up.
> Tortoiseshell mats are spread,
> In order to enjoy the revels.

To the tune "River-bobbed Oars":

A Powerful Family Blocks Its Gate in Order to Enjoy Fireworks

Decorated lanterns are suspended on either side,
On top of which, a skyful of moon and stars[13]
  shine bright.
Everywhere we look, the pendants of embroidered sashes
  are flying in the wind,
Jeweled canopies sway gently,
On hills of lanterns, the lamplight
  is scintillating,
Paper cutouts of spring moths quiver atop chignons.

To the tune "Seven Brothers":

On the one hand, there is dancing,
There is singing,
And there is instrumental music.
The astonishing vaudeville acts
  are truly marvelous;
The terrifying aerial performances
  are utterly inimitable;
The comical yüan-pen farces
  are truly comical.

To the tune "Plum Blossom Wine":

Ah! On one hand, they do the dance of the old crone.
The wellborn young ladies are dolled up
  to look their best,
Displaying their seductiveness in a myriad ways,[14]
With a hundred allurements and a thousand coquetries.[15]
On the one hand, hoofers parade to the drum,
On the other hand, mummers parade on stilts.
It is truly a comical sight.
The fine haze is redolent of orchid and musk.
With broad smiles we drink the fragrant wine.

To the tune "Enjoying the South":

Ah! Today, in joyous abandon, we feast in order to
  celebrate the Lantern Festival.
Slender jade fingers gently strum
  the rosewood instruments.
The light of the lanterns and the bright moon
  illuminate each other,
Shining on towers and terraces, halls and chambers.

Distinguished Guests in a High Chamber Appreciate the Lanterns

Today is a time to relax, become intoxicated,
    and devote ourselves to pleasure.[16]

When the singing was over, they ate the Lantern Festival dumplings, and
then Han Tao-kuo was the first to go home. Shortly thereafter, Hsi-men Ch'ing
ordered Lai-chao to open up the twelve-foot-wide lower room, hang up the
blinds, and carry the rack of fireworks outside. Hsi-men Ch'ing and his guests
looked on from the second-story, while Wang Liu-erh, along with the two
singing girls and Lai-chao's wife, "The Beanpole," were able to watch the
show from the floor below.

Tai-an and Lai-chao set up the rack of fireworks in the middle of the street
and, moments later, proceeded to set them off. The bystanders on either side
who crowded around to see the show:

Rubbing shoulders and nudging elbows,
Were incalculable in number.[17]

They all said, "When His Honor Hsi-men Ch'ing chooses to put on a fireworks display here, who wouldn't come to see it. Truly, they have been set up
just right. What fine fireworks!" Behold:

The rack of fireworks soars up
    fifteen feet high;
On all sides hill-shaped booths
    bustle with activity.
On the highest point there stands
    an immortal's crane,
Holding a vermilion edict suspended
    from its mouth,
Which turns out to be a "high-rising rocket."[18]
When it first takes off,
With a sudden rush, it creates
    a trail of cold light,[19]
Boring its way right up beside the
    Herd Boy and the Dipper.
Only after that,
In the middle distance, a "watermelon bomb"
    explodes into sight,
Showering sparks on the spectators
    in all four directions,
Pi po-po, a myriad thunderclaps
    all resound at once.
"Lotus-gathering boats" and "brighter than moonlights,"[20]
One chasing after the other,
Are just like "golden lanterns"[21] dispersing
    the "stars in the azure sky."

"Purple grapes,"[22] by the thousands and ten thousands,
Resemble a cascade of "black dragon pearls,"
   a "portiere of beaded crystal."
The "whips of the Hegemon-King"[23]
   crack everywhere;
The "earthbound rats"[24] scurry about
   under peoples' clothes.
"Alabaster cups" and "jade saucers,"
Whirl about in a way that is
   truly spectacular;
"Silver moths" and "golden cicadas,"
Display ingenuity that could scarcely
   be improved upon.
The "Eight Immortals bearing birthday gifts,"
Severally display their magic powers;[25]
The "Seven Sages subduing demons,"[26]
Appear completely shrouded in flames.
"Yellow sparklers"[27] and "green sparklers,"
Produce enveloping mists resembling
   a "myriad sunset clouds;"
"Quick- and slow-blooming lotus blossoms,"[28]
Flare resplendently, vying to display
   a "montage of brocades."[29]
"Ten-foot chrysanthemums"[30] and "smoky orchids"[31]
   confront each other;
"Big pear blossoms"[32] and "fallen peach blossoms"
   contest the spring.
"Towers and terraces," "halls and chambers,"
In but a trice cease to exhibit
   their lofty eminence;
The drumming of the "parading village mummers,"
Seems to subside, its joyful hubbub
   no longer heard.
The "peddler's basket,"
Above and below, shines crystal clear;
The "old crone's cart,"
Both head and tail, explodes to bits.
The "Five Devils plaguing the Assessor,"[33]
With scorched heads and singed scalps[34]
   manifest their bellicosity;
As a result of the "tenfold ambuscade,"[35]
Horses collapse, men gallop away, and
   the outcome remains in doubt.

Despite the fact that infinite ingenuity
    may have been expended
In the end:
The fire burns out and the smoke dissolves,[36]
    leaving nothing but ashes.

The jade clepsydra with its bronze tanks
    should not hurry one along;[37]
The starry bridges and trees of lanterns[38]
    will scintillate until dawn.[39]
The ten thousand varieties of puppetry
    are nothing but illusions;
Providing an excuse for the revellers to
    return home with a smile.

Ying Po-chüeh saw that Hsi-men Ching was drunk, and when he went downstairs to relieve himself immediately after the fireworks were over, he noticed that Wang Liu-erh was there, so he took Hsieh Hsi-ta and Chu Jih-nien by the hand and left without bidding his host farewell.

"Where are you off to?" asked Tai-an.

"My clever child," Ying Po-chüeh whispered into his ear, "it's that matter I asked you about before. If I were not to go, those others would stick around indefinitely, which would look as though I didn't know the score. When your master asks, just tell him that we've all left."

Later on, when Hsi-men Ch'ing realized that the fireworks were over and asked where Ying Po-chüeh and the others had gotten to, Tai-an said, "Master Ying the Second and Master Hsieh all went off together. I wasn't able to hold them back. They told me to convey their thanks."

Hsi-men Ch'ing did not inquire any further but summoned Li Ming and Wu Hui, rewarded each of them with a large bumper of wine, and said, "I won't pay you the fee for your performance right now, because I'd like the two of you to come and help out again, early on the sixteenth. I'll be entertaining those three, Master Ying the Second and the others, along with my managers and employees, for a drinking party at the front gate that evening."

Li Ming knelt down, and said, "I'm bound to report to Your Honor that on the sixteenth, I, along with the other three, Wu Hui, Tso Shun, and Cheng Feng, all have to report for duty at the installation ceremony for the newly promoted prefect of Tung-p'ing prefecture, His Honor Hu Shih-wen, so we couldn't show up before some time in the afternoon."

"In any case," said Hsi-men Ch'ing, "we won't begin drinking until evening. Just be sure you don't fail to appear, that's all."

"We would never dare let you down," the two of them said.

Thereupon, they knelt down to consume the wine that was offered them and then prepared to go out the door and make their farewells.

Hsi-men Ch'ing then said to the two singing girls, "Tomorrow, I'm entertaining some female guests at home. Li Kuei-chieh and Wu Yin-erh will also be there. Be sure that the two of you come along as well."

The two boy actors and the two singing girls then went out the gate together. But no more of this.

Hsi-men Ch'ing, after ordering Lai-chao, Tai-an, and Ch'in-t'ung to see that everything was properly cleared away, and to put out the lamps and candles, retired to the bedroom in the rear of the house.

To resume our story, Lai-chao's son, Little Iron Rod, had been outside watching the fireworks display when he saw that Hsi-men Ch'ing had withdrawn to the interior. Thereupon, he went upstairs, where he found his old man putting together a platter of leftover meat and other fare, along with a goblet of wine, and a few Lantern Festival dumplings, to take into their room. When he asked his mother, "The Beanpole," for some of it, she saw that he was still holding a singed firecracker in his hand and gave him a couple of slaps for his pains, but she did not prevent him from going into the rear courtyard to play.

Upon hearing the sound of laughter coming from the main room on the courtyard, he thought, "It must be the singing girls who haven't left yet." Noticing that the door was closed, he thereupon proceeded to peer inside through a crack and saw that the interior was brightly lit by lamps and candles. It so happens that Hsi-men Ch'ing and Wang Liu-erh were engaged in intercourse on the edge of the bed. Hsi-men Ch'ing, who was already the worse for wear, had bent the woman over the edge of the bed where, by the light of the lamp, he had stripped off her drawers, fastened the clasp on his organ, and was busy plucking the flower in her rear courtyard. Once he got started, he slammed away at her, back and forth, being good for no less than several hundred thrusts at a time. As he slammed away:

The reiterated sounds reverberated loudly.

The noise of their panting, and their back and forth movements, sounded, for all the world, as though they were engaged in breaking up the bed and could be heard everywhere. The little boy was too preoccupied by staring at this sight to notice when his mother, "The Beanpole," happened to come into the rear courtyard.

When she saw what her child was up to, she grabbed him by the tuft of hair on top of his head, dragged him back to the front of the house, gave him a couple of sharp raps on the head with her knuckles, and scolded him, saying, "You lousy mischief-making little slave! All you need is to risk your life a second time by going and eavesdropping on him once again!"

Thereupon, she gave him several Lantern Festival dumplings to eat, refused to let him out of the room, and threatened him into getting onto the k'ang and going to sleep.

Hsi-men Ch'ing and the woman kept at it for about the time it would take to eat two meals before finally calling it quits. Tai-an, who had taken care of providing food and wine for the chair bearers, then escorted her back to her home and returned to join Ch'in-t'ung in carrying lanterns as they accompanied Hsi-men Ch'ing back to his residence. Truly:

> Do not fear lest the bright moon should set,
> It will be succeeded by a subtle fragrance.[40]

There is a poem that testifies to this:

> Enjoying the view from the Southern Tower,
>   he forgets to go back;
> However romantic the occasion may be,
>   how long can it last?[41]
> By his return, the bright moon will be down
>   at the third watch;
> Obsessed with pleasure, before he knows it,
>   he is utterly sloshed.

> If you want to know the outcome of these events,
> Pray consult the story related in the following chapter.

Chapter 43

BECAUSE OF THE MISSING GOLD
HSI-MEN CH'ING CURSES CHIN-LIEN;
AS A RESULT OF THE BETROTHAL
YÜEH-NIANG MEETS MADAME CH'IAO

Scrutiny of the events of past and present
　　can only induce sorrow;
The exalted and the humble alike return
　　to a mere mound of earth.
Where are the occupants of the Jade Hall
　　of Emperor Wu of the Han?[1]
Within the Golden Valley of Shih Ch'ung[2]
　　the river flows aimlessly on.
Light and darkness continue to alternate
　　as dawn turns into dusk;
The luxurious foliage of spring inexorably
　　gives way to that of autumn.
Since mundane affairs, like time itself,
　　will never come to an end;
One might as well become a sojourner in
　　the Land of Drunkenness.[3]

THE STORY GOES that it was already the third watch by the time Hsi-men Ch'ing returned home. When he went back to the rear compound, he found that Wu Yüeh-niang had not yet gone to bed, but was sitting up with her sister-in-law, Wu K'ai's wife, and the others, having a chat. He also noticed that Li P'ing-erh was still in attendance, helping to serve the wine. As soon as Sister-in-law Wu saw that Hsi-men Ch'ing had come home, she moved into another room. Yüeh-niang, observing that he was inebriated, helped him off with his outer clothes and merely had Li P'ing-erh kowtow to him, after which they sat down together, and he asked a few questions about how things had gone at the party that day. After Yü-hsiao had served him with tea, because Sister-in-law Wu was there, he went to Meng Yü-lou's room to spend the night.

The next day, the chef arrived early in order to take care of the arrangements for the catered banquet. It was a day on which Hsi-men Ch'ing had to go to the yamen to perform the ceremonies of bowing before the imperial tablet and presiding over the general disposition of pending cases. When Judicial Commissioner Hsia Yen-ling saw him, he expressed his thanks for the pains he had expended for the entertainment of his wife the previous day.

"I fear the fare was extremely meager," said Hsi-men Ch'ing. "Forgive me. Forgive me."

When he arrived home, he found that Ch'iao Hung's household had sent Auntie K'ung to escort a servant from Madame Ch'iao the Fifth's establishment, who delivered gifts of a jug of southern wine and four kinds of delicacies for the occasion. Hsi-men Ch'ing accepted the gifts and saw that the servant was provided with food and wine. Auntie K'ung made her way to the rear compound where she was given a seat in Yüeh-niang's room. The sedan chair of Wu Shun-ch'en's wife, Third Sister Cheng, was the first to arrive, and after she had paid her respects to Yüeh-niang, she joined the others in keeping Auntie K'ung company while tea was served.

Just at this juncture, Li Chih and Huang the Fourth showed up with the sum of a thousand taels of silver that they had received in payment for the consignment of incense and wax that they had purveyed for the use of the imperial household and had arranged with Pen the Fourth to convey to Hsi-men Ch'ing's residence from Tung-p'ing prefecture. When Ying Po-chüeh got wind of this, he also hurried over to assist in seeing it duly transferred to Hsi-men Ch'ing. Ch'en Ching-chi was ordered to weigh it out with a steelyard in the reception hall, and when this process was completed, it was put away for safekeeping. They still owed Hsi-men Ch'ing five hundred taels of capital and a hundred and fifty taels of interest. On this occasion, Huang the Fourth brought out four gold bracelets, weighing thirty ounces altogether, as payment of the hundred and fifty taels of interest and proposed that they renegotiate the contract for the remainder of the debt.

"Wait until after the Lantern Festival is over," Hsi-men Ch'ing told the two of them. "You can come back and discuss it then. I'm tied up at home for the next few days."

At this, Li Chih and Huang the Fourth, reiterating, "Your Honor this, and Your Honor that," went out the gate with:

A thousand thanks and ten thousand
expressions of gratitude.

Ying Po-chüeh, preoccupied with the thought that since they had promised him something in the way of a karmic encumbrance, this would be a good opportunity to ask them about it, wanted to follow after them, but Hsi-men Ch'ing called him to a halt in order to have a word with him.

"Yesterday," he proceeded to ask, "how come the three of you ran off that way, before anyone was aware of it, without telling me what you were doing? I sent a page boy after you, but he fell behind and was unable to catch up with you."

"Yesterday," said Ying Po-chüeh, "I fear we imposed upon you egregiously and consumed more than enough wine. When I saw that you were in your cups and recalled that your wife was entertaining today and must be waiting up to discuss things with you, I realized that if we didn't take ourselves off, there was no telling how late we would keep at it. As it is, my guess would be that you haven't made it to the yamen today. You've been wearing yourself out for days on end."[4]

"By the time I got home yesterday," said Hsi-men Ch'ing, "it was already the third watch. Today I had to go to the yamen early to participate in the ceremony of bowing before the imperial tablet, take my place in court, and preside over the general disposition of pending cases, as well as spending some time on other public business. At the moment I'm preoccupied with the preparations for the party for the womenfolk here at home. And later today, after coming back from offering incense at the temple in connection with the *chiao* rites in celebration of the Festival of the First Prime, I've got to go to a party at the home of Commandant Chou Hsiu. Who knows what time it will be before I get home."

"It's a good thing you've got the temperament for it," said Ying Po-chüeh. "Such great good fortune as yours, and I'm not just flattering you to your face, is something that nobody else could hope to handle."

The two of them talked for a while, and Hsi-men Ch'ing wanted to keep him there to share a meal with him, but Ying Po-chüeh said, "I won't have anything to eat. I'm on my way."

"Why hasn't your wife shown up for the party?" Hsi-men Ch'ing went on to ask.

"The sedan chair for my wife has already been ordered," Ying Po-chüeh said. "She'll be here any minute now."

Whereupon, raising his hand in salute and saying goodbye, he went out the gate and hastened after Li Chih and Huang the Fourth. Truly:

Even if you command the art of driving the fog
and mounting the clouds;[5]
You cannot hope to obtain fire by drilling ice[6]
without the aid of money.

When Hsi-men Ch'ing had seen off Ying Po-chüeh, he fondled the four blazing yellow gold bracelets in his hand, which he found to be very worthy of admiration.

From his mouth no word was uttered, but
In his heart he thought to himself,

"This baby boy that Sister Li has borne is certainly starting out on a firm footing. No sooner was he born than I had this official position unexpectedly conferred upon me, and now I have formed a marriage alliance with the Ch'iao family, and made all this money to boot."

Thereupon, he secreted the four gold bracelets in his sleeve and, instead of going back to the rear compound, went straight into the garden, headed for Li P'ing-erh's quarters.

Just as he passed by the postern gate of P'an Chin-lien's quarters, Chin-lien happened to come out and, catching sight of him, called him to a halt, saying, "What's that you've got in hand there? Come over and let me have a look."

"Wait until I come back," said Hsi-men Ch'ing. "I'll let you see what it is then."

Whereupon, carrying his burden as before, he continued on his way to Li P'ing-erh's quarters.

The woman, on seeing that she had failed to call him back, was more than a little mortified and said, "What sort of rare object could it be that he should be in such a frightful hurry over, refusing to let me see it? May he break his leg, the lousy three-inch good-for-nothing of a ruffian! When he sets foot on her threshold, may he come a cropper, fracture both his legs, and thereby:

Suffer the consequences before my very eyes."

To resume our story, Hsi-men Ch'ing, carrying the gold bracelets in hand, went into Li P'ing-erh's quarters and saw that she had just finished combing her hair, and that the wet nurse was holding the baby and playing with him. He went straight over to them and, putting the four gold bracelets into the baby's hands, encouraged him to play with them.

"Where did those come from?" Li P'ing-erh asked. "I'm afraid they may be too cold for his hands."

Hsi-men Ch'ing told her all about how Li Chih and Huang the Fourth had shown up that day in order to repay the silver they had borrowed from him, and that he had agreed to accept these gold bracelets in lieu of interest. Li P'ing-erh, fearful lest the baby's hands should be chilled, insisted on chafing the bracelets with a figured handkerchief before letting him continue to play with them.

Whom should they see at this juncture but Tai-an, who came in and reported, "Manager Yün Li-shou has ridden over with two horses and is waiting outside. He'd like Father to go out and take a look at them."

"Where did Manager Yün come by these horses?" asked Hsi-men Ch'ing.

"He says that his elder brother, Assistant Regional Commander Yün, sent the horses from his post on the frontier," replied Tai-an. "He claims that they can really step along pretty well."

As they were speaking, whom should they see but Li Chiao-erh, and Meng Yü-lou, accompanying Sister-in-law Wu, and her daughter-in-law, Third Sister Cheng, who had all come from the rear compound to Li P'ing-erh's quarters to see Kuan-ko.

Hsi-men Ch'ing left the four gold bracelets behind and went out to the main gate to see the horses.

On observing that a crowd of visitors had arrived, Li P'ing-erh was so preoccupied by the need to greet them and offer them seats that she forgot what
the baby was doing. He continued to play with the gold bracelets, pulling
them about this way and that, until one of them got lost in the process.

At this juncture, the wet nurse, Ju-i, said to Li P'ing-erh, "Mother, did you
happen to pick up one of the gold bracelets the baby was playing with? There
are only three of them left, so one of them is missing."

"I haven't picked any of them up," said Li P'ing-erh, "but I wrapped them
in a handkerchief for him."

"The handkerchief has also fallen on the floor," said Ju-i. "I've shaken it
out, but the gold bracelet is nowhere to be found."

At this, consternation broke out in the room. The wet nurse interrogated
Ying-ch'un, and Ying-ch'un, in turn, interrogated Old Mother Feng.

"Ai-ya! Ai-ya!" Old Mother Feng exclaimed. "I'm not so blind as to be
unable to see anything. In all the years I've been here, I've never presumed
to pick up so much as a broken needle. As Mother knows perfectly well, even
if it were made of gold, it wouldn't be anything I'm enamored of. It's you two
who are in charge of looking after the baby. You'd better not try to pin any
unjust accusations on me."

"Just listen to the nonsense this old crone talks," laughed Li P'ing-erh. "If
the missing object weren't gold, what would all the fuss be about?"

She also took Ying-ch'un to task, saying, "You lousy little stinker! Why are
you making such a to-do about it for no good reason? When your father comes
in, I'll ask him about it. I imagine he may have picked it up, but I don't know
why he only picked up one of them."

"Where did this gold object come from?" asked Meng Yü-lou.

"Father brought it in and gave it to the baby to play with," replied Li P'ing-
erh. "Who knows where it came from?"

Who could have anticipated that Hsi-men Ch'ing would spend some time
looking over the horses in front of the main gate. His managers and servants
were all gathered there. He had page boys ride the horses back and forth and
put them through their paces for two trial runs.

"Although these two horses may come from the Eastern Circuit," opined
Hsi-men Ch'ing, "their manes and tails are not much to look at, and they
can't really step along as well as they should. When it comes to trotting, they
do all right, but that's all."

Turning to Manager Yün, he asked, "How much does your elder brother
want for these horses?"

"He's only asking seventy taels of silver for the two of them," replied Yün
Li-shou.

"That's not a lot to ask," said Hsi-men Ch'ing, "but they don't seem able to
really step along. You'd better take them back with you. If you happen to

come up with any better horses in the future, ride them over. I won't haggle about the price."

When he had finished speaking, Hsi-men Ch'ing came inside.

Whom should he see at this juncture but Ch'in-t'ung, who had come looking for him, saying, "The Sixth Lady would like to see you in her quarters."

Hsi-men Ch'ing thereupon went into Li P'ing-erh's quarters, where she asked him, "Did you, by any chance, take one of those gold bracelets with you? There are only three of them here now."

"I left them behind when I went outside to look at the horses," said Hsi-men Ch'ing. "Who could have taken it?"

"If you didn't take it," said Li P'ing-erh. "Where could it have gotten to? We've been looking for it all this time, and it's nowhere to be found. The wet nurse tried to blame it on Old Mother Feng, who is so upset that:
> Swearing by the gods and uttering oaths,
all she can do is cry."

"Who could actually have taken it?" said Hsi-men Ch'ing. "Let it be for now. You can search for it at your leisure."

"I was going to start looking for it just now," said Li P'ing-erh, "but because I was interrupted when the people from the rear compound, along with Sister-in-law Wu and her daughter-in-law, dropped in, I forgot all about it. I imagined that you must have taken it when you went out. Who could have known that you didn't take it after all, so the matter has been doubly delayed. When I did start to search for it, it frightened everyone off."

Thereupon, she returned the three remaining bracelets to Hsi-men Ch'ing for safe keeping.

Just at this juncture, Pen the Fourth arrived with a hundred taels of newly minted silver to turn over to Hsi-men Ch'ing, who went to the rear compound to see to weighing it out and putting it away.

To resume our story, when P'an Chin-lien heard that there had been a ruckus in Li P'ing-erh's quarters over the disappearance of a gold bracelet that the baby was playing with:
> Before she even got wind of anything,
> She was ready for the rain,
and headed straight for the master suite to tell Yüeh-niang about it, saying, "Elder Sister, just see what that three-inch good-for-nothing has been up to! No matter how rich you may be, you ought not to give gold objects to children to play with."

"Someone just told me about it," said Yüeh-niang. "They say that her quarters have been turned upside down, and that they can't find a gold bracelet. I really don't know where this gold bracelet came from."

"Who knows where it came from?" said Chin-lien. "You didn't see it, but, a little while ago, he brought it in from outside, concealing it in the sleeve of his jacket, for all the world as if it were a case of:

The Eight Tribes coming to offer their tribute.
I asked him what it was and said, 'Bring it over here so I can have a look at it.' But, without even turning his head, he took off straight for her quarters as though his life depended on it. A little while later, pandemonium broke out, and it was claimed that a gold bracelet had disappeared. The way she explained it to that three-inch good-for-nothing, all he had to say was, 'Let it be for now. You can search for it at your leisure.'

> Even if you were as rich as Moneybags Wang,
> That wouldn't do.

A gold object like that must weigh some ten ounces at the least, and be worth fifty or sixty taels of silver. And you'd let it go at that, for no good reason!

> If a pet turtle should escape from the jar,
> It could only be with the connivance of someone at hand.

Who else would have had access to her quarters?"

As she was speaking, whom should they see but Hsi-men Ch'ing, who came in after weighing and putting away the newly minted silver that Pen the Fourth had brought.

Turning over the three remaining gold bracelets to Yüeh-niang to be put away, he explained to her, "These are four gold bracelets that Li Chih and Huang the Fourth paid me in lieu of interest on a loan I made to them. I gave them to the baby to play with, but one of them has disappeared."

Then he instructed Yüeh-niang, "I want you to call out the maidservants from each person's quarters and subject them to an interrogation. I've sent a page boy out on the street to buy a wolf's sinew.[7] If the missing object is promptly produced, I'll leave it at that. But if it is not, I'll start applying the wolf's sinew."

"If you consider the matter," said Yüeh-niang, "gold objects like these should not be handed over to a baby. They're heavy and might give him a chill. And what would you do if it should ever happen that his hands or feet should be crushed?"

P'an Chin-lien, from her vantage point to one side, picked up where Yüeh-niang had left off, saying, "You ought not to have given them to the baby to play with, indeed! Your only regret was that you couldn't get them into her quarters fast enough. When I called to you a while ago, you wouldn't so much as turn your head, but acted just like a red-eyed soldier protecting his loot, not wanting anyone to know what you were up to. And now that one of the gold bracelets has disappeared, it's a wonder you have the face to come and complain to Elder Sister, instructing her to interrogate the maidservants from each of our quarters. As for the maidservants from our quarters:

> If they don't laugh at you with their mouths,
> They'll certainly laugh through their cunts."

These few words upset Hsi-men Ch'ing so much that he strode forward, bent Chin-lien over Yüeh-niang's k'ang, and, brandishing his fist, cursed her, saying, "How hateful can you get! If I didn't care for the opinion of the world, you little splay-legged whore, I'd finish you off with a few blows of my fist. You're never anything but:

Bad-mouthed and sharp-tongued,[8]

sticking your foot in where it's none of your business."

P'an Chin-lien, putting on quite a scene, began to cry, saying, "I'm well aware that:

Relying on your office to flaunt your power, and

Depending on your wealth to play the master,

you have hardened your heart against me. I seem to be the only person you take advantage of. No doubt the idea of taking a person's, or even half a person's, life doesn't carry any weight with you. Well, what's holding you back? Go ahead and beat me. I'm right here, at your disposal. No matter how badly you beat me, chances are I'll still retain a breath of life. But if I should die, never fear but that my frail old mother will demand that you pay the penalty. No matter how much money and influence your household may have, she'll lodge a complaint against you. You may think yourself immune as a judicial commissioner in the yamen, but what will that avail you? You're no more than an impoverished functionary, hiding under an empty shell of debt and the battered silk hat of an official. How many charges of murder do you think you can sustain? For that matter, even the emperor would hardly dare to murder his subordinates with impunity."

These few words, contrary to expectation, produced a guffaw of laughter from Hsi-men Ch'ing, who sputtered out, "Why you! This actually. You little splay-legged whore! What a wicked mouth you've got! You say I'm an impoverished functionary hiding under the battered silk hat of an official. Have a maidservant bring out that silk hat of mine. Just where does it show any signs of wear? You may ask around here in this district of Ch'ing-ho whether I'm indebted to anyone or not, though you say that I'm an empty shell of debt."

"How can you call me splay-legged?" Chin-lien demanded to know, lifting one of her legs into the air. "Just take a look at my leg here and tell me what's crooked about it. You may abuse me for being splay-legged, but there's nothing wrong with these legs of mine."

Yüeh-niang, from her vantage point to one side, laughed, saying, "The two of you are like:

A brass basin meeting up with a steel brush.[9]

As the saying goes:

One wicked person will be ground down
    upon encountering another;[10]
Upon encountering such another person
    he will be utterly undone.[11]

It has always been true that:

P'an Chin-lien Exchanges Caustic Taunts with Hsi-men Ch'ing

It is the strongmouthed who get ahead.
Luckily for you, Sixth Sister, you've got that mouth of yours. Otherwise, if you were slow of speech, you'd never make it."

Hsi-men Ch'ing, realizing that he could not get the better of her, put on his outside clothes and started to leave, when he encountered Tai-an, who said, "Commandant Chou's household has sent someone to urge you on your way. The horse is ready for you. Let me ask, are you planning to go participate in the *chiao* ceremonies first, or are you going straight to Commandant Chou's place?"

"As for the *chiao* ceremonies," Hsi-men Ch'ing instructed him, "have my son-in-law go in my stead and then come right home after burning some incense. You can look to my horse. I might as well go straight to the party at Commandant Chou's place."

Turning to Shu-t'ung, he said, "Fetch my official cap and girdle."

As he was putting these on and fastening his girdle, what should he see but the two instructors from the dramatic troupe belonging to Wang the Second, the distaff relative of the imperial family, leading the whole troupe in to kowtow to him.

Hsi-men Ch'ing instructed Shu-t'ung to see that they were fed, and said to them, "All of you do your best to entertain the ladies today, and I will see that you are properly rewarded. There's no need for you to go before them and pass the collection box around."[12]

The two instructors knelt down and said, "If we don't do our best to entertain them, how could we expect a reward?"

Hsi-men Ch'ing then instructed Shu-t'ung, "They will have been performing for two days. Including the gratuity, set aside five taels of silver as their remuneration."

"I understand," Shu-t'ung assented.

Hsi-men Ch'ing then proceeded to mount his horse and set off to attend the party at Commandant Chou Hsiu's place.

Let us return to the story of P'an Chin-lien, who continued to sit in the master suite, keeping company with Sister-in-law Wu.

Wu Yüeh-niang then said to her, "You'd better go back to your quarters and redo your makeup, hadn't you? You've rubbed your eyes until they're all red. In a little while the guests will arrive, and you'll only make a spectacle of yourself. Whoever taught you to cross him that way? I actually broke into a sweat on your behalf. If I hadn't been there to dissuade him, even without any other funny business, you'd have suffered a few blows on your body for sure.

The male of the species has dog's hair
    growing on his face.[13]
But, just as though you:
    Didn't know any better,[14]

you adamantly insisted on picking a quarrel with him. If a gold bracelet has disappeared, let it go at that. Whether to look for it or not is not up to you. After all, it wasn't in your quarters that it disappeared. Why should you stick your neck out and try to tough it out with him, for no good reason? You're just wasting your breath."

With these few words, she succeeded in reducing Chin-lien to silence, and she returned to her quarters to redo her makeup.

A little while later, Li P'ing-erh, along with Wu Yin-erh, both of them in formal dress, came into Yüeh-niang's room, and she asked them, "How did that gold bracelet come to disappear? Just now, it was the occasion for a real altercation between Father and Sister Six, in which they became so upset with each other they almost came to blows. I had to intervene between them, after which Father went off to attend a party at someone's place. He has ordered a page boy to buy a wolf's sinew, and when he gets home this evening, he's going to apply it to the maidservants from each of our quarters. What were the maidservants and Old Mother Feng in your quarters doing? If they were watching the baby play, how could a gold bracelet disappear just like that? After all, it's not as though it were a mere bauble, worth a candareen, or half a candareen, or anything like that"

"Father just happened, out of the blue, to come in carrying four gold brace-lets," said Li P'ing-erh, "and gave them to the baby to play with. I was busy talking to Sister-in-law Wu and Third Sister Cheng, who had come for a visit along with the Second Lady. Who knows how one of the bracelets happened to disappear? Right now, the maidservants are blaming the wet nurse, and the wet nurse is blaming Old Mother Feng, who is so upset by it all that, weeping and wailing, she is threatening to commit suicide. It is one of those things that is:

Difficult to clear up without eyewitnesses.[15]

As things stand, whom would it be appropriate to blame?"

"My Heavens!" exclaimed Wu Yin-erh. I have played with the baby often enough. It's a good thing that today I was in another room of Mother's comb-ing my hair and hadn't come over yet. Otherwise, I'd be implicated too. Even if Father and Mother were not to say anything about it, how could we help being ill at ease with each other? After all:

Who is there who doesn't care about money?

We denizens of the licensed quarter are particularly sensitive about such things. If such an imputation were to be noised abroad, it wouldn't bear lis-tening to."

As they were speaking, whom should they see but Han Yü-ch'uan and Tung Chiao-erh, who came in carrying their costume bags with them.

With ingratiating smiles, they kowtowed first to Yüeh-niang, Sister-in-law Wu, and Li P'ing-erh, after which they stood up and made a bow to Wu Yin-erh, saying, "Sister Wu, you must have come yesterday, without returning home."

"How did the two of you come to know that?" asked Wu Yin-erh.

"Yesterday," said Tung Chiao-erh, "the two of us were singing in the house on the Lantern Market, and His Honor mentioned it. He told us to come and sing today, in order to entertain the ladies."

Yüeh-niang then invited the two of them to take a seat. In a little while, Hsiao-yü brought in two cups of tea, at which Han Yü-ch'uan and Tung Chiao-erh hastily stood up to accept the tea and responded to Hsiao-yü with a bow.

Wu Yin-erh then asked, "How late did the two of you sing yesterday before the party broke up?"

"It was already past the second watch by the time we got home," said Han Yü-ch'uan. "We came back to the quarter along with your brother and Li Ming."

After they had chatted for a bit, Yüeh-niang instructed Yü-hsiao, "See to it that the tea is served as soon as possible. In a little while, I fear that we will have our hands full when the guests arrive."

A table was then set up, and two square containers, each holding four boxes of delicacies, were placed upon it.

Yüeh-niang then directed Hsiao-yü, "Go to the Second Lady's quarters and invite Li Kuei-chieh to come and have tea with us."

Before long, she appeared, accompanied by her aunt, and the two of them saluted the company, sat down, and joined them for tea, after which the tea things were cleared away.

Who should suddenly appear at this point but Ying-ch'un, all dressed up and carrying Kuan-ko, whose head was adorned with a gilt-ridged satin cap decorated with the eight auspicious symbols, whose body was clad in a loosely cut crimson robe, and whose lower limbs were dressed in white damask socks and satin shoes. On his chest an amulet on its cord was displayed, and on his hands he was wearing little gold bracelets.

When Li P'ing-erh saw him, she said, "Little gentleman, no one invited you. What are you doing here?"

Then, taking him from the maidservant, she placed him on her knee, from which vantage point he surveyed the roomful of people, looking uninterruptedly, first at one of them and then at another.

Li Kuei-chieh, who was sitting on Yüeh-niang's k'ang, smiled and, playfully teasing the baby for the fun of it, said, "The child keeps looking over here. It must be that he wants me to hold him."

Thereupon, she reached out to him with her hands, and the baby fell into her arms and allowed her to hold him.

Sister-in-law Wu laughed at this, saying, "Such a wee bit of a child, but he already knows how to demonstrate his affections."

Yüeh-niang, picking up on this, said, "Who is his father, after all? In the future, when he grows up, he's sure to be a little lady-killer."

"If he turns into a little lady-killer," said Meng Yü-lou, "his First Mother will have to give him a real spanking."

"My child," said Li P'ing-erh, "while your elder sister is holding you, see that you don't go wee-wee on her clothes, or you'll get the spanking of your life, quick enough."

"Ai-ya!" exclaimed Li Kuei-chieh. "What is there to worry about? If he goes wee-wee, what of it? It doesn't matter. I just love holding Little Brother and playing with him."

Whereupon, she continued to play with him, nuzzling him mouth to mouth.

Who should appear at this juncture but P'an Chin-lien,[16] who came in to join the group.

Tung Chiao-erh and Han Yü-ch'uan got up from their seats to greet her and then sat down, saying, "The two of us have been here some time already, but we haven't sung a single song to entertain the ladies, as yet."

Then, turning to the maidservant, they said, "Sister Hsiao-yü, if you fetch our musical instruments, we can perform a song."

Hsiao-yü then fetched a psaltery and a p'i-p'a and handed them over to the two of them. Thereupon, with Han Yü-ch'uan[17] playing the p'i-p'a, Tung Chiao-erh playing the psaltery, and Wu Yin-erh chiming in from the side, they proceeded to sing the song suite, the second song of which begins with the words:

Luxuriant blossoms spread before my eyes,[18]

to the tune "A Golden Chain Hangs from the Phoenix Tree." The very first line that they sang, truly possessed:

A timbre that causes dust to fall and
lingers around the rafters:
A sound that causes rocks to split and
sets the clouds in motion.

Kuan-ko was so frightened by the noise that he hid his face in Li Kuei-chieh's bosom:

Not daring to raise his head,[19]

or take another breath.

When Yüeh-niang saw what was happening, she called out, "Sister Li, you'd better take the child, and have Ying-ch'un take him back to your room. What a hopeless little rascal. Just see how frightened his face looks."

Li P'ing-erh promptly took the child and said to Ying-ch'un, "Cover up his ears and take him into another room."

Thereupon, the four entertainers, singing in ensemble, proceeded with the performance of the song suite on which they had embarked.

Luxuriant blossoms spread before my eyes;
My embroidered quilt pointlessly remains.
That wretched lover of mine has treated me
    altogether too cruelly.
In my last incarnation I must have owed him
    a love debt due in this life.[20]
Neglecting to sleep, forgetting to eat;[21]
Lingering at the door I wait for him.[22]
The bedchamber is silent;[23] how am I
    ever to endure it?

To the tune "Cursing One's Lover":

Coldly deserted, the bedchamber is silent;
    how am I ever to endure it?
All by myself I lean against the screen.
Who knows what his feelings may be.
I recall how originally, we walked together,
    sat together,[24] and rejoiced together.
But now, left all alone, how am I to
    cope with the situation?
In my desolation, I am too listless to pour wine;
In my discomfiture, I am too lazy to wear flowers.

To the tune "Wen-chou Song":

I am too lazy to wear flowers;
I am too listless to pour wine.
Now, though we make a swallow's tryst or oriole's
    assignation, he fails to come.
It must be that he is somewhere else, somewhere else,
    seeking gratification.
His keepsakes are here, but where is he?[25]
In vain do I task my dreaming soul[26] to transport me
    to the Radiant Terrace.
All I can do is let the tears cover my cheeks.

To the tune "Moved by Imperial Favor":

Ah! All I can do is let two streams of tears
    cover my cheeks.[27]
It must be that it is something
    determined by fate.[28]
No doubt your destiny is meager, and
    my allotment is shallow.

It must be that our fortunes are askew
    and the times out of joint.[29]
How can we avoid the trouble caused by
    the gossip of idle folk;
Who employ artful schemes to frustrate us;
Tearing to shreds our girdle of communion;[30]
Insistently separating the phoenix hairpins;
And inundating the Radiant Terrace of Ch'u?

To the tune "Needlework Box":

The strings of my musical instruments
    are covered with dust.
The twin peaks of my eyebrows remain knitted.
My fragrant flesh is emaciated,[31] due to
    this hopeless sorrow.
Too listless for embroidery,
I sit by my dressing mirror.
Beset by old resentment and new sorrow,[32]
How am I ever to endure it?
My only fear is lest the butterfly ambassadors
    and bee go-betweens[33] not return.
Confronting the phoenix mirror, I ask, "If
    my pink cheeks were unaltered,[34]
Would he already have had a change of heart?"

To the tune "Tea-picking Song":

My pink cheeks have been altered, my body
    has become emaciated.
Coldly deserted, how am I ever to endure it?
My only fear is that Liang Shan-po is no longer
    enamored of his Chu Ying-t'ai.[35]
If he should perfidiously break faith and forget favor,[36]
    seeking a pretext to criticize me,
I'll bring up the oaths we swore by the hills and seas,[37]
    reiterating them in clear-cut terms.

To the tune "Relieving Three Hangovers":

He has utterly forgotten the oaths we swore
    by the hills and seas.
He has utterly forgotten the promised letters
    which he has not sent.

He has utterly forgotten the kindness and love
    shared at my pillow side.
He has utterly forgotten the intimate contact
    of our unclothed bodies.
He has utterly forgotten the thousands of times
    we bowed before the gods.
He has utterly forgotten my keepsake, a fragrant
    silk red embroidered shoe.
If I were to mention it, even bystanders would find
    their cheeks flooded with pearly tears.[38]

To the tune "Crows Cry at Night":

Right now, having been disunited for three months,
    it feels like a separation of years.
If we are to meet again, on what day of what year[39]
    will it ever take place?
As for me, I am so utterly emaciated my body is
    like a stick of kindling.[40]
When will I ever pay back completely the love debt
    I owe from my last life?
I fail to see any blue bird conveying
    his love letter.[41]
The dog Yellow Ear has brought no news.[42]
Every day I am sick with depression, too lazy
    to sit by my dressing mirror.
But if we are ever reunited, we will sacrifice
    a consecrated lamb.
Our affinities will be fulfilled;
Our hearts be mutually inclined.
We will soon become as inseparable as
    male and female phoenix mates;[43]
And thereby avoid derisive butterflies
    and suspicious honeybees.[44]

Coda:

The scene is assuredly set.
My lover, sooner or later,
    will surely return;
And as loving husband and wife[45] we will
    live happily ever after.[46]

While the four singing girls were still performing, whom should they see come
in but Tai-an.

Yüeh-niang asked him, "Why is it that the group of ladies you went to invite still haven't shown up?"

"When I went to Kinswoman Ch'iao's place for that purpose," said Tai-an, "the wives of Censor Chu and Provincial Graduate Shang had already forgathered there and were only awaiting the arrival of Madame Ch'iao, the widow of Ch'iao the Fifth, before setting out to come here."

Yüeh-niang instructed him, "Tell the page boy P'ing-an to keep a lookout at the main gate and come in to give us advance notice as soon as the sedan chairs of the ladies arrive."

"Drum music will be struck up to welcome them, both at the front gate and in the main reception hall," said Tai-an, "so you will have ample time to prepare to receive them."

Yüeh-niang further instructed Tai-an, "See to it that brocade carpets are laid down in the parlor of the rear reception hall, that the seats are properly arranged, and that the blinds are rolled up."

Golden curtain hooks are hung in pairs;[47]
The fragrance of orchid and musk swirls.[48]

Ch'un-mei, Ying-ch'un, Yü-hsiao, and Lan-hsiang were all dressed up for the occasion. The wives of the servants were all:

Studded with gold and decked with silver;
Sporting red and trailing green;

as they prepared to receive their new relatives by marriage.

Who should appear at this juncture but Ying Po-chüeh's wife, whose sedan chair was the first to arrive, escorted by Ying Pao. Yüeh-niang and the others welcomed her in, and, after the customary amenities had been exchanged, she took a seat in the parlor.

Bowing repeatedly to Yüeh-niang, she said, "My husband is constantly imposing upon you, I fear. We are grateful for your patronage."

"How can you say such a thing?" Yüeh-niang responded. "We are much indebted to the help of Master Ying the Second."

After some time, what should they hear but the approach of an escort shouting to clear the way, and as:

Drums and music began to sound,

in the front reception hall, P'ing-an came in to report that Madame Ch'iao's sedan chair had arrived. In no time at all, the whole area was rendered black by the number of servitors accompanying the five large sedan chairs as they came to rest at the front gate. The sedan chair of Madame Ch'iao, the widow of Ch'iao the Fifth, was in the van. It had a silver finial on top, from which pearls were suspended; was invested in an ultramarine, double-fringed, gold lamé, waterproof canopy; and was accompanied by an escort of retainers, armed with rattan canes, who shouted to clear the way. Behind it came the wives of her servants, ensconced in smaller sedan chairs; four commandants, bearing her dressing case and brazier; and two black-clad servants, riding on ponies. The remainder of the procession consisted of the wife of Ch'iao Hung, Censor Chu's wife, the wife of Provincial Graduate Shang, Ts'ui Pen's wife, Big Sister Tuan, and the wife of Ch'iao T'ung, the head servant in Ch'iao Hung's household, who accompanied her mistress in a smaller sedan chair, in order to look after her clothes.

Wu Yüeh-niang was attired in a full-sleeved robe of scarlet variegated satin, decorated with a motif of the four animals representing the cardinal directions[49] paying homage to the *ch'i-lin*.[50] Around her waist she wore a girdle of gold inlaid with assorted jewels. On her head:

> Her chignon was of an imposing height;
> Phoenix pins protruded to either side;
> And pearls and trinkets rose in piles.

On her breast:

> Gold pendants hung on embroidered cords;
> And a profusion of amulets scintillated.

Beside her skirt were suspended:

> Decorative pendants of lustrous pearls.

Along with Li Chiao-erh, Meng Yü-lou, P'an Chin-lien, Li P'ing-erh, and Sun Hsüeh-o, all of whom were dressed up to look as though they were:

> Modeled in plaster, carved of jade,
> Producing brocade effects that dazzle the eye,

Wu Yüeh-niang came out as far as the gate that led into the second courtyard to greet their guests.

What should they see but the crowd of female guests, gathered around Madame Ch'iao the Fifth as she made her entrance. She was petite in stature, more than seventy years old, wore a head-dress bedecked with kingfisher feathers, jewels, and pearls, and a scarlet robe decorated with palace-style embroidery. When looked at close up, it was apparent that her hair was all white. Truly:

> Her eyebrows are two streaks of snow,
> Her chignon is tied into a bag of silk;
> Her eyes resemble autumn waters, somewhat disturbed,
> Her hair is like the hills of Ch'u, veiled in clouds.[51]

Once she had been ushered into the rear reception hall, she first exchanged salutations with Sister-in-law Wu and after that proceeded to do the same with Yüeh-niang and the others.

Yüeh-niang reiterated, "Madame, pray accept my salutation," but her guest refused to accede, and it was only after they had dickered politely for a while that she agreed to accept a half kowtow from her.

After that, Yüeh-niang proceeded to exchange the courtesies appropriate between new relatives by marriage with Ch'iao Hung's wife, each of them in turn expressing her satisfaction with their new relationship and thanking the other for the lavish gifts they had received.

As a Result of the Betrothal Yüeh-niang Meets Madame Ch'iao

When these amenities were concluded, Madame Ch'iao the Fifth was ushered to the place of honor, where she was invited to take her seat upon a chair
covered with a brocade cushion in front of a standing brocade screen.

Ch'iao Hung's wife was invited to take the seat next to hers, but she repeatedly demurred, saying, "As the wife of Madame's nephew, I could scarcely
presume to take such a liberty."

She deferred to the wives of Censor Chu and Provincial Graduate Shang,
but the two of them also declined, and it was only after they had dickered
politely for some time that Madame Ch'iao the Fifth consented to take her
place in the seat of honor, and the rest of the company sat down in two rows,
with the guests on the east and the hosts on the west.

In the center of the room was a large square box stove in which a fire was
blazing, so that:

     The atmosphere was as genial as that of spring.[52]

The four maidservants, Ch'un-mei, Ying-ch'un, Yü-hsiao, and Lan-hsiang,
all of whom were dressed in jackets of scarlet figured satin, blue gold lamé
skirts, and green brocaded vests, waited upon the company and served them
with tea.

After some time, Madame Ch'iao the Fifth said to Yüeh-niang, "Why not
invite His Honor Hsi-men to come out and meet us, so we can exchange the
courtesies appropriate to relatives by marriage."

"My poor husband has had to go to the yamen to conduct public business
today," explained Yüeh-niang, "and he hasn't come home yet."

"What office does His Honor hold?" asked Madame Ch'iao the Fifth.

"Though nothing but:

     A humble villager,"

said Yüeh-niang, "thanks to our sovereign's grace, he has been granted a substantive appointment as battalion commander, and currently occupies a post
in the legal system. For our humble household to aspire to a marriage alliance
with these relatives of yours is truly presumptuous."

"How can you talk that way?" responded Madame Ch'iao the Fifth. "Such
an exalted position as His Honor has achieved is more than sufficient. The
other day when I heard that the daughter of my nephew had been betrothed
to the scion of your household, my heart was filled with delight. Today I have
come in order to get acquainted, so that we will be comfortable addressing
each other on social occasions in the future."

"My only fear is," said Yüeh-niang, "that such an alliance can only detract
from your reputation."

"What kind of talk is that?" replied Madame Ch'iao the Fifth. "Do you
suppose that the sovereign himself never deigns to form marriage alliances
with commoners?

     It's a long story,[53]

but the honored consort, née Cheng, of the present emperor, who resides in
the Eastern Palace, happens to be a niece of mine.[54] Her father and mother
are both dead, so I am the only relative she has left. When my old man was
still alive he held the hereditary title of commander, but, unfortunately, he
died without issue at the age of forty-nine, so the title passed to a nephew of
his from another branch of the family. As for this nephew of mine, although
he didn't have any money to start with, he has now become a well-to-do householder. Although he may have started out as a corvée laborer, he now has
enough to live on quite comfortably, so he would not detract in any way from
the reputation of your family."

After they had talked for some time, Sister-in-law Wu said to Yüeh-niang,
"Why don't you have the baby brought out so our venerable visitor can have
a look at him and he can solicit a share of her longevity?"

Li P'ing-erh hastily went back to her room and told the wet nurse, "Bring
Kuan-ko out so he can pay his respects to Madame Ch'iao."

When Madame Ch'iao saw him, she exclaimed hyperbolically, "What a
perfectly formed little fellow!"

Then, calling over one of her attendants, she opened her felt bag and took
out a length of purple brocade material, shot with yellow, of the kind purveyed
for use in the palace, and a pair of gilded bracelets for the child to wear.

Yüeh-niang hastily got up from her place to thank her, and then invited her
to retire to her boudoir in order to change her clothes.

Before long, four tables were set up in the summerhouse in the front garden, where tea was to be served. Upon each table were arrayed forty saucers of
every kind of condiment and sweetmeat, mouth-watering appetizers, steamed-
shortcake pastries, and the finest deep-fried patisserie, while to either side
maidservants and the wives of household retainers stood by to wait upon the
company. But no more of this.

After they were finished with tea, Yüeh-niang opened the gate which led
into the garden behind them, with its artificial hill, and they all went in for a
tour of the premises. By that time Ch'en Ching-chi had come back from the
chiao rites of cosmic renewal, where he had stayed only for the noon vegetarian repast, and, along with Shu-t'ung and Tai-an, had made all the necessary
preparations for the feast in the front reception hall, where the ladies were
now invited to partake of wine and inaugurate the festivities. Truly it was a
fine feast. Behold:

> Screens display their peacocks' tails,
> Cushions conceal their hibiscus blossoms.
> Platters are piled with exotic fruits and rare viands,
> Vases are studded with gold flowers and emerald leaves.[55]
> Braziers burn animal-shaped briquettes,
> Incense diffuses the odor of ambergris.[56]
> The table service is an array
>   of exotic antiques from Hsiang-chou;[57]

The hanging blinds are adorned with
    shining pearls from Ho-p'u.[58]
White jade saucers are piled high with
    preserved *ch'i-lin* meat;[59]
Golden flagons are filled to the brim with
    carnelian-hued nectar.
There are stewed chimpanzee lips,
And baked leopard embryos;
Truly, one has but to use one's chopsticks
    to exhaust ten thousand cash.
There are deep-fried dragon livers,
And roast phoenix marrow;
Indeed, when they are all displayed,
    seasonal delicacies abound.
The denizens of the Pear Garden,[60]
Crowd around with their phoenix pipes
    and phoenix flutes.[61]
The courtesans from the inner palace,
Urgently tune their silver psalteries
    and ivory clappers.[62]
The beauties proffering wine are duplicates of
    the Goddess of the Lo River;[63]
The incense-burning serving girls are replicas of
    Ch'ang-o, the Goddess of the Moon.[64]

Truly:

Two ranks of pearls and trinkets[65] are
    arrayed beneath the steps;
The tones of pipes and voices[66] hover
    about the banquet hall.[67]

In due course, Wu Yüeh-niang offered Li P'ing-erh a goblet of wine, and after the players beneath the steps had concluded a flourish of the drums, Madame Ch'iao and the rest of the assembled relatives toasted Li P'ing-erh and wished her a long life in honor of her birthday. The four singing girls, Li Kuei-chieh, Wu Yin-erh, Han Yü-ch'uan, and Tung Chiao-erh, took their places before the company, struck up their instruments:

Patterned cithara, silver psaltery,
Jade-surfaced *p'i-p'a*, and
Clappers inlaid with red ivory,[68]

and sang the song suite that begins with the words:

May you live as long as the Southern Hills.[69]

After which, from beneath the steps:

Drums and music began to sound,

and the players presented the accordion-bound album listing the names of the dramas they were prepared to perform. Madame Ch'iao the Fifth instructed them to put on the play entitled *Wang Yüeh-ying Leaves her Shoe Behind on the Lantern Festival.*[70] The chef then came out and presented the minor entrée of roast goose, for which Madame Ch'iao rewarded him with five mace of silver.

By the time:

> Five carved entrées had been consumed,
> Three courses of soup had been served,

and the four scenes of the drama were concluded, it began to grow late.

> Painted candles dispersed their light,

from mountainous banks of sconces; every variety of decorative taper was lit up.

> Brocade sashes fluttered,[71]
> Gaudy ropes hung pendulously.
> The wheel of the bright moon,[72]
> Arose out of the east, and
> Illuminated the chamber,
> Under the flickering lamplight.

Lai-hsing's wife Hui-hsiu and Lai-pao's wife Hui-hsiang attended upon the company, each of them bearing a square platter of stuffed Lantern Festival dumplings. The tea that was served in cups inlaid with silver, provided with gold teaspoons in the shape of apricot leaves, was flavored with rose hips and crystallized sugar and exuded a mouth-watering fragrance. The four senior maidservants, Ch'un-mei, Ying-ch'un, Yü-hsiao, and Lan-hsiang, divided the task of waiting upon the company between them:

> Observing the demands of propriety,
> Dignified and stately in demeanor.

Meanwhile, beneath the steps, the music started up again. Playing a *p'i-p'a,* a psaltery, and a mandola, accompanied by pipes and flutes, the musicians performed a song suite in celebration of the Lantern Festival, beginning with the tune "Prelude to Painted Eyebrows," the first line of which is:

Blossoms and moonlight pervade the spring metropolis.[73]

When the performance was over, Madame Ch'iao the Fifth and Ch'iao Hung's wife called the players before them and rewarded them with two packages, each of which contained a tael of silver. The four singing girls were also awarded two mace of silver apiece.

Yüeh-niang had also set up many saucers full of delicacies in the parlor of the master suite in the rear compound, where the guests were invited to retire after the formal entertainment was over. The four tables were loaded with refreshments.

The singers performed,
The musicians played,
and another round of wine was served.

Madame Ch'iao the Fifth repeatedly remarked that it was getting late, and that she should be on her way. Yüeh-niang and the others were unable to persuade her to stay any longer and accompanied her to the main gate, where she was detained for a parting cup of wine and invited to view the fireworks. The onlookers on either side of the street were as closely arrayed as:

Fish scales or swarming bees.

P'ing-an, together with a contingent of orderlies with sticks in hand, tried to hold back the crowds, but they surged forward repeatedly. After a little while, when a rack of fireworks had been set off, the onlookers to either side scattered. Only then did Madame Ch'iao the Fifth and the other ladies bid farewell to Yüeh-niang, mount their sedan chairs, and make their departure. By that time, it was already the third watch. Subsequently they also had to see Ying Po-chüeh's wife on her way.

When Yüeh-niang and her sister wives returned to the rear compound, they instructed Ch'en Ching-chi, Lai-hsing, Shu-t'ung, and Tai-an to put away the tableware from the reception hall, see that the players and their two instructors were provided with food and wine, pay them five taels of silver for their services, and send them on their way.

Yüeh-niang gave instructions that the remaining table's worth of leftovers and half a jug of wine, should be set aside for the delectation of Manager Fu, Pen the Fourth, and Ch'en Ching-chi.

"They must be worn out," she said. "Let them all have a drink together. Set up a table for them in the main reception hall. Who knows how late it will be before your father returns home."

Thereupon, there still remaining some lamps that had not burnt out, Manager Fu, Pen the Fourth, Ch'en Ching-chi, and Lai-pao took the positions of honor, while Lai-hsing, Shu-t'ung, Tai-an, and P'ing-an ranged themselves to either side, and the wine was poured.

Lai-pao called out, "P'ing-an, you ought to depute someone to cover the main gate, lest Father should return and find no one tending the door."

"I've told Hua-t'ung to take care of it," replied P'ing-an. "That's not a problem."

Thereupon the eight of them fell to playing at guess-fingers while drinking their wine.

"Let's not play at guess-fingers," said Ch'en Ching-chi. "If we:

Create such a commotion,

we'll only disturb the people in the rear compound. Let's quietly play a game of forfeits instead. Each player must come up with a line of poetry. Those who are able to do so will escape paying a forfeit, but those who fail to do so will have to drink a large cup of wine.

Manager Fu started off with the line:

How comical are the trappings of the Lantern Festival,

Pen the Fourth continued:

The occasions for pleasure in man's life are numbered.

Ch'en Ching-chi said:

Availing ourselves of this moonshine and lantern light,

to which Lai-pao responded:

We must, on no account, allow them to go unappreciated.

Lai-hsing said:

Our trysts with our girls may have failed to come off,

To which Shu-t'ung responded:

But we have complied with the wishes of the First Lady.

Tai-an said:

Though we have only leftover wine and waning lamplight,

and P'ing-an concluded:

It may still constitute "a fling in the spring breeze."

When the group of them had finished their joint composition, they broke into loud laughter. Truly:

> After finishing their drinking, when the wine
>   is exhausted and the party is over;[74]
> There is no one to notice that the moonlight
>   is illuminating the plum branches.

> If you want to know the outcome of these events,
> Pray consult the story related in the following chapter.

Chapter 44

WU YÜEH-NIANG DETAINS

LI KUEI-CHIEH OVERNIGHT;

HSI-MEN CH'ING DRUNKENLY

INTERROGATES HSIA-HUA

In straitened circumstances, I continue to be
   mired in the muck day by day;
While the resplendence of the imperial park
   is perennially renewed.
Brambles do not encroach on the carriageways
   and riding paths;
Pipes and strings forever enhance the homes
   of the silk-clad.
Patrician youths roam the greensward like
   fluttering butterflies;
Budding damsels disport in the breeze like
   proliferating blossoms.
But I am reluctant to go out, let the vagrant
   youths scoff as they will;
For, once back inside the gate, the old life
   will go on just as before.[1]

THE STORY GOES that while Ch'en Ching-chi, Manager Fu, and the others were drinking in the front compound, Sister-in-law Wu's sedan chair arrived, and she prepared to return home.

Wu Yüeh-niang did her best to detain her, saying repeatedly, "Stay another night, Sister-in-law, and go home tomorrow."

"Including the time I spent at Kinsman Ch'iao Hung's place," Sister-in-law Wu replied, "I've been away for three or four days already. There's no one to look after the place at home, and your brother is tied up at the yamen, so he's not there either. I'd better go home. Tomorrow all of you ladies are invited, whatever you do, to come to our place for a holiday visit. In the evening, you can walk off the hundred ailments on your way home."

"Tomorrow," said Yüeh-niang, "we won't be able to make it before evening."

"You really ought to come by sedan chair a little earlier," said Sister-in-law Wu. "That will give you time to walk back together later in the evening."

When they had finished speaking, Yüeh-niang had two gift boxes made up for her, one of Lantern Festival dumplings, and one of steamed dumplings, and ordered Lai-an to escort her sister-in-law on her way home.

The four singing girls, Li Kuei-chieh and company, then kowtowed to Yüeh-niang and bade her farewell as they also prepared to return home.

"What's the hurry?" said Yüeh-niang. "Are you that anxious to be off? Wait till your father gets home and dismisses you. On his way out he told me to keep you here. I expect he has something else to say to you. I wouldn't presume to let you go."

"Father has gone out to a drinking party," said Li Kuei-chieh. "Who knows when he'll get home? We've been waiting for some time already. Mother, why don't you let me and Wu Yin-erh leave before the others. The two of them only came today, while we've been here for two days already. Who knows how anxious my mother back at home is to see me?"

"Is your mother really so anxious to see you," said Yüeh-niang, "that she can't bear to wait another night?"

"That's a fine thing to say," protested Li Kuei-chieh. "There's no one to look after the place at home, and moreover my elder sister's services have been engaged elsewhere. Mother, if we get out our instruments and sing another song for you, surely you'll let us go home."

As they were speaking, whom should they see but Ch'en Ching-chi, who came in to turn over the unused gratuities to Yüeh-niang.

"The one-candareen gratuities for the chair carriers of the Ch'iao family and the others came to ten packets in all, amounting to three taels," he reported. "There are still ten packets left over."

As Yüeh-niang was putting these away, Li Kuei-chieh took the opportunity to ask, "Son-in-law, when you were outside just now, did you notice whether our sedan chairs had come for us or not?"

"Only the sedan chairs for the other two are here," replied Ch'en Ching-chi. "Those for you and Wu Yin-erh have not arrived. It seems that a while ago someone sent them away."

"Son-in-law," exclaimed Li Kuei-chieh, "did you really send them away? You're fooling me."

"If you don't believe me, go see for yourself," said Ch'en Ching-chi. "As though I would try to fool you."

Before he had finished speaking, whom should they see but Ch'in-t'ung, who came in carrying his master's felt bag and announced, "Father has come home."

"It's a good thing the two of you haven't left," said Yüeh-niang. "It turns out your father has shown up after all."

Before long, Hsi-men Ch'ing came in, still wearing his official hat on his head, and 70 or 80 percent inebriated. Striding into the room, he assumed his place in the seat of honor.

"Tung Chiao-erh and Han Yü-ch'uan are still here," Yüeh-niang reported, and the two of them proceeded to step forward and kowtow.

"Everyone has left," said Hsi-men Ch'ing, "and it is already late at night. Do you still want me to have them sing for us?"

"They've been asking me to let them go home," said Yüeh-niang.

To resume our story, Hsi-men Ch'ing turned to Li Kuei-chieh and said, "You and Yin-erh might as well wait until the festival is over before going home. It's all right to let the other two go."

"You see," said Yüeh-niang. "I told you so, but you wouldn't believe me and acted as though I were fooling you, or something."

Li Kuei-chieh merely lowered her head with a disgruntled expression and had nothing further to say.

Hsi-men Ch'ing asked Tai-an, "Are the sedan chairs for those two here or not?"

"Only the two sedan chairs for Tung Chiao-erh and Han Yü-ch'uan are waiting for them," Tai-an responded.

"I'll not have anything more to drink," said Hsi-men Ch'ing. "You can each get out your instruments and sing the medley called 'Ten Strips of Brocade' for us, after which I'll let those two go home before the others."

Thereupon, with Li Kuei-chieh playing the *p'i-p'a*, Wu Yin-erh playing the psaltery, Han Yü-ch'uan strumming the mandola, and Tung Chiao-erh beating a quick tempo on the drum, the four singing girls, performing in relay, sang the twenty halves of the ten songs that made up "Ten Strips of Brocade." Wu Yüeh-niang, Li Chiao-erh, Meng Yü-lou, P'an Chin-lien, and Li P'ing-erh all sat down in the room to listen to the performance.

Li Kuei-chieh started off with the first half of a song to the tune "Sheep on the Mountain Slope":

My handsome lover naturally stands out
    among his kind,[2]
But my halcyon-hued coverlet is cold and
    I am desolate and alone.
Since we parted, I think of him by day
    and yearn for him at night.[3]
I yearn for him, wondering when we will
    ever meet again.
When I do meet with my lover, it will be
    just as before,
Just as before.

It was then Wu Yin-erh's turn to sing the first half of a song to the tune "Sutra in Letters of Gold":

Where has the flower-lover gone?
The red petals have fallen, spring is over.
I have already climbed the lofty tower and
    leaned over all twelve balustrades,
All twelve balustrades.[4]

Han Yü-ch'uan then sang the first half of a song to the tune "Stopping the Clouds in Flight":

Depressed, I lean over the balustrade.[5]
The swallows and orioles, I am
    reluctant to watch.
Who has broken the commandment against adultery?
Who has grown accustomed to spectral visitations?[6]

Tung Chiao-erh continued with the first half of a song to the tune "River Water, with Two Variations":

My flowerlike countenance and moonlike allure[7]
    have faded completely away.
The double gates are always closed.
It is just the time when the east wind is chilly,[8]
Fine rain sprinkles continuously,[9] and
Fallen red petals by the thousands dot the ground.[10]

Li Kuei-chieh continued with the first half of a song to the tune "Prelude to Painted Eyebrows":

Since the last time I met my handsome lover,
My silver psaltery is covered with dust and
    I am reluctant to touch it.
Although we are only separated by
    a matter of feet,
It feels as though we are at opposite ends of the sky.
I remember a hundred instances of his kindness,
And cannot recall the slightest case of deceptive
    conduct on his part.

Wu Yin-erh continued with the first half of a song to the tune "Red Embroidered Slippers":

On the surface of the water there was
    a pair of mandarin ducks,
Beside the bank of the river, following
    each other in close formation.[11]
How could they have foreseen that a fishing
    boat would separate them,
Making them fly off in different directions?

Han Yü-ch'uan continued with the first half of a song to the tune "Playful Children":

> Ever since he left, I have become
> > haggard and emaciated.
> I have never before been sick for so long.
> When my talented lover went away[12]
> > it had just become spring;
> But before I know it, the geese have flown,
> > and it is already midautumn.[13]

Tung Chiao-erh continued with the first half of a song to the tune "Confronting the Dressing Mirror":

> At the present time,
> The strings on the jasper-inlaid zither are broken,[14]
> > there is no one to listen to them.
> When the blossoms are most beautiful,
> Who is there with whom to enjoy them?

Li Kuei-chieh continued with the first half of a song to the tune "Shrouding the Southern Branch":

> Outside my gauze window,
> The moon is setting.
> I am always yearning for that man of mine,
> Unable to get him out of my mind.
> On my behalf, you utterly exhaust
> > your strength and heart;
> On your behalf, I secretly wipe away
> > the pearly tears.

Wu Yin-erh continued with the first half of a song to the tune "The Cassia Sprig Is Fragrant":

> His heart is like a willow catkin,[15]
> Flying wherever the wind takes it.
> It turns out that his intentions are false
> > and his reputation undeserved;
> But he has induced me to cater to him
> > with sincere devotion.[16]

Han Yü-ch'uan then resumed by singing the second half of the song to the tune "Sheep on the Mountain Slope":

> He is solicitous of jade and considerate of fragrance.[17]
> He and I lay face to face underneath
> > the hibiscus bed curtains,[18]

Where we revealed every detail of our innermost
　　feelings to each other.
Speaking of our emotions at separation, how could
　　you have abandoned me?
It makes me so mad I'm half drunk
　　and half crazy.
How could you have had such a change of heart as to
　　pick up with another soul mate?
When will we ever be able to arrange another
　　assignation, another assignation?
If we really meet again, it will be
　　just like a dream.

Tung Chiao-erh then sang the second half of the song to the tune "Sutra in
Letters of Gold":

Though I wipe them away,
Tears have stained my silk handkerchief.
On the southern bank of the river,
The setting sun reveals hills beyond the hills.[19]

Li Kuei-chieh then sang the second half of the song to the tune "Stopping
the Clouds in Flight":

Ch'a!
I have sent him letters two or three times,
But it has been difficult to see him.
I'd better take up my frosty brush,
And write out another dubious indictment;
But the ink is not dry on the page of loving feelings
　　I have already expressed.[20]

Wu Yin-erh then sang the second half of the song to the tune "River Water,
with Two Variations":

I am too indolent to burn another coil of incense,
And reluctant to pick up my needle.
My emaciated body is cadaverous,
Beset as it is by spectral visitations.[21]
When I reexamine the old feelings that
　　we had for each other,
Sorrow weighs down the turquoise peaks
　　of my painted eyebrows;
Which only serves to arouse the distaste
　　of my young lover,
So that, for some time, despite the orioles and the flowers,
　　I have not bothered to roll up my curtain.

Han Yü-ch'uan then sang the second half of the song to the tune "Prelude to Painted Eyebrows":

> When I think of the affectionate words he uttered
>   when we shared the same pillow,
> I can't help feeling a shuddering of the flesh
>   and benumbing of the body.

Tung Chiao-erh then sang the second half of the song to the tune "Red Embroidered Slippers":

> One of us headed for the east,
> The other flew toward the west;
> Which left me languishing
>   in the south,
> While he set off for the north.

Li Kuei-chieh then sang the second half of the song to the tune "Playful Children":

> While you're there within the bed-curtains of gold lamé
>   cuddling the red and hugging the turquoise,[22]
> I'm here clandestinely letting the tears flow as I
>   keep solitary vigil in my fragrant boudoir.[23]
> I remember the vows of fidelity that you swore,
> But they have faded from your fickle mind as quickly
>   as the lantern gutters out.
> The evidence against you is still on record
>   in the Temple of the God of the Sea.[24]

Wu Yin-erh then sang the second half of the song to the tune "Confronting the Dressing Mirror":

> Who is there with whom to pour the vintage wine?
> Our feelings have come to naught, like a pitcher
>   that has fallen down a well.
> We are as unlikely to see each other as Orion and Antares.[25]
> Since we became separated years and months have gone by.
> I have calculated the date of your return so often
>   I have worn away the golden tip of my comb.

Han Yü-ch'uan then sang the second half of the song to the tune "Shrouding the Southern Branch":

> On either side we have been
>   disturbed at heart.
> How could we have known that the wind
>   would sweep the clouds away,

So that tonight the full moon would
   shine forth once more,
Permitting my lover once again to unfasten
   my fragrant silk raiment?
In discussing our feelings, the question of
   who was unfaithful to whom,
Is something I will have to demand a
   clarification of from you.

Tung Chiao-erh then sang the second half of the song to the tune "The Cassia
Sprig Is Fragrant":

How could he ever have forgotten that time in the past
   when he swore to be as faithful as the hills?
He has buried me alive,
That lover of mine.
Since he has abandoned me here,
When will we be able to make love again?

Li Kuei-chieh then concluded by singing the Coda:

Embroidered silk slippers, but half a span in length;
When his eyes catch sight of them, his amorous
   feelings are aroused.
My delectable and talented lover, let's forgo
   any further recriminations.
Hurry up and embrace this shapely body of mine.

When they had finished singing, Hsi-men Ch'ing paid Han Yü-ch'uan and
Tung Chiao-erh for their services, and the two of them said their farewells and
departed, but he instructed Li Kuei-chieh and Wu Yin-erh to stay overnight.

All of a sudden, a commotion became audible in the front compound and,
before they knew it, Tai-an and Ch'in-t'ung came in, dragging Hsia-hua, the
maidservant from Li Chiao-erh's quarters, along with them, and reported to
Hsi-men Ch'ing, saying, "After escorting the two singing girls to the gate just
now, we took a lantern into the stable to prepare the fodder for the horses,
when what should we see but Hsia-hua hiding under the manger, which gave
us quite a start. We don't know what she was doing there, and when we asked
her, she refused to answer."

When Hsi-men Ch'ing heard this, he said, "Where is that slave? Bring her
over here."

Thereupon, he strode into the corridor outside the parlor and sat down in
a chair, while the maidservant was hustled into his presence and forced to
kneel down in front of him.

Hsia-hua Is Found under the Manger with the Stolen Gold

When Hsi-men Ch'ing demanded to know why she had gone out to the front compound, she refused to answer.

Li Chiao-erh chimed in from the sidelines, saying, "I didn't send you on any errand. Whatever were you up to, going out to the stable, for no good reason?"

When Hsi-men Ch'ing saw what a state of panic the girl was in, he assumed that she had been trying to run away and ordered the servants to search her person, but she resisted being searched. Thereupon, Ch'in-t'ung dragged her down with a tug, when what should they hear but a tinkling sound as an object that had been concealed in her waist fell to the ground. Hsi-men Ch'ing asked what it was, and when Tai-an handed it to him:

Strange as it may seem,
it turned out to be a gold bracelet.

When Hsi-men Ch'ing had examined it by lamplight, he said, "It's that gold bracelet that disappeared a while ago and couldn't be found anywhere. So it turns out that this slave had stolen it."

Hsia-hua protested that she had only picked it up, but when Hsi-men Ch'ing demanded to know where she had picked it up, she remained silent. This enraged Hsi-men Ch'ing, and he forthwith ordered Ch'in-t'ung to go to the front compound and fetch the finger squeezers. In no time at all, the maidservant's fingers were put in the squeezers and squeezed until she:

Howled like a stuck pig.

After she had been squeezed for a while, he ordered that the squeezers should be struck twenty times. Yüeh-niang saw that her husband was drunk and did not dare to interfere.

Unable to bear the pain any longer, the maidservant finally said, "I picked it up off the floor in the Sixth Lady's quarters."

Only then did Hsi-men Ch'ing order the squeezers removed, after which he instructed Li Chiao-erh, "Take her back to your room and, tomorrow, call in a go-between to take her away and sell her. What would we want to keep a slave like this around for anyway?"

Li Chiao-erh was initially at a loss for words, after which she finally said, "You lousy slave! Whoever told you to go out to the front compound? As long as I'm maintaining you, you should ask my permission before doing anything, instead of sneaking out there without anyone knowing about it. If you picked up that gold bracelet in her room, you should have told me about it."

When Hsia-hua merely continued to cry, Li Chiao-erh said to her, "Slave that you are, you might just as well have been squeezed to death, for all I care. Still crying are you?"

"That's enough of that," said Hsi-men Ch'ing, after which he turned the gold bracelet over to Yüeh-niang to put away and went out to Li P'ing-erh's quarters in the front compound.

When the page boys had all left, Yüeh-niang ordered Hsiao-yü to close the ceremonial gate between the front and rear compounds and then turned to Yü-hsiao and asked, "Did that maidservant actually go out to the front compound on that occasion?"

"When the Second Lady and the Third Lady," reported Yü-hsiao, "accompanied Sister-in-law Wu and her daughter-in-law, Third Sister Cheng, to the Sixth Lady's place, she went along with them. Who could have anticipated that she would steal this gold bracelet without anyone's knowing it? A while ago, when she overheard Mother saying that Father had sent a page boy out to buy a wolf's sinew, she was frightened to death. She asked me in the kitchen what a wolf's sinew was, which gave all of us a laugh, and we told her, 'A wolf's sinew, no doubt, is a sinew from the body of a wolf. If anyone has stolen something, and the wolf's sinew is applied to him, it will wrap itself around the guilty person's body and bind his hands and feet together.' I imagine that, when she heard what we said, she panicked, and took advantage of the departure of the singing girls tonight, to sneak out there in the endeavor to run away. When she saw that there were people at the front gate, she must have ducked into the stable and tried to hide under the manger, but ended up being spotted by the page boys and dragged out into the open."

Yüeh-niang said:
"How is one to judge what people are really like?[26]
Who would have thought that such a young maidservant would turn out to be:
Like a furtive thieving rat,
and not a proper person at all?"

To resume our story, Li Chiao-erh led Hsia-hua back to her quarters, and, that evening, Li Kuei-chieh took her severely to task, saying, "It turns out that you're nothing but an uncouth youngster. For someone who is fourteen or fifteen years old, and knows something about human behavior, how could you be so stupid? Even in the licensed quarter where I work, that sort of thing would never be countenanced. There's no one else here, so I can speak frankly. If you pick up something, you should bring it back to your room and turn it over inconspicuously to your mistress. Then, if the matter should come to light, she would be able to intervene on your behalf. How could you fail to say so much as a word to her about it? What did it feel like to be put in the squeezers and beaten like that just now? A fine maidservant you are! As the saying goes:
If you don the black livery of a servant,
You must cling to even the blackest post.
If you weren't assigned to her quarters, it wouldn't matter, but when you are subjected to the third degree the way you just were, how do you suppose it reflects on your mistress's standing in the household?"

She then went on to take her aunt to task, saying, "You're really hopeless! If it had been me, I would never have let him subject a maidservant of mine to the squeezers in front of everybody that way. If she were at fault, I would drag her back to my own room and give her a caning myself. How is it that none of the maidservants from the front compound were put in the squeezers, and it was only a maidservant from your quarters that was subjected to the third degree? You allow yourself to be taken advantage of, as though:

You haven't any breath in your own nostrils.[27]

If you wait until tomorrow, are you really going to let him get rid of your maidservant that way, without saying a word about it? If you won't say anything about it, I will. Anything would be better than letting her be taken off that way, and making yourself a laughingstock to the others. Just take a look at the one named Meng and the one named P'an. The two of them are just like a pair of vixens. You're not very likely to get the better of them."

She then called Hsia-hua over and asked her, "Do you want to leave, or not to leave?"

"I don't want to leave," the maidservant replied.

"If you don't leave," said Li Kuei-chieh, "in the future, you'll have to pay closer attention to your mistress's interests. In all matters, you must strive to be:

Of one heart and one mind,

with her. No matter what you might pick up, turn it over to her, so that she will treat you with the same favor that she does Yüan-hsiao."

"Your instructions are duly noted," said Hsia-hua.

Let us put the chiding addressed to Hsia-hua aside for a moment and say no more about it.

To resume our story, when Hsi-men Ch'ing went out to Li P'ing-erh's quarters in the front compound, what should he find but Li P'ing-erh and Wu Yin-erh sitting together on the k'ang.

All he wanted to do was to get undressed and go to bed, but Li P'ing-erh said, "Since Wu Yin-erh is here, there's no place to put you. You'd better go next door."

"What do you mean there's no place to put me?" said Hsi-men Ch'ing. "The two of you, mother and daughter, can lie down on either side, and I'll go to sleep between you."

Li P'ing-erh gave him a look, saying, "Now you're getting vulgar."

"Well, where am I to sleep then?" asked Hsi-men Ch'ing.

"You can go next door to Sister Six's place to sleep tonight," said Li P'ing-erh.

After sitting with them for a while, Hsi-men Ch'ing got up to go, saying, "All right. All right. At least that will prevent me from disturbing the two of you any further. I might as well go over there to sleep then."

Thereupon, he went straight over to Chin-lien's quarters. When Chin-lien realized that Hsi-men Ch'ing had come in, she felt:

Just as though he had fallen from Heaven.

She came forward to help him off with his outer garments and girdle, provided a clean set of bedding:

Spread out the mermaid silk covers, and

Deftly positioned the coral pillow.

After a serving of tea, the two of them went to bed for the night. But no more of this.

Meanwhile, at Li P'ing-erh's place, after she had seen Hsi-men Ch'ing on his way, she and Wu Yin-erh sat down, face to face, at a k'ang table, set out the black and white pieces on the board, and proceeded to play a game of elephant chess by lamplight.

"Prepare two cups of tea," she instructed Ying-ch'un, "bring a box of assorted delicacies, and decant a flagon of that sweet Chin-hua wine for me to share with Sister Yin-erh."

"Would you like some rice, Sister Yin-erh?" she went on to ask. "I can have her bring some rice for you to eat."

"Mother, I'm not hungry," Wu Yin-erh replied. "Don't have her bring anything for me."

"All right," said Li P'ing-erh. "Since Sister Yin-erh doesn't want any rice, get four of those stuffed pastries out of my cabinet, and bring them here in a box lid for Yin-erh to eat."

In a little while, Ying-ch'un brought in four saucers of side dishes, one of the fermented brawn from a set of pig's trotters, one of salted chicken, one of poached eggs, and one of sautéed bean sprouts and jellyfish, in addition to which there were also a box of assorted fancy nuts, and a box of stuffed pastries, which were all put down beside them.

It did not take long for Li P'ing-erh and Wu Yin-erh to finish three games of elephant chess, after which the wine was poured, and the two of them proceeded to drink together from silver cups.

At this point, Wu Yin-erh said, "Sister Ying-ch'un, if you would hand me my p'i-p'a, I'll sing a song for your mistress's entertainment."

"Sister, I'd rather you didn't sing," said Li P'ing-erh. "The little gentleman is asleep, and if his father should happen to hear the singing from next door, he'd scold me for it. We can play at dice instead."

Thereupon, she told Ying-ch'un to fetch the dice box, and the two of them proceeded to enjoy themselves casting dice, with the loser having to down a cup of wine as a forfeit.

After they had played with the dice for a while, Wu Yin-erh said, "Sister Ying-ch'un, why don't you step into the other room and invite the wet nurse to come over here and have a cup of wine."

Two Beauties Enjoy a Game of Elephant Chess by Lamplight

"She's lying on the k'ang in there with the baby in her arms," said Ying-ch'un.

"Tell her to stay where she is with the baby in her arms," said Li P'ing-erh, "but take a cup of wine over there for her. That ought to do. You don't know about it, but this little gentleman is rather hypersensitive. If you try to leave him, he's sure to wake up. One day, when he was asleep on my side of the k'ang, and his father presumed to start something with me, he opened his eyes wide and woke up, just as if he was aware of what was going on. I had the wet nurse take him into the other room, but all he would do was cry, and insist on my holding him."

"Now that you've got this baby boy," Wu Yin-erh laughed, "it seems that Father and you can't even spend a satisfactory night together any more. How often does Father pay a visit to your room?"

"There's no telling," said Li P'ing-erh. "He doesn't always stop at one, or even two visits, but drops in to see him all the time. It ought not to matter that he comes to see the child this way, but the fact that he comes here so often has had the effect of filling certain persons to bursting with rage, and induced them to utter the direst imprecations against the child and his father behind their backs. As for me, it goes without saying that I am nothing but an object of obloquy. It's not as though he and I are up to anything in particular. I'd really rather he didn't come here so often. Whenever he does, the next day people indicate by looks and grimaces that they think I'm monopolizing their husband. Why do you suppose, when he came in here just now, I urged him to go somewhere else?

"Sister Yin-erh, you may not know it, but in this household:

When people are many, tongues are many.[28]

Take today, for instance. When that gold bracelet disappeared, fortunately you were here to see it yourself, a certain person, out of spite, went to the rear compound and did her best to incite the First Lady against me, raising suspicions about the fact that the gold was brought into my quarters, and it was in my room that the bracelet disappeared. Later on, it was only after it was disclosed that the maidservant from the Second Lady's quarters had stolen it, that the:

Blue or red, black or white,

of the situation finally became clear. Had that not been the case, even without any other funny business, things looked bad enough for the maidservants in my room and the wet nurse. And Old Mother Feng was so upset she started to cry, threatening to commit suicide, and saying, 'If the gold bracelet is not found, I'm not going to go anywhere.' And, in fact, it was not until the bracelet turned up, later on, that she consented to leave the premises, and, taking a lantern, set off for home."

"Mother," said Wu Yin-erh, "if that's the way it is, out of consideration for
Father, all you can do is look after the child as best you can, and let things
take their course. Whatever happens, you'll just have to:

Deal with matters as they occur.[29]

As for the First Lady in the rear compound, so long as she doesn't have anything to say against you, that's that. The problem is that the others, on seeing
that you have given birth to a son, can't help being somewhat put out. As long
as Father takes charge of the situation, things ought to be all right."

"If it weren't for the consideration shown by Father and the First Lady,"
said Li P'ing-erh, "the child would not have lived to this day."

As they were talking together, what with:

First a cup for you,

Then a cup for me,

without their realizing it, it was the third watch of the night before they went
to bed. Truly:

When a favored guest arrives, one's feelings
can never be satiated;

When a real confidante shows up, conversation
is mutually agreeable.[30]

There is a poem that testifies to this:

Within the painted boudoir a bright moon
traverses the shutters;

As beauties, keeping each other company,
spend the night together.

Who could be anything but enamored of their
jade bones and icy flesh?

A sprig of plum blossoms projects its shadow
through the unending night.

If you want to know the outcome of these events,
Pray consult the story related in the following chapter.

Chapter 45

LI KUEI-CHIEH REQUESTS

THE RETENTION OF HSIA-HUA;

WU YÜEH-NIANG IN A FIT OF ANGER

CURSES AT TAI-AN

As a fancy name, it has been designated
    the king of all the flowers;[1]
The miraculous appearance of its icy flesh
    sets it apart from its rivals.
Its seductiveness enhanced by the sunlight,
    it displays its pure allure;
Its cool limpidity transported by the wind
    diffuses a chaste fragrance.
Its jade countenance need not envy the ladies
    who affect teary complexions;[2]
Its snowy visage cannot help but remind one of
    the powder-faced gentleman.[3]
With sandalwood clappers and golden goblets[4]
    its qualities are celebrated;
What need is there to boast of Mr. Wei's Purples
    and Mr. Yao's Yellows?[5]

THE STORY GOES that because Hsi-men Ch'ing was on holiday he did not go to the yamen that day. When he got up in the morning, he went to the front reception hall to look on as Tai-an prepared two table settings of food for the Ch'iao family, one of them to be delivered to Madame Ch'iao the Fifth, and the other to the wife of Ch'iao Hung. Both of them were replete with:
    High-stacked pyramids of square-shaped confectionery,
assortments of the giblets of domestic fowl, seasonal fruits, and the like. Madame Ch'iao the Fifth rewarded Tai-an with two handkerchiefs and three candareens of silver, and Ch'iao Hung's wife gave him a bolt of black silk, but there is no need to describe this in detail.

It so happens that Ying Po-chüeh, upon taking leave of Hsi-men Ch'ing the day before, had gone straight to the home of Huang the Fourth. Huang the Fourth, for his part, had already arranged with his associates to seal up the sum of ten taels of silver to thank Ying Po-chüeh for his services.

"His Honor told us to come back after the Lantern Festival is over," said Huang the Fourth. "From what he said, it sounded as though he might be willing to renegotiate the contract for the remaining five hundred taels that we owe him. We can hardly manage without the use of that sum of money."

"How much more do you need right now?" asked Ying Po-chüeh.

"Brother Li the Third doesn't know any better," said Huang the Fourth, "and wants to try to borrow it from some eunuch or other. But it would still cost us 5 percent interest per month. It seems to me that it would be better if we could borrow it here, and thereby take advantage of the prestige of his yamen. Even if we have to expend something, both high and low, it would still end up costing us less. Right now, if he can be induced to put up another fifty ingots of silver, it would make it a contract for an even thousand taels, and simplify the calculation of the monthly interest payments."

When Ying Po-chüeh had heard him out, he nodded his head and said, "That's no problem. But if I succeed in persuading him to do this on your behalf, how will you and your associates, the six of you, reward me for my efforts?"

"I will take it up with Li the Third," said Huang the Fourth, "and persuade our associates to give you an additional five taels of silver."

"You can forget about any five taels," said Ying Po-chüeh. "With the skills that I possess, those five taels of yours mean nothing to me. But if you rely on my ingenuity to persuade him with a single word, I'll have to be included in the deal. Today, my wife has gone to his place to attend a party, but I won't be going there myself. Tomorrow evening, however, I've been invited to a lantern-viewing party there. The two of you, first thing tomorrow morning, should supply yourselves with four kinds of delicacies, and also a jug of Chin-hua wine. Don't bother to engage the services of any singing girls, because Li Kuei-chieh and Wu Yin-erh are already there and haven't gone home yet. You can hire six players of wind and percussion instruments from the licensed quarter. If I escort you over there, he's sure to invite you to sit down for a visit. Then, by putting in no more than:

A single word or half a sentence,[6]

from the sidelines, I guarantee that I will persuade him to do as you wish. If he agrees to come up with another five hundred taels of silver and renegotiate the contract for an even thousand taels, at the very most you'll owe him fifty taels of silver per month. What does that amount to after all? It would cost you that much to keep a mistress for a month. As the saying goes:

An undissembling scholar may well exist, but there is
no such thing as unadulterated varnish.[7]

When you turn over the consignment of goods you have contracted to purvey, you can mix some sawdust in with the incense and adulterate the wax with juniper oil. Who will know the difference? After all:

> You're not out to catch fish,
> But only to muddy the waters.[8]

The best way to proceed is to avail yourself of his reputation."

Thereupon, their plan having been decided upon, the next day, Li the Third and Huang the Fourth actually purchased the wine and gifts and turned them over to Ying Po-chüeh, who escorted their two servants on the way to deliver them to Hsi-men Ch'ing's residence.

Hsi-men Ch'ing was still in the front reception hall taking care of the dispatch of the complimentary table settings, when Ying Po-chüeh showed up and said, "My wife put you to a lot of trouble yesterday and was late returning home."

"I went to a party at Commandant Chou Hsiu's place yesterday," said Hsi-men Ch'ing, "and it was already the first watch of the night before I got home. So I didn't even have a chance to see my new relatives, who, I was told, had departed some time earlier. This morning, being on holiday, I did not have to go to the yamen, but, rather than going to see them, I have sent two table settings to the houses of my Ch'iao relatives."

When he had finished speaking, he sat down.

Ying Po-chüeh then called for Li Chin, the servant from Li the Third's household who had accompanied him, and said, "Bring in the gifts."

The two servants then carried in the gifts and put them down just inside the ceremonial gate leading into the second courtyard.

"Brothers Li the Third and Huang the Fourth," said Ying Po-chüeh, "have repeatedly told me of their sense of obligation for the great favor they have received from you. On this festive occasion, not having anything else to offer, they have purchased some insignificant gifts as a humble offering for you to give away to someone if you like."

What should they see at this juncture, but the two servants, who proceeded to come forward, prostrate themselves on the ground, and kowtow.

"What did you have to bring these gifts for?" said Hsi-men Ch'ing. "It would not be right for me to accept them. Tell them to carry them back where they came from."

"Brother," said Ying Po-chüeh, "for you to refuse to accept these gifts of theirs, and insist on having them returned to the donors, would be a very ugly gesture. They also wanted to engage the services of some singing girls to come and wait on you, but I put a stop to that. They have, however, hired six players of wind and percussion instruments, who are waiting outside at this moment."

Hsi-men Ch'ing then ordered, "Have them called inside for me."

In no time at all, the six musicians were summoned into their presence and knelt down in front of him.

"Since their services have already been engaged," said Hsi-men Ch'ing to Ying Po-chüeh, "I can hardly send them back where they came from. The appropriate thing to do would be to invite the two of them over for a visit."

This was just the signal Ying Po-chüeh had been waiting for, and he promptly called Li Chin over and instructed him, "When you get home, tell your master that His Honor has accepted his gifts and is not going to send anyone with a formal invitation, but that he would like your master and Master Huang the Fourth to come over as soon as possible for a visit."

Li Chin assented to these instructions and withdrew. Before long, the gifts were duly put away, Hsi-men Ch'ing ordered Tai-an to reward the two servants with a candareen of silver apiece, and they kowtowed and departed. The six players of wind and percussion instruments stood in attendance in the courtyard below.

In a little while, Ch'i-t'ung brought in a serving of tea, and Hsi-men Ch'ing kept Ying Po-chüeh company as they drank it.

Ch'i-t'ung then said, "The food is ready. Where would you like to eat it?"

Hsi-men Ch'ing responded by ushering Ying Po-chüeh over to the anteroom on the west side of the courtyard, where they took their seats.

He then went on to ask Ying Po-chüeh, "You didn't happen to run into Hsieh Hsi-ta today, did you?"

"I had no sooner gotten up this morning," said Ying Po-chüeh, "than Li the Third showed up at my place and arranged with me to take care of having the gifts delivered here. How could I have had the spare time to meet with him?"

Hsi-men Ch'ing then directed Ch'i-t'ung, "Quickly go and invite Master Hsieh to come join us."

In no time at all, Shu-t'ung set up a table and prepared it for their repast, while Hua-t'ung brought in four portions of appetizers in a square box coated with translucent lacquer. These were served in dainty diminutive picnic saucers, decorated with patterns both inside and out. There was one saucer of delectably tasty squash and eggplant julienne marinated with ten spices, one saucer of a sweet-flavored assortment of pickled beans, one saucer of redolently fragrant orange conserve, and one saucer of fragrant bamboo shoots preserved in fermented red mash. There were also four large serving bowls containing main dishes. One bowl of stewed singed sheep's head, one bowl of marinated broiled duck, one bowl of blanched celery cabbage, egg, and wonton soup, and one bowl of yams with red-cooked minced-pork meatballs. At either end of the table there were set out ivory chopsticks inlaid with gold. In front of Ying Po-chüeh there was a bowl of fresh polished white rice, and in front of Hsi-men Ch'ing there was a cup of fragrant congee made from nonglutinous rice.

After the two of them had consumed their repast, the utensils were cleared away, and the table was wiped clean, Hsi-men Ch'ing and Ying Po-chüeh continued to sit where they were, playing at backgammon, with the loser having to down a cup of wine as a forfeit.

Taking advantage of the fact that Hsieh Hsi-ta had not showed up yet, Ying Po-chüeh seized the occasion to ask, "Brother, how much silver do you propose to advance to Li Chih and Huang the Fourth tomorrow?"

"I plan to retrieve the old contract and renegotiate a new one for the five hundred taels of silver they still owe me," said Hsi-men Ch'ing. "That ought to do it."

"That would be all right, I guess," opined Ying Po-chüeh, "but it would really be better if you could see your way to advance them enough additional capital to make a round thousand taels. It would make it easier to calculate the interest in the future. And I also have another suggestion. Since you really have no use for those gold bracelets they gave you, if you were to throw them in at a valuation of a hundred and fifty taels, you wouldn't have to come up with much in the way of additional cash."

When Hsi-men Ch'ing had heard him out, he said, "What you say makes a lot of sense. I'll advance them another three hundred and fifty taels tomorrow, then, and renegotiate the contract for an even thousand taels. That way I won't be so improvident as to let the gold sit idly at home."

As the two of them were playing backgammon together, Tai-an suddenly came in and announced, "Pen the Fourth has brought in a large marble standing screen, inlaid with mother-of-pearl, together with a bronze gong, and a bronze drum, complete with their stands and knockers. He says that they belong to the household of that distaff relative of the imperial family, Hsiang the Fifth, who wants to pawn them for thirty taels of silver. Is Father willing to agree to that or not?"

"Tell Pen the Fourth to bring them in for me to see," said Hsi-men Ch'ing.

Before long, Pen the Fourth, with the aid of two assistants, carried them in and set them down in the reception hall. Hsi-men Ch'ing and Ying Po-chüeh gave up their game of backgammon and came over to look at them. It so happens that the principal object was a three-foot-wide, five-foot-tall, marble standing screen, suitable for being displayed upon a table, inlaid with mother-of-pearl and decorated with gold tracery, the pattern in the marble being such that:

The black and white were distinctly defined.[9]

After Ying Po-chüeh had contemplated the objects for a while, he said deliberately to Hsi-men Ch'ing, "Brother, just take a good look at these things. The pattern in the marble resembles a lion couchant, protector of the house, and the two stands for the bronze gong and the bronze drum are sumptuously decorated with varicolored designs and cloud patterns carved in relief, the workmanship of which is truly outstanding."

Doing his best to expedite things from the sidelines, he continued, "Brother, you really ought to accept these objects that he is offering to pawn with

Hsi-men Ch'ing Accepts the Pawning of a Bronze Gong and Drum

you. Even leaving out of account the bronze gong and drum with their two stands, this screen alone is something you could hardly hope to buy for fifty taels of silver."

"There is no way of knowing whether or not he is likely to redeem them in the future," said Hsi-men Ch'ing.

"Needless to say," opined Ying Po-chüeh, "he is hardly likely to redeem them. His affairs are like a cart on the downward slope. And if he waits as long as three years, the accumulated interest would probably be equal to the capital."

"All right then," said Hsi-men Ch'ing. "Have my son-in-law in the shop up front weigh out thirty taels of silver for him."

As soon as he had sent Pen the Fourth on his way, Hsi-men Ch'ing had the standing screen wiped clean, positioned it at the upper end of the large reception hall, and proceeded to examine it from left and right. Indeed, he found, the golds and greens of the varicolored clouds blended their hues harmoniously.

"Have those musicians had something to eat yet?" he then went on to ask.

"They're being fed down below right now," said Ch'in-t'ung.

"Tell them, when they're finished eating," said Hsi-men Ch'ing, "to come and let us hear them play."

Thereupon, a great drum was carried into the reception hall, the bronze gong and bronze drum were set up in the corridor, and the musicians commenced to play. Truly:

The sound shakes the cloudy empyrean;
The tones startle both fish and birds.[10]

As they were playing, who should appear but Ch'i-t'ung, with Hsieh Hsi-ta in his wake, who came in and bowed to the two of them.

"Hsieh Hsi-ta," said Hsi-men Ch'ing, "come over here and see what you think this standing screen is worth."

Hsieh Hsi-ta stepped up and proceeded to examine it for some time, uttering no end of exaggerated praise as he did so, saying, "Brother, even if you were able to strike a bargain, you must have paid at least a hundred taels of silver for this standing screen. If you had offered any less, they would have refused to sell it."

"Would you believe it?" said Ying Po-chüeh. "Even with that bronze gong and bronze drum out there thrown in, complete with their two stands and knockers, he paid only thirty taels of silver for them altogether."

Clapping his hands together, Hsieh Hsi-ta exclaimed, "Amitābha be praised! Where could one ever find such a bargain? Including capital and interest, even if you leave the standing screen out of account, thirty taels of silver would hardly suffice to purchase this bronze gong and bronze drum, together with their stands. Just look at the workmanship of these stands. The cinnabar-red painted lacquer is all done in accord with official specifications, and the instruments themselves must contain, at the very least, some forty catties of resounding bronze, which must be worth a pretty penny. No wonder they say:

Every object has its rightful owner.[11]

Who else could hope to have such great good fortune as yours, that a bargain like this should just happen to come your way?"

After they had chatted for a while, Hsi-men Ch'ing invited them to have a seat in his studio, and, before long, Li Chih and Huang the Fourth also showed up.

"Why did the two of you go to the trouble of sending me gifts?" said Hsi-men Ch'ing. "It would hardly be right for me to accept them."

This threw Li Chih and Huang the Fourth into such a state of consternation that they kowtowed, saying, "Pray don't embarrass us. These insignificant things are only indiscriminate tokens for you to give away to someone if you like. We could hardly presume not to respond to Your Honor's summons."

Thereupon, seats were provided for them, and they sat down to one side. Shortly thereafter, the page boy Hua-t'ung brought in five cups of tea, and, after they had drunk them, he took the cups and their raised saucers away.

A little later, Tai-an came up and asked, "Father, where would you like me to set up the table?"

"Bring the table in here," directed Hsi-men Ch'ing. "We might as well remain where we are."

Thereupon, Tai-an and Hua-t'ung between them managed to carry in an Eight Immortals table finished with agateware lacquer and set it down on the floor over a charcoal brazier. Ying Po-chüeh and Hsieh Hsi-ta took the seats of honor at the head of the table, Hsi-men Ch'ing occupied the host's position opposite them, and Li Chih and Huang the Fourth sat down at either side. Shortly thereafter, a plate of assorted cold hors d'oeuvres suitable to accompany a drinking party was brought in, along with soup, rice, and other delicacies, served in:

Large platters and large bowls,

consisting of goose, duck, chicken feet, and every other kind of side dish.

The finest of Yang-kao vintages is decanted;

The soup appears afloat with peach blossoms.

The musicians continued to play outside the windows, and Hsi-men Ch'ing asked Wu Yin-erh to serve the wine. But we will say no more, for the time being, about this drinking party in the front compound.

To continue our story, the male servant from Li Kuei-chieh's establishment and the maidservant, La-mei, from Wu Yin-erh's place, having engaged sedan chairs for the purpose, came to take their mistresses back home. When Li Kuei-chieh heard that the servant had arrived, she hurried out to the front gate and engaged him in a surreptitious conversation for some time, after which she returned to the master suite to say goodbye and explain that she needed to go home.

Wu Yüeh-niang repeatedly urged her to stay, saying, "We're all about to go to the home of my sister-in-law and are prepared to take both of you with us. If it gets too late, you can set off from their place, without any need for sedan chairs, and make your way home by joining the rest of us in 'walking off the hundred ailments.' "

"Mother, you don't understand," said Li Kuei-chieh. "There's no one to be relied upon at home. My elder sister is not there, and moreover, my fifth maternal aunt has invited a lot of people for a 'hamper party.'[12] My mother is really anxious to have me there and was expecting me all day yesterday. If she weren't so concerned, she wouldn't have sent the servant to fetch me. Under ordinary circumstances, if you invited me to stay several days, I'd be happy to do so."

When Yüeh-niang realized that she would not stay, she told Yü-hsiao to take the two trays from the gift box she had originally brought with her, fill one of them with Lantern Festival dumplings, and the other with sugar crisps, and then give it to the servant from her establishment to carry. She also gave Li Kuei-chieh a tael of silver and allowed her to make an early departure. After Kuei-chieh had said goodbye to Yüeh-niang and the others, her aunt accompanied her to the front compound and told Hua-t'ung to carry her felt bag for her. When she came by the door to the studio in the front courtyard, she told Tai-an to ask Hsi-men Ch'ing to come out and speak to her.

Cautiously lifting aside the portiere, Tai-an went inside the studio and extended the invitation to Hsi-men Ch'ing, saying, "Kuei-chieh is about to go home and would like to have a word with you."

"Do you mean to say that little whore Li Kuei-chieh hasn't left yet?" said Ying Po-chüeh.

"She's not going home until today," explained Hsi-men Ch'ing.

He then stepped outside, where he saw that Li Kuei-chieh was wearing a jacket that opened down the middle, made of lilac-colored Lu-chou silk with purfled edging, over a skirt of white glazed damask with a wide varicolored drawnwork border, and had a white satin kerchief shot with turquoise wrapped around her head.

Like a sprig of blossoms swaying in the breeze;
Sending the pendants of her embroidered sash flying,

she knelt down in front of him and kowtowed four times, saying, "I've put Father and Mother to a lot of trouble."

"Why don't you go home tomorrow?" said Hsi-men Ch'ing.

"There's no one to look after things at home," said Kuei-chieh. "My mother has sent the servant with a sedan chair to fetch me."

"There is also another matter that I'd like to take up with you," she went on to say. "With regard to that child in my aunt's quarters, you really oughtn't to have her taken away. My aunt has already punished her last night with a few strokes of the cane. If you consider the situation, she's still young and doesn't really understand how to behave. I gave her a real talking to, and from now on her conduct will be reformed. She won't dare do anything like that again. It's not so much that I object to your getting rid of her, but if my aunt is left with no one to wait on her during a major festival like this, wouldn't you be troubled by it? It's always been the case that:

> Though the wooden ladle or the fire tongs may be short,
> They're still better than having to use your hands.[13]

Father, whatever you do, for my sake, allow this maidservant to remain in your household."

"Since you have spoken up for her," said Hsi-men Ch'ing, "I'll keep the slave after all."

Turning to Tai-an, he said, "Go to the rear compound and tell the First Lady not to send for a go-between."

Noticing that Hua-t'ung was standing by with Kuei-chieh's felt bag, Tai-an said, "Have him give me Kuei-chieh's felt bag to hold, and send him back to the rear compound to deliver the message."

Hua-t'ung assented and headed straight back to the rear compound.

When Kuei-chieh had finished speaking to Hsi-men Ch'ing, she raised her voice outside the east window and called out, "Beggar Ying, I won't bother to pay my respects to you. Your mother is on her way home."

"Drag that lousy little whore back in here," exclaimed Ying Po-chüeh. "Don't let her go. Have her sing a song suite for my delectation."

"You'll have to wait until your mother has the leisure to sing for you," said Kuei-chieh.

"What kind of chaste schemes are the two of you hatching," asked Ying Po-chüeh, "that you insist on carrying on a private conversation without letting me in on it? If you let her go home in broad daylight like this, you'll only be benefiting the lousy little whore. She'll have time to take on any number of customers before it gets dark."

"You're delirious, you beggar!" said Kuei-chieh, as she made her exit with a laugh.

Tai-an accompanied her on the way out and saw her into her sedan chair. When he had finished speaking with Kuei-chieh, Hsi-men Ch'ing went back to the rear compound to adjust his toilet.

During his absence, Ying Po-chüeh said to Hsieh Hsi-ta, "This little whore, Li Kuei-chieh, is carrying on just like an escaped convict. Her meretriciousness is more beguiling than ever. As though on a major festival like this she would ever consent to remain at one place if she could help it. She has arranged for the procuress of her establishment to send for her. I wonder who it might be that is waiting for her there."

"Take a guess," said Hsieh Hsi-ta, as he surreptitiously whispered no more than a few sentences:

Thus and thus, and
So and so,
into Ying Po-chüeh's ear.

"Keep your voice down," said Ying Po-chüeh. "Our brother doesn't know anything about it."

In no time at all, they heard the sound of Hsi-men Ch'ing's footsteps, and the two of them ceased speaking.

Taking Wu Yin-erh onto his lap, Ying Po-chüeh then proceeded to pass the same cup of wine back and forth between them, saying as he did so, "This adopted daughter of mine is both gentle and soft, a hundred times better than that little whore from the Li Family Establishment, that not even a dog would want to mess around with."

"What a thing to say, Master Two!" laughed Wu Yin-erh.

Every single person is a unique individual,
A hundred persons are a hundred individuals.
In the space of any particular quarter,
There are both the wise and the foolish.[14]

Why insist on comparing one with another? What has Kuei-chieh ever done to annoy you?"

"There's no point in interrogating that lousy dog!" said Hsi-men Ch'ing. "All he utters is the same old:

Ridiculous blatherskite."

"Don't you worry yourself about anyone else," said Ying Po-chüeh. "Just let me live out my days with this adopted daughter of mine. Daughter, come over here, take up your *p'i-p'a*, and sing me a song."

Thereupon, Wu Yin-erh:

Neither hastily nor hurriedly,
Deftly extended her jade fingers,
Gently strummed the silken strings,

placed the *p'i-p'a* on her knees, and sang in a low voice a song to the tune "The Willows Dangle Their Gold":

In my heart I am preoccupied,
Unable to eat food or drink tea.[15]
It is not easy to relinquish
    my handsome lover.
I am desolate because I can't get him
    out of my mind.
I don't even know whose establishment
    you are visiting now.
If you want to part company with me, at least you could
    give me a clear statement.
You have utterly abandoned me;

You have utterly deceived me;
But you'd better not think you've
heard the last of me.

After Ying Po-chüeh had downed a cup of wine, Wu Yin-erh proffered another
to Hsieh Hsi-ta and then proceeded to sing, to the same tune as before:

I am constantly depressed.
When will I ever achieve my heart's desire?
I am preoccupied with the thought of
my tender-hearted lover.
My sisters do their best to keep me
under tight control;
My old mother will not let up on me;
Which makes it look as if I am
unable to keep my word.
I don't love you for your jewels or your gold.
The thing that I love, the thing that I love,
is just your handsome face.
If we could only be man and wife,
I could die happy,
Because then you and I could satisfy
each other's desires.

But we will say no more, for the moment, about how Wu Yin-erh served
wine, played her instrument, and sang in the front compound.

To resume our story, Hua-t'ung went back to the rear compound on his
errand, where he found that Wu Yüeh-niang was sitting in the master suite
together with Meng Yü-lou, Li P'ing-erh, Hsi-men Ta-chieh, Sun Hsüeh-o,
and the abbess of the Kuan-yin Nunnery.

On seeing Hua-t'ung come in, Yüeh-niang was just about to send him after
Old Mother Feng in order to take Hsia-hua away, when Hua-t'ung said, "Father has sent me to tell you that he doesn't want you to have her taken away."

"Your father told me to sell her off," said Yüeh-niang. "Why should he not
want to sell her now? Tell me the truth. Who was it who suggested to your
father that she not be taken away?"

"Just now," said Hua-t'ung, "I was standing by, holding Kuei-chieh's felt bag
for her. But when she was just about to leave, she spoke to Father, begging
him to let Hsia-hua stay, to deal with her leniently, and not to allow her to be
taken away. Father told Tai-an to come back and tell you about it, but Tai-an
refused to come inside and, right in front of Father, sent me to come in his
stead, took her felt bag away from me, and then proceeded to see Kuei-chieh
on her way himself."

When Yüeh-niang heard this, she was more than a little annoyed and cursed Tai-an, saying, "Why that double-dealing, ingratiating, treacherous slave! No wonder, when I was originally told to send for a go-between, he said it was Father who had ordered that she be taken away, when all along he was just up to his tricks. And now he's contrived to be the one who sees Kuei-chieh on her way. When he comes back here, I'll have something to say to him."

As she was speaking, whom should she see but Wu Yin-erh, who came in after she had finished singing in the front compound.

"La-mei, the maidservant from your place, has come to fetch you," Yüeh-niang said to her. "Li Kuei-chieh has already gone home. No doubt, you're planning to go home yourself."

"Since you have urged me to stay," said Wu Yin-erh, "if I were to go home, it would only show that:

　　I wouldn't know a favor if I saw one."

Then, turning to La-mei, she went on to ask, "What did you come for?"

"Mother sent me to see how you were doing," said La-mei.

"There isn't anything going on at home, is there?" Wu Yin-erh asked.

"Nothing at all," La-mei replied.

"Since there's nothing going on," said Wu Yin-erh, "what did you come to fetch me for? You might as well return home. Mother here has urged me to stay, and to join her and the other ladies this evening in visiting her sister-in-law's place and then 'walking off the hundred ailments' together. I won't come home until getting back from that excursion."

When she had finished speaking, La-mei was about to depart, but Yüeh-niang said, "Call her back so I can see that she has something to eat."

"The First Lady is offering you something to eat," said Wu Yin-erh. If you wait a little, you can take my clothes bag home with you. Tell Mother not to send a sedan chair for me. This evening I'll make my way home on foot."

"Why didn't Wu Hui come?" she went on to ask.

"He's at home suffering from an eye ailment," La-mei said.

"Take La-mei back to the rear compound," Yüeh-niang instructed Yü-hsiao, "and see that she gets provided with two dishes of pork, a plate of steamed dumplings, and a cup of wine. And also take the gift box that she brought with her and replenish it with a tray of Lantern Festival dumplings, and a tray of tea cakes, to take back with her."

It so happens that Wu Yin-erh had left her clothes bag in Li P'ing-erh's quarters, and Li P'ing-erh had already sought out a set of first-class silk brocade clothing, two gold lamé handkerchiefs, and a tael of silver and put them in her felt bag as a gift.

But Wu Yin-erh blithely declined them, saying, "Mother, I don't want these clothes."

"The truth of the matter is, Mother," she continued with an ingratiating smile, "that I don't have a white jacket to wear. If you would take back these silk clothes, could you possibly seek out any kind of old white satin jacket and give it to me instead?"

"My white jackets are all too big for you," said Li P'ing-erh. "You could scarcely wear any of them."

Thereupon, she said to Ying-ch'un, "Take the keys and get a whole bolt of white satin out of my large trunk to give to Yin-erh."

"Tell your mother," she said, "to have a tailor make up two dress jackets for you."

"By the way," she went on to ask, "did you want figured satin or plain?"

"Mother, I'd prefer the plain," replied Wu Yin-erh. "I want something that will go well with a vest."

Then, turning to Ying-ch'un, she said with an ingratiating smile, "I'm putting you to the trouble of going upstairs again on my behalf. In the future, though I have nothing else to offer, I can always entertain you with a song."

In a little while, Ying-ch'un brought down from upstairs a bolt of fine plain white satin, manufactured on a wide loom in Sung-chiang, the label attached to the end of which indicated that it weighed thirty-eight ounces, and handed it to Wu Yin-erh. Yin-erh hastily:

> Like a sprig of blossoms swaying in the breeze;
> Sending the pendants of her embroidered sash flying;
> Just as though inserting a taper in its holder;

kowtowed to Li P'ing-erh four times. After which, she got to her feet and also bowed deeply to Ying-ch'un eight times.

"Yin-erh," said Li P'ing-erh, "Wrap up this silk clothing and take it along with you too. Sooner or later you may have occasion to wear it to a party."

Wu Yin-erh said, "Mother has not only bestowed this white satin on me to make a jacket out of, but also persuaded me to take this other clothing as well."

Thereupon, she kowtowed to her again to express her gratitude. In no time at all, when La-mei had finished her meal, the gift box and felt bag were entrusted to her, and she set off for home.

Yüeh-niang took the occasion to say, "Yin-erh, this conduct of yours is just the kind I like. See that you don't imitate those meretricious tricks of Li Kuei-chieh. Yesterday, and again this morning, she carried on just like:

> A recalcitrant tiger that refuses to lie down,

declining our invitation to stay, and insisting on going home. What's happening at her place that requires her to be there so urgently? She didn't even want to put herself out to sing. When she saw that the servant from her place had come for her, she didn't even have anything to eat before running off, without even waiting to say goodbye to you. See that you don't imitate that conduct of hers."

"Dear Mother!" exclaimed Wu Yin-erh. "What sort of a place is this after all, the residence of Father and Mother? If she had any excess wind in her

Li P'ing-erh Contributes a Gift of White Satin to Wu Yin-erh

colon, she should have saved it for somewhere else, rather than presuming to let it off here. But Kuei-chieh is still young, and doesn't know what's what. Mother shouldn't allow herself to be bothered by her."

As they were talking, who should appear but the page boy Lai-ting, who had been sent by Sister-in-law Wu to urge them on their way, saying, "My mistress respectfully requests that Sister-in-law Three, and the other ladies, including Li Kuei-chieh and Wu Yin-erh, should come over as soon as possible, and that Sun Hsüeh-o should also come along for a visit."

"When you get home," said Yüeh-niang, "say to your mistress, 'We're in the process of getting ready right now. The Second Lady is suffering from pain in her legs, and will not be coming, but stay behind to look after the house. Your brother-in-law is entertaining some guests in the front compound today, leaving hardly anyone in the residential part of the house. The lady from the rear compound will not be coming, and Li Kuei-chieh has already gone home, so that, including Hsi-men Ta-chieh and Wu Yin-erh, there will be six of us in all. You oughtn't to go to any trouble on our behalf. After visiting together a while longer, we'll come over at nightfall.' "

"Who have your master and mistress engaged to sing for us?" she went on to ask Lai-ting.

"Big Sister Yü," Lai-ting replied and, when he had finished speaking, set off ahead of them.

Wu Yüeh-niang then, along with Meng Yü-lou, P'an Chin-lien, Li P'ing-erh, Hsi-men Ta-chieh, and Wu Yin-erh, having spoken to Hsi-men Ch'ing about their arrangements, and instructed the wet nurse to stay at home and look after Kuan-ko, all dressed themselves up to befit the occasion and set off in six sedan chairs. Escorted by Tai-an, Ch'in-t'ung,[16] and Lai-an, along with four orderlies, they proceeded on their way to the home of Sister-in-law Wu. Truly:

> In myriads of courtyards the spring prospects
>   are conspicuous;
> In thousands of households the lantern lights[17]
>   blaze all night.
> In this life nights such as this are seldom
>   to be seen;
> Next year where will we see the bright moon
>   on this night?[18]

> If you want to know the outcome of these events,
> Pray consult the story related in the following chapter.

Chapter 46

RAIN AND SNOW INTERRUPT A WALK

DURING THE LANTERN FESTIVAL;

WIFE AND CONCUBINES LAUGHINGLY

CONSULT THE TORTOISE ORACLE

In the imperial precincts the prospects are fine
   during the Lantern Festival,
Surpassing those in the immortal Isles of the Blest.
Jade dust is stirred into flight,
Escorts clamor around decorated chariot hubs,
Moonlight illuminates the towers and terraces.

In the three palaces[1] this night is a time for rejoicing.
A myriad golden lotus lanterns,
Are scattered about the streets of the capital.
Hoofers parade to the drum all night.
Citizens compete to put up decorated lanterns,
Which are displayed for five consecutive nights.[2]

THIS LYRIC was composed by a poet of former times in order to celebrate the sights of the Lantern Festival and the prosperity of the people.[3]

To resume our story, on that day Hsi-men Ch'ing saw Wu Yüeh-niang and the others off on their way to the party at Sister-in-law Wu's place, while asking Li Chih and Huang the Fourth to keep their seats.

Ying Po-chüeh took advantage of his host's absence while he was seeing off the ladies to address them, thus and so, saying, "I have already spoken to him on behalf of you two gentlemen, and he has positively agreed to advance you another five hundred taels of silver tomorrow."

Li Chih and Huang the Fourth bowed in gratitude to Ying Po-chüeh again and again, and, when it became dusk, said goodbye and departed. Ying Po-chüeh, for his part, along with Hsieh Hsi-ta, continued to drink with Hsi-men Ch'ing in the antechamber where his studio was located. Whom should they see at this juncture but Li Ming, who lifted aside the portiere and came in.

When Ying Po-chüeh saw him, he said, "So Li Ming has come."

Li Ming knelt down on the floor and kowtowed to the company, after which Hsi-men Ch'ing asked him, "Why has Wu Hui not come with you?"

"Today," said Li Ming, "Wu Hui was not even able to report for duty at the installation ceremony for the new prefect of Tung-p'ing prefecture. He's at home suffering from an eye ailment. I've engaged Wang Chu to come in his stead."

He then called out to Wang Chu, "Come in and kowtow to His Honor."

Wang Chu then proceeded to lift aside the portiere and come into the room, where he kowtowed to the company and then stood to one side with Li Ming.

Addressing himself to the latter, Ying Po-chüeh then said, "Li Kuei-chieh from your establishment has just left to return home. Did you not know about it?"

"When I got home from my duty assignment in Tung-p'ing," said Li Ming, "I only had time to wash my face before coming over here. I don't know anything about it."

Turning to Hsi-men Ch'ing, Ying Po-chüeh said, "I fear the two of them have probably not had a chance to eat yet. Brother, why don't you direct that the two of them be given something to eat?"

"Master Two," said Shu-t'ung, who was standing in attendance, "let them wait a little, and they can eat together with the other musicians. That will obviate the need to fetch food for them a second time."

Ying Po-chüeh told Shu-t'ung to provide him with a tray, to which he transferred two saucers of hors d'oeuvres and a plate of roast lamb from the table top and gave it to Li Ming, saying, "If you wait until they come with the rice, the two of you can take a couple of bowls worth and eat in the parlor here."

Then, turning his attention to Shu-t'ung, he said, "My good nephew! As the saying goes:

Affairs come together according to their tendencies;
Things are differentiated according to their classes.[4]

You don't understand the fact that this category of people, even though they may only be boy actors from the licensed quarter, are not the same as musicians. Although one may treat them alike, it will only serve to show that you and I do not know the score."

This disquisition caused Hsi-men Ch'ing to give Ying Po-chüeh a rap on the head as he admonished him with a laugh, saying, "Dog that you are, since:

People in that line of trade,
Always stand up for each other,

it's no wonder that you know all about the pains and pleasures of those who are subject to performance on demand."

"My good child!" said Ying Po-chüeh. "What do you know about it? You've been a devotee of the licensed quarters for nothing if you don't even understand the four characters that mean:

Solicitous of jade and considerate of fragrance.

How should they be explicated? Girls with painted faces and boy actors are just like fresh flowers. If you are solicitous and considerate of them, they will respond by being more vivacious. But if you mistreat them, it will be a case of 'Eight Beats of a Kan-chou Song':

Listlessly, listlessly withering away,[5]

and they will be hard to keep alive."

"I yield to my son," said Hsi-men Ch'ing with a laugh, "in his understanding of principle."

In a short time, Li Ming and Wang Chu finished eating, and Ying Po-chüeh called them over to ask, "Do the two of you know the song suite that begins with the line:

Together we used to descant upon the snow and moon,
     the breeze and flowers,

or not?"

"That's a suite in the Huang-chung mode,"[6] said Li Ming. "We do know it."

Thereupon, he picked up his psaltery, after which, with Wang Chu playing the *p'i-p'a* and Li Ming playing the psaltery:

Commencing to sing in full voice,

they sang the song suite that begins with the tune "Drunk in the Flowers' Shade" in the Huang-chung mode:

Together we used to descant upon the snow and moon,
     the breeze and flowers;[7]
In our dreams of clouds and rain, the fragrance
     was alluring, the jade soft.[8]
Though the blossoms are now splendid, the moon just full;
They are weighed down with snow and tossed by the wind;
While my lover is as out of reach as the horizon.
For some time I have wanted to send him
     a broken-hearted message,
But I find that this boundless
     longing of mine,
Is nearly impossible to communicate.

To the tune "Rejoicing at the Oriole's Ascent":

Choosing the blue sea as an inkwell,
And a rabbit-haired brush,[9] sturdy
     as a beam;
For pine soot ink,
I will grind down Mount T'ai itself;

And use the infinite expanse of azure Heaven[10]
    as brocade notepaper,
In order to display the art of the sage
    of cursive calligraphy.[11]
Though I write for a while,
I cannot write out the feelings in my heart;
Though I explain for a while,
I cannot explain the extent of my suffering.

To the tune "Dancers' Ensemble":

I remember the first time we met,
When I first caught sight of my romantic
    young karmic encumbrance.
In our two hearts we mutually acknowledged
    a life and death affinity;
For a whole year our relationship was as close
    as glue and lacquer.
Who could have anticipated that you would have
    a change of heart along the way,
Turning our case into a Heaven of Frustrated Separation?[12]

To the same tune:

When I haven't seen him for two or three days,
It feels just as though we have been separated
    for more than ten years.
Not a meal goes by without my feeling
    preoccupied with him;
Not a quarter of an hour passes without
    my calling him to mind;
Not a watch of the night transpires without
    my dreaming of him.

To the tune "Four Gates Students":[13]

There is not a traveler from whom I do not
    ask for news of him.
This lovesickness is really
    driving me crazy.
My acquaintances on seeing the state I am in
    urge me to desist;
But I can't help being preoccupied with him
    in my heart.

I long for him until he appears vividly
    before my eyes;[14]
I yearn for him so hard the saliva in
    my mouth dries up.
The fronts of my lapels,
The sides of my sleeves,
Are completely covered with tearstains.
I think of that time in the past when
    he and I exchanged vows.
In those days he was attractively young
    while I was in my prime;
As for his intelligence, who had ever
    seen the like?
And he seemed to exhibit an abundance
    of genuine sincerity.

To the tune "Ground Scouring Wind":

For my part, my feelings for him have
    never diminished.
My tears flow in rivers, I love him so much.
We used to sit knee to knee,
And chat shoulder to shoulder.
Amid the fragrance of the caltrops and lotuses we used to
    entwine our necks like mandarin ducks.
We used to walk hand in hand,
And sleep on the same pillow.
Heavens! It seems that my destiny is meager,
    and my allotment shallow.[15]

To the tune "The Water Nymphs":

It's not a case of my being capricious,
And merely seeking "phoenix glue with which to
    mend the broken string."[16]
I recall the oaths we swore upon our pillow;[17]
I think of the vows we made before the gods.
One whose heart is firm can wear through stone.[18]
Surreptitiously, I importune
    azure Heaven:[19]
If I am guilty of failing his expectations
    in a former incarnation,
So that my handsome lover cannot fulfill
    his desires in this life,

May we be able to be reunited in
    the life to come.

CODA

I enjoin you not to let your innermost
    feelings change.
If we are to meet again, it will not be until
    ages have passed and years gone by.
Though you may be distant in the flesh,
Do not allow your heart to be distant.[20]

The story goes that, when they had finished singing it was gradually growing dark. Truly:

The gold raven slowly sinks behind
    the western hills;
The jade rabbit gradually climbs above
    the painted balustrade.[21]
A beautiful lady comes gently in to
    report the fact that:
"The moon has moved the flower shadows[22]
    onto the gauze window."[23]

Hsi-men Ch'ing ordered that the utensils be cleared away and then sent someone to invite Manager Fu Ming, Han Tao-kuo, Manager Yün Li-shou, Pen the Fourth, and Ch'en Ching-chi to join them at the front gate, where a standing screen had been erected, two tables had been set up, a pair of rams-horn lanterns were suspended, and a party spread had been laid out, replete with a plate of assorted cold hors d'oeuvres and boxes containing every kind of delicacy. Hsi-men Ch'ing, along with Ying Po-chüeh and Hsieh Hsi-ta, occupied the positions of honor at the head of the seating arrangement, while the employees and managers sat down to either side. Outside the front gate there were twelve golden lotus lanterns arrayed on either side, in addition to which there was a small stand of fireworks, which Hsi-men Ch'ing had ordered should not be set off until the womenfolk arrived home.

Before this, the six musicians had carried the bronze gong and bronze drum to the front gate, where they now started to play. After performing for a while on the bronze gong and bronze drum, they followed up with an interlude of more refined music on their wind instruments. The boy actors, Li Ming and Wang Chu, then came forward with their psaltery and *p'i-p'a* and sang a song suite in celebration of the Lantern Festival, beginning with the tune "Prelude to Painted Eyebrows," the first line of which is:

Blossoms and moonlight pervade the spring metropolis,[24]

etc. etc.

The passersby in the street, who crowded around to see the show:
    Scarcely dared to gaze upon them.
Hsi-men Ch'ing was wearing a "loyal and tranquil hat,"[25] a velvet robe decorated with a crane motif, and a white satin jacket. Tai-an and P'ing-an took
turns setting off sparklers one at a time. A pair of orderlies, holding staves in
their hands, used them to fend off the crowd and prevent any idlers from
getting too close for comfort.
    In no time at all, when it was observed that:
    The clouds were tranquil in the azure heavens,
    As the wheel of a bright moon[26] rose in the east,
crowds of sightseers congregated in the street, and:
    The merrymaking was at its height.
Behold:
    At every doorway, the beating of gongs and drums;[27]
    In every house, the airs of woodwinds and strings.
    Troupe after troupe, the sightseers tread
        to the sound of singing;
    All of a flutter, the wellborn young ladies
        trail undulating sleeves.
    Hills of lanterns decorated with bunting,[28]
    Soar majestically to a hundred feet,
        piercing the clear sky;
    Aromatic incense from phoenix censers,
    Drifts hazily in a thousand layers,
        investing the silken throngs.
    Empty courtyards, both inside and out,
    Are awash in the brilliance of the precious moon;
    Painted bowers, both above and below,
    Are iridescent in the glow of decorated lanterns.[29]
    In the three markets and six streets[30]
        the people are making merry;
    On this festive day in the metropolis
        we enjoy the Lantern Festival.[31]
    To resume our story, in the rear compound Ch'un-mei, Ying-ch'un, Yü-
hsiao, Lan-hsiang, Hsiao-yü, and company, on observing that Yüeh-niang was
not at home, and hearing the sound of the bronze drum and other forms of
musical performance at the front gate, as well as the fact that there were to
be fireworks, all got dressed up and concealed themselves behind the standing
screen to see what was going on. Shu-t'ung and Hua-t'ung were also behind
the standing screen, heating wine over the brazier.
    It so happens that Yü-hsiao and Shu-t'ung had been carrying on an affair
for some time and were constantly flirting with each other. The two of them,
on finding themselves together on this occasion, helped themselves to some

melon seeds to crack, and in the process of doing so managed to knock over a pewter flagon of wine that was resting on the brazier. The fire in the brazier flared up conspicuously, scattering ashes all over the area, but Yü-hsiao merely continued to laugh about it.

When Hsi-men Ch'ing heard this, he sent Tai-an to ask who was laughing, and why the ashes had been scattered in such a way.

That day Ch'un-mei was wearing a new white satin jacket with a brocaded scarlet vest and was sitting sedately in a chair. When she saw the two of them knock over the wine, she immediately raised her voice and berated Yü-hsiao, saying, "What a wondrously wanton whore you are! No sooner do you catch sight of a man than you start carrying on with him in an unheard of way. It's enough that the two of you knocked over the wine, but how can you continue to guffaw over it? What are you laughing at? You've not only managed to put out the fire, but covered us all with ashes to boot."

When Yü-hsiao realized that she was being taken to task, she was too frightened to say anything and headed back toward the rear compound.

Shu-t'ung was thrown into consternation and came forward to explain, saying, "I was heating some wine on the brazier and happened to knock over the pewter flagon of wine."

When Hsi-men Ch'ing heard this explanation, he didn't pursue the matter any further and let it drop.

Before this happened, on that particular day, Pen the Fourth's wife, on learning that Yüeh-niang would not be at home, and having been aware for some time that Ch'un-mei, Yü-hsiao, Ying-ch'un, and Lan-hsiang were favorite body servants of Hsi-men Ch'ing, had laid in all kinds of holiday dishes and delicacies and sent her daughter Chang-chieh to invite the four of them to her house to relax and visit together.

They took her to see Li Chiao-erh, but she said, "I'm only:
> A walking stick made of rush:
> Not to be relied upon.[32]
You'd better ask Father's permission."

They also went to ask Sun Hsüeh-o, but she was even less willing to take responsibility for the decision. They procrastinated until after lamplighting time, when Pen the Fourth's wife again sent Chang-chieh to invite the four of them. Lan-hsiang pressed Yü-hsiao, Yü-hsiao pressed Ying-ch'un, and Ying-ch'un pressed Ch'un-mei to go back to Li Chiao-erh as a group and ask her, in her turn, to go to Hsi-men Ch'ing and request permission for them to go.

But Ch'un-mei just sat there:
> Without turning a hair,
and upbraided Yü-hsiao and the others, saying, "The lot of you are like a bunch of good-for-nothings who:

Have never even attended a banquet.
Though you've never been to a feast,
You can't wait to get a sniff of one.

Even if it means I don't get to go, I won't go begging someone else for the privilege. Each and every one of you is carrying on as though you were ghost-driven. What's the big hurry, anyway? I can't bring myself to countenance such things with even half an eye."

Ying-ch'un, Yü-hsiao, and Lan-hsiang had all dressed themselves up to befit the occasion, and come out to the front compound, but did not dare to depart, while Ch'un-mei refused to budge from her seat.

Shu-t'ung, on seeing that Pen the Fourth's wife had again sent Chang-chieh to invite them, said, "Even if Father takes me to task, so be it. Let me go out and petition him on your behalf."

Going straight out to Hsi-men Ch'ing's side, he covered his mouth and whispered into his ear, "Pen the Fourth's wife, on this festival occasion, has invited my sister maidservants over for a visit, and they have asked me to inquire whether they may go or not."

When Hsi-men Ch'ing heard this, he instructed him, "Tell your sister maid-servants to get themselves ready and go, but to come home early. There isn't anyone to be relied on at home."

Shu-t'ung promptly went inside and said, "Thanks to my initiative in approaching him, he has consented to your request. He says that you should get yourselves ready and go, but to come home early."

Only then did Ch'un-mei nonchalantly betake herself to her room, make herself up, and prepare to depart.

Before long, the four of them passed through the gate together, after Shu-t'ung had adjusted the placement of the standing screen so as to partially conceal their exit, and proceeded on their way to the house of Pen the Fourth.

When Pen the Fourth's wife caught sight of them, she felt:
    Just as though they had fallen from Heaven,
and invited them into an inner room, from the ceiling of which hung lighted hydrangea-shaped gauze lanterns, and which featured a table replete with a meticulously laid out and sumptuous display of comestibles, as well as platters of cold hors d'oeuvres.

Pen the Fourth's wife addressed Ch'un-mei as Elder Sister, Ying-ch'un as Second Sister, Yü-hsiao as Third Sister, and Lan-hsiang as Fourth Sister. When they had all exchanged salutations, she also invited Auntie Han, the wife of Mohammedan Han, to come over and help keep her guests company, having directed that she be provided with a separate selection of foodstuffs that would not violate her dietary restrictions.

Ch'un-mei and Ying-ch'un were seated in the positions of honor, with Yü-hsiao and Lan-hsiang facing them, while Pen the Fourth's wife and Auntie Han sat to either side, and Chang-chieh went back and forth to heat the wine and wait upon them. But let us put this aside for a moment and say no more about it.

Hsi-men Ch'ing meanwhile proceeded to call over the musicians and instructed them, saying, "Sing that song suite for us, the first words to the prelude of which are:

The east wind is chilly,[33]

beginning with the tune "A Happy Event Is Imminent."

Just at this juncture, individual servings of rose-flavored Lantern Festival dumplings, provided with silver spoons in the shape of apricot leaves, were brought out from the rear compound, and the company proceeded to pick them up and enjoy them together. Truly, they were:

Fragrant, sweet, and delectable,
And melted on entering the mouth;
Most appropriate for the occasion.

In front of the gathering, Li Ming and Wang Chu took up their instruments and accompanied themselves as they sang the words of this song suite. Truly:

The rhythm was slow and lingering,
The beat melodious and harmonious.

They sang to the tune "A Happy Event Is Imminent":

In the eastern fields the blue mist has dissipated.
We delight in this clear morning of a fragrant day.
Our disposition to love flowers,[34]
Has caused us to get up, this spring,
    earlier than usual.
Our curiosity aroused,
We inquire of the Lord of the East, "How much spring
    are you going to allow us?"
To which our maidservant responds
    with a smile,
"Last night the flowering crab apples have bloomed."

To the tune "May You Live a Thousand Years":

Amid sprigs of apricot blossoms,
Interspersed with snowy pear blossoms,
Tiny green plums may be seen
    sparsely scattered.
Beside the bridge over flowing water,[35]
Beside the bridge over flowing water,
All one can hear is the reiterated calls
    of the flower sellers.
Beyond the swing, along the road,

All we can hear from within the walls,
Is the happy laughter of beautiful maidens,
Joyously exclaiming, "What a wonderful spring."
Eagerly we strive to fill up
    our flower baskets,
While bearing our picnic hampers on high.

To the tune "Better than Ever":

Where the flowers are at their thickest,[36]
A wine flag flutters to attract
    our attention.
Beside the Peony Pavilion,
We seek female companions to compare botanical specimens.
From amid the lofty green willow branches,
With a flicker of wings[37] the morning oriole
    flies over the treetops.
The cascading red blossoms, and
    flittering butterflies,
Fly over the painted bridge.
Out of the whole year,
With its four seasons,
Spring alone is the most wonderful.
Amid the flowers we drink lustily;
Beneath the moon we laugh joyously.[38]

To the tune "Red Embroidered Slippers":

Listening to the strains of phoenix pipes
    and phoenix flutes;
We ogle the sight of kingfisher ornaments
    and clustering pearls.
Raising our jade goblets,
We stumble in drunkenness,
Singing "Golden Threads,"[39]
We do the "Liu-yao" dance.[40]
Let the bright moon climb the flowering branches;[41]
The moon climb the flowering branches.[42]

CODA:

Completely inebriated, let us recline
    amid the fragrant verdure,
Suspending our silver lanterns on high
    underneath the flowers.

The fullness of youth turns all too easily to age.[43]
Let us not permit the wonders of spring to
     escape us unappreciated.[44]

But let us say no more for the moment about the playing and singing as the
party continued.

To resume our story, Tai-an and Ch'en Ching-chi, with lots of firecrackers
in their sleeves, called for a pair of orderlies to carry lanterns for them and set
out for Sister-in-law Wu's house to escort Wu Yüeh-niang and the others on
their way home. They found them in the parlor, together with Yüeh-niang's
elder sister, the wife of Mr. Shen, the wife of Yüeh-niang's second brother,
Wu the Second, and Wu Shun-ch'en's wife, Third Sister Cheng, where they
were drinking wine and being entertained by the playing and singing of Big
Sister Yü.

When their hostess saw that Ch'en Ching-chi had arrived, she arranged for
him to be seated together with Wu the Second and her son, Wu Shun-ch'en,
and said, "My husband is not at home today. He's at battalion headquarters
supervising the compilation of the guard registers."

She also had a table set up for them and provided with a platter of cold
hors d'oeuvres, an assortment of other dishes, and wine, so they could keep
Ching-chi company.

Tai-an then came forward and said to Yüeh-niang, "Father sent me to escort
you ladies on your way, and to ask you to come home early. He is worried that
the crowds may get rowdy later in the evening. I came together with your
son-in-law."

Because she had been annoyed with him earlier, Yüeh-niang had not a
word to say to him in response.

Sister-in-law Wu then said to her page boy Lai-ting, "Get something for
Tai-an to eat."

"Wine and meat, soup and rice, are all laid out up front," said Lai-ting.
"He can eat with us there."

"What's the need," said Yüeh-niang, "for someone who's:
     Newly come and just arrived,
to be fed right away? Tell him to go stand out front. We're about to get started."

"What's the hurry, kinswoman?" said Sister-in-law Wu. "How can you bring
yourself to start:
     Waxing supercilious before you enter the door,
as it were? At present, with all you ladies here, and on this festival occasion,
we sisters ought to be able to have a relaxed visit together. In any case, you
left the Second Lady and the other lady at home; so what is there to worry
about, that you should want to set off so early? If it were someone else's place,
that would be another story."

She then turned to Big Sister Yü and said, "Sing a good song to entertain us. The ladies here have been critical of you."

"The Sixth Lady has really been upset with her," said Meng Yü-lou, "for not showing up to celebrate her birthday."

Big Sister Yü promptly got up from her place and kowtowed to Li P'ing-erh four times, saying, "Ever since I got home after celebrating the Fifth Lady's birthday, I haven't been feeling well. It was only yesterday, when your sister-in-law sent someone to summon me, that I've been able to pull myself together sufficiently to come out. If I'd been feeling better, how could I have failed to come pay my respects to you?"

"Big Sister Yü," said Chin-lien, "The Sixth Lady has been out of sorts. Sing a good song for her, and she won't be upset with you anymore."

Li P'ing-erh merely sat where she was and smiled, without making a sound.

"That's no problem," said Big Sister Yü. "Bring my *p'i-p'a* over here, and I'll sing something for you."

Sister-in-law Wu turned to Third Sister Cheng, the wife of Wu Shun-ch'en, saying, "Pour out some more wine for your two aunts and the other ladies. It's been a long time since their cups have been refilled."

Big Sister Yü then took her *p'i-p'a* in hand and proceeded to sing a set of songs to the tune "The Windswept River":

Midnight has come.
How is this feeling of desolation to be borne?
Within silk screens and brocaded curtains[45]
    I lie down in my clothes.
My naughty lover,
You promised me that you'd show up
    between twelve and two,
But it's already past four.
I can only await him with a painful heart,
    but what can I do?
He has abandoned me.
I hope the gods will see fit to visit him
    with an appropriate disaster.

It is already six.
I idly do up my raven locks in a chignon.
Ashamed to gaze into the caltrop-patterned mirror,[46]
I think of him.
I am unable to put on my
    brocade clothes;
Reluctant to don my kingfisher
    ornaments and pearls;

Unable to dispel my melancholy.
   eight o'clock has already past;
There is no sign of him at ten.
All on your account, my sorrow is
   making me sick.

It is noon.
I am really afflicted with lovesickness,
So afflicted that my soul has taken leave of me.
I think of my talented lover.
Do you remember how, under the moon,
   beneath the stars,
We swore oaths of fidelity by the hills and seas?
Who has ever taken you for granted?
If he should show up by two,
It would relieve my sorrowing breast.
If he makes it by four, I'll purchase
   a pig's head to sacrifice.

It's already six o'clock.
I can't help being disturbed at heart.
Who is there to share a few understanding words?
My equivocating lover,
You're probably in the houses of pleasure,[47]
Hugging the turquoise and cuddling the red;
Your lust as big as the sky.
At eight o'clock I light my candles,
But there is no sign of him, early or late.
At ten o'clock I must resign myself to
   consulting the tortoise oracle.[48]

As she was singing, Yüeh-niang remarked, "How is it that just now it's begun
to get so chilly in here?"

Lai-an, who was standing in attendance at one side, reported, "The weather
has turned cold outside, and it's started to snow."

"Sister," said Meng Yü-lou, "the clothes you're wearing are too thin. I've
brought a padded cloak with me. After all, by this time of night, it's bound to
be cold."

"Since it's snowing," said Yüeh-niang, "we'd better call for a page boy to go
home and bring us our fur coats to wear."

Lai-an promptly left the room and said to Tai-an, "Mother has directed that
someone go home and fetch the fur coats of the ladies."

Tai-an, in turn, called for Ch'in-t'ung and said, "You go get them, and let
me stay here to attend upon them."

Ch'in-t'ung, without inquiring any further, headed straight off for home.

In a little while, Yüeh-niang remembered the problem about a fur coat for Chin-lien and asked Lai-an, "Who went to fetch the fur coats?"

"Ch'in-t'ung went to get them," replied Lai-an.

"He just went off without inquiring any further, did he?" said Yüeh-niang.

"Something was forgotten in his instructions, just now," said Meng Yü-lou, "when he was told to fetch our fur coats. The Fifth Lady doesn't have a fur coat. It would have sufficed if he had been told just to fetch yours, Sister."

"It isn't really the case that there aren't any at home," said Yüeh-niang. "There's a fur coat that somebody pawned, which could have been brought for Sister Six to wear."

Yüeh-niang then asked, "Why didn't that slave Tai-an go on this errand himself, rather than sending that other slave in his stead? Tell him to come here."

Tai-an was duly called into her presence, where Yüeh-niang took him severely to task, saying, "A fine slave you are! When you're told to do something, you refuse to bestir yourself, but depute another officer to act in your stead. You sent that slave off without so much as mentioning it to me, so that he was gone before anyone knew it. All you do is presume to:

Sit at the altar dispatching your generals,[49]

like a Taoist priest. No wonder that:

Having assumed the position of a high official,
You were reluctant to set the fins on your
    silk hat aflutter,[50]

but dispatched him on the errand instead."

"Mother is mistaken in her criticism of me," protested Tai-an. "If you had originally directed me to go, would I have dared not to go? But when you sent Lai-an out with the message, all he said was that someone should be dispatched to go home on this errand."

"How would that lowly slave Lai-an dare to order the likes of you around?" said Yüeh-niang sarcastically. "Even legitimate wives such as myself hardly dare tell you what to do. Right now all you slaves have been indulged to the point that you seem to have lost all sense of decorum. I suppose, where your masters are concerned:

If a smoke-stained Buddhist effigy,
Is displayed on your wall:
When you have such a benefactor,
You'll get a monk to match.[51]

Do you suppose that I'm unaware of the tricks you've been up to, what with your double-dealing, ingratiating, officious, two-faced, meretricious, lazy, gluttonous, and mercenary conduct:

Duping your superiors while engaging in malfeasance,[52]

behind their backs? Just a while ago, your master did not send you to escort Li Kuei-chieh on her way home, so how did you come to escort her? Someone was already there, holding her felt bag, when you unceremoniously grabbed it out of his hands. Whether to retain the maidservant, or not to retain the maidservant, was not up to you. When you were told to come in and tell me about it, why did you refuse to come in, but set off that way to escort Kuei-chieh to the licensed quarter, no doubt in hopes of getting something to eat for your pains, and send someone else to come inside in your stead? You must have anticipated that if I were upset about it, I would take it out on the other person instead of you. And you still deny that:

You're a practiced old hand."

"It couldn't have been anyone else," protested Tai-an. "That must have been Hua-t'ung's story. Father saw him holding her felt bag and ordered me, 'You escort your sister Kuei-chieh on her way home.' It was he who sent him inside. As Mother said, whether to retain the maidservant, or not to retain the maidservant, was not up to me; so what have I got to do with it?"

Yüeh-niang became very angry and cursed him, saying, "You lousy slave! Still shooting off your mouth, are you? I don't have the leisure to bandy words with you here. Slave that you are, you've gone altogether too far with your stiff-necked, recalcitrant ways. When I tell you to do something, you refuse to move and have the nerve to talk back to me. Believe you me, if I don't tell him about it tomorrow, so that he takes you, deceitful slave that you are, and:

Pounds you into a bloody sheep's head,
I might as well quit."

"Tai-an," interposed Sister-in-law Wu, "Why don't you get a move on, and fetch the ladies' fur coats for them. Can't you see she's upset?"

"Sister," she went on to say, "tell him where to find that other fur coat for the Fifth Lady to wear."

P'an Chin-lien picked up where she left off, saying, "Sister, don't bother to have him fetch it for me. I don't have to wear a fur coat. Just tell him to bring that cloak of mine from home for me to wear. If it's something that's been pawned, who knows what kind of shape it's in? If it looks like a yellow dog's pelt[53] and I put it on, it will only make me a laughingstock. Besides it's not propitious, since sooner or later it will be redeemed."

"The fur coat I have in mind was not really pawned," said Yüeh-niang. "It was actually given to us in lieu of payment for a debt of sixteen taels of silver by that man Li Chih. The fur coat that was pawned with us by the household of Imperial Commissioner Wang has already been given to Li Chiao-erh to wear."

She then went on to instruct Tai-an, "The fur coat in question is in the large cabinet. Have Yü-hsiao find it for you. And bring Mistress Ch'en's cloak while you're at it."

Pouting with his lips, Tai-an went outside, where Ch'en Ching-chi asked him, "Where are you off to?"

"What a purely provoking business!" complained Tai-an.

"A single errand has to be performed twice.
At this hour of the night I've got to run home again."

He went straight home, where he found Hsi-men Ch'ing still partying at the front gate. Manager Fu Ming and Manager Yün Li-shou had already left, but Ying Po-chüeh, Hsieh Hsi-ta, Han Tao-kuo, and Pen the Fourth were still drinking and had not yet gone home.

They asked Tai-an, "Are the ladies coming?" and he replied, "No, they haven't started out yet. They've sent me to fetch their fur coats."

He then headed for the rear compound.

Before this, when Ch'in-t'ung had arrived home, he looked for Yü-hsiao in the master suite, to find the fur coats for him.

There he found Hsiao-yü sitting on the k'ang, not in the best of moods, who said, "Today those four whores have all gone off to Pen the Fourth's wife's place to have a party. I don't know where the fur coats are kept. You'll have to go to her place and ask them to find them for you."

Ch'in-t'ung went straight to Pen the Fourth's house, where, rather than announcing himself, he surreptitiously eavesdropped outside the windows.

What should he hear but Pen the Fourth's wife, saying, "Elder Sister and Second Sister, how is it that it's been such a long time since you've had a drink? And you haven't even been using your chopsticks to help yourselves to the dishes. Is it that you turn up your noses at the fare provided by such mean folk as ourselves, or what?"

"Sister-in-law Four," said Ch'un-mei, "we've had enough to drink."

"Ai-ya!" exclaimed Pen the Fourth's wife. "It scarcely needs saying, but how can you start:

Waxing supercilious before you enter the door,
that way?"

Then, turning to the wife of Mohammedan Han, she said, "As my next-door neighbor, you're just like an assistant host. Urge Third Sister and Fourth Sister to avail themselves of the wine in front of them on my behalf. How can you be so wooden?"

Instructing her daughter Chang-chieh to serve the wine, she went on to say, "Pour some more for Third Sister, but go a little easy in refilling Fourth Sister's cup."

"I've never been able to drink much," said Lan-hsiang.

"I fear you sisters will end up being famished today, since we've failed to provide any tasty dishes for your entertainment. Please don't make fun of us. We were going to engage a minstrel to come and sing for you ladies as you drank your wine, but we were afraid that the noise might be overheard at

Father's place. Our lodgings are so inadequate. The inconveniences such mean folk as ourselves have to put up with can scarcely be described."

As she was speaking, Ch'in-t'ung gave a knock on the door, and everyone fell silent.

After a considerable pause, Chang-chieh was heard asking, "Who is it?"

"It's me," said Ch'in-t'ung. "I need to have a word with my sisters."

The door was duly opened, and Ch'in-t'ung came in, at which Yü-hsiao asked, "Have the ladies come home?"

Ch'in-t'ung looked at them and nearly burst out laughing but refrained from speaking for some time.

"What are you showing your teeth in such a crazy grin for?" demanded Yü-hsiao.

"When I ask you a question," she went on to say, "what are you grinning like that for, without deigning to reply?"

"The ladies are still at Sister-in-law Wu's place drinking wine," responded Ch'in-t'ung. "When they saw that the sky had become overcast and it had started to snow, they sent me home to fetch their fur coats. I was instructed to wrap them all up and take them back with me."

"Mother's fur coat," said Yü-hsiao, "is in that cabinet with the gold tracery in the outer room, isn't it. You can get Hsiao-yü to give it to you."

"Hsiao-yü told me I should come ask you for it," said Ch'in-t'ung.

"How could you believe that little whore?" said Yü-hsiao. "As though she didn't know where it was."

"Those of you whose mistresses have fur coats can get them for him," said Ch'un-mei. "Since my mistress doesn't have a fur coat, I'm the only one who doesn't have to bestir herself."

Lan-hsiang said to Ch'in-t'ung, "You can ask Hsiao-luan for the Third Lady's fur coat."

Ying-ch'un then reached for the keys she carried at her waist and gave them to Ch'in-t'ung, saying, "Get Hsiu-ch'un to open the door to the inner room and get her coat for you."

Ch'in-t'ung went back to the rear compound, where Hsiao-yü in the master suite, and Hsiao-luan in Meng Yü-lou's quarters, wrapped up the fur coats in question and turned them over to him.

Just as he was carrying them out to the front compound, he ran into Tai-an and asked him, "What have you come back home for?"

"You might well ask!" said Tai-an. "All on account of the fact that I sent you on this errand, I've been subjected to a real dressing down by the First Lady. On top of which, she's sent me back to fetch a fur coat for the Fifth Lady."

"Right now, I'm on my way to fetch the Sixth Lady's fur coat," said Ch'in-t'ung.

"When you've fetched it, wait for me here," said Tai-an, "so we can go back together. It shouldn't really matter if you get there ahead of me, but I don't want to give the First Lady any excuse for cursing me out again."

When he had finished speaking, he proceeded to the master suite, where he found Hsiao-yü sitting on the k'ang, warming herself over the frame of the brazier, and cracking melon seeds with her teeth.

When she caught sight of Tai-an, she asked, "So you've come too, have you?"

"You might well ask!" said Tai-an. "I'm suffering from:

A bellyful of anger."

Thereupon, he related the whole episode of how Yüeh-niang had cursed him out, from first to last, saying, "I told Ch'in-t'ung to come fetch the fur coats, and she got angry with me for not coming myself, claiming that I was deputing officers to act in my stead. Then, because the Fifth Lady doesn't have a fur coat of her own, she sent me to come after one. She said that in the large cabinet there was a fur coat that had been left in lieu of a debt by Li the Third, and that I should ask you for it to take back with me."

"Yü-hsiao has the key to the inner room with her," said Hsiao-yü, "and they're all having a party at Pen the Fourth's place. You'll have to have her come and get it for you."

"Ch'in-t'ung has gone to the Sixth Lady's quarters to fetch her fur coat but will be back directly," said Tai-an. "We can get him to go after her. That will give me a chance to give my legs a rest and warm myself at the brazier."

Hsiao-yü then made a place for him at the head of the k'ang, and they sat down next to each other, shoulder to shoulder, and warmed themselves at the brazier.

"There's some wine in the flagon," said Hsiao-yü. "Let me pour a cup for you."

"That's the spirit," said Tai-an. "I accept your largess."

Hsiao-yü got down off the k'ang, put the flagon to heat on the brazier, pulled open a drawer from which she extracted a bowl of preserved goose meat, and poured out some wine for him. There being no one else present, the two of them fell to kissing and sucking each other's tongues.

As they were drinking, Ch'in-t'ung came in, and Tai-an offered him a drink, after which, he told him, "Go fetch Sister Yü-hsiao, so she can locate the fur coat for the Fifth Lady to wear."

Ch'in-t'ung put down the felt bag and went to Pen the Fourth's place to get Yü-hsiao.

Yü-hsiao cursed him, saying, "You lousy jailbird! What have you come back for?"

She refused to come herself but gave him a key and told him to get Hsiao-yü to open the door. Hsiao-yü opened the door to the inner room with it and tried the key in the lock of the cabinet, but, though she tried for some time, she was unable to get the lock to open, and Ch'in-t'ung had to go back to Pen the Fourth's place again.

"That's not the key," said Yü-hsiao. "The key to Mother's cabinet is kept under the mattress on her bed."

When Hsiao-yü heard this, she cursed Yü-hsiao, saying, "That whore! It's just as though her bottom were nailed in place over there. She refuses to budge herself and, after two trips back and forth, still continues to order me around instead."

When she finally succeeded in getting the cabinet open, it turned out not to contain any fur coats, so Ch'in-t'ung had to make yet another trip to Pen the Fourth's place to ask about it.

This constant running back and forth had aroused Ch'in-t'ung's resentment, and he muttered, "Even if I were to die, I ought to have three days and three nights without this kind of provocation. It's just my luck to run into these pestilential ghosts of small-time ladies, on the lookout for someone to plague."

Turning to Tai-an, he said, "What do you say? When we go back this time, we'll only provoke another tongue-lashing from Mother, who won't take into consideration the fact that the room was locked, but just blame us for the delay."

Returning to Pen the Fourth's place, he said to Yü-hsiao, "We looked in the cabinet in Mother's room, but it didn't contain any fur coats."

Yü-hsiao thought to herself for a while and then laughed, saying, "I forgot. It must be in the large cabinet in the outer room."

When he made his way back to the rear compound, Hsiao-yü started cursing again, saying, "That whore must have been fucked silly by her lover! So the fur coat was here all the time, while we've been looking everywhere for it."

She then proceeded to get it out and wrap it up in a package, together with Hsi-men Ta-chieh's cloak, and handed it over to Tai-an and Ch'in-t'ung to take back to Sister-in-law Wu's house.

When they got there, Yüeh-niang started cursing again, saying, "You lousy slaves! You've been in cahoots so that neither of you came back without the other. That's all there is to it."

Tai-an was too perturbed to answer, but Ch'in-t'ung spoke up, saying, "The fur coats for the other ladies were all there, but we had to wait while sister looked for this fur coat with the black fabric facing."

Thereupon, they opened up the package and took it out.

Sister-in-law Wu examined it under the lamp light and said, "This is also a good fur coat. Fifth Lady, why did you run it down that way, describing it as a yellow dog's pelt? Where would you find a yellow dog's pelt like that? I'd be happy to wear a coat like this myself."

"It's practically a new fur coat," said Yüeh-niang. "The only thing is that the lapels in front are a little worn. In the future if you replace them with two new brocaded panels, it will look just fine."

Meng Yü-lou picked it up and joked with Chin-lien, saying, "My child, come over here and try on this yellow dog's pelt so your mother can see how well it looks on you."

"If I'm up to snuff," said Chin-lien, "make no mistake about it, I ought to be able to ask my husband to give me one of my own in the future. Who wants to pick up someone else's used fur coat to wear, for no good reason?"

Meng Yü-lou continued to joke with her, saying, "How can you hope to repudiate your karma that way? Since this fur coat of somebody's is available, you ought to be grateful enough to put it on and recite the Buddha's name."

Thereupon, she proceeded to help her on with the coat, and when Chin-lien realized that it had an ample and substantial look to it, she had nothing more to say.

At this point, Wu Yüeh-niang, Meng Yü-lou, and Li P'ing-erh all donned their sable fur coats and prepared to bid farewell to Sister-in-law Wu and the wife of Wu the Second and set out for home. Yüeh-niang gave Big Sister Yü a package containing two candareens of silver.

"I, too, will bid farewell to the sisters-in-law and you other ladies," said Wu Yin-erh, and she proceeded to kowtow to them in turn.

At this point, Sister-in-law Wu presented her with a pair of silver flower ornaments, and Yüeh-niang and Li P'ing-erh each pulled a tael of silver out of their sleeves and gave them to her, for which she kowtowed to them in thanks.

Sister-in-law Wu, Wu the Second's wife, and Third Sister Cheng all expressed a desire to see Yüeh-niang and company on their way, but when they saw that it was snowing, Yüeh-niang insisted that they go back inside.

"It was still snow that was falling a little while ago," reported Ch'in-t'ung, "but now it's turned to drops of water that moisten the body. I'm afraid the clothing of you ladies may get wet. You'd better see if you can borrow an umbrella from Sister-in-law Wu's place, to give you some protection on the way home."

Wu the Second promptly fetched an umbrella, and Ch'in-t'ung put it up. The two orderlies that had accompanied them on their way there held lanterns, and the cluster of men and women set out in their wake. After traversing several narrow lanes, they came out on Main Street.

At this point, Ch'en Ching-chi, who had been setting off numerous firecrackers along the way, said, "Sister Yin-erh, your place is not far from here. We might as well escort you to your home."

"Just where is her place located?" Yüeh-niang then asked.

"If you go straight down this alley here," said Ching-chi, "that establishment with the imposing gateway halfway down is her place."

Rain and Snow Interrupt a Walk during the Lantern Festival

"I'll say goodbye to you ladies here," said Wu Yin-erh, "and go on home."

"The ground is wet," said Yüeh-niang. "Go on home. You have already performed your kowtows. I'll send a page boy to escort you the rest of the way."

She then called for Tai-an and said, "You escort Sister Yin-erh on her way home."

"Mother," said Ching-chi, "let me and Tai-an, the two of us, go with her."

"All right," said Yüeh-niang, "Sister, you can go on home with the two of them to escort you."

This was just the signal Ch'en Ching-chi had been waiting for, and he set off with Tai-an to see her to her place, while Wu Yüeh-niang and the others continued on their way home.

Along the way, P'an Chin-lien said, "Elder Sister, originally you said something about our seeing her home. How is it that we didn't end up doing it?"

"You're just like a child," Yüeh-niang laughed. "When someone jokes with you, you take it seriously. What sort of a place is the Verdant Spring Bordello,[54] that the likes of you and me should accompany her there?"

"It seems to me unlikely," said Pan Chin-lien, "if someone's husband were out whoring in the licensed quarter, that his wife would never come looking for him, or never endeavor to:
Beat him into a pot of porridge."

"There you go again!" said Yüeh-niang. "If our husband goes into the quarter some time in the future, just you go looking for him and give it a try. You might well end up being mistaken for a painted face yourself, and dragged off by someone else's husband, if he deigned to give you so much as a second look."

As they were speaking, they gradually approached the entrance to East Street, not far from the gateway of Ch'iao Hung's house, where they saw that Ch'iao Hung's wife and Big Sister Tuan, the wife of her nephew Ts'ui Pen, were standing in the doorway. When the latter two persons observed from a distance that Yüeh-niang and the cluster of men and women accompanying her were approaching, they insisted upon inviting them to come in.

Yüeh-niang declined repeatedly, saying, "Although we very much appreciate our kinswoman's lavish hospitality, it is already late, and we'd better not come in."

But Ch'iao Hung's wife refused to let them go, saying, "My good kinswoman, how can you start:
Waxing supercilious before you enter the door?"

She insisted on dragging them inside, where, in the parlor, they found lanterns suspended, an array of wine and delicacies set out, and two female entertainers to play and sing for them as they enjoyed the wine. But no more of this.

To resume our story, Hsi-men Ch'ing was still drinking with Ying Po-chüeh and company at his front gate, but the party was about to break up. Before this, Ying Po-chüeh and Hsieh Hsi-ta, who had been stuffing themselves all day, had long since reached the point where they couldn't have swallowed another bite. But when they noticed that Hsi-men Ch'ing had fallen asleep in his chair, they took advantage of the fact that he wasn't looking to dump whatever remained on the saucers and serving dishes into their sleeves, clearing them off completely, and then decamped, along with Han Tao-kuo, leaving only Pen the Fourth behind, who was afraid to return home on his own initiative. He remained to keep Hsi-men Ch'ing company until he finally arranged for the musicians to have something to drink, paid them for their services, and sent them on their way, saw that the things were put away, and the lanterns and candles extinguished, and made his way back to the rear compound.

Meanwhile, at Pen the Fourth's house, P'ing-an came in and said, "Sisters, haven't you gotten a move on yet? Father's already gone inside."

When Ch'un-mei heard this, along with Ying-ch'un, Yü-hsiao, and company, they were in such a hurry to return that they didn't even pay their proper respects to Pen the Fourth's wife, but took their leave and ran off in a cloud of dust.

Lan-hsiang, who had gotten one of her feet twisted in her shoe, was unable to keep up with them and cursed, saying, "The way the lot of you have taken off, as though you were:
      Picking up your coffins and fleeing for your lives,
has made me twist my foot in its shoe, so I can't seem to get it on right."

When they arrived in the rear compound, they heard that Hsi-men Ch'ing had gone to Li Chiao-erh's quarters, and all trooped in to kowtow to him. The abbess of the Kuan-yin Nunnery, on seeing that Hsi-men Ch'ing had come to retire in Li Chiao-erh's quarters, had retreated to the master suite and the company of Hsiao-yü.

When Yü-hsiao came in and saluted her, Hsiao-yü took her to task, saying, "Yü-hsiao, when Mother sent the page boy back from over there to fetch that fur coat, you refused to come take care of it yourself but directed that I should do it. But I didn't know which key it was that opened the door of the cabinet. And then, when we finally got it open, the coat wasn't there. Later on, it turned out to be in the large cabinet in the outer room. You were the one who put it there in the first place, but it seems you were so confused you didn't know what was going on. The lot of you must have had more than enough to eat and drink over there. Each and every one of you looks as though she's put on an additional bulge or two."

Yü-hsiao was so affected by this tirade that the blood flew to her cheeks, and she responded, "Why you crazy little whore! Has the dog scratched your face, or what? Just because you weren't invited, are you going to take it out on those of us who were?"

"As though I cared anything about an invitation from that whore!" exclaimed Hsiao-yü.

The abbess of the Kuan-yin Nunnery, from her position on the sidelines, remarked, "You two sisters ought to be more accommodating in the way you talk to each other, or your master in the other room will overhear you. The ladies are likely to return any minute now. You would do better to prepare some tea for them."

As they were speaking, whom should they see but Ch'in-t'ung, who came in carrying a felt bag.

"Has Mother come home?" Yü-hsiao asked.

"The ladies were almost here," reported Ch'in-t'ung, "but the wife of Kinsman Ch'iao was standing in her doorway and invited them in for a drink. They should be getting up to go by now."

Only then did the two maidservants stop bandying words.

Before long, Yüeh-niang and the others took their leave of Ch'iao Hung's wife and arrived at the front gate, where Pen the Fourth's wife came out to greet them. Ch'en Ching-chi and Pen the Fourth then got out a rack of miniature fireworks, and they all stopped to watch them being set off before coming inside. When they had bowed in salutation to Li Chiao-erh and the abbess of the Kuan-yin Nunnery, Sun Hsüeh-o came out to kowtow to Yüeh-niang and exchange greetings with Meng Yü-lou and her two companions.

"Where is Father?" Yüeh-niang went on to ask.

"He came into my room just now," said Li Chiao-erh, "where I've already tucked him in for the night."

When Yüeh-niang heard this, she hadn't a word to say.

Whom should they see at this juncture but Ch'un-mei, Ying-ch'un, Yü-hsiao, and Lan-hsiang, who came in to kowtow.

Li Chiao-erh then explained, "Today Pen the Fourth's wife from up front invited the four of them to come visit for a while, and they've just gotten back."

When Yüeh-niang heard this, she remained silent for some time and then took them to task, saying, "The preternatural bitches! What did they go out there for, for no good reason? Who said they could go?"

"They got permission from Father before they went," replied Li Chiao-erh.

"So they asked him, did they?" said Yüeh-niang. "A fine good-for-nothing to take charge of anything he is! Your household is getting to be like:

The temple that opens its gates early
    on the first and fifteenth;
Only to let a bunch of insignificant
    ghosts expose themselves."

"Dear Lady!" exclaimed the abbess of the Kuan-yin Nunnery. "Each of these four sisters is as pretty as a picture. How can you refer to them as insignificant ghosts?"

"If they're as pretty as pictures," said Yüeh-niang, "they must be only half-length portraits. What need is there to let them out for no good reason, only to allow outsiders to feast their eyes on them?"

Meng Yü-lou, realizing that Yüeh-niang was not in a good mood, was the first to make her departure. After that, Chin-lien, on seeing her get up to go, also went off, together with Li P'ing-erh and Hsi-men Ta-chieh, leaving only the abbess to spend the night with Yüeh-niang. The snow and sleet continued to fall until the fourth watch of the night before stopping. Truly:

> It is night in the storied bowers, the incense
>   has dissipated, the candles are cold;
> It is a time for cutting vegetables by lantern
>   light, and sweeping away the snow.

Of the events of that evening there is no more to tell.

The next day, Hsi-men Ch'ing went to the yamen. Around lunch time, Yüeh-niang, along with Meng Yü-lou and Li P'ing-erh, saw the abbess off on her way to the nunnery.

As they were standing inside the front gate, they caught sight of an old country woman who made her living telling fortunes by means of the tortoise oracle. She was wearing a patchwork jacket and a blue cotton skirt, her forehead was enclosed in a black headband, and she was carrying a pouch on her back as she came along the street.

Yüeh-niang sent a page boy to invite her to come inside the second gate, where, after she had laid out her fortune-telling diagrams and put her consecrated tortoise in place, she said to her, "How about telling our fortunes?"

The old woman knelt down on the ground and kowtowed to her four times, after which she said, "May I ask how old you are, madame?"

"Tell the fortune of a woman who was born in the year of the dragon," said Yüeh-niang.

"If it's the greater dragon, you'd be forty-one," said the woman. "If it's the lesser dragon, you'd be twenty-nine."

"I'm twenty-nine," said Yüeh-niang. "I was born at midnight on the fifteenth day of the eighth month."

The old woman gave the consecrated tortoise a nudge, and after it had made a circuit of the diagrams, it came to rest on one, which, when it was picked up, turned out to depict an official and a lady formally seated and surrounded by servitors, some of them seated and some of them standing, guarding a hoard of gold and silver and other valuables.[55]

"This lady," said the old woman, "is the mistress of the household and was born in the year *wu-ch'en*.

> Those born in *wu-ch'en* or *chi-ssu* are like
>   trees from a great forest;
> Throughout her life she will be characterized
>   by humanity and righteousness.

Wife and Concubines Laughingly Consult the Tortoise Oracle

She is magnanimous by nature;
Benevolent and given to good works;[56]
Recites scripture and bestows alms;
And distributes her favors widely.
Throughout her life she will labor
    to maintain the household;
Even at the cost of taking the blame
    for the faults of others.[57]
But it may not be said that,
Her joy and anger are constant, and
She is inept in managing her servants.

Truly:

When she is happy, she is all
    ingratiating smiles;
When she is angry, she is all
    reverberating wrath.
Others may sleep till the sun is high in the sky
    before getting out of bed;
But you are up betimes, superintending the maids
    as they do the pots and pans.
Though your temper may occasionally flare up
    like windblown fire;[58]
In the twinkling of an eye, you'll be talking
    and laughing once more.
The only problem is the presence of adverse signs
    in your 'palace of illness and adversity,'[59]
Indicating that you are ever beset with bickering,
Though your goodness of heart will enable
    you to overcome it.
In the end, you will live to the ripe
    old age of sixty-nine."

"Can you tell whether this lady is fated to have any sons?" asked Meng
Yü-lou.

"Pray don't take it amiss," said the old woman, "but there's something indis-
tinct about her 'palace of sons and daughters.'[60] In the end she will have to
depend on a son who has taken the tonsure to support her in her old age.
This is not something she can do anything about, but chances are she will
not be able to keep him."

Meng Yü-lou smiled at Li P'ing-erh, saying, "That must refer to your son
Wu Ying-yüan who has had a religious name bestowed upon him as a Taoist
priest."

Yüeh-niang then pointed to Meng Yü-lou and said, "You, too, ought to get her to tell your fortune."

"Tell the fortune," said Yü-lou, "of a thirty-three-year-old woman who was born at 4:00 AM on the twenty-seventh day of the eleventh month."

The old woman once again laid out her fortune-telling diagrams and put the consecrated tortoise in place, where, after making a circuit, it came to rest on a diagram designated "palace of fate."[61] When the old woman picked up this second diagram, it turned out to depict a woman, accompanied by three men, one of whom was dressed like a travelling merchant in his skullcap, the second was an official dressed in red, and the third was a scholar, who was also guarding a hoard of gold and silver. They were surrounded by servitors to wait upon them.

The old woman said, "This lady was born in the year *chia-tzu*.

> Those born in *chia-tzu* or *i-ch'ou* are
>   like gold in the sea;
> But her fate is crossed by the 'three
>   penalties' and 'six banes.'[62]
> Only by gaining ascendancy over her husband
>   will she be all right."

"I already have," said Meng Yü-lou.

The old woman continued:

> "You are gentle and congenial by nature,[63]
> And possess a good disposition.
> When you are annoyed at anyone,
>   they don't know it;
> When you are pleased by anyone,
>   they don't know it;
> You do not display your feelings.
> Throughout your life you will please your superiors,
>   be respected by your inferiors,
> And gain the love and favor of your husband.

But there is one problem.

> No matter how many good turns you
>   may do for others,
> You will often fail to win their hearts.
> Throughout your life you are fated to take the blame
>   for the faults of others;
> No matter how much trouble petty persons
>   may make for you,
> You will not be praised for your forbearance.
> But since your heart is in the right place,
> Even though petty persons should annoy you,
> They will not succeed in making you give way."

"Just now," said Yü-lou with a smile, "when I took the heat for that ruckus with Father over the page boy's demand for money,[64] I guess that was an example of my:

Taking the blame for the faults of others."

"Can you tell whether or not this lady will have any sons in the future?" asked Wu Yüeh-niang.

"If she navigates her vicissitudes safely," the old woman said, "she may have a daughter, though it does not appear that she will have a son. As for longevity, that she will have."

"Now tell the fortune of this lady," said Yüeh-niang. "Sister Li, tell her the eight characters of your horoscope."

"I was born in the year of the sheep," said Li P'ing-erh with a smile.

"If it's the lesser sheep," said the old woman, "you would be twenty-six, and have been born in the year *hsin-wei*. What month were you born in?"

"I was born at noon on the fifteenth day of the first month," Li P'ing-erh replied.

The old woman started the tortoise on its circuit, and it came to an abrupt halt on another diagram designated "palace of fate." When the old woman picked up this diagram, it turned out to depict a woman accompanied by three officials, the first of whom was dressed in red, the second of whom was dressed in green, and the third of whom was dressed in blue. She was holding a child in her arms and was guarding a hoard of gold and silver and other valuables. Beside her there stood a demon with a blue face, protruding fangs, and red hair.[65]

The old woman said, "As for this lady:

Those born in *keng-wu* or *hsin-wei* are
    like earth beside the road;
Throughout her life she will enjoy glory
    and luxury, wealth and honor.
She will have all she wants to eat, and
    all she needs to wear;
The husbands whom she attracts will be
    persons of distinction.
Her heart will be characterized by
    humanity and righteousness.
Gold and silver, riches and silk,[66] will
    not be a matter of concern.
She is content to let herself be taken
    advantage of or exploited;
Indeed, she is disappointed if they do
    not take advantage of her.
But she will suffer from the 'matched
    shoulders' in her horoscope,

And find that, in everything, others will
    requite kindness with enmity.
Truly:

'Matched shoulders,' 'penalties,' and 'banes,'
    will make difficulties for her;
In the twinkling of an eye, they will exhibit
    a heartless knack for knavery.
It is preferable to encounter a tiger blocking
    the road to your 'three births,'[67]
Than to meet someone, before your very eyes,
    with two faces and three knives.

Pray don't take what I say amiss, lady, but you're just like a bolt of fine red silk that is, unfortunately, a little shorter than it ought to be. You should try not to let yourself get so upset over things. And, as for the prospects of your son, it's hard to say."

"He has already had a religious name bestowed upon him as a Taoist priest," said Li P'ing-erh.

"If he has already left lay life," said the old woman, "he should be safe. But there is another problem. This year the planet Ketu[68] impinges on your fate,[69] meaning that you may suffer a bloody catastrophe.[70] Only if you can avoid hearing the sound of weeping in the seventh and eighth months, will you be all right."

When she had finished speaking, Li P'ing-erh fished a five-candareen lump of silver out of her sleeve, and Yüeh-niang and Meng Yü-lou each gave her fifty cash.

Just after they had sent the old woman who told fortunes by means of the tortoise oracle on her way, whom should they see but P'an Chin-lien, who came out from the rear compound with Hsi-men Ta-chieh and said with a laugh, "I was just saying that you were not to be found in the back, and it turns out that you have all come out to the front here."

"We came out just now to see off the abbess of the Kuan-yin Nunnery," explained Yüeh-niang. "Since then, all this while, we've been having our fortunes told by the tortoise oracle. If you had come a step earlier, we could have had her tell your fortune as well."

"Fortune-telling is not for me," said Chin-lien, with a shake of her head. "As the saying goes:
    You may calculate a person's fate,
    But you can't predict his conduct.
I remember that previous occasion when the Taoist practitioner was physiognomizing us and said that I would suffer a premature death. Who needs it? It only serves to make one depressed. What will be, will be.

If I die in the street, bury me in the street;
If I die on the highroad, bury me on the road;
And if I should fall into an open drain,
It will just have to serve as my coffin."

When she had finished speaking, she returned to the rear compound with
Yüeh-niang and the others. Truly:

The myriad affairs are things that one
    cannot argue with;
One's whole life is entirely determined
    by one's destiny.[71]

There is a poem that testifies to this:

Kan Lo's[72] success came early, while Chiang
    Tzu-ya's[73] came late;
P'eng-tsu[74] and Yen Hui[75] attained longevities
    of differing length.
Fan Jan[76] was impoverished, while Shih Ch'ung[77]
    was a rich man;
However calculated, the differences were only
    in the timing.[78]

If you want to know the outcome of these events,
Pray consult the story related in the following chapter.

Chapter 47

WANG LIU-ERH PEDDLES INFLUENCE

IN PURSUIT OF PROFIT;

HSI-MEN CH'ING ACCEPTS A BRIBE

AND SUBVERTS THE LAW

The wind agitates unruly waves, making
    the breakers turbulent;
Aboard a lonely craft, obliquely moored,
    one's sleep is anxious.
The cry of the isolated bird is shrill
    beyond the cold clouds;
The drum of the relay station interrupts
    the traveller's dreams.
Poetic fancy only enhances the greenness
    of the poolside grass;
The river boats, without prearrangement,
    rise on the evening tide.
Gazing into the void, I enumerate those
    who truly understand me;
But there is only my old friend the moon
    up there in the sky.

THIS POEM merely reiterates the fact that on the northern frontier carts and horses are the norm, whereas in the Chiang-nan region boats and oars are more convenient. Hence, it is certainly true that:

> Southerners ride boats, and
> Northerners ride horses.[1]

The story goes that in the ancient city of Kuang-ling, or Yang-chou, in the Chiang-nan region, there dwelt a well-to-do commoner named Miao T'ien-hsiu, who possessed property worth ten thousand strings of cash and was devoted to poetry and ritual.[2] He was thirty-nine years old and had no sons, but an only daughter, who had not yet been married. His wife, née Li, was bedridden with an intractable disease, so the affairs of the household had been entrusted to his favorite concubine, née Tiao, who was known as Tiao the Seventh. She was formerly a singing girl from a brothel on the main Yang-chou dock, whom Miao T'ien-hsiu had purchased for three hundred taels of silver and installed as a secondary wife in his household, where she reigned supreme in his affections.

Suddenly one day, an old Buddhist monk appeared at his door, claiming to be from the Pao-en Temple, or Temple of Kindness Requited, in the Eastern Capital, who stated that because his temple hall lacked a gilded bronze effigy of an arhat, he had arrived here in the course of his peregrinations, in the hope of calling on the faithful and raising a subscription. Miao T'ien-hsiu was not stingy but promptly agreed to donate fifty taels of silver to the monk for this purpose.

"It scarcely requires so much," the monk said. "Half of that amount would suffice to finish the image in question."

"Master, pray don't take offense at the meagerness of my donation," said Miao T'ien-hsiu. "If there is anything left over after the completion of the Buddhist effigy, you can expend it on the customary oblations."

The monk folded his hands in front of his chest and made him a bow in the Buddhist manner to thank him for his gift.

Before taking his leave, he said to Miao T'ien-hsiu, "Under the socket of your left eye there is a white emanation, which is a fatal sign and indicates that before this year is out you will suffer a great calamity. Because you have shown such a generous affinity for me, how could I refrain from warning you of this impending event? From now on, no matter what may come up, you should on no account venture outside of this locality. Take heed! Take heed!"[3]

Having finished speaking, he took his leave of Miao T'ien-hsiu and departed.

Less than half a month later, Miao T'ien-hsiu happened to wander into his back garden, where he caught sight of his servant Miao Ch'ing,[4] who had always been a dissolute scamp, embracing and whispering to his concubine, née Tiao, beside a pavilion. Not having anticipated Miao T'ien-hsiu's abrupt arrival, they did not have time to conceal themselves. Having caught sight of them:

Without permitting any further explanation,
Miao T'ien-hsiu proceeded to give Miao Ch'ing a severe beating and swore to expel him from the household. Miao Ch'ing was intimidated by this threat and begged the neighbors to intercede on his behalf, which they had to do more than once before he was finally allowed to remain. But he continued to harbor acute resentment in his heart.

Unexpectedly, a certain maternal cousin of Miao T'ien-hsiu's named Huang Mei, a native of Yang-chou, who had obtained office as a provincial graduate, who currently served as assistant prefect of K'ai-feng, the Eastern Capital, and who was a man possessed of:

Broad erudition and extensive knowledge,
sent a man to Yang-chou one day to deliver a letter to his cousin, inviting him to come to the Eastern Capital for a visit. On the one hand, he could enjoy

the sights; and on the other, something might be done to improve his future prospects.

When Miao T'ien-hsiu received this letter, he was:

Unable to contain his delight,

and addressed his wife and concubine, saying, "The Eastern Capital is:

The purlieu of the imperial equipage,

a place where splendor and luxury are concentrated. I have long harbored the wish to see it but have lacked an opportunity. Now that my maternal cousin has sent me this invitation, it will truly serve to fulfill the wish of a lifetime."[5]

To this his wife, née Li, responded, "The other day, when that monk examined your features, he detected a portent of calamity and enjoined you not to leave the premises. Moreover, the capital is a long way from here, your property is a weighty responsibility, and if you leave your young child and sick wife at home, there is no telling whether this trip will actually improve your prospects. It would be better not to go."

Miao T'ien-hsiu did not accept her argument but instead angrily rebuked her, saying, "For a:

Man of mettle, inhabiting the space between

Heaven and Earth,[6]

Whose will is symbolized by a mulberry bow

and rubus arrows,[7]

to be unable to:

Journey at will about the empire, and

Appreciate the sights of the capital,

but be content merely to:

Grow old and die beneath his own windows,[8]

is to have lived in vain. Moreover, for someone like myself, who:

Harbors talent in his breast,[9]

and whose:

Purse is abundantly supplied,[10]

what reason is there to worry that success will not come my way? If I pay this visit, my maternal cousin is sure to have something good in store for me. Don't say another word about it."

Thereupon, he ordered his servant Miao Ch'ing to get together his baggage and accoutrements, provided himself with two trunks of silver, loaded a boat with merchandise, and prepared to embark for the Eastern Capital, taking a page boy and Miao Ch'ing with him. Thinking that:

Achieving success and fame would be like

picking up a mustard stalk;[11]

Obtaining a desirable post would be like

spitting into one's hand,

he admonished his wife and concubine to take care of the household and set off on the appointed day.

It was at the end of autumn and the beginning of winter that he boarded his boat and departed from the dock in Yang-chou. After travelling for several days, they arrived at the Hsü-chou Rapids. Behold:

>The stretch of white water,
>Looked extremely menacing.

For a myriad li the water of the long rapids
   seems to be cascading;
As it strikes the islands on its way east
   they resound like thunder.[12]
The endless billowing of the snowy whitecaps[13]
   causes people to fear;
When travelling merchants encounter it
   who is not affrighted?[14]

When they had proceeded to a place called Shan-wan, Miao T'ien-hsiu saw that it was getting late and ordered the boatmen to lay to for the night. It was one of those occasions on which:

>His fated lot was running out;
>Something was destined to happen.

Unbeknownst to him, the boat he had hired was a pirate boat, and the two boatmen were both evildoers, one of whom was named Ch'en the Third and the other Weng the Eighth. As the saying goes:

>Without the help of an insider,
>A household cannot be broached.[15]

Now this Miao Ch'ing held a deep grudge against his master, Miao T'ien-hsiu, for the beating he had previously received at his hands. He had wanted to get revenge for some time but had not had an opportunity to do so.

>From his mouth no word was uttered, but
>In his heart he thought to himself,

"Why don't I:

>Thus and thus, and
>So and so,

collaborate with these two boatmen in seizing my master, killing him, shoving his body into the water, and then dividing his property between us? If I return home and manage to plot the death of his invalid wife, his whole estate, together with his concubine, née Tiao, will all be mine."

Truly:

>Flowering branches, beneath their leaves,
>   conceal their thorns;
>How can one know for sure the human heart
>   contains no poison?[16]

This Miao Ch'ing, thereupon, proceeded to consult secretly with the two boatmen, saying, "In my master's leather trunks, in addition to a thousand taels of silver, there are two thousand taels worth of satin piece goods, and an ample quantity of clothing and so forth. If the two of you are willing to conspire with me against him, I am willing to agree to an equitable division of the spoils."

Ch'en the Third and Weng the Eighth laughed, saying, "Since you have spoken, we need not deceive you, but we have had the same idea for some time."

That night, the sky was overcast and dark. Miao T'ien-hsiu and the page boy, An-t'ung, were asleep in the middle cabin, and Miao Ch'ing was in the stern sheets behind the scull. When it was nearly the third watch, around midnight, Miao Ch'ing deliberately started calling out, "Thief! Thief!"

Miao T'ien-hsiu, upon being startled out of his dreams, stuck his head out of the cabin door to see what was up, and Ch'en the Third, who was holding a sharp knife in his hand, stabbed him in the throat with a single thrust, and then shoved the body into the turbulent waves of the shallow. An-t'ung tried to escape, but Weng the Eighth struck him a blow from behind, which knocked him into the water.

The three conspirators then went into the cabin, where they extracted all the victim's property and money, satin goods and clothing, and proceeded to sort things out before dividing them up among themselves.

The two boatmen then said, "Brother, if we were to keep these piece goods, we would surely be caught. But, because you are a servant in his employ, if you transport these goods to market and offer to sell them, no one will suspect anything."

On this account, the two boatmen, after dividing the thousand ounces of silver in the leather trunk, and Miao T'ien-hsiu's clothing, etc., between them, proceeded to punt their boat back in the direction they had come from. Miao Ch'ing, on the other hand, engaged another boat, on which he conveyed his booty as far as the dock at Lin-ch'ing,[17] where he saw it through the customs station, and then had it transported by land to Ch'ing-ho district, and stored in a licensed warehouse outside the city wall. When he encountered merchants from Yang-chou with whom he was familiar, he merely explained that his master was on another boat, behind his, and would soon arrive. But we will say no more for the moment about how Miao Ch'ing endeavored to dispose of his merchandise.

As the saying goes:
Though men may plan to do thus and so:
Heaven's principles may yet deny them.[18]
Alas for Miao T'ien-hsiu! Although:
He had always been a good man,
one fine day, he was done in by his own servant, and:
Failed to achieve a good death.[19]
Though it is true that he had:

Miao Ch'ing Connives in the Murder of His Master

Disregarded a well-meant admonishment,
it is also the case that:
One's allotted years are hard to evade.[20]
Who could have anticipated that, although An-t'ung was knocked uncon-
scious by the boatman and fell into the water, he fortunately escaped death.
After bobbing up and down for a while among the reeds in the cove, he was
able to climb ashore, where he proceeded to loudly lament his fate on the
embankment.

Gradually:
The dawn began to glimmer,[21]
and there suddenly appeared a fishing boat, coming downstream from the
upper reaches of the river, with an old man sitting on it, dressed in a hat of
woven bamboo and a short coir rain cape. Upon hearing the sound of lamentation coming from deep among the reeds along the bank, he moved his boat
closer to investigate and found that it was a sixteen- or seventeen-year-old boy,
whose body was completely soaked with water. When he enquired into the
story behind this, from first to last, he learned that his interlocutor was a page
boy from Miao T'ien-hsiu's household who had suffered a criminal assault on
the rapids. The old fisherman took him aboard his boat, poled it back to his
home, provided him with a change of clothing, and gave him something to
eat and drink.

He then went on to ask him, "Would you prefer to go back where you came
from, or would you like to stay here and live with me?"

An-t'ung wept, saying, "My master has met with a calamity, and I don't
know what has become of him.[22] What home have I got to return to? I would
prefer to stay here with you, sir."

"That's all right," said the old fisherman. "You can stay here with me for
the time being. I'll gradually make inquiries into who your assailants might
be, and we can decide what to do then."[23]

An-t'ung bowed in gratitude to the old man and resigned himself to trying
to make a go of it with him henceforth.

One day, it was one of those occasions on which:
Something was destined to happen.
On the last day of the year, the old fisherman, taking An-t'ung with him, had
just come out to the port on the New Canal to sell his catch, when Ch'en
the Third and Weng the Eighth, who had been drinking aboard their boat,
happened to come ashore, dressed in Miao T'ien-hsiu's clothes, in order to
buy fish.

An-t'ung recognized them and surreptitiously communicated this to the old
fisherman, saying, "My master's wrong is about to be righted."

The old fisherman said, "Why don't you prepare a deposition and lodge
a complaint against them with the proper authorities? That ought to settle
the case."

An-t'ung then proceeded to prepare a deposition and presented it to the office of the Regional Military Command, which was responsible for security along that section of the Grand Canal, but Commandant Chou Hsiu rejected the complaint for lack of material evidence. He then presented his complaint to the office of the Provincial Surveillance Commission, and when Hsia Yen-ling saw that it involved accusations of armed robbery and murder on the part of criminal elements, he agreed to hear the case.

On the fourteenth day of the first month, he sent detectives, taking An-t'ung with them, to arrest the suspects. When they arrived at the port on the New Canal, they took Ch'en the Third and Weng the Eighth into custody and brought them before the bench. Upon interrogation, the two boatmen saw that An-t'ung was standing by to give evidence against them and, without even being subjected to torture, admitted to every particular of the charges. Their deposition stated that at the time of the crime, the victim's servant, Miao Ch'ing, was also present and had conspired with them to murder his master, after which, he had taken his share of the booty and departed. All three persons, both accused and accuser, were incarcerated pending the arrest of Miao Ch'ing, at which time the sentencing of the guilty parties would take place.

Because of the New Year's holiday, the officials and staff of the Provincial Surveillance Commission did not report to the yamen for the next two days in a row. Well before this time was up, however, a hanger-on at the gate of the yamen who specialized in leaking news had covertly tipped Miao Ch'ing off. Miao Ch'ing was panic-stricken by this news, locked the door of his room, and surreptitiously hid out in the home of the proprietor of the warehouse, a broker named Yüeh the Third.

Now this Yüeh the Third lived in a house, with a six-foot-wide frontage and three interior courtyards, receding along a vertical axis, that was located right next door to that of Han Tao-kuo on the east[24] side of the stone bridge on Lion Street, and his wife was on very good terms with Wang Liu-erh. She constantly came over to Wang Liu-erh's place to visit, and when Wang Liu-erh had nothing else to do, she would visit her in return, so that the two of them had become quite intimate with each other.

When Yüeh the Third took a look at Miao Ch'ing and saw that:

His face exhibited a worried hue,

he asked what the trouble was and then said, "It's no big deal. The wife of the house next door is the mistress of His Honor Hsi-men Ch'ing of the Provincial Surveillance Commission, and her husband is the manager of one of his business enterprises. The wife is on such good terms with my spouse that, in all things, she is:

Obedient to her every whim.

If you want to ensure that nothing will come of this trouble of yours, as long as you're willing to spend what it takes, you should get my wife to go over and negotiate things with her counterpart next door."

When Miao Ch'ing heard this, he promptly got down on his knees and said, "If there is any way you can enable me to escape this predicament I am in:

> Your kindness will be amply rewarded,
> I will never dare to forget it."

Thereupon, he proceeded to write out an explanatory note and sealed up a packet of fifty taels of silver, along with two outfits of figured satin clothing, while Yüeh the Third directed his wife to go next door and explain the matter, thus and so, to Wang Liu-erh. The latter was as pleased as could be and took possession of the clothing, the silver, and the explanatory note, in order to await Hsi-men Ch'ing's next visit, but he failed to turn up.

On the seventeenth, when the sun began to set in the west, who should appear but Tai-an, riding along the middle of the street on horseback, with his master's felt bag under his arm.

Wang Liu-erh, who was standing at her front door, called him to a halt and asked, "Where are you headed?"

"I've been accompanying Father on a long trip to deliver some presents in Tung-p'ing prefecture," replied Tai-an.

"Where's your master right now?" asked Wang Liu-erh. "Has he come back already, or not?"

"Father and Pen the Fourth," said Tai-an, "have gone home ahead of me."

Wang Liu-erh then invited him inside, explained the matter to him, thus and so, and showed him the explanatory note.

"Auntie Han," said Tai-an, "don't underestimate the gravity of this case you are proposing to meddle with. Right now, the two boatmen who are in custody at the yamen have confessed, and he is the only other party implicated. If you come up with only these few taels of silver, they will not even suffice to take care of the servants in the case. Even if I were to do nothing else but broach the subject to him, Auntie Han, I would demand twenty taels of silver from you. Then, if I should manage to get Father to come over here, you can take the matter up with him however you like."

"You crazy oily mouth!" laughed Wang Liu-erh.

> "If you want something to eat,
> You shouldn't offend the cook.[25]

If the endeavor succeeds, taking care of you will not be a problem. Even if we were not to get anything out of it ourselves, we would see to it that you were not shortchanged."

"Auntie Han," said Tai-an, "that's not it at all. As the saying goes:

> The superior man is not ashamed to speak face to face.[26]
> Once the prior conditions are determined,
> There may be room for further discussion."

Wang Liu-erh, thereupon, provided a selection of delicacies and invited Tai-an to have a drink.

"If I drink until my head and face are red," said Tai-an, and Father asks me about it, what am I to say?"

"What is there to be afraid of?" said Wang Liu-erh. "Just say that this is where you were."

Thereupon, Tai-an, after drinking only a single goblet of wine, prepared to depart.

"Whatever you do, I'm much indebted to you for speaking on my behalf," said Wang Liu-erh. "I'll be waiting here for the result."

Tai-an then proceeded to mount his horse and go straight home, where he handed over the felt bag he had been carrying and stood in attendance in the rear compound until Hsi-men Ch'ing, who had been taking a nap in his room, came out and sat down in an anteroom.

Tai-an casually approached him and, having nothing else to report, said, "As I was on my way home, Auntie Han called me to a halt and wanted me to ask you to go over there as soon as possible, because she has something important to say to you."

"What could that be?" said Hsi-men Ch'ing. "I'll do as she suggests."

No sooner had he finished speaking than a certain school official named Liu came by to negotiate a loan for some silver. After he had taken care of this School Official Liu, Hsi-men Ch'ing mounted his horse, put on his eye shades and an informal skullcap, directed Tai-an and Ch'in-t'ung to accompany him, and made his way to Wang Liu-erh's house. Once there, he dismounted, went inside, and sat down in the parlor, and Wang Liu-erh came out to greet him.

That day, because it was his turn to spend the night in the shop across the street, Han Tao-kuo had not come home, but his wife had bought a lot of provisions and arranged for Old Mother Feng to prepare them in the kitchen, in anticipation of Hsi-men Ch'ing's arrival. The maidservant, Chin-erh, brought in the tea, and the woman served it to him. Hsi-men Ch'ing then ordered Ch'in-t'ung to take his horse to the house across the street, and close the front door after him.

The woman, who was circumspect about plunging right into the matter at hand, merely started out by saying, "Father, you must be exhausted by the successive days of entertaining at your place. I've heard that your son has been betrothed. Congratulations."

"It all started with the proposal of my Sister-in-law Wu," said Hsi-men Ch'ing, "as a result of which we have arranged his betrothal with the Ch'iao family. Their household also has only this single daughter. If you stop to consider it, it's not an entirely appropriate match, but we decided, for better or for worse, to:

Add another tie to the existing ties,[27]
between our families, that's all."

"It's fine enough that you should form a marriage alliance with them," said Wang Liu-erh, "the only thing is that since you now occupy such a high office, when you get together socially it could be embarrassing."

"What a suggestion!" said Hsi-men Ch'ing.

After they had chatted for a while, the woman said, "I'm afraid you might be getting cold here. Why don't we go into my room."

On the one hand, she ushered him into her room, while on the other, she set out a chair next to the brazier for him, and Hsi-men Ch'ing sat down.

In due course, the woman took out Miao Ch'ing's explanatory note and handed it to Hsi-men Ch'ing, saying, "He asked the wife of the broker Yüeh the Third, next door, to come over and speak to me about it. This Miao Ch'ing has been putting up at his warehouse and has been implicated, thus and so, by the two boatmen. His only hope is that his name may be eradicated from the case, so that he will not have to appear in court. He has presented me with some gifts in return for my good offices. For better or for worse, I hope that you will see fit to do what you can for him."

Hsi-men Ch'ing perused the explanatory note and then asked, "What were the gifts he offered you?"

Wang Liu-erh got the fifty taels of silver out of her trunk and showed them to Hsi-men Ch'ing, saying, "In the future, if his overture should prove successful, he has also promised me two outfits of clothing."

Hsi-men Ch'ing looked at the silver and laughed, saying, "Is that all? What can you hope to do with such a paltry sum? You may not know it, but this Miao Ch'ing is the servant of a wealthy commoner from Yang-chou named Miao T'ien-hsiu, who conspired with the two boatmen on their boat to murder his master and dump him in the river, a case of conspiracy to commit murder with larcenous intent. Right now they are trying to dredge up the body but have not yet recovered it. Moreover, the evidence provided by the two boatmen before the bench has led to the finding of the page boy, An-t'ung, who had originally accompanied him, who has also given testimony, so that there are three witnesses against him. If he is brought before the court, he is sure to be judged guilty of a crime for which the penalty is death by slow slicing,[28] while the other two offenders will only be subject to decapitation.[29] At present, the two boatmen have also testified that he has two thousand taels worth of merchandise in his possession. What does he expect to accomplish with this paltry amount of silver? You might just as well return it to him immediately."

Wang Liu-erh thereupon went into the kitchen and sent the maidservant, Chin-erh, to call over Yüeh the Third's wife, to whom she returned the original gifts and explained the situation, thus and so.

If Miao Ch'ing had not heard about this nothing might have happened, but having heard about it, he felt as though he had been:

> Doused with a bucket of water,
> All the way from the crown of his head
>   to the soles of his feet.

Truly:

> The shock affected all six of his vital organs,
>   including liver and gall;
> The fright damaged the three ethereal and seven
>   material souls in his heart.

Without more ado, he invited Yüeh the Third to a conference and said, "Even if I have to give up this two thousand taels worth of merchandise, I am willing to do that, if I can only manage to save my life and get home safely."

"If that's what His Honor has to say from his exalted vantage point," opined Yüeh the Third, "it would seem that halfway measures will simply not suffice to influence the two officials involved. You'll have to set aside a thousand taels worth of merchandise for them, and at least half of what is left over will be needed to take care of the adjutants, and the detectives who originally arrested the culprits."

"On top of everything else," said Miao Ch'ing, "I haven't yet arranged the sale of the merchandise. How am I going to come up with the requisite silver?"

He then sent Yüeh the Third's wife over to speak to Wang Liu-erh, saying, "If His Honor is willing to accept merchandise, I can deliver a thousand taels worth to him. If that does not suit him, I respectfully hope that he will allow me two or three days of grace, which will enable me to sell off the merchandise at a reduced price, after which I will come in person and present the proceeds at His Honor's residence."

Wang Liu-erh took the note containing this proposal back into her room and showed it to Hsi-men Ch'ing.

"If that's the way it is," said Hsi-men Ch'ing, "I'll order the original detectives involved in the case to put off arresting him for a few days. But tell him to present the list of his proposed gifts immediately."

Thereupon, the wife of Yüeh the Third, on receiving this oral instruction, went back to report to Miao Ch'ing, who was delighted by the news.

Hsi-men Ch'ing realized that there were people right next door, and thought it prudent not to extend his visit. After drinking a few goblets of wine and engaging in intercourse with the woman for a while, on seeing that his servant had come back to fetch him with his horse, he got up and returned home.

The next day, upon going to the yamen, at the early session of the court he did not bring up this case for a hearing, but instead ordered the detectives not to make any further arrests. Miao Ch'ing, on his part, sought the assistance of the broker, Yüeh the Third, in making contact with buyers that very night, in order to unload his merchandise. In less than three days he managed to dispose of it all and realized the sum of one thousand seven hundred taels of silver. Without touching his original gift to Wang Liu-erh, he augmented it with another fifty taels of silver and, in addition, presented her with four outfits of first-class clothing.

To resume our story, on the nineteenth, Miao Ch'ing counted out a thousand taels of silver, which he concealed in four wine jars, purchased a freshly butchered pig, and, waiting until after the lamps were lighted, had them carried to the gate of Hsi-men Ch'ing's residence. The servants were all in on it, so Tai-an, P'ing-an, Shu-t'ung, Ch'in-t'ung, and the four prison guards who made the delivery were paid off with ten taels of silver. Tai-an also demanded another ten taels of silver for himself from Wang Liu-erh.

In a little while, Hsi-men Ch'ing came out and took a seat in the summerhouse. No lamps were lit, and:
> The light of the moon was dusky,[30]
for it had just arisen.

The gifts were carried into his presence, and Miao Ch'ing, wearing black clothing, proceeded to kowtow to Hsi-men Ch'ing, saying, "Your humble servant has been the recipient of your life-saving grace. Though:
> My body should be pulverized and my bones shattered,[31]
> I can hardly hope to repay you either dead or alive."[32]

"As for this case in which you are involved," said Hsi-men Ch'ing, "I haven't even properly looked into it yet. Those two boatmen are adamant in implicating you. If you should appear in court, you would be charged with a very serious crime. But since people have intervened on your behalf, I'm allowing you to escape with your life. If I were not to accept this gift of yours, you would not be reassured. I intend to give half of it to Judicial Commissioner Hsia Yen-ling, so the two of us will both participate in doing you this favor. You cannot afford to stick around any longer, but should set out for home this very night."

"Where do you live in Yang-chou?" he went on to ask.

Miao Ch'ing kowtowed in reply, saying, "Your humble servant lives inside the city walls of Yang-chou."

Hsi-men Ch'ing ordered that tea should be brought from the rear compound, and Miao Ch'ing stood underneath the pine trees as he drank it and then kowtowed once again, took his leave, and departed.

But Hsi-men Ch'ing called him back, saying, "Have you spoken to the detectives involved in the original arrest, or not?"

"I have already settled things satisfactorily with all the other people involved," said Miao Ch'ing.

"In that case," Hsi-men Ch'ing directed him, "you had better set out for home immediately."

Miao Ch'ing accordingly went out the gate, returned to Yüeh the Third's house, and proceeded to get his baggage ready for the journey. He found that he still had a hundred and fifty taels of silver on hand, of which he took fifty

Hsi-men Ch'ing Takes a Bribe and Subverts the Law

taels, together with a few remaining bolts of satin, and gave them to Yüeh the Third and his wife out of gratitude for their help. At the fifth watch, around 4:00 AM, they hired a long-distance pack animal for him, and he set out on his way to Yang-chou. Truly, he was:

> As flustered as a dog who has
>   lost his way home;[33]
> As flurried as a fish who has
>   escaped the net.[34]

We will say no more for the moment about how Miao Ch'ing escaped with his life, but return to the story of Hsi-men Ch'ing.

He and Hsia Yen-ling came out of the yamen together when the court session was over and rode along with their horses side by side until they arrived at the entrance to Main Street, where Hsia Yen-ling was about to take his leave as they parted company.

But Hsi-men Ch'ing, without dismounting, raised his whip and said, "If my colleague has no objections, would you condescend to drop by my place for a chat?"

Having succeeded in inviting Judicial Commissioner Hsia to his home, Hsi-men Ch'ing dismounted with him outside the gate and proceeded into the reception hall, where, after they had exchanged the appropriate amenities, Hsi-men Ch'ing conducted him to the summerhouse, and they loosened their clothing as the attendants served them with tea. Shu-t'ung and Tai-an then came in and set up a table for their entertainment.

"I really ought not to barge in this way and put my colleague to such trouble," said Hsia Yen-ling.

"Whoever heard of such a thing," responded Hsi-men Ch'ing.

Before long, the two page boys brought in an assortment of refreshments in square boxes and set them down to one side. They consisted of chicken feet, goose, duck, fresh fish, and other appetizers, making a total of sixteen bowls in all. After they had consumed this repast, and the utensils had been cleared away, another selection of savories suitable to accompany wine drinking was brought out, as well as little gold goblets with handles, on silver saucers, and gold-inlaid ivory chopsticks.

As they were drinking wine together, Hsi-men Ch'ing casually brought up the subject of Miao Ch'ing's case, saying, "This rascal yesterday importuned a member of the gentry to come and intercede with me insistently on his behalf, and also presented me with something in the way of an inducement. Your pupil would certainly:

> Not presume to take matters into his own hands,[35]

and that is why I have invited my colleague here today, in order to consult with him about it."

Thereupon, he handed the gift card to Hsia Yen-ling, who read it and then said, "My colleague should feel free to decide the matter as he sees fit."

"As I see it," said Hsi-men Ch'ing, "tomorrow we might as well continue proceedings against those two culprits on the basis of the actual booty in their possession. There is no need to proceed any further against this Miao Ch'ing. As for the original plaintiff, that page boy, An-t'ung, we can release him on bond until such time as the corpse of Miao T'ien-hsiu comes to light. It will not be too late to settle the case at that time. The gifts I propose to send over to your place."

"This last proposal of my colleague's is not right," said Judicial Commissioner Hsia. "Your view of the case is quite appropriate, and it is you who have taken the trouble to deal with it. Why should you have to share anything with me? That will never do."

They dickered about it, back and forth, for some time before Hsi-men Ch'ing, seeing no alternative, agreed to split the gratuity evenly between them and arranged to have five hundred taels put into food boxes.

Judicial Commissioner Hsia got up from his seat and bowed in thanks, saying, "Since my colleague has chosen to favor me in this way, to refuse yet again would be to display a fastidious response to your lavish generosity.

I will never be able to thank you enough.
It is really quite embarrassing."

Only after accepting a few more cups of wine did he say goodbye and leave. For his part, Hsi-men Ch'ing forthwith ordered Tai-an to take charge of the boxes, which still appeared to contain wine, and have them carried to Hsia Yen-ling's home. When they arrived there, Judicial Commissioner Hsia came out to the door in person to receive them, produced a return note, and presented Tai-an with two taels of silver, and the two orderlies with four mace apiece. But no more of this. Truly:

> When heat reaches the proper level,
>   the pig's head is dissolved;
> When money reaches the right hands,
>   the case is resolved.[36]

To resume our story, Hsi-men Ch'ing and Hsia Yen-ling had already colluded on a plan of action, and, the next day, when they went to the yamen and took their places on the bench, the clerks, adjutants, detectives, and inspectors, high and low, had all been taken care of by Yüeh the Third on Miao Ch'ing's behalf. The instruments of torture were conspicuously displayed, and Ch'en the Third and Weng the Eighth were brought out of the lockup and subjected to interrogation.

When their depositions reiterated that they had conspired with the servant of the deceased, Miao Ch'ing, Hsi-men Ch'ing became enraged, and shouted to the attendants, "Put them to the question. You two bandits have been active on the rivers and waterways for years, pretending to be engaged in riverine transportation, while actually devoting yourselves to plundering the property of your passengers, holding up merchants, and committing murder with larcenous intent.[37] Right now there is this page boy who testifies that you stabbed Miao T'ien-hsiu to death with a knife and threw him overboard, after which you wounded him by a blow with a stick that knocked him into the water as well. There is also the evidence provided by the fact that you are wearing items of his master's clothing. How can you have the nerve to try to implicate anyone else?"

He then had An-t'ung brought forward and asked him, "Who was it who stabbed your master to death and pushed him overboard?"

An-t'ung testified, "On the day in question, at the third watch of the night, Miao Ch'ing started calling out, 'Thief!' At which, when my master came out of the cabin to investigate, he was stabbed to death with one thrust of a knife by Ch'en the Third, and pushed overboard. I was then struck a blow with a stick by Weng the Eighth, which knocked me into the water, and barely escaped with my life. I do not know anything about the whereabouts of Miao Ch'ing."

"The testimony of this page boy has the ring of truth," said Hsi-men Ch'ing. "How can the two of you get around it?"

Thereupon, he had a pair of ankle-squeezers put on each of them and had them struck thirty blows with a cudgel, with the result that their shinbones were crushed, and they:

Howled and writhed like stuck pigs.

More than half of their thousand taels worth of booty had been recovered, and the remainder had all been spent.

That very day, the judicial commissioners saw to the drafting of the necessary documents, sequestered the recovered booty, and forwarded the records of the case to Tung-p'ing prefecture. The prefect of Tung-p'ing prefecture, Hu Shih-wen,[38] who was also on good terms with Hsi-men Ch'ing, made out the formal indictment according to the terms of the documents he had received and provisionally sentenced Ch'en the Third and Weng the Eighth to decapitation for the crimes of armed robbery and murder, while releasing An-t'ung on bond pending further developments.

One day, An-t'ung made his way to the Eastern Capital, where he sought out the yamen of the assistant prefect, Huang Mei, and lodged a complaint accusing Miao Ch'ing of having stolen his master's property and then bribed the judicial commissioners to remove his name from the case, and asking when this miscarriage of justice at his master's expense could be righted.

When the assistant prefect, Huang Mei, had heard him out, he wrote a letter on his behalf that very night, sealed it up with his written complaint, provided him with travelling expenses, and told him to deliver it to the office of the regional investigating censor of Shantung.

As a direct result of this act, the wrongdoing of Miao Ch'ing would be reinvestigated from the beginning, and:

> Though Hsi-men Ch'ing's deeds were done in the past,
> Today the chickens would come home to roost.

There is a poem that testifies to this:

> Good and evil, in the end, always turn out
>   to have their causes;
> Good luck and bad, misfortune and fortune,
>   travel hand in hand.[39]
> If, all your life, you have done nothing
>   to be ashamed of;
> The midnight sound of knocking at the door
>   will not disturb you.[40]

> If you want to know the outcome of these events,
> Pray consult the story related in the following chapter.

Chapter 48

INVESTIGATING CENSOR TSENG IMPEACHES

THE JUDICIAL COMMISSIONERS;

GRAND PRECEPTOR TS'AI SUBMITS

A MEMORIAL REGARDING SEVEN MATTERS

Some words of admonition:

Be alert to danger and recognize peril,
And you will finally avoid the meshes of the law.
Praise the good and recommend the worthy,
And you will attain a secure place for yourself.
Bestow kindness and practice virtue,[1]
And you will ensure the success of your posterity.
Harbor venom and conceal treachery,
And your whole life will be subject to catastrophe.
To injure others for your own advantage,[2]
Is not, in the final analysis, a far-reaching plan.
To hurt your fellows to achieve success,[3]
Can scarcely be considered a long-range strategy.
Use of pseudonyms and disguised appearance,
Are always necessitated by resort to specious words.
Exposure to lawsuits and loss of property,
Are the inevitable consequences of inhumane conduct.[4]

THE STORY GOES that An-t'ung accepted the document and letter, took his leave of Assistant Prefect Huang Mei, and set out on the highroad to Shantung. Upon inquiry, he learned that the regional investigating censor was currently in residence at his office in Tung-ch'ang prefecture, that his name was Tseng Hsiao-hsü,[5] that he was the son of the former censor-in-chief, Tseng Pu,[6] had passed the *chin-shih* examination in the year 1115, and that he was an official of absolute integrity and honor.

An-t'ung thought to himself, "If I say that I am delivering a letter, the gate-keepers are certain not to let me in. I had better stay here until they hang up the tablet announcing the category of cases to be heard, at which point I can make my way in on my knees and present both the letter and my complaint at the same time. When His Honor sees them, he will surely consent to adjudicate the case."

Thereupon, he put the text of the complaint, which he had long since prepared, in his breast pocket and remained outside the gate of the regional investigating censor's office. After he had waited there for some time, he heard the sounding of the cloud-shaped gong that announced the sessions of the court. The main gate and the inner gate were opened, and Investigating Censor Tseng took his place on the bench. When the first tablet was displayed, it stated, in large characters, "Accusations against imperial princes, distaff relatives of the imperial family, consorts of imperial princesses, and members of influential households." When the second tablet was displayed, it read, "Complaints against the regional military commission, the provincial administration commission, the provincial surveillance commission, and the officers and functionaries of the armies and guards." Finally, when the third tablet was displayed, it read, "Lawsuits among commoners over census registration, marriage, land ownership, and other subjects of litigation."

An-t'ung, accordingly, followed in the wake of this tablet as it was carried inside, and it was only after all the other cases had been disposed of, that he knelt down at the foot of the red steps leading up to the dais. The attendants standing to either side demanded to know what his business was, and only then did An-t'ung present his letter, holding it up with both hands as high as he could.

From his position on the bench, Investigating Censor Tseng was heard to call out, "Bring it up here."

The docket officers in attendance hurriedly came down from the dais and, taking the letter back up with them, placed it on the table before him, after which Tseng Hsiao-hsü proceeded to open and peruse it. Truly, what did the contents of the document say? The letter read:

> Earnestly indited by his junior fellow graduate in the capital, Huang Mei, for the perusal of his mentor and fellow graduate the distinguished censor Tseng, courtesy name Shao-t'ing:
>
> Since I forsook your illustrious countenance,[7] a year has abruptly elapsed.[8] Those who truly understand one are difficult to meet.[9] The most satisfying intercourse is easily interrupted. This heart of mine is ardent,[10] ever endeavoring to keep at your side. Last autumn, upon the unexpected receipt of your elegant epistle, when I opened and reverently perused it, my spirit was transported, and I felt exactly as though we were face to face in the capital as of old. Whenever I am feeling melancholy, I recite it once again, and find that it relieves my spirits. Not long after that, you returned south to visit your parents, and I heard the good news that you had been appointed regional investigating censor of Shantung. I am quite:
>
> > Unable to contain my satisfaction.[11]
>
> Congratulations! Congratulations!

In consideration of the fact that my fellow graduate is an exemplar of the great virtues of loyalty and filiality, whose integrity is like the wind and frost, whose mind is ever subject to the grindstone of self-cultivation, who is a shining light in the imperial court, and a frequent topic of remark in the discourse of the gentry, now that you have taken up your position as an investigating censor, it is truly the season for you to expose examples of official malfeasance, with a view to the reformation of public morality. In the light of my humble admiration for you, this is something that I cannot forget.

I venture to observe that my fellow graduate, who has always possessed a capacity for significant deeds, and who finds himself at an appropriate time for action, it being an era of sage enlightenment and rectitude, and a day when his venerable father is still alive and well, should take advantage of the opportunity to greatly extend his talent and faculties in the cause of improving law and morals, so as not to allow pettifogging functionaries to manipulate the statutes, or treacherous malefactors to practice their deceits.

How is it then that in the prefecture of Tung-p'ing there should be such an egregious lawbreaker as Miao Ch'ing, and such a victim of unrequited injustice as Miao T'ien-hsiu? I would not have thought that in an era of sage enlightenment such demons could exist. Since this falls within my fellow graduate's jurisdiction, it is to be hoped that he will adjudicate this miscarriage of justice and set the record straight.

The bearer, An-t'ung, is the body servant of the victim, and the carrier of a written complaint that I hope you will condescend to consider. I am unable to express myself more fully. Composed on the sixteenth day of the middle month of spring.

When Investigating Censor Tseng Hsiao-hsü had finished reading the letter, he asked, "Does he have a written complaint or not?"

The attendants hurriedly came down from the dais and said, "His Honor wants to know whether you have a written complaint or not."

An-t'ung thereupon reached into his breast, pulled out the complaint, and formally presented it.

When Tseng Hsiao-hsü had perused it, he picked up his brush and endorsed it with the words, "The prefectural officials of Tung-p'ing prefecture are hereby adjured to conduct an honest inquiry in order to ascertain the facts of the case, examine the corpse of the deceased, and submit a report with all the relevant documents."

He then ordered that An-t'ung should proceed to Tung-p'ing prefecture in order to await the outcome of the proceedings. An-t'ung hastily kowtowed, got up from his knees, and was allowed to exit through a side door, while Tseng Hsiao-hsü, for his part, put the written complaint, along with his endorsement, in a dispatch case, sealed it with his official seal, and sent someone to deliver it to Tung-p'ing prefecture.

When the prefect, Hu Shih-wen, saw that the case had been remanded to him by a higher authority, he was thrown into such consternation that:

He did not know where to put hand or foot,[12]

and delegated the problem to the vice-magistrate of Yang-ku district, Ti Ssu-pin.[13] This individual was a native of Wu-yang in Honan province, was rigid and upright by nature, and did not solicit bribes, but was so muddleheaded in hearing cases that everyone called him Turbid Ti.

Sometime before this mandate came down, he had set out to reconnoiter the banks of the canal in the hope of locating the corpse of Miao T'ien-hsiu. It turned out to be one of those occasions on which:

Something was destined to happen.

Who could have anticipated that when Vice-Magistrate Ti Ssu-pin led his entourage in reconnoitering the banks of the canal to the west of the district seat of Ch'ing-ho, as they were going about their task, a whirlwind[14] suddenly appeared in front of his mount, that refused to dissipate but kept pace with his horse as he proceeded.

"How uncanny!" remarked Ti Ssu-pin, reining in his horse, "You go follow this whirlwind wherever it goes," he ordered the runners in his entourage. "It's essential that we get to the bottom of this."

The runners did, indeed, follow in the wake of the whirlwind until it came to a halt just as they approached the port on the New Canal, and they went back to report this information to Ti Ssu-pin. The latter ordered them to take the local community elder into custody, and when they had used spades to excavate the soil of the embankment to a depth of several feet, they discovered a corpse, which actually displayed the scar of a knife wound on its throat. After ordering the coroner's assistant to complete his examination, he asked what the place that lay before them might be.

"The Tz'u-hui Ssu, or Temple of Compassionate Wisdom, is located not far from here," the runners reported.

Vice-Magistrate Ti then ordered that the resident monks of the temple be taken into custody and interrogated. They testified unanimously that during the tenth month of the preceding winter, when the temple was engaged in setting water lanterns afloat, they had found a corpse that had drifted into the inlet from upstream; that the abbot, out of compassion, had retrieved and buried it; and that they had no knowledge of the circumstances of the death.

"It is obvious," pronounced Vice-Magistrate Ti Ssu-pin, "that you monks conspired to kill this man and bury him here. No doubt he had valuables on his person, so you are unwilling to testify to the truth."

Thereupon:

Without permitting any further explanation,

he had the abbot subjected to a session with the head-press, two applications of the finger-squeezers, and then put into ankle-squeezers which were struck a hundred blows. The remaining monks were each given twenty strokes with the heavy bamboo, after which he ordered that they all be incarcerated in the lockup.

When this information was conveyed to Tseng Hsiao-hsü, he ordered that the matter be reinvestigated and reported back to him, but the monks all claimed to be victims of injustice and refused to alter their testimony.

Tseng Hsiao-hsü thought to himself, "If these monks had really conspired to do him in, they would surely have thrown the corpse into the river. Why should they have buried it on the embankment instead? Moreover, there would have been too many people involved. There is something suspicious about this."

He therefore ordered that the monks should be kept in custody, and they had already been incarcerated for nearly two months when this formal complaint of An-t'ung's unexpectedly came into the picture, as a consequence of which, officers were deputed to escort An-t'ung to the site where the body had been discovered in order to identify the corpse.

When An-t'ung saw the body, he wept grievously, saying, "It truly is my master, and the wound inflicted by the knife of those bandits is still visible."

Thereupon, once the examination was completed, the results were reported back to Tseng Hsiao-hsü, who immediately released the monks in custody, while, on the other hand, he ordered a review of the documents in the case and had Ch'en the Third and Weng the Eighth interrogated once again. When they persisted in testifying that Miao Ch'ing had been the instigator of the plot, Tseng Hsiao-hsü was greatly angered and sent someone with an arrest warrant to go to the relevant prefecture in his jurisdiction and hale Miao Ch'ing before the court. At the same time he drafted a memorial impeaching the two judicial commissioners who had heard the case for having accepted bribes and put justice up for sale. Truly:

Corrupt functionaries and venal officials
    subvert the nation's laws;
But Tseng Hsiao-hsü's review of this case
    righted an injustice.
Yet, though his orders were as stringent
    as the wind or thunder;
The wins and losses occurring in a dream
    are always unreliable.[15]

At this point the story divides into two. To resume our story, no sooner had Wang Liu-erh obtained the hundred taels of silver and four outfits of clothing for intervening on Miao Ch'ing's behalf, than she consulted with her husband, Han Tao-kuo, that very night and then busied herself all day and remained sleepless the following night, planning to have head ornaments, hairpins, and bracelets fashioned for herself, calling in a tailor to design clothes for her, and ordering the manufacture of a new fret of silver filigree. She also expended sixteen taels of silver to purchase an additional maidservant, named Ch'un-hsiang, to wait upon her, and, sooner or later, also serve the sexual needs of Han Tao-kuo. But no more of this.

One day Hsi-men Ch'ing dropped by Han Tao-kuo's home and Wang Liu-erh ushered him inside and served him with tea. When he had finished drinking his tea, Hsi-men Ch'ing went back to the rear of the house to relieve himself and happened to notice that there was a terrace on the second floor of the adjacent house.

"Who does that belong to?" he asked.

"It's the terrace on the house of Yüeh the Third next door," replied Wang Liu-erh.

Hsi-men Ch'ing directed Wang Liu-erh, "You tell him that he'd better take it down, or else. How can you allow him to interfere with the geomantic situation of your residence that way? If you won't, I'll have the local constable order him to do it."

Wang Liu-erh consulted with Han Tao-kuo about this, saying, "They're our neighbors. How can we broach the subject with them?"

"The best thing to do," said Han Tao-kuo, "would be to keep His Honor in the dark, buy a few sticks of lumber at the temple fair, and put up a terrace behind our own place over here. We can benefit by sun-drying bean paste on top of it, and using the room below for either a stable or a privy."

"Phooey!" his wife exclaimed. "What a louse of a senseless creature you are! Rather than erecting a terrace, wouldn't it be better to lay in some bricks and tiles, and construct two upper-story sheds?"

"If we merely put up two sheds," said Han Tao-kuo, "they won't be much use to us. We'd only use them for storage purposes. We might as well put up a single story, containing two small regular rooms."

Thereupon, they proceeded to lay out thirty taels of silver and had two flat-roofed rooms added to the back of their property. Hsi-men Ch'ing sent Tai-an in charge of a considerable quantity of wine, meat, and baked wheat cakes for them to use in rewarding the artisans for their efforts. Among the residents of the street there were none who were unaware of this.

Judicial Commissioner Hsia Yen-ling, upon obtaining these several hundred taels of silver, used them to enroll his seventeen-year-old son, Hsia Ch'eng-en, as a degree candidate in the military school of the local guard, where he became a government student. Every day he entertained his instructors and friends, with whom he practiced archery and horsemanship. Hsi-men Ch'ing got together with Eunuch Director Liu and Eunuch Director Hsüeh, Commandant Chou Hsiu, Battalion Commander Ching Chung, Militia Commander Chang Kuan, and the entire officers corps of the guard battalion to contribute toward the cost of presenting him with a commemorative scroll in celebration of the occasion. But there is no need to describe this in detail.

Hsi-men Ch'ing had recently arranged for the construction of an artificial hill, summerhouses, and additional buildings on the site of his family grave-yard, but, since the birth of Kuan-ko and his appointment as a battalion com-mander, he had not yet visited the family graves in order to sacrifice to his ancestors. After ordering Master Hsü, the yin-yang master, to assess the geo-mantic configuration of the site, he had a new gateway erected, a paved cause-way leading to the tombs of his ancestors built, a mausoleum constructed, willows placed about the gate, pines and cypresses planted all around, and raised embankments situated on either side.

In anticipation of his visit to the graves of his ancestors on the Ch'ing-ming Festival, he planned to install a new plaque announcing his status as a mem-ber of the Embroidered-Uniform Guard, slaughter pigs and sheep, and order the appropriate table settings. Prior to the festival itself, which fell on the sixth day of the third month that year, he sent out invitations to a lot of people, arranged for the transportation of the requisite accoutrements, wine, rice, and other culinary supplies, and engaged the services of musicians and tumblers, a troupe of players, the boy actors Li Ming, Wu Hui, Wang Chu, and Cheng Feng, and the singing girls Li Kuei-chieh, Wu Yin-erh, Han Chin-ch'uan, and Tung Chiao-erh. The male guests he invited included Militia Commander Chang Kuan, Ch'iao Hung, his brothers-in-law Wu K'ai and Wu the Second, Hua Tzu-yu, Brother-in-law Shen, the husband of Wu Yüeh-niang's elder sis-ter, Ying Po-chüeh, Hsieh Hsi-ta, Manager Fu, Han Tao-kuo, Yün Li-shou, Pen Ti-ch'uan, and his son-in-law Ch'en Ching-chi, more than twenty people in all. The females invited were Militia Commander Chang Kuan's wife, Kinswoman Chang, Ch'iao Hung's wife, Censor Chu's wife, the wife of Pro-vincial Graduate Shang, Wu K'ai's wife, Wu the Second's wife, Aunt Yang, Old Mrs. P'an, Hua Tzu-yu's wife, Wu Yüeh-niang's elder sister, Meng Yü-lou's elder sister, Wu Shun-ch'en's wife, Third Sister Cheng, Ts'ui Pen's wife, Big Sister Tuan, and, from his own household, Wu Yüeh-niang, Li Chiao-erh, Meng Yü-lou, P'an Chin-lien, Li P'ing-erh, Sun Hsüeh-o, Hsi-men Ta-chieh, Ch'un-mei, Ying-ch'un, Yü-hsiao, Lan-hsiang, and the wet nurse, Ju-i, holding Kuan-ko in her arms. Altogether, twenty-four or twenty-five sedan chairs were required to accommodate them all.

Before the day in question, Yüeh-niang had spoken to Hsi-men Ch'ing, saying, "There's no need to have the child taken out to the graveyard. On the one hand, he's not even a year old, and on the other hand, Dame Liu says that his parietal bones are not yet completely formed, and that he has a timorous disposition. It's a long way to the graveyard, and I fear he could become fright-ened. In my view, it would be better not to have him go, but to leave him here at home, where the wet nurse and Old Mother Feng can look after him, and let his mother go without him."

But Hsi-men Ch'ing would not listen to her, saying, "Really! Why shouldn't the two of them, mother and child, both go to the graveyard to kowtow to my ancestors? You put too much stock in the nonsense put out by that crone. The old whore! Even if it be true that the child's parietal bones are not yet completely formed, as long as you have the wet nurse wrap him up securely in a quilt while they are in the sedan chair, what is there to be afraid of?"

"Since you refuse to take anyone's advice," said Yüeh-niang, "you may do as you please."

Early on the morning of the day in question, the female guests all left their homes to forgather for the occasion, mounted their sedan chairs, and set off. But no more of this.

When they approached the family graveyard, five li outside the South Gate, they beheld from a distance that:

The verdant pines were luxuriant,
The emerald cypresses were dense.

The graveyard had been enhanced by the newly erected gateway, the two raised embankments on either side, and a stone wall surrounding the entire site. The paved causeway in the middle, the mausoleum, the spirit platform, the incense burners, and the candlesticks were all hewn out of white alabaster. The newly replaced plaque on the gate was inscribed in large characters, reading: The Ancestral Graveyard of Master Hsi-men, Commandant for Military Strategy of the Embroidered-Uniform Guard. The main facade of the mausoleum was:

Encompassed by raised earthen embankments, and
A copse of trees with interlacing branches.

Hsi-men Ch'ing, clad in scarlet official attire, having seen to the setting out of the slaughtered pigs and sheep and other sacrificial offerings, and table settings, proceeded to pay formal homage to his ancestors. Only after the male guests had followed suit did the female guests do likewise.

As these acts of worship took place, percussion instruments, gongs, and drums were all sounded simultaneously, and the resulting din so frightened Kuan-ko that he hid himself in the wet nurse's breast, started to choke, and did not dare to move a muscle.

Yüeh-niang then called out, "Sister Li, how come you haven't had the wet nurse take the child back to the rear yet? Just see how frightened he is. I said there was no need to bring the child, but that obstinate good-for-nothing of ours insisted on having him wrapped up and brought along anyway. Just see how frightened he is."

Li P'ing-erh promptly came down from her seat, ordered Tai-an to have them stop beating the gongs and drums, and directed the wet nurse to quickly cover the baby's ears and take him back to the rear of the premises.

In a little while, after the sacrifices were finished, Master Hsü had recited the elegy to the dead, and the paper money had been burnt, Hsi-men Ch'ing invited the male guests to join him in the front reception hall, while Yüeh-

niang invited the female guests to come with her to the summerhouse in the
rear. They proceeded through the garden to get there.

To either side of the juniper hedges,
Were arrayed bamboo-lined walks and balustrades;
In all directions the flowering trees,
Stretched before them as far as the eye could see.

Truly:

The red peach blossoms and the green willows[16]
    are traversed by shuttling orioles;
All of which were brought into being by the
    creativity of the Lord of the East.

Thereupon, the troupe of players put on a performance for the female
guests in the summerhouse, while the four boy actors sang for a time in the
front reception hall for the entertainment of the male guests, and the four
singing girls took turns serving the wine. The four senior maidservants, Ch'un-
mei, Yü-hsiao, Lan-hsiang, and Ying-ch'un, waited on the female guests, holding flagons and pouring wine, after which they stood beside Hsi-men Ta-
chieh's table and had something to eat.

After the female guests had feasted for some time, P'an Chin-lien, along
with Meng Yü-lou, Hsi-men Ta-chieh, Li Kuei-chieh, and Wu Yin-erh, went
into the garden together, where they enjoyed themselves on the swing for
a while.

It so happens that behind the summerhouse Hsi-men Ch'ing had put a
structure consisting of three compartments, one well-lighted parlor, and two
less well-lighted inner rooms, each provided with a k'ang frame. Inside they
were furnished with bed-curtains, and supplied with tables and chairs, comb-
boxes, dressing mirrors, toilet stands, and the like, in order that female visitors
to the graveyard would have a place to make themselves up and rest, or that
casual visitors from the demimonde could be entertained. The rooms had
been plastered so that they were as spotless as snow grottoes and were embellished with calligraphy, painting, zither, and chessboard,[17] all of which were
elegantly displayed.

The wet nurse Ju-i, who was looking after Kuan-ko, happened to be reclining just then on the gold-flecked k'ang frame, on which she had placed a little
sleeping mat for the baby, with whom Ying-ch'un, who was standing by her
side, was playing. What should they see at this juncture but P'an Chin-lien,
who suddenly came in from the garden, all by herself, holding a sprig of peach
blossoms in her hand.

Upon entering the room and seeing Ying-ch'un, she remarked, "So you've
been here all this time, instead of waiting on us up front."

"Ch'un-mei, Lan-hsiang, and Yü-hsiao are all up front," protested Ying-
ch'un. "Mother told me to come back here to see how the baby is doing, and
to bring two saucers of delicacies for Ju-i to eat."

Chin-lien noticed that there was a saucer of goose meat, a saucer of pig's trotters, and some pieces of fruit on the table.

When the wet nurse saw Chin-lien come in, she picked up Kuan-ko, and Chin-lien proceeded to tease him, saying, "Little oily mouth! When they struck up the gongs and drums a little while ago, you were so frightened you were speechless. Are you really as timorous as all that?"

Thereupon, she opened up her jacket of pale lavender silk and her gold lamé blouse, took the baby in her arms, held him fast in her embrace, and proceeded to kiss him, mouth to mouth. All of a sudden, Ch'en Ching-chi came in, and, seeing that Chin-lien was playing with the child, proceeded to do likewise.

"Little Taoist," said Chin-lien, "give your brother-in-law a kiss."

At which:

> Strange as it may seem,

Kuan-ko actually giggled at him, and Ching-chi:

> Without permitting any further explanation,

took the child into his arms and proceeded to give him a series of kisses.

"You crazy short-life!" protested Chin-lien. "It's all right to show your affection to the child, but you're mussing the hair over my temples."

Ching-chi flirted with her, saying, "You don't say. It's a good thing I didn't kiss the wrong person by mistake."

When Chin-lien heard this, fearing that the maidservants would catch on, she facetiously turned over the fan in her hand and proceeded to hit him with the handle, to such effect that Ching-chi wriggled like a carp.

"You crazy short-life!" she berated him. "Who has the patience to:

> Bandy words or waggle tongues,

with you?"

"That's not the problem," protested Ching-chi. "You ought to pay more attention to other peoples' feelings. I'm wearing too thin a layer of clothing for you to hit me like that."

"Why should I pay any attention to your feelings for no good reason?" vociferated Chin-lien. "If you pester me that way again, I'll hit you just as hard."

When Ju-i saw the way they were mixing it up with each other, she took Kuan-ko into her arms and let Chin-lien and Ching-chi carry on as they liked. Chin-lien bent the sprig of peach blossoms in her hand into a wreath, which she surreptitiously stuck on top of Ching-chi's cap. When they came outside, they happened to encounter Meng Yü-lou, along with Hsi-men Ta-chieh and Li Kuei-chieh, the three of whom were coming toward them from the other direction.

When Hsi-men Ta-chieh caught sight of the wreath, she asked, "Who's responsible for this bit of funny business?"

Chin-lien Puts a Wreath of Peach Blossoms on Ching-chi's Cap

Ching-chi took it off and went his way, without saying another word about it.

When four long scenes from a hsi-wen drama had been performed for the female guests, it was observed that:

The sunlight outside the window goes its way
in a snap of the fingers;
The flower shadows in the banquet hall move
among the revellers' seats.[18]

Evening was gradually coming on. Hsi-men Ch'ing ordered Pen the Fourth to provide each of the chair carriers with a bowl of wine, four baked wheat cakes, and a plate of precooked pork. Only after these viands had been properly distributed did the female guests prepare to mount their sedan chairs and set off, with the male guests following behind them on horseback, while Lai-hsing and the caterers, carrying their food boxes, slowly brought up the rear. Tai-an, Lai-an, Hua-t'ung, and Ch'i-t'ung accompanied the sedan chairs of Wu Yüeh-niang and company; Ch'in-t'ung and four orderlies followed after Hsi-men Ch'ing on his horse; while the wet nurse, Ju-i, all by herself in a small sedan chair, carried the baby in her arms, wrapped up tightly in a quilt.

As they entered the city, Yüeh-niang was still concerned enough about the baby to send Hua-t'ung back, instructing him, "Stick close to the wet nurse's sedan chair. I'm afraid the crowds may get rowdy as we enter the city."

When Yüeh-niang's sedan chair had entered the city, she parted ways with the sedan chairs of the female guests from the Ch'iao family and made her way home, where she descended from her chair and went inside. It was some time after that before Hsi-men Ch'ing and Ch'en Ching-chi arrived home and dismounted from their horses.

Whom should they encounter there but P'ing-an, who met them at the gate and reported, "Today His Honor Judicial Commissioner Hsia came in person, dismounted, went into the reception hall, asked for you, and then left. After that, he has sent people to ask after you twice. I don't know what it's all about."

When Hsi-men Ch'ing heard this, he was troubled in his heart. When he arrived in the reception hall, whom should he see but Shu-t'ung, who came up to take his outer clothes.

Hsi-men Ch'ing then asked him, "When His Honor Hsia came today, what message did he leave for me?"

"He didn't divulge anything," said Shu-t'ung. "He merely asked where you had gone, saying, 'Send someone after him. I've got something important to say to him.' I told him, 'Today they've all paid a visit to the family graveyard to burn paper money to the ancestors and won't return until evening.' At which, His Honor Hsia said, 'I'll come back at noontime.' After that, he sent people to ask after you twice, and I told them that you had not returned yet."

Hsi-men Ch'ing's mind was not put to rest by this information, and he wondered all the more, "What could it be about?"

Just as he was in this perplexity, whom should he see but P'ing-an, who came in to report, "His Honor Hsia is here."

It was already dusk when Judicial Commissioner Hsia appeared, wearing informal clothes and a Tung-p'o hat,[19] with two servitors in attendance.

He dismounted, came into the reception hall, exchanged the customary social amenities, and said, "So my colleague has paid a visit to his country estate today."

"Today we have been sweeping the graves and making sacrifices at my ancestral tombs," said Hsi-men Ch'ing. "Not knowing that my colleague would condescend to pay us a visit, I was not here to greet you myself. Forgive me. Forgive me."

"I have ventured to come," said Judicial Commissioner Hsia, "on account of a matter that I need to report to you."

"Let's go to the guest room over there and sit down," he went on to say.

Hsi-men Ch'ing ordered Shu-t'ung to open the door of the summerhouse and invited his guest to accompany him there for a chat, after which he dismissed all his attendants.

"Today," said Judicial Commissioner Hsia, "His Honor Li Ta-t'ien of the district yamen came to my place and reported, thus and so, that recently the regional investigating censor has submitted an impeachment to the Eastern Capital, in which both my colleague and myself are implicated. I ordered someone to make a copy of the draft for your perusal."

When Hsi-men Ch'ing heard this, he:

Turned pale with consternation,

hastily took the copy of the draft, and proceeded to read it by lamplight. What did the text actually say?

Memorial Submitted by Tseng Hsiao-hsü, Regional Investigating Censor of Shantung

In re: An Impeachment of Venal, Refractory, and Unqualified Military Officials, Requesting that They Be Dismissed from Office with a View toward the Rectification of Law and Morals

Your servant has heard that to make a circuit of the four quarters in order to monitor the state of public morality is the responsibility of the Son of Heaven in making his tours of inspection. To impeach and repress official malfeasance in order to improve law and morals is the task of the censor in his endeavor to rectify government. In ancient times, according to the *Spring and Autumn Annals*, when the ruler went on his tours of inspection, the myriad states felt cherished and protected, the morals of the populace were ameliorated, the way of the ruler was made manifest, the four classes of people were rendered obedient, and the advantages of the sage king's administration were illuminated. Since the day last year that your servant accepted appointment as regional investigating censor of Shantung, the land of the ancient states of Ch'i and Lu, until the present time when my assignment is about to expire,

I have successively inquired into the worthiness, or lack thereof, of all the regional officials, both civil and military, who hold office in my jurisdiction, and am confident that I have succeeded in ascertaining the truth about them. Now that the end of my assignment is imminent, it is incumbent upon me to differentiate among them according to precedent, and report my conclusions to Your Majesty. In addition to the separate memoranda I have submitted regarding other regional officials from this jurisdiction, I ask that Your Majesty take cognizance of the following cases.

The judicial commissioner of the Ch'ing-ho office of the Shantung Provincial Surveillance Commission, and concurrently, battalion commander in the Imperial Insignia Guard, Hsia Yen-ling, is a man whose mediocre talents and corrupt conduct have long excited public comment and besmirched the reputation of his unit. In the past, when he was in charge of herds in the horse pasturages of the imperial domain, he created so much trouble with his flagrant depredations that his peculations were exposed by one of his own subordinates. Now that he is a judicial commissioner in Shantung, his rapacious greed is once more so blatant that it has had to be restrained by his colleagues. He allowed his son, Hsia Ch'eng-en, to assume a false district of origin when taking the military examination, and then hired a stand-in to take the qualifying test for him, with the result that:

> The esprit of the officer class is debased.[20]

He permitted his servant, Hsia Shou, to appropriate funds while responsible for the payroll, thereby giving rise to the vituperation of the troops in his command, and exposing his ignorance of proper administration. In his relations with others he exhibits such a:

> Servile countenance and obsequious posture,[21]

that his coevals call him "The Maidservant." In adjudicating cases he is so:

> Equally indifferent to the pros and cons,[22]

that his subordinates deride him as "The Puppet."

The assistant judicial commissioner, and concurrently battalion vice-commander, Hsi-men Ch'ing, was originally no more than a "bare stick" from the marketplace, who took advantage of his connections to obtain office, and has laid false claim to military accomplishment, while being so ignorant that he is:

> Incapable of telling beans from wheat, and
> Unable to recognize the simplest character.[23]

He lets his wife and concubines roam the streets and alleys for their pleasure, thereby failing to maintain the purity of his household. He invites female musicians to join him for drinking bouts in the marketplace, thereby blemishing the reputation of the official class. He has even gone to the extreme of maintaining the wife of Mr. Han as his mistress, for the purpose of indulging his lusts, thus failing to regulate his conduct;[24] and taking the clandestine bribe of Miao Ch'ing, in order to cover up his crime, though the evidence of his guilt is manifest.

These two venal and incompetent officials have long been the objects of principled criticism, and should not be permitted to remain in office another hour. I respectfully hope that Your Majesty, in his sage enlightenment, will deign to take note of this matter by ordering the appropriate board to conduct a thorough reinvestigation; and, if your servant's words prove not to be unfounded, direct that Hsia Yen-ling and his associate be promptly removed from office,[25] so that the norms of official conduct may be relied upon, and Your Majesty's sage virtue may be made eternally manifest.

When Hsi-men Ch'ing had finished perusing this document, he was so agitated that he and his companion could only:

> Gaze at each other in consternation,
> Too dumbstruck to utter a single word.

"My colleague," Hsia Yen-ling finally said, "in this situation, what are we to do?"

Hsi-men Ch'ing replied, "As the saying goes:

> When armies come the general confronts them;
> When waters overflow earthworks arrest them.[26]
> Once things have come to a head,[27]
> The Way is what man makes of it.

The only thing you and I can do is to prepare gifts and send people to the Eastern Capital as soon as possible, in order to entreat His Honor to intercede on our behalf."

Thereupon, Judicial Commissioner Hsia bid him a hasty farewell and went home, where he came up with two hundred taels of silver and two silver flagons for the purpose, while Hsi-men Ch'ing, on his hand, came up with a girdle of gold, inlaid with jade and assorted jewels, and three hundred taels of silver. The Hsia household chose their servant Hsia Shou for this assignment, while Hsi-men Ch'ing entrusted the job to Lai-pao. By the time these gifts had been properly wrapped up, and Hsi-men Ch'ing had written a covering letter to the majordomo Chai Ch'ien, the two deputies had hired mounts for themselves and proceeded to set off on their mission to the Eastern Capital that very night. But no more of this.

To resume our story, from the time that Kuan-ko returned home from the visit to the family graveyard, he kept crying from fright all night and would not allow himself to be breast-fed, spitting up whatever milk he swallowed. This threw Li P'ing-erh into such consternation that she came and told Yüeh-niang about it.

"It's just as I said," responded Yüeh-niang. "The child is not even a year old and should not have been taken on an excursion outside the city walls. But that obstinate good-for-nothing of ours would not agree, no matter what the consequences might be. His only response was to say, 'Really! Why shouldn't the two of them, mother and child, go to the graveyard today to sacrifice to my ancestors? If you don't allow the mother and child to go, it will look as if you're afraid she might want to replace you or something like that.' He actually opened his eyes wide and shouted at me. And now, what are we to do?"

Li P'ing-erh really didn't know what to do. Moreover, because of the impeachment lodged against him by the regional investigating censor, Hsi-men Ch'ing was busy talking to Judicial Commissioner Hsia in the front compound about sending someone to the Eastern Capital to try to fix things up and was too preoccupied to pay any attention to the fact that the child of the house was unwell again. Yüeh-niang sent a page boy after Dame Liu to come and examine him and also engaged the services of a licensed pediatrician, with the result that, what with the:

Opening of gates and closing of doors,[28]
the household was in a state of disruption all night long.

When Dame Liu had examined him, she said, "The child is suffering from the colic brought on by a fright and must have encountered the General of the Five Ways[29] along the road. It doesn't matter. Just burn some paper money on his behalf to send the General on his way and he'll be all right."

She also left behind two doses of medicine in the form of cinnabar pills. Only after he had swallowed these, together with a decoction of field mint and bog rush, did he quiet down and go to sleep, no longer crying from fright and spitting up his milk, but his fever had not yet receded. Li P'ing-erh promptly produced a tael of silver and gave it to Dame Liu with which to buy paper money. That afternoon she came back with her husband, Stargazer Liu, and a shamaness, who proceeded to burn paper money and perform a shamanistic dance on behalf of Kuan-ko in the summerhouse.

Hsi-men Ch'ing was up at the fifth watch to send Lai-pao and Hsia Shou on their way, after which he and Judicial Commissioner Hsia were preoccupied with going to Tung-p'ing prefecture to get news from Prefect Hu Shih-wen on whether or not Miao Ch'ing had been arrested.

When Yüeh-niang heard Dame Liu say that the child had been subjected to a fright along the road, she expressed resentment at the wet nurse, Ju-i, saying, "You didn't look after the child carefully enough, but must have allowed him to become frightened in the sedan chair along the way. Otherwise, why should he have taken ill this way?"

"I had him inside the sedan chair, wrapped up tightly in a quilt," protested Ju-i. "And he was not jounced about. When you sent Hua-t'ung back to accompany my sedan chair, he was perfectly all right, and I held him as he slept. It was only after we had entered the city, and were almost at the door of the house, that I felt a cold shiver go up his spine. Then, when we got home, he rejected his milk and started to cry."

Let us put aside for the moment the events in the household as they burnt paper money and invoked the gods on behalf of the child.

To resume our story, Lai-pao and Hsia Shou hastened on their way and in only six days found themselves in the Eastern Capital, where they went to the grand preceptor's mansion, gained access to the majordomo Chai Ch'ien, and completed the process of turning over the gifts proffered by their two households.

When Chai Ch'ien had read Hsi-men Ch'ing's letter, he said, "Censor Tseng's bill of impeachment has not yet been delivered, so you had better stick around for a few days. At present, the situation here is that His Honor has just submitted a memorial laying out proposals with regard to seven matters, but the imperial rescript in response to it has not yet come down. You might as well wait until this document comes down. After that, when Censor Tseng's memorial arrives, I'll be able to speak to him about it, and get him to issue a verbal notation in the Grand Secretariat, ordering that it be:

Directed to the attention of the appropriate board.[30]

On my part, I'll then send someone with my card, instructing the minister of war, Yü Shen,[31] to suppress the memorial so that it is not resubmitted. Your master can relax. I guarantee that nothing will ever come of it."

Thereupon, after the two men had been entertained with food and drink, they returned to their inn to rest and await further developments.

One day, the imperial rescript approving the memorial laying out proposals with regard to seven matters that had been submitted by Grand Preceptor Ts'ai Ching duly came down. Lai-pao prevailed upon one of the gatekeepers at the grand preceptor's mansion to copy the relevant material from the government gazette so that he could take it home and show it to Hsi-men Ch'ing. What seven matters did this memorial actually propose the implementation of?

Memorial Submitted by Ts'ai Ching, Grand Academician of the Hall for Veneration of Governance, Minister of Personnel, and Duke of Lu

In Re: The Exposition of His Ignorant Views, the Realization of His Modest Hopes, the Recruitment of Human Talent, the Achievement of Effective Results, the Amplification of Fiscal Resources, the Amelioration of the People's Condition, and the Strengthening of Your Majesty's Sage Administration

Proposal number one:[32] The abolition of the system of recruiting scholars by examination, replacing it by allowing local schools to recommend candidates for bureaucratic appointment.

I venture to observe that the deterioration of cultural standards and the decay of public morals[33] are all due to the failure of the existing system of recruiting scholars to select candidates of genuine talent, with the result that cultural standards lack anything on which to rely. The *Book of Documents* says, "Heaven in giving birth to the people, made for them rulers, and made for them instructors."[34] In the Han dynasty candidates were recommended for being filial and incorrupt. The T'ang dynasty established government schools. It was our dynasty that first established a system which combined examination and recommendation, but due to bias and corruption in its administration the candidates selected lack genuine talent, and the people are unable to rely upon their guidance. Your Majesty seeks after talent both awake and asleep, and strives for good government both early and late. Now, good government depends upon the cultivation of worthy men, and nothing contributes more toward the cultivation of worthy men than schools. From now on, in recruiting scholars, we should adhere to the precedents of antiquity, and allow local schools to recommend candidates for bureaucratic appointment, while abolishing the system of having prefectures and districts send candidates to the capital for examination by the Ministry of Rites. Every year an examination administrator can be designated to examine the students in the Superior College of the National University, in a fashion similar to that employed by the Ministry of Rites.[35] A system should also be established for recruiting scholars renowned for eight kinds of virtuous conduct. These eight kinds of virtuous conduct are filiality, brotherly love, cordiality with agnatic kin, good relations with affinal kin, trustworthiness with friends, kindness toward neighbors, loyalty to the ruler, and judiciousness in differentiating the right from the profitable. Scholars who possess these virtues should be admitted to the Superior College of the National University without examination.[36]

Proposal number two: The abolition of the Financial Advisory Bureau.

I venture to observe that at the inception of the present reign, when the institutional structure was being determined, a Financial Advisory Bureau was set up under the Department of State Affairs,[37] the purpose of which was, on behalf of the ruler, to limit superfluous expenditure, and conserve the wealth of the people. Now, since Your Majesty acceded to the throne, you have neither valued exotic products from afar, nor overtaxed the resources of your subjects, but have set a personal example of frugality[38] in supplying your own needs. As a result, the empire is without customs that cannot be corrected, or expenses that cannot be reduced, while those in authority devote themselves to accomplishing the reformation of morals, and establishing the inviolability of the prohibitions, being neither lax in the beginning nor negligent in the end. The government is flourishing, morals are honest, and the state of the realm is characterized by the words abundance, prosperity, contentment, and greatness.[39] That being the case, what need is there for a Financial Advisory Bureau. Let it be completely abolished.[40]

Proposal number three: The reform of the salt voucher system.

I venture to observe that the salt voucher system is a means of raising tax revenue for the state in order to supply the needs of border defense. At the present time, would it not be appropriate for Your Majesty to restore the salt administration system of your ancestors by ordering that the merchants who have received old salt vouchers in return for delivering grain and fodder to the Three Border Regions of Yün-chung, Shensi, and Shansi be required to exchange them for new salt vouchers from the southeastern Huai-Che region? The price of the new vouchers should be thirty percent of their face value in cash, with the remainder payable in old vouchers at seventy percent of their face value.[41] Now merchants should go to the salt production areas designated on the vouchers in order to take delivery of the salt, and then, as in the case of the tea voucher system, after undergoing official weighing and inspection of their consignments, pay the required duty, receive their duly authorized certificates, and then proceed, within the designated time limits, to the areas in which they trade in order to sell the salt. If they exceed the time limits, their salt should be subject to confiscation, and they should be required to purchase new certificates. If they try to sell more than their certificates entitle them to, they should be subject to the penalties for salt smugglers. If this proposal is enacted, the tax revenues of the state will be regularly enhanced, and the logistic needs of border defense will be met.[42]

Proposal number four: The standardization of the currency.

I venture to observe that currency is the blood and pulse of the state. It is essential that it circulate freely and not be subject to blockage. If it is subject to obstruction or blockage, so that it fails to circulate, how will the common people be able to cope, and on what will the tax revenues of the state depend? From the minting of "goose-eye" coins[43] in the latter days of the Chin dynasty[44] to the early years of the present reign, the coinage has been unacceptably heterogeneous, sometimes even being debased by adulteration with lead, iron, or tin. The residents along the border sell these coins to the barbarians, who melt them down in order to cast weapons, the harm resulting from which is not insignificant.[45] Would it not be appropriate to completely prohibit the circulation of these heterogeneous coins, and require them to be redeemed for the larger denomination coins that Your Majesty has minted during the Ch'ung-ning and Ta-kuan reign periods,[46] at an exchange ratio of ten to one, so that the common people will be supplied with a viable currency and the price of goods will not be subject to sudden inflation.[47]

Proposal number five: The reinstitution of the system of government sale and distributive purchase of grain in order to alleviate scarcity.[48]

I venture to observe that the government sale of grain at reduced prices is for the purpose of relieving the victims of famine. In recent years, whenever floods and droughts have succeeded each other, and the people have lacked sufficient food, Your Majesty has issued rescripts ordaining this method of relief. Recently, the vice-minister of the Ministry of Revenue, Han Lü,[49] has submitted a memorial requesting the reinstitution of this system, which has elicited imperial assent. It is recommended that each of the subprefectures and districts affected should establish community institutions to carry out this system of government sale of grain at a reduced price and purchase of grain before it is harvested. The security groups within each ward, the wards within each village, and the villages within each township should promote the establishment of these community institutions. The households of each township should be divided into three categories, upper, middle, and lower, with the upper households required to contribute a quota of grain, the middle households half as much, and the lower households entitled to receive an appropriate allotment. The amount of money advanced to farmers for specified quantities of grain prior to the harvest is what is referred to as distributive purchase. If this method is followed, a system for government acquisition and distribution of grain for the benefit of the people will be implemented, and Your Majesty will be able to augment Your benevolence at little cost. It only remains to authorize the relevant prefects and district magistrates to rigorously carry it out. The benefit to be derived from this policy is not insignificant.

Proposal number six: The promulgation of a rescript ordering the subprefectures and prefectures of the empire to exact a commutation tax in lieu of corvée labor.

I venture to observe that at the inception of the present reign, because the threat of foreign invasion had not yet been put to rest, conscript soldiers and able-bodied males were assembled in the capital in order to provide logistic transport and strengthen the defenses of the state. Now that we have enjoyed peace for an extended period,[50] and the people are content with their occupations, it would be appropriate to promulgate a rescript ordering the subprefectures and prefectures of the empire to exact an annual commutation tax in lieu of corvée labor, at the rate of thirty strings of cash per capita, and transmit the proceeds to the capital in order to defray the cost of provisioning the border regions. By so doing we would achieve two ends with a single action,[51] and thus somewhat relieve the demands on the people's strength.[52]

Proposal number seven: The establishment of a Supervisorate of Palace Transport.

I venture to observe that since Your Majesty acceded to the throne you have refused to accept the presentation of musicians, beauties, dogs, and horses. The flowers and rocks for which You have expressed appreciation are all products of the mountains and forests in which most people have no interest. It is simply due to the excessive zeal with which the authorities have sought them out for presentation to the throne that the populace has been disturbed, which has injured the reputation of Your sage administration. If Your Majesty sees fit to curtail these excesses, it is proposed that a Supervisorate of Palace Transport be established, the expenses of which would all be defrayed out of the Palace Treasury, so that designated officials could be dispatched to obtain the desired products without disturbing the people of the subprefectures and prefectures.[53]

An imperial decision with regard to these matters is hereby humbly requested.

The imperial rescript elicited by this memorial read as follows:

Your proposals are highly relevant to the problems of the times, and serve both to augment Our feeling of delight, and demonstrate your penchant for loyal counsel. Let them all be enacted as proposed, and directed to the attention of the appropriate board.

Lai-pao had a copy made of the relevant material from the government gazette, after which, when Majordomo Chai Ch'ien had written a reply to Hsi-men Ch'ing's letter, and provided them with five taels of silver for their traveling expenses, he and Hsia Shou took to the road and headed back toward

Ch'ing-ho district. When they arrived there in due course, Hsi-men Ch'ing was at home, where he was:

Unable to get the matter off his mind,

while Judicial Commissioner Hsia had been sending someone over twice a day to inquire after the news. As soon as Hsi-men Ch'ing learned that Lai-pao and his companion had arrived, he summoned them into the rear compound and interrogated them about the facts of the case.

Lai-pao gave him a complete report on the above-mentioned events, saying, "When we saw Master Chai Ch'ien in the ministerial mansion, after reading your letter, he said, 'This affair should not be a problem. You can tell your master to relax. Right now, the regional investigating censor's term of office has already expired, and a new investigating censor has been appointed. And moreover, his bill of impeachment has not yet arrived in the capital. When his memorial arrives, I'll mention it to His Honor, and, no matter how serious the charges it contains may be, he'll merely issue a notation directing that it be:

Directed to the attention of the appropriate board.

His Honor can then send someone with his card instructing the minister of war, Yü Shen, to file the memorial without resubmitting it. In that case, even if he should have the ability to breach the gates of Heaven, it would be to no avail.'"

Only after hearing this report was Hsi-men Ch'ing's anxiety relieved.

He then went on to ask, "How did it happen that his memorial had not yet been delivered?' "

"When we left," Lai-pao explained, "we traveled on horseback by day and night and succeeded in getting to the capital in only five days. It's not surprising that we got there first. On starting back, we encountered a group of mounted couriers, with jangling bells, one of whom was carrying a yellow dispatch case on his back, with a pair of pheasant tails stuck in it, as well as two serrated pennants. No doubt it was the sealed text of the memorial from the office of the regional investigating censor that was only then arriving."

"If his memorial was that late in getting there," said Hsi-men Ch'ing, "everything ought to be all right. I was afraid we might not have acted in time."

"You can relax, master," said Lai-pao. "I guarantee that nothing will ever come of it. But that is not the only thing I accomplished. I also learned of two other favorable developments that I can report to you."

"Really," said Hsi-men Ch'ing, "and what might they be?"

"His Honor the grand preceptor," said Lai-pao, "has recently submitted a memorial laying out proposals regarding seven matters, all of which have already been approved for enactment by imperial rescript. At present, His Honor's relative by marriage, the vice-minister of the Ministry of Revenue, Han Lü, has been authorized according to precedent to encourage salt production in the Three Border Regions of Yün-chung, Shensi, and Shansi by setting up

Lai-pao Passes the Mounted Courier Conveying the Impeachment

charity granaries in every prefecture, subprefecture, commandary, and district for the government sale of grain at reduced prices. Among the common people, the top rank of the upper grade households will be required to contribute a quota of grain to these granaries for which they will receive granary vouchers that may be exchanged for salt certificates which entitle the holder to take delivery of specified quantities of salt. The old vouchers may be exchanged for new vouchers at seventy percent of their face value plus thirty percent in cash. The thirty thousand taels worth of vouchers that you formerly received, in partnership with your kinsman, Ch'iao Hung, for delivering grain to the Kao-yang customs station⁵⁴ can be exchanged for thirty thousand taels worth of salt certificates, to be allocated by the Ministry of Revenue. You might as well take advantage of the fact that His Honor Ts'ai Yün has been appointed salt-control censor there to send someone to the designated salt production area and take delivery of the specified quantity of salt. It should turn out to be a highly profitable transaction."

When Hsi-men Ch'ing heard this, he said, "Is this information really true?"

"If you don't believe me," said Lai-pao, "I've got a copy of the relevant material from the government gazette right here."

Pulling it out of his letter case, he handed it to Hsi-men Ch'ing to read. Upon glancing over the extensive vocabulary of characters in the text, Hsi-men Ch'ing called Ch'en Ching-chi in from the front compound to read it out loud to him. Ch'en Ching-chi succeeded in reading part way through it before coming to a halt, stumped by several unfamiliar characters. Consequently, Shu-t'ung was called in to read it. Now Shu-t'ung, having gotten his start in life as a "gate-boy,"⁵⁵ was able to read it through, all the way to the end, as fluently as flowing water, without making a single mistake. The seven proposals contained in the memorial were those enumerated above.

When Hsi-men Ch'ing heard them, he was delighted. He went on to read Majordomo Chai Ch'ien's letter, from which he learned that their gifts had all been safely delivered, and that the principal graduate Ts'ai Yün, upon an audience with the emperor, had, indeed, been appointed salt-control censor of the Liang-Huai region. In his heart he felt:

Unable to contain his delight.

On the one hand, he sent Hsia Shou home with the injunction to, "Give your master the good news," while, on the other hand, he rewarded Lai-pao with five taels of silver, two bottles of wine, and a side of pork. After which, he went back to the master suite to rest. But no more of this.

Truly:

When a tree is tall it attracts the wind,⁵⁶
    and the wind damages the tree;
When a man's name becomes too prominent,
    his prominence will do him in.⁵⁷

There is a poem that testifies to this:

Success and failure, flourishing and decay,
  are controlled by fate;
Everything is determined by the year, month,
  day, and hour of birth.
Those who harbor ambition in their breasts
  may achieve their goals;
But those whose purses are devoid of money
  cannot depend on talent.[58]

If you want to know the outcome of these events,
Pray consult the story related in the following chapter.

Chapter 49

HSI-MEN CH'ING WELCOMES INVESTIGATING CENSOR SUNG CH'IAO-NIEN; IN THE TEMPLE OF ETERNAL FELICITY HE ENCOUNTERS AN INDIAN MONK

With relaxed temperament and relaxed bosom
  let the years go by;
People are dying and people are being born
  before your eyes.
Whether it be exalted or whether it be lowly,[1]
  submit to your fate;
Though it be long or though it be short,[2]
  do not repine.
Though you possess much or possess nothing,
  forgo your sighs;
Whether you be wealthy or whether you be poor
  is Heaven's decree.
Be content to accept your lifetime allotment
  of clothing and wages;
Even a single day of undisturbed leisure[3]
  is a day of immortality.[4]

THE STORY GOES that when Hsia Shou returned home and reported on his mission, Judicial Commissioner Hsia Yen-ling immediately came over to express his gratitude to Hsi-men Ch'ing, saying, "My colleague has done me:
        The favor of saving my life.[5]
Had I not been able to rely upon the powerful influence of your diffracted radiance, how could this affair ever have been brought to an end?"

"My colleague can relax," said Hsi-men Ch'ing with a smile. "I figure that you and I did not do anything inappropriate. Let the censor criticize our conduct however he likes. His Honor will have a clear understanding of the case."

He then ordered that a table be set up in the reception hall and entertained his visitor with a meal. They chatted and laughed together until evening before Hsia Yen-ling said goodbye and went home. The next day they both went to the yamen and conducted their business as usual. But no more of this.

To resume our story, when the regional inspecting censor Tseng Hsiao-hsü saw that his memorial of impeachment had been submitted without eliciting any result, he realized that the two officials had succeeded in putting in the fix, and his heart was filled with ire. Because there were so many points in the seven proposals submitted by Grand Preceptor Ts'ai Ching that he deemed to be:

Either illegitimate or wrongheaded;

and because all of them were:

Injurious to those below while benefiting those above;[6]

when he returned to the capital for an audience in order to report on his assignment, he submitted a memorial in which he argued forcefully as follows:

The wealth of the empire should be allowed to circulate freely. To seize the economic resources of the people and accumulate them in the capital is not, I fear, the way to obtain a just administration.[7] The proposed system of government sale and distributive purchase of the people's grain should not be instituted. The requirement that the coins currently in circulation be redeemed for larger denomination coins at an exchange ratio of ten to one should not be implemented. The salt voucher system should not be repeatedly changed. I have heard it said that if the people's resources are exhausted, who will there be to protect the country for You?[8]

Ts'ai Ching was enraged by this and submitted a memorial to Emperor Hui-tsung in which he accused Tseng Hsiao-hsü of "giving vent to slanderous words, and interfering with national affairs."

At this juncture, Tseng Hsiao-hsü was turned over to the Ministry of Personnel for investigation, and subsequently demoted to the position of prefect of Ch'ing-chou in Shensi. The regional investigating censor of Shensi at the time was Sung Sheng-ch'ung,[9] who was the elder brother of Ts'ai Yu's wife. Ts'ai Ching secretly suborned him into traducing Tseng Hsiao-hsü for an alleged private transgression, as a result of which his servants were arrested and:

Tortured into giving evidence to substantiate the case.[10]

Ts'ai Ching consequently succeeded in having him removed from office and:

Banished to the southern extremity of the country,

in order to accomplish his revenge. But this is a subsequent event; having mentioned it, we will say no more about it.

To resume our story, Hsi-men Ch'ing, back at home, had already entrusted his granary vouchers to Han Tao-kuo, along with Ch'iao Hung's nephew, Ts'ui Pen, and sent them to report to the office of Vice-Minister Han Lü of the Ministry of Revenue at the Kao-yang customs station, in order to have them properly registered.

Meanwhile, he kept Lai-pao at home to take charge of ordering the provisions for an elaborate feast and then deputed him to ascertain when the salt-control censor Ts'ai Yün's boat would arrive in the vicinity.

One day Lai-pao learned that Ts'ai Yün's boat had left the capital at the same time as that of the new regional investigating censor, Sung Ch'iao-nien,[11] and that they were about to arrive in the neighborhood of Tung-ch'ang prefecture. When he sent someone home to report this news, Hsi-men Ch'ing, together with Hsia Yen-ling, set out to meet them, while keeping the magistrates of the various prefectures, subprefectures, and districts, and the officers of the various guards, who had all gotten their attendants, men and horses, together for the same purpose, as completely in the dark as if they had been:

Locked tight in an iron bucket.

Lai-pao paid an advance visit to Salt-Control Censor Ts'ai Yün's boat when it arrived at Tung-ch'ang prefecture and delivered a gift for the road from his master. It was only after this that Hsi-men Ch'ing and Hsia Yen-ling came out some fifty li beyond the suburbs to meet them at the port on the New Canal, at a place called Pai-chia Ts'un, or Hundred Family Village. They first went aboard Ts'ai Yün's boat to pay their respects, and to communicate the fact that they wished to extend an invitation to Sung Ch'iao-nien as well.

"I understand," responded Salt-Control Censor Ts'ai Yün. "You can be sure that he will accompany me on a visit to your mansion."

It was only then that the presiding magistrate of Tung-p'ing prefecture, Hu Shih-wen, together with the regional officials from all the subprefectures and districts in his jurisdiction, the officers of the various guards, the docket officers and government students, the Buddhist and Taoist authorities and Yin-yang masters, with their respective curricula vitae in hand, arrayed themselves in attendance to receive the new regional investigating censor. Commandant Chou Hsiu of the Regional Military Command, Military Director-in-Chief Ching Chung, and Militia Commander Chang Kuan, in command of contingents of men and horse, dressed in armor and carrying weapons, cleared the way so effectively that even chickens and dogs stayed out of sight, as they escorted Sung Ch'iao-nien, to the music of drums and wind instruments, into the office of the regional investigating censor in Tung-ch'ang prefecture. After all the attending officials had been introduced and given the chance to hand in their documents, the newly arrived censor was finally allowed to rest for the night.

The next day, who should appear but the gatekeeper, who announced that His Honor, the salt-control censor, Ts'ai Yün had come to pay him a visit. Sung Ch'iao-nien hurriedly ordered that the cases he had been examining be put away, while he straightened his headgear and came out to meet his visitor. When the two of them had finished exchanging amenities, they sat down in the positions of guest and host.

A little later, after tea had been served, Sung Ch'iao-nien asked, "Since my fellow graduate must make the deadline for reporting to his new post, when are you going to set out?"

"I plan to stay another day or two," Ts'ai Yün replied.

Hsi-men Ch'ing Meets the Boat of the Salt-Control Censor

He then went on to say, "There is an acquaintance of mine, Battalion Commander Hsi-men Ch'ing, who resides in Ch'ing-ho district and belongs to one of the great lineages of that place. He is honest and scrupulous by nature, is one of those who are:
> Wealthy yet observant of the rites,[12]
and is also a protégé of His Honor the venerable Ts'ai Ching. Since I have a nodding acquaintance with him, and he has been good enough to come out to welcome me at a distance, I would like to pay a visit to his residence in order to pay my respects."

"Just who is this Battalion Commander Hsi-men Ch'ing?" asked Sung Ch'iao-nien.

"At present he is a battalion commander in the local guard and a judicial commissioner in the Ch'ing-ho office of the Provincial Surveillance Commission," replied Ts'ai Yün. "He is one of those who came to pay their respects to my fellow graduate yesterday."

Sung Ch'iao-nien ordered his attendants to fetch the curricula vitae that had been submitted to him the day before and, when he had located the names of Hsi-men Ch'ing and Hsia Yen-ling, said, "This must be the person who has some relationship with Chai Ch'ien, is it not?"

"That's the one," replied Ts'ai Yün. "Right now he is waiting outside and has asked me to accompany my fellow graduate in paying a visit to his place for a meal. But I don't know how my fellow graduate feels about it."

"I have only just arrived here," said Sung Ch'iao-nien. "It would hardly be appropriate for me to go."

"What is there to be afraid of?" said Ts'ai Yün. "It would be doing a favor to Chai Ch'ien for the two of us to visit him. What harm could it do?"

Thereupon, orders were given to prepare their sedan chairs, and the fact that the two of them were about to depart for this purpose was duly promulgated.

No sooner was Hsi-men Ch'ing apprised of this news than he set out for home, together with Lai-pao and Pen the Fourth, riding fast horses, in order to arrive there ahead of his guests, and have time to make the necessary preparations for the feast. A hill-shaped screen-wall and gaily decorated bowers were erected outside his front gate. Musicians from the two Music Offices were engaged to provide music, and a troupe of Hai-yen[13] actors, as well as a troupe of tumblers, were engaged to provide the entertainment.

It so happens that Regional Investigating Censor Sung Ch'iao-nien dismissed most of the men and horse in his entourage, only retaining several squads of soldiers bearing blue flags to clear the way, along with the officials and functionaries in his suite, and set out, together with Salt-Control Censor Ts'ai Yün, seated in two large palanquins, protected by double-tiered canopies, in order to pay a visit to Hsi-men Ch'ing's residence.

At the time, this had the effect of:

Dumbfounding Tung-p'ing prefecture,
While elevating Ch'ing-ho district.

Everyone said, "Even His Honor the regional investigating censor is sufficiently familiar with the Honorable Hsi-men Ch'ing to attend a banquet at
his residence."

Commandant Chou Hsiu, Director-in-Chief Ching Chung, and Militia
Commander Chang Kuan all felt compelled to put in an appearance by leading contingents of the men and horse under their respective commands to
station themselves at the mouths of the streets to left and right of the Hsi-men
residence in order to maintain order. Hsi-men Ch'ing, dressed in black and
attired in his official cap and girdle, came out a considerable distance to welcome his guests. On either side of the street, musicians struck up their drums
and stringed instruments as his visitors made their way to the main gate and
dismounted from their palanquins.

As they proceeded inside, Regional Investigating Censor Sung Ch'iao-nien
and Salt-Control Censor Ts'ai Yün were both garbed in robes of scarlet brocade, decorated with an embroidered *hsieh-chih*, a mythical one-horned goat
that was said to gore wrongdoers, black silk caps, black shoes, and official
girdles featuring plaques of "crane's crest red,"[14] and were accompanied by
attendants bearing two large flabella.

They saw before them a thirty-foot-wide reception hall, in which:

Speckled bamboo blinds were rolled high,[15] and
Brocaded standing screens were arrayed,

while in the place of honor there stood two fancy table settings, of a kind
intended as much for display as for eating, replete with:

High-stacked pyramids of square-shaped confectionery,
Ingot-shaped cakes, and cone-shaped piles of fruit,

all of them meticulously arranged.

The two officials, politely deferring to each other, entered the reception
hall in order to exchange amenities with Hsi-men Ch'ing. Salt-Control Censor Ts'ai Yün ordered his retainers to proffer:

The customary presentation gifts,

consisting of two bolts of Hu-chou silk, the collected literary works of a well-
known author, four bags of tender leaf tea, and an inkstone from Tuan-ch'i.[16]
Regional Investigating Censor Sung Ch'iao-nien merely presented a single
calling card on safflower red paper,[17] which read, "Your devoted servant Sung
Ch'iao-nien pays his respects."

Addressing himself to Hsi-men Ch'ing, he said, "Your pupil has long been
aware of your illustrious reputation but, having just arrived in this region, has
not yet had an opportunity to fully express the extent of his admiration. I really
ought not to impose upon you, but had it not been for my fellow graduate,
Ts'ai Yün, who invited me to join him in paying our respects, how could I
have been fortunate enough to gaze upon your distinguished countenance?"

This threw Hsi-men Ch'ing into such consternation that he knelt down to kowtow, saying, "Your servant is but an insignificant military official who is subject to your jurisdiction. The fact that, today, I have been fortunate enough to be the beneficiary of your disinterested attention, has had the effect of:
Shedding glory on my humble abode."[18]
Thereupon, he prostrated himself in order to pay his respects, exhibiting the utmost modesty in his courteous demeanor. Censor Sung Ch'iao-nien returned his salutation, and they exchanged the customary amenities.

At this point, Censor Ts'ai allowed Censor Sung to take the position of honor on the left, while he took that on the right, and Hsi-men Ch'ing obsequiously kept them company with lowered head. After tea had been served:
Classical melodies saturate the ears;[19]
Drums and music resound to the heavens,
as the musicians began to play. After Hsi-men Ch'ing had seen to the serving of the wine, and sat down to preside over the feast, the various courses were presented from below.

Words are inadequate to describe the scene:
Only the rarest delicacies are arrayed;[20]
The soup shows off its peach-red waves;
The wine overflows with golden ripples.[21]
Truly:
The singers and dancers display voice and color;
The tables, ten-foot square, are laden with food.[22]

Hsi-men Ch'ing was aware of the large number of attendants that had accompanied his visitors, so, for the retinues of each of the two sedan chairs, he set aside fifty bottles of wine, five hundred snacks, and a hundred catties of precooked pork, which were duly accepted and taken outside. The personal servants, secretaries, "gate-boys," etc. were separately entertained in an antechamber, but there is no need to describe this in detail. Suffice it to say that it cost Hsi-men Ch'ing all of a thousand taels of silver to put on the banquet that day.

This Regional Investigating Censor Sung Ch'iao-nien, being a native of Nan-ch'ang in Kiangsi province, was impatient by nature. Without having stayed very long, after listening to the performance of but a single scene from a hsi-wen drama, he got up to go. This threw Hsi-men Ch'ing into such consternation that he repeatedly insisted upon his remaining a while longer.

Censor Ts'ai Yün chimed in from the side, saying, "Since my fellow graduate has nothing else to do, you might as well stay for a while. What need is there to return in such haste?"

"My fellow graduate can stay if he likes," responded Censor Sung, "but I need to get back to the Investigation Bureau in order to take care of some public business."

Hsi-men Ch'ing promptly ordered his servants to pack up the contents of the two table settings, including the gold and silver utensils, in food boxes, making twenty carrier loads in all, and summoned the servitors of his visitors to take charge of them. Censor Sung Ch'iao-nien's lavish table setting consisted of two jugs of wine, two carcasses of mutton, two pairs of ornamental flowers fashioned out of gold filigree, two bolts of red satin, a set of gold salvers, two silver flagons, ten silver wine cups, two silver ewers with hinged lids, and a pair of ivory chopsticks. That of Censor Ts'ai Yün was the same. Lists of the contents of both table settings were duly presented.

Censor Sung Ch'iao-nien repeatedly demurred, saying, "How could your pupil presume to accept these things?"

Thereupon, he directed his gaze at Censor Ts'ai Yün, who said, "This falls within my fellow graduate's distinguished jurisdiction.

It is only natural,[23]

that he should accept. But how could I be worthy of such an honor?"

"It is but a paltry gift," said Hsi-men Ch'ing, "no more than something to enhance a drinking bout, that's all. Why be so standoffish?"

By the time the two officials had done with their demurrals the table settings had long since been carried out the gate. Only then did Censor Sung, seeing that there was no help for it, order his attendants to accept the list of gifts and express his thanks.

"Today," he said, "on the occasion of my first visit in order to make your acquaintance, I have not only put you to the trouble of providing a lavish entertainment, but have also accepted your magnanimous gifts.

What can I do to be worthy of such largess?[24]

It remains for me to find some way of repaying your generosity without fail."

Then, turning to Censor Ts'ai, he said, "My fellow graduate, stay a little longer if you like, but your pupil must announce his departure."

Then and there, he bade farewell and got up to go. Hsi-men Ch'ing expressed the wish to escort him for some distance, but Censor Sung would not allow it and, urgently pressing him to return, raised his hand in salute, got into his sedan chair, and went his way.

When Hsi-men Ch'ing had returned inside to keep Censor Ts'ai company, he urged his visitor to join him in divesting themselves of their official caps and girdles and invited him back to the summerhouse in the interior of the garden where they could be more relaxed. He then ordered that the musicians be dismissed, and that only the actors need remain. Hsi-men Ch'ing directed his servants to provide new table settings for them, and to set out appropriate delicacies and viands so they could drink wine together.

"Today," said Censor Ts'ai, "it was presumptuous of me to join my fellow graduate Sung Ch'iao-nien in paying you a visit. On top of which, you have bestowed these wine vessels from your abundant storehouse upon me.

What can I do to be worthy of such largess?"

"The paltry nature of these gifts is embarrassing," responded Hsi-men
Ch'ing.

"They are no more than tokens of my esteem."[25]

He then went on to ask, "What is His Excellency Sung Ch'iao-nien's courtesy name?"

"His courtesy name is Sung-yüan," replied Censor Ts'ai. "That is to say,
the sung of the expression sung-shu, or 'pine tree,' and the yüan of the expression yüan-ch'üan, or 'fountainhead.'"

He then went on to say, "Originally he repeatedly refused to come. It was
only after your pupil had extolled your surpassing virtue, and intimated that
you were acquainted with the venerable minister, that he finally agreed. He
is also aware that your household has some kind of marriage relationship with
that of Chai Ch'ien."

"I think it must be true," observed Hsi-men Ch'ing, "that Kinsman Chai
has spoken to him about me, but it appears that this gentleman, Sung Ch'iao-
nien, has a somewhat strange personality."

"Although he is, to be sure, a native of Kiangsi province," said Censor Ts'ai,
"there really isn't anything strange about him. It's simply that this was his first
meeting with you. It's not surprising that he should want to put on something
of a show."

When he had finished speaking, he laughed.

"It's getting rather late today," Hsi-men Ch'ing then said. "There's really
no reason for the venerable gentleman to return to his boat."

"Early tomorrow morning," said Censor Ts'ai, "I have to set sail on a long
journey."

"If you do not see fit to reject me," said Hsi-men Ch'ing, "why don't you
stay overnight in my humble abode? Tomorrow morning your pupil will undertake to see you off with an appropriate libation at the roadside pavilion ten
li outside of town."

"I have already benefited excessively from your generous regard." said Censor Ts'ai.

Then, turning to his retainers, he directed them, "All of you return outside
the city gate, and come back to get me first thing tomorrow morning."

The crowd of his retainers all assented and took themselves off, leaving
behind only two household servants to wait on him.

When Hsi-men Ch'ing saw that his guest's retainers had all departed, he
got up from his place at the table, summoned Tai-an, and proceeded to:

Whisper into his ear in a low voice,
thus and so, "Go right away into the licensed quarter, single out Tung Chiao-
erh and Han Chin-ch'uan by name, and have them delivered to the rear door
of the house by sedan chair, without letting anyone know what you are doing."

Tai-an, for his part, departed on his mission, while Hsi-men Ch'ing returned
to his place at the table, in order to keep Censor Ts'ai company while they

drank together, and listened to the singing of the troupe of Hai-yen actors who stood to one side and performed for their entertainment.

Hsi-men Ch'ing then asked his visitor, "Venerable Sir, how long were you able to remain at home before returning to the capital? And is your venerable mother still able to get around, and in good health?"

"My elderly mother, as it happens, is doing all right," said Censor Ts'ai. "As for your pupil's sojourn at home, the half year passed by swiftly before I knew it. But, upon my return to the capital for an audience with the emperor, who would have thought that I would be impeached by Ts'ao Ho,[26] as a result of which your pupil, along with fourteen of his fellow graduates who were serving in the Historiography Institute, were all simultaneously demoted to provincial offices. In my case, I was appointed to the Censorate, and, most recently, selected for the post of salt-control censor of the Liang-Huai region, while my fellow graduate, Sung Ch'iao-nien, was appointed to the position of regional investigating censor in your distinguished province. He is also a protégé of the venerable minister, Ts'ai Ching."

"At the present time," asked Hsi-men Ch'ing, "what post is the venerable gentleman, An Ch'en, occupying?"

"An Ch'en," responded Ts'ai Yün, "has already been promoted to the position of secretary in the Ministry of Works and has been sent to Ching-chou to expedite the delivery of imperial lumber. He is doing all right for himself."

When they had finished speaking, Hsi-men Ch'ing summoned the troupe of Hai-yen actors to come over and serve them with wine.

Censor Ts'ai instructed them, "Sing a song suite beginning with the tune 'Fisherman's Pride' for us."

The actors, standing beside them, clapped their hands to keep time and proceeded to sing to the tune "Fisherman's Pride":

Since our parting we are distant and there are no letters.
This ailment that causes no physical hurt or pain[27]
    is hard to get rid of.
Alas, in this desolate inn, who is there
    who knows me?
The message-bearing fish are submerged and
    the geese bring no letters.
As for that beauty from the three Isles of the Blest,
    who knows where she is to be found.
I yearn for her asleep and long for her in dreams.[28]
On whose behalf do I endure these feelings?
Listlessly, listlessly wasting away,
I am just like a willow catkin tossed in the breeze.
Who knows when we will ever be able
    to meet again?

To the tune "Black Silk Robe"

Before my eyes the yellow chrysanthemums have just bloomed.
I wonder why that T'ao Yüan-ming[29] of mine
    has not returned home.
It makes me gaze into the distance until
    my eyes are worn out.
Lover of mine, why can't you
    do me a good turn?
Ever since he left,
I've been beset by lovesickness,[30]
As confused as though drunk,
My tears continually flowing.
Who knows when we will ever be able
    to see each other again?

To the same tune

I love the peach blossoms that
    make up her face;
The bamboo shoots that form her
    ten slender fingers;[31]
I love the faint spring peaks of her eyebrows,
    like willows tangled in the mist;
I love the bright clarity of her pair of eyes,
    that remind me of autumn ripples;
The raven locks that adorn her temples;
The black silk filaments tied in a bun;
The pendant crescents of her sickle brows;
The sunset glow suffusing her countenance.
I can't help longing for her until my liver
    and intestines are sundered.

To the same tune

The drum on the battlements has begun to sound the watch.
I listen to the dying notes of the bugle[32] as it
    plays taps on the watchtower.
Banging on my bed and pounding my pillow[33]
    several thousand times;
I give vent to long sighs as well as short[34]
    on a myriad occasions.
My spirits are distraught;
My words are inarticulate;[35]

Forgetting to eat, neglecting to sleep,[36]
I lie down in my clothes as my tears flow.
All day long I remain in a stupor,
   too tired to do anything.

To the same tune

Only on your account, all the livelong day
   I am given over to longing;
While you are there, playing and laughing
   in pursuit of pleasure.
Whenever I happen to call it to mind,
   my thoughts are suspended;
Every time the subject comes up, I am
   only the more resentful.
My regard for you is as deep as the sea;
My feelings are as weighty as mountains.[37]
Our assignation was scarcely accidental;[38]
Separation is the hardest thing to bear.
As the saying goes, "The lotus root may be broken,
   but the threads remain connected."[39]

As they were singing, who should appear but Tai-an, who asked Hsi-men
Ch'ing to step aside for a word with him.

"I have summoned Tung Chiao-erh and Han Chin-ch'uan," Tai-an reported. "They came in through the back door and are sitting in Mother's room
at the moment."

"You'd better give orders that their sedan chairs be carried out of the way
somewhere," said Hsi-men Ch'ing.

"They've already been carried out of the way," said Tai-an.

Hsi-men Ch'ing then proceeded back to the master suite, where the two
singing girls stepped forward and kowtowed to him.

"I've invited the two of you here today," explained Hsi-men Ch'ing, "so
that you'll be available to wait upon His Honor Ts'ai Yün in the grotto underneath the artificial hill this evening. At present he holds the post of regional
inspector, so you can't afford to be remiss with him. If you do your best to
accommodate him, I'll reward the two of you independently of whatever he
may give you."

Han Chin-ch'uan laughed, saying, "There's no need for you to instruct us.
We'll know what to do."

Hsi-men Ch'ing then went on to say, with a wink, "He's one of those south-
erners, you know, who are enamored of the 'southern breeze.'[40] You mustn't
be squeamish with him."

"Mother, just listen to him!" exclaimed Tung Chiao-erh. "Father, you're just like:

> The ramshorn scallion that grows by the southern wall;
> The longer it stays there the hotter it gets.
> Since we've already kowtowed before the prince's palace;
> Would we refuse to drink the water from his well?"

Hsi-men Ch'ing laughed at this as he made his way back toward the front compound. Just as he arrived at the ceremonial gate that separated the compounds, whom should he encounter but Lai-pao and Ch'en Ching-chi, who were carrying a card to show to him.

Would we refuse to drink the water from his well?"
tion that you take advantage of the fact that His Honor Ts'ai Yün is at leisure here at the moment, to broach this matter with him. I fear that tomorrow when he's getting ready to go, he'll be too busy to consider it. I've gotten your son-in-law to write our two names down on the card here."

"You come along with me," said Hsi-men Ch'ing.

Lai-pao then followed him as far as the summerhouse, where he knelt down outside the latticework partition.

In the course of drinking with his guest, Hsi-men Ch'ing brought the subject up, saying, "There's a certain matter here that I'm reluctant to trouble you with."

"My dear Ssu-ch'üan,"[41] responded Censor Ts'ai, "what have you got in mind? Just tell me what you'd like me to do. Your pupil would not presume to reject your command."

"Last year," said Hsi-men Ch'ing, "in partnership with my kinsman Ch'iao Hung, we delivered a consignment of grain to the border, in return for which we were issued salt certificates that entitle us to take delivery of the specified quantity of salt at the seat of your distinguished jurisdiction in Yang-chou. All we are hoping for is that when our agents show up there, you will look upon the matter favorably, and allow them to take early delivery of the salt, as a token of your generous regard."

He then proceeded to proffer the card to him, and when Censor Ts'ai looked at it, he saw that it read, "The merchants Lai-pao and Ts'ui Pen, who hold previously issued salt certificates entitling them to thirty thousand taels worth of salt from the Liang-Huai region, request that upon presentation of the said certificates, they may take early delivery."

When Censor Ts'ai had perused it, he laughed, saying, "A thing like this is no big deal."

Hsi-men Ch'ing then called for Lai-pao to come inside and kneel down, instructing him, "Perform a kowtow to His Honor Ts'ai."

"After I get to Yang-chou," said Censor Ts'ai, "the two of you can come straight to the Investigation Bureau and ask to see me. I'll let you take delivery of your salt a month before any of the other merchants."

"Venerable Sir," said Hsi-men Ch'ing, "if you are considerate enough to let them have it ten days earlier than the rest, that will be sufficient."

Censor Ts'ai Yün proceeded to put the card in question into his sleeve, while Shu-t'ung served them with wine, and the actors continued with their song suite, to the tune "The Tiger Descends the Mountain":

As the Mid-autumn Festival draws near,
I realize that my feelings have turned sour.
All I can see is the moon in the window;
I do not see the return of my lover.
The dinning sound of pounding laundry bats
    resounds in my ears;
With strident cries, the northern geese
    return to the south.
How could these things fail to increase
    the sadness in my heart?
I anticipate that this lovesickness,
Will be the ruination of my youth.
After the dusk has fallen,
As the night watches recede,
Only after trimming the silver lamp
    am I able to sleep.

To the same tune

Originally, when we held hands together,
Standing side by side beneath the moon,
We swore to be as faithful as the hills and seas;
And made an oath before Heaven,
That whoever should break faith and forget favor[42]
    should revert apace to the Nine Springs.
How is it then that, all this time, news of you
    has been so inaccessible,
That all I can do is cast my lot in coins?
Neglecting to sleep, forgetting to eat,
Who is there to express concern for me?
After the dusk has fallen,
As the night watches recede,
Only after trimming the silver lamp
    am I able to sleep.

CODA

If azure Heaven is only willing to
    do me a good turn,

Send my lover back to my pillow side
    as soon as possible,[43]
So that this student will no longer
    have to sleep alone.

By the time they had finished singing it was lamplighting time, and Censor Ts'ai said, "I have put you to a great deal of trouble all day. I think we had better call a halt to the drinking."

Whereupon, he got up from his place at the table, and his attendants prepared to light him on his way.

"There's no need to light the lamps yet," said Hsi-men Ch'ing. May I invite you, Venerable Sir, to adjust your toilet in the interior."

Thereupon, he conducted his visitor on a tour of the garden. When they arrived back at the Kingfisher Pavilion, they found that:

    Speckled bamboo blinds were hanging low,
    Candles burned brightly in silver stands,[44]
and a complete new feast had already been laid out for them. In the interim, Hsi-men Ch'ing had arranged for his servants to provide the troupe of Hai-yen actors with food and wine, reward them for their services with two taels of silver, and send them on their way; and Shu-t'ung had cleared away the used utensils from the summerhouse and closed the postern gate.

What should they observe at this point but the two singing girls, resplendently dressed, waiting for them beneath the steps, who now came forward and;

    Like sprigs of blossoms swaying in the breeze,
kowtowed to them. Behold:

Graceful of figure, comely of countenance,
    garbed in golden threads,
Without even disturbing the fragrant dust,
    she descends the stairs.
When her time comes, the sprinkling water
    will moisten her silk skirt,
Just like the Goddess of Witches' Mountain
    returning from her rainmaking.

When Censor Ts'ai Yün caught sight of them:
    Though he wished to advance, he couldn't;
    Though he wished to retire, he was unable.[45]
"Ssu-ch'üan," he protested, "how can you show me such generous regard? I fear that it will never do."

Hsi-men Ch'ing laughed, saying, "How does this differ from the way in which, in former times, Hsieh An enjoyed himself in the Eastern Mountains?"[46]

"I fear that I do not measure up to the genius of Hsieh An," said Censor Ts'ai. "But you, Sir, do possess the discriminating taste of Wang Hsi-chih."[47]

Thereupon, he held hands with the two singing girls beneath the moon, looking for all the world like Liu Ch'en or Juan Chao upon their arrival in the T'ien-t'ai Mountains.[48] Upon entering the pavilion, and seeing that it contained all the cultural artifacts that he remembered from his previous visit, he asked for paper and writing brush that he might compose a memorial of the occasion.

Hsi-men Ch'ing directed Shu-t'ung to comply with his wishes, and he promptly supplied an inkstone from Tuan-ch'i, ground the ink until it was appropriately dark, and spread out a sheet of brocade notepaper before him.

Now this Censor Ts'ai Yün possessed the talent of a principal graduate, after all, so:

> Taking the writing brush in hand,[49]
> Without altering a single stroke,[50]
> Engendering characters like dragons and serpents,

under the lamplight, he:

> Dashed off a composition with a single flourish,[51]

producing a poem, which read:

> It has been more than half a year
>   since I visited your home;
> The cultured decor of your studio
>   is just the same as before.
> When the rain is over, Shu-t'ung
>   opens up the herb garden;
> As the breeze returns, immortals
>   pace among the flower beds.
> As we near a state of inebriation,
>   how swiftly the cups fly;
> When our poems are finally composed,
>   the clepsydra urges us on.
> Our impending separation only adds
>   another source of regret;
> Who knows when the day will come
>   that I visit you again?

When he had finished his composition, he had Shu-t'ung paste it on the wall in order to commemorate the occasion.

He then asked the two singing girls, "What are your names?"

"My surname is Tung," one of them replied, "and my given name is Chiao-erh. My companion's name is Han Chin-ch'uan."

"Do the two of you have courtesy names?" Censor Ts'ai went on to ask.

"We are but unknown singing girls," replied Tung Chiao-erh. "Where would we get courtesy names from?"

"There is no call for you two to be so modest," said Censor Ts'ai.

Only after he had enquired repeatedly did Han Chin-ch'uan respond, "My courtesy name is Yü-ch'ing, or Jade Darling."

"And my humble courtesy name is Wei-hsien, or Crape Myrtle Fairy," said Tung Chiao-erh.

When Censor Ts'ai heard the words "Crape Myrtle Fairy," his heart was filled with delight, and he consequently devoted special attention to her. After Shu-t'ung had been ordered to bring in a table with an inlaid chessboard on its surface, they laid out the pieces, and Censor Ts'ai played a game with Tung Chiao-erh, while Hsi-men Ch'ing kept them company, and Han Chin-ch'uan stood to one side, holding a flagon with which to serve them with wine.

Clapping his hands to keep time, Shu-t'ung sang a song for them, to the tune "Jade Lotus Blossoms":

The east wind sends willow catkins flying;
By jade flagstones orchid shoots are small.
The resplendence of the spring scene would tax
    the skill of an artist to depict.
Over the top of the wall, red-rouged beauties[52]
    are seen to smile.
Once finished with their swinging,[53] they are
    drenched in perfumed sweat.
In pursuit of fragrant flowers,
One does not repine over the distance.
Behold, at last I see the banner of the wine shop
    fluttering beyond the apricot blossoms.

By the time he finished singing, Censor Ts'ai had won the chess game with Tung Chiao-erh. After drinking a cup of wine as a forfeit, she toasted Censor Ts'ai in turn. Han Chin-ch'uan, for her part, replenished Hsi-men Ch'ing's wine, and he drank a cup to keep them company. Shu-t'ung then continued to sing, to the same tune:

The wind turns over the trailing plantain fronds;
The rain scatters the pearls on the lotus leaves.
I see a beauty with spit curls like cicada wings
    adorning her temples.
Her beige silk fan coquettishly half conceals her
    lotus blossom cheeks;
The art with which her variegated sleeves flutter
    rivals that of Hsiao-man.[54]

Her eyes are autumn ripples.
It is hard for us both to cope with our emotions;
Which makes me so despondent and lonely that
    tears lie crisscross on my face.

When they had finished their drinks, the two of them proceeded to play
another game, and this time Tung Chiao-erh was the winner, whereupon she
promptly proffered a cup of wine to Censor Ts'ai. Hsi-men Ch'ing, in his
position on the sidelines, again drank a cup of wine to keep him company.
Shu-t'ung then continued to sing, to the same tune:

Yellow chrysanthemums are blooming everywhere;[55]
As other varieties of verdure begin to wither.
Little crickets chirrup incessantly
    on the empty steps.
The Herd Boy, as always, is at his post
    night after night;
Why is it, then, that the Weaving Maid
    is not to be seen?[56]
Lovesick as I am,
What am I to make of my confused dreams?
On her account, my tears have soaked the memento
    of her phoenix-toed shoes.

When he finished the song, Censor Ts'ai said, "Ssu-ch'üan, it's getting
late, and:
        I cannot handle the effects of the drink."[57]
Thereupon, he walked outside and stood under the flowering trees. At the
time, it was around the middle of the fourth lunar month, and the moon had
just arisen.

"Venerable Sir," said Hsi-men Ch'ing, "it's early yet, and Han Chin-ch'uan
has not yet had a chance to offer you a cup of wine."

"That's true," said Censor Ts'ai. "Call her out, and I'll drink a cup while
standing under the flowers here."

Thereupon, Han Chin-ch'uan took a large gold goblet in the shape of a
peach, filled it with wine, and proffered it to him with her slender hands,
while Tung Chiao-erh stood by his side and offered him some fruit. Shu-
t'ung, clapping his hands to keep time, then sang a fourth song to the
same tune:

The snow falls like scattered pear blossoms;
The wings of roving bees are no longer seen.
In front of the small window, magpies
    perch on withered branches.

It is disheartening to learn of the advent of those who
  brave the snow to look for plum blossoms.
One suddenly becomes aware that the bronze tanks of the
  clepsydra are marking extended intervals.
These heartbreaking events,
Make me think of the sadness of separation.
On her account, I cannot set aside the writing brush
  with which I compose love letters.

When Censor Ts'ai had finished his drink, he poured out a cup to reward
Han Chin-ch'üan and then begged off, saying, "Ssu-ch'üan, the wine is too
much for me today. Have your esteemed servant take it away."

Thereupon, taking Hsi-men Ch'ing by the hand, he said, "Worthy Sir, your:
  Lavish hospitality and surpassing virtue,
are:
  Forever suspended in this heart of mine.[58]
If you were not:
  Bone and flesh of this culture of ours,[59]
  How could you ever have come thus far?[60]
As for that loan that you formerly made to me:
  It is a conspicuous burden on my mind.[61]
and I have already said as much to Chai Ch'ien in the capital. If, at some
future date, I should:
  Advance so much as an inch in my career,
I could hardly fail to repay your surpassing virtue."

"Venerable Sir," said Hsi-men Ch'ing:
  "How can you say such a thing?[62]
  You need not give it a thought."

When Han Chin-ch'üan saw the way that Ts'ai Yün was holding hands with
Tung Chiao-erh, she understood the situation and tactfully withdrew to the
rear compound.

Upon her arrival in the master suite, Yüeh-niang asked her, "Why have you
come back here instead of spending the night with him?"

"He chose to keep Tung Chiao-erh with him," Han Chin-ch'üan said with
a laugh. "If I had not come back here, what would I have done with myself
over there?"

After some time, Hsi-men Ch'ing also said good night and returned to the
front compound, where he summoned Lai-hsing and instructed him, saying,
"Early tomorrow morning, at the fifth watch, prepare food boxes with the
requisite wine and rice, snacks and other refreshments, and hire a chef to
accompany them to the Temple of Eternal Felicity outside the South Gate,
where I plan to provide a farewell collation for His Honor Ts'ai Yün. Also
engage the services of two boy actors, and see that nothing goes amiss."

"Tomorrow is the eve of the Second Lady's birthday," said Lai-hsing, "and there won't be anyone here at home to take care of things."

"Have Ch'i-t'ung stay behind to buy the necessary provisions," said Hsi-men Ch'ing, "and engage a cook to prepare things on the big stove in the rear compound."

In no time at all, Shu-t'ung and Tai-an had cleared away the used utensils and procured a pot of high-grade tea, which they took into the garden for Ts'ai Yün to rinse out his mouth with. In the studio within the Kingfisher Pavilion, quilts and pillows were all properly laid out on the bed. Censor Ts'ai noticed that Tung Chiao-erh was holding a folding fan made of speckled bamboo with a gold-flecked surface, on which there was depicted in ink-wash a variety of aquatic orchid beside the flowing water of a level stream.

"Might I trouble Your Honor," said Tung Chiao-erh, "to do me the favor of writing a poem on the face of this fan for me?"

"I don't have any subject at hand," said Censor Ts'ai, "so I'll allude to your courtesy name, Crape Myrtle Fairy."

Thereupon, under the lamplight, he was inspired to take up a writing brush, with which he indited a quatrain on the fan.

> The little courtyard with its empty portico[63]
>   is silent and undisturbed;
> Above the garden pool the moon has arisen,
>   bathing the window gauze.
> Having encountered each other by chance,[64]
>   the time is not yet too late;
> The Secretary of the Hall of Purple Myrtle
>   confronts the myrtle blossom.[65]

When he had finished writing out the poem, Tung Chiao-erh hastily kow-towed to him in gratitude, and the two of them, after performing the necessary preliminaries:

> Got into bed and prepared to sleep.

Shu-t'ung and Tai-an, together with Ts'ai Yün's personal servants, retired to sleep together in the parlor. Of the events of that evening there is no more to tell.

Early the next morning, Censor Ts'ai presented Tung Chiao-erh with a single tael of silver, sealed up in an ostentatious packet of red paper.

When she returned to the rear compound and showed it to Hsi-men Ch'ing, he laughed, saying, "That's the typical behavior of a civil official. Where would he come up with the big money to reward you more appropri-ately? This is the very best you could hope for if you were to consult your fortune with the bamboo sticks."[66]

He then went on to instruct Yüeh-niang to give each of the singing girls five mace of silver, and see that they were sent on their way through the rear door.

Shu-t'ung, meanwhile, fetched some water for Ts'ai Yün to wash his face with, and helped him perform his toilet and put on his clothes, after which, Hsi-men Ch'ing came out to the front compound to keep him company as he ate his breakfast congee in the reception hall. By this time, his subordinates were already standing by with his sedan chair and horse, ready to accompany him on his way. As he took his leave of Hsi-men Ch'ing, he thanked him again and again.

Hsi-men Ch'ing responded by saying, "As for that matter that your pupil mentioned to you yesterday, after you arrive at your post, Venerable Sir, were I to send you a letter about it, if you should see fit to pay it some attention, I would be much indebted to you."

"Worthy Sir," said Censor Ts'ai, "even if you should not deign to honor me with an elegant epistle, if your esteemed servant were to show up with the merest note:

There is nothing I would not do on your behalf."[67]

When they had finished speaking, the two of them mounted their horses together and, followed by their attendants, proceeded to the Temple of Eternal Felicity outside the city, where Hsi-men Ch'ing had borrowed the abbot's quarters in which to provide a farewell libation before seeing off his visitor. Lai-hsing and the chef that he had hired for the occasion had long since made all the necessary preparations, and the two boy actors, Li Ming and Wu Hui, played and sang for their entertainment. After a few cups of wine had been consumed, without sitting very long, Censor Ts'ai got up to go. His chair-bearers, horse, and palanquin were waiting for him outside the temple gate.

As Ts'ai Yün was about to set out, Hsi-men Ch'ing brought up the matter of Miao Ch'ing, saying, "He is an acquaintance of your pupil's. Because he was falsely implicated in a case adjudicated by the former regional investigating censor, Tseng Hsiao-hsü, a warrant for his arrest has been sent to Yang-chou, and the final disposition of the litigation awaits his apprehension. Since this matter has already been adequately dealt with, if you should happen to run into His Honor Sung Ch'iao-nien, I hope that you will:

Put in a word on his behalf,[68]

for which we would both be very grateful."

"That's no problem," said Censor Ts'ai. "When I see my fellow graduate Sung Ch'iao-nien, I'll mention it to him, and, even if he has been taken into custody, he'll be released. That's all there is to it."

Hsi-men Ch'ing once again expressed his gratification with a bow.

Gentle reader take note: Later on, while Censor Sung Ch'iao-nien was on his way to Chi-nan to take up his post, he happened to be in conference with Censor Ts'ai Yün aboard his boat on the canal, when the arresting officers brought Miao Ch'ing before him. "This has to do with a case adjudicated by His Honor Tseng Hsiao-hsü," said Censor Ts'ai, "so why should you concern yourself with it?" As a result, he was released and allowed to return home. At

the same time, a directive was sent down to Tung-p'ing prefecture, ordaining
that the two boatmen should be:

Executed without waiting for the customary season,[69]

and that An-t'ung should be set at liberty. Truly:

Though men may plan to do thus and so:
Heaven's principles may yet deny them.

There is a poem, designed to explicate the difficulties that human feelings
make for people, which goes as follows:

Justice and human feelings are
    frequently in conflict;
Human feelings and justice[70] are
    difficult to reconcile.
If one insists upon doing justice,
    human feelings will suffer;
If one gives way to human feelings,
    justice will lose out.

The prefect of Tung-P'ing prefecture, Hu Shih-wen, had already been suborned by Hsi-men Ch'ing and Hsia Yen-ling in connection with this case,
so there was nothing he would not do on their behalf. I would say more about
it, but this is a subsequent event.

That day, Hsi-men Ch'ing wanted to see his visitor off as far as his boat,
but Censor Ts'ai would not permit it, saying, "Worthy Sir, there is no need
for you to escort me for such a distance. I will simply bid you farewell here
and now."

"Pray take care of yourself," said Hsi-men Ch'ing, "and permit me to ask
after you by means of my paltry servant in the future."

When they had finished speaking, Censor Ts'ai got into his sedan chair
and departed.

Hsi-men Ch'ing returned to the abbot's quarters and took a seat. The abbot
then came in to offer him some tea. He wore a Vairocana hat on his head
and was attired in a cassock. A young novice brought in the cups of tea in
their raised saucers, and after presenting them withdrew. The abbot saluted
his visitor by pressing his palms together in front of his chest and bowing to
him in the Buddhist fashion. Hsi-men Ch'ing returned the compliment by
saluting him in return.

Noticing that:

His snowy eyebrows were glistening white,

he asked the abbot, "How old are you?"

"This humble monk is seventy-four," the abbot replied.

"You're still looking remarkably healthy," exclaimed Hsi-men Ch'ing.

"And what is your religious name?" he went on to ask.

"This humble monk's religious name is Tao-chien,[71] or Stand Hard," replied the abbot.

"And how many disciples do you have?"

"I have only two young acolytes," the abbot replied. "But there are thirty-odd monks in this temple."

"This temple of yours," said Hsi-men Ch'ing, "is certainly capacious enough. But it is sadly in need of repair."

"There is no need for me to dissemble," said the abbot. "This temple was originally erected by His Honor Chou Hsiu. But the monastic treasury does not contain enough in the way of money or grain to maintain it. So it is in danger of falling down."

"So this is the family temple of His Honor Chou Hsiu of the Regional Military Command," said Hsi-men Ch'ing. "I noticed that his country estate is not far from here. This shouldn't be a problem. If you petition His Honor for permission to prepare a subscription list, and circulate it elsewhere in the usual way, when you come to my place, I will undertake to contribute something toward its upkeep."

Tao-chien promptly pressed his palms together and expressed his gratitude by saluting him in the Buddhist manner.

Hsi-men Ch'ing ordered Tai-an to extract a single tael of silver from his letter case, with which he thanked the abbot, saying, I've put you to a good deal of trouble here today."

"This humble monk did not know that you were coming," said Tao-chien. "So I was unable to prepare a vegetarian repast."

"I would like to go inside in order to adjust my toilet," said Hsi-men Ch'ing.

Tao-chien promptly called for a young novice to show him the way to a side door.

When Hsi-men Ch'ing had finished adjusting his toilet, he observed that behind the abbot's quarters there was a large thirty-foot-wide meditation hall, occupied by a considerable number of itinerant monks, who were beating on wooden fish and reciting sutras. Hsi-men Ch'ing:

> Without premeditation or forethought,

strolled inside to take a look and noticed a monk whose physique was out of the ordinary, and whose appearance was grotesque. His leopard-shaped head with its sunken eyes was the color of purple liver and was crowned with a cock's comb-like chaplet. He wore a long flesh-colored gown. The whiskers beneath his chin bristled unevenly, and he had a shiny annular ridge around the base of his head. Truly, he was:

> An authentic arhat, of the most
>   extraordinary aspect;[72]
> A one-eyed dragon, undivested of
>   his fiery temperament.

In the Temple of Eternal Felicity He Meets an Indian Monk

He had fallen into a trance on his meditation couch, so that his head was drooping, his neck had subsided into his upper trunk, and a trickle of jade-white mucus was dribbling from his nostrils.

When Hsi-men Ch'ing had finished observing him:

From his mouth no word was uttered, but
In his heart he thought to himself,

"This priest must surely be a monk of high attainments, possessed of extraordinary powers. If not, how could he exhibit such an unusual appearance? I might as well wake him up and ascertain the truth of the matter."

Thereupon, raising his voice, he called out to the monk, "Where do you come from, and what temple are you attached to, that you have arrived here in the course of your peregrinations?"

The first time he called out to him, there was no response; and the second time, he also failed to reply; but the third time, behold, that monk on his meditation couch jerked himself erect, gave his torso a stretch, opened his one good eye, sprang up from his relaxed position, nodded his head toward Hsi-men Ch'ing, and said, in a coarse voice, "Why are you interrogating me?

I neither alter my given name when abroad,
Nor change my surname when at home.

I am a foreign monk from the land of India in the Western Regions, who has descended into the mundane world from Cold Shivers Temple, beneath Navel Waist Peak, in Dense Sperm Forest.[73] Having come here in the course of my peregrinations I plan to distribute medicine in order to cure people. In calling upon me this way, sir, what have you got to say?"

"Since you plan to distribute medicine in order to cure people," said Hsi-men Ch'ing, "were I to ask you for some restorative medication, might you have such a thing, or not?"

"I do! I do!" exclaimed the monk.

Hsi-men Ch'ing then went on to ask, "Were I to invite you to my home, would you come, or not?"

"I'll come! I'll come!" asseverated the monk.

"Since you say you'll come," said Hsi-men Ch'ing, "we might as well start out at once."

The Indian monk straightened himself erect, picked up his iron staff from the head of the bed to support himself with, hitched the leather pouch containing his two medicine gourds onto his back, stepped down from the meditation hall, and strode outside.

Hsi-men Ch'ing directed Tai-an, saying, "Hire two donkeys, and escort His Reverence back home right away. You can wait for me there. I'll be along directly."

"There's no need to go to all that trouble, sir," said the Indian Monk. "You can mount your horse and go right ahead. Even without the aid of a donkey, I guarantee I'll be there before you."

"He certainly must be a monk of high attainments, possessed of extraordinary powers," said Hsi-men Ch'ing to himself. "If not, how could he talk so bluntly?"

Fearing that he might get away, he ordered Tai-an, "Make sure, whatever you do, not to let him out of your sight."

Thereupon, he took his leave of the abbot, mounted his horse, and, accompanied by his retinue, headed straight into the city on his way home.

That day was the seventeenth day of the fourth month, which happened to be Wang Liu-erh's birthday. It was also the eve of Li Chiao-erh's birthday, and some female guests had been invited to the house to celebrate it. That afternoon, Wang Liu-erh, having no one else at hand to send, deputed her younger brother, Wang Ching, to come and invite Hsi-men Ch'ing to visit her. She instructed him that when he got to the gate of the house, he should seek out Tai-an, and no one else, in order to deliver her message.

When he failed to find Tai-an at the gate, he decided to stand and wait, and he remained standing there for a good two hours. At this juncture, Wu Yüeh-niang and Li Chiao-erh came out to see off Auntie Li the Third as she got into her sedan chair. When they noticed a fourteen- or fifteen-year-old boy, with his hair done up in a topknot, standing there, they asked who he was.

The young man, unthinkingly, came up to them and kowtowed to Yüeh-niang, saying, "I'm from the Han household, looking for Brother An, to have a word with him."

"What Brother An is that?" asked Yüeh-niang.

P'ing-an, who was standing to one side, was afraid that Yüeh-niang would realize that he came with a message from Wang Liu-erh if he said anything amiss, so he stepped forward and pulled him aside, explaining to Yüeh-niang, "He's been sent from Manager Han's place to speak to Tai-an, and find out when Manager Han will be coming home."

By so doing, he managed to pull the wool over Yüeh-niang's eyes, so that she said nothing more about it, and returned to the rear compound.

Not long after this, Tai-an and the Indian monk arrived at the gate before Hsi-men Ch'ing did. Tai-an had been constrained to walk so fast that his two legs ached, and:

     His whole body was covered with sweat,[74]

which made him as resentful as could be; whereas, the Indian monk seemed to be completely relaxed and was not even short of breath.

P'ing-an told Tai-an all about how Wang Liu-erh had sent Wang Ching to speak to him and explained, "Who could have anticipated that the First Lady happened to come out just then in order to see off Auntie Li from the licensed quarter as she got into her sedan chair. Catching sight of her, he:

     Recklessly and impulsively,[75]

came right up to the First Lady and kowtowed to her. When the First Lady asked who he was, he said he was from the Han household. Fortunately, I was standing nearby and was able to pull him aside. After that, when the First Lady asked me, I explained that he had been sent from Manager Han's place to find out when Manager Han would be coming home. At that, the First Lady had nothing further to say, so that, luckily, no horse's hoof was exposed to view. Later on, if Mother asks you anything about it, you'd better say the same thing."

Tai-an had been put through his paces until his eyes were staring out of his head, and all he could do was fan himself with his fan.

"Has this turned out to be my unlucky day, or hasn't it!" he complained. "Father insisted that I escort this lousy baldpated jailbird home, for no good reason. It's some distance, I can tell you! From that temple outside the city gate all the way here, I never once had a chance to rest my legs along the road. I've been walking so fast:

> Each new breath has not had a chance
> to catch up with the last.

Father wanted me to hire donkeys for us, but he refused to ride one. If he preferred to walk, that's no matter, no matter at all, but it has really been hard on these two legs of mine. The soles of my shoes are worn through, and my feet are blistered. What a provoking business!"

"What has Father invited him home for, anyway?" said P'ing-an.

"Who knows?" said Tai-an. "He tells me he's hoping to obtain some kind of medicine from him."

As they were speaking, what should they hear but the sound of an escort shouting to clear the way, as Hsi-men Ch'ing arrived home.

When Hsi-men Ch'ing saw that the Indian monk was at his gate, he exclaimed, "Master, you must really be a god among men to have actually gotten here before me."

As he spoke, he ushered him inside and offered him a seat in the large reception hall. Hsi-men Ch'ing called for Shu-t'ung to take his outer garments and changed into an informal skullcap, before sitting down to keep him company.

The Indian monk opened his eyes wide and observed that:

> The chamber was lofty and spacious, and
> The courtyard was secluded and imposing.[76]

Over the door there was suspended:

> A glossy-green beaded portiere,
>   woven of shrimp's whiskers,
>   with a tortoiseshell pattern.

On the floor there was positioned:

> A rug fashioned of woolen yarn,
>   displaying a pair of lions,
>   playing with a brocade ball.[77]

In the center of the room there was:
>   A soap-colored table in raised relief,
>   on bulging "mantis belly" legs,
>   with cabriole "dragonfly feet."[78]

On the table there was displayed:
>   A vertical marble monolith,
>   mounted on a ringlike stand,
>   like the base of Mount Sumeru.

All around it there were placed:
>   Folding armchairs of swollen shape,
>   with backs of nan wood,
>   and loach-head finials.

On the two walls were displayed:
>   Hanging scrolls, replete with
>   damask borders and agate knobs,
>   adorning purple bamboo rollers.

Truly:
>   While painted drums of alligator hide,
>   resound in courts and halls;
>   The banquet table, wrought of ebony,
>   is loaded with wine vessels.

When the Indian monk had seen his fill, Hsi-men Ch'ing asked him, "Master, do you drink wine, or not?"

"I consume both wine and meat," proclaimed the monk.

Hsi-men Ch'ing accordingly directed a page boy, "When you go back to the kitchen, don't bother to bring any vegetarian fare, but serve us with regular food and wine."

That day, being the eve of Li Chiao-erh's birthday, there were delicacies of every kind to be had in the kitchen. Once the table was set in place, all that had to be done was to serve the feast.

To begin with, there were four saucers of nuts, and four saucers of appetizers. Then there were another four dishes to complement the wine, namely, one saucer of bullhead, one saucer of duck preserved in a fermented wine mash, one saucer of black-bone chicken, and one saucer of still wriggling male sculpin. Still another four dishes to go with the rice were then served, to wit, a saucer of walnut kernels blanched with ramshorn scallions, a saucer of finely minced goat-meat hash, a saucer of fatty stuffed sheep's-gut sausage, and a saucer of shiny smooth slippery loach. Yet another two courses were then forthcoming. One of which was a soup served in a bowl containing two meatballs straddling a gristly roulade of pork, and called "The Lone Dragon Toys with a Pair of Pearls," while the other was a large platter of overstuffed steamed pork buns, the heads of which were bursting open.

Hsi-men Ch'ing encouraged the Indian monk to eat his fill. He then ordered Ch'in-t'ung to fetch a round-handled chicken-crop flagon, open the red clay stopper, and pour gush after gush of the whitish, yin-replenishing, liquor, painstakingly distilled in the Province of the Loins, into a high-stemmed goblet in the shape of a drooping lotus seedpod, which he presented to the Indian monk. The Indian monk put it to his lips and drank it off with one gulp.

Thereupon, after the table had been cleared, another two courses were presented. One, a saucer of inch-thick horseback sausages, and the other, a saucer of salt-cured goose necks. These were supplemented by two more stimulating dishes for the enjoyment of the Indian monk as he drank his wine. One, a saucer of bitter melon, and the other, a saucer of oozing overripe red plums. After these had been consumed, a large bowl of eel noodles, along with a serving of spring rolls, was also provided for the Indian monk to dispose of.

In no time at all, the Indian monk was so stuffed that the eyes were starting out of his head, and he said, "I'm already:

Drunk on wine and satiated with food.

It's time to call a halt."

Hsi-men Ch'ing summoned his attendants and had them remove the table at which they had been drinking, after which he besought his visitor to supply him with the promised medication to enhance his performance of the arts of the bedchamber.

The Indian monk responded, "I have in my possession a remedy that was:

Perfected by the Lord Lao-tzu himself, and

Transmitted by the Queen Mother of the West.

For the wrong person it will not prove effective;

To the wrong person it must never be transmitted.

It will work only for one with the right affinity.

Since you have entertained me so lavishly, Sir, I will provide you with a few pills thereof."

Thereupon, he groped out one of the gourds in his pouch, from which he decanted some hundred or so pills, saying, "You must only take one pill at a time, not any more than that, and wash it down with a draft of distilled spirits."

Shifting then to the other gourd, he squeezed out a glob of about two-tenths of an ounce of pink ointment, saying, "Be sure to use no more than two-thousandths of an ounce at a time. Don't use too much of it. If your organ becomes uncomfortably congested, use your hands to knead your thighs on either side of it, and slap them a hundred or so times. Only then will you be able to ejaculate. You must employ these medications sparingly, and not lightly let them fall into the hands of other people."

Hsi-men Ch'ing respectfully received the proffered items with both hands, saying, "Permit me to inquire, what efficacy does this medication possess?"

The Indian monk said:

"Its shape is like a hen's egg;
Its coloring is gosling yellow.
It has been thrice refined by the Lord Lao-tzu;
And transmitted by the Queen Mother of the West.
Examined externally, it is as worthless as dung;
Inspected internally, it is rarer than carnelian.
It may be compared to gold, but not acquired with gold;
It may be compared to jade, but not procured with jade.
Though you be girdled with gold and garbed in purple,[79]
Though you occupy spacious structures and high halls,[80]
Though you own the lightest furs and sleekest horses,[81]
Though you manifest the talents of a pillar of state,
Once you have this medication firmly in your grasp,
Your body will be impelled into the bridal chamber.
Within the chamber, spring reigns eternally;
Beyond the mundane, vistas are ever-fragrant.
Your jade pinnacle will never be impaired;
Your cinnabar field will glow in the dark.
After one battle, your spirits remain valiant;
As the duel continues, your vigor is enhanced.
No matter how captivating and voluptuous your favorites,
Though you possess twelve beauties in their rosy makeup;
You may engage with them however you wish,
Remaining stiff as a spear all night long.
If used for long, your appetite will be insatiable;
It will stir your testicles and stiffen your organ.
In a hundred days your hair will regain its color;
In a thousand days your stamina will be augmented.
It will strengthen your teeth and brighten your eyes;
Only when yang is in the ascendant will yin diminish.
If you are not able to believe these claims,
Mix it in with rice and feed it to your cat.
For three days it will indulge itself without restraint;
On the fourth day it will be too overheated to stand it.
A white cat will be transformed into a black one,
Its excretory functions will stop and it will die.
In the summer months you should sleep in the breeze,
In the winter you should submerge yourself in water;
But should you ever be unable to ejaculate,
Your hair will drop out and leave you bald.
If you use a thousandth or so of an ounce at a time,
Your organ will become erect and stronger than ever;
You will be able to handle ten women in one night,

And your reservoir of sperm will not be exhausted.
Older women will contract their brows in dismay;
Prostitutes will find it hard to accommodate you.
If you should ever lose interest in the battle,
Wishing to retire your warriors from the field,
Swallow a mouthful of cold water,
So as to retain your sperm intact.
Your pleasures may thus extend throughout the night,
And spring colors will pervade your nuptial chamber.
This present is offered only to the cognoscenti,
As a recipe for their lasting self-preservation."

When Hsi-men Ch'ing heard this, he wanted to ask him for the prescription, saying:

"In engaging a physician you should engage only the best;
In prescribing drugs you should impart the prescription.

Master, if you do not give the prescription to me, should I happen to run out of it at a later date, where could I hope to find you? No matter how much you want for it, I will be happy to comply."

He then ordered Tai-an, "Go back to the rear compound as quick as you can and fetch me twenty taels of silver to give to this Indian monk in exchange for the prescription for this medication."

The Indian monk laughed, saying, "I am someone who has left home to become a priest, and:

Wanders like a cloud among the four quarters.

What would I want this money for? Pray take it back, Sir."

He then got up to take his leave.

When Hsi-men Ch'ing realized that he would not give him the prescription, he said, "Master, if you won't accept money, I have a forty-foot-long bolt of muslin, which you could use to clothe yourself with."

So saying, he immediately ordered his attendants to fetch it and proffered it to the Indian monk with both hands. Only then did the monk express his thanks by pressing his palms together in front of his chest and bowing to him in the Buddhist fashion.

As he was about to go out the gate, he enjoined him one more time, "Don't use too much of it. Take heed! Take heed!"

When he had finished speaking, he hitched his pouch onto his back, fastened his staff to it, went out the gate, and proceeded nonchalantly on his way. Truly:

Suspended from his staff he bears on high
        the dyad sun and moon;
In his straw sandals he traverses all nine
        divisions of the realm.

There is a poem that testifies to this:

Maitreya Buddha,[82] as a mendicant monk, has
   appeared in China;
His calico bag is hanging from the tip of
   his walking staff.[83]
No matter how many myriad transformations
   you can perform;
Every incarnation must cope with its own
   burden of sorrow.[84]

   If you want to know the outcome of these events,
   Pray consult the story related in the following chapter.

Chapter 50

CH'IN-T'UNG EAVESDROPS
ON THE JOYS OF LOVEMAKING;
TAI-AN ENJOYS A PLEASING RAMBLE
IN BUTTERFLY LANE

Heaven has bestowed the rouge with which
    to dab their ruby lips;
Their faces, blithe as the eastern breeze,
    are wreathed in smiles.
Their fragrant hearts, needless to say,
    are replete with delight;
Their inebriated faces constantly suggest
    new forms of satisfaction.
Kingdom-toppling beauties are oft disposed
    to agitate their patrons;
Inclining toward the sun, without a word,
    they flirt with but a smile.
How many men in the world of the Red Dust,
    with sorrow-laden brows,
Are wont to visit flowery groves, to seek
    for intimate companions?

THE STORY GOES that the day in question was the eve of Li Chiao-erh's birthday, and Nun Wang from the Kuan-yin Nunnery, as she had promised, had invited Nun Hsüeh of the Lotus Blossom Nunnery and her two disciples, Miao-feng and Miao-ch'ü, to come help celebrate the occasion. Wu Yüeh-niang, on hearing that Reverend Hsüeh had arrived, and having heard her to be a nun renowned for her exemplary conduct, hastened out to welcome her.

She was attired in the headdress of an immaculate nun, was clothed in a dull brown tea-leaf-colored cassock, had been shaved so closely as to produce a bluish, finely polished pate, and presented an imposingly corpulent figure, with a pondlike mouth and piglike cheeks. As she came in, she pressed her palms together in front of her chest and saluted Yüeh-niang and the others in the Buddhist fashion.

As she did so, Nun Wang said, "This is the mistress of the household, and these are her fellow ladies."

This threw Yüeh-niang and the others into such consternation that they made haste to return her salutation. Impressed by her proclivity for:

Raising her brows and batting her eyes,[1]
Assuming attitudes and putting on airs;[2]

and observing that she was given to:

Hairsplitting and logic-chopping;

in speaking to her, the words "Reverend Hsüeh" were seldom out of their mouths; while she, in turn, addressed Yüeh-niang with the words "Lay Bodhisattva,"[3] or "My Lady." Yüeh-niang treated her with the greatest possible respect.

That day Sister-in-law Wu and Aunt Yang were also present. Yüeh-niang had prepared tea for her guests, as well as vegetarian fare in the form of various dishes and treats, all of which were laid out on a large table, making a more than ordinarily sumptuous repast. Nun Hsüeh's two young disciples, Miaoch'ü and Miao-feng, were only thirteen or fourteen years old and were naturally very good-looking. They stood by her side and helped themselves to the refreshments on the table.

When they were finished with their tea, they all sat down in the master suite, along with Yüeh-niang, Li Chiao-erh, Meng Yü-lou, P'an Chin-lien, Li P'ing-erh, and Hsi-men Ta-chieh, in order to listen to Nun Hsüeh expound on the Buddhist Dharma. What should they see at this juncture but Huat'ung, who came in from the front compound carrying a load of used utensils.

Yüeh-niang took the occasion to ask him, "Has that meat- and wine-consuming Buddhist priest left yet?"

"He has just gotten up to go," reported Hua-t'ung. "Father has gone out to see him off."

"Where did he invite that priest to come here from?" asked Sister-in-law Wu.

"He is a priest that Father brought back with him after going to a temple outside the South Gate to see off Censor Ts'ai Yün," replied Yüeh-niang. "He consumes both meat and wine. Father wanted to get the prescription for some medication from him and offered him silver for it, but he said he had no need for it and refused to take any money. Who knows what sort of business he's up to? He's been gorging himself all day, before taking himself off."

When Nun Hsüeh heard this, she said, "As for eating meat and drinking wine,[4] these two acts are hard to justify. In the final analysis, it is we Buddhist nuns who are more likely to keep our vows. What do these male monks care about such things? Is it not stated in the Great Buddhist Canon that for every mouthful of such substances that you consume you will be required to make recompense in a subsequent incarnation?"

When Sister-in-law Wu heard this, she said, "For people like us who eat meat all day long, there's no telling how much evil karma we will have accumulated by the time we're reincarnated."

"As for venerable bodhisattvas such as yourself," Nun Hsüeh asserted, "it's all due to the good fortune you have cultivated for yourselves in former incarnations that you are destined to bask in glory and luxury, and enjoy wealth and distinction.[5] It is just as it is with the five grains; if you do not plant them in the spring, when autumn comes, how can you hope to reap a harvest?"

We will say no more about this conversation for the moment.

To resume our story, when Hsi-men Ch'ing came inside after seeing off the Indian monk, whom should he see but Tai-an, who quietly stepped forward and said, "A little while ago, Auntie Han sent her younger brother over here to extend you an invitation. She said that today is her birthday, and that she hoped, whatever happens, that you will be able to come over and pay her a visit."

Ever since acquiring the aphrodisiac from the Indian monk, Hsi-men Ch'ing had made up his mind to go there in order to try it out with the woman, but how could he have anticipated that she would actually send him an invitation. Since this development coincided precisely with his own wishes, he immediately ordered Tai-an to prepare his horse and sent Ch'in-t'ung ahead to deliver a jug of wine in honor of the occasion.

Thereupon, he went straight into P'an Chin-lien's quarters, picked up the bag of sexual implements, attired himself in casual clothes and an informal skullcap, put on his eye shades, and headed straight for Wang Liu-erh's house, with Tai-an in attendance.

Upon dismounting and going inside, he gave directions, saying, "I'll keep Ch'in-t'ung here to wait on me, while Tai-an can go home with the horse. If anyone at home asks, just say that I'm in the shop on Lion Street going over the accounts."

Tai-an assented with the words, "I understand," after which he mounted the horse and went home.

When Wang Liu-erh came out to greet her visitor, she was wearing her chignon enclosed in a fret of silver filigree, held in place with gold filigree pins and combs, along with ornaments with kingfisher feather inlays, and a pair of earrings adorned with two pearls apiece. Her head was uncovered, and she was attired in a jade-colored silk vest, over a linen blouse, and a white-waisted drawnwork skirt with a single border.

After kowtowing to Hsi-men Ch'ing, and sitting down beside him, she said, "Having some free time, I've invited you to come relax and visit together. Also, thank you very much for the wine you sent over."

"I had forgotten that it was your birthday," said Hsi-men Ch'ing. "I was obliged to go outside the South Gate to see someone off today and have only just gotten back."

He then pulled a pair of hairpins out of his sleeve and presented them to her, saying, "This is in honor of your birthday."

The woman, accepting them and looking them over, saw that they were a pair of gold hairpins in the shape of the character for long life, and exclaimed, "What fine workmanship!"

She then hastened to bow to him in thanks.

Hsi-men Ch'ing also gave her five mace of silver and said to her, "Weigh out five candareens, and get my page boy to buy a bottle of southern distilled spirits for me to drink."

Wang Liu-erh laughed at this, saying, "Father, you've grown tired of other wines have you? So now you've come up with the idea of trying southern distilled spirits."

Thereupon, she promptly weighed out five candareens of silver and sent Ch'in-t'ung out with a bottle in hand to buy it for him.

Wang Liu-erh then helped Hsi-men Ch'ing off with his outer garments and invited him into her room to sit down, while she took the trouble to:

Wash her hands and trim her nails,

before personally shelling some nuts for him. She had ordered her maidservant to brew some fine tea, which she brought out for Hsi-men Ch'ing to drink. A small table was set up in the room so they could play cards together. Only after they had played for a while did they put the cards away and fall to drinking. But let us put this aside for the moment and say no more about it.

Let us now return to the story of Tai-an. By the time he returned home with the horse, he had been hard at work all day and was utterly exhausted from trying to keep up with the Indian monk. He went straight to his room in the front compound and lay down for a nap. It was not until lamplighting time that he woke up, rubbed his eyes, and, seeing that it was already late in the day, went to the rear compound to fetch a lantern with which to go back for Hsi-men Ch'ing.

As he was standing there, Yüeh-niang said to him, "Earlier today, after Father had seen off the Indian monk, he didn't even come inside to change his clothes, but took off somewhere before anyone was aware of it. Really now, whose place has he gone off to drink at?"

Tai-an was at a loss for words but finally said, "Father hasn't gone to anyone else's place. He's at the shop on Lion Street going over the accounts with Lai-pao."

"Even if he were going over the accounts," said Yüeh-niang, "it wouldn't take him all day."

"After finishing the accounts," said Tai-an, "he's probably having himself a drink."

"Without anyone to keep him company?" said Yüeh-niang. "No doubt he's drinking all by himself, for no good reason! It's obvious that your story is duplicitous. What was that young man up to who came looking for you from Han Tao-kuo's household a while ago?"

"He came to ask when Uncle Han was coming home," said Tai-an.

"You lousy jailbird!" Yüeh-niang vociferated. "Who knows what kind of mischief you're up to?"

Tai-an did not dare say any more on the subject.

Yüeh-niang told Hsiao-yü to fetch a lantern for him, saying, "You tell him that the Second Lady is waiting for him at home to celebrate the eve of her birthday."

Hsiao-yü accordingly fetched a lantern and turned it over to Tai-an, who made his way out to the shop in the front compound.

What should he see there but Shu-t'ung and Manager Fu, sitting together at the counter, on which there were laid out a bottle of wine, two sets of cups and chopsticks, several bowls and saucers, and a platter of beef tripe, while P'ing-an was on the way in from outside with two bottles of preserved fish in fermented mash.

Just as they were settling down to enjoy their wine, whom should they see but Tai-an, who came in, put his lantern down, and said, "Great! I've arrived just in the nick of time."

Then, catching sight of Shu-t'ung, he said in jest, "What a fine wanton you are! What are you doing here? I've been looking all over for you, and it turns out you've been hiding in here all the time drinking wine."

"Just what did you want me for?" said Shu-t'ung. "Have you been harboring the wish to be my grandson for a spell?"

"Why you 'sweetie' of a page boy!" cursed Tai-an. "You have the nerve to talk back to me, do you? I was looking for you so I could fuck you in the ass."

Thereupon, stepping forward, he held him down on his chair and gave him a kiss.

Shu-t'ung pushed him away with both hands, complaining, "You crazy good-for-nothing! I'd just be wasting my breath on you! You've not only scraped the tartar right off my teeth, but knocked the hat off my head."

When Manager Fu saw that his hat was lying on the floor, he exclaimed, "It's a brand new lantern-shaped hat."

Then, turning to P'ing-an, he said, "Pick it up, or, I fear, it might get stepped on."

Shu-t'ung grabbed it out of his hands and threw it onto the k'ang, his face turning bright red as he did so.

"What a fine wanton you are!" said Tai-an. "I was just teasing you, and you're all hot and bothered."

Whereupon:

Without permitting any further explanation,

he lifted him up by the legs, forced him down onto the k'ang, and spit a mouthful of saliva into his mouth, as hard as he could, knocking the wine over in the process, so that it ran all over the surface of the counter.

Manager Fu was afraid the account books would get wet, so he promptly grabbed a towel and started mopping it up, saying, "You can be sure it won't be long before the way the two of you are horsing around will turn nasty."

"A fine wanton you are!" said Tai-an. "Whose countenance have you procured that's made you so squeamish today?"

Shu-t'ung, whose hair had gotten all rumpled, complained:

"A game's a game;
A joke's a joke,

but you've spit a mouthful of filthy jizz all over me."

"Why you lousy hick of a 'sweetie'!" said Tai-an. "As though this were the first time you've ever swallowed jizz. From first to last, who knows how much jizz you may have swallowed?"

P'ing-an poured out a goblet of wine and gave it to Tai-an, saying, "You drink this off, and then go on to fetch Father. If you have anything left to say, you can say it to him when you get back."

"Just wait till I've come back from fetching Father," said Tai-an, "and I'll have something to say to him. If I don't fix it so that 'sweetie' of a page boy starts:

Seeing spirits and seeing ghosts,[6]

he won't take me seriously. As for my saliva, am I someone:

Not sired by a human being,[7]

that I must be expected to keep my mouth sucked dry?"

Thereupon, having drunk the wine, he picked up a houseboy from the duty room in the gatehouse to carry the lantern for him and rode on horseback to Wang Liu-erh's place.

After calling for someone to open the door, he asked Ch'in-t'ung, "Where's Father?"

"Father's asleep in the bedroom," replied Ch'in-t'ung.

Thereupon, the two of them closed the door and made their way back to the kitchen in the rear of the house.

Old Mother Feng said to him, "So Master Tai-an has finally shown up. Your Auntie Han has been expecting you, but you were not to be seen. She has set aside a portion of something for you."

She then opened a kitchen cabinet and pulled out a platter of donkey meat, a saucer of preserved roast chicken, two bowls of birthday noodles, and a carafe of wine for him.

Tai-an ate for a while and then offered Ch'in-t'ung some wine, saying, "Come over here. I can't manage all of this wine. The two of us might as well finish this carafe off between us."

"It was set aside for you," said Ch'in-t'ung. "Drink it yourself."

"I've just had a goblet a little while ago," said Tai-an.

Thereupon, the two of them proceeded to finish it off together.

When they were done, Tai-an said, "Old Mother Feng, I've got something to say to you. Don't be offended. It seems to me that you're supposed to be keeping house for the Sixth Lady, and yet here you are, right now, keeping house for Auntie Han. When I get home, just see if I speak to the Sixth Lady about it, or not."

Old Mother Feng gave him a playful slap, saying, "You crazy monkey! You'll drop dead in your tracks someday! Cut it out!

Those may be words but they don't make utterances.

If you go home and say that sort of thing, you'll have her upset with me for the rest of my life, and I won't dare go near her."

While Tai-an and Old Mother Feng were bandying words, who would have thought that Ch'in-t'ung had stationed himself under the window of the bedroom in order to surreptitiously eavesdrop on the events within.

It so happens that Hsi-men Ch'ing had swallowed a dose of the Indian monk's medicine, and washed it down with distilled spirits. After taking off all his clothes, he had gone to bed in order to engage in sexual intercourse with the woman. Sitting down on the edge of the bed, he opened the bag of sexual implements, fastened the silver clasp around the base of his penis, fitted the sulfur-imbrued ring around his turtle head, and, pinching up one and a half thousandths of an ounce of the pink ointment the Indian monk had given him, which he kept in a little silver box, daubed it in the eye of his urethra. In no time at all, the medication began to take effect. His organ became engorged with rage,

Its protuberances swelled and its head sprang up,

Its sunken eye grew round, and

Its distended blood vessels were all exposed.

It was the color of purple liver, was six or seven inches long, and more than ordinarily thick and large.

Hsi-men Ch'ing was:

Secretly delighted in his heart,[8]

thinking to himself, "Sure enough, this Indian monk's medicine is something else."

The woman, who had stripped herself stark naked, sat in his lap and pumped his organ with her hand, saying, "No wonder you wanted distilled spirits to drink, since it turns out that this is what you're up to."

She then went on to ask, "Where did you get this medication?"

Hsi-men Ch'ing hastily recounted the whole story, from the beginning, of how he had obtained the medicine from the Indian monk.

He then started out by telling the woman to recline faceup on the bed, supporting her back on a pair of pillows, while she guided his organ to its destination with her hand. His turtle head was proud and large, so that, even with moistening and reaming, it was some time before he was able to achieve any penetration. The woman's vaginal secretions then began to overflow, until, in a little while, it felt smoother, and the knob of his glans was completely submerged.[9] Hsi-men Ch'ing was exhilarated by the spirits he had consumed and gave himself over to a series of shallow retractions and deep thrusts,[10] until he felt a melting sensation the pleasure of which was indescribable.[11]

The woman, for her part, was drunk with lecherous desires. Reclining languidly on the pillows, she gave vent to incessant groans of satisfaction, protesting again and again, "My big-dicked daddy! This whore of yours is going to die at your hands today."

She then went on to say, "Whatever else you do, save some energy to play around with my backside."

Hsi-men Ch'ing, thereupon, turned the woman over so she was kneeling on the edge of the bed, plunged his organ into her orifice, lifted up her haunches, and slammed away at her with all his might. As he slammed away at her:

The reiterated sounds reverberated loudly.

"Daddy," the woman said to him. "Keep on slamming away at this whore of yours. Don't stop. Better yet, why don't you move the lamp over, so you can get a better view of the fun?"

Hsi-men Ch'ing, thereupon, moved the lamp closer, told the woman to stick her two feet straight back, and then straddled them, while he lifted up her thighs, assumed a squatting position, and proceeded to thrust away. The woman, from her position below him, stimulated her clitoris with one hand, while raising her haunches to meet him, and making quavery noises without end.

Hsi-men Ch'ing then said to the woman, "When your husband gets home, I'll send him to Yang-chou, along with Lai-pao and Ts'ui Pen, in order to take delivery of a consignment of salt. Then, after they have taken delivery of the salt, and sold it, I'll send him to Hu-chou to arrange a shipment of woven silk goods. How would that be?"

"My good daddy!" exclaimed the woman, "Send him wherever you want, just so he's out of the way. What's the point of keeping the cuckold idle at home?"

She then went on to ask, "As for the shop, who will you put in charge of it?"

"I'll keep Pen the Fourth at home," said Hsi-men Ch'ing, "and have him take care of the business in his stead."

"That's all right, then," said Wang Liu-erh. "Let Pen the Fourth take care of it."

While the two of them were engaging in sexual intercourse, who would have thought that Ch'in-t'ung, from his vantage point outside the window, heard everything so clearly that he might well have ejaculated:

"Is it not delightful?"

Tai-an, who happened to come in from the back and noticed him eaves-
dropping beneath the window, gave him a playful slap, saying, "What's the
point of listening to them for no good reason? We'd do better to take advantage
of the time before they get up to go out somewhere on our own."

Ch'in-t'ung, accordingly, accompanied him outside.

"You don't know about it," said Tai-an, "but in the little lane right behind
here, two fine young girls have recently shown up. When I was riding over on
horseback just now, I went by there and got a look at them. They're working
at that place, the madam of which is called Lu Ch'ang-t'ui, or Longleg Lu.
One of them is named Chin-erh, and the other is named Sai-erh, and they're
both no more than fifteen or sixteen years old. If we get the houseboy I brought
with me to act as a lookout for us here, we can go over there and have some
fun for a while."

He then instructed the houseboy, saying, "You stay here and listen at the
gate. We're going out onto the street to relieve ourselves. If they start looking for us inside, just step over to the mouth of the little lane there and call
for us."

When he had finished giving his instructions, the two of them, traversing
the moonlit ground, strode into the little lane.

It so happens that this lane was called Butterfly Lane, and there were ten
or more establishments along it whose owners made their living by operating
unlicensed houses of prostitution. Tai-an was already inebriated, and it
seemed like half a day before his calls succeeded in getting anyone to open
the gate.

It so happened that the procurer and the madam, Longleg Lu, were engaged, just then, under the lamplight, in weighing out the day's take of silver
on a big scale with its yellow yard. When they saw that two intruders had
barged in like avenging spirits, they promptly blew out the lamp in their inner
room. The procurer, who recognized that Tai-an was a head servant in the
household of His Honor Hsi-men Ch'ing of the Provincial Surveillance Commission, came out and offered him a seat.

"Call out the two girls," demanded Tai-an, "so they can sing a song for us,
and then we'll go."

"I'm afraid you've come a step too late, sir," explained the procurer. "The
two of them are both engaged with customers just now."

Without permitting any further explanation,
Tai-an swept into the interior in large strides, where he found it to be as dark
as a cave, since none of the lamps were lit. On the k'ang there were two senior
wine-making artisans, wearing white felt caps.

One of them had already lain down on the k'ang, while the other had
just finished taking off his foot-bindings and asked, "Who is that coming into
the room?"

Ch'in-t'ung Eavesdrops on the Joys of Lovemaking

"I'll fuck your mother's hole!" exclaimed Tai-an, and, without any warning, he sent a clenched fist whistling into him, leaving the wine-maker with no alternative but to complain vociferously as he flew outside, without even putting on his foot-bindings and stockings. The other one, also, crawled up off the surface of the k'ang, and:

Stumbling at every step,

followed him outside.

"Light up the lamps!" called out Tai-an, and he cursed, saying, "Those lousy uncivilized vagrants! They actually had the nerve to ask who I am, did they! It's lucky for them I didn't choose to pluck them clean, just now, but let them get away, for no good reason. How do you suppose they would have liked it if I had them dragged into the yamen and given a taste of our new ankle-squeezers?"

Longleg Lu came forward at this point, lit the lamps, and, bowing repeatedly, said, "Temper your rage, my good brethren. They're from out of town and don't know who's who. You've got to make allowances for them."

Then she instructed Chin-erh and Sai-erh, "Come on out and sing a song for your two uncles."

Lo and behold, the two of them, with their hair done up in casual "bag of silk" spiral buns, wearing bleached white blouses, and red and green silk skirts, came forward and said, "We didn't know that our two uncles were coming today, and it's already late at night, so we have been caught unprepared."

Four saucers of pickled vegetables were then laid out, in addition to which there were saucers of duck eggs, dried shrimp, preserved fish mash, salted fish, the meat from a braised pig's head, dried sausage, and the like.

Tai-an proceeded to embrace Sai-erh where he was sitting, while Ch'in-t'ung, for his part, hugged Chin-erh. Tai-an noticed that Sai-erh was wearing a pink silk scent bag, so he reached into his sleeve for a handkerchief, and the two of them exchanged love tokens. In a little while, wine was decanted, and Sai-erh poured out a cup and offered it to Tai-an.

Before this, Chin-erh had already taken up a *p'i-p'a*, and, after proffering a cup of wine to Ch'in-t'ung:

Commencing to sing in full voice,

she sang a song to the tune "Sheep on the Mountain Slope":

The camp of mist and flowers,
Is truly difficult to endure.
One simply never has the spare time
    to sit down and relax.
One's days are spent welcoming visitors
    and treating guests.
The livelihood of the entire establishment
    is totally dependent on me alone.

Tai-an Enjoys a Pleasing Ramble in Butterfly Lane

When night falls, I am also the one under
    pressure from the loan sharks.
As for the old procuress,
She doesn't care whether I am dead or alive.
I have to stand outside the door until
    the late watches of the night;
But, when evening comes, who bothers to ask
    whether I am hungry or full?
If I manage to last another three to five years
    in the camp of mist and flowers,
The chances of my surviving are few, while the
    chances of my dying are many.
I can't help the fact that the tears in my eyes
    come and go like shuttles.[12]
Only when the iron tree shall blossom forth,[13]
Will I ever be able to harvest my garden
    and reap my just reward.[14]

When Chin-erh had finished singing, Sai-erh poured another cup of wine and offered it to Tai-an, after which she took over the *p'i-p'a* and sang another song to the same tune:

When I enter my room,
And look around me,
All I can see is that *p'i-p'a* hanging
    on the plastered wall.
I notice that the *p'i-p'a* is
    covered with dust.
Reaching into my sleeve and pulling out
    a handkerchief,
I brush away the dust.
Holding it in my arms, I tune the strings,
    and play a lonesome melody,
My tears gushing like a spring.
When I possessed that lover of mine,
    how happy we were,
But now that my lover has gone, he's abandoned me
    just like that neglected *p'i-p'a*.
When he was here, how we used to sing together
    and play together;
But at the present time, I am left
    all by myself.
I can't help shedding tears
    of desolation.

The keepsake remains, and I will hold on to it,
But I don't know where that man of mine
   is to be found.

Just as she was in full voice, the houseboy suddenly appeared to call them away.

The two of them hastily got up to go, and Tai-an said to Sai-erh, "We'll come to see you again another day."

When he had finished speaking, they went out the door and returned to Wang Liu-erh's place, where they learned that Hsi-men Ch'ing had just gotten up, and the woman was having a drink of wine with him.

The two of them went into the kitchen, and Tai-an asked, "Old Mother Feng, has Father been looking for us?"

"Father has not been looking for you," said Old Mother Feng. "He merely asked if the horse had come back, to which I replied that it had. That's all he had to say."

The two of them sat down in the kitchen and asked Old Mother Feng for some tea. After each of them had drunk a cup of tea, they had the houseboy light the lantern and lead the horse outside.

As Hsi-men Ch'ing was about to get up and go, the woman said to him, "Father, this is nice heated wine. Have another cup. Or, perhaps, you're going to have more to drink when you get home."

"I'm not going to drink any more when I get home," said Hsi-men Ch'ing.

Thereupon, he picked up the wine and drained another cup.

"Now that you're going," the woman asked him, "when will you come by for another visit?"

"I won't come back until I've sent your husband and the others off," said Hsi-men Ch'ing.

When he had finished speaking, a maidservant brought him a cup of tea to rinse out his mouth with, and Wang Liu-erh saw him to the door. Only then did Hsi-men Ch'ing mount his horse and go home.

To resume our story, P'an Chin-lien and the rest had assembled in Yüeh-niang's room to listen to Nun Hsüeh's two disciples sing Buddhist songs for their entertainment, and it was only after the first watch that she returned, temporarily, to her own quarters.

Upon her arrival there, she thought to herself, "A while ago, when Yüeh-niang accused Tai-an of being duplicitous in his response to her, I wonder what he was up to."

With this in mind, she looked in the bedroom for the bag of sexual implements but couldn't find it.

She called for Ch'un-mei and interrogated her, but she said she hadn't taken it.

"A while ago, when you weren't here," she reported, "Father came into the room and fumbled about in the drawers of the cabinet on the rear wall of the bedstead, before going off somewhere. Who knows where that bag is to be found?"

"When did he come in here," Chin-lien asked, "without my knowing about it?"

"Mother had just gone back to the rear compound to see Nun Hsüeh," said Ch'un-mei, "when Father came in, wearing an informal skullcap. I asked him what he was up to, but he didn't reply."

"He must have taken those things off to the place of some whore in the licensed quarter," opined Chin-lien. "When he gets home, I'll subject him to a thorough interrogation."

Who could have anticipated that when Hsi-men Ch'ing arrived home, seeing that it was late at night, he didn't even go back to the rear compound. Ch'in-t'ung, carrying the lantern, escorted him as far as the postern gate leading into the garden, from which point he made his way to Li P'ing-erh's quarters. Ch'in-t'ung then took the lantern back to the rear compound and turned it over to Hsiao-yü, who put it away.

At this time, Wu Yüeh-niang, along with Li Chiao-erh, Meng Yü-lou, P'an Chin-lien, Li P'ing-erh, Sun Hsüeh-o, Hsi-men Ta-chieh, and the two nuns, were sitting together in the master suite.

Yüeh-niang asked Ch'in-t'ung, "Has Father come home?"

To which Ch'in-t'ung replied, "Father is here. He's gone to the Sixth Lady's quarters in the front compound."

"Just look at him!" exclaimed Yüeh-niang. "How unprincipled can you get? Everyone is waiting for him here, and he doesn't even bother to come in."

Li P'ing-erh hastened out to the front compound and said to Hsi-men Ch'ing, "The Second Lady is in the rear compound, waiting for you to come celebrate the eve of her birthday. Why have you come into my quarters for no good reason?"

Hsi-men Ch'ing merely laughed, saying, "I'm drunk. Tomorrow will do just as well."

"Even if you're drunk," said Li P'ing-erh, "you could go back to the rear compound and share a cup with her. If you refuse to go, you can hardly avoid upsetting the Second Lady."

Thereupon, by means of vigorous urging, she succeeded in getting Hsi-men Ch'ing to go back to the rear compound.

After Li Chiao-erh had offered him a cup of wine, Yüeh-niang said, "What were you doing today, drinking all by yourself at the house over there, until this time of night?"

"I was drinking with Brother Ying the Second," said Hsi-men Ch'ing.

"There you are," said Yüeh-niang. "Just as I said, without a companion, how could anyone drink all by himself?"

Having said this, she dropped the matter and made an end of it.

Hsi-men Ch'ing did not sit around very long before picking up his feet and stealing off to Li P'ing-erh's quarters in the front compound.

It so happens that, as a result of taking the Indian monk's medicine at Wang Liu-erh's place, he was still so much in the grip of the aphrodisiac that, even after fooling around with the woman all day, although he was on the verge of ejaculation, he had been unable to get himself off. His organ was stiffer and harder than ever and resembled an iron pestle.

When he arrived in her quarters, he had Ying-ch'un help him off with his clothes and then climbed into bed, intending to sleep with Li P'ing-erh. Li P'ing-erh had not expected him to return and was already asleep on the bed with Kuan-ko.

Turning her head around, and seeing who it was, she said, "You might as well have gone to sleep in the rear compound. What are you coming back here for? The child has just dropped off and is sleeping soundly. I'm really not in the mood for it, and besides, my period has come on, and it wouldn't be convenient. Go and sleep in someone else's quarters, why don't you, instead of coming here to pester me."

Before she knew it, Hsi-men Ch'ing embraced her by the neck, held her down, and gave her a kiss, saying, "You crazy slave! Your daddy has it in his heart to sleep with you."

Hsi-men Ch'ing accordingly exposed his organ for Li P'ing-erh to see.

Li P'ing-erh was frightened to death and exclaimed, "Ai-ya! How did you ever manage to make it that big?"

Hsi-men Ch'ing laughed and explained how he had taken the Indian monk's medicine, saying, "If you refuse to sleep with me, I'll be so randy it will be the death of me."

"What am I to do?" said Li P'ing-erh. "My period came on two days ago and isn't over yet. It would be better to wait a while until it's over, and then I'll sleep with you. Today, you might just as well spend the night at the Fifth Lady's place. It's all the same."

"Today," said Hsi-men Ch'ing, "I don't know why, but the only thing I want to do is sleep with you. Right now, do I have to:

  Sacrifice a chicken in order to
    plead with you?

On the other hand, you could get a maidservant to fetch some water, and wash yourself before sleeping with me. That ought to take care of it."

"You make me laugh," said Li P'ing-erh. "Where have you been drinking today, to make you drunk enough to come home and give me such a hard time? Even if I were to wash myself, I still wouldn't be clean. For a man's body to be contaminated by a woman's menses is not only filthy, but bad luck as well. If I should die as a result of this, you'll look for me in vain."

Thereupon, unable to resist his pressure any longer, she had Ying-ch'un fetch some water and washed her private parts clean before getting into bed in order to engage in sexual intercourse with Hsi-men Ch'ing.

Strange as it may seem,
when Li P'ing-erh finally succeeded in coaxing Kuan-ko to sleep, no sooner did she crawl over to the other side of the bed, than the child woke up. After this had happened three times in a row, Li P'ing-erh told Ying-ch'un to get the child's toy clapper-drum[15] to keep him amused, and take him over to the wet nurse's room. Only then were the two of them able to:

Enjoy themselves to their heart's content.

Hsi-men Ch'ing seated himself inside the bed curtains, while Li P'ing-erh got down on all fours beside him, allowing Hsi-men Ch'ing to insert his organ into her vagina from the rear. This position enabled him, under the lamplight, to observe his organ, as well as her snow-white bottom. Using both hands, he embraced her haunches in order to:

Observe the sight as he went in and out.

Half of his organ had already been engulfed, and he could hardly contain his excitement. Li P'ing-erh was afraid that his organ would carry blood out with it, so she continually wiped it off with a handkerchief. Hsi-men Ch'ing engaged in thrusting and retracting for a long time, gripping her around the hips with both hands, and kneading away at her. His organ penetrated her all the way to the root, without leaving even a hairsbreadth outside, while the pubic hair beneath his navel prickled her bottom, and he felt a melting sensation the pleasure of which was indescribable.

Li P'ing-erh said, "Daddy! Slow down a bit. You're thrusting so hard it really hurts inside."

"If you're hurting," said Hsi-men Ch'ing, "I'll let go and be done with it."

Thereupon, he reached for the tea on the bedside table, and swallowed a mouthful of cold tea. Instantaneously, his semen arose and he:

Ejaculated like a geyser.

Truly:

His four limbs are suffused with pleasure;
His entire body a mass of spring feelings.

Only now did Hsi-men Ch'ing fully realize what a marvelous medicine he had obtained from the Indian monk. By the time they went to sleep, it was the third watch.

To resume our story, when P'an Chin-lien saw that Hsi-men Ch'ing had gone to spend the night in Li P'ing-erh's quarters, she merely assumed that he had taken the bag of sexual implements in order to enjoy himself with her, and failed to ascertain what he had been up to on the outside. That night she could only:

Silently gnash her silvery teeth,
close the door, and go to sleep.

Wu Yüeh-niang invited Nun Hsüeh and Nun Wang to spend the night with her in the master suite. Nun Wang took the afterbirth of a firstborn male child that she had procured, along with the medication concocted by Nun Hsüeh, and surreptitiously handed them over to Yüeh-niang.

Nun Hsüeh instructed Yüeh-niang, saying, "If you select a *jen-tzu* day,[16] take these preparations with some wine, and then sleep with your husband that night, you will be sure to conceive. But you must not let even a single person know what you are doing."

Yüeh-niang promptly put the medications away and bowed in gratitude to the two nuns.

"I waited expectantly for you throughout the first month," Yüeh-niang said to Nun Wang, "but you never came."

"That's a fine thing to say!" protested Nun Wang. "I was going to come and see you, but then I said to myself, 'I might as well wait until the Second Lady's birthday in the fourth month, when I'll be able to come together with Reverend Hsüeh.' Who would have thought that, thanks to the Reverend here, I was able to procure the critical ingredient. It is the afterbirth of the firstborn child of a certain family's daughter-in-law. It just so happened that Reverend Hsüeh was there and was able to obtain it surreptitiously from the midwife, with whom she was familiar, for three mace of silver. We have brought it here after cleansing it with alum water, dehydrating it according to formula in a vessel containing a new pair of coupled male and female tiles, sifting it through a heavy gauze sieve, and then mixing it into the talismanic potion provided by Reverend Hsüeh."

"I fear I have put the two of you, Reverend Hsüeh and Reverend Wang, to a lot of trouble," said Yüeh-niang.

Thereupon, she brought out two taels of silver for each of them and said, "In the future, if I should in fact conceive, I will also provide Reverend Hsüeh with a bolt of dark brown silk with which to make a cassock."

Nun Hsüeh placed her palms together and saluted her in the Buddhist fashion, saying, "I am most grateful for the Bodhisattva's good-heartedness."

As the saying goes:

> You may peddle a load of truths for ten days
>   without making a sale;
> While, in a single day, a load of falsehoods
>   will actually sell out.[17]

Truly:

> If persons of this ilk were really capable
>   of attaining Buddhahood;
> The monks and nuns dwelling in this world
>   would overflow like water.

> If you want to know the outcome of these events,
> Pray consult the story related in the following chapter.

Chapter 51

YÜEH-NIANG LISTENS TO THE

EXPOSITION OF THE DIAMOND SUTRA;

LI KUEI-CHIEH SEEKS REFUGE

IN THE HSI-MEN CH'ING HOUSEHOLD

Too ashamed to face the phoenix mirror,
    I grieve over my pink face;
Propping my fragrant cheek upon my hand,[1]
    I am too indolent to sleep.
My slender waist is so emaciated that
    my turquoise belt is loose;
As tears flow over my powdered face,[2]
    my golden hairpin falls out.
The annoying conduct of my fickle lover
    produces an aching sorrow;
It disturbs my fragrant heart[3] until
    my resentment is unending.
When will I be able to avail myself
    of the eastern wind;
To blow my handsome lover all the way
    to my pillow side?

THE STORY GOES that when P'an Chin-lien realized that Hsi-men
Ch'ing had taken the bag of sexual implements and gone to spend the night
in Li P'ing-erh's quarters, she was so upset that she was unable to sleep all
night long and secretly stored up resentment in her heart.

The next day, upon learning that Hsi-men Ch'ing had gone to the yamen,
and that Li P'ing-erh was still combing her hair in her quarters, she lost no
time in going back to the rear compound, where she said to Yüeh-niang, "Li
P'ing-erh has been criticizing you severely behind your back. She said, 'Elder
Sister puts on the airs of a grande dame, ordering people around as though
she were holding court. It was someone else's birthday, but you insisted on
taking charge. It was your husband who got drunk and came into my quarters
when I was not there, but you shamed me before the others for no good
reason, causing me to lose face. I was so upset by this that I went back up
front and insisted that Father return to the rear compound, but after a while,

somehow or other, he didn't remain there, but chose to come back to my quarters.' The two of them engaged in intimate conversation all night long and managed to expose everything but their hearts and entrails to me in the process."

When Yüeh-niang heard this, how could she help but be upset.

Turning to Sister-in-law Wu and Meng Yü-lou, she expostulated, "Luckily the two of you were here yesterday and saw what happened. I didn't say anything against her. When the page boy brought in the lantern, I merely asked him, 'Why hasn't Father come inside?' To which he replied, 'He's gone into the Sixth Lady's quarters.' I then said, 'The Second Lady is waiting here. How can he be so unprincipled as not to come inside?' If you stop to consider it, there was nothing intended to reflect upon her. How can she say that I put on the airs of a grande dame, or order people around as though I were holding court? She may think of me as a whorish wife, but I have always treated her as a decent person. It so happens that:

> In knowing people, you can know their faces,
>   but you can't know their hearts.[4]

How is one to judge what people are really like?

She turns out to be nothing but:

> A needle in a wad of cotton;
> A thorn in the flesh.

Who knows what tales she may have told our husband about me behind my back? No wonder she departed so resolutely for the front compound yesterday. My clever sister! Never fear! Even if our husband should choose to spend all his days in your quarters, without coming out, don't think that it would affect this heart of mine one way or the other. I relinquish him to the lot of you. You can do whatever you like. It's not as though I can't abide maintaining my widowhood. Remember how it was, not long after he married me, when for some time that lousy ruffian and I:

> Had nothing to do with each other,
>   either indoors or out.[5]

How do you suppose I managed to survive that?"

Sister-in-law Wu intervened from the sidelines, saying, "Sister-in-law, that's enough! Take the child into consideration. It has always been true that:

> A grand councilor must have enough room
>   in his gut to float a boat;[6]
> The head of a household is a receptacle
>   for catching dirty water.[7]
> The good things that take place should be
>   kept to yourself;
> The bad things that happen should also be
>   kept to yourself."[8]

"Sooner or later," said Yüeh-niang, "I'm going to confront her about those two charges of hers. I'll demand to know just how it is that I put on the airs of a grande dame, or order people around as though I were holding court."

This statement flustered Chin-lien so much that she blurted out, "Elder Sister! You'd better be magnanimous with her. As the saying goes:

> A great person does not deign to notice
> the faults of petty persons;[9]
> What petty person is there who has never
> committed some indiscretion?

As for the things she says about us to our husband behind our backs when she's got him in her room, who is there among the rest of us who hasn't been victimized by her allegations? After all, my quarters and hers are separated by only a common wall. If I didn't make allowances for her, there'd never be an end to it. Whatever she does, she depends upon that child of hers to take advantage of the rest of us. And she has fine things to say too. For example, she says that in the future, when that child of hers grows up, he will:

> Requite favor with favor, and
> Requite enmity with enmity.[10]

So it looks like the rest of us are fated to die of starvation. You don't know the half of it."

"My dear lady!" said Sister-in-law Wu. "How could she have said any such thing?"

Yüeh-niang had nothing further to say about it, but, as the saying goes:

> When an injustice is witnessed on the road,[11]
> Someone will always try to shed light on it.[12]

Who could have anticipated that Hsi-men Ta-chieh had been, for some time, on extremely good terms with Li P'ing-erh. Whenever she was out of needles and thread, or shoe uppers, Li P'ing-erh would supply her with what she needed, giving her even the best quality satins and silks, or two or three fine handkerchiefs at a time. It goes without saying that she also surreptitiously supplied her with cash when the need arose. On that day, when she overheard these allegations about her, how could she help telling her about it.

Li P'ing-erh was in her quarters at the time, engaged in making a silk cord and amulet for her child to wear on the Dragon Boat Festival, along with different-colored little silk *tsung-tzu*, and tigers adorned with apotropaic artemisia leaves.[13] When she saw Hsi-men Ta-chieh come in, Li P'ing-erh offered her a seat, so she could look on with her as she continued with her work.

"Bring some tea for the young lady to drink," Li P'ing-erh instructed Ying-ch'un.

As they drank the tea, Hsi-men Ta-chieh said, "When you were invited back to the rear compound for tea a while ago, why didn't you come?"

"After seeing Father off," said Li P'ing-erh, "I thought I would take advantage of the morning coolness to start making up these miscellaneous things for the child to wear."

"This is not just talebearing,
mind you," said Hsi-men Ta-chieh, "but something has come up that I thought I should tell you about. It is reported that you said that Mother puts on the airs of a grande dame. You must have done something to annoy the Fifth Lady. In the rear compound, while speaking, thus and so, to Mother, she lodged a whole string of accusations against you. Right now, Mother wants to confront you about this. You mustn't say that I told you about it or she might take it amiss, but you ought to prepare something to say about it when you have to explain it to her."

Nothing might have happened if Li P'ing-erh had not heard about this, but having heard these words, she could not even lift the needle she was holding in her hand. Her two arms went soft on her, and she was rendered speechless for some time.

Facing Hsi-men Ta-chieh with the tears falling from her eyes, she said, "Young lady, I never said so much as a word of idle talk on this subject. Last night, while I was in the rear compound, on hearing the page boy say that Father had gone to my quarters, I came out front and urged him to go back to the master suite. Since when did I ever say a word against anybody? Your mother has always been so kind to me, do you really think that I'm so:
    Unconscious of right and wrong,[14]
as to say that sort of thing? And even if I were to have done so, to whom would I have said it? There has to be some evidence for such an allegation."

Hsi-men Ta-chieh said, "When she heard Mother say that sooner or later she was going to confront you about these charges, she became flustered. If it were up to me, the two of you ought to have it out between you, like:
    The gong on the one hand,
    And the drum on the other."

"As though I could hope to contend with that mouth of hers!" exclaimed Li P'ing-erh. "All I can do is leave it to Heaven. One way or the other, she is constantly plotting against me. Mother and son, it won't come to an end until she manages to underhandedly do away with one or the other of us."

When she had finished speaking, she started to cry. Hsi-men Ta-chieh sat down and endeavored to comfort her for a while.

Whom should they see at this point but Hsiao-yü, who came in and said, "The Sixth Lady and the young mistress are invited to come and eat."

She then returned to the rear compound. Li P'ing-erh dropped her needlework and accompanied Hsi-men Ta-chieh back to the master suite. She did not eat anything, however, but returned to her quarters and went to bed. When Hsi-men Ch'ing came home from the yamen, he found her asleep and asked Ying-ch'un about it.

"Mother hasn't eaten a thing all day," reported Ying-ch'un.

This threw Hsi-men Ch'ing into such consternation that he went over to her and demanded, "Why haven't you eaten anything? Tell me what's the matter."

He also noticed that her eyes were red with weeping and asked insistently, "What's troubling you? Tell me about it."

Li P'ing-erh promptly got up, rubbed her eyes, and said, "My eyes are sore. That's all. There's nothing wrong with me. I just didn't feel like eating anything today."

She did not utter a word about what had happened. Truly:

> A whole breastful of intimate concerns,
> Resides in what is not expressed in words.

There is a poem that testifies to this:

> Do not suppose that a beautiful woman
>   is always foolish;
> No amount of brightness and cleverness[15]
>   may do her any good.
> It is only because she is so well versed
>   in human affairs,
> That she has brought a bellyful of grief
>   upon herself.[16]

While Hsi-men Ta-chieh was in the rear compound, she said to Yüeh-niang, "I asked her about it, and she asserted, 'I never said anything of the sort. And to whom am I alleged to have said it?' Moreover:

> Swearing by the gods and uttering oaths,

she turned to me and wept, repeating that, in view of the kindness that Mother has always shown her, how could she ever have brought herself to say such a thing?"

"I simply don't believe it," said Sister-in-law Wu. "Sister Li is such a good person. How could she ever have said such a thing?"

"I imagine," said Yüeh-niang, "that the two of them must have had some minor falling out over who knows what, and that, when she was unable to induce our husband to act on her behalf, she came back to the rear compound and made these groundless allegations, making me out to be an object of obloquy. I've got one shadow too many around here as it is."

"Sister-in-law," said Wu K'ai's wife, "from now on you must be on your guard lest you do her an injustice. It's not that I'm just engaging in gossip behind her back, but she's worth more than a hundred P'an Chin-liens. She's good-hearted by nature. In the two or three years since she became a member of our family she hasn't made so much as a false step."

As they were talking, whom should they see but Ch'in-t'ung, who came in carrying a large bag made of blue cloth on his back.

"What have you got there?" asked Yüeh-niang.

"Thirty thousand taels worth of salt certificates," said Ch'in-t'ung. "Han Tao-kuo and Ts'ui Pen have just arrived back from registering the granary vouchers in exchange for them at the Kao-yang customs station. Father said to see they were given something to eat. Right now, they're weighing out the silver and packing things up. Day after tomorrow, on the twentieth, which is an auspicious day, the two of them, along with Lai-pao, are to set off for Yang-chou.

"I fear my brother-in-law will be coming inside," said Sister-in-law Wu. "The two nuns and I will go visit for a while in the Second Lady's quarters."

Before she had even finished speaking, who should appear but Hsi-men Ch'ing, who lifted aside the portiere and came in. This so flustered Sister-in-law Wu, along with Nun Hsüeh and Nun Wang, that they lost no time in running off to Li Chiao-erh's quarters.

But they were not quick enough to avoid being seen by Hsi-men Ch'ing, who interrogated Yüeh-niang, saying, "That was Nun Hsüeh, the lousy fat shaven-pated whore! What's she doing here?"

Yüeh-niang replied, "How can you persist in being so:

Bad-mouthed and evil-tongued?

It's really outrageous. What's she ever done to annoy you? And how do you know that her name is Hsüeh?"

"You don't know the feats she's capable of," said Hsi-men Ch'ing. "She inveigled the daughter of Vice Commissioner Ch'en into visiting the Ksitigarbha Nunnery, of which she was the abbess, on the fifteenth day of the seventh month, where she engaged in illicit intercourse with a young scamp named Juan the Third. Who could have anticipated that this Juan the Third died on top of the young woman's body. Nun Hsüeh was an accessory before the fact, having received ten taels of silver for her cooperation. When the matter came to light, and she was brought into the yamen, I saw to it that she was stripped of her clothing, given twenty strokes of the bamboo, and ordered to marry a husband and return to lay life.[17] How is it now that she has not returned to lay life? How do you suppose she would like it if I had her dragged into the yamen and given another taste of the squeezers?"

"As though you didn't know any better!" expostulated Yüeh-niang. "You persist in:

Blaspheming gods and profaning Buddhas.

Since she is a devoted Buddhist, I imagine that:

Her good roots continue to exist.

Why should she return to lay life for no good reason? You may not be aware of it, but she is known for her exemplary conduct."

"Just ask her," said Hsi-men Ch'ing, "if she exhibits such exemplary conduct, how many men she can take on in a single night?"

"Stop talking so deliriously," said Yüeh-niang, "or you'll provoke me into a real tirade."

She then went on to ask, "When are you sending those three off on their mission?"

"I have just now dispatched Lai-pao to confer with our kinsman Ch'iao Hung," said Hsi-men Ch'ing. "He's going to put up five hundred taels, and I'm going to put up five hundred taels. The twentieth is an auspicious day, so they can start off then."

"Who will you put in charge of the silk goods store?" Yüeh-niang asked.

"I'll get Pen the Fourth to substitute for him," replied Hsi-men Ch'ing.

When they had finished speaking, Yüeh-niang opened a trunk and got out the silver, which was duly weighed out and turned over to the three servants, who were in the summerhouse at the time, looking after the packing for their trip. Five taels of silver were weighed out for each of them, and they were told to return to their homes and take care of packing their personal belongings. But no more of this.

Who should appear at this juncture but Ying Po-chüeh, who walked into the summerhouse and saw that Hsi-men Ch'ing was supervising the packing.

"What are you having packed up, Brother?" he inquired.

Hsi-men Ch'ing then explained to him all about how, on the twentieth, he was sending Lai-pao and the others to Yang-chou to take delivery of the salt.

Raising his hand in salute, Ying Po-chüeh said, "Congratulations, Brother. When they get back from this trip you're sure to reap a large profit."

Hsi-men Ch'ing offered him a seat, on the one hand, while calling for tea, which they proceeded to drink together.

He then went on to ask, "When are Li the Third and Huang the Fourth going to receive payment of the silver that is due them?"

"They should receive payment no later than the end of this month," said Ying Po-chüeh. "They said to me the other day that right now, in Tung-p'ing prefecture, there is another contract being let for the purveying of twenty thousand taels worth of incense, and they would like to ask if you couldn't help them out in this temporary exigency[18] with the loan of another five hundred taels of silver. When they receive the payment for their current contract, they will bring it over to you, without touching so much as a candareen of it."

"As you can see," said Hsi-men Ch'ing, "I'm in the process of preparing to send my agents off to Yang-chou, but I'm so strapped for cash that I've had to borrow five hundred taels of silver from my kinsman Ch'iao Hung. Where would I come up with any additional silver?"

"They have repeatedly urged me," said Ying Po-chüeh, "to remind you that:
   One guest does not trouble two hosts.
If you refuse to help them out in this exigency, where else would you have them go?"

"The shop of Hsü the Fourth, on the east side of the street outside the city gate," said Hsi-men Ch'ing, "owes me some money. I could transfer five hundred taels of what he owes me to them. How would that be?"

"That's the spirit," said Ying Po-chüeh.

As they were speaking, whom should they see but P'ing-an, who came in carrying a card and said, "His Honor Hsia Yen-ling has sent Hsia Shou with an invitation for Father to pay him a visit tomorrow."

Hsi-men Ch'ing opened the invitation, which read, "So and so."

"The reason I have presumed to come visit you today," said Ying Po-chüeh, "is because there is something I want to tell you about. You know about this affair concerning Li Kuei-chieh from the quarter, I suppose. Has she not come to see you?"

"She hasn't been here since she left in the first month," said Hsi-men Ch'ing. "I don't know about any affair concerning her."

Ying Po-chüeh then set out to explain matters, saying, "It so happens that the third son in the household of the late Imperial Commissioner Wang I-hsüan is married to the niece of Defender-in-Chief Huang Ching-ch'en[19] in the Eastern Capital. In the first month of this year, when they went to the Eastern Capital to wish him a happy new year, the old eunuch gave the two of them a thousand taels of silver as a new year's present. You may not know it, but this niece of Defender-in-Chief Huang's is as pretty as a picture. Really, if an artist were able to depict even half of her beauty, she would still present an elegant appearance. With someone like that at home, one would expect you to stick to her, but every day he allows Blabbermouth Sun, Pockmarked Chu, and Trifler Chang, the three or four of them, to inveigle him into carrying on in the licensed quarter. He has deflowered Ch'i Hsiang-erh, that little slavey from the Ch'i Family Establishment on Second Street, and has also been frequenting Li Kuei-chieh's place. He has even taken to pawning his wife's head ornaments, which has angered her so much that she has tried to hang herself at home. Who would have thought that the other day, earlier this month, she went to the Eastern Capital to celebrate the old eunuch's birthday and told him all about it. The old gentleman was so angry that he sent the names of these fellows to Chu Mien, the defender-in-chief of the Embroidered Uniform Guard, and Chu Mien has issued a mandate to the authorities of Tung-p'ing prefecture ordering that they be taken into custody. Yesterday Blabbermouth Sun, Pockmarked Chu, and Trifler Chang were all apprehended at Li Kuei-chieh's place. Li Kuei-chieh, herself, managed to hide out at Greenhorn Chu's place next door, where she spent the night, but today, she says, she is going to come to your place to beg for your help."

"As I have said," remarked Hsi-men Ch'ing, "during the first month they had already latched onto him and were inveigling him into trying to borrow money under false pretenses, first from this place, and then from that. Pockmarked Chu was trying out his new tricks right in front of me even then."

When he had finished speaking, Ying Po-chüeh said, "I'm going. In a little while, I fear, Li Kuei-chieh is likely to show up. No matter whether you agree to help her out or not, she'll accuse me of interfering with you if she knows I've been here."

"Why not stay a little longer," said Hsi-men Ch'ing. "I've got something else to say to you. As far as Li the Third is concerned, don't promise him anything until I've had a chance to collect that silver that's owed to me outside the city gate, and given you the go-ahead."

"I understand," said Ying Po-chüeh.

By the time he went out the front door, Li Kuei-chieh's sedan chair was there, and she had already gotten out of it and gone inside.

Hsi-men Ch'ing was in the act of instructing Ch'en Ching-chi to ride a mule outside the city gate to Hsü the Fourth's place and dun him for the money, when whom should he see but Ch'in-t'ung, who came into the summerhouse to fetch him, saying, "The First Lady would like you to come back to the master suite. Li Kuei-chieh has come to pay a call."

Hsi-men Ch'ing went back to the rear compound where whom should he see but Li Kuei-chieh, who was wearing plain tea-colored clothing, without any makeup, and had a white drawn-work kerchief fastened around her head.

With her:

> Cloudy locks in disarray, and her
> Flowery countenance dispirited,

she kowtowed to Hsi-men Ch'ing and started to weep, saying, "Father, I don't know how it is that I've been implicated in this unlucky business. Truly:

> Though you sit in your house behind closed doors,
> Catastrophe may yet strike you out of the blue.

This Wang the Third is someone we weren't even acquainted with, but Pockmarked Chu and Blabbermouth Sun, for no good reason, brought him by our place looking for a cup of tea. My elder sister was not at home, and I figured that we'd be better off having nothing to do with them, but my mother, who is getting more demented by the day, was just setting out for your place that day to celebrate my aunt's birthday. It would have been better if she had just gotten into her sedan chair and gone her way, but when she saw the way that Pockmarked Chu was groveling about on his knees to her, she came back inside and said to me, 'Sister, wouldn't it be treating them shabbily not to go out and serve them a cup of tea?' After which she headed off for your place here. I had just locked the door and refused to come out, when who could have anticipated that a crowd of men should come bursting in from outside and:

> Without permitting any further explanation,

apprehended the three of them and took them away. Wang the Third managed to bolt out the gate and escape, while I succeeded in hiding out in the house next door, so there was nobody left in the place. When I sent the male servant here to fetch my mother, she was so frightened when she got home that her soul fled, and all she wanted to do was commit suicide. And today the black-robed lictors from the district yamen, with an arrest warrant in hand, raised a hue and cry about the place all morning before finally taking off. Right now, it seems, I am wanted by name to answer to interrogation in the Eastern Capital. Father, if you refuse to take pity on me and do something to rescue me, what am I to do? Mother, for your part, won't you say something to him on my behalf?"

Hsi-men Ch'ing laughed, and said, "Get up."

He then went on to ask, "What other names are there on the arrest warrant?"

"The other name is that of Ch'i Hsiang-erh," said Li Kuei-chieh. "He has deflowered Ch'i Hsiang-erh, and spent his money at her establishment, so that is only appropriate. But if our place has ever seen so much as a candareen of his money, may the pupils of our eyes drop out. If he ever laid a hand on me, may I develop an abscess in every hair follicle."

Turning to Hsi-men Ch'ing, Yüeh-niang said, "That's enough of that. Lest she continue making these horrific oaths, why don't you speak up on her behalf?"

"At the present time," asked Hsi-men Ch'ing, "has Ch'i Hsiang-erh been arrested or not?"

"Ch'i Hsiang-erh is hiding out in the home of Wang the Second, the distaff relative of the imperial family," said Li Kuei-chieh.

"If that's the case," said Hsi-men Ch'ing, "you can stay at our place here for a few days. If anyone comes looking for you, I'll send someone to the district yamen to plead on your behalf."

Thereupon, he called for Shu-t'ung and instructed him, "Quickly, write out a calling card and deliver it to His Honor Li Ta-t'ien in the district yamen. Just say that Li Kuei-chieh's services are constantly required here, and ask him to see if there isn't some way to avoid having her haled into court."

Shu-t'ung assented and went off on his errand wearing his livery of black silk. It was not long before he returned with a reply from District Magistrate Li.

"His Honor Li," reported Shu-t'ung, "sends his greetings to you but says that, although with regard to any other matter he would not presume to reject your command, this is a case of a certified document issued by his superiors in the Eastern Capital, ordering the district authorities to take the designated persons into custody. The district is only responsible for apprehending the persons named. As a favor to you, he would be willing to relax the deadline by a couple of days, but if you want to avoid having her haled into court altogether, you will have to address yourself to his superiors in the Eastern Capital."

When Hsi-men Ch'ing heard this he thought to himself silently for a while and then said, "Right now Lai-pao is due to set out in a day or two, so there's no one available to send to the Eastern Capital."

"That's all right," said Yüeh-niang. "If you were to send the other two ahead and keep Lai-pao here, so he could go to the Eastern Capital and address himself to this matter on Kuei-chieh's behalf and then catch up with them later, it wouldn't be too late. Just look at the state this fright has put her in."

At this, Li Kuei-chieh hastened to kowtow to Yüeh-niang and Hsi-men Ch'ing.

Hsi-men Ch'ing then sent someone to summon Lai-pao and told him, "You are not to go on the twentieth after all. I'm going to send the other two ahead of you. Tomorrow you can set out for the Eastern Capital instead and negotiate this matter on behalf of Li Kuei-chieh. When you see Majordomo Chai Ch'ien, make sure that whatever he does he sends someone to speak about this matter at the headquarters of the Embroidered Uniform Guard."

Kuei-chieh promptly prostrated herself before Lai-pao, which threw him into such consternation that he kowtowed in return and backed off, saying, "Sister Kuei, I'll go."

Hsi-men Ch'ing then told Shu-t'ung to write a letter for him, thanking Majordomo Chai Ch'ien for all the trouble he had been put to earlier in connection with Regional Investigating Censor Tseng Hsiao-hsü, and also sealed up twenty taels of silver in lieu of a seasonal gift and entrusted it to Lai-pao along with the letter.

This pleased Li Kuei-chieh so much that she took out five taels of silver and offered it to Lai-pao to defray his expenses on the road, saying, "When you come back, Brother Pao, both my mother and I will see that you are amply rewarded."

Hsi-men Ch'ing would not allow this and told Kuei-chieh to take back her money, while he directed Yüeh-niang to provide another five taels of silver for Lai-pao's expenses.

"That doesn't make any sense," said Kuei-chieh. "Since I'm the one who's begging Father to intervene on my behalf, am I to put him to extra expense?"

"Do you take me for such a laughingstock," protested Hsi-men Ch'ing, "that I can't come up with five taels of silver for his traveling expenses, but have to get the money from you?"

Only then did Li Kuei-chieh put her silver away, bowing to Lai-pao again and again, while saying, "I'm imposing on you, Brother Pao, but I hope, whatever happens, you'll be able to start out tomorrow, or it may be too late."

"I'll be on the road by the fifth watch tomorrow morning," said Lai-pao.

Thereupon, he took the letter and went off to Han Tao-kuo's home on Lion Street. Wang Liu-erh was in the house at the time, engaged in sewing up some underwear for her husband.

When she saw through the window that it was Lai-pao, she promptly said, "If you have something to say, please come inside and sit down. He's not at home right now, having gone to the tailor's to pick up some clothes, but he'll be back any moment."

She then summoned Chin-erh and said, "Why don't you go across the street to Tailor Hsü's place and fetch your master? Tell him that Mr. Lai-pao is here."

"I have presumed to come over," explained Lai-pao, "in order to tell you that it turns out I won't be able to go off with your husband tomorrow. Another karmic impediment has come up, and the master has decided to send me off to the Eastern Capital in order to intercede on behalf of Li Kuei-chieh from the licensed quarter. Just now, she kowtowed repeatedly in front of Father in an act of formal obeisance and supplication, at which Mother consulted with Father, and then said, 'That's all right. If you are willing to make a trip to the Eastern Capital to intercede in this matter on her behalf, we can let Han Tao-kuo and Ts'ui Pen go on ahead, and it won't be too late for you to catch up with them after you get back.' So I'll have to set out early tomorrow morning, and the letter has even been entrusted to me just now."

He then went on to ask, "Sister-in-law, what's that you're working on?"

"It's his underwear," replied Wang Liu-erh.

"You can tell him there's no need to take a lot of clothes with him," said Lai-pao. "That area is the cradle of production for silks and gauzes, satins and damasks, so he needn't worry about not having clothes to wear."

As they were speaking together, Han Tao-kuo arrived home.

After the two of them had exchanged salutations, and the above matters had been explained to him, Lai-pao went on to ask, "When the day comes, where am I to look for you two in Yang-chou?"

"The master has directed," said Han Tao-kuo, "that we should put up right on the docks at the inn of a merchant named Wang Po-ju. He says that his own late father and the father of Wang Po-ju were on good terms with each other, that the rooms in his inn are spacious and can accommodate many traders, and that it is a safe place to store merchandise without having to worry about it. The best thing to do would be to look for us there."

Lai-pao then went on to say, "Sister-in-law, when I set out for the Eastern Capital tomorrow, do you have any shoes and foot-bindings, or things like that, that I can deliver to your daughter in the minister's residence?"

"I don't have anything," said Wang Liu-erh, "except for two pairs of hairpins that her father has had made for her, and two pairs of shoes, if we could trouble you to deliver them to her."

Thereupon, she wrapped these items up in a handkerchief and handed them to Lai-pao, on the one hand, while on the other, she called for Ch'un-hsiang to prepare something to eat and decant some wine. The woman then hastily set aside the needlework she had been doing and saw to the setting up of a table.

"Sister-in-law," said Lai-pao, "don't go to all that trouble. I can't stay for long. I've got to go home and pack my bag so that I'll be ready to start off tomorrow."

"Ai-ya!" exclaimed Wang Liu-erh with an ingratiating smile, "how can you start:

> Waxing supercilious before you enter the door?

When your fellow employee's household offers you such a farewell collation, you ought to have a cup to drink."

She then went on to complain, "Han Tao-kuo, how can you be so sober-sided? The table isn't steady on its feet. See if you can't steady it, and offer Uncle Pao a seat. You're acting like a mere bystander."

Thereupon, dishes of food were brought out, and wine was poured and offered to Lai-pao. Wang Liu-erh joined them at the side of the table, and the three of them sat down to drink.

After Lai-pao had drunk a few cups, he said, "I'd better get home. If I stay any later, I'm afraid the gate back there will already be closed."

"Have you hired your mount or not?" asked Han Tao-kuo.

"I'll hire it first thing tomorrow morning," said Lai-pao.

He then went on to say, "You might as well turn over the keys to the shop, and the account books, to Pen the Fourth, so you won't have to spend the night there. A good night's rest at home will prepare you for the journey."

"What you say is true enough," said Han Tao-kuo. "I'll hand them over to him tomorrow."

Wang Liu-erh poured out another goblet of wine and said, "Uncle Pao, if you'll just finish off this cup, we won't presume to keep you any longer."

"Sister-in-law," said Lai-pao, "if you want me to drink it, could you warm it up a little?"

Wang Liu-erh promptly poured it back into the flagon and told Chin-erh to reheat it, after which she filled his cup and proffered it to Lai-pao with both hands, saying, "I'm afraid we don't have anything worth eating in order to go with Uncle Pao's wine."

"That's a fine thing to say, Sister-in-law!" protested Lai-pao. "After all:

> The normal formalities do not apply in the home."[20]

So saying, he lifted up his wine in order to toast the woman, and the two of them drained their cups together, before he got up to take his leave.

Wang Liu-erh then handed the gifts for her daughter back to him, saying, "Might I trouble you, Uncle Pao, whatever happens, when you get to the minister's mansion, to ask how my daughter is getting along? I'll be relieved to know."

Thereupon, she bowed to him, saying, "Many felicitations," after which she and her husband saw him to the door.

We will say no more for the moment about how Lai-pao went home, packed his baggage, and set out for the Eastern Capital the next day, but return to the story of Yüeh-niang, who was in the master suite engaged in serving tea to Li Kuei-chieh. Sister-in-law Wu, Aunt Yang, and the two nuns were all visiting together with her there.

At this juncture, Brother-in-law Wu K'ai showed up and said to Hsi-men Ch'ing, "A document has been sent down from Tung-p'ing prefecture, deputing the seal-holding officers of the Left and Right Battalions of our Ch'ing-ho Guard to supervise the repair of the local Charity Granary. The edict of authorization states that if the work is completed by the deadline in the sixth month, they will be promoted one grade, but that if they fail to meet the deadline, they will be subject to investigation and impeachment by the provincial regional inspector. If my brother-in-law has the silver to spare and could lend me a few taels to defray the cost of the work, I would be able to return every bit of it as soon as I receive reimbursement for these expenses."

"Brother-in-law," said Hsi-men Ch'ing, "whatever you need is yours for the asking."

"If you'll deign to help me out," said Wu K'ai, "twenty taels ought to do the trick."

They then went back to the rear compound and spoke to Yüeh-niang about it. Hsi-men Ch'ing had her get out twenty taels and turn them over to Wu K'ai. After drinking a cup of tea, they came out again. Because there were female guests being entertained in the master suite and it was inconvenient to accommodate them there, Yüeh-niang had suggested that he invite her brother to stay a while and have some wine with him in the main reception hall.

As they were drinking their wine, whom should they see but Ch'en Ching-chi, who came in to report, saying, "As for that debt that you're trying to collect from Hsü the Fourth outside the city gate, he sends you his regards but asks that you give him another couple of days' grace."

"Nonsense!" exclaimed Hsi-men Ch'ing. "I need the money here right now. Why should I give him another couple of days' grace? You go right back there and give that dog of a whore's spawn a piece of my mind."

When Ch'en Ching-chi had agreed to do so, Wu K'ai offered him a seat, and he bowed to him in response before sitting down to one side. Ch'in-t'ung promptly provided him with chopsticks and a wine cup, and they continued to drink together in the front compound.

To resume our story, in the rear compound, Sister-in-law Wu, Aunt Yang, Li Chiao-erh, Meng Yü-lou, P'an Chin-lien, Li P'ing-erh, and Hsi-men Ta-chieh were all keeping Li Kuei-chieh company as they drank wine in Yüeh-niang's room. To begin with, Big Sister Yü, who had been performing the story of Chang Chün-jui's sightseeing visit to the Temple of Universal Salvation[21] for a while, finally put down her p'i-p'a.

Meng Yü-lou, who was located at her side, poured out some wine and offered her a serving of food, saying, "What a lousy blind millstone-turning donkey you are! You've been singing for us all day, and you'll probably say we don't even take care of you."

P'an Chin-lien, for her part, picked up a piece of pork shank with her chopsticks and teased her by dangling it provocatively in front of her nose.

Li Kuei-chieh then said, "Sister Yü-hsiao, if you'll hand me Big Sister Yü's *p'i-p'a*, I'll sing a song for my aunt and Sister-in-law Wu."

"Kuei-chieh," said Yüeh-niang, "you've got enough on your mind as it is. There's no need for you to sing."

"It's no problem," said Kuei-chieh. "Let me sing. Now that Mother and Father have agreed to intervene on my behalf, I'm not anxious about things any more."

Meng Yü-lou smiled at this, saying, "Li Kuei-chieh is a true child of the quarter. She can alter her demeanor at will. When she first arrived just a little while ago, her brows were knit, and she was so anxious she couldn't even drink her tea. But now:

She talks, and she laughs."

Thereupon, Li Kuei-chieh:

Deftly extended her slender fingers,
Impulsively plucked the icy strings,

and proceeded to sing for a while. As she was still singing, who should appear but Ch'in-t'ung, who was engaged in bringing in the utensils from the front compound.

Yüeh-niang asked him, "Has Brother-in-law Wu left yet?"

"He has already left," replied Ch'in-t'ung.

"I fear Brother-in-law will soon be coming inside," said Sister-in-law Wu. "We'd better bestir ourselves."

"Father won't be coming back to the rear compound," said Ch'in-t'ung. "He's gone to the Fifth Lady's quarters."

When P'an Chin-lien heard that he had gone to her quarters, she was unable to remain in her seat and could hardly wait to take off, but she felt embarrassed to leave too precipitously.

Yüeh-niang, without even waiting for her to make a move, said, "Since he's gone to your quarters, you'd better get going, lest you end up as a kinswoman with an empty womb."

"A likely story!" protested P'an Chin-lien; but although her mouth remained adamant, her feet carried her quickly away.

When she arrived in the front compound and went into her quarters, she found that Hsi-men Ch'ing had already taken a dose of the Indian monk's medicine, gotten Ch'un-mei to help him off with his clothes, and was sitting inside the bed curtains on the bed.

On seeing this, Chin-lien laughed, saying, "My child, what a good boy you are today, going to bed without even waiting for your mother. I've been in the rear compound, just now, keeping company with Sister-in-law Wu and Aunt Yang, while listening to Li Kuei-chieh sing, and being compelled to have a few cups too many. All by myself, in the dark shadows, staggering along with:

> One step high, and
> One step low,[22]

I've only just managed, somehow or other, to make it home."

Then, calling to Ch'un-mei, she said, "If you've got some tea, pour out a cup for me."

Ch'un-mei proceeded to pour a cup of tea for her, and Chin-lien drank it; after which she gave her a meaningful moue, which Ch'un-mei correctly understood. She had long since heated some water for her in the adjacent room, where the woman shook some sandalwood and alum into it, washed her private parts, took down her hair under the lamplight, retaining only a single gold hairpin, took up the mirror with which to apply a new coat of rouge to her lips, and put a breath-sweetening lozenge into her mouth, before coming back into the bedroom. Ch'un-mei fetched her sleeping shoes from the head of the bed, helped her exchange them for the ones she had on, put the latch on the door, and went out.

The woman then proceeded to move the lampstand closer to the bed, where she placed it on a table, let down half of the silk bed curtain with one hand:

> Took off her red drawers, and
> Exposed her jadelike body.

Hsi-men Ch'ing, who was sitting on the pillow, with two clasps fastened around his organ, which had caused it to swell to a prodigious size, exposed it for her to see. When the woman caught sight of it under the lamplight, it gave her quite a start. It was so thick she could hardly get her hand around it, empurpled and tumid, it was more than she could encircle with her thumb and forefinger.

Casting an amorous glance at Hsi-men Ch'ing, she said, "My guess would be that you can hardly deny having already taken a dose of that monk's medicine in order to work it up to such dimensions, with the sole intention of giving me a hard time. But:

> The best wine and the finest meat,
> Get eaten by Community Head Wang.

Whoever it is that you've tried it on first has reduced you to no more than:

> The bested general of a defeated army,[23]

by the time you bother to show up in my room here. Am I only fit to be fucked by what's left of that spent prick of yours? And you claim not to be practicing favoritism! No wonder the other day, when I wasn't in my room, you made off to her quarters with that bag of implements without anyone being the wiser. So it turns out that she was the one you were up to your business with that night. And yet she contrives to protest her own virtue in front of others. As for you, you're simply nothing but an incorrigible three-inch good-for-nothing! Come to think of it, I'd be better off if I refused to have anything to do with you though I live to be a hundred."

"You little whore," Hsi-men Ch'ing exclaimed with a laugh, "come over here. If you have the talent to suck it to ejaculation, I'll forfeit a tael of silver to you."

"You're delirious," the woman said. "No matter what it is that you've imbibed, you expect me to put up with it."

Thereupon, she lay down diagonally across the mat, grasped his organ with both hands, and engulfed it with her ruby lips, saying as she did so, "What a big thing it is! It stretches my mouth till it hurts."

When she had finished speaking, she either:

Sucked it audibly as it moved in and out; or
Explored the mouth of his urethra with
   the tip of her tongue; or
Licked the frenum underneath his turtle head; or
Held it in her mouth to nibble and toy with
   as it came and went; or
Brushed it back and forth against her powdered cheek;
Titillating it in a hundred different ways.

His organ was stiffer and harder than ever and stood up, tumid and perpendicular.

In the bursting melon-head the sunken eye
   grows round;
Trailing its side whiskers the body swells
   itself erect.

Hsi-men Ch'ing bent his head in order to observe the woman's fragrant flesh by the flickering light underneath the silk bed curtains. With her slender fingers, she took hold of his limber organ with both hands and popped it into her mouth, moving back and forth as she did so under the lamplight.

Who could have anticipated that a white long-haired leonine cat[24] that was crouching by their side was attracted by the motion, and, not knowing what kind of an object it was, pounced forward and batted at it with her claws. Hsi-men Ch'ing, from his superior vantage point, took to playfully teasing it with the gold-flecked black fan in his hand, at which the woman grabbed the fan away from him and hit the cat as hard as she could with the handle of the fan, driving it outside the bed curtains.

Giving Hsi-men Ch'ing an amorous glance, she said, "What a crazy excuse for a lover you are! On top of the fact that she's sticking her paws in where they don't belong in such an obnoxious[25] way, you would humor her into:

Assuming privileges above her station.

If she should happen to scratch my face, what would you do then? I might as well call this business to a halt here and now. How would that be?"

"You crazy little whore!" exclaimed Hsi-men Ch'ing. "You'll do me in yet with all your objections."

Chin-lien Hits the Cat while Sucking Off Hsi-men Ch'ing

"Why don't you get Li P'ing-erh to suck it off for you then?" said the woman. "It's always my room you come to when you want someone to submit to your pestering. I don't know what it is that you've imbibed, but I've been sucking you off all day to no avail."

Hsi-men Ch'ing thereupon took the little silver box out of his handkerchief, picked out some of the pink ointment it contained with a toothpick, and daubed it in the mouth of his urethra. After which, adopting a prone position, he had the woman sit astride his body.

"Let me stretch it open," the woman said, "so you can get inside more easily."

His turtle head was proud and large, so that, even with moistening and reaming, it was some time before the knob of his glans was completely submerged. The woman in her superior position rubbed her body back and forth against his, while seeming to be unable to overcome her distress.

"My own daddy!" she exclaimed. "I feel completely stuffed inside. It's really hard to bear."

While fondling it with her hand, she saw under the lamplight that half of his jade chowrie handle[26] had already been engulfed by her vagina, the labia of which were stretched to capacity on either side. No longer moving back and forth, the woman used her saliva to moisten her labia until it felt somewhat smoother, whereupon she resumed her motions, alternately raising and lowering herself, until his organ finally penetrated her to the root.

The woman addressed herself to Hsi-men Ch'ing, saying, "That aphrodisiac you usually use, called 'The Quavery Voices of Amorous Beauties,'[27] induces a hot and itchy sensation inside that is hard to stand. How can it be compared to this monk's medication? When it penetrates all the way to the womb, it produces a cool shivery feeling that reaches all the way up to the heart. Right now:

My whole body, from top to bottom,[28]

is infused with a melting sensation. I foresee that today I may die at your hands, but it's a hard thing to bear."

"Fivey," said Hsi-men Ch'ing, "I've got a joke to tell you, which I heard from Brother Ying the Second. A certain man died, and King Yama enveloped his body in a donkey's skin in order to change him into a donkey. Later, however, the Assessor consulted his ledgers and found that he still had thirteen years in the human realm allotted to him, so he was allowed to return to life. His wife noticed that although the rest of his body had reverted to human form, his male organ was still that of a donkey and had not returned to its former dimensions. 'Let me go back to the nether regions and get it changed,' the man said. But this threw his wife into consternation and she replied, 'Brother, if you undertake this journey, I fear that you may not be allowed to return, and what would we do then? Just leave it as it is, and I'll gradually learn to put up with it.' "[29]

When the woman heard this, she laughed, gave him a whack with the handle of the fan, and said, "No wonder Beggar Ying's two wives are so inured to that donkey's prick of his. You filthy-mouthed good-for-nothing! If I didn't care for the opinion of the world, I'd really let you have it!"

The two of them went at it for a full two hours, but Hsi-men Ch'ing had still not ejaculated. He merely lay underneath her with his eyes closed, and let the woman squat on top of him, thrusting and retracting for all she was worth. These efforts of hers caused his turtle head to make a weird noise, *kua-ta kua-ta*, as it went in and out. After she had been at it for a long time, she stooped forward so that she was looking right at Hsi-men Ch'ing. Hsi-men Ch'ing lifted up her haunches with both hands and alternately submerged and exposed the knob of his glans, moving back and forth with abandon.[30] Although Hsi-men Ch'ing's body was in contact with hers, and he was able to observe the action with his eyes, he seemed to remain completely unaffected. After some time, the woman's feelings came to a climax, and, stooping down again, she embraced Hsi-men Ch'ing around the neck with both hands, resting her body on his, and sticking her tongue into his mouth. His organ had penetrated all the way to the interior of her vagina, as he continued kneading away at her.

"My own daddy!" she cried out inarticulately. "That's enough. Your Fivey is dying."

A moment afterwards:

> She swooned completely away,[31]
> The tip of her tongue became ice-cold, and
> She gave way to an orgasm.

Hsi-men Ch'ing became aware of a wave of warmth within her vagina that penetrated all the way to his cinnabar field, while in his heart, he felt a melting sensation the pleasure of which was indescribable. Meanwhile, her vaginal secretions overflowed, and the woman wiped them up with a handkerchief. The two of them continued:

> Hugging and embracing each other,
> With entwined necks, thigh over thigh,
> Audibly sucking each other's tongues,

while his organ remained embedded in her. After napping for an hour, the woman, whose lascivious feelings were still unsatisfied, climbed back on top of his body, and the two of them went at it again.

The woman had two orgasms in a row and began to feel somewhat fatigued, but Hsi-men Ch'ing:

> Feigning total indifference,[32]

thought to himself, "This medication of the Indian Monk's is truly supernatural."

Before long:

> The cock crowed outside the window, and
> The eastern horizon began to grow light.

"Dear heart," the woman said. "You still haven't ejaculated. What should we do? This evening, if you come again, I'll be sure, whatever happens, to suck it off for you."

"Even if you suck it, I won't ejaculate," said Hsi-men Ch'ing. "I can assure you, there's only one thing that will bring about an ejaculation."

"Tell me," the woman said, "what might that be?"

Hsi-men Ch'ing said:

"The dharma must not be divulged to six ears.[33]

Wait until I come back this evening, and I'll tell you."

That morning he got up, combed his hair, and performed his ablutions, after which Ch'un-mei helped him on with his clothes. Han Tao-kuo and Ts'ui Pen were already outside, waiting for him. When Hsi-men Ch'ing came out, he burnt some paper money to ensure a safe journey and prepared to send them on their way.

Turning over a pair of letters to them, he said, "One of these is addressed to Wang Po-ju at his inn on the docks at Yang-chou. The other is addressed to Miao Ch'ing. You must go into the city of Yang-chou to find him, discover how his affair has turned out, and send the information back to me post haste. If your funds prove insufficient, I'll send Lai-pao with some more later on."

"Do you also have a letter for His Honor Ts'ai Yün?" asked Ts'ui Pen.

"His Honor Ts'ai Yün's letter hasn't been written yet," said Hsi-men Ch'ing. "I'll have Lai-pao bring it with him later on."

The two men then got onto their mounts and set off on their journey. But no more of this.

Hsi-men Ch'ing, having donned his official cap and girdle, set out for the yamen, where he met with Judicial Commissioner Hsia and thanked him for his invitation of the day before.

"Today," said Hsia Yen-ling, "in presuming to hope that my colleague will deign to come over for a chat, I have not invited any other guests."

When they had finished disposing of the business at hand, the two of them separated and returned to their homes.

Wu Yüeh-niang had long since prepared a meal in the master suite and invited Hsi-men Ch'ing to partake of some congee.

Who should appear at this juncture but a black-liveried lictor, mounted on a swift steed, and carrying a felt dispatch case, who arrived at the front gate with his face bathed in sweat and asked P'ing-an, "Is this the home of the judicial commissioner, His Honor Hsi-men?"

"Where have you come from?" asked P'ing-an.

The man hastily dismounted from his steed, made a bow, and said, "I have been sent ahead by His Honor An Ch'en, who is engaged in expediting the delivery of imperial lumber, in order to present some gifts to His Honor Hsi-men Ch'ing. My master, together with His Honor Huang, who is in charge of the imperial brickyard, are on their way to attend a drinking party in Tung-p'ing prefecture at the invitation of His Honor Hu Shih-wen. Taking advantage of the opportunity, they would like to stop off for a visit with His Honor on the way. So I have been sent ahead to find out if His Honor is at home or not."

"Do you have a card or not?" asked P'ing-an.

The man reached into his felt bag and pulled out a card, which he turned over to P'ing-an, along with the presents. P'ing-an took them inside and delivered them to his master.

Hsi-men Ch'ing seeing that the list of gifts read:

Two bolts of Chekiang silk,

Four catties of Hu-chou silk floss,

One girdle with a decorative plaque of aromatic wood, and

One antique mirror,

ordered that five mace of silver be wrapped up and presented to the courier, together with a reply, stating that he would respectfully await the impending visit. The lictor, then, went swiftly on his way.

Hsi-men Ch'ing had wine and food prepared in his home for the event and waited until noon, when the two officials duly arrived, preceded by escorts shouting to clear the way. On this occasion, they were riding in palanquins, protected from the sun by elaborate baldachins. Upon arrival, they sent in their calling cards, one of which read, "Your devoted servant An Ch'en pays his respects," and the other read, "Your devoted servant Huang Pao-kuang[34] pays his respects." Both of them wore robes emblazoned with mandarin squares portraying a silver pheasant against a background of azure clouds,[35] black silk caps, and black shoes. They deferred politely to each other as they came in, and Hsi-men Ch'ing went out to the main gate to welcome them. Upon arriving in the main reception hall, and exchanging the customary amenities, they each expressed:

The sentiments they had felt while apart,[36]

and then sat down in the positions appropriate for guests and host. Secretary Huang took a place on the left, Secretary An took a place on the right, while Hsi-men Ch'ing assumed the host's position in order to keep them company.

Secretary Huang initiated the proceedings by raising his hand, and saying, "Having long been an admirer of your worthy name, surpassing virtue, and illustrious reputation, I fear I have been tardy in paying my respects."

"You do me too much honor," responded Hsi-men Ch'ing. "I fear I am guilty, Venerable Sir, of putting you to the trouble of paying me an initial visit. You must allow me to return the favor in the future. May I venture to enquire as to your distinguished courtesy name?"

"My fellow graduate Huang's courtesy name is T'ai-yü, or Vast Vision," said Secretary An. "It is derived from the line, 'He whose vision is vast and serene emits a Heavenly light.'"[37]

"May I venture to enquire as to your distinguished courtesy name?" said Secretary Huang.

"Your pupil's courtesy name is Ssu-ch'üan, or Four Springs," replied Hsi-men Ch'ing. "It was chosen because my country estate has four wells on it."

"The other day," said Secretary An, "I met with my fellow graduate Ts'ai Yün, who reported that he and Sung Ch'iao-nien had put you to the trouble of entertaining them at your distinguished mansion."

"In consideration of Chai Ch'ien's esteemed request," replied Hsi-men Ch'ing, "and the fact that he is also the superior official in my humble jurisdiction, I could hardly fail to make him welcome. While my paltry servant was in the capital, he learned of your illustrious appointment, but I have not, heretofore, been able to congratulate you in person."

He then went on to ask, "When did you take leave of your native place?"

"After departing from your distinguished mansion last year," said Secretary An, "your pupil returned to his home in order to remarry. After the New Year's celebrations, I came back to the capital in the first month and have been appointed to the position of secretary in the Ministry of Works, where I have been put in charge of expediting the delivery of imperial lumber, a task that requires me to travel to Ching-chou. Since my route takes me by this place, I could hardly fail to pay my respects."

Hsi-men Ch'ing went on to say, "As for your lavish gifts:
    My gratitude knows no bounds."[38]

When he had finished speaking, Hsi-men Ch'ing invited his guests to loosen their formal clothing and relax, while ordering his attendants to set up tables for them.

Secretary Huang wished to depart immediately, and Secretary An explained, "To tell the truth, my fellow graduate Huang and I are currently on our way to attend a banquet at the invitation of Prefect Hu Shih-wen in Tung-p'ing prefecture. Since our route took us past your distinguished mansion, we could hardly fail to pay our respects. On another day we will come again and impose upon your hospitality."

"If you are proceeding to Hu Shih-wen's place," said Hsi-men Ch'ing, "you still have some distance to go. Even if you two gentlemen are not hungry yourselves, what about your attendants? Your pupil would not presume to provide a formal libation. I have merely prepared a meal here, with which to regale your subordinates and attendants."

Thereupon, platters of viands were sent out for the chair bearers, and table settings were simultaneously arrayed in the reception hall.

    The rare dainties and exotic delicacies,[39]
    Were the finest the season could provide,
consisting of soup, rice, sweetmeats, and delectable fresh seafood. After Hsi-men Ch'ing had toasted his visitors with but three small golden goblets of wine, these table settings were carried out for the refreshment of the personal attendants and docket officers in their entourage.

After a little while, the two officials bade farewell and got up to go, saying to Hsi-men Ch'ing, "Tomorrow your pupils will dispatch a paltry missive, presuming to hope, Worthy Sir, that you will deign to pay a visit to the estate of my fellow graduate Huang's colleague, Eunuch Director Liu, for a chat. But we don't know whether you will consent to order out your equipage or not."

"As the recipient of your magnanimous summons," said Hsi-men Ch'ing, "I could but hasten to comply."

When they had finished speaking, he escorted his visitors to the main gate, where they got into their sedan chairs and departed.

Whom should he encounter at this juncture, but a servant sent by Judicial Commissioner Hsia to remind him of his invitation.

"I'm leaving right away," Hsi-men Ch'ing told him.

Having ordered his horse to be prepared, he went back to the rear compound, changed his clothes, came out again, mounted his horse, and set out for the residence of Judicial Commissioner Hsia, accompanied by Tai-an and Ch'in-t'ung, and preceded by orderlies who shouted to clear the way, holding aloft a black flabellum to shield him from the sun.

After he arrived in the reception hall, and they had greeted each other, he said, "Just now, Secretary An Ch'en of the Ministry of Works, who is expediting the delivery of imperial lumber to the capital, and Secretary Huang Pao-kuang, who is in charge of the imperial brickyard, paid me a visit and stayed for half a day before departing. Otherwise, I would have come over earlier."

When they had run through the customary amenities, he was helped off with his outer clothes, which Tai-an directed an orderly to fold up and put into his felt bag, together with his official girdle. There were two table settings arrayed in the reception hall. Hsi-men Ch'ing was ushered to the position of honor at the one on the left, while the position next to his was occupied by Licentiate Ni, a tutor employed in the household of Hsia Yen-ling.

In the course of the ensuing conversation, Hsi-men Ch'ing said to him, "Might I enquire as to your distinguished courtesy name, Venerable Sir?"

"Your pupil is named Ni P'eng, or Familiar Ni," replied the licentiate. "My informal name is Shih-yüan, and my courtesy name is Kuei-yen. At present I occupy a position in the prefectural school and also serve as a tutor in the residence of my venerable patron Hsia Yen-ling, where I am engaged in preparing the young gentleman, his worthy son, for the civil service examinations. I fear I have been remiss in failing to make your acquaintance."

As they were speaking, two boy actors came forward and kowtowed before the company. When they had finished their soup and rice, the chef came out and carved the entrée, after which Hsi-men Ch'ing directed Tai-an to reward him with an appropriate gratuity.

"Bring me my informal cap to wear," Hsi-men Ch'ing said to Tai-an. "Take my official cap, girdle, and robe home with you, and come back to fetch me this evening."

Tai-an assented, ate the snack that had been provided for him, and went home with the horse. But no more of this.

To resume our story, P'an Chin-lien, after seeing Hsi-men Ch'ing off that morning, slept until noon before crawling out of bed. And once she was up, she was too lazy to comb her hair. Fearing that this would subject her to criticism by the denizens of the rear compound, when Yüeh-niang invited her to join them for lunch, she refused on the grounds that she was not feeling well. It was late afternoon before she ventured out the door of her quarters and made her way to the rear compound.

Yüeh-niang, taking advantage of Hsi-men Ch'ing's absence, planned to listen to Nun Hsüeh expound the Buddhist dharma by performing the *Chin-kang k'o-i*, or *Liturgical Exposition of the Diamond Sutra*. With this end in view, a lectern for the sutra recitation had been set up in the parlor of the master suite, incense had been ignited, Nun Hsüeh and Nun Wang sat facing each other, while Nun Hsüeh's two disciples, Miao-ch'ü and Miao-feng, stood to either side, ready to chime in by reciting the Buddha's name in unison. Sister-in-law Wu, Aunt Yang, Wu Yüeh-niang, Li Chiao-erh, Meng Yü-lou, P'an Chin-lien, Li P'ing-erh, Sun Hsüeh-o, and Li Kuei-chieh, one and all, seated themselves around them, prepared to listen to the performance.

Nun Hsüeh began the recitation as follows:[40]

I have heard tell that:
The flash of lightning is quickly extinguished;
The spark from a flint is difficult to sustain.
Fallen blossoms are not fated to
return to the tree;
Flowing water is not destined to
return to its source.[41]
Though you dwell in painted hall and brocade room,[42]
When your life is over, they are like
the infinite void;
Though you possess supreme rank and lofty office,
When your salary stops, they resemble
nothing but dreams.
Yellow gold and white jade,[43]
Are merely prerequisites for disaster;
Red powder and light furs,
Are but the expenses of mundane labor.
Wives and children cannot ensure
a lifetime of happiness;

The darkness of the grave entails
    a myriad forms of grief.
One fine day, while sleeping on your pillow,
You'll end up underneath the Yellow Springs.[44]
An empty epitaph will proclaim
    your specious fame;
The yellow earth will entomb
    your fragile bones.
Your hundred acres of fields and gardens,
Will only create dissension among your
    sons and daughters;
Your thousand trunks of satin and brocade,[45]
Will not furnish you an inch of thread
    after your death.[46]
Before the springtime of youth is half over,
White hair will encroach upon your head;
No sooner will your well-wishers be heard,
Than they will come to condole at your wake.[47]
It is bitter! Bitter! Bitter!
The breath is transformed into a clear breeze,
    the dust returns to earth;
The wheel of transmigration turns inexorably,
    it cannot be called back;
The head is altered and the face replaced[48]
    an infinite number of times.[49]

Homage to the Three Jewels, the Buddha, the Dharma, and the San-
gha, that permeate the empty void, and pervade the dharma realm,
past, present, and future.[50]

The subtle and mysterious dharma
    of utmost profundity,
Is difficult to encounter even
    in myriads of kalpas.
Now that we have heard it, and
    are able to keep it,
We wish to understand the true
    meaning of the Tathāgata.[51]

Nun Wang said, "In those days of yore, how did Śākyamuni Buddha,
the patriarch of all the Buddhas, and founder of the Buddhist faith, come to
leave home in order to take up the religious life? We would like to hear you
expound it."
Nun Hsüeh then sang, to the tune "Five Offerings":

Śākyamuni Buddha,
The Indian prince,
Relinquished his kingdom in order to
    meditate in the Himalayas.
Severing his flesh to feed the eagles,[52]
    magpies nested on his crown.[53]
He cultivated himself until,
Nine dragons sprayed him with water,[54]
    turning his body to gold.
Only then was he revered as the
World-honored Śākyamuni,
Lord of the Greater Vehicle and
    supreme enlightenment.

Nun Wang continued, "Now that we have heard you expound the story of Śākyamuni Buddha, in those days, how did the bodhisattva Avalokiteśvara engage in religious practice until attaining the glorious realization of multi-form transformations and vast numinous powers? We would like to hear you explain it."

Nun Hsüeh then continued, to the same tune:

The great and glorious,
Princess Miao-shan,[55]
Forsook the imperial palace in order to
    dwell in Hsiang-shan.
Devas brought her offerings[56] as she
    sat in meditation.
She cultivated herself until,
She was able to manifest the fifty-three forms[57]
    of her transformation body.
Only then was she revered as Kuan-shih-yin,
    the bodhisattva who,
Perceives the sounds of the world and saves people
    from suffering and disaster.

Nun Wang said, "Now that we have heard the dharma of the bodhisattva Avalokiteśvara, in days of yore there were the Six Patriarchs, Buddhas who transmitted the lamp. The first of them, Bodhidharma, since the Western Regions had already been converted, turned to the East, in order to transmit the ineffable teaching that does not rely on written words.[58] What arduous austerities did he undergo? We would like to hear the details."

Nun Hsüeh then continued, to the same tune:

Master Bodhidharma, from whom the Dharma passed
To the Sixth Patriarch, whose lay surname was Lu,[59]

Meditated with his face to the wall for nine years,[60]
    so arduous were his austerities.
He remained so still reeds grew between his knees,[61]
    while subduing dragons and tigers.
He cultivated himself until,
With the aid of a single shoe or a plucked reed[62]
    he was able to go where he willed.
Only then was he revered as the Buddha Vairocana,
    who, with supreme compassion,
Swore the great vow to work for the salvation
    of all sentient beings.

Nun Wang said, "Now that we have heard the details about how the Six Patriarchs transmitted the lamp, I venture to ask for an explanation of how, in days of yore, the layman P'ang Yün disposed of all his worldly wealth by sending it to the bottom of the sea[63] and thereby reaped the true fruit?"

Nun Hsüeh then sang, to the same tune:

The layman P'ang Yün,
An enlightened being,
Invested in his future life by coming to the aid
    of the impoverished and wretched,
After overhearing the complaints against him of
    donkeys and horses one night.[64]
He cultivated himself until,
Abandoning his wife and children,[65] he was able
    to embark upon the dharma boat.
Only then was he revered as the guardian of
    the monastic establishment,
The abode of the wonderful vehicle
    and its wonderful dharma.

Just as Yüeh-niang was fully absorbed in listening to the performance, whom should she see but P'ing-an, who appeared in a state of obvious agitation and said, "The household of His Honor the regional investigating censor Sung Ch'iao-nien has sent two couriers and a gate-boy to deliver some presents."

Yüeh-niang was flustered and said, "Father has gone to have a drink at Judicial Commissioner Hsia's house. Whoever can we send to fetch him?"

As they were in the very midst of perturbation over this problem, who should appear but Tai-an, who had come in to put away his master's felt bag and said, "That's no problem. I'll just take his card and go explain the situation to Father. Simply have Brother-in-law invite the gate-boy in and give him something to eat and drink."

Tai-an then turned over the felt bag, took the card in hand, mounted the horse, and took off for Judicial Commissioner Hsia's house like a cloud scudding before the wind.

Upon arrival, he reported, thus and so, saying, "His Honor the regional investigating censor Sung Ch'iao-nien has had some gifts delivered to you."

Hsi-men Ch'ing looked at the accompanying card, on which the list of presents read, "One freshly slaughtered pig, two flagons of Chin-hua wine, four hundred sheets of official-quality stationery, and a miniature book," underneath which was written, "Your devoted servant Sung Ch'iao-nien pays his respects."

Hsi-men Ch'ing promptly ordered, "When you get back home, have Shu-t'ung send an acknowledgment in a double-folded accordion-bound album that states my official rank. Reward the gate-boy with three taels of silver and a pair of handkerchiefs, and the bearers with five mace of silver each."

When Tai-an arrived home, he looked everywhere for Shu-t'ung, but he was nowhere to be found. This made him so anxious all he could do was:

> Turn round and round like a millstone.

Ch'en Ching-chi was also not at home, so he got Manager Fu to keep the messenger company while he had a drink. Tai-an then fetched the handkerchiefs and silver from the second floor room in the rear compound, but there was no one available to seal them properly, so he had to seal them up on the shop counter himself and get Manager Fu to write the superscriptions on the three large and small gift packages.

He then asked P'ing-an, "Have you no idea where they've gone?"

"Originally, before Brother-in-law had left," said P'ing-an, "he was still here; but, later on, when Brother-in-law went outside the city gate to collect a debt of silver, he disappeared."

"Don't bother to mention it!" exclaimed Tai-an. "No doubt that 'sweetie' of a page boy has gone out on the town in order to:

> Careen about rather recklessly,

or even to keep a mistress."

Just as they were all in a stew about it, whom should they see but Ch'en Ching-chi and Shu-t'ung, who arrived back riding tandem on a mule. Tai-an gave Shu-t'ung a piece of his mind, after which he had him write the acknowledgment in the accordion-bound album that indicated Hsi-men Ch'ing's official rank and sent it off with the messenger who had delivered the gifts.

"You lousy 'sweetie' of a page boy!" railed Tai-an. "On the one hand you:

> Lie down with spread legs to solicit trade,

while on the other you:

> Clamber on top in order to drop your load.[66]

When Father's not at home, rather than looking after the house, you go off with someone else to service your mistress. Father never told you to accompany Brother-in-law in going outside the city gate to collect a debt. What induced you to go off with him for no good reason? Just see if I tell Father about it or not."

"Go ahead and tell him if you want," said Shu-t'ung. "Do you think I'm afraid of you? If you don't tell him, you'll only show me what a good son you are."

"Why you lousy dog-fucked 'sweetie' of a page boy!" exclaimed Tai-an. "You think you can call my bluff, do you?"

Thereupon, he actually stepped forward, tripped Shu-t'ung up with a single kick at his ankles, and the two of them ended up rolling on top of each other on the floor. Only after Tai-an had taken advantage of the upper hand to spit a mouthful of saliva into his mouth did he call it quits.

"I've got to go back after Father," he announced, "but when I get home, I'll settle accounts with the whore."

Having said which, he mounted the horse and set straight off on his errand.

Meanwhile, in the rear compound, Yüeh-niang saw to it that the two nuns were served some tea and refreshments and then continued to listen to them as they sang Buddhist songs and recited gathas. P'an Chin-lien grew restless, first tugging at Meng Yü-lou, and then, having failed to dislodge her, pulling at Li P'ing-erh, all the while afraid that Yüeh-niang would criticize her.

Yüeh-niang finally said, "Sister Li, she's trying to get your attention. You might as well go off with her, so she won't have to remain here, where she doesn't know what to do with herself."

Only then did Li P'ing-erh consent to go outside with her.

As they departed, Yüeh-niang gave Chin-lien a look, saying:

"When you weed out the turnips, there is
　　room for other things.[67]
Now that she's gone, we won't have to put up with her hopping around the place like a rabbit any more. She's just not the sort of person to listen to the Buddhist dharma."

P'an Chin-lien, with Li P'ing-erh in tow, went out through the inner gate, saying, "Elder Sister really goes for that stuff. No one in your household is dead. So what's the point of having nuns in to recite precious scrolls, for no good reason; not to mention hovering around them like that? We might as well take a walk out to the front courtyard and see what Hsi-men Ta-chieh is up to in her quarters."

Thereupon, they went out through the main reception hall and found that lamps had been lit in the antechamber where they lived, and Hsi-men Ta-chieh and Ch'en Ching-chi could be heard inside bickering over the loss of a sum of silver.

Chin-lien gave a rap on the latticework of their window and said, "Not having gone back to the rear compound to listen to Buddhist songs, what are the two of you quarreling about here in your room?"

Ch'en Ching-chi came outside to see who was there and, on catching sight of the two of them, said, "It's a good thing I didn't start to swear just now. It turns out to be the Fifth Lady and the Sixth Lady. Please come in and have a seat."

"You might as well go ahead and swear if you have the nerve," said Chin-lien.

Going inside, and seeing that Hsi-men Ta-chieh was engaged in stitching the sole of a shoe by lamplight, she said, "At this hour of the day, in such hot weather, you're still stitching shoes, are you?"

She then went on to ask, "What were the two of you squabbling about?"

"You ask her," said Ch'en Ching-chi. "Father sent me outside the city gate to collect a debt, and she gave me three mace of silver and asked me to bring back some gold lamé handkerchiefs for her. But who could have anticipated that when I got there and groped in my sleeve for the silver, there was nothing there, so I was unable to bring back the handkerchiefs. Then, when I got home, she maintained that I had been carrying on with a mistress and started to rail at me. She's been abusing me all this while, which got me so agitated that I was reduced to:

Swearing by the gods and uttering oaths.

Who would have thought that a maidservant, in sweeping the floor, happened to pick up the missing silver, but she has confiscated it and refuses to give it to me, while still demanding that I buy the handkerchiefs for her tomorrow. Let you two ladies be the judge. Who is at fault in this matter?"

"Why you lousy jailbird, shut your mouth!" exclaimed Hsi-men Ta-chieh. "If you haven't been carrying on with a woman, why should you have taken Shu-t'ung with you, for no good reason? Just now, Tai-an didn't mince words in giving you a piece of his mind. I imagine the two of you must have been in cahoots to make out with some woman. Otherwise you wouldn't have gotten home so late. And where is that debt of silver you were sent to collect."

"Is the missing silver in your possession or not?" asked Chin-lien.

"I've got the silver," said Hsi-men Ta-chieh. "Just now, a maidservant was sweeping the floor and picked it up. I'm holding on to it."

"It's no problem," said Chin-lien. "If I give you the money, you can also bring me back two gold lamé handkerchiefs tomorrow."

"Brother-in-law," inquired Li P'ing-erh, "if there are gold lamé handkerchiefs for sale outside the city gate, would you bring back a few for me as well?"

"Outside the city gate, on Handkerchief Lane," said Ch'en Ching-chi, "the well-known Wang family shop specializes in:

Every color and variety,

of gold lamé, shot with turquoise, handkerchiefs and kerchiefs. No matter how many you might want, they would have them in stock. If you'll just tell me what color and pattern you want, I can bring them all back to you tomorrow."

"I'd like one gold lamé, shot with turquoise, handkerchief," said Li P'ing-erh, "the color of old gold, and decorated with a motif of 'phoenixes traversing the flowers.' "

"Sixth Lady," said Ch'en Ching-chi, "gold lamé work on a ground the color of old gold will not show the gold to advantage."

"Mind your own business," said Li P'ing-erh. "I also want one pink satin handkerchief with a motif of 'waves splashing on the shore,' and decorated with the symbolic representations of the 'eight treasures,' as well as one gold lamé handkerchief with a sesame flower design in shot silk."

"Fifth Lady," Ch'en Ching-chi then asked, "what kind would you like for yourself?"

"I'm short of money," said Chin-lien, "so two handkerchiefs is all I can afford. I'd like one gold lamé handkerchief of jade-colored satin, with a diapered ground."

"You're not an elderly person yet," said Ch'en Ching-chi. "What would you want with something as white as that?"

"What's it to you?" said Chin-lien. "If I can't use it yet, I'll save it for some time in the future when I'm in mourning."

"What color do you want the other one to be?" Ch'en Ching-chi asked.

"As for the other one," said Chin-lien, "I want a gold lamé handkerchief, intermittently shot with turquoise, of delicate, purple grape-colored, Szechwanese satin, with a variegated brocade insert displaying the motif of 'joined hearts' in the form of interlocking lozenges, enclosing a roundel with a pair of magpies face to face, a rebus for the words 'happy reunion,' and with the symbolic representations of the 'eight treasures' worked into the borders on either side in beadwork."

"Ai-ya! Ai-ya!" exclaimed Ch'en Ching-chi. "That's enough of that. You're just like:

> The melon seed peddler who opens his box
> and then sneezes into it:
> What a giant hodgepodge of a mess!"

"You crazy short-life!" exclaimed Chin-lien.

> "Those who have the means to purchase
> their hearts' desires,
> Ought to feel perfectly free to buy
> whatever they want.

What's it to you, anyway?"

Li P'ing-erh then reached into her purse and pulled out a piece of silver, which she handed to Ch'en Ching-chi, saying, "You can include the cost of the Fifth Lady's purchases in this."

Chin-lien shook her head, saying, "Let me take care of it."

"We might as well have Brother-in-law make a single purchase out of it," said Li P'ing-erh. "What need is there to make a separate undertaking?"

Ching-chi Loses at Cards and Consents to Stand a Treat

"Even if I include the cost of the Fifth Lady's items," said Ch'en Ching-chi, "there's more than enough silver here to cover it all."

He then put it on the scales, and it turned out to weigh one tael and nine mace.

"Take whatever's left over," said Li P'ing-erh, "and bring back two handkerchiefs for Hsi-men Ta-chieh."

Hsi-men Ta-chieh hastily expressed her gratitude with a bow.

"Since the Sixth Lady is offering to buy handkerchiefs for you," said Chin-lien to Hsi-men Ta-chieh, "you'd better produce those three mace of silver you're holding onto, and the two of you can play cards to see who will stand treat with it. If it isn't enough, you can ask the Sixth Lady to supplement it. Tomorrow, when Father's not at home, you can use it to buy a roast duck and some distilled spirits to entertain us with."

"Since the Fifth Lady has spoken," said Ch'en Ching-chi, "you'd better come up with it."

Hsi-men Ta-chieh gave it to Chin-lien, who turned it over to Li P'ing-erh to hold while they got out a deck of cards and had Hsi-men Ta-chieh and Ch'en Ching-chi play forfeits against each other. Chin-lien stood at her side and advised Hsi-men Ta-chieh, with the result that, in no time at all, she had defeated Ching-chi in three hands.

Just at this juncture, they heard a knocking at the front gate, indicating that Hsi-men Ch'ing had come home. Only then did P'an Chin-lien and Li P'ing-erh return to their quarters.

Ch'en Ching-chi went out to welcome Hsi-men Ch'ing and reported on his errand, saying, "As for the debt that Hsü the Fourth owes you, he will send you a preliminary payment of two hundred fifty taels the day after tomorrow, and repay the remainder at the end of the month."

Hsi-men Ch'ing uttered a few imprecations, after which, being:

Half inebriated with wine,[68]

he did not even go back to the rear compound but headed straight for the quarters of P'an Chin-lien. Truly:

Past mistress of the intimate arts,
 she caters to her lover's whim;
What need is there to fear that tomorrow
 the flower will refuse to open.

If you want to know the outcome of these events,
Pray consult the story related in the following chapter.

Chapter 52

YING PO-CHÜEH INTRUDES ON

A SPRING BEAUTY IN THE GROTTO;

P'AN CHIN-LIEN INSPECTS A MUSHROOM

IN THE FLOWER GARDEN

On the flowering crab apples deep in the courtyard[1]
    the rain has just let up;
With no breeze sweeping over the mossy paths
    the butterflies make free.
The hundred-budded clove blossoms blazon forth
    their exquisite beauty;
The thrice dormant weeping willows[2] manipulate
    their supple branches.
The red of the peach blossoms, lustrous as wine,
    is of a lighter shade;
The green of the foliage, in the lingering chill,
    grows more luxuriant.
Silently making their way through beaded curtains
    the swallows return;
The cry of the cuckoo carries with it the sorrow
    of the departing spring.[3]

THE STORY GOES that while Hsi-men Ch'ing was drinking at the home of Judicial Commissioner Hsia Yen-ling that day and received the information that the regional investigating censor Sung Ch'iao-nien had sent a set of gifts to him, he was as delighted as could be. Hsia Yen-ling also treated him with a degree of respect:

    Different from that of former days,[4]
blocking the door and urging him to have another drink, so that it was the second watch before he permitted him to go home.

P'an Chin-lien had long since taken off her headdress under the lamplight, revealing her:

    Powdered face and glossy hair,
and ordered Ch'un-mei to lay out the quilts and pillows on the bed and wipe off the cool bamboo bed mat, after which she proceeded to:

Light incense and wash her private parts,

in expectation of Hsi-men Ch'ing's arrival. When he came in the door, she observed that he was:

Half inebriated with wine,

and hastened to help him off with his clothes. After drinking the tea that Ch'un-mei served them, they proceeded straight to bed.

Hsi-men Ch'ing saw that the woman, who had stripped herself stark naked, was sitting on the edge of the bed, with her head bent low, as she adjusted the foot binding on one of her fresh, white legs, which was resting horizontally over her knee, preparatory to changing into her scarlet flat-soled sleeping shoes, that were:

Barely three inches long,

But half a span in length.

Upon observing this sight, Hsi-men Ch'ing's:

Lecherous desires were suddenly aroused,

and his jade chowrie handle became conspicuously erect. He then asked the woman for the bag of sexual implements, and she promptly groped it out from underneath the mattress and handed it to him.

Hsi-men Ch'ing, having fastened both of the clasps in place, pulled the woman onto his lap with one hand and said, "Today your daddy would like to pluck the flower in your rear courtyard. Are you willing to agree to that?"

The woman gave him a look, saying, "What an utterly shameless lover you are! After screwing around with that page boy Shu-t'ung until you're tired of it, you've come to pester me. Just continue carrying on with that slave, why don't you?"

"What a crazy little oily-mouth!" Hsi-men Ch'ing laughed. "That's enough of that. If you'll agree to go along with me, what would I hanker after that page boy for? You may not know it, but what your daddy delights in the most is this very thing. You can be sure that if I just get it inside, I'll ejaculate."

The woman was unable to withstand his pestering and said, "My only fear is that I'll not be able to accommodate that great big thing of yours. If you'll remove the ring from your glans I'll consent to try it out with you."

Hsi-men Ch'ing actually did remove the sulfur-imbrued ring and left only one of the silver clasps around the base of his organ. He then ordered the woman to get down on all fours on the surface of the bed, with her bottom raised high, while he used saliva to moisten his turtle head, and then moved back and forth, moistening and reaming, before attempting to plunge it into her orifice. His turtle head was proud and firm, so that it was some time before he succeeded in immersing the knob of his glans. The woman, in her abject position, knit her brows and silently endured the pain, biting on a handkerchief in her mouth when it became too difficult to bear.

"Daddy!" she cried. "Slow down a bit. This is not like it is in front. You're stretching me so tightly inside that it hurts as though I'm being:

Seared with heat or scorched with fire."

"Dear heart!" exclaimed Hsi-men Ch'ing. "Keep on calling me 'Daddy.' It's not a problem. Tomorrow I'll buy a set of patterned silk clothing for you to wear."

"The sort of clothing I want is readily available," said Chin-lien. "Yesterday I noticed that Li Kuei-chieh was dressed in a drawnwork silk skirt of glossy gosling-yellow with silver stripes, and an inset of gold-spangled sheepskin, trimmed with varicolored thread, that really looked nice. She said that it was purchased in the licensed quarter, and that they all possessed them. But I alone don't have a skirt of that kind. I don't have any idea how much they cost, but if you buy one for me to wear, I'll stop complaining."

"That's no problem," said Hsi-men Ch'ing. "Tomorrow I'll buy one for you."

In the meantime, while this conversation was taking place, from his superior vantage point, he began to thrust and retract in earnest, alternately submerging and exposing the knob of his glans, as he gave himself over to a series of shallow retractions and deep thrusts, as if there were no end in sight.

The woman:

Turning her head around with an amorous glance,

called out, "Daddy! It's tight in there. You're really hurting me. How can you insist on carrying on so strenuously? I beg of you, whatever else you do, ejaculate as quickly as possible, and be done with it."

Hsi-men Ch'ing paid no attention, but lifted her haunches in order to:

Savor the sight as he went in and out,

while, at the same time, crying out, "P'an the Fifth, you little whore, devote yourself to wantonly calling me 'Daddy,' in order to coax out your daddy's spunk."

The woman, in fact, in her abject position:

As her starry eyes grew dim,

Her oriole's voice all a quaver,

Gently wriggled her willowy waist,[5]

Half responding with her fragrant flesh,

while:

The lascivious sounds and complaisant words,

that issued from her mouth:

Were too multifarious to describe in detail.

After some time, Hsi-men Ch'ing, feeling that he was about to ejaculate, grasped her haunches with both hands and proceeded to ram away at her with all his strength, so that, as his body collided with her bottom:

The noise was incessant.

Meanwhile the woman, in her abject position below him, moaned inarticulately:

Unable to control herself.[6]

As he was on the brink of ejaculation, Hsi-men Ch'ing grasped the woman's bottom, inserted his jade chowrie-handle all the way to the root, so that it reached straight into the most deep and marvelous region, producing a pleasurable sensation that could hardly be endured. Thereupon:

> Responding to her with abandon,
> He ejaculated like a geyser.

The woman, for her part, received his semen, and their two bodies remained glued to each other.

After some time, when the jade chowrie-handle was withdrawn, the stalk was seen to be stained blood-red, and fluid was still oozing from the mouth of the urethra. Only after the woman had wiped it off with her handkerchief did they go to sleep. Of the events of that evening there is no more to tell.

The next day, when Hsi-men Ch'ing returned home after going to the yamen in the morning, a messenger came from Secretary An Ch'en and Secretary Huang Pao-kuang, in order to deliver an invitation to a banquet, on the twenty-second, at the estate of Eunuch Director Liu, the manager of the Imperial Brickyard, and to urge him to come as early as possible.

Hsi-men Ch'ing sent the messenger on his way and was just coming out of the reception hall after eating some congee in the master suite, when he encountered Little Chou, the barber, who prostrated himself before him, kowtowed, and then stood in waiting to one side.

"You've arrived in the nick of time," said Hsi-men Ch'ing. "I was just going to look for you to do my hair."

Thereupon, Hsi-men Ch'ing led him into the garden, as far as the small summerhouse, the Kingfisher Pavilion, where he sat down on a cool chair, took off his cap and headband, and let his hair fall loose. Little Chou then laid out his combs and implements on a table behind him and proceeded to comb out his hair, examining his dandruff as he did so, as a way of assessing his prospects.

Kneeling down in expectation of a tip, he said, "Your Honor is sure to receive a major promotion in the course of the coming year. The coloration of your hair is very propitious."[7]

Hsi-men Ch'ing was greatly pleased, and, after his hair had been combed, also had him clean the wax from his ears, and give him a massage. He possessed a complete set of implements for this purpose and gave Hsi-men Ch'ing a thorough going over, in addition to which he had him engage in some of the therapeutic gymnastic techniques called *tao-yin*, or "guiding and pulling,"[8] that gave:

> His entire body a feeling of well-being.[9]

He rewarded him with five mace of silver and told him to have something to eat, and then stay in attendance so that he could cut Kuan-ko's hair. Hsi-men Ch'ing then went into his studio, where he collapsed on the bed, inlaid with Yunnanese marble, and went to sleep.

On that day, Aunt Yang departed, and Nun Wang and Nun Hsüeh also prepared to go home. Wu Yüeh-niang had the gift boxes that they had brought with them filled with steamed-shortcake pastries and saw them off, presenting each of them with five mace of silver, and Nun Hsüeh's two young disciples with a narrow bolt of cotton fabric apiece.

As Yüeh-niang ushered them out the front gate, Nun Hsüeh once more enjoined her, "When the next *jen-tzu* day occurs, if you take that potion, you will be sure to conceive."

"Reverend Hsüeh," said Yüeh-niang, "after you leave today, whatever you do, come for another visit on my birthday in the eighth month. I'll be expecting you."

Nun Hsüeh placed her palms together and saluted her in the Buddhist fashion, saying, "We have put the lay Bodhisattva to a lot of trouble already. I will be sure to come when that day arrives."

Thereupon, they took their leave of Yüeh-niang, and the rest of the women-folk, who had all come out to the main gate to see them off, and Yüeh-niang and Sister-in-law Wu then returned to the rear compound.

However, Meng Yü-lou, P'an Chin-lien, Li P'ing-erh, and Hsi-men Ta-chieh, along with Li Kuei-chieh, who was wearing a white silver-striped silk blouse that opened down the middle, over a gosling-yellow drawnwork silk skirt, embellished with gold thread, a chignon enclosed in a fret of silver filigree, a hair ornament displaying a motif of turquoise water and auspicious clouds, gold filigree hairpins, pendant amethyst earrings, and scarlet shoes, and was carrying Kuan-ko in her arms, seized the occasion to take a walk in the garden.

"Kuei-chieh," said Li P'ing-erh, "hand him over. Let me carry him."

"Sixth Lady, it's no problem," responded Li Kuei-chieh. "I'm enjoying the chance to carry the youngster."

"Kuei-chieh," said Meng Yü-lou, "you haven't yet been to the new studio that Father has fixed up for himself. Come take a look at it."

As they entered the garden, Chin-lien noticed that the crape myrtle blossoms were in full flower and picked two of them for Li Kuei-chieh to stick in her hair.

Thereupon, they proceeded along the juniper hedge to the Kingfisher Pavilion, where they observed that the interior of the studio was furnished with a curtained bed and standing screens, and further embellished with calligraphy, painting, zither, and chessboard, all of which were elegantly displayed. The bed was arrayed with chiffon curtains, held in place by silver hooks, cool matting, and a coral pillow. Hsi-men Ch'ing was lying collapsed upon the bed:

In a state of slumbering oblivion.

A skein of burning ambergris incense wafted from a small gilded censer. The green gauze window was half closed, and the plantains outside the casement[10] bent to catch the light.

P'an Chin-lien picked up the incense case on the table and fiddled with it, while Meng Yü-lou and Li P'ing-erh sat down on chairs.

All of a sudden, Hsi-men Ch'ing turned over and, observing the womenfolk in the room, said, "What are you doing here?"

"Li Kuei-chieh wanted to see your studio," said Chin-lien, "so we brought her along to take a look at it."

Hsi-men Ch'ing saw that she was carrying Kuan-ko with her and playfully teased him for a while, when Hua-t'ung suddenly appeared and said, "Master Ying the Second has come."

The crowd of womenfolk hastily got out of the way and headed toward Li P'ing-erh's quarters.

When Ying Po-chüeh got as far as the juniper hedge and saw Li Kuei-chieh carrying Kuan-ko, he said, "Wonderful! So Li Kuei-chieh is here."

He then went on meaningfully to ask her, "How long have you been here?"

Li Kuei-chieh continued on her way, saying, "That's enough, you crazy beggar! It's none of your business. What do you want to know for?"

"What a consummate little whore you are!" said Ying Po-chüeh. "If it's none of my business, that's that. Just give me a kiss and I'll call it quits."

Thereupon, he embraced her and endeavored to give her a kiss, but Kuei-chieh pushed him away with her hand and swore at him, "You lousy, obnoxious, crazy chunk of knife-bait! If I weren't afraid of frightening the baby, I'd give you a rap with the handle of my fan."

Hsi-men Ch'ing came outside at this point and, observing that Ying Po-chüeh was holding on to Li Kuei-chieh, said, "You crazy dog! Be careful or you'll scare the baby."

Then he turned to Shu-t'ung and said, "You take the baby and carry him to the Sixth Lady's place."

Shu-t'ung promptly took the baby in his arms. The wet nurse, Ju-i, who was waiting by the corner of the juniper hedge, then took charge of him and bore him away.

Ying Po-chüeh, who remained standing in parley with Kuei-chieh, asked her, "How has that affair of yours turned out?"

"I am much indebted to Father here," said Kuei-chieh, "who has taken pity on me and sent Brother Lai-pao to the Eastern Capital to intervene on my behalf."

"Wonderful! Wonderful!" exclaimed Ying Po-chüeh. "That should take care of it. In that case, you ought to be able to relax a little."

When he had finished speaking, Kuei-chieh started off for the rear compound, but Ying Po-chüeh said, "Come back here, you crazy little whore! I've still got something to say to you."

"I've got to go now, but I'll be back," said Kuei-chieh.

Thereupon she went over to Li P'ing-erh's quarters to join the others. Only then did Ying Po-chüeh salute Hsi-men Ch'ing with a bow, and the two of them sat down in the studio together.

"Yesterday," said Hsi-men Ch'ing, "while I was having a drink at Hsia Yenling's place, His Excellency Sung Ch'iao-nien, the regional investigating censor, sent someone to deliver some gifts, including a freshly slaughtered pig. Fearing that it wouldn't keep, I engaged a cook, this morning, to come and dismember it, season it with pepper, and braise the whole thing, including the head. If you will stay a while, I'll invite Hsieh Hsi-ta to join us, so we can play backgammon and enjoy it together."

He then directed Ch'in-t'ung, "You go, right away, and invite Master Hsieh to join us. Tell him that Brother Ying the Second is also here."

Ch'in-t'ung assented and went straight off on his errand.

Ying Po-chüeh then asked, "With regard to that debt that Hsü the Fourth owes you, have you collected it yet?"

"That lousy unprincipled dog-bone," exclaimed Hsi-men Ch'ing, "claims he won't be able to come up with the whole amount until tomorrow, but he made me an initial payment of two hundred and fifty taels. You can tell those two to come here the day after tomorrow. If I'm still short, I'll make up the amount out of my household funds, that's all."

"That will be fine," said Ying Po-chüeh. "I expect they'll buy some fresh things in season and come to pay their respects to you later today."

"There's really no need for them to go to so much trouble," said Hsi-men Ch'ing.

After they had chatted for a while, Hsi-men Ch'ing asked, "Have those two, Blabbermouth Sun and Pockmarked Chu, already set out for the capital, or not?"

"By this time they're on their way," replied Ying Po-chüeh. "After they were apprehended at Li Kuei-chieh's place, they were incarcerated in the lockup at the district yamen overnight. The next day, the three of them were linked together on a single length of iron chain and escorted off to the Eastern Capital. Once they get there, it's not likely that any of them will return home unscathed. You thought you could help yourselves to:

Wine by the bowl and meat by the hunk,

day after day, just like a bug on the pantry shelf, and now your efforts have earned you a tasty treat. This sort of suffering is only their just deserts. They're on the road in this hot weather, weighed down by iron chains, and without any traveling expenses, but what does it matter."

"You crazy dog!" laughed Hsi-men Ch'ing. "If they're not up to standing guard duty when condemned to military exile, whoever was it, in the first place, who induced them to hang out and fool around all day with that youngster from the Wang household? It's really a case of their suffering the consequences of trouble they made for themselves."

"Brother, you've got a point there," said Ying Po-chüeh. "After all:

> Flies don't cluster on eggs
> > unless they're cracked.

Why do you suppose they didn't come after me or Hsieh Hsi-ta, if not because:

> The clear is ever clear,
> The turbid ever turbid?"[11]

As they were speaking, Hsieh Hsi-ta arrived and, after bowing in greeting, sat down and devoted himself to fanning himself with his fan.

"How have you managed to work up such a faceful of sweat?" asked Hsi-men Ch'ing.

"Don't even mention it, Brother," replied Hsieh Hsi-ta. "If your servant had shown up so much as a step later, I wouldn't have been at home. I had just come out the front gate when he happened to arrive at the same time. I've had:

> A bellyful of anger,

out of the blue today."

"What have you had to be angry about?" asked Ying Po-chüeh.

"Early this morning," said Hsieh Hsi-ta, "Blabbermouth Sun's wife showed up at my place, claiming that I had been responsible for getting him into such a pickle. What reason would I have had to do that? The unreasonable old whore! 'It was your husband who inveigled him into the licensed quarter day after day, scrounging:

> Wine by the bowl and meat by the hunk,

and bringing home silver by the handful for you to expend on your own gratification. Everyone knows that you were getting a kickback for his pains, but since when did you ever share a candareen of it with anyone else?' I had just told her off with a sentence or two, and come outside, when I unexpectedly received a summons from Brother's place over here."

Ying Po-chüeh said, "Didn't I just say to Brother here that:

> If newly fermented wine is put in separate containers,
> The clear is ever clear,
> The turbid ever turbid?

It could hardly avoid turning out just as we predicted. As I said, if they continued to hang out with that youngster from the Wang household, sooner or later they would come a cropper, and now see how they've managed to stumble into this net. They've no one to blame but themselves."

"What sort of great prowess does that youngster from the Wang household possess?" said Hsi-men Ch'ing. "How old is he, after all? His parietal bones are not yet fully formed. He hardly has what it takes to satisfy the sort of women that we rejected in our early days. It's enough to embarrass a ghost."

"What's he ever seen of the great world," said Ying Po-chüeh, "that could stand comparison with your doings in those days? If he even heard tell of them, he'd be scared to death."

When they had finished speaking, a page boy served them with tea, and they proceeded to drink it.

"Why don't the two of you play a game of backgammon?" said Hsi-men Ch'ing. "They're cooking up some noodles in the rear compound. I'll have a page boy bring some out for us to eat."

Before long, Ch'in-t'ung came in to set up a table, and Hua-t'ung brought in four square boxes, that enclosed four diminutive picnic saucers, containing four different delicacies. There was one saucer of squash and eggplant julienne marinated with ten spices, one saucer of an assortment of pickled beans, one saucer of fresh fagara marinated in soy sauce, and one saucer of candied garlic. These were accompanied by three saucers of garlic extract, for dipping purposes, and a large bowl of pork pot roast, along with three pairs of ivory chopsticks, all of which were laid out in proper order. Only after Hsi-men Ch'ing had joined his guests at the table were three bowls of noodles placed before them, each person pouring onto his noodles as much of the pot roast, garlic, and vinegar as he liked.

Ying Po-chüeh and Hsieh Hsi-ta picked up their chopsticks and disposed of the contents of their bowls in:

Three mouthfuls and two swallows.

In no time at all, the two of them had wolfed down seven bowls apiece.

Hsi-men Ch'ing, who had not even been able to finish his second bowl, said, "My sons, the two of you certainly know how to put it away."

"Brother," said Ying Po-chüeh, "which of your womenfolk is responsible for preparing these noodles today? They're both tasty and delicious."

"This pot roast has been braised to perfection," said Hsieh Hsi-ta. "Were it not for the fact that I had just eaten at home before coming over here, I'd be prepared to suffer another bowl."

The two of them, who had gotten overheated from eating so fast, took off their outer clothes and hung them over their chairs.

On seeing Ch'in-t'ung clearing away the utensils, Ying Po-chüeh said, "Young gentleman, when you get back to the rear compound, bring some water for us to rinse out our mouths with."

"Some warm tea would be good too," said Hsieh Hsi-ta. "If it's too hot, it will only bring out the smell of the garlic."

In a little while, Hua-t'ung arrived with the tea, and the three of them drank it, after which they came outside and strolled among the flower beds on the other side of the juniper hedge.

Who should appear at this point but P'ing-an, who brought in four boxes of gifts that had just been delivered from the household of Huang the Fourth for Hsi-men Ch'ing to see. One box contained fresh black caltrops, one contained fresh water chestnuts, one contained four large iced shad, and one contained loquats.

When Ying Po-chüeh saw them, he said, "What fine stuff! Who knows where he dug it up to send over here? Let me take a taste."

Snatching up a number of items with one hand, he handed two of them to Hsieh Hsi-ta, saying, "There are those who:
                    Live to old age and death,
without knowing that such things as this exist."

"You crazy dog!" exclaimed Hsi-men Ch'ing.
                    "Even before they're offered to Buddha,
                    You snatch them for your own enjoyment."

"Who accuses me of failing to offer them to Buddha?" said Ying Po-chüeh.
                    "Upon entering my mouth the evidence is destroyed."

Hsi-men Ch'ing directed that the gifts be taken to the rear compound and put away, adding, "Ask the Third Lady for three candareens of silver to give the messenger."

Ying Po-chüeh inquired, "Was it Li Chin who delivered them, or was it Huang Ning?"

"It was Huang Ning," replied P'ing-an.

"It must be that dog-bone's lucky day," said Ying Po-chüeh, "to be rewarded with these three candareens of silver."

Hsi-men Ch'ing continued to look on as the two of them played a game of backgammon. But no more of this.

To resume our story, Li Kuei-chieh, along with her aunt, Li Chiao-erh, Meng Yü-lou, P'an Chin-lien, Li P'ing-erh, and Hsi-men Ta-chieh, had all eaten in the parlor of the master suite and were sitting in the veranda outside, when they noticed that Little Chou could be seen:
                    Sticking out his head and craning his neck,
on the other side of the screen-wall.

"Little Chou," said Li P'ing-erh, "you've come at a good time. Come in and cut the little master's hair, which has been allowed to grow too long."

Little Chou hastily came forward and kowtowed to all of them, saying, "Just a while ago, His Honor directed that I should come inside to cut little brother's hair."

"Sister Six," said Yüeh-niang, "take a look at the almanac and see whether this is an auspicious day or an inauspicious day to cut the child's hair."

Chin-lien told Hsiao-yü to fetch an almanac, opened it up and perused it for a while, and then said, "Today is the twenty-first day of the fourth month, a *keng-hsü* day, for which the descriptive character is *ting*, or steady. It is governed by the constellation *lou-chin-kou*, or Aries, and is an auspicious day for making sacrifices, donning official cap and girdle, setting out on a journey, having clothes made, performing ablutions, getting one's hair cut, repairing or constructing, and for breaking ground. The best time to initiate these activities is the period from 11:00 AM to 1:00 PM It is an auspicious day."[12]

"Since it's an auspicious day," said Yüeh-niang, "I'll have a maidservant heat water, and you can also shampoo the child's hair."

She then admonished Little Chou to proceed cautiously and coax the child into letting him cut his hair. Hsiao-yü stood to his side in order to catch the hair in a handkerchief. But before the barber had made more than a few cuts with the scissors, Kuan-ko, with the sound of a gurgling cry, started to howl in earnest. Little Chou continued to cut away hastily even as the child cried out, but who could have anticipated that the boy would choke on himself, falling silent, as his face became swollen and red.

Li P'ing-erh, who became panic-stricken at this, hastily exclaimed, "Don't cut any more! Don't cut any more!"

Little Chou, for his part, was thrown into such consternation that he abandoned the tools of his trade and fled outside as fast as his legs would carry him.

"As I've observed before," said Yüeh-niang, "this child is rather a hopeless case, forever anxious to protect his head. We should have cut his hair ourselves instead of calling someone in to do it for no good reason. What sort of a job can he do?"

As providence would have it,

after the child had remained choked up for what seemed like half a day, he let out a cry. Only then did Li P'ing-erh feel as though:

The stone on her head had finally fallen to the ground.

Taking the child in her arms, she devoted herself to petting him, saying as she did so, "What a fine thing for Little Chou to do! What a nerve, to come in here for no good reason, and insist on cutting your hair. On top of which, he's taken advantage of you by leaving the job only half-finished. Why don't I drag him back in here and give him a drubbing, in order to vent your spleen?"

Thereupon, she carried him over to Yüeh-niang, who said, "What a hopeless little beggar! The haircut was originally intended for your benefit, but it's only resulted in a crying fit. With no more hair than this left, you're likely to be mistaken for a shaven-headed convict."

After she had playfully teased him for a while, Li P'ing-erh turned him over to the wet nurse, and Yüeh-niang instructed her, "Don't breast-feed him right away, but wait until he's had a nap before feeding him."

The wet nurse then carried him back to the front compound.

Who should appear at this juncture but Lai-an, who came in to collect Little Chou's implements and reported, "Little Chou is at the front gate, so frightened that his face has turned a scorched shade of brown."

"Has he had anything to eat?" asked Yüeh-niang.

"He has eaten," said Lai-an, "and Father has rewarded him with five candareens of silver."

"Take a goblet of wine out and give it to him," said Yüeh-niang. "He's been so frightened that these few candareens must seem hard-earned."

Hsiao-yü promptly poured out a cup of wine, fetched a saucer of cured meat, and told Lai-an to give them to Little Chou and send him on his way.

Wu Yüeh-niang then turned to Chin-lien and said, "Take a look at the almanac and see when the next *jen-tzu* day will be."

Chin-lien examined it and said, "The twenty-third is a *jen-tzu* day. It falls within the solar term *mang-chung*, or 'Grain in Ear,'[13] which also includes the Fifth Month Festival, or Dragon Boat Festival."

She then went on to ask, "Sister, why do you ask?"

"For no particular reason," said Yüeh-niang. "I just thought I'd ask."

Li Kuei-chieh then picked up the almanac to look at and said, "The twenty-fourth, I regret to say, is my mother's birthday, and I won't be able to be at home for it."

"The tenth day of the last month," said Yüeh-niang, "was your elder sister's birthday and has already been celebrated. And now the twenty-fourth day of the current month just happens to be your mother's birthday. It would seem that you denizens of the quarter suffer from two ailments a day, while celebrating three birthdays as well. During the daylight hours, you suffer from the ailment of yearning for money, while, during the night, you suffer from the ailment of yearning for customers. In the morning it's your mother's birthday, at noon it's your elder sister's birthday, and in the evening it's your own birthday. How do they all come to occur so close together? As long as your patrons have money, you might as well contrive to make every day a birthday."

Li Kuei-chieh merely smiled at this, without making a sound.

Who should appear at this juncture but Hua-t'ung, who had been sent by Hsi-men Ch'ing to invite Li Kuei-chieh to join him. Only then did Kuei-chieh go into Yüeh-niang's room to put on new makeup and redo her face, after which she headed off for the summerhouse in the garden, where an Eight Immortals table had already been set up, the blinds had been lowered both in front and in back, and the table had been spread with a variety of delicacies.

There were two large platters of roast pork, two platters of roast duck, two platters of newly pan-fried fresh shad, four saucers of rose-flavored pastries, two saucers of boiled chicken and bamboo shoots, and two saucers of boiled squab. These were followed by four saucers of chitterlings, blood pudding, pork tripe, fermented sausage, and the like.

As the company proceeded to eat for a while, Kuei-chieh stood by their side, replenishing the wine cups.

"I say this in your father's hearing," Ying Po-chüeh said to her, "and I'm not just giving you a hard time, but that affair of yours has already been taken care of satisfactorily. Your father has also spoken on your behalf to the district yamen, so they're no longer looking for you. And who do you have to thank for this but yours truly? It was only after I had repeatedly begged your father to intervene that he consented to do so. Do you suppose he would ever have taken the initiative in pulling strings on your behalf for no good reason? Choose whatever you like from your repertoire of songs, and sing one for me to enjoy as I drink my wine. It would be a case of making up for my efforts with one of your own."

Kuei-chieh laughed at this and cursed him, saying, "You crazy indecent beggar!

> With the bigness of a flea,
> How much face have you got,

that Father would believe anything you said?"

"Why you lousy little whore!" retorted Ying Po-chüeh.

> "Before the sutra has even been recited,
> You start to take the stick to the monk.
> If you want something to eat,
> You shouldn't offend the cook.

You may think that since:

> A monk has no mother-in-law,
> Being but a solitary male,

I can't handle the likes of you. You little whore! You'd better not take me for a joke.

> Though only half functional,[14]
> I'd still be up to the job."

At this, Kuei-chieh whacked him twice, as hard as she could, with the handle of the fan in her hand.

Hsi-men Ch'ing laughed and cursed him, saying, "You dog! In the future:

> Your sons will be thieves and your daughters whores,

thanks only to the example you set for them."

They laughed at this for a while before Kuei-chieh finally picked up her p'i-p'a, held it horizontally across her knees:

> Opened her ruby lips,
> Exposed her white teeth,

and proceeded to sing a song suite beginning with the tune "Three Terraces Song from I-chou":

> I think of how flagrantly you have betrayed my love,
> How you have forgotten our vows of devotion.
> On fine occasions such as flowery mornings
>   and moonlit evenings,[15]
> You have caused me to waste the springtime
>   of my youth.
> Depressed as can be, I lean upon
>   the balustrade,
> Gazing fixedly into the distance, but there is
>   no news of you at all.

Again and again I think to myself,
It must just be that my lot is meager
   and my fate fickle.

To the tune "Yellow Oriole":

Who could have anticipated such a thing?

Ying Po-chüeh interpolated, "Though a boat were to capsize in your open drain, ten years might pass without your knowing it."

My fragrant flesh has been reduced,
Distress has rendered me emaciated.

Ying Po-chüeh said, "No matter how much you love him, and yearn for him, he's left you in the gutter."

My image in the mirror is covered with dust,
   and I am loath to improve it.
I am sparing of rouge and powder,
And too indolent to stick flowers in my hair.
The mascara on my eyebrows vainly accentuates
   the resentment of spring peaks.

Ying Po-chüeh said, "You remember the sayings:
   Though I've taken a thousand comers,
   My feelings are concentrated on one.
   Silently I face the mirror, giving vent
      to long sighs.
   I am half enamored of you, and
      half resentful of you.[16]
The two of you got along well enough at the outset, but now you're anticipating surprise and suffering fear on his account. Enough of that. Give over your resentment."

"You're delirious," protested Kuei-chieh. "How can you talk such nonsense?"

The hardest thing to bear,

"If you can't bear it," interjected Ying Po-chüeh, "how could anyone else be expected to?"

Is the bugle on the watchtower,
The dying notes of which are enough to break one's heart.

"It's not your heart that's broken," said Ying Po-chüeh, "but the strings by which your puppeteer manipulates you. The two of you are no longer able to perform together."

At this, Kuei-chieh gave him a whack as hard as she could and cursed him, saying, "You lousy dog-fucked beast! You're delirious today. All you do is try to provoke people."

To the tune "A Gathering of Worthy Guests":

All is silent within my secluded window
    and the moon is bright;
In my resentment, I lean alone against the standing screen.[17]
Suddenly I hear a solitary wild goose
    cry outside my bower,
Which only serves to reawaken the sorrow
    of separation.
The watches are long and the clepsydra never-ending.[18]
Before I know it, the lamp grows dim, the incense burns out,[19]
    and I am unable to get to sleep,
While, wherever he may be, he is
    sleeping soundly.

"You silly little whore!" remarked Ying Po-chüeh. "Why shouldn't he be sleeping soundly? Not having been hustled off anywhere, he's happily asleep at home, while you've had to hide out at someone else's place, feeling as agitated as a sheepskin drum every day, awaiting the arrival of someone from the Eastern Capital before you can feel that:

The stone on your head has finally fallen to the ground."

Kuei-chieh was so disturbed by this banter that she exclaimed, "Father, just look at the way Beggar Ying here is carrying on, persisting in pestering me, I don't know why."

"It's about time you got around to acknowledging your father," said Ying Po-chüeh; but Kuei-chieh ignored him and, plucking her *p'i-p'a*, continued to sing.

To the tune "Alliterations and Rhymes":

When I think of him,
When I think of him,
How can I help taking it to heart?

"Since he scratches you where you itch," interjected Ying Po-chüeh, "you can't help taking it to heart."

When there is no one around,
When there is no one around,
My teardrops silently cascade.

"There was once a man," said Ying Po-chüeh, "who habitually wet his bed. One day his mother died, and, as an expression of his filiality, he set up a bunk in front of her spirit tablet. Having gotten to sleep late, who could have anticipated that he would, once again, wet his bed. When someone came in and, noticing that the mattress was wet, asked how it had happened, he was at a loss for words and only replied, 'You wouldn't understand, but I consigned my tears to my stomach, and they overflowed.' Your case is analogous to his. Since you can't refer to him in the open, all you can do is cry over him in secret."

"You shameless pip-squeak!" protested Kuei-chieh. "You were an eyewitness, I suppose. You're delirious."

> I blame him,
> I blame him,
> More than words can tell.

"As to that," said Ying Po-chüeh, "I've got something else to say. You might just as well blame Heaven. Who knows how much money you've made off him already? And today, now that you're reduced to hiding out at someone else's place, your business has been disrupted 'more than words can tell.' Your affectation is about as incongruous as a left-hand Gate God masquerading with a white face.[20] Who do you think you're going to fool with that rigmarole?"

> Who could have known, when he was here,
>   that he would be so elusive?

"You might have known," commented Ying Po-chüeh, "that though you thought you had him in hand, he might still fly away."

> My only regret is that, to begin with, I ought not
>   to have taken him so seriously.

"You silly little whore!" remarked Ying Po-chüeh. "Nowadays, around here, you couldn't fool a three-year-old child with that stuff, let alone a habitué of the world of breeze and moonlight. So you took him seriously, did you? Just you wait a minute, while I sing a song for you, to the tune 'A Southern Branch':

> As for the realm of breeze and moonlight,
>   let me explain it to you.
> Nowadays, there is no distinguishing
>   between true and false.
> Each and every denizen of that world is
>   a downright degenerate;
> Each and every denizen of that world is
>   a practiced old hand.
> Their arts are designed only to bury you alive,
>   making blind scapegoats of you.

The old procuress is only out
   to make money;
While the young whore has no choice but to
   stick her neck out and forge ahead.
It is bitter enough to make her jump into the river;
It is sad enough to make her want to seek out a well.
She wonders when her crock of bad karma
   will ever be full,
So that even if she is reborn as a donkey or horse,
She will not have to continue
   in this line of work."

By this time, his raillery had reduced Kuei-chieh to tears, and Hsi-men Ch'ing intervened by giving Ying Po-chüeh a whack on the head with his fan, laughing as he cursed him, saying, "You insensitive dog! You simply insist on plaguing people to death."

He then turned to Kuei-chieh and said, "Go ahead and sing. Don't pay any attention to him."

"Brother Ying," chimed in Hsieh Hsi-ta, "Don't be such a killjoy. Today:
   Trying first this and then that,
you've devoted yourself exclusively to offending this goddaughter of mine. If you say another word, may you develop a huge boil on your mouth."

After some time had elapsed, Li Kuei-chieh picked up her *p'i-p'a* and continued to sing, to the tune "Mustering the Palace Guard":

Everyone said that he was trustworthy,

Ying Po-chüeh was about to say something, but Hsieh Hsi-ta put his hand over his mouth and said, "Kuei-chieh, go ahead and sing. Don't pay any attention to him."

Li Kuei-chieh then continued to sing:

But he turns out to have been bent only on seduction.
His eyes were wide open,
But his heart and his mouth were not in agreement.[21]

Hsieh Hsi-ta having removed his hand, Ying Po-chüeh resumed his commentary, saying, "If they had been in agreement it would have been a good thing. This affair might never have occurred. Your hearts and mouths may not have been in agreement, but your tiger's mouths[22] were certainly responsive enough. Though not many, at least two or three cones of moxa were burnt there."[23]

"How can you be so:
   Barefaced and red-eyed?"
protested Kuei-chieh. "You were an eyewitness, I suppose."

"I may not have seen it with my own eyes," said Ying Po-chüeh, "but it took place in the Star of Joy Bordello, did it not?"

The whole company, including Hsi-men Ch'ing, couldn't help laughing at this.

Swearing to be as faithful as the hills and seas,
He spoke falsehood while alleging truth.[24]
I nearly made the mistake of contracting a case of
    lovesickness on his account.

"What a silly creature!" said Ying Po-chüeh.
    "People may buy things by mistake,
    But nobody sells things by mistake.
You denizens of the quarter are hardly likely to contract any diseases by mistake."

That unfaithful lover;
Judging from the way he's been carrying on,
What kind of a future will he
    allow me to have?

"You may not be able to expect much in the way of a future," remarked Ying Po-chüeh, "but someday he is bound to inherit the rank of Imperial Commissioner."

To the tune "An Amber Cat Pendant":

Every day we are estranged we grow further apart.[25]
How will we ever meet again?
It is in vain that, in my infatuation, I have
    been content to patiently wait.

"How long must you wait, after all?" asked Ying Po-chüeh. "In the days to come, once this affair in the Eastern Capital is taken care of, it won't be too late to relight the furnace."

My dreams of clouds and rain on Witch's Mountain[26]
    are unlikely to be fulfilled.
You fickle fellow,
As far as this life is concerned,
The phoenix and its mate are destined to part,[27]
The phoenix and its mate are destined to part.

Coda:

Lover of mine, you've shown yourself to be
    altogether too fickle.

You've found it possible to give me up,
　　leaving me all alone.
Our love in a previous incarnation has turned
　　into nothing but a painted pastry.[28]

When she had finished singing, Hsieh Hsi-ta said, "That's enough. That's enough. Let Hua-t'ung take away her *p'i-p'a*, so I can reward her labors by presenting her with a cup of wine."

"And I'll offer her a serving of food," said Ying Po-chüeh. "My talents may not amount to much, but at least it would be a case of making up for her efforts with one of my own."

"Get out of here, you beggar!" said Li Kuei-chieh. "Why should anyone pay attention to you?

First you beat a person with your big fists,
And then you rub the bruises with your hand."

At this juncture, Hsieh Hsi-ta proffered Kuei-chieh three cups of wine in a row and then pulled Ying Po-chüeh aside, saying, "We still have those two games of backgammon to complete."

Thereupon, the two of them resumed playing backgammon, while Hsi-men Ch'ing tipped Kuei-chieh a wink and then got up to leave the room.

"Brother," said Ying Po-chüeh, "if you're going to the rear compound, send some breath-sweetening lozenges out to us, would you. We ate all that garlic a little while ago, and now it's paying us back by eructing in an unpleasant way."

"Where would I get any breath-sweetening lozenges from?" said Hsi-men Ch'ing.

"Brother, who do you think you're fooling?" said Ying Po-chüeh. "I happen to know that school official named Liu from Hang-chou has sent you a considerable quantity of them. It would hardly be fitting for you to consume them all by yourself."

Hsi-men Ch'ing laughed at this and proceeded to head for the rear compound. Li Kuei-chieh also disappeared outside, where she stood next to the T'ai-hu rockery and pretended to busy herself picking flowers to wear in her hair. Ying Po-chüeh and Hsieh Hsi-ta played three games of backgammon in a row while waiting for Hsi-men Ch'ing to return, but he did not appear.

When they asked Hua-t'ung, "What is your father doing in the rear compound?" he replied, "Father went back to the rear compound but came right out again."

"If he came right out again," said Ying Po-chüeh, "where could he have gone?"

Then, turning to Hsieh Hsi-ta, he said, "You stay sitting here while I go have a look for him."

Hsieh Hsi-ta then proceeded to play a game of elephant chess with Shu-t'ung on the surface of the desk.

It so happens that Hsi-men Ch'ing, after paying a visit to Li P'ing-erh's quarters, had come outside and was standing under the banksia rose arbor, when he caught sight of Li Kuei-chieh, pulled her into the "snow cave" in the Hidden Spring Grotto, and closed the door; whereupon the two of them sat down on a low couch to chat. The fact is that Hsi-men Ch'ing, upon ducking into Li P'ing-erh's quarters, had taken a dose of the aphrodisiac before coming out again. Taking Kuei-chieh onto his lap and settling her down upon his thighs, he proceeded, without more ado, to expose his organ for her to see, which gave her quite a start.

"How on earth did you make it as big as that?" she asked.

Hsi-men Ch'ing told her the whole story about the Indian monk's medication and then started out by having her:

> Bend low her powdered neck,
>
> Gently part her scarlet lips,

and suck him off for a while. After that, he lightly lifted her two tiny golden lotuses, that were:

> But half a span in length,
>
> Barely three inches long,
>
> With handsome heel lifts,
>
> Vying with lotus buds,
>
> Fit to tread fragrant dust, or
>
> Pirouette upon an emerald disk,[29]
>
> Beloved of thousands,
>
> Craved by tens of thousands,

and hung them over his arms to either side. She had on scarlet shoes of plain silk with high white satin heels, and figured ankle leggings with gold borders, the ends of which were tied in place with lengths of sand-green cord. He then carried her over to a chair, where the two of them started to go at it.

Who would have thought that Ying Po-chüeh, having looked for Hsi-men Ch'ing in every one of the pavilions in the garden without finding him, passed through the miniature Dripping Emerald Cavern, came down to the banksia rose arbor, went around the grape arbor, and arrived at the Hidden Spring Grotto, deep among the pines and bamboos. Here he faintly overheard the sound of people laughing, though he wasn't sure where it was coming from. Ying Po-chüeh then slowly proceeded with:

> Skulking step and lurking gait,[30]

to lift aside the portiere, exposing the fact that the two leaves of the door were ajar, and, taking his stand immediately outside, devoted himself to eaves-dropping on the scene within.

Ying Po-chüeh Intrudes on a Spring Beauty in the Grotto

He overheard Kuei-chieh, calling out in a quavery voice as she responded with her body to the movements of Hsi-men Ch'ing, "Daddy, finish off as quickly as you can. I'm afraid someone may come along."

At this, Ying Po-chüeh, giving vent to a loud cry, suddenly pushed open the door and burst in. Seeing that Hsi-men Ch'ing, who had Kuei-chieh's legs hoisted over his arms as she laid back on the chair, was just in the thick of things, he said, "Quickly, fetch some water to splash on them. The two rutting creatures have gotten themselves stuck together."

"You crazy chunk of knife-bait!" protested Li Kuei-chieh. "Breaking in on us that way, you've given me quite a start."

"Finish off as quickly as you can, eh?" said Ying Po-chüeh. "It's not as easy as all that. You've got to wait until things run their course, after all. You no sooner expressed the fear that someone might catch you in the act, than I turned up. Come over here, and let me have a share of the take."

"You crazy dog!" exclaimed Hsi-men Ch'ing. "Get out of here immediately, and stop pestering me. I fear a page boy may come by and see us."

"You little whore!" said Ying Po-chüeh. "You'd better consent to entreat me nicely, or I'll raise such a hue and cry that even the ladies in the rear compound will hear what's going on. You've already been acknowledged as an adopted daughter by the First Lady, and she's kindly agreed to let you hide out here for a day or two, and here you are carrying on an affair with her husband. If she were to find out, you'd never hear the end of it."

"Get out of here, you crazy beggar!" responded Kuei-chieh.

"I'll go," said Ying Po-chüeh, "but not before snatching a kiss."

Thereupon, holding Kuei-chieh in place, he gave her a kiss before starting outside.

"You crazy dog!" said Hsi-men Ch'ing. "Aren't you even going to put the latch on the door?"

Ying Po-chüeh came back to put the latch on the door and said, "My son, the two of you can just fuck away, fuck away to your heart's content. You can knock the bottom out of her for all I care. It's no concern of mine."

He had gotten no further than the pine tree outside, when he came back and said, "As for those breath-sweetening lozenges that you promised me a while ago, where are they?"

"You crazy dog!" said Hsi-men Ch'ing. "Just wait a little while and I'll see that you get them, that's all. Why continue to pester us?"

Only then did Ying Po-chüeh take his leave, laughing as he went.

"What an obnoxious chunk of knife-bait!" exclaimed Kuei-chieh.

Hsi-men Ch'ing and Li Kuei-chieh continued to carry on with each other in the "snow cave" for a good two hours until, by eating a red date,[31] he was finally able to finish off, with the result that:

The rain evaporated and the clouds dispersed.[32]

There is a poem that testifies to this:

Among the crab apple boughs, orioles
    dart quickly to and fro;
In the shade of green bamboos, swallows
    parley incessantly.
Even if one were to entrust the scene to
    a skillful painter;
This picture of spring beauty could never
    be properly depicted.[33]

In a little while, the two of them straightened their clothing and ventured
outside. Kuei-chieh reached into Hsi-men Ch'ing's sleeve and groped out a
quantity of breath-sweetening lozenges, which she proceeded to secrete in her
own sleeve. Hsi-men Ch'ing, who had so exerted himself that:
    His whole body was bathed in fragrant sweat,[34]
    And he couldn't help panting and puffing,
went over under the flowering lantana to urinate, while Kuei-chieh, for her
part, groped out a mirror from about her person, put it on the sill of the moon
window, in order to:
    Arrange her cloudy locks and adjust her tresses,
after which, she went back to the rear compound. Hsi-men Ch'ing went into
Li P'ing-erh's quarters to wash his hands, and when he came out to rejoin his
company, Ying Po-chüeh demanded the breath-sweetening lozenges.
    "You crazy beggar!" responded Hsi-men Ch'ing. "You must be splenetic!
How can you persist in pestering people so?"
    He then handed a few lozenges to each of them, at which Ying Po-chüeh
complained, "You're only giving me these measly couple of them, are you?
Never mind. Never mind. I'll just have to ask that little whore from the Li
Family Establishment for some."
    As they were speaking, who should they see but Li Ming, who came in and
kowtowed to them.
    "Li Ming," said Ying Po-chüeh, "where have you come from? You haven't
heard anything about how this affair of theirs is going, have you?"
    "As for this Kuei-chieh of ours," said Li Ming, "thanks to the intervention
of Father here, no one has come pressing us about her for the last couple of
days. They are just waiting for word from the capital of the final disposition
of the case."
    "Has that young woman from the Ch'i Family Establishment come out of
hiding yet?" asked Ying Po-chüeh.
    "Ch'i Hsiang-erh is still hiding out in the home of Wang the Second, the
distaff relative of the imperial family," said Li Ming. "It's a good thing that Kuei-
chieh is here at Father's place. Who would dare to come looking for her here?"
    "Were that not the case," said Ying Po-chüeh, "she'd be in a pretty pickle.
She has only to thank myself and Master Hsieh here, who repeatedly pointed

out to your patron that if he didn't consent to intervene on her behalf, where
was she to go for succor?"

"If Father here had refused to intervene," said Li Ming, "there would have
been no end to the matter. This Auntie Li the Third of ours conducts her
business in such a haphazard way, there's no telling what the outcome might
have been."

"I recollect," said Ying Po-chüeh, "that her birthday is coming up any day
now. We'll get together with your patron here, and help to celebrate her
birthday."

"There's no need for you gentlemen to do that," said Li Ming. "Once this
affair is concluded, you can be sure that Auntie Li the Third and Kuei-chieh
will ask you gentlemen over for a visit."

"When the time comes, then," said Ying Po-chüeh, "we can celebrate her
birthday after the fact."

He then summoned Li Ming to come forward and said to him, "You drink
this cup of wine for me. I've been drinking all day and can't handle any more."

Li Ming accepted the silver goblet with handles that was proffered to him,
knelt down, and:

Drained it in one gulp.

Hsieh Hsi-ta also told Ch'in-t'ung to pour out a goblet of wine and offer it
to him.

"You probably haven't had anything to eat yet," said Ying Po-chüeh.
"There's still a plate of pastries left over on the table there."

Hsieh Hsi-ta also picked up two platters of braised pig's head and roast duck
and handed them to him.

Li Ming accepted them with both hands and was in the process of retiring
to eat them, when Ying Po-chüeh detached a half-section of shad with his
chopsticks and offered it to him, saying, "It seems to me that you are unlikely
to have eaten anything like this so far this year. Have a taste of something new."

"You crazy dog!" said Hsi-men Ch'ing. "You might as well let him have the
whole thing to eat. What do you want to keep it around for?"

"In a little while," said Ying Po-chüeh, "if the wine should run out, I might
be hungry and wouldn't be satisfied to eat rice. This fish of yours from Chiang-
nan is only in season once a year. If it gets stuck in the cracks between your
teeth, when you manage to extricate it, it is still fragrant. It's not easy to come
by. To tell the truth, I doubt if it is available even at court. Where else are you
likely to find it except at Brother's place here?"

As they were speaking, whom should they see but Hua-t'ung, who came in
carrying four saucers of fresh things in season, one saucer of black caltrops,
one saucer of water chestnuts, one saucer of snowy lotus root, and one saucer
of loquats. Before Hsi-men Ch'ing even had a chance to put any of these in
his mouth, Ying Po-chüeh proceeded to snatch away whole saucers full and
dump them into his sleeve.

"You'd better leave a couple of them for me," protested Hsieh Hsi-ta, taking advantage of the opportunity to appropriate the saucer of black caltrops, leaving only the lotus root on the table.

Hsi-men Ch'ing managed to pick up a single piece and put it in his mouth, leaving the remainder for Li Ming to eat.

He then directed Hua-t'ung, "Bring another two loquats back from the rear compound and give them to Li Ming."

Li Ming put these in his sleeve, saying, "When I get home I'll share them with Auntie Li the Third."

Only after Li Ming had finished eating the fare provided for him did he rejoin the company, take up his psaltery, and prepare to sing.

"Sing us that song suite that begins with the tune "The Herbaceous Peony Enclosure," said Ying Po-chüeh.

After tuning the strings of his psaltery, Li Ming, doing his best to show off the quality of his voice, sang:

By the pond with its new verdure,
I suddenly strike the balustrade;
With whom can I discuss what's in my heart?
The flowers have nothing to say,
The butterflies have nothing to say;
The frustration of separation fills my breast,[35]
    entangling my feelings.
I resent the Lord of the East's unwillingness
    to retain the parting guest.
I sigh at the dancing red blossoms and drifting catkins,
Lightly sprinkled with the powder of butterfly wings.
The scene remains the same,
Things remain the same,
But, sadly, I no longer see my lover's face.

To the tune "Autumn Geese on the Frontier":

When we parted from each other
    it was early spring.
The flowering crab apples had just begun to bloom,
Their buds barely open and intermittently visible.
Imperceptibly, the pomegranate blossoms burst,
The red lotus flowers were in bloom,
Iced fruits were submerged,
And silk fans were waved to avoid the heat.
In no time at all, the chrysanthemums were yellow,
The metallic autumn wind began to blow,
The dead leaves were scattered,

And the foliage of the phoenix tree changed color.
Before long, the wintersweet was in bloom,
Frozen flakes were falling,
And people were mulling wine within
    heated chambers.
The scenes presented by the four seasons are multifarious,
Even to think of them is to be enraptured.
But I don't know where that handsome lover of mine,
Out in the cold,
All by himself,
Deeply depressed,
Is enduring his lonely resentment.

To the tune "Redoubled Joy in the Golden Palace":

I sigh with resentment.
It has always been true that romance leads
    young people astray.
How can I bear that it is late spring again?
I dread the twilight hours,
Grieve at the twilight hours;
All by myself, I am too depressed
    to enjoy anything.
Though I were to fumigate my bedding with rare incense,
    with whom would I share it?
I sigh that the night is long, my pillow is cold,
    and my coverlet is chill.[36]
You sleep alone,
I sleep alone,
Only in dreams can we meet.

To the tune "The Peddler":

One day, should our lifelong desires
    ever be fulfilled,
We will be united as husband and wife;
Heaven be thanked.
That would make a happy marriage affinity
    in this incarnation,
Rather than being out in the cold,
    suffering from loneliness,
Or being sunk deep in depression,
    enduring misfortune.

To the tune "Exhilarated by Peace" (Coda):[37]

Solely on account of that impassioned
   karmic encumbrance of mine,
I am today troubled with resentment
   and entangled in emotion.[38]
I think how, beneath the stars, we first swore oaths
   of fidelity by the hills and seas,
Which only served as an impediment during
   the romantic years of my youth.
If, one day, we should ever be united in wedlock
   like the morning clouds and evening rain,[39]
Enjoy the singing and dancing in decorated halls[40]
   during a joyous wedding feast,
Celebrate a perpetual reunion within silk screens
   and brocaded curtains,
Where our enamored branches may intertwine amidst
   the painted candles of the nuptial chamber,[41]
We must never forget the abundance of misfortunes
   that we have had to endure.[42]

That day the three of them continued to drink until the lamps were lighted and, even then, waited until some congee made with polished rice, flavored with mung beans, had been brought out from the rear compound for them to eat before preparing to depart.

"Brother," said Ying Po-chüeh, "are you busy tomorrow?"

"Tomorrow," said Hsi-men Ch'ing, "I'm going to pay a visit to the estate of Eunuch Director Liu, the manager of the Imperial Brickyard. Yesterday, Secretary An Ch'en and Secretary Huang Pao-kuang invited me there for a banquet, and I have to get an early start."

"With regard to that matter concerning Li the Third and Huang the Fourth," said Ying Po-chüeh, "I'll arrange with them to come the day after tomorrow then."

Hsi-men Ch'ing nodded his head and instructed him to have them come on the afternoon of that day, and not to show up any earlier. His two guests then made their departure, without waiting to be seen off. Hsi-men Ch'ing told Shu-t'ung to clear away the utensils and then went back to the rear compound, where he spent the night in Meng Yü-lou's quarters. Concerning that evening there is nothing more to relate.[43]

The next day, Hsi-men Ch'ing got up early and did not go to the yamen. Having eaten some congee, he donned his official cap and girdle, mounted his horse, holding a gold-flecked fan in his hand, and, followed by a retinue of servants, made his way to Eunuch Director Liu's estate thirty li outside the

South Gate to attend the banquet. On this occasion, both Shu-t'ung and Tai-an accompanied him. But no more of this.

P'an Chin-lien, taking advantage of Hsi-men Ch'ing's absence from the house, made plans with Li P'ing-erh to take the three mace of silver that Ch'en Ching-chi had forfeited, together with the seven mace that Li P'ing-erh had agreed to add, and get Lai-hsing to buy one roast duck, two chickens, a mace of silver's worth of other dishes to go with the rice, a jug of Chin-hua wine, a bottle of distilled spirits, and a mace of silver's worth of square, stuffed glutinous rice cakes, to be served cold. These foodstuffs were all properly prepared by Lai-hsing's wife, Hui-hsiu.

Chin-lien said to Yüeh-niang, "The other day Hsi-men Ta-chieh won three mace of silver from our son-in-law, Ch'en Ching-chi, at a game of cards, and our sister Li P'ing-erh has augmented this with an additional seven mace of silver. Today we would like to play host, and invite our sister to enjoy a repast with us in the garden."

Wu Yüeh-niang, accordingly, along with Meng Yü-lou, Li Chiao-erh, Sun Hsüeh-o, Hsi-men Ta-chieh, and Li Kuei-chieh, joined P'an Chin-lien and Li P'ing-erh and started out by feasting for a while in the summerhouse. Afterward, taking what was left of the food and wine with them, they made their way up the artificial hill to the highest point in the garden, the Cloud Repose Pavilion, where they proceeded to amuse themselves by playing board games and "pitch-pot."

Meng Yü-lou, along with Li Chiao-erh, Hsi-men Ta-chieh, and Sun Hsüeh-o, then ascended the Flower-Viewing Tower, where they leaned over the balustrade, from which they could see extending below them, in front of the artificial hill:

> The tree peony grove,
> The garden peony bed,
> The crab apple bower,
> The seven sisters trellis,
> The banksia rose arbor,
> And the rosa rugosa shrubs.

Truly:

> All four seasons produce their
>   never-fading flowers;
> All eight festivals appear one
>   everlasting spring.

After they had enjoyed the scene for a while, they came back down to the Cloud Repose Pavilion, where Hsiao-yü and Ying-ch'un were waiting on Yüeh-niang, pouring the wine and serving the food.

Yüeh-niang suddenly remarked, "Today I forgot to invite Master Ch'en."

"Today," said Hsi-men Ta-chieh, "Father has once again sent him to Hsü the Fourth's shop outside the city gate, to dun him for the silver he owes him. He should be back any time now."

It was not long before Ch'en Ching-chi presented himself:

> His body clad in a gown of jet velour,
> His feet shod in sandals and white socks,
> His head adorned with a tasseled "tile-ridge" hat,
> Held in place with a gold hairpin.

After making his bow of greeting to Yüeh-niang and the rest, he pulled Hsi-men Ta-chieh aside and sat down with her.

Addressing himself to Yüeh-niang, he said, "I've brought the final payment of silver from Hsü the Fourth's place back with me. It's in five sealed packages, two hundred fifty taels in all. I delivered it to the master suite, and Yü-hsiao has put it away."

Thereupon:

> With the raising of glasses and passing of cups,
> Several rounds of wine were consumed, and
> Their faces all took on the glint of spring.[44]

Yüeh-niang went back to playing board games with Li Chiao-erh and Li Kuei-chieh, while Meng Yü-lou, Li P'ing-erh, Sun Hsüeh-o, Hsi-men Ta-chieh, and Ch'en Ching-chi sauntered about enjoying the flowers and verdant foliage.

Chin-lien wandered off by herself, behind the artificial hill, among a thick grove of plantains, where she amused herself by batting at the butterflies with the round white-silk fan in her hand.

Unexpectedly, Ch'en Ching-chi, who had surreptitiously crept up behind her, abruptly addressed her, saying, "Fifth Lady, you don't know how to go about batting a butterfly. Let me show you how it's done. These butterflies are just like you, they've got:

> The mind of a ball,
> Bobbing up, bobbing down,

elusive creatures that they are."

Chin-lien swiveled her powdered neck, gave him a sidelong glance, and berated him with a laugh, saying, "You dead duck of a lousy short-life! Who needs you to bat butterflies for them? If anyone should overhear you, you'd be done for: though I suppose you're too far gone to care. Having knocked back several goblets of wine, you've come here to pester me, have you?"

She then went on to ask, "What about those handkerchiefs you undertook to buy for me?"

Ch'en Ching-chi, with an ingratiating smile, reached into his sleeve, pulled them out, and handed them to her, saying, "I've got the Sixth Lady's here too."

"Now that I've delivered the handkerchiefs," he went on to say, "what are you prepared to give me in return?"

Thereupon, he put his face up to hers; to which Chin-lien responded by giving him a shove.

Though neither of them realized it, Li P'ing-erh, carrying Kuan-ko in her arms, and accompanied by the wet nurse, happened to come along from the other side of the juniper hedge and caught sight of Chin-lien and Ch'en Ching-chi flirting together and batting butterflies.

When she saw that no one was looking, she stepped nimbly into the grotto in the artificial hill, from which she suddenly emerged, crying out, "Why don't the two of you bat a butterfly for Kuan-ko's amusement?"

This threw P'an Chin-lien into such consternation, fearing that Li P'ing-erh might have caught them out, that she calculatedly inquired, "Has Son-in-law Ch'en given you the handkerchiefs you requested from him, or not?"

"No, he hasn't given them to me yet," Li P'ing-erh replied.

"He had them in his sleeve," said Chin-lien, "but didn't feel comfortable giving them to us in front of Hsi-men Ta-chieh, so he slipped them to me unobtrusively, just now."

The two of them then sat down together on the stone border of the flower bed, opened the package, and divided the handkerchiefs between them.

Chin-lien, having noticed that Kuan-ko had a white drawnwork handkerchief fastened around his neck, while he sucked on a plum that he was holding in his hand, asked, "Is that one of your handkerchiefs?"

Li P'ing-erh said, "It's one that his senior mother put around his neck, just now, when she saw that he was sucking on a plum, the juice of which was dripping onto him."

The two of them continued to sit together beneath the grove of plantains.

"This place is really quite shady and cool," said Li P'ing-erh. "Let's sit here and enjoy it for a while."

She then directed Ju-i, "You go and get Ying-ch'un to fetch the child's little pillow from my quarters, and also bring the cool bamboo bed mat, so we can put him down here for a nap. Also tell her to bring a set of dominoes, so I can play a game of dominoes with the Fifth Lady here. You can stay there and look after the place."

Ju-i went off on this errand, and, before long, Ying-ch'un showed up with the pillow and mat, as well as the set of dominoes. Li P'ing-erh arranged the mat and laid Kuan-ko down on his little pillow, where he was left to amuse himself while she played dominoes with Chin-lien. After they had been playing for a while, she told Ying-ch'un to go back to her quarters and boil a pot of fine tea for them.

Who could have anticipated that Meng Yü-lou, from her vantage point at the balustrade of the Cloud Repose Pavilion, caught sight of them and waved to Li P'ing-erh with her hand, saying, "Elder Sister has something to say to you. She'll be right there."

Li P'ing-erh, abandoning her child, whom she entrusted to Chin-lien's care, responded, "I'll be right there."

Chin-lien, however, who was preoccupied by the fact that Ch'en Ching-chi was still lurking in the grotto, was scarcely concerned about the welfare of the child, but seized the opportunity to step nimbly through the door of the grotto, locate Ch'en Ching-chi, and say to him, "There's no one else around. You can come out now."

Ch'en Ching-chi then called to the woman to come inside and see the mushroom, saying, "Some mushrooms with enormous heads have sprung up in here."[45]

Having thus inveigled the woman into the grotto, he bent his knees, knelt down before her, and proposed that they indulge in the play of clouds and rain together. The two of them then embraced and began to kiss each other.

It so happens that:

As providence would have it,

when Li P'ing-erh arrived at the Cloud Repose Pavilion, Wu Yüeh-niang said to her, "Sister Meng the Third has just lost a game of pitch-pot with Hsi-men Ta-chieh. Why don't you come and try your hand at a couple of pitches on her behalf?"

"There's no one down below to look after the child," said Li P'ing-erh.

"After all, Sister Six is there," said Meng Yü-lou. "What is there to be afraid of?"

"Sister Meng the Third," said Yüeh-niang, "why don't you go look after the child for her?"

"Third Lady," said Li P'ing-erh, "might I also trouble you to bring the baby back with you?"

She then turned to Hsiao-yü and said, "You go along with her, and bring the mat and his little pillow back with you."

When Hsiao-yü and Meng Yü-lou arrived beneath the grove of plantains, they found the baby lying on his back on the mat:

Gesticulating with both hands and feet,

and screaming at the top of his voice, while Chin-lien was nowhere to be found. What should they see beside him but a large black cat, which, on seeing them arrive, disappeared in a puff of smoke.

"Where has the Fifth Lady gone?" exclaimed Meng Yü-lou. "Ai-ya! Ai-ya! She's left the child here all alone, and he's been terrified by a cat."

Chin-lien then emerged from the grotto to one side, saying, "I've just been in here relieving myself. Who's gone off anywhere? And how could any cat have terrified him? How can you be so:

Barefaced and red-eyed?"

Meng Yü-lou did not go into the grotto for a look but merely took Kuan-ko in her arms and devoted herself to petting him, as she made her way back up to the Cloud Repose Pavilion, while Hsiao-yü followed her with the pillow

P'an Chin-lien Inspects a Mushroom in the Flower Garden

and mat. Chin-lien, who was afraid she might tell tales about her, stuck right to her tail.

"Why is the child crying?" asked Yüeh-niang.

"When I got there," said Meng Yü-lou, "there was a large black cat, from who knows where, crouched right beside the child's head."

"It must clearly have terrified the child," said Yüeh-niang.

"The Fifth Lady was looking after him," said Li P'ing-erh.

"Sister Six had gone into the grotto to relieve herself," said Meng Yü-lou.

Chin-lien stepped up at this point and said, "Yü-lou, how can you be so:

> Barefaced and red-eyed?

Where would I have gotten a cat from? I imagine he must have been hungry and was crying to be breast-fed. You're just trying to lay the blame on me."

Li P'ing-erh saw that Ying-ch'un had come back with the tea and said to her, "Go summon the wet nurse so she can breast-feed the child."

Meanwhile, Ch'en Ching-chi, on seeing that the coast was clear, sneaked out of the grotto, made his way along the juniper hedge, rounded the corner of the summerhouse, and headed straight out the postern gate into the front compound. Truly:

> With both hands he tore open the road
> > between life and death;
> Flopping over and leaping out through
> > the gate to perdition.

Yüeh-niang, on seeing that the baby would not allow himself to be breast-fed but continued to cry, said to Li P'ing-erh, "You carry him back to your quarters, and do what you can to get him to go to sleep."

Thereupon, the wine drinking came to an end, and the party broke up.

It so happens that Ch'en Ching-chi had failed in his attempt to make out with P'an Chin-lien.

> Though they may have wished to emulate the
> > billing swallows and cooing orioles;
> The bee's antennae had no more than grazed
> > the corolla of the flower.

His endeavor had not turned out propitiously, and when he returned to his anteroom in the front compound, he couldn't help muttering unhappily to himself. Truly:

> Unable to help themselves,[46]
> > the blossoms fall;
> Conveying a sense of deja vu,[47]
> > the swallows return.[48]

There is a song to the tune "Plucking the Cassia" that testifies to this:

I saw her rakishly sporting a spray of blossoms;
Smiling as she toyed with her spray of blossoms.

On her ruby lips she wore no rouge;
But looked as though she did wear rouge.
When we met the other day,
And then met again today;
She seemed to have feelings for me,
But displayed no feelings for me.
Though she wished to consent,
She never gave her consent.
It looked as though she refused me;
But she really never did refuse me.
When can we make another assignation;
When will we ever see each other again?
If we don't meet,
She may long for me;
When we do meet,
I still long for her.[49]

If you want to know the outcome of these events,
Pray consult the story related in the following chapter.

Chapter 53[1]

WU YÜEH-NIANG ENGAGES IN COITION

IN QUEST OF MALE PROGENY;

LI P'ING-ERH FULFILLS A VOW

IN ORDER TO SAFEGUARD HER SON

In this life, to have a son is the consummation
   of a myriad desires;[2]
After death, to leave behind no male heir is to
   have lived in vain.
If one should produce a dragon steed, one must
   endeavor to protect it;
If one hopes to bear a unicorn, one must enact
   good deeds in secret.
Praying to the gods, she is anxious to fulfill
   the promise of her vow;
By imbibing a potion, she hopes to be able to
   make her womb receptive.
Parents would do well to carry out their human
   obligations to the full;
But the good or bad luck that may result must
   be left to Azure Heaven.

THE STORY GOES that Wu Yüeh-niang, having spent some time amusing herself along with Li Chiao-erh, Li Kuei-chieh, Meng Yü-lou, Li P'ing-erh, Sun Hsüeh-o, P'an Chin-lien, and Hsi-men Ta-chieh, began to feel somewhat fatigued, retired to her room, and took a nap.

When she awoke, around the first watch, she sent Hsiao-yü to say to Li P'ing-erh, "Has Kuan-ko stopped that unnatural crying of his? Have the wet nurse wrap him up carefully and coax him to sleep. Don't let anything disturb him into crying again."

The wet nurse, who was eating her supper on the k'ang, did not get down from her position but kept the child there beside her.

Li P'ing-erh said, "Thank the First Lady for me, and tell her that when we came back to my quarters, he kept on crying out loud and suffering from the cold shivers continuously, and he has only now stopped crying, cuddled up

against the wet nurse's body, and fallen asleep. His forehead feels rather feverish, and the wet nurse is unwilling to move for fear of disturbing him. In a
little while, I'm going to wake him, so he can have his evening feeding and
relieve himself."

Hsiao-yü returned to the master suite and reported this information to
Yüeh-niang.

"They're not taking things as seriously as they should," said Yüeh-niang.
"How could she have left a little baby like that under the plantains, and just
gone off somewhere else, so that he was scared to death by a cat? Only now
are they:
  Lamenting before the gods and weeping to ghosts.
At this rate, they're likely to do him some real harm before they come to their
senses."

At that time, after expressing these few words of criticism, she washed her
face and went to sleep for the night.

The next morning, when she got up:
  Having nothing else to say,
she sent Hsiao-yü to ask if Kuan-ko had been able to get any sleep during the
remainder of the night, or not?

She also reported, "As soon as the First Lady has eaten her congee, she is
planning to drop by and see how Kuan-ko is doing."

Li P'ing-erh said to Ying-ch'un, "The First Lady is about to come over here.
Quickly, fetch me some water, so I can wash my face."

Ying-ch'un flew off on this errand and returned with the water for her to
wash her face. Li P'ing-erh hastily combed her hair and ordered Ying-ch'un
to heat some water for tea as quickly as possible, and to light some benzoin
incense in the room.

Before they knew it, Hsiao-yü came in and announced, "The First Lady
has entered your quarters."

This had the effect of causing Li P'ing-erh to jump up in consternation to
greet Yüeh-niang and lead her to the wet nurse's bed, where she caressed
Kuan-ko, saying as she did so, "What a hopeless little oily mouth! You're constantly taking your own mother and:
  Dunking her in a water crock,
for no good reason."

At this, Kuan-ko, with the sound of a gurgling cry, started to howl in earnest.
Yüeh-niang made haste to playfully tease him for a while before he finally
stopped.

Yüeh-niang then turned to Ju-i and said, "Since I haven't been able to have
a child myself, this little bit of a boy is the only issue of our family. You can't
afford to underestimate his importance. To get right down to it, you've simply
got to look after him conscientiously."

The wet nurse Ju-i replied, "As to that, there is no need for the First Lady
to instruct me any further."

Yüeh-niang was about to take her leave, when Li P'ing-erh said, "Now that the First Lady is here, I have had a cup of tea prepared. Won't you visit a while before leaving?"

Yüeh-niang then sat down and asked, "Sixth Lady, how is it that your hair is so mussed?"

Li P'ing-erh said, "It's all on account of the way this heartless enemy of mine has been:

　　Acting up and making trouble,

that I haven't even had a chance to comb my hair. Then, when I heard that you were coming, I hastily twisted it into a knot and fitted the fret over it, without realizing what sort of laughable shape it was in."

"Just look at you!" exclaimed Yüeh-niang. "How unprincipled can you get? He's your own flesh and blood, to whom you've given birth, and yet you refer to him as your heartless enemy. While, as for me, though I long for such a heartless enemy all day long, I haven't been able to have one."

"It's just a manner of speaking," said Li P'ing-erh. "If only he weren't beset by all these spectral visitations, everything would be all right. But nowadays, I hardly get two or three days of peace without the occurrence of such an outbreak. The other day, when we visited the family graveyard, he was frightened by the gongs and drums. Not long after that, he started to cry like anything when he had his hair cut. And now he's been frightened once again by a cat. Other people's babies seem easy enough to raise, but this creature of mine turns out, contrarily, to be as fragile as a rush."

After they had chatted for a while, Yüeh-niang walked out of the room, and Li P'ing-erh followed behind her to see her off.

"Don't bother to see me off," said Yüeh-niang. "Go back inside and look after Kuan-ko."

Li P'ing-erh, accordingly, returned inside, while Yüeh-niang made her way back to the master suite.

As she did so, she overheard someone talking, as furtively as a thief trying to destroy evidence, on the other side of the screen-wall.

Yüeh-niang stopped to listen and, on peeking through a crack between the boards, saw that one of them was P'an Chin-lien, who was leaning on the balustrade, together with Meng Yü-lou, while she chattered away,[3] in a subdued voice, saying, "Our elder sister really has no sense of decorum. Having no child of her own, when someone else bears a son, she insists to the point of befuddlement on claiming a specious intimacy, and sucking up to her in the most egregious way.[4] It seems to me that:

　　Even the indigent should maintain their indigent spirit,

　　Just as the eminent should display their eminent spirit.

What's the point of playing up to her that way? When the child grows up, he will only acknowledge his natural mother, why should he acknowledge you?"

Who should pass by at this point but Ying-ch'un, which caused the two of them to slip off toward the rear compound, pretending to be looking for the cat in order to feed it.

Nothing might have happened if Yüeh-niang had not overheard this conversation, but having overheard these words:

> Anger arose in her heart, and
> Resentment stiffened her jaw.

At the time, she would have liked to interrupt the conversation and call them to account, but since it was not something that could be solved by making a fuss, and would, instead, only have the effect of detracting from her own dignity, she chose to restrain herself. She went directly into her room and lay down on the bed, but she did not feel free to cry over the situation, lest the maidservants overhear her. All she could do was:

> Complain silently to herself,[5]

giving vent to:

> Long sighs as well as short.

Truly:

> Even in her own home she dared not risk
>   crying out too loudly,
> Fearing lest the gibbons on hearing her
>   should break their hearts.[6]

At that time, it was just high noon, and she had not yet gotten up.

Hsiao-yü stood beside her bed and said, "First Lady, won't you get up and have something to eat?"

"I'm not feeling well," said Yüeh-niang, "and don't want to eat anything, but you can close the door of the room, and prepare some tea for me."

Only after Hsiao-yü had brought in the tea did Yüeh-niang get up and sit disconsolately in her room, saying to herself, "Simply because I don't have a son of my own, I have to put up with all this annoyance at other people's hands. I have:

> Besought Heaven and worshipped Earth,

in the hope of obtaining one, so that I can shame those lousy whores to their fucking faces."

Thereupon, she went to the comb box on the dressing table in her inner room and got out the afterbirth of a firstborn male child that Nun Wang had provided, as well as the medication that Nun Hsüeh had procured for her, and saw that the sealed container in which they were enclosed was engraved with four characters that read:

> An efficacious elixir for conceiving sons.

There was also an eight-line poem, which read:

> Like Ch'ang-o who mischievously fled to the moon
>   with the elixir of immortality;

This potion has obligingly appropriated the horn
   on the striped dragon's crown.
It has been sanctioned by the Peach Blossom Mandate
   of an emperor of the Han dynasty;[7]
And has also been ordained by the Bamboo Leaf Edict
   of a ruler of the Liang dynasty.[8]
In no time at all, once the medication starts to act,
   it will produce enviable results;
Even the elderly and decrepit will be rejuvenated,
   such are its praiseworthy effects.
Do not take it as something to enhance the joys of
   snow and flowers, breeze and moon;
Even the smallest amount will enable you to conceive
   a handsomely black-bearded son.

After this there was an encomium, which read:

     Its flaming red color sparkles,
     Exactly like coral that has been
        ground to powder;
     Its fragrant redolence is dense,
     Resembling that of newly ignited
        sandalwood or musk.
     If you hold it in your mouth,
     A sweet exudation will rise up about
        the base of your teeth;
     If you place it in your palm,
     A warm sensation will suffuse the
        area beneath your navel.
     It will enable you to retain your essence
        and replenish your fluid;[9]
     What need is there to seek the Magic Frost
        Pounded with a Jade Pestle?[10]
     It will allow you to change a female embryo
        into a male embryo;[11]
     What need is there to look elsewhere for
        the Divine Bower Powder?[12]
     Do not waste it on the chickens and dogs by
        your alchemical furnace;[13]
     It is meant to enhance the joys of mandarin
        ducks beneath the quilt.
     If you ingest it when the spirit moves you,
     It will produce the dream of an azure dragon;[14]
     If you act upon it when the time is ripe,

> It will engender the omen of a flying swallow.[15]
> Those who seek to bear a son may accomplish
>   their objective with a single try;
> Those who wish to achieve transcendence can
>   become immortals in a hundred days.

After this there were some further directions, which read:

> Anything damaging to the brain, or
>   harmful to the blood stream,
> Should be strictly avoided.
> Radishes as well as spring onions
>   should also be avoided.
> If you engage in intercourse on an odd day
>   you will conceive a son;
> If you engage in intercourse on an even day
>   you will conceive a daughter;
> You may do as your heart desires.
> If you take this medication for a year,
> You may achieve everlasting life.

When Yüeh-niang had finished reading this material, she felt a sense of pleasure gradually arise in her heart. Observing that the container was tightly sealed:

> With slender tapering fingers,
> She delicately prized it open.

When she unfolded the packet within and took a look, she found that it consisted of three or four layers of "black gold paper,"[16] wrapped around a single bolus of medication, the exterior of which was attractively decorated with gold-flecked vermilion. Yüeh-niang placed it in the palm of her hand and, sure enough, she felt a warm sensation arise below her navel. She then held it next to her nose and, sure enough, becoming moist:

> Her mouth was filled with sweet spittle.

With a smile, Yüeh-niang said to herself, "This Nun Hsüeh must really be a person of exemplary conduct. Who knows where she must have gone to locate such a:

> Marvelous medicine and efficacious elixir?

It must be that I am fated to conceive, since I have come upon such a fine medication, but who knows?"

After toying with the medication for a while, fearing lest it might lose its efficacy, she hastily fetched some paste and sealed it up tightly as before, went back into her inner room, and locked it up inside her comb box.

Strolling out onto the veranda, she gazed up to Heaven and gave a long sigh, saying, "Should this woman, née Wu, tomorrow, which is a *jen-tzu* day, take this medication of Nun Hsüeh's and succeed in conceiving a son to perpetuate the ancestral rites of the Hsi-men house, so that she does not end up as a ghost with no one to sacrifice to it, my gratitude to August Heaven will know no bounds."

By that time, the day was drawing to a close, and Yüeh-niang finally had something to eat, but there is nothing more to say about this.

When Hsi-men Ch'ing arrived at Eunuch Director Liu's estate that day, he sent in his card, and the servants informed Secretary Huang Pao-kuang and Secretary An Ch'en, who came out together to meet him. They were both formally attired in their official caps and girdles.

When they had exchanged the customary greetings and sat down, Secretary Huang Pao-kuang opened the proceedings by saying, "The other day, motivated by admiration of your great fame, we presumed to visit you unceremoniously but did not expect to put you to such great expense."

"I fear I was guilty of treating you remissly," said Hsi-men Ch'ing.

"On that occasion," said Secretary An Ch'en, "we were on our way to respond to an invitation from our fellow graduate, Prefect Hu Shih-wen, and were therefore compelled to take our leave rather precipitously. But:

The profound sentiments of our host,[17]

still resonate in our hearts. Today it is only appropriate that we should enjoy ourselves fully until break of day."

"I am deeply affected by your lavish hospitality," responded Hsi-men Ch'ing.

After a "gate boy" had announced in a low voice that the feast was fully prepared, Hsi-men Ch'ing was invited to repair to the summerhouse, where they divested themselves of their official caps and girdles and proceeded to take their seats. Hsi-men Ch'ing was ushered to the seat of honor where, after a pro forma demurral, he consented to sit down.

A singing boy then came forward and sang a song to the tune "Embroidered Oranges and Plums":

The fragrant redness of her face is suffused with
    the glow of sunset clouds;
The glossy blackness of her raven locks is heaped
    in piles about her temples.
I expect that she,
Must be a denizen of the quarter,
Dressed up as she is, a fit subject
    for an artist's brush.
Quiveringly, she is wearing a turquoise
    ornament in her hair;
Ostentatiously, she is clad in garments
    of the thinnest silk.

The stylishness she exhibits is enough
    to slay the beholder.
Ch'a!
Whose establishment does she hail from,
That she should secretly look me over so
    unceasingly with her eyes?[18]

Hsi-men Ch'ing praised this performance, and Secretary An Ch'en and
Secretary Huang Pao-kuang presented him with cups of wine. When Hsi-men
Ch'ing had returned the compliment, the singing boy once again:
        Accompanying himself with a sandalwood clapper,
sang a song to the tune "Vanquishing the Yellow Dragon, Quick Tempo":

Since there is no convenient way to correspond,
I am too lazy to inscribe my brocade notepaper.
The gold bracelet about my wrist is loose;
The jade of my flesh has become emaciated;
My silken garments droop completely slack.
Tears have encroached upon,
The makeup on my two cheeks.
I am too sorrowful to look into my precious mirror,
And ashamed to wear my halcyon-feathered ornaments.

To the same tune:

I have pointlessly squandered,
The good days and fine nights.[19]
In my jade incense burner,
On the silver candlestick,
The incense has dissipated and the candle gone out.[20]
The phoenix bed curtains have been forsaken,[21]
The mandarin duck quilt is supplied in vain.
I incessantly fidget with my jade fingers,
And repeatedly stamp my embroidered shoes.[22]

On this occasion, they continued drinking until after 6:00 o'clock:
        With the raising of glasses and passing of cups;
but we have already said enough about this.
    To resume our story, back at home, P'an Chin-lien, having failed on the
previous day in her attempt in the "snow cave" to make out with Ch'en Ching-
chi, took advantage of the opportunity presented by the fact that Hsi-men
Ch'ing was away at Eunuch Director Liu's estate, drinking with Secretary
Huang Pao-kuang and Secretary An Ch'en, and that Wu Yüeh-niang was staying in her room, to:

Run in and run out,
of her quarters, just like:
An ant on a hot plate.[23]
As for Ch'en Ching-chi, after escaping from the "snow cave," he had gone
to sleep in the shop, where his organ remained stiff all night long. On this
occasion, while Hsi-men Ch'ing was not at home, he and P'an Chin-lien
uninhibitedly:
Exchanged looks with eyes and eyebrows,
This went on until after dusk, when the lamps were about to be lighted in the
various quarters. At this point Chin-lien proceeded with:
Skulking step and lurking gait,
to tiptoe out behind the summerhouse, where Ch'en Ching-chi just happened to come by. When he perceived by the dim light that it was Chin-lien,
he proceeded without more ado to embrace her tightly and put his face next
to hers, whereupon the two of them exchanged some ten or more kisses.
"My darling," said Ch'en Ching-chi, "yesterday when that pain in the neck,
Meng the Third, interrupted us, I had such a stiff erection that it stayed up
all night. And today, when I saw how:
Seductively and bewitchingly,[24]
you swayed as you strolled by, my whole body was infused with a melting
sensation."
"You dead duck of a lousy short-life!" said Chin-lien. "You must be utterly
devoid of principles to grab hold of your own mother-in-law and kiss
her. Aren't you afraid that someone might come along and hear what you're
up to?"
"If I spot a lantern light coming in this direction," said Ch'en Ching-chi,
"I'll have time to get out of the way."
Ch'en Ching-chi kept on uttering the word "darling" with his mouth, while
beneath the single thickness of his gown, his organ, like a bar of red-hot iron,
surged forward beneath the fabric. Chin-lien, for her part, couldn't help
thrusting her body forward to meet the overheated organ beneath his gown.
Unable to restrain herself, Chin-lien lifted Ch'en Ching-chi's gown aside with
her hand and firmly gripped his male organ. Ch'en Ching-chi was so flustered
that in trying to pull down Chin-lien's waistband, he only succeeded, with a
rending sound, in ripping out one of the pleats in her skirt.
"You lousy slave!" expostulated Chin-lien with a laugh. "How clumsy can
you get? You're still so unused to snitching your food, and so timorous in going
about it, that all you've done, in your flusteration, is to rip out one of the
pleats in my skirt."
So saying, she pulled down her own waistband, exposing the mouth of her
vagina, lifted one of her legs onto the balustrade, and proceeded to stuff Ch'en
Ching-chi's male organ into the orifice. It so happens that, because Chin-lien
had been fooling around for some time, her vagina was already sopping wet,

so that when Ch'en Ching-chi gave a single forceful thrust, he succeeded immediately in effecting penetration.

"My darling," said Ch'en Ching-chi, "standing up like this, it's hard to get in all the way. What should we do?"

"If you just keep on retracting and thrusting so impetuously," said Chin-lien, "we'll come up with something."

Ch'en Ching-chi was about to resume retracting and thrusting, when they suddenly heard the dogs outside start to bark noisily, and realized that Hsi-men Ch'ing must have arrived home from his drinking party. This threw the two of them into such consternation that they disappeared in a puff of smoke.

It turned out to be Shu-t'ung and Tai-an, carrying Hsi-men Ch'ing's official cap and girdle, and his gold-flecked fan, who came into the compound, creating quite a stir as they exclaimed, "We've really been put through our paces today!"

Yüeh-niang sent Hsiao-yü out to investigate, and she observed that the two page boys were both befuddled with drink.

"Why has Father not returned?" Hsiao-yü asked.

"Just now," explained Tai-an, "because we were afraid we wouldn't be able to keep up with his horse on foot, we got Father's permission to start back ahead of him. His horse is fast, so he should be right behind us."

Hsiao-yü went back to the rear compound to report this, and before long, Hsi-men Ch'ing arrived at the gate and dismounted.

He had originally intended to spend the night in Chin-lien's quarters, but who could have anticipated that he was so drunk that he went into Yüeh-niang's room by mistake.

Yüeh-niang thought to herself, "Tomorrow is the twenty-third, which is a *jen-tzu* day. If I keep him here tonight, it might spoil my opportunity with regard to that important matter tomorrow. Moreover, my period is coming to an end today, so tomorrow it would be more sanitary."

"You're too groggy with drink tonight," she said to Hsi-men Ch'ing. "I don't want you fooling around here. My period is not quite over yet. It would be better if you slept in someone else's quarters, and came back here tomorrow night."

As she spoke, she pushed Hsi-men Ch'ing, who was smiling bemusedly, out of her room, and he headed straight for Chin-lien's quarters.

Pinching Chin-lien's cheeks, he said to her, "This is the little whore I've been looking for. Just now, I was intending to come over here, but who would have thought that, because I've had a few cups of wine, without knowing what I was doing, I went into the First Lady's room instead."

"What an inveterate oily-mouthed creature you are!" said Chin-lien. "No doubt you'll tell me some story about having originally intended to sleep in Elder Sister's room tomorrow. What a filthy braggart!

A Tryst between Chin-lien and Ching-chi Is Interrupted

> You wouldn't hesitate to tell a bold-faced lie
>   to a Perfected Being.

And you expect me to believe you!"

"You crazy oily mouth!" said Hsi-men Ch'ing. "All you ever do is give people a hard time. That's the way it really is. What reason would I have to lie about it?"

"Just tell me, then," said Chin-lien, "why didn't Elder Sister keep you there tonight?"

"I don't know," said Hsi-men Ch'ing. "She kept claiming that I was drunk and pushed me out of her room, saying, 'Come back tomorrow night.' So I came over here as fast as I could."

Chin-lien was about to wash her private parts, when Hsi-men Ch'ing reached over to feel her there.

Covering herself with both hands, Chin-lien upbraided him, saying, "You short-life! Cut it out. I've had enough of your tricks around here."

Hsi-men Ch'ing, embracing her with one hand, stuck his other hand into her crotch, where, after feeling it, he said, "You crazy good-for-nothing! How does it happen that, night after night, it's perfectly dry, whereas tonight, it's sopping wet inside? No doubt you've been hankering after a man, so that your vaginal secretions have started to flow."

It so happens that Chin-lien had, in fact, been so preoccupied with Ch'en Ching-chi that she had neglected to wash her private parts. And now that Hsi-men Ch'ing had unintentionally hit upon what was on her mind, her face turned bright red in an instant, and she was reduced to covering up as best she could, half smiling and half objecting, as she bathed her private parts and washed her face before the two of them retired for the night. But no more of this.

To resume our story, when Wu Yüeh-niang got up the next morning, it being a *jen-tzu* day, she thought to herself, "As Nun Hsüeh was about to take her leave, she enjoined me repeatedly, in no uncertain terms, that if I took this potion of hers on a *jen-tzu* day, I would be sure to conceive. Today is a *jen-tzu* day, so I really ought to take her medication. Moreover, it's fortunate that last night:

> By a providential coincidence,[25]

Hsi-men Ch'ing came home drunk and made his way into my room, so I was able to arrange for him to return tonight."

For this reason, Yüeh-niang secretly rejoiced in her heart. Upon arising, early in the morning, after performing her ablutions and completing her toilet, she proceeded to pay obeisance to Buddha and recited the *Sutra of the White-Robed Kuan-yin*.[26] It is essential that those who wish to conceive sons should recite this sutra, and that is why Yüeh-niang recited it. Moreover, Nun Wang had also urged her to recite it. The day in question was also a *jen-tzu* day, a

Wu Yüeh-niang Recites a Sutra in Quest of Male Progeny

day of critical importance. That is why, early in the morning, she closed the
door to her room;

Ignited incense and lit candles,[27]

and recited this text, before going back to her inner room to fetch the medication.

Instructing Hsiao-yü to heat some wine, she did not take any congee but
prepared herself by eating some cakes, biscuits, and the like. First, after having
held the nostrum up reverently with both hands, and:

Uttered a prayer to Heaven,[28]

she dissolved Nun Hsüeh's bolus of medication in the wine, producing a
potion, of which:

The exotic fragrance assailed the nostrils,

and finished it off in two or three mouthfuls. When she then turned her
attention to the afterbirth of a firstborn male child that Nun Wang had provided, although it had been rendered into powdered form, it nevertheless
made her feel somewhat skittish. It exuded a perceptible odor of incineration
and was not something easy to swallow.

"If I don't take it," Yüeh-niang thought to herself, "it won't have the desired
effect. While, if I do take it, I can't overcome my misgivings. But enough
of this:

Once things have come to a head,
They are out of one's control.[29]

I'll simply have to force myself to swallow it, that's all."

First taking a handful of the talismanic potion and forcing it into her
mouth, she urgently swallowed half a bowl of wine and almost regurgitated
it, her eyes turning red as she did so. Hastily washing this down with more
wine, she still felt as though something were sticking in her throat and
followed up with another few mouthfuls of wine. After which she called
for some warm tea with which to rinse out her mouth and then lay down on
her bed.

Hsi-men Ch'ing happened to come by her room just then and, noticing
that the door was closed, called for Hsiao-yü to open it, asking, "How come
everything is so quiet, and the door to the room is closed? Could it be that
the First Lady is somewhat annoyed[30] with me for having left her alone
last night?"

"How would I know?" responded Hsiao-yü.

Hsi-men Ch'ing went into the room and called to her several times, but
Yüeh-niang, who had had wine to drink that morning, was fast asleep facing
the interior of the bed and did not answer him.

"You lousy slave!" Hsi-men Ch'ing said to Hsiao-yü. "Just now I called to
the First Lady and she refused to answer. Why should she do that unless she
were annoyed with me?"

Not knowing what to do with himself, he walked out of the room, only to encounter Shu-t'ung coming in, who reported, "Master Ying the Second is outside."

When Hsi-men Ch'ing came out, Ying Po-chüeh said to him, "Brother, when you went to Eunuch Director Liu's estate the other day to attend the party hosted by Messrs. An Ch'en and Huang Pao-kuang, were you able to enjoy yourself fully? How late did you continue to drink before the party broke up?"

"I am grateful for the lavish affection the two gentlemen have shown me," said Hsi-men Ch'ing. "When they condescended to visit me on that former occasion, because they were on their way to a party hosted by Prefect Hu Shih-wen, they didn't stay long. But when I arrived at their place, I found that:

Our feelings were genial, our thoughts in accord.[31]

They kept me there for some time and insisted upon my having quite a few cups of wine, right up until the time the night watches began. It was a long way home, and I was so drunk I hardly knew what I was doing."

"For people from other places," opined Ying Po-chüeh, "they are gentlemen of real feeling. You ought to send them something in the way of gifts for the road."

"You've got a point there," said Hsi-men Ch'ing.

There and then, he summoned Shu-t'ung and told him to fill out a pair of red gift cards, and to direct the people in the rear compound to prepare two equally sumptuous sets of gifts, consisting of litchis, longans, peaches, dates, geese, ducks, legs of lamb, fresh fish, and two jugs of southern wine. He also had him write messages on two of his own calling cards, expressing his gratitude for their hospitality. When these tasks were completed, he called for Shu-t'ung once again and directed him to deliver the gifts himself. Shu-t'ung duly assented and went off on his errand.

At this point, Ying Po-chüeh moved closer to Hsi-men Ch'ing, sat down beside him, and asked, "Do you remember what you said to me the day before yesterday?"

"What is there to remember?" responded Hsi-men Ch'ing.

"I guess you've been so busy you've forgotten all about it," said Ying Po-chüeh. "It's what I said to you just before we left when Hsieh Hsi-ta and I were having a drink with you here the day before yesterday."

Hsi-men Ch'ing stared vacantly into space and thought for a while before saying, "It must have been something to do with that affair of Li the Third and Huang the Fourth, wasn't it?"

Ying Po-chüeh responded, with a laugh, "Just as they say:

When the rainwater from the eaves
   drips down from above:
Every drop hits the mark."

Hsi-men Ch'ing knit his brows and said, "Where would you have me come up with the necessary silver? You saw how it was the other day when I was arranging to take delivery of that salt and was so strapped for cash that I had to borrow five hundred taels of silver from my kinsman Ch'iao Hung in order to complete the transaction. Where would I come up with all this additional silver to invest?"

"In any event," said Ying Po-chüeh, "it's an investment that is bound to be profitable. Why don't you see if you can dig out something from the corner of one of your trunks, or somewhere, to give to them? Brother, you said that yesterday you got an initial payment of two hundred fifty taels from Hsü the Fourth's place outside the city gate, so the remaining half of what they need should be easy enough to get together."

"That's as may be," said Hsi-men Ch'ing, "but where am I to scrape it up from? You'd better tell them to wait until I've received the entire sum that Hsü the Fourth owes me, and I'll turn it over to them then in a lump sum."

Ying Po-chüeh adopted a serious expression and said, "Brother:

A single word from a gentleman, is like
A single whip stroke to a fleet steed.[32]
If a man is untrustworthy,
How can that be tolerated?[33]

It would have been better if you had not made that promise to me the day before yesterday. I've already told them that it's:

As certain as certain can be,

they'll get the money today, so what am I to say to them? They have complete faith in your reputation for magnanimity. Over such a trivial matter, would you have these businessmen bad-mouthing you behind your back?"

"If Master Ying the Second says so," responded Hsi-men Ch'ing, "I might as well give it to them, and be done with it."

He then went back to the rear compound, where he got together two hundred thirty taels of silver, and asked Yü-hsiao for the two hundred fifty taels that had been received from Hsü the Fourth's place the day before, which weighed out to a total of exactly four hundred eighty taels.

Coming outside again, he said to Ying Po-chüeh, "I have only been able to scrape together four hundred eighty taels, so I am still twenty taels short. But I can supply some satin piece goods to make up the difference. Will that do?"

"That would make things difficult," said Ying Po-chüeh. "They require ready cash in order to fulfill their part of this contract for the purveying of incense. You don't have any of the best grade of satin piece goods in stock right now, and those pieces of pink satin you do have aren't good enough to fill the bill. You might as well scrape up the ready money, and save me a lot of legwork."

"That's enough! That's enough!" said Hsi-men Ch'ing.

So saying, he went back inside, weighed out twenty taels of good-quality silver, and told Tai-an to take the whole amount out with him.

Li the Third and Huang the Fourth had been sitting in a neighbor's house for a long time, just waiting for a signal from Ying Po-chüeh before putting in an appearance, and Hsieh Hsi-ta happened to come in at the same time.

Having first greeted Hsieh Hsi-ta, Li the Third and Huang the Fourth saluted Hsi-men Ch'ing, saying, "On a former occasion we were the recipients of your great kindness, and it is only because the silver that is due us has not yet been disbursed that we have been so dilatory in paying you back. And now, in Tung-p'ing prefecture, there is another contract being let for the purveying of twenty thousand taels worth of incense, and we have once again made bold to ask you for the loan of another five hundred taels of silver, in order to temporarily relieve this:

Eyebrow singeing exigency.[34]

When we receive the payment for our current contract, we will bring it over to you, without touching so much as a candareen of it, and repay you in full, including the interest due."

Hsi-men Ch'ing then called for Tai-an and sent him to fetch the steelyard from the shop, and invite his son-in-law, Ch'en Ching-chi, to join them. After which, he weighed out, first, the twenty-five packets of ten taels each that he had collected from Hsü the Fourth's place, and then, the two hundred fifty taels that he had provided himself, and turned them over to Huang the Fourth and Li the Third. The two of them, after seemingly never ending expressions of gratitude, finally took their leave.

Hsi-men Ch'ing wanted to keep Ying Po-chüeh and Hsieh Hsi-ta for a further parley, but the two of them had no stomach for an extended visit, wishing, instead, to leave forthwith in order to divvy up the brokerage fee they expected to receive from Li the Third and Huang the Fourth. Claiming falsely to have other engagements, they hastily took their leave, but on their way out, Ying Po-chüeh was pestered by Tai-an and Ch'in-t'ung, who demanded something for themselves with which to buy sweetmeats.

Ying Po-chüeh waved them off with his hand, saying, "I've got nothing for you! I've got nothing for you! This is something I undertook on my own initiative. I didn't bring anything for the likes of you. Dogs of a whore's spawn that you are!" And he and his companion took themselves off.

Who should appear at this juncture but Shu-t'ung, who came in to deliver thank-you notes from Secretary Huang Pao-kuang and Secretary An Ch'en and reported, "The two gentlemen protested that they really ought not to accept such gifts from you, but agreed to receive them for fear of offending you. They asked me to convey their gratitude to you, and each of them gave me a tip in a sealed envelope."

Hsi-men Ch'ing told him to keep these gratuities for himself and also weighed out some silver for the carriers who had been hired to deliver the gifts, and sent them on their way. It being lamp-lighting time already, Hsi-men Ch'ing then went into Yüeh-niang's room and sat down.

Yüeh-niang said, "Hsiao-yü tells me that you came into my room earlier today and called to me, but I was asleep at the time and didn't know that you were calling me."

"There you go again," said Hsi-men Ch'ing. "I knew all along that you were not too pleased with me."

"Who says that I'm not pleased with you?" protested Yüeh-niang, and then she ordered Hsiao-yü to prepare some tea and fetch some supper for them to eat.

After downing several cups of tea, Hsi-men Ch'ing, whose body was affected by several successive days of heavy drinking, would have been happy enough simply to go to sleep. But since it had been some time since he spent the night in Yüeh-niang's room, he was anxious to please her, and had used some of the Indian monk's ointment, so that his male organ was swollen into the shape of an iron pestle.

When Yüeh-niang saw it, she said out loud, "That Indian monk was so unprincipled that he would spring this kind of frightening trick on someone, would he?"

But:

In her heart she thought to herself,[35]
"He may have the Indian monk's techniques on his side, but I've got the Nun's transcendent elixir on mine. Something good is bound to come out of this."

Consequently, they both got into bed and spent a pleasurable night together, and it was nearly noon before they got up the next day.

This fact did not fail to attract the attention of P'an Chin-lien, who:

Exercised her lips and waggled her tongue,
to Meng Yü-lou, saying, "The other day, Elder Sister asked me to look up when the next jen-tzu day would occur, and that must be why she was so anxious to sleep with our husband last night. It could hardly be a mere coincidence."

"Whoever heard of such a thing?" laughed Meng Yü-lou.

As they were speaking, Hsi-men Ch'ing came by, at which Chin-lien grabbed hold of him with one hand and said, "Whoever heard of anyone going to bed so early and getting up so late? The sun is already well on its way toward setting. So where are you off to now?"

Hsi-men Ch'ing was subjected to her bantering for some time, which only had the effect of causing his organ to grow stiff again, so they simply abandoned Meng Yü-lou, leaving her to return to her quarters by herself.

Once Hsi-men Ch'ing had thrust Chin-lien through the portal of her bed, the two of them proceeded to dally with each other in earnest. Ch'un-mei fetched them something to eat, and they ate it together. But no more of this.

To resume our story, ever since Yüeh-niang had overheard Chin-lien criticizing her behind her back for being overprotective of Kuan-ko, she had refrained from visiting him in his room for two days.

Who should appear at this juncture but Li P'ing-erh, who came into her room and told her, "The child keeps on crying, day and night, and suffering from the cold shivers continuously. What are we to do?"

"Do whatever should occur to you," said Yüeh-niang, "and if his condition improves, it will be all right. You might try making vows to burn incense on his behalf, or even a vow to sacrifice to the gods. Such steps ought to alleviate his condition."

"The other day," said Li P'ing-erh, "he was running a fever, and I vowed to make propitiatory offerings to the God of Walls and Moats and the local Tutelary God, and those vows are now due to be fulfilled."

"That sounds all right," said Yüeh-niang. "After all, they're your vows to make. But you ought also to invite Dame Liu over for a consultation, and see what she has to suggest."

Just as Li P'ing-erh was about to take her leave, Yüeh-niang said to her, "Why do you suppose it was that all day yesterday I failed to come over to your place to see the child? It was all because the day before yesterday, after coming to see the child, as I passed by the screen-wall in front of the summer-house, I overheard P'an Chin-lien saying to Meng the Third that since I had no child of my own, I was reduced to playing up to someone else who did. It's no big deal that she should talk such rot, but I was so upset by it for half a day that I was unable to eat anything."

"What can you expect from that crazy good-for-nothing of a splay-legged whore!" said Li P'ing-erh. "How unprincipled can you get? She's been the frequent recipient of your good intentions. What have you ever done to her that she should be up to such nasty tricks as that?"

"You keep it to yourself," said Yüeh-niang. "In order to protect yourself from her, you'd better not say a word about it."

"So that's what happened," said Li P'ing-erh. "Day before yesterday Ying-ch'un said that when she went outside she saw her standing there talking to Meng the Third, and that when they saw her, they slipped off pretending to look for the cat."

As they were speaking, whom should they see but Ying-ch'un, who came running in, panting for breath, and said, "Mother, you'd better come at once. For no evident reason, Kuan-ko's two eyes have started to turn up incessantly, and there is some white foam dribbling from his mouth."

Li P'ing-erh was thrown into such consternation that:

> Her mouth clamped shut without a word,[36] and
> She knitted her brows on the verge of tears.

On the one hand, she sent Hsiao-yü to inform Hsi-men Ch'ing, and on the other, she hastily returned to her quarters. When she arrived there, she found that the wet nurse Ju-i and the others had all turned pale.

She had barely had time to assess the situation when Hsi-men Ch'ing also came into the room and, being startled to find that Kuan-ko seemed to be:
        Hovering between life and death,
exclaimed, "It looks bad! It looks bad! What are we to do? You women have not been adequately protective of him, allowing him to get to such a state before informing me about it. Now, what is to be done?"

Pointing his finger at Ju-i, he said, "Wet nurse, you've not been taking proper care of him, until, today, it's come to this. If, by any chance, something untoward should occur:
        It would not be deemed outlandish,
if you were to be pounded into mincemeat."

Ju-i was thrown into such consternation by this outburst that she dared not open her mouth, while:
        The tears flowed from both her eyes,
and Li P'ing-erh could only gaze at the child while crying to herself.

"Crying won't do any good," said Hsi-men Ch'ing. "We might as well invite Shih Cho-kuei, or Plastromancer Shih, to prognosticate on his behalf by applying heat to the plastron of a tortoise shell. Once we've determined what the prognosis for good or ill may be, we can decide what to do next."

He then asked Shu-t'ung to take out one of his calling cards and fly on his way to request the attendance of Shih Cho-kuei.

When the latter had sat down, Ch'en Ching-chi kept him company for a serving of tea, while Ch'in-t'ung and Tai-an:
        Lit candles and ignited incense,[37]
provided some purified water, and set up a table. Hsi-men Ch'ing then came out to greet him and, taking the plastron in his hands:
        Uttered a prayer to Heaven,
saluted him, and ushered him into the reception hall, where he placed the plastron on the table. Shih Cho-kuei then took it up in both hands, applied some medication to certain spots on its surface, and applied fire to them, after which they had another cup of tea.

As Hsi-men Ch'ing was sitting there, they heard a sharp sound of crepitation as the plastron cracked. Shih Cho-kuei proceeded to examine it and then paused for a while, without saying anything.

"What does it portend for good or ill?" asked Hsi-men Ch'ing.

"What sort of problem is it that you are concerned about?" asked Shih Cho-kuei.

"My young son is ill," said Hsi-men Ch'ing. "How does the general configuration look? Are there sufficient indications for a prognosis or not?"

"The general configuration does not show anything much to worry about at the present time," said Shih Cho-kuei, "but there is reason to fear that later on the malady may recur and linger on, so that there will be no possibility of a complete cure. When parents divine about their children or grandchildren, the lines for their children or grandchildren should not be unfavorable. Moreover, you see that the line for the Red Bird has been markedly disturbed, which indicates that sacrifices should be offered to the Red-Robed Guardian, the God of Walls and Moats, etc. You should slaughter a pig and a sheep to sacrifice to them. In addition you should take offerings of three bowls of soup and rice, together with effigies of one prematurely deceased male and two prematurely deceased females, and dispatch them to escort the malevolent influences responsible for the malady off to the south in a straw boat."

Hsi-men Ch'ing rewarded him for his services with a mace of silver, at which Shih Cho-kuei, who was a past master in the arts of flattery and ingratiation, bent his body into the shape of a shrimp and departed with:

A thousand thanks and ten thousand
    expressions of gratitude.

Hsi-men Ch'ing then went into Li P'ing-erh's quarters and said, "Just now, the plastromancer said the general configuration indicates that the malady may be protracted, and that we should be on our guard for recurrences, but that in the present exigency we should sacrifice to the Lady of the God of Walls and Moats."

"I made a vow to that effect the other day," said Li P'ing-erh, "but I haven't fulfilled it yet, because the child has been such a source of trouble."

"Can such things be?"

exclaimed Hsi-men Ch'ing, and he immediately ordered Tai-an to go summon Ch'ien T'an-huo, or Phlegm-fire Ch'ien, a Taoist healer, experienced at burning petitions to the gods.

Tai-an promptly went out the gate on this errand.

Hsi-men Ch'ing then joined Li P'ing-erh, who embraced Kuan-ko and said, "My child, I'm going to sacrifice to the gods on your behalf, and if you get any better, I can only:

Thank Heaven and thank Earth."[38]

No sooner had she said this, than:

Strange to relate,

the pupils of the child's eyes fell back into their normal position, as he cuddled up against his mother's body and fell asleep.

"How very strange!" said Li P'ing-erh to Hsi-men Ch'ing. "No sooner did I promise to sacrifice to the gods on his behalf, than he got significantly better."

Only then did Hsi-men Ch'ing feel in his heart that:

The stone on his head had finally fallen to the ground.

When Yüeh-niang heard about it, she also was:

Unable to contain her pleasure,

and sent Ch'in-t'ung off to summon Dame Liu.

Dame Liu lost no time in bustling on her way, with:

One step high, and

One step low.

Hsi-men Ch'ing did not have any faith in such female practitioners but, out of his love for Kuan-ko, felt that he was compelled to give her the benefit of the doubt.

Dame Liu headed straight for the kitchen, where she proceeded to rub the door of the stove.

"This old crone must be delirious," Ying-ch'un laughed at her. "Rather than attending to Kuan-ko, what do you think you're doing heading into the kitchen instead, and rubbing the door of the stove?"

"Little slave," responded Dame Liu, "what do you know about it? That's enough of your lip. Old-timer that I am:

I've got three hundred sixty days for every year

that I'm older than you.

As I came along the road, I fear I may have come in contact with some noxious influences, which I have sought to counteract by approaching the door of the stove."

Ying-ch'un made a face at her but, on hearing that Li P'ing-erh was calling for her, accompanied Dame Liu to her quarters.

When Dame Liu had kowtowed, Hsi-men Ch'ing, who needed to order Tai-an to weigh out the silver with which to purchase the necessary items for the offerings to the gods, and slaughter the pig and sheep for this purpose, strode out of the room.

"Is Kuan-ko any better?" asked Dame Liu.

"On the contrary, his condition is critical," said Li P'ing-erh. "That's why I have invited you over for a consultation."

"As I recommended on a former day," said Dame Liu, "once you made an offering to the General of the Five Ways, he was all right. On the present occasion, judging by his coloration, if you offer propitiatory rites to the Tutelary Gods of the Three Worlds, he should recover."

"Just now," said Li P'ing-erh, "Shih Cho-kuei suggested that we ought to make an offering to the Lady of the God of Walls and Moats."

"He is consistently off the mark," said Dame Liu. "What does he know about it? This is a case of convulsions brought on by a fright. The best thing to do would be for me to exorcise the fright."

"How would you exorcise the fright?" asked Li P'ing-erh.

"Sister Ying-ch'un," said Dame Liu, "if you go fetch some rice and dip out a bowl of water for me, I'll show you how it's done."

Ying-ch'un duly went to fetch the rice and water for her.

Dame Liu proceeded to take a high-stemmed earthenware goblet and fill it to capacity with grains of rice. She then groped an old green chiffon handkerchief out of her sleeve, wrapped the rice from the goblet up in it, and kneaded it with her hands, after which she proceeded to shake it in the air as she moved it back and forth over the length of Kuan-ko's body, from his face and head to his hands and feet.

Kuan-ko was asleep at the time, and the wet nurse said, "Be careful not to wake him up."

Dame Liu gave a negative wave of her hand and said in a low voice, "I know. I know."

After moving the rice-filled handkerchief back and forth for a while, she began to mutter something incomprehensible under her breath, but one or two passages were a little more audible than the rest.

Li P'ing-erh managed to catch the words, "Affrighted by Heaven, affrighted by Earth, affrighted by humans, affrighted by ghosts, affrighted by cats, affrighted by dogs," at which point she said, "It all started when the child was frightened by a cat."

When Dame Liu had finished her incantation, she shook open the handkerchief, placed the goblet on the table, and contemplated the results for a while. Then, selecting two grains of rice from the heap created by shaking it out of the handkerchief, she dropped them into the bowl of water, by doing which she was able to prognosticate that the malady would be cured by the end of the month. She likewise recommended that the effigies of one prematurely deceased male and two prematurely deceased females should be dispatched to escort the malevolent influences responsible for the malady off in a southeasterly direction. But she argued that, rather than sacrificing to the God of Walls and Moats, she should make a propitiatory offering to the local Tutelary God.

Li P'ing-erh was perplexed by this, but finally said, "I'll just make an additional propitiatory offering to the local Tutelary God. That won't be a problem."

She then told Ying-ch'un to go outside and tell Hsi-men Ch'ing that Dame Liu, after "prognosticating with a bowl of water," had said that they ought to make an offering to the local Tutelary God; and that, since it was too late to go to the temple of the God of Walls and Moats tonight anyway, they should lay in all the proper offerings, and be prepared to hold a devout ceremony in the morning.

Hsi-men Ch'ing consequently instructed Tai-an to take care of procuring all the necessary paraphernalia for the sacrifice, as well as the pig and sheep, and be prepared to go take care of it in the morning; and that, in addition, he should purchase what was needed for an offering to the local Tutelary God, including fried rice and cocoon-shaped pastries, earthenware writing brushes and ink cakes, as well as live sparrows, loaches, eels, and the like, to be released in honor of the occasion.

> No item was left unsupplied;
> Each object was of the best.

Dame Liu then took leave of Li P'ing-erh's place and headed inside to Yüeh-niang's quarters in the rear compound, where Yüeh-niang kept her for supper.

To resume our story, when Ch'ien T'an-huo arrived, he sat down in the small reception hall, and Ch'in-t'ung and Tai-an hastily prepared to assist him in the ceremony of making a propitiatory offering to the local Tutelary God. As soon as Ch'ien T'an-huo had finished his tea, he asked for the purport of the petition he was to present, and Hsi-men Ch'ing had Shu-t'ung write it out for him.

Ch'ien T'an-huo then donned his collapsible thunder cap, put on his customary vestments:

> Brandished his sword with philter in hand,

started to pace the dipper, and began to recite the altar-cleansing invocation. The invocation read:

> From the mysterious void of the grotto heavens,
> To the refulgent realm of the great primordial,
> May the prepotent gods of the eight directions,
> Assure my consonance with the forces of nature.
> These Numinous Treasure talismans,
> Are addressed to the Nine Heavens.
> The celestial net extends its awe-inspiring sway,
> Over the mysterious realms of grottoes and stars,
> Decapitating demons and shackling monsters,[39]
> Killing devils by the myriads and thousands.
> This sanctified invocation of the polestar,
> This jade writ of the primordial beginning,
> When duly incanted but a single time,
> Dispels disease and lengthens years;
> When dispatched to the Five Sacred Peaks,
> And made known throughout the Eight Seas,
> The demon-kings will be compelled,
> To stand as bodyguards at my side;
> Misfortune and pestilence will be dispelled,
> And the force of the Tao remain ever present,[40]

etc., etc.

He then asked the ordainer of the ceremony to burn incense. Hsi-men Ch'ing accordingly washed his hands, rinsed out his mouth, donned his official cap and girdle, and put on his kneepads. Sun Hsüeh-o, Meng Yü-lou, Li Chiao-erh, and Li Kuei-chieh all helped him on with his clothes, clucking with approbation as they did so. When Hsi-men Ch'ing emerged and proceeded to burn incense and pay obeisance to Buddha, a page boy followed at his heels to straighten his garments. It was all done with conspicuous formality.

On seeing that his patron had come outside, Ch'ien T'an-huo started to declaim his texts twice as loudly as before, while the womenfolk, concealing themselves behind a standing screen, peeked at Hsi-men Ch'ing, pointed at Ch'ien T'an-huo, and fell into a heap with laughter. When Hsi-men Ch'ing heard the sound of their raucous laughter, kneeling as he was before the effigy of the god, he was not in a position to say anything about it but could only survey the scene with his eyes. Only after Shu-t'ung became aware of the situation and made a gesture with his mouth did the womenfolk quiet down a bit.

Meanwhile, Chin-lien, who was coming out from the rear compound by herself, upon turning a corner, suddenly ran into Ch'en Ching-chi, who fell to kissing her and feeling her breasts.

Groping a handful of sweetmeats out of her sleeve, and giving them to him, she went on to ask, "Would you like to have a drink of distilled spirits?"

"I wouldn't mind having a little," responded Ch'en Ching-chi.

Consequently, he allowed Chin-lien to take advantage of this interval during which the others were busy, by pulling him into her quarters, and telling Ch'un-mei to shut the door.

After sharing a couple of cups with him, she said, "You'd better get going. I'm afraid someone might turn up, which would be the death of me."

Ch'en Ching-chi wanted to kiss her again, but Chin-lien said, "You indecent short-life! Aren't you afraid that the maidservants will catch on?"

Then she facetiously gave him a resounding whack, upon which Ch'en Ching-chi prepared to make his escape. Chin-lien told Ch'un-mei to precede him outside, and she saw him safely out of the way. Truly:

> With two hands he tore open the road
>   between life and death;
> Flopping over and leaping out through
>   the gate to perdition.

Chin-lien also went outside at the same time to see if the coast was clear. But no more of this.

Hsi-men Ch'ing, in paying his respects to the local Tutelary God, had been kneeling for what seemed like half a day, before he was able to get to his feet again. Thus far, the ceremony had only progressed as far as the initial invocation, and Ch'ien T'an-huo was about to proceed to the ritual of penance.

Hsi-men Ch'ing went behind the standing screen and admonished the womenfolk there, saying, "You've got to stop giggling like that. It's so contagious that several times I've barely been able to prevent myself from following suit."

"That Ch'ien T'an-huo," said the womenfolk, "is no more than a paperburning ghoul. He's not a proper Taoist priest. When he dons his collapsible cap and puts on his vestments, he's being both bold-faced and shameless. In the course of his babbling, who knows how many buckets of stinking spittle he's managed to expectorate."

Hsi-men Ch'ing said:

"Sacrifice to the gods as if the gods are present.[41]

You really oughtn't to bad-mouth or ridicule him so cruelly."

Ch'ien T'an-huo then requested his presence for the ritual of penance, and Hsi-men Ch'ing returned to the carpeted altar space. Ch'ien T'an-huo, having started off with the introit, proceeded to recite the text of the ritual of penance, beginning with the statement of his sincere intentions in seeking an audience. As he did so, the spittle around the edges of his mouth:

Curled in and curled out,

while his head:

Bobbed up and bobbed down,

like that of the kowtowing bug, or click beetle, which caused the eaves-dropping women to fall into a heap with laughter. Hsi-men Ch'ing was quite unable to keep up with the pace of his kowtowing. Ch'ien T'an-huo addressed himself to a different Divine Lord with each kowtow, but by the time Hsi-men Ch'ing had performed one kowtow, he had already kowtowed to several additional Divine Lords. Thereupon, being unable to keep track of things, he simply fell to kowtowing at random, which caused the eavesdropping women to laugh even harder.

Just at this juncture, Hsiao-yü came out to invite Li Kuei-chieh to the rear compound for dinner, saying, "The First Lady is sitting all by herself back there, engaged in idle chatter with Hsi-men Ta-chieh and Dame Liu, while out here the rest of you are having a merry time of it."

Li Chiao-erh and Li Kuei-chieh promptly went back inside, and the rest of them all wished to follow suit, with the exception of P'an Chin-lien, who wanted to continue eavesdropping, until, in the end, when she saw that they had all gone inside, she felt compelled to come inside as well.

Wu Yüeh-niang remarked to Hsi-men Ta-chieh, "If you have a mind to sacrifice to the gods, you ought to be appropriately devout about it. What's the point of having all these crazy womenfolk crowding around out there? It's not as though there were any real spectacle to be seen, such as live lions devouring each other, or anything like that."

She had hardly finished speaking when Li Kuei-chieh came in to join Yüeh-niang and Hsi-men Ta-chieh for dinner. But no more of this.

To resume our story, Hsi-men Ch'ing had kowtowed until his entire body was bathed with sweat, when he came inside, took off his robe and cap, boots and girdle, went in to Kuan-ko's bedside, and caressed him, saying, "My son, I've made a propitiatory offering to the local Tutelary God on your behalf."

He then turned to Li P'ing-erh and said, "It's amazing. Come and feel his forehead. It's a lot cooler than before. Heaven be thanked! Heaven be thanked!"

Li P'ing-erh laughed, saying:

"Strange as it may seem,

ever since I promised to make a propitiatory offering to the local Tutelary God, he's been getting better. Right now, his fever has receded, his eyes are no longer turning up, and his cold shivers have subsided somewhat. How can you say that Dame Liu is without merit?"

"Tomorrow," said Hsi-men Ch'ing, "we might as well follow up by completing the sacrifice at the temple of the God of Walls and Moats."

"The only problem is that his father has been wearing himself out," said Li P'ing-erh. "You'd better dry yourself off, and have some dinner before you go."

"If I stay here, I'm afraid I'll disturb the child," said Hsi-men Ch'ing. I'll go somewhere else to eat."

Upon making his way to Chin-lien's place, he sat down in a chair and said, "The area around my kidneys hurts as though they were about to drop out."

Chin-lien laughed, saying, "Why should anyone with such a filial heart have to feel pain? Right now, you might as well get someone to do the kowtowing in your place."

"That makes sense. That makes sense," said Hsi-men Ch'ing.

He then told Ch'un-mei to summon Ch'in-t'ung and instruct him, "Go invite Son-in-law Ch'en to do the kowtowing, and the seeing off of the paper effigies of the spirits on Father's behalf."

Who would have thought that Ch'en Ching-chi, after having downed several cups of distilled spirits in Chin-lien's quarters, was afraid that his face was red enough for the page boys to spot, so he endeavored to account for it by buying some weak wine, and drinking several cups of it in the shop. His capacity, however, was inadequate, so that he soon became drunk and fell asleep where he was, snoring stertorously.

Ch'in-t'ung found it impossible to rouse him and flew back like an arrow to report to Hsi-men Ch'ing, saying, "He's fast asleep there, and I was unable to rouse him."

Hsi-men Ch'ing was annoyed by this and exclaimed, "How unprincipled can you get? Quite aside from his neglect of the family business, what sort of a spectacle does it present to our neighbors for him to fall asleep so early in the day?"

He then told Ch'un-mei to go to the First Lady's room and say to Hsi-men Ta-chieh, "Father has developed a sore back from all the kowtowing and asked our son-in-law to continue the kowtowing, and the seeing off of the paper effigies of the spirits on his behalf. He wants to know why it is that he refuses to come, but insists on remaining there asleep?"

"What a hopeless case he is!" exclaimed Hsi-men Ta-chieh, and she started out of the room.

Yüeh-niang, however, sent Hsiao-yü to go to the shop and wake up Ch'en Ching-chi.

Still rubbing his eyes, Ch'en Ching-chi came back to the rear compound, where he saw Hsi-men Ta-chieh and said, "What's the big rush in calling for me, as though my life depended on it?"

"You've been asked to participate in the propitiatory offering to the local Tutelary God, and the seeing off of the paper effigies of the spirits on Father's behalf," explained Hsi-men Ta-chieh. "Just now, when Ch'in-t'ung went to summon you, you failed to respond, and now you're trying to give me a hard time about it. This time it was Mother who sent Hsiao-yü to summon you. In any case, you'd better start kowtowing, hadn't you?"

Thereupon:

Half pushing him and half supporting him,

she hustled Ch'en Ching-chi out to the reception hall, after which she returned to her room. Hsiao-yü first reported this development back to Yüeh-niang, and then to Hsi-men Ch'ing. Hsi-men Ch'ing ordered Ch'in-t'ung and Tai-an to continue waiting upon Ch'ien T'an-huo until the ceremony was completed, and then went to sleep on Chin-lien's bed. But no more of this.

To resume our story, it was only when Ch'en Ching-chi arrived in the reception hall and saw that it was:

Blazing with lamps and candles,[42]

that he finally sobered up. Opening his eyes wide, he observed that Ch'ien T'an-huo was waiting to receive his "flower-scattering fee" for officiating over the ceremony. After they had exchanged the customary greetings, Ch'ien T'an-huo took the offering of soup and rice and, telling Ch'in-t'ung to light the way, proceeded to the door of Li P'ing-erh's quarters, where Ying-ch'un took it inside, along with some incense, and gave it to Ju-i, who blew on it on Kuan-ko's behalf, before handing it back out again. Ch'ien T'an-huo:

Alternately impersonating gods and ghosts,

recited a spell over it, after which he came back to the reception hall to preside over the ceremony of seeing off the paper effigies of the spirits. After Ch'en Ching-chi had kowtowed for a while, Ch'ien T'an-huo duly finished seeing off the paper effigies of the spirits and dispatched the proclamation, along with a talismanic transcription of the hexagram ch'ien.[43]

Having done so, he said, "Once the proclamation has been delivered to the Gate of Heaven, his condition should improve within a day or two. Even if the malady should recur, it won't amount to anything."

By the time Ch'ien T'an-huo had finished the rituals of releasing the living creatures provided for the occasion, seeing off the paper effigies of the spirits, offering a libation, and dismissing the gods:

His mouth was dry, his stomach was empty,

and he was ready to have something to eat. Tai-an cleared away the utensils, and Ch'in-t'ung set up a table so that Ch'en Ching-chi could keep him company in consuming a share of the foodstuffs that remained from the preceding ceremony. Ch'ien T'an-huo was profuse in his thanks, and, after he had departed, Ch'en Ching-chi went back to his quarters. Li P'ing-erh also sent Ying-ch'un to deliver some of the leftover fruits and other sacrificial offerings to Hsi-men Ta-chieh's room, for which she expressed her gratitude. But no more of this.

To resume our story, Dame Liu, who was being entertained in Yüeh-niang's quarters, thanked her for her hospitality and took her leave. She had just emerged from the main gate when whom should she encounter but Ch'ien T'an-huo, who staggered up behind her, holding a lantern, and reeking of alcohol.

"Master Ch'ien," said Dame Liu, "you really ought to share that 'flower-scattering fee' with me, shouldn't you?"

"What's that got to do with you?" demanded Ch'ien T'an-huo.

"It was my 'prognosticating with a bowl of water' that set up this job for you, old man," said Dame Liu. "Are you totally:
        Unconscious of right and wrong?
The next time the opportunity comes my way, I won't recommend you."

Ch'ien T'an-huo adamantly refused, saying, "What an inveterate oily mouth you are, you old whore! You're shooting your mouth off without foundation. Since when did you ever recommend me? He's a longstanding client of mine. Whoever heard of sharing a 'flower-scattering fee'?"

Dame Liu pointed her finger at him and cursed, saying, "May you starve to death, you lousy paper-burning ghoul, before you ever expect another favor from me!"

The two of them mixed it up together, continuing their verbal dual for some time before finally separating. But no more of this.

To resume our story, when Hsi-men Ch'ing got up the next morning, he ordered a page boy to follow him and set out for the temple of the God of Walls and Moats. The carriers of the pig and sheep carried the pig and sheep, while the bearer of his official cap and girdle bore his official cap and girdle. He went straight into the temple, throwing the Taoist priests there into a flurry as they put down a carpet and proceeded to intone the memorial. Hsi-men Ch'ing donned his official cap and girdle and, when he had finished paying obeisance to the god, proceeded to divine about Kuan-ko's condition by means of selecting a prognosticatory bamboo stick, which he then asked a Taoist priest to interpret.[44] The priest took the bamboo stick and, after tea had been served, went on to interpret it.

The inscription on the stick in question indicated medium good luck, and the priest interpreted it by saying, "The party who is ill should recover, but, in order to guard against a recurrence, it is appropriate that you should take additional precautions."

After distributing the "incense money" for the ceremony, Hsi-men Ch'ing returned home. When he dismounted and came inside, he found Ying Po-chüeh sitting in the summerhouse.

"Have a seat," said Hsi-men Ch'ing. "I'll go inside and come right out."

He then went into Li P'ing-erh's quarters and told her about how he had consulted the bamboo sticks on behalf of Kuan-ko:

Thus and thus, and

So and so.

After doing which, he went straight back to the summerhouse and said to Ying Po-chüeh, "Was the brokerage fee you received for that transaction the other day adequate? You really ought to treat me to something or other."

Ying Po-chüeh laughed and said, "Hsieh Hsi-ta also made a little something out of it. Why should I alone be expected to treat you? But that's all right. I'll buy some things for Brother to eat, that's all."

Hsi-men Ch'ing laughed at this, saying, "Who wants to eat anything of yours? I was only testing you."

"That being the case," said Ying Po-chüeh, "inasmuch as you went to the temple today with a pig and a sheep, there must be quite a lot in the way of sacrificial offerings left over. Since your younger brother is here, why don't you share some of the bounty with me?"

"You've got a point there," said Hsi-men Ch'ing.

He then summoned Ch'in-t'ung to go invite Hsieh Hsi-ta to come over so they could enjoy it together and, at the same time, sent directions to the kitchen to prepare the foodstuffs in question and bring them out so he could share them with Brother Ying the Second over a cup of wine.

Ying Po-chüeh seated himself to wait for the arrival of Hsieh Hsi-ta, but he failed to show up, so he finally said, "Why don't we go ahead and settle down to it? Who has the patience to wait for such a slippery operator?"

Hsi-men Ch'ing and Ying Po-chüeh then proceeded to enjoy a drink together.

When Ch'in-t'ung returned, he reported, "Master Hsieh is not at home."

"What took you so long?" asked Hsi-men Ch'ing.

"I went looking all over for him," said Ch'in-t'ung.

Ying Po-chüeh then initiated a game of forfeits, the import of which was the wish for Kuan-ko's recovery, which pleased Hsi-men Ch'ing so much he was:

Unable to contain his delight.

"I am so constantly imposing on your hospitality," said Ying Po-chüeh, "that I really:

Feel uneasy at heart.

Tomorrow or the next day, I would like to play a paltry role as host in inviting the members of our brotherhood to share a cup of wine with you. How would that be?"

Hsi-men Ch'ing laughed, saying, "So, having scrounged a little something in the way of a brokerage fee, you're ready to squander your silver. But there's no need for you to lay out anything. I've got this pig and sheep left over, which I'll donate to you in order to supply the necessary ingredients."

Ying Po-chüeh thanked him, saying, "I feel that you're doing more than friendship requires."

"As for the singing girls and the boy actors," said Hsi-men Ch'ing, "I'll leave those arrangements to you."

"That goes without saying," said Ying Po-chüeh. "The only thing is, there'll be no one to wait on us. What are we to do?"

"We are all brothers, after all," said Hsi-men Ch'ing. "The servants of any one of us will do as well as another. We might as well make use of Ch'in-t'ung and Tai-an from my place."

"That will take care of everything," said Ying Po-chüeh.

After drinking a while longer, he said farewell and departed. Truly:

Even if you were to drink all day for a hundred years,
It would only amount to thirty-six thousand occasions.[45]

If you want to know the outcome of these events,
Pray consult the story related in the following chapter.

Chapter 54

YING PO-CHÜEH CONVENES HIS FRIENDS
IN A SUBURBAN GARDEN;
JEN HOU-CH'I DIAGNOSES AN ILLNESS
FOR A POWERFUL FAMILY

Whether the morrow will be overcast or clear
　is not possible to predict;[1]
As the saying goes, "The pinnacle of delight
　begets sorrow and distress."
While the gallivanting youth is captivated by
　the red thoroughfares;
The neglected damsel vents her resentment by
　her green gauze window.
Having just visited Apricot Blossom Village[2]
　to procure vintage wine;
One must now resort to the Orange Tree Well[3]
　to seek a rare prescription.
How many are the occasions for sorrow and joy
　in the life of man;
Yet routinely the spring breeze gives way to
　a spell of frost.

THE STORY GOES that when Hsi-men Ch'ing got out of bed in Chin-lien's room the next morning, he told Ch'in-t'ung and Tai-an to deliver the pig's feet and mutton to Ying Po-chüeh's home. When the two page boys arrived on this errand, Ying Po-chüeh was just coming home from inviting the other guests and, upon seeing them, went into the house, where he wrote a reply, couched in terms that were:

　　　Half demanding and half inviting,
and read:

Yesterday, I imposed egregiously on your hospitality, and now I am once again the recipient of your lavish magnanimity. Thank you. Thank you. At this moment, I pray that my elder brother will deign to visit my humble abode, so that we may proceed together upon a pleasure excursion to the suburbs.

When he had finished writing it, he came outside and was about to hand it to Tai-an, when Tai-an said, "There's no need for you to write a note in reply. Father sent the two of us to wait on you here, so we're not going back."

Ying Po-chüeh laughed and said, "It's hardly right for me to put you two familiar oily mouths to so much trouble. You'll be the death of me yet." Upon saying which, he put the note back into his sleeve.

"Master Two," said Tai-an, "where are you going to be holding your drinking party today? Shouldn't we start setting the tables out? They're covered with dust."

"A fine one you are!" said Ying Po-chüeh. "I was just going to wipe them off. We'll begin by setting things up for an ordinary repast here at my place, after which, we'll repair to a suburban garden somewhere and enjoy ourselves there."

"It makes a lot of sense to eat at home first," said Ch'in-t'ung. It will save you the trouble of having to eat again once you get there. The only things we'll have to take with us, then, are the partitioned picnic boxes, the wine, and the saucers."

"The two of you are real smart asses, aren't you," remarked Ying Po-chüeh. "What you say just happens to coincide with my own crude ideas. I imagine:

You've been bored into so often,
    both day and night,
That the holes in your smart asses
    have been reamed out."[4]

"There's no need to bandy idle words," said Tai-an. "We'll help you get things ready."

To this Ying Po-chüeh responded, "That is what could be said to describe:

Three shrines to the goddess Kuan-yin
    lined up in a row:
Wonderful! Wonderful! Wonderful!"[5]

Just as the two page boys had completed 70 or 80 percent of their preparations, who should come swaggering through the gate but Pai Lai-ch'iang, or Scrounger Pai.

After saluting Ying Po-chüeh with clasped hands, he caught sight of Ch'in-t'ung and Tai-an and exclaimed, "These two little darlings are certainly playing up to their Master Two."

"Don't you be jealous now," responded Ying Po-chüeh, at which everyone had a good laugh.

"Who all have you invited today, Brother?" asked Scrounger Pai.

"Only the members of our brotherhood are getting together," said Ying Po-chüeh. "It will be just like a meeting of the club. No one else has been invited."

"That's great," said Scrounger Pai. "What I am most put off by is having to drink with people I don't know. If we have a little gathering of the members of our brotherhood today, it will be a perfect occasion for drinking wine and having fun together. But the party will not be complete without the company of singing girls, along with Li Ming and Wu Hui, to play and sing for us, and help us down with our wine."

"There's no need for you to instruct me on that head," said Ying Po-chüeh. "You're talking to someone who knows the score, after all. Surely you don't mean to suggest that I would arrange for us to merely share a melancholy drink together, and then call it a day. When have you ever known me to do anything like that?"

"That's fine. That's fine," said Scrounger Pai. "Leave it to you, old hand that you are. The only thing is, in a little while, if the occasion should arise, don't make me drink too many forfeits of wine. The other night I had a little too much of some fiery spirits, and my throat is still as sore as can be. I'd better confine myself to tea, and rice, and vermicelli soup."

Ying Po-chüeh said:

"The best cure for a hangover is a dose of wine.

You might as well have a little. What harm can it do? The other day I also had a rather sore throat, and, after downing a few cups of wine, it felt much better. You'd better take this prescription of mine. It's absolutely marvelous."

"Brother," said Scrounger Pai, "so far, you've only proposed a cure for my sore throat. You don't happen to have a cure for my stomach, do you?"

"I imagine," said Ying Po-chüeh, "that you haven't had any breakfast."

"That's not far off the mark," said Scrounger Pai.

"What am I to do?" said Ying Po-chüeh, and he ran inside and came out with a saucer of cakes, a saucer of sandalwood-flavored biscuits, and a pot of tea for Scrounger Pai's consumption.

Scrounger Pai polished off the sandalwood-flavored biscuits:

One per mouthful,

and praised them, saying, "These biscuits are great."

"The cakes are not bad either," said Ying Po-chüeh.

Scrounger Pai, audibly smacking his lips as he did so, went on to finish them off as well. It became apparent at this juncture that Ch'in-t'ung and Tai-an had finished the task of getting the utensils together, cleaning the windows, and wiping off the tables.

"Everything is in proper order," said Scrounger Pai. "The only thing is that our brothers have not all shown up yet. The earlier we forgather the more fun we can have. Why should they insist on skulking at home this way? What are they up to?"

Just as Ying Po-chüeh was gazing outside, whom should he see but Ch'ang Shih-chieh, or Cadger Ch'ang, who made his way into the room and was met by Ch'in-t'ung, coming out with a serving of tea.

After Cadger Ch'ang had saluted the company with clasped hands, he looked at Ch'in-t'ung and said, "So you're here, are you?"

Ch'in-t'ung:

> Smiled but did not respond.[6]

After finishing their tea, the three of them had just stood up to stretch their legs when Scrounger Pai noticed that there was a go board on the cabinet and said to Cadger Ch'ang, "I'll play a game of go with you."

"I'm still overheated from walking over here just now," said Cadger Ch'ang. "I was about to loosen my clothing and fan myself, and now you want me to play a game of go. Well all right, I'll play a casual game with you if you like."

Having said which, they took down the go board and began to play a game of go.

"Is the loser going to treat the rest of us?" asked Ying Po-chüeh.

"We're putting our elder brother to enough trouble today," said Scrounger Pai. "Winner takes all would be a better way to do it. It's more convenient and would save us the need to pretend to be hungry when there's more than we can eat. Winner takes all is better all the way round."

"I'm the host," said Ying Po-chüeh, "so I won't participate. The two of you can surely come up with something to treat each other with, can't you?"

Everyone laughed at this.

"Now that we're agreed," said Cadger Ch'ang, "shall we play for objects, or for silver?"

"I didn't happen to bring any silver with me," said Scrounger Pai. "All I have here is a fan, which I pawned for two or three mace of silver and have only recently been able to redeem."

"I've got an embroidered velour handkerchief here that I won from somebody else," said Cadger Ch'ang. "It's worth a good deal, but I guess I'd be willing to hazard it."

The two of them together handed over their stakes to Ying Po-chüeh, who, upon examining them, saw that one of them was a gold-flecked folding fan, with plain bamboo slats, decorated with a painting and an accompanying poem, though the state of the slats indicated its age; while the other was a brand new embroidered handkerchief.

"They'll do," said Ying Po-chüeh. "Go ahead and play."

Ying Po-chüeh held onto the stakes while the two of them faced off against each other and began their game. Ch'in-t'ung and Tai-an, seeing that their master was not present, went back and forth incessantly behind their chairs to look on as they played.

"Little oily mouths," said Ying Po-chüeh, "I've a mind to ask if you wouldn't brew another cup of tea for me?"

Ch'in-t'ung surreptitiously made a face at Tai-an but duly headed to the back of the house to heat the tea.

To resume our story, Scrounger Pai and Cadger Ch'ang were fairly evenly matched at go, but Cadger Ch'ang had a slight edge. Scrounger Pai was an inveterate reneger. As they were playing, lo and behold, a block of Scrounger

Pai's stones was on the verge of being taken, and Cadger Ch'ang anticipated that he might renege.

Sure enough, Scrounger Pai wanted to retract several of his moves, so he knocked the last few stones Cadger Ch'ang had played aside with one hand, saying, "That won't do. That won't do. I didn't mean to make that move."

"Brother, come here. This conduct is unacceptable," exclaimed Cadger Ch'ang.

Ying Po-chüeh came running out, saying, "What happened? What's the row all about?"

"The last three or four stones he played were ill-considered moves," said Cadger Ch'ang, "and now he wants to retract them. That isn't fair. Brother, you be the judge. How can one be so nonchalant about such things?"

Scrounger Pai's face turned crimson, the blue veins on his temples became distended, and saliva spurted all over his face, as he shouted, "I hadn't yet made my move when he suddenly played his stone. I was just trying to get a good view of the configuration when he began moving his hand back and forth over the board, which confused me so much that:

My eyes were playing tricks on me.[7]

I was just in the process of making a move, and my hand had not even let go of the stone, when he claimed that I was reneging. You decide. How can he claim that I was doing anything wrong?"

"As for the move in question," said Ying Po-chüeh, "we might as well compromise by letting you play it where you like, without calling it a case of reneging. But you'd better not do that kind of thing again."

"All right," said Cadger Ch'ang. "I'll let you renege on that move. But I won't let you grab any stones of mine with impunity in the future."

"You're a perennial loser yourself," said Scrounger Pai, "yet you have the nerve to criticize me."

As they were speaking, Hsieh Hsi-ta, or Tagalong Hsieh, also showed up, and Ch'in-t'ung brought him some tea.

When he had drunk it, he said, "You two go ahead and finish your game. I'll look on while you play."

As he was observing the game, Wu Tien-en, or Heartless Wu, also came into the house and, after the conventional amenities about the weather had been exchanged, asked, "What have they staked on this game?"

Ying Po-chüeh brought out the two objects in question and showed them to the assembled company, at which, they all said, "In that case, they must see the game to its conclusion."

"Brother Nine," said Scrounger Pai, "the game is as good as over. What are you pondering over?"

Cadger Ch'ang was still engaged in scrutinizing the situation, while Heartless Wu and Tagalong Hsieh made a bet with each other on the side.

Tagalong Hsieh said, "Brother Nine has won."

"He's already lost," said Heartless Wu. "How can you claim he's won? Let's bet a cup of wine on it."

"Just you watch while yours truly wraps up the victory," said Cadger Ch'ang.

Scrounger Pai's face turned crimson, and he said, "You don't mean to say that I've already ceded this fan to you, do you?"

"That's about it," responded Cadger Ch'ang.

Thereupon, the end game having been completed, they proceeded to count up the stones. Scrounger Pai had taken possession of five areas on the board, while Cadger Ch'ang had taken only two.

Scrounger Pai, however, had forfeited three stones to Cadger Ch'ang and muttered to himself, "It was those three moves that cost me the game."

When he hurriedly counted up the stones in his possession, he found that he had lost by five stones.

"Just what I predicted," said Tagalong Hsieh, and, pointing at Heartless Wu, he continued, "You owe me the consumption of a cup of wine. In a little while you'll have to pay me off by drinking it."

Heartless Wu:

Smiled but did not respond.

Ying Po-chüeh took the fan, along with the handkerchief that he had originally pledged, and turned them over to Cadger Ch'ang, who tucked the handkerchief back into his sleeve and then made a show of opening the fan and critically evaluating the poem and the painting on it. Everyone had a laugh at this.

Tai-an then came running in from outside to report some new arrivals, who turned out to be Wu Yin-erh and Han Chin-ch'uan. The two of them:

Tugging each other by the hand,

came in laughing merrily and saluted each member of the gathering with a deep bow. Scrounger Pai expressed the wish to play another game of go but only elicited the laughter of the company.

"That's enough of that," said Ying Po-chüeh. "As soon as our elder brother arrives, and we've had something to eat, we'll head for a garden in the suburbs. How long do you intend to play? Don't start another game."

Thereupon, Ch'in-t'ung cleared away the stones, and they all had a cup of tea.

"Our elder brother ought to be here by now," said Ying Po-chüeh. "We oughtn't to delay our departure too long, or we won't have time to really enjoy ourselves."

He had hardly finished speaking when Hsi-men Ch'ing arrived, dressed to befit the occasion, and accompanied by four page boys. The members of the company all got up from their places to welcome him and, after exchanging the customary amenities, offered him a seat, while the two singing girls kowtowed to him, and Li Ming and Wu Hui also showed up and came in to kowtow.

Ying Po-chüeh then urged Ch'in-t'ung and Tai-an to bring in eight diminutive picnic saucers. There was one saucer of squash julienne marinated with ten spices, one saucer of an assortment of pickled beans, one saucer of fagara marinated in soy sauce, one saucer of corydalis sprinkled with strong vinegar, one saucer of candied garlic, one saucer of bamboo shoots preserved in fermented mash, one saucer of Chinese cabbage seasoned with red pepper, one saucer of Ta-t'ung ginger in a preservative sauce, and a saucer of fragrant mushrooms. Once these appetizers had been properly laid out, the two page boys, observing that Hsi-men Ch'ing had joined the company, were more careful than ever, feeling the need, more than before, to be as attentive as a groom at the horse's head.

When Ying Po-chüeh noticed that Hsi-men Ch'ing was observing the way they went about setting out the utensils, he said, "I am indebted to the two of them for taking care of a host of matters, and thereby saving me a lot of trouble."

"I fear they may not be up to the task of waiting upon you," said Hsi-men Ch'ing.

"They're extremely adept at it," said Ying Po-chüeh.

"As the saying goes," remarked Tagalong Hsieh:

"Under an effective commander there are
    no incompetent troops.[8]

Once they've undergone the proper training, it's only natural that they should perform satisfactorily."

The two page boys, having laid out the appetizers, brought out a large flagon of wine, after which, in uninterrupted succession, they served up twenty bowls of delicacies to go with it, including diced roast rump of pork, seasoned with garlic and designed to resemble litchi nuts; braised mutton, seasoned with spring onions, pepper, and cinnamon; roast fish; roast chicken; glazed duck; pork tripe; and the like. Altogether, there were too many culinary specialties to enumerate in detail.

It so happens that Ying Po-chüeh, in the course of his sponging at other people's tables, had picked up some pointers about the art of cooking, with the result that:

Every single dish was done to perfection;
    There was not one that was not marvelous.

The members of the company all picked up their chopsticks and proceeded to gorge themselves, making a gobbling sound as they did so. After several large cups of wine had been consumed, the rice was served. Han Chin-ch'uan was on a vegetarian diet that did not permit her to eat anything with meat in it, so she only picked at the appetizers.

"Today is neither the first nor the fifteenth of the month," said Ying Po-chüeh, "so what are you being so fastidious about? Once upon a time, there was a person who had been a vegetarian all his life. When he died and went before King Yama in the nether world, he said, 'I've been a vegetarian all my life, and expect to be reborn as a human being of good status.' 'How is one to know whether you confined yourself to vegetarian fare or not?' said King Yama. 'We'll have to cut open your belly to find out.' When he was cut open, all they found was a bellyful of saliva. It turns out that every time he had seen anyone else eating meat, he had started to salivate."

Everyone doubled over with laughter at this.

"Where do you come up with these annoying turns of yours?" said Han Chin-ch'uan. "Aren't you afraid of having your tongue plucked out in Hell?"[9]

"Only little whores like you have their tongues plucked out in Hell," said Ying Po-chüeh. "The charge being that when they kiss their tongues are overly active."

Everyone had a laugh at this.

"Let's set out on our excursion to the suburbs, shall we?" said Ying Po-chüeh.

"That would be really great," said Hsi-men Ch'ing.

Everyone else agreed that it would be great.

Ying Po-chüeh then asked Tai-an and the other servants to take charge of the two picnic boxes and a jug of wine, and carry them down to the riverside, where a small boat was hired, and they were loaded aboard. He also hired another empty boat to carry the company, and, once they were all aboard, they were sculled more than thirty li outside the south gate, where they passed right in front of the estate of Eunuch Director Liu.

Ying Po-chüeh ordered the boatmen to moor the boats and then climbed ashore, after which he helped Han Chin-ch'uan and Wu Yin-erh to disembark.

"Whose garden do you think would be best to visit?" asked Hsi-men Ch'ing.

"We might as well avail ourselves of Eunuch Director Liu's garden," said Ying Po-chüeh.

"All right," said Hsi-men Ch'ing. "His place ought to do."

The group of them accordingly headed there. After entering a reception hall, they turned into a:

Secluded walk along a zigzag gallery,

leading through:

Luxuriant forests and lofty bamboos.[10]

Words are inadequate to describe the beauty of the scene. Behold:

The emerald cypresses are dense,
The lofty bamboo groves whisper.
The fragrant verdure evenly spreads
    its mat of green brocade;
The weeping willows delicately wave
    their green silk braids.
Along zigzag paving and multiple balustrades,
A myriad varieties of famous flowers
    exhibit a profusion of hues;

Beyond secluded windows and hidden casements,
The varied notes of frolicsome birds
   resound like reed instruments.
Truly it resembles the fabled Gardens of Paradise,
Nothing less than the Pure Metropolis of the gods.
Leisured gentlemen of lofty status,
Daily frequent it in search of entertainment;
Wandering ladies on vagrant outings,
Ever enjoy it enough to forget their fatigue.
Surely it belongs to the category of rare sights,
This is not an instance of inflated commendation.

Hsi-men Ch'ing, leading Han Chin-ch'uan and Wu Yin-erh by the hand, set out to explore the various sights, in order to enjoy them to the full. Upon arriving under a banksia rose arbor, they found a spot that was both well-shaded and cool, to either side of which there were arrayed extensive:

Stone benches and zither stands,

making it ideally suited for a casual conclave. The entire company, accordingly, sat down. Ying Po-chüeh then went back and directed Ch'in-t'ung and the two boatmen to bring the wine, picnic boxes, comestibles, portable stove, and utensils up from the boat and put them down under the green shade.

During an initial round of tea, a casual conversation started up about the predicament of Blabbermouth Sun and Pockmarked Chu, which led Cadger Ch'ang to remark, "Were it not for that, they would both be here today. What can one say about it?"

Hsi-men Ch'ing said, "It's only another illustration of the fact that:

One must suffer the consequences of one's own acts."[11]

"Let's all take our seats," said Ying Po-chüeh.

"That's a good idea," chimed in Scrounger Pai.

Thereupon, they proceeded to arrange themselves in appropriate order and sit down, with Hsi-men Ch'ing in the place of honor, flanked on either side by the two singing girls, while Li Ming and Wu Hui, standing beside a T'ai-hu rockery:

Lightly plucking their *p'i-p'a*,[12] and
Idly raising their sandalwood clappers,

sang a song to the tune "The Water Nymphs":

My old mother's temperament being what it is,
She was only waiting for the flames from the fire
   in the Zoroastrian Temple to flare up:[13]
   kua-kua tsa-tsa;[14]
Forcing the mandarin ducks floating on the water
   to disentangle their necks:
   t'e-leng-leng-t'eng;[15]

For the surcingle on the embossed saddle
   to come loose:
   Shu-la-la-sha;
For the lovers' tryst to be interrupted
   by the night watchman,
   shouting the hour and ringing his bell:[16]
   Ssu-lang-lang-t'ang;
For the string on the green jade psaltery
   to break, never to be mended:
   chih-leng-leng-cheng;
For the caltrop-patterned mirror to be smashed
   to pieces on the glazed bricks:
   chi-ting-ting-tang;
And for the silver vase to drop to
   the bottom of the well:[17]
   p'u-t'ung-t'ung-tung.[18]

When the two musicians had finished singing, the company moved their party to the edge of a pond, where they put down felt carpets and sat down together, after which:

   With the raising of glasses and passing of cups,

they fell to:

   Playing at guess-fingers and gambling with dice.

Just as the party was at its height, Hsi-men Ch'ing said, "Why isn't that little whore, Tung Chiao-erh, here?"

"Yesterday I went to invite her in person," said Ying Po-chüeh. "She said that she was committed to escorting a patron on his way out the city gate today and consequently would not be able to show up until just before noon. I imagine that by this time, knowing that we're here enjoying ourselves, she must surely be on her way to join us."

"It's all our second brother's fault," said Scrounger Pai. "Why didn't you make absolutely certain that she'd be here?"

Hsi-men Ch'ing then turned to Scrounger Pai and whispered into his ear, saying, "Let's make a bet with this beggar. Just say that if Tung Chiao-erh hasn't shown up by noon, each of us will make our host pay a forfeit by drinking three large cups of wine."

When Scrounger Pai communicated this proposal to Ying Po-chüeh, he said, "That's all right. But if she should turn up before noon, each one of you will have to pay a forfeit by drinking three large cups of wine."

Once this bet had been made, nothing was to be seen of Tung Chiao-erh, and Ying Po-chüeh was thrown into such consternation that all he could do was to smile apprehensively. Scrounger Pai, along with Tagalong Hsieh, Hsi-men Ch'ing, and the two singing girls, colluded on a plan, so and so. Hsi-

men Ch'ing pretended to get up in order to relieve himself and instructed
Tai-an to come in and falsely proclaim that Tung Chiao-erh had arrived and
was waiting outside, thus and thus.

Tai-an got the idea, and, a little while later, just as Ying Po-chüeh was
beginning to get perturbed, whom should they see but Tai-an, who came
rushing into their midst, saying, "Sister Tung is here. She hasn't known where
to look for us."

"That thrills me to death, old matron that I am!" exclaimed Ying Po-chüeh.
"I told you that she'd be here soon. Quickly, fetch the wine. I must invite
each of you to down three cups."

"If we had won the bet," said Hsi-men Ch'ing, "and demanded that you
drink your forfeit, would you have consented to do so?"

"If I were to lose, and refuse to pay my forfeit," said Ying Po-chüeh, "I would
not be a human being."

"That's as may be," they all said. "But you'd better go out and call her in
before we'll undertake to drink our forfeits."

"All right," said Ying Po-chüeh.

"A man is as good as his word."

Having gone outside, he proceeded to scan the scene, east, west, south, and
north, until his eyes grew dim, without catching so much as a glimpse of Tung
Chiao-erh's soul.

Gazing into space, he cursed, saying, "You lousy whore! You've made your
Master Two lose face, pulling the stepladder out from under him, while assuming the right to do as you please."

When he went back inside, his companions laughed uproariously at his
discomfiture and crowded around him, saying, "It's already past noon now.
You'll have to pay off each one of us by drinking three cups of wine."

"Thanks to the trickery of that little oily mouth," complained Ying Po-
chüeh, "the lot of you have made sure that I'll be stuck with the wine. How
am I to handle it?"

Hsi-men Ch'ing:

Without permitting any further explanation,

filled a large cup of wine to the brim and proffered it to Ying Po-chüeh, saying,
"Just now you said that if you refused to drink your forfeit you would not be
a human being."

Ying Po-chüeh took the cup in his hand, while Tagalong Hsieh poured
another cup for him. Before he was able to finish this, Heartless Wu followed
up by pouring out another large cup of wine.

This threw Ying Po-chüeh into such consternation that he called out, "It's
no good. It's making me retch. You'd better get me some appetizers to help
me get it down."

Scrounger Pai responded by bringing him some sweetmeats, at which Ying
Po-chüeh blurted out, "You lousy short-life! Instead of bringing me something

sour, you're deliberately making trouble for me by bringing me something sweet."

"You'll get something sour with the next cup of wine," said Scrounger Pai. "One way or another, you'll have a chance to savor the salty, the sour, the bitter, and the peppery before you're through. There's no need to get flustered about it."

"What an inveterate oily mouth you are," exclaimed Ying Po-chüeh, "as good a filthy braggart as ever!"

Next it was the turn of Cadger Ch'ang to proffer him a cup of wine, and Ying Po-chüeh tried to run out in the hope of gaining a temporary respite, but Hsi-men Ch'ing and the two singing girls surrounded him so that he was unable to get away.

"Tung Chiao-erh, you lousy short-life, you little whore!" exclaimed Ying Po-chüeh. "You've really done your old man in this time!"

This outburst only had the effect of causing the rest of the company to fall all of a heap with laughter.

Scrounger Pai once again directed Tai-an to fetch the wine flagon and fill another bumper to the brim. Tai-an accordingly stuck the spout of the flagon an inch or more inside the cup and poured away with a gurgling sound, showing no sign of restraint.

When Ying Po-chüeh saw this, he said:

> "Only a demented guest would attempt
> to ply his host with wine.[19]

That's enough of that. The lousy little whore, confirmed bugger that he is, is sticking his spout right into the mouth of the cup. You just wait and see. Even in a thousand years, your Master Two will never urge your owner to find you a wife."

Han Chin-ch'uan and Wu Yin-erh then each poured out a cup of wine and proffered it to Ying Po-chüeh.

"I'll get down on my knees to you, like a chicken on the chopping block," pleaded Ying Po-chüeh.

"You can skip the obeisance as long as you drink the wine," said Han Chin-ch'uan.

"Why didn't you abase yourself like a chicken on the chopping block to Sister Tung, and beg her to come?" asked Wu Yin-erh.

"Don't jest with me," said Ying Po-chüeh. "I've got enough to contend with as it is."

The two of them held their cups of wine right up to his mouth. Ying Po-chüeh found this difficult to handle, so, on the one hand, he took one cup in each hand and gulped them down, and then hastily ate some appetizers.

In no time at all, his face turned crimson, and he called out, "I've been had by the lot of you. Wine is better consumed slowly. Why should you want to get me hopelessly befuddled?"

His companions were about to pour out more wine for him, when Ying Po-
chüeh knelt down in front of Hsi-men Ch'ing and said, "Elder Brother, I beg
you to put in a word on my behalf and thereby save my poor life. After all,
you'll need to preserve me in a fit state to entertain my guests. If I should
become so drunk that I:

> Don't know whether it's a fine day
>   or an overcast one,

what fun can we have together?"

"That's all right," said Hsi-men Ch'ing. "We can postpone the payment of
the additional two cups per person that you still owe until another time, and
not demand that you make good on them now."

Ying Po-chüeh then got up and thanked him, saying, "If you were to exempt
me from my remaining obligations altogether, it would be a manifestation of
your great kindness."

"All right," said Hsi-men Ch'ing, "we'll forgive you. The only thing is that,
just now, you said that anyone who refused to pay his forfeit would not be a
human being. So that, right now, it would seem that your humanity is gradually ebbing away."

"I'm the one who's ended up inebriated," said Ying Po-chüeh, "while I
don't know where that whore is up to her usual tricks."

Wu Yin-erh had a laugh at Ying Po-chüeh's expense, saying, "Hey, how is
it that even when His Honor is here playing the role of master of the revels,
Sister Tung Chiao-erh is unwilling to put in an appearance?"

Ying Po-chüeh responded meretriciously, "As a celebrated courtesan, who
is fit to appear in the best company, she's not that easy to engage."

"She's merely off pursuing her own interests somewhere," said Han Chin-
ch'uan. "What kind of a creature is she to be entitled to be called a celebrated
courtesan?"

"I understand," said Ying Po-chüeh. "I imagine you must be feeling a bit
jealous about some event in the past."

Hsi-men Ch'ing recognized that this must refer to the night when the young
gentleman Ts'ai Yün had preferred Tung Chiao-erh's company to her own,
and he gave Han Chin-ch'uan a meaningful look. But no more of this.

By this time Ying Po-chüeh was already stinking drunk. The two singing
girls, for their part, were not the sort to put up with the doldrums and fell to:

> Moving their lips and waggling their tongues,[20]

exchanging quips at each other's expense.

When the drinking began to taper off, Scrounger Pai said to Han Chin-
ch'uan, "Would the two of you consent to favor us with a song?"

"That we could," said Wu Yin-erh. "Let Han Chin-ch'uan go first."

"That fan that I won off Younger Brother Pai," said Cadger Ch'ang, "has
sturdy slats that would make it a good thing to keep time with."

"Lend it to me to keep time with then," said Han Chin-ch'uan.

Having taken it and looked it over, she said, "I don't happen to possess this kind of a fan to keep time with. Why don't you pretend that it was I who won that game of go, and give it to me?"

"That's a good idea," pronounced Hsi-men Ch'ing.

Cadger Ch'ang was unable to resist the pressure of his peers and felt constrained to give it to her.

"Wu Yin-erh is here too," said Han Chin-ch'uan. "It wouldn't be right for me to simply appropriate it myself. Let's cast a die for it, and whoever comes up with the higher number can have it."

"That makes sense," said Cadger Ch'ang, and when they had each cast a die, Wu Yin-erh was the winner, and Han Chin-ch'uan handed it over to her.

"That's hardly fair," said Cadger Ch'ang, with a false air of gentility. "I still have that handkerchief of mine, and I'll give it to Han Chin-ch'uan to make up for the loss of the fan."

He then proceeded to hand it over to her, and Han Chin-ch'uan accepted it, saying, "This is really extravagant of you."

"It's a pity I didn't bring one of my fine Szechwan fans with me," said Hsi-men Ch'ing, "so I could also make a display of my munificence."

"I realize that's a hit at me," said Cadger Ch'ang.

Tagalong Hsieh suddenly cried out, saying, "I almost forgot about it until this mention of the fan came up."

After directing Tai-an to pour out a large cup of wine and give it to Heartless Wu, he said, "Be so kind as to pay me off for our side bet on the game of go by drinking this cup of wine."

"Well all right," said Heartless Wu, "but it sure took you a long time to remember it. Since the other two have forfeited their goods, what should I care about a cup of wine."

Unable to resist the pressure of Tagalong Hsieh, he had no alternative but to swallow it down.

At that point, Han Chin-ch'uan proceeded to entertain them with a song to the tune "Rose-leaved Raspberry Fragrance":

I remember how, when we first started going together,
More or less by chance, we achieved
    a casual consummation,[21]
Expecting, in our bliss, to remain inseparable.
Together we feasted and enjoyed the flowery
    mornings and moonlit nights,[22]
Feeling that fine festivals deserve to be celebrated;
But today, it has all come to an abrupt end.
As the saying goes: Heaven is niggardly
    with its blessings.[23]

Our happy marriage affinity has been
    damnably obstructed;
The male and female phoenix mates have been
    forcibly separated.

To the same tune:

I long for him as I sit and yearn for him as I walk,[24]
My breast disturbed by thoughts of our old feelings.
He has betrayed all of those heartfelt vows
    beneath the stars, under the moon.[25]
If he has not violated his oaths,
Or suppressed his sorrow at our parting,
Heaven and the gods may still protect him.
But if we should encounter each other
    unexpectedly someday,
And speak of our separation,
He is sure to see that I am wasting away.[26]

When she had finished singing, Wu Yin-erh took over from her by singing a song to the tune "The Green Apricot":

The wind and rain feel sorry for the flowers,[27]
Once the wind and rain are over, the flowers
    will also be finished.
I urge you, do not scruple to get drunk
    amid the flowers.[28]
The flowers may fade today, or
The flowers may fade tomorrow;[29]
It is enough to turn one's hair white.[30]

Whenever the spirit moves you, indulge yourself
    in two or three cups.
Select lovely spots amid the streams and hills
    for pleasure excursions.
As long as you have an adequate supply of wine,
    and nothing else to do;
If there are flowers, that is fine;[31]
If there are no flowers, that is fine;
Who cares whether it be spring or autumn?[32]

When she had finished singing, Li Ming and Wu Hui were standing there next in line, and Tagalong Hsieh said, "There still remain these talents that have not yet been displayed."

Lo and behold:
>Strumming their strings, and
>Playing their woodwinds,

they proceeded to accompany themselves:
>With *p'i-p'a* and flute,

as they sang a song to the tune "Shorter Liang-chou":

The red dust outside the gates of the city[33] flies
>in ever-rolling clouds,
But it does not fly as far as the clear streams,
>where fish and birds reside.
In the green shade of the tall willows,
>one listens to the golden oriole.
The significance of this perching in seclusion,
Is not something that ordinary people understand.

The mountains and forests are the places to which
>one must finally retire,
That one may serve when required, and seclude
>oneself when not wanted.[34]
Grieving for posterity and emulating one's forebears,
On the fifth day of the fifth lunar month,
One sings the *Songs of Ch'u* and commiserates over
>the tragedy on the River Hsiang.[35]

By the time they finished singing, the company's enthusiasm for drinking had begun to wane. Scrounger Pai discovered that there was a small, two-sided, barbarian drum on a stand in the garden reception hall and took it behind the T'ai-hu rockery, where he also picked a sprig of blossoms, so they could play the game of:
>Passing the Flower to the Beat of the Drum.[36]

Hsi-men Ch'ing told Li Ming and Wu Hui to beat the drum and tipped them a wink, which they understood to mean that they should peek through a hole in the rockery, and stop drumming when the flower passed into the hands of whomever he thought ought to have a drink.

Scrounger Pai objected to this, saying, "You can be sure those lousy oily mouths will be up to their usual tricks. I'll go beat the drum myself."

As a result, he was able to rig it so that Hsi-men Ch'ing had to drink several cups of wine.

Just as the drinking was at its merriest, whom should they see but Shu-t'ung, who came rushing in unceremoniously, approached Hsi-men Ch'ing, and proceeded to:
>Whisper into his ear in a low voice,

saying, "The Sixth Lady has fallen quite ill and requests that you return home as quickly as possible. I've brought a horse with me, which is waiting for you outside the gate."

When Hsi-men Ch'ing heard this, he immediately got up and prepared to take his leave. By this time, the entire company was inebriated.

Everyone stood up together, and Ying Po-chüeh said, "Brother, I haven't had a chance to toast you yet today. How can you simply take off? This sort of whispered communication is no good."

He was all set to detain him, but Hsi-men Ch'ing told him the truth of the situation, thanked him, and departed on horseback.

Ying Po-chüeh, who tried to prevent the party from breaking up, saw that Han Chin-ch'uan had taken advantage of the distraction to disappear and set out to look for her with:

Skulking step and lurking gait.

Lo and behold, he found her squatting under the T'ai-hu rockery, in the process of taking a piss:

Revealing a single strand of red thread,
That emitted a myriad glistening pearls.

From his vantage point on the other side of the fence, Ying Po-chüeh proceeded to stick a blade of grass through a hole, with which he tickled the mouth of her vagina. Han Chin-ch'uan was not even able to finish what she was about but jumped up in surprise, getting the waist of her drawers all wet in the process.

"You indecent short-life!" cursed Han Chin-ch'uan. "How diabolically unprincipled can you get?"

Her face turned completely crimson as:

Half smiling and half cursing,

she rejoined the company. Ying Po-chüeh told everyone what had happened, and they all had another laugh over it.

Hsi-men Ch'ing had left Ch'in-t'ung to help Ying Po-chüeh take care of the impedimenta, and, once he had loaded the portable stove and picnic gear into the boat, they all returned to the city, where they thanked Ying Po-chüeh and went their separate ways. Ying Po-chüeh paid off the two boatmen, while Ch'in-tung carried the picnic things into his house, after which he invited Ch'in-t'ung to have a drink. But no more of this.

To resume our story, when Hsi-men Ch'ing arrived home, he hastened:

Covering two steps with every one,

to make his way straight to Li P'ing-erh's quarters.

"Mother is as sick as can be," reported Ying-ch'un. "You had better go see her right away."

Having arrived at her bedside, he found that Li P'ing-erh was groaning aloud with pain, and that the pain was in the area of her stomach.

Ying Po-chüeh Tickles Han Chin-ch'uan in an Indecorous Way

When Hsi-men Ch'ing heard her calling out in distress, he promptly said, "We've got to send for Dr. Jen Hou-ch'i immediately to come and examine you."

He then turned to Ying-ch'un and said, "Summon Shu-t'ung and have him write out a card and go with it to invite the attendance of Dr. Jen."

Ying-ch'un went outside and did as she was told, whereupon Shu-t'ung wrote out a formal calling card and went off to invite the attendance of Dr. Jen.

Hsi-men Ch'ing embraced Li P'ing-erh and sat down on the bed beside her, whereupon Li P'ing-erh complained, "You're reeking of alcohol."

"It's only because your stomach's empty," explained Hsi-men Ch'ing, "that you object so to the smell of wine."

He then turned to Ying-ch'un and asked, "Has she had any congee or soup to eat?"

"From this morning until now," replied Ying-ch'un, "she hasn't eaten so much as a grain of rice. All she's had is two or three cups of soup. The areas around her heart, her stomach, and her two kidneys have all been hurting to an unusual extent."

Hsi-men Ch'ing knitted his brows, screwed up his eyes, and sighed several times, after which he asked Ju-i, "Has Kuan-ko recovered?"

"Last night," said Ju-i, "he still had a feverish sensation in the head and cried a lot."

"What bad luck," said Hsi-men Ch'ing. "Both mother and son are sick. What can we do to restore the mother's spirits, so she will be better able to look after the child?"

Li P'ing-erh started to groan aloud with pain again, and Hsi-men Ch'ing said, "Try to bear it as best you can. The doctor will be here soon. After he's examined your pulse, and you've had a couple of cups of medicine, you should be all right."

Ying-ch'un swept the room, dusted off the tables and chairs, lit some incense, prepared tea, and helped the wet nurse to coax Kuan-ko to sleep. By this time, the night watches had begun, and the dog outside began to bark incessantly, which turned out to be occasioned by Ch'in-t'ung's return from Ying Po-chüeh's house.

Before long, Shu-t'ung also came back, escorting Dr. Jen Hou-ch'i, and holding a lantern to light him on his way. The doctor, who was wearing a four-cornered square-cut scholar's cap and a wide-sleeved gown, arrived on horseback, entered the gate, and sat down under the portico.

Shu-t'ung came inside and reported, "I succeeded in inviting him, and he's sitting under the portico."

"That's good," exclaimed Hsi-men Ch'ing. "Quickly, take some tea out for him."

Tai-an promptly picked up the tea and accompanied Hsi-men Ch'ing outside to welcome Dr. Jen.

"I don't know," the doctor said, "which resident of your distinguished mansion it is whose pulse I am to examine. I have been remiss in calling upon you, for which I am truly much at fault."

"It makes me very uncomfortable," said Hsi-men Ch'ing, "to put you to so much trouble late at night. I very much hope that you will deign to forgive me."

The doctor bowed to the ground, saying, "I would not be so presumptuous."

After drinking a cup of tea steeped with cured beans, the doctor asked, "Whose honorable indisposition is it that I am to diagnose?"

"That of my sixth insignificant concubine," replied Hsi-men Ch'ing.

After the first cup of tea had been replaced with another, flavored with salted cherries, and the exchange of a few more sentences of small talk, Tai-an started to clear away the cups, and Hsi-men Ch'ing said to him, "Have things inside been straightened up? You go in to give them the word, and bring a lantern out to light us on our way."

Tai-an went into Li P'ing-erh's quarters to give them the word and then came back out to report, with lantern in hand.

Hsi-men Ch'ing then stood up with a bow and invited the doctor to accompany him to Li P'ing-erh's quarters. The doctor followed him there, making a half bow at every gateway, the head of every flight of stairs, and every turning point, while:
>   His whole body expressed the utmost deference, and
>   His mouth was full of conventional platitudes.

When he entered Li P'ing-erh's quarters, what should he see but:
>   A nimbus of incense encompassing a golden tripod,
>   Orchidaceous flames smoldering in a silver vessel;
>   Brocaded curtains surrounding the bed,
>   With jade hooks symmetrically suspended.
>   Truly, a secluded realm of splendor and luxury;
>   It turned out to be yet another grotto heaven.

Hsi-men Ch'ing offered the doctor a chair, to which the doctor responded, "There's no need of that," as he offered his host a chair in return.

When they had both taken their seats, Ying-ch'un propped up Li P'ing-erh's hand on an embroidered cushion, wrapped her jade arm in a brocade handkerchief, and enclosed her slender fingers in her own sleeve, before exposing a segment of her powder-white arm from underneath the bed curtains, so that the doctor could examine her pulse.

The doctor, after:
>   Cleansing his mind and stabilizing his vital energy,
began to evaluate her pulse, finding that her stomach was depleted and her vital energy weak, that her blood was deficient while her liver conduit was hyperactive, that her heart was not clear, that an inflammation had affected her *tricalorium*, or triple burner,[37] and that it was necessary to reduce the inflammation and fortify the blood. He then proceeded:

Citing the appropriate texts and relevant principles,
to propound his diagnosis to Hsi-men Ch'ing.

"Doctor," said Hsi-men Ch'ing, "it is just as though you had been observing the course of her ailment with your own eyes. You have described her symptoms exactly. This insignificant concubine of mine is possessed of an exceedingly long-suffering disposition."

"That is precisely the source of the problem," said the doctor. "That is why her liver conduit is hyperactive. People do not understand what goes on inside her. The element wood in her liver has overcome the element earth in her stomach, so that the vital energy of her stomach has been weakened. As a result, there is no way for her vital energy to be replenished, or for her blood to be regenerated. The element water in her kidneys cannot sustain the element fire in her heart, so that the fire has ascended into her upper body, and the area of her chest beneath the diaphragm feels congested and painful. She also suffers from periodic pains in the stomach. Because her blood is depleted, her two kidneys and the joints throughout her body all ache, and she has lost her appetite for food and drink. Does that describe her situation?"

"Her symptoms are just as you have described them," said Ying-ch'un.

"You may truly be described as Immortal Jen," exclaimed Hsi-men Ch'ing. "Where the four diagnostic methods of your noble profession are concerned, namely:

Inspection, auscultation, interrogation, and palpation,[38]
the fact that you understand the principles of pulse taking so thoroughly that you are able to describe the patient's symptoms without prior interrogation, is my insignificant concubine's good fortune."

The doctor responded with a deep bow and said, "What does your pupil know about anything? It was mostly guesswork on my part."

"You are altogether too modest," said Hsi-men Ch'ing.

He then went on to ask, "At the present time, what medications should my insignificant concubine take?"

"It is a matter of reducing the inflammation and fortifying the blood," said the doctor. "Once the inflammation has been reduced, the area of her chest beneath the diaphragm will naturally be more comfortable, and when her blood has been regenerated, the pains in her waist and the area of her ribs should cease. Do not assume that this is an ailment of exogenous origin. It is not that at all. The symptoms are all those of deficiency."

He then went on to ask, "Have her menses been regular or not?"

"They have not been dependable," said Ying-ch'un.

"How often do they occur?" asked the doctor.

"Ever since she gave birth to Kuan-ko," said Ying-ch'un, "they have not been what they should be."

"Her original store of vital energy was weak," said the doctor, "and her postpartum conditions have not been stabilized, with the result that her blood

Jen Hou-ch'i Diagnoses an Illness for a Powerful Family

has become depleted. It is not a case of blockage that would require purgative medications. Only if she is treated gradually with a regimen of pills can she be induced to come round and make a recovery. Otherwise, her condition will only become worse."

"You have certainly made a perspicacious assessment of the situation," said Hsi-men Ch'ing. "Right now, I hope that you can first provide a decoction that will alleviate her present pain, after which we can ask for whatever pills you may prescribe."

"That is only appropriate," said the doctor. "After your pupil has returned to his humble abode, he will deliver them immediately. It is not a serious case. It is only necessary to know that these are the symptoms of a deficiency. The pain in her chest beneath the diaphragm is caused by an inflammation and is not of exogenous origin. The unusual pains afflicting her waist and the area of her ribs are due to a depletion of her blood, and not to stagnation of the blood. Once she has taken the prescribed medications, these conditions should naturally be alleviated, one by one. There is no cause for alarm."

Hsi-men Ch'ing:

Expressed his gratitude without ceasing,

and had just gotten up to leave the room, when Kuan-ko woke up and started to cry again.

"This young gentleman has a healthy voice," said the doctor.

"That may be so," said Hsi-men Ch'ing, "but he is too prone to become ill, which is most unfortunate, and poses a hardship for my insignificant concubine, who is:

Unable to rest comfortably on her pillow,

both day and night."

He then proceeded to escort the doctor on his way out.

To resume our story, Shu-t'ung said to Ch'in-t'ung, "When I went to request his attendance just now, he had already gone to bed. I had to knock on the gate for what seemed like half a day before anyone came out to let me in. That oldster was still rubbing his eyes as he came outside, and when he mounted his horse, he kept dozing off so frequently that I was afraid he would fall off the saddle."

"You had a rough job of it," said Ch'in-t'ung, "while I had as good a time as could be today. On top of which, I got to drink a bellyful of wine."

As they were engaged in this idle chat, Tai-an appeared, holding a lantern to light the way for Hsi-men Ch'ing as he escorted the doctor on his way out.

When they got as far as the portico, the doctor wanted to continue on his way, but Hsi-men Ch'ing said, "Please relax and sit down long enough for me to offer you another cup of tea. I can also provide something in the way of ordinary fare or a snack."

The doctor shook his head and said, "Many thanks for your lavish hospitality, but I cannot presume to accept any more of it," as he headed straight outside.

Hsi-men Ch'ing saw him onto his horse and deputed Shu-t'ung to hold a lantern and light him on his way home. As soon as he had taken leave of the doctor, he flew inside and directed Tai-an to take a tael of silver and catch up with them, in order to take receipt of the prescribed medications.

They proceeded straight to Dr. Jen's house, where the doctor dismounted and said to the two of them, "Uncles, take a seat and have a cup of tea while I go inside to prepare the medications."

Tai-an took out the gift box and handed it to the doctor, saying, "Please accept this payment for the medications."

"We are friends," said the doctor. "I would not presume to accept any remuneration from your master."

"I beseech you to accept it before we can feel comfortable about taking possession of the medications," said Shu-t'ung. "Otherwise, we can hardly agree to accept them. I fear that if we go home with them, we will certainly only be required to deliver them back to you, which will mean an extra trip for nothing. It would be better all the way round if you were to make no bones about accepting the payment, so we can wait for the medications and take them home with us."

"A fortune told for nothing, is worth nothing,"[39]
said Tai-an. "I beseech you to accept it."

The doctor felt compelled to assent, and, seeing that the payment was lavish, he went inside and hastily got together the ingredients for a decoction and poured out a little less than half the pills in a bottle. By the time the two page boys had finished their tea, a reply was sent out from inside for Tai-an and Shu-t'ung to deliver, after which the gate was closed behind them.

When the two page boys arrived home, Hsi-men Ch'ing noticed that the pouch containing the medicine was bulky and said, "Why should there be so much?"

When he tore it open and took a look, he found that the pills were also inside and laughed, saying:
"If you have the money you can make a ghost
     turn the millstone for you.[40]
Just now, he said that he would first send the ingredients for a decoction, but now he has sent everything at once. That's fine. That's fine."

Looking at the pouch containing the ingredients for the decoction, he saw that the inscription on the label read:

Decoction for reducing inflammation and fortifying the blood

Boil in two cups of water, without adding ginger, until reduced to eight parts. Take on an empty stomach. The dregs may be used a second time. Avoid eating bran or wheat flour, or anything greasy, roasted, or fried.

Affixed to the label there was also the imprint of a seal that read:

Dispensary of the hereditary physician, Dr. Jen

The crimson label on the other container read:

Pills of foxglove root to enhance appetite

Hsi-men Ch'ing turned the medications over to Ying-ch'un and directed her to start out by decocting one packet of the powdered medicine. Li P'ing-erh drank some hot water, while Ying-ch'un boiled the medicine, and Hsi-men Ch'ing personally oversaw its preparation.

After straining the dregs out of it, he carried it to Li P'ing-erh's bedside and said, "Sixth Lady, your medicine is here."

Li P'ing-erh turned over:

Unable to overcome a beguiling tremor,

while Hsi-men Ch'ing, holding the decoction in one hand, supported her head and neck with the other. Li P'ing-erh complained that it tasted bitter, and Ying-ch'un promptly fetched some hot water, with which she rinsed out her mouth. Hsi-men Ch'ing ate some congee and washed his feet, after which he lay down to sleep with Li P'ing-erh. Ying-ch'un heated some more water and put something over the kettle to keep it hot, after which she lay down to sleep in her clothes.

Strange to relate,

after Li P'ing-erh had taken this medication, she was able to sleep. Hsi-men Ch'ing also fell fast asleep, but Kuan-ko persisted in wanting to cry. Ju-i was afraid that he would wake Li P'ing-erh, so she gave him her breast to suck, and, before long, they were all sleeping quietly.

The next morning, when Hsi-men Ch'ing was about to get up, he asked Li P'ing-erh, "Are you feeling any better since last night?"

"Strange as it may seem,"

said Li P'ing-erh, "no sooner did I take that medicine than, somehow or other, I fell fast asleep. This morning, I no longer feel any particular pain in my innards. If the condition I was in late last evening had continued unabated, the pain would have been the death of me."

"Heaven be thanked! Heaven be thanked!" exclaimed Hsi-men Ch'ing, with a smile. "Right now, if we boil another two cups of water, so you can take a second dose of that decoction, you'll be all well."

Ying-ch'un, accordingly, boiled some more water for her, and she took it as directed. As for Hsi-men Ch'ing, only then did:

His affrighted soul fly off to Java.

How is one to describe such a situation? There is a poem that testifies to this:

Hsi-shih, from time to time, may be wont to knit
    her turquoise brows;[41]

But, luckily, she possesses a transcendent elixir
  of divine efficacy.
Verily, medicine cures only those diseases
  which are not fatal;
Beyond a doubt, the Buddha saves only those
  destined to be saved.[42]

> If you want to know the outcome of these events,
> Pray consult the story related in the following chapter.

Chapter 55

HSI-MEN CH'ING OBSERVES A BIRTHDAY

IN THE EASTERN CAPITAL;

SQUIRE MIAO FROM YANG-CHOU SENDS

A PRESENT OF SINGING BOYS

Myriad-year peaches of immortality are brought,
    while still bedecked with dew;
Brought to the chambers of the grand councilor,
    to wish him a hundred years of life.
It is a day for the Eight Immortals to descend,
    in order to proffer their toasts;
A time for presentation of brocades, featuring
    seven phoenixes in flowered roundels.
From the six directions and the five waterways[1]
    come congratulatory scrolls;
From the four barbarian tribes and three isles[2]
    are presented exotic rarities.
Hsi-ho should not send the two orbs too swiftly
    along their appointed paths;[3]
To allow time to celebrate the birthday of the
    emperor's grand preceptor.

THE STORY GOES that after Doctor Jen had palpated Li P'ing-erh's pulse, he returned to the reception hall and sat down.[4]

Hsi-men Ch'ing then initiated the consultation by saying, "I do not know what your interpretation of her symptoms might be. Is it nothing to be worried about?"

"This illness of your wife's," said Doctor Jen, "is the result of inadequate care in the treatment of her postpartum conditions. That is the etiology of her ailment. At present, she is suffering from lochiorrhea, her complexion is sallow, she has an indifferent appetite, and she is easily fatigued. In your pupil's ignorant opinion, she needs to be treated with diligent care. Generally speaking, the hardest things to treat from a medical standpoint are the postpartum ailments of women and the complications of children who have contracted smallpox. If the slightest mistake is made in these circumstances, the roots of further pathology may be planted. Right now, the pulses on your wife's two wrists are feeble rather than replete. When palpated, they are both scattered and large, as well as flaccid, and unable to recuperate themselves. These symptoms are all indications of inflammation, resulting from the fact that in the liver the element earth is deficient and the element wood is in the ascendant, causing an abnormal circulation of the depleted blood. If these conditions are not treated at once, they will only grow worse in the future."

When he had finished speaking, Hsi-men Ch'ing asked, "Under the present circumstances, what medications are called for?"

"The situation requires medications that will reduce the inflammation and arrest the lochiorrhea," said Dr. Jen. "The principal drugs should be Amur cork-tree bark and anemarrhena, which may be supplemented with foxglove root, skullcap, and the like. If the doses of these ingredients are increased or decreased as observation directs, she should recover."

When Hsi-men Ch'ing heard this, he told Shu-t'ung to seal up a tael of silver and give it to Dr. Jen as a down payment for the prescribed medications. After expressing his gratitude, Dr. Jen took his leave, and, before long, the prescribed medications were duly delivered, decocted, and administered to Li P'ing-erh in her bedroom. But no more of this.

To resume our story, after seeing Dr. Jen off, Hsi-men Ch'ing came back inside and sat down for a chat with Ying Po-chüeh. It suddenly occurred to him that the time for the celebration of Grand Preceptor Ts'ai Ching's birthday in the Eastern Capital was fast approaching. In anticipation of this event, he had already sent Tai-an to Hang-chou to procure the dragon robes, brocades, floral ornaments of gold, and other precious objects appropriate to offer as birthday gifts, and they had all been duly assembled, so that he could proceed forthwith to the Eastern Capital in order to offer his congratulations in person. Upon calculating that the day in question was drawing near, and that it would take a good half a month's journey to get from Shantung to the Eastern Capital, he realized that he could just make it if he got his baggage together that night and set off the next morning, and that there was no room for further delay. Consequently, he went back to the master suite and explained the situation to Yüeh-niang, thus and so.

"All this time," said Yüeh-niang, "you've neglected to bring the subject up. And now you seem to be all in a rush about it. Just when do you plan to start out?"

"I'll have to start out tomorrow in order to get there in time, and leave myself a few days leeway," said Hsi-men Ch'ing.

When Hsi-men Ch'ing had finished speaking, he went outside and directed Tai-an, Ch'in-t'ung,[5] Shu-t'ung, and Hua-t'ung to start getting their clothes and baggage ready, so they could accompany him to the Eastern Capital the next day. Each of the four page boys proceeded to prepare his baggage without delay.

Yüeh-niang then instructed Hsiao-yü, "Go ask your various mistresses to come and help pack your father's bags."

At this juncture, only Li P'ing-erh, because she had to look after her child, on the one hand, and because she was taking medicine, on the other, was unable to leave her quarters. Among the other ladies of the household, Meng Yü-lou and P'an Chin-lien, showed up and set about the task of packing the python robes, dragon robes, bolts of silk, and other birthday presents into leather trunks and rattan boxes, making more than twenty carrier loads in all. They also completed the task of getting together the official caps and girdles and other articles of clothing that would be needed in the course of the trip.

That evening, the three ladies provided a feast of wine and delicacies in order to see Hsi-men Ch'ing off. During the feast, Hsi-men Ch'ing communicated several words of instruction to each of the ladies, after which he went into Yüeh-niang's room and retired for the night.

The next day, the twenty carrier loads of baggage were sent ahead, together with a waybill authorizing the shipment and an official tally entitling the bearer to the provision of carriers and horses at the relay stations along the way. Only after all the necessary arrangements had been made did Hsi-men Ch'ing go into Li P'ing-erh's quarters, where he looked in on Kuan-ko and then said a few words to Li P'ing-erh.

"Be diligent in treating your illness," he said. "I'll return home to see you before long."

Li P'ing-erh, with tears in her eyes, said, "Be careful and look after yourself on the road."

Then she escorted him out to the reception hall, where she joined Wu Yüeh-niang, Meng Yü-lou, and P'an Chin-lien in seeing him off at the front gate.

There Hsi-men Ch'ing got into an open sedan chair, accompanied by the four page boys on horseback, and proceeded to set off for the Eastern Capital. By the time they had wended their way for about a hundred li, evening was approaching, and Hsi-men Ch'ing ordered that they should stop for the night. The station master of the relay station received him and provided for their needs.

After spending the night there, early the next morning, Hsi-men Ch'ing urged the carriers and horses to take up their loads and proceed on their way as expeditiously as possible. Along the way they enjoyed gazing at the:

Lucent hills and limpid streams.[6]

At noon they stopped to prepare a midday meal and then continued on their journey. Those they encountered along the road consisted entirely of regional officials, both civil and military, who were on their way to the capital to congratulate the grand preceptor on his birthday. Those among them who presided over birthday gift convoys for this purpose were without number.

After traveling for another ten days or so, they calculated that there was not much farther to go, and that if they continued their current pace they should be able to arrive at their destination precisely on time. They spent the night on the road and, after another two days of travel, arrived in the Eastern Capital, which they entered through the Myriad Years Gate.

By the time they arrived:

The light was beginning to wane,[7]

and they proceeded directly to Majordomo Chai Ch'ien's quarters in Grand Preceptor Ts'ai Ching's residence beneath the commemorative arch on Dragon's Virtue Street, where they expected to be put up for the night.

When Majordomo Chai Ch'ien learned that Hsi-men Ch'ing had arrived, he hastened out to welcome him. After they had exchanged the customary amenities about the weather and had a cup of tea, Hsi-men Ch'ing told Tai-an to take care of the luggage and see that each and every load was carried into Chai Ch'ien's quarters, where Chai Ch'ien directed a member of the household staff to take charge of them. Chai Ch'ien then laid on a feast in order to refresh Hsi-men Ch'ing after the hardships of the road.

Before long, a carved lacquer table of the kind manufactured for official use made an appearance, laden with several tens of culinary specialties, as well as several tens of side dishes. All of them were:

Delicacies of the most delectable variety,[8]

such as swallow's nest and shark's fin, dishes of the very finest kind. The only items lacking were:

Dragon's liver and phoenix marrow.[9]

Everything displayed:

The utmost discrimination and opulence.

Even the fare provided for the enjoyment of Grand Preceptor Ts'ai Ching himself:

Did not surpass this.[10]

The attendants on duty provided goblets made of "Heaven penetrating rhinoceros horn,"[11] which they filled with Ma-ku wine.[12] They handed one of them to Chai Ch'ien, who first poured a libation to Heaven and then refilled it and offered a toast to Hsi-men Ch'ing, who responded in kind. After the two of them had resumed their seats, a profusion of candied fruits and hot dishes to go with the wine were served to them, one after another:

Like a stream of flowing water.

After:

Two rounds of wine had been consumed,

Hsi-men Ch'ing said to Chai Ch'ien, "This visit on your pupil's part is motivated solely by the desire to offer his birthday congratulations to the venerable grand preceptor. I have seen fit to provide a few insignificant gifts to show my filial feelings for the grand preceptor, which I anticipate that he will not refuse. But it has been your pupil's wish for some time to become even more closely attached to him. If my kinsman would be so kind as to broach the matter with him in advance, so that I might become a protégé of the grand preceptor's, and be acknowledged by him as an adopted son, I would feel that:

The entire span of my natural life,[13]

will not have been lived in vain. I don't know whether you might be willing to propose this matter to him in order to accommodate your pupil, or not."

"Where's the difficulty in that?" replied Chai Ch'ien. "This patron of ours, although he may be a high official at court, is extremely susceptible to flattery. Upon seeing the lavish gifts that you have provided today, he is certain to augment your office and rank, let alone acknowledge you as an adopted son. He is sure to agree to it."

When Hsi-men Ch'ing heard this:

His delight could not be contained.[14]

After they had been drinking for some time, Hsi-men Ch'ing suggested, "Let's not drink any more."

"Have another cup," urged Majordomo Chai Ch'ien. "Why should we stop?"

"Tomorrow there is serious business to attend to," said Hsi-men Ch'ing, "so I don't dare have too much to drink."

Only after repeated urging did he consent to have one more cup.

Majordomo Chai Ch'ien saw to it that Hsi-men Ch'ing's attendants were provided with food and wine, and he ordered that the horses should be led back to the stables in the rear. At this point the utensils were cleared away, and he invited Hsi-men Ch'ing to his studio in the back of the mansion where he was to rest for the night. There he found prepared for him an ornate gilt lacquer canopy bed with mermaid silk curtains, held open with silver hooks, revealing a fine embroidered quilt within, that was redolent of incense. After his band of page boys had helped Hsi-men Ch'ing off with his clothes and stockings, he got into bed to:

Sleep by himself in solitary slumber.[15]

This was something that Hsi-men Ch'ing had never been used to, and he found it difficult to get through the night. Waiting it out until dawn, he was prepared to get up, but since in Chai Ch'ien's quarters:

The gates and doors were all closed,

where was he to get any water with which to wash his face? It was not until 10:00 AM that someone with a key came through to unlock the doors. After this, one page boy came in with a towel, while another came into the studio with a wash basin and filled it with perfumed water. After Hsi-men Ch'ing had finished washing up and combing his hair, he donned his "loyal and tranquil hat," put on his formal outer garments, and sat down all by himself in the studio.

Who should appear at this juncture but Majordomo Chai Ch'ien, who came in, greeted Hsi-men Ch'ing, and sat down. An attendant then brought in a crimson box containing some thirty delectable delicacies, and a silver flagon, from which he poured out wine to go with their breakfast.

"Please go ahead and enjoy your breakfast," said Chai Ch'ien. "Your pupil is going to go into the residence beforehand, and say a word to the master, after which it will be appropriate for you to bring in your gifts."

"You are putting yourself to a lot of trouble on my behalf," said Hsi-men Ch'ing.

After:

> Several cups of wine had been consumed,

breakfast was served and eaten, and the utensils were cleared away.

"If you will just sit here for the time being," said Majordomo Chai Ch'ien, "I will go ahead into the residence and be back in no time at all."

After Majordomo Chai Ch'ien had gone on this errand, it was not long before he hurried back to his own quarters and reported to Hsi-men Ch'ing, "His Honor is still in his studio, washing up and combing his hair, while outside, the officials, both civil and military, from the entire court, are waiting in vain for the chance to congratulate him on his birthday. Your pupil has already spoken to His Honor about it. Right now, you can proceed in to offer your congratulations ahead of the rest, so as not to be lost in the crowd, while your pupil will follow right behind you."

On hearing this, Hsi-men Ch'ing was:

> Unable to contain his delight,

and ordered his attendants, along with several servants from Chai Ch'ien's household, to transport the twenty carrier loads of silver and gold, bolts of silk, etc., out to the front of the grand preceptor's residence. The entire retinue responded with one voice and set about their task without delay, while Hsi-men Ch'ing donned his official cap and girdle and proceeded after them in a sedan chair.

What should he encounter but a confused hubbub created by the crowds of officials, both high and low:

> Rubbing shoulders and nudging backs,

as they gathered to offer their birthday congratulations. From a distance, Hsi-men Ch'ing caught sight of another official, riding in a sedan chair, on his way into the Dragon's Virtue precinct, whom he recognized, after taking a closer look, to be none other than the now well-to-do gentleman and holder of a supernumerary title as squire, Miao Ch'ing. Who could have anticipated that Miao Ch'ing had also caught sight of Hsi-men Ch'ing. The two of them got out of their sedan chairs, bowed to each other, and exchanged the customary amenities about the weather.

It so happens that Miao Ch'ing was now a substantial man of property and had also acquired a prestige title for himself, in addition to which, he had earlier contrived to become a protégé of Grand Preceptor Ts'ai Ching. That is why he had come to offer his birthday congratulations and happened to run into his old friend. On this occasion, the two of them hastily exchanged a few words by the roadside before taking leave of each other.

When Hsi-men Ch'ing arrived in front of the grand preceptor's mansion, what should he see? Behold:

The hall extends like P'ei Tu's Green Wilderness Hall,[16]
Seeming to reach into the cloudy empyrean;
The pavilion rises like T'ai-tsung's Ling-yen Pavilion,[17]
As though extending right up to the stars.
The area in front of the gate is spacious enough
    for horses to wheel around;
The memorial posts outside the entrance are fit
    for the display of banners.
Throughout the forest of brocades,[18]
The wind carries the brilliance
    of the thrushes' cries;
Amid the piles of gold and silver,[19]
The sun enhances the fragrance
    of the flowering trees.
The rafters and beams are crafted
    out of sandalwood;
The steps and stairs are paved with
    "sobering stones."[20]
To either side the ladies forming "fleshly screens,"[21]
    are all Hsi-shihs or Red-dusters;[22]
Throughout the halls are arrayed valuable antiques,
    all Chou tripods or Shang vessels.
Shining ever so brightly,
There are twelve luminescent pearls suspended on high;
So that even in the dark of night no lamp oil is needed.
Prestigious in appearance,
Three thousand retainers gather in pearl-studded shoes;[23]
Those strumming their sword hilts are all eminent men.[24]
Though they hail from the Nine Provinces and Four Seas,[25]
The teeming crowds of officials, both high and low,
Have all come to proffer congratulations.
Even among the grand secretaries of the Six Ministries,
And the supreme commanders of the Three Border Regions,
There are none who do not bow their heads.

Truly:

Second only to the respect due the Son of Heaven,
    Lord of Ten Thousand Years,
Is the veneration extended to the chief councilor
    who presides over the court.

Hsi-men Ch'ing made a respectful bow as he approached the main gateway. He noticed that the door in the center was closed, and that the officials all went in through a side door.

"Why is it," Hsi-men Ch'ing asked, "that on such a special day as this, the main door in not open?"

"It so happens," explained Majordomo Chai Ch'ien, "that the main door has been used by the emperor when favoring the grand preceptor with a visit. For this reason, no one else presumes to go in or out through that door."

Hsi-men Ch'ing and Majordomo Chai Ch'ien proceeded through a number of doors, all of which were guarded by military officers, who did not permit the slightest irregularity.

Upon seeing Chai Ch'ien, each of them asked, "Majordomo, where does your guest come from?"

"My kinsman is from Shantung," replied Majordomo Chai Ch'ien. "He has come to congratulate His Honor on his birthday."

After this interrogation, they proceeded through several more doors and turned a number of corners. Everywhere they looked they saw nothing but:

Painted beams and carved rafters,[26]

as befitted:

The residence of a Chin or Chang.[27]

They also became aware of the faint sound of drums and music, that

Seemed to come from Heaven itself.

Once again, Hsi-men Ch'ing asked about this, saying, "Since, in this location, we are:

Isolated from the homes of the people,

where does this:

Resounding clamor of drums and music,

come from?"

"It is created by the female musicians that His Honor is training," replied Majordomo Chai Ch'ien. "They form a troupe of twenty-four persons in all. They know how to perform the Dance of the Daughters of Māra,[28] the Dance of Rainbow Skirts,[29] and the Dance of Kuan-yin.[30] They perform before His Honor during breakfast, at lunch, and at evening banquets. I imagine that at present they are entertaining him at breakfast."

Before Hsi-men Ch'ing had heard him out, his nose sensed:

The aroma of an exotic fragrance,[31]

and the sound of the music drew ever nearer.

"We are now approaching His Honor's studio," said Majordomo Chai Ch'ien. "Walk a little more softly."

After they had traversed a zigzag gallery, what should they see but a large reception chamber that resembled:

A temple hall or an immortal's palace.

In front of this chamber there were cranes such as those ridden by immortals, as well as peacocks and other varieties of rare birds. In addition:

All four seasons produced their
never-fading flowers,

including alabaster blossoms, night-blooming cereus, and Chinese hibiscus. The entire scene:

Glittered and scintillated,[32]

to such effect that:

It is impossible to do it justice.[33]

Hsi-men Ch'ing was too diffident to barge in unannounced and asked Majordomo Chai Ch'ien to precede him, after which, he also made his way:

Hesitatingly and punctiliously,

to the front of the hall. In the position of honor at the upper end of the chamber, there was placed a grand preceptor's folding armchair,[34] covered with a tiger skin, on which there sat a figure, garbed in a crimson python robe. It was the grand preceptor himself. Behind a standing screen, there were arrayed thirty or forty beautiful women, all of whom were dressed in palace style, holding towels and fans, in order to minister to his needs.

Majordomo Chai Ch'ien stood to one side, while Hsi-men Ch'ing faced the upper end of the chamber and kowtowed four times. Grand Preceptor Ts'ai Ching then stood up and, availing himself of a velvet mat, responded to the homage of his visitor with a single obeisance, in recognition of the fact that this was the first time they had met. After this, Majordomo Chai Ch'ien went up close to Grand Preceptor Ts'ai Ching, whispered a few words into his ear, and then came back down again.

Recognizing that this colloquy must have pertained to his request, Hsi-men Ch'ing, once again, faced the upper end of the chamber and kowtowed four times, while, this time, Grand Preceptor Ts'ai Ching did not reply in kind. These four kowtows signified that he recognized the recipient as his adoptive father. From that time on, the two of them addressed each other as father and son.

Hsi-men Ch'ing then initiated the conversation by saying, "Your son has no way to adequately express his filial feelings for his father. But since today is your birthday, I have brought a few insignificant gifts from home, merely to express the meaning of:

A goose feather conveyed a thousand li,[35]

and to say to Your Honor:

May you live as long as the Southern Hills."

"How could I be worthy to accept what you have to offer?" said Grand Preceptor Ts'ai Ching. "Please have a seat."

An attendant brought in a chair for him, and Hsi-men Ch'ing bowed toward the upper end of the chamber, announced, "I am taking my seat," and then sat down on the west side of the room to have some tea.

Hsi-men Ch'ing Observes a Birthday in the Eastern Capital

Meanwhile, Majordomo Chai Ch'ien ran hastily out to the gate and called for the bearers of the gifts to bring their twenty-odd loads inside, where he had the lids taken off the rattan boxes, and handed up a list of the presents. These consisted of a crimson python robe, a dragon robe of statutory green, twenty bolts of brocade in Han dynasty patterns, twenty bolts of Szechwan brocade, twenty bolts of asbestos fabric, and twenty bolts of cloth imported from the Western Ocean.[36] In addition, there were forty bolts of fabrics in flowered and plain patterns, a girdle with a jade plaque depicting the king of the Lion Barbarians,[37] a girdle with a plaque of aloeswood enchased with gold, ten pairs each of jade cups and cups of rhinoceros horn, eight goblets of pure gold enchased with floral designs, ten luminescent pearls, and two hundred ounces of gold for his personal expenditures. All of these things were being offered to Grand Preceptor Ts'ai Ching as:

> The customary presentation gifts.

When Grand Preceptor Ts'ai Ching had finished perusing the list of presents and observed that some twenty carrier loads had been brought in, he was exceedingly pleased. On the one hand, he expressed his gratitude repeatedly, while telling Majordomo Chai Ch'ien to have them moved into the storehouse, and, on the other hand, he ordered that wine should be served for the entertainment of his guest.

Hsi-men Ch'ing, observing how busy his host was, put forward a pretext for taking leave of Grand Preceptor Ts'ai, to which the grand preceptor responded, "In that case, be sure to come back early this afternoon."

Hsi-men Ch'ing bowed to his host and got up to leave, while Grand Preceptor Ts'ai saw him off for a few steps but did not continue any further. Hsi-men Ch'ing, as before, was accompanied on his way out by Majordomo Chai Ch'ien, who, because he had further business to conduct inside the mansion, then bade him farewell and went back inside.

Hsi-men Ch'ing returned to Chai Ch'ien's quarters, where he doffed his official cap and girdle, consumed another fine repast that had been prepared for him, and then went back to the studio to take a nap.

In due course, Grand Preceptor Ts'ai Ching sent a houseman to invite him to a party, and Hsi-men Ch'ing rewarded him with some "fan money" and told him, "You go ahead back. I'll follow along shortly."

He then brushed off his official cap and girdle, directed Tai-an to prepare a considerable number of sealed envelopes containing tips and put them into a calling card case, and set off for the grand preceptor's residence in a sedan chair, accompanied by his four page boys. But no more of this.

To resume our story, Grand Preceptor Ts'ai Ching had invited each and every one of the officials, both civil and military, from the entire court, who had come to tender their congratulations, to attend a drinking party. Beginning with the next day, they were to come in three contingents. The first day was to be for the distaff relatives of the imperial family and palace eunuchs.

The second day was to be for the grand secretaries of the Six Ministries and officials from other prestigious offices. The third day was to be for other officials, both high and low, from the Inner and Outer Courts. An exception was made in the case of Hsi-men Ch'ing alone. On the one hand, because he was a guest who had come from afar, and on the other hand, because he had presented so many gifts, Grand Preceptor Ts'ai Ching was particularly pleased with him. For this reason, on the actual day of his birthday, he had invited only Hsi-men Ch'ing to come all by himself.

Upon hearing that his newly adopted son, Hsi-men Ch'ing, had arrived, he hastened out to the portico to welcome him in.

Hsi-men Ch'ing repeatedly demurred, saying, "Pray precede me, Father," before bending his back and circumspectly stepping over the threshold.

"I have put you and your entourage to the trouble of coming a great distance," said Grand Preceptor Ts'ai Ching, "and occasioned you the expense of your magnanimous gifts. The fact that I have invited you over for a brief visit today is merely:

A paltry expression of my heartfelt feelings."[38]

"The fact that your son is still able to:

Bear Heaven above and tread the Earth below,"[39]

said Hsi-men Ch'ing, "is entirely owing to his father's abundant grace. These insignificant expressions of his respect are:

Scarcely worthy of consideration."[40]

The two of them went on to engage in:

Intimate laughter and conversation,

just as though they were really father and son. Meanwhile, the twenty female musicians simultaneously struck up a tune, and the members of the household staff who were on duty served them with wine. Grand Preceptor Ts'ai Ching wished to offer Hsi-men Ch'ing a preliminary toast, which Hsi-men Ch'ing stalwartly declined, on the grounds that he was unworthy of the honor, but was finally induced to accept, remaining on his feet as he drained it to the bottom. After this, they sat down to the feast.

Hsi-men Ch'ing ordered Shu-t'ung to bring him a gold goblet in the shape of a peach, which he filled to the brim with wine, and then, approaching Grand Preceptor Ts'ai Ching's seat, got down on his knees before him and said, "May my father live for a thousand years."

Grand Preceptor Ts'ai Ching's face was suffused with joy as he said, "Get up my son," and, accepting the proffered cup, drained it to the bottom.

Only then did Hsi-men Ch'ing get back to his feet and then sit down in his place as before. On this occasion, it being a lavish feast in the residence of the grand councilor, a myriad varieties of exotic rarities were served up, but there is no need to describe all of this.

Hsi-men Ch'ing continued drinking with his host until dusk, when he distributed the sealed envelopes containing tips to the various servitors and then expressed his gratitude and took his leave, saying, "Father, I know how busy you are. Your son would like to hereby express his humble thanks. In the days to come I will not presume to seek another meeting with you."

He then proceeded out the gate of the mansion and returned to the quarters of Chai Ch'ien to rest overnight.

The next day he wanted to go pay his respects to Miao Ch'ing and sent Tai-an to find out where he was staying. After the better part of the day, Tai-an succeeded in tracking him down and ascertained that he was living in the residence of Eunuch Director Li Yen,[41] which was located behind the Forbidden City.

Upon making his way there, he sent Tai-an ahead with a calling card to announce his visit, and Miao Ch'ing came out to welcome him, saying, "Your pupil has been sitting here all by himself and was just thinking how nice it would be to have an intimate friend with whom to chat. Your arrival is providential."

He then insisted on entertaining his visitor with a feast, and Hsi-men Ch'ing could not refuse but consented to remain for the occasion. There and then:

Rare viands from the hills and seas,

too many to describe, were laid before them. There were also two singing boys, with:

Clear-cut brows and sparkling eyes,[42]

who opened up their throats and sang several song suites for their entertainment.

During the course of their performance, Hsi-men Ch'ing pointed to Tai-an, Ch'in-t'ung, Shu-t'ung, and Hua-t'ung and remarked to Miao Ch'ing, "Just look at that bunch of imbeciles. All they care about is their food and drink. How can they be compared to these two of yours?"

Miao Ch'ing laughed and said, "My only fear is that they might not be able to serve you satisfactorily. But if you admire them that much, I would have no problem making you a present of them."

Hsi-men Ch'ing demurred, saying, "How could I presume to:

Appropriate the source of another's pleasure?"[43]

They continued drinking until the late watches of the night, when Hsi-men Ch'ing took leave of Miao Ch'ing and returned, as before, to Chai Ch'ien's dwelling to sleep.

During the days that followed, each and every one of the officers on the staff of the grand councilor's mansion insisted on inviting him for a drink, so that he was detained for another eight or nine days.

Hsi-men Ch'ing was:

Anxious to return as swiftly as an arrow,[44]

so he told Tai-an to get his baggage together, but Majordomo Chai Ch'ien tried as hard as he could to get him to prolong his stay. As a result, he felt compelled to spend another evening drinking with him, during which they

Miao Ch'ing Presents Hsi-men Ch'ing with Two Singing Boys

reiterated their gratification at the fact that they were united by the ties of marriage and felt the greatest affection for each other.

The next day, Hsi-men Ch'ing got up bright and early, took leave of his host, and headed back for Shantung. Along the way they suffered the usual vicissitudes of travel:

Sleeping by the waters and dining in the wind,[45]
but no more of this.

To resume our story, ever since Hsi-men Ch'ing had set off for the Eastern Capital to offer his birthday congratulations, the sisterhood of his wife and concubines had anxiously awaited his return, concerned as they were for his safety. For the most part they kept to their quarters, doing needlework, and not coming out to engage in idle pastimes.

Among them, only P'an Chin-lien dressed herself up to look:

As lovely as a flower or a piece of jade,[46]
Making a captivating spectacle of herself,
as she sallied forth to join the maidservants in playing at guess-fingers, or competing at dominoes.

She talked, and she laughed,
with total abandon, guffawing raucously, heedless of whether anyone saw her or not. All she could think about was how to hook up with Ch'en Ching-chi, the thought of which produced turmoil in her heart and got her all hot and bothered, so that she:

Gave vent to long sighs as well as short,
propped her cheek upon her hand, and stared vacantly into space. She kept hoping that Ch'en Ching-chi would come back inside, so they could get down to business together, but what she did not realize was that he was on duty in the shop every day and didn't have time for such things. She would have liked to go out looking for him herself, but there were so many maidservants going back and forth that it was not convenient for her to do so. During the daylight hours, just like:

An ant on a hot plate,
she constantly:

Ran in and ran out,
without being content to sit in her quarters.

One day, when:

The breeze was genial and the sun was warm,[47]
Chin-lien enhanced her person with quantities of aromatic musk and liquid-ambar, walked out behind the summerhouse, and gazed longingly in the direction of the "snow cave." But Ch'en Ching-chi was doing his daily stint in the shop up front and was unable to get away and come into the garden. After gazing for a while without seeing him, all she could do was to return to her quarters:

Take her writing brush in hand,

and incant a few lines to herself before jotting them down in the form of a letter, sealing it, and giving it to Ch'un-mei to deliver to Ch'en Ching-chi.

When Ching-chi received it, he tore open the envelope and read it over from the beginning. It turned out to be not an ordinary letter, but the words of a song. When Ching-chi finished reading it, he was so flustered he dropped his business in the shop and rushed inside to the back of the summerhouse, where he proceeded to look around. Lo and behold, when Ch'un-mei had gone back to her quarters and reported to P'an Chin-lien, she lost no time in running out to the summerhouse herself, so the two of them ran into each other there. Just like someone whose:

> Hungry eyes have alighted on a melon skin,

she couldn't help throwing herself into Ching-chi's arms, pinching his cheeks, and giving him a succession of kisses, in the course of which they sucked each other's tongues so assiduously that the sound of the sucking was quite audible.

"You fickle short-life of a lousy jailbird!" she complained. "Ever since you had to leave after our rendezvous in my room was broken up by Hsiao-yü,[48] it's been some time since we've been able to meet. In the last few days, since your father-in-law went off to the Eastern Capital, I've been sitting on the k'ang all by myself, longing for you, with the tears streaming from my eyes. Do you mean to say that your ears haven't even gotten hot? I've been thinking things over carefully, and concluded that if you're going to be so fickle, even if you should desert me, I'd simply have to give you up. But when it comes to the crunch, I just can't let you go. It's the old story of:

> The fond female and the
> fickle lover,

only you seem to be completely devoid of feeling."

Just as they were beginning to get into it together, who could have anticipated that Meng Yü-lou should catch sight of what they were up to with her sardonic eye. When Chin-lien happened to look up and see that they were being observed, she responded by giving him a shove with her free hand that nearly knocked Ching-chi head over heels, and the two of them hastily went their separate ways. But no more of this.

Later that same day, Wu Yüeh-niang, Meng Yü-lou, and Li P'ing-erh were sitting together, when whom should they see but Tai-an, who came agitatedly running through the door, kowtowed upon seeing Yüeh-niang, and said, "Father is about to get back. I've been riding ahead on horseback, carrying the official tally authorizing the provision of fresh mounts at the relay stations along the way, which is why I've arrived ahead of him. By this time, he must be no more than twenty li from here."

"Have you had anything to eat?" asked Yüeh-niang.

"I had breakfast this morning," said Tai-an, "but I haven't had any lunch."

"Go to the kitchen and get something to eat," said Yüeh-niang, "and tell them to prepare some food for when the master gets home. At that time, our entire sisterhood of wives from all six chambers will go as a group to welcome him in the reception hall."

Truly:

> Though the poet may have grown old,
>> Ying-ying remains at hand;
> When the gentleman comes home again,
>> Yen-yen will bestir herself.[49]

The four of them engaged in idle chat for some time, when, before they knew it, Hsi-men Ch'ing arrived in front of the gate and dismounted from his sedan chair. The crowd of his wife and concubines welcomed him inside together. Hsi-men Ch'ing and Yüeh-niang exchanged greetings first, after which, Meng Yü-lou, Li P'ing-erh, and P'an Chin-lien greeted him in turn. When Hsi-men Ch'ing had finished exchanging the customary amenities about the weather with his wife and concubines from all six chambers, Shu-t'ung, Ch'in-t'ung, and Hua-t'ung also came in and kowtowed to the ladies, after which, they went to the kitchen to get something to eat.

Hsi-men Ch'ing told them in detail about the hardships he had encountered on the road, about how he had put up at Chai Ch'ien's residence, about Grand Preceptor Ts'ai Ching's lavish kindness the next day, and about how he had been invited to drinking parties day after day by various palace eunuchs.

He then asked Li P'ing-erh, "How has the child been doing all this time? And how have you been treating your own ailments? Have the medications prescribed for you by Dr. Jen Hou-ch'i proven to be at all effective? Although I made the trip to the Eastern Capital, I haven't been able to get our household affairs off my mind. And I haven't known how business has been going in my various shops. For all these reasons, I've been anxious to get home."

"Nothing has happened so far as the child is concerned," said Li P'ing-erh, "and as for my own state, after taking the prescribed medicine, I've been feeling somewhat better."

Yüeh-niang, on the one hand, directed everyone to help stow away the luggage, in addition to the gifts for the road he had received from Grand Preceptor Ts'ai Ching, while, on the other hand, she arranged to have a meal prepared for Hsi-men Ch'ing to eat. That evening, she also saw to it that wine was served in order to welcome Hsi-men Ch'ing back home from his trip. Hsi-men Ch'ing elected to spend that night, as well as the next, making two nights in all, in Yüeh-niang's quarters. Truly, their feelings of mutual affection were like:

> Encountering sweet rain after a prolonged draught, or
> Meeting an old acquaintance when traveling abroad.[50]

But there is no need to describe all of this.

The next day, Ch'en Ching-chi and Hsi-men Ta-chieh came to see him and discussed the accounts for the shop. When Ying Po-chüeh and Ch'ang Shih-chieh heard that he had returned home, they also came to see him.

When Hsi-men Ch'ing came out to greet them, the two of them said with one voice, "Brother, you must have had:

A hard time of it on the road."

Hsi-men Ch'ing told them in detail about the opulence of the Eastern Capital, and about the kindness with which he had been treated by the grand preceptor, to which the two of them responded by expressing no end of wonderment and admiration. That day, Hsi-men Ch'ing retained the two of them and drank with them all day.

When Ch'ang Shih-chieh, or Cadger Ch'ang, was on the verge of getting up to go, he said to Hsi-men Ch'ing, "I have a request I'd like to make of you, Brother, but I don't know whether you will accede to it or not."

As he spoke, he lowered his face:

Half choking on his words and half spitting them out.

"Pray express yourself without constraint," said Hsi-men Ch'ing.

"The fact is," said Cadger Ch'ang, "that the house I'm living in is not convenient, and I'd like to find another one to move into, but I don't have the necessary silver. For this reason, I'd like to ask you, Brother, if you'd be willing to help me out. At a future date, of course, Brother, I'd pay you back with interest."

"Among companions like ourselves," said Hsi-men Ch'ing, "what need is there to speak of interest? At the moment, however, I'm rather pressed for cash and have no way to come up with the silver. You'll have to wait until my manager, Han Tao-kuo, gets back with his boatload of goods. I should be able to manage it then."

When they had finished speaking, Cadger Ch'ang and Ying Po-chüeh expressed their thanks and departed. But no more of this.

To resume our story, when Miao Ch'ing met with Hsi-men Ch'ing in front of the grand preceptor's mansion, he had invited him to a party, and at the party he had promised to make him a present of the two singing boys. On a later day, Hsi-men Ch'ing had been:

Anxious to return as swiftly as an arrow,

and consequently had departed for home without saying goodbye to him. Thinking that Hsi-men Ch'ing was still in the capital, Miao Ch'ing sent one of his retainers to Chai Ch'ien's residence to ask after him, only to be told that His Honor Hsi-men Ch'ing had set out for home three days before.

Only after this retainer reported back to him did Miao Ch'ing understand what had happened, and he thought to himself, "As the saying goes:

A single word from a gentleman, is like

A single whip stroke to a swift steed.

Under the circumstances, if I don't give them to him, it really wouldn't matter, but if he should hold it against me, it would be hard to remain on speaking terms with him in the future."

Consequently, he called out the two singing boys and said to them, "The other day, when I invited His Honor Hsi-men Ch'ing from Shantung to come over for a drink, in the course of the party, I promised to make him a present of the two of you, but I find that he has already left the Eastern Capital to return home. It is, therefore, now my intention to send you to him there. You must pack up your things right away, so that, as soon as I've prepared a letter for him, I can send you on your way."

The two singing boys pled with him together, saying, "We have served you faithfully for some years already, so how can you now consent to get rid of us so callously? Besides, we don't know a thing about the disposition of this Honorable Hsi-men Ch'ing. We hope that you will make an appropriate decision on our behalf."

"You don't know it," said Miao Ch'ing, "but the household of His Honor Hsi-men Ch'ing is possessed of:

Wealth enough to splash against the sky,
and is:

Copiously supplied with gold and silver.
The position he occupies:

Combines both civil and military duties.
And at present he has been acknowledged as an adopted son under the patronage of Grand Preceptor Ts'ai Ching. Even among the palace eunuchs and court officials there are few who are not on intimate terms with him. Out of his home he operates two shops selling silk and satin piece goods, and currently he is also thinking of opening a commercial armed escort service for the protection of goods in transit. The profits he takes in from these enterprises are truly incalculable. Moreover, he is:

Good-natured and agreeable in disposition,[51]
given to:

Saluting the breeze and invoking the moon.[52]
In his home he supports some seventy or eighty maidservants, every one of which is:

Dressed in satins and affects a jacket;
while in his inner apartments he has at his disposal some five or six wives, every one of which is:

Studded with pearls and draped in gold.
Each one of the boy actors and adult troupers that he patronizes borrows money from him and does his bidding. Virtually all of the courtesans from the different streets of the licensed quarter are also the recipients of his favor. All of this goes without saying. The problem is that at that drinking party the other day I promised to make him a present of the two of you, and now you can hardly expect me to go back on my word."

To this the singing boys responded by saying, "Master, over the last few years, who knows how much effort you have expended in training us to play music and sing; and now that we have finally begun to master our stringed instruments, rather than keeping us at home for your own enjoyment, how can you bring yourself to give us away to minister to the pleasure of someone else?"

When they had finished speaking, before they knew it, with a gush, the tears began to flow from their eyes.

Miao Ch'ing, who also felt himself to be:

> Wretched and unhappy,[53]

said, "My little ones, what you say is true enough. I also have wondered why I should feel compelled to do such a thing. But:

> If a man is untrustworthy,
> How can that be tolerated?[54]

I can scarcely disregard these words, uttered by the sage Confucius himself. Under the present circumstances, there is nothing you can do about it. I'll depute a retainer to escort you there, and write a letter enjoining him to look upon you with a favorable eye. When you get there, you'll have an even happier time of it than you've had in my service here."

He then had his private secretary draft a conventional letter inquiring about the health of the recipient on eight-columned note paper, to which he appended the fact that he was sending him the singing boys and asked him to look favorably upon them. He also had him write out a list of presents, including a bolt of silk and the customary book and kerchief, to serve as indications of his good will, and ordered his servants, Miao Hsiu and Miao Shih, to take charge of these documents, and escort the two singing boys on their journey. In no time at all, their mounts were saddled, and, taking their bags of bedding and luggage with them, they set out for the home of Hsi-men Ch'ing in Shantung.

At the time of their departure, they were unable to suppress their feelings, with the result that:

> The tears dripped down their cheeks.[55]

But since:

> A master's order is hard to disobey,

there was no alternative, so:

> Just as though inserting a taper in its holder,

they kowtowed several times, bade Miao Ch'ing farewell:

> Vaulted onto their horses,

and proceeded to wend their way forward. Behold:

> Blue mountains encompass the horse's head,
> Green waters surround the traveler's whip;
> A wine flag is visible deep in the forest,
> Before a thatched hut among sunset clouds.

> Only due to the fact that,
> Diverting the moving clouds,
> The sound of their singing is peerless;

Before they are aware of it,
They must leave a kind master,
To brave the winds and mists of a trip.
The two of them,
Longing for home and thinking of their master,
Have taken the,
Romantic overtones of sandalwood clappers,
The classic tunes "Warm Spring" and "White Snow,"[56]
And completely forgotten them.
The two of them,
Hasting to their goal and speeding on their way,
Think only of,
The early accomplishment of their mission,
Enveloped in stars, proceeding by moonlight,[57]
Forgetting to sleep at night.

Truly:

In the morning they were gifted singing boys
    in Miao Ch'ing's residence;
But by evening they were merely entertainers
    in the Hsi-men establishment.

Gazing into the distance, they observed that there was a wine flag suspended deep in a forest of green trees before them.

One of the boy-singers said to the other, "Brother, we've been traveling all
day long and are getting rather hungry. Let's stop for a cup of wine before
going any further."

Lo and behold, the four of them promptly:

Rolled out of their saddles,[58]

and walked into the wine shop. On the signboard were displayed two lines
that put it very well:

Spirits and immortals have deposited
    their jade girdles;
Ministers and councilors have pawned
    their golden sables.[59]

Truly, it was a fine wine shop.

The four of them sat down and called for the waiter, telling him, "Draw us
two ewers of wine, pound some scallions and garlic, and serve us a large side
of pork, together with a few saucers of bean curd and other side dishes."

Just as they were about to:

Unburden themselves and drink lustily,

all of a sudden they happened to look around and saw that on the whitewashed
wall there were two columns of characters in "flying white"[60] calligraphy, that
read:

A thousand li is not a great distance,
To return after ten years is not late.
So long as we remain in this universe,
Why need we mourn over our separation?

When the eyes of the two singing boys were confronted with these sentiments,
they couldn't help feeling affected by them, like:
    The apothecary who finds himself to be ill.
Before they knew it, with a gush, two rows of tears began to flow from their
eyes.
    One of them said to the other, "Brother, we served Squire Miao faithfully,
in the expectation that we'd remain together till the end, like:
    A plant-stem that reaches all the way to the ground.[61]
Who would have thought that in the course of a drinking party:
    With a single word or a couple of sentences,[62]
he would casually give us away to someone else?
    People away from home are at a disadvantage.[63]
Who knows what will happen to us after leaving him?"
    Miao Hsiu and Miao Shih attempted to reassure them with soothing words
for a while, after which, having eaten a meal, they remounted their horses
and resumed their journey.
    What with their:
    Four horses, and
    Sixteen hooves,
they made decidedly good progress. In no more than a few days, they arrived
in the vicinity of Ch'ing-ho district in Tung-p'ing prefecture. The four of them,
after dismounting and tethering their horse, inquired for directions and eventually found their way to Hsi-men Ch'ing's residence on Amethyst Street.
    To resume our story, ever since Hsi-men Ch'ing had returned home from
the Eastern Capital, he had been kept busy every day by people sending gifts
to him, or inviting him to parties, so that day after day was spent carousing
with his:
    Three friends and four companions.
Not only did Wu Yüeh-niang provide an entertainment to welcome him back
from his trip, but he was also obliged to resume intimate relations with each
of his concubines in their various quarters, so that, for days on end, he was:
    Entranced by the clouds and intoxicated by the rain.
For this reason, he had not even reported to the yamen, or canceled the cer-
tificate entitling him to time off from his official duties.
    On this particular day, finding himself at leisure, he went to the yamen,
where he took his place on the bench, held roll call, reheard the cases of all
the defendants who had been brought to court for the crimes of rape, assault,
gambling, or larceny, and took the time to sign the documents that had accu-

mulated during his absence. He then got into an open sedan chair and headed for home, escorted by a number of jailers who shouted to clear the way.

Whom should he see upon his arrival but Miao Hsiu, Miao Shih, and the two singing boys, who had been waiting at the gate for some time and now followed his sedan chair to the front reception hall, where they got down on their knees and explained, "We come from Squire Miao Ch'ing of Yang-chou and are the bearers of a letter asking after Your Honor's health."

Having kowtowed to him, they got up and stood to one side. Hsi-men Ch'ing, after acknowledging their salutation by raising his hand, and telling them to get up, spent some time running through the customary formalities of inquiring about Squire Miao's doings since they parted, and discussing the weather. He then summoned Shu-t'ung and had him cut open the protective outer envelope with a pair of silver scissors, after which he tore open the inner envelope, unfolded the enclosed note, and carefully perused it.

What should he observe at this juncture but Miao Hsiu and Miao Shih, who got down on their knees as before, in order to present the numerous gifts they had brought with them, saying, "These are just a few tokens of our squire's filial sentiments, which we beg that Your Honor will deign to accept."

Hsi-men Ch'ing, who was:

Unable to contain his delight,

promptly told Tai-an to take charge of the gifts, while he invited Miao Hsiu and Miao Shih to get up, saying, "Who would have thought that when your master and I:

Encountered each other a thousand li from home,[64]

Our feelings were genial, our thoughts in accord,

to such an extent that the squire, in his boundless good will, promised to make me a present of these singing boys? Thinking at the time that these were merely:

Words uttered in his cups,

I had long since forgotten them. Because I was anxious to get home without delay, I failed to call upon him in order to say goodbye. And now, just as I was thinking about this, who would have thought that, for the squire:

A word of assent is worth a thousand pieces of gold,[65]

so that, even at a distance, he has remembered his promise. I recall that among famous examples of fidelity between men of yore, the pledge of friendship that led Fan Shih to honor his promise to visit Chang Shao at an appointed time though they were a thousand li apart,[66] in both ancient and modern times:

Is considered to be an exemplary tale.[67]

And nowadays, truly, men such as this squire of yours are not easily come by."

Praising his strong points and acclaiming his virtue,

he continued expressing his gratitude in fulsome detail for some time.

Lo and behold, at this juncture, the two singing boys once again approached him and kowtowed several times, saying, "The squire enjoined us to serve Your Honor faithfully and expressed the hope that you would look upon us with a favorable eye."

Hsi-men Ch'ing observed that the two singing boys were clean-cut in appearance, and truly:

> Both slender and seductive.

Although they may not have been females, who:

> Wear their clothes in two pieces;[68]

they were superior to mere girls, whose:

> Lips are red and teeth are white.[69]

Hsi-men Ch'ing felt:

> As though nothing in Heaven or Earth could
> > make him happier,

and celebrated the occasion by inviting his four managers to a party in the front reception hall. On the one hand, he prepared generous gifts of silks and satins and other valuables, and wrote a letter to thank Squire Miao for his consideration, while, on the other hand, he had a room prepared for the two singing boys and told them that he would expect them to wait upon him in his studio.

Lo and behold, when Ying Po-chüeh and company:

> Got wind of this affair, and
> Were apprised of this event,

they all came to see for themselves. Hsi-men Ch'ing accordingly told Tai-an to obtain some dishes of food, appetizers, snacks, and new wine from the rear compound, and lay them out on an Eight Immortals table for the entertainment of his guests. In the course of the proceedings, he called upon the two singing boys to come out and sing for them.

Lo and behold:

> Holding up their sandalwood clappers,

they started to sing, performing a song suite beginning with the tune "Fresh Water Song":

> In the little garden last night
> > the river plum blossomed,
> Bringing with it an intoxicating
> > aura of a different kind.
> I welcome the smiles of the pear blossom,
> But envy the lissome waist of the willow,
> And inquire of the rose-leaved raspberry,
> If it blooms till the crab apple flowers.

To the tune "Stopping the Horse to Listen":

> Over the sparse hedge along the country road,
> Gust after gust of fragrant breeze
> > attracts the swallows.
> By the secluded paving in the little garden,
> Flurry after flurry of clearing rain
> > moves past the woods.

Her fragrant heart remains undetected
   by the butterflies;
Her subtle fragrance has not yet been
   scented by the bees.
As she leans over every balustrade,
Who knows how many heartbreaking thoughts
   she is beset by?

To the binary tunes "Wild Geese Alight" and "Victory Song":

Lo and behold: in the azure shade, Hsi Shih
   knits her brows.
With red drops, petals are stained by the
   cuckoo's pearly tears;
Dancing about, sprigs of flowers adorn
   shiny silken caps;
Fluttering airily, blossoms cascade down
   before the belvedere.

As ever, their fragrant aura permeates
   one's garments;
But their alluring forms are easily
   soiled in the mud.
Where they fall the fish are startled;
As they flutter hither, the butterflies
   become confused.
She wonders to herself,
"To whom can I entrust my yearning?"
And sorrows that,
The Peach Blossom Spring remains
   beyond her reach.

Hsi-men Ch'ing nodded with approval and exclaimed, "Sure enough, your singing is superb."

The two singing boys made a half obeisance by falling to one knee before him and said, "We've also learned the words to a set of four lyrics, which we can perform for you while we're at it, if you like."

"That would be even better," said Hsi-men Ch'ing, and directed them to proceed. To the tune "The Whole River Is Red":

Tearing off a strip of Shantung silk,
With the aid of pigments and backing,
One depicts the scene of a herd boy in the spring.
The grass is short,
Spread out evenly over the level fields.

He sits idly on his brown water buffalo calf.
With a tattered volume in one hand, perched securely
   on the buffalo's back,
He sounds a few notes on his short flute, while
   traversing the emerald mist.
Thinking to indite a verse to go with the picture,
   one tries to compose a new lyric,
Putting the imagination to work.

If the composition is good enough,
It may be preserved in the Palace Library.
If the tune is sufficiently catchy,
It may be set to woodwinds and strings.
If sung without accompaniment,
Though the classic tune "Warm Spring" is hard to match,
The connoisseurs of a generation
   may yet praise it.
It will appeal to every taste, and people may
   compete to transcribe it.
If one can only emulate the master who imagined
   the writing of the "Kao-t'ang fu,"[70]
The sentiment of the lyric will suffice.

To the same tune:

One delineates a scene of summer plowing.
Beyond the suburban plain,
The paths between the fields run east and west.[71]
The village commons are irregular,
Encircled by the turquoise hues of the hills.
The embankments and dikes are interconnected.
The color green pervades the enclosed fields,
   teeming with millet and rice.
The ears of wheat are densely clustered;
   silkworms fill their frames.
And there also appears to be a stream
   circling the wattled gate,
By the sheer slopes of the hills.

Someone is leaning on a bamboo staff,
Skirting the hills and valleys,
Traversing the woods and marshes,
Listening to the gibbons and cranes.
His son is plowing, his wife brings a hamper,
As they cooperate in the work of cultivation.

The tall trees provide ample shade where
    they settle down to rest.
Stroking their bulging bellies, they relax
    by stretching out their feet.
If one can only emulate the master who imagined
    the composing of the "Airs of Pin,"[72]
The pleasures of rural life will be conveyed.

To the same tune:

When one has finished applying the colors,
The new picture turns out well,
Embellished as it is with streams and hills.
Faintly discernible,
There are sand spits beyond the riverbanks,
Green clover fern and red smartweed.
A stream of autumn light seems to connect
    the shorelines.
A figure in a short rain cape and bamboo hat
    is perceptible amid misty waves,
Trying to estimate how many fresh fish
    he has netted by this time;
But the perch are small.

Fishermen's songs arise,
Flying geese are remote,
The river moon is white,
Returning clouds are few.
Leaning by his matted window, he looks out for,
His sworn friends, the sea gulls.
One is tempted to ask how the forgotten
    concerns of the past,
Can be compared with the tranquillity of
    his present situation.
If one can only emulate the master who imagined,
    the singing of the song "Blue Waters,"[73]
One will rise above the dust of the world.

To the same tune:

On all sides the clouds are lowering;
The frozen flakes scatter,
Evenly covering the thatched dwelling.
The red brazier is warm,

In which his wife is baking sweet potatoes.
Pouring out vintage wine for himself,
The cottager tasks a servant to fetch fuel
    from outside the gate,
And calls to his son, who is playing with
    a crane in the courtyard.
If one can succeed in capturing this scene,
    and conveying it in a picture,[74]
It will gladden the mind's eye.

Wealth and distinction,
Are bestowed by Heaven;
To keep clear of excess,
Is one's only ambition.
Giving beauty and wonder free expression,
One adorns the scroll with fine lyrics.
Fearing lest one's own talent for poetic
    effusions be lacking,
One gives way to one whose literary devices
    are up to the task.
If one can only emulate the master who imagined
    the joys of "mulberry and elm,"[75]
One's countenance will be like jade.[76]

Sure enough:

    Their tones divert the moving clouds;[77]
    Their songs create a new "White Snow."

The quality of their performance induced the ladies from the rear compound, Wu Yüeh-niang, Meng Yü-lou, P'an Chin-lien, and Li P'ing-erh, to come and listen. They were all exceedingly delighted by it and exclaimed, "How well they sing!"

Lo and behold, from her vantage point amid the crowd, P'an Chin-lien focused her gaze directly on the two singing boys and quietly muttered to herself, "These two youngsters not only sing well, but, in appearance, they are as handsome as can be."

In her heart, she had already registered something of a partiality for them.

At the time, Hsi-men Ch'ing arranged for the two singing boys to stay in an anteroom on the eastern side of the front courtyard. On the one hand, he directed that a meal should be provided for Miao Hsiu and Miao Shih, while, on the other hand, he prepared appropriate presents, and a reply, expressing his gratitude to Squire Miao Ch'ing.

    If you want to know the outcome of these events,
    Pray consult the story related in the following chapter.

Chapter 56

HSI-MEN CH'ING ASSISTS CH'ANG SHIH-CHIEH;

YING PO-CHÜEH RECOMMENDS LICENTIATE SHUI

Those who endeavor to amass gold by the peck, emulating
    the luxury of the "untitled nobility,"[1]
Are as deluded as was Chuang Chou in the dream in which
    he imagined himself to be a butterfly.[2]
One has heard tell that the magnificence of the Citadel
    at Mei proved difficult to perpetuate;[3]
Who would have thought that the wealth extracted from
    the Copper Mountains could be exhausted?[4]
Nowadays Pao Shu-ya is praised for the way in which he
    divided the proceeds with Kuan Chung;[5]
In former times P'ang Yün was laughed at for choosing
    to sink his entire fortune in the sea.[6]
As one approaches the inevitable end of life's journey,
    who can be said to be a bosom friend?
It is only such a noble friend who can continue to pay
    due honor to the customs of antiquity.

THE BURDEN of the above eight lines of regulated verse is simply that:
    For humans residing in this world,[7]
    Glory and luxury, wealth and honor,
cannot be retained forever. One fine day, when:
    Impermanence, or death, visits you,[8]
no matter how much you may have in the way of:
    Piled up gold and accumulated jade,[9]
you will wind up:
    Returning to the shades empty-handed.
Because Hsi-men Ch'ing was so:
    Chivalrous by nature and open-handed with his wealth,
as well as being:
    Willing to lend aid to those in poverty and distress,
everyone sang his praises. But no more of this.

    That day, Hsi-men Ch'ing retained the two singing boys to await his pleasure, telling them, "When I have occasion to call upon you:

You must not be disobedient."[10]

The two of them nodded their assent and withdrew.

He then saw to the preparation of a reply and return gifts to entrust to the retainers from the Miao household, and he also rewarded them with some silver. Miao Shih and Miao Hsiu kowtowed to him in gratitude and then made their departure.

Later on, because Hsi-men Ch'ing found no use for the two singing boys, he ended up making a present of them to the grand preceptor's household. Truly:

> When one has spent thousands in gold[11] teaching
>> her how to sing and dance;
> One must bequeath her to someone else to provide
>> pleasure during his youth.[12]

To resume our story, Ch'ang Shih-chieh, or Cadger Ch'ang, from the time he had asked for Hsi-men Ch'ing's assistance at the party on a previous occasion, did not yet have anything to show for it. Moreover, day and night, his landlord had been pressing him incessantly for his arrears. It so happened that, ever since Hsi-men Ch'ing had come home from the Eastern Capital, he had been invited out to parties to celebrate his return day after day, so that ten days in a row had gone by without Cadger Ch'ang's having a chance to meet with him. As the saying goes:

> Even when people meet face to face, it is
>> hard to express everything.

If one cannot even arrange a meeting, to whom is one to make an appeal? Every day, he asked Ying Po-chüeh to accompany him in going to Hsi-men Ch'ing's front gate and asking after him; only to be told that he was not at home, and having to return empty-handed.

Moreover, when he arrived home, his wife berated him, saying, "You claim to be a male of the species, a man of mettle, and yet you don't even have a house to call your own and have to put up with all this annoyance. You customarily boast of your friendship with His Honor Hsi-men Ch'ing, yet today, when you ask a favor of him, it's like a pitcher falling into the water."

She railed at Cadger Ch'ang so effectively that:

> Though he had a mouth he was left speechless,

and could only stare vacantly into space, without daring to utter a word.

The next day, he got up early, sought out Ying Po-chüeh, and invited him to join him in a visit to a wine shop. What should they see there but a small thatched hut, situated by a bend in a flowing stream.[13] In front of the door, amid the shade of the green trees, a wine flag was visible, and five or seven workers were seen to be busily engaged in carrying in supplies of wine and meat. Across the front of the shop there was a counter, over which there were suspended fresh fish, geese, ducks, and the like. It was really a nice clean place to sit, so he invited Ying Po-chüeh to share three cups of wine with him in the shop.

"I really ought not to put you to the trouble," demurred Ying Po-chüeh, but Cadger Ch'ang dragged him into the shop, and they sat down together.

The waiter measured out some wine for them and laid out a platter of smoked pork, and a platter of fresh fish.

After:

>Two rounds of wine had been consumed,

Cadger Ch'ang said, "With regard to that matter that I have asked you to speak to His Honor Hsi-men Ch'ing about, for some days now we haven't been able to arrange a meeting with him. Meantime, my landlord has been pressing me hard for my arrears, and last evening my wife bickered with me about it for half the night. Not being able to put up with it anymore, I extricated myself at the fifth watch this morning, only to implore you, Brother, to join me in taking advantage of the earliness of the hour to wait patiently outside his gate and waylay him before he goes out. What do you think of this proposal, Brother?"

Ying Po-chüeh replied:

>"Once one has acceded to someone's request,
>It is imperative to see the job through to the end.[14]

Today, for better or for worse, I'll make sure that His Honor helps you out, that's all there is to it."

The two of them shared another few cups of wine, after which Ying Po-chüeh protested, "We'd better not drink any more so early in the morning."

Cadger Ch'ang urged him to have another cup, after which he settled the score, and they left together, going straight to the residence of Hsi-men Ch'ing.

At that time, it was early in the fall, and:

>The metallic autumn wind was brisk.

Hsi-men Ch'ing, who had gotten drunk for several days in a row and was feeling somewhat under the weather, had received yet another invitation to a drinking party from Eunuch Director Chou, which he had found some pretext for refusing. Instead, he was relaxing in the Hidden Spring Grotto in his garden.

It so happens that the Hidden Spring Grotto in the rear of Hsi-men Ch'ing's garden was surrounded by fruit-bearing trees and fresh flowers, which:

>Flourished throughout the four seasons.

At this time, although it was early autumn, an incalculable number of flowers were blooming in the garden. Hsi-men Ch'ing, being at home with nothing to do, was enjoying himself in the flower garden with Wu Yüeh-niang, Meng Yü-lou, P'an Chin-lien, and Li P'ing-erh, five of them in all. On his head, Hsi-men Ch'ing wore a "loyal and tranquil hat." On his body he wore a long gown of willow-green moiré, and white-soled boots. Yüeh-niang was wearing a willow-green jacket of Hang-chou chiffon that opened down the middle, over a light blue skirt of water-patterned pongee, and gold-red phoenix-toed, high-heeled shoes. Meng Yü-lou was wearing a raven-black satin jacket, over a skirt of gosling-yellow pongee, and peach-red high-heeled shoes of plain silk with purfled gold-spangled edging. P'an Chin-lien was wearing a pink crepe blouse that opened down the middle with a white chiffon lining, and a vest of gold-red material with a bright green border, over a skirt of white Hang-chou chiffon with a decorated border, and high-heeled shoes of pink patterned silk. Only Li P'ing-erh was wearing a wide-lapelled jacket of plain blue Hang-chou chiffon, a skirt of finished pale blue moon-colored chiffon, and light blue plain silk high-heeled shoes. The four of them:

Seductively and bewitchingly,

kept Hsi-men Ch'ing company while he enjoyed himself:

Scanning the flowers and inspecting the willows.[15]

To resume our story, when Cadger Ch'ang and Ying Po-chüeh got as far as the reception hall and learned that His Honor was at home, they sat down happily and waited for what seemed like half a day, but no one appeared. What should they see at this juncture but Shu-t'ung and Hua-t'ung, who came in the gate from outside, panting for breath, and carrying a trunk full of satin and chiffon clothing.

Calling out agitatedly, "We waited half a day and were only able to pick up half the order," they set the trunk down in the reception hall.

"Where has your master gotten to?" Ying Po-chüeh asked them.

"Father is in the garden enjoying himself," replied Shu-t'ung.

"May I trouble you to say a word to him?" said Ying Po-chüeh.

The two of them, carrying the trunk as before, then proceeded inside.

Before long, Shu-t'ung came out and said, "Father requests Master Ying the Second and Uncle Ch'ang the Second to wait a bit. He'll be right out."

The two of them sat down and waited a while longer before Hsi-men Ch'ing finally came out. After they had saluted him with a bow, they were asked to resume their seats.

"For days on end, it seems," said Ying Po-chüeh, "Brother has been so busy attending drinking parties that he hasn't had any time to himself. How do you happen to be at home today?"

"Ever since the last time I saw you," said Hsi-men Ch'ing, "I've been invited out to drinking parties every day and have been as drunk as can be, which has left me completely enervated. I was invited out to another party today, but I concocted a pretext for not going."

"Where did that trunkful of clothing that was carried in just now come from?" asked Ying Po-chüeh.

"At the present time, autumn has already begun," said Hsi-men Ch'ing, "and everyone needs to be supplied with autumn clothing. That trunkful just now was for your senior sister-in-law, but they haven't finished completing the order. That was only the first half of it."

Cadger Ch'ang stuck out his tongue in disbelief and said, "In that case the six chambers of my sisters-in-law will require six trunkloads. What a lot of expense that will entail. As for such mean folk as ourselves, we can hardly afford a single bolt of cotton. The fact that you can arrange to have so many clothes of satin and chiffon made up for you is an indication, Brother, that you have become a real plutocrat."

This remark induced a fit of laughter on the part of Hsi-men Ch'ing and Ying Po-chüeh.

"How is it," asked Ying Po-chüeh, "that during these last few days your boatload of goods from Hang-chou has not yet been seen to arrive? I wonder how the business is going. As for that money that you promised the other day to Li the Third and Huang the Fourth, you agreed that when the money owed you by Hsü the Fourth outside the gate came into your hands, you would use it to make up the sum you promised to turn over to them."

"That boatload of goods," said Hsi-men Ch'ing, "seems to have been delayed somewhere or other, and they haven't even sent me a letter about it. It's a real cause for concern. As far as the money for Li the Third and Huang the Fourth is concerned, I have done as you suggested."

Ying Po-chüeh moved his seat closer to that of Hsi-men Ch'ing and took advantage of the occasion to say, "Regarding that matter that Brother Ch'ang the Second besought your help about the other day, you have been so busy since then that he hasn't had a chance to speak to you about it. Brother Ch'ang the Second's landlord has been pressing him so hard for his arrears that he is being driven to distraction. His wife, too, is berating him about it every day, so that he has been reduced to paralysis and doesn't know what to do. Right now, the autumn days are getting colder, and the fur coat he would normally wear is in hock in the pawnshop. Brother, if you are goodhearted about it, as the saying goes:

> If you want to help someone, you must do it
> when they need it the most.[16]

That would also spare him the:

> Incessant bickering,[17]

that his wife subjects him to in their room, day and night. What is more, if he can find a proper house to live in, the figure that he cuts in society will only serve to enhance your prestige. For this reason, Brother Ch'ang the Second has asked me to come here for the sole purpose of beseeching you to come to his assistance as soon as possible."

"I originally promised him that I would do so," said Hsi-men Ch'ing. "But, because my trip to the Eastern Capital cost me a lot of silver, I had planned to wait until Manager Han Tao-kuo returned from his excursion before taking care of it. Since he is in need of a house, I will weigh out the silver required for him to buy it if it is now such an urgent matter."

"It's not so much an urgent matter for Brother Ch'ang the Second," said Ying Po-chüeh, "as it is that he can't stand his wife's nagging. That is why he feels compelled to ask you to take care of it as soon as possible."

Hsi-men Ch'ing hesitated for some time before saying, "If that's the case, it won't be all that difficult. Let me ask you, though, how much of a house will suffice for him to live in?"

"The two of them," responded Ying Po-chüeh, "will need a front room opening onto the street, a sitting room for the entertainment of guests, a bedroom, and a kitchen, those four rooms at a minimum. As for the price, it will certainly amount to more than three or four taels of silver. Brother, see if you can't, sooner or later, get together an appropriate amount, and enable him to complete this transaction."

"Today," said Hsi-men Ch'ing, "I'll give him a few pieces of loose silver to start off with. He can use them to buy himself a coat, purchase some furniture, and take care of his current expenses. After he has located a suitable house for himself, of course I'll weigh out the required amount of silver for him, so that he can complete the transaction. How would that be?"

The two of them thanked him with one voice, saying, "Brother, such good-heartedness is a rare thing."

Hsi-men Ch'ing then called for Shu-t'ung and told him, "Go ask the First Lady for the packet of loose silver in the leather case, and bring it back with you."

Shu-t'ung nodded assent and went off on his errand. Before long he came back out with a packet of silver and handed it to Hsi-men Ch'ing.

Hsi-men Ch'ing said to Cadger Ch'ang, "This packet of loose silver contains twelve taels of silver left over from the sealed envelopes containing tips that I took with me on my visit to the grand preceptor's mansion in the Eastern Capital. You take them and use them for your miscellaneous expenses."

He then opened up the packet and showed the contents to Cadger Ch'ang, which consisted entirely of loose lumps of inscribed silver weighing three to five mace apiece. Cadger Ch'ang accepted them, put them in the sleeve of his gown, and bowed his thanks.

"These last few days," said Hsi-men Ch'ing, "it has not been my intention to delay the fulfillment of my promise. I have only been waiting for you to locate a suitable house, at which time I would complete the transaction with you at one stroke. And you haven't located a house yet. Right now, you should do your best to locate one as soon as possible, and then, when I have the silver in hand, I'll be prepared to weigh it out for you, that's all."

Cadger Ch'ang, once again, expressed his gratitude repeatedly. The three of them sat down as before, and Ying Po-chüeh said, "There are numerous cases among the men of old who:

Hsi-men Ch'ing Comes to the Assistance of Cadger Ch'ang

Disdained wealth and practiced philanthropy,[18]
in which, later on, their descendants succeeded in:
Enhancing the height and size of their gates,[19]
significantly increasing the estates of their ancestors. Among the stingy, on the
other hand, who were only interested in accumulating gold and valuables for
themselves, there are many cases in which, later on, their descendants turned
out badly, and not even the graves of their ancestors were preserved. From
this it is clear that:
The Way of Heaven favors reversion."[20]
"Money," said Hsi-men Ch'ing, "is something which:
Likes movement and dislikes inertia.
It will not allow itself to be immured in any one place. And it is designed by
Heaven for human use. For every person who accumulates a surplus there
will be another who suffers a deficiency. It is very wrong, therefore, merely to
pile up wealth and valuables."
There is a poem that testifies to this:

There are those who are not happy unless they can
accumulate jade and pile up gold;[21]
They remain unaware that wealth and valuables are
merely the roots of catastrophe.
They treasure every single cash as though it were
a part of their flesh and blood;
While those who are chivalrous by nature can only
laugh at them for their inanity.
They treat each one of their relatives and friends
as if they were total strangers;
They preserve a facade, but their hearts are dead,
which is certainly regrettable.
One can anticipate that one fine day impermanence,
or death, will pay them a visit;
And they will proceed, empty-handed and all alone,
to the abode of everlasting night.

As they were speaking, who should appear but Shu-t'ung, who brought out
some refreshments for them. When they had finished eating, Cadger Ch'ang
thanked his host, stood up to go, and went happily home with the silver tucked
in his sleeve.
He had scarcely entered the door, when his wife came noisily out to meet
him and berated him in a strident voice, saying:
"When the leaves fall off the phoenix tree,[22]
Nothing is left but a trunk of 'bare sticks.'
You good-for-nothing! You've been gone the whole day, leaving your wife to
starve at home. And now you come back with:

A thousand or ten thousand signs of joy.[23]
How can you be anything but ashamed of yourself? You don't have a house
to call your own, which only elicits the contumely of our neighbors, but you
leave it to the ears of your wife to suffer their abuse."

Cadger Ch'ang did not even open his mouth but waited until his wife had
finished her tirade before gently groping the silver out of his sleeve and placing
it on the table.

Opening up the packet and gazing at it, he said, "My 'square-holed brothers'! My 'square-holed brothers'![24] You are truly:

A priceless treasure,

and when I contemplate your shining and jingling qualities:

My whole body turns numb with delight.[25]

I only wish I could swallow you whole, like a mouthful of water. If you had
only come my way a little earlier, I wouldn't have had to put up with all the
quarreling this whore has subjected me to."

When the woman clearly saw that there was a pile of twelve or thirteen
taels of silver in the packet, she started forward in her excitement, as though
she intended to seize it from the hands of her old man.

"You're congenitally given to abusing your husband," exclaimed Cadger
Ch'ang, "but, no sooner do you see silver in the picture, than you want to
cozy up to him. Tomorrow, I'll take this silver to buy a new outfit of clothes
for myself, and go live somewhere else, so I won't have to fool around with
you anymore."

Putting a smile on her face, the woman said, "My dear, where did it ever
come from, all this silver?"

Cadger Ch'ang did not deign to reply.

"My dear," the woman went on to say, "no doubt you resent all I've had to
say to you. But my only desire has been for your success. Now that you have
the silver, we ought to discuss what to do, buy a house for ourselves, and settle
down. Wouldn't that be the best thing to do, instead of carrying on like this?
As your wife, I haven't been remiss in any way. You can resent me if you like,
but it isn't just."

Cadger Ch'ang, again, did not deign to open his mouth.

The woman continued to chatter away, but, when she noticed that Cadger
Ch'ang was not paying any attention to her, she began to feel some compunction about the situation and couldn't help giving way to tears.

When Cadger Ch'ang saw this, he sighed, saying, "For a woman, who:

Neither plows nor weaves,[26]

you certainly give your old man a hard time!"

At this, the woman wept even more copiously, and the two of them lapsed
into silence. There being no one there to admonish them to make up, they
simply sat there, sunk in depression.

Cadger Ch'ang with Silver in Hand Lords It over His Wife

Finally, Cadger Ch'ang thought to himself, "It is not easy to be a woman. She has had to put up with a lot of hardship and can hardly be blamed if she resents me for it. Now that I have some silver today, if I don't pay her any attention, people will say that I'm hardhearted. Even His Honor, if he finds out about it, will judge me to be in the wrong."

Turning to the woman with a smile, he said, "I was only having some fun with you. I don't hold anything against you, it's just that you're constantly nagging me. This morning, I couldn't stand it any longer, so I made a point of inviting Brother Ying the Second to join me for three cups of wine in a tavern, and then accompany me on a visit to His Honor's place. Providentially, he happened to be at home and had not gone out drinking anywhere. It was only thanks to the efforts of Brother Ying the Second, who gave his lips and tongue a real workout on my behalf, that I ended up with this silver in hand. And he also elicited a promise from His Honor that when we find a house, he will weigh out the necessary silver in order to close the deal for us. These twelve taels, he told me, were merely an advance that we can use to cover our daily expenses."

"So it turns out that this is really a gift to you from His Honor," the woman said. "We mustn't allow it to be wasted. You must find a winter coat for yourself, in order to fend off the cold."

"That's just what I wanted to discuss with you," said Cadger Ch'ang. "If we use these twelve taels of incised silver to buy a few items of clothing, and a few articles of furniture, once we have a new house to move into, we'll look a little better off. We can't thank His Honor enough for his generosity. On a later day, when we have moved into our new house, we'll have to invite him over for a visit."

"We'll have to wait until the time comes," said the woman. "We can decide what to do then."

Truly:

> It has always been true that gratitude for kindness
> and festering resentment;
> Even in a thousand or ten thousand years
> will never be allowed to gather dust.

After Cadger Ch'ang and his wife had talked things over for a while, the woman asked, "Did you have anything to eat while you were over there?"

"I did have something to eat at His Honor's place," said Cadger Ch'ang. "If you haven't had anything to eat, let's take some of this silver and buy some rice with it."

"Be careful how you keep that packet of silver fastened up," the woman said. "I'll wait for you. Come back right away."

Cadger Ch'ang took a wicker basket and went out onto the street. Before long, when he came back after buying the rice, there was also a large hunk of mutton lying in the basket.

When he came rushing back, laughing out loud, the woman met him in the doorway and said, "This hunk of mutton! What on earth did you buy that for?"

"Just now you were complaining about all the hardships you had suffered," said Cadger Ch'ang with a smile. "Not to mention this bit of mutton, I really ought to have had several oxen slaughtered in order to treat you."

"You heartless louse!" the woman scolded Cadger Ch'ang with a laugh. "Today I'll just store up the resentment in my heart and wait to see how you treat me in the future."

"I can foresee," said Cadger Ch'ang, "that one of these days, though you may plead with me ten thousand times, saying, 'Darling, spare this little whore of yours,' I'll refuse to spare you. Just try your luck and see."

When the woman heard this, she merely laughed while she went out to the well to draw some water.

There and then, the woman cooked up some rice, cut up a bowl of mutton, and placed them on the table, saying, "Come have something to eat, dear."

"I've already eaten at His Honor's place," said Cadger Ch'ang. "I don't want anything. You're as hungry as can be. Just help yourself."

The woman then proceeded to eat it all up by herself, and clear away the utensils, before sending Cadger Ch'ang out to buy the clothes.

Cadger Ch'ang put the silver in his sleeve and headed straight for Main Street, where he looked over the wares in several shops before finding anything that suited him. In the end, he merely bought a blue woman's jacket of Hang-chou chiffon, a green pongee skirt, a pale blue moon-colored blouse of cloud-patterned silk, a red satin jacket, and a skirt of white pongee, five items in all. To match these purchases, he bought for himself a gosling-yellow satin jacket, a long robe of lavender-colored pongee, and several items of coarse cotton clothing. Altogether, he spent six taels and five mace of silver.

Wrapping all of these items up in a single package, he came home carrying it on his back and told the woman to open it up and see what it contained.

The woman promptly opened it up to take a look and then asked, "How much did it cost?"

"I was able to get it all for six taels and five mace of silver," replied Cadger Ch'ang.

"Although they weren't cheap," the woman said, "they were good value for that amount of silver. On the one hand, we should get out a trunk and pack them safely away, while tomorrow we can go and buy some furniture."

That day the woman went about her daily tasks:

> As though nothing in Heaven or Earth could
> make her happier;

while all her customary complaints were:

> Relegated to that great sea, the Eastern Ocean.

But no more of this.

To resume our story, after Ying Po-chüeh and Hsi-men Ch'ing had sent Cadger Ch'ang on his way, the two of them continued to sit together in the reception hall as before.

Hsi-men Ch'ing then reopened the conversation, saying, "Though I am merely a military official and am only able to maintain the sort of front that I do, I have managed to become acquainted with quite a few officials serving both inside and outside the capital. And recently I have also been acknowledged as a protégé of the grand preceptor. As a consequence, the number of letters and cards going back and forth has become:

> Like a stream of flowing water.

I don't have the spare time to devote to it, so that a good deal of it is not properly dealt with. I would very much like to find a live-in social secretary, to whom I could turn over the task of handling this correspondence for me. It would be very helpful to be spared this expenditure of effort. The only trouble is, I haven't been able to locate anyone with the requisite talent and learning. If you happen to know of such a person, let me know about it. I will undertake to find an empty room to accommodate him and will also provide him with an annual stipend of several taels of silver for the support of his family. If it should turn out to be someone with whom you are on intimate terms, so much the better."

"Brother," said Ying Po-chüeh:

> "If you had not spoken, I would not have known.[27]

If you were looking for any other sort of person, they would be readily available, but this particular sort of person is hard to find. Why is this the case? In the first place, it must be someone with the requisite talent and learning. In the second place, it must be someone of personal integrity, and also someone with whom you can get along. You're better off without anyone who:

> Engages in the pros and cons of idle tattle,[28]

or:

> Wiggles his lips and waggles his tongue;[29]

and, as for persons of mediocre talent and learning, who are old hands at chicanery, what use would you have for them?

"The only person I can think of is the grandson of an old friend of my grandfather's. At present he holds the rank of a licentiate in this subprefecture. He has taken the provincial examinations several times but did not succeed in passing. The talent and learning he has acquired actually make him superior to Pan Ku or Ssu-ma Ch'ien, while, as for his personal integrity, he is in a class with Confucius and Mencius. Because of the long-standing relationship between our families, he is like a brother to me. We are extremely close.

"I remember that when he took the provincial examinations ten years ago, the examining official praised his two essays on public policy to the skies. But, who could have anticipated that there was another candidate whose essays were even better, so that he did not pass. Since then, he has taken the examinations several more times but has been unsuccessful, with the inevitable result that the hair on his head and around his temples has become speckled with white. Right now, he is:

A scholar at large with his books and sword.[30]

But his family still possesses more than fifteen acres of arable land, and three or four houses, which are fit to live in."

"That ought to be more than enough to maintain his family," remarked Hsi-men Ch'ing. "Why should he be willing to hire himself out as a live-in secretary in someone else's place?"

"The land and houses that he formerly possessed," said Ying Po-chüeh, "have all been purchased by more affluent families, so that, right now, he has nothing left but the skin on his two hands."

"So the land that you mentioned has already been sold off," said Hsi-men Ch'ing. "What does that amount to?"

"True enough, that doesn't amount to anything," said Ying Po-chüeh. "But he has a wife who is only about nineteen years old and is exceedingly attractive, as well as two children who are just two or three years old."

"If he's got an attractive wife," said Hsi-men Ch'ing, "why should he be willing to take a job away from home?"

"The good news on that front," said Ying Po-chüeh, "is that two years ago his wife, who was addicted to extramarital affairs, ran off to the Eastern Capital with someone, and his two children have died of smallpox, so he is the only member of the household left. Of course, he'd be willing to take a job away from home."

"In that case," laughed Hsi-men Ch'ing, "you're really doing a job on him. It's all folderol. Tell me, what is his surname?"

"His surname is Shui," said Ying Po-chüeh. "His talent and learning are really incomparable. If you were to employ him, Brother, I guarantee that every last one of the poems, lyrics, songs, or rhapsodies that he might compose would serve to augment your stature. When people saw them, they would all say to themselves, 'His Honor Hsi-men Ch'ing is certainly possessed of talent and learning.' "

"The first two things you mentioned about him just now," said Hsi-men Ch'ing, "turned out to be humbug. I don't believe this humbug of yours. If you happen to remember any compositions of his, recite them for me. If they impress me favorably, I'll invite him to become a member of my household, and set aside a room for him to live in. Since it's only a matter of a single individual, it should be easy to manage. We can just pick an auspicious day and invite him over, that's all."

"I can remember something of a letter he sent me," said Ying Po-chüeh, "asking if I could help him find an employer. I recall a few lines of it, which I'll recite for your delectation. To the tune 'Yellow Oriole':

This letter is addressed to Brother Ying.
My thoughts of you since we parted go without saying.
Thanks to your kindness, my whole family
   is in good health.
The character *she* and the character *kuan*,
Combine to mean the post of live-in secretary.[31]
If you hear of such an opening, I will, of course,
   beseech your help.
If anyone is desirous of a brush sturdy as a beam,
To compose his correspondence,
My brush is capable of engendering clouds and mist."

When Hsi-men Ch'ing heard this, he started to laugh out loud, saying, "If he were wholeheartedly serious about wanting you to find him an employer, why didn't he send you a regular letter, instead of putting his request into a song, which is not even very well written? It's obvious that his talent and learning are inadequate to the task, and his personal integrity leaves something to be desired."

"You ought not to be so sure of that," said Ying Po-chüeh. "It's only because our families have been close to each other for three generations. When I was one or two years old, he was no more than three or four. In those days, when we shared candy and cake, biscuits and fruit, or the like, we didn't even quarrel over them. Later on, when we had both grown up and started to school in order to learn to read and write, the teacher used to say, 'Scholar Ying and Scholar Shui are both as smart as can be and are sure to be successful in their future lives.' And later still, when we took up composition, we would compete in writing essays together, without a trace of jealousy or envy. By day, we walked together, and sat together, and at night, we sometimes even slept together. And when we reached adulthood and donned hairnets, we remained as fast friends as ever. Consequently, the two of us are almost like one person and are fond brothers to each other. For this reason, ignoring convention, he felt free to express his ideas to me in the form of a song.

"When I first saw it, I was also somewhat annoyed. But later, when I thought about it, I concluded that it was only because he was making his appeal to a friend that he presumed to do what he did, and I was no longer annoyed by it. Moreover, that song of his is actually rather cleverly done, though you may not have noticed it. The first line, where he says 'This letter is addressed to Brother Ying,' is the salutation, just like when people write, 'For the perusal of so-and-so.' Isn't that appropriate? The second line, where he says, 'My thoughts of you since we parted go without saying,' is like the conventional amenities about the weather. It is both concise and literary. Is that not appropriate also? The third line reads, 'Thanks to your kindness, my whole family is in good health.' That is simply to say that his family is all right. After that it gets even better."

"What are the fourth and fifth lines intended to convey?" asked Hsi-men Ch'ing.

"Brother, you may not get it," said Ying Po-chüeh, "but this is an example of the word game of breaking characters down into their component parts, which people often find difficult. 'The character *she* and the character *kuan*, combine to mean the post of live-in secretary.' That is to say, if they are written together, do they not form the character *kuan*, meaning the post of live-in secretary? If such a post becomes available, he is anxious that I should recommend him for it, which is why he says, 'If you hear of such an opening, I will, of course, beseech your help.' The line, 'If anyone is desirous of a brush sturdy as a beam,' means that his brush is as sturdy as a beam, and that in handling correspondence, he has but to put his brush to work in order to fill the paper with clouds and mist.

"Brother, if you examine this composition of his, is there so much as a single word that is wasted? With just these few lines, he has succeeded perfectly in putting the feelings in his mind on paper. Isn't that a worthy accomplishment?"

Hsi-men Ch'ing was so affected by Ying Po-chüeh's praise of Licentiate Shui's composition that he was unable to respond further.

All he could do was to say to Ying Po-chüeh, "Since you have been emphasizing all his good points, let me ask you, do you have any serious communications of his? If you can show me one, I'll consider hiring him."

"I do have some examples of lyrics and rhapsodies that he has written at my place," said Ying Po-chüeh, "but I didn't bring any with me to show you. I happen to have memorized a composition of his, however, that is very well written. Let me recite it for you.

When I first donned a scholar's cap, my heart was
    filled with delight;
How was I to know that today, it is this very cap
    that has done me in.[32]
Others generally manage to wear you for no more
    than three to five years;
But you have chosen to remain enamored of my head
    for a good thirty years.
Now that I wish to don an official black silk hat,
    I pray your indulgence;
I have composed these lines of verse in order to
    bid Your Honor farewell.
On this occasion it is not to be understood that
    my feelings are fickle;
It is the white hair that encroaches on my head
    that I find hard to bear.
This autumn if I fail to pass the examinations
    with the highest honors;

I will trample my enemy to pieces under my feet
    and take up husbandry.
It is the year for the triennial
    provincial examinations,
And the time has come for the results
    to be publicly announced.
In order to divulge the feelings in my heart,
I hereby lodge a complaint against you, my cap.
With your help I aspired to mount to the blue clouds
    and thereby bring glory on myself;
Who could have known that now, despite my white hair,
    you remain true to your old friend.
Alas!
I recall when I first donned a scholar's cap,
"Blue, blue was my student's collar."[33]
Thanks to your condescending favor,
I was proud of my newly acquired dignity.
But you did not permit me to gain early success
    while still a young man;
Nor allow me to remain stooped for long, only to
    stand upright in the end.
Above, I do not hold a position as senior official
    or grand master;
Below, as a citizen, I am not a farmer, an artisan,
    nor a merchant.
Year after year, I dwell in the house of a commoner;
Day after day, I report for duty at the local school.
Whenever the education intendant comes to inspect us,
My heart is filled with nervousness and trepidation.
Whenever it is necessary to entertain superiors,
I am compelled to run around, now east, now west.[34]
On your account, I spend my lifetime,
In anxiety and perturbation,
Suffering from a multitude of hardships.
During all four seasons of the year,[35]
In scattered bits and pieces,[36]
My teacher's salary has remained unpaid.
When I have sued for aid on the grounds of poverty,
I have been allotted five pecks of grain.
At the biannual sacrifices I have received coupons,[37]
Entitling me to obtain half a pound of meat.
When officials encounter me,

They can't help being irritated.
When yamen runners refer to me,
They designate me an instructor.
Upon the road to the Eastern Capital,
I have accompanied others several times.
Among the prefects in the schoolroom,
I, alone, am the most venerated of all.[38]
You see that my black boots are
    both down at the heel,
While my blue scholar's gown is
    completely threadbare.
Having buried my head in the books for many years,
I cannot completely describe all the hardships
    and vicissitudes I have suffered.
What hope is there of ever getting a start in life?
I have undergone all of this forsaken solitude
    and painful suffering for nothing.
Though I have approached all the established figures,
In my entire career, I have yet to gain any
    advantage from my compositions;
Not having known the benefit of imperial benevolence,
For years on end, I have continued to harbor
    the hope of conspicuous success.
Alas and alack!
I bemoan this scholar's cap.
If you only look at its shape,
It is something to be proud of.
Vertical behind and horizontal in front,
What sort of an object are you anyway?
With seven fissures and eight holes,
You are truly the root of catastrophe.
Alas!
The cloud-soaring bird has not yet
    folded its wings;
But the fish with dragon potential
    has lost its scales.
Have you not heard that:
The bird that has not flown for long,
Once it does, will soar to the clouds;
The bird that has not cried for long,
Once it cries, will startle everyone?[39]
Early on, I entreated you to help me
    make a new person of myself;[40]

This is not a case of my abandoning
   the old in favor of the new.
As a famed exemplar of this culture of ours,
I thought you possessed supernatural powers.
If only from now on we are forever separated,
Then will I be grateful for your magnanimity.
Of these few words and this meager libation,
I would prevail upon you to come and partake.
Your rationale and your destiny are exhausted;
I cannot overstate the urgency of my request.
From this point on, I would bid you farewell;[41]
Please take yourself off as soon as possible."[42]

When Ying Po-chüeh had finished his recitation, Hsi-men Ch'ing clapped his hands and laughed loudly, saying, "Well, Brother Ying the Second, so you really consider this sort of talent and learning the equivalent of that of Pan Ku or Yang Hsiung?"[43]

"His personal integrity ranks even higher than his talent and learning," said Ying Po-chüeh. "Now let me tell you something of his personal integrity."

"Go ahead and tell me about it," said Hsi-men Ch'ing.

"Some years ago," said Ying Po-chüeh, "he held a position as live-in secretary in the establishment of Vice Minister Li. The Li household had several tens of maidservants, each and every one of which was attractive and clever. Moreover, there were also a number of page boys, each and every one of which was a good-looking catamite. This Licentiate Shui resided there for four or five years, without getting any improper ideas. But, later on, who would have anticipated that several mischief-making maidservants and page boys, seeing that he put on the airs of a saint, actually devoted themselves, day and night, to tempting him. This Licentiate Shui, who is extremely magnanimous by nature, eventually allowed his resistance to soften so far as to be enticed into an affair, for which his employer drove him out the door. This created quite a stir in the neighborhood, and everyone accused him of immoral conduct.

"The fact is that this Licentiate Shui is actually:
   Impervious to the temptations of the flesh.
If you were to employ him in your home, Brother, no matter how many maidservants and page boys you might have, even if they were to:
   Sleep together or share the same quarters,[44]
would this Licentiate Shui resort to disorderly conduct? He would never do so."

"Since he was driven out the door by his previous employer," said Hsi-men Ch'ing, "there must definitely be something not quite right about him. Even though you and I are on the best of terms, I am not prepared to accept this recommendation of yours. The other day, a friend of my colleague Hsia Yen-ling, the venerable gentleman Ni P'eng, mentioned that he was acquainted with a fellow licentiate surnamed Wen. I'll wait until he comes to see me before deciding what to do."

If you want to know the outcome of these events,
Pray consult the story related in the following chapter.

Chapter 57

ABBOT TAO SOLICITS FUNDS TO REPAIR

THE TEMPLE OF ETERNAL FELICITY;

NUN HSÜEH ENJOINS PAYING FOR

THE DISTRIBUTION OF THE *DHĀRANĪ SUTRA*

If one's basic nature is perfected,[1] one can
    comprehend the Way;
Turning over a new leaf, one may jump free of
    the entangling net.
Disciplining oneself to achieve dhyāna is not
    an easy thing to do;
Refining oneself in order to achieve no-birth
    is no ordinary task.
Let the clear and the turgid alternate as the
    wheel of dharma turns;
Break open the kalpas, so that one may travel
    either east or west.
One may wander free and easy for myriads of
    aeons without number;
One's single ray of divine light[2] will forever
    illuminate the void.[3]

THE STORY GOES that in Tung-p'ing prefecture of Shantung province,
there was in former times a Ch'an Buddhist temple called the Temple of
Eternal Felicity. It was erected in the second year of the P'u-t'ung reign period,[4] during the reign of Emperor Wu of the Liang dynasty,[5] and its founder
was the venerable patriarch Wan-hui.[6]

Why do you suppose he was called the venerable patriarch Wan-hui? It was
because, when the old master was only six or seven years old, he had an elder
brother who had joined the army and was stationed on the frontier. Since:

The normal communication of news was difficult,[7]
They did not know whether he was alive or dead.[8]

For this reason, his aged mother could not get concern for her eldest son out
of her mind and constantly wept about the house.

Suddenly one day, the child questioned his mother, saying, "Mother, at a time like this:

> The world is at perfect peace,[9]

and your children are not troubling you. Though we have nothing to eat but meal after meal of millet, we are able to get by. Why is it, then, that you are constantly giving way to tears? Tell me about it Mother, and perhaps I will be able to share the burden of your sorrow with you."

"As a little child," his aged mother replied, "you do not yet comprehend the sorrows of your elders. During the four or five years since your father died, and your elder brother was dispatched to the frontier to serve as a senior officer, he has not sent a single letter home. I don't know whether he is dead or alive, or whether he exists or not. How can I ever get it off my mind?"

As she spoke, she started to cry again.

"Fortunately," the child responded, "if that's all it is, what's the difficulty about it? Mother, if you'll just tell me where my elder brother is stationed right now, I, his younger brother, will simply go there, sooner or later find my elder brother, get a letter from him, and come home to report back to you. Wouldn't that be a good idea?"

The old lady, crying on the one hand, and laughing on the other, said, "What a crazy simpleton you are! To take up the question of where your elder brother is located, if it were a trip of no more than a hundred or two hundred li, you might be able to make it. But he's somewhere in Liao-tung, more than ten thousand li from here. Even a stalwart young man, making the best possible time, would take four or five months to get there. I'm laughing because a child like you could hardly be expected to make such a trip."

"Aha!" said the child. "If it's only Liao-tung where he is, it's not as though he were up in the sky, or anything like that. I'm going to set out, find my elder brother, and come right back."

Lo and behold, he proceeded to fasten on his sandals, adjust his long gown, bow to his mother, and disappear in a cloud of dust. The old lady, finding that:

> Though she might call after him, he did not respond;
> Though she might pursue him, she could not catch up,

became even more depressed than before.

Among her neighbors in the locality, there were women, both old and young, who:

> Rubbing shoulders and nudging backs,
> Providing soup and supplying water,
> Praising here and faultfinding there,[10]

came forward to comfort her in her distress.

Some among them endeavored to reassure her, saying, "How could the child have gone very far? Sooner or later, before long, he is bound to return."

As a result, the old lady allowed the tears flowing from her two eyes to dry up and sat down in a state of depression. After a while:

> The red sun began to set in the west.[11]

While, as for her:

> Neighbors to the east and the west,[12]

each and every one of them:

> Heated her soup and cooked her rice, or
> Mounted her k'ang and shut the gate.

The old lady continued to:

> Stick out her head and crane her neck,[13]

while the two pupils of her eyes were habitually directed outside, as though she only wished she could follow in his footsteps. Lo and behold, at this juncture, as she gazed into the distance, she saw the figure of a youngster emerging from the darkening shadows.

At this, the old lady exclaimed:

> "Thanks to Heaven and thanks to Earth,

and thanks to:

> The light of the sun, moon, and stars,[14]

if this is really my youngest child coming, my resolution:

> To fast and maintain a vegetarian diet,

will not have been in vain."

Lo and behold, before she knew it, the venerable patriarch Wan-hui knelt down in front of her and said, "Mother, before you have even gone to sleep on the k'ang, I have been to Liao-tung, found my elder brother, and brought back a family letter indicating that all is well with him."

At this, the old lady laughed and said, "My child, it's a good thing you haven't actually gone, leaving your old mother behind to worry about you. But you really oughtn't to indulge in such a whopper in order to fool your old mother. Since when is it possible to travel a distance of ten thousand li and back between the morning and evening of a single day?"

"Mother," the child responded, "can it really be that you don't believe me?"

He then proceeded straightaway to put down his clothes bag and take out the family letter indicating that all was well with his elder brother, and, sure enough, it turned out to be in his elder brother's handwriting. He also took out an undershirt that he was bringing back to be laundered, which had been hand-stitched by the old lady herself, so that she could identify it as authentic:

> Without the slightest possibility of error.[15]

This event created quite a stir in the neighborhood, and he came to be referred to as Wan-hui, or "The one who returned from a journey of ten thousand li." Later, when he had:

> Abandoned lay life to take up a religious vocation,

he became known as the Venerable Wan-hui. To be sure, it turned out that:

> His prowess and virtue were lofty and marvelous,
> His superhuman powers were both broad and great.[16]

On one occasion, during an audience before Shih Hu, the emperor of the
Later Chao dynasty,[17] he demonstrated his prowess by swallowing two pints of
iron needles.[18] On another occasion, in the audience hall of Emperor Wu of
the Liang dynasty, he extracted three relics from the crown of his head. That
is why the Ch'an Buddhist temple called the Temple of Eternal Felicity was
established by imperial decree on behalf of the venerable patriarch Wan-hui,
and dedicated to the perpetuation of his memory. There is no knowing how
much money was expended on this project. Truly:

> The divine monk was born into this world
>> with vast supernatural powers;
> He was highly regarded by the sage ruler
>> whose generosity was profound.

Who would have thought that:

> The years and months resemble shuttles;[19]
> The times change and circumstances differ.[20]

Lo and behold, in due course, the venerable patriarch Wan-hui:

> Returned to Heaven, having achieved parinirvana,

and those monks of superior attainments in his entourage, who:

> Still retained their skin and flesh,

one by one, passed away. Eventually the temple fell into the hands of a bunch
of shiftless monks who repudiated the monastic code of conduct known as
Pai-chang ch'ing-kuei, or *Pai-chang's Rules of Purity*,[21] maintaining mistresses,
drinking distilled spirits, and engaging in every kind of forbidden activity.
Even going so far as incitement to homosexual venery, there was no conduct
in which they refused to indulge. But they ended up falling victim to crooked
swindlers and profiteers who provided them with illicit liquor at inflated
prices. When they were unable to pay their debts, it was not long before they
started to pawn their cassocks, and hock their bells and chimes. They tried to
sell the rafters from the main hall of the temple, but nobody wanted them, so
they were reduced to burning them for fuel, and even bartered the bricks and
tiles of the structure for liquor. Exposed to:

> The drizzling rain and blustering wind,

the Buddhist idols began to tumble down, leaving the premises in:

> A state of utter bleakness and desolation,[22]

with the result that those who had been wont to burn incense there ceased to
come. And, as for the former patrons and disciples, and those who had spon-
sored religious ceremonies or services for the salvation of the departed, it was
just like:

> Kuan Yü, the God of War, trying to
>> peddle bean curd:
> Not even a ghost would venture to
>> come to the door.[23]

What had been the site of:

Sacred rites performed to bell and drum,
was suddenly transformed into a place of:
Desolate mists and withered vegetation.[24]
Before anyone knew it, thirty or forty years had elapsed, and there was no one
prepared to:
Deal with the destruction or renovate the ruins.
It so happens that in this temple there was an Abbot Tao-chien. He was
originally a native of western India who so admired the splendor of the Middle
Kingdom that he formed the wish to make a pilgrimage to that exalted place.
Traversing the River of Flowing Sands, the Sea of Stars, and the basin of the
Kuan River, he traveled for eight or nine years before finally reaching Chinese
territory. Wending his way forward, he finally reached the region of Shantung
and chose to stick his staff into the soil on the grounds of this dilapidated temple.
He meditated for nine years with his face to the wall,[25]
Without saying anything or uttering so much as a word.[26]
Truly:
The Buddhist dharma originally dispenses with
the impediment of written words;
The fruits of ritual performance are only won
in the practice of meditation.
Suddenly one day, a thought occurred to him, and he said to himself, "Even
a temple of these dimensions has been allowed to fall into such a state of
dilapidation. If one contemplates these shaven-pated donkeys, with their:
Muddled heads and uncouth brains,
all they are capable of is:
Drinking wine and devouring food.
Is it not a pity that they have taken this sanctuary of an ancient Buddha
and reduced it to the barest ruins? If only someone could be induced to come
up with:
A single brick or half a tile,
in order to:
Resurrect its former grandeur.
I remember that a man of yore put it very well when he said about a certain
place:
Its men are superlative and its territory is numinous.[27]
Now that things have come to the present pass:
If I don't take responsibility,
Who will take responsibility?
If I don't stick my neck out,
Who will stick his neck out?
Moreover, nowadays in this region of Shantung there is a prominent official
named Hsi-men Ch'ing, who holds a post in the Embroidered-Uniform
Guard.

His family property runs into the tens of thousands,[28]
His wealth is similar to that of princes and nobles.

There is scarcely anything that his household does not possess. The other day, when he was seeing off Censor Ts'ai Yün, he chose this spot at which to provide a farewell libation for him. Because he noticed that the temple was in a dilapidated state, he expressed a desire to:

Contribute some money as a charitable donation,

for the purpose of:

Rebuilding and refurbishing the original edifice.

At the time, although I didn't say anything definite, something in the way of a plan began to develop in my mind. Now today, if I should only prove able to induce that donor to:

Take responsibility for promoting the idea,

I am sure that, sooner or later, my expectations may be realized. But I will have to arrange to pay him a visit myself."

At this juncture, he proceeded to summon his:

Dharma heirs and disciples,

and had them:

Strike the bells, and
Beat the drums,

in order to convene the entire assembly, after which he ascended the hall and announced this idea of his. How was this abbot dressed? Behold:

The Ch'an cassock that envelops his body
　　is dyed bloodred;
The two rings that dangle from his ears
　　are made of gold.
The metal staff he holds in his hand is as
　　bright as a mirror;
The hundred and eight pearls of his rosary
　　shine like the sun.
He reveals the golden cords that line the
　　way to enlightenment;
And inspires even ordinary men to awaken
　　from their dreams.
With bushy eyebrows, jet-black hair, and
　　eyes like bronze bells;
He is reputed to be a venerable sage monk
　　from the Western Heaven.

When the abbot had finished his announcement, he told an acolyte to bring him:

The four treasures of the writer's studio,[29]

whereupon he ground the fragrant ink known as "ambergris balm,"[30] moistened his "rat's whisker brush,"[31] spread out a sheet of stationery with "black thread columns,"[32] and proceeded to draft a petition, in which he started out by explaining:

The background of the matter from beginning to end,[33]

and ended by urging the recipients to:

Donate money and create good fortune for themselves.

His calligraphy was such that:

Every line was straight, and

Every character was clear.

Truly, this worthy abbot was an avatar of an ancient Buddha or bodhisattva.

At this juncture, he took his leave of the assembly, put on his Ch'an sandals, donned a hooded cloak and bamboo hat, and betook himself straight to Hsi-men Ch'ing's residence.

To resume our story, after Hsi-men Ch'ing had said goodbye to Ying Po-chüeh, he headed back toward the rear compound, shedding his outer garments at the summerhouse on the way, and went straight into Wu Yüeh-niang's room, where he told her about Ying Po-chüeh's recommendation of Licentiate Shui.

He then went on to say, "The other day, after my trip to the Eastern Capital, all of those relatives and friends of ours were kind enough to come and share a drink with me. Now we can hardly avoid arranging a little party for them in order to reciprocate. Since I happen to be at leisure today, with no other obligations, we might as well take care of this matter."

There and then, he instructed Tai-an to take a basket, go to the marketplace, and buy some fresh fruits in season, pork, mutton, fish, salted and preserved chicken and goose, and other foodstuffs. When he had finished with these instructions, he sent page boys off in different directions to invite the guests.

He then took Yüeh-niang by the hand, and the two of them went to Li P'ing-erh's quarters in order to see Kuan-ko. Li P'ing-erh welcomed Yüeh-niang and Hsi-men Ch'ing with an ingratiating smile.

"His mother has come to see the child," said Hsi-men Ch'ing.

Li P'ing-erh told the wet nurse to bring Kuan-ko out, and they observed that his eyebrows were straggly, and he looked just as though he had been molded out of a lump of flour. Smiling happily, he crawled right into Yüeh-niang's arms.

Yüeh-niang took him in hand and embraced him, saying, "My child, how clever you are. When you grow up you're sure to be as smart as can be."

She then addressed him again, saying, "When you grow up, my child, how are you going to look after your old mother?"

To this Li P'ing-erh responded, "Mother, how can you say such a thing? If our son should grow up to adulthood, and succeed in obtaining:

An official post or even half of one,[34]

the honors bestowed upon his family as a consequence would start at the top.

You would surely be the first person to be granted the privilege of wearing:
    The phoenix cap and roseate shawl,[35]
and he would be in an excellent position to look after his old mother."

Hsi-men Ch'ing picked up on this, saying, "My son, when you grow up, you must strive to obtain a position as a celestial official in the civil bureaucracy, rather than following in the footsteps of your old man, and serving in the western ranks of the military bureaucracy, in which, though you may achieve some success, you will never be fully respected."

As they were speaking, they were unaware that P'an Chin-lien was eavesdropping outside the room. Before she knew it:
    Anger flared up in her heart,
and she started to curse, saying, "Why you shameless, stinking whore, with your empty pretensions! So you think you're the only one that can raise a child successfully, do you? He hasn't even lived through three rainy seasons or four summer solstices yet, let alone survived to the age of fourteen or fifteen, passed through the gate of puberty, or started to attend school and learn to read. He's still as fragile as a bubble, subsisting here in the company of King Yama. How can anyone foresee that he will become an official, or that official honors will be bestowed on the venerable matriarch? And as for that crazy louse of a jailbird, that shameless good-for-nothing of ours, how can he expect him to become a civil official rather than following in his footsteps?"

Just as she was grumbling and muttering away, cursing on the one hand, and expressing her annoyance on the other, who should appear but Tai-an, who came waltzing in and addressed her, saying, "Fifth Lady, where is Father?"

"You crazy, sharp-beaked louse of a jailbird!" Chin-lien cursed him. "Who knows where that so-called Father of yours may be? And what would he be doing coming to my quarters anyway? He's already got a grand lady with a patent of nobility inscribed on patterned damask, a venerable noblewoman, ready to wait upon him with:
    Eight culinary delicacies in five tripods.[36]
So what are you asking me for?"

Tai-an, who realized that he was barking up the wrong tree, simply said, "You're right," and headed off in the direction of the Sixth Lady's quarters.

When he arrived in front of the door to her room, he coughed discreetly and addressed Hsi-men Ch'ing, saying, "Master Ying the Second is in the reception hall."

"I just saw Master Ying the Second off a little while ago," said Hsi-men Ch'ing. "So what's he up to now?"

"Father, you'd better go find out for yourself," said Tai-an.

Hsi-men Ch'ing felt compelled to abandon Wu Yüeh-niang and Li P'ing-erh, stopped by the summerhouse to put on his outer garments, and went out to the front compound to receive Ying Po-chüeh.

Just as he was about to interrogate him, it transpired that the venerable abbot Tao-chien arrived at his gate to seek a subscription and called out in a loud voice, "Amitābha Buddha! Is this the gate to the residence of His Honor Hsi-men Ch'ing? Would one of you responsible servitors announce my arrival? Just say that if you wish to:

> Support your cassia-like sons, and
> Protect your orchid-like grandsons,

So that:

> Those for whom you seek good fortune obtain good fortune,
> And those for whom you seek long life obtain long life,

the venerable abbot Tao-chien from the Eastern Capital has come to seek an interview."

It so happens that Hsi-men Ch'ing was a man who was accustomed to squandering silver and spending money, and he had only recently acquired an heir in the person of Kuan-ko, so he was exceedingly pleased to hear this and wished to perform some charitable deeds for the benefit of his infant son. Since his servants were quite aware of this, they did not:

> Respond angrily or make difficulties,

but went inside and reported the visitor's arrival to Hsi-men Ch'ing.

"Have him come in. I'll see him," said Hsi-men Ch'ing.

Lo and behold, the servants:

> Covering three steps with every two,[37]

made haste to invite the abbot inside, as respectfully as though they were dealing with a living Buddha.

The abbot proceeded directly to the elaborately furnished reception room, where he saluted his host by pressing his hands together in front of his chest and bowing to him in the Buddhist fashion, saying, "I am a native of western India who, in the course of my peregrinations, has visited the Eastern Capital, Pien-liang, and has chosen to stick my staff into the soil on the grounds of the Ch'an Buddhist temple called the Temple of Eternal Felicity, where:

> I meditated for nine years with my face to the wall,
> And labored to transmit the mind-seal of the Buddha.

Because:

> The halls of the sanctuary are falling down,
> And the temple is in a state of dilapidation,

it has occurred to me that as a disciple of the Buddha, it is appropriate that I should:

> Exert myself on the Buddha's behalf.

Were I not to do so, on whose person should the responsibility devolve? For this reason, I have formed a resolution. On a prior occasion, when my venerable benefactor chose to come there in order to provide a farewell libation for some gentlemen, you expressed regret that the temple was in such a dilapidated state, and also exhibited:

A good conscience and admirable intentions,

by volunteering to take some responsibility for its maintenance. At that time, the various Buddhas and bodhisattvas authenticated the covenant. I recollect that in the Buddhist sutras it is well said that if pious men and pious women contribute alms for the refurbishment of Buddhist effigies, it will ensure that they will be recompensed when their:

Cassia-like sons and orchid-like grandsons,[38]

are born with:

Well-proportioned and good-looking features,[39]

and in days to come:

Achieve early success in the examinations,

so that, in turn, their:

Sons are privileged and their wives ennobled.[40]

It is for this reason that I have chosen to knock at your exalted gate. It matters not whether it be five hundred or a thousand taels. I merely beseech my venerable benefactor to:

Open the subscription book and reveal your intentions,

In order to realize the ripening of these good fruits."

He then proceeded to open up an embroidered wrapper, take out the subscription book with its accompanying petition, and proffer them to Hsi-men Ch'ing with both hands. Who could have anticipated that the preceding speech had already had such an effect on Hsi-men Ch'ing that his heart was moved. Before he knew it:

As though nothing in Heaven or Earth could
make him happier,

he had accepted the petition and the subscription book, and told a page boy to fetch some tea.

When he opened the petition, he saw that it read as follows:

I respectfully submit that:

The white horse bearing sutras[41] introduced the
religion of symbols into China;

Chu Fa-lan and Mātanga explicated the Dharma
and founded the Buddhist sect.[42]

Of the living beings in the entire realm,[43]

None fail to confess their allegiance[44]
to the Buddhist patriarchs.

Everywhere within the three chiliocosms,

There are found Buddhist temples that
are elaborately decorated.[45]

But if one observes the dilapidated rubble
of this establishment,

How can it be considered a famous temple
  in a scenic location?[46]
If one does not compassionately contribute
  alms for its restoration,
How can the votaries of Buddha be described
  as charitable to others?
Now with regard to this Ch'an Temple of Eternal Felicity:
It is the sanctuary of an ancient Buddha,
A blessed place dedicated to religious practice.
Erected in the time of Emperor Wu
  of the Liang dynasty,
It was founded by the ancestral
  patriarch Wan-hui.
Magnificent in scale,
It resembled the Jetavana Park,[47]
The grounds of which were paved with gold.[48]
Exquisitely sculpted,
It was like the Jetavana Vihara,
The steps of which were made of white jade.
Its lofty chambers grazed the void,
The aroma of its sandalwood extending
  beyond the nine heavens;
Its layered base covered the ground,
The Buddha's Hall able to accommodate
  a thousand Ch'an monks.
Its two wings were majestic,
Consisting entirely of resplendent halls
  and purple buildings.[49]
Its corridors were immaculate,
Truly, even more magnificent than those
  of the grotto heavens.
At that time, when the bells and drums sounded,
Everyone said it was a Buddhist kingdom
  within the human world;
Verily, the serried ranks of black-robed monks,
Gave the impression of a human paradise
  within our mundane realm.
Who could foresee that, during the passage of
  the everlasting years,[50]
In the blink of an eye, times would change and
  circumstances alter?
Uncouth monks indulged in drunkenness
  and wreaked havoc,

Utterly ignoring the Rules of Purity.
Empty-headed lay workers were indolent
    and coveted sleep,
Refusing to sweep out the premises.
Eventually the temple was deserted,
No longer attracting any disciples.
Finally it became so desolate that,
Those who looked up to it were few.
Moreover, it became infested with birds and rodents;
How could it withstand the beating of wind and rain?
The buildings were dilapidated,
One and then two, two and then three,
Until they could not be maintained.
The walls began to disintegrate,
Day after day, and year after year,
But there was nobody to rebuild them.
Vermilion latticework partitions,
Were used to heat wine or heat tea.
Armloads of rafters and railings,
Were bartered for salt or for rice.
Wind has assailed the arhats until the gold
    is all washed away;
Rain has fallen upon the effigy of Amitābha
    reducing it to dust.
Alas! The brilliance of golds and greens,
Has one day turned into overgrown jungle.
Though success may eventuate in disaster,[51]
The nadir will be followed by the zenith.[52]
Fortunately, the zealous devotion of Abbot Tao
    is such that,
He cannot bear to see the temple of the Brahman
    prince collapse.
He has sworn a noble-minded vow,
To canvass all potential donors,
In the hope that they will all exhibit benevolence,
By uniformly displaying a compassionate disposition.
Rafters and pillars, beams and columns,
Without regard to their dimensions,[53]
When they are given, will be inscribed prominently
    with the names of their donors;
Silver bullion, cloth or paper currency,
No matter how munificent or meager,

Once in the till, will be recorded with the donors'
    names in the subscription book.
Relying upon the awesome efficacy of
    the Buddhist patriarchs,
Fortune, emolument, and longevity,
Will be yours for ever and ever,
Even for a hundred or a thousand years.
Thanks to the clear discernment of
    the guardian spirits,
Your fathers, sons, and grandsons,
Each and every one of them,
Will obtain high emolument and office.
Your posterity will proliferate,[54]
Engendering three locust and five cassia trees.[55]
Your forecourts will be imposing,
Refulgent with golden walls and hills of coins.
Everything that you exert yourself to pursue,
Will turn out auspiciously just as you wish.[56]
When you are presented with the text of this petition,
May each of you overcome the parsimony in your hearts.
Respectfully petitioned.

When he had finished reading the petition, Hsi-men Ch'ing straightened up the pages of the fascicle, put them back in their brocaded case, fastened it by inserting the pins into their clasps, further secured it by wrapping the attached brocade ribbon around it, and then:

Respectfully and reverentially,[57]
placed it on the table.

Folding his hands in front of him, he addressed the abbot, saying, "There is no reason for me to deceive you. Though my family may not amount to much, I do possess property worth several tens of thousands. Although merely a military official, I am not unacquainted with men of contemporary renown. Who could have anticipated that even at my age I should remain without an heir? Though there are five or six women in my household, I had remained worried about this and had determined to perform some charitable deeds, when, last year, my sixth consort gave birth to a son, thereby consummating my myriad desires. Then, by chance, the need to see off a friend of mine brought me to your exalted quarters, where I noticed that the temple buildings were dilapidated, and I formed a resolution to donate some money for their restoration. Since my venerable preceptor has condescended to approach me on this matter, how could I presume to refuse."

Taking a fine rabbit-hair brush in hand, Hsi-men Ch'ing was just hesitating over what to contribute, when Ying Po-chüeh said to him, "Brother, since you have formed this good-hearted resolution to make a pledge on my nephew's behalf, why don't you undertake to:

Accomplish the whole task singlehandedly?
It wouldn't be that much of a commitment for you."

Hsi-men Ch'ing, while still holding the brush in his hand, laughed, saying, "My resources are limited! My resources are limited!"

"At the very least you ought to contribute a thousand taels," said Ying Po-chüeh.

Hsi-men Ch'ing laughed again, saying, "My resources are limited! My resources are limited!"

At this point, the abbot spoke up, saying, "With all due respect, venerable benefactor, I don't wish to be intrusive, but it is our Buddhist practice to let people bestow alms as they see fit, rather than making demands upon them that are difficult to fulfill. Your Honor should feel free to contribute only as much as you wish. If there are relatives or friends besides yourself that might be potential contributors, I hope that you will be good enough to recommend this cause to them."

"My venerable preceptor is most understanding," said Hsi-men Ch'ing. "It would not do to contribute too little."

So saying, he wrote himself down for five hundred taels and then laid his rabbit-hair brush aside, while the abbot expressed his gratitude by pressing his palms together in front of his chest and bowing to him in the Buddhist fashion.

Hsi-men Ch'ing then went on to say, "The palace eunuchs and eunuch directors around here, as well as the granary heads, and patrolling inspectors from the local prefectures and districts, are all on good terms with me. In the days to come, I'll take the subscription book around to them and ask them to put down their names. No matter whether they put themselves down for three hundred, two hundred, one hundred, or fifty taels, I can guarantee that this good work of my venerable preceptor will be successfully completed."

That day, he detained the abbot for a vegetarian meal, before seeing him off at the gate. Truly:

> Acts of compassion and good works are the stock
>   in trade of influential families;
> Preserving good fortune and dispelling disaster
>   are the considerations of parents.

There is a poem on this subject of charitable donations:

> The Buddhist dharma is not very complicated,
>   it merely resides in the heart;
> The planting of melons or planting of fruit
>   is what constitutes its basis.
> As for pearls and jade, amber, and other
>   such valuables and rarities;

Hsi-men Ch'ing Subscribes a Sum for the Temple's Repair

Who is able to take them with him when he
  comes to confront King Yama?
Those who accumulate good deeds are content
  even if they live in poverty;
Powerful families that accumulate property
  throw their money away in vain.
If it were possible to purchase longevity
  by the expending of one's wealth;
The wicked dictator Tung Cho[58] might well
  have lived until the present day.

To resume our story, as soon as Hsi-men Ch'ing had seen off the abbot, he returned to the reception hall, sat down with Ying Po-chüeh, and said, "Brother, I was just planning to send someone to invite you over. You've arrived in the nick of time. The other day, after my trip to the Eastern Capital, all of my relatives and friends were kind enough to come and share a drink with me. Today I have sent a servant to buy the necessary provisions, so that your sister-in-law and I may hold a little party for them in order to reciprocate. I wanted you to be here to help keep them company. I could scarcely have anticipated the arrival of this abbot, whose visit has consumed a good deal of time."

"He seems to be a very fine cleric," said Ying Po-chüeh. "No doubt he is really someone of virtuous attainments. In the course of his conversation with you, even my heart was sufficiently moved to make me a benefactor."

"Brother," said Hsi-men Ch'ing, "since when did you become a benefactor? When did you inscribe your name in the subscription book?"

Ying Po-chüeh laughed and said, "So! Do you mean to say that my intervention was not the act of a benefactor? Brother, you are not familiar with the Buddhist sutras. In the Buddhist sutras the greatest weight is placed on giving of the heart, which is followed in importance by giving of the dharma, and then giving of property. Do you mean to say that my:
      Urging from the sidelines,[59]
did not constitute a giving of the heart?"

"Brother," laughed Hsi-men Ch'ing, "in your case I fear that:
      The words are mouthed but the heart isn't in it."

The two of them clapped their hands and had a good laugh over this.

Ying Po-chüeh then went on to say, "I am content to wait here until the guests come. If you have anything important to take care of, Brother, you might as well go and discuss it with my sister-in-law."

Hsi-men Ch'ing, thereupon, took leave of Ying Po-chüeh and returned to the inner courtyard.

It so happened that P'an Chin-lien:
      Mumbling and muttering to herself,
      Feeling listless and discontented,[60]

had fallen victim, before she knew it, to a compulsive desire to sleep. After sneezing a couple of times, she had gone into her room, fallen onto her ivory bedstead, and promptly fallen asleep. Li P'ing-erh, for her part, concerned as she was about her child's crying, was sitting in her quarters, together with the wet nurse and her maidservants, looking after Kuan-ko and trying to get him to laugh. Only Wu Yüeh-niang and Sun Hsüeh-o, together with two servants, were in the rear compound preparing a meal.

Hsi-men Ch'ing went up to them, sat down, and proceeded to give Yüeh-niang a detailed account of how Abbot Tao-chien had come to solicit funds for the repair of the temple, and how he had seen fit to enter his name in the subscription book. He also related how Ying Po-chüeh had made a joke out of the matter, and they all had a laugh over it:

> As though nothing in Heaven or Earth could
> make them happier.

Now it so happened that Wu Yüeh-niang was basically a serious person, and she was moved on this occasion:

> Neither hurriedly nor hastily,
> Without thought or meditation,

to say a few words that affected Hsi-men Ch'ing like:

> The insertion of a needle in the cranium.[61]

Truly:

> A worthy wife will admonish her husband
> as often as the cock crows;
> Her intimate words will regularly convey
> doses of therapeutic advice.

Just what were the words that she addressed to him?

"Brother," said Yüeh-niang, "you've had the great good luck to sire a son and have also developed the virtuous intention to:

> Extensively contract good affinities.[62]

How can this be anything but an earnest of good fortune for our entire family? The only thing is, I fear that your virtuous intentions are not many, and your evil intentions have not been completely eliminated. Brother, in days to come, it would be a good idea if you would engage in fewer of these meaningless casual liaisons, and eschew the petty deeds that suggest you are:

> Covetous of wealth and given to lust.[63]

If you were to do a few good deeds in secret, it would benefit the little one."

"Mother," said Hsi-men Ch'ing with a laugh, "you're expressing your jealousy again. As the saying goes:

> Even Heaven and Earth are characterized
> as yin and yang;
> It is only natural that male and female
> should mate.

Those who engage in secret trysts and illicit affairs in this life are all persons whose:

Fates were ordained in a previous life.[64]

Their names were entered in:

The register of amorous affinities,[65]

and they are merely fulfilling their fates in this life. You don't mean to say that they are merely acting on impetuous and reckless impulse, do you? I've heard it said of the Jetavana Park, in the western realm of the Buddhist patriarch himself, that it was only acquired after:

The grounds were paved with gold;

and that even in the Ten Courts of the Underworld,[66] something in the way of paper money is required if one is to survive. As long as I expend this property of mine in the doing of extensive good works, even if I were to rape Ch'ang-o, fornicate with the Weaving Maid, kidnap Hsü Fei-ch'iung,[67] or abduct the daughter of the Queen Mother of the West, it would do nothing to diminish the Heaven-splashing wealth and distinction that I now possess."

Yüeh-niang laughed, saying, "Brother, you're just like:

The dog who devours hot shit;

Taking it to be fragrant and sweet.

Once you get the taste of fresh blood between your teeth;

How can your carnivorous nature ever be altered?"

Just as they were laughing over this, who should appear but Nun Wang, bringing Nun Hsüeh along with her, who barged in carrying a box, flew forward to salute Yüeh-niang, and also kowtowed to Hsi-men Ch'ing, saying, "Your Honor, we're fortunate to have found you at home. Since we parted the other day, I've been preoccupied with various paltry matters that have prevented me from coming to look in on you. But I haven't been able to get you out of my mind, so today I've brought Nun Hsüeh along with me to pay you a visit."

It so happens that this Nun Hsüeh had not left home to take up a religious vocation in her early years. In her youth she had married a husband who lived across the street from the Kuang-ch'eng Monastery and peddled steamed wheat cakes for a living. Who could have anticipated that, earnings from his business being meager, Nun Hsüeh, finding herself in this:

Unsatisfactory predicament,[68]

should have resorted to:

Bandying words and wagging her tongue,[69]

with the monks and acolytes in the monastery.

Exchanging looks with eyes and eyebrows,

Approving this and disapproving that,[70]

she managed to work these monks up into such a state that each and every one of them developed a stiff erection in his groin. Taking advantage of her husband's absence from the house, while:

Anticipating tea or recovering from wine,
she contrived to seduce some four, five, or six of them. They would constantly
drop by and present her with baked wheat cakes, stuffed pastries, steamed
dumplings, or chestnuts. Some of them would even give her the fees they
earned for their religious services to enable her to buy flowers, while others
would donate the fabric they received as payment for celebrating the ritual
Destruction of Hell for her to make footbindings out of. Her husband remained oblivious to all this, and when, sometime later, he contracted an
illness and died, because she was so intimately acquainted with the Buddhist
establishment she opted to take the tonsure and become a nun. As such, she
spent her time frequenting the homes of the gentry in the endeavor to corner
the market for the recitation of Buddhist sutras and litanies of repentance.
There were also good-for-nothing women who hankered after illicit affairs and
engaged her to smuggle monks into their homes, for whom she acted as a
procuress, which turned out to be a lucrative trade.

When she learned that Hsi-men Ch'ing's household was extremely wealthy
and observed that he had a plethora of concubines and serving maids at his
disposal, she thought she could contrive to reap a profit from this situation
and took to frequenting his house accordingly. Hsi-men Ch'ing, for his part,
was unaware that:

The three female professionals and the six dames,[71]
are persons whom people should do everything in their power to prevent from
frequenting their homes. Truly:

Originally, her conduct was that of
    an unlicensed prostitute.
Setting up shop as a Buddhist monk or preceptor,
She dresses up accordingly, and recites
    the name of Amitābha.
Every time she opens her mouth, she speaks of
    the way to the Western Paradise.
Wrapping her head in a length of cloth,
Draping her body in a long gown,
And girdling herself with a yellow sash,
Early and late, she loiters by the gate
    or lingers beside the door.
She regards relieving others of their gold and silver
    as acceptable conduct;
While, in the final analysis, in her heart
    she is utterly benighted.
Any way you look at it, she is
    scarcely a decent nun.
How many fine reputations have been
    besmirched by her?[72]

There is also another song that puts it very well:

Buddhist nuns, of course, are known for
    their shiny bald heads.
Enticing monks into their quarters, they
    are busy night after night.
When three shiny knobs congregate,
They resemble a master and his two disciples.
But what are they doing rubbing their
    cymbals together in bed?[73]

When Nun Hsüeh had taken a seat, she opened the little box, saying, "We have no way of adequately expressing our respect for you, but we have brought some fruits that were offered to the Buddha by our benefactors, as a makeshift way of presenting you with something fresh."

"If you wish to visit us," said Yüeh-niang, "simply come and visit us. What need is there for you to go to all this trouble?"

It so happened that P'an Chin-lien had awoken from her nap and heard people talking outside. Thinking that it was merely a continuation of what had been going on before, she went outside to see what was up. She saw that Li P'ing-erh was in her quarters playing with her child. When the latter found out that Nun Wang was here, she wanted to have a talk with her about doing something for the protection of Kuan-ko, so she went back to Yüeh-niang's room together with Chin-lien. After everyone had greeted each other, they all sat down.

Hsi-men Ch'ing, realizing that Li P'ing-erh had not heard about it, repeated the story of how Abbot Tao-chien had come to solicit a subscription, and how he had signed the subscription book and agreed to make a donation, in the hope of acquiring good fortune for Kuan-ko. Who could have anticipated that this would have the effect of annoying P'an Chin-lien so much that she took herself off in a puff of smoke, muttering to herself as she went.

At this juncture, Nun Hsüeh stood up, pressed her palms together in front of her chest, and exclaimed, "Buddha be praised! As long as Your Honor has:
    The benign intention of creating good fortune,
there is no doubt but that you will enjoy:
    A lifetime of a thousand years,
beget:
    Five sons and two daughters,[74]
and remain:
    United with your seven children.[75]
But there is another opportunity I would like to recommend to you, venerable sir. This instance of karmic cause and effect costs very little to initiate, yet it will:
    Procure immeasurable good fortune.[76]

So, venerable benefactor! If you were to perform this act of merit, even the deeds of the venerable Gautama Buddha when he:

Practiced austerities in the Himalayas,[77]

or of the honorable Kāśyapa when he:

Spread his hair to cover the ground,[78]

or of the second Ch'an patriarch Hui-k'o[79] when he:

Plunged from a cliff to feed a tiger,[80]

or of the venerable Anātapindika[81] when he:

Paved the entire grounds with gold,[82]

would not equal this act of merit on your part."

Hsi-men Ch'ing laughed at this and said, "Reverend Sister, pray remain seated and tell me in detail just what this meritorious deed might be, that I may accede to your suggestion."

Nun Hsüeh then said, "Our Buddhist patriarchs have bequeathed to us the text of the *Dhāranī Sutra* in one scroll, that is solely devoted to exhorting us to seek the way to the Pure Land of the Western Paradise. The Buddha has told us that the Third Dhyāna Heaven, the Fourth Dhyāna Heaven, the Thirty-third Heaven, the Tusita Heaven, the Grand Veil Heaven, and the Imperfect Heaven are all places to which one cannot expect to gain immediate admission whenever one wants. The only such place is the Western Paradise presided over by Amitābha. There are no seasons of spring, summer, autumn, or winter there; no frigid winds or summer heat. Rather, one always enjoys:

The temperate weather,[83]

of the three months of spring. Moreover, there are no distinctions between husbands and wives, or men and women there. One is reborn:

In the Pool of the Seven Treasures,[84]

On the Terrace of the Golden Lotus."[85]

"How large is that lotus blossom?" asked Hsi-men Ch'ing. "If one were reborn on top of it and were struck by a gust of wind, would one not be in danger of tumbling off and falling into the pond?"

"My good sir," said Nun Hsüeh, "you still don't understand. Let me explain it to you on the basis of what the scripture says. The Buddhists call a distance of five hundred li a yojana.[86] That lotus blossom is really something. It is very large, very large; in fact, five hundred yojanas in diameter. When one is reborn there:

Precious garb is furnished to order;

Fine repasts are provided by Heaven;

in addition to which:

Songbirds harmonize with each other,

sounding just like the reeds of a panpipe. Truly, it is a wondrous realm. Only because:

The ordinary man with fleshly eyes,[87]

Does not realize where he is going,

And lacks both reverence and faith,

the Buddhist patriarch chose to promulgate this sutra, urging people to:

Devotedly recite the Buddha's name,[88]

And be reborn in the western realm,

that they might behold the Buddha Amitābha himself. From that time on, from one age to the next, even unto a hundred, a thousand, or a myriad ages, they will never again fall subject to the wheel of transmigration. The Buddhist patriarch put it very well when he said, 'Anyone who recites this sutra, arranges to have this sutra printed, or copies this sutra, and thus persuades a single person, or a thousand, or a myriad persons to recite this sutra, will thereby:

Procure immeasurable good fortune.'

Moreover, included in this sutra there are sacred incantations for the protection of male offspring. All families that give birth to boys and girls must devote themselves to this in order to insure that:

Their growth and upbringing will both be easy,

and that:

Mishap may be avoided and good fortune assured.

Right now, the printing blocks for this sutra already exist. All that is needed is for someone to take care of their printing and distribution. Venerable sir, all you need to do is to pay for the labor and materials required to produce a print run of several thousand copies, have them properly bound, and distributed in all ten directions. The merit accruing to such an act would be great indeed."

"That would not be difficult," said Hsi-men Ch'ing. "But I don't know how many sheets of paper would be required for the reproduction of this sutra, or the cost of having it bound and printed. Only on the basis of a detailed estimate would it be appropriate for me to proceed."

"Venerable sir," said Nun Hsüeh, "you're being unreasonable. How can you say such a thing, or demand a detailed estimate? All you need to do is to give the sutra printing establishment an advance of nine taels of silver; tell them to print several thousand, or several tens of thousands, of copies; and promise to settle accounts with them by paying a lump sum for the cost of labor and paper after the binding has been completed. That's all there is to it. What need is there for such a thing as a detailed estimate?"

Just as they were in the thick of their discussion, lo and behold, Ch'en Ching-chi had something to say to Hsi-men Ch'ing and had been looking for him for some time without finding him. He asked Tai-an where he was and was told that he was in Yüeh-niang's quarters. As he made his way past the summerhouse, as luck would have it, he ran into P'an Chin-lien, who had been leaning on the balustrade sniggering to herself. When she suddenly lifted her head and saw that it was Ch'en Ching-chi, she reacted just like:

A cat upon catching sight of some fresh seafood:

Her only thought was to gobble it up immediately.

Before she knew it, the depression she had been suffering from all day changed into:

P'an Chin-lien and Ch'en Ching-chi Enjoy a Furtive Tryst

The genial atmosphere of a spring breeze.[89]

The two of them, taking advantage of the fact that there was no one about, fell to holding hands and snuggling up against each other, puckering up their lips and sucking each other's tongues, carrying on in the most disgusting way for some time. Because they were afraid that Hsi-men Ch'ing might come out and catch them at it, they were unable to consummate the matter that really counted. Their two pairs of eyes were like those of rats on catching sight of a cat:

Looking left and glancing right,[90]

forever on the lookout. Their tryst having proven abortive, they ended up scurrying their separate ways in a puff of smoke.

To resume our story, when Hsi-men Ch'ing had done listening to Nun Hsüeh's spiel, his heart was moved imperceptibly to a benign intent.

Calling for Tai-an, he had him fetch his card case, opened it with the little key attached to his handkerchief, and got out a sealed packet of silver, consisting of precisely thirty taels of the highest grade of incised silver stamped with the mark of the Sung-chiang mint, which he handed over to Nun Hsüeh and Nun Wang, saying, "The two of you should go together to the sutra printing establishment of your choice and have them print five thousand copies of this sutra for me. When the job is finished, I will settle accounts with them, and pay whatever remains due."

While they were still speaking, who should appear but Shu-t'ung, who came in hurriedly to report, "The guests whom you have invited have all arrived."

Needless to say, this group consisted of Wu K'ai, Hua Tzu-yu, Hsieh Hsi-ta, Ch'ang Shih-chieh, the whole bunch of them in fact, all of whom arrived together, properly attired for the occasion. Hsi-men Ch'ing hurriedly straightened his clothing, went outside to greet them, and ushered them into the reception hall. Tables had already been set up there, with an appropriate array of appetizers.

Wu K'ai was invited to assume the place of honor, after which the rest of them:

Segregating themselves by order of precedence, and
Indicating their relative degrees of seniority,

all proceeded to sit down in their places. Whereupon, whether salted, preserved, fried, or stewed, unlimited quantities of fish and meat, roast chicken, roast duck, and fresh fruits in season were all brought out together. Hsi-men Ch'ing also ordered that Ma-ku wine should be opened up and heated for their consumption.

Behold:

When drinking wine with one's bosom friends,[91]
Demeanor and deportment are often forgotten.
Some play at guess-fingers;

Some beat the drum, while
Others pass the flower;[92]
Two out of three moves are bluffs.
Ballads are performed,
Dramatic arias are sung.
Those telling of breeze and moonlight
   speak of how,
Tu Fu and Ho Chih-chang[93] appreciated
   the spring season.[94]
Those showing off their book learning
   also recall how,
Su Shih and Huang T'ing-chien roamed
   below the Red Cliff.[95]
Those playing pitch-pot want to make
   the variations known as,
Regular Geese in Flight,
Irregular Geese in Flight, or
The Eight Immortals Cross the Sea.[96]
Those playing at dice want to throw
   the combinations known as,
The Regular Cavalry,
The Irregular Cavalry,[97] or
Loaches Entering a Clump of Caltrops.[98]
Those who lose a forfeit of wine,
Must drain their cups to the last drop;
Even if it induces them to,
Collapse like a jade pinnacle.[99]
Those who are the winners at dice,
Must hang up congratulatory red banners;
Would anyone permit them to,
Wear their caps upside down?[100]
Inexhaustible,
Are the scenes on the Stage of Youthful Festivity;
Indescribable,
Are the days and months in the Land of Drunkenness.[101]
Truly:

The autumn moon and the spring flowers[102]
   are to be found everywhere;
Occasions for enjoyment and happy events[103]
   tend to occur then as well.

If one fails during one's hundred years
    to be drunk a thousand times;
All the hustle and bustle of one's life
    will simply amount to nothing.

      If you want to know the outcome of these events,
      Pray consult the story related in the following chapter.

Chapter 58

INSPIRED BY A FIT OF JEALOUSY
CHIN-LIEN BEATS CH'IU-CHÜ;

BEGGING CURED PORK THE MIRROR POLISHER
TELLS A SOB STORY

All alone within the embroidered bed curtains,
 her thoughts are subdued;
A myriad reasons for new melancholy beset her,
 both by day and by night.
A solitary goose calls after its mates, as it
 crosses the autumn frontier;
A distracting cricket bemoans its sorrows, as
 the moon hovers in the eaves.
Having lost her way en route to Blue Bridge,[1]
 she despairs of the red cord;[2]
Without anybody to share her golden boudoir,
 she lets down the green blind.
Her fate can be compared to the bamboos that
 grow along the Hsiang River;
That are to this day speckled with the tears
 shed by those nymphs of old.[3]

THE STORY GOES that on that day Hsi-men Ch'ing continued drinking wine with his friends and relatives in the front reception hall until he became stinking drunk, after which he made his way toward Sun Hsüeh-o's quarters in the rear compound. Sun Hsüeh-o herself was in the kitchen at the time, overseeing the cleaning up of the utensils. When she heard that Hsi-men Ch'ing was headed for her place, she hastened back to it:

Covering two steps with every one.

The blind entertainer Big Sister Yü had been sitting on the k'ang in her quarters, and she hustled her off to spend the night with Yü-hsiao and Hsiao-yü in the room with the k'ang in Yüeh-niang's quarters.

It so happens that, like the other women in the rear compound, Sun Hsüeh-o occupied quarters consisting of three compartments, one well-lighted parlor and two less well-lighted inner rooms, one of which was furnished with a bed, and the other with a k'ang. Hsi-men Ch'ing had not ventured into her quarters for more than a year. When she realized that he had come to see her today, on the one hand, she hastened forward to help Hsi-men Ch'ing off with his clothes and provided a chair in the center of the parlor for him to sit on, while on the other hand, she wiped off the cool bamboo bed mat in her room, proceeded to:

Light incense and wash her private parts,

and then went back out to serve Hsi-men Ch'ing some tea. When they were finished with the tea, she helped him into her room and onto the bed, took off his boots, unfastened his girdle, and saw to it that he was resting comfortably. Concerning that evening there is nothing more to relate.

The next day was the twenty-eighth, the actual date of Hsi-men Ch'ing's birthday. They had just finished burning some paper money in honor of the occasion when, lo and behold, who should appear but Hu Hsiu, a young man employed by Han Tao-kuo, who arrived at the front gate, dismounted, and had the attendants announce his arrival to Hsi-men Ch'ing. Hsi-men Ch'ing ordered that he be ushered into the reception hall, where, after Hu Hsiu had kowtowed to him, he inquired about the whereabouts of the boatload of goods.

Hu Hsiu then proceeded to hand him a letter with a statement of account and told him how Uncle Han Tao-kuo had managed to purchase a cargo of ten thousand taels worth of silk goods in Hang-chou, how they had now gotten as far as the customs station in Lin-ch'ing but lacked sufficient silver to pay the customs duty, and how only after paying the duty would they be able to transship the merchandise and transport it into the city.

On the one hand, when Hsi-men Ch'ing had read the letter with the statement of account he was delighted and ordered Ch'i-t'ung, "See to it that some food is provided for Hu Hsiu to eat."

On the other hand, he directed Hu Hsiu to go over to kinsman Ch'iao Hung's place and report the news to him. It was not long before Hu Hsiu finished his meal and went off on this errand.

Hsi-men Ch'ing then went inside and reported to Yüeh-niang, thus and so, saying, "Manager Han Tao-kuo's boatload of goods has reached Lin-ch'ing, and he has sent his young man, Hu Hsiu, to deliver a letter with a statement of account. Right now, we'll have to sweep out the place across the street, store the goods there, find a manager to take care of it, construct an underground storehouse, and open up a shop for business."

When Yüeh-niang heard this, she said, "You'd better start looking for someone right away. It's not exactly early days yet, that would allow you to take your time about it."

"Right now I'm just waiting for Brother Ying the Second to come by," said Hsi-men Ch'ing. "I plan to take up the matter with him, and get him to find someone as quickly as possible."

In due course, when Ying Po-chüeh showed up, Hsi-men Ch'ing joined him in the reception hall and said, "Manager Han Tao-kuo's boatload of goods from Hang-chou has arrived, but I am in need of a manager to take charge of selling the merchandise."

"Brother," said Ying Po-chüeh, "you are to be congratulated. Not only is today your birthday, but your boatload of goods has arrived. You are sure to reap a tenfold profit in this enterprise, since this is a case of:

One happy event occurring on top of another.

Brother, if it's a sales manager you want, that's no problem. I know someone who is a friend of mine because:

When fathers associate, their sons are acquainted.

He was originally a salesperson in the silk trade who has been down on his luck for several years and is sitting idle at home. This year he is forty-some years old, truly, a man in the prime of life. That he has a good eye for judging the quality of silver goes without saying. He is proficient at writing and arithmetic, and a good hand at business transactions. This person's surname is Kan, his given name is Jun, and his courtesy name is Ch'u-shen. He is currently living in Stonebridge Alley and resides in a house of his own."

"If he is agreeable," said Hsi-men Ch'ing, "ask him to come see me tomorrow."

As they were speaking, who should appear but Li Ming, Wu Hui, and Cheng Feng, all three of them, who prostrated themselves on the ground and kowtowed before getting up and standing to one side. Before long the tumblers and musicians all arrived, and preparations were made to feed them in an antechamber. Tables were set up and they were fed, along with Li Ming, Wu Hui, and Cheng Feng.

Who should appear at this juncture but the adjutant on duty, with a summons in hand, who came back and reported, "Among the singing girls that I was sent to summon, only Cheng Ai-yüeh is not coming. The madam of her establishment said that she had made her preparations and was all set to come when she was commandeered by a servant from the household of the distaff relative of the imperial family, Wang the Second, who carried her off to perform there. Thus, I was only able to summon Ch'i Hsiang-erh, Tung Chiao-erh, and Hung the Fourth, who have all gotten themselves ready and will be here before long."

When Hsi-men Ch'ing heard that she was not coming, he said, "What nonsense! Why should she not come?"

He then called over Cheng Feng and asked him, "How is it that your younger sister, when I have called for her services, has refused to come? Is it really true that she has been commandeered by the household of Wang the Second?"

Cheng Feng knelt down in front of him and said, "I live apart from her and don't know anything about it."

Hsi-men Ch'ing said, "You may think that if she's gone off to Wang the Second's place to sing, that's that. No doubt you assume that, in that case, I won't be able to get hold of her."

He then called for Tai-an and, when he came forward, ordered him, "Take two orderlies with you, and one of my calling cards, and go to the residence of those distaff relatives of the imperial family surnamed Wang. When you see His Honor Wang the Second, tell him that I have invited some people for a drinking party, and that I engaged the services of Cheng Ai-yüeh for the occasion some two or three days ago and, whatever the case may be, would be obliged if he would let her come and fulfill her engagement. Should any objections be made to this, have her put in chains, along with the madam of her establishment, and lock them up in my gatehouse. How provoking can you get! Does she think that if she plays hard to get, I'll let it go at that?"

He then turned to Cheng Feng, and said, "You go along with him."

Cheng Feng did not dare to refuse and, going outside, appealed to Tai-an, saying, "Brother, when we get there you go on in, while I wait for you outside. If it is really true that His Honor Wang the Second sent for her, I imagine she may not have completed her preparations and gone over there yet. I'd be much indebted to you, Brother, if she hasn't left yet, if you'd contrive some way of persuading her to make the best of it and come along with us."

"If she's actually gone to Wang the Second's place," said Tai-an, "I'll take Father's calling card and try to get her. If she's still hiding out at home, on the other hand, you should go inside and tell her mother that she had better get herself ready and come along with us. If I put in a good word for her on your behalf, Father will let it go at that. You people don't seem to understand his temperament. He engaged her for this occasion while at His Honor Hsia Yen-ling's place the other day. If she failed to come, it's no wonder that he should be annoyed."

Cheng Feng, on the one hand, set off for the Cheng Family Establishment to investigate the situation, while Tai-an, with the two orderlies and the adjutant, followed after him.

To resume our story, after Hsi-men Ch'ing had sent Tai-an and Cheng Feng off on this errand, he turned to Ying Po-chüeh, and said, "How provoking can this little whore be? She's willing enough to sing at other people's places, but when I engage her services, she refuses to come."

"The little baggage!" said Ying Po-chüeh. "What does she understand? She doesn't yet know what you're capable of."

"I noticed at that drinking party," said Hsi-men Ch'ing, "that she had a way with words. I engaged her to come here and sing for a couple of days as a means of testing her. And she comes up with such a provoking response."

"Brother," said Ying Po-chüeh, "these four painted faces that you've selected to perform today are conspicuous for the way in which they:

Stand out among their kind.
There are not any better to be found."

"You haven't even seen Ai-yüeh, have you?" said Li Ming.

"The last time I joined your master for a drink at her place," said Ying Po-chüeh, "she was still a child. I haven't seen her for the last several years, so I don't know how she's developed."

"This little painted face," said Li Ming, "may have a good enough figure, but she's altogether too preoccupied with dolling herself up. Although she may be capable of singing a song, she can't do it even half as well as Kuei-chieh. What kind of a place does she think Father's is that she should be so presumptuous as not to show up? Were she to come, it could only redound to her advantage. How can she be so:

Oblivious to the true value of things?"[4]

Who should appear at this juncture but Hu Hsiu, who came back and reported, "I've been to Master Ch'iao Hung's place, and he says that he will await your instructions."

Hsi-men Ch'ing then instructed Ch'en Ching-chi, "Go back to the rear compound and get fifty taels of silver; have Shu-t'ung write a letter and stamp it with my seal; and depute an adjutant to set out early tomorrow morning together with Hu Hsiu and deliver it to His Honor Ch'ien Lung-yeh at the Lin-ch'ing customs station, requesting that, so far as the customs duties are concerned, he should:

Look upon the matter with favorable eyes."

In no time at all Ch'en Ching-chi fetched a packet of silver and turned it over to Hu Hsiu.

"I'm going to Uncle Han Tao-kuo's house to spend the night," reported Hu Hsiu.

He then took possession of the letter and customs statement, and left with the adjutant early the next morning. But no more of this.

Suddenly the sound of orderlies shouting to clear the way became audible, and P'ing-an came in to report, "Eunuch Director Liu and Eunuch Director Hsüeh have arrived."

Hsi-men Ch'ing promptly donned his official cap and girdle and went out to welcome them into the main reception hall. After they had exchanged the customary amenities, he invited them to the summerhouse, where they divested themselves of their python robes and sat down on two folding chairs that had been set out in the place of honor at the head of the chamber, while Ying Po-chüeh joined Hsi-men Ch'ing at the foot of the chamber in playing the role of hosts.

"Who is this gentleman here?" Eunuch Director Hsüeh inquired.

"You met him once before, last year," said Hsi-men Ch'ing. "He is your pupil's old friend Ying the Second."

"So it's that Mr. Ying who is so given to making a joke out of everything, is it?" said Eunuch Director Hsüeh.

Ying Po-chüeh bowed in his direction and said, "So you still remember, do you, sir? Your humble servant is that very one."

In no time at all tea was served and duly consumed.

Who should appear at this juncture but P'ing-an, who came in and reported, "His Honor Chou Hsiu of the Regional Military Command has sent a servant with a card indicating that he has another party to attend today and will consequently arrive a bit late. He says that you should start without him. There is no need to wait."

When Hsi-men Ch'ing had finished reading the card, he said, "I understand."

"Your Honor Hsi-men," said Eunuch Director Hsüeh, "who is it that's coming late today?"

"Chou Hsiu has another party to attend," explained Hsi-men Ch'ing. "He has sent someone to say that we should go ahead and not wait for him, since he fears he may be a little late."

"Since he's sent someone to inform you," said Eunuch Director Hsüeh, "we might as well leave a place for him and proceed."

At this juncture, two page boys made their way to the upper end of the chamber and stood one to either side of the guests of honor, cooling them with their fans.

As the conversation proceeded, Wang Ching came in with two calling cards and announced that the two licentiates had arrived. Hsi-men Ch'ing, upon glancing at the cards and seeing that one of them read, "Your devoted servant Ni P'eng," and the other, "Wen Pi-ku," realized that Licentiate Ni had come with the friend and fellow student whom he had recommended to him, and he hastened out to welcome them.

He saw that each of them was attired in the cap and gown of a scholar. Having ushered them inside, he did not bother to inspect Licentiate Ni but, turning his attention to Wen Pi-ku, or Pedant Wen, observed that he was not more than forty years old, was possessed of:

> Bright eyes and white teeth,[5]
> A three-forked beard,
> An uninhibited demeanor,[6] and
> An elegant carriage.
> If you don't know what he might be capable of,
> You must observe what he does and does not do.

There are a few lines that describe him very well:

> Though possessed of an unbridled talent,[7]
> He is given to visiting unsavory places.
> Having stumbled in his pursuit of success,
> His heroic ambitions have turned to ashes.
> His property having been allowed to dribble away,[8]

His spirit of nobility[9] was the first thing to go.[10]
His literary efforts and Confucian principles,
Have all been handed back to Confucius himself.
He has taken the task of supporting the ruler
    and benefiting the people,
As well as the desire to glorify his ancestors
    and elevate his relatives,
And relegated them, in their entirety, to that
    great sea, the Eastern Ocean.
Concealing his light and following the crowd,[11]
His only concern is for his own advantage.[12]
Conforming indifferently to square and round,[13]
He no longer takes shame to be significant.
Affecting both a high hat and a broad belt,
He acts as though no one else were present.[14]
In company his speeches are long and lofty,
But in his breast he harbors nothing at all.
For three years he has answered the roll call,
But failed to pass the entrance examination;
The cassia in the moon will forever remain
    beyond his reach.
Among convivial companions he enjoys his cups,
Undisturbed by his withdrawal from the world;
He is content to dwell as a recluse within
    his cliffside cave.

Hsi-men Ch'ing ushered his guests into the reception hall where they saluted each other, upon which they each presented him with the customary book and kerchief in honor of his birthday.

After they had bowed to each other and sat down in the positions of guest and host, Hsi-men Ch'ing said, "I have long been an admirer of the venerable Master Wen's great talents. May I venture to enquire as to your distinguished courtesy name?"

Licentiate Wen replied, "Your pupil's given name is Pi-ku, my informal name is Jih-hsin, and my courtesy name is K'uei-hsüan."

"Venerable Master K'uei-hsüan," said Hsi-men Ch'ing, "may I also ask in which government school you are enrolled, and what classic you specialize in?"

"Though your pupil is deficient in talent," Licentiate Wen replied, "I am enrolled in the prefectural school and am engaged in a rudimentary study of the I-ching, or Book of Changes. I have long been an admirer of your household's great reputation but have not presumed to pay you a visit. Only because, the other day, my fellow student Ni P'eng brought up the subject of your surpassing virtue, have I ventured to ascend your hall in order to pay my respects."

"You do me too much honor," said Hsi-men Ch'ing. "Since you have taken the initiative in calling upon me, venerable sir, your pupil will not fail to return the favor when time allows. The fact is that your pupil, being but a military official, is too uncouth to comprehend the literary niceties and stands in need of someone qualified to handle his social correspondence for him. Because, some time ago, when visiting the home of a colleague of mine, I encountered the venerable gentleman, Ni P'eng, who praised you, venerable sir, for your great talent and surpassing virtue, I resolved to pay you a visit and seek your instruction. How could I have anticipated that you would condescend to drop in on me, and present me with such a handsome gift to boot?

I will never be able to thank you enough."

"Your pupil," responded Licentiate Wen, "is possessed of but:

Paltry talent and meager virtue.

I am unworthy of such extravagant praise."

When they had finished their tea, Hsi-men Ch'ing invited them to the summerhouse, where Eunuch Director Hsüeh and Eunuch Director Liu were already seated.

"Pray invite the two venerable gentlemen to come in and divest themselves of their formal clothes," said Eunuch Director Hsüeh.

Hsi-men Ch'ing accordingly invited them to loosen their blue gowns. Once inside, they were as deferential as could be, before sitting down, one on either side, with lowered heads.

As they were chatting, Hsi-men Ch'ing's brother-in-law Wu K'ai and Battalion Commander Fan Hsün arrived, exchanged greetings with the company, and sat down.

Before long, Tai-an, along with some fellow servants and Cheng Feng, came in and reported that the four singing girls engaged for the occasion had all been summoned.

Hsi-men Ch'ing asked, "Was she at Imperial Relative Wang's place or not?"

"I had to go to Imperial Relative Wang's place to call for her," said Tai-an, "but she had not made any preparations to leave. It was only when I threatened to truss up the madam of her place and have her locked up that she became flustered and consented to get into her sedan chair and come along with the others."

Hsi-men Ch'ing then went outside and stood on the stylobate of the reception hall in order to observe the four singing girls as they came in together. Thereupon, each of them:

Like a sprig of blossoms swaying in the breeze,
Sending the pendants of her embroidered sash flying,
Just as though inserting a taper in its holder,

proceeded to kowtow to him.

Cheng Ai-yüeh was wearing a purple gauze blouse over a white gauze drawnwork skirt. On her head:

> A phoenix hairpin is half askew,
> The jewels in her chignon tinkle.[15]
> Her slender waist is lissome,[16]
> Resembling the lithe branches of the willow;
> Her flowery face is pleasing,
> With the voluptuousness of the lotus blossom.

Truly:

> The myriad forms of her seductiveness[17]
>   are nowhere to be bought;
> Even at a thousand taels for one night[18]
>   her like cannot be found.[19]

Hsi-men Ch'ing, addressing himself to Cheng Ai-yüeh, said, "I engaged you for this occasion, so why did you fail to come? How provoking can you get? No doubt you thought I would be unable to get hold of you."

Cheng Ai-yüeh stood up after kowtowing to him, without saying a word in response, and merely smiled as she joined her companions in trooping off toward the rear compound. Upon arriving there, and kowtowing to Yüeh-niang and the rest of the company, they noticed that Li Kuei-chieh and Wu Yin-erh were already in attendance.

After greeting them with a bow, they remarked, "The two of you are here early."

"We haven't been home for the last two days," Li Kuei-chieh said.

She then went on to ask, "How come the four of you are so late?"

"It was Sister Cheng Ai-yüeh who prevented us from coming any earlier," said Tung Chiao-erh. "We were all ready and waiting for her, but she refused to start out."

Cheng Ai-yüeh merely covered her face with her fan and smiled, without saying a word.

Yüeh-niang then asked, "Whose establishment does this young lady belong to?"

"You may not know her," Tung Chiao-erh explained, "but she's the younger sister of Cheng Ai-hsiang. It's not even half a year since she was deflowered."

"She does indeed have a nice figure," said Yüeh-niang.

Tea was ordered for them to drink, and a table was set up for the purpose.

Meanwhile, P'an Chin-lien amused herself by lifting up Cheng Ai-yüeh's skirt and displaying her feet, saying as she did so, "It seems that you denizens of the quarter favor straight pointed toes to your shoes, rather than the turned up tips that we outsiders prefer. The shoes we outsiders wear have level soles, while you denizens of the quarter prefer high heels."

Yüeh-niang turned to her sister-in-law, Wu K'ai's wife, and said, "Just see how she insists on playing the role of the superior know-it-all. Why should she concern herself with such things?"

A little later, Chin-lien pulled a stickpin with a dangling goldfish out of Cheng Ai-yüeh's hairdo and asked her, "Where did you have this particular piece made?"

"It was designed by one of the silversmiths in the quarter," replied Cheng Ai-yüeh.

Before long, tea was served, and Yüeh-niang suggested that Li Kuei-chieh and Wu Yin-erh join the other four in partaking of the tea.

In no time at all, the six singing girls finished their tea, and Li Kuei-chieh and Wu Yin-erh said to Tung Chiao-erh and the others, "Why don't you come and take a stroll in the garden with us?"

"We'll come join you," said Tung Chiao-erh, "after making another visit in the rear compound."

Li Kuei-chieh and Wu Yin-erh then followed P'an Chin-lien and Meng Yü-lou out through the ceremonial gate that separated the front and rear compounds and into the garden. Because there were people in the large summer-house, they did not go that way, but, skirting it, enjoyed the flowery vegetation for a while and then went into Li P'ing-erh's quarters to see Kuan-ko.

Kuan-ko was feeling somewhat out of sorts. He had awakened from a dream, crying from fright, and would not allow himself to be breast-fed. Li P'ing-erh was in the room, looking after him, and had not come out. When she saw that Li Kuei-chieh and Wu Yin-erh, along with Meng Yü-lou and P'an Chin-lien, had come in, she hastily invited them to sit down.

"Is little brother asleep?" Li Kuei-chieh asked.

"He's been crying for some time," said Li P'ing-erh. "Only after I put him down facing the interior of the bed just now, has he fallen asleep."

Meng Yü-lou said, "The First Lady told you to send for Dame Liu to take a look at him. Why don't you send a page boy right now to summon her?"

"Today is Father's birthday," said Li P'ing-erh. "I'll send for her tomorrow."

As they were talking, they saw the four singing-girls, along with Hsi-men Ta-chieh and Hsiao-yü, come in.

"So this is where you all are," said Hsi-men Ta-chieh. "We've been looking for you in the garden."

"Since there are male guests being entertained in the garden," said Meng Yü-lou, "we didn't feel it right to linger there, but just took a look, and then came over here."

Li Kuei-chieh asked Hung the Fourth, "What were the four of you doing in the rear compound that delayed you in getting here for so long?"

"We were drinking tea in the Fourth Lady's quarters in the rear compound," explained Hung the Fourth, "and have been visiting there all this time."

When P'an Chin-lien heard this, she smiled meaningfully at Meng Yü-lou and Li P'ing-erh and said to Hung the Fourth, "Who told you to call her the Fourth Lady?"

"She asked us into her quarters for some tea," said Tung Chiao-erh. "When one of us enquired of her, saying, 'We haven't previously had the opportunity to kowtow to you, so we don't know which lady you are,' she replied, 'I am your Fourth Lady.' "

"Why the shameless concubine!" exclaimed Chin-lien. "If other people choose to address you that way, it's all right, I suppose. But whoever heard of anyone referring to herself as the Fourth Lady? Who is there in this entire household who deigns to show you any favor, or considers you to count for anything? Who is there who refers to you as the Fourth Lady? Merely because our husband spent a night in your room, you think that:

> Having obtained some pigments,
> You're ready to start up a dyer's establishment.

If it weren't for the fact that Sister-in-law Wu was staying overnight in the First Lady's room, Li Kuei-chieh was staying in the Second Lady's room, Aunt Yang was staying in the Third Lady's room, Wu Yin-erh was staying in Li P'ing-erh's room, and I had Old Mrs. P'an in my room, it never would have occurred to him to go into your room."

"You haven't even seen everything that happened," said Meng Yü-lou. "This morning, after sending Father off to the front compound, she made quite a spectacle of herself in the courtyard:

> Summoning this one and calling for that."[20]

"As the saying goes," said Chin-lien:

> "Slaves should never be indulged, and
> Children ought not to be humored."

She then proceeded to interrogate Hsiao-yü, saying, "I hear that your master told your mistress that she really ought to find a maidservant for her. Last night when he went into her quarters and saw that she hadn't finished cleaning things up, that little whore put on quite a show, saying to your master, 'I didn't have the spare time yesterday to put the room in order, and now you've seen fit to come spend the night here at my place.' To which your master responded, 'That's not a problem. Tomorrow, I'll tell your mistress to find a maidservant for you.' Is that really what happened?"

"I don't know," said Hsiao-yü. "No doubt it was something that Yü-hsiao overheard."

Chin-lien explained to Li Kuei-chieh, "Except when there are visitors in each of our quarters, Father doesn't ordinarily go into her place in the rear compound. No doubt we may appear to be disparaging her behind her back, but the fact of the matter is that she is so:

> Ignorant of the ways of the world,[21]

that she is constantly given to harming other people with that tongue of hers, so that the rest of us are not ordinarily on speaking terms with her."

As they were speaking, Hsiu-ch'un came in with some tea, and each person was served a cup of tea, flavored with fruit kernels.

While they were drinking their tea, all of a sudden, in the front compound:
> Drums and music began to sound,

as Director-in-Chief Ching Chung and the other guests all arrived together. As soon as they had been seated and served with wine, Tai-an came to call for the four singing girls, and they duly trooped off to the front compound. Ch'iao Hung did not attend the party that day.

First there was a show by the tumblers, and vaudeville acts, while the musicians:
> Played wind and percussion instruments and sang.

Then, after the ensemble dances were finished, a comic farce of the genre known as hsiao-lo yüan-pen was performed. The chef then came in and presented the first course, along with soup and rice.

Who should appear at this juncture but Dr. Jen Hou-ch'i, who came in wearing his official cap and girdle. Hsi-men Ch'ing got up to welcome him into the chamber, where, after they had exchanged the customary amenities, Dr. Jen ordered his attendants to reach into his felt bag and extract a handkerchief embroidered with the character for long life, in which were wrapped two mace of silver, as a birthday gift for Hsi-men Ch'ing.

"Only yesterday," he said, "did Han Ming-ch'uan mention to me that today is your birthday. Please excuse your pupil for his tardiness."

"How could I presume to put you to the trouble of mounting your equipage on my behalf," said Hsi-men Ch'ing. "And many thanks for your lavish gift. I am much obliged to you for the efficacious prescriptions you have provided in the past."

When they had finished saluting each other, Dr. Jen wanted to offer his host a drink, but Hsi-men Ch'ing said, "There is no need for that. The salutation you offered me just now is sufficient."

After Dr. Jen had divested himself of his outer garments, he was offered a seat at the fourth table setting on the left side, next to that of Wu K'ai. Soup and rice were served to him, and platters of viands were also provided for his servitors. Dr. Jen thanked Hsi-men Ch'ing for his hospitality, directed his servitors to take the food provided for them outside, and then sat down.

After the four singing girls had lined up to one side, struck up their instruments, and sung a birthday song in celebration of the occasion, Hsi-men Ch'ing ordered them to join the company and divide up the job of serving the guests with wine.

The performers at the foot of the chamber then came forward to where Eunuch Director Liu and Eunuch Director Hsüeh were sitting and presented them with the program, from which they selected the tsa-chü drama entitled *Han Hsiang-tzu tu Ch'en Pan-chieh sheng-hsien hui* (Han Hsiang-tzu induces Ch'en Pan-chieh to ascend to the realm of the immortals).[22]

Only one scene of this drama had been performed when they heard the sound of orderlies shouting to clear the way gradually approach, and P'ing-an came in to announce that His Honor Commandant Chou Hsiu had arrived. Hsi-men Ch'ing put on his official cap and girdle and went out to welcome him. Before even exchanging formal greetings with him, he suggested to his guest that he divest himself of his formal outer garments.

"I have not come for any other reason," said Chou Hsiu, "than to offer my brother Ssu-ch'üan[23] a cup of wine."

Eunuch Director Hsüeh came forward at this point and said, "Your Honor Chou, there is no need to offer him a cup of wine. It will suffice to exchange salutations with him."

The two of them bowed to each other, after which Chou Hsiu went on to say, "Your pupil has arrived late. Forgive me. Forgive me."

Only after running through the customary amenities did Chou Hsiu divest himself of his outer garments, loosen his girdle, and salute the assembled guests. A goblet and chopsticks were provided for him at the third place setting on the left, after which he was supplied with soup and rice, and a new main course was served. In the presence of the gathering, two platters of snacks, two platters of baked meats, and two bottles of wine were provided for each of the servitors who had accompanied Chou Hsiu to tend the horses.

Chou Hsiu raised his hand in acknowledgment and thanked his host, saying, "You are too generous."

Only after calling in his attendants to take the proffered viands outside did he consent to sit down in his place, whereupon Eunuch Director Liu and Eunuch Director Hsüeh each toasted him with a large bumper of wine.

The festivities lasted until:
> Drinking vessels and game tallies lay helter-skelter,

accompanied by:
> Song and dance and wind and string instruments,
> Amid clustering blossoms and clinging brocade.

Truly:
> The dancing continued till the moon in the pavilion
>   amid the willows hung low;
> The singing went on until the breeze underneath the
>   peach-blossom fans expired.[24]

The party continued until evening, when Dr. Jen Hou-ch'i, because he lived outside the city gate, was the first to leave.

As Hsi-men Ch'ing saw him off, Dr. Jen asked him, "Is your venerable consort's ailment any better?"

"My humble housemate did feel appreciably better after taking your excellent prescription," said Hsi-men Ch'ing, "but during the last few days, for some reason or other, she is once again somewhat indisposed. I hope that you will come by another day, venerable sir, in order to examine her."

When they had finished speaking, Dr. Jen said goodbye, mounted his horse, and went his way. Subsequently, Licentiate Ni P'eng and Licentiate Wen Pi-ku also got up to go.

When Hsi-men Ch'ing's repeated urgings that they should stay a little longer proved unsuccessful, he saw them out to the front gate, where he said to Wen Pi-ku, "On another day, I will pay you a visit to seek your instruction. Across the street from my humble abode, I have prepared a studio in which you may reside, venerable sir, along with your dependents, if that is convenient. Each month I will respectfully offer you a stipend to provide for your sustenance."

"I am much indebted to you for your gracious appreciation," said Licentiate Wen.

"I will never be able to thank you enough."

"This is an example, venerable sir," said Licentiate Ni, "of your civilized endeavor to support this culture of ours."

When Hsi-men Ch'ing had seen the two licentiates on their way, he continued drinking with his guests until late at night before the party broke up. The four singing girls had returned to Yüeh-niang's apartment, where they sang for the entertainment of Yüeh-niang, Wu K'ai's wife, Aunt Yang, and the others. Hsi-men Ch'ing remained in the front compound, where he asked Wu K'ai and Ying Po-chüeh to remain so they could sit down again and resume their drinking. They looked on as the musicians were supplied with food and wine, after consuming which they departed. The utensils from the party were all cleared away, and the fresh fruit and left over comestibles were divided up among the servants.

At this point, new saucers of delicacies were called for from the rear compound, and Li Ming, Wu Hui, and Cheng Feng played their instruments and sang for their entertainment, after which they were rewarded with large goblets of wine.

"Brother," said Ying Po-chüeh, "at this feast that you put on in celebration of your illustrious birthday, everyone had a good time."

"This day," said Li Ming, "His Honor Hsüeh and His Honor Liu expended a good deal in the way of gratuities. And later, when they saw Li Kuei-chieh and Wu Yin-erh come out, they provided each of them with a packet as well. The only thing is, His Honor Hsüeh, being younger than His Honor Liu, is more given to mischief."

It was not long before Hua-t'ung brought out the new saucers of delicacies. These consisted of candied deep-fried sweetmeats, hazelnut and pine nut kernels, red caltrops and snowy lotus roots, lotus seeds and water chestnuts, butterfat "abalone shell" sweets, candied plums frosted with crystallized sugar, rose-flavored pastries, and the like.

When Ying Po-chüeh set eyes on the two varieties of butterfat "abalone shell" sweets, one pure white and the other pink in color, and both of them flecked with gold, he selected one for himself and popped it into his mouth, whereupon:

Sweet dew suffused his heart, and
It melted on entering his mouth.

"These are really delicious!" he exclaimed.

"My son," said Hsi-men Ch'ing, "it's only appropriate that you should like them. Your Sixth Lady made them with her own hands."

"I see, they're a product of my daughter's filial sentiments," laughed Ying Po-chüeh.

Turning to Wu K'ai, he went on to say, "Venerable Brother-in-law, you must have one of these."

Whereupon, he selected one of them and put it into Wu K'ai's mouth. He also called Li Ming, Wu Hui, and Cheng Feng before him, and rewarded one to each of them.

As the drinking continued, Ying Po-chüeh turned to Tai-an, and said, "You go back to the rear compound and tell those four little whores to come out here. If they don't wish to oblige me, that's that, but they really ought to sing something for our venerable brother-in-law. If we wait any longer, they'll be ready to go home. They've scarcely earned their pay today, having sung no more than two song suites for us. We ought not to let them off so easily."

Tai-an did not stir from his place but said, "I've already called for them. They're in the rear compound, entertaining Sister-in-law Wu and the other ladies. They'll be here presently."

"You lousy little oily mouth!" said Ying Po-chüeh. "Since when did you go back there. You can't fool me."

He then called up Wang Ching and said, "You go."

Wang Ching, also, refused to budge.

"Since I see that none of you are willing to go," said Ying Po-chüeh, "I'll go myself."

Thereupon, he started out toward the rear compound.

"You'd better not go in there," said Tai-an. "There's a dog in the rear compound who's really fierce. He's likely to bite you in the thigh."

"If I'm bitten," said Ying Po-chüeh, "I'll end up recuperating on your mother's k'ang."

Tai-an went back to the rear compound. After some time had elapsed, they became aware of a whiff of fragrance, accompanied by the sound of laughter, and the four painted faces came out, with their kerchiefs wrapped around their heads.

When Ying Po-chüeh saw them, he said, "My children, whoever taught you to be so disingenuous? If you've already put your headgear on, it looks as though you think you're on the way out. You're certainly bent on having an easy time of it, hoping to get away without singing a single song for us. At the very least, the charge for your services, including the fare for your sedan chair, is four candareens of silver. That would suffice to buy a picul and seven or eight pecks of unhusked red rice, enough to feed you, your madam, and the entire staff of your establishment, great and small, for a month."

"Brother," said Tung Chiao-erh, "if you think our expenses for food and clothing are so low, you might as well become a licensed entertainer yourself."

"Your Honor," said Hung the Fourth, "by this time it must be almost the second watch of the night. You ought to let us go."

"Tomorrow," said Ch'i Hsiang-erh, "we have to get up early in order to attend a funeral outside the city gate."

"Whose funeral is that?" asked Ying Po-chüeh.

"It's someone from that household the door of which opens practically under our eaves." said Ch'i Hsiang-erh.

"Do you mean to say that it's someone from the household of Wang the Third?" said Ying Po-chüeh. "The other day, when you got into trouble on his account, it was only thanks to His Honor's intervention on behalf of Li Kuei-chieh that you, too, were spared. This time:

The sparrow is no longer in that nest.[25]

That's all there is to it."

"Why you crazy old oily mouth!" exclaimed Ch'i Hsiang-erh. "You're delirious. What nonsense you talk."

"You may scoff at me for being old," responded Ying Po-chüeh, "but what part of me is old?

Though only half functional,

I'd have no trouble handling the likes of you four little whores."

"Brother," laughed Hung the Fourth, "as I see it, your ball-handling is not that great. All you can do is brag about it."

"My child," said Ying Po-chüeh, "when it comes to that:

I pay only what the performance is worth."

He then went on to say, "That lousy little whore from the Cheng Family Establishment seems to have gorged herself with the candied effigies of the Five Ancients,[26] thrones and all. Her mouth is so stuffed she can't get a word out. She has a distracted look about her. I dare say she's preoccupied with the thought of some customer back home."

"After listening to your braggadocio just now," said Tung Chiao-erh, "she's a little skittish about what may ensue."

"Skittish or not," said Ying Po-chüeh, "each of you must get your instruments out and sing a song suite for us. After that, you can go. I won't try to keep you."

"That's enough," said Hsi-men Ch'ing. "Two of you can serve us with wine, while the other two sing a song suite for him."

"Sister Cheng Ai-yüeh and I will sing for you then," said Ch'i Hsiang-erh.

At this, Cheng Ai-yüeh took up her *p'i-p'a*, and Ch'i Hsiang-erh her psaltery, as they seated themselves on a folding bench. Thereupon, the two of them:

> Deftly extended their slender fingers,
> Gently strummed the silken strings,
> Opened their ruby lips,
> Exposed their white teeth,
> Interpreted the melodious tunes, and
> Displayed their coquettish voices,

as they sang the song suite in the Yüeh-tiao mode, starting with the tune "Fighting Quails," that begins with the words:

> Had you but gone by night and returned at dawn,[27]
> Your affair could have been as everlasting as Heaven
>   and as enduring as Earth.[28]

During the performance, Tung Chiao-erh served wine to Wu K'ai, and Hung the Fourth served wine to Ying Po-chüeh. As the party continued:

> Exchanging cups as they drank,
> Hugging the turquoise and cuddling the red,
> Blue-green sleeves were raised assiduously,[29]
> Golden goblets were filled to overflowing.[30]

Truly:

> In the morning he attends feasts in Golden Valley,
> In the evening he favors beauties in ornate houses.
> But do not consider these to be occasions for joy,
> Time's flowing light only chases the sunset clouds.[31]

On this occasion, after:

> Three rounds of wine had been consumed; and
> Two suites of songs had been performed,

the four singing girls were allowed to go. Hsi-men Ch'ing still urged his brother-in-law, Wu K'ai, to stay a while and instructed Ch'un-hung to come forward and sing him a southern song. After which, he ordered Ch'i-t'ung to get a horse ready and take a lantern with which to see his brother-in-law home.

"Brother-in-law," said Wu K'ai, "there's no need for you to provide a horse. I'll just walk home together with Brother Ying the Second. It's gotten rather late."

"There's no reason for you to refuse," said Hsi-men Ch'ing. "But in that case, I'll still have Ch'i-t'ung take a lantern and see you to your home."

Thereupon, after a song suite had been performed, Wu K'ai and Ying Po-chüeh got up and took their leave, saying, "We've imposed egregiously on your hospitality."

Hsi-men Ch'ing saw them off as far as the front gate, where he said to Ying Po-chüeh, "Tomorrow, whatever else you do, make sure to contact that manager Kan Jun that you recommended, and have him come to see me, so we can sign a contract. I've already agreed with my kinsman Ch'iao Hung to get the house over there ready, so that we can unload the merchandise within the next couple of days."

"Brother," responded Ying Po-chüeh, "there's no need for you to instruct me. I know what to do."

So saying, he took his leave and departed together with Wu K'ai, while Ch'i-t'ung lighted them on their way with a lantern.

Along the way, Wu K'ai asked him, "What house is that which my brother-in-law spoke of getting ready just now?"

Ying Po-chüeh then told him the whole story of how Han Tao-kuo's boat-load of goods had arrived, how Hsi-men Ch'ing was in need of someone to take charge of selling the merchandise, how he intended to open a silk goods shop, how he was getting the house across the street ready for that purpose, and how he had asked him to recommend a manager to whom he could entrust the enterprise.

"When do you suppose they will open for business?" asked Wu K'ai. "We relatives and friends must surely not fail to provide artificial flowers, red bunting, and boxes of candied fruit in celebration of the occasion."

Before long, they emerged onto Main Street and arrived at the mouth of the little alley on which Ying Po-chüeh lived.

Wu K'ai told Ch'i-t'ung, "Take the lantern and see your uncle Ying the Second to his home."

Ying Po-chüeh demurred, saying, "Ch'i-t'ung, you see Brother-in-law Wu to his home. I don't need a lantern. My place is just inside the alley."

So saying, they said goodbye to each other and went their separate ways, with Ch'i-t'ung escorting Wu K'ai.

Hsi-men Ch'ing took care of paying Li Ming and company the fees for their performance, locked the gate, went back to Yüeh-niang's room in the rear compound, and retired for the night.

The next day, sure enough, Ying Po-chüeh brought Kan Jun over, dressed in black livery, to meet Hsi-men Ch'ing. After discussing business with him for a while, Hsi-men Ch'ing called for Ts'ui Pen and sent him to confer with Ch'iao Hung about getting the house ready for the unloading of the merchandise, and the construction of an underground storehouse and shop front, so that they could settle on a date for the opening of the business.

Ch'iao Hung said to Ts'ui Pen, "In the future, with regard to all things, great and small, I am content to let our kinsman decide. There is no need to consult me about it any further."

Thereupon, Hsi-men Ch'ing signed a contract with Kan Jun, which established Ying Po-chüeh as his guarantor, and determined that as far as the profits of the enterprise were concerned, Hsi-men Ch'ing was entitled to 50 percent, and Ch'iao Hung to 30 percent, with the remainder to be divided evenly among Han Tao-kuo, Kan Jun, and Ts'ui Pen. It was also decided that they should lay in the necessary bricks, tiles, lumber, and stone, proceed with the construction of an underground storehouse and shop front, and design a plaque for the door of the establishment, so that when the cartloads of merchandise arrived, they would be prepared to accommodate them.

Space in the rear was also set aside as a studio in which Licentiate Wen Pi-ku could reside as his private tutor, or social secretary, who would take responsibility for dealing with his employer's correspondence with his peers, in return for a stipend of three taels of silver per month, and appropriate gifts on festival occasions. It was also arranged that Hua-t'ung would wait on him for half of every evening, in order to provide for his food and drink, and fetch water for his inkstone, and, if he should go out to visit his friends, accompany him in order to carry his card case. It was also expected that when Hsi-men Ch'ing entertained guests he would be invited to help keep them company as they drank their wine, but there is no need to describe this in detail.

On the same day, Hsi-men Ch'ing's birthday being over, Dr. Jen Hou-ch'i was invited to come examine Li P'ing-erh and prescribe appropriate medications for her, while Hsi-men Ch'ing dealt with the alterations being made to the house across the street. Aunt Yang was the first to go home, but Li Kuei-chieh and Wu Yin-erh had not yet done so. Wu Yüeh-niang purchased some crabs for three mace of silver and had them cooked at noontime, when she invited Sister-in-law Wu, Li Kuei-chieh, Wu Yin-erh, and the rest to enjoy them in the courtyard of the rear compound, where they gathered round to consume them. While they were still eating, Dame Liu, whom Yüeh-niang had engaged to come and see Kuan-ko, arrived, and, after she had been served with tea, Li P'ing-erh accompanied her to her quarters in the front compound.

"Little brother has suffered from a fright," said Dame Liu, "and is rejecting his milk."

She provided several doses of medicine, after which Yüeh-niang gave her three mace of silver and sent her on her way.

Meanwhile, Meng Yü-lou and P'an Chin-lien, together with Li Kuei-chieh, Wu Yin-erh, and Hsi-men Ta-chieh, set up a small table under the flower arbor, covered it with a strip of felt, and amused themselves by playing dominoes for forfeits of wine. Whoever lost a hand had to consume a large cup of wine. Sun Hsüeh-o lost seven or eight times to the others and had to down as many cups of wine. Consequently, she did not dare to continue playing and, after sitting a while longer, took herself off. Hsi-men Ch'ing, who was engaged in overseeing the preparations in the house across the street, was drinking there along with Ying Po-chüeh, Ts'ui Pen, and his new manager, Kan Jun, and sent a page boy back home to fetch some food for them. This threw Sun Hsüeh-o into such a state of consternation that she felt compelled to bustle off to the kitchen to take care of it, leaving Li Chiao-erh to take her place in the game of dominoes.

At this point, Chin-lien said to Wu Yin-erh and Li Kuei-chieh, "Why don't you sing us that song suite celebrating the evening of the seventh day of the seventh month."

Thereupon, accompanying themselves on the *p'i-p'a*, they sang the song suite in the Shang mode that begins with a song to the tune "A Gathering of Worthy Guests":

Summer is just beginning to recede, as the star Antares
    gradually moves toward the west.
The handle of the Dipper is moving toward
    the Northern Palace.
A single leaf of the phoenix tree[32] flutters down,
And everywhere a hint of autumn can be detected.
The evening clouds float idly as the stridulation
    of the cicadas resounds;
The nighttime breeze is gentle as the coruscating
    fireflies begin to fly.
On the Celestial Stairs the coolness of the night
    is as clear as water;
Most appropriately, paintings of the Magpie Bridge[33]
    are suspended on high.
In golden basins five sprouts are planted;[34]
In alabaster towers banquets are prepared.[35]

That day the sisterhood of womenfolk continued drinking until evening, when Yüeh-niang filled their gift boxes and saw Li Kuei-chieh and Wu Yin-erh off on their way home.

P'an Chin-lien was completely inebriated by the time she returned to her quarters. Because she observed the frequency with which Hsi-men Ch'ing chose to spend the night in Li P'ing-erh's quarters, and that he had once again invited Dr. Jen Hou-ch'i to come and examine her that very morning, her heart was filled with rancor. She was also aware that her rival's child was not well.

As she entered her courtyard:
    As providence would have it,
amid the dark shadows, she stepped into a pile of dog shit with one of her feet. As soon as she got inside, she had Ch'un-mei light a lamp to examine the damage and saw that the entire vamp of her brand new scarlet silk shoe had been soiled. Immediately, she:
    Pricked up her willow brows,
    Opened wide her starry eyes,[36]
called for Ch'un-mei to bring a lantern, locked the postern gate, picked up a big stick, and proceeded indiscriminately to beat the offending dog, beating him until he howled outlandishly.

Li P'ing-erh, in her adjacent quarters, sent Ying-ch'un over to say, "My mistress says to tell you that the baby has just taken Dame Liu's medicine and fallen asleep, and asks that the Fifth Lady refrain from beating the dog any longer."

Chin-lien sat down and had nothing to say for some time, after which, she beat the dog a little more, opened the gate, and let him out. She then turned her attention to finding fault with Ch'iu-chü. When she examined her shoe, she was:

Angry on the left, and
Angry on the right.

Calling Ch'iu-chü before her, she said, "If you consider the matter, by this time of day, the dog ought to have been let out. What were you keeping him in here for, anyway? I suppose, slave that you are, he serves you as a clandestine lover. By not letting him out, you caused him to leave his shit all over the place, so that by stepping into it, this brand new pair of shoes of mine, which, including today, I haven't worn for more than three or four days, is all covered with shit. You knew I would be coming home and should have lit a lantern and come out to meet me. How can you expect to get away with:

Pretending to be both deaf and dumb,[37]
and playing the fool this way?"

"I told her some time ago," said Ch'un-mei, "you ought to take advantage of the fact that Mother isn't home yet to feed him and put him out in the back courtyard. But she pretended to be deaf and paid me no attention at all, even giving me a dirty look."

"There you are!" exclaimed Chin-lien. "The lousy, audacious, death-defying slave! How is it that she's so reluctant to get her ass in motion? I'm aware that you think you're the boss around here. As they say, you're such a hardened convict that a beating no longer means anything to you."

Thereupon, she called her up in front of her and told Ch'un-mei to bring a lamp over so she could see better, saying as she did so, "Just look at the filth on my shoe. It's a shoe that I just made, and one that I really liked, and now it's been ruined by a slave like you."

Having tricked her into lowering her head in order to see better, she took up the shoe by its heel lift and slapped her right in the face several times with the sole. She hit her so hard that Ch'iu-chü's lips were broken, and, rubbing away the blood with her hand, she stepped out of reach.

"You lousy slave!" the woman cursed at her. "Trying to get away, are you?"

"Drag her over here, and make her kneel down," she said to Ch'un-mei. "Fetch the riding crop, and strip off her clothing for me. I'll give her a good thirty strokes with the whip before I'm through. Merely grabbing hold of her and giving her a few random strokes will hardly do the job."

Ch'un-mei accordingly stripped off Ch'iu-chü's clothing. The woman then told Ch'un-mei to tie her hands, after which she swung the riding crop into

P'an Chin-lien Beats a Dog at the Expense of a Human Being

the air, and the strokes of the whip began to fall on Ch'iu-chü like rain. She whipped the slave girl until she:

Howled like a stuck pig.

In the adjacent quarters, Kuan-ko had just closed his eyes in sleep when he was startled back awake, and Li P'ing-erh once again sent Hsiu-ch'un over to say, "My mistress respectfully requests that the Fifth Lady let Ch'iu-chü off for now, and stop whipping her. She's afraid that the commotion will startle the baby awake."

When Old Mrs. P'an, who was lying on the k'ang in the inner room, heard Chin-lien whipping Ch'iu-chü until she screamed, she hastily crawled to her feet and admonished her from the sidelines, but Chin-lien paid no attention.

Later, when she saw that Li P'ing-erh had sent Hsiu-ch'un over to plead with her, she stepped forward and attempted to pry the whip from her daughter's hand, saying, "My child, spare her a few strokes. You've annoyed the young lady next door into complaining. I'm afraid you may frighten the baby.

You may break off a switch to beat the donkey,
So long as you don't injure the redbud tree."[38]

When Chin-lien, who was already in a state of rage, heard her mother admonish her with these words, it was just as though a torch had been applied to her heart.

In an instant her whole face was purple.
Giving her a shove with one hand, she very nearly knocked Old Mrs. P'an down.

"You crazy old baggage!" she cried. "What do you know about it? Get out of my way and sit down somewhere. It's none of your business. What the fuck are you trying to admonish me for? What's all this about the redbud tree, and taking a switch to the donkey? Whose side are you on, anyway, with this two-faced interference of yours?"

"Why you lousy death-bound short-life!" expostulated Old Mrs. P'an. "How can you call me two-faced? I come to visit you in the hope of picking up a few morsels of cold food, and you treat me as roughly as this!"

"Tomorrow," said Chin-lien, "you can just squeeze your old cunt between your legs and take it out of here, for all I care. It's not as though any one in this house would dare to:

Stew me in a pot and eat me."

When Old Mrs. P'an heard the way in which her own daughter defied her, she went back into the inner room, and gave way to:

Sobbing and wailing,[39]

while the woman continued to whip Ch'iu-chü. She gave her a good twenty or thirty strokes with the riding crop and then finished her off with ten criss-cross strokes of the cane. She beat her until:

The skin was broken and the flesh was split,

before letting her up. She also used her sharp fingernails to gouge the cheeks of her face until they were a bloody mess.

All Li P'ing-erh, in her adjacent quarters, could do was to cover the baby's ears with both hands, while tears of distress rolled down her cheeks.

Though she dared to be angry,
She dared not speak.

Who could have anticipated that on that day, when Hsi-men Ch'ing's drinking party in the house across the street broke up, he went straight to Meng Yü-lou's quarters and spent the night.

The next day, Commandant Chou Hsiu invited him to a belated drinking party in honor of his birthday, so he was not at home.

Li P'ing-erh observed that, though Kuan-ko had taken Dame Liu's medicine, it had produced no visible effect, and that the fright he had been subjected to during the night had caused his eyeballs to roll up and remain dangling there out of sight. Because Nun Hsüeh and Nun Wang were about to go home that day, she took a pair of silver lions that were used to hold her bedspread in place from her room and went to see Yüeh-niang, proposing that Nun Hsüeh be commissioned to arrange the printing of copies of the *Fo-ting-hsin t'o-lo ching* (Dhāraṇī sutra of the Buddha's essence),[40] in time for the Mid-Autumn Festival on the fifteenth day of the eighth month, so that they could be distributed at the Temple of the God of the Eastern Peak.

Nun Hsüeh was about to take them, and go on her way, when Meng Yü-lou spoke up from one side, saying, "Reverend, hold on a minute. First Lady, you ought to send a page boy to call in Pen the Fourth so he can weigh these lions and determine what they're worth, and then accompany her to the sutra printing shop and settle on the number of copies to be printed, the cost per copy, the amount we're willing to contribute, and the date by which the job will be done. That's the right way to do it. If you send Reverend Hsüeh off to do it all by herself, how can we be sure that she will be able to handle it correctly?"

"What you say is right," said Yüeh-niang.

She then dispatched Lai-an, saying, "Go see if Pen the Fourth is at home or not, and get him to come here."

Lai-an went straight off on this errand, and, before long, Pen the Fourth showed up and bowed to Yüeh-niang and the others. When he put the two silver lions on the scale, they turned out to weigh forty-one taels and five mace.

Yüeh-niang then instructed him, "Accompany Reverend Hsüeh to the sutra printing shop and request them to print the appropriate number of copies."

Chin-lien thereupon said to Meng Yü-lou, "Why don't we see the two reverends off, and, while we're at it, we can drop in on Hsi-men Ta-chieh and see if she is still in her room making shoes."

The two of them then took each other by the hand and set off for the front compound, while Pen the Fourth, along with Lai-an, accompanied Nun Hsüeh and Nun Wang on their way to the sutra printing shop.

When P'an Chin-lien and Meng Yü-lou arrived in front of the main reception hall, they saw that Hsi-men Ta-chieh was sitting under the eaves at the door of her anteroom on the east side of the courtyard, with her sewing basket, engaged in stitching a shoe. Chin-lien picked it up to take a look and saw that the upper was made of sand-green Lu-chou silk.

"Young lady," said Meng Yü-lou, "you really ought not to use this red chain stitching. The fact is, it would be more dignified to use blue thread. And, when the time comes, you can attach a scarlet heel lift."

"I already have a pair with scarlet heel lifts," said Hsi-men Ta-chieh. "For this pair, I intend to use blue heel lifts. That's why I'm chain stitching this one with scarlet thread."

After Chin-lien had looked over her handiwork, the three of them sat down on the stylobate of the reception hall, and Meng Yü-lou asked Hsi-men Ta-chieh, "Is your husband in your room, or not?"

"He's had a couple of cups of wine, I don't know where," said Hsi-men Ta-chieh, "and he's sleeping it off in the room."

Meng Yü-lou then said to Chin-lien, "Just now, if I hadn't intervened from the sidelines, that muddleheaded baggage, Sister Li, would simply have turned her silver over to the nuns in order to get some copies of a sutra printed. The sutra might never have been printed, and, legless crab of a creature that she is, if they chose to hide out in some prominent household, where would she ever find them? Luckily, after I intervened, Pen the Fourth was summoned to accompany them."

"Look here," said Chin-lien. "If I were asked to do it, where such a wealthy sister is concerned, if I didn't make something out of it, I'd be a fool. It would be no more than:

Plucking a single hair from the body of an ox.

If your child is not fated to live, quite aside from donating sutras, if you were to donate the entire realm, with its:

Myriad leagues of rivers and mountains,[41]

it would be of no avail. Truly:

Though you may have money enough to worship
    the Northern Dipper,
Who is able to buy a guarantee that nothing
    untoward will happen?

Right now, in this room of hers, she carries on like the magistrate who:

Authorizes himself alone to ignite fires,
But won't let the rest of us light lamps.[42]

Young lady, listen to what I'm saying. You're not an outsider.

She's painted herself so white that she won't
    take on any other color.
You think that you alone can get away with being:
    So flippant in your hundred ways.
At the crack of dawn, she inveigles our husband into calling in the doctor to examine her. Well, she can do what she wants because she knows that we won't dare to interfere.

"Whenever she's in front of other people, she is forever protesting her own virtue. 'I'm not in the mood for it,' she says. 'Father is constantly coming into my quarters, pretending that he only wants to see the baby, and then pestering me to sleep with him. Who can be bothered? I end up having to urge him to go and sleep in someone else's quarters.' In front of us, she puts on such a show of virtue, while behind our backs, she engages in bad-mouthing us. And our eldest sister insists on paying heed to her one-sided words.

"If you claim not to be competing with the rest of us for his favors, how is it that the other day, when our husband did not come into your room, you sent your maidservant out to the postern gate to waylay him, allegedly to see the baby? And then, because you were taking medicine, you actually went so far as to arrange for him to spend the night in the other room with Wu Yin-erh, thereby showing just how clever you are at getting your husband to like you. And our eldest sister has nothing to say about it.

"Last night, when I came back to my room, I soiled my shoe by stepping into a pile of dog shit, and when I beat the maidservant and drove the dog out, she got upset and sent her maidservant over to complain that I was frightening her baby. My mother, the old baggage, who didn't understand the situation, having scrounged something to eat from her in the past, elected to play the role of her lackey, and admonished me by saying:
    'You may break off a switch to beat the donkey,
    So long as you don't injure the redbud tree.'
I was already annoyed at her:
    Simpleminded officiousness,
so, when she continued to argue with me, I told her off in no uncertain terms, and, today, she has gone home in a huff.

"Her departure caused me to say to her, 'His household does not feel overburdened by such poor relatives as yourself, and will not feel diminished without you. If you're so quick to lose your temper, in the future, you might just as well stay away. If you're afraid that someone in this house might:
    Stew me in a pot and eat me,
just let me handle it for myself.' "

"What an ill-bred offspring you are!" laughed Meng Yü-lou. "How can you talk that way to your own mother?"

"That's not it at all," said Chin-lien. "What really annoys me is the fact that:

She may be a brown cat, but she's got a black tail.

She's so two-faced about things, always taking the other person's side, on the principle that:

If you've eaten a bowl and a half of someone's food,

You're obligated to do whatever they want you to do.[43]

If she manages to pick up so much as a sweet date from someone, she'll sing her praises a thousand times, if not ten thousand times. From the very outset, once she'd borne this child, she has manipulated our husband to such effect that it's just as though he's taken root in her place. He treats her the same way he would if she had been formally raised to the status of legitimate wife, while she can hardly wait for the chance to trample the rest of us into the mud.

"But today, thanks to the fact that:

Heaven also has eyes,[44]

your child has fallen ill. As I have said all along:

The sun may be at high noon,

But the time will come when it will pass its zenith."[45]

As they were speaking, who should appear but Pen the Fourth and Lai-an, who had been to the sutra printing shop to hand over the silver lions and had returned to report to Yüeh-niang. When they saw that Meng Yü-lou, P'an Chin-lien, and Hsi-men Ta-chieh were sitting on the stylobate of the reception hall, they came to a halt outside the ceremonial gate, hesitating to come inside.

Lai-an stepped forward and said, "Ladies, get out of the way if you please. Pen the Fourth is here."

"You crazy jailbird!" said Chin-lien. "Tell him to go ahead in. It's not as though we've never seen him before."

When Lai-an repeated this to him, Pen the Fourth lowered his head and went straight back to the rear compound, where he reported to Yüeh-niang and Li P'ing-erh, saying, "I took the aforementioned silver lions, weighing forty-one taels and five mace, and, in the presence of the two nuns, turned them over to Chai Ching-erh, or Sutra Chai, the proprietor of the sutra printing shop. He agreed to print five hundred copies of the *Dhāraṇī sutra* with damask bindings, for five candareens apiece, and a thousand copies with plain silk bindings, for three candareens apiece, which comes to a total of fifty-five taels of silver. In addition to the forty-one taels and five mace which he has already accepted, he is still due thirteen taels and five mace, in return for which, he promises to deliver the sutras on the morning of the fourteenth."

Li P'ing-erh promptly went back to her quarters and returned with a silver incense burner, which, when she had Pen the Fourth put it on the scale, turned out to weigh fifteen taels.

"You take it to him," said Li P'ing-erh, "and keep the surplus over what he is due in order to cover your expenses when the sutras are distributed at the temple fair on the fifteenth. That way you won't have to come and ask me for anything more."

Pen the Fourth, thereupon, took the incense burner and headed out the door, while Yüeh-niang told Lai-an to see him out.

"Brother Four," said Li P'ing-erh, "I'm much indebted to you."

Pen the Fourth bowed deferentially and said, "How could I presume?"

He then went back to the front compound, where Chin-lien and Meng Yü-lou once again called him to a halt and asked him, "Did you turn the silver lions over to the sutra printing shop?"

"It's all been properly settled," said Pen the Fourth. "They agreed to print one thousand five hundred copies of the sutra for a fee of fifty-five taels of silver. In addition to the forty-one taels and five mace that they have already received, the Sixth Lady, just now, has provided this silver incense burner."

Meng Yü-lou and Chin-lien looked it over but had nothing to say, after which Pen the Fourth continued on his way home.

Turning to Chin-lien, Meng Yü-lou said, "Sister Li in carrying on this way is simply wasting her money. If he is really destined to be your child, even a blow with a cudgel would not kill him. If he is not destined to be your child, no matter what you do in the way of donating sutras and creating effigies, it will not preserve him. She puts too much faith in these nuns, who are capable of anything. Just now, if I hadn't intervened, she would have simply turned these things over to them to take away. It was better to send someone from our household to accompany them, wasn't it?"

"Even if they made something out of the transaction," said Chin-lien, "it wouldn't amount to much."

The two of them chatted for a while and then stood up.

"Let's go out to the front gate," proposed Chin-lien.

She then went on to ask Hsi-men Ta-chieh, "Will you go out with us?"

"I won't go," Hsi-men Ta-chieh replied.

P'an Chin-lien then took Meng Yü-lou by the hand, and the two of them went and stood just inside the main gate.

They then asked P'ing-an, "Have the renovations in the house across the street been completed yet?"

"By this time?" said P'ing-an. "Yesterday, Father was over there supervising the work, and the place has been properly swept out. The merchandise is going to be temporarily stored on the upper floor of the building in the rear. Yesterday he had the yin-yang master come to preside over the ceremony of breaking ground. They are constructing a three-roomed underground store-house beneath the building in order to store the silk goods and are opening up an eighteen-foot-wide frontage of three rooms in a row, to serve as the shop front. Artisans have been engaged to repaint and varnish the interior, pave the floor, and put up shelving, so that they can open for business next month."

Meng Yü-lou went on to inquire, "Have the dependents of that secretary, Licentiate Wen, moved in yet, or not?"

"They moved in yesterday," said P'ing-an. "And this morning Father directed that the summer bedstead in storage in the rear compound should be allocated to them, and that two tables and four chairs should be moved over for them to sit on."

"Did you happen to notice what his wife looked like?" asked Chin-lien.

"She was sitting in a sedan chair in the dark shadows," said P'ing-an. "Nobody got a good look at her."

As they were speaking, what should they hear in the distance but the *ssu-lang-lang* sound made by an old gentleman as he came along shaking the distinctive mirror polisher's clapper by means of which he alerted housewives to his presence.

"The mirror polisher is coming this way," said Chin-lien.

She then said to P'ing-an, "You call him to a halt so that he can polish our mirrors for us. My mirrors, these last few days, have gotten tarnished. I told you, jailbird that you are, to be on the lookout for him, but you haven't done anything about it. And now, how does it happen that we haven't been standing out here any time at all, and the mirror polisher shows up?"

P'ing-an, accordingly, called the mirror polisher to a halt. The old man set down his load of equipment, and, seeing that there were two women standing just inside the gate, stepped forward to salute each of them with a bow and then stood to one side.

Chin-lien then asked Meng Yü-lou, "If you're planning to have your mirrors polished too, why not have the page boy bring them out as well, so we can have them all polished at the same time?"

Thereupon, she directed Lai-an, "Go to my quarters, and get your sister Ch'un-mei to find my large face mirror, my two small mirrors, and also the large rectangular dressing mirror; then bring them all out here so that he can give them a good polishing."

Meng Yü-lou instructed Lai-an, "Go to my quarters, and get Lan-hsiang to find my mirrors, so you can bring them out to me."

Lai-an had not been gone for long, when he came out, carrying eight mirrors in all, the ordinary mirrors, large and small, in his two hands, and the rectangular dressing mirror hugged against his breast.

"You lousy little piece!" exclaimed Chin-lien. "You can't handle them all. You should have made two trips out of it. How can you manage to bring them all out at once this way? If you should happen to dent one of my mirrors, what then?"

"I haven't seen this large mirror of yours before," said Meng Yü-lou. "Where did it come from?"

"Someone left it at the pawnshop," said Chin-lien. "I like it because it's so bright. I've put it in my room and use it to look at myself both day and night."

She then went on to say, "Only three of these mirrors actually belong to me."

"And only two of them, one large and one small, are mine," said Meng Yü-lou.

"Then who do these other two belong to?" asked Chin-lien.

"Those two belong to sister Ch'un-mei," said Lai-an. "She sent them out in the hope that he would be able to polish them too."

"The lousy little piece!" said Chin-lien. "She leaves her own mirrors hidden away, unused, while picking up my mirrors to look at herself all the time. No wonder they've gotten so tarnished."

All eight mirrors, large and small, were turned over to the old mirror polisher, who was told to polish away. Thereupon, he fastened them to his workbench, applied mercury to their surfaces, and, in less time than it takes to eat a meal, polished them until they:

Shone brightly enough to dazzle the eyes.[46]

When Chin-lien picked one up and examined her flowery countenance, it was like gazing into:

A stretch of limpid autumn water.

There is a poem that testifies to this:

When the lotus blossom and the caltrop-patterned
    mirror confront each other,
The breeze blows, the countenance is disturbed,
    and the image becomes blurred.
Exposed to the limpid autumn water of her gaze,
    the lotus blossom reveals itself,
Resembling the appearance of the Goddess Ch'ang-o
    in the Palace of the Moon.
With turquoise sleeves she wipes away the dust,
    as the frosty tarnish recedes,
When she breathes upon it with her ruby lips,
    the azure clouds thicken.
If, in their flight, the powdered butterflies
    come to impinge upon it,
One will believe that the blossom's fragrance
    resides in the picture.

When the old mirror polisher, in no time at all, finished polishing the mirrors, he turned them over to the women to look over, and they, in turn, entrusted them to Lai-an to take back inside and put away. Meng Yü-lou told P'ing-an to ask manager Fu Ming, who was tending counter in the shop, for fifty candareens to give to the mirror polisher. That oldster took the money in one hand but remained standing where he was, without leaving.

P'an Chin-lien and Meng Yü-lou Patronize a Mirror Polisher

Meng Yü-lou told P'ing-an to ask the old man, "Why aren't you going? No doubt you think the money is insufficient."

Before they knew it, with a gush, the tears began to flow from his eyes, as he started to weep.

"My mistress wants to know why you are so distressed," said P'ing-an.

"There is no reason to deceive you, Brother," said the old man. "I have led a futile existence for sixty years. Early on, I was left with a son by my first wife, who is now twenty-one years old and is not yet married. All he does is scrounge around like a dog looking for garbage, rather than trying to make a living. I have to go out every day and labor for the money with which to support him, while he, on the other hand:

Is not the sort to abide by his lot,

and is constantly gambling with the knockabouts on the street. The other day, he got himself into trouble and was trussed up with his companions and taken before the commandant's yamen, where he was arraigned for petty larceny, and given twenty strokes with the heavy bamboo. When he came home, he took all of his stepmother's skirts and jackets and pawned them, which upset his stepmother so much that she came down with convulsions and was confined to her bed for half a month. When I said a few words of criticism to him, he simply took off and stopped coming home, so that I now spend every day looking for him, but so far without success. I'm tempted to vent my spleen by giving up on trying to find him at all, but I'm already an old man, and he is my only son, so that, in the future, I would have no one to support me in my old age. But if he were at home, and I saw that he was not turning out to be a decent human being, that would only upset me further. The way things are, he's simply my karmic encumbrance, and all I can do about it is to:

Suffer injustice and harbor resentment,

with no place to lodge a complaint. That's why:

The tears flow from my wounded heart."[47]

Meng Yü-lou said to P'ing-an, "You ask him, 'How old is your second wife this year?' "

"This year she has led a futile existence for fifty-four years," said the old man. "She has neither a son nor daughter of her own, and, now that she has just recovered somewhat from her convulsions, I lack the means to properly nurture her. She has her heart set on a chunk of cured pork, and I have spent the last two or three days scouring through ten or more streets and alleys but have been unable to find any. It's really enough to make one sigh in despair."

"That's no problem," said Meng Yü-lou with a smile. "I've got a chunk of cured pork in a drawer in my quarters."

She then said to Lai-an, "You go speak to Lan-hsiang about it. There are also two leftover scones. Get her to give them to you as well."

Chin-lien then called to the old man, asking him, "Does your old lady eat millet gruel, or not?"

"Why wouldn't she eat it?" said the old man. "That would be just the thing for her."

Chin-lien then called over Lai-an and said, "Tell Ch'un-mei to measure out two pints of that new millet that my mother brought the other day, and also bring out two pickled cucumbers, to give to his old lady to eat."

Lai-an had not been gone for long when he brought out half a leg of cured pork, two scones, two pints of millet, and two pickled cucumbers and called out, "Come over here, old man. You're in luck. If your old lady isn't craving these things because of illness, no doubt she's recuperating from childbirth and feels the need for a 'heart stabilizing potion.' "[48]

The old man promptly received these things with both hands, stowed them in his load, bowed to Meng Yü-lou and Chin-lien, and then, shouldering his burden and shaking his clapper, proceeded nonchalantly on his way.

"You two ladies," remarked P'ing-an, "ought not to have given him all those things. The old oily mouth has contrived to cheat you out of them. His old lady is a go-between, whom I happened to notice walking by on this very street just yesterday. Since when is she convalescing at home?"

"You lousy jailbird!" said Chin-lien. "Why didn't you tell us any earlier?"

"Leave it alone," said P'ing-an. "Let him have his piece of luck. It was just a coincidence that you two ladies had come out, called him to a halt, and patronized him with all those things."

Truly:

Having nothing better to do, they came out
    and idled at the gateway,
Just as the old codger happened to come by
    shaking his clapper.
Not only can even the most trivial things
    be of help to people,
But if you lack the affinity, a drop of water
    will prove hard to get.

If you want to know the outcome of these events,
Pray consult the story related in the following chapter.

Chapter 59

HSI-MEN CH'ING DASHES "SNOW LION" TO DEATH;

LI P'ING-ERH CRIES OUT IN PAIN FOR KUAN-KO

As the sun sets, the rivers flow, returning
    ever from west to east;
So long as the glory of spring is not over,
    the willows will endure.
In the temple of the Goddess of Witch's Mountain,[1]
    they bend to hold the rain;
Before the gate of Sung Yü's residence,
    they flutter in the wind.
There is no comparing the color of elm pods
    to their blue-green hues;
One is profoundly moved by the way they set off
    the red of the apricot blossoms.
On the Pa River in Han-nan there are a thousand
    or ten thousand willow trees;[2]
How many travelers have plucked their branches
    as they said their farewells?[3]

THE STORY GOES that Meng Yü-lou and P'an Chin-lien were still standing at the front gate after sending the mirror polisher on his way, when they suddenly saw a man coming toward them from the east, wearing a large hat and eye shades, and riding a mule. He rode at a fast clip right up to the gateway and dismounted, which sent the two women scurrying inside. When he took off his eye shades, it turned out to be Han Tao-kuo reporting back home.

"Have the cartloads of merchandise arrived, or not?" P'ing-an hastily inquired.

"They're already inside the city," replied Han Tao-kuo. "I've come to ask Father where to unload them."

"Father isn't at home," said P'ing-an. "He's attending a party at the residence of His Honor Chou Hsiu. Space has already been prepared for the merchandise to be unloaded on the second floor of the building across the street. Please go ahead inside."

Before long, Ch'en Ching-chi came out and accompanied Han Tao-kuo to the rear compound, where he reported to Yüeh-niang and then came back outside to the reception hall, brushed the dust of the journey off his clothes, and asked Wang Ching to take his baggage and wallet home for him. Yüeh-niang meanwhile sent something out for him to eat.

It was not long before the cartloads of merchandise arrived. Ch'en Ching-chi took the keys and opened the door to the building across the street, where-upon the carriers who had been hired to unload the carts took their tallies and carried the merchandise, one box at a time, to unload on the second floor of the building. There were ten large cartloads of silk goods, as well as some wine and rice for the use of the family, so the unloading process lasted right up till lamplighting time. Ts'ui Pen also assisted by supervising the com-pletion of the unloading, checking to see that the numbers tallied, locking the door, sealing it with a strip of paper, paying off the carriers, and seeing them off the premises.

While this was going on, Tai-an had gone to Commandant Chou Hsiu's residence to report the news to Hsi-men Ch'ing. When Hsi-men Ch'ing heard that the goods were being unloaded at home, he drank several more cups of wine before leaving and arrived home somewhat after lamplighting time. Han Tao-kuo was sitting in the reception hall waiting for him and gave him a complete recital of the events of the trip, from beginning to end, both going and coming.

Hsi-men Ch'ing then asked him, "When the letter I sent to His Honor Ch'ien Lung-yeh was delivered, did he respond favorably to my request, or not?"

"Thanks entirely to your letter to His Honor Ch'ien Lung-yeh," replied Han Tao-kuo, "we saved a good deal in the way of customs duties. By treating two crates as one, I got away with reporting no more than two-thirds of the merchandise, which I also passed off as consisting merely of tea leaves and mirabilite for the making of incense. As a result, when it came time to compute the charges, for all ten large cartloads of goods we were only assess-ed thirty taels and five mace of silver in the way of customs duties. And when His Honor accepted the affidavit, he did not send any customs offi-cers to inspect the merchandise but merely waved the cartloads of goods on their way."

When Hsi-men Ch'ing heard this, he was utterly delighted and said, "In the future we must purchase a substantial gift to thank His Honor Ch'ien Lung-yeh for his pains."

Thereupon, he ordered Ch'en Ching-chi to keep company with Han Tao-kuo and Ts'ui Pen and also had some food sent out from the rear compound, so that they could have a drink together before breaking up and going home.

When Wang Liu-erh heard that Han Tao-kuo had returned, and that Wang Ching had brought his baggage and wallet home for him, she promptly took charge of the luggage and asked, "So your brother-in-law is back, is he?"

"Brother-in-law is supervising the unloading of the goods," said Wang Ching, "and is waiting to see Father before coming home."

The woman told her maidservants Ch'un-hsiang and Chin-erh to prepare some good tea and good food for the occasion. That night, when Han Tao-kuo finally returned home, he paid his respects before the family shrine, took off his traveling clothes, and washed his face, before husband and wife exchanged accounts of the events that had transpired during their separation. Han Tao-kuo told his wife how pleased he was with the way his business had gone, and his wife observed how heavy and ponderous the silver in his wallet felt.

When she asked him about it, he said, "I also picked up some two or three hundred taels worth of goods, including wine and rice, for myself. I've unloaded it in the shop across the street, and we can sell it off for silver at our leisure."

His wife was utterly delighted by this and went on to say, "I've also heard Wang Ching report that His Honor has found someone named Kan Jun to act as sales manager, and that we will divide a share of the profits with him and Ts'ui Pen, which is good news. I hear that the shop is slated to open for business next month."

"He may have engaged someone to act as sales manager here," said Han Tao-kuo, "but someone will still be needed down south to set up an office and take charge of purchasing at that end. I think His Honor is almost certain to appoint me to that post."

"You've got a good eye for evaluating merchandise," said his wife. "It's always been true that:
The abler you are, the more is demanded of you.[4]
Look you, if you weren't good at this business, would His Honor entrust it to you? As the saying goes:
Unless you are prepared to exert yourself to the utmost;
You will never make any money off the men of this world.[5]
It will probably entail your being away from home for three years. But if you're reluctant to go, I'll speak to His Honor and have him send Kan Jun and Lai-pao to take care of the outside business, and let you stay at home as the sales manager. That ought to do it."

"I'm already habituated to being away from home," said Han Tao-kuo. "Let's leave it at that."

"There you are," said his wife. "As far as you're concerned:
When the physiognomist has lost his touch,
It's all one whether he stays home or not."

When they had finished speaking, she served some wine, and the two of them, husband and wife, drank several cups to celebrate their reunion, after which, they cleared up the utensils and went to bed. That night, they:
Indulged in pleasure without restraint,
but there is no need to describe this in detail.

The next day was the first day of the eighth month. Han Tao-kuo arrived early, and Hsi-men Ch'ing had him join Ts'ui Pen and Kan Jun in supervising the provision of the necessary bricks, tiles, lumber, and stone for the construction of the underground storehouse. But no more of this.

To resume our story, Hsi-men Ch'ing, having already overseen the unloading of the merchandise, and having nothing to occupy him at home, suddenly bethought himself that he would like to pay a visit to the house of Cheng Ai-yüeh. With this end in view, he surreptitiously sent Tai-an to deliver three taels of silver and a set of silk clothing to her. When the madam of the Cheng family bordello heard that His Honor Hsi-men Ch'ing was coming to engage the services of one of her girls, she felt:

> Just as though he had fallen from Heaven.

Making haste to take charge of the presents, she blurted out to Tai-an, "Express my utmost gratitude to His Honor, and tell him that both of my girls will await him here, and urge him to drop in as soon as possible."

Tai-an went back home and reported this to Hsi-men Ch'ing in his studio. Early that afternoon, Hsi-men Ch'ing directed Tai-an to prepare a wickerwork sedan chair for him. He then donned a Tung-p'o hat on his head, a long gown of jet moiré with a muted mandarin square woven inconspicuously into the fabric, and white-soled black boots.

He first went to the house across the street and watched the progress on the construction of the underground storehouse for a while, after which he stood up, took his seat in the wickerwork sedan chair, and let down the speckled bamboo blinds. He arranged for Ch'in-t'ung and Tai-an to accompany him, left Wang Ching at home, taking only Ch'un-hung to carry his dispatch case, and headed straight for Cheng Ai-yüeh's establishment in the licensed quarter. Truly:

> The Weaving Maid, positioned at her loom,
>   adjusts the fragrant silk;
> Injecting his hand, he manages to tear off
>   a bolt of the snowy fabric.
> Not satisfied to seek the ford leading to
>   the Peach Blossom Spring;
> He prefers to come to the Moon Grotto for
>   a liaison with Ch'ang-o.[6]

To resume our story, Cheng Ai-hsiang, sporting on her head a chignon enclosed in a fret of silver filigree with plum-blossom-shaped ornaments, fastened in place all round with gold filigree pins; made up in such a way as to enhance her:

> Powdered face and glossy hair,
> Flowery visage and moon-like features;[7]

wearing a blouse of pale lavender silk above, and a beige skirt below; upon seeing Hsi-men Ch'ing arrive, stood just inside the open upper half of the doorway[8] with a broad smile on her face, ushered him inside to the parlor, and saluted him with a bow.

Hsi-men Ch'ing sat down and instructed the page boy Ch'in-t'ung, "Take the sedan chair home with you now, and come back to get me with a horse this evening."

Ch'in-t'ung accordingly went home with the sedan chair. But no more of this. Hsi-men Ch'ing kept only Tai-an and Ch'un-hung to wait upon him.

After some time, the madam came out to pay her respects and said, "The other day, at your place, my girl put you to a lot of trouble. No doubt Your Honor was bored silly at home and has simply come here in search of diversion. What need was there for you to worry about sending any gifts? But, many thanks for the clothing you have provided for my girl."

"When I engaged her services for that day," said Hsi-men Ch'ing, "why didn't she come? Is it that you only recognize the household of that distaff relative of the imperial family, Wang the Second?"

"We are still upset," explained the madam, "that Tung Chiao-erh and Li Kuei-chieh failed to inform us that it was Your Honor's birthday that their services were being engaged for. They each had presents for the occasion, while only my girl had not prepared anything. If I had known it was your birthday, I certainly would never have agreed to let her go perform at Wang the Second's place but would have had her go to Your Honor's residence first, despite the fact that the engagement for her to sing at Your Honor's place was made later. My girl was just getting herself ready to start out when someone from Wang the Second's household showed up and proposed to make off with her costume bag. Right after that, Your Honor sent someone here, along with her elder brother Cheng Feng, who said, 'If you don't go to his place, His Honor will be moved to anger.' This threw me into such a fluster that I hustled my girl out the back door and into her sedan chair behind the back of the servant from the Wang household."

"The other day," said Hsi-men Ch'ing, "while I was attending a party at the residence of His Honor Hsia Yen-ling, I engaged her services. If she had failed to show up for the occasion, needless to say, I would have been annoyed. How is it that on that day she conducted herself:

Without saying anything or uttering so much as a word,
Conveying the clear impression that she was not happy?[9]
Really, how do you account for it?"

"The little baggage!" responded the madam. "Ever since she was deflowered, she has been reluctant to go out and perform in public. When she found herself in Your Honor's residence and saw all the people there, who knows how frightened she may have been? Ever since she was a child, she has been sparing of words and has been spoiled enough to get away with it. Look how late in the day it is already, and she has just gotten up. I pressed her several times, saying, 'His Honor is coming today, you ought to get up and get yourself ready,' but she paid me no heed and continued to lie in bed to this hour."

Before long, a maidservant brought in some tea, and Cheng Ai-hsiang came forward to serve it.

When they had finished the tea, the madam said, "Will Your Honor please come into the interior and have a seat."

It so happens that Cheng Ai-hsiang's establishment consisted of a twenty-four-foot-wide frontage opening onto the street and five interior courtyards, receding along a vertical axis. Just inside the hanging screen, there was a fence of woven bamboo splints, behind which there was an eighteen-foot-wide courtyard, with four anterooms ranged along either side. The main suite at the far end of the courtyard consisted of three compartments, one well-lighted parlor, and two less well-lighted inner rooms, and was the dwelling place of Cheng Ai-yüeh. The quarters in which her elder sister Cheng Ai-hsiang lived were located further back, in the fourth courtyard.

Hsi-men Ch'ing observed that:

The screens and lattices were redolent of incense.

As he entered the parlor, he saw that there was a hanging scroll depicting Kuan-yin of the Ocean Tides in the place of honor on the facing wall, while on the walls to either side there were hung four scrolls depicting beautiful women in the four seasons, spring, summer, autumn, and winter, inscribed with the poetic lines:

Concerned for the flowers, one rises early in spring.
Enamored of the moon, one goes to sleep late at night.
Scooping up water, one finds the moon in one's hands.
Fondling the flowers, fragrance infuses one's clothes.[10]

Above everything was suspended a couplet that read:

Rolling up the blind, one invites the moon to look in;
Tuning the cithara, one waits for the clouds to enter.

At the head of the room there were arrayed four Tung-p'o chairs,[11] and on either side were placed two wide benches finished with translucent varnish of the kind used in the making of zithers.[12] Hsi-men Ch'ing sat down and saw that there was a plaque over the room inscribed with three characters in formal script designating it as "The Moon-loving Studio."

After he had waited for what seemed like half a day, he suddenly became aware of the rustle of the portiere as Cheng Ai-yüeh came in. She was not wearing a fret but had done up her hair in a casual "bag of silk" chignon in the Hang-chou style. Her raven locks were combed in such a way as to set off their blackness and glossiness. Two tufts of hair were allowed to escape at either temple. Her cloudy locks were piled up in disarray, suggesting a range of effects from light mist to dense fog, and were further enhanced with judiciously placed gold-flecked trinkets, and plum-blossom-shaped ornaments

with kingfisher feather inlays, fastened in place all round with gold filigree
pins neatly stuck into the hair behind her temples.

A phoenix hairpin was half askew.

Her ears were adorned with pendant amethyst earrings. Above, she wore a
blouse, fit for an immortal, of pale lavender silk that opened down the middle.
Below, she wore a skirt of purple chiffon, decorated with turquoise figures:

Beneath which there peeked out a pair of tiny shoes,
The points of which bore the beaks of red phoenixes.

On her breast there was suspended a necklace of sculpted jade stones that
tinkled when she moved. On her face she wore three turquoise beauty patches
that served to enhance the lotus blossom of her painted face. All around her:

There floated a fragrant aura;[13]

serving to set off:

Her willowlike slender waist.[14]

Truly:

If she is not the image of a portrait of
Kuan-yin by Wu Tao-tzu;[15]
She must be the subject of a painting of
a beauty by Mao Yen-shou.[16]

After having faced in his direction and:

Neither correctly nor precisely,

made a bow to Hsi-men Ch'ing, she concealed her powdered face behind a
gold-flecked fan and sat down next to him.

Hsi-men Ch'ing:

Focused his eyes on her with a fixed stare,

and felt that she appeared even more stunning than when he had seen her
for the first time. Involuntarily:

His heart was agitated and his eyes disturbed,

to such an extent that:

He was unable to control himself.

Before long, a maidservant brought in another serving of tea, at which the
painted face:

Lightly flaunted her silken sleeves,
Slightly exposed her slender fingers,

brought a cup of tea over to him, brushed away a few drops of water from the
rim of the cup, and presented it to Hsi-men Ch'ing with both hands. After
this, she and Cheng Ai-hsiang each took a cup for themselves and kept him
company as they drank it together. When the tea was finished, and the cups
and raised saucers had been taken away, they suggested that he loosen his
outer garments and take a seat in the inner room.

Hsi-men Ch'ing called Tai-an to come forward, help him off with his black
silk outer garment, and put it on a chair for him; after which he entered into
the painted face's bedroom. Behold:

Because the green windows were curtained
   with white gauze,
The pale moonlight barely invaded them;
Because the brocade hangings were exposed
   to the night light,
They glowed with an auspicious luster.[17]
Inside the room there was a black lacquer bedstead
   with incised gold ornamentation:
The curtains of which were of embroidered brocade;
The coverlet of which concealed a patterned quilt.
To one side there was a low table of carved red lacquer,
   and a small Po-shan incense burner,[18]
From which the aroma of aloeswood and sandalwood
   assailed the nostrils.[19]
On the wall there hung a brocade bag that held
   a "Tinkling Spring" zither;[20]
In a silver vase there were displayed blossoms
   of "Purple Shoots" camellia.[21]
In front of the bed there stood two low chairs
   with embroidered cushions;
Beside which there hung a pair of brocaded
   curtains of mermaid silk.
Upon a mica screen, was depicted a landscape
   in varying shades of ink;
On a shelf of the nuptial couch, was a pile
   of ancient and modern books.[22]
When Hsi-men Ch'ing sat down, he felt that:
   An exotic aroma invaded his person;[23]
   As refined and elegant as could be.[24]
It was just what is conventionally described as:
   A grotto palace of spirits and immortals,[25]
   A destination inaccessible to human feet.[26]
   As they engaged each other in conversation,
   While laughing and joking with each other,
who should they see but a maidservant, who came in and set up a small table,
on which she laid out four small turquoise saucers containing exquisitely pre-
pared julienned vegetables, shredded celery, minced and marinated sturgeon,
phoenix entrails and puree. After this, she brought out two servings of:
   Perfectly round,
   Like the bright moon,
   Thin as paper,
   White as snow,
   Fragrant, sweet, and delectable,

> Butterfat and honey,
> Sesame, pepper, and salt flavored,
> Thin lotus-blossom pancakes.

Cheng Ai-hsiang and Cheng Ai-yüeh then proceeded with their own hands to make selections of the various shredded meats and vegetables, wrap them in the pancakes into spring rolls, place them in small gilded saucers, and present them to Hsi-men Ch'ing to eat. To one side, cups of gold-inlaid cloisonné were filled with strong cinnamon and osmanthus flavored tea.

Before long, after the two sisters had joined him in consuming the spring rolls, and the utensils had been put away, and the table wiped off, a madder red strip of felt was placed over a bed table, a set of thirty-two ivory dominoes was extracted from a sandalwood box decorated with carved lacquer, and the two of them proceeded to play dominoes with Hsi-men Ch'ing. In due course, Hsi-men Ch'ing melded the combinations known as "Heaven and Earth Separated"[27] and "Ten Pricks with a Sword,"[28] Cheng Ai-hsiang melded the combinations known as "Earth"[29] and "Flowers Blossom and Butterflies Fill the Branches,"[30] and Cheng Ai-yüeh melded the combinations known as "Man"[31] and "Mounts a Ladder to Gaze at the Moon."[32]

After a while, they put the dominoes away, and wine was served. Behold:

> Platters are piled with exotic fruits,
> The wine overflows with golden ripples.

The table was spread with goose, duck, chicken feet, fried dragon, and roasted phoenix.

> The scarce fruits were:
> Seldom seen in this world;[33]
> The rare repast was:
> Unmatched in Heaven itself.[34]

Truly:

> Their dancing waylays the bright moon
>   into shining on the pleasure-houses of Ch'in;
> Their singing diverts the moving clouds
>   into hovering atop the bordellos of Ch'u.[35]
> In mandarin duck goblets,
> And turquoise wine cups,
> They drink the jade hued liquids,
> And carnelian nectars of the gods.

The two sisters plied him with wine and then positioned themselves to one side, where Cheng Ai-hsiang, with:

> The bridges on her psaltery ranged like wild geese,
> Gently strummed the silken strings.

Thereupon, with Cheng Ai-hsiang playing the psaltery, and Cheng Ai-yüeh playing the p'i-p'a, they sang the song suite, beginning with the tune "A Happy Event Is Imminent," that opens with the words:

Insistently he comes into my mind.[36]

Truly:

> When words emerge from the mouth of a beauty,[37]
> They have a timbre that causes rocks to split
> and lingers around the rafters.

When they had finished singing, another twelve saucers of assorted nuts and other delicacies were served, and the two sisters:

> Moving their seats closer together,[38]

got out a dicebox with twenty dice and fell to playing "Competing for the Red"[39] and guess-fingers with Hsi-men Ch'ing.

After they had been drinking for some time, Cheng Ai-hsiang, alleging that she had to go to the bathroom, disappeared, leaving Cheng Ai-yüeh alone to continue drinking with Hsi-men Ch'ing.

To begin with, Hsi-men Ch'ing reached into his sleeve and pulled out a white satin handkerchief with a double-patterned border, to one end of which was attached a chatelaine with three pendant charms, including a toothpick, and, to the other end, a cylindrical gold pillbox.

Cheng Ai-yüeh assumed that it contained breath-sweetening lozenges and wanted to open it, but Hsi-men Ch'ing said, "It doesn't contain breath-sweetening lozenges, but a restorative medication that I use every day. My breath-sweetening lozenges are not kept there but are wrapped in a paper packet."

Thereupon, he reached into his sleeve, pulled out a packet of cinnamon-flavored breath-sweetening lozenges, and handed it to her.

Cheng Ai-yüeh, who was still unsatisfied, stuck out her hand to grope inside his other sleeve and discovered a purple crepe handkerchief, with a low-grade gold toothpick attached to it, which she held in her hand to admire, saying, "I've noticed that Li Kuei-chieh and Wu Yin-erh both have handkerchiefs like this. So it was you they got them from."

"They were part of my boatload of goods that just arrived from Yang-chou," said Hsi-men Ch'ing. "If they didn't get them from me, who else could they have gotten them from? If you like it, you can have it, and tomorrow I'll send another like it to your sister."

When they had finished speaking, Hsi-men Ch'ing swallowed a dose of the medication in his cylindrical pillbox, washed it down with a cupful of wine, and took the painted face onto his lap. The two of them then passed the same cup back and forth between them as they drank and sucked each other's tongues.

> There was no length to which they would not go.

Hsi-men Ch'ing then stuck out his hand and proceeded to fondle her fragrant breasts, which were:

> Tight and squeezy,

and as smooth as sesame seed glutinous rice dumplings. Opening up her blouse to take a look at them, he saw that they were:

Pale and fragrant,

and as lustrous as jade. After he had played with them for some time, his:

Lecherous desires were suddenly aroused,

and the organ that lay between his loins abruptly sprang to life. Loosening his pant strings, he suggested that she grasp it with her slender fingers.

When the painted face saw how long and thick it was, she was so perturbed she stuck her tongue out in fear and, putting her arms around Hsi-men Ch'ing's neck, said, "My darling, since this is our first tryst, please bear with me, and only insert it halfway. If you stick it all in, it will be the death of me. That must have been an aphrodisiac you took to make it as big as this. Otherwise, how on earth could you ever have produced anything so monstrous, deep red, and purple? It's really enough to give one the creeps."

Hsi-men Ch'ing laughed and said, "My child, get down on your knees and suck it for me."

"What's the hurry?" said Cheng Ai-yüeh. "After all:

There are as many days ahead of us as there are
    leaves on the trees.

This is our first tryst today.

We are newly acquainted and hardly know each other.[40]

If you come again, I'll suck it for you."

When they had finished speaking, Hsi-men Ch'ing sought to take his pleasure with her.

"Do you not want any more wine?" asked Cheng Ai-yüeh.

"I've had enough," said Hsi-men Ch'ing. "Let's go to bed."

Cheng Ai-yüeh then called for a maidservant to move the table at which they had been drinking out of the way and help Hsi-men Ch'ing off with his boots, while she went inside to relieve herself and wash her private parts. When Hsi-men Ch'ing's boots had been removed, he rewarded the maidservant with a piece of silver, after which, he got into bed while the maidservant lit some incense and put it in the burner.

After a while, the woman came back into the room and asked Hsi-men Ch'ing, "Would you like some tea, or not?"

To which Hsi-men Ch'ing replied, "I don't want any."

She then closed the door to the room, let down the satin chiffon bed curtains, put a handkerchief under the bedding, took off her clothes, and got into bed. The two of them then proceeded to cavort like:

Mandarin ducks upon the pillow,

Water birds under the coverlet.

Hsi-men Ch'ing saw that when the painted face took off her clothes, her skin was delicate and fine, and her vagina was clean and devoid of pubic hair, as soft and delectable as a white steamed bun. When he embraced her waist, it was hardly a handful. In truth, she was just like:

Soft jade and warm incense;[41]

Not to be bought for a thousand pieces of gold.[42]

Hsi-men Ch'ing Exposes His Organ and Startles Cheng Ai-yüeh

Thereupon, he wrapped her two fresh, white, tender legs, like bars of silver, around his waist, fastened the clasp on his organ, and plunged it into the heart of the flower. His turtle head was proud and large, so that, even with moistening and reaming, it was some time before the knob of his glans was submerged. Cheng Ai-yüeh knitted her brows together and gripped the pillow with both hands, finding her distress hard to bear.

Her starry eyes grew dim and she pled with him, "Pray spare your Cheng Ai-yüeh today."

Hsi-men Ch'ing then hoisted her two golden lotuses over his shoulders and devoted himself to retracting and thrusting:

> Unable to contain his pleasure.[43]

Truly, it is a case of:

> When spring touches the apricot and peach trees,
>   their new buds burst into red flower;
> When the breeze plays among the willow fronds,
>   they are made to bend their green waists.[44]

There is a poem about the flowering crab apple that testifies to this:

> Bearing raindrops, shrouded in mist,
>   this sapling is remarkable;
> Beguiling in stance, it appears to be
>   unable to support itself.
> Its red reminds one of the matchless
>   blooms of the West Park;[45]
> In spring it wins first place among
>   the flowers of Ho-yang.[46]
> Its gaudy coloring inspires comparison
>   with that of Master Cheng;[47]
> The skill demonstrated belies analogy
>   with the work of Wang Wei.[48]
> Replete with feeling, it deliberately
>   keeps its heart in check;
> Holding onto the east wind to prevent
>   it from returning home.[49]

On this occasion, Hsi-men Ch'ing dallied with Cheng Ai-yüeh until the third watch before going home.

The next day, Wu Yüeh-niang, after seeing him off to the yamen, remained seated in the master suite along with Meng Yü-lou, P'an Chin-lien, and Li Chiao-erh. Who should appear at this juncture but Tai-an, who came in to fetch a gift box for bolts of fabric and the like, in which to deliver the birthday presents for Judicial Commissioner Hsia Yen-ling, consisting of four varieties of fresh delicacies, a jug of wine, and a bolt of brocade.

Yüeh-niang took advantage of the occasion to ask Tai-an, "Whose place was it that your father took a sedan chair to go drinking at yesterday and remained drinking so late before coming home? I imagine he must have gone to Han Tao-kuo's house to look in on that wife of his. You lousy jailbird! It seems that you keep me in the dark all the time, while abetting him in these tricks behind my back."

"That's not the case," said Tai-an. "After all, her husband has come home. How could Father do anything like that?"

"If he didn't go there," said Yüeh-niang, "where did he go?"

Tai-an did not reply but merely smiled, picked up the gift box, and went off to deliver the presents.

"Mother," said Chin-lien, "there's no point in your asking that lousy jailbird anything. He'll never tell you the truth. But I've heard that that southern page boy also accompanied Father on his expedition yesterday. The thing to do is to call in that southern page boy and ask him about it."

She then proceeded to summon Ch'un-hung into their presence.

"When you accompanied your father's sedan chair yesterday," said Chin-lien, "whose place did he go drinking at? If you tell the truth, we'll leave it at that. But if you fail to tell the truth, the First Lady will see that you get a beating on the spot."

Ch'un-hung knelt down and said, "Mother, don't beat me. I'll tell you all about it, that's all. Your servant, along with Tai-an and Brother Ch'in-t'ung, the three of us, accompanied Father in going through a great gateway, after which we traversed several streets and alleys and came to a house with a door, inlaid with a sawtooth pattern, only the lower half of which was closed, inside which there stood a lady who was all made up in a flashy fashion."

When Chin-lien heard this, she laughed, saying, "The jailbird! He doesn't even recognize the horizontal half-doors of the licensed quarter, and he refers to a painted face as a lady."

"And what did that lady look like?" Chin-lien went on to ask. "Did you recognize her or not?"

"I didn't recognize her," said Ch'un-hung. "She looked like a veritable Bodhisattva and was wearing a fret on her head just like the ones you ladies wear. When we went inside, an old crone with white hair came out and saluted Father with a bow, after which we were invited into the interior, which was protected by a fence of woven bamboo splints. Once inside, another young lady appeared, who was not wearing a fret, but had a silver salver face, shaped like a melon-seed, and whose lips were daubed with red. She kept Father company while he drank."

"And where were you allowed to sit all this time?" asked Chin-lien.

"Tai-an, Brother Ch'in-t'ung, and I," replied Ch'un-hung, "were entertained in the room of the old crone, who provided us with wine and pork dumplings, and kept us company as we consumed them."

This caused Yüeh-niang and Meng Yü-lou to laugh without restraint.

They then went on to ask, "Did you recognize this lady, or not?"

"It seemed to me that she has performed at our place," replied Ch'un-hung.

"Then it must have been Li Kuei-chieh," laughed Meng Yü-lou.

"So it seems that's where he snuck off to," said Yüeh-niang.

"Our establishment doesn't have horizontal half-doors," said Li Kuei-chieh. "And it doesn't have a fence woven of bamboo splints either."

"I fear you may not know about it," said Chin-lien. "Perhaps your place has recently put in horizontal half-doors."

After they had interrogated Ch'un-hung for a while, Hsi-men Ch'ing came home from the yamen and then set out for the residence of Hsia Yen-ling to celebrate his birthday.

To resume our story, P'an Chin-lien kept a white long-haired leonine cat in her quarters, whose entire body was pure white, except for a streak of tortoiseshell-patterned black fur on its forehead. It was named "Coal in the Snow"[50] and was also called "Snow Lion," and it could pick up handkerchiefs and fans in its mouth. When Hsi-men Ch'ing was not in her quarters, the woman would go to sleep with the cat cuddled in her arms underneath the quilt, and it never soiled her garments with urine or feces. When the woman ate, it would often perch on her shoulder and allow her to feed it.

> When summoned, it would come;
> When dismissed, it would go.[51]

The woman commonly referred to it as "Snow Bandit." Its daily diet consisted, not of calves' liver or dried fish, but of half a pound of raw meat, as a result of which, it was as fat and sturdy as could be, and its fur was so thick you could hide an egg in it. She was extremely fond of it and petted it on her lap all day long, but not with benevolent intent. Knowing that Li P'ing-erh's child, Kuan-ko, had previously shown a fondness for cats, she would frequently, when no one else was around, wrap the meat in a piece of red silk and encourage the cat to pounce on it, tear it open, and eat it.

This was one of those occasions on which:

> Something was destined to happen.

Kuan-ko had not been feeling very well. For some days he had been taking the medications prescribed by Dame Liu, and he felt a little better. Li P'ing-erh had dressed him in a shirt of red chiffon and put him on a little sleeping mat on the k'ang in the outer room to play. Ying-ch'un was looking after him, while the wet nurse was holding a bowl in her hand and eating to one side. Unexpectedly, this "Snow Lion" from Chin-lien's quarters, which had been perched on the bedrail, upon seeing Kuan-ko lying on the k'ang dressed in a red shirt and fidgeting as he played, was reminded of the way in which its meat was customarily prepared for it, and suddenly pounced down onto Kuan-ko's body and tore at him with its claws.

All that could be heard was:

> The sound of a gurgling cry,

as Kuan-ko choked up and then fell silent, while his hands and feet went into convulsions. This threw the wet nurse into such consternation that she dropped her rice bowl, picked Kuan-ko up and cuddled him on her lap, while devoting herself to prophylactic spitting, in the endeavor to exorcise the fright. Meanwhile the cat continued to claw at him until Ying-ch'un drove it out of the room. Ju-i expected that the child would merely undergo a fit of convulsions, and then be all right, but who could have anticipated that they went on continuously, one fit being succeeded by another.

Li P'ing-erh was back in the rear compound at the time, so Ju-i sent Ying-ch'un there to fetch her, saying, "Little brother is unwell and is suffering from convulsions. Mother had better come quickly."

Nothing might have happened if Li P'ing-erh had not heard this, but having heard it, truly:

> The shock affected all six of her vital organs,
>   including liver and lungs;
> The fright damaged the three bristles and seven
>   apertures of her heart.[52]

Yüeh-niang also was thrown into such consternation that:

> Covering two steps with every one,

she too rushed straight to Li P'ing-erh's quarters. What they found when they got there was that the convulsions had caused the child's eyeballs to roll straight up so that their black pupils were completely invisible, white foam was dribbling from his mouth, he was making inarticulate sounds like the chirping of a young chick, and his hands and feet were moving spasmodically. Li P'ing-erh no sooner saw this than she felt as though her heart were being lacerated with a knife.

Hastily picking him up and holding him in her arms, she brushed her cheek against his mouth and wept loudly, saying, "My little child, you were doing fine when I went out. Why should you have gone into convulsions?"

Ying-ch'un and the wet nurse then told her all about how he had been frightened by the cat from the Fifth Lady's quarters.

Li P'ing-erh wept all the more, saying, "My little child, you have simply failed to live up to the expectations of your father and mother. And today, there's no gainsaying the fact that there's no other road for you to take."

When Yüeh-niang heard this, she said not a word, but sent for Chin-lien and interrogated her, saying, "They say that it was the cat from your quarters that frightened the child."

"Who says so?" demanded Chin-lien.

Yüeh-niang indicated that it was the wet nurse and Ying-ch'un who had said so.

"Just look at the goggle-eyed way the old woman is staring at me," said Chin-lien. "My cat is happily asleep in my room, isn't it. You're talking nonsense. How could it have frightened the child? You'd better not try to blame it on me:

> Snitching only those melons whose
> stems are soft.[53]

It seems that only the inhabitants of my quarters are fit to be taken advantage of."

"What was her cat doing in this room?" asked Yüeh-niang.

"It constantly comes over here to play," said Ying-ch'un.

Chin-lien picked up where she left off, saying, "It's a good thing you said that. If it's constantly over here, why hadn't it scratched him before, instead of picking on this particular day to start scratching him? You slavey! You're just following in her footsteps, what with your:

> Knitted brows and staring eyes,

and your:

> Ridiculous blatherskite.

Take it easy, will you! There's no call for you to:

> Pull your bow all the way taut,[54]

like that. I guess we're just doomed to be out of favor."

Whereupon, she took herself off to her quarters in a huff.

Gentle reader take note: As the saying goes:

> Flowering branches, beneath their leaves,
> conceal their thorns;
> How can one know for sure the human heart
> contains no poison?[55]

This P'an Chin-lien, having been aware for some time that ever since Li P'ing-erh had borne Kuan-ko, Hsi-men Ch'ing had been:

> Obedient to her every whim,

that:

> Whatever she asked for, she received tenfold,

and that every day she was:

> Contending in beauty and competing for favor,[56]

had developed feelings of jealousy and anger in her heart over this favoritism. On this day, therefore, she had deliberately set this secret plot in motion, training her cat for the purpose, out of a desire to frighten her rival's child to death, and thereby diminish Li P'ing-erh's favor, and cause Hsi-men Ch'ing to resume his intimacy with her. It was just like the way in which, in ancient times, T'u-an Ku trained his dog, Shen-ao, with the intent to murder the grand councilor, Chao Tun.[57] Truly:

> Azure Heaven, in its profundity,[58]
> cannot be deceived;[59]
> Before intentions are even formed
> it is aware of them.[60]

Say not that timely retribution
  seems not to occur;
From ancient times until today[61]
  who has been spared?[62]

When Yüeh-niang and the rest of them saw that the child was continuing to suffer from convulsions, on the one hand, they decocted some ginger extract and poured it into his mouth, while, on the other hand, they sent Lai-an off to summon Dame Liu as quickly as possible.

Before long, Dame Liu showed up, examined his pulse, and then, stamping her feet in frustration, said, "This time the fright he has been subjected to is serious. It has resulted in a case of tetany, which is difficult to cure."

She urgently directed them to prepare a decoction of bog rush, field mint, and honeysuckle, after which she pulled out a bolus of gold foil and dissolved it in a cup of the decoction. The baby's jaws were tightly closed, but Yüeh-niang promptly extracted a gold pin from her hair and pried his mouth open with it in order to pour the decoction into his mouth.

"If this proves effective," said Dame Liu, "that will be that. But, if it does not, as I've already told you, Madame, we'll have to resort to moxabustion at several points before there will be any hope of recovery."

"Who would be willing to take responsibility for that?" said Yüeh-niang. "We'll have to wait until his father gets home, and consult with him about it. Otherwise, if we go ahead with the moxabustion on our own, he's likely to raise a hue and cry when he gets home."

"First Lady, his life is at stake," said Li P'ing-erh. "If we wait till he gets home, it may be too late. If his father should get abusive about it, I'm willing to take the heat."

"It's your child, after all" said Yüeh-niang. "Proceed with the moxabustion if you like. I won't presume to take a stand on the issue."

Thereupon, Dame Liu proceeded to apply moxabustion to the glabella between his eyebrows, the nape of his neck, the wrists of his two hands, and his precordium, five points in all, after which he was put down to sleep. The child, who was:

  Both torpid and comatose,[63]

slept right up until the time when Hsi-men Ch'ing returned home that evening, without waking up.

When Dame Liu saw that Hsi-men Ch'ing had come home, she took the five mace of silver that Yüeh-niang paid her for her services and disappeared through the enclosed passageway in a puff of smoke.

When Hsi-men Ch'ing arrived back in the master suite, Yüeh-niang told him how the child had fallen ill and suffered from convulsions. He immediately went out to the front compound to see for himself and observed that Li P'ing-erh's eyes were red with weeping.

"What caused the child to go into convulsions?" he asked.

Li P'ing-erh's eyes brimmed over with tears, but she did not have a word to say. When he asked the maidservant and the wet nurse, they did not dare to reply. When Hsi-men Ch'ing saw the spots on Kuan-ko's hands where the skin had been torn off, and the scars that the moxabustion had left on the other parts of his body, he became furious and strode back to the rear compound to question Yüeh-niang about it. Yüeh-niang felt unable to conceal the facts and told him how the cat from Chin-lien's quarters had frightened the child.

"Dame Liu had no sooner examined him," she explained, "than she said that it was an extreme case of tetany, that if we did not resort to acupuncture and moxabustion it was doubtful if he would recover, and that if we waited until you got home, it might be too late. His mother decided in favor of moxabustion, and it was applied to five points on the child's body, after which he was put down to sleep. It's been half a day now, and he hasn't yet waked up."

If Hsi-men Ch'ing had not heard these words nothing might have happened, but having heard them:

> The spirits of his Three Corpses became agitated;
> The breaths of his Five Viscera ascended to Heaven.[64]
> Anger flared up in his heart, and
> Malice accrued in his gall.

Heading straight for P'an Chin-lien's quarters:

> Without permitting any further explanation,

he sought out the cat and, dangling it by one foot, strode out to the veranda, took aim at the stone stylobate, swung the cat up into the air, and dashed it against it. All that could be heard was:

> A single resounding report,

at which:

> The contents of its brain burst into
>   ten thousand peach blossoms;[65]
> Its mouthful of teeth were reduced to
>   scattered fragments of jade.[66]

Truly:

> No longer able in the world of light
>   to capture rats or mice,
> It reverts to the abode of the dead
>   to become a fox fairy.[67]

When P'an Chin-lien saw that he had taken her cat out and dashed it to death, she sat on her k'ang:

> Without turning so much as a hair,

and waited until he had vacated her quarters, muttering to herself, as she cursed him, saying, "You lousy death-defying ruffian! If you had only dragged me out and killed me, it would have been more heroic of you. Did the cat really get in the way of your shit-eating business so much that you felt compelled to barge in here, like a madman, and dash it to death? When it comes before the authorities in the nether world, it's likely to demand your life in compensation. What are you so exercised about? You'll come to a bad end, you lousy fickle ruffian!"

Hsi-men Ch'ing went back to Li P'ing-erh's quarters and berated the wet nurse and Ying-ch'un, saying, "I instructed you to take special care of the child. How could you have allowed the cat to frighten it so, and even claw the skin off its hands? And how could you have had such confidence in that old whore, Dame Liu, as to allow her to subject him to such a course of moxabustion, for no good reason? If he recovers, that will be that; but if he doesn't, I'll have that old whore dragged off to the yamen and subjected to a finger-squeezing or two."

"Look you," expostulated Li P'ing-erh, "the child's life was at stake, and yet you carry on this way. After all, compassion is a prerequisite for medical practitioners. She was as concerned for his welfare as anyone."

From that time on, all Li P'ing-erh could do was to hope for the child's recovery. Unexpectedly, however, the effect of the moxabustion had been to internalize the disorder so that it became a case of chronic mild convulsions of the stomach and intestines, and the discharge of both urine and feces. The stools that he extruded were variegated in color, his eyes opened and closed irregularly, he remained torpid and comatose all day long, and he would not allow himself to be breast-fed.

Li P'ing-erh became panicked about the situation. Everywhere she could think of:

The gods were besought and diviners consulted,
but the results of these prognostications were all:
Ominous and inauspicious.[68]
Yüeh-niang, behind Hsi-men Ch'ing's back, once again invited Dame Liu to come and perform a shamanistic dance on behalf of Kuan-ko. She also invited a licensed pediatrician to come and examine him.

He recommended that they try a powdered nasal decongestant on him, saying, "If it causes him to sneeze when insufflated into his nostrils, he may recover; but if no mucus is dislodged, all you can do is keep vigil over him and hope that the good deeds you have done in secret will avail."

Thereupon, they insufflated the powder into his nostrils, but he remained:
Insensibly oblivious,[69]
without so much as a sneeze. As a result, Li P'ing-erh kept vigil over him day and night, even more assiduously than before, while:
Weeping and sniffling unceasingly,
and even reducing her food and drink to a minimum.

As the fifteenth day of the eighth month gradually approached, Yüeh-niang, on account of Kuan-ko's indisposition, decided to abandon the celebration of her own birthday. Even those relatives who had sent presents to her were not invited for the occasion. The only people in the house to keep her company were Sister-in-law Wu, Aunt Yang, and the abbess of Kuan-yin Nunnery.

Meanwhile, Nun Hsüeh and Nun Wang were engaged in a dispute over the division of the profits they had reaped on the money Li P'ing-erh had provided to the sutra printing shop and were hurling angry accusations at each other.

On the fourteenth, Pen the Fourth and Nun Hsüeh went to the shop to demand the promised delivery, and all fifteen hundred copies of the sutra were carried back to the house. Li P'ing-erh also donated a string of cash for the purchase of paper money, incense, and candles. Early on the morning of the fifteenth, Pen the Fourth accompanied Ch'en Ching-chi to the Temple of the God of the Eastern Peak to present the incense and paper money and oversee the disposition of the sutras, all of which were duly distributed, and then came back to report to Li P'ing-erh.

The family of Ch'iao Hung sent Auntie K'ung over every day to see how Kuan-ko was doing and also recommended a pediatrician named Dr. Pao, who came to examine him and said, "This is a case in which the baleful star Tiao-k'o, or Condoler, has been offended. No cure is possible."

Li P'ing-erh gave him five mace of silver and sent him on his way. When she tried to pour the medication he had prescribed into Kuan-ko's mouth, he rejected it and spit it up. Keeping his eyes closed, he cried out in such a manner that the edges of his teeth chattered against each other. Li P'ing-erh:

Without taking the trouble to undress,[70]

held him on her lap day and night, weeping the while, so that:

Her tears never dried.

Hsi-men Ch'ing also abstained from all social engagements, coming in to see the child every day as soon as he arrived home from the yamen.

At this time, one day in the final decade of the eighth month, Li P'ing-erh was lying on her bed, holding Kuan-ko in her arms, while a silver lamp burned on the table. The maidservants and the wet nurse were all fast asleep. Observing that:

The window was illuminated by moonlight,[71]

While the clepsydra dripped interminably,

and that her child was comatose, and:

Oblivious to human affairs,[72]

she felt for some time as though:

Her sorrow-laden bowels were tied in a myriad knots,[73]

While her fears of separation took a thousand forms.

Truly:

When one confronts happy events, one's
    spirits are exhilarated;[74]
When melancholy invades one's bowels,
    one is prone to nod off.[75]

Behold:

> The silver river shines resplendent;[76]
> The jade clepsydra drips unendingly.[77]
> The bright moon penetrates the window,
>   blazing with cold light;
> The cool breeze infiltrates the door,
>   blowing its night breath.
> The cries of the wild geese resonate,
> Disturbing the dreams of men of talent
>   who sleep alone.
> The chirring of crickets is desolate,
> Embittering the feelings of beauties
>   in solitary slumber.
> The watch-marking drums on the watchtower,
> Before a single watch is done with,
>   sound a new one;
> The laundry bats in an adjacent courtyard,
> Before a thousand blows are finished,
>   strike up another.
> Before painted eaves, the ding-donging
>   of the wind chimes,
> Causes wellborn young ladies to
>   break their hearts;
> On silver lampstands, the glimmering
>   of the lamplight,
> Succeeds merely in illuminating
>   the beauty's sighs.
> Her sole concern is with the welfare
>   of her child;
> Who could foresee that sorrow comes
>   often in a dream.[78]

At this juncture, Li P'ing-erh was lying on her bed:

> Seemingly asleep yet not asleep,[79]

when she dreamed that Hua Tzu-hsü came in the front door, dressed entirely in white, and looking just as he did while still alive.

When he caught sight of Li P'ing-erh, he condemned her in a harsh voice, saying, "You lousy wanton whore! How could you have misappropriated my property and turned it over to Hsi-men Ch'ing? Right now I'm on my way to lodge a formal complaint against you."

Li P'ing-erh grasped the sleeve of his garment with one hand and pled with him, saying, "Good Brother, pray forgive me."

But Hua Tzu-hsü broke loose, causing her to:
> Wake up with a jerk,[80]

revealing it to be but:
> A dream of the Southern Branch.[81]

When she woke up, what she was grasping in her hand was the sleeve of Kuan-ko's garment.

After gasping several times, she said, "How strange! How strange!"

When she listened, she heard the watchman striking the third quarter of the third watch. Li P'ing-erh was so disturbed that:
> Her whole body broke into a cold sweat,[82]

and her hair stood on end.

When Hsi-men Ch'ing came into her quarters the next day, she told him about her dream.

"Who knows where he has gone after his death," said Hsi-men Ch'ing. "This is just a case of your:
> Remembering your former situation in a dream.

Just set your mind at rest, and pay no attention to it. There's no reason for you to be upset. Under the circumstances, I'll send a page boy with a sedan chair to fetch Wu Yin-erh, so she can keep you company at night. And I'll summon Old Mother Feng to come and wait on the two of you."

Tai-an, accordingly, went to the licensed quarter and brought Wu Yin-erh back with him. Even before the sun began to set in the west, Kuan-ko, whom the wet nurse was holding on her lap, began to breathe irregularly.

This threw the wet nurse into such consternation that she called to Li P'ing-erh, saying, "You'd better come and see. The black pupils of Little Brother's eyes have rolled out of sight, and in his mouth, he is:
> Only breathing out, but
> Not breathing in."[83]

Li P'ing-erh came over, embraced the child in her arms, began to cry, and called out to the maidservant, saying, "Quickly, go and fetch Father. Tell him that the child is about to stop breathing."

It so happened that, just at this juncture, Ch'ang Shih-chieh had come to visit Hsi-men Ch'ing in order to tell him that he had found the house he was looking for, that it had a twelve-foot-wide frontage and a second floor, making four rooms in all, both large and small, and that the price was only thirty-five taels of silver.

When Hsi-men Ch'ing heard the news from the interior that Kuan-ko was in serious condition, he sent Ch'ang Shih-chieh on his way, saying, "I won't bother to see you off. I'll send someone with the silver to go look at the house with you another day."

He then urgently made his way to Li P'ing-erh's quarters. Yüeh-niang and the others, including Wu Yin-erh and Sister-in-law Wu, were all in the bedroom looking at the child, who was breathing only irregularly, clasped in his mother's arms. Hsi-men Ch'ing could not bear to see it and went into the parlor, where he sat down on a chair, giving vent to:

Long sighs and short breaths.[84]

As for Kuan-ko, after less time than it would take to drink half a cup of tea:

Alas and alack;

He stopped breathing and died.

At the time it was 4:00 PM on the twenty-third day of the eighth month. He had lived a scant one year and two months.

All the members of the household, from top to bottom, started to cry out loud, while Li P'ing-erh:

Grasping her ears and scratching her cheeks,[85]

in consternation, threw herself on the floor and wept until she fainted away.

It was some time before she recovered consciousness, whereupon she embraced Kuan-ko and gave vent to loud weeping, saying, "My child, have you no saving star? You've broken my heart. It would have been better if I could have died with you. I also am:

Not long for this world.[86]

My darling, you're abandoning me to my fate, forsaking me only too cruelly."

The wet nurse, Ju-i, and Ying-ch'un, who were in attendance upon her, also wept until they were:

Unable to speak, and

Unable to move.

Hsi-men Ch'ing, thereupon, ordered the page boys to clean out an anteroom on the west side of the front courtyard, and set up two wide benches in it, intending to have the child, along with his bedding, carried out there for his laying out. But Li P'ing-erh placed herself over the child's body, hugging it in both arms, and was unwilling to relinquish it.

She continued to protest, again and again, crying out, "My heartless enemy, who lacks a saving star! My darling son! You've ripped my innards out and taken them with you. You've forsaken me, so that all the pains I've taken on your behalf have been in vain.

I've suffered everything for nothing.[87]

I'll never be able to see you again, my darling!"

Yüeh-niang and the others wept with her for a while and tried to admonish her to look after herself without success.

Hsi-men Ch'ing came over and, seeing that she had scratched the skin open on her face and rolled on the floor until her:

Jeweled chignon had been disheveled,[88]

Leaving her raven locks in disarray,

said, "Think of him as an alien rascal. Seeing that:

He is not fated to be our child,

we have raised him in vain. Since he was fated to die an early death:

Weep for him a couple of times and forget it.[89]
Why continue crying that way?
You can't cry him back to life again.[90]
Your health is more important. I want to have him carried out now so that I
can send a page boy to summon the yin-yang master to come and assess his
situation. What time was it that he died?"

"It was around 4:00 o'clock," said Yüeh-niang.

"Just as I suggested before," said Meng Yü-lou, "he was sure to wait for that
time before slipping away. He was born at 4:00 PM, and he died at 4:00 PM;
and even the dates are the same. Both events occurred on the twenty-third.
Only the months were different. He lived exactly a round one year and two
months."

When Li P'ing-erh observed that the page boys were waiting on either side
to take him away, she wept again, saying, "What need is there to carry him
out so hastily? First Lady, reach out your hand and feel him. His body is
still warm."

Then she cried out, saying, "My son! How can I bear to let you go? You're
treating me too cruelly!"

She then threw herself down on the floor once again and gave vent to her
tears. There is a song to the tune "Sheep on the Mountain Slope" that testifies
to this:

I utter a single cry,
"Oh Azure Heaven,
How can you so ruin my life?"
I call out, "My darling boy,
If only with this one cry,
I could get you to respond.
It is all due to an earlier affinity from a previous life,[91]
In which incarnation I must have owed you a love debt
    that I have failed to repay.
And now it transpires that, in this life
    in this world,[92]
The tears I shed over you will never
    come to an end."
Every day I have been on tenterhooks,
Doing everything I could think of.
From the very beginning, I have never done anything
    to hurt or to harm anyone else.
"Azure Heaven, how can you so fail to
    keep your eyes open?"
"It's not that you and I had no affinity,
It must simply be that I am

fated to be unlucky.
Your abandonment of me has left me
   on the ground on all fours;[93]
The fallen tree no longer provides shade.[94]
I am reduced to trying to dip up water
   with a bamboo basket;[95]
All my labors are in vain."
I call out, "My heartbreaking darling boy,
I am more than willing to travel with you
   along the road to the shades."

At this juncture, after Li P'ing-erh had wept for a while, Kuan-ko was carried out to the anteroom on the west side of the front courtyard for his laying out.

Yüeh-niang consulted with Hsi-men Ch'ing, saying, "We also ought to send word to our kinfolk, and to the abbess at the Kuan-yin Nunnery."

"We can send word to the abbess tomorrow morning," said Hsi-men Ch'ing.

On the one hand, he sent Tai-an to convey the news to the members of Ch'iao Hung's household, and, on the other, he sent someone to invite Yin-yang Master Hsü to come and interpret his divinatory texts about Kuan-ko's fate. In addition, he produced ten taels of silver and gave them to Pen the Fourth, instructing him to go immediately to acquire a set of deal planks and have artisans construct a little coffin out of them as quickly as possible, so that it would be ready for the encoffining.

No sooner was the news conveyed to Ch'iao Hung's household than his wife set out in a sedan chair to offer her condolences, and she began to weep as soon as she came in the door. Yüeh-niang and the others joined her in lamenting grievously for some time and told her about the preceding events. Before long, it was announced that Yin-yang Master Hsü had arrived.

After surveying the situation, he said, "So the child passed away at exactly 4:00 PM."

Yüeh-niang instructed him to proceed with consulting the *Black Book*[96] about his fate.

Master Hsü:
   Calculated on the joints of his fingers,
consulted his esoteric yin-yang texts for a while, and pronounced:

The eight characters that determine the child's horoscope indicate that he was born at 4:00 PM on the twenty-third day of the sixth month in the *ping-shen* year of the Cheng-ho reign period; and died at 4:00 PM on the twenty-third day of the eighth month of the *ting-yu* year of the same reign period. The fact that his death took place during a *ting-yu* month on a *jen-tzu* day indicates a conflict between the celestial stems and earthly branches that portends a double bereavement. The members of his immediate family should abstain from crying, although relatives by marriage need not do so. On the day of the encoffining ceremony, it would be auspicious if people born in the year of the snake, the year of the dragon, the year of the rat, and the year of the hare would stay out of the way. Moreover, the *Black Book* says that those who die on a *jen-tzu* day are governed by the zodiacal palace Precious Vase[97] above, which corresponds to the area of Shantung below. In his former life, he was the scion of a family named Ts'ai in Yen-chou. Relying on his influence, he seized other people's property, drank away his inheritance, failed to revere Heaven and Earth as well as his six relations, became implicated in a criminal offense, caught a chill, was confined to his bed for some time, and died in his own filth. In this life, while still an infant, he became epileptic, and, ten days ago, he was frightened out of his wits by a domestic animal. Moreover, because the Earth Spirit and Year God[98] were offended, his soul was extracted from his body, resulting in a premature death. He will be reborn as the scion of a family named Wang in Cheng-chou, will rise to the rank of battalion commander, and will live to the age of sixty-seven before dying.

A little later, after once again consulting his *Black Book*, Master Hsü enquired, "Your Honor, do you wish to remove his body from the premises for either burial or cremation tomorrow?"

"How can we send him away tomorrow?" said Hsi-men Ch'ing. "Sutras will need to be recited for him on the third day, and we will escort him out to the family graveyard for burial on the fifth day."

"The twenty-seventh is a *ping-ch'en* day," said Master Hsü. "The horoscopes of the entire family will not create any conflicts on that day. It would be appropriate for the interment to take place at 12:00 noon."

When Master Hsü had finished interpreting his texts, and they began to prepare for the encoffining, it was already the third watch at night. Li P'ing-erh, weeping as she went, returned to her quarters to fetch his little Taoist robe, his Taoist cap, his shoes and stockings, etc., and put them into the coffin with him. The "longevity nails" were driven into the lid of the casket, and all the members of the household, from top to bottom, wept for a while, after which the yin-yang master was sent on his way.

The next day, Hsi-men Ch'ing was too busy to go to the yamen. When Judicial Commissioner Hsia Yen-ling heard the news, he came to offer his condolences after the morning session of the court was over and presented the customary consolatory contribution to the funeral expenses. Hsi-men Ch'ing also sent someone to inform Abbot Wu of the Taoist Temple of the Jade Emperor and arranged for eight monks from the Buddhist Temple of Kindness Requited to come and recite sutras on the third day. Abbot Wu of the Taoist temple and the household of Ch'iao Hung each contributed the cost of a table with portions of the three sacrificial animals, the cow, the sheep, and the pig, for the funeral oblation.

On the third day, Brother-in-law Wu K'ai, Mr. Shen, the husband of Wu Yüeh-niang's elder sister, Mr. Han, the husband of Meng Yü-lou's elder sister, from outside the city gate, and Hua the Elder all contributed offertory tables of the three sacrificial animals and came to burn paper money. Ying Po-chüeh, Hsieh Hsi-ta, Licentiate Wen, Ch'ang Shih-chieh, Han Tao-kuo, Kan Jun, Pen Ti-ch'uan, Li Chih, and Huang the Fourth all clubbed together to make a joint contribution and came to keep Hsi-men Ch'ing company during the overnight wake. When the monks had been sent on their way, a troupe of puppeteers was engaged to entertain the company. After the ritual sacrifice before Kuan-ko's spirit tablet had been performed, Hsi-men Ch'ing presided over a feast for his guests in the large reception hall. On the day in question, the three houses of Li Kuei-chieh, Wu Yin-erh, and Cheng Ai-yüeh in the licensed quarter also sent people to bring gifts and burn paper money in honor of the occasion.

Li P'ing-erh, in her grieving over Kuan-ko, grew sallower by the day and was disinclined to take either tea or nourishment. Whenever the subject came up, she gave herself over to weeping and sniffling until her voice grew hoarse. Hsi-men Ch'ing was afraid that in her grief for her child she might resort to the foolish way out of suicide, so he gave orders that during the day the wet nurse, maidservants, and Wu Yin-erh should keep her company:
> Without ever leaving her side.[99]
As for the evening hours, Hsi-men Ch'ing spent three successive nights in her room, trying as best he could to comfort her in her distress.

Nun Hsüeh also kept evening vigil with her, reciting the Śūraṅgama Sutra,[100] and a spell for dispelling enmity, and urging her to cease her weeping.

"As it is well said in the sutras," she remarked:
> "The head is altered and the face replaced, as
>   the wheel of transmigration turns;
> It is unavailing to consider what awaits you
>   in the predestined life to come.[101]
In the life to come:
> He is not fated to be your child.
He is your:
> Enemy or creditor,[102]
from a previous existence, who has been reborn in order to seek restitution by defrauding you of your property. He may die in his first year, he may die in his second year, he may die in his third, sixth, or ninth year.
> In the space of a single day and a single night,[103]
> Men die and are reborn by the tens of thousands.[104]
As it is well said in the Dhāraṇī Sutra:

In former days there was a woman who constantly adhered to the Fo-ting-hsin t'o-lo ching[105] and made offerings to the Bodhisattva Kuan-yin every day without fail, but who, three incarnations ago, had poisoned someone to death. This enemy of hers had never departed from her side but sought a means by which he might accomplish his revenge by committing matricide. Thus he was reincarnated in her body and so squeezed his mother's entrails that when the time came for her to give birth, the parturition was so difficult that her life was imperiled.[106] On emerging from the womb, he was appropriately well formed, but in less than two years he died. His mother was stricken with grief, and, giving vent to loud lamentation, threw her child into the river. Three times in a row, he was reincarnated in his mother's womb and sought a means by which he might terminate his mother's life. The third time, he was reincarnated in his mother's womb as before and did his best to squeeze his mother's entrails, in order to imperil her life,[107] causing her to faint away and cry out during childbirth, only to emerge from the womb as handsome as could be, with all his features intact. But, once again, in less than two years he died. When his mother saw this, she could not help weeping out loud, "What sort of evil karma has resulted in this?" As before, she took her child right up to the river bank but hesitated for some time, unable to bear the thought of abandoning him. Her grief so moved the Bodhisattva Kuan-yin that she transformed herself into the guise of a monk, dressed in his patched cassock, came straight to the river bank, and addressed the woman, saying, "There is no need for you to weep. This is not your child, but your enemy from three incarnations ago. He has been reincarnated three times, seeking to gain revenge by killing his mother, but has been unable to do so. It is because you have constantly recited the Fo-ting-hsin t'o-lo ching, and made offerings to the Bodhisattva Kuan-yin without fail, that he has been prevented from killing you. If you wish to see this enemy of yours, just look in the direction to which I point." When she had done speaking, she used her superhuman powers to point with her finger, at which the child was transformed into the guise of a yaksha, standing in the water, who said to her, "Because you murdered me, I have come with the intent to exact revenge. However, because your heart is set on supreme enlightenment, and you constantly adhere to the Fo-ting-hsin t'o-lo ching, good devas have protected you day and night, so that I have been unable to kill you. I have now been converted by the Bodhisattva Kuan-yin and, from now on, will forever cease to be your enemy." When he had finished speaking, he plunged into the water and disappeared. The woman, as two streams of tears crisscrossed her face,[108] paid obeisance to the bodhisattva, went home, and devoted herself even more fervently to good works. In the end, she lived to the age of ninety-six before dying and was transformed by reincarnation from a woman into a man.[109]

Although it may be inappropriate for me to say so, this son of yours must surely have been:
> An enemy of yours from a previous existence,[110]

who was reborn in order to seek restitution and wished to do you bodily harm. It is only because of your meritorious deeds in making offerings and adhering to the doctrine, as well as donating the cost of reproducing fifteen hundred copies of this sutra, that he was unable to kill you. Now that he has left your side, it is only when you give birth to another child in the future that it will truly be your own child."

When Li P'ing-erh heard this, in the end:

Her love affinity was not broken,

so that, every time the subject came up, she wept and sniffled unceasingly.

In no time at all, five days passed by. On the morning of the twenty-seventh, eight young professional mourners were hired, who were dressed in black robes with white caps. The coffin was encased in crimson lacquer ornamented with gold tracery and was accompanied in the funeral procession by a heraldic pennant and cloud-adorned baldachin, replete with the artificial floral embellishments known as "jade plum blossoms" and "snowy willows,"[111] and preceded by a crimson banner inscribed with the words, "Casket of the Eldest Son of the Hsi-men Family." Abbot Wu of the Temple of the Jade Emperor also sent twelve black-robed young Taoist acolytes to recite the *Sheng-shen yü-chang* (Jade Stanzas of the Vitalizing Spirits)[112] during the procession, and perform sacred music on the way to the funeral.

The relatives and friends of the family, dressed in white mourning-clothes, all accompanied Hsi-men Ch'ing in the funeral procession. It was only after they had walked as far as the east end of Main Street and were approaching the city gate that they got onto their mounts for the rest of the journey. Hsi-men Ch'ing feared that Li P'ing-erh would be overcome by grief if she went to the grave site, so he forbade her to go. Only Wu Yüeh-niang, Li Chiao-erh, Meng Yü-lou, P'an Chin-lien, and Hsi-men Ta-chieh, in five sedan chairs, accompanied Ch'iao Hung's wife, Wu K'ai's wife, Li Kuei-chieh, Cheng Ai-yüeh, and Wu Shun-ch'en's wife, Third Sister Cheng, to the family graveyard. Sun Hsüeh-o, Wu Yin-erh, and Nun Hsüeh were left at home to keep Li P'ing-erh company.

When Li P'ing-erh realized that she would not be allowed to go and saw the coffin starting on its way, she accompanied it as far as the front gate.

Approaching the coffin, she broke into loud lamentation, crying out again and again, "My ungrateful son, who will never come home again!"

She continued crying out this way until her voice broke, upon which, without knowing what she was doing, she fell down underneath the gateway:

Breaking the skin on her powdered forehead, and

Scattering her gold hairpins on the ground.[113]

This threw Wu Yin-erh and Sun Hsüeh-o into such consternation that they came forward to help her to her feet and persuaded her to return inside. When she arrived back in her quarters and saw that the k'ang was desolately empty, and that only the toy clapper-drum decorated with the portrait of the God of Longevity that her child had been accustomed to play with was still hanging on the bedstead, she was reminded of him and couldn't help crying out again.

Li P'ing-erh on Seeing the Clapper-Drum Grieves for Kuan-ko

There is a full-length song to the tune "Sheep on the Mountain Slope" that testifies to this:

When I come into the room,
Quiet reigns on all sides,
And I can't help sighing quietly.
When I think of my darling boy,
I weep until the energy in my vitals
    is completely exhausted.
"I remember how, in giving birth to you,
I suffered a thousand trials and
    a myriad tribulations.[114]
Not to mention the nights when I moved you to the
    dry spots while I occupied the wet,[115]
All the livelong day, I was preoccupied with
    looking after you.
It is aggravating enough to
    break my heart,
That you and I should end up
    as antagonists.
I really expected that as you developed
    you would stand up for me,
That we would remain together for a long time.
Who could have known that Heaven
    should be so blind,
As to bring what was left of
    your life to an end;
Leaving me betwixt and between,
Unable to reach the village ahead,
Or make it back to the inn behind?"[116]
I am aware that before long I am doomed,
To end up underneath the Yellow Springs.
The two of us, mother and son, are reduced to,
Reposing together in the Gateway to the Shades.[117]
I call out, "My darling sweetheart,
It is because you lacked karmic affinity in your past life,
    that this life of yours has been cut short."

Wu Yin-erh, who was standing by her side, took her hand and endeavored to comfort her, saying, "Mother, try not to cry. Little Brother has already forsaken you. You can hardly cry him back to life again. You must assume the responsibility for dealing with your own distress. You mustn't simply give way to your grief."

"After all, you're still:
    In the springtime of your youth,"[118]
said Sun Hsüeh-o. "Surely there is no reason to fear that you won't be able to
have another child in the future. But hereabouts:
    Walls have cracks,
    Fences have ears,
so we've got to be careful what we say. As far as she's concerned:
    Those who devote their every thought to scheming,
    Only end up bringing calamity on their own heads.[119]
Who doesn't know that she resented the fact that you gave birth to this child?
If she really is responsible for doing him in, surely, in the life to come, since:
    Every act brings its own retribution,[120]
he will demand her life in return. Who knows how many times she has done
her best to bury the rest of us alive? She is never content unless she is able to
monopolize the attentions of our husband. But if he chooses to spend the
night in anyone else's room, she gets:
    So angry she scarcely cares whether she is
        dead or alive.
Fortunately you are all aware that in the past our husband seldom ventured
into my place in the rear compound. But when he happened to do so on one
occasion recently, you all saw the way in which she was all of a heap engaging
in chitter-chatter at my expense with those singing girls behind my back. Does
she think she can simply:
    Wrap it up in a paper bag?
I may not say anything about it, but every day, I'm going to keep my eyes
peeled where she's concerned. Who knows what sort of a bad end that whore
will come to in the future?"

"That's enough of that," said Li P'ing-erh. "Though I'm still here, I've contracted an ailment that is likely to kill me, if not today, then some day soon.
I can't contend with her any longer. Let her do as she pleases."

As she was speaking, who should appear but the wet nurse Ju-i, who came
forward and knelt down before her, saying in a tearful voice, "I have something
to say that I hardly dare mention to you, Mother. The fact that Little Brother
has died is also a misfortune for me. I'm afraid that in the days to come Father
and the First Lady will dismiss me. My husband is dead, and I'll have nowhere
to go."

When Li P'ing-erh heard what she had to say, she felt a pang of sympathy
in her heart and thought to herself, "As long as I've got that dear enemy of
mine around, I might as well make use of him. I can't imagine he would
threaten such a thing."

"You crazy woman, " she said to her, "you can relax on that score. Although
the child is dead, I'm not dead yet. And even if I should die tomorrow, you've
served me well, and I'll see to it that no one will show you the gate. In the

future, if the First Lady should give birth to a son or a daughter, you would be able to take over the nursing of the child, just as you've been doing for me. So what are you so agitated about?"

Only then was Ju-i content to say no more about it.

After some time had elapsed, Li P'ing-erh, once again, was overcome by her grief and broke into tears. To the same tune as before:

> Yearning for my darling boy,
> I yearn for you until,
> I am all topsy-turvy.[121]
> Gazing after my darling boy,
> Unless it be in dreams, you will
> no longer appear.
> During the day, when I see your things
> I am distressed,[122]
> As though a knife were disemboweling me;
> And at night, when I awake from sleep
> I no longer find you,
> Safely embraced in my arms.
> I can't prevent the pearly tears from
> falling from my eyes.
> No longer will you lie playing on my ornate bed
> with its gold tracery;
> No longer will you let me lift you in my hands
> and induce you to smile;
> No longer will you come and cuddle up
> against my breast.
> You have managed to inflict a stab wound
> in my ardently beating heart.
> I have suffered in vain on your behalf,
> And it has all proven to be effort
> expended for nothing.
> Though you may have satisfied the wishes of another,
> You have left me with no future in sight.

Sun Hsüeh-o and Wu Yin-erh remained by her side and attempted to console her, saying, "You really ought to have something to eat, rather than merely continuing to cry this way."

Hsiu-ch'un went to the rear compound and brought some food back for her, setting it out on a table and helping her to eat. But Li P'ing-erh could hardly swallow anything and, after eating only half a bowl, put it down and refused to eat anything more.

Meanwhile, Hsi-men Ch'ing, at the family graveyard, asked Yin-yang Master Hsü to determine the proper geomantic orientation of the grave and then had Kuan-ko buried next to the grave site of his first wife, née Ch'en, so that she could hold the infant in her arms, as it were. That day Ch'iao Hung and the other relatives all assembled at the grave side and offered sacrifices, after which they were entertained in the newly erected summerhouse, where they enjoyed a libation for the rest of the day.

When the funeral party arrived home, Li P'ing-erh kowtowed to Yüeh-niang, Ch'iao Hung's wife, and Sister-in-law Wu and, weeping as she did so, addressed herself to Ch'iao Hung's wife, saying, "My kinswoman, who could be compared to me in raising such an unlucky child, who has died before his time? Now that he has died, your daughter will be a virgin widow, and all that you have done turns out to have been:

Labor expended in vain.[123]
Please don't hold it against me."

"Kinswoman, how can you say such a thing?"protested Ch'iao Hung's wife. "Every child has a predetermined number of years to live. Who can be sure of what the future holds in store? As the saying goes:

A betrothal, once made, should not be altered.[124]
And moreover, Kinswoman, you are not old. There is no reason to worry about not being able to have children and grandchildren in the future. You must take it easy, Kinswoman, and not distress yourself so."

When she had finished speaking, she took her leave and went home.

Hsi-men Ch'ing, in the front reception hall, arranged for Yin-yang Master Hsü to scatter ashes around the premises to prevent the soul of the departed from coming back, and to paste pollution-dispelling spells on all the doors, which read:

The baleful spirit of the departed is thirty feet high and is headed in a northeasterly direction. If it encounters the Wandering Day Spirit, it will be forced to return and be unable to escape. If it is executed, all will be well. Relatives of the departed need not avoid the site.

Hsi-men Ch'ing then brought out a bolt of muslin and two taels of silver with which to thank Master Hsü for his services and then escorted him to the gate.

That evening, he went to Li P'ing-erh's quarters and slept with her. During the night, he said everything he could think of to comfort her. He noticed that Kuan-ko's playthings were still in evidence and, fearing that Li P'ing-erh would be distressed on seeing them, ordered Ying-ch'un to take them all back to the rear compound. Truly:

Thinking of her darling boy, she weeps
    both by day and by night;
Her heart feels lacerated[125] so much that
    her life hangs by a thread.

Of the ten thousand things that create
  grief in this human world;
Nothing exceeds the severance of death
  and separation of the living.[126]

If you want to know the outcome of these events,
Pray consult the story related in the following chapter.

Chapter 60

LI P'ING-ERH BECOMES ILL

BECAUSE OF SUPPRESSED ANGER;

HSI-MEN CH'ING'S SILK GOODS STORE

OPENS FOR BUSINESS

> The marriage affinity bound with red cord[1]
>   is over, without hope of renewal;
> When one's luck runs out for no good reason,[2]
>   whom does one presume to blame?
> Her lingering tears, alarmed at the advent
>   of autumn, fall with the leaves;
> Her alienated soul, trailing after the moon,
>   is slow to approach the window.
> As the metallic autumn wind brushes her face,
>   she yearns for her son;
> When the jade candle burns itself to ashes,
>   her doleful tears fall.
> Even if her viscera should be fashioned
>   out of iron or stone;
> Though unable to engender sorrow, yet they
>   would engender sorrow.

THE STORY GOES that on that day Sun Hsüeh-o and Wu Yin-erh stayed by her side and endeavored to comfort Li P'ing-erh for some time, thus and so, before returning to the rear compound.

When P'an Chin-lien saw that the child was no more, and that Li P'ing-erh had lost her son to death, every day she plucked up her spirits and expressed her gratification in a hundred different ways.

Pointing at one of the maidservants, she railed away at Li P'ing-erh by indirection, saying, "You lousy whore! As I have said all along:

> The sun may be at high noon,
> But the time will come when it will pass its zenith.
> When the turtledove has dropped its egg:
> It has no recourse but to pout.[3]
> When the bench's back is broken:

You have nothing left to lean on.
Like Dame Wang who sold her grindstone:
You've no way to grind your axe anymore.
Like the old procuress whose painted face has died:
You've nothing more to hope for.
How do you like it, now that you're no better off than I am?"

Li P'ing-erh, in her adjacent quarters, overheard all this invective but did not dare say anything in response. All she could do was to shed tears behind Chin-lien's back. Suffering from this:

Suppressed anger and suppressed resentment,
on top of her accumulated vexation and sorrow; gradually:
Her heart and spirit were disoriented, and
Her dreaming soul turned topsy-turvy.[4]
With every day her intake of tea and food diminished.

The day after the funeral party returned from the graveyard after burying Kuan-ko, Wu Yin-erh went back to her establishment, and Old Mother Feng brought in a twelve-year-old maidservant, whom she sold to Sun Hsüeh-o for five taels of silver, and whose name was changed to Ts'ui-erh. But no more of this.

As for Li P'ing-erh, in the first place, because she was longing for her child, and in the second place, because she was afflicted with suppressed rage, her former ailment reappeared, and, as before, her menses flowed unceasingly from her lower body. Hsi-men Ch'ing invited Dr. Jen Hou-ch'i to come and examine her and obtained a prescription from him, but when she took it, it was about as effectual as if she had:

Attempted to irrigate a stone with water.[5]
The more of his medication she took, the worse the hemorrhaging became. In the space of less than half a month:

Her countenance lost color,
Her flesh became emaciated,[6]
and her radiant good looks were no longer what they used to be. Truly:

Her flesh and bones shrunk to
no more than a handful;
How could she hope to sustain
such a load of sorrow?[7]
One day, in the first decade of the ninth month, when:

The weather becomes threatening, and
The autumn wind begins to sough,
Li P'ing-erh was sleeping by herself at night.

The pillow was cold within her silver bedstead,
The moonlight flooded her gauze-covered window.

Li P'ing-erh Dreams of Hua Tzu-hsü Demanding Her Life

She couldn't help thinking of her child and gave herself over to prolonged sighs.

Seemingly asleep yet not asleep,

she became indistinctly aware of the noise made by someone tapping on the window frame. Li P'ing-erh called to her maidservants, but they were both fast asleep and did not respond. Consequently, she got out of bed herself:

Scuffed around with her slippers on backwards,
Tried to put her brocaded gown on upside down,

opened the door to the room, and went outside to see who was there. She seemed to see Hua Tzu-hsü, holding Kuan-ko in his arms, and calling out that he had found a new abode, and that she should join him in going there to live. Li P'ing-erh was not yet ready to relinquish Hsi-men Ch'ing and refused to go with him, but she reached out with both hands to embrace the child, at which Hua Tzu-hsü gave her a shove that knocked her to the ground, causing her to:

Wake up with a jerk,

revealing it to be but:

A dream of the Southern Branch.

She was so frightened that:

Her entire body broke into a cold sweat,[8]

and she gave way to:

Sobbing and wailing,

continuing to cry until dawn. Truly:

In possessing emotions we are surely all alike, but
To be fixated on appearances is to delude oneself.

There is a poem that testifies to this:

Slender, slender, is the new moon as it
    shines on the silver screen;
While the woman in the secluded boudoir
    is about to break her heart.
Regretting ever more that romantic ardor
    is often not sufficient;
She is increasingly aware that affection
    may be the root of sorrow.[9]

At that time, Lai-pao's boatload of goods from Nanking also arrived, and he sent the young employee Wang Hsien ahead to get the silver for the cartage fee. Hsi-men Ch'ing wrote a letter and deputed his young employee Jung Hai to take it, together with a hundred taels of silver, and the customary gifts of mutton, wine, and satin brocade, to the secretary of the Ministry of Revenue in charge of the Lin-ch'ing customs station, requesting that, so far as the customs duties were concerned, he should:

Look upon the matter with favorable eyes.

Meanwhile, at home, the preparations for the new shop were completed, and he selected the fourth day of the ninth month for the grand opening. On that very day, the goods were unloaded, consisting of twenty large cartloads, including personal baggage.

On the day in question, the relatives and friends who brought boxes of candied fruit and congratulatory red banners to celebrate the occasion numbered more than thirty persons, and Ch'iao Hung engaged twelve musicians, as well as acrobats, to perform for the company. On Hsi-men Ch'ing's part, the three boy actors, Li Ming, Wu Hui, and Cheng Ch'un, were engaged to play their musical instruments and sing. The managers, Kan Jun and Han Tao-kuo, worked behind the counter, selling the merchandise, one of them taking charge of the cash, and the other bargaining with the customers, while Ts'ui Pen was responsible for handling the goods. Whoever showed up, whether they were businessmen or customers, were ushered inside and offered two cups of wine.

When Hsi-men Ch'ing, who was dressed in a crimson robe and his official cap and girdle, had finished the ceremony of burning paper money, and his friends and relatives had all presented their boxes of candied fruit and toasted him with a drink, fifteen banquet tables were set up in the rear reception hall, replete with the customary:

Five appetizers, five dishes,
Three soups and five courses;
a new round of drinks was served, and, as the guests took their places:
Drums and music resounded to the heavens.

That day, the household of Judicial Commissioner Hsia Yen-ling sent someone to deliver a present and the customary red bunting in honor of the occasion, and Hsi-men Ch'ing sent the messenger back with a gift in return. Among those present were Ch'iao Hung, Wu K'ai, Wu the Second, Hua Tzu-yu, Brother-in-law Shen, Han Ming-ch'uan, Abbot Wu, Licentiate Ni P'eng, Licentiate Wen Pi-ku, Ying Po-chüeh, Hsieh Hsi-ta, and Ch'ang Shih-chieh.

With regard to the latter, it so happens that, in recent days, Hsi-men Ch'ing had given him fifty taels of silver, of which he had spent thirty-five taels for the mortgage on a house, while setting aside fifteen taels as the capital with which to open a small general store in his home, which enabled him to make ends meet. But no more of this.

On the present occasion, he had joined the others in making a contribution toward the cost of the celebration and had come along with them to congratulate Hsi-men Ch'ing. In addition, there were Li Chih, Huang the Fourth, Fu Ming, and the other entrepreneurs and managers, along with the neighbors in the area, all of whom filled the seats at the banquet tables. The three boy actors came before the feast and performed a song suite in the Nan-lü mode, beginning with the tune "Red Jacket," the first line of which was:

Hsi-men Ch'ing's Silk Goods Store Opens for Business

When primordial chaos first engendered the supreme ultimate,[10]

etc., etc. It was not long before:

> Five rounds of wine had been consumed; and
> Three main courses had been served.

By the time that the musicians below the hall had done performing, and the acrobatics and vaudeville acts were concluded, atop the banquet tables:

> Drinking vessels and game tallies lay helter-skelter.

On that day, Ying Po-chüeh and Hsieh Hsi-ta outdid themselves in raising large goblets, as they:

> Passed their winecups back and forth.

The drinking continued until sunset before the party broke up.

Hsi-men Ch'ing asked Wu K'ai, Brother-in-law Shen, Licentiate Ni, Wen Pi-ku, Ying Po-chüeh, and Hsieh Hsi-ta to remain, and new tables were set up for another round of drinks. On that day when the new shop opened for business, the managers did a quick job of reckoning the accounts and found that they had sold more than five hundred taels worth of goods, which delighted Hsi-men Ch'ing no end. After the shop closed that evening, he invited Manager Kan Jun, Han Tao-kuo, Fu Ming, Ts'ui Pen, Pen the Fourth, and Ch'en Ching-chi to join the party. After the musicians had performed for some time, they were allowed to go home, and only the three boy actors were retained to entertain the company.

Ying Po-chüeh, who had been drinking all day, was already inebriated and came out to the front compound to relieve himself. On the way, he called over Li Ming and asked him, "Whose place is that boy actor with the clear-cut appearance and his hair done up in a topknot from?"

"Do you mean to say you don't know, Master Two?" said Li Ming. Then, discreetly covering his mouth with his hand, he said, "He's Cheng Feng's younger brother. The other day, when Father was in the licensed quarter drinking at their establishment, he engaged the services of his elder sister Cheng Ai-yüeh."

"Really?" exclaimed Ying Po-chüeh. "No wonder, the other day, she contributed toward the burning of the paper money, and attended the funeral ceremony."

Thereupon, rejoining the party, he said to Hsi-men Ch'ing, "Brother, you are once again to be congratulated. You've managed to pick up another little brother-in-law."

"You crazy dog!" laughed Hsi-men Ch'ing. "Don't talk such nonsense."

He then called over Wang Ching and said to him, "Pour Master Two another large cup of wine."

Turning to Wu K'ai, Ying Po-chüeh said, "Venerable Brother-in-law, what do you think? I'm being fined this goblet of wine for no stated reason."

"You dog!" said Hsi-men Ch'ing. "I'm fining you for:

Violating protocol by speaking out of turn."

Ying Po-chüeh lowered his head to consider this and then laughed, saying, "It doesn't matter. I'll drink it. I'll drink it. After all:

It's not going to kill me."

He then went on to say, "But I've never been able to abide drinking wine without a song to accompany it. Only if you get Cheng Ch'un to come up here and sing a song for me, will I go along with it."

At this, the three boy actors all came forward and offered to play their instruments and sing.

Ying Po-chüeh dismissed Li Ming and Wu Hui, saying, "I don't want the two of you. I only want Cheng Ch'un to provide a solo accompaniment on the psaltery, and sing a short song, to help me get down the wine."

"Cheng Ch'un," said Hsieh Hsi-ta, "come over here and do as Master Two says."

"I've already explained the rules to Beggar Ying," said Hsi-men Ch'ing. "For every song, he must down a goblet of wine."

Thereupon, Tai-an proceeded to fetch two large silver goblets and place them in front of Ying Po-chüeh, while Cheng Ch'un:

Gently strummed the silver psaltery,
and sang in a low voice a song to the tune "Clear River Prelude":

A young lady of fifteen or sixteen,
Sees a pair of butterflies playing together.
Leaning against the wall with her fragrant shoulder,
Her slender fingers brush away her tears.
She calls out, "Maidservant,
Chase them away to fly somewhere else."[11]

When Cheng Ch'un had finished singing this song, he invited his auditor to have a drink, and no sooner did Ying Po-chüeh down it, than Tai-an poured out another cup for him. Cheng Ch'un then proceeded to sing another song to the same tune:

Skirting the carved balustrade, he catches sight of her,
Leaning against the rose-leaved raspberry trellis.
Coyly adjusting her phoenix hairpin,
She says nothing of last night's events,
But, smiling ingratiatingly,
Plucks a blossom and tosses it at him.[12]

When Ying Po-chüeh had finished drinking his cup of wine, he made haste to push the responsibility for continuing onto Hsieh Hsi-ta, saying, "That's enough. I can't handle any more. I can't handle any more. These two large goblets have done me in."

"You clever beggar!" exclaimed Hsieh Hsi-ta. "When you can't handle any more, you try to push the responsibility onto me. Do you take me to be a pushover of an encunted southerner like that wife of yours?"

"Clever beggar, is it!" responded Ying Po-chüeh. "If I become a senior official someday in the future, you'll be in line to take my place with her."

"You dog!" said Hsi-men Ch'ing. "If you ever get an official post, it will only be that of a ceremonial dancer."

"My clever child!" laughed Ying Po-chüeh. "If I ever become a ceremonial dancer, I'll cede the position of senior official to you, that's all."

Hsi-men Ch'ing laughed at this and ordered Tai-an, "Give this lousy beggar a whack with the slapstick."

Hsieh Hsi-ta surreptitiously gave him a sounding rap on the head, saying, "You beggar! The venerable Licentiate Wen is here, and yet you continue to spout such rubbish."

"The venerable Mr. Wen," said Ying Po-chüeh, "is a man of culture, who doesn't concern himself with such trivial affairs."

"You two gentlemen," said Licentiate Wen, "are obviously on good terms with our venerable host. If one were really to prohibit this kind of badinage at a drinking party, it wouldn't be any fun. When pleasure resides in the heart, it is appropriate that it find external expression, and before one knows it, one finds oneself:

Miming it with one's hands, and
Dancing it with one's feet,[13]

just like this."

Among those present, Brother-in-law Shen turned to Hsi-men Ch'ing and said, "Brother-in-law, this is not the way to do it. Why don't you invite your senior brother-in-law Wu K'ai to take charge of the situation by choosing a game of forfeits. The outcome could be determined by throwing dice, by playing at guess-fingers, or by playing cards; or it could be by reciting poems, lyrics, songs, or rhapsodies; or playing the game of 'thimble-stitching' in which lines of verse are joined together by beginning each new line with the last word of the preceding one;[14] or even by reciting tongue twisters. Whoever fails at his task would have to drink a cup of wine as a forfeit. That would be more evenhanded, and less likely to create disputes."

"Brother-in-law, your suggestion is just the thing," said Hsi-men Ch'ing, and he proceeded to pour a cup of wine and present it to Wu K'ai to initiate the proceedings.

Wu K'ai picked up the dice box and said, "I'll start things off then, and if I get anything wrong, I'll pay the penalty by drinking a cup of wine. I'll begin with only a single die, after which I'll use a pair. If I throw a number that corresponds to those in any of the following lines, I'll pay the forfeit.

1: Amid the *hundred* myriads of men,
   the *white* flag is furled.

2: As for the heroes under *Heaven*,
few *men* recognize them.

3: The Prince of *Ch'in* has executed
Generalissimo *Yü*;

4: Having *cursed* him for not providing
a *horse* for him to ride.

5: This so frightened me that *I* lack
the *mouth* to respond.

6: The *seething* crowds on the street
remove his *clothes*.

7: The black-clad *lictors* haven't any
white hair on their heads.

8: After *splitting* up the corpse, they
leave their *knives* behind.

9: There is a *bolus* of good medicine, but
no one wants a *dab* of it.

10: A *thousand* years of accomplishment is
negated with a single *stroke*."[15]

When Wu K'ai had finished throwing the dice, two of his throws corresponded
to the numbers in the lines, and he drank the penalty cups of wine accordingly.

It was then the turn of Brother-in-law Shen to call the game, and he said,
"I will throw a pair of dice six times, and if I throw a number that corresponds
to those in any of the following lines, I'll pay the forfeit

The image of Heaven is a double six; the image
of Earth is a pair of twos;

The image of Man is conveyed by the red pair
of ones and the double four.

A double three suggests Witch's Mountain; a double
five evokes plum blossoms;

Few indeed are those who really understand the
import of these symbols."

When he played, one of his throws resulted in a red double four, and he drank
his cup of wine accordingly. He then turned the dice box over to Licentiate
Wen.

"Your pupil will propose a game," said Licentiate Wen. "For each of the six
numbers I will name an appropriate flower, and follow it with a line from the
Four Books,[16] that begins with the last character of the flower named above.

1: Spot of Red.[17] 'The red plum blossom confronts
the white plum blossom.'[18]

2: Double-headed Lotus. 'Amid the ripples,
mandarin ducks play.'[19]

3: Willow of the Three Springs. 'Under the willow
one does not adjust one's hat.'[20]
4: Principal Graduate's Red.[21] 'Red and violet coloured
silks were not used for informal dress.'[22]
5: Wintersweet Blossom. 'Blossoms brush against sword
pendants as the stars begin to sink.'[23]
6: Sky Full of Stars.[24] 'The stars and other heavenly
bodies are so distant.' "[25]

Licentiate Wen was only required to drink one cup of wine, after which it was
the turn of Ying Po-chüeh to call the game.

"Your humble servant can hardly recognize a single character," said Ying
Po-chüeh, "so I'll recite a tongue twister:
A hurrying-scurrying housewife,
Holding a basket of soybeans in her left hand,
And a sack of cotton in her right hand,
Was only intent upon forging ahead,
When she ran into a yellow and white spotted dog,
Which took a bite out of the sack of cotton.
At which the hurrying-scurrying housewife,
Put down the basket of soybeans in her right hand,
And tried to beat off the yellow and white spotted dog.
But I don't know whether her hand overcame the dog,
Or whether the dog overcame her hand."

"You god-damned louse!" laughed Hsi-men Ch'ing derisively. "You'll bust
your gut coming up with such nonsense. Who would ever undertake to beat
off a dog with his hand without getting bitten for his pains?"

"Who would have anyone take on a dog without a stick in hand?" said Ying
Po-chüeh. "I'm in the same boat as:
The beggar who has misplaced his stick:
I have to confront the rancor of a dog."[26]

"Your Honor," said Hsieh Hsi-ta. "Notice how the beggar has acknowledged
his own downfall by describing himself as a beggar."

"He ought to be made to drink a penalty cup," said Hsi-men Ch'ing. "His
effort is hardly up to snuff. Hsieh Hsi-ta, it's your turn now."

"This tongue twister of mine is better than his," said Hsieh Hsi-ta. "If I don't
get it right, I'll drink a penalty cup.
On top of the wall there is a broken tile.
Below the wall there is a mule.
The broken tile falls down,
And lands on the mule.
I don't know whether the broken tile wounded the mule,
Or whether the mule stamped the broken tile to pieces."

"You ridiculed my tongue twister as inferior," said Ying Po-chüeh, "as though this broken tile of yours were any better. That wife of yours, Sister Liu, may be a mule, and I may be a broken tile, but the two of us are as well matched as a broken millstone and a lame donkey."

"As for that wife of yours, née Tu," said Hsieh Hsi-ta, "old whore of a southern hag that she is, she's just like a handful of black beans, fit only to feed to a pig. Even a dog would turn up his nose at her."

The two of them sparred verbally with each other for a while, after which each of them was made to drink a cup of wine.

It was then the turn of Manager Fu Ming, who said, "I'll call a game current on the rivers and lakes. If I throw a number that corresponds to those in any of the following lines, I'll pay the forfeit. I'll begin with a single die, and later switch to a pair.

> Aboard a single boat with a pair of oars,
> Three men row out into a waterway in the
>   Province of the Four Rivers.
> Employing the five notes and six semitones,[27]
> Seven men sing together a song about the
>   Eight Taoist Immortals.
> The nine times ten days of springtime[28]
>   are all equally enjoyed.
> During the eleventh and twelfth months
>   we celebrate primal harmony."[29]

When he had done, none of his throws corresponded to the numbers in the lines that he recited.

"None of the other games proposed have come up to this game of Manager Fu's," opined Wu K'ai. "It's more appropriate to the occasion than any of the others."

"In that case," said Ying Po-chüeh, "he ought to drink a 'Cup of Peace,' rather than a penalty cup."

Thereupon, he got up from his place, poured out a cup, and gave it to Fu Ming to drink, after which he said, "It's now the turn of Manager Han."

"Since Your Honor is present," said Han Tao-kuo, "how could I presume to precede you?"

"After all of you have done," said Hsi-men Ch'ing, "I'll call a game of my own."

Thereupon, Han Tao-kuo said, "I propose a game in which the first line must contain the name of a flying fowl, the second line the name of a fruit, the third line the name of a domino, and the fourth line the name of an official, all of which must be strung together in such a way as to make some kind of sense. If I throw a number that corresponds to that in any of the following six quatrains, I'll drink a penalty cup in front of the company.

From up in the sky there flies down
  an immortal crane,
Which alights in the garden and
  eats a fresh peach.
But it ends up being apprehended
  by a solitary goose,
And then taken to be presented to
  an education-intendant.

From up in the sky there flies down
  a sparrow hawk,
Which alights in the garden and
  eats a red cherry.
But it ends up being apprehended
  by a pair of nuns,
And then taken to be presented to
  a senior official.

From up in the sky there flies down
  an aged stork,
Which alights in the garden and
  eats water chestnuts.
But it ends up being apprehended
  by 'The Three Bonds,'
And taken to be presented to
  an assistant prefect.

From up in the sky there flies down
  a turtledove,
Which alights in the garden and
  eats a pomegranate.
But it ends up being apprehended
  by a red foursome,
And taken to be presented to
  a noble marquis.

From up in the sky there flies down
  a golden pheasant,
Which alights in the garden and
  eats bitter bamboo.
But it ends up being apprehended
  by the Five Peaks,
And taken to be presented to
  an imperial minister.

From up in the sky there flies down
  a pelican,
Which alights in the garden and
  eats an apple.
But it ends up being apprehended
  by the six spots,
And taken to be presented to
  a record keeper."

When he had finished with his game, it was the turn of Hsi-men Ch'ing.

"I'll just make four throws," said Hsi-men Ch'ing, "and if any of them correspond to the numbers in any line of the following quatrain, I'll drink a penalty cup

All six mouths convey a single touch
  of glowing sunset clouds,
Not to mention the colors of spring
  displayed by plum blossoms.
I elect to embrace red Hung-niang
  and give her a kiss,
Leaving the double-named Ying-ying
  to grieve by herself."

When he recited the line about the red Hung-niang, sure enough he threw a red four.

When Ying Po-chüeh saw this, he said, "Brother, this coming winter you are bound to be promoted to a higher office. This throw of a lucky red four indicates an impending cause for celebration."

Thereupon, he poured out a large cup of wine and gave it to Hsi-men Ch'ing to drink, while, at the same time, summoning the three boy actors, Li Ming and company, to play and sing for their entertainment in honor of the occasion. The party continued until the late watches of the night before breaking up.

Hsi-men Ch'ing saw the boy actors off and then looked on as the servants cleared things away. He gave directions that Han Tao-kuo, Kan Jun, Ts'ui Pen, and Lai-pao should take turns staying overnight in the newly opened shop, and he admonished them to be careful who they let into the house, after which, he returned to his own residence across the street. Of the events of that evening there is no more to tell.

To resume our story, the next day Ying Po-chüeh brought Li Chih and Huang the Fourth with him to turn over some of the silver they owed Hsi-men Ch'ing.

"On this occasion," they reported, "we only received a payment from the authorities of one thousand four hundred and fifty or sixty taels, which is not enough to meet all our obligations. So we have only been able to set aside these three hundred fifty taels of silver toward the payment of our debt to Your Honor. When we receive the next payment from the authorities, we should be able to pay off what is left of our obligation to you and will not dare to be remiss."

Ying Po-chüeh, from the sidelines, also put in a good word on their behalf. Hsi-men Ch'ing accordingly took the proffered silver and directed Ch'en Ching-chi to bring the steelyard and weigh it out properly, after which he sent Li Chih and Huang the Fourth on their way. The silver remained lying on the table.

Hsi-men Ch'ing then said to Ying Po-chüeh, "Brother Ch'ang the Second tells me that he has found the house he has been looking for, consisting of four rooms in all, front and back, and that the owner is willing to sell it for only thirty-five taels of silver.[30] When he came to speak to me about it, it happened to be just the time when I learned that the illness of my little boy was at a crisis stage, and I was too flustered to deal with it and sent him away. I don't know whether he has mentioned this to you or not."

"He did speak to me about it," said Ying Po-chüeh, "and I said to him, 'You approached him at a bad time. His son was in critical condition, and he was all flustered about it. How could he have spared the attention to listen to what you had to say? You ought to hold the owner off until I have a chance to speak to our elder brother about it.' "

When Hsi-men Ch'ing heard this, he said, "That's all right then. You have something to eat, and then I'll entrust you with a sealed packet of fifty taels of silver. Today is an auspicious day for an undertaking of this kind. You can take this money and go with him to close the deal on the house, and tell him to use what is left over to open a limited-capital business in the front of his new house. The income he can realize every month ought to be enough for the two of them to get by on."

"This is a case of Brother's condescending to help him out in a scrape," said Ying Po-chüeh.

Before long, a table was set up, and a meal was laid out upon it.

Hsi-men Ch'ing partook of the repast with him and then said, "I won't detain you any longer. You can take the silver, and take care of this job for me."

"You ought to depute one of your servants to accompany me in delivering this silver," said Ying Po-chüeh.

"Don't talk such rot!" said Hsi-men Ch'ing. "All you have to do is put it in your sleeve and get on with it."

"It's not that," said Ying Po-chüeh. "It's just that today I've got another little obligation to take care of. The fact of the matter is, Brother, that today is the birthday of my cousin Tu the Third, and when I sent a present to him this morning, he sent a servant back to invite me over for a visit this afternoon. So I won't be able to report back to you on the completion of my errand. If you send a servant to accompany me, after the deal on the house is closed, I can send him back to report to you."

When he had finished explaining the situation, Hsi-men Ch'ing said, "In that case, I'll have Wang Ching go with you."

He then summoned Wang Ching, and he set out with Ying Po-chüeh for the home of Ch'ang Shih-chieh. Ch'ang Shih-chieh was at home, and when he saw that Ying Po-chüeh had come, he invited him to come in and have a seat.

Ying Po-chüeh accordingly brought out the silver and showed it to Ch'ang Shih-chieh, saying, "His Honor, thus and thus, asked me to go with you today in order to close the deal on your house. But I don't have much free time because I've been invited for a drink by my cousin Tu the Third. Right now, as soon as I've finished with this business of yours, I'll have to go. That's why His Honor's servant has come with me. Once the deal on the house is concluded, I won't be able to report back to His Honor, but his servant will be able to report back to him instead."

"Quick. Bring some tea," Ch'ang Shih-chieh called out to his wife, and then he remarked, "Who could there be as magnanimous as our elder brother?"

As soon as they had finished their tea, he contacted the housing agent, and they set out together for New Market Street to weigh out the silver for the seller of the house, and draw up the deed of ownership. Ying Po-chüeh then told Wang Ching to take the deed and go home and show it to Hsi-men Ch'ing, and he confirmed to Ch'ang Shih-chieh that he was authorized to hold on to the remaining silver. Having done so, he took leave of Ch'ang Shih-chieh and went off to his engagement at the home of Tu the Third. When Hsi-men Ch'ing had looked over the deed for the house, he sent Wang Ching to give it back to Ch'ang Shih-chieh to keep. But no more of this. Truly:

> If you seek help from someone, you must do it
>   from a man of mettle;
> If you want to help someone, you must do it
>   when he needs it the most.[31]
> Everything else among the myriad possibilities
>   must be adjudged inferior;[32]
> But who is there who understands that secret
>   acts of virtue are the best?

Truly:

> The three luminaries cast shadows, but
>   who can catch them;
> The ten thousand things have no roots, they
>   just arise of themselves.[33]

If you want to know the outcome of these events,
Pray consult the story related in the following chapter.

NOTES

CHAPTER 41

1. This formulaic four-character expression occurs in an anonymous Sung dynasty lyric, *Ch'üan Sung tz'u* (Complete *tz'u* lyrics of the Sung), comp. T'ang Kuei-chang, 5 vols. (Hong Kong: Chung-hua shu-chü, 1977), 5:3767, upper register, l. 12; *Shen-hsiang ch'üan-pien* (Complete compendium on effective physiognomy), comp. Yüan Chung-ch'e (1376–1458), in *Ku-chin t'u-shu chi-ch'eng* (A comprehensive corpus of books and illustrations ancient and modern), presented to the emperor in 1725, fac. repr. (Taipei: Wen-hsing shu-tien, 1964), section 17, *i-shu tien*, *chüan* 634, p. 25b, l. 5; the ch'uan-ch'i drama *Wu Lun-ch'üan Pei* (Wu Lun-ch'üan and Wu Lun-pei, or the five cardinal human relationships completely exemplified), by Ch'iu Chün (1421–95), in *Ku-pen hsi-ch'ü ts'ung-k'an, ch'u-chi* (Collectanea of rare editions of traditional drama, first series) (Shanghai: Shang-wu yin-shu kuan, 1954), item 37, *chüan* 4, scene 29, p. 36a, l. 4; the ch'uan-ch'i drama *Huai-hsiang chi* (The stolen perfume), by Lu Ts'ai (1497–1537), *Liu-shih chung ch'ü* ed. (Taipei: K'ai-ming shu-tien, 1970), scene 23, p. 72, l. 3; *Ch'üan-Han chih-chuan* (Chronicle of the entire Han dynasty), 12 *chüan* (Chien-yang: K'o-ch'in chai, 1588), fac. repr. in *Ku-pen hsiao-shuo ts'ung-k'an, ti-wu chi* (Collectanea of rare editions of traditional fiction, fifth series) (Peking: Chung-hua shu-chü, 1990), vol. 2, *chüan* 3, p. 3b, l. 5; *San-ming t'ung-hui* (Comprehensive compendium on the three fates), comp. Wan Min-ying (cs 1550), in *[Ying-yin Wen-yüan ko] Ssu-k'u ch'üan-shu* ([Facsimile reprint of the Wen-yüan ko Imperial Library copy of the] Complete library of the four treasuries), 1,500 vols. (Taipei: T'ai-wan Shang-wu yin-shu kuan, 1986), vol. 810, *chüan* 1, p. 5b, ll. 6–7; the long sixteenth-century literary tale *T'ien-yüan ch'i-yü* (Celestial destinies remarkably fulfilled), in *Kuo-se t'ien-hsiang* (Celestial fragrance of national beauties), comp. Wu Ching-so (fl. late 16th century), pref. dated 1587, 3 vols., fac. repr. in *Ming-Ch'ing shan-pen hsiao-shuo ts'ung-k'an, ti-erh chi* (Collectanea of rare editions of Ming-Ch'ing fiction, second series) (Taipei: T'ien-i ch'u-pan she, 1985), vol. 3, *chüan* 7, p. 5a, lower register, l. 10; *Hai-fu shan-t'ang tz'u-kao* (Draft lyrics from Hai-fu shan-t'ang), by Feng Wei-min (1511–80), pref. dated 1566 (Shanghai: Shang-hai ku-chi ch'u-pan she, 1981), *chüan* 2b, p. 134, l. 10; *Mu-lien chiu-mu ch'üan-shan hsi-wen* (An exhortatory drama on how Maudgalyāyana rescued his mother from the underworld), by Cheng Chih-chen (1518–95), author's pref. dated 1582, in *Ku-pen hsi-ch'ü ts'ung-k'an, ch'u-chi*, item 67, *chüan* 3, p. 32a, l. 5; and a set of songs by Hsüeh Lun-tao (c. 1531–c. 1600), *Ch'üan Ming san-ch'ü* (Complete nondramatic song lyrics of the Ming), comp. Hsieh Po-yang, 5 vols. (Chi-nan: Ch'i-Lu shu-she, 1994), 3:2848, l. 4.

2. Wang Tao (276–339) held a succession of high offices during three reigns of the Eastern Chin dynasty (317–420). For his biography, see *Chin shu* (History of the Chin dynasty [265–420]), comp. Fang Hsüan-ling (578–648) et al., 10 vols. (Peking: Chung-hua shu-chü, 1974), vol. 6, *chüan* 65, pp. 1745–54.

3. See *The Plum in the Golden Vase or, Chin P'ing Mei. Volume One: The Gathering*, trans. David Tod Roy (Princeton: Princeton University Press, 1993), prefatory lyrics, n. 2.

4. This formulaic four-character expression occurs in *Hsüan-ho i-shih* (Forgotten events of the Hsüan-ho reign period [1119–25]) (Shanghai: Shang-hai ku-tien wen-hsüeh ch'u-pan she, 1955), p. 10, l. 7, and p. 67, l. 10, where it is used, in both cases, to describe the self-indulgent lifestyle of Emperor Hui-tsung of the Sung dynasty (r. 1100–25), the ruler in whose reign the story of the *Chin P'ing Mei* is set. It also occurs in the anonymous Yüan-Ming ch'uan-ch'i drama *Sha-kou chi* (The stratagem of killing a dog), *Liu-shih chung ch'ü* ed., scene 3, p. 9, l. 6; the early vernacular story *Sung Ssu-kung ta-nao Chin-hun Chang* (Sung the Fourth raises hell with Tightwad Chang), in *Ku-chin hsiao-shuo* (Stories old and new), ed. Feng Meng-lung (1574–1646), 2 vols. (Peking: Jen-min wen-hsüeh ch'u-pan she, 1958), vol. 2, *chüan* 36, p. 526, l. 9; the early vernacular story *Cheng Chieh-shih li-kung shen-pi kung* (Commissioner Cheng wins merit with his magic bow), in *Hsing-shih heng-yen* (Constant words to awaken the world), ed. Feng Meng-lung (1574–1646), first published in 1627, 2 vols. (Hong Kong: Chung-hua shu-chü, 1958), vol. 2, *chüan* 31, p. 668, l. 14; the early vernacular story *Pai Niang-tzu yung-chen Lei-feng T'a* (The White Maiden is eternally imprisoned under Thunder Peak Pagoda), in *Ching-shih t'ung-yen* (Common words to warn the world), ed. Feng Meng-lung (1574–1646), first published in 1624 (Peking: Tso-chia ch'u-pan she, 1957), *chüan* 28, p. 432, l. 2; *Chien-teng yü-hua* (More wick-trimming tales), by Li Ch'ang-ch'i (1376–1452), author's pref. dated 1420, in *Chien-teng hsin-hua [wai erh-chung]* (New wick-trimming tales [plus two other works]), ed. and annot. Chou I (Shanghai: Ku-tien wen-hsüeh ch'u-pan she, 1957), *chüan* 5, p. 291, ll. 3–4; the Ming dynasty ch'uan-ch'i drama *Yü-huan chi* (The story of the jade ring), *Liu-shih chung ch'ü* ed., scene 5, p. 11, l. 10; a song suite by Ch'en To (fl. early 16th century), *Ch'üan Ming san-ch'ü*, 1:681, l. 7; a song suite by Shen Shih (1488–1565), ibid., 2:1384, l. 6; the ch'uan-ch'i drama *Huan-sha chi* (The girl washing silk), by Liang Ch'en-yü (1519–91), *Liu-shih chung ch'ü* ed., scene 4, p. 10, l. 2; the ch'uan-ch'i drama *Mu-tan t'ing* (The peony pavilion), by T'ang Hsien-tsu (1550–1616), ed. and annot. Hsü Shuo-fang and Yang Hsiao-mei (Peking: Chung-hua shu-chü, 1959), scene 15, p. 74, l. 6; and *Hai-ling i-shih* (The debauches of Emperor Hai-ling of the Chin dynasty [r. 1149–61]), in *Ssu wu-hsieh hui-pao* (No depraved thoughts collectanea), comp. Ch'en Ch'ing-hao and Wang Ch'iu-kuei, 45 vols. (Taipei: Encyclopedia Britannica, 1995–97), vol. 1, p. 73, l. 12.

5. This custom is attested as early as the tenth century, although it is probably older. See the biography of Wang Jung (874–921) in *Chiu Wu-tai shih* (Old history of the Five Dynasties), comp. Hsüeh Chü-cheng (912–81) et al., 6 vols. (Peking: Chung-hua shu-chü, 1976), vol. 3, *chüan* 54, p. 728, l. 15. It was prohibited by statute in 1269 under the Yüan dynasty but continued in practice down to the present time. See *Yüan tien-chang* (Institutions of the Yüan), fac. repr. of 1303 ed. (Peking: Chung-kuo shu-tien, 1990), *chüan* 30, p. 3a, ll. 2–5. It is referred to in the early vernacular story *Chang Yü-hu su nü-chen kuan chi* (Chang Yü-hu spends the night in a Taoist nunnery), in *Yen-chü pi-chi* (A miscellany for leisured hours), ed. Lin Chin-yang (fl. early 17th century), 3 vols., fac. repr. of Ming ed., in *Ming-Ch'ing shan-pen hsiao-shuo ts'ung-k'an*, ch'u-pien (Collectanea of rare editions of Ming-Ch'ing fiction, first series) (Taipei: T'ien-i ch'u-pan she, 1985), vol. 2, *chüan* 6, p. 24a, lower register, l. 4; *Yüan-ch'ü hsüan wai-pien* (A supplementary anthology of Yüan tsa-chü drama), comp. Sui Shu-sen, 3 vols. (Peking: Chung-hua shu-chü, 1961), 2:670, l. 20; the anonymous ch'uan-ch'i drama *Chin-ch'ai chi* (The gold hairpin), manuscript dated 1431, modern ed. ed. Liu

Nien-tzu (Canton: Kuang-tung jen-min ch'u-pan she, 1985), scene 43, p. 76, ll. 1–2; and *Mu-tan t'ing*, scene 53, p. 261, l. 6.

6. This four-character expression occurs in the ch'uan-ch'i drama *Ssu-hsi chi* (The four occasions for delight), by Hsieh Tang (1512–69), *Liu-shih chung ch'ü* ed., scene 31, p. 76, l. 9.

7. The following song suite is a truncated version of the suite from scene 3 of the fourteenth-century tsa-chü drama *Liang-shih yin-yüan* (Two lives of love), by Ch'iao Chi (d. 1345). See *Yüan-ch'ü hsüan*, 3:977–82. The story relates how the historical figure Wei Kao (746–806) falls in love with a singing girl named Yü-hsiao before going to the capital to take the examinations and promises to marry her. However, immediately after passing the examinations he is sent on a distant mission, and Yü-hsiao dies of unfulfilled longing for him. Eighteen years later, when Wei Kao has become a victorious military commander, he visits his former acquaintance Chang Yen-shang (727–87), the military commissioner of Ching-chou, on his way back to the capital and encounters the latter's adopted daughter, who is also named Yü-hsiao, is just eighteen years old, and is the spitting image of his former love. When Yü-hsiao and Wei Kao exchange words and glances at a feast in his honor, Chang Yen-shang becomes enraged, and it is only the intervention of the emperor that enables the protagonist and his reincarnated lover to be married at the end of the play. Scene 3, from which this song suite is taken, occurs at the banquet at which Wei Kao and Yü-hsiao recognize each other and is sung by Yü-hsiao, who describes the developing situation as she sees it. One of the songs that is omitted from this suite, as quoted in the novel, decries the impropriety of making matches on the spur of the moment without resort to a go-between and may thus be interpreted as a critical comment on the casual betrothal of the infants in the story. See *Yüan-ch'ü hsüan*, 3:981, ll. 3–4.

8. This four-character expression occurs in a song suite by Wang T'ien (15th century), *Ch'üan Ming san-ch'ü*, 1:1016, l. 9.

9. This four-character expression occurs in a song by T'ang Fu (14th century), in *Yüeh-fu ch'ün-chu* (A string of lyric pearls), ed. Lu Ch'ien (Shanghai: Shang-wu yin-shu kuan, 1957), *chüan* 4, p. 279, l. 8.

10. This four-character expression occurs in a lyric by Kao Ssu-sun (cs 1184), *Ch'üan Sung tz'u*, 4:2271, lower register, l. 14; a lyric by Yüan Hao-wen (1190–1257), *Ch'üan Chin Yüan tz'u* (Complete lyrics of the Chin and Yüan dynasties), comp. T'ang Kuei-chang, 2 vols. (Peking: Chung-hua shu-chü, 1979), 1:76, lower register, l. 11; a lyric by Yeh-lü Chu (1221–85), ibid., 2:623, lower register, l. 16; a song suite by Kuan Han-ch'ing (13th century), *Ch'üan Yüan san-ch'ü* (Complete nondramatic song lyrics of the Yüan), comp. Sui Shu-sen, 2 vols. (Peking: Chung-hua shu-chü, 1964), 1:178, l. 1; a lyric by Sa-tu-la (cs 1327), *Ch'üan Chin Yüan tz'u*, 2:1092, upper register, l. 3; the tsa-chü drama *Wang Lan-ch'ing chen-lieh chuan* (The story of Wang Lan-ch'ing's heroic refusal to remarry), by K'ang Hai (1475–1541), in *Ku-pen Yüan Ming tsa-chü* (Unique editions of Yüan and Ming tsa-chü drama), ed. Wang Chi-lieh, 4 vols. (Peking: Chung-kuo hsi-chü ch'u-pan she, 1958), vol. 2, scene 1, p. 3a, l. 1; and a song suite by Chang Lien (cs 1544), *Ch'üan Ming san-ch'ü*, 2:1689, l. 8.

11. This four-character expression occurs in the ch'uan-ch'i drama *Shuang-lieh chi* (The heroic couple), by Chang Ssu-wei (late 16th century), *Liu-shih chung ch'ü* ed., scene 16, p. 45, l. 1.

12. This four-character expression occurs in *Yüan-ch'ü hsüan*, 2:801, l. 13; a song by Chao Shan-ch'ing (14th century), *Ch'üan Yüan san-ch'ü*, 1:744, l. 12; a song suite by Yang Li-chai (14th century), ibid., 2:1273, l. 7; an anonymous Yüan dynasty set of songs, ibid., 2:1739, l. 7; a song suite by Chu Yu-tun (1379–1439), *Ch'üan Ming san-ch'ü*, 1:377, l. 14; a song suite by Ch'ang Lun (1493–1526), ibid., 2:1553, ll. 4–5; and *Ta-T'ang Ch'in-wang tz'u-hua* (Prosimetric story of the Prince of Ch'in of the Great T'ang), 2 vols., fac. repr. of early 17th-century edition (Peking: Wen-hsüeh ku-chi k'an-hsing she, 1956), vol. 2, *chüan* 5, ch. 35, p. 21b, l. 7.

13. This four-character expression occurs in a set of songs by Wang Chiu-ssu (1468–1551), *Ch'üan Ming san-ch'ü*, 1:878, l. 9.

14. This idiomatic expression occurs in *Tung Chieh-yüan Hsi-hsiang chi* (Master Tung's western chamber romance), ed. and annot. Ling Ching-yen (Peking: Jen-min wen-hsüeh ch'u-pan she, 1962), *chüan* 4, p. 86, l. 13; the tsa-chü drama *T'ung-lo Yüan Yen Ch'ing po-yü* (In T'ung-lo Tavern Yen Ch'ing gambles for fish), in *Shui-hu hsi-ch'ü chi, ti-i chi* (Corpus of drama dealing with the *Shui-hu* cycle, first series), ed. Fu Hsi-hua and Tu Ying-t'ao (Shanghai: Ku-tien wen-hsüeh ch'u-pan she, 1957), scene 3, p. 29, l. 1; a song suite by Ching Kan-ch'en (13th century), *Ch'üan Yüan san-ch'ü*, 1:140, l. 11; a song by Sun Chou-ch'ing (14th century), ibid., 2:1061, l. 12; [*Chi-p'ing chiao-chu*] *Hsi-hsiang chi* (The romance of the western chamber [with collected commentary and critical annotation]), ed. and annot. Wang Chi-ssu (Shanghai: Shang-hai ku-chi ch'u-pan she, 1987), play no. 1, scene 2, p. 22, ll. 10–11; *Yüan-ch'ü hsüan*, 2:838, l. 2; a song suite by T'ang Shih (14th–15th centuries), *Ch'üan Yüan san-ch'ü*, 2:1502, l. 6; a song suite by T'ang Fu (14th century), *Ch'üan Ming san-ch'ü*, 1:229, l. 12; the tsa-chü drama *Cho Wen-chün ssu-pen Hsiang-ju* (Cho Wen-chün elopes with [Ssu-ma] Hsiang-ju), by Chu Ch'üan (1378–1448), in *Ming-jen tsa-chü hsüan* (An anthology of Ming tsa-chü drama), comp. Chou I-pai (Peking: Jen-min wen-hsüeh ch'u-pan she, 1958), scene 2, p. 121, l. 9; and a song by Ch'en To (fl. early 16th century), *Ch'üan Ming san-ch'ü*, 1:449, l. 9.

15. This four-character oxymoron occurs ubiquitously in Chinese literature. See, e.g., a lyric by Ma Yü (1123–83), *Ch'üan Chin Yüan tz'u*, 1:284, upper register, l. 1; *Ju-ju chü-shih yü-lu* (The recorded sayings of layman Ju-ju), by Yen Ping (d. 1212), pref. dated 1194, xerox copy of manuscript in the Kyoto University Library, *chia-chi* (first collection), *chüan* 1, p. 8b, l. 6; a song suite by T'ung-t'ung (14th century), *Ch'üan Yüan san-ch'ü*, 2:1263, l. 12; *Yüan-ch'ü hsüan*, 2:801, l. 16; a set of songs by Chu Yu-tun (1379–1439), *Ch'üan Ming san-ch'ü*, 1:281, l. 9; a song by K'ang Hai (1475–1541), ibid., 1:1175, l. 11; *Huai-hsiang chi*, scene 17, p. 49, l. 10; a song suite by Ch'en Ho (1516–60), *Ch'üan Ming san-ch'ü*, 2:2160, l. 2; a song suite by Tsung Ch'en (1525–60), ibid., 2:2391, l. 7; and *Ssu-hsi chi*, scene 5, p. 14, l. 7.

16. Variants of this conceit occur in a song by Ch'iao Chi (d. 1345), *Ch'üan Yüan san-ch'ü*, 1:625, ll. 1–2; the early vernacular story *San hsien-shen Pao Lung-t'u tuan-yüan* (After three ghostly manifestations Academician Pao rights an injustice), in *Ching-shih t'ung-yen*, *chüan* 13, p. 173, l. 17–p. 174, l. 1; and *Chien-teng hsin-hua* (New wick-trimming tales), by Ch'ü Yu (1341–1427), in *Chien-teng hsin-hua* [*wai erh-chung*], *chüan* 2, p. 54, l. 14.

17. Variants of this line occur in *Mu-tan t'ing*, scene 28, p. 150, l. 10; and the *Chin P'ing Mei tz'u-hua*, vol. 1, ch. 8, p. 2a, ll. 5–6. See Roy, *The Plum in the Golden Vase*, vol. 1, chap. 8, p. 150, ll. 19–20.

18. See ibid., chap. 2, n. 47.

19. This four-character expression occurs in a lyric by Chou Hsün (14th century), *Ch'üan Chin Yüan tz'u*, 2:1134, upper register, ll. 12–13.

20. This line occurs in a lyric by Ma Hung (15th century), *Ch'üan Ming tz'u* (Complete *tz'u* lyrics of the Ming), comp. Jao Tsung-i and Chang Chang, 6 vols. (Peking: Chung-hua shu-chü, 2004), 1:251, upper register, ll. 11–12; a set of songs by Chu Yün-ming (1460–1526), *Ch'üan Ming san-ch'ü*, 1:774, l. 7; a song by Wang Chiu-ssu (1468–1551), ibid., 1:858, l. 5; a set of songs by Yang Shen (1488–1559), ibid., 2:1444, l. 9; a song by Ch'ang Lun (1493–1526), ibid., 2:1549, l. 2; a song suite by Shih Li-mo (cs 1521), ibid., 2:1777, l. 12; a song suite by Chang Feng-i (1527–1613), ibid., 3:2610, l. 9; and a song by Mei Ting-tso (1549–1615), ibid., 3:3197, l. 10.

21. This line occurs in a lyric by Yüan Hao-wen (1190–1257), *Ch'üan Chin Yüan tz'u*, 1:86, upper register, l. 8; a song suite by Ch'iao Chi (d. 1345), *Ch'üan Yüan san-ch'ü*, 1:644, l. 1; and a song suite by Chu Yu-tun (1379–1439), *Ch'üan Ming san-ch'ü*, 1:377, l. 15.

22. This line occurs in *[Chi-p'ing chiao-chu] Hsi-hsiang chi*, play no. 3, scene 3, p. 123, ll. 9–10; *Yüan-ch'ü hsüan*, 4:1341, l. 14; and recurs in the *Chin P'ing Mei tz'u-hua*, vol. 4, ch. 80, p. 9a, ll. 7–8.

23. This idiomatic expression occurs in *Yüan-ch'ü hsüan*, 1:17, l. 14; and 3:1275, l. 14; and a song by Ch'en To (fl. early 16th century), *Ch'üan Ming san-ch'ü*, 1:489, l. 3.

24. This line alludes to a famous episode of 207 B.C., in which the wicked eunuch Chancellor Chao Kao (d. 207 B.C.) demonstrates his power to the Second Emperor of the Ch'in dynasty (r. 210–207 B.C.) by deliberately calling a deer a horse. See *Shih-chi* (Records of the historian), by Ssu-ma Ch'ien (145–c. 90 B.C.), 10 vols. (Peking: Chung-hua shu-chü, 1972), vol. 1, *chüan* 6, p. 273, ll. 7–9. This passage has been translated by Burton Watson as follows:

Chao Kao was contemplating treason but was afraid the other officials would not heed his commands, so he decided to test them first. He brought a deer and presented it to the Second Emperor but called it a horse. The Second Emperor laughed and said, "Is the chancellor perhaps mistaken, calling a deer a horse?" Then the emperor questioned those around him. Some remained silent, while some, hoping to ingratiate themselves with Chao Kao, said it was a horse, and others said it was a deer. Chao Kao secretly arranged for all those who said it was a deer to be brought before the law. Thereafter the officials were all terrified of Chao Kao.

See *Records of the Grand Historian: Qin Dynasty*, trans. Burton Watson (New York: Columbia University Press, 1993), p. 70. Variants of this expression occur in *San-kuo chih* (History of the Three Kingdoms), comp. Ch'en Shou (233–97), 5 vols. (Peking: Chung-hua shu-chü, 1973), vol. 2, *chüan* 12, p. 386, l. 5; *Hou-Han shu* (History of the Later Han dynasty), comp. Fan Yeh (398–445), 12 vols. (Peking: Chung-hua shu-chü, 1965), vol. 3, *chüan* 23, p. 812, l. 5; *Chou shu* (History of the Chou dynasty [557–81]), comp. Ling-hu Te-fen (583–666), 3 vols. (Peking: Chung-hua shu-chü, 1971), vol. 1, *chüan* 1, p. 11, l. 15; *Chiu T'ang shu* (Old history of the T'ang dynasty), comp. Liu Hsü (887–946) et al., 16 vols. (Peking: Chung-hua shu-chü, 1975), vol. 11, *chüan* 121, p. 3486, l. 15; the collection of literary tales entitled *Hsiao-p'in chi* (Emulative frowns collection), by Chao Pi, author's postface dated 1428 (Shanghai: Ku-tien wen-hsüeh ch'u-pan she, 1957), p. 91, l. 7; and the anonymous Ming ch'uan-ch'i drama *Hsün-ch'in chi* (The quest for the father), *Liu-shih chung ch'ü* ed., scene 13, p. 40, l. 3. It occurs in the same form as in the novel in a set of songs by Ch'en To (fl. early 16th century), *Ch'üan Ming san-ch'ü*, 1:519, l. 10; *P'u-ching ju-lai yao-shih pao-chüan* (Precious volume of the Tathāgatha P'u-ching: The Buddha of the Key [to salvation]), by P'u-ching (d. 1586), in *Pao-chüan ch'u-chi* (Precious volumes, first collection), comp. Chang Hsi-shun et al., 40 vols. (T'ai-yüan: Shan-hsi jen-min ch'u-pan she, 1994), 5:163, ll. 4–5; and *Ch'üan-Han chih-chuan*, vol. 1, chüan 1, p. 9a, l. 2.

25. A variant of this four-character expression occurs in a set of songs by Chu Yu-tun (1379–1439), *Ch'üan Ming san-ch'ü*, 1:333, l. 9. It occurs in the same form as in the novel in *Yüan-ch'ü hsüan*, 1:127, l. 6.

26. Kung-sun Hung (200–121 B.C.), a famous chancellor of the Han dynasty, is said to have offered entertainments in the Eastern Vestibule in order to attract worthy men. See *Han-shu* (History of the Former Han dynasty), comp. Pan Ku (32–92), 8 vols. (Peking: Chung-hua shu-chü, 1962), vol. 6, *chüan* 58, p. 2621, ll. 2–3.

27. This entire line occurs in *Chin-t'ung Yü-nü Chiao Hung chi* (The Golden Lad and the Jade Maiden: The story of Chiao-niang and Fei-hung), attributed to Liu Tui (fl. early 15th century), in *Ming-jen tsa-chü hsüan*, p. 34, l. 12. The idiomatic expression that forms the second half of the line occurs ubiquitously in Chinese vernacular literature. See, e.g., a song suite by Kuan Han-ch'ing (13th century), *Ch'üan Yüan san-ch'ü*, 1:180, l. 12; an anonymous Yüan dynasty song, ibid., 2:1662, l. 6; [*Chi-p'ing chiao-chu*] *Hsi-hsiang chi*, play no. 3, scene 3, p. 125, l. 11; *Yüan-ch'ü hsüan*, 3:898, l. 8; *Yüan-ch'ü hsüan wai-pien*, 2:351, l. 12; a song by Chu Yu-tun (1379–1439), *Ch'üan Ming san-ch'ü*, 1:291, l. 7; a song suite by Ch'en To (fl. early 16th century), ibid., 1:588, l. 4; *Huai-hsiang chi*, scene 16, p. 44, ll. 4–5; a song suite by Wu Kuo-pao (cs 1550), *Ch'üan Ming san-ch'ü*, 2:2279, l. 12; the ch'uan-ch'i drama *Yen-chih chi* (The story of the rouge), by T'ung Yang-chung (16th century), in *Ku-pen hsi-ch'ü ts'ung-k'an, ch'u-chi*, item 49, *chüan* 2, scene 39, p. 30b, l. 8; and *Hai-fu shan-t'ang tz'u-kao*, *chüan* 3, p. 150, l. 9.

28. For the famous story of Cho Wen-chün, the daughter of Cho Wang-sun, and her elopement with Ssu-ma Hsiang-ju, see Roy, *The Plum in the Golden Vase*, vol. 1, chap. 3, n. 29.

29. In addition to its dramatic version, this song suite is preserved in the anthologies *Sheng-shih hsin-sheng* (New songs of a surpassing age), pref. dated 1517, fac. repr. (Peking: Wen-hsüeh ku-chi k'an-hsing she, 1955), pp. 396–98; *Tz'u-lin chai-yen* (Select flowers from the forest of song), comp. Chang Lu, pref. dated 1525, 2 vols., fac. repr. (Peking: Wen-hsüeh ku-chi k'an-hsing she, 1955), vol. 2, pp. 1201–4; and *Yung-hsi yüeh-fu* (Songs of a harmonious era), pref. dated 1566, 20 ts'e, fac. repr. (Shanghai: Shang-wu yin-shu kuan, 1934), ts'e 13, pp. 60a–61a. This song suite is also quoted in extenso in *Tz'u-nüeh* (Pleasantries on lyrical verse), by Li K'ai-hsien (1502–68), in *Chung-kuo ku-tien hsi-ch'ü lun-chu chi-ch'eng* (A corpus of critical works on classical Chinese drama), comp. Chung-kuo hsi-ch'ü yen-chiu yüan (The Chinese Academy of Dramatic Arts), 10 vols. (Peking: Chung-kuo hsi-chü ch'u-pan she, 1959), 3:304–6. The text as given in the novel is closer to those in the above anthologies than to those in the dramatic version or in *Tz'u-nüeh*.

30. This four-character expression occurs in a collection of poetic riddles by Li K'ai-hsien (1502–68), the author's pref. to which is dated 1555. See *Li K'ai-hsien chi* (The

collected works of Li K'ai-hsien), ed. Lu Kung, 3 vols. (Peking: Chung-hua shu-chü, 1959), 3:1019, l. 10.

31. For the Spirit of the Perilous Paths, see Roy, *The Plum in the Golden Vase*, vol. 1, chap. 4, n. 22. The God of Longevity is conventionally depicted as a short, roly-poly, old man and thus presents a striking contrast with the unusual height of the Spirit of the Perilous Paths. This saying is thus a Chinese equivalent of the pot calling the kettle black.

32. Variants of this idiomatic expression occur in *Yüan-ch'ü hsüan*, 1:241, l. 9; 376, l. 18; 3:1014, l. 9; and 4:1654, l. 16. It also recurs in the *Chin P'ing Mei tz'u-hua*, vol. 3, ch. 43, p. 3a, l. 3.

33. Tang Chin (929–79) is a historical figure. For his biography, see *Sung shih* (History of the Sung dynasty), comp. T'o-t'o (1313–55) et al., 40 vols. (Peking: Chung-hua shu-chü, 1977), vol. 26, *chüan* 260, pp. 9018–19. He was an illiterate military commander who became a byword for his uncouth manners.

34. The eight auspicious symbols, decorative motifs of Buddhist origin, are the jar, the conch, the umbrella, the canopy, the lotus, the wheel of the law, the fish, and the mystic knot. For an illustration, see C.A.S. Williams, *Encyclopedia of Chinese Symbolism and Art Motives* (New York: The Julian Press, 1960), p. 157.

35. This couplet is from a poem by Li She (fl. early 9th century) on the subject of Su Wu (140–60 B.C.), the heroic Han dynasty official who endured nineteen years of captivity in Hsiung-nu territory, during part of which he survived by herding sheep, rather than becoming a turncoat, for which he was offered every inducement. The couplet contrasts the sybaritic life of the Han nobility, who were intent on enjoying their privileges, with the plight of Su Wu, who sacrificed everything for the sake of loyalty to his country. See *Ch'üan T'ang shih* (Complete poetry of the T'ang), 12 vols. (Peking: Chung-hua shu-chü, 1960), vol. 7, *chüan* 477, p. 5426, l. 3.

CHAPTER 42

1. This four-character expression occurs ubiquitously in Chinese literature. See, e.g., a quatrain by Li Po (701–62), *Ch'üan T'ang shih*, vol. 3, *chüan* 167, p. 1723, l. 8; a quatrain by Ts'ao T'ang (c. 802–c. 866), ibid., vol. 10, *chüan* 641, p. 7348, l. 3; a lyric by Liu Yung (cs 1034), *Ch'üan Sung tz'u*, 1:31, lower register, l. 9; a lyric by Su Che (1039–1112), ibid., 1:355, lower register, l. 10; the biography of Śākyamuni Buddha in *Wu-teng hui-yüan* (The essentials of the five lamps), comp. P'u-chi (1179–1253), 3 vols. (Peking: Chung-hua shu-chü, 1984), vol. 1, *chüan* 1, p. 7, l. 10; a lyric by Chi I (1193–1269), *Ch'üan Chin Yüan tz'u*, 2:1219, lower register, l. 2; a song by Ch'iao Chi (d. 1345), *Ch'üan Yüan san-ch'ü*, 1:621, ll. 9–10; [*Chi-p'ing chiao-chu*] *Hsi-hsiang chi*, play no. 1, scene 2, p. 20, l. 8; *Yüan-ch'ü hsüan*, 1:176, l. 13; *Yüan-ch'ü hsüan wai-pien*, 3:793, l. 15; *T'ien-pao i-shih chu-kung-tiao* (Medley in various modes on the forgotten events of the T'ien-pao [742–56] reign period), by Wang Po-ch'eng (fl. late 13th century), in *Chu-kung-tiao liang-chung* (Two exemplars of the medley in various modes), ed. and annot. Ling Ching-yen and Hsieh Po-yang (N.p.: Ch'i-Lu shu-she, 1988), p. 141, l. 2; a lyric by Liu Chi (1311–75), *Ch'üan Ming tz'u*, 1:90, upper register, l. 11; a song suite by T'ang Shih (14th–15th centuries), *Ch'üan Yüan san-ch'ü*, 2:1484, l. 9; a song suite by Chu Yün-ming (1460–1526), *Ch'üan Ming san-ch'ü*, 1:779, l. 1; a song suite by Yang Shen (1488–1559), ibid., 2:1409, l. 12; a song by his

wife Huang O (1498–1569), ibid., 2:1767, l. 6; *Hai-fu shan-t'ang tz'u-kao*, *chüan* 3, p. 180, l. 2; and *Mu-tan t'ing*, scene 34, p. 181, l. 4.

2. This line, with one insignificant variant, has already occurred in the *Chin P'ing Mei tz'u-hua*, vol. 1, ch. 15, p. 1a, l. 5. See Roy, *The Plum in the Golden Vase*, vol. 1, chap. 15, p. 298, ll. 14–15.

3. The final clause of this line occurs in *Yüan-ch'ü hsüan*, 3:1132, l. 13.

4. This formulaic four-character expression occurs ubiquitously in Chinese literature. See, e.g., a lyric by Su Shih (1037–1101), *Ch'üan Sung tz'u*, 1:291, lower register, l. 13; a lyric by Ch'ao Tuan-li (1046–1113), ibid., 1:424, lower register, l. 1; a lyric by Ma Yü (1123–83), *Ch'üan Chin Yüan tz'u*, 1:286, upper register, l. 12; *Yüan-ch'ü hsüan wai-pien*, 2:371, l. 1; the Yüan-Ming ch'uan-ch'i drama *Yu-kuei chi* (Tale of the secluded chambers), *Liu-shih chung ch'ü* ed., scene 29, p. 89, l. 9; *P'i-p'a chi* (The lute), by Kao Ming (d. 1359), ed. Ch'ien Nan-yang (Peking: Chung-hua shuchü, 1961), scene 18, p. 109, l. 3; *Chin-ch'ai chi*, scene 14, p. 28, l. 21; an anonymous set of poems on the story of *The Romance of the Western Chamber* included in the front matter of *Hsi-hsiang chi* (The romance of the western chamber), fac. repr. of 1498 edition (Taipei: Shih-chieh shu-chü, 1963), p. 26b, l. 9; *Shui-hu ch'üan-chuan* (Variorum edition of the *Outlaws of the Marsh*), ed. Cheng Chen-to et al., 4 vols. (Hong Kong: Chung-hua shu-chü, 1958), vol. 2, ch. 30, p. 469, l. 8; and *Huan-sha chi*, scene 25, p. 87, l. 5.

5. This formulaic four-character expression occurs ubiquitously in Chinese vernacular literature. See, e.g., a lyric composed in 1227 by Yüan Hao-wen (1190–1257), *Ch'üan Chin Yüan tz'u*, 1:83, lower register, l. 1; a lyric by Wei Ch'u (1231–92), ibid., 2:706, upper register, l. 4; *[Chi-p'ing chiao-chu] Hsi-hsiang chi*, play no. 2, scene 3, p. 73, l. 5; a song suite by Ma Chih-yüan (c. 1250–c. 1325), *Ch'üan Yüan san-ch'ü*, 1:256, l. 13; *Yüan-ch'ü hsüan*, 2:709, ll. 8–9; *Yüan-ch'ü hsüan wai-pien*, 1:44, l. 5; *T'ien-pao i-shih chu-kung-tiao*, p. 167, l. 5; a song by Chung Ssu-ch'eng (c. 1279–c. 1360), *Ch'üan Yüan san-ch'ü*, 2:1359, l. 1; *Yü-huan chi*, scene 34, p. 130, l. 9; a song suite attributed to Li Tung-yang (1447–1516), *Ch'üan Ming san-ch'ü*, 1:426, ll. 10–11; a set of songs by Wang Chiu-ssu (1468–1551), ibid., 1:913, l. 4; *Shui-hu ch'üan-chuan*, vol. 4, ch. 118, p. 1776, l. 10; *Ssu-hsi chi*, scene 31, p. 78, l. 1; the anonymous ch'uan-ch'i drama *Pa-i chi* (The story of the eight righteous heroes), *Liu-shih chung ch'ü* ed., scene 11, p. 26, l. 5; *Hsi-yu chi* (The journey to the west), 2 vols. (Peking: Tso-chia ch'u-pan she, 1954), vol. 2, ch. 96, p. 1087, l. 17; the Ming novel *Ts'an-T'ang Wu-tai shih yen-i chuan* (Romance of the late T'ang and Five Dynasties) (Peking: Pao-wen t'ang shutien, 1983), ch. 18, p. 69, ll. 16–17; and the novel *Sui-T'ang liang-ch'ao shih-chuan* (Historical chronicle of the Sui and T'ang dynasties), 12 *chüan* (Su-chou: Kung Shao-shan, 1619), microfilm of unique copy in Sonkeikaku Bunko, Tokyo, *chüan* 11, ch. 105, p. 33a, l. 3.

6. The proximate source of this couplet is *Shui-hu ch'üan-chuan*, vol. 2, ch. 33, p. 516, l. 10, but it is ultimately derived, with considerable textual variation, from the final couplet of a quatrain on the Lantern Festival by Ts'ui Yeh (fl. early 8th century), *Ch'üan T'ang shih*, vol. 1, *chüan* 54, p. 667, l. 15. It also recurs, with insignificant textual variation, in the *Chin P'ing Mei tz'u-hua*, vol. 4, ch. 79, p. 4a, l. 2.

7. According to the recollections of a contemporary of the author of the *Chin P'ing Mei*, in the years between 1567 and 1582, clove-shaped earrings made of gold or jade and inset with pearls were in fashion. See *Yün-chien chü-mu ch'ao* (Jottings on matters

eyewitnessed in Yün-chien), by Fan Lien (b. 1540), pref. dated 1593, in *Pi-chi hsiao-shuo ta-kuan* (Great collectanea of note-form literature), 17 vols. (Yang-chou: Chiang-su Kuang-ling ku-chi k'o-yin she, 1984), vol. 6, *ts'e* 13, *chüan* 2, p. 2a, l. 4.

8. See *The Plum in the Golden Vase or, Chin P'ing Mei. Volume Two: The Rivals*, trans. David Tod Roy (Princeton: Princeton University Press, 2001), chap. 32, n. 31.

9. This four-character expression occurs in *Yüan-ch'ü hsüan wai-pien*, 3:826, ll. 3–4.

10. The Chinese text here splits the two characters of the common word for "slave" into their left and right components, which are then used as a slang term for the same word. I have tried to suggest this by combining the initial sl/ of the word "slimy" with the final /ave of the word "knave" to indicate the word "slave."

11. Variants of this idiomatic expression occur in *Yüan-ch'ü hsüan*, 1:338, l. 20; 2:465, l. 17; 2:836, l. 10; *Yüan-ch'ü hsüan wai-pien*, 3:905, ll. 17–18; an anonymous song in *Ch'üan Yüan san-ch'ü*, 2:1751, l. 1; and a song suite by Shen Ching (1553–1610), *Ch'üan Ming san-ch'ü*, 3:3267, l. 9.

12. This line recurs in the *Chin P'ing Mei tz'u-hua*, vol. 3, ch. 46, p. 4a, l. 5.

13. This four-character expression occurs in a lyric by Li Kang (1083–1140), *Ch'üan Sung tz'u*, 2:904, upper register, l. 15.

14. This four-character expression occurs in *T'ien-pao i-shih chu-kung-tiao*, p. 240, l. 7; and in the early vernacular story *Hsiao fu-jen chin-ch'ien tseng nien-shao* (The merchant's wife offers money to a young clerk), in *Ching-shih t'ung-yen*, *chüan* 16, p. 224, l. 9.

15. This formulaic four-character expression is ubiquitous in Chinese vernacular literature. See, e.g., a lyric composed in the year 1200 by Ch'iu Ch'ung (1135–1209), *Ch'üan Sung tz'u*, 3:1741, upper register, l. 12; a song by K'ung Wen-sheng (13th century), *Ch'üan Yüan san-ch'ü*, 1:136, l. 10; a set of songs by Liu T'ing-hsin (14th century), ibid., 2:1429, l. 3; *Wu-wang fa Chou p'ing-hua* (The p'ing-hua on King Wu's conquest of King Chou), originally published in 1321–23 (Shanghai: Chung-kuo ku-tien wen-hsüeh ch'u-pan she, 1955), p. 9, l. 12; *Pai Niang-tzu yung-chen Lei-feng T'a*, p. 430, l. 7; the long fifteenth-century literary tale *Chung-ch'ing li-chi* (A pleasing tale of passion), in *Yen-chü pi-chi*, vol. 2, *chüan* 6, upper register, p. 19a, l. 14; the long mid-Ming literary tale *Huai-ch'un ya-chi* (Elegant vignettes of spring yearning), in ibid., vol. 3, *chüan* 9, upper register, p. 23b, l. 4; the middle period vernacular story *Feng-yüeh hsiang-ssu* (A tale of romantic longing), in *Ch'ing-p'ing shan-t'ang hua-pen* (Stories printed by the Ch'ing-p'ing Shan-t'ang), ed. T'an Cheng-pi (Shanghai: Ku-tien wen-hsüeh ch'u-pan she, 1957), p. 82, l. 5; a song by Wang Chiu-ssu (1468–1551), *Ch'üan Ming san-ch'ü*, 1:914, l. 2; a song suite by K'ang Hai (1475–1541), ibid., 1:1222, l. 4; the anonymous Ming tsa-chü drama *Shih Chen-jen ssu-sheng so pai-yüan* (Perfected Man Shih and the four generals subdue the white gibbon), in *Ku-pen Yüan-Ming tsa-chü*, vol. 4, scene 2, p. 5b, ll. 10–11; the sixteenth-century ch'uan-ch'i drama *Ming-feng chi* (The singing phoenix), *Liu-shih chung ch'ü* ed., scene 23, p. 98, l. 5; *Hai-fu shan-t'ang tz'u-kao*, *chüan* 3, p. 154, l. 7; *Ssu-sheng yüan* (Four cries of a gibbon), by Hsü Wei (1521–93), originally published in 1588, ed. and annot. Chou Chung-ming (Shanghai: Shang-hai ku-chi ch'u-pan she, 1984), p. 32, l. 8; *San-pao t'ai-chien Hsi-yang chi t'ung-su yen-i* (The romance of Eunuch Cheng Ho's expedition to the Western Ocean), by Lo Mao-teng, author's preface dated 1597, 2 vols. (Shanghai: Shang-hai ku-chi ch'u-pan she, 1985), vol. 2, ch. 96, p. 1243, l. 6; and *Hai-ling i-shih*, *chüan* 2, p. 106, l. 7.

16. This anonymous song suite is preserved in *Sheng-shih hsin-sheng*, pp. 357–58; *Tz'u-lin chai-yen*, vol. 2, pp. 642–43; and *Yung-hsi yüeh-fu*, ts'e 11, pp. 3a–3b. The version in the novel is closer to those in *Sheng-shih hsin-sheng* and *Tz'u-lin chai-yen* than to that in *Yung-hsi yüeh-fu*.

17. This formulaic four-character expression occurs ubiquitously in Chinese litera-ture. See, e.g., *Chan-kuo ts'e* (Intrigues of the Warring States), comp. Liu Hsiang (79–8 B.C.), 3 vols. (Shanghai: Shang-hai ku-chi ch'u-pan she, 1985), vol. 1, *chüan* 7, p. 283, l. 10; *Shih-chi*, vol. 7, *chüan* 71, p. 2319, l. 10; *San-kuo chih p'ing-hua* (The p'ing-hua on the history of the Three Kingdoms), originally published in 1321–23 (Shanghai: Ku-tien wen-hsüeh ch'u-pan she, 1955), p. 10, l. 1; the early vernacular story *Lü Tung-pin fei-chien chan Huang-lung* (Lü Tung-pin beheads Huang-lung with his flying sword), in *Hsing-shih heng-yen*, vol. 2, *chüan* 21, p. 464, l. 3; *P'o-hsieh hsien-cheng yao-shih chüan* (Precious volume on the key to refuting heresy and presenting evidence [for correct doctrine]), by Lo Ch'ing (1442–1527), originally published in 1509, in *Pao-chüan ch'u-chi*, 2:70, l. 2; *Shui-hu ch'üan-chuan*, vol. 1, ch. 20, p. 294, l. 14; the middle period vernacular story *Yüeh-ming Ho-shang tu Liu Ts'ui* (The monk Yüeh-ming converts Liu Ts'ui), in *Ku-chin hsiao-shuo*, vol. 2, *chüan* 29, p. 433, l. 13; the anonymous Ming tsa-chü drama *Wang Wen-hsiu Wei-t'ang ch'i-yü chi* (The story of Wang Wen-hsiu's remarkable encounter in Wei-t'ang), in *Ku-pen Yüan Ming tsa-chü*, vol. 4, scene 1, p. 1a, l. 5; *Lieh-kuo chih-chuan* (Chronicle of the feudal states), by Yü Shao-yü (fl. mid-16th century), 8 *chüan* (Chien-yang: San-t'ai kuan, 1606), fac. repr. in *Ku-pen hsiao-shuo ts'ung-k'an*, ti-liu chi (Collectanea of rare editions of tradi-tional fiction, sixth series) (Peking: Chung-hua shu-chü, 1990), vol. 1, *chüan* 2, p. 29b, l. 4; *Huang-Ming k'ai-yün ying-wu chuan* (Chronicle of the heroic military exploits that initiated the reign of the imperial Ming dynasty) (Nanking: Yang Ming-feng, 1591), fac. repr. in *Ku-pen hsiao-shuo ts'ung-k'an*, ti san-shih liu chi (Collectanea of rare editions of traditional fiction, thirty-sixth series) (Peking: Chung-hua shu-chü, 1991), vol. 1, *chüan* 2, p. 11b, l. 6; the ch'uan-ch'i drama *Yü-ching t'ai* (The jade mirror stand), by Chu Ting (16th century), *Liu-shih chung ch'ü* ed., scene 28, p. 74, ll. 1–2; and *Ta-T'ang Ch'in-wang tz'u-hua*, vol. 1, *chüan* 2, ch. 11, p. 25a, l. 8.

18. This term appears in a description of fireworks displays in Peking during the late sixteenth century. See *Wan-shu tsa-chi* (Miscellaneous records concerning the magistracy of Wan-p'ing), by Shen Pang, pref. dated 1592 (Peking: Pei-ching ku-chi ch'u-pan-she, 1980), *chüan* 17, p. 190, l. 13. Recipes for the making of this pyrotechnic device may be found in *Huo-hsi lüeh* (An outline of pyrotechnics), comp. Chao Hsüeh-min (c. 1719–c. 1805), author's pref. dated 1780, 2 vols., fac. repr. (N.p.: T'ien-chin Library, n.d.), *chüan* 2, pp. 14a–15a.

19. This four-character expression occurs in an anonymous Yüan dynasty song suite, *Ch'üan Yüan san-ch'ü*, 2:1653, l. 13; *T'ang-shu chih-chuan t'ung-su yen-i* (The romance of the chronicles of the T'ang dynasty), by Hsiung Ta-mu (mid-16th century), 8 *chüan* (Chien-yang: Ch'ing-chiang t'ang, 1553), fac. repr. in *Ku-pen hsiao-shuo ts'ung-k'an*, ti-ssu chi (Collectanea of rare editions of traditional fiction, fourth series) (Peking: Chung-hua shu-chü, 1990), vol. 1, *chüan* 3, p. 22b, l. 7; and *Nan Sung chih-chuan* (Chronicle of the Sung conquest of the south), attributed to Hsiung Ta-mu (mid-16th century), 10 *chüan* (Nanking: Shih-te t'ang, 1593), fac. repr. in *Ku-pen hsiao-shuo ts'ung-k'an*, ti san-shih ssu chi (Collectanea of rare editions of traditional fiction, thirty-fourth series) (Peking: Chung-hua shu-chü, 1991), vol. 1, *chüan* 5, p. 23b, l. 12.

20. A recipe for this type of pyrotechnic device may be found in *Huo-hsi lüeh, chüan* 2, p. 17a, ll. 3–6.

21. A recipe for this type of pyrotechnic device may be found in ibid., *chüan* 2, p. 9a, ll. 2–3.

22. Recipes for this type of pyrotechnic device may be found in ibid., *chüan* 4, p. 15a, ll. 4–7. Fireworks of this kind were still in use in twentieth-century Peking. See H. Y. Lowe, *The Adventures of Wu: The Life Cycle of a Peking Man*, 2 vols. (Princeton: Princeton University Press, 1983), 2:152.

23. For the Hegemon-King, see Roy, *The Plum in the Golden Vase*, 1:462, n. 5. A pyrotechnic device of this name is mentioned in *Ti-ching sui-shih chi-sheng* (Record of the outstanding seasonal observances in the imperial capital), by P'an Jung-pi (18th century), author's pref. dated 1758 (Peking: Pei-ching ku-chi ch'u-pan she, 1981), p. 11, l. 1. On the significance of the word "whip" in this name, see Lowe, *The Adventures of Wu*, 2:150.

24. This type of pyrotechnic device figures in an anecdote dated to the period 1225–32. See *Ch'i-tung yeh-yü* (Rustic words of a man from eastern Ch'i), by Chou Mi (1232–98), pref. dated 1291 (Peking: Chung-hua shu-chü, 1983), *chüan* 11, p. 208, ll. 1–6; and the translation in Joseph Needham et al., *Science and Civilisation in China*, Volume 5, part 7: *Military Technology; The Gunpowder Epic* (Cambridge: Cambridge University Press, 1986), pp. 135–36. It is also mentioned in *Wan-shu tsa-chi, chüan* 17, p. 190, l. 13; and recipes for its manufacture may be found in *Huo-hsi lüeh, chüan* 2, pp. 16b–17a.

25. This four-character expression occurs in *San-pao t'ai-chien Hsi-yang chi t'ung-su yen-i*, vol. 1, ch. 38, p. 494, l. 4.

26. The Seven Sages referred to here are probably the seven demigods associated with the hunt that figure prominently in chapters 6 and 63 of *Hsi-yu chi*, where they are called the Seven Sages of Mei-shan. See ibid., vol. 1, ch. 6, p. 62, l. 16. They are also referred to as the Seven Sages in *San-chiao yüan-liu sou-shen ta-ch'üan* (Complete compendium on the pantheons of the three religions), pref. dated 1593, fac. repr. (Taipei: Lien-ching ch'u-pan shih-yeh kung-ssu, 1980), p. 113, l. 6.

27. Recipes for this type of pyrotechnic device may be found in *Huo-hsi lüeh, chüan* 2, p. 4a, ll. 2–4, and p. 7a, ll. 4–5.

28. A recipe for the second of these types of pyrotechnic devices may be found in ibid., *chüan* 3, pp. 26a–26b.

29. Recipes for this type of pyrotechnic device, under a slightly different name with the same meaning, may be found in ibid., *chüan* 2, pp. 29a–29b.

30. Recipes for this type of pyrotechnic device may be found in ibid., *chüan* 3, p. 14b, ll. 1–4.

31. A recipe for this type of pyrotechnic device may be found in ibid., *chüan* 3, p. 23a, ll. 2–4.

32. Recipes for this type of pyrotechnic device may be found in ibid., *chüan* 3, pp. 1b–3a.

33. The Five Devils are variously defined in different sources, and the Assessor is an important figure in the bureaucracy of the underworld. For differing versions of the story behind this topos, see the anonymous Ming tsa-chü drama, probably written for performance during the New Year's celebrations at the imperial court, entitled *Ch'ing feng-nien Wu-kuei nao Chung K'uei* (Celebrating a prosperous year, the

Five Devils plague Chung K'uei), in *Ku-pen Yüan Ming tsa-chü*, vol. 4; and *San-pao t'ai-chien Hsi-yang chi t'ung-su yen-i*, vol. 2, ch. 90. Pyrotechnic devices of this name were still in use in Peking in the twentieth century. See Lowe, *The Adventures of Wu*, 2:150.

34. This four-character expression occurs in an anecdote about Ch'un-yü K'un (4th century B.C.) recorded by Huan T'an (c. 43 B.C.–A.D. 28) in his *Hsin-lun* (New treatise), which is extant only in fragmentary form. See *Ch'üan Shang-ku San-tai Ch'in Han San-kuo Liu-ch'ao wen* (Complete prose from High Antiquity, the Three Dynasties, Ch'in, Han, the Three Kingdoms, and the Six Dynasties), comp. Yen K'o-chün (1762–1843), 5 vols. (Peking: Chung-hua shu-chü, 1965), vol. 1, *Ch'üan Hou-Han wen* (Complete prose of the Later Han dynasty), *chüan* 13, p. 9a, l. 13; and *Hsin-lun (New Treatise) and Other Writings by Huan T'an*, trans. Timoteus Pokora (Ann Arbor: Center for Chinese Studies, University of Michigan, 1975), p. 39, l. 24. It occurs ubiquitously in later Chinese literature. See, e.g., *Han-shu*, vol. 6, *chüan* 68, p. 2958, l. 5; a literary tale set in the year 872 entitled *Wang Chih-ku wei hu chao-hsü* (Wang Chih-ku is selected as a son-in-law by a lair of foxes), by Huang-fu Mei (10th century), in his *San-shui hsiao-tu* (Short pieces by the man from San-shui), completed in 910 (Peking: Chung-hua shu-chü, 1960), *chüan* 1, p. 17, l. 1; a poem by Lu Yu (1125–1210), *Ch'üan Sung shih* (Complete poetry of the Sung), comp. Fu Hsüan-ts'ung et al., 72 vols. (Peking: Pei-ching ta-hsüeh ch'u-pan she, 1991–98), 39:24376, l. 12; *Hsüan-ho i-shih*, p. 130, l. 8; *[Hsin-pien] Wu-tai shih p'ing-hua* ([Newly compiled] p'ing-hua on the history of the Five Dynasties), originally published in the 14th century (Shanghai: Chung-kuo ku-tien wen-hsüeh ch'u-pan she, 1954), p. 51, l. 3; *San-kuo chih t'ung-su yen-i* (The romance of the Three Kingdoms), attributed to Lo Kuan-chung (14th century), preface dated 1522, 2 vols. (Shanghai: Shang-hai ku-chi ch'u-pan she, 1980), vol. 1, *chüan* 8, p. 398, l. 13; *Shui-hu ch'üan-chuan*, vol. 3, ch. 79, p. 1309, l. 14; *Ta-Sung chung-hsing yen-i* (The romance of the restoration of the great Sung dynasty), by Hsiung Ta-mu (mid-16th century), 8 *chüan* (Chien-yang: Ch'ing-pai t'ang, 1552), fac. repr. in *Ku-pen hsiao-shuo ts'ung-k'an, ti san-shih ch'i chi* (Collectanea of rare editions of traditional fiction, thirty-seventh series) (Peking: Chung-hua shu-chü, 1991), vol. 1, *chüan* 1, p. 16a, l. 2; *Lieh-kuo chih-chuan*, vol. 1, *chüan* 3, p. 19a, l. 12; *Hai-fu shan-t'ang tz'u-kao*, *chüan* 4, p. 192, l. 15; *Mu-lien chiu-mu ch'üan-shan hsi-wen*, *chüan* 2, p. 86, l. 6; *Ch'üan-Han chih-chuan*, vol. 2, *chüan* 6, p. 14a, l. 12; *San-pao t'ai-chien Hsi-yang chi t'ung-su yen-i*, vol. 1, ch. 34, p. 438, l. 14; and *Ch'eng-yün chuan* (The story of the assumption of the mandate [by the Yung-lo emperor]), in *Ku-pen hsiao-shuo ts'ung-k'an, ti-pa chi* (Collectanea of rare editions of traditional fiction, eighth series) (Peking: Chung-hua shu-chü, 1990), vol. 3, *chüan* 3, p. 15b, l. 9.

35. This four-character expression for an elaborate ambush is ubiquitous in Chinese vernacular literature. See, e.g., *Ch'ien-Han shu p'ing-hua* (The p'ing-hua on the history of the Former Han dynasty), originally published in 1321–23 (Shanghai: Ku-tien wen-hsüeh ch'u-pan she, 1955), *chüan* 2, p. 27, l. 12; *Yüan-ch'ü hsüan*, 1:71, l. 15; *Yüan-ch'ü hsüan wai-pien*, 1:234, l. 9; a song suite by Liu T'ing-hsin (14th century), *Ch'üan Yüan san-ch'ü*, 2:1438, l. 1; the ch'uan-ch'i drama *Ch'ien-chin chi* (The thousand pieces of gold), by Shen Ts'ai (15th century), *Liu-shih chung ch'ü* ed., scene 38, p. 122, l. 8; *San-kuo chih t'ung-su yen-i*, vol. 1, *chüan* 6, p. 306, l. 8; *Shui-hu ch'üan-chuan*, vol. 3, ch. 77, p. 1280, l. 1; *T'ang-shu chih-chuan t'ung-su yen-i*, vol. 1, *chüan*

4, p. 24a, l. 8; *Ch'üan-Han chih-chuan*, vol. 2, *chüan* 2, p. 32a, l. 3; a song about fireworks by Hsüeh Lun-tao (c. 1531–c. 1600), *Ch'üan Ming san-ch'ü*, 3:2773, l. 10; *Ta-T'ang Ch'in-wang tz'u-hua*, vol. 1, *chüan* 1, ch. 3, p. 34b, l. 5; and *Sui-T'ang liang-ch'ao shih-chuan*, *chüan* 1, ch. 7, p. 43b, l. 2.

36. This four-character expression is from a poem by Fu Hsüan (217–78), *Hsien-Ch'in Han Wei Chin Nan-pei ch'ao shih* (Complete poetry of the Pre-Ch'in, Han, Wei, Chin, and Northern and Southern dynasties), comp. Lu Ch'in-li, 3 vols. (Peking: Chung-hua shu-chü, 1983), 1:576, l. 2. It occurs ubiquitously in later Chinese literature. See, e.g., a lyric by Ma Yü (1123–83), *Ch'üan Chin Yüan tz'u*, 1:296, lower register, l. 16; a poem by T'an Ch'u-tuan (1123–85), *Ch'üan Chin shih* (Complete poetry of the Chin dynasty [1115–1234]), comp. Hsüeh Jui-chao and Kuo Ming-chih, 4 vols. (Tientsin: Nan-k'ai ta-hsüeh ch'u-pan she, 1995), 1:337, l. 14; a song suite by Wang Po-ch'eng (fl. late 13th century), *Ch'üan Yüan san-ch'ü*, 1:326, l. 10; the allegorical Taoist drama on internal alchemy entitled *Hsing-t'ien Feng-yüeh t'ung-hsüan chi* (The Master of Breeze and Moonlight utilizes his Heaven-bestowed nature to penetrate the mysteries), by Lan Mao (1403–76), pref. dated 1454, in *Ku-pen hsi-ch'ü ts'ung-k'an, wu-chi* (Collectanea of rare editions of traditional drama, fifth series) (Shanghai: Shang-hai ku-chi ch'u-pan she, 1986), item 1, scene 12, p. 32a, l. 1; *Mu-lien chiu-mu ch'üan-shan hsi-wen*, *chüan* 2, p. 62, l. 7; *Hsi-yu chi*, vol. 1, ch. 28, p. 316, l. 13; a set of songs by Hsüeh Lun-tao (c. 1531–c. 1600), *Ch'üan Ming san-ch'ü*, 3:2741, ll. 3–4; *San-pao t'ai-chien Hsi-yang chi t'ung-su yen-i*, vol. 1, ch. 41, p. 531, l. 13; and *Ta-T'ang Ch'in-wang tz'u-hua*, vol. 1, *chüan* 1, ch. 3, p. 28b, l. 8.

37. The purport of this line is expressed in a pentasyllabic poem on the Lantern Festival by Su Wei-tao (648–705), *Ch'üan T'ang shih*, vol. 2, *chüan* 65, p. 753, ll. 1–2.

38. This four-character expression occurs in a lyric by Chang Hsien (990–1078), *Ch'üan Sung tz'u*, 1:78, lower register, l. 8; a song by Ma Chih-yüan (c. 1250–c. 1325), *Ch'üan Yüan san-ch'ü*, 1:230, l. 11; a lyric by Ku Hsün (1418–1505), *Ch'üan Ming tz'u*, 1:284, lower register, l. 16; the Ming ch'uan-ch'i drama *Shuang-chu chi* (The pair of pearls), by Shen Ch'ing (15th century), *Liu-shih chung ch'ü* ed., scene 2, p. 3, l. 12; the prose preface to a song suite by Liang Ch'en-yü (1519–91), *Ch'üan Ming san-ch'ü*, 2:2200, l. 9; and a song by Tu Tzu-hua (16th century), ibid., 3:3018, l. 9.

39. The proximate source of this couplet is *Shui-hu ch'üan-chuan*, vol. 2, ch. 33, p. 516, l. 10, but it is ultimately derived, with considerable textual variation, from the initial couplet of a quatrain on the Lantern Festival by Ts'ui Yeh (fl. early 8th century), *Ch'üan T'ang shih*, vol. 1, *chüan* 54, p. 667, l. 15. This poem also occurs in *Mu-lien chiu-mu ch'üan-shan hsi-wen*, *chüan* 3, p. 4a, l. 6; and, with some textual variation, in *Yen-chih chi*, *chüan* 2, scene 32, p. 19b, l. 1.

40. This couplet is derived, with some textual variation in the second line, from the final couplet of a poem by Sung Chih-wen (cs 675, d. 712), *Ch'üan T'ang shih*, vol. 1, *chüan* 53, p. 647, l. 5. It recurs in the *Chin P'ing Mei tz'u-hua*, vol. 4, ch. 78, p. 11a, l. 4.

41. This line occurs in the Ming ch'uan-ch'i drama *Chiang Shih yüeh-li chi* (The story of Chiang Shih and the leaping carp), by Ch'en P'i-chai (fl. early 16th century), in *Ku-pen hsi-ch'ü ts'ung-k'an, ch'u-chi*, item 36, *chüan* 1, scene 2, p. 4a, l. 9.

CHAPTER 43

1. The Jade Hall was the name of an audience chamber in the palace complex of Emperor Wu of the Han dynasty (r. 141–87 B.C.).

2. On Shih Ch'ung (249–300), see Roy, *The Plum in the Golden Vase*, 1:464, n. 2. This four-character expression occurs in a poem by Ch'iao Chih-chih (d. 697), *Ch'üan T'ang shih*, vol. 2, *chüan* 81, p. 876, l. 1; a poem by Wang Yin (cs 737), ibid., vol. 2, *chüan* 145, p. 1471, l. 4; a poem by Yin Yao-fan (cs 814), ibid., vol. 8, *chüan* 492, p. 5576, l. 15; a song suite by Ch'en So-wen (d. c. 1604), *Ch'üan Ming san-ch'ü*, 2:2575, l. 9; and a set of songs by Ch'en Yü-chiao (1544–1611), ibid., 3:3167, l. 12.

3. This poem is by the ninth-century poet Hsüeh Feng (cs 841), *Ch'uan T'ang shih*, vol. 8, *chüan* 548, p. 6327, ll. 6–7. It also occurs in *T'ang-shu chih-chuan t'ung-su yen-i*, vol. 2, *chüan* 6, p. 1a, ll. 5–8; and, with some textual variation in the last line, in *Ta-T'ang Ch'in-wang tz'u-hua*, vol. 1, *chüan* 1, ch. 6, p. 58a, ll. 7–9.

4. This four-character expression occurs in *Shui-hu ch'üan-chuan*, vol. 3, ch. 84, p. 1389, l. 14; *Ta-T'ang Ch'in-wang tz'u-hua*, vol. 2, *chüan* 8, ch. 59, p. 26b, l. 6; and the ch'uan-ch'i drama *Chin-chien chi* (The brocade note), by Chou Lü-ching (1549–1640), *Liu-shih chung ch'ü* ed., scene 25, p. 78, l. 4.

5. This formulaic four-character expression occurs in a quatrain by Ch'iu Ch'u-chi (1148–1227), *Ch'üan Chin shih*, 2:159, l. 12; *Yüan-ch'ü hsüan wai-pien*, 2:536, l. 13; the ch'uan-ch'i drama *Ming-chu chi* (The luminous pearl), by Lu Ts'ai (1497–1537), *Liu-shih chung ch'ü* ed., scene 14, p. 41, l. 5; *Shui-hu ch'üan-chuan*, vol. 1, ch. 15, p. 221, l. 4; *Mu-lien chiu-mu ch'üan-shan hsi-wen*, *chüan* 2, p. 63b, l. 7; and *San-pao t'ai-chien Hsi-yang chi t'ung-su yen-i*, vol. 1, ch. 22, p. 289, l. 11.

6. Variants of this four-character expression, with the components in reverse order, occur in the Buddhist compendium *Tsung-ching lu* (The mirror of the source), comp. Yen-shou (904–75), in *Taishō shinshū daizōkyō* (The newly edited great Buddhist canon compiled in the Taishō reign period [1912–26]), 85 vols. (Tokyo: Taishō issaikyō kankōkai, 1922–32), vol. 48, no. 2016, *chüan* 2, p. 425, middle register, l. 21; the Taoist compendium *Yün-chi ch'i ch'ien* (Seven lots from the bookbag of the clouds), comp. Chang Chün-fang (c. 965–c. 1045), ed. and annot. Chiang Li-sheng et al. (Peking: Hua-hsia ch'u-pan she, 1996), *chüan* 102, p. 620, right-hand column, l. 19; an anonymous Yüan dynasty song in *Ch'üan Yüan san-ch'ü*, 2:1699, l. 6; and *Hsi-yu chi*, vol. 1, ch. 28, p. 319, l. 9.

7. The belief that something called a *lang-chin*, literally "wolf's sinew," variously defined as a sinew from the thigh of a wolf, or a weblike tissue secreted by an insect, could be used to detect the culprit in cases of theft is attested as early as the ninth century. See *Yu-yang tsa-tsu* (Assorted notes from Yu-yang), comp. Tuan Ch'eng-shih (803–63) (Peking: Chung-hua shu-chü, 1981), ch'ien-chi (first collection), *chüan* 16, p. 160, ll. 11–12. Further information on this mysterious object may be found in *Hsü Po-wu chih* (Supplement to Record of the investigation of things), comp. Li Shih (1108–81), in *Pai-tzu ch'üan-shu* (Complete works of the hundred philosophers), fac. repr., 8 vols. (Hang-chou: Che-chiang jen-min ch'u-pan she, 1984), vol. 7, *chüan* 3, p. 1b, ll. 8–10; and *Pen-ts'ao kang-mu* (Materia medica arranged by categories and topics), by Li Shih-chen (1518–93), 6 vols. (Hong Kong: Shang-wu yin-shu kuan, 1974), vol. 6, *chüan* 51, p. 52, ll. 12–13.

8. A variant of this formulaic four-character expression occurs in *Yüan-ch'ü hsüan*, 2:486, ll. 5–6; and it occurs in the same form as in the novel in a song about the mosquito by Chin Luan (1494–1583), *Ch'üan Ming san-ch'ü*, 2:1589, l. 5.

9. Variants of this idiomatic expression occur in *Shui-hu ch'üan-chuan*, vol. 4, ch. 104, p. 1596, l. 16; and *Hsi-yu chi*, vol. 1, ch. 22, p. 249, l. 1; and vol. 2, ch. 77, p. 878, l. 3.

10. Variants of this line occur in the thirteenth-century hsi-wen drama *Chang Hsieh chuang-yüan* (Top graduate Chang Hsieh), in *Yung-lo ta-tien hsi-wen san-chung chiao-chu* (An annotated recension of the three hsi-wen preserved in the *Yung-lo ta-tien*), ed. and annot. Ch'ien Nan-yang (Peking: Chung-hua shu-chü, 1979), scene 8, p. 45, l. 2; *Yüan-ch'ü hsüan*, 1:79, l. 3; and 3:1025, l. 21; *Sha-kou chi*, scene 14, p. 54, l. 7; the ch'uan-ch'i drama *Hsiang-nang chi* (The scent bag), by Shao Ts'an (15th century), *Liu-shih chung ch'ü* ed., scene 14, p. 40, l. 5; the ch'uan-ch'i drama *Shuang-chung chi* (The loyal pair), by Yao Mao-liang (15th century), in *Ku-pen hsi-ch'ü ts'ung-k'an, ch'u-chi*, item 33, *chüan* 1, scene 16, p. 33a, l. 3; *Shui-hu ch'üan-chuan*, vol. 2, ch. 30, p. 460, l. 7; and the *Chin P'ing Mei tz'u-hua*, vol. 5, ch. 93, p. 2a, l. 5.

11. A variant of this proverbial couplet occurs in *San-pao t'ai-chien Hsi-yang chi t'ung-su yen-i*, vol. 2, ch. 88. p. 1138, l. 15.

12. The term *ta-hsiang*, which I have translated as "pass the collection box around," is defined in a contemporary source as "to ask for a gratuity in return for performing some special skills." See *Nan-tz'u hsü-lu* (A preliminary account of southern-style drama), by Hsü Wei (1521–93), in *Chung-kuo ku-tien hsi-ch'ü lun-chu chi-ch'eng*, 3:246, l. 12; and K. C. Leung, *Hsü Wei as Drama Critic: An Annotated Translation of the Nan-tz'u Hsü-lu* (N.p.: University of Oregon Asian Studies Program, 1988), p. 81, ll. 3–4.

13. This idiomatic saying suggests that men are as sensitive to slights as dogs, which are likely to bite if you approach them in the wrong way. It recurs in the *Chin P'ing Mei tz'u-hua*, vol. 4, ch. 73, p. 9b, l. 4.

14. This formulaic four-character expression is ubiquitous in Chinese vernacular literature. See, e.g., *Yüan-ch'ü hsüan wai-pien*, 1:190, l. 17; *Cheng Chieh-shih li-kung shen-pi kung*, p. 670, l. 8; *Shui-hu ch'üan-chuan*, vol. 4, ch. 103, p. 1586, l. 11; *Huan-sha chi*, scene 22, p. 75, l. 12; *Hsi-yu chi*, vol. 1, ch. 3, p. 30, l. 9; and *San-pao t'ai-chien Hsi-yang chi t'ung-su yen-i*, vol. 1, ch. 36, p. 469, l. 15.

15. This four-character expression occurs in a set of songs by Liu Hsiao-tsu (1522–89), *Ch'üan Ming san-ch'ü*, 2:2314, l. 13.

16. The text actually reads Meng Yü-lou at this point, but the context indicates that P'an Chin-lien must have been meant.

17. The text here actually reads Han Chin-ch'uan, but the context makes it clear that Han Yü-ch'uan must have been meant.

18. The first four characters of this line occur in *Ta-T'ang Ch'in-wang tz'u-hua*, vol. 1, *chüan* 1, ch. 2, p. 15b, ll. 4–5.

19. This formulaic four-character expression occurs ubiquitously in Chinese vernacular literature. See, e.g., *Wu-wang fa Chou p'ing-hua*, p. 34, l. 11; *Yüan-ch'ü hsüan wai-pien*, 3:993, l. 16; the Yüan-Ming hsi-wen drama *Pai-yüeh t'ing chi* (Moon prayer pavilion), in *Ku-pen hsi-ch'ü ts'ung-k'an, ch'u-chi*, item 9, *chüan* 1, scene 7, p. 11b, l. 6; *Cheng Chieh-shih li-kung shen-pi kung*, p. 267, l. 12; the middle period vernacular story *Cheng Yüan-ho*, in *Tsui yü-ch'ing* (Superlative delights), pref. dated 1647, fac.

repr. in *Ku-pen hsiao-shuo ts'ung-k'an*, *ti erh-shih liu chi* (Collectanea of rare editions of traditional fiction, twenty-sixth series) (Peking: Chung-hua shu-chü, 1991), 4:1439, upper register, l. 9; *Shui-hu ch'üan-chuan*, vol. 1, ch. 9, p. 140, l. 5; *Hsi-yu chi*, vol. 1, ch. 21, p. 236, l. 11; and *Ta-T'ang Ch'in-wang tz'u-hua*, vol. 1, *chüan* 4, ch. 27, p. 24a, l. 8.

20. Variant versions of this conventional sentiment occur in *Yüan-ch'ü hsüan wai-pien*, 1:211, ll. 9–10; a song by T'ang Shih (14th–15th centuries), *Ch'üan Yüan san-ch'ü*, 2:1600, ll. 10–11; an anonymous set of songs published in 1471, *Ch'üan Ming san-ch'ü*, 4:4521, l. 13; an anonymous set of songs in *Tz'u-lin chai-yen*, 1:53, l. 2; and the *Chin P'ing Mei tz'u-hua*, vol. 5, ch. 94, p. 12b, l. 2.

21. A variant of this four-character expression occurs as early as the sixth century. See *Yen-shih chia-hsün [chi-chieh]* (Family Instructions for the Yen clan [with collected commentaries]), by Yen Chih-t'ui (531–91), ed. Wang Li-ch'i (Shanghai: Shang-hai ku-chi ch'u-pan she, 1980), *chüan* 3, ch. 8, p. 179, l. 5. It occurs ubiquitously in the same form as in the novel in Chinese vernacular literature. See, e.g., a lyric by Chao Ling-chih (1051–1134), *Ch'üan Sung tz'u*, 1:493, upper register, l. 8; *Tung Chieh-yüan Hsi-hsiang chi*, *chüan* 5, p. 100, l. 10; a song suite by Shang Tao (cs 1212), *Ch'üan Yüan san-ch'ü*, 1:22, l. 6; *[Chi-p'ing chiao-chu] Hsi-hsiang chi*, play no. 2, scene 5, p. 94, l. 6; *Yüan-ch'ü hsüan*, 3:975, l. 19; *Yüan-ch'ü hsüan wai-pien*, 2:427, l. 2; *T'ien-pao i-shih chu-kung-tiao*, p. 187, l. 9; the early vernacular story *Feng-yüeh Jui-hsien T'ing* (The romance in the Jui-hsien Pavilion), in *Ch'ing-p'ing shan-t'ang hua-pen*, p. 40, l. 12; the early vernacular story *Hua-teng chiao Lien-nü ch'eng-Fo chi* (The girl Lien-nü attains Buddhahood in her bridal palanquin), in *Ch'ing-p'ing shan-t'ang hua-pen*, p. 201, l. 1; the early vernacular story *Yü Chung-chü t'i-shih yü shang-huang* (Yü Chung-chü composes a poem and meets the retired emperor, Sung Kao-tsung [r. 1127–62]), in *Ching-shih t'ung-yen*, *chüan* 6, p. 64, l. 7; a song by Chu Yu-tun (1379–1439), *Ch'üan Ming san-ch'ü*, 1:283, l. 6; *Chung-ch'ing li-chi*, *chüan* 6, p. 6a, l. 8; a song suite by Ch'en To (fl. early 16th century), *Ch'üan Ming san-ch'ü*, 1:581, l. 8; the long six-teenth-century literary tale *Shuang-ch'ing pi-chi* (A record of the two Ch'ing [Chang Cheng-ch'ing and Chang Shun-ch'ing]), in *Kuo-se t'ien-hsiang*, vol. 2, *chüan* 5, lower register, p. 13a, l. 13; *Ming-chu chi*, scene 12, p. 35, l. 8; *Shui-hu ch'üan-chuan*, vol. 3, ch. 60, p. 1013, ll. 16–17; the middle period vernacular story *Chieh-chih-erh chi* (The story of the ring), in *Ch'ing-p'ing shan-t'ang hua-pen*, p. 249, l. 7; *Hai-fu shan-t'ang tz'u-kao*, *chüan* 3, p. 141, l. 7; and *Pa-i chi*, scene 21, p. 45, l. 6. It also recurs in the *Chin P'ing Mei tz'u-hua*, vol. 3, ch. 49, p. 7b, l. 9.

22. This line occurs in *[Chi-p'ing chiao-chu] Hsi-hsiang chi*, play no. 4, scene 1, p. 142, l. 3; an anonymous set of songs published in 1471, *Ch'üan Ming san-ch'ü*, 4:4521, l. 5; and a set of songs by Wang Chiu-ssu (1468–1551), ibid., 1:924, l. 12.

23. This four-character expression occurs in a song suite attributed to T'ang Shih (14th–15th centuries), *Ch'üan Yüan san-ch'ü*, 2:1548, l. 2; an anonymous Yüan dynasty song suite, ibid., 2:1875, l. 13; a song suite by Chu Yün-ming (1460–1526), *Ch'üan Ming san-ch'ü*, 1:780, ll. 12–13; and a song suite by Ch'en So-wen (d. c. 1604), ibid., 2:2552, l. 1.

24. This four-character expression occurs in a lyric by Yang Wu-chiu (1097–1171), *Ch'üan Sung tz'u*, 2:1202, upper register, l. 8; a poem by Wang Che (1112–70), *Ch'üan Chin shih*, 1:220, l. 1; a quatrain by Ma Yü (1123–83), ibid., 1:255, l. 12; the early hsi-wen drama *Hsiao Sun-t'u* (Little Butcher Sun), in *Yung-lo ta-tien hsi-wen san-*

chung chiao-chu, scene 10, p. 296, l. 6; a song suite by Tseng Jui (c. 1260–c. 1330), *Ch'üan Yüan san-ch'ü*, 1:514, l. 12; a song suite by Chao Yen-hui (14th century), ibid., 2:1233, l. 7; *Yüan-ch'ü hsüan wai-pien*, 1:4, l. 3; *T'ien-pao i-shih chu-kung-tiao*, p. 253, l. 4; and *Yu-kuei chi*, scene 22, p. 61, l. 6. It also recurs in the *Chin P'ing Mei tz'u-hua*, vol. 3, ch. 56, p. 9a, ll. 9–10.

25. This line occurs in *Yüan-ch'ü hsüan*, 3:1271, l. 7; the Yüan-Ming ch'uan-ch'i drama *Ching-ch'ai chi* (The thorn hairpin), *Liu-shih chung ch'ü* ed., scene 48, p. 138, ll. 8–9; a set of song lyrics by Li K'ai-hsien (1502–68) written in 1531, *Li K'ai-hsien chi*, 3:909, l. 7; and the ch'uan-ch'i drama *Pao-chien chi* (The story of the precious sword), by Li K'ai-hsien (1502–68), in *Shui-hu hsi-ch'ü chi, ti-erh chi* (Corpus of drama dealing with the *Shui-hu* cycle, second series), ed. Fu Hsi-hua (Shanghai: Ku-tien wen-hsüeh ch'u-pan she, 1958), scene 39, p. 69, ll. 16–17.

26. This four-character expression occurs in a quatrain by Kao P'ien (d. 887), *Ch'üan T'ang shih*, vol. 9, chüan 598, p. 6920, l. 14.

27. This four-character expression occurs in *Tung Chieh-yüan Hsi-hsiang chi*, chüan 6, p. 130, l. 9; the early Ming hsi-wen drama *Pai-she chi* (The story of the white snake), by Cheng Kuo-hsüan (14th century), in *Ku-pen hsi-ch'ü ts'ung-k'an, ch'u-chi*, item 43, chüan 2, scene 35, p. 37a, l. 1; an anonymous set of songs published in 1471, *Ch'üan Ming san-ch'ü*, 4:4521, l. 12; and *Chiang Shih yüeh-li chi*, chüan 3, scene 28, p. 11a, l. 10.

28. This four-character expression occurs in an anonymous Yüan dynasty song, *Ch'üan Yüan san-ch'ü*, 2:1666, l. 6; *Yüan-ch'ü hsüan wai-pien*, 1:223, l. 17; and a song suite by Chang Lien (cs 1544), *Ch'üan Ming san-ch'ü*, 2:1688, l. 13.

29. This four-character expression occurs in an anonymous Yüan dynasty song suite, *Ch'üan Yüan san-ch'ü*, 2:1842, l. 6; *Yüan-ch'ü hsüan*, 1:372, l. 10; and *Yüan-ch'ü hsüan wai-pien*, 1:127, l. 5.

30. The "girdle of communion" is a type of love token, consisting of a belt or girdle made up of interwoven strands of material of two different colors, to symbolize harmonious union, and may be worn by either men or women. It is mentioned in a poem by Chu Hsi (1130–1200), *Ch'üan Sung shih*, 44:27465, l. 1. See the entry in *Chung-kuo i-kuan fu-shih ta tz'u-tien* (Comprehensive dictionary of Chinese costume and its decorative motifs), comp. Chou Hsün and Kao Ch'un-ming (Shanghai: Shang-hai tz'u-shu ch'u-pan she, 1996), p. 439.

31. This four-character expression occurs in *Tung Chieh-yüan Hsi-hsiang chi*, chüan 7, p. 141, l. 3; a lyric by Wang Yüan-liang (13th century), *Ch'üan Sung tz'u pu-chi* (Supplement to Complete tz'u lyrics of the Sung), comp. K'ung Fan-li (Peking: Chung-hua shu-chü, 1981), p. 88, upper register, l. 10; a song suite by Wang Chiu-ssu (1468–1551), *Ch'üan Ming san-ch'ü*, 1:989, l. 12; and an anonymous set of songs published in 1553, ibid., 4:4552, l. 5.

32. This four-character expression occurs ubiquitously in Chinese vernacular literature. See, e.g., a lyric by Chao Ling-chih (1051–1134), *Ch'üan Sung tz'u*, 1:496, upper register, l. 6; a lyric by Hsin Ch'i-chi (1140–1207), ibid., 3:1919, upper register, l. 14; a song by Tseng Jui (c. 1260–c. 1330), *Ch'üan Yüan san-ch'ü*, 1:474, l. 10; a song suite by Sui Ching-ch'en (14th century), ibid., 1:545, l. 14; *Yu-kuei chi*, scene 36, p. 105, l. 8; a lyric by Liu Chi (1311–75), *Ch'üan Ming tz'u*, 1:94, upper register, l. 4; a song suite attributed to T'ang Shih (14th–15th centuries), *Ch'üan Yüan san-ch'ü*, 2:1546, l. 10; a set of songs by Ch'en To (fl. early 16th century), *Ch'üan Ming san-*

ch'ü, 1:478, l. 11; the ch'uan-ch'i drama *Lien-huan chi* (A stratagem of interlocking rings), by Wang Chi (1474–1540) (Peking: Chung-hua shu-chü, 1988), *chüan* 2, scene 26, p. 69, l. 1; *Huai-hsiang chi*, scene 17, p. 46, l. 8; a song suite by Shen Shih (1488–1565), *Ch'üan Ming san-ch'ü*, 2:1380, l. 15; a set of songs by Hsüeh Lun-tao (c. 1531–c. 1600), ibid., 3:2866, l. 2; and a set of songs by Chao Nan-hsing (1550–1627), ibid., 3:3218, ll. 10–11.

33. This four-character expression occurs in a poem by the famous Sung dynasty poetess Chu Shu-chen (fl. 1078–1138), *Ch'üan Sung shih*, 28:17955, l. 17. It has become ubiquitous in later Chinese literature. See, e.g., a lyric by Shao Shu-ch'i (12th century), *Ch'üan Sung tz'u*, 2:995, lower register, l. 2; *Yüan-ch'ü hsüan*, 2:800, l. 19; *Yüan-ch'ü hsüan wai-pien*, 2:374, l. 8; a song suite by Hsüeh Ang-fu (14th century), *Ch'üan Yüan san-ch'ü*, 1:723, l. 12; a song suite by Sung Fang-hu (14th century), ibid., 2:1306, l. 8; a song suite by T'ang Shih (14th–15th centuries), ibid, 2:1514, l. 1; a song suite by Chu Yu-tun (1379–1439), *Ch'üan Ming san-ch'ü*, 1:359, l. 9; the tsa-chü drama *Hsiang-nang yüan* (The tragedy of the scent bag), by Chu Yu-tun (1379–1439), author's pref. dated 1433, in *Sheng-Ming tsa-chü, erh-chi* (Tsa-chü dramas of the glorious Ming dynasty, second collection), comp. Shen T'ai (17th century), fac. repr. of 1641 edition (Peking: Chung-kuo hsi-chü ch'u-pan she, 1958), scene 2, p. 14a, l. 3; a lyric by Ku Hsün (1418–1505), *Ch'üan Ming tz'u*, 1:287, lower register, l. 8; *Huai-hsiang chi*, scene 24, p. 74, l. 6; a song suite by Wang Chiu-ssu (1468–1551), *Ch'üan Ming san-ch'ü*, 1:941, l. 2; a set of songs by Li K'ai-hsien (1502–68), *Li K'ai-hsien chi*, 3:910, l. 10; *Pao-chien chi*, scene 31, p. 59, l. 10; and *Ssu-sheng yüan*, play no. 4, scene 5, p. 101, l. 3.

34. This four-character expression occurs in a lyric by Liu K'o-chuang (1187–1269), *Ch'üan Sung tz'u*, 4:2601, lower register, l. 10; and a song suite by Wu Ch'eng-en (c. 1500–82), *Ch'üan Ming san-ch'ü*, 2:1799, ll. 6–7.

35. Liang Shan-po and Chu Ying-t'ai, somewhat like Romeo and Juliet, are the names of the protagonists of a tragic love story, conventionally set in the Eastern Chin dynasty (317–420), in which the two lovers are united only in death. Their names have become eponymous for frustrated young lovers, and their story exists in many different generic forms. A succinct and representative account may be found in the prologue to story number 28 in *Ku-chin hsiao-shuo*, vol. 2, *chüan* 28, pp. 417–18; and *Stories Old and New: A Ming Dynasty Collection*, comp. Feng Menglong (1574–1646), trans. Shuhui Yang and Yunqin Yang (Seattle: University of Washington Press, 2000), pp. 490–92.

36. This four-character expression occurs ubiquitously in Chinese vernacular literature. See, e.g., *Ju-ju chü-shih yü-lu, chia-chi* (first collection), *chüan* 2, p. 3b, ll. 9–10; *[Chi-p'ing chiao-chu] Hsi-hsiang chi*, play no. 4, scene 2, p. 150, l. 14; *Yüan-ch'ü hsüan*, 2:606, l. 17; *Yüan-ch'ü hsüan wai-pien*, 1:51, l. 18; *Sha-kou chi*, scene 20, p. 75, l. 10; *Feng-yüeh Jui-hsien T'ing*, p. 43, l. 15; *Ch'ien-chin chi*, scene 39, p. 127, l. 11; *San-kuo chih t'ung-su yen-i*, vol. 1, *chüan* 7, p. 308, l. 9; the anonymous Ming tsa-chü drama *Ch'ang-an ch'eng ssu-ma t'ou-T'ang* (In Ch'ang-an city four horsemen surrender to the T'ang), in *Ku-pen Yüan Ming tsa-chü*, vol. 3, scene 4, p. 16b, l. 9; *Huan-sha chi*, scene 12, p. 37, l. 5; *Mu-lien chiu-mu ch'üan-shan hsi-wen*, *chüan* 1, p. 43b, l. 3; *Hsi-yu chi*, vol. 1, ch. 9, p. 96, l. 9; a set of songs by Hsüeh Kang (c. 1535–95), *Ch'üan Ming san-ch'ü*, 3:2954, l. 4; *Ta-T'ang Ch'in-wang tz'u-hua*, vol. 1, *chüan* 3, ch. 17, p. 2a, l. 6; and *Sui-T'ang liang-ch'ao shih-chuan*, *chüan* 4, ch. 38, p. 50a, l. 6.

37. This four-character expression occurs in *T'ien-pao i-shih chu-kung-tiao*, p. 216, l. 4; *Yu-kuei chi*, scene 35, p. 101, l. 1; a song suite by Lu Teng-shan (14th century), *Ch'üan Yüan san-ch'ü*, 2:1084, l. 11; a set of songs by Chu Yu-tun (1379–1439), *Ch'üan Ming san-ch'ü*, 1:323, l. 13; a song suite by Ch'en To (fl. early 16th century), ibid., 1:605, l. 13; a song suite by Ch'ang Lun (1493–1526), ibid., 2:1554, l. 1; a song suite by Chang Lien (cs 1544), ibid., 2:1687, l. 7; a song suite by Wu Kuo-pao (cs 1550), ibid., 2:2285, l. 8; and *Shuang-lieh chi*, scene 3, p. 6, l. 7.

38. This four-character expression occurs in *P'i-p'a chi*, scene 6, p. 45, l. 13; and scene 37, p. 209, l. 13.

39. This four-character expression occurs in a song by Kuan Yün-shih (1286–1324), *Ch'üan Yüan san-ch'ü*, 1:360, l. 6; a song suite by Li Ai-shan (14th century), ibid., 2:1187, l. 11; and an anonymous set of songs published in 1471, *Ch'üan Ming san-ch'ü*, 4:4503, l. 7.

40. This four-character expression occurs in *Yüan-ch'ü hsüan wai-pien*, 3:989, l. 10; and a set of songs included in the front matter of the 1498 edition of *Hsi-hsiang chi*, p. 11b, l. 3.

41. See Roy, *The Plum in the Golden Vase*, vol. 2, chap. 36, n. 27.

42. A fabled dog belonging to Lu Chi (261–303), Yellow Ear was said to understand human speech, and to carry letters for his master over great distances. See the biography of Lu Chi in *Chin shu*, vol. 5, *chüan* 54, p. 1473, ll. 9–11. This four-character expression occurs in *[Chi-p'ing chiao-chu] Hsi-hsiang chi*, play no. 4, scene 1, p. 142, l. 3; and *Huai-ch'un ya-chi*, *chüan* 10, p. 12b, ll. 2–3.

43. This formulaic four-character expression occurs ubiquitously in Chinese vernacular literature. See, e.g., a set of songs by Hsü Yen (d. 1301), *Ch'üan Yüan san-ch'ü*, 1:81, ll. 1–2; *[Chi-p'ing chiao-chu] Hsi-hsiang chi*, play no. 4, scene 2, p. 152, l. 13; *Yüan-ch'ü hsüan*, 1:7, l. 11; *Yüan-ch'ü hsüan wai-pien*, 1:74, l. 18; a song suite by Kao Ming (d. 1359), *Ch'üan Yüan san-ch'ü*, 2:1463, l. 9; a song suite by T'ang Shih (14th–15th centuries), ibid., 2:1516, l. 9; *Yü-huan chi*, scene 8, p. 24, l. 11; a song by Chu Yün-ming, *Ch'üan Ming san-ch'ü*, 1:773, l. 6; the ch'uan-ch'i drama *Hsiu-ju chi* (The embroidered jacket), by Hsü Lin (1462–1538), *Liu-shih chung ch'ü* ed., scene 9, p. 23, l. 5; a song suite by K'ang Hai (1475–1541), *Ch'üan Ming san-ch'ü*, 1:1221, l. 4; *Mu-lien chiu-mu ch'üan-shan hsi-wen*, *chüan* 3, p. 23a, l. 7; *Hsi-yu chi*, vol. 2, ch. 54, p. 630, l. 2; the ch'uan-ch'i drama *Kuan-yüan chi* (The story of the gardener), by Chang Feng-i (1527–1613), *Liu-shih chung ch'ü* ed., scene 20, p. 43, l. 9; and *San-pao t'ai-chien Hsi-yang chi t'ung-su yen-i*, vol. 1, ch. 47, p. 609, l. 4. It also recurs in the *Chin P'ing Mei tz'u-hua*, vol. 3, ch. 54, p. 9b, l. 10; and vol. 4, ch. 64, p. 1a, l. 5.

44. This four-character expression occurs in a song suite by Liu T'ing-hsin (14th century), *Ch'üan Yüan san-ch'ü*, 2:1446, l. 8.

45. This four-character expression occurs in *Tung Chieh-yüan Hsi-hsiang chi*, *chüan* 8, p. 158, l. 3; a song suite by Shang Tao (cs 1212), *Ch'üan Yüan san-ch'ü*, 1:18, l. 8; *Yüan-ch'ü hsüan*, 2:684, l. 20; *Yu-kuei chi*, scene 40, p. 114, l. 5; *P'u-tung Ts'ui Chang chu-yü shih-chi* (Collection of poetic gems about [the affair of] Ts'ui [Ying-ying] and Chang [Chün-jui] in P'u-tung), included as part of the front matter in the 1498 edition of *Hsi-hsiang chi*, p. 19a, l. 17; and *Wang Lan-ch'ing chen-lieh chuan*, scene 1, p. 2b, l. 14.

46. This entire line occurs verbatim in *Yüan-ch'ü hsüan*, 3:1168, l. 10. The above song suite, which for some unknown reason omits the first tune, has been questionably

attributed to Wang Shih-fu (13th century), the author of *Hsi-hsiang chi*. See *Ch'üan Yüan san-ch'ü*, 1:294–95. It is preserved in the following anthologies: *Sheng-shih hsin-sheng*, pp. 287–89; *Tz'u-lin chai-yen*, 2:1042–45; *Yung-hsi yüeh-fu*, ts'e 9, pp. 70a–71b; *Nan-pei kung tz'u-chi* (Anthology of southern- and northern-style song lyrics), comp. Ch'en So-wen (d. c. 1604), ed. Chao Ching-shen, 4 vols. (Peking: Chung-hua shu-chü, 1959), vol. 4, *chüan* 6, pp. 665–66; and *Ch'ün-yin lei-hsüan* (An anthology of songs categorized by musical type), comp. Hu Wen-huan (fl. 1592–1617), 4 vols., fac. repr. (Peking: Chung-hua shu-chü, 1980), 3:1951–54.

47. This four-character expression occurs in *[Chi-p'ing chiao-chu] Hsi-hsiang chi*, play no. 2, scene 5, p. 92, l. 3; and *Hai-fu shan-t'ang tz'u-kao*, *chüan* 3, p. 142, l. 1.

48. This four-character expression occurs in a song suite by Wang Tzu-i (14th century), *Ch'üan Ming san-ch'ü*, 1:2, l. 3; and a song suite attributed to T'ang Shih (14th–15th centuries), *Ch'üan Yüan san-ch'ü*, 2:1475, l. 13.

49. The four animals representing the cardinal directions are the dragon of the east, the phoenix of the south, the tiger of the west, and the tortoise of the north.

50. On the *ch'i-lin*, see Roy, *The Plum in the Golden Vase*, vol. 1, chap. 7, n. 16. This motif is mentioned again in the *Chin P'ing Mei tz'u-hua*, vol. 4, ch. 78, p. 28a, l. 4; and vol. 5, ch. 96, p. 1b, l. 7.

51. These four lines occur verbatim in the Ming novel *San Sui p'ing-yao chuan* (The three Sui quash the demons' revolt), fac. repr. (Tokyo: Tenri daigaku shuppan-bu, 1981), *chüan* 1, ch. 2, p. 16b, ll. 2–3. A variant of these four lines occurs in the early vernacular story *Chien-t'ieh ho-shang* (The Monk's billet-doux), in *Ch'ing-p'ing shan-t'ang hua-pen*, p. 14, l. 14. The first two lines also occur verbatim in the early vernacular story *Tsao-chiao Lin Ta-wang chia-hsing* (A feat of impersonation by the King of Tsao-chiao Wood), in *Ching-shih t'ung-yen*, *chüan* 36, p. 552, l. 3. A variant of the third line occurs in the early vernacular story *Lo-yang san-kuai chi* (The three monsters of Lo-yang), in *Ch'ing-p'ing shan-t'ang hua-pen*, p. 69, l. 14; and a variant of the third and fourth lines occurs in the early vernacular story *Hsi-hu san-t'a chi* (The three pagodas at West Lake), in ibid., p. 26, l. 7.

52. This four-character expression recurs twice in the *Chin P'ing Mei tz'u-hua*, vol. 4, ch. 68, p. 11b, l. 2; and ch. 69, p. 6b, ll. 4–5.

53. Variants of this common storyteller's phrase occur in *Yüan-ch'ü hsüan*, 4:1450, ll. 20–21; and *San-pao t'ai-chien Hsi-yang chi t'ung-su yen-i*, vol. 2, ch. 91, p. 1174, l. 15.

54. Consort Cheng (1081–1132) is a historical figure. For her biography, see *Sung shih*, vol. 25, *chüan* 243, pp. 8639–40.

55. This four-character expression occurs in *Shui-hu ch'üan-chuan*, vol. 4, ch. 110, p. 1652, l. 1.

56. This four-character expression occurs in a song by Hsü Yen (d. 1301), *Ch'üan Yüan san-ch'ü*, 1:82, l. 1; and *Yüan-ch'ü hsüan*, 3:1226, l. 20.

57. See Roy, *The Plum in the Golden Vase*, vol. 1, chap. 10, n. 14.

58. See ibid., n. 15.

59. This four-character expression occurs in *Shui-hu ch'üan-chuan*, vol. 3, ch. 82, p. 1359, ll. 2–3.

60. See Roy, *The Plum in the Golden Vase*, vol. 1, chap. 11, n. 21. This four-character expression occurs in a poem by Tu Fu (712–70), *Ch'üan T'ang shih*, vol. 4, *chüan* 222, p. 2357, l. 1; a palace poem by Hua-jui Fu-jen (Lady Flower Stamen) (10th

century), ibid., vol. 11, *chüan* 798, p. 8977, 1. 6; a lyric by Wang Yüan-liang (13th century), *Ch'üan Sung tz'u*, 5:3342, upper register, 1. 4; a lyric by Chang Yen (1248–1322), ibid., 5:3499, lower register, 1. 5; *Yüan-ch'ü hsüan*, 1:349, 1. 1; a lyric by Ku Hsün (1418–1505), *Ch'üan Ming tz'u*, 1:293, upper register, 1. 16; and *Sui-T'ang liang-ch'ao shih-chuan*, *chüan* 11, ch. 101, p. 5b, 1. 2.

61. This four-character expression occurs in the early vernacular story *K'an p'i-hsüeh tan-cheng Erh-lang Shen* (Investigation of a leather boot convicts Erh-lang Shen), in *Hsing-shih heng-yen*, vol. 1, *chüan* 13, p. 241, ll. 2–3; an anonymous Yüan dynasty song suite, *Ch'üan Yüan san-ch'ü*, 2:1806, 1. 3; a lyric by Liu Ping (14th century) written in the year 1377, *Ch'üan Ming tz'u*, 1:135, lower register, 1. 7; a song suite by Wang Chiu-ssu (1468–1551), *Ch'üan Ming san-ch'ü*, 1:963, 1. 10; a song suite by Wu T'ing-han (cs 1521), ibid., 2:1792, 1. 5; and the sixteenth-century tsa-chü drama *Tung-t'ien hsüan-chi* (Mysterious record of the grotto heaven), attributed to Yang Shen (1488–1559), in *Ku-pen Yüan Ming tsa-chü*, vol. 2, scene 2, p. 9b, 1. 2. It also recurs in the *Chin P'ing Mei tz'u-hua*, vol. 3, ch. 46, p. 6b, 1. 4.

62. This four-character expression occurs in a song suite by Ch'iao Chi (d. 1345), *Ch'üan Yüan san-ch'ü*, 1:645, 1. 12; a song suite by Liu T'ing-hsin (14th century), ibid., 2:1444, ll. 14–15; a song suite by T'ang Shih (14th–15th centuries), ibid., 2:1491, 1. 15; a set of songs by Chu Yu-tun (1379–1439), *Ch'üan Ming san-ch'ü*, 1:273, 1. 9; a set of songs by Wang Chiu-ssu (1468–1551), ibid., 1:862, 1. 5; a song suite by Chang Lien (cs 1544), ibid., 2:1697, 1. 1; the ch'uan-ch'i drama *Yü-chüeh chi* (The jade thumb-ring), by Cheng Jo-yung (16th century), *Liu-shih chung ch'ü* ed., scene 12, p. 36, 1. 6; a set of songs by Hsüeh Lun-tao (c. 1531–c. 1600), *Ch'üan Ming san-ch'ü*, 3:2786, 1. 6; and a song suite by Li Wei-chen (1547–1626), ibid., 3:3183, ll. 10–11.

63. The Goddess of the Lo River is celebrated in a famous rhapsody by Ts'ao Chih (192–232) entitled *Lo-shen fu* (Rhapsody on the Goddess of the Lo River). See *Wen-hsüan* (Selections of refined literature), comp. Hsiao T'ung (501–31), 3 vols., fac. repr. (Peking: Chung-hua shu-chü, 1981), vol. 1, *chüan* 19, pp. 11b–16a; and *Wen xuan or Selections of Refined Literature*, trans. and annot. David R. Knechtges, 3 vols. (Princeton: Princeton University Press, 1982–96), 3:355–65. This line occurs verbatim in *Ts'an-T'ang Wu-tai shih yen-i chuan*, ch. 13, p. 44, 1. 12.

64. These two goddesses are paired together in similar poetic couplets in a poem by Liang Huang (8th century), *Ch'üan T'ang shih*, vol. 3, *chüan* 202, p. 2114, 1. 7; a poem by Yang Chü-yüan (755–c. 833), ibid., vol. 5, *chüan* 333, p. 3740, 1. 2; *Chang Hsieh chuang-yüan*, scene 45, p. 189, ll. 9–10; *Feng-yüeh Jui-hsien T'ing*, p. 41, 1. 16; the early vernacular story *Ch'ien-t'ang meng* (The dream in Ch'ien-t'ang), included as part of the front matter in the 1498 edition of the *Hsi-hsiang chi*, p. 4a, ll. 5–6; and the early vernacular story *Fo-yin shih ssu t'iao Ch'in-niang* (The priest Fo-yin teases Ch'in-niang four times), in *Hsing-shih heng-yen*, vol. 1, *chüan*, 12, p. 236, 1. 14. A variant of this couplet also recurs in the *Chin P'ing Mei tz'u-hua*, vol. 4, ch. 78, p. 29a, ll. 2–3.

65. This four-character expression occurs in a poem by Lo Yin (833–909), *Ch'üan T'ang shih*, vol. 10, *chüan* 658, p. 7557, 1. 1; a lyric by Liu Yung (cs 1034), *Ch'üan Sung tz'u*, 1:20, lower register, 1. 3; a lyric by Wang Chih-tao (1093–1169), ibid., 2:1164, lower register, 1. 3; two anonymous Sung dynasty lyrics, ibid, 5:3804, lower register, 1. 13; and 5:3813, upper register, 1. 4; and the early vernacular story *Yang Wen*

lan-lu hu chuan (The story of Yang Wen, the road-blocking tiger), in *Ch'ing-p'ing shan-t'ang hua-pen*, p. 169, l. 15.

66. This four-character expression occurs ubiquitously in Chinese vernacular literature. See, e.g., a song suite by Liu T'ing-hsin (14th century), *Ch'üan Yüan san-ch'ü*, 2:1444, l. 13; *Yüan-ch'ü hsüan*, 2:804, l. 18; *Yüan-ch'ü hsüan wai-pien*, 2:655, l. 4; *Ching-ch'ai chi*, scene 12, p. 36, l. 10; a song suite by T'ang Shih (14th–15th centuries), *Ch'üan Yüan san-ch'ü*, 2:1512, l. 3; the anonymous Yüan-Ming tsa-chü drama *Liang-shan wu-hu ta chieh-lao* (The five tigers of Liang-shan carry out a great jailbreak), in *Ku-pen Yüan Ming tsa-chü*, vol. 3, scene 4, p. 7b, ll. 5–6; *Chin-ch'ai chi*, scene 32, p. 59, l. 10; *Hsing-t'ien Feng-yüeh t'ung-hsüan chi*, scene 10, p. 26, l. 6; a song suite by K'ang Hai (1475–1541), *Ch'üan Ming san-ch'ü*, 1:1178, l. 13; a set of songs by Ch'ang Lun (1493–1526), ibid., 2:1523, l. 2; the ch'uan-ch'i drama *Hung-fu chi* (The story of Red Duster), by Chang Feng-i (1527–1613), *Liu-shih chung ch'ü* ed., scene 5, p. 9, l. 10; *Yen-chih chi*, chüan 2, scene 41, p. 34b. l. 4; the sixteenth-century ch'uan-ch'i drama *Su Ying huang-hou ying-wu chi* (The story of Empress Su Ying's parrot), in *Ku-pen hsi-ch'ü ts'ung-k'an*, ch'u-chi, item 45, chüan 2, scene 22, p. 7b, l. 8; *Hsi-yu chi*, vol. 2, ch. 54, p. 628, l. 3; *Huang-Ming k'ai-yün ying-wu chuan*, chüan 7, p. 5a, l. 1; *Pa-i chi*, scene 11, p. 26, l. 9; a song by Wang K'o-tu (c. 1526–c. 1594), *Ch'üan Ming san-ch'ü*, 2:2457, l. 8; a set of songs by Hsüeh Lun-tao (c. 1531–c. 1600), ibid., 3:2730, l. 4; a song suite by Wang Chih-teng (1535–1612), ibid., 3:2913, l. 14; and *Ta-T'ang Ch'in-wang tz'u-hua*, vol. 1, chüan 2, ch. 15, p. 60b, l. 1. It also recurs in the *Chin P'ing Mei tz'u-hua*, vol. 4, ch. 76, p. 20a, l. 5.

67. A close variant of this couplet occurs in *Shui-hu ch'üan-chuan*, vol. 1, ch. 2, p. 17, ll. 15–16.

68. This four-character expression occurs in a set of songs by Wang Yüan-heng (14th century), *Ch'üan Yüan san-ch'ü*, 2:1378, l. 15; a song suite by T'ang Shih (14th–15th centuries), ibid., 2:1486, l. 6; and a song by Shen Shih (1488–1565), *Ch'üan Ming san-ch'ü*, 2:1369, l. 3.

69. This song suite is preserved in the following anthologies: *Sheng-shih hsin-sheng*, pp. 551–52; *Tz'u-lin chai-yen*, 1:262–64; and *Yung-hsi yüeh-fu*, ts'e 16, pp. 18a–19a. Significantly, it is a song suite written to celebrate the emperor's birthday. This four-character expression occurs in a speech attributed to Hsiao I (444–92) in his biography in *Nan shih* (History of the Southern dynasties), comp. Li Yen-shou (7th century), completed in 659, 6 vols. (Peking: Chung-hua shu-chü, 1975), vol. 4, chüan 42, p. 1065, l. 9; a lyric by Wang Kuan (cs 1057), *Ch'üan Sung tz'u pu-chi*, p. 5, upper register, l. 15; *Ching-ch'ai chi*, scene 3, p. 6, l. 11; *Hua-teng chiao Lien-nü ch'eng-Fo chi*, p. 204, l. 1; a song by Chu Yu-tun (1379–1439), *Ch'üan Ming san-ch'ü*, 1:282, l. 10; *Wu Lun-ch'üan Pei*, chüan 1, scene 6, p. 31b, l. 5; a song suite by K'ang Hai (1475–1541), *Ch'üan Ming san-ch'ü*, 1:1179, l. 12; *Mu-lien chiu-mu ch'üan-shan hsi-wen*, chüan 1, p. 30a, l. 8; and *Hsi-yu chi*, vol. 1, ch. 45, p. 517, l. 13. It also recurs in the *Chin P'ing Mei tz'u-hua*, vol. 3, ch. 55, p. 6a, l. 5.

70. This anonymous tsa-chü drama entitled *Wang Yüeh-ying yüan-yeh liu-hsieh chi* is included in *Yüan-ch'ü hsüan*, 3:1265–79. It is a tale of an illicit love affair that almost ends tragically but is brought to a happy conclusion thanks to the intervention of the famous Sung dynasty magistrate Pao Cheng (999–1062). Despite the fact that the play ends happily, the illegitimate nature of the relationship makes it an ironic choice for performance during the celebration of a betrothal. For a plot summary and a further

elaboration of this point, see Katherine Carlitz, *The Rhetoric of Chin p'ing mei* (Bloomington: Indiana University Press, 1986), pp. 102–105.

71. This four-character expression occurs in the ch'uan-ch'i drama *Chieh-hsia chi* (The steadfast knight errant), by Hsü San-chieh (fl. late 16th century), *Liu-shih chung ch'ü* ed., scene 14, p. 33, l. 9.

72. This four-character expression occurs ubiquitously in Chinese literature. See, e.g., a lyric by Liu Yung (cs 1034), *Ch'üan Sung tz'u*, 1:43, upper register, l. 4; a poem by Sa-tu-la (cs 1327), *Yüan shih hsüan, ch'u-chi* (An anthology of Yüan poetry, first collection), comp. Ku Ssu-li (1665–1722), 3 vols. (Peking: Chung-hua shu-chü, 1987), 2:1255, l. 4; *Yüan-ch'ü hsüan*, 3:1161, l. 2; *Chien-teng hsin-hua, chüan* 3, p. 72, l. 15; *Hsiao fu-jen chin-ch'ien tseng nien-shao*, p. 228, ll. 6–7; a set of songs by Chu Yu-tun (1379–1439), *Ch'üan Ming san-ch'ü*, 1:328, l. 8; *Chung-ch'ing li-chi*, vol. 2, *chüan* 6, p. 14a, l. 6; *Shui-hu ch'üan-chuan*, vol. 2, ch. 31, p. 474, l. 13; *Hsi-yu chi*, vol. 1, ch. 36, p. 411, l. 13; *San-pao t'ai-chien Hsi-yang chi t'ung-su yen-i*, vol. 1, ch. 15, p. 189, l. 4; and an abundance of other occurrences, too numerous to list. It also recurs in the *Chin P'ing Mei tz'u-hua*, vol. 5, ch. 81, p. 3b, l. 11; and ch. 100, p. 10b, l. 7.

73. This song suite by Ch'en To (fl. early 16th century) is preserved in the following anthologies: *Sheng-shih hsin-sheng*, pp. 559–61; *Tz'u-lin chai-yen*, 1:279–84; *Nan-pei kung tz'u-chi*, vol. 1, *chüan* 2, pp. 77–78; and *Ch'ün-yin lei-hsüan*, 4:2141–44. It is a celebration of the Lantern Festival in the Ming capital of Peking and ends with an expression of gratitude to the reigning emperor.

74. This four-character expression occurs ubiquitously in Chinese vernacular literature. See, e.g., a lyric by Yen Shu (991–1055), *Ch'üan Sung tz'u*, 1:92, upper register, l. 12; a lyric by Su Shih (1037–1101), ibid., 1:293, lower register, l. 7; a lyric by Lü Wei-lao (12th century), ibid., 2:1119, lower register, l. 11; the prose introduction to a lyric by Wang Yün (1228–1304), *Ch'üan Chin Yüan tz'u*, 2:654, lower register, l. 7; a lyric by Wang Hsü (13th century), ibid., 2:889, upper register, l. 15; a lyric by Chang Yeh (13th–14th centuries) written in the year 1318, ibid., 2:902, lower register, l. 15; a song by Wu Hung-tao (14th century), *Ch'üan Yüan san-ch'ü*, 1:729, l. 10; a song by Chang K'o-chiu (1270–1348), ibid., 1:839, l. 3; *Hsiao Sun-t'u*, scene 3, p. 267, l. 8; *Ching-ch'ai chi*, scene 3, p. 8, l. 2; a song by Ch'en To (fl. early 16th century), *Ch'üan Ming san-ch'ü*, 1:465, l. 3; *Hsiu-ju chi*, scene 33, p. 94, l. 7; a song suite by Ho T'ang (1474–1543), *Ch'üan Ming san-ch'ü*, 1:1117, l. 1; a song by Yang Shen (1488–1559), ibid., 2:1416, l. 9; *Ssu-hsi chi*, scene 20, p. 54, l. 7; *Sui-T'ang liang-ch'ao shih-chuan*, *chüan* 1, ch. 10, p. 58b, l. 8; and *Ta-T'ang Ch'in-wang tz'u-hua*, vol. 1, *chüan* 1, ch. 7, p. 78b, l. 1.

CHAPTER 44

1. This poem is by the ninth-century poet Hsüeh Feng (cs 841), *Ch'üan T'ang shih*, vol. 8, *chüan* 548, p. 6323, l. 16–p. 6324, l. 1.

2. The locus classicus for this four-character expression is a passage in *Mencius*, which D. C. Lau translates: "The Sage, too, is the same in kind as other men.

Though one of their kind
He stands far above the crowd."

See *Meng-tzu yin-te* (A Concordance to Meng-tzu) (Taipei: Chinese Materials and Research Aids Service Center, 1966), Book 2A, ch. 2, p. 12, ll. 5–6; and *Mencius*, trans. D. C. Lau (Baltimore: Penguin Books, 1970), p. 80, ll. 13–15. It also occurs in *San-kuo chih*, vol. 4, *chüan* 44, p. 1058, l. 3; *Yüan-ch'ü hsüan wai-pien*, 3:955, l. 14; and *Chien-teng yü-hua, chüan* 1, p. 141, l. 7; and recurs in the *Chin P'ing Mei tz'u-hua*, vol. 3, ch. 58, p. 3b, l. 3.

3. This formulaic four-character expression occurs in a lyric by Liu Yung (cs 1034), *Ch'üan Sung tz'u*, 1:16, lower register, l. 15. It is ubiquitous in Chinese vernacular literature. See, e.g., *Yüan-ch'ü hsüan wai-pien*, 1:215, l. 1; *Chien-teng yü-hua, chüan* 5, p. 294, l. 11; *Chin-ch'ai chi*, scene 24, p. 46, l. 12; *Wu Lun-ch'üan Pei, chüan* 1, scene 8, p. 38a, l. 1; the ch'uan-ch'i drama *San-yüan chi* (Feng Ching [1021–94] wins first place in three examinations), by Shen Shou-hsien (15th century), *Liu-shih chung ch'ü* ed., scene 34, p. 88, l. 3; *Shuang-chu chi*, scene 34, p. 118, l. 2; *Hsün-ch'in chi*, scene 34, p. 113, l. 7; *Chung-ch'ing li-chi, chüan* 6, p. 20b, l. 9; a song suite by T'ang Yin (1470–1524), *Ch'üan Ming san-ch'ü*, 1:1076, ll. 1–2; *Yü-huan chi*, scene 34, p. 128, l. 12; *Pao-chien chi*, scene 30, p. 56, l. 20; *Chiang Shih yüeh-li chi, chüan* 2, scene 25, p. 21b, l. 8; *Mu-tan t'ing*, scene 40, p. 204, l. 14; and *Ssu-hsi chi*, scene 17, p. 42, l. 11. It also recurs in the *Chin P'ing Mei tz'u-hua*, vol. 4, ch. 61, p. 12b, l. 9.

4. This is the first half of a song by Chang K'o-chiu (1270–1348), *Ch'üan Yüan san-ch'ü*, 1:820, l. 7. It is also preserved in *Yung-hsi yüeh-fu, ts'e* 19, p. 53b, ll. 7–8. The version in the novel is closer to that in *Yung-hsi yüeh-fu*.

5. This four-character expression occurs in an anonymous Yüan dynasty song suite, *Ch'üan Yüan san-ch'ü*, 2:1853, l. 16; the anonymous early Ming ch'uan-ch'i drama *P'o-yao chi* (The dilapidated kiln), in *Ku-pen hsi-ch'ü ts'ung-k'an, ch'u-chi*, item 19, *chüan* 1, scene 10, p. 29b, l. 4; *Hsiu-ju chi*, scene 27, p. 74, l. 11; a song suite by Ch'en To (fl. early 16th century), *Ch'üan Ming san-ch'ü*, 1:580, ll. 12–13; a set of songs by Liu Hsiao-tsu (1522–89), ibid., 2:2319, l. 1; and *Hai-fu shan-t'ang tz'u-kao, chüan* 1, p. 6, l. 2.

6. This is the first half of a song by Ch'en To (fl. early 16th century), *Ch'üan Ming san-ch'ü*, 1:524, ll. 2–3. It is also preserved in *Tz'u-lin chai-yen*, 1:48, ll. 6–8; *Yung-hsi yüeh-fu, ts'e* 15, *hou-chi*, p. 5a, ll. 6–8; *[Hsin-pien] Nan chiu-kung tz'u* ([Newly compiled] Anthology of song lyrics in the nine southern modes), fac. repr. of Wan-li (1573–1620) edition (Taipei: Shih-chieh shu-chü, 1961), *chung-lü*, p. 7b, ll. 8–9; and *Nan-tz'u yün-hsüan* (An anthology of southern style song lyrics arranged by rhyme), comp. Shen Ching (1553–1610), ed. Cheng Ch'ien (Taipei: Pei-hai ch'u-pan kung-ssu, 1971), p. 46, ll. 4–5.

7. This four-character expression occurs in *Hai-fu shan-t'ang tz'u-kao, chüan* 3, p. 143, l. 3.

8. This four-character expression occurs in a poem by Lu Kuei-meng (fl. 865–881), *Ch'üan T'ang shih*, vol. 9, *chüan* 624, p. 7179, l. 8; a lyric by Wang Chih-tao (1093–1169), *Ch'üan Sung tz'u*, 2:1144, lower register, ll. 4–5; a lyric by Wang Yen (1138–1218), ibid., 3:1853, lower register, l. 6; *Chang Hsieh chuang-yüan*, scene 41, p. 177, l. 6; a lyric by T'ao Tsung-i (c. 1316–c. 1403), *Ch'üan Chin Yüan tz'u*, 2:1132, upper register, l. 2; *Hsiu-ju chi*, scene 13, p. 36, l. 4; a set of songs by Wang Chiu-ssu (1468–1551), *Ch'üan Ming san-ch'ü*, 1:937, l. 11; and recurs in the *Chin P'ing Mei tz'u-hua*, vol. 3, ch. 46, p. 5b, l. 11.

9. This four-character expression occurs in a lyric by Wang Tan-kuei (12th century), *Ch'üan Chin Yüan tz'u*, 1:491, lower register, l. 3; and a lyric by Pei Ch'iung (c. 1297–1379), *Ch'üan Ming tz'u*, 1:19, lower register, l. 4.

10. This line occurs in a poem by Chu Shu-chen (fl. 1078–1138), *Ch'üan Sung shih*, 28:17956, l. 2; and a lyric by Shao Heng-chen (1309–1401) written in the year 1348, *Ch'üan Chin Yüan tz'u*, 2:1117, lower register, l. 14. This is the first half of another song by Ch'en To (fl. early 16th century), *Ch'üan Ming san-ch'ü*, 1:475, l. 13–476, l. 2. It is also preserved in *Nan-pei kung tz'u-chi*, vol. 2, *chüan* 4, p. 234, ll. 9–11; and *Wu-sao ho-pien* (Combined anthology of the songs of Wu), comp. Chang Ch'i (fl. early 17th century) and Chang Hsü-ch'u (fl. early 17th century), pref. dated 1637, 4 *ts'e*, fac. repr. (Shanghai: Shang-wu yin-shu kuan, 1934), *ts'e* 4, *chüan* 4, p. 31a, ll. 5–9. It is performed again in the *Chin P'ing Mei tz'u-hua*, vol. 4, ch. 75, p. 13a, ll. 5–8.

11. This four-character expression occurs in a lyric by Ch'ao Pu-chih (1053–1110), *Ch'üan Sung tz'u*, 1:576, lower register, l. 14; a lyric by Chao Ch'ang-ch'ing (12th century), ibid., 3:1776, lower register, l. 8; a song by Chao Yen (13th century), *Ch'üan Yüan san-ch'ü*, 1:138, l. 10; a song suite by Teng Yü-pin (13th century), ibid., 1:307, l. 14; a song by Wu Hung-tao (14th century), ibid., 1:730, l. 11; *Hsiao Sun-t'u*, scene 9, p. 286, l. 5; the anonymous Ming tsa-chü drama *Feng-yüeh Nan-lao chi* (Romance in the South Prison), in *Ku-pen Yüan Ming tsa-chü*, vol. 4, scene 1, p. 3b, l. 8; the collection of literary tales entitled *Hua-ying chi* (Flower shadows collection), by T'ao Fu (1441–c. 1523), author's pref. dated 1523, in *Ming-Ch'ing hsi-chien hsiao-shuo ts'ung-k'an* (Collectanea of rare works of fiction from the Ming-Ch'ing period) (Chi-nan: Ch'i-Lu shu-she, 1996), p. 881, l. 10; and a song by Chang Lien (cs 1544), *Ch'üan Ming san-ch'ü*, 2:1653, l. 2.

12. This four-character expression occurs in a song by Pai P'u (1226–c. 1306), *Ch'üan Yüan san-ch'ü*, 1:195, l. 8.

13. This is the first half of a song from a song suite attributed to T'ang Fu (14th century), *Ch'üan Ming san-ch'ü*, 1:225, l. 13–226, l. 1. It is also preserved in *Sheng-shih hsin-sheng*, p. 256, ll. 9–12; *Tz'u-lin chai-yen*, 1:444, ll. 3–6; and *Yung-hsi yüeh-fu*, *ts'e* 7, pp. 19a, l. 9–19b, l. 3. The version in the novel is closest to that in *Yung-hsi yüeh-fu*.

14. This four-character expression occurs in an anonymous Yüan dynasty song suite, *Ch'üan Yüan san-ch'ü*, 2:1835, l. 14.

15. This four-character expression occurs in a song by Chang K'o-chiu (1270–1348), *Ch'üan Yüan san-ch'ü*, 1:950, l. 3; a song by Yang Shen (1488–1559), *Ch'üan Ming san-ch'ü*, 2:1427, l. 11; a song suite by Ch'en Ho (1516–60), ibid., 2:2161, l. 1; a set of songs by Hsüeh Lun-tao (c. 1531–c. 1600), ibid., 3:2754, l. 11; and the ch'uan-ch'i drama *Shih-hou chi* (The lion's roar), by Wang T'ing-no (fl. 1593–1611), *Liu-shih chung ch'ü* ed., scene 9, p. 27, l. 9.

16. This is the first half of an anonymous song that is preserved in *Yung-hsi yüeh-fu*, *ts'e* 15, hou-chi, p. 15a, ll. 1–3.

17. This formulaic four-character expression is ubiquitous in Chinese vernacular literature. See, e.g., *[Chi-p'ing chiao-chu] Hsi-hsiang chi*, play no. 5, scene 3, p. 187, l. 10; *Yüan-ch'ü hsüan*, 2:532, l. 21; *Yüan-ch'ü hsüan wai-pien*, 2:390, l. 12; a song suite by Sa-tu-la (cs 1327), *Ch'üan Yüan san-ch'ü*, 1:700, l. 4; a song by Chang K'o-chiu (1270–1348), ibid., 1:871, l. 5; the fourteenth-century description of the demimonde *Ch'ing-lou chi* (Green bower collection), by Hsia T'ing-chih (c. 1316–c. 1368), in

Chung-kuo ku-tien hsi-ch'ü lun-chu chi-ch'eng, 2:20, l. 11; the Yüan-Ming ch'uan-ch'i drama *Chin-yin chi* (The golden seal), by Su Fu-chih (14th century), in *Ku-pen hsi-ch'ü ts'ung-k'an, ch'u-chi*, item 27, *chüan* 2, scene 15, p. 10b, l. 4; a song suite by Chu Yu-tun (1379–1439), *Ch'üan Ming san-ch'ü*, 1:350, l. 1; *Huai-hsiang chi*, scene 21, p. 63, l. 6; *Hsiu-ju chi*, scene 4, p. 10, l. 1; *Pao-chien chi*, scene 26, p. 48, l. 20; the long sixteenth-century literary tale *Liu sheng mi Lien chi* (The story of Liu I-ch'un's quest of Sun Pi-lien), in *Kuo-se t'ien-hsiang*, vol. 1, *chüan* 2, lower register, p. 21a, l. 5; *Huan-sha chi*, scene 28, p. 102, l. 4; *Hsi-yu chi*, vol. 2, ch. 55, p. 636, l. 4; a song suite by Chang Feng-i (1527–1613), *Ch'üan Ming san-ch'ü*, 3:2606, l. 2; and *Mu-tan t'ing*, scene 10, p. 47, l. 8. It also recurs in the *Chin P'ing Mei tz'u-hua*, vol. 3, ch. 46, p. 2a, l. 3.

18. This four-character expression occurs in a poem by Li Po (701–62), *Ch'üan T'ang shih*, vol. 3, *chüan* 184, p. 1881, l. 10.

19. This line occurs in a poem by Tai Fu-ku (1167–c. 1246), *Ch'üan Sung shih*, 54:33531, l. 1; a set of songs by Hsüeh Ang-fu (14th century), *Ch'üan Yüan san-ch'ü*, 1:718, l. 7; and a song by Jen Yü (14th century), ibid., 1:1006, l. 6.

20. This line is from a lyric by Yüan Hao-wen (1190–1257), *Ch'üan Chin Yüan tz'u*, 1:99, upper register, l. 5. It also occurs in the 1498 edition of *Hsi-hsiang chi*, play no. 3, scene 2, p. 101a, ll. 10–11; and in *Nan Hsi-hsiang chi* (A southern version of the *Romance of the western chamber*), usually attributed to Li Jih-hua (fl. early 16th century), *Liu-shih chung ch'ü* ed., scene 22, p. 63, l. 11.

21. This formulaic four-character expression occurs in a song suite by Tu Jen-chieh (13th century), *Ch'üan Yüan san-ch'ü*, 1.32, l. 13; a song suite by Ch'en Tzu-hou (14th century), ibid., 2:1143, l. 5; *Yüan-ch'ü hsüan*, 4:1532, l. 14; a song by Sheng Ts'ung-chou (14th century), *Ch'üan Ming san-ch'ü*, 1:250, l. 6; an anonymous set of poems included as part of the front matter in the 1498 edition of the *Hsi-hsiang chi*, p. 27b, l. 11; a song by Ch'en To (fl. early 16th century), *Ch'üan Ming san-ch'ü*, 1:448, l. 3; a song suite by Wang Chiu-ssu (1468–1551), ibid., 1:984, l. 9; a song suite by T'ang Yin (1470–1524), ibid., 1:1091, l. 9; *Pao-chien chi*, scene 22, p. 42, l. 25; a song by Huang O (1498–1569), *Ch'üan Ming san-ch'ü*, 2:1759, l. 8; a song suite by Chang Feng-i (1527–1613), ibid., 3:2609, l. 10; the ch'uan-ch'i drama *Chu-fa chi* (Taking the tonsure), by Chang Feng-i (1527–1613), completed in 1586, in *Ku-pen hsi-ch'ü ts'ung-k'an, ch'u-chi*, item 61, *chüan* 2, scene 17, p. 2b, l. 5; a set of songs by Hsüeh Lun-tao (c. 1531–c. 1600), *Ch'üan Ming san-ch'ü*, 3:2876, l. 2; a song suite by Shen Ching (1553–1610), ibid., 3:3259, l. 7; and *Chin-chien chi*, scene 38, p. 113, l. 1.

22. The first seven characters of this line occur in a song suite by Kao Shih (14th century), *Ch'üan Yüan san-ch'ü*, 2:1025, l. 4.

23. This four-character expression occurs in *Yüan-ch'ü hsüan*, 3:1266, l. 9; a set of songs by Wang Ai-shan (14th century), *Ch'üan Yüan san-ch'ü*, 2:1191, ll. 13–14; and an anonymous set of songs published in 1471, *Ch'üan Ming san-ch'ü*, 4:4521, l. 8.

24. On the Temple of the God of the Sea, see Roy, *The Plum in the Golden Vase*, vol. 1, chap. 8, n. 19.

25. Because the asterisms Orion and Antares are at opposite ends of the zodiac they are never visible in the sky at the same time and have thus become symbolic of permanent separation.

26. This proverbial rhetorical question recurs in the *Chin P'ing Mei tz'u-hua*, vol. 3, ch. 51, p. 1b, l. 10. A close variant also occurs in *San-pao t'ai-chien Hsi-yang chi t'ung-su yen-i*, vol. 1, ch. 35, p. 452, l. 6.

27. A variant of this idiomatic expression recurs in the *Chin P'ing Mei tz'u-hua*, vol. 5, ch. 93, p. 2a, l. 4.

28. This idiomatic expression recurs in ibid., ch. 85, p. 7b, l. 2.

29. This idiomatic expression recurs in ibid., vol. 4, ch. 76, p. 16b, l. 2.

30. Variants of this proverbial couplet occur in the middle-period vernacular story *Hsin-ch'iao shih Han Wu mai ch'un-ch'ing* (Han Wu-niang sells her charms at New Bridge Market), in *Ku-chin hsiao-shuo*, vol. 1, *chüan* 3, p. 73, l. 14; a scene from the lost ch'uan-ch'i drama *Ch'a-ch'uan chi* (The tea-merchant's boat), in *Yüeh-fu hung-shan* (The red coral anthology of dramatic excerpts), comp. Chi Chen-lun (fl. early 17th century), pref. dated 1602, fac. repr. in *Shan-pen hsi-ch'ü ts'ung-k'an* (Collectanea of rare editions of works on dramatic prosody), 36 vols. (Taipei: Hsüeh-sheng shu-chü, 1984–87), 11:441, l. 8; and the vernacular story *Kuei-chien chiao-ch'ing* (An intimate bond between the exalted and the humble), in *Tsui-yü ch'ing*, p. 1545, upper register, ll. 8–9. A close variant also recurs in the *Chin P'ing Mei tz'u-hua*, vol. 4, ch. 72, p. 35a, l. 2; and vol. 5, ch. 98, p. 13a, l. 2.

CHAPTER 45

1. This line is taken almost verbatim from the second line of a quatrain attributed to P'i Jih-hsiu (c. 834–c. 883). See *Yüan-chien lei-han* (A comprehensive encyclopedia arranged by categories), compiled under the aegis of the K'ang-hsi emperor (r. 1661–1722) by Chang Ying (1638–1708) et al., 7 vols., fac. repr. of the Palace edition of 1710 (Taipei: Hsin-hsing shu-chü, 1967), vol. 7, *chüan* 405, p. 8a, ll. 6–7.

2. Sun Shou (d. 159), the extravagant wife of the powerful chief minister Liang Chi (d. 159), is said to have initiated the fashion of making up the area under the eyes to look as though one had been weeping, a caprice that was widely imitated by society at large. See *Hou-Han shu*, vol. 5, *chüan* 34, p. 1180, l. 1; and vol. 11, *chih* (treatises), no. 13, pp. 3270–71.

3. For the powder-faced gentleman, see Roy, *The Plum in the Golden Vase*, vol. 2, chap. 31, n. 17. This couplet is derived from the first two lines of a quatrain by Wei Chuang (836–910). See *Wei Chuang chi chiao-chu* (A collated and annotated edition of the works of Wei Chuang), ed. Li I (Ch'eng-tu: Ssu-ch'uan sheng she-hui k'o-hsüeh yüan ch'u-pan she, 1986), p. 403, l. 7.

4. This four-character expression is derived from the final line of a famous poem on plum blossoms by Lin Pu (968–1028). See *Ch'üan Sung shih*, 2:1218, l. 2; and the translation by Hans H. Frankel in Maggie Bickford et al., *Bones of Jade, Soul of Ice: The Flowering Plum in Chinese Art* (New Haven: Yale University Art Gallery, 1985), p. 165. It occurs in a lyric by Liu Ch'en-weng (1232–97), *Ch'üan Sung tz'u*, 5:3199, lower register, l. 13; a song by Chang K'o-chiu (1270–1348), *Ch'üan Yüan san-ch'ü*, 1:786, l. 11; a lyric by Wu Ching-k'uei (1292–1355), *Ch'üan Chin Yüan tz'u*, 2:1050, upper register, l. 12; and a set of songs by Chu Yu-tun (1379–1439), *Ch'üan Ming san-ch'ü*, 1:334, l. 2.

5. Mr. Wei's Purples and Mr. Yao's Yellows were the names of two highly prized varieties of peonies in the Lo-yang area that were named after Wei Jen-p'u (911–69)

and a certain commoner named Yao, who were allegedly the first to cultivate them. See *Lo-yang mu-tan chi* (A record of the peonies of Lo-yang), by Ou-yang Hsiu (1007–72), written in 1034, in *Ou-yang Yung-shu chi* (The collected works of Ou-yang Hsiu), 3 vols. (Shanghai: Shang-wu yin-shu kuan, 1958), vol. 2, *ts'e* 9, *chü-shih wai-chi* (additional works), *chüan* 22, p. 5. These two varieties of peonies are often mentioned together. See, e.g., a poem by Ou-yang Hsiu, *Ch'üan Sung shih*, 6:3680, l. 6; a lyric by Mao P'ang (1067–c. 1125), *Ch'üan Sung tz'u*, 2:665, upper register, l. 15; a lyric by Hung K'uo (1117–84), ibid., 2:1376, lower register, l. 2; a lyric by Chao Pi-hsiang (1245–94), ibid., 5:3381, upper register, l. 4; a lyric in a literary tale included in *Tsui-weng t'an-lu* (The old drunkard's selection of tales), comp. Lo Yeh (13th century) (Taipei: Shih-chieh shu-chü, 1972), *kuei-chi* (10th collection), *chüan* 2, p. 119, l. 1; a lyric by Shen Hsi (14th century), *Ch'üan Chin Yüan tz'u*, 2:1042, upper register, ll. 5–6; *Chang Hsieh chuang-yüan*, scene 53, p. 214, l. 1; *Hsiao Sun-t'u*, scene 2, p. 261, l. 15; a song suite by Hsia Wen-fan (16th century), *Ch'üan Ming san-ch'ü*, 1:826, l. 12; a song by Wang Chiu-ssu (1468–1551), ibid., 1:861, l. 3; a set of songs by Liu Liang-ch'en (1482–1551), ibid., 2:1324, l. 4; and *Hsi-yu chi*, vol. 2, ch. 82, p. 940, l. 16. A close variant of this entire line occurs in a song by Ch'en So-wen (d. c. 1604), *Ch'üan Ming san-ch'ü*, 2:2491, l. 11.

6. This four-character expression occurs in a speech attributed to the Buddhist monk Ta-t'ung (819–914), *Wu-teng hui-yüan*, vol. 1, *chüan* 5, p. 298, l. 2; the *Chu-tzu yü-lei* (Classified sayings of Master Chu), comp. Li Ching-te (13th century), 8 vols. (Taipei: Cheng-chung shu-chü, 1982), vol. 1, *chüan* 11, p. 6a, l. 4; a speech attributed to the Buddhist monk Chih-yü (1185–1269), *Hsü-t'ang Ho-shang yü-lu* (Recorded sayings of the Monk Hsü-t'ang), in *Taishō shinshū daizōkyō*, vol. 47, no. 2000, *chüan* 1, p. 993, upper register, ll. 15–16; *Kuan-shih-yin p'u-sa pen-hsing ching* (Sutra on the deeds of the bodhisattva Avalokiteśvara), also known as *Hsiang-shan pao-chüan* (Precious scroll on Hsiang-shan), attributed to P'u-ming (fl. early 12th century), n.p., n.d. (probably 19th century), p. 93b, l. 9; and *Ch'in ping liu-kuo p'ing-hua* (The p'ing-hua on the annexation of the Six States by Ch'in), originally published in 1321–23 (Shanghai: Ku-tien wen-hsüeh ch'u-pan she, 1955), p. 12, l. 12.

7. This proverbial saying occurs in *Shuang-chu chi*, scene 32, p. 111, l. 3.

8. This idiomatic couplet recurs in the *Chin P'ing Mei tz'u-hua*, vol. 5, ch. 86, p. 5b, l. 4.

9. The locus classicus for this four-character expression is a passage in the *Ch'un-ch'iu fan-lu* (Luxuriant dew of the Spring and autumn annals), attributed to Tung Chung-shu (c. 179–c. 114 B.C.). See *Ch'un-ch'iu fan-lu chu-tzu so-yin* (A concordance to the *Ch'un-ch'iu fan-lu*) (Hong Kong: Shang-wu yin-shu kuan, 1994), *chüan* 6, ch. 7, p. 27, l. 19. It also occurs in a memorial submitted to the throne in A.D. 30 by Chu Fu (1st century A.D.), *Hou-Han shu*, vol. 4, *chüan* 33, p. 1142, l. 2; a quatrain by Wang Chien (c. 767–c. 830), *Ch'üan T'ang shih*, vol. 5, *chüan* 301, p. 3427, l. 9; a poem by Han Wo (844–923), ibid., vol. 10, *chüan* 681, p. 7808, l. 4; a quatrain by T'an Ch'u-tuan (1123–85), *Ch'üan Chin shih*, 1:339, l. 11; and the early vernacular story *Yin-chih chi-shan* (A secret good deed accumulates merit), in *Ch'ing-p'ing shan-t'ang hua-pen*, p. 119, l. 10.

10. These two lines occur in close proximity in *Shui-hu ch'üan-chuan*, vol. 3, ch. 82, p. 1359, l. 17; and recur together in the *Chin P'ing Mei tz'u-hua*, vol. 4, ch. 71, p. 2b, l. 6.

11. This four-character expression occurs in *Yüan-ch'ü hsüan wai-pien*, 3:855, l. 13; and recurs, in a variant form, in the *Chin P'ing Mei tz'u-hua*, vol. 4, ch. 62, p. 10a. l. 11.

12. A "hamper party" was an occasion on certain festival days at which courtesans assembled to celebrate among themselves, without the presence of their male patrons, and competed with each other to see who could produce the fanciest hamper of holiday delicacies. The custom is described in the preface to a poem on the subject by Shen Chou (1427–1509). See *Shih-t'ien hsien-sheng chi* (The collected literary works of Shen Chou), by Shen Chou (1427–1509), 2 vols., fac. repr. of Wan-li edition, pref. dated 1615 (Taipei: Kuo-li Chung-yang t'u-shu kuan, 1968), 1:275–76. This preface and poem are translated in A *Feast of Mist and Flowers: The Gay Quarters of Nanking at the End of the Ming Dynasty*, trans. Howard S. Levy (Yokohama: Mimeographed private edition, 1966), pp. 102–4. For a vivid description of the same custom in a famous seventeenth-century ch'uan-ch'i drama, see *T'ao-hua shan* (The peach blossom fan), by K'ung Shang-jen (1648–1718), ed. Wang Chi-ssu and Su Huan-chung (Peking: Jen-min wen-hsüeh ch'u-pan she, 1958), scene 5, p. 37, ll. 2–11; and *The Peach Blossom Fan*, trans. Chen Shih-hsiang and Harold Acton with the collaboration of Cyril Birch (Berkeley: University of California Press, 1976), pp. 39–40.

13. A variant of this idiomatic saying occurs in *Yüan-ch'ü hsüan wai-pien*, 3:814, l. 15.

14. This proverbial couplet recurs in the *Chin P'ing Mei tz'u-hua*, vol. 4, ch. 64, p. 6b, l. 10.

15. A variant of this formulaic six-character expression, in which the two components are reversed, occurs ubiquitously in Chinese vernacular literature. See, e.g., *Yüan-ch'ü hsüan*, 1:267, l. 21; *Yüan-ch'ü hsüan wai-pien*, 3:992, ll. 4–5; a song suite attributed to a fourteenth-century courtesan née Wang, *Ch'üan Yüan san-ch'ü*, 2:1275, l. 5; *Chin-t'ung Yü-nü Chiao Hung chi*, part 2, p. 24, l. 9; a song suite by Chu Yu-tun (1379–1439), *Ch'üan Ming san-ch'ü*, 1:361, l. 7; *Wu Lun-ch'üan Pei*, scene 3, p. 9a, l. 2; a song suite by Ch'en To (fl. early 16th century), *Ch'üan Ming san-ch'ü*, 1:597, l. 4; a song by Huang O (1498–1569), ibid., 2:1754, l. 8; and *Yen-chih chi*, scene 7, p. 8a, column 3. It occurs in the same form as in the novel in *K'u-kung wu-tao chüan* (Precious volume on awakening to the Way through bitter toil), by Lo Ch'ing (1442–1527), originally published in 1509, in *Pao-chüan ch'u-chi*, 1:126, l. 4; and a song suite by Ku Hsien-ch'eng (1550–1612), *Ch'üan Ming san-ch'ü*, 3:3234, l. 9.

16. The text here reads Ch'i-t'ung, but the events of the next chapter indicate that this is a mistake for Ch'in-tung.

17. This four-character expression occurs in a lyric by Ch'ao Ch'ung-chih (11th century), *Ch'üan Sung tz'u*, 2:654, lower register, l. 8; a poem by Chu Shu-chen (fl. 1078–1138), *Ch'üan Sung shih*, 28:17957, l. 12; a lyric by Pei Ch'iung (c. 1297–1379), *Ch'üan Ming tz'u*, 1:21, upper register, l. 14; and *Shuang-chu chi*, scene 2, p. 5, l. 2.

18. These two lines are derived, with one textual variant, from the final couplet of a quatrain by Su Shih (1037–1101), *Su Shih shih-chi* (Collected poetry of Su Shih), 8 vols. (Peking: Chung-hua shu-chü, 1982), vol. 2, *chüan* 15, p. 753, ll. 4–5. This poem of Su Shih's also occurs, without attribution, in *Pai-chia kung-an* (A hundred court cases), 1594 ed., fac. repr. in *Ku-pen hsiao-shuo ts'ung-k'an, ti-erh chi* (Collectanea of rare editions of traditional fiction, second series) (Peking: Chung-hua shu-chü, 1990), vol. 4, *chüan* 10, ch. 88, p. 2b, ll. 9–10. The proximate source of all four lines,

with some textual variation in the first couplet, is probably *Hsiu-ju chi*, scene 29, p. 80, ll. 10–11.

CHAPTER 46

1. The three palaces are those of the emperor, the empress dowager, and the empress.

2. The proximate source of this lyric to an unidentified tune is *Hsüan-ho i-shih*, p. 72, ll. 10–11, where it is introduced in the course of a description of the Lantern Festival as celebrated in the Sung capital of K'ai-feng in 1124.

3. This four-character expression occurs in the Sung dynasty literary tale *Hung-hsiao mi-yüeh: Chang Sheng fu Li-shih niang* (The secret tryst [arranged by means of] a red silk [handkerchief]: How Chang Sheng betrayed Ms. Li), in *Tsui-weng t'an-lu*, *jen-chi* (9th collection), *chüan* 1, p. 98, l. 7; the early vernacular story *Chao Po-sheng ch'a-ssu yü Jen-tsung* (Chao Po-sheng encounters Emperor Jen-tsung in a tea shop), in *Ku-chin hsiao-shuo*, vol. 1, *chüan* 11, p. 166, l. 2; *Shui-hu ch'üan-chuan*, vol. 3, ch. 61, p. 1023, l. 6; and the long sixteenth-century literary tale *Hua-shen san-miao chuan* (The flower god and the three beauties), in *Kuo-se t'ien-hsiang*, vol. 2, *chüan* 6, p. 1a, lower register, ll. 8–9.

4. These two lines are from the opening paragraph of the *Hsi-tz'u* (Attached commentary) in the *I-ching* (Book of changes). See *Chou-i yin-te* (A concordance to the I-ching) (Taipei: Chinese Materials and Research Aids Service Center, 1966), p. 39, column 2, l. 3. They also occur in *Li-chi* (The book of rites), in *Shih-san ching ching-wen* (The texts of the thirteen classics) (Taipei: K'ai-ming shu-tien, 1955), ch. 17, p. 73, ll. 7–8; and *Hsi-yu chi*, vol. 2, ch. 62, p. 711, l. 15.

5. This is the opening line of the first song at the beginning of play number two of *Hsi-hsiang chi*, in which Ts'ui Ying-ying bemoans her lovesick plight. See *[Chi-p'ing chiao-chu] Hsi-hsiang chi*, play no. 2, scene 1, p. 48, l. 12; and *The Moon and the Zither: The Story of the Western Wing*, by Wang Shifu; trans. Stephen H. West and Wilt L. Idema (Berkeley: University of California Press, 1991), p. 219, l. 10. The same line also occurs in *Yu-kuei chi*, scene 34, p. 98, l. 8; a song suite by Chu Yün-ming (1460–1526), *Ch'üan Ming san-ch'ü*, 1:781, l. 1; and a set of songs by Hsüeh Lun-tao (c. 1531–c. 1600), ibid., 3:2730, l. 12.

6. For technical discussions of what the modes of Chinese music meant in musical terms, see Rulan Chao Pian, *Sonq Dynasty Musical Sources and Their Interpretation* (Cambridge: Harvard University Press, 1967), ch. 2, pp. 43–58; and Dale R. Johnson, *Yuarn Music Dramas: Studies in Prosody and Structure and a Complete Catalogue of Northern Arias in the Dramatic Style* (Ann Arbor: Center for Chinese Studies, University of Michigan, 1980), pp. 74–86.

7. This four-character expression, which refers to the beauties of natural scenery or the pleasures of romantic attachments, occurs in a poem written by Shao Yung (1011–77) in 1074, *Ch'üan Sung shih*, 7:4585, l. 9. It is ubiquitous in Chinese vernacular literature. See, e.g., a lyric by Huang T'ing-chien (1045–1105), *Ch'üan Sung tz'u*, 1:395, upper register, l. 20; the poetical exegesis of the *Diamond Sutra* by the Buddhist monk Tao-ch'uan (fl. 1127–63), *Chin-kang pan-jo-po-lo-mi ching chu* (Commentary on the *Vajracchedikā prajñāpāramitā sutra*), by Tao-ch'uan (fl. 1127–63), pref. dated 1179, in *[Shinzan] Dai Nihon zokuzōkyō* ([Newly compiled] great Japanese continuation of the Buddhist canon), 100 vols. (Tokyo: Kokusho kankōkai, 1977), vol. 24, no.

461, p. 550, lower register, l. 19; *Tung Chieh-yüan Hsi-hsiang chi*, *chüan* 1, p. 1, l. 9; *Yüan-ch'ü hsüan*, 2:806, l. 7; *Yüan-ch'ü hsüan wai-pien*, 2:381, l. 16; a song suite by Kuan Yün-shih (1286–1324), *Ch'üan Yüan san-ch'ü*, 1:379, l. 7; a song by Ch'iao Chi (d. 1345), ibid., 1:629, l. 8; a set of songs by Wang Yüan-heng (14th century), ibid., 2:1385, l. 11; *Sha-kou chi*, scene 21, p. 78, l. 3; *Nan Hsi-hsiang chi* (Li Jih-hua), scene 7, p. 21, l. 12; a song suite by Wang P'an (d. 1530), *Ch'üan Ming san-ch'ü*, 1:1053, l. 3; *Hsiu-ju chi*, scene 4, p. 7, l. 8; the middle-period vernacular story *Chang Sheng ts'ai-luan teng chuan* (The story of Chang Sheng and the painted phoenix lanterns), in *Hsiung Lung-feng ssu-chung hsiao-shuo* (Four vernacular stories published by Hsiung Lung-feng [fl. c. 1590]), ed. Wang Ku-lu (Shanghai: Ku-tien wen-hsüeh ch'u-pan she, 1958), p. 5, ll. 8–9; a song suite by Cheng Jo-yung (16th century), *Ch'üan Ming san-ch'ü*, 2:1514, l. 13; a song suite by Wu T'ing-han (cs 1521), ibid., 2:1795, l. 3; *Hai-fu shan-t'ang tz'u-kao*, *chüan* 2a, p. 107, l. 4; a song suite by Chin Luan (1494–1583), *Ch'üan Ming san-ch'ü*, 2:1618, l. 1; a song suite by Yin Shih-tan (1522–82), ibid., 2:2336, l. 3; a set of songs by Hsüeh Lun-tao (c. 1531–1600), ibid., 3:2821, l. 6; and a song suite by Chou Lü-ching (1542–1632), ibid., 3:3120, l. 10.

8. This formulaic four-character expression occurs in a lyric by Kao Kuan-kuo (fl. early 13th century), *Ch'üan Sung tz'u*, 4:2363, upper register, l. 4; *Yüan-ch'ü hsüan*, 4:1423, l. 11; *Yüan-ch'ü hsüan wai-pien*, 3:783, l. 17; *T'ien-pao i-shih chu-kung-tiao*, p. 128, l. 3; a song suite by Lan Ch'u-fang (14th century), *Ch'üan Yüan san-ch'ü*, 2:1628, l. 6; a song suite by T'ang Shih (14th–15th centuries), ibid., 2:1481, l. 5; a song suite by Li Tung-yang (1447–1516), *Ch'üan Ming san-ch'ü*, 1:426, l. 4; a song suite by Ch'en To (fl. early 16th century), ibid., 1:669, l. 9; a song by Wang Chiu-ssu (1468–1551), ibid., 1:918, l. 1; and a song suite by Huang O (1498–1569), ibid., 2:1762, l. 6. It recurs in the *Chin P'ing Mei tz'u-hua*, vol. 4, ch. 68, p. 16a, l. 5.

9. A literal translation of the preceding three characters would be "the hair of [the Baron of] Kuan-ch'eng [Tube City]." This is an allusion to a famous jeu d'esprit by Han Yü (768–824) entitled *Mao Ying chuan* (The biography of Mao Ying), which is an elaborate and punning description of a writing brush, presented in a form that parodies that of a historical biography. See *Han Ch'ang-li wen-chi chiao-chu* (The prose works of Han Yü with critical annotation), ed. Ma T'ung-po (Shanghai: Ku-tien wen-hsüeh ch'u-pan she, 1957), *chüan* 8, p. 327, l. 2. This work has been translated by James R. Hightower, who points out that Kuan-ch'eng was an actual Han dynasty place name, although it is employed here for its literal meaning, and that a Chinese writing brush is made by inserting a clip of rabbit hair into a bamboo tube. See James R. Hightower, "Han Yü as Humorist," *Harvard Journal of Asiatic Studies*, vol. 44, no. 1 (June 1984), p. 12, n. 27.

10. This four-character expression occurs in a quatrain by Tu Mu (803–52), *Ch'üan T'ang shih*, vol. 8, *chüan* 522, p. 5974, l. 11; a lyric by Huang T'ing-chien (1045–1105), *Ch'üan Sung tz'u*, 1:385, lower register, l. 13; a lyric by Li Tseng-po (1198–c. 1265), ibid., 4:2807, upper register, l. 16; a song by Chang K'o-chiu (1270–1348), *Ch'üan Yüan san-ch'ü*, 1:805, l. 3; and *Su Ying huang-hou ying-wu chi*, *chüan* 2, scene 31, p. 26b, l. 6.

11. Among the various figures who have been called sages of cursive calligraphy, Chang Hsü (8th century) is the most famous.

12. In popular Buddhist lore there were thirty-three heavens, the highest of which was the Heaven of Frustrated Separation, the abode of lovers condemned never to

meet again. It is mentioned frequently in Chinese vernacular literature. See, e.g., *[Chi-p'ing chiao-chu] Hsi-hsiang chi*, play no. 1, scene 1, p. 7, l. 10; *Yüan-ch'ü hsüan*, 1:179, l. 14; *Yüan-ch'ü hsüan wai-pien*, 1:210, l. 15; *Hsi-yu chi*, vol. 1, ch. 5, p. 52, l. 7; and the ch'uan-ch'i drama *Yü-tsan chi* (The story of the jade hairpin), by Kao Lien (1527–c. 1603), probably written in 1570, ed. and annot. Huang Shang (Shanghai: Shang-hai ku-tien wen-hsüeh ch'u-pan she, 1956), scene 11, p. 41, l. 17.

13. The School of the Four Gates was the name of an educational institution in the capital that existed, at least nominally, from the fifth to the thirteenth centuries. See Charles O. Hucker, *A Dictionary of Official Titles in Imperial China* (Stanford: Stanford University Press, 1985), p. 453, no. 5719.

14. This four-character expression occurs in a song by Wu Hung-tao (14th century), *Ch'üan Yüan san-ch'ü*, 1:731, l. 3; and *Yüan-ch'ü hsüan wai-pien*, 2:584, l. 1.

15. This formulaic four-character expression occurs ubiquitously in Chinese vernacular literature. See, e.g., a song suite by Li Ai-shan (14th century), *Ch'üan Yüan san-ch'ü*, 2:1188, l. 3; an anonymous Yüan dynasty song suite, ibid., 2:1786, l. 10; *Yüan-ch'ü hsüan*, 3:974, ll. 12–13; *Yüan-ch'ü hsüan wai-pien*, 3:784, ll. 4–5; *Chin-t'ung Yü-nü Chiao Hung chi*, p. 21, l. 13; *Hsiang-nang yüan*, scene 4, p. 23a, l. 2; *Yü-huan chi*, scene 8, p. 26, l. 8; a song suite by Ch'en To (fl. early 16th century), *Ch'üan Ming san-ch'ü*, 1:626, l. 11; a set of songs by Ch'ang Lun (1493–1526), ibid., 2:1532, l. 3; a song suite by Huang O (1498–1569), ibid., 2:1762, l. 11; *Hai-fu shan-t'ang tz'u-kao*, chüan 3, p. 143, l. 2; and *[Hsiao-shih] Chen-k'ung sao-hsin pao-chüan* ([Clearly presented] Precious volume on [the Patriarch] Chen-k'ung's [instructions for] sweeping clear the mind), published in 1584, in *Pao-chüan ch'u-chi*, 19:146, l. 2.

16. Phoenix glue is a legendary substance so adhesive that it is capable of permanently reattaching the broken ends of bowstrings or the strings of musical instruments. The idiom "to mend a broken string" means to find a replacement for a lost spouse or lover. The locus classicus for this five-character expression is a line from a lyric attributed to T'ao Ku (903–70). See *Yü-hu ch'ing-hua* (Elegant anecdotes from Yü-hu), by Wen-ying (11th century), in *Pi-chi hsiao-shuo ta-kuan*, vol. 1, ts'e 2, chüan 4, p. 5b, l. 10. It is ubiquitous in Chinese vernacular literature. See, e.g., a lyric by Hsin Ch'i-chi (1140–1207), *Ch'üan Sung tz'u*, 3:1974, upper register, l. 7; *Yüan-ch'ü hsüan*, 1:22, l. 20; *P'i-p'a chi*, scene 21, p. 124, ll. 10–11; *Yu-kuei chi*, scene 39, p. 11, l. 12; the middle-period vernacular story *Feng Po-yü feng-yüeh hsiang-ssu hsiao-shuo* (The story of Feng Po-yü: a tale of romantic longing), in *Hsiung Lung-feng ssu-chung hsiao-shuo*, p. 45, l. 6; the long sixteenth-century literary tale *Hsün-fang ya-chi* (Elegant vignettes of fragrant pursuits), in *Kuo-se t'ien-hsiang*, vol. 2, chüan 4, lower register, p. 51b, l. 11; *Ming-chu chi*, scene 31, p. 97, l. 11; *Ssu-hsi chi*, scene 34, p. 85, l. 8; *Hsün-ch'in chi*, scene 23, p. 77, l. 5; and *Chin-chien chi*, scene 35, p. 107, l. 10.

17. This four-character expression occurs in a lyric by Su Mao-i (13th century), *Ch'üan Sung tz'u*, 4:2560, upper register, ll. 8–9.

18. This proverbial idiom is derived from a story contained in an early Taoist work according to which a certain Mr. Fu spent seven years in the mountains cultivating the Tao when Lao-tzu appeared to him and gave him a wooden drill and a five-foot-thick stone disk, promising him that if he succeeded in wearing a hole all the way through the disk he would attain the Tao. The man worked night and day at this task for forty-seven years until he finally succeeded in wearing all the way through the stone disk, after which he ascended to Heaven and became a part of the Taoist pantheon.

See *Chen-kao* (Declarations of the perfected), comp. T'ao Hung-ching (452–536), in *Cheng-t'ung Tao-tsang* (The Cheng-t'ung [1436–49] Taoist canon) (Shanghai: Shang-wu yin-shu kuan, 1926), *ts'e* 637, *chüan* 5, p. 7b, ll. 3–8. Variants of this idiom occur in the long literary tale *Yu hsien-k'u* (Excursion to the dwelling of the goddesses), by Chang Cho (cs 675) (Shanghai: Chung-kuo ku-tien wen-hsüeh ch'u-pan she, 1955), p. 13, l. 10; and the anonymous fifteenth-century ch'uan-ch'i drama *Ts'ai-lou chi* (The gaily colored tower), ed. Huang Shang (Shanghai: Shang-hai ku-tien wen-hsüeh ch'u-pan she, 1956), scene 6, p. 21, l. 1. It occurs in the same form as in the novel in a lyric by Ts'ai Shen (1088–1156), *Ch'üan Sung tz'u*, 2:1023, upper register, l. 7; *Yeh-k'o ts'ung-shu* (Collected writings of a rustic sojourner), by Wang Mao (1151–1213) (Peking: Chung-hua shu-chü, 1987), *chüan* 28, p. 327, l. 3; *Chang Hsieh chuang-yüan*, scene 25, p. 129, l. 7; *Yüan-ch'ü hsüan*, 1:313, l. 1; *Yüan-ch'ü hsüan wai-pien*, 2:392, l. 15; two anonymous Yüan dynasty songs, *Ch'üan Yüan san-ch'ü*, 2:1763, l. 12; and 2:1769, l. 8; the tsa-chü drama *Huang T'ing-tao yeh-tsou Liu-hsing ma* (Huang T'ing-tao steals the horse Shooting Star by night), by Huang Yüan-chi (14th century), in *Ming-jen tsa-chü hsüan*, scene 2, p. 100, l. 10; *Chung-ch'ing li-chi*, *chüan* 6, p. 6a, l. 14; and *Hsün-ch'in chi*, scene 23, p. 77, l. 2.

19. This four-character expression occurs in *Yüan-ch'ü hsüan wai-pien*, 3:785, l. 8; a song suite by Lan Ch'u-fang (14th century), *Ch'üan Yüan san-ch'ü*, 2:1629, l. 1; and a song suite by Huang O (1498–1569), *Ch'üan Ming san-ch'ü*, 2:1763, l. 10.

20. This anonymous song suite, thought to date from the Yüan dynasty, is preserved in *Sheng-shih hsin-sheng*, pp. 84–86; *Tz'u-lin chai-yen*, 2:1133–36; *Yung-hsi yüeh-fu*, *ts'e* 1, pp. 10a–11a; *Ts'ai-pi ch'ing-tz'u* (Emotive lyrics from variegated brushes), comp. Chang Hsü (early 17th century), pref. dated 1624, fac. repr. in *Shan-pen hsi-ch'ü ts'ung-k'an*, vol. 76, pp. 773–76; and *Ch'üan Yüan san-ch'ü*, 2:1782–83. The version in the novel is closer to those in *Sheng-shih hsin-sheng* and *Tz'u-lin chai-yen* than to those in the other anthologies.

21. "Gold raven" and "jade rabbit" are kennings for the sun and moon, respectively.

22. This four-character expression occurs in a quatrain by Wang An-shih (1021–86), *Ch'üan Sung shih*, 10:6716, l. 11; a lyric attributed to Li Ch'ing-chao (1084–c. 1151), *Ch'üan Sung tz'u*, 2:934, upper register, ll. 7–8; a lyric by Ts'ai Shen (1088–1156), ibid., 2:1010, lower register, l. 15; *Tung Chieh-yüan Hsi-hsiang chi*, *chüan* 4, p. 82, l. 13; a lyric by Hung Tzu-k'uei (1176–1236), *Ch'üan Sung tz'u*, 4:2463, upper register, l. 8; a lyric by Li P'eng-lao (13th century), ibid., 4:2970, lower register, l. 13; [Chi-p'ing chiao-chu] *Hsi-hsiang chi*, play no. 4, scene 1, p. 142, l. 2; *Yüan-ch'ü hsüan*, 1:176, l. 9; a song suite by Tseng Jui (c. 1260–c. 1330), *Ch'üan Yüan san-ch'ü*, 1:527, l. 12; an anonymous Yüan dynasty song, ibid., 2:1760, l. 14; the early vernacular story *Su-hsiang T'ing Chang Hao yü Ying-ying* (In Su-hsiang T'ing Chang Hao meets [Li] Ying-ying), in *Ching-shih t'ung-yen*, *chüan* 29, p. 454, l. 1; *P'u-tung Ts'ui Chang chu-yü shih-chi*, p. 20a, l. 3; a set of songs by Yang T'ing-ho (1459–1529), *Ch'üan Ming san-ch'ü*, 1:745, l. 10; a song suite by Chu Ying-ch'en (16th century), ibid., 2:1271, l. 2; a song suite by Chang Feng-i (1527–1613), ibid., 3:2608, l. 11; and a song suite by Chou Lü-ching (1542–1632), ibid., 3:3123, l. 5.

23. This line occurs verbatim in *Cheng Chieh-shih li-kung shen-pi kung*, p. 666, l. 6. A version of this entire quatrain, with some textual variation, occurs in *Ch'ien-t'ang meng*, p. 3a, ll. 9–10.

24. See chapter 43, note 73.

25. On this type of headgear, see Roy, *The Plum in the Golden Vase*, vol. 2, chap. 37, n. 5.

26. This four-character expression occurs in a quatrain by Hou Shan-yüan (12th century), *Ch'üan Chin shih*, 2:290, l. 3; *Yüan-ch'ü hsüan wai-pien*, 2:595, l. 2; a song suite by Fan K'ang (14th century), *Ch'üan Yüan san-ch'ü*, 1:469, l. 5; a song suite by Li Chih-yüan (14th century), ibid., 2:1257, l. 1; a set of songs by Chung Ssu-ch'eng (c. 1279–c. 1360), ibid., 2:1355, l. 7; and *San-pao t'ai-chien Hsi-yang chi t'ung-su yen-i*, vol. 1, ch. 3, p. 26, l. 4.

27. This formulaic four-character expression occurs in [*Chi-p'ing chiao-chu*] *Hsi-hsiang chi*, play no. 2, scene 1, p. 48, l. 8; *Yüan-ch'ü hsüan wai-pien*, 2:487, l. 16; *Pai-chia kung-an, chüan* 7, ch. 64, p. 28a, ll. 8–9; and *San-pao t'ai-chien Hsi-yang chi t'ung-su yen-i*, vol. 1, ch. 41, p. 534, l. 4.

28. This four-character expression occurs in a lyric by Ku Hsün (1418–1505), *Ch'üan Ming tz'u*, 1:285, upper register, l. 5.

29. This four-character expression occurs in *Ta-T'ang Ch'in-wang tz'u-hua*, vol. 1, *chüan* 2, ch. 9, p. 10b, l. 9. The proximate source of the above set piece of descriptive parallel prose, with some textual variation, is the middle-period vernacular story *Wen-ching yüan-yang hui* (The fatal rendezvous), in *Ch'ing-p'ing shan-t'ang hua-pen*, p. 161, ll. 14–15.

30. This four-character expression occurs in *Shui-hu ch'üan-chuan*, vol. 1, ch. 6, p. 101, l. 12; and vol. 3, ch. 66, p. 1129, l. 16.

31. This line has already occurred in the *Chin P'ing Mei tz'u-hua*, vol. 3, ch. 42, p. 9b, l. 10. See above, chapter 42, note 12.

32. See Roy, *The Plum in the Golden Vase*, vol. 2, chap. 26, n. 6.

33. This song suite is from a lost Yüan dynasty hsi-wen drama entitled *Tzu-mu yüan-chia* (Mother and son as dearest enemies), the plot of which is unknown, although the title is suggestive of incest. See *Sung-Yüan hsi-wen chi-i* (Collected fragments of Sung and Yüan hsi-wen drama), comp. Ch'ien Nan-yang (Shanghai: Shang-hai ku-tien wen-hsüeh ch'u-pan she, 1956), pp. 5–6.

34. This four-character expression occurs in a lyric by Lu Ping (fl. early 13th century), *Ch'üan Sung tz'u*, 3:2169, lower register, l. 5; a lyric by Ch'en Yün-p'ing (13th century), ibid., 5:3100, lower register, l. 3; a lyric by Ch'iu Yüan (1247–1326), ibid., 5:3411, upper register, l. 14; and a set of songs by Wang Yin (16th century), *Ch'üan Ming san-ch'ü*, 3:2669, l. 11.

35. This four-character expression occurs in a lyric by Yüan Ch'ü-hua (cs 1145), *Ch'üan Sung tz'u*, 3:1494, upper register, ll. 7–8; a song by Wang P'an (d. 1530), *Ch'üan Ming san-ch'ü*, 1:1034, l. 9; a song suite by Shen Shih (1488–1565), ibid., 2:1374, l. 14; a set of songs by Liu Hsiao-tsu (1522–89), ibid., 2:2307, l. 12; and a set of songs by Wang K'o-tu (c. 1526–c. 1594), ibid., 2:2453, l. 9.

36. This four-character expression occurs in a lyric by Ts'ao Hsün (1098–1174), *Ch'üan Sung tz'u*, 2:1219, upper register, l. 10; a lyric by Tseng Ti (1109–80), ibid., 2:1322, upper register, l. 11; a lyric by Ch'en Liang (1143–94), ibid., 3:2108, lower register, l. 16; *Yüan-ch'ü hsüan*, 4:1427, l. 9; and the tsa-chü drama *Ssu-shih hua-yüeh sai chiao-jung* (The flowers and moonlight of the four seasons compete in loveliness), by Chu Yu-tun (1379–1439), in *Ku-pen Yüan Ming tsa-chü*, vol. 2, scene 3, p. 6b, l. 7.

37. This onomatopoetic expression occurs in *Mu-tan t'ing*, scene 55, p. 276, l. 15.

38. This song did not originally belong to this song suite but has been interpolated from another lost hsi-wen drama entitled *Chang Ts'ui-lien*. See *Sung-Yüan hsi-wen chi-i*, p. 157, ll. 8–11.

39. See Roy, *The Plum in the Golden Vase*, vol. 2, chap. 27, n. 37.

40. "Liu-yao" was the name of a popular tune, at least as old as the T'ang dynasty, the exact meaning of which is uncertain.

41. This five-character expression occurs in *Yüan-ch'ü hsüan*, 3:1161, l. 2; 4:1315, ll. 9–10; and *Ming-feng chi*, scene 4, p. 16, l. 11.

42. This four-character expression occurs in a lyric by Yao Shu-yao (cs 1154), *Ch'üan Sung tz'u*, 3:1556, lower register, l. 1; *Yüan-ch'ü hsüan*, 3:1160, l. 13; 4:1671, l. 3; a set of songs by Chung Ssu-ch'eng (c. 1279–c. 1360), *Ch'üan Yüan san-ch'ü*, 2:1358, l. 12; a set of songs by Yang T'ing-ho (1459–1529), *Ch'üan Ming san-ch'ü*, 1:745, l. 10; a song suite by Wang Ch'ung (1494–1533), ibid., 2:1571, l. 10; and *Pao-chien chi*, scene 3, p. 10, l. 2.

43. This four-character expression occurs in a song suite by Chu Ch'üan (1378–1448), *Ch'üan Ming san-ch'ü*, 1:262, l. 7; *Huai-ch'un ya-chi, chüan* 9, p. 24b, l. 11; *Ming-feng chi*, scene 20, p. 85, l. 1; and a song by Wang K'o-tu (c. 1526–c. 1594), *Ch'üan Ming san-ch'ü*, 2:2456, l. 8.

44. See note 33 above. Versions of the above song-suite close to that in the novel are preserved in *Sheng-shih hsin-sheng*, pp. 521–22; *Tz'u-lin chai-yen*, 1:255–57; *Chiu-pien nan chiu-kung p'u* (Formulary for the old repertory of the nine southern musical modes), comp. Chiang Hsiao (16th century), pref. dated 1549, fac. repr. in *Shan-pen hsi-ch'ü ts'ung-k'an*, 26:119–21; *Nan-pei kung tz'u-chi*, vol. 1, *chüan* 2, pp. 85–86; and *Nan-tz'u yün-hsüan*, *chüan* 11, p. 61. Expanded versions that interpolate northern-style songs between those in the original version are included in *[Hsin-pien] Nan chiu-kung tz'u*, *chüan* 3, pp. 1a–3a; *Ch'ün-yin lei-hsüan*, vol. 4, pp. 2059–62; and 2297–2300; *Wu-yü ts'ui-ya* (A florilegium of song lyrics from Wu), comp. Chou Chih-piao (fl. early 17th century), pref. dated 1616, fac. repr. in *Shan-pen hsi-ch'ü ts'ung-k'an*, 12:300–304; *Tz'u-lin i-hsiang* (Lingering notes from the forest of song), comp. Hsü Yü (fl. early 17th century), pref. dated 1623, fac. repr. in *Shan-pen hsi-ch'ü ts'ung-k'an*, 17:221–27; *Wu-sao ho-pien, ts'e* 2, *chüan* 2, pp. 5b–7b; and *Nan-yin san-lai* (Three kinds of southern sound), comp. Ling Meng-ch'u (1580–1644), 4 *ts'e*, fac. repr. of late Ming edition (Shanghai: Shang-hai ku-chi shu-tien, 1963), *ts'e* 1. pp. 47a–48b.

45. This formulaic four-character expression occurs in *Yüan-ch'ü hsüan*, 2:529, l. 9; 4:1697, l. 5; an anonymous Yüan dynasty song suite, *Ch'üan Yüan san-ch'ü*, 2:1824, l. 2; *Chung-ch'ing li-chi, chüan* 6, p. 18a, l. 7; a song suite by Ku Meng-kuei (1500–58), *Ch'üan Ming san-ch'ü*, 2:1788, l. 8; a song suite by Wu Kuo-pao (cs 1550), ibid., 2:2283, l. 6; *Su Ying huang-hou ying-wu chi, chüan* 2, scene 28, p. 18b, l. 6; and a set of songs by Hsüeh Lun-tao (c. 1531–c. 1600), *Ch'üan Ming san-ch'ü*, 3:2708, l. 7.

46. This line occurs in the literary tale *P'eng-lai hsien-sheng chuan* (The story of Mr. P'eng-lai), in *Hsiao-p'in chi*, p. 72, l. 7; a song suite by Cheng Jo-yung (16th century), *Ch'üan Ming san-ch'ü*, 2:1511, l. 8; and an anonymous song, in *Nan-kung tz'u-chi* (Anthology of southern-style lyrics), comp. Ch'en So-wen (d. c. 1604), in *Nan-pei kung tz'u-chi*, vol. 2, *chüan* 4, p. 218, l. 4.

47. This formulaic four-character expression for bordellos is ubiquitous in Chinese vernacular literature. See, e.g., a song suite by Shang Tao (cs 1212), *Ch'üan Yüan san-ch'ü*, 1:20, l. 9; a song suite by Kuan Han-ch'ing (13th century), ibid., 1:178, l. 2; a

song by Wu Hung-tao (14th century), ibid., 1:731, l. 8; a song suite by Chu T'ing-yü (14th century), ibid., 2:1204, l. 7; a song suite by Liu T'ing-hsin (14th century), ibid., 2:1446, l. 10; *Yüan-ch'ü hsüan*, 4:1430, l. 14; *Yüan-ch'ü hsüan wai-pien*, 2:389, l. 21; a song by Chia Chung-ming (1343–c. 1422), *Ch'üan Ming san-ch'ü*, 1:173, l. 2; and a set of songs by Hsüeh Lun-tao (c. 1531–c. 1600), ibid., 3:2786, l. 8.

48. This method of fortune telling is mentioned in passing in *Yüan-ch'ü hsüan*, 2:713, l. 19; 4:1355, l. 4; 4:1392, l. 4; 4:1532, l. 16; *Yüan-ch'ü hsüan wai-pien*, 2:498, l. 4; a song suite by Lan Ch'u-fang (14th century), *Ch'üan Yüan san-ch'ü*, 2:1626, l. 7; and an abundance of other occurrences, too numerous to list. It is described in considerable detail in the ch'uan-ch'i drama *Tzu-ch'ai chi* (The story of the purple hairpin), by T'ang Hsien-tsu (1550–1616), originally completed in 1587, author's pref. dated 1595, ed. and annot. Hu Shih-ying (Peking: Jen-min wen-hsüeh ch'u-pan she, 1982), scene 44, pp. 162–63; and later in this chapter of the *Chin P'ing Mei*.

49. This four-character expression occurs in a song suite by Su Tzu-wen (16th century), *Ch'ün-yin lei-hsüan*, 4:2037, l. 3; and *Ku-chin t'an-kai* (A representative selection of anecdotes ancient and modern), comp. Feng Meng-lung (1574–1646), pref. dated 1620 (Fu-chou: Hai-hsia wen-i ch'u-pan she, 1985), *chüan* 29, p. 917, l. 6.

50. The black silk hats worn by officials in the Ming dynasty had a pair of fins attached to them at the back that extended to the left and right, came in various shapes and sizes, and quivered when the official walked or moved his head. For an illustration of this type of headgear, reproduced from a contemporary portrait, see *Chung-kuo fu-shih wu-ch'ien nien* (Five thousand years of Chinese costume), comp. Chou Hsün and Kao Ch'un-ming (Hong Kong: Shang-wu yin-shu kuan, 1984), p. 153.

51. A close variant of these four lines occurs in a song suite composed of proverbial sayings by Su Tzu-wen (16th century), *Ch'ün-yin lei-hsüan*, 4:2039, ll. 1–2.

52. This four-character expression occurs in *Pao-chien chi*, scene 12, p. 25, l. 17.

53. This may be an allusion to a line attributed to Ch'un-yü K'un (4th century B.C.), who said, "A fox fur may be inferior, but you would not choose to mend it with a yellow dog's pelt." See *Shih-chi*, vol. 6, *chüan* 46, p. 1890, l. 6.

54. On the Verdant Spring Bordello, see Roy, *The Plum in the Golden Vase*, vol. 1, chap. 15, n. 1.

55. This formulaic four-character expression occurs in a lyric by Wang Che (1112–70), *Ch'üan Chin Yüan tz'u*, 1:231, lower register, l. 7; a lyric by Ma Yü (1123–83), ibid., 1:326, lower register, l. 16; a lyric by Hou Shan-yüan (12th century), ibid., 1:534, upper register, l. 5; an anonymous Yüan dynasty song, *Ch'üan Yüan san-ch'ü*, 2:1892, l. 9; *Wu-wang fa Chou p'ing-hua*, p. 82, l. 1; the tsa-chü drama *Hei Hsüan-feng chang-i shu-ts'ai* (The Black Whirlwind is chivalrous and openhanded), by Chu Yu-tun (1379–1439), in *Shui-hu hsi-ch'ü chi, ti-i chi*, scene 3, p. 107, l. 25; *Yü-huan chi*, scene 18, p. 71, l. 6; *T'an-shih wu-wei pao-chüan* (Precious volume on Nonactivism in lamentation for the world), by Lo Ch'ing (1442–1527), originally published in 1509, in *Pao-chüan ch'u-chi*, 1:323, l. 3; and *Cheng-hsin ch'u-i wu hsiu cheng tzu-tsai pao-chüan* (Precious volume of self-determination needing neither cultivation nor verification which rectifies belief and dispels doubt), by Lo Ch'ing (1442–1527), originally published in 1509, in *Pao-chüan ch'u-chi*, 3:138, l. 3.

56. This four-character expression occurs in *Yüan-ch'ü hsüan*, 4:1587, l. 8; and the middle-period vernacular story *Cha-ch'uan Hsiao Ch'en pien Pa-wang* (In Cha-ch'uan Hsiao Ch'en rebukes the Hegemon-King), in *Ch'ing-p'ing shan-t'ang hua-pen*, p. 314, l. 3.

57. This four-character expression occurs in *Hsi-yu chi*, vol. 1, ch. 25, p. 284, l. 4; and ch. 37, p. 426, l. 8.

58. This five-character expression occurs in *Mu-tan t'ing*, scene 47, p. 231, l. 3.

59. The "palace of illness and adversity" is the name of one of the "twelve palaces" found on the face, according to some schools of physiognomy. It is located on the bridge of the nose. See *Shen-hsiang ch'üan-pien, chüan* 631, pp. 50b, l. 4–51a, l. 3; and the illustration in William A. Lessa, *Chinese Body Divination: Its Forms, Affinities, and Functions* (Los Angeles: United World, 1968), p. 49.

60. The "palace of sons and daughters" is the name of one of the "twelve palaces" found on the face, according to some schools of physiognomy. It refers to the hollows underneath the left and right eyes. See *Shen-hsiang ch'üan-pien, chüan* 631, pp. 48b, l. 1–49a, l. 7; and the illustration in Lessa, *Chinese Body Divination*, p. 49.

61. The "palace of fate" is the name of one of the "twelve palaces" that are found on the face, according to some schools of physiognomy. It is located on the lower forehead in the space between the eyebrows. See *Shen-hsiang ch'üan-pien, chüan* 631, pp. 45b, l. 2–46a, l. 4; and the illustration in Lessa, *Chinese Body Divination*, p. 49.

62. The "three penalties" and "six banes" refer to cases in which the earthly branches that occur in a person's horoscope, and the five phases that are correlated with them, are thought to conflict with each other. These terms occur together in *Shen-hsiang ch'üan-pien, chüan* 641, p. 6a, l. 7; and recur in the *Chin P'ing Mei tz'u-hua*, vol. 4, ch. 62, p. 22a, l. 7.

63. This four-character expression occurs in *Pai Niang-tzu yung-chen Lei-feng T'a*, p. 436, l. 15.

64. Since no such episode occurs in the text of the novel as we now have it, the author, or an editor, must have deleted it without remembering to alter this allusion to it.

65. This six-character description of the typical demon occurs verbatim in *Shui-hu ch'üan-chuan*, vol. 4, ch. 117, p. 1760, l. 13. The first four characters occur together ubiquitously in Chinese vernacular literature. See, e.g., *Yüan-ch'ü hsüan*, 4:1385, l. 10; *Hsi-yu chi*, vol. 1, ch. 6, p. 63, l. 13; and *San-pao t'ai-chien Hsi-yang chi t'ung-su yen-i*, vol. 1, ch. 1, p. 7, l. 1. A close variant, with identical meaning, also occurs in *Mu-tan t'ing*, scene 55, p. 274, l. 12.

66. This formulaic four-character expression occurs in *Shui-hu ch'üan-chuan*, vol. 1, ch. 20, p. 289, l. 17; and *Hsi-yu chi*, vol. 1, ch. 19, p. 218, l. 16.

67. "Three births" is a Buddhist term for one's past, present, and future incarnations.

68. Ketu is the name of one of two imaginary "dark stars," or invisible planets, introduced into China during the T'ang dynasty through the translation of works on Indian astronomy, as part of a theory to account for lunar eclipses. In Chinese astrology and fortune-telling it was regarded as a baleful influence.

69. This five-character expression recurs in the *Chin P'ing Mei tz'u-hua*, vol. 4, ch. 61, p. 25b, l. 3.

70. This four-character expression meaning a bloody catastrophe occurs ubiquitously in Chinese vernacular literature. See, e.g., *Yüan-ch'ü hsüan*, 1:386, l. 6; *Yüan-ch'ü hsüan wai-pien*, 1:197, l. 7; *Shen-hsiang ch'üan-pien, chüan* 642, p. 27a, l. 3; *Shui-hu ch'üan-chuan*, vol. 3, ch. 61, p. 1025, ll. 3–4; *Nan Sung chih-chuan*, vol. 1, *chüan* 3, p. 30a, ll. 4–5; *Pei Sung chih-chuan* (Chronicle of the Sung conquest of the north), attributed to Hsiung Ta-mu (mid-16th century), 10 *chüan* (Nanking: Shih-te t'ang, 1593), fac. repr. in *Ku-pen hsiao-shuo ts'ung-k'an, ti san-shih ssu chi*, vol. 3, *chüan* 7, p. 28b, l. 7; *Pai-chia kung-an, chüan* 3, ch. 28, p. 21a, ll. 2–3; *Yang-chia fu shih-tai*

chung-yung yen-i chih-chuan (Popular chronicle of the generations of loyal and brave exploits of the Yang household), pref. dated 1606, 2 vols., fac. repr. (Taipei: Kuo-li chung-yang t'u-shu kuan, 1971), vol. 2, *chüan* 5, p. 6b, ll. 4–5; and *Ta-T'ang Ch'in-wang tz'u-hua*, vol. 1, *chüan* 3, ch. 20, p. 42b, l. 10.

71. A close variant of this proverbial couplet occurs in *Chang Hsieh chuang-yüan*, scene 2, p. 14, l. 15. In the same form in which it appears in the novel it is ubiquitous in Chinese vernacular literature. See, e.g., the early (13th or 14th century) hsi-wen drama *Huan-men tzu-ti ts'o li-shen* (The scion of an official's family opts for the wrong career), in *Yung-lo ta-tien hsi-wen san-chung chiao-chu*, scene 5, p. 233, l. 11; *Sha-kou chi*, scene 8, p. 26, l. 2; *Ching-ch'ai chi*, scene 23, p. 71, l. 5; the anonymous Yüan-Ming ch'uan-ch'i drama *Chao-shih ku-erh chi* (The story of the orphan of Chao), in *Ku-pen hsi-ch'ü ts'ung-k'an, ch'u-chi*, item 16, *chüan* 2, scene 38, p. 29a, ll. 1–2; *P'o-yao chi*, *chüan* 1, scene 2, p. 3a, l. 5; *Chin-yin chi*, *chüan* 1, scene 7, p. 11a, l. 10; the fourteenth-century anthology of moral aphorisms entitled *Ming-hsin pao-chien* (A precious mirror to illuminate the mind), pref. dated 1393 (microfilm copy of a Ming edition in the East Asian Library, University of Chicago), *chüan* 1, p. 3b, l. 6; *Ch'ien-chin chi*, scene 5, p. 12, l. 1; *Shuang-chu chi*, scene 38, p. 135, l. 9; *Huai-hsiang chi*, scene 23, p. 72, l. 12; *Ming-chu chi*, scene 7, p. 19, l. 5; *Pao-chien chi*, scene 20, p. 40, l. 17; *Chu-fa chi*, *chüan* 1, scene 5, p. 9a, l. 5; *Kuan-yüan chi*, scene 27, p. 60, l. 3; and *Ta-T'ang Ch'in-wang tz'u-hua*, *chüan* 4, ch. 26, p. 17a, l. 8. The first line of this couplet also appears independently in *Ssu-sheng yüan*, play no. 1, p. 6, l. 11.

72. Kan Lo (3rd century B.C.) was an infant prodigy who is said to have successfully carried out a demanding diplomatic mission at the age of eleven. See *Shih-chi*, vol. 7, *chüan* 71, pp. 2319–21; and Watson, *Records of the Grand Historian: Qin Dynasty*, pp. 110–12.

73. On Chiang Tzu-ya (11th century B.C.), see Roy, *The Plum in the Golden Vase*, vol. 2, appendix, n. 19.

74. P'eng-tsu is a legendary figure from early Chinese history, sometimes called the Chinese Methuselah, who is said to have lived for more than eight hundred years. See *Le Lie-sien Tchouan*, trans. Max Kaltenmark (Peking: Université de Paris, Publications du Centre d'études sinologiques de Pékin, 1953), pp. 82–84.

75. On Yen Hui (521–490 B.C.), see Roy, *The Plum in the Golden Vase*, vol. 1, chap. 4, n. 12.

76. Fan Jan (112–85) was a man who chose to endure a life of poverty and support himself by fortune-telling rather than compromising his integrity by going along with the corrupt values of his time. See *Hou-Han shu*, vol. 9, *chüan* 81, pp. 2688–90.

77. On Shih Ch'ung (249–300), see Roy, *The Plum in the Golden Vase*, vol. 1, prefatory lyrics, n. 2.

78. Versions of this poem occur in *San hsien-shen Pao Lung-t'u tuan-yüan*, p. 196, l. 2; and *Shui-hu ch'üan-chuan*, vol. 3, ch. 61, p. 1023, l. 17.

CHAPTER 47

1. A variant of these two lines occurs in *San-kuo chih t'ung-su yen-i*, vol. 1, *chüan* 11, p. 522, l. 4.

2. This episode, which occupies most of chapter 47 and continues into chapter 48, is adapted, with many significant changes, from a crime-case story, the earliest extant

version of which is found in chapter 50 of *Pai-chia kung-an*. See Patrick Hanan, "Sources of the *Chin P'ing Mei*," *Asia Major*, n.s., vol. 10, part 1 (1963), pp. 40–42. The best study of this adaptation and its function in the novel is in Indira Satyendra, "Toward a Poetics of the Chinese Novel: A Study of the Prefatory Poems in the *Chin P'ing Mei tz'u-hua*," Ph.D. dissertation, University of Chicago, 1989, pp. 53–70.

3. This repeated admonition occurs in *Mencius*. See *Meng-tzu yin-te*, p. 8, 1B.12, l. 4; and Lau, *Mencius*, p. 70, l. 31. It also occurs in *San-kuo chih t'ung-su yen-i*, vol. 2, *chüan* 19, p. 916, l. 24; and recurs in the *Chin P'ing Mei tz'u-hua*, vol. 3, ch. 49, p. 17a, ll. 6–7; and vol. 4, ch. 66, p. 8b, l. 7.

4. The name Miao Ch'ing may be significant because it is made up, in reverse order, of the two characters *ch'ing-miao*, literally "green sprouts," the name of a notorious system of agricultural loans introduced by the controversial institutional reformer Wang An-shih (1021–86) in 1069. This system, although intended to benefit farmers, was so abused by government bureaucrats and functionaries in the way it was administered that, along with many of the other reforms introduced by Wang An-shih, it was later considered to have contributed significantly to the fall of the Northern Sung dynasty in 1127. For a detailed description of the "green sprouts" policy and a judicious assessment of its pros and cons, see H. R. Williamson, *Wang An Shih: A Chinese Statesman and Educationalist of the Sung Dynasty*, 2 vols. (London: Arthur Probstain, 1935–37), 1:142–76; and 2:171–78. The choice of this name for this particular character must have represented a conscious decision on the part of the author of the *Chin P'ing Mei*, since in the original story on which this episode is based the servant in question is only referred to by his surname of Tung. For an insightful study of the significance of this name change, see Satyendra, "Toward a Poetics of the Chinese Novel: A Study of the Prefatory Poems in the *Chin P'ing Mei tz'u-hua*," pp. 60–65.

5. This four-character expression occurs in *Chin-chien chi*, scene 32, p. 96, l. 11.

6. A close variant of this line occurs in *San-kuo chih t'ung-su yen-i*, vol. 1, *chüan* 2, p. 80, l. 23. It occurs in the same form as in the novel in *Yüan-ch'ü hsüan*, 3:1155, l. 8; and *Ts'an-T'ang Wu-tai shih yen-i chuan*, ch. 13, p. 44, ll. 21–22.

7. It was customary in ancient China to provide the sons of the aristocracy with these objects upon birth, in order to symbolize what their ambitions should be as men. This four-character expression occurs twice in *The Book of Rites*. See *Li-chi*, ch. 10, p. 58, l. 2; and ch. 44, p. 131, l. 8; and *Li Chi: Book of Rites*, trans. James Legge, 2 vols. (New Hyde Park, N.Y.: University Books, 1967), 1:472, ll. 14–15; and 2:452, ll. 11–12. The latter passage is translated by James Legge as follows: "Hence, when a son is born, a bow of mulberry wood, and six arrows of the wild raspberry plant (are placed on the left of the door), for the purpose of shooting at heaven, earth, and the four cardinal points. Heaven, earth, and the four points denote the sphere wherein the business of a man lies." This expression also occurs in a letter by Lu Yün (262–303), *Ch'üan Shang-ku San-tai Ch'in Han San-kuo Liu-ch'ao wen*, vol. 2, *Ch'üan Chin wen* (Complete prose of the Chin dynasty), *chüan* 103, p. 5b, l. 12; a letter by Li Po (701–62), *Ch'üan T'ang wen* (Complete prose of the T'ang), 20 vols. (Kyoto: Chūbun shuppan-sha, 1976), vol. 8, *chüan* 348, p. 13b. l. 2; a poem by Hua Chen (b. 1051, cs 1079), *Ch'üan Sung shih*, 18:12347, l. 11; a lyric by Li Liu (b. 1175, cs 1208), *Ch'üan Sung tz'u*, 4:2320, lower register, ll. 12–13; a lyric by Hsü Ching-sun (1192–1273), ibid., 4:2720, lower register, l. 13; a lyric by Sung Chiung (1292–1344) written in the year 1338, *Ch'üan Chin Yüan tz'u*, 2:1056, upper register, l. 14; *Chien-teng hsin-hua, chüan*

3, p. 73, l. 6; *Shuang-chu chi*, scene 31, p. 105, l. 12; *Huai-hsiang chi*, scene 2, p. 2, l. 9; *Shuang-lieh chi*, scene 2, p. 3, l. 11; and *Ta-T'ang Ch'in-wang tz'u-hua*, vol. 1, *chüan* 3, ch. 24, p. 77a, l. 4.

8. This four-character expression occurs in *Hsiao-p'in chi*, *chüan* 2, p. 52. l. 13.

9. This four-character expression occurs in *Yüan-ch'ü hsüan wai-pien*, 2:363, ll. 16–17; and 3:768, l. 5.

10. This four-character expression occurs in *San-yüan chi*, scene 3, p. 5, l. 1; and *Yü-chüeh chi*, scene 6, p. 15, l. 3.

11. This line occurs verbatim in the ch'uan-ch'i drama *Tuan-fa chi* (The severed tresses), by Li K'ai-hsien (1502–68), in *Ku-pen hsi-ch'ü ts'ung-k'an*, *wu-chi*, item 2, *chüan* 1, scene 16, p. 40a, l. 5. Slightly different versions occur in *P'o-yao chi*, *chüan* 1, scene 15, p. 46a, l. 5; and *San-pao t'ai-chien Hsi-yang chi t'ung-su yen-i*, vol. 1. ch. 37, p. 474, l. 4.

12. A very similar couplet occurs in the early vernacular story *Fu Lu Shou san-hsing tu-shih* (The three stellar deities of Fortune, Emolument, and Longevity visit the mundane world), in *Ching-shih t'ung-yen*, *chüan* 39, p. 583, l. 9.

13. This four-character expression occurs in the early vernacular story *Yang Ssu-wen Yen-shan feng ku-jen* (Yang Ssu-wen encounters an old acquaintance in Yen-shan), in *Ku-chin hsiao-shuo*, vol. 2, *chüan* 24, p. 372, ll. 3–4.

14. Very similar poems occur in *Shui-hu ch'üan-chuan*, vol. 2, ch. 41, p. 657, l. 17; and vol. 4, ch. 111, p. 1665, l. 3.

15. A variant of this proverbial saying recurs in the *Chin P'ing Mei tz'u-hua*, vol. 5, ch. 90, p. 7a, l. 2.

16. This proverbial couplet occurs in the early vernacular story *Chi Ya-fan chin-man ch'an-huo* (Duty Group Leader Chi's golden eel engenders catastrophe), in *Ching-shih t'ung-yen*, *chüan* 20, p. 284, l. 12. It also recurs in the *Chin P'ing Mei tz'u-hua*, vol. 3, ch. 59, p. 11a, l. 1; and, with an insignificant variant, in ibid., vol. 5, ch. 92, p. 7b, ll. 4–5.

17. During the Ming dynasty Lin-ch'ing was an important port on the Grand Canal, where a customs station to collect duty on goods transported on inland waterways was established in 1435. For a map showing the position of Lin-ch'ing on the Grand Canal in the sixteenth century, and a discussion of the inland customs duty, see Ray Huang, *Taxation and Governmental Finance in Sixteenth-Century Ming China* (Cambridge: Cambridge University Press, 1974), pp. 54, and 226–31.

18. A variant of this proverbial couplet occurs in *Ming-hsin pao-chien*, *chüan* 1, p. 3a, l. 4; and other variants recur in the *Chin P'ing Mei tz'u-hua*, vol. 3, ch. 49, p. 12a, ll. 2–3; and vol. 5, ch. 88, p. 3a, l. 7.

19. This four-character expression occurs in *Yüan-ch'ü hsüan*, 4:1571, l. 19; and *San-pao t'ai-chien Hsi-yang chi t'ung-su yen-i*, vol. 1, ch. 40, p. 518, l. 13.

20. This four-character expression occurs in *Pei Sung chih-chuan*, vol. 3, *chüan* 9, p. 22a, l. 2; and a set of songs by Hsüeh Lun-tao (c. 1531–c. 1600), *Ch'üan Ming san-ch'ü*, 3:2742, l. 11.

21. This formulaic four-character expression is ubiquitous in Chinese vernacular literature. See, e.g., *Shui-hu ch'üan-chuan*, vol. 1, ch. 6, p. 101, l. 1; *Ta-Sung chung-hsing yen-i*, vol. 2, *chüan* 7, p. 13b, l. 10; *T'ang-shu chih-chuan t'ung-su yen-i*, vol. 1, *chüan* 5, p. 30b, ll. 8–9; *Ch'üan-Han chih-chuan*, vol. 2, *chüan* 5, p. 32b, ll. 13–14; *Nan Sung chih-chuan*, vol. 1, *chüan* 5, p. 13a, ll. 8–9; *Ts'an-T'ang Wu-tai shih yen-i*

chuan, ch. 18, p. 66, l. 18; *Pai-chia kung-an, chüan* 6, ch. 55, p. 17a, l. 9; *San-pao t'ai-chien Hsi-yang chi t'ung-su yen-i*, vol. 2, ch. 83, p. 1068, l. 9; *Yang chia fu shih-tai chung-yung yen-i chih-chuan*, vol. 1, *chüan* 1, p. 14a, l. 2; and *Sui-T'ang liang-ch'ao shih-chuan, chüan* 3, p. 51b, ll. 8–9.

22. This four-character expression occurs in *Huang-ch'ao pien-nien kang-mu pei-yao* (Chronological outline of the significant events of the imperial [Sung] dynasty), comp. Ch'en Chün (c. 1165–c. 1236), pref. dated 1229, 2 vols., fac. repr. (Taipei: Ch'eng-wen ch'u-pan she, 1966), vol. 2, *chüan* 25, p. 17b, l. 6; *Wu Lun-ch'üan Pei, chüan* 3, scene 22, p. 38a, l. 7; and *Yang-chia fu shih-tai chung-yung yen-i chih-chuan*, vol. 2, *chüan* 8, p. 49a, l. 3.

23. This formulaic four-character expression occurs in *K'an p'i-hsüeh tan-cheng Erh-lang Shen*, p. 247, l. 9; *Shui-hu ch'üan-chuan*, vol. 2, ch. 34, p. 535, l. 16; *Hung-fu chi*, scene 7, p. 13, l. 12; *Kuan-yüan chi*, scene 15, p. 31, l. 9; *Hsi-yu chi*, vol. 1, ch. 22, p. 247, l. 1; *Pa-i chi*. scene 28, p. 60, ll. 11–12; *Hai-ling i-shih*, p. 111, ll. 5–6; and the ch'uan-ch'i drama *I-hsia chi* (The righteous knight-errant), by Shen Ching (1553–1610), *Liu-shih chung ch'ü* ed., scene 8, p. 20, l. 10.

24. The text here reads "west" rather than "east," but I have emended it to conform with the information in chapter 39, where we are told that Han Tao-kuo's house was located on the east side of the stone bridge on Lion Street. See *Chin P'ing Mei tz'u-hua*, vol. 2, ch. 39, p. 1a, l. 10; and Roy, *The Plum in the Golden Vase*, 2:405, l. 2.

25. This proverbial saying recurs in the *Chin P'ing Mei tz'u-hua*, vol. 3, ch. 52, p. 9a, l. 9.

26. This proverbial saying occurs in *Yüan-ch'ü hsüan*, 1:124, l. 10; *Yüan-ch'ü hsüan wai-pien*, 3:812, l. 3; and the tsa-chü drama *Seng-ni kung-fan* (A monk and a nun violate their vows), by Feng Wei-min (1511–80), in *Ming-jen tsa-chü hsüan*, scene 2, p. 342, l. 8.

27. This four-character expression occurs in *[Chi-p'ing chiao-chu] Hsi-hsiang chi*, play no. 5, scene 3, p. 187, l. 5.

28. This is indeed the penalty prescribed for this crime in the Ming penal code according to a provision enacted in 1497. See *Ming-tai lü-li hui-pien* (Comprehensive edition of the Ming penal code and judicial regulations), comp. Huang Chang-chien, 2 vols. (Taipei: Academia Sinica, 1979), vol. 1, *chüan-shou* (preliminary *chüan*), p. 170, l. 7.

29. See ibid., p. 172, ll. 2 and 5.

30. This four-character expression occurs in an anonymous Yüan dynasty song suite, *Ch'üan Yüan san-ch'ü*, 2:1804, l. 4; *Shui-hu ch'üan-chuan*, vol. 2, ch. 42, p. 674, ll. 9–10; *Lieh-kuo chih-chuan*, vol. 1, *chüan* 2, p. 18b, l. 9; *Ssu-hsi chi*, scene 6, p. 16, l. 7; and recurs in the *Chin P'ing Mei tz'u-hua*, vol. 4, ch. 69, p. 5a, l. 8.

31. This formulaic four-character expression occurs in *Yeh Chia chuan* (Biography of Yeh Chia), by Su Shih (1037–1101), in *Su Shih wen-chi* (Collected prose of Su Shih), 6 vols. (Peking: Chung-hua shu-chü, 1986), vol. 2, *chüan* 13, p. 430, l. 6; the Yüan-Ming hsi-wen drama *Su Wu mu-yang chi* (Su Wu herds sheep), in *Ku-pen hsi-ch'ü ts'ung-k'an, ch'u-chi*, item 20, *chüan* 1, scene 8, p. 18a, ll. 6–7; *Wu Lun-ch'üan Pei, chüan* 1, scene 5, p. 25b, l. 3; *T'ang-shu chih-chuan t'ung-su yen-i*, vol. 2, *chüan* 6, p. 43b, l. 11; *Hai-fu shan-t'ang tz'u-kao, chüan* 4, p. 194, l. 9; *Huan-sha chi*, scene 27, p. 94, l. 12; *Yü-ching t'ai*, scene 26, p. 69, l. 3; and *Huang-Ming k'ai-yün ying-wu chuan, chüan* 2, p. 3a, l. 8.

32. This formulaic four-character expression occurs in *P'i-p'a chi*, scene 19, p. 114, l. 5; the Yüan-Ming ch'uan-ch'i drama *Huang hsiao-tzu* (The filial son Huang [Chüeh-ching]), in *Ku-pen hsi-ch'ü ts'ung-k'an, ch'u-chi*, item 23, *chüan* 2, scene 24, p. 36a, l. 7; and *Pao-chien chi*, scene 23, p. 43, l. 12.

33. The locus classicus for this four-character expression is a description of Confucius (551–479 B.C.) reported in his biography in the *Shih-chi*. See ibid., vol. 6, *chüan* 47, p. 1921, l. 15; and *Records of the Historian*, trans. Yang Hsien-yi and Gladys Yang (Hong Kong: Commercial Press, 1974), p. 11, l. 22. It occurs frequently in later literature. See, e.g., a document by Hsia-hou Chan (243–91) included in his biography in *Chin shu*, vol. 5, *chüan* 55, p. 1493, l. 7; *Lieh-kuo chih-chuan*, vol. 2, *chüan* 6, p. 42a, l. 3; *Chiang Shih yüeh-li chi*, *chüan* 2, scene 22, p. 14b, l. 6; *Yü-chüeh chi*, scene 32, p. 99, l. 12; and *Su Ying huang-hou ying-wu chi*, *chüan* 1, scene 17, p. 36a, l. 5.

34. This four-character expression occurs independently in *Yüan-ch'ü hsüan wai-pien*, 1:105, l. 1; *Pao-chien chi*, scene 19, p. 36, l. 15; and *San-pao t'ai-chien Hsi-yang chi t'ung-su yen-i*, vol. 1, ch. 36, p. 465, l. 11. Variants of this couplet occur in *San-kuo chih t'ung-su yen-i*, vol. 1, *chüan* 3, p. 133, ll. 18–19; *Shui-hu ch'üan-chuan*, vol. 1, ch. 3, p. 53, l. 10; *San-pao t'ai-chien Hsi-yang chi t'ung-su yen-i*, vol. 2, ch. 54, p. 694, l. 10; *Ta-T'ang Ch'in-wang tz'u-hua*, vol. 1, *chüan* 2, ch. 11, p. 27a, l. 9; and recur in the *Chin P'ing Mei tz'u-hua*, vol. 5, ch. 92, p. 11a, l. 4; ch. 94, p. 6a, ll. 1–2; and ch. 100, p. 7b, ll. 3–4. The entire couplet occurs as given here in *Yüan-ch'ü hsüan*, 3:934, l. 11.

35. This four-character expression occurs in the *Shih-chi* in a passage describing the conduct of King Wu (r. 1045–1043 B.C.), the founder of the Chou dynasty. See ibid., vol. 1, *chüan* 4, p. 120, l. 6. It also occurs in *Huang-ch'ao pien-nien kang-mu pei-yao*, vol. 2, *chüan* 29, p. 12a, l. 1; [*Chi-p'ing chiao-chu*] *Hsi-hsiang chi*, play no. 4, scene 2, p. 150, l. 14; *Yüan-ch'ü hsüan wai-pien*, 1:245, l. 15; *Ch'ien-Han shu p'ing-hua*, p. 43, l. 13; *Huang T'ing-tao yeh-tsou Liu-hsing ma*, scene 3, p. 106, l. 9; *Ch'ang-an ch'eng ssu-ma t'ou-T'ang*, scene 4, p. 19a, l. 12; *Hsing-t'ien Feng-yüeh t'ung-hsüan chi*, scene 8, p. 21b, l. 5; *Shui-hu ch'üan-chuan*, vol. 3, ch. 83, p. 1369, l. 8; *T'ang-shu chih-chuan t'ung-su yen-i*, *chüan* 2, p. 42b, l. 5; and *Ta-T'ang Ch'in-wang tz'u-hua*, vol. 1, *chüan* 2, ch. 12, p. 37b, l. 9.

36. This proverbial couplet occurs verbatim in *K'an p'i-hsüeh tan-cheng Erh-lang Shen*, p. 245, l. 3. The second line also occurs independently in the Ming tsa-chü drama *Yao-ch'ih hui Pa-hsien ch'ing-shou* (Meeting at the Jasper Pool the Eight Immortals celebrate longevity), by Chu Yu-tun (1379–1439), pref. dated 1432, in *Mai-wang kuan ch'ao-chiao pen ku-chin tsa-chü* (Ancient and modern tsa-chü: manuscripts and collated editions of Mai-wang hall), 84 *ts'e*, fac. repr. in *Ku-pen hsi-ch'ü ts'ung-k'an, ssu-chi* (Collectanea of rare editions of traditional drama, fourth series) (Shanghai: Shang-wu yin-shu kuan, 1958), *ts'e* 40, scene 2, p. 10a, l. 7.

37. This four-character expression occurs in *Yüan-ch'ü hsüan*, 1:399, l. 17; and *Yüan-ch'ü hsüan wai-pien*, 1:78, l. 18.

38. Hu Shih-wen (fl. early 12th century) is a historical figure who was both a relative by marriage and a protégé of Ts'ai Ching. His name is mentioned three times, always pejoratively, in *Sung shih*, vol. 7, *chüan* 94, p. 2334, l. 12; vol. 13, *chüan* 175, p. 4257, l. 14; and vol. 39, *chüan* 472, p. 13724, l. 4.

39. This line occurs in *Shui-hu ch'üan-chuan*, vol. 4, ch. 113, p. 1692, l. 3; and recurs in the *Chin P'ing Mei tz'u-hua*, vol. 5, ch. 93, p. 1a, l. 3.

40. Variants of this proverbial couplet occur in *Yüan-ch'ü hsüan*, 1:45, l. 6; 4:1396, l. 2; *Yüan-ch'ü hsüan wai-pien*, 2:639, l. 17; 3:945, ll. 16–17; *K'an p'i-hsüeh tan-cheng Erh-lang shen*, p. 257, l. 12; the early vernacular story *Shih-wu kuan hsi-yen ch'eng ch'iao-huo* (Fifteen strings of cash: a casual jest leads to uncanny disaster), in *Hsing-shih heng-yen*, vol. 2, *chüan* 33, p. 699, l. 1; the early vernacular story *Wang K'uei* (The story of Wang K'uei), in *Tsui yü-ch'ing*, 4:1513, upper register, ll. 1–2; the middle-period vernacular story *Jen hsiao-tzu lieh-hsing wei shen* (The apotheosis of Jen the filial son), in *Ku-chin hsiao-shuo*, vol. 2, *chüan* 38, p. 578, l. 6; and *San-pao t'ai-chien Hsi-yang chi t'ung-su yen-i*, vol. 1, ch. 47, p. 613, ll. 3–4.

CHAPTER 48

1. This four-character expression occurs in *San-kuo chih t'ung-su yen-i*, vol. 2, *chüan* 24, p. 1155, ll. 23–24; and *Yüan-ch'ü hsüan wai-pien*, 1:60, l. 6.

2. This four-character expression occurs in a lyric by Yin Chih-p'ing (1169–1251), *Ch'üan Chin Yüan tz'u*, 2:1183, upper register, l. 15; *Yüan-ch'ü hsüan*, 1:36, l. 11; *Yüan-ch'ü hsüan wai-pien*, 1:102, l. 19; *Shih Chen-jen ssu-sheng so pai-yüan*, scene 1, p. 4b, l. 1; *San-yüan chi*, scene 7, p. 17, l. 9; *Ts'an-T'ang Wu-tai shih yen-i chuan*, ch. 10, p. 31, l. 11; a song by Kao Ying-ch'i (16th century), *Ch'üan Ming san-ch'ü*, 2:2299, l. 3; *Hsi-yu chi*, vol. 1, ch. 16, p. 187, l. 16; *Mu-lien chiu-mu ch'üan-shan hsi-wen*, *chüan* 3, p. 17a, l. 2; *Su Ying huang-hou ying-wu chi*, *chüan* 1, scene 13, p. 27a, l. 2; *San-pao t'ai-chien Hsi-yang chi t'ung-su yen-i*, vol. 1, ch. 28, p. 363, l. 11; and *Ch'ün-yin lei-hsüan*, 4:2490, l. 7.

3. This four-character expression occurs in a lyric by Yin Chih-p'ing (1169–1251), *Ch'üan Chin Yüan tz'u*, 2:1183, upper register, l. 15; *Yüan-ch'ü hsüan*, 2:505, ll. 2–3; an anonymous Yüan dynasty song suite, *Ch'üan Yüan san-ch'ü*, 2:1659, l. 3; *Shih Chen-jen ssu-sheng so pai-yüan*, scene 4, p. 13a, l. 1; *Hai-fu shan-t'ang tz'u-kao*, *chüan* 4, p. 188, l. 13; and *Mu-lien chiu-mu ch'üan-shan hsi-wen*, *chüan* 3, p. 47a, l. 1.

4. A version of this entire admonitory passage of parallel prose that is very close to that in the novel occurs in *Ming-hsin pao-chien*, where it is attributed to Emperor Chen-tsung (r. 997–1022) of the Sung dynasty. See ibid., *chüan* 2, p. 5a, ll. 3–6. Much of it also occurs, with considerable variation, in *Shui-hu ch'üan-chuan*, vol. 2, ch. 31, p. 474, ll. 3–6.

5. Tseng Hsiao-hsü (1049–1127) is a historical figure, classified by traditional histo-riographers as an exemplar of loyalty and righteousness. For his biography, see *Sung shih*, vol. 38, *chüan* 453, pp. 13319–20. He is the only incorruptible official portrayed in the entire novel, and it is probably no accident that the author chose this particular figure to fulfill this role since his given name *Hsiao-hsü* consists of two words that mean "filiality" and "hierarchy," two of the most important values in traditional Confu-cianism.

6. Tseng Pu (1036–1107) is a historical figure, though he was not the father of Tseng Hsiao-hsü. For his biography, see *Sung shih*, vol. 39, *chüan* 471, pp. 13714–17.

7. This four-character expression recurs in the *Chin P'ing Mei tz'u-hua*, vol. 4, ch. 67, p. 4b, l. 10.

8. This four-character expression occurs in *Yüan-ch'ü hsüan*, 4:1359, l. 21.

9. This four-character expression occurs in a lyric by Chang Po-ch'un (1242–1302), *Ch'üan Chin Yüan tz'u*, 2:746, lower register, l. 7.

10. This four-character expression occurs in a lyric by Wei Ch'u (1231–92), *Ch'üan Chin Yüan tz'u*, 2:699, upper register, 1. 10.

11. This four-character expression occurs in *Hua-shen san-miao chuan*, p. 41b, l. 3; *Liu sheng mi Lien chi, chüan* 3, p. 24a, l. 5; and *Ming-feng chi*, scene 41, p. 175, l. 11.

12. This four-character expression is ultimately derived from a famous passage in Book 13 of the *Lun-yü* (The analects of Confucius). See *Lun-yü yin-te* (A concordance to the *Analects*) (Taipei: Chinese Materials and Research Aids Service Center, 1966), Book 13, p. 25, paragraph 3, l. 4. The passage in question is translated by D. C. Lau as follows: "When names are not correct, what is said will not sound reasonable; when what is said does not sound reasonable, affairs will not culminate in success; when affairs do not culminate in success, rites and music will not flourish; when rites and music do not flourish, punishments will not fit the crimes; when punishments do not fit the crimes, the common people will not know where to put hand and foot." See *The Analects*, by Confucius, trans. D. C. Lau (New York: Penguin Books, 1979), p. 118. This expression occurs in the same form as in the novel in *Shui-hu ch'üan-chuan*, vol. 3, ch. 64, p. 1096, l. 6.

13. There is a sixteenth-century figure of this name who passed the *chin-shih* examinations in 1547 and probably lived into the Wan-li reign period (1573–1620). See Liu Chung-kuang, "*Chin P'ing Mei* jen-wu k'ao-lun" (A study of the historical figures in the *Chin P'ing Mei*), in Yeh Kuei-t'ung et al., eds., *Chin P'ing Mei tso-che chih mi* (The riddle of the authorship of the *Chin P'ing Mei*) (N.p.: Ning-hsia jen-min ch'u-pan she, 1988), pp. 154–58.

14. It is a Chinese folk belief that discontented ghosts sometimes manifest themselves in the form of miniature whirlwinds, or dust devils. See the commentary by Li Pi (1159–1222) on a poem by Wang An-shih (1021–86), in *Wang Ching-wen kung shih Li Pi chu* (The poetry of Wang An-shih with commentary by Li Pi), 2 vols., fac. repr. of Korean movable type edition (Shanghai: Shang-hai ku-chi ch'u-pan she, 1993), vol. 2, *chüan* 46, p. 6b, ll. 6–7.

15. The last line of this quatrain occurs verbatim in a poem by Li Shan-fu (9th century), *Ch'üan T'ang shih*, vol. 10, *chüan* 643, p. 7364, l. 12. It also occurs in a set of songs by Yang Shen (1488–1559), *Ch'üan Ming san-ch'ü*, 2:1415, l. 6; *Su Ying huang-hou ying-wu chi, chüan* 1, scene 14, p. 30b, l. 1; and *Huang-Ming k'ai-yün ying-wu chuan, chüan* 3, p. 16b, l. 1.

16. This formulaic four-character expression, which literally means "the red of the peach blossoms and the green of the willows," occurs in a lyric by Shih Hao (1106–94), *Ch'üan Sung tz'u*, 2:1275, upper register, l. 7; a song by Kuan Yün-shih (1286–1324), *Ch'üan Yüan san-ch'ü*, 1:358, l. 12; *Yüan-ch'ü hsüan*, 3:1151, l. 7; *Yüan-ch'ü hsüan wai-pien*, 2:697, l. 5; a lyric by Feng Tsun-shih (14th century), *Ch'üan Chin Yüan tz'u*, 2:1245, upper register, ll. 8–9; the early vernacular story *Chin-ming ch'ih Wu Ch'ing feng Ai-ai* (Wu Ch'ing meets Ai-ai at Chin-ming Pond), in *Ching-shih t'ung-yen, chüan* 30, p. 460, l. 1; *Liang-shan wu-hu ta chieh-lao*, scene 4, p. 7a, l. 14; *Yüeh-ming Ho-shang tu Liu Ts'ui*, p. 433, l. 7; *Pai-chia kung-an, chüan* 3, ch. 28, p. 21b, l. 1; a song suite by Hu Wen-huan (fl. 1592–1617), *Ch'üan Ming san-ch'ü*, 3:2931, l. 13; and *Ta-T'ang Ch'in-wang tz'u-hua*, vol. 1, *chüan* 3, ch. 18, p. 16a, l. 3.

17. This four-character expression, referring to four of the arts most highly valued by persons of cultivated taste, occurs in *Yüan-ch'ü hsüan*, 3:971, l. 5; *Chien-teng yü-hua, chüan* 2, p. 179, ll. 12–13; a song suite by Lü Ching-ju (16th century), *Ch'üan*

Ming san-ch'ü, 1:849, l. 9; *Huai-ch'un ya-chi, chüan* 9, p. 17a, upper register, l. 5; *Hsi-yu chi*, vol. 2, ch. 96, p. 1082, l. 10; and *Ssu-sheng yüan*, play no. 4, scene 1, p. 62, l. 11.

18. This proverbial couplet is ubiquitous in Chinese vernacular literature. Versions of it occur in *Wu-wang fa Chou p'ing-hua*, p. 19, ll. 13–14; *Hsüan-ho i-shih*, p. 52, ll. 7–8; *Shui-hu ch'üan-chuan*, vol. 1 ch. 2, p. 25, ll. 13–14; and the *Chin P'ing Mei tz'u-hua*, vol. 4, ch. 74, p. 9b, ll. 3–4. Other variants of the couplet occur in *Yüan-ch'ü hsüan wai-pien*, 1:116, l. 21; *Sha-kou chi*, scene 19, p. 72, l. 2; and *Ching-ch'ai chi*, scene 34, p. 103, ll. 6–7. It occurs exactly as in the novel in *Yüan-ch'ü hsüan*, 2:557, l. 19; *P'i-p'a chi*, scene 3, p. 18, l. 9; the middle-period vernacular story *Ch'en Hsün-chien Mei-ling shih-ch'i chi* (Police Chief Ch'en loses his wife in crossing the Mei-ling Range), in *Ch'ing-p'ing shan-t'ang hua-pen*, p. 129, l. 9; and *Yüeh-ming Ho-shang tu Liu Ts'ui*, p. 434, l. 3. A close variant of the first line occurs independently in *San-pao t'ai-chien Hsi-yang chi t'ung-su yen-i*, vol. 2, ch. 96, p. 1230, l. 7; and the second line also occurs independently in a song suite by Chou Wen-chih (d. 1334), *Ch'üan Yüan san-ch'ü*, 1:563, l. 14; a song suite by Lü Chih-an (14th century), in ibid., 2:1131, l. 8; *Yüan-ch'ü hsüan*, 3:1266, l. 16; and *Yüan-ch'ü hsüan wai-pien*, 2:348, l. 3.

19. This type of informal headgear, which continued to be popular through the Ming dynasty, was traditionally believed to have been either designed or favored by Su Shih (1037–1101), one of whose courtesy names was Tung-p'o. For excellent pictures of what this type of headgear looked like, see the illustrations reproduced in Shen Ts'ung-wen, *Chung-kuo ku-tai fu-shih yen-chiu* (A study of traditional Chinese costume) (Hong Kong: Shang-wu yin-shu kuan, 1981), pp. 326–27.

20. This four-character expression occurs in *Huai-ch'un ya-chi, chüan* 10, p. 23a, l. 9.

21. This four-character expression occurs in a poem by Lu Kuei-meng (fl. 865–881), *Ch'üan T'ang shih*, vol. 9, *chüan* 621, p. 7147, l. 3. It is ubiquitous in later Chinese literature. See, e.g., a memorial by Ch'en Chung-wei (1212–83), *Sung shih*, vol. 36, *chüan* 422, p. 12619, l. 10; *San-kuo chih t'ung-su yen-i*, vol. 2, *chüan* 19, p. 901, l. 9; a song by Ch'en To (fl. early 16th century), *Ch'üan Ming san-ch'ü*, 1:462, l. 11; a song suite by Lü Ching-ju (16th century), ibid., 1:849, l. 2; *Huan-sha chi*, scene 7, p. 17, l. 5; *Ming-feng chi*, scene 4, p. 12, l. 9; *Hai-fu shan-t'ang tz'u-kao, chüan* 2a, p. 81, l. 13; a literary tale in *Yüan-chu chih-yü: hsüeh-ch'uang t'an-i* (Supplementary guide to Mandarin Duck Island: tales of the unusual from the snowy window) (Peking: Chung-hua shu-chü, 1997), *chüan* 2, p. 56, l. 2; *San-pao t'ai-chien Hsi-yang chi t'ung-su yen-i*, vol. 1, ch. 33, p. 432, l. 2; and a song suite by Ch'en So-wen (d. c. 1604), *Ch'üan Ming san-ch'ü*, 2:2544, l. 9.

22. This four-character expression occurs under the year 944 in the *Tzu-chih t'ung-chien* (Comprehensive mirror for aid in government), comp. Ssu-ma Kuang (1019–86), 4 vols. (Peking: Ku-chi ch'u-pan she, 1957), vol. 4, *chüan* 284, p. 9272, ll. 10–11; and a letter by Kuei Yu-kuang (1507–71), in *Chen-ch'uan hsien-sheng chi* (Collected works of Kuei Yu-kuang), by Kuei Yu-kuang, 2 vols. (Shanghai: Shang-hai ku-chi ch'u-pan she, 1981), vol. 1, *chüan* 8, p. 170, l. 9.

23. This four-character expression occurs in a lyric attributed to a Sung dynasty figure named Editor Wu (dates unknown), *Ch'üan Sung tz'u*, 5:3550, upper register, l. 12; a lyric by a Sung dynasty figure named Jen Hsiang-lung (dates unknown), ibid., 5:3588, upper register, l. 5; and *Pao-chien chi*, scene 50, p. 89, l. 9.

24. This four-character expression occurs in *Feng-yüeh Nan-lao chi*, scene 4, p. 9a, l. 14.

25. This four-character expression recurs in the *Chin P'ing Mei tz'u-hua*, vol. 4, ch. 77, p. 19b, l. 6.

26. Variants of this proverbial couplet, the lines of which sometimes occur in reverse order, are ubiquitous in Chinese popular literature. See, e.g., *Yüan-ch'ü hsüan*, 1:279, l. 20; *Yüan-ch'ü hsüan wai-pien*, 1:164, ll. 7–8; and 3:749, l. 11; the anonymous Yüan-Ming tsa-chü drama *Yün-t'ai Men chü erh-shih pa chiang* (The twenty-eight generals gather at Yün-t'ai Gate), in *Ku-pen Yüan Ming tsa-chü*, vol. 2, scene 1, p. 3b, l. 11; the anonymous Yüan-Ming tsa-chü drama *Shou-t'ing hou nu chan Kuan P'ing* (The Marquis of Shou-t'ing angrily executes Kuan P'ing), in *Ku-pen Yüan Ming tsa-chü*, vol. 3, scene 1, p. 3b, l. 11; *Ch'ang-an ch'eng ssu-ma t'ou-T'ang, hsieh-tzu* (wedge), p. 4a, ll. 1–2; *San-kuo chih t'ung-su yen-i*, vol. 2, *chüan* 15, p. 707, l. 18; and *chüan* 23, p. 1090, ll. 19–20; *Shui-hu ch'üan-chuan*, vol. 1, ch. 20, p. 290, l. 17; *T'ang-shu chih-chuan t'ung-su yen-i*, vol. 2, *chüan* 6, p. 32b, l. 5; *Nan Sung chih-chuan*, vol. 1, *chüan* 8, p. 14a, l. 11; *Pei Sung chih-chuan*, vol. 2, *chüan* 4, p. 11b, ll. 5–6; *Ta-Sung chung-hsing yen-i*, vol. 1, *chüan* 2, p. 51a, ll. 2–3; *Ch'üan-Han chih-chuan*, vol. 3, *chüan* 3, p. 20b, l. 10; *Huang-Ming k'ai-yün ying-wu chuan*, *chüan* 4, p. 22b, l. 4; and *Ta-T'ang Ch'in-wang tz'u-hua*, vol. 1, *chüan* 1, ch. 3, p. 29a, l. 6. The second line also occurs independently in *San-pao t'ai-chien Hsi-yang chi t'ung-su yen-i*, vol. 2, ch. 55, p. 709, l. 2.

27. This four-character expression occurs in *Chin-t'ung Yü-nü Chiao Hung chi*, p. 30, l. 6; *Ming-chu chi*, scene 28, p. 88, l. 12; *Huan-sha chi*, scene 26, p. 92, l. 1; *Hung-fu chi*, scene 16, p. 30, l. 10; and *Hai-ling i-shih*, p. 161, l. 3.

28. This four-character expression recurs in the *Chin P'ing Mei tz'u-hua*, vol. 5, ch. 90, p. 6a, l. 2.

29. On the General of the Five Ways, see Roy, *The Plum in the Golden Vase*, vol. 1, chap. 2, n. 25.

30. This four-character expression occurs in *San-pao t'ai-chien Hsi-yang chi t'ung-su yen-i*, vol. 1, ch. 16, p. 203, l. 7.

31. Yü Shen (d. 1132) is a historical figure. For his biography, see *Sung shih*, vol. 32, *chüan* 352, pp. 11121–22.

32. The following seven proposals are all derived from standard historical sources, which are, in many cases, selectively quoted verbatim, but they are anachronistic, in that they were originally presented at different times rather than in a single document. The author of the novel has combined them for narrative convenience.

33. These two consecutive four-character expressions are quoted verbatim from Chu Hsi's (1130–1200) preface to his commentary on the *Ta-hsüeh* (The great learning), which was written in 1189, and would have been familiar to every educated reader in sixteenth-century China. See *Ssu-shu chang-chü chi-chu* (Collected commentary on the paragraphed and punctuated text of the Four books), by Chu Hsi (Peking: Chung-hua shu-chü, 1983), p. 1, l. 14.

34. This is a slightly modified quotation from the *Shu-ching* (Book of documents), where the first phrase reads, "Heaven in order to protect the people below," instead of, "Heaven in giving birth to the people." See *The Shoo King or The Book of Historical Documents*, trans. James Legge (Hong Kong: University of Hong Kong Press, 1960), p. 286. The same passage is also cited by Mencius (c. 372–c. 289 B.C.), where he

quotes the first phrase as, "Heaven in giving birth to the people below." See *Meng-tzu yin-te*, p. 6, 1B. 3. The same passage, again with an insignificant variation in the opening phrase, occurs in *Lieh-kuo chih-chuan*, vol. 3, *chüan* 8, p. 2b, l. 10; and the first phrase as given in the novel occurs independently in *Su Ying huang-hou ying-wu chi*, *chüan* 2, scene 31, p. 26b, l. 10.

35. The wording of the above two sentences is very close to that in an imperial rescript issued by Emperor Hui-tsung (r. 1100–25) in response to a recommendation by Ts'ai Ching (1046–1126) in 1104. See *Sung shih*, vol. 11, *chüan* 155, p. 3622, ll. 8–9; *chüan* 157, p. 3664, ll. 1–2; and *Hsü Tzu-chih t'ung-chien* (A continuation of the Comprehensive mirror for aid in government), comp. Pi Yüan (1730–97), 4 vols. (Peking: Ku-chi ch'u-pan she, 1958), vol. 2, *chüan* 89, p. 2278, ll. 2–4.

36. This measure was enacted by imperial rescript in 1107. See *Sung shih*, vol. 2, *chüan* 20, p. 378, l. 1; and vol. 11, *chüan* 157, pp. 3666–67.

37. This institution was established in 1102. See *Huang-ch'ao pien-nien kang-mu pei-yao*, vol. 2, *chüan* 26, pp. 18a–18b; *Sung shih*, vol. 2, *chüan* 19, p. 364, l. 11; and vol. 39, *chüan* 472, p. 13723, ll. 5–7.

38. This four-character expression occurs in *Ch'üan-Han chih-chuan*, vol. 2, *chüan* 6, p. 1a, l. 13.

39. For Ts'ai Ching's use of these four words, see *Sung tsai-fu pien-nien lu [chiao-pu]* ([Collated and supplemented recension of] A chronological record of the rescripts appointing and demoting the chief ministers of the Sung dynasty), comp. Hsü Tzu-ming (fl. early 13th century), ed. Wang Jui-lai, 4 vols. (Peking: Chung-hua shu-chü, 1986), vol. 2, *chüan* 13, p. 836, ll. 6, and 14–15; *Huang-ch'ao pien-nien kang-mu pei-yao*, *chüan* 26, p. 18a, l. 3; *chüan* 27, p. 20a, l. 5; *chüan* 28, p. 13b, l. 9; and the biography of Ts'ai Ching in *Sung shih*, vol. 39, *chüan* 472, p. 13724, l. 12.

40. The abolition of this institution took place in 1104. See *Huang-ch'ao pien-nien kang-mu pei-yao*, vol. 2, *chüan* 26, p. 18b, ll. 4–5; and *Sung shih*, vol. 2, *chüan* 19, p. 369, l. 7. For a detailed appraisal of this government agency, see *Sung-tai ch'ao-yen chih-tu yen-chiu* (A study of the salt voucher system of the Sung dynasty), by Tai I-hsüan (Shanghai: Shang-wu yin-shu kuan, 1957), pp. 312–18.

41. On the somewhat unclear exchange rate between old and new salt vouchers, see *Hsüan-ho i-shih*, p. 14, ll. 3–4; and *Huang-ch'ao pien-nien kang-mu pei-yao*, vol. 2, *chüan* 26, p. 25b, ll. 2–3. According to the latter source, this measure was enacted in 1105.

42. For a detailed analysis of Ts'ai Ching's changes in the salt administration, see Tai I-hsüan, *Sung-tai ch'ao-yen chih-tu yen-chiu*, ch. 5, pp. 307–35.

43. For "goose-eye" coins, see Roy, *The Plum in the Golden Vase*, vol. 2, chap. 33, n. 33.

44. This is technically incorrect, since the Chin dynasty ended in 420, and "goose-eye" coins were not minted until 465.

45. This formulaic four-character expression occurs in *Yang-chia fu shih-tai chung-yung yen-i chih-chuan*, vol. 2, *chüan* 7, p. 21a, l. 5; and *Shih-hou chi*, scene 22, p. 77, l. 2.

46. The Ch'ung-ning reign period lasted from 1102 through 1106, and the Ta-kuan reign period from 1107 through 1110.

47. For an illustrated survey of Sung dynasty coinage and an analysis of Ts'ai Ching's monetary policies and their results, see Peng Xinwei, *A Monetary History of*

China, trans. Edward H. Kaplan, 2 vols. (Bellingham: Center for East Asian Studies, Western Washington University, 1993), 1:332–56; and 397–403.

48. The fact that Tseng Hsiao-hsü (1049–1127) objected to this policy initiative of Ts'ai Ching's is mentioned in his biography in *Sung shih*, vol. 38, *chüan* 453, p. 13319, l. 8.

49. Han Lü (fl. early 12th century) is a historical figure, the brother-in-law of Ts'ai Ching's son Ts'ai T'ao (d. after 1147), who was appointed vice-minister of the Ministry of Personnel in 1124. See *Sung shih*, vol. 39, *chüan* 472, p. 13727, l. 4; and *Hsü Tzu-chih t'ung-chien*, vol. 2, *chüan* 95, p. 2480, l. 8.

50. This four-character expression occurs in the biography of An Lu-shan (d. 757) in *Chiu T'ang shu*, vol. 16, *chüan* 200a, p. 5370, l. 4; *San-kuo chih t'ung-su yen-i*, vol. 1, *chüan* 1, p. 16, l. 6; and *Sui-T'ang liang-ch'ao shih-chuan*, *chüan* 11, p. 9b, l. 1.

51. This four-character expression occurs in *Yüan-ch'ü hsüan*, 4:1499, ll. 6–7; and *Hai-ling i-shih*, p. 156, l. 3.

52. This measure was enacted by imperial rescript in 1124. See *Huang-ch'ao pien-nien kang-mu pei-yao*, vol. 2, *chüan* 29, p. 18a; *Sung shih*, vol. 2, *chüan* 22, p. 414, ll. 4–5; and *Hsü Tzu-chih t'ung-chien*, vol. 2, *chüan* 95, p. 2475, ll. 7–10.

53. This measure was enacted in 1117, and much of the language of this proposal is taken straight from the standard historical sources. See *Huang-ch'ao pien-nien kang-mu pei-yao*, vol. 2, *chüan* 28, p. 16a, ll. 7–8; and *Hsü Tzu-chih t'ung-chien*, vol. 2, *chüan* 92, p. 2389, l. 15–p. 2390, l. 1.

54. During the Sung dynasty this was located east of what is now Kao-yang district in Hopei province.

55. See Roy, *The Plum in the Golden Vase*, vol. 2, chap. 31, n. 16.

56. A variant of this four-character expression occurs in a speech attributed to the Buddhist monk Shou-hsün (1079–1134) in *Wu-teng hui-yüan*, vol. 3, *chüan* 19, p. 1305, l. 15. It occurs in the same form as in the novel in *Hai-fu shan-t'ang tz'u-kao*, *chüan* 1, p. 27, l. 14.

57. A variant of this couplet occurs in *Hsi-yu chi*, vol. 1, ch. 33, p. 381, l. 4.

58. The same poem, with two insignificant variants, recurs in the *Chin P'ing Mei tz'u-hua*, vol. 5, ch. 95, p. 14b, ll. 2–3.

CHAPTER 49

1. This four-character expression occurs in an anonymous Yüan dynasty lyric, *Ch'üan Chin Yüan tz'u*, 2:1282, lower register, l. 12.

2. This four-character expression occurs in a set of songs by Liu Hsiao-tsu (1522–89), *Ch'üan Ming san-ch'ü*, 2:2314, ll. 14–15.

3. This four-character expression occurs independently in a song by Yang Ch'ao-ying (c. 1270–c. 1352), *Ch'üan Yüan san-ch'ü*, 2:1296, l. 6; *Shui-hu ch'üan-chuan*, vol. 4, ch. 90, p. 1472, l. 16; and a set of songs by Hsüeh Lun-tao (c.1531–c. 1600), *Ch'üan Ming san-ch'ü*, 3:2748, ll. 10–11.

4. This poem occurs in *Ming-hsin pao-chien*, *chüan* 2, p. 4a, l. 14–p. 4b, l. 2. The last line occurs independently in *Yung-hsi yüeh-fu*, *ts'e* 5, p. 22a, ll. 9–10, in an anonymous song suite composed entirely of stock expressions and proverbial sayings; a poem by Li K'ai-hsien (1502–68), *Li K'ai-hsien chi*, 1:151, l. 4; a set of song lyrics by the same author, the pref. to which is dated 1544, ibid., 3:878, l. 10; and a set of songs by Hsüeh

Lun-tao (c. 1531–c. 1600), *Ch'üan Ming san-ch'ü*, 3:2851, ll. 4–5. A variant version of this line also occurs in *Sui-T'ang liang-ch'ao shih-chuan*, *chüan* 12, p. 23b, l. 7.

5. This formulaic four-character expression is ubiquitous in Chinese vernacular literature. See, e.g., *Tung Chieh-yüan Hsi-hsiang chi*, *chüan* 4, p. 88, l. 12; *Yüan-ch'ü hsüan*, 3:933, l. 12; *Chin-ming ch'ih Wu Ch'ing feng Ai-ai*, p. 469, l. 13; *Ch'ien-chin chi*, scene 39, p. 127, l. 12; *San-kuo chih t'ung-su yen-i*, vol. 2, *chüan* 18, p. 850, l. 3; *Ssu-hsi chi*, scene 40, p. 102, l. 2; *Hsi-yu chi*, vol. 1, ch. 8, p. 86, l. 7; *San-pao t'ai-chien Hsi-yang chi t'ung-su yen-i*, vol. 1, ch. 14, p. 175, l. 15; *Yang-chia fu shih-tai chung-yung yen-i chih-chuan*, vol. 2, *chüan* 8, p. 27a, l. 4; *Sui-T'ang liang-ch'ao shih-chuan*, *chüan* 8, p. 9a, ll. 2–3; and *Ta-T'ang Ch'in-wang tz'u-hua*, vol. 1, *chüan* 1, ch. 5, p. 48b, l. 6. It also recurs in the *Chin P'ing Mei tz'u-hua*, vol. 4, ch. 68, p. 1a, ll. 10–11; vol. 5, ch. 81, p. 1a, l. 10; and ch. 84, p. 10a, l. 5.

6. This four-character expression occurs in the *I-ching* (Book of changes). See *Chou-i yin-te*, p. 25, col. 2, l. 15.

7. The wording of these two sentences is drawn, almost verbatim, from the biography of Tseng Hsiao-hsü in the *Sung shih*, vol. 38, *chüan* 453, p. 13319, ll. 7–8. See also *Huang-ch'ao pien-nien kang-mu pei-yao*, vol. 2, *chüan* 27, p. 6a, l. 8–p. 6b, l. 1.

8. This sentence is also derived from the biography of Tseng Hsiao-hsü in the *Sung shih*, vol. 38, *chüan* 453, p. 13319, l. 9. See also *Huang-ch'ao pien-nien kang-mu pei-yao*, vol. 2, *chüan* 27, p. 6b, l. 4. For an interpretation of the significance of this passage for the understanding of the novel as a whole, see Roy, *The Plum in the Golden Vase*, 1:xxxviii–xl.

9. The given name of this character as it appears in the text is P'an-chiu, which makes no sense as a name and is clearly an orthographic error for Sheng-ch'ung, as indicated by the relevant historical records. Sung Sheng-ch'ung (fl. early 12th century) is a historical figure whose role in framing Tseng Hsiao-hsü is described in *Huang-ch'ao pien-nien kang-mu pei-yao*, vol. 2, *chüan* 27, p. 6b, ll. 4–5; and *Sung shih*, vol. 38, *chüan* 453, p. 13319, ll. 9–10. For a discussion of the need for this textual emendation, see Lu Ko and Ma Cheng, *Chin P'ing Mei jen-wu ta-ch'üan* (Great compendium of the characters in the *Chin P'ing Mei*) (Ch'ang-ch'un: Chi-lin wen-shih ch'u-pan she, 1991), pp. 368–69.

10. This four-character expression occurs in *Shuang-chu chi*, scene 26, p. 85, l. 2; and in a memorial by Wang Yung-chi (1528–93), as quoted in *Kuo-se t'ien-hsiang*, vol. 1, *chüan* 1, p. 40b, upper register, l. 6.

11. Sung Ch'iao-nien (1047–1113) is a historical figure who became a protégé of Ts'ai Ching late in life despite the fact that he had been cashiered early in his career for consorting with prostitutes and employing public functionaries for private purposes. For his biography, see *Sung shih*, vol. 32, *chüan* 356, pp. 11207–208.

12. See Roy, *The Plum in the Golden Vase*, vol. 2, chap. 36, n. 10.

13. Hai-yen is the name of a coastal town in Chekiang province that gave its name to one of the four most important styles of southern opera performance that competed with each other for popularity in the course of the sixteenth century. It was a style, thought to have originated in the fifteenth century, that featured northern Mandarin pronunciation despite its southern provenance and emphasized the singing, which was accompanied by percussion instruments only, without woodwinds or strings. This made it especially suitable for performance in private settings, and it was much favored by members of the official class.

14. On "crane's crest red," see Roy, *The Plum in the Golden Vase*, vol. 2, chap. 31, n. 1.

15. This formulaic four-character expression occurs in *P'u-tung Ts'ui Chang chu-yü shih-chi*, p. 13b, l. 17; a song by P'eng Tse (cs 1490), *Ch'üan Ming san-ch'ü*, 1:835, l. 12; a song suite attributed to Wang Chiu-ssu (1468–1551), ibid., 1:986, l. 1; a song suite by Liang Ch'en-yü (1519–91), ibid., 2:2210, l. 2; *Ssu-hsi chi*, scene 36, p. 89, l. 10; and a song suite by Ch'en So-wen (d. c. 1604), *Ch'üan Ming san-ch'ü*, 2:2570, l. 2.

16. See Roy, *The Plum in the Golden Vase*, vol. 2, chap. 27, n. 15.

17. On this type of paper, see ibid., chap. 39, n. 79.

18. This formulaic four-character expression occurs in *Yüan-ch'ü hsüan wai-pien*, 2:575, l. 4; *Hsing-t'ien Feng-yüeh t'ung-hsüan chi*, scene 15, p. 36b, l. 5; and *Ch'üan-Han chih-chuan*, vol. 2, *chüan* 1, p. 5b, l. 4.

19. This formulaic four-character expression occurs in *Hsüan-ho i-shih*, p. 48, l. 13, where it is part of the description of Emperor Hui-tsung's clandestine visit to a house of prostitution. It also recurs in the *Chin P'ing Mei tz'u hua*, vol. 4, ch. 70, p. 12a, ll. 10–11; and ch. 76, p. 7b, ll. 1–2.

20. This formulaic four-character expression recurs in the *Chin P'ing Mei tz'u-hua*, vol. 4, ch. 77, p. 8a, l. 9.

21. This formulaic four-character expression recurs four times in ibid., vol. 3, ch. 59, p. 6a, l. 4; vol. 4, ch. 78, p. 9a, l. 8; vol. 5, ch. 96, p. 5b, ll. 1–2; and ch. 97, p. 2b, l. 11.

22. The locus classicus for this four-character expression is a passage in *Mencius*, which D. C. Lau translates as follows: "Mencius said, 'When speaking to men of consequence it is necessary to look on them with contempt and not be impressed by their lofty position. Their hall is tens of feet high; the capitals are several feet broad. Were I to meet with success, I would not indulge in such things. Their tables, laden with food, measure ten feet across, and their female attendants are counted in the hundreds. Were I to meet with success, I would not indulge in such things. They have a great time drinking, driving and hunting, with a retinue of a thousand chariots. Were I to meet with success I would not indulge in such things. All the things they do I would not do, and everything I do is in accordance with ancient institutions. Why, then, should I cower before them?'" See *Meng-tzu yin-te*, p. 58, 7B.34; and Lau, *Mencius*, p. 201. This expression also occurs in *Yüan-ch'ü hsüan*, 2:812, l. 13; *Yüan-ch'ü hsüan wai-pien*, 1:231, l. 18; [*Chi-p'ing chiao-chu*] *Hsi-hsiang chi*, play no. 1, wedge, p. 1, l. 9; *P'o-yao chi*, *chüan* 1, scene 10, p. 29b, l. 8; *Huai-hsiang chi*, scene 8, p. 20, l. 5; *Tung-t'ien hsüan-chi*, scene 2, p. 9a, l. 7; *Lieh-kuo chih-chuan*, vol. 3, *chüan* 8, p. 48a, l. 5; *Hai-fu shan-t'ang tz'u-kao*, *chüan* 1, p. 24, l. 11; *Yü-ching t'ai*, scene 25, p. 64, ll. 2–3; and recurs in the *Chin P'ing Mei tz'u-hua*, vol. 4, ch. 70, p. 12a, l. 11.

23. This four-character expression occurs in a lyric by Ma Yü (1123–83), *Ch'üan Chin Yüan tz'u*, 1:284, lower register, l. 15; a lyric by T'an Ch'u-tuan (1123–85), ibid., 1:399, lower register, l. 3; a poetic encomium by Liu Ch'u-hsüan (1147–1203), *Ch'üan Chin shih*, 2:116, l. 11; a quatrain by Hou Shan-yüan (12th century), ibid., 2:288, l. 8; *San-ming t'ung-hui*, *chüan* 2, p. 28a, l. 6; and recurs in the *Chin P'ing Mei tz'u-hua*, vol. 4, ch. 62, p. 16b, l. 5; ch. 70, p. 8b, ll. 1–2; and p. 15a, ll. 4–5; and ch. 78, p. 19b, ll. 5–6.

24. This formulaic four-character expression occurs in a letter by Ssu-k'ung T'u (837–908), *Ch'üan T'ang wen*, vol. 17, *chüan* 807, p. 11b, l. 9. It is ubiquitous in

Chinese vernacular literature. See, e.g., *Yüan-ch'ü hsüan*, 2:801, l. 20; *Yüan-ch'ü hsüan wai-pien*, 1:23, ll. 9–10; *P'i-p'a chi*, scene 42, p. 225, l. 4; *Chang Yü-hu su nü-chen kuan chi*, p. 9b, l. 11; *Su Wu mu-yang chi, chüan* 1, scene 5, p. 9a, l. 1; *Cho Wen-chün ssu-pen Hsiang-ju*, scene 2, p. 123, l. 10; *Hsin-ch'iao shih Han Wu mai ch'un-ch'ing*, p. 70, l. 9; *Shui-hu ch'üan-chuan*, vol. 2, ch. 40, p. 641, l. 9; *San-pao t'ai-chien Hsi-yang chi t'ung-su yen-i*, vol. 1, ch. 50, p. 649, l. 11; and an abundance of other occurrences, too numerous to list.

25. This formulaic four-character expression occurs in *Pai Niang-tzu yung-chen Lei-feng T'a*, p. 424, l. 12.

26. Ts'ao Ho (cs 1547) is a historical figure who served for a time in the mid-sixteenth century as supervising secretary of the Ministry of Works. See Lu Ko and Ma Cheng, *Chin P'ing Mei jen-wu ta-ch'üan*, pp. 370–71.

27. This formulaic four-character expression for the feelings associated with love-sickness is ubiquitous in Chinese vernacular literature. See, e.g., *Yüan-ch'ü hsüan*, 1:333, l. 8; a song suite by Tseng Jui (c. 1260–1330), *Ch'üan Yüan san-ch'ü*, 1:523, l. 9; the early vernacular story *Chang Ku-lao chung-kua ch'ü Wen-nü* (Chang Ku-lao plants melons and weds Wen-nü), in *Ku-chin hsiao-shuo*, vol. 2, *chüan* 33, p. 491, l. 13; *Hua-teng chiao Lien-nü ch'eng-Fo chi*, p. 201, l. 9; the middle-period vernacular story *Tu Li-niang mu-se huan-hun* (Tu Li-niang yearns for love and returns to life), in Hu Shih-ying, *Hua-pen hsiao-shuo kai-lun* (A comprehensive study of promptbook fiction), 2 vols. (Peking: Chung-hua shu-chü, 1980), 2:534, l. 29; a song suite attributed to T'ang Yin (1470–1524), *Ch'üan Ming san-ch'ü*, 1:1081, l. 5; a song suite by Liang Ch'en-yü (1519–91), ibid., 2:2221, l. 13; a rhapsody entitled *Nü hsiang-ssu fu* (Rhapsody on female lovesickness), in *Kuo-se t'ien-hsiang*, vol. 1, *chüan* 3, upper register, p. 2b, ll. 6–7; and a song by Shen Ching (1553–1610), *Ch'üan Ming san-ch'ü*, 3:3251, ll. 8–9.

28. This formulaic four-character expression is ubiquitous in Chinese vernacular literature. See, e.g., a lyric by Yen Chi-tao (c. 1031–c. 1106), *Ch'üan Sung tz'u*, 1:257, lower register, l. 1; *T'ien-pao i-shih chu-kung-tiao*, p. 249, l. 10; a song by Hsü Tsai-ssu (14th century), *Ch'üan Yüan san-ch'ü*, 2:1043, l. 2; *Yüan-ch'ü hsüan*, 3:967, ll. 20–21; *Yüan-ch'ü hsüan wai-pien*, 2:628, ll. 1–2; a song attributed to Chu Yu-tun (1379–1439), *Ch'üan Ming san-ch'ü*, 1:283, l. 6; *Shuang-chu chi*, scene 10, p. 28, l. 7; *Ming-chu chi*, scene 12, p. 35, l. 8; *Huai-hsiang chi*, scene 10, p. 26, l. 4; and an abundance of other occurrences, too numerous to list.

29. T'ao Ch'ien (365–427), better known by his courtesy name as T'ao Yüan-ming, was a poet particularly famous for his love of chrysanthemums.

30. This four-character expression occurs in a song suite by Liang Ch'en-yü (1519–91), *Ch'üan Ming san-ch'ü*, 3:2608, l. 2.

31. This four-character expression occurs in a quatrain by Chang Hu (c. 792–c. 854), *Ch'üan T'ang shih*, vol. 8, *chüan* 511, p. 5844, l. 9; a poem by Wang Che (1112–70), *Ch'üan Chin shih*, 1:191, l. 15; and an anonymous Ming dynasty set of songs published in 1471, *Ch'üan Ming san-ch'ü*, 4:4515, l. 9.

32. This four-character expression occurs in a set of songs on the frontier moon by Hsüeh Lun-tao (c. 1531–c. 1600), *Ch'üan Ming san-ch'ü*, 3:2892, l. 4.

33. Variants of this four-character expression occur in *Yüan-ch'ü hsüan*, 4:1534, l. 19; [*Chi-p'ing chiao-chu*] *Hsi-hsiang chi*, play no. 1, scene 2, p. 22, l. 9; *Yüan-ch'ü hsüan wai-pien*, 1:86, l. 6; and 1:209, l. 18; *Tuan-fa chi, chüan* 2, scene 29, p. 19a, l.

6; a set of songs by Liu Hsiao-tsu (1522–89), *Ch'üan Ming san-ch'ü*, 2:2318, l. 6; and a set of songs by Hsüeh Lun-tao (c. 1531–c. 1600), ibid., 3:2759, l. 3.

34. This formulaic four-character expression is ubiquitous in Chinese vernacular literature. See, e.g., a song suite by Kuan Han-ch'ing (13th century), *Ch'üan Yüan san-ch'ü*, 1:174, l. 12; a song suite by Kuan Yün-shih (1286–1324), ibid., 1:375, l. 12; *Yüan-ch'ü hsüan*, 4:1450, l. 14; [*Chi-p'ing chiao-chu*] *Hsi-hsiang chi*, play no. 1, scene 2, p. 22, l. 9; *Yüan-ch'ü hsüan wai-pien*, 1:209, l. 18; *Ching-ch'ai chi*, scene 31, p. 98, l. 1; *Yu-kuei chi*, scene 22, p. 60, l. 7; *K'an p'i-hsüeh tan-cheng Erh-lang Shen*, p. 242, l. 9; *Wu Lun-ch'üan Pei*, chüan 3, scene 21, p. 35b, l. 4; *Chung-ch'ing li-chi*, vol. 2, chüan 6, p. 10b, l. 8; *San-kuo chih t'ung-su yen-i*, vol. 1, chüan 2, p. 71, ll. 22–23; *Chiang Shih yüeh-li chi*, chüan 1, scene 10, p. 16a, l. 10; *Huai-hsiang chi*, scene 9, p. 25, l. 6; *Sui-T'ang liang-ch'ao shih-chuan*, chüan 5, p. 29b, ll. 6–7; and an abundance of other occurrences, too numerous to list.

35. A variant of this four-character expression occurs in *Hsi-yu chi*, vol. 1, ch. 25, p. 282, l. 11.

36. This formulaic four-character expression is ubiquitous in Chinese vernacular literature. See, e.g., *Yüan-ch'ü hsüan*, 4:1432, ll. 10–11; [*Chi-p'ing chiao-chu*] *Hsi-hsiang chi*, play no. 2, scene 4, p. 82, l. 14; *Chin-t'ung Yü-nü Chiao Hung chi*, p. 33, l. 3; *P'o-yao chi*, chüan 2, scene 23, p. 20a, l. 2; a song by Ch'en To (fl. early 16th century), *Ch'üan Ming san-ch'ü*, 1:466, l. 1; *Chiang Shih yüeh-li chi*, chüan 3, scene 32, p. 20b, l. 7; *Huai-hsiang chi*, scene 8, p. 22, l. 2; *Mu-lien chiu-mu ch'üan-shan hsi-wen*, chüan 3, p. 56b, l. 5; and an abundance of other occurrences, too numerous to list.

37. Variants of this couplet occur in *Kuan-shih-yin p'u-sa pen-hsing ching*, p. 65a, l. 4; and *Yüan-ch'ü hsüan*, 4:1699, l. 15. Variants of the first line occur independently in *Lieh-kuo chih-chuan*, vol. 3, chüan 8, p. 40a, l. 6; and *San-pao t'ai-chien Hsi-yang chi t'ung-su yen-i*, vol. 1, ch. 19, p. 251, l. 14. The first line occurs in the same form as in the novel in *Ching-ch'ai chi*, scene 42, p. 124, l. 5.

38. This four-character expression occurs in a set of songs on amorous encounters by Hsüeh Lun-tao (c. 1531–c. 1600), *Ch'üan Ming san-ch'ü*, 3:2899, l. 6.

39. The force of this proverbial expression depends upon a pun between the word *ssu*, meaning "thread," and the word *ssu*, meaning "thought," "longing," or "yearning." Variants of this saying occur in a lyric by Weng Yüan-lung (13th century), *Ch'üan Sung tz'u*, 4:2943, lower register, l. 5; *Chiang Shih yüeh-li chi*, chüan 4, scene 36, p. 6b, l. 9; a song by Li K'ai-hsien (1502–68), *Tz'u-nüeh*, 3:275, l. 4; and a song by Liu Hsiao-tsu (1522–89), *Ch'üan Ming san-ch'ü*, 2:2315, l. 2. It occurs in the same form as in the novel in a song suite by Yang Shen (1488–1559), ibid., 2:1451, l. 12.

40. See Roy, *The Plum in the Golden Vase*, vol. 2, chap. 36, n. 25.

41. Ssu-ch'üan, or Four Springs, is the courtesy name that Hsi-men Ch'ing had adopted because there were four wells on his country estate. See *Chin P'ing Mei tz'u-hua*, vol. 3, ch. 51, p. 15b, l. 10. It has already been mentioned in Roy, *The Plum in the Golden Vase*, vol. 2, p. 351, ll. 26–27.

42. An orthographic variant of this four-character expression occurs in *Yüan-ch'ü hsüan wai-pien*, 1:83, l. 4; and *Wang K'uei*, 4:1518, upper register, l. 8. It occurs in the same form as in the novel in *Huang-chi chin-tan chiu-lien cheng-hsin kuei-chen huan-hsiang pao-chüan* (Precious volume of the golden elixir and nine-petaled lotus of the Imperial Ultimate period that leads to rectifying belief, reverting to the

real, and returning to our true home), originally published in 1498, in *Pao-chüan ch'u-chi*, 8:228, l. 1; and a set of songs by Liu Hsiao-tsu (1522–89), *Ch'üan Ming san-ch'ü*, 2:2312, l. 9.

43. A close variant of this line occurs in an anonymous Ming dynasty song, *Ch'üan Ming san-ch'ü*, 4:4546, l. 10.

44. This four-character expression occurs in a poem by Li Ch'ün-yü (c. 813–c. 861), *Ch'üan T'ang shih*, vol. 9, *chüan* 569, p. 6604, l. 2; and twice in *T'ien-pao i-shih chu-kung-tiao*, p. 100, l. 6; and p. 128, l. 5.

45. A variant of this couplet occurs in *Pai-chia kung-an*, *chüan* 10, ch. 94, p. 12a, l. 13.

46. Hsieh An (320–85), one of the most famous statesmen of the Eastern Chin dynasty (317–420), is said to have kept a female entertainer in his entourage while he was living in retirement in the Eastern Mountains of Chekiang before taking office in 360. See *Shih-shuo Hsin-yü: A New Account of Tales of the World*, by Liu I-ch'ing, trans. Richard B. Mather (Minneapolis: University of Minnesota Press, 1976), p. 207, item 21.

47. Wang Hsi-chih (321–79) is China's most renowned calligrapher. This conversational exchange between a corrupt merchant-official and a venal bureaucrat is surely intended to be ironic since Hsieh An and Wang Hsi-chih are two of the most admired arbiters of taste from the Eastern Chin period.

48. See Roy, *The Plum in the Golden Vase*, vol. 1, chap. 6, n. 28.

49. This four-character expression occurs in *Ta-T'ang Ch'in-wang tz'u-hua*, vol. 1, *chüan* 1, ch. 8, p. 85a, l. 2.

50. This four-character expression occurs in the preface to the *Ying-wu fu* (Rhapsody on the parrot), by Mi Heng (173–98), in *Wen-hsüan*, vol. 1, *chüan* 13, p. 20b, l. 9. It occurs ubiquitously in later literature. See, e.g., *Wen-shih chuan* (Biographies of literary figures), comp. Chang Yin (4th century), in *Shuo-fu san-chung* (*The frontiers of apocrypha*: Three recensions), 10 vols. (Shanghai: Shang-hai ku-chi ch'u-pan she, 1988), 5:2694, p. 2a, l. 5; the preface to a poem by Li Po (701–62), *Ch'üan T'ang shih*, vol. 3, *chüan* 171, p. 1764, l. 1; *T'ang chih-yen* (A gleaning of T'ang anecdotes), by Wang Ting-pao (870–c. 954) (Shanghai: Ku-tien wen-hsüeh ch'u-pan she, 1957), *chüan* 13, p. 145, l. 6; the preface to a lyric by Huang T'ing-chien (1045–1105), *Ch'üan Sung tz'u*, 1:385, lower register, l. 11; an anecdote set in the year 1204 in *T'ing-shih* (Tabletop notes), by Yüeh K'o (1183–c. 1240) (Peking: Chung-hua shu-chü, 1981), *chüan* 11, p. 131, l. 6; the early vernacular story *Shih Hung-chao lung-hu chün-ch'en hui* (Shih Hung-chao: The meeting of dragon and tiger, ruler and minister), in *Ku-chin hsiao-shuo*, vol. 1, *chüan* 15, p. 213, l. 7; *Chien-teng hsin-hua*, *chüan* 1, p. 11, l. 13; *Chien-teng yü-hua*, *chüan* 3, p. 233, l. 15; *Chung-ch'ing li-chi*, vol. 3, *chüan* 7, upper register, p. 29a, l. 12; *San-kuo chih t'ung-su yen-i*, vol. 2, *chüan* 15, p. 681, l. 16; *Hua-ying chi*, p. 877, l. 5; the middle-period vernacular story *K'uei-kuan Yao Pien tiao Chu-ko* (At K'uei-kuan Yao Pien commemorates Chu-ko Liang), in *Ch'ing-p'ing shan-t'ang hua-pen*, p. 307, l. 14; *Huai-ch'un ya-chi*, *chüan* 10, p. 6a, l. 15; *Ch'ien-t'ang hu-yin Chi-tien Ch'an-shih yü-lu* (The recorded sayings of the lakeside recluse of Ch'ien-t'ang, the Ch'an master Crazy Chi [Tao-chi (1148–1209)]), fac. repr. of 1569 edition, in *Ku-pen hsiao-shuo ts'ung-k'an, ti-pa chi*, vol. 1, p. 25b, l. 9; and *Sui-T'ang liang-ch'ao shih-chuan*, *chüan* 9, p. 21a, ll. 7–8.

51. This four-character expression occurs in *Ch'ü-wei chiu-wen* (Old stories heard in Ch'ü-wei), by Chu Pien (d. 1144), in *Pi-chi hsiao-shuo ta-kuan*, vol. 4, *ts'e* 8, *chüan* 7, p. 4a, l. 9; *Yü Chung-chü t'i-shih yü shang-huang*, p. 76, l. 3; *Chien-teng hsin-hua*, *chüan* 1, p. 11, l. 13; *Chien-teng yü-hua*, *chüan* 5, p. 292, l. 6; *Hua-ying chi*, p. 877, ll. 5–6; *Hsün-fang ya-chi*, vol. 2, *chüan* 4, p. 7a, l. 13; *T'ien-yüan ch'i-yü*, vol. 3, *chüan* 8, p. 10b, l. 10; and *Ch'ien-t'ang hu-yin Chi-tien Ch'an-shih yü-lu*, p. 36b, l. 9.

52. This four-character expression occurs three times in lyrics by Ou-yang Hsiu (1007–72), *Ch'üan Sung tz'u*, 1:127, upper register, l. 3; 1:134, upper register, l. 16; and 1:143, lower register, l. 10. It also occurs in a preface to the recorded sayings of the Buddhist monk Fa-yen (d. 1104), by Chang Ching-hsiu (cs 1067), in *Ku tsun-su yü-lu* (The recorded sayings of eminent monks of old), comp. Tse Tsang-chu (13th century), in *Hsü Tsang-ching* (Continuation of the Buddhist canon), 150 vols., fac. repr. (Hong Kong: Hsiang-kang ying-yin *Hsü Tsang-ching* wei-yüan hui, 1967), 118:227a, upper register, l. 1; *Hsiao fu-jen chin-ch'ien tseng nien-shao*, p. 230, l. 1; *Ming-chu chi*, scene 3, p. 5, l. 8; and *Mu-lien chiu-mu ch'üan-shan hsi-wen*, *chüan* 1, p. 44b, l. 3.

53. This four-character expression occurs in an anonymous Sung dynasty lyric, in *Ch'üan Sung tz'u*, 5:3837, lower register, l. 3; and *Ssu-shih hua-yüeh sai chiao-jung*, scene 1, p. 3a, l. 9.

54. See Roy, *The Plum in the Golden Vase*, vol. 2, chap. 35, n. 31.

55. This line occurs in *Pai-yüeh t'ing chi*, *chüan* 1, scene 25, p. 45a, l. 1.

56. On the Herd Boy and the Weaving Maid, see Roy, *The Plum in the Golden Vase*, vol. 1, chap. 2, n. 40.

57. This four-character expression occurs in *San-kuo chih t'ung-su yen-i*, vol. 1, *chüan* 7, p. 339, l. 12; *T'ang-shu chih-chuan t'ung-su yen-i*, vol. 1, *chüan* 5, p. 53a, l. 9; and *Hua-shen san-miao chuan*, p. 10b, l. 8.

58. A variant of this four-character expression, with the addition of another word, occurs in *T'ien-yüan ch'i-yü*, vol. 3, *chüan* 8, p. 2a, ll. 5–6. It occurs in the same form as in the novel in a letter to Li K'ai-hsien (1502–68) by Liu Hui (cs 1535), *Li K'ai-hsien chi*, 3:921, ll. 2–3.

59. This four-character expression occurs in *Kuei-chien chiao-ch'ing*, 4:1548, upper register, ll. 9–10. The term "this culture of ours" stands for the value system of the educated Confucian elite. For a book-length exposition of the concept, see Peter K. Bol, *"This Culture of Ours": Intellectual Transitions in T'ang and Sung China* (Stanford: Stanford University Press, 1992), passim.

60. This four-character expression occurs in *Pei Sung chih-chuan*, vol. 3, *chüan* 9, p. 17b, l. 8; *T'ien-yüan ch'i-yü*, vol. 3, *chüan* 7, p. 25b, l. 7; *Liu sheng mi Lien chi*, *chüan* 2, lower register, p. 6a, l. 3; *Huang-Ming k'ai-yün ying-wu chuan*, *chüan* 7, p. 2a, l. 14; and *Hai-ling i-shih*, p. 74, l. 12.

61. This four-character expression occurs in *San-kuo chih t'ung-su yen-i*, vol. 1, *chüan* 12, p. 534, l. 18.

62. This four-character expression occurs in *Hsiu-ju chi*, scene 15, p. 41, l. 9; and *Pa-i chi*, scene 28, p. 61, ll. 3–4.

63. This four-character expression occurs in a lyric by Chou Pang-yen (1056–1121), *Ch'üan Sung tz'u*, 2:613, upper register, l. 3; a song by Kuan Yün-shih (1286–1324), *Ch'üan Yüan san-ch'ü*, 1:374, l. 9; and a song by Ch'iao Chi (d. 1345), ibid., 1:621, ll. 1–2.

64. A variant of this four-character expression occurs in the *Shih-ching* (Book of songs). See *Mao-shih yin-te* (Concordance to the Mao version of the *Book of Songs*) (Tokyo: Japan Council for East Asian Studies, 1962), song no. 94, p. 19. It is ubiquitous, in the form in which it appears in the novel, in later Chinese literature. See, e.g., a quatrain by Liu Shang (fl. late 8th century), *Ch'üan T'ang shih*, vol. 5, *chüan* 304, p. 3458, l. 14; a lyric by Chou Pang-yen (1056–1121), *Ch'üan Sung tz'u*, 2:596, upper register, l. 13; a song by Hsü Yen (d. 1301), *Ch'üan Yüan san-ch'ü*, 1:80, l. 10; a song suite by Shih Tzu-an (14th century), *Ch'üan Ming san-ch'ü*, 1:246, l. 11; *Wu Lun-ch'üan Pei*, *chüan* 3, scene 18, p. 20a, l. 6; *P'u-tung Ts'ui Chang chu-yü shih-chi*, p. 14b, l. 14; *Chang Sheng ts'ai-luan teng chuan*, p. 7, l. 10; *Sui-T'ang liang-ch'ao shih-chuan*, *chüan* 7, p. 39a, l. 6; *Yen-chih chi*, *chüan* 1, scene 8, p. 11b, l. 11; *Hai-fu shan-t'ang tz'u-kao*, *chüan* 3, p. 186, l. 6; *Hsi-yu chi*, vol. 1, ch. 36, p. 418, l. 7; *Shuang-lieh chi*, scene 11, p. 31, l. 1; *San-pao t'ai-chien Hsi-yang chi t'ung-su yen-i*, vol. 1, ch. 39, p. 506, l. 7; and an abundance of other occurrences, too numerous to list.

65. This line is derived from the last line of a quatrain by Po Chü-i (772–846), which reads, "The purple myrtle blossom confronts the Secretary of the Hall of Purple Myrtle." See *Ch'üan T'ang shih*, vol. 7, *chüan* 442, p. 4934, l. 7. The Hall of Purple Myrtle was a literary name for the Central Drafting Office, in which Po Chü-i held a post as secretary at the time the poem was written. The entire quatrain by Po Chü-i is quoted in *Yüan-ch'ü hsüan wai-pien*, 3:899, ll. 8–9; and the last line is quoted independently in ibid., 2:356, l. 17. This poem, as given in the novel, may be a reworking of a frequently anthologized quatrain by Hung Tzu-k'uei (1176–1236), which contains a good deal of similar language and imagery. See *Ch'üan Sung shih*, 55:34610, l. 17.

66. This refers to a variety of Chinese fortune-telling that is still commonly practiced today, in which a set of numbered bamboo sticks with meaningful inscriptions on them are shaken in a tube until one of them emerges from the rest and is then interpreted for its mantic significance. For a detailed description of this practice, see Richard J. Smith, *Fortune-tellers and Philosophers: Divination in Traditional Chinese Society* (Boulder: Westview Press, 1991), pp. 235–44.

67. This four-character expression occurs in *Hsi-yu chi*, vol. 1, ch. 12, p. 135, l. 5.

68. This four-character expression occurs in *Ching-ch'ai chi*, scene 40, p. 120, l. 7.

69. Executions were customarily carried out in the autumn because, according to the traditional system of correlative correspondences, autumn was regarded as the season of death. This four-character expression occurs twice in the subcommentary to the T'ang penal code, attributed to Chang-sun Wu-chi (d. 659). See *T'ang-lü shu-i* (The T'ang code with subcommentary), comp. Chang-sun Wu-chi (Taipei: Shang-wu yin-shu kuan, 1973), *chüan* 1, p. 16, ll. 12–13; and *chüan* 3, p. 55, l. 7. It also occurs in *Yüan-ch'ü hsüan*, 3:1125, l. 8; and 4:1654, l. 6; *Shih-wu kuan hsi-yen ch'eng ch'iao-huo*, p. 705, l. 14; *Shui-hu ch'üan-chuan*, vol. 2, ch. 40, p. 644, l. 5; and *Ming shih* (History of the Ming dynasty), comp. Chang T'ing-yü (1672–1755) et al., 28 vols. (Peking: Chung-hua shu-chü, 1974), vol. 8, *chüan* 93, p. 2292, l. 7.

70. This four-character expression occurs in the early Ming tsa-chü drama *Yü-ch'iao hsien-hua* (A casual dialogue between a fisherman and a woodcutter), in *Ku-pen yüan Ming tsa-chü*, vol. 4, scene 4, p. 12b, l. 7; and *Pao-chien chi*, scene 18, p. 36, l. 12.

71. A Buddhist monk named Tao-chien (fl. early 12th century) is mentioned in *Lin Ling-su chuan* (The story of Lin Ling-su), by Keng Yen-hsi (fl. early 12th century), as quoted in *Pin-t'ui lu* (Records written after my guests have left), by Chao Yü-shih

(1175–1231) (Taipei: Kuang-wen shu-chü, 1970), *chüan* 1, p. 6b, ll. 3–5. The same passage also appears in *Hsüan-ho i-shih*, p. 68, ll. 3–4.

72. This formulaic four-character expression occurs in *Chang Ku-lao chung-kua ch'ü Wen-nü*, p. 499, l. 8; *Shen-hsiang ch'üan-pien*, *chüan* 636, p. 22b, l. 9; *Ta-Sung chung-hsing yen-i*, *chüan* 2, p. 17a, l. 4; *Hsi-yu chi*, vol. 2, ch. 67, p. 762, l. 11; *Sui-T'ang liang-ch'ao shih-chuan*, *chüan* 12, p. 47b, l. 8; *Ts'an-T'ang Wu-tai shih yen-i chuan*, ch. 6, p. 15, l. 2; and *San-pao t'ai-chien Hsi-yang chi t'ung-su yen-i*, vol. 1, ch. 26, p. 340, l. 3.

73. These three fanciful place names are given in more innocent form in the text of the novel, a literal translation of which would be Cold Court Temple, beneath Waist-High Peak, in Dense Pine Forest. However, the key words *t'ing* (court), *ch'i* (high, as in waist-high), and *sung* (pine) pun with the words *t'ing* (shiver), *ch'i* (navel), and *sung* (sperm). I have chosen to translate the puns since they were obviously intended to alert readers, if they have not already caught on, to the double entendre in the description of the appearance and behavior of the Indian monk.

74. This formulaic four-character expression occurs in *Hsi-yu chi*, vol. 1, ch. 33, p. 379, l. 7; *Ts'an-T'ang Wu-tai shih yen-i chuan*, ch. 31, p. 124, l. 1; and *San-pao t'ai-chien Hsi-yang chi t'ung-su yen-i*, vol. 1, ch. 13, p. 163, l. 6. It also recurs in the *Chin P'ing Mei tz'u-hua*, vol. 5, ch. 100, p. 15a, l. 2.

75. Orthographic variants of this reduplicative compound occur in *Hsi-yu chi*, vol. 1, ch. 36, p. 416, l. 11; and *Hai-ling i-shih*, p. 116, l. 4.

76. This formulaic four-character expression is ubiquitous in Chinese popular literature. See, e.g., a lyric by Yang Tse-min (13th century), *Ch'üan Sung tz'u*, 4:3013, upper register, l. 10; an anonymous Yüan dynasty song suite, *Ch'üan Yüan san-ch'ü*, 2:1855, l. 4; *Cheng Chieh-shih li-kung shen-pi kung*, p. 665, l. 7; the long literary tale *Chiao Hung chuan* (The Story of Chiao-niang and Fei-hung), by Sung Yüan (14th century), in *Ku-tai wen-yen tuan-p'ien hsiao-shuo hsüan-chu, erh-chi* (An annotated selection of classic literary tales, second collection), ed. Ch'eng Po-ch'üan (Shanghai: Shang-hai ku-chi ch'u-pan she, 1984), p. 309, l. 14; a song suite by Ch'en To (fl. early 16th century), *Ch'üan Ming san-ch'ü*, 1:666, l. 11; and an anonymous song suite in *Yung-hsi yüeh-fu*, *ts'e* 12, p. 57a, l. 5.

77. For a discussion of the significance of this motif and an illustration of what a typical example looked like, see *Chung-kuo chi-hsiang t'u-an* (Chinese auspicious art motifs), comp. Nozaki Seikin (Taipei: Chung-wen t'u-shu ku-fen yu-hsien kung-ssu, 1979), pp. 504, and 508. This motif is referred to in *Shui-hu ch'üan-chuan*, vol. 3, ch. 56, p. 944, l. 13; and *San-pao t'ai-chien Hsi-yang chi t'ung-su yen-i*, vol. 1, ch. 35, p. 458, l. 9.

78. On these features of cabriole legs, see Roy, *The Plum in the Golden Vase*, vol. 2, chap. 34, n. 5, and n. 6.

79. This formulaic four-character expression is ubiquitous in Chinese vernacular literature. See, e.g., a lyric by Yüan Shih-yüan (14th century), *Ch'üan Chin Yüan tz'u*, 2:1060, upper register, l. 4; *Ch'ien-Han shu p'ing-hua*, p. 57, ll. 2–3; *Hsiao Sun-t'u*, scene 2, p. 261, l. 4; *Yüan-ch'ü hsüan*, 3:1221, l. 8; *Yüan-ch'ü hsüan wai-pien*, 1:93, l. 4; a song by Yang Ch'ao-ying (c. 1270–c. 1352), *Ch'üan Yüan san-ch'ü*, 2:1292, l. 8; *P'i-p'a chi*, scene 33, p. 184, l. 9; *Ching-ch'ai chi*, scene 35, p. 107, l. 6; the earliest extant printed edition of the Yüan-Ming ch'uan-ch'i drama *Pai-t'u chi* (The white rabbit), *[Hsin-pien] Liu Chih-yüan huan-hsiang Pai-t'u chi* ([Newly compiled] Liu Chih-

yüan's return home: The white rabbit), in *Ming Ch'eng-hua shuo-ch'ang tz'u-hua ts'ung-k'an* (Corpus of prosimetric tz'u-hua narratives published in the Ch'eng-hua reign period [1465–87] of the Ming dynasty), 12 *ts'e* (Shanghai: Shanghai Museum, 1973), *ts'e* 12, p. 4b, l. 9; *P'o-yao chi, chüan* 2, scene 26, p. 30a, l. 3; a song by Wang Chiu-ssu (1468–1551) written in 1528, *Ch'üan Ming san-ch'ü*, 1:876, l. 10; *Shui-hu ch'üan-chuan*, vol. 4, ch. 85, p. 1401, l. 10; *Ch'üan-Han chih-chuan*, vol. 2, *chüan* 4, p. 3b, l. 14; and an abundance of other occurrences, too numerous to list.

80. This four-character expression occurs in *Yüan-ch'ü hsüan*, 4:1434, l. 17; *Yüan-ch'ü hsüan wai-pien*, 2:518, l. 14; *Shui-hu ch'üan-chuan*, vol. 2, ch. 41, p. 659, l. 12; and *Hsi-yu chi*, vol. 1, ch. 23, p. 266, l. 7.

81. This four-character expression is ultimately derived from a passage in the *Lun-yü* (The analects of Confucius), in which it is said that when a certain well-to-do disciple of Confucius went to Ch'i, he drove sleek horses and was clothed in light furs. See *Lun-yü yin-te*, Book 6, p. 10, l. 4. This expression occurs ubiquitously in later Chinese literature. See, e.g., a lyric by Hsin Ch'i-chi (1140–1207), *Ch'üan Sung tz'u*, 3:1894, upper register, l. 6; *Yüan-ch'ü hsüan*, 1:136, l. 9; *Ching-ch'ai chi*, scene 8, l. 12; *Shen-hsiang ch'üan-pien, chüan* 639, p. 12b, l. 7; *Hsiu-ju chi*, scene 7, p. 18, l. 1; *Chiang Shih yüeh-li chi, chüan* 1, scene 5, p. 7b, l. 8; a song suite by K'ang Hai (1475–1541), *Ch'üan Ming san-ch'ü*, 1:1180, l. 11; *Shui-hu ch'üan-chuan*, vol. 3, ch. 85, p. 1397, l. 7; *Pao-chien chi*, scene 11, p. 24, l. 15; *Ta-Sung chung-hsing yen-i*, vol. 2, *chüan* 7, p. 33a, l. 6; *Tung-t'ien hsüan-chi*, scene 2, p. 7a, l. 14; the collection of literary tales entitled *Mi-teng yin-hua* (Tales told while searching for a lamp), by Shao Ching-chan (16th century), author's pref. dated 1592, in *Chien-teng hsin-hua [wai erh-chung]*, *chüan* 1, p. 327, l. 1; *Shih-hou chi*, scene 26, p. 90, l. 3; and an abundance of other occurrences, too numerous to list.

82. On Maitreya Buddha, see Alan Sponberg and Helen Hardacre, eds., *Maitreya, the Future Buddha* (Cambridge: Cambridge University Press, 1988).

83. The Calico Bag Monk, also known as the Laughing Buddha, of Chinese popular religion is said to have been an avatar of the Buddha Maitreya, who was active in the Ning-po area of Chekiang in the late T'ang period and died in the year 916. See *Wu-teng hui-yüan*, vol. 1, *chüan* 2, pp. 121–23; E.T.C. Werner, *A Dictionary of Chinese Mythology* (New York: The Julian Press, 1961), pp. 303–305; and Meir Shahar, *Crazy Ji: Chinese Religion and Popular Literature* (Cambridge: Harvard University Press, 1998), pp. 39–40.

84. A version of this quatrain occurs in *Cheng Chieh-shih li-kung shen-pi kung*, p. 656, l. 2; and another version recurs in the *Chin P'ing Mei tz'u-hua*, vol. 5, ch. 90, p. 12a, ll. 4–5. The last line also occurs independently in *Ming-hsin pao-chien, chüan* 2, p. 6a, l. 2.

CHAPTER 50

1. This four-character expression occurs in *Yüan-ch'ü hsüan*, 2:540, l. 20; and 2:783, l. 20; *Yüan-ch'ü hsüan wai-pien*, 1:19, l. 5; and 3:908, l. 21; a song by Chang Ming-shan (14th century), *Ch'üan Yüan san-ch'ü*, 2:1282, l. 11; a set of songs by Chao Nan-hsing (1550–1627), *Ch'üan Ming san-ch'ü*, 3:3217, l. 12; and recurs in the *Chin P'ing Mei tz'u-hua*, vol. 5, ch. 88, p. 9a, l. 1. Orthographic variants of the same expression also occur in an anecdote included in *Shan-chü hsin-hua* (New tales recorded while

dwelling in the mountains), comp. Yang Yü (1285–1361), in *Pi-chi hsiao-shuo ta-kuan*, vol. 5, *ts'e* 11, p. 2b, l. 4; and a song by K'ang Hai (1475–1541), *Ch'üan Ming san-ch'ü*, 1:1124, l. 1.

2. This four-character expression occurs in *Hai-fu shan-t'ang tz'u-kao, chüan* 3, p. 146, l. 12; and a song suite by Wang K'o-tu (c. 1526–c. 1594), *Ch'üan Ming san-ch'ü*, 2:2475, l. 13; and recurs three times in the *Chin P'ing Mei tz'u-hua*, vol. 4, ch. 75, p. 11a, l. 6; p. 12a, l. 6; and p. 16a, ll. 6–7. Orthographic variants of the same expression also occur in song suites by Ch'en To (fl. early 16th century), *Ch'üan Ming san-ch'ü*, 1:605, l. 14; and 1:612, l. 13; and *[Hsiao-shih] Chen-k'ung sao-hsin pao-chüan*, 19:178, ll. 2–3.

3. This four-character expression occurs in the biography of P'ang Yün (d. 808), in *Tsu-t'ang chi* (Patriarchal hall collection), ed. Wu Fu-hsiang and Ku Chih-ch'uan, originally published in 952 (Ch'ang-sha: Yüeh-lu shu-she, 1996), *chüan* 15, p. 348, l. 14; a commentary on the *Vajracchedikā prajñāpāramitā sutra*, by Chang Shang-ying (1043–1121), as quoted in *Chin-kang ching chi-chu* (The *Vajracchedikā prajñāpāramitā sutra* with collected commentaries), comp. by the Yung-lo emperor of the Ming dynasty (r. 1402–24), pref. dated 1424, fac. repr. of original edition (Shanghai: Shanghai ku-chi ch'u-pan she, 1984), p. 143a, column 3; another commentary on the same work by the Buddhist monk Yüan-wu (1063–1135), ibid., p. 73a, column, 4; *Ju-ju chü-shih yü-lu, chia-chi, chüan* 1, p. 3b, l. 4; an anonymous Sung dynasty lyric, *Ch'üan Sung tz'u*, 5:3765, upper register, l. 6; *K'u-kung wu-tao chüan*, 1:86, l. 2; *P'o-hsieh hsien-cheng yao-shih chüan*, 2:27, l. 2; and *P'u-ming ju-lai wu-wei liao-i pao-chüan* (Precious volume of the Tathāgatha P'u-ming who thoroughly comprehends the meaning of Nonactivism), by P'u-ming (d. 1562), completed in 1558, in *Pao-chüan ch'u-chi*, 4:590, l. 5.

4. This four-character expression is ultimately derived from a passage on the subject of fasting in *Chuang-tzu*, which Burton Watson translates as follows: "Yen Hui said, 'My family is poor. I haven't drunk wine or eaten any strong foods for several months.' " See *Chuang-tzu yin-te* (A concordance to *Chuang-tzu*) (Cambridge: Harvard University Press, 1956), ch. 4, p. 9, l. 15; and *The Complete Works of Chuang Tzu*, trans. Burton Watson (New York: Columbia University Press, 1968), ch. 4, p. 57, ll. 25–26.

5. These two three-character phrases occur together in *Yüan-ch'ü hsüan wai-pien*, 2:423, l. 16; *Hsi-yu chi*, vol. 1, ch. 23, p. 261, l. 1; *Pa-i chi*, scene 40, p. 85, l. 2; and recur in the *Chin P'ing Mei tz'u-hua*, vol. 4, ch. 74, p. 12a, l. 4.

6. This four-character expression occurs in a speech attributed to the Buddhist monk I-hsüan (d. 867), the founder of the Lin-chi sect of Ch'an Buddhism, in *Ku tsun-su yü-lu, chüan* 4, p. 101a, lower register, l. 5; *Chin-ming ch'ih Wu Ch'ing feng Ai-ai*, p. 469, l. 10; the ch'uan-ch'i drama *Yüeh Fei p'o-lu tung-ch'uang chi* (Yüeh Fei defeats the barbarians: the plot at the eastern window), by Chou Li (15th century), in *Ku-pen hsi-ch'ü ts'ung-k'an, ch'u-chi*, item no. 21, *chüan* 2, scene 36, p. 27a, l. 6; and the anonymous Ming tsa-chü drama *Li Yün-ch'ing te-wu sheng-chen* (Li Yün-ch'ing attains enlightenment and achieves transcendence), in *Ku-pen Yüan Ming tsa-chü*, vol. 4, scene 2, p. 8a, l. 12.

7. This line occurs in *Su Wu mu-yang chi, chüan* 1, scene 9, p. 22a, l. 6.

8. This formulaic four-character expression is ubiquitous in Chinese vernacular literature. See, e.g., *Chin-ming ch'ih Wu Ch'ing feng Ai-ai*, p. 468, l. 14; *K'an p'i-hsüeh tan-cheng Erh-lang Shen*, p. 259, l. 5; *Chao Po-sheng ch'a-ssu yü Jen-tsung*, p. 166, l.

3; *Jen hsiao-tzu lieh-hsing wei shen*, p. 577, l. 11; *Shui-hu ch'üan-chuan*, vol. 2, ch. 39, p. 619, l. 5; *Ta-Sung chung-hsing yen-i*, vol. 1, *chüan* 1, p. 41a, l. 2; *T'ang-shu chih-chuan t'ung-su yen-i*, vol. 1, *chüan* 2, p. 46a, ll. 10–11; *Pei Sung chih-chuan*, vol. 3, *chüan* 8, p. 25b, l. 3; *Lieh-kuo chih-chuan*, vol. 2, *chüan* 5, p. 44a, l. 6; *Hsi-yu chi*, vol. 1, ch. 3, p. 28, ll. 15–16; *Ch'üan-Han chih-chuan*, vol. 2, *chüan* 4, p. 15a, l. 11; *Huang-Ming k'ai-yün ying-wu chuan*, *chüan* 4, p. 15a, l. 13; *Pai-chia kung-an*, *chüan* 1, p. 4b, l. 12; and *San-pao t'ai-chien Hsi-yang chi t'ung-su yen-i*, vol. 1, ch. 23, p. 305, l. 12.

9. This sentence is probably derived from the scurrilous mid- sixteenth-century novelette *Ju-i chün chuan* (The tale of Lord As You Like It), Japanese movable type edition, colophon dated 1880, p. 9b, l. 2. For a critical study and an annotated translation of this work, see Charles R. Stone, *The Fountainhead of Chinese Erotica: The Lord of Perfect Satisfaction (Ruyijun zhuan)* (Honolulu: University of Hawai'i Press, 2003).

10. This four-character expression occurs in *Ju-i chün chuan*, p. 9b, ll. 9–10.

11. This clause is derived verbatim from ibid., p. 11a, l. 9.

12. This four-character expression occurs in *[Hsiao-shih] Chen-k'ung sao-hsin pao-chüan*, 19:222, l. 4.

13. Versions of this idiom for events that are rare or unlikely, if not impossible, occur in a lyric by Huang T'ing-chien (1045–1105), *Ch'üan Sung tz'u*, 1:397, upper register, l. 5; a deathbed gatha by the Buddhist monk Shih-t'i (1108–79), *Wu-teng hui-yüan*, vol. 3, *chüan* 20, p. 1364, l. 13; and *Mu-tan t'ing*, scene 23, p. 118, l. 9.

14. This four-character expression occurs in an anonymous Sung dynasty lyric, *Ch'üan Sung tz'u*, 5:3663, upper register, l. 14; *Yüan-ch'ü hsüan*, 1:78, l. 21; *Hsing-t'ien Feng-yüeh t'ung-hsüan chi*, scene 4, p. 12b, l. 6; *[Hsiao-shih] Chen-k'ung sao-hsin pao-chüan*, 19:56, ll. 2–3; a set of songs by Liu Hsiao-tsu (1522–89), *Ch'üan Ming san-ch'ü*, 2:2321, l. 2; a set of songs by Hsüeh Lun-tao (c. 1531–c. 1600), ibid., 3:2766, l. 9; and recurs in the *Chin P'ing Mei tz'u-hua*, vol. 5, ch. 89, p. 5a, ll. 5–6. The same expression, with an orthographic variant, also occurs twice in *Huang-chi chin-tan chiu-lien cheng-hsin kuei-chen huan-hsiang pao-chüan*, 8:35, l. 4; and 8:209, l. 3.

15. See Roy, *The Plum in the Golden Vase*, vol. 2, chap. 32, n. 5.

16. See ibid., chap. 40, n. 2.

17. Variants of these two lines occur in *San-pao t'ai-chien Hsi-yang chi t'ung-su yen-i*, vol. 2, ch. 61, p. 789, l. 10; and the *Chin P'ing Mei tz'u-hua*, vol. 5, ch. 93, p. 11b, l. 11.

CHAPTER 51

1. This formulaic four-character expression occurs in *K'an p'i-hsüeh tan-cheng Erh-lang shen*, p. 246, l. 3; *Chin-ch'ai chi*, scene 24, p. 46, l. 17; an anonymous set of songs published in 1471, *Ch'üan Ming san-ch'ü*, 4:4511, l. 5; *Chiang Shih yüeh-li chi*, *chüan* 4, scene 39, p. 14b, l. 6; *Yung-hsi yüeh-fu*, ts'e 19, p. 33b, l. 2; and *Hai-fu shan-t'ang tz'u-kao*, *chüan* 3, p. 170, l. 8.

2. This four-character expression occurs in *P'u-tung Ts'ui Chang chu-yü shih-chi*, p. 15b, l. 2.

3. This four-character expression occurs in a lyric by Han Piao (1159–1224), *Ch'üan Sung tz'u*, 4:2248, upper register, l. 13; *Yü-ching t'ai*, scene 5, p. 11, l. 12; and recurs in the *Chin P'ing Mei tz'u-hua*, vol. 4, ch. 73, p. 20b, ll. 6–7.

4. This proverbial saying is ubiquitous in Chinese vernacular literature. See, e.g., *Yüan-ch'ü hsüan*, 3:1178, l. 11; *P'i-p'a chi*, scene 28, p. 161, l. 5; *Sha-kou chi*, scene 2, p. 4, l. 3; *Ming-hsin pao-chien*, *chüan* 2, p. 2a, ll. 4–5; *Hsiang-nang chi*, scene 33, p. 101, l. 6; the ch'uan-ch'i drama *Huan-tai chi* (The return of the belts), by Shen Ts'ai (15th century), in *Ku-pen hsi-ch'ü ts'ung-k'an*, *ch'u-chi*, item 32, *chüan* 1, scene 14, p. 40b, l. 3; the middle-period vernacular story *Ts'ao Po-ming ts'o-k'an tsang chi* (The story of Ts'ao Po-ming and the mistaken identification of the booty), in *Ch'ing-p'ing shan-t'ang hua-pen*, p. 211, l. 14; *Jen hsiao-tzu lieh-hsing wei shen*, p. 577, l. 9; *Shui-hu ch'üan-chuan*, vol. 2, ch. 45, p. 745, l. 6; *Li K'ai-hsien chi*, 3:1024, l. 6; *Liu sheng mi Lien chi*, *chüan* 2, p. 39b, ll. 3–4; *Shuang-lieh chi*, scene 38, p. 105, l. 3; and *Pai-chia kung-an*, *chüan* 7, ch. 59, p. 12a, l. 6. It also recurs twice in the *Chin P'ing Mei tz'u-hua*, vol. 4, ch. 76, p. 25a, l. 1; and ch. 80, p. 12a, ll. 3–4.

5. This idiomatic expression recurs in the *Chin P'ing Mei tz'u-hua*, vol. 5, ch. 97, p. 4b, l. 10.

6. Versions of this proverbial saying occur in *Chin-yin chi*, *chüan* 4, scene 41, p. 19b, l. 2; the volume of historical notes entitled *Shui-tung jih-chi* (Daily jottings east of the river), by Yeh Sheng (1420–74) (Peking: Chung-hua shu-chü, 1980), *chüan* 15, p. 157, l. 14; *Wu Lun-ch'üan Pei*, *chüan* 4, scene 27, p. 24a, l. 1; *Yü-huan chi*, scene 4, p. 8, l. 1; *Yung-hsi yüeh-fu*, ts'e 5, p. 22a, ll. 6–7; and *Mu-lien chiu-mu ch'üan-shan hsi-wen*, *chüan* 2, p. 78a, l. 5.

7. A variant form of this proverbial saying recurs in the *Chin P'ing Mei tz'u-hua*, vol. 4, ch. 76, p. 2b, l. 11.

8. A variant form of this proverbial saying recurs in ibid, vol. 4, ch. 62, p. 5a, l. 10.

9. This proverbial saying occurs in *Yü-chien* (Meaningful notes), by Shen Tso-che (cs 1135), author's pref. dated 1174, in *Ts'ung-shu chi-ch'eng* (A corpus of works from collectanea), 1st series (Shanghai: Shang-wu yin-shu kuan, 1935–37), vol. 296, *chüan* 5, p. 40, l. 9. Variants of this saying also recur in the *Chin P'ing Mei tz'u-hua*, vol. 4, ch. 72, p. 23a, ll. 2–3; and vol. 5, ch. 83, p. 4b, ll. 9–10.

10. This couplet occurs in *Yüan-ch'ü hsüan wai-pien*, 1:141, l. 1; and the Ming tsa-chü drama *Jen chin shu ku-erh hsün-mu* (Identifying the gold [hairpins] and the [jade] comb an orphan seeks his mother), in *Ku-pen Yüan-Ming tsa-chü*, vol. 3, scene 1, p. 3b, ll. 2–3.

11. This four-character expression, occurring either independently or followed by another line, is ubiquitous in Chinese vernacular literature. See, e.g., a speech attributed to the Buddhist monk I-ts'ung (10th century), *Wu-teng hui-yüan*, vol. 2, *chüan* 8, p. 488, l. 4; *Ch'in ping liu-kuo p'ing-hua*, p. 50, l. 10; *Yüan-ch'ü hsüan*, 1:121, l. 7; *Yüan-ch'ü hsüan wai-pien*, 2:424, l. 2; *Yang Wen lan-lu hu chuan*, p. 184, l. 10; *Shih Hung-chao lung-hu chün-ch'en hui*, p. 230, l. 8; the early vernacular story *Wan Hsiu-niang ch'ou-pao shan-t'ing-erh* (Wan Hsiu-niang gets her revenge with a toy pavilion), in *Ching-shih t'ung-yen*, *chüan* 37, p. 563, l. 8; *Sha-kou chi*, scene 23, p. 87, l. 10; *Hei Hsüan-feng chang-i shu-ts'ai*, scene 1, p. 98, l. 28; the middle period vernacular story *Shen Hsiao-kuan i-niao hai ch'i-ming* (Master Shen's bird destroys seven lives), in *Ku-chin hsiao-shuo*, vol. 2, *chüan* 26, p. 400, l. 6; *Ming-chu chi*, scene 31, p. 95, l. 2; *Shui-hu ch'üan-chuan*, vol. 1, ch. 17, p. 244, l. 10; a set of songs by Hsüeh Lun-tao (c. 1531–c. 1600), *Ch'üan Ming san-ch'ü*, 3:2802, l. 14; and *I-hsia chi*, scene 30, p. 80, l. 8.

12. These two lines recur together in the *Chin P'ing Mei tz'u-hua*, vol. 5, ch. 96, p. 8b, ll. 10–11.

13. See Roy, *The Plum in the Golden Vase*, vol. 1, chap. 16, n. 15.

14. This formulaic four-character expression is ubiquitous in Chinese vernacular literature. See, e.g., *Sha-kou chi*, scene 3, p. 7, ll. 4–5; *Huan-sha chi*, scene 24, p. 85, l. 3; *Ming-feng chi*, scene 5, p. 20, l. 12; *Hsi-yu chi*, vol. 2, ch. 52, p. 604, ll. 1–2; and *San-pao t'ai-chien Hsi-yang chi t'ung-su yen-i*, vol. 2, ch. 84, p. 1083, l. 9.

15. This four-character expression occurs in a lyric by Wang Che (1112–70), *Ch'üan Chin Yüan tz'u*, 1:247, l. 1; and a quatrain by Ma Yü (1123–83), *Ch'üan Chin shih*, 1:288, l. 3.

16. This couplet occurs verbatim in *San hsien-shen Pao Lung-t'u tuan-yüan*, p. 171, l. 3.

17. See Roy, *The Plum in the Golden Vase*, vol. 2, chap. 34, pp. 302–3, and n. 18.

18. This four-character expression occurs in *San-kuo chih t'ung-su yen-i*, *chüan* 4, p. 174, l. 15; and *Sui-T'ang liang-ch'ao shih-chuan*, *chüan* 4, p. 20a, l. 8.

19. The eunuch Huang Ching-ch'en (d. 1126) is a historical figure who exercised considerable power during the reign of Emperor Hui-tsung (r. 1100–25). He is mentioned in *Sung-shih*, vol. 9, *chüan* 128, p. 2998; vol. 31, *chüan* 345, p. 10963; vol. 32, *chüan* 351, p. 11103; and *chüan* 363, pp. 11349–50. He is referred to here as Liu-huang t'ai-wei, a designation that I do not know how to translate, and which also occurs in *Hsüan-ho i-shih*, p. 73, l. 2. An anecdote about his death in 1126 is included in *I-chien chih* (Records of I-chien), comp. Hung Mai (1123–1202), 4 vols. (Peking: Chung-hua shu-chü, 1981), vol. 4, *pu* (supplement), *chüan* 1, p. 1549.

20. This four-character expression occurs in *Hsi-yu chi*, vol. 1, ch. 42, p. 484, l. 3.

21. This story is the subject matter of the first scene of play no. 1 of *Hsi-hsiang chi* and provides the occasion for Chang Chün-jui's first meeting with Ts'ui Ying-ying. See *[Chi-p'ing chiao-chu] Hsi-hsiang chi*, play no. 1, scene 1; and West and Idema, *The Moon and the Zither*, pp. 171–81.

22. This idiomatic expression occurs in *Shui-hu ch'üan-chuan*, vol. 1, ch. 10, p. 157, l. 10; and *Hai-fu shan-t'ang tz'u-kao*, *chüan* 2a, p. 93, l. 13.

23. This four-character expression occurs in *Yüan-ch'ü hsüan wai-pien*, 3:735, l. 13.

24. This is a type of long-haired and bushy-tailed cat that was probably introduced into China from Southeast Asia. Twenty of them were allegedly presented to the Chinese throne by the kingdom of Lavo, in what is now Thailand, during one of the famous maritime expeditions of the eunuch Cheng Ho (1371–1433). See *San-pao t'ai-chien Hsi-yang chi t'ung-su yen-i*, vol. 1, ch. 33, p. 432, l. 13.

25. The four-character expression *pu-te jen-i*, which I have translated as "obnoxious," literally means "unable to obtain the approbation of others." It occurs in the transmitted text of the Taoist work *T'ai-p'ing ching* (Scripture on great peace), much of the content of which is thought to date from the second century A.D. See *T'ai-p'ing ching ho-chiao* (A collated text of the Scripture on great peace), ed. Wang Ming (Peking: Chung-hua shu-chü, 1985), *chüan* 50, p. 174, l. 5. It recurs three times in the *Chin P'ing Mei tz'u-hua*, vol. 3, ch. 52, p. 4b, l. 2; p. 13a, l. 11; and vol. 4, ch. 68, p. 12b, l. 4. In its occurrences in the novel it is employed exclusively as a pejorative expression in passages of vituperation.

26. See Roy, *The Plum in the Golden Vase*, vol. 2, chap. 27, n. 59.

27. An aphrodisiac of this name is mentioned in a list of sexual stimulants in *Hai-ling i-shih*, p. 54, l. 3. It is mentioned three more times in the *Chin P'ing Mei tz'u-hua*, vol. 4, ch. 73, p. 1b, l. 7, where it is described as a medicinal powder; ch. 77, p. 16b, l. 4; and vol. 5, ch. 83, p. 9a, l. 3.

28. This formulaic four-character expression is ubiquitous in Chinese vernacular literature. See, e.g., *Huan-men tzu-ti ts'o li-shen*, scene 5, p. 233, l. 4; *Yüan-ch'ü hsüan*, 4:1402, l. 18; *Yüan-ch'ü hsüan wai-pien*, 3:940, l. 21; *Hsi-hu san-t'a chi*, p. 25, l. 15; *Sha-kou chi*, scene 13, p. 45, l. 1; *Yü-ch'iao hsien-hua*, scene 4, p. 11a, l. 11; *San-kuo chih t'ung-su yen-i*, vol. 2, *chüan* 15, p. 688, l. 6; *Shui-hu ch'üan-chuan*, vol. 1, ch. 24, p. 355, l. 11; *Yüeh-ming Ho-shang tu Liu Ts'ui*, p. 438, l. 3; *Hung-fu chi*, scene 31, p. 64, l. 12; *Hsi-yu chi*, vol. 1, ch. 37, p. 421, l. 11; *San-pao t'ai-chien Hsi-yang chi t'ung-su yen-i*, vol. 1, ch. 49, p. 628, l. 7; and a song by Chao Nan-hsing (1550–1627), *Ch'üan Ming san-ch'ü*, 3:3220, l. 12.

29. There is an anecdote about Li K'ai-hsien (1502–68) that shows he was probably familiar with some version of this joke. See *Li K'ai-hsien chi*, 3:1030, ll. 14–16; and Pu Chien, *Chin P'ing Mei tso-che Li K'ai-hsien k'ao* (An inquiry into Li K'ai-hsien's authorship of the *Chin P'ing Mei*) (Lan-chou: Kan-su jen-min ch'u-pan she, 1988), pp. 276–78.

30. This four-character expression occurs in *Ju-i chün chuan*, p. 13a, l. 10.

31. This four-character expression occurs in a set of songs on the subject of lovesickness by Hsüeh Lun-tao (c. 1531–c. 1600), *Ch'üan Ming san-ch'ü*, 3:2876, l. 6.

32. This formulaic four-character expression, with some variation in orthography, occurs in the early vernacular story *Ts'ui Ya-nei pai-yao chao-yao* (The white falcon of Minister Ts'ui's son embroils him with demons), in *Ching-shih t'ung-yen*, *chüan* 19, p. 266, l. 10; *Chang Sheng ts'ai-luan teng chuan*, p. 6, l. 3; *Hsi-yu chi*, vol. 1, ch. 23, p. 260, l. 11; and *Hai-fu shan-t'ang tz'u-kao*, *chüan* 2a, p. 94, l. 6.

33. This dictum, which is presumably of Buddhist origin and means "the secret must not be shared with a third person," recurs twice in the *Chin P'ing Mei tz'u-hua*, vol. 4, ch. 68, p. 17a, l. 8; and ch. 73, p. 2b, l. 1.

34. Huang Pao-kuang (fl. early 12th century) is a historical figure. For his biography, see *Sung shih*, vol. 32, *chüan* 348, pp. 11028–30.

35. During the Ming dynasty mandarin squares with the motif of the silver pheasant were badges of rank worn by civil officials of the fifth rank. See *Ming shih*, vol. 6, *chüan*, 67, p. 1638, l. 3. For a recent study of this subject, with numerous color photographs of actual examples, primarily dating from the Ch'ing dynasty, see Beverley Jackson and David Hugus, *Ladder to the Clouds: Intrigue and Tradition in Chinese Rank* (Berkeley: Ten Speed Press, 1999).

36. This formulaic four-character expression occurs in *Chung-ch'ing li-chi*, vol. 2, *chüan* 6, p. 16a, l. 11; and recurs twice in the *Chin P'ing Mei tz'u-hua*, vol. 4, ch. 70, p. 4b, ll. 4–5; and ch. 75, p. 7a, l. 11.

37. This line is a slightly corrupted version of one that occurs in the *Chuang-tzu*. See *Chuang-tzu yin-te*, ch. 23, p. 63, l. 4; and Watson, *The Complete Works of Chuang Tzu*, ch. 23, p. 254, ll. 13–14. The precise meaning of the original line is obscure, and my translation differs somewhat from Watson's in order to make sense out of the name.

38. This formulaic four-character expression occurs in *Chin-ming ch'ih Wu Ch'ing feng Ai-ai*, p. 469, l. 11; *Tsao-chiao Lin Ta-wang chia-hsing*, p. 554, l. 11; *San-kuo chih t'ung-su yen-i*, vol. 1, *chüan* 4, p. 161, ll. 5–6; *Hsi-yu chi*, vol. 1, ch. 12, p. 140, l. 13;

San-pao t'ai-chien Hsi-yang chi t'ung-su yen-i, vol. 1, ch. 27, p. 347, l. 10; *I-hsia chi*, scene 30, p. 79, ll. 11–12; and recurs in the *Chin P'ing Mei tz'u-hua*, vol. 4, ch. 71, p. 11a, l. 6.

39. This four-character expression occurs in *Ta-T'ang Ch'in-wang tz'u-hua*, vol. 2, *chüan* 8, ch. 60, p. 32, ll. 4–5.

40. The text that follows does not correspond to any of the extant versions of the *Chin-kang k'o-i*, although some of the language does appear in that work, as indicated in the notes.

41. These four lines, with some textual variants, occur in Chüeh-lien's commentary to the *Chin-kang k'o-i* (Liturgical exposition of the Diamond Sutra). See *[Hsiao-shih] Chin-kang k'o-i [hui-yao chu-chieh]* ([Clearly presented] liturgical exposition of the Diamond sutra [with critical commentary]), ed. and annot. Chüeh-lien (16th century), preface dated 1551, in *[Shinzan] Dai Nihon zoku zōkyō*, 24:711, middle register, ll. 12–13.

42. This four-character expression occurs in a lyric by Liu Yung (cs 1034), *Ch'üan Sung tz'u*, 1:13, lower register, l. 3.

43. This four-character expression occurs in the early literary tale *Chao Fei-yen wai-chuan* (Unofficial biography of Chao Fei-yen), attributed to Ling Hsüan (1st century), but probably dating from the Six Dynasties period (222–589), in *Ssu wu-hsieh hui-pao wai-pien* (Supplement to No depraved thoughts collectanea), comp. Ch'en Ch'ing-hao and Wang Ch'iu-kuei, 2 vols. (Taipei: Encyclopedia Britannica, 1997), vol. 1, p. 64, l. 7; the eighth- or ninth-century manuscript from Tun-huang entitled *Wang Chao-chün pien-wen* (The pien-wen on Wang Chao-chün), in *Tun-huang pien-wen chi* (Collection of pien-wen from Tun-huang), ed. Wang Chung-min et al., 2 vols. (Peking: Jen-min wen-hsüeh ch'u-pan she, 1984), 1:105, l. 9; a song by Wang Yüeh (1423–98), *Ch'üan Ming san-ch'ü*, 1:405, l. 4; and *Shih Chen-jen ssu-sheng so pai yüan*, scene 4, p. 13a, l. 9.

44. This formulaic four-character expression occurs in *Yüan-ch'ü hsüan*, 2:569, l. 14; *Yüan-ch'ü hsüan wai-pien*, 1:54, l. 3; a lyric attributed to Cheng I-niang (12th century), *Ch'üan Sung tz'u*, 5:3891, upper register, l. 10; a song by Chia Chung-ming (1343–c. 1422), *Ch'üan Ming san-ch'ü*, 1:177, l. 9; and *Shih Chen-jen ssu-sheng so pai-yüan*, scene 4, p. 12a, l. 2.

45. This formulaic four-character expression occurs in *Yüan-ch'ü hsüan wai-pien*, 3:973, l. 7; *Yao-shih pen-yüan kung-te pao-chüan* (Precious volume on the original vows and merit of the Healing Buddha), published in 1544, in *Pao-chüan ch'u-chi*, 14:210, l. 1; a song suite, composed entirely of familiar sayings, by Su Tzu-wen (16th century), *Ch'üan Ming san-ch'ü*, 4:4012, l. 6; and *Pa-i chi*, scene 8, p. 16, l. 11.

46. These twenty-two lines, with some textual variation, recur as part of a funeral eulogy for Hsi-men Ch'ing recited by a Buddhist priest in the *Chin P'ing Mei tz'u-hua*, vol. 4, ch. 80, p. 7a, ll. 3–9.

47. These four lines, with some textual variation, occur in *Ju-ju chü-shih yü-lu, chia-chi, chüan* 1, p. 4a, ll. 1–2; and *[Hsiao-shih] Chin-kang k'o-i [hui-yao chu-chieh]*, 24:656, lower register, l. 16.

48. This formulaic four-character expression occurs in a poem attributed to the legendary Buddhist poet Han-shan (8th century), *Ch'üan T'ang shih*, vol. 12, *chüan* 806, p. 9089, l. 12; a fragment of a tenth-century *ya-tso wen* (seat-settling text) discovered at Tun-huang, *Tun-huang pien-wen chi*, 2:840, l. 5; a lyric by the Taoist Celestial

Master Chang Chi-hsien (1092–1126), *Ch'üan Sung tz'u*, 2:760, lower register, l. 11; *Kuan-shih-yin p'u-sa pen-hsing ching*, p. 19b, l. 8; a lyric by Wang Che (1112–70), *Ch'üan Chin Yüan tz'u*, 1:258, lower register, ll. 14–15; a lyric by Ma Yü (1123–83), ibid., 1:304, lower register, l. 8; a letter by Chu Hsi (1130–1200), in *Hui-an hsiensheng Chu Wen-kung wen-chi* (The collected literary works of Chu Hsi), *Ssu-pu pei-yao* (Collectanea of works from the four treasuries) ed. (Shanghai: Chung-hua shu-chü, 1936), *chüan* 63, p. 20b, l. 12; a lyric by Liu Ch'u-hsüan (1147–1203), *Ch'üan Chin Yüan tz'u*, 1:424, upper register, ll. 12–13; *Ju-ju chü-shih yü-lu, chia-chi*, p. 1a, l. 7; a lyric by Ch'iu Ch'u-chi (1148–1227), *Ch'üan Chin Yüan tz'u*, 1:468, upper register, l. 7; *Yüan-ch'ü hsüan*, 3:1072, ll. 15–16; *Huang-chi chin-tan chiu-lien cheng-hsin kuei-chen huan-hsiang pao-chüan*, 8:371, l. 1; *Yao-shih pen-yüan kung-te pao-chüan*, 14:236, l. 5; *[Hsiao-shih] Chen-k'ung pao-chüan* ([Clearly presented] Precious volume on [the teaching of the Patriarch] Chen-k'ung), in *Pao-chüan ch'u-chi*, 19:265, l. 4; *Shui-hu ch'üan-chuan*, vol. 2, ch. 29, p. 455, l. 3; and *Hsi-yu chi*, vol. 2, ch. 94, p. 1061, ll. 14–15.

49. These four lines, with some textual variation, recur twice in the *Chin P'ing Mei tz'u-hua*, vol. 4, ch. 65, p. 7b, ll. 10–11; and ch. 80, p. 7a, ll. 9–10. In the first instance, they occur in a funeral eulogy for Li P'ing-erh recited by the Taoist priest, Abbot Wu; and in the second instance, they occur in a funeral eulogy for Hsi-men Ch'ing recited by a Buddhist priest.

50. This invocation occurs verbatim in numerous early sectarian *pao-chüan* (precious scrolls or precious volumes). See, e.g., *Yao-shih pen-yüan kung-te pao-chüan*, 14:194, ll. 3–5; *P'u-ming ju-lai wu-wei liao-i pao-chüan*, 4:377, ll. 4–6; *[Hsiao-shih] Chen-k'ung sao-hsin pao-chüan*, 18:391, ll. 1–3; and *[Hsiao-shih] Chen-k'ung pao-chüan*, 19:265, l. 1.

51. This quatrain, sometimes designated as a sutra-opening gatha, occurs in many Buddhist and sectarian texts. See, e.g., *Pai-i Ta-pei wu yin-hsin t'o-lo-ni ching* (Dhāraṇī sutra of five mudrās of the Great Compassionate White-Robed Kuan-yin), a stele inscription the calligraphy of which is attributed to Ch'in Kuan (1049–1100), reproduced in Chün-fang Yü, *Kuan-yin: The Chinese Transformation of Avalokiteśvara* (New York: Columbia University Press, 2001), p. 128; *[Hsiao-shih] Chin-kang k'o-i [hui-yao chu-chieh]*, 24:670, middle register, ll. 9–10; *Fo-shuo Huang-chi chieh-kuo pao-chüan* (Precious volume expounded by the Buddha on the karmic results of the era of the Imperial Ultimate), originally published in 1430, in *Pao-chüan ch'u-chi*, 10:223, ll. 5–6; *T'an-shih wu-wei pao-chüan*, 1:302, ll. 1–2; *Yao-shih pen-yüan kung-te pao-chüan*, 14:195, ll. 2–3; *[Hsiao-shih] Chen-k'ung sao-hsin pao-chüan*, 18:392, ll. 1–2; and *[Hsiao-shih] Chen-k'ung pao-chüan*, 19:262, ll. 1–2. This quatrain also recurs in the *Chin P'ing Mei tz'u-hua*, vol. 4, ch. 74, p. 13a, ll. 2–3.

52. This four-character expression, with an insignificant variant, occurs in *Kuan-shih-yin p'u-sa pen-hsing ching*, p. 44b, l. 4; and *San-pao t'ai-chien Hsi-yang chi t'ung-su yen-i*, vol. 1, ch. 11, p. 143, l. 9.

53. The legend that while Śākyamuni Buddha was meditating in the mountains he sat so still that magpies nested on his crown is alluded to in the tenth-century manuscript from Tun-huang entitled *Pa-hsiang pien* (Pien-wen on the eight aspects [of Śākyamuni Buddha's life]), in *Tun-huang pien-wen chi*, 1:341, l. 2; and *Ju-ju chü-shih yü-lu, chia-chi, chüan* 2, p. 7a, l. 13.

54. This four-character expression occurs in *Pa-hsiang pien*, 1:331, l. 12; and the biography of Śākyamuni Buddha in *Tsu-t'ang chi, chüan* 1, p. 6, l. 26.

55. According to a widely disseminated Chinese tradition, probably originating in the eleventh century, the Goddess Kuan-yin was originally a princess named Miao-shan. For a definitive study of this story and its later development, see Glen Dudbridge, *The Legend of Miao-shan* (London: Ithaca Press, 1978).

56. This four-character expression occurs in *Fo-shuo Huang-chi chieh-kuo pao-chüan*, p. 373, ll. 1–2.

57. On the fifty-three forms of Kuan-yin, see Chün-fang Yü, *Kuan-yin: The Chinese Transformation of Avalokiteśvara*, p. 88.

58. This four-character expression occurs in the biography of Śākyamuni Buddha in *Wu-teng hui-yüan*, vol. 1, *chüan* 1, p. 10, l. 6; a statement attributed to Bodhidharma (fl. 470–528) in *Tsu-t'ang chi, chüan* 2, p. 46, l. 18; a statement about Bodhidharma in *Pi-yen lu* (Blue cliff record), comp. Yüan-wu (1063–1135), first published in 1128, in *Taishō shinshū daizōkyō*, 48:140, middle register, l. 1; the 1291 edition of *Liu-tsu ta-shih fa-pao t'an-ching* (The Dharma treasure of the platform sutra of the Sixth Patriarch), ed. Tsung-pao (13th century), in ibid., 48:360, middle register, l. 26; *Ju-ju chü-shih yü-lu, chia-chi, chüan* 3, p. 1b, l. 13; *Yüan-ch'ü hsüan*, 4:1337, l. 17; Chüeh-lien's (16th century) commentary on the *Chin-kang k'o-i, [Hsiao-shih] Chin-kang k'o-i [hui-yao chu-chieh]*, 24:695, middle register, l. 13; and a reference to Bodhidharma in *Hsü Fen-shu* (Supplement to A book to be burned), by Li Chih (1527–1602) (Peking: Chung-hua shu-chü, 1961), *chüan* 4, p. 96, l. 9.

59. This is Hui-neng (638–713), the Sixth Patriarch of Ch'an Buddhism. He is referred to in this way in *Shui-hu ch'üan-chuan*, vol. 2, ch. 31, p. 484, l. 11; and *San-chiao yüan-liu sou-shen ta-ch'üan*, p. 81, l. 2.

60. Legend has it that after Bodhidharma arrived in the state of Wei he sat facing a wall for nine years. See a lyric on Bodhidharma by Huang T'ing-chien (1045–1105), *Ch'üan Sung tz'u*, 1:397, lower register, l. 10; and *Pi-yen lu*, 48:140, lower register, l. 5. This four-character expression, in the form in which it appears here, occurs in a speech attributed to the Buddhist monk Ching-hsüan (943–1027), *Wu-teng hui-yüan*, vol. 3, *chüan* 14, p. 871, l. 4; a lyric by Shih Hao (1106–94), *Ch'üan Sung tz'u*, 2:1282, lower register, l. 4; *Ju-ju chü-shih yü-lu, chia-chi, chüan* 2, p. 9a, l. 14; *[Hsiao-shih] Chin-kang k'o-i [hui-yao chu-chieh]*, 24:731, lower register, l. 4; *Yüan-ch'ü hsüan*, 3:1241, l. 14; and a song suite attributed to the legendary Taoist master Chang Ch'üan-i (fl. 14th century), *Ch'üan Ming san-ch'ü*, 1:237, l. 7.

61. Legend has it that Śākyamuni Buddha, during the course of his austerities, remained still for so long that reeds grew up between his knees. Variants of this four-character expression occur in *Pa-hsiang pien*, 1:341, l. 2; and *San-pao t'ai-chien Hsi-yang chi t'ung-su yen-i*, vol. 1, ch. 11, p. 143, l. 9. It occurs in the same form as in the novel in *Ju-ju chü-shih yü-lu, chia-chi, chüan* 2, p. 7a, l. 13; and p. 9a, l. 14.

62. This line refers to two legends about Bodhidharma: first, that three years after his death he was encountered crossing the Pamirs on a single shoe; and second, that after an unsatisfactory meeting with Emperor Wu of the Liang dynasty (r. 502–49), he crossed the Yangtze River on a plucked reed. Both of these legends are alluded to in a lyric on the subject of Bodhidharma by Huang T'ing-chien (1045–1105), *Ch'üan Sung tz'u*, 1:397, lower register, ll. 9–12. For reproductions of three paintings depicting the second of these legends, see Jan Fontein and Money L. Hickman, *Zen Painting*

and Calligraphy (Boston: Museum of Fine Arts, 1970), pp. 54–55; and Marsha Weidner, ed., *Latter Days of the Law: Images of Chinese Buddhism 850–1850* (Lawrence, Kansas: Spencer Museum of Art, 1994), pp. 395 and 425.

63. P'ang Yün (d. 808) was a devout Buddhist layman who is said to have loaded all his worldly possessions onto a boat and sunk it in a body of water; accounts differ as to whether it was a river, a lake, or the sea. On this figure, and this incident in particular, see *The Recorded Sayings of Layman P'ang: A Ninth-Century Zen Classic*, trans. Ruth Fuller Sasaki, Yoshitaka Iriya, and Dana R. Fraser (New York: Weatherhill, 1971), p. 40 and passim. The career of P'ang Yün is also the subject of the tsa-chü drama entitled *P'ang Chü-shih wu-fang lai-sheng chai* (Layman P'ang mistakenly incurs debts in a future life), by Liu Chün-hsi (14th century), in *Yüan-ch'ü hsüan*, 1:294–314.

64. This incident is dramatized in scene 2 of *P'ang Chü-shih wu-fang lai-sheng chai*, 1:302–7.

65. This four-character expression occurs in *Hsin-ch'iao shih Han Wu mai ch'un-ch'ing*, p. 76, l. 11.

66. These two lines of invective recur in the *Chin P'ing Mei tz'u-hua*, vol. 5, ch. 81, p. 2a, l. 1.

67. This idiomatic saying occurs in the anonymous Yüan-Ming tsa-chü drama *T'ao Yüan-ming tung-li shang-chü* (T'ao Yüan-ming enjoys the chrysanthemums by the eastern hedge), in *Ku-pen Yüan Ming tsa-chü*, vol. 3, scene 2, p. 8b, l. 4; and recurs in the *Chin P'ing Mei tz'u-hua*, vol. 4, ch. 76, p. 2b, ll. 5–6.

68. This formulaic four-character expression occurs in *Ch'ien-Han shu p'ing-hua*, p. 29, l. 6; *San-kuo chih p'ing-hua*, p. 1, l. 12; *Ch'üan-Han chih-chuan*, vol. 2, *chüan* 1, p. 5b, ll. 12–13; and recurs twice in the *Chin P'ing Mei tz'u-hua*, vol. 3, ch. 52, p. 1a, l. 11; and vol. 4, ch. 78, p. 3b, ll. 6–7.

CHAPTER 52

1. This four-character expression occurs in *Yüan-ch'ü hsüan wai-pien*, 3:707, l. 10.

2. According to tradition, there was a type of willow in the imperial park during the Han dynasty the branches of which reclined three times a day before springing up again. This four-character expression occurs in a song suite by T'ang Shih (14th–15th centuries), *Ch'üan Yüan san-ch'ü*, 2:1496, l. 2.

3. This poem is by Chu Shu-chen (fl. 1078–1138), *Ch'üan Sung shih*, 28:17950, ll. 14–15.

4. This four-character expression recurs in the *Chin P'ing Mei tz'u-hua*, vol. 4, ch. 65, p. 10a, l. 11.

5. This four-character expression occurs in *[Chi-p'ing chiao-chu] Hsi-hsiang chi*, play no. 4, scene 1, p. 143, l. 15.

6. This formulaic four-character expression occurs in *Jen hsiao-tzu lieh-hsing wei shen*, p. 573, l. 1; *T'ang-shu chih-chuan t'ung-su yen-i*, vol. 2, *chüan* 7, p. 23b, l. 8; *Lieh-kuo chih-chuan*, vol. 1, *chüan* 1, p. 37b, ll. 6–7; *Ch'üan-Han chih-chuan*, vol. 2, *chüan* 6, p. 28a, l. 2; *Hsi-yu chi*, vol. 2, ch. 79, p. 909, l. 8; and recurs twice in the *Chin P'ing Mei tz'u-hua*, vol. 3, ch. 59, p. 5a, ll. 6–7; and vol. 4, ch. 78, p. 28b, l. 6.

7. A very similar passage involving a barber's assessment of a woman's prospects on the basis of the condition of her hair occurs in *Hai-ling i-shih*, 1:92–93.

8. On these techniques, see Catherine Despeux, "Gymnastics: The Ancient Tradition," in Livia Kohn, ed., *Taoist Meditation and Longevity Techniques* (Ann Arbor: Center for Chinese Studies, University of Michigan, 1989), pp. 225–61.

9. This four-character expression occurs in *[Chi-p'ing chiao-chu] Hsi-hsiang chi*, play no. 4, scene 1, p. 144, l. 7.

10. This four-character expression occurs in a lyric by Tu An-shih (11th century), *Ch'üan Sung tz'u*, 1:185, lower register, l. 12; a lyric by Mo-ch'i Yung (12th century), ibid., 2:811, upper register, l. 10; an anonymous Sung dynasty lyric, ibid., 5:3664, upper register, l. 16; an anonymous Yüan dynasty song suite, *Ch'üan-Yüan san-ch'ü*, 2:1778, l. 1; and a lyric by Chu Yu-tun (1379–1439), *Ch'üan Ming tz'u*, 1:239, upper register, ll. 6–7.

11. Variants of these two lines recur in the *Chin P'ing Mei tz'u-hua*, vol. 3, ch. 52, p. 6a, l. 2; vol. 5, ch. 91, p. 5b, l. 11–6a, l. 1; and ch. 92, p. 6a, l. 7.

12. For a brief description of the hemerological features of the traditional Chinese almanac, which is still in use today, see Martin Palmer, *T'ung Shu: The Ancient Chinese Almanac* (Boston: Shambhala, 1986), pp. 185–94 and passim.

13. The solar term *mang-chung* extends from June 6th through June 20th in the solar calendar.

14. This line recurs in the *Chin P'ing Mei tz'u-hua*, vol. 3, ch. 58, p. 11a, l. 4.

15. This formulaic four-character expression occurs in the biography of Ts'ui Hsien (d. 834), *Chiu T'ang shu*, vol. 15, *chüan* 190c, p. 5060, l. 6; the biography of Lo Wei (fl. early 10th century), ibid., vol. 14, *chüan* 181, p. 4693, l. 2; a lyric by Liu Yung (cs 1034), *Ch'üan Sung tz'u*, 1:42, lower register, l. 11; a lyric by Tseng Ti (1109–80), ibid., 2:1325, upper register, l. 8; a lyric by Hsia Yüan-ting (fl. early 13th century), ibid., 4:2714, lower register, l. 9; an anonymous Yüan dynasty song suite, *Ch'üan Yüan san-ch'ü*, 2:1799, l. 5; *Yu-kuei chi*, scene 8, p. 23, l. 7; *P'o-yao chi*, *chüan* 1, scene 3, p. 9a, l. 6; *T'ao Yüan-ming tung-li shang-chü*, scene 4, p. 13b, l. 9; a song suite by Ch'en To (fl. early 16th century), *Ch'üan Ming san-ch'ü*, 1:646, l. 11; *Ming-chu chi*, scene 6, p. 16, l. 12; *Hsiu-ju chi*, scene 10, p. 24, l. 6; and *Hsi-hu yu-lan chih-yü* (Supplement to the Guide to the West Lake), comp. T'ien Ju-ch'eng (cs 1526) (Peking: Chung-hua shu-chü, 1958), *chüan* 20, p. 358, l. 2, where the two components of the expression are said to refer to the fifteenth day of the second month and the fifteenth day of the eighth month.

16. This line may be derived from the second line of a quatrain attributed to a singing girl from T'ai-yüan, written to her lover Ou-yang Chan (cs 792), *Ch'üan T'ang shih*, vol. 11, *chüan* 802, p. 9024, l. 12.

17. This four-character expression occurs in a lyric by Shen Hsi (14th century), *Ch'üan Chin Yüan tz'u*, 2:1042, lower register, l. 1.

18. This formulaic four-character expression occurs in *[Chi-p'ing chiao-chu] Hsi-hsiang chi*, play no. 2, scene 5, p. 93, l. 4; *Yüan-ch'ü hsüan*, 4:1358, l. 12; *Yüan-ch'ü hsüan wai-pien*, 1:208, l. 17; a song suite by Chou Wen-chih (d. 1334), *Ch'üan Yüan san-ch'ü*, 1:566, l. 2; a song suite by T'ung-t'ung (14th century), ibid., 2:1262, l. 1; a song suite by K'ang Hai (1475–1541), *Ch'üan Ming san-ch'ü*, 1:1221, l. 1; a song by Yang Shen (1488–1559), ibid., 2:1409, l. 14; *Hai-fu shan-t'ang tz'u-kao*, *chüan* 3, p. 183, l. 13; and *Shih-hou chi*, scene 4, p. 9, l. 9.

19. This four-character expression occurs in a quatrain by Chu Shu-chen (fl. 1078–1138), *Ch'üan Sung shih*, 28:17965, l. 9.

20. The Gate God pasted on the left-hand panel of the front gate has a red face, which, in the symbolism of Chinese opera, stands for loyalty, bravery, and generosity; whereas a white painted face stands for cunning, treachery, and licentiousness. See Anne S. Goodrich, *Peking Paper Gods: A Look at Home Worship* (Nettetal: Steyler Verlag, 1991), p. 43; and A. C. Scott, *The Classical Theatre of China* (New York: Macmillan, 1957), p. 168.

21. This line occurs in a quatrain by Wang Che (1112–70), *Ch'üan Chin shih*, 1:220, l. 6; a song by Liu Hsiao-tsu (1522–89), *Ch'üan Ming san-ch'ü*, 2:2314, l. 5; and an anonymous Ming dynasty set of songs, ibid., 4:4577, l. 11.

22. See Roy, *The Plum in the Golden Vase*, vol. 1, chap. 15, n. 19.

23. See ibid., chap. 8, n. 41.

24. This four-character expression occurs in a song suite by Wen Cheng-ming (1470–1559), *Ch'üan Ming san-ch'ü*, 1:1025, l. 9; and a set of songs by Hsüeh Lun-tao (c. 1531–c. 1600), ibid., 3:2724, l. 5.

25. This four-character expression occurs in a lyric by Ch'ao Tuan-li (1046–1113), *Ch'üan Sung tz'u*, 1:440, lower register, l. 9; and *Sha-kou chi*, scene 4, p. 9, l. 9.

26. This four-character expression occurs in a poem by Chang Yüeh (667–731), *Ch'üan T'ang shih*, vol. 2, chüan 87, p. 956, l. 14; a poem by Li Po (701–62), ibid., vol. 3, chüan 173, p. 1775, l. 16; a quatrain by Ch'üan Te-yü (761–818), ibid., vol. 5, chüan 328, p. 3675, l. 2; *Hua-ying chi*, p. 898, l. 3; a song suite by Liang Ch'en-yü (1519–91), *Ch'üan Ming san-ch'ü*, 2: 2221, l. 10; and *Mu-lien chiu-mu ch'üan-shan hsi-wen*, chüan 2, p. 72b, l. 7.

27. This formulaic four-character expression occurs in *Ching-ch'ai chi*, scene 18, p. 56, l. 5; *Pai-yüeh t'ing chi*, chüan 2, scene 43, p. 43b, l. 1; *Shuang-chu chi*, scene 27, p. 86, l. 12; a song by Ch'en To (fl. early 16th century), *Ch'üan Ming san-ch'ü*, 1:472, l. 11; *Hai-fu shan-t'ang tz'u-kao*, chüan 2b, p. 137, l. 13; *Mu-lien chiu-mu ch'üan-shan hsi-wen*, chüan 3, p. 23a, l. 4; and a song suite by Hsü Chieh (1503–83), *Ch'üan Ming san-ch'ü*, 2:1877, l. 10.

28. Variants of this idiomatic expression occur in *Ching-ch'ai chi*, scene 28, p. 89, ll. 4–5; and *Shui-hu ch'üan-chuan*, vol. 3, ch. 67, p. 1142, l. 17. Versions of this song suite are preserved in *Sheng-shih hsin-sheng*, pp. 519–20; *Tz'u-lin chai-yen*, 1:251–53; *[Hsin-pien] Nan chiu-kung tz'u'u*, chüan 8, pp. 2b–3b; *Yung-hsi yüeh-fu*, ts'e 16, pp. 39b–40a; and *Ch'ün-yin lei-hsüan*, 4:2194–96, where it is attributed to Ch'en Wan (1359–1422). Although the variations are slight, the version in the novel is closest to those in *Sheng-shih hsin-sheng* and *Tz'u-lin chai-yen*.

29. See Roy, *The Plum in the Golden Vase*, vol. 1, chap. 9, n. 8.

30. This formulaic four-character expression occurs in the anonymous thirteenth-century prosimetric narrative *Liu Chih-yüan chu-kung-tiao [chiao-chu]* (Medley in various modes on Liu Chih-yüan [collated and annotated]), ed. Lan Li-ming (Ch'eng-tu: Pa-Shu shu-she, 1989), part 2, p. 67, l. 2; *[Chi-p'ing chiao-chu] Hsi-hsiang chi*, play no. 3, scene 3, p. 124, l. 15; *Yüan-ch'ü hsüan*, 3:1245, l. 13; a song composed in 1531 by Li K'ai-hsien (1502–68), *Li K'ai-hsien chi*, 3:913, l. 14; a song suite composed in 1570 by Feng Wei-min (1511–80), *Hai-fu shan-t'ang tz'u-kao*, chüan 1, p. 38, l. 14; and a set of songs by Hsüeh Lun-tao (c. 1531–c. 1600), *Ch'üan Ming san-ch'ü*, 3:2872, l. 10.

31. The act of eating a red date recurs at the climax of Hsi-men Ch'ing's fatal bout of sexual overindulgence in chapter 79. See *Chin p'ing Mei tz'u-hua*, vol. 4, ch. 79, p. 9b, l. 7.

32. This formulaic four-character expression is ubiquitous in Chinese popular literature. See, e.g., a poem by Wen T'ing-yün (c. 812–c. 870), *Ch'üan T'ang shih*, vol. 9, *chüan* 578, p. 6725, l. 11; a lyric by Chou Pang-yen (1056–1121), *Ch'üan Sung tz'u*, 2:623, upper register, l. 2; a lyric by Tseng Ti (1109–80), ibid., 2:1325, upper register, l. 10; a lyric by Chao Yung (b. 1289), *Ch'üan Chin Yüan tz'u*, 2:1032, lower register, l. 11; a song suite by Kao Ming (d. 1359), *Ch'üan Yüan san-ch'ü*, 2:1463, l. 10; *Chien-teng yü-hua*, *chüan* 4, p. 256, l. 5; *Chung-ch'ing li-chi*, vol. 2, *chüan* 6, p. 27b, l. 8; a song by Ch'en To (fl. early 16th century), *Ch'üan Ming san-ch'ü*, 1:472, l. 12; a song by Wang P'an (d. 1530), ibid., 1:1031, l. 10; *Huai-ch'un ya-chi*, *chüan* 10, p. 34b, ll. 1–2; *Tung-t'ien hsüan-chi*, scene 3, p. 10b, l. 13; *Hung-fu chi*, scene 3, p. 5, l. 3; *Hsi-yu chi*, vol. 1, ch. 45, p. 526, l. 11; and *San-pao t'ai-chien Hsi-yang chi t'ung-su yen-i*, vol. 1, ch. 6, p. 80, l. 15.

33. This line occurs verbatim in *Chung-ch'ing li-chi*, vol. 2, *chüan* 6, p. 33a, l. 1.

34. This four-character expression occurs in *Chung-ch'ing li-chi*, vol. 2, *chüan* 6, p. 32a, l. 14; a song suite by Chin Luan (1494–1583), *Ch'üan Ming san-ch'ü*, 2:1627, l. 4; and *San-pao t'ai-chien Hsi-yang chi t'ung-su yen-i*, vol. 1, ch. 20, p. 259, l. 12.

35. This four-character expression occurs in a song by Tseng Jui (c. 1260–c. 1330), *Ch'üan Yüan san-ch'ü*, 1:495, ll. 6–7.

36. This four-character expression occurs in *Yüan-ch'ü hsüan*, 4:1413, ll. 7–8; *Shih Chen-jen ssu-sheng so pai-yüan*, scene 2, p. 6a, l. 8; *Feng-yüeh hsiang-ssu*, p. 90, l. 2; *Yü-ching t'ai*, scene 22, p. 55, l. 5; and a set of songs by Hsüeh Lun-tao (c.1531–c. 1600), *Ch'üan Ming san-ch'ü*, 3:2869, l. 6.

37. The author of the novel has chosen to end the song suite with this tune, which is why he has appended the word "coda" to the tune title, although in the original there are four additional songs.

38. This four-character expression occurs in a song suite by Ching Yüan-ch'i (14th century), *Ch'üan Yüan san-ch'ü*, 2:1152, l. 6; a song suite by Li Ai-shan (14th century), ibid., 2:1187, l. 13; an anonymous Yüan dynasty song suite, ibid., 2:1840, l. 12; and *Shih Chen-jen ssu-sheng so pai-yüan*, scene 4, p. 12a, l. 12.

39. This four-character expression is an allusion to the prose preface to the "Kao-t'ang fu," in which, after an overnight tryst with King Huai of Ch'u (r. 328–299 B.C.), the Goddess of Witch's Mountain tells him, "At dawn I am the morning clouds, and at dusk the driving rain." See Roy, *The Plum in the Golden Vase*, vol. 1, chap. 2, n. 47. It occurs ubiquitously in later Chinese literature. See, e.g., a poem by Li Po (701–62), *Ch'üan T'ang shih*, vol. 3, *chüan* 184, p. 1879, l. 16; a poem by Tu Fu (712–70), ibid., vol. 4, *chüan* 234, p. 2586, l. 8; a quatrain by Li Shang-yin (c. 813–58), ibid., vol. 8, *chüan* 540, p. 6186, l. 14; a lyric by Liu Yung (cs 1034), *Ch'üan Sung tz'u*, 1:22, lower register, l. 2; *Hsiao Sun-t'u*, p. 305, l. 15; *Yüan-ch'ü hsüan*, 4:1343, l. 10; *Yüan-ch'ü hsüan wai-pien*, 1:333, l. 6; *T'ien-pao i-shih chu-kung-tiao*, p. 151, l. 7; a lyric by Kao Yung (13th century), *Ch'üan Chin Yüan tz'u*, 1:71, upper register, l. 7; a song by Yü T'ien-hsi (13th century), *Ch'üan Yüan san-ch'ü*, 1:223, l. 11; a petition by Lu Chü-jen (14th century), in *Ch'o-keng lu* (Notes recorded during respites from the plough), by T'ao Tsung-i (c. 1316–c. 1403), preface dated 1366 (Peking: Chung-hua shu-chü, 1980), *chüan* 12, p. 148, l. 7; *Chiao Hung chuan*, p. 309, l. 3; *Pai-yüeh t'ing chi*, *chüan*

2, scene 35, p. 23b, l. 5; *P'eng-lai hsien-sheng chuan*, p. 72, l. 4; a song by Chu Yu-tun (1379–1439), *Ch'üan Ming san-ch'ü*, 1:315, l. 12; *Chung-ch'ing li-chi*, vol. 2, *chüan* 6, p. 10a, l. 5; *Wang Lan-ch'ing chen-lieh chuan*, scene 1, p. 2a, l. 14; *San-pao t'ai-chien Hsi-yang chi t'ung-su yen-i*, vol. 1, ch. 24, p. 315, l. 12; *Shih-hou chi*, scene 2, p. 4, l. 1; and an abundance of other occurrences, too numerous to list.

40. This formulaic four-character expression occurs in a poem by Liu Yü-hsi (772–842) about an incident that occurred in the year 816, *Ch'üan T'ang shih*, vol. 6, *chüan* 365, p. 4120, l. 8; a quatrain by Tu Mu (803–52), ibid., vol. 8, *chüan* 522, p. 5973, l. 15; a lyric by Chang Hsien (990–1078), *Ch'üan Sung tz'u*, 1:84, upper register, l. 13; a lyric by Wang Yün (1228–1304), *Ch'üan Chin Yüan tz'u*, 2:686, upper register, l. 9; a song by Ch'ang Lun (1493–1526), *Ch'üan Ming san-ch'ü*, 2:1521, l. 10; and a song by Chang Lien (cs 1544), ibid., 2:1673, l. 4.

41. This formulaic four-character expression occurs in *Yüan-ch'ü hsüan wai-pien*, 1:327, l. 5; *P'i-p'a chi*, scene 23, p. 137, ll. 6–7; *Hua-teng chiao Lien-nü ch'eng-Fo chi*, p. 205, l. 9; a song suite by Chao Yen-hui (14th century), *Ch'üan Yüan san-ch'ü*, 2:1234, l. 1; a song suite by Wang T'ien (15th century), *Ch'üan Ming san-ch'ü*, 1:1013, l. 7; *Hsiu-ju chi*, scene 41, p. 110, l. 6; and *Yen-chih chi*, *chüan* 2, scene 24, p. 7b, l. 7.

42. Versions of this anonymous song suite, with some textual variations, are preserved in *Sheng-shih hsin-sheng*, pp. 45–47; *Tz'u-lin chai-yen*, 2:802–6; *Yung-hsi yüeh-fu*, ts'e 2, pp. 37b–39a; and *Ch'ün-yin lei-hsüan*, 4:2317–20.

43. This formulaic four-character expression occurs in *Shui-hu ch'üan-chuan*, vol. 4, ch. 93, p. 1502, l. 17.

44. This four-character expression recurs in the *Chin P'ing Mei tz'u-hua*, vol. 4, ch. 77, p. 9b, l. 9.

45. Although the text does not say so in so many words, the implication of this passage is that she is being invited to inspect his erect penis.

46. This four-character expression occurs ubiquitously in Chinese literature. See, e.g., *Chan-kuo ts'e*, vol. 3, *chüan* 31, p. 1135, l. 4; *Shih-chi*, vol. 1, *chüan* 4, p. 147, l. 13; a song by Po Chü-i (772–846), *Ch'üan T'ang shih*, vol. 7, *chüan* 461, p. 5248, l. 13; and *Shui-hu ch'üan-chuan*, vol. 1, ch. 14, p. 200, ll. 10–11.

47. This four-character expression occurs in a lyric by Wu Wen-ying (13th century), *Ch'üan Sung tz'u*, 4:2875, upper register, l. 7; a lyric by Chou Mi (1232–98), ibid., 5:3272, upper register, l. 15; a song suite by Liang Ch'en-yü (1519–91), written in 1563, *Ch'üan Ming san-ch'ü*, 2:2223, l. 6; and *Mu-tan t'ing*, scene 26, p. 138, l. 9.

48. This couplet is from a poem by Yen Shu (991–1055), *Ch'üan Sung shih*, 3:1943, l. 16; and also occurs in a lyric by the same author, *Ch'üan Sung tz'u*, 1:89, upper register, l. 8. The same couplet occurs in *Chieh-hsia chi*, scene 5, p. 9, l. 12; and, with one insignificant variant, in *Pao-chien chi*, scene 31, p. 60, l. 5.

49. This song has already occurred in the *Chin P'ing Mei*. See Roy, *The Plum in the Golden Vase*, vol. 1, chap. 19, pp. 380–81, and chap. 19, n. 14. The description of the abortive flirtation between Ch'en Ching-chi and P'an Chin-lien in this chapter replicates, in many of its details, the similar scene in chap. 19.

CHAPTER 53

1. As noted on page xix of my introduction, chapters 53–57 are not extant in their original form. Textual evidence and linguistic analysis indicate that they must have

been supplied by two or more editors, on the basis of the clues contained in the chapter titles, which are probably genuine. They are demonstrably inferior to the rest of the work in terms of both internal consistency and literary quality. For a detailed study of these five chapters and their relationship to the remainder of the text, see Patrick Hanan, "The Text of the *Chin P'ing Mei*," *Asia Major*, n.s. vol. 9, part 1 (1962): 14–39.

2. This five-character expression, which has become proverbial, occurs in a penta-syllabic poem by Su Shih (1037–1101), written in 1098, *Su Shih shih-chi*, vol. 7, *chüan* 42, p. 2303, l. 12; the title of a set of ten poems by Tai Piao-yüan (1244–1310), *Ch'üan Sung shih*, 69:43649, l. 9; *Hsiu-ju chi*, scene 18, p. 51, l. 3; *Ming-feng chi*, scene 3, p. 9, l. 8; *Mu-tan t'ing*, scene 16, p. 78, l. 15; and *Shih-hou chi*, scene 25, p. 88, l. 3.

3. This four-character reduplicative expression occurs in *Yüan-ch'ü hsüan*, 1:59, l. 15; *[Chi-p'ing chiao-chu] Hsi-hsiang chi*, play no. 3, scene 3, p. 125, l. 2; and a set of songs by Chu Yu-tun (1379–1439), *Ch'üan Ming san-ch'ü*, 1:273, l. 11.

4. An orthographic variant of this three-character expression occurs in *Ming-feng chi*, scene 4, p. 14, l. 5.

5. This four-character expression occurs in *Yüan-ch'ü hsüan*, 3:879, l. 19.

6. Variants of this proverbial couplet occur ubiquitously in Chinese vernacular liter-ature. See, e.g., *Hsiao Sun-t'u*, scene 14, p. 308, ll. 12–13; *Yüan-ch'ü hsüan*, 3:966, ll. 20–21; *Ching-ch'ai chi*, scene 30, p. 95, l. 11; *Sha-kou chi*, scene 16, p. 59, l. 7; and scene 22, p. 78, l. 10; *Yu-kuei chi*, scene 26, p. 80, ll. 6–7; the anonymous Yüan-Ming ch'uan-ch'i drama *Pai-t'u chi* (The white rabbit), *Liu-shih chung ch'ü* ed., scene 12, p. 40, l. 8; *Chao-shih ku-erh chi*, *chüan* 2, scene 26, p. 3a, l. 7; *P'i-p'a chi*, scene 20, p. 120, ll. 6–7; and scene 23, p. 137, l. 7; *Shuang-chung chi*, *chüan* 2, scene 29, p. 20a, l. 10; *Shuang-chu chi*, scene 18, p. 58, l. 1; *Huai-hsiang chi*, scene 35, p. 118, l. 8; *Hsiu-ju chi*, scene 30, p. 83, l. 4; *Pao-chien chi*, scene 15, p. 32, l. 17; *Ming-feng chi*, scene 10, p. 45, l. 4; and *Mu-lien chiu-mu ch'üan-shan hsi-wen*, *chüan* 1, p. 32a, l. 1. A variant of the first line occurs independently in *[Hsin-pien] Liu Chih-yüan huan-hsiang Pai-t'u chi*, p. 28a, l. 7; and variants of the second line occur independently in *Hsiang-nang chi*, scene 33, p. 99, l. 10; and *San-pao t'ai-chien Hsi-yang chi t'ung-su yen-i*, vol. 2, ch. 82, p. 1055, ll. 4–5.

7. This line almost certainly refers to Emperor Wu of the Han dynasty (r. 141–87 B.C.), a ruler who was obsessed by the quest for immortality, although I have been unable to identify the specific allusion to the Peach Blossom Mandate.

8. This line must refer to Emperor Wu of the Liang dynasty (r. 502–49), who was a credulously devout patron of Buddhism, although I have been unable to identify the specific allusion to the Bamboo Leaf Edict.

9. This four-character expression is a variant of the more common term *huan-ching pu-nao* (retain your essence and replenish your brain), an important concept in Taoist sexual hygiene. See, e.g., *Fei-lung p'ien* (The flying dragon), by Ts'ao Chih (192–232), in *Ts'ao Chih chi chiao-chu* (Ts'ao Chih's collected works collated and annotated), ed. Chao Yu-wen (Peking: Jen-min wen-hsüeh ch'u-pan she, 1984), *chüan* 3, p. 397, l. 13; and *Pao-p'u tzu* (The master who embraces simplicity), by Ko Hung (283–343), in *Chu-tzu chi-ch'eng* (A Corpus of the philosophers), 8 vols. (Hong Kong: Chung-hua shu-chü, 1978), vol. 8, *nei-p'ien* (inner chapters), ch. 8, p. 34, l. 6. For discussions of this term and its significance, see Henri Maspero, *Taoism and Chinese Religion*, trans. Frank A. Kierman, Jr. (Amherst: University of Massachusetts Press, 1981), pp. 522–40;

and Joseph Needham and Lu Gwei-djen, *Science and Civilisation in China*, Vol. 5, part 5, *Spagyrical Discovery and Invention: Physiological Alchemy* (Cambridge: Cambridge University Press, 1983), pp. 184–218.

10. This is an allusion to the literary tale entitled *P'ei Hang*, by P'ei Hsing (825–80), in which the protagonist wins an immortal wife by pounding an elixir of immortality with a jade mortar and pestle for a hundred days. See *P'ei Hsing Ch'uan-ch'i* (P'ei Hsing's Tales of the marvelous), ed. and annot. Chou Leng-ch'ieh (Shanghai: Shanghai ku-chi ch'u-pan she, 1980), pp. 54–57; and "Pei Hang," in *Ladies of the Tang*, trans. Elizabeth Te-chen Wang (Taipei: Heritage Press, 1961), pp. 53–68.

11. This four-character expression occurs in *Ch'ien-chin yao-fang* (Essential prescriptions worth a thousand pieces of gold), comp. Sun Ssu-miao (581–682). See *Ch'ien-chin fang* (Prescriptions worth a thousand pieces of gold), comp. Sun Ssu-miao, ed. Liu Keng-sheng and Chang Jui-hsien (Peking: Hua-hsia ch'u-pan she, 1996), *chüan* 2, p. 16, right-hand column, l. 12. It was a folk belief that during the first three months of pregnancy it was possible by various devices to alter the sex of the embryo. Several methods for doing so are described in the above source.

12. This is the name of a miraculous medication said to have saved the life of the alchemist Li Shao-chün (2nd century B.C.) when bestowed upon him by the legendary immortal Master An-ch'i. See *Han Wu-ti nei-chuan* (Esoteric traditions regarding Emperor Wu of the Han dynasty), traditionally attributed to Pan Ku (32–92) but more probably dating from the fifth or sixth century, in *Ts'ung-shu chi-ch'eng*, 1st series, vol. 3436, *fu-lu* (appendix), p. 27, l. 8.

13. Legend has it that Liu An (179–122 B.C.), the Prince of Huai-nan, succeeded in concocting the elixir of immortality and made enough of it so that there was a sufficient amount left over to enable even his chickens and dogs to ascend with him into the heavens. See *Lun-heng* (Discourses weighed in the balance), by Wang Ch'ung (27–c. 97), in *Chu-tzu chi-ch'eng*, vol. 7, ch. 24, p. 68, ll. 16–17; and *Lun-Heng: Philosophical Essays of Wang Ch'ung*, trans. Alfred Forke, 2 vols. (New York: Paragon Book Gallery, 1962), 1:335.

14. The dream of an azure dragon alludes to the story of Empress Dowager Po (d. 155 B.C.), the mother of Emperor Wen of the Han dynasty (r. 179–157 B.C.). See *Shih-chi*, vol. 6, *chüan* 49, p. 1971, ll. 1–5; and *Records of the Grand Historian of China*, trans. Burton Watson, 2 vols. (New York: Columbia University Press, 1961), 1:382. Watson translates the relevant passage as follows: "The emperor [Kao-tsu (r. 202–195 B.C.)] was deeply moved and, out of pity for Lady Po, summoned her that very day and favored her. 'Last night,' said Lady Po, 'I dreamed that an azure dragon lay upon my belly.' 'This is a wonderful sign,' replied the emperor, 'and for your sake I will make it come true!' From her one moment of favor a son was born who became the King of Tai [the future Emperor Wen]."

15. This line alludes to the legend that Chang Yüeh's (667–731) mother dreamed that a jade swallow flew into her breast from the southeast, as a consequence of which she became pregnant and bore Chang Yüeh, who became a distinguished poet and high official. See *K'ai-yüan T'ien-pao i-shih* (Forgotten events of the K'ai-yüan [713–41] and T'ien-pao [742–56] reign periods), comp. Wang Jen-yü (880–942), in *K'ai-yüan T'ien-pao i-shih shih-chung* (Ten works dealing with forgotten events of the K'ai-yüan and T'ien-pao reign periods), ed. Ting Ju-ming (Shanghai: Shang-hai ku-chi ch'u-pan she, 1985), *chüan* 1, p. 74, l. 2.

16. This was a type of glossy black paper used in the process of making gold leaf and favored by pharmacists for the packaging of medications. See *T'ien-kung k'ai-wu* (The exploitation of the works of nature), by Sung Ying-hsing (1587–c. 1666) (Hong Kong: Chung-hua shu-chü, 1978), *chüan* 14, p. 339, l. 11–p. 340, l. 5; and *T'ien-kung k'ai-wu: Chinese Technology in the Seventeenth Century*, trans. E-tu Zen Sun and Shiou-chuan Sun (University Park: Pennsylvania State University Press, 1966), p. 237, ll. 14–22.

17. This four-character expression is from a famous lyric by Su Shih (1037–1101), *Ch'üan Sung tz'u*, 1:278, lower register, l. 5. It occurs ubiquitously in later Chinese literature. See, e.g., a lyric by Huang T'ing-chien (1045–1105), ibid., 1:403, lower register, l. 13; a lyric by Ch'in Kuan (1049–1100), ibid., 1:481, upper register, l. 8; a lyric by Fang Yüeh (1199–1262), ibid., 4:2849, lower register, l. 6; *[Chi-p'ing chiao-chu] Hsi-hsiang chi*, play no. 2, scene 5, p. 91, l. 11; *Yüan-ch'ü hsüan*, 3:1192, l. 15; a lyric by Wang Yün (1228–1304), *Ch'üan Chin Yüan tz'u*, 2:657, upper register, l. 3; a song by Chang K'o-chiu (1270–1348), *Ch'üan Yüan san-ch'ü*, 1:813, l. 5; a song by Ch'ang Lun (1493–1526), *Ch'üan Ming san-ch'ü*, 2:1547, l. 9; *Ming-chu chi*, scene 1, p. 1, l. 4; and the anonymous sixteenth-century literary tale *Ku-Hang hung-mei chi* (The story of the red plum of old Hang-chou), in *Kuo-se t'ien-hsiang*, vol. 3, *chüan* 8, upper register, p. 9a, l. 12.

18. This song is by Chang K'o-chiu (1270–1348). See *T'ai-ho cheng-yin p'u* (Formulary for the correct sounds of great harmony), comp. Chu Ch'üan (1378–1448), in *Chung-kuo ku-tien hsi-ch'ü lun-chu chi-ch'eng*, 3:115, ll. 6–8; and *Ch'üan Yüan san-ch'ü*, 1:982, ll. 10–12.

19. This four-character expression occurs in a lyric by Liu Yung (cs 1034), *Ch'üan Sung tz'u*, 1:19, lower register, l. 8. It is ubiquitous in later Chinese literature. See, e.g., a lyric by the 30th Taoist Celestial Master Chang Chi-hsien (1092–1126), ibid., 2:757, lower register, l. 14; a lyric by Hsin Ch'i-chi (1140–1207), ibid., 3:1922, upper register, l. 5; *Tung Chieh-yüan Hsi-hsiang chi*, *chüan* 1, p. 2. ll. 9–10; a song by Lu Chih (cs 1268), *Ch'üan Yüan san-ch'ü*, 1:132, l. 3; a song suite by Pai P'u (1226–c. 1306), ibid., 1:207, l. 11; a song suite by Ma Chih-yüan (c. 1250–c. 1325), ibid., 1:269, l. 7; *Yüan-ch'ü hsüan*, 3:1150, l. 4; *Cho Wen-chün ssu-pen Hsiang-ju*, scene 2, p. 123, l. 9; *Feng-yüeh Nan-lao chi*, scene 1, p. 2a, l. 1; a song by K'ang Hai (1475–1541), *Ch'üan Ming san-ch'ü*, 1:1172, l. 4; *Hai-fu shan-t'ang tz'u-kao*, *chüan* 2a, p. 73, l. 8; and an abundance of other occurrences, too numerous to list.

20. This four-character expression occurs in a song suite by Tseng Jui (c. 1260–c. 1330), *Ch'üan Yüan san-ch'ü*, 1:523, l. 14; and an anonymous Yüan dynasty song, ibid., 2:1717, l. 1.

21. This four-character expression occurs in a lyric attributed to Cheng I-niang (12th century), *Ch'üan Sung tz'u*, 5:3891, upper register, l. 5.

22. These two songs are from a song suite by Kuan Han-ch'ing (13th century). See *T'ai-ho cheng-yin p'u*, 3:72, ll. 3–7; and *Ch'üan Yüan san-ch'ü*, 1:168, ll. 9–12.

23. This idiomatic expression recurs in the *Chin P'ing Mei tz'u-hua*, vol. 3, ch. 55, p. 8b, l. 1.

24. This reduplicative four-character expression occurs in *Chin-ming ch'ih Wu Ch'ing feng Ai-ai*, p. 462, l. 16; *Chiang Shih yüeh-li chi*, *chüan* 2, scene 22, p. 14b, l. 7; *Shui-hu ch'üan-chuan*, vol. 4, ch. 101, p. 1571, l. 15; *Yü-chüeh chi*, scene 12, p. 36,

ll. 5–6; *Chieh-hsia chi*, scene 12, p. 27, l. 10; and *Chin-chien chi*, scene 12, p. 34, l. 11. It also recurs in the *Chin P'ing Mei tz'u-hua*, vol. 3, ch. 56, p. 2b, l. 10.

25. This four-character expression occurs in *Yü-kuei chi*, scene 22, p. 64, ll. 11–12.

26. This is the generic title for a number of short indigenous Chinese Buddhist texts dealing with Kuan-yin as a fertility goddess that date from as early as the eleventh century. A typical example would be the *Pai-i Ta-pei wu yin-hsin t'o-lo-ni ching*, cited in chap. 51, n. 51. This text is translated in Chün-fang Yü, *Kuan-yin: The Chinese Transformation of Avalokitesvara*, pp. 126–27; and this and other examples are described and discussed in ibid., pp. 118–41 and 258.

27. This formulaic four-character expression occurs in *Kuan-shih-yin p'u-sa pen-hsing ching*, p. 41a, l. 9; *Yüan-ch'ü hsüan*, 3:1093, l. 9; *Hua-teng chiao Lien-nü ch'eng-Fo chi*, p. 195, l. 12; *Hsiu-ju chi*, scene 18, p. 49, l. 11; *Ming-chu chi*, scene 23, p. 66, l. 4; and *Chieh-chih-erh chi*, p. 255, l. 3.

28. This four-character expression occurs in *Yüan-ch'ü hsüan*, 4:1461, l. 9; *Yüan-ch'ü hsüan wai-pien*, 2:427, l. 1; *K'an p'i-hsüeh tan-cheng Erh-lang Shen*, p. 246, l. 4; *Wu Lun-ch'üan Pei*, chüan 4, scene 23, p. 3b, l. 8; *San-pao t'ai-chien Hsi-yang chi t'ung-su yen-i*, vol. 2, ch. 82, p. 1058, l. 5; and *Shih-hou chi*, scene 25, p. 87, l. 12. It also recurs in the *Chin P'ing Mei tz'u-hua*, vol. 3, ch. 53, p. 11b, l. 10.

29. This four-character expression occurs in a song suite by Hsü Yen (d. 1301), *Ch'üan Yüan san-ch'ü*, 1:84, l. 12; *Ching-ch'ai chi*, scene 8, p. 24, l. 7; and *Shih Chen-jen ssu-sheng so pai-yüan*, scene 3, p. 8b, l. 14. It also occurs in conjunction with the preceding line in *Hai-ling i-shih*, p. 161, l. 3.

30. The expression that I have translated as "annoyed" literally means "twenty-four" and is an example of the type of wordplay called *hsieh-hou yü*. It is the first part of the expression *erh-shih ssu ch'i* (the twenty-four solar terms), with the final *ch'i* omitted. This word, which literally means "breath," has the common meaning of "anger," or "annoyance," and is meant to be suggested by its omission from the end of the expression *erh-shih ssu ch'i*.

31. This four-character expression occurs in *Hung-fu chi*, scene 13, p. 24, l. 2; *Hsi-yu chi*, vol. 1, ch. 27, p. 304, l. 2; and recurs in the *Chin P'ing Mei tz'u-hua*, vol. 3, ch. 55, p. 13a, l. 7.

32. A variant form of this couplet is attributed to the Buddhist monk Tao-ming (8th century), *Wu-teng hui-yüan*, vol. 1, chüan 3, p. 161, l. 7; and also occurs in a speech attributed to the Buddhist monk Fa-ch'üan (11th century), ibid., vol. 3, chüan 16, p. 1030, ll. 10–11. A version closer to that in the novel, with only one insignificant variant, occurs in *Ming-hsin pao-chien*, chüan 2, p. 12b, l. 2. A variant of the second line occurs independently in *Yang Wen lan-lu hu chuan*, p. 178, l. 5; and the couplet as given here recurs in the *Chin P'ing Mei tz'u-hua*, vol. 3, ch. 55, p. 10b, l. 4.

33. This is a quotation from Book 2 of the *Lun-yü* (The analects of Confucius). See *Lun-yü yin-te*, Book 2, p. 3, l. 20. It also occurs in *Yüan-ch'ü hsüan*, 3:1158, ll. 18–19; *[Chi-p'ing chiao-chu] Hsi-hsiang chi*, play no. 4, scene 2, p. 150, l. 9; *Hsi-yu chi*, vol. 1, ch. 1, p. 5, l. 5; and recurs in the *Chin P'ing Mei tz'u-hua*, vol. 3, ch. 55, p. 11a, l. 11.

34. A variant of this idiomatic four-character expression, with the identical meaning, occurs in *San-yüan chi*, scene 3, p. 6, l. 8; and *Shui-hu ch'üan-chuan*, vol. 2, ch. 35, p. 552, l. 16. It occurs in the same form as in the novel in a commemorative inscription by Li K'ai-hsien (1502–68), *Li K'ai-hsien chi*, 2:418, ll. 10–11; *Ts'an-T'ang*

Wu-tai shih yen-i chuan, ch. 16, p. 55, ll. 4–5; and *San-pao t'ai-chien Hsi-yang chi t'ung-su yen-i*, vol. 1, ch. 36, p. 470, l. 10.

35. This four-character expression occurs in *Shui-hu ch'üan-chuan*, vol. 3, ch. 64, p. 1092, l. 14; *Ts'an-T'ang Wu-tai shih yen-i chuan*, ch. 37, p. 151, l. 8; and *Ta-T'ang Ch'in-wang tz'u-hua*, vol. 2, *chüan* 8, ch. 60, p. 5b, l. 2.

36. This formulaic four-character expression occurs in *Lü Tung-pin fei-chien chan Huang-lung*, p. 463, l. 6; *Hsin-ch'iao shih Han Wu mai ch'un-ch'ing*, p. 67, l. 11; *Cheng Yüan-ho*, 4:1443, l. 7; *Shui-hu ch'üan-chuan*, vol. 4, ch. 103, p. 1586, l. 11; and *Hsi-yu chi*, vol. 1, ch. 27, p. 312, l. 5.

37. This four-character expression occurs in *Yüan-ch'ü hsüan wai-pien*, 1:33, l. 11; and *Shui-hu ch'üan-chuan*, vol. 2, ch. 45, p. 734, l. 9.

38. This formulaic four-character expression is ubiquitous in Chinese vernacular literature. See, e.g., a poem by Shao Yung (1011–77), *Ch'üan Sung shih*, 7:4701, l. 15; a lyric by Wang Ch'u-i (1142–1217), *Ch'üan Chin Yüan tz'u*, 1:446, upper register, l. 16; *Yüan-ch'ü hsüan*, 4:1613, l. 6; *Pai-yüeh t'ing chi*, *chüan* 1, scene 7, p. 11a, l. 6; *Hsing-t'ien Feng-yüeh t'ung-hsüan chi*, p. 6b, l. 5; *Wu Lun-ch'üan Pei*, *chüan* 2, scene 13, p. 12a, l. 4; *Chiang Shih yüeh-li chi*, *chüan* 1, scene 12, p. 20b, l. 8; *Ssu-hsi chi*, scene 17, p. 45, l. 3; *Ming-feng chi*, scene 4, p. 16, l. 12; *Hsi-yu chi*, vol. 1, ch. 10, p. 103, l. 16; *Hai-fu shan-t'ang tz'u-kao*, *chüan* 1, p. 11, l. 11; *Mu-tan t'ing*, scene 54, p. 270, l. 8; and an abundance of other occurrences, too numerous to list.

39. This four-character expression occurs in *Shih Chen-jen ssu-sheng so pai-yüan*, scene 2, p. 5a, l. 4.

40. Versions of this invocation, with some textual variation, may be found in *T'ai-shang chu-kuo chiu-min tsung-chen pi-yao* (Secret essentials of the assembled perfected of the Most High for the relief of the state and the deliverance of the people), comp. Yüan Miao-tsung (fl. 1086–1116), pref. dated 1116, in *Cheng-t'ung Tao-tsang*, ts'e 986–87, *chüan* 8, p. 9b, ll. 4–8; and *Tao-men t'ung-chiao pi-yung chi* (Anthology of essentials on the comprehensive teachings of the Taoist sect), comp. Lü T'ai-ku (fl. late 12th–early 13th century), introduction dated 1201, in ibid., ts'e 984–85, *chüan* 7, p. 4b, ll. 4–8. Another version of the same invocation that is even closer to the one in the novel is quoted in *Chung-hua tao-chiao ta tz'u-tien* (Encyclopedia of the Chinese Taoist religion), comp. Hu Fu-ch'en et al. (Peking: Chung-kuo she-hui k'o-hsüeh ch'u-pan she, 1995), p. 667, left column, ll. 29–33, but the source is not indicated. This invocation is still in use in Taiwan today. See Kristofer M. Schipper, *Le Fen-teng: rituel taoiste* (Paris: École Française D'Extrême-Orient, 1975), p. 1 of the Chinese text, ll. 8–13.

41. This is a quotation, with one insignificant textual variant, from the *Lun-yü* (The analects of Confucius). See *Lun-yü yin-te*, Book 3, p. 4, l. 19. This quotation also occurs in the same form as in the novel in *Chang Hsieh chuang-yüan*, scene 16, p. 83, l. 15.

42. This formulaic four-character expression occurs in *Yüan-ch'ü hsüan*, 4:1541, l. 10; *Fo-yin shih ssu t'iao Ch'in-niang*, p. 233, l. 6; *Chien-teng hsin-hua*, *chüan* 3, p. 67, l. 3; *Chien-teng yü-hua*, *chüan* 4, p. 244, l. 8; *Shui-hu ch'üan-chuan*, vol. 4, ch. 92, p. 1490, l. 14; *Huan-sha chi*, scene 30, p. 108, l. 12; *Hsi-yu chi*, vol. 1, ch. 30, p. 341, l. 15; *Kuei-chien chiao-ch'ing*, 4:1534, ll. 1–2; and *Hai-ling i-shih*, p. 105, l. 7.

43. This is the first hexagram in the *Book of Changes*. It stands for Heaven and the male element and is regarded as particularly potent and auspicious.

44. On this method of fortune-telling, see chap. 49, n. 66.

45. The ultimate inspirations for these two lines, although they are not worded in precisely the same way, are a couplet in a poem by Li Po (701–62), *Ch'üan T'ang shih,* vol. 3, *chüan* 166, p. 1715, l. 5; and a further elaboration of the same idea in three lines of a lyric by Su Shih (1037–1101), *Ch'üan Sung tz'u,* 1:278, lower register, l. 14. Close variants of this couplet occur in *Yüan-ch'ü hsüan wai-pien,* 1:132, l. 12; a song by Kuan Yün-shih (1286–1324), *Ch'üan Yüan san-ch'ü,* 1:357, l. 11; *Pao-chien chi,* scene 2, p. 7, l. 22; and *Mu-lien chiu-mu ch'üan-shan hsi-wen, chüan* 1, p. 57a, l. 9. The proximate source is probably *Yü-chüeh chi,* scene 6, p. 17, l. 1, where it occurs in the same form as in the novel. The second line, occurring independently, is ubiquitous in Chinese popular literature. See, e.g., the lyric by Su Shih cited above, *Ch'üan Sung tz'u,* 1:278, lower register, l. 14; a lyric by Li Kuang (1078–1159), ibid., 2:787, upper register, l. 5; a lyric by Hsin Ch'i-chi (1140–1207), ibid., 3:1902, upper register, l. 12; a lyric by Li Chün-ming (1176–c. 1256), *Ch'üan Chin Yüan tz'u,* 1:68, upper register, l. 9; a lyric by Tuan Ch'eng-chi (1199–1279), ibid., 1:154, lower register, l. 11; a lyric by Yao Sui (1238–1313), ibid., 2:740, lower register, ll. 10–11; a lyric by Ch'eng Wen-hai (1249–1318), ibid., 2:788, upper register, l. 1; *Liu Chih-yüan chu-kung-tiao [chiao-chu],* part 1, p. 5, l. 3; *Yüan-ch'ü hsüan wai-pien,* 2:369, l. 18; a song suite by Yang Wen-k'uei (14th century), *Ch'üan Ming san-ch'ü,* 1:214, l. 15; *Chung-ch'ing li-chi, chüan* 6, p. 10a, upper register, ll. 7–8; a song by K'ang Hai (1475–1541), *Ch'üan Ming san-ch'ü,* 1:1164, l. 4; a song by Chang Lien (cs 1544), ibid., 2:1678, l. 2; a song by Wu Kuo-pao (cs 1550), ibid., 2:2258, l. 10; *Hai-fu shan-t'ang tz'u-kao, chüan* 2a, p. 100, l. 8; a song by Hsüeh Lun-tao (c. 1531–c. 1600), *Ch'üan Ming san-ch'ü,* 3:2751, l. 13; and *San-pao t'ai-chien Hsi-yang chi t'ung-su yen-i,* vol. 1, ch. 1, p. 1, l. 5.

CHAPTER 54

1. Variants of this line occur in *Shuang-chu chi,* scene 6, p. 15, ll. 7–8; *Huai-hsiang chi,* scene 3, p. 5, l. 9; and *Yü-chüeh chi,* scene 20, p. 64, l. 12.

2. This is an allusion to a famous quatrain on the Ch'ing-ming festival, traditionally attributed to Tu Mu (803–52), although it does not appear in his collected works. The last two lines of this poem read: "When I enquire where a tavern is to be found, / The herd boy points to the distant Apricot Blossom Village." See *Hou-ts'un Ch'ien-chia shih chiao-chu* (Liu K'o-chuang's poems by a thousand authors edited and annotated), comp. Liu K'o-chuang (1187–1269), ed. and annot. Hu Wen-nung and Wang Hao-sou (Kuei-yang: Kuei-chou jen-min ch'u-pan she, 1986), *chüan* 3, p. 98, l. 8. The term Apricot Blossom Village has since come to stand for any rural tavern.

3. This is an allusion to a shadowy figure in Taoist lore named Su Hsien-kung, who is alleged to have told his mother, before leaving her to become an immortal, that there would be an epidemic the following year, but she could support herself by curing people with a potation made from the water of her well and the leaves of the adjacent orange trees. When the predicted epidemic occurred, this prophecy was fulfilled. See *T'ai-p'ing kuang-chi* (Extensive gleanings from the reign of Great Tranquility), comp. Li Fang (925–96) et al., first printed in 981, 10 vols. (Peking: Chung-hua shu-chü, 1961), vol. 1, *chüan* 13, p. 91, ll. 9–13. The term Orange Tree Well has since come to stand for any source of effective remedies.

4. A variant of this line occurs in *Hai-ling i-shih,* p. 89, l. 3.

5. This *hsieh-hou yü* hinges on a pun between the word *miao*, meaning "wonderful," and its homophone, meaning "temple."

6. This four-character expression occurs in *Ming-hsiang chi* (Signs from the unseen realm), comp. Wang Yen (fl. late 5th–early 6th centuries), in *Ku hsiao-shuo kou-ch'en* (Rescued fragments of early fiction), comp. Lu Hsün (Peking: Jen-min wen-hsüeh ch'u-pan she, 1955), p. 383, l. 8; a quatrain by Li Po (701–62), *Ch'üan T'ang shih*, vol. 3, *chüan* 178, p. 1813, l. 4; the literary tale *Li-wa chuan* (The story of Li Wa), by Po Hsing-chien (776–826), in *T'ang Sung ch'uan-ch'i chi* (An anthology of literary tales from the T'ang and Sung dynasties), ed. Lu Hsün (Peking: Wen-hsüeh ku-chi k'an-hsing she, 1958), p. 100, ll. 11–12; *Hsüan-ho i-shih*, p. 139, l. 8; *Fo-yin shih ssu t'iao Ch'in-niang*, p. 235, l. 7; *Chung-ch'ing li-chi, chüan* 6, p. 4b, l. 9; *Hua-ying chi*, p. 850, l. 17; *Ju-i chün chuan*, p. 18b, l. 7; *Feng-yüeh hsiang-ssu*, p. 80, l. 9; *Huai-ch'un ya-chi, chüan* 10, p. 16b, l. 1; *Hua-shen san-miao chuan, chüan* 6, p. 9a, l. 11; *Hsün-fang ya-chi, chüan* 4, p. 43a, l. 8; *Liu sheng mi Lien chi, chüan* 2, p. 14b, l. 9; the sixteenth-century literary tale *Chin-lan ssu-yu chuan* (The story of the four ardent friends), in *Kuo-se t'ien-hsiang*, vol. 3, *chüan* 9, upper register, p. 6a, l. 4; *Hai-fu shan-t'ang tz'u-kao, chüan* 1, p. 44, l. 2; the novel *Tung-yu chi: shang-tung pa-hsien chuan* (Journey to the east: the story of the eight immortals of the upper realm), comp. Wu Yüan-t'ai (16th century), appendix dated 1596, fac. repr. of Chien-yang edition published by Yü Hsiang-tou (c. 1550–1637), in *Ku-pen hsiao-shuo ts'ung-k'an, ti san-shih chiu chi* (Collectanea of rare editions of traditional fiction, thirty-ninth series) (Peking: Chung-hua shu-chü, 1991), 1:35, l. 3; and *Hai-ling i-shih*, p. 67, ll. 6–7. It also recurs in the *Chin P'ing Mei tz'u-hua*, vol. 3, ch. 54, p. 4b, l. 1.

7. This four-character expression occurs in *[Chi-p'ing chiao-chu] Hsi-hsiang chi*, play no. 1, scene 1, p. 7, ll. 8–9; *Ta-Sung chung-hsing yen-i, chüan* 8, p. 22a, l. 9; *Hsi-yu chi*, vol. 1, ch. 24, p. 269, ll. 8–9; *Mu-lien chiu-mu ch'üan-shan hsi-wen, chüan* 1, p. 13a, l. 6; *Pa-i chi*, scene 39, p. 82, l. 9; and a song by Chao Nan-hsing (1550–1627), *Ch'üan Ming san-ch'ü*, 3:3218, l. 13.

8. A variant of this idiomatic saying is quoted as proverbial by Su Shih (1037–1101), *Su Shih wen-chi*, vol. 5, *chüan* 71, p. 2258, l. 9. Other variants occur in *Shou-t'ing hou nu-chan Kuan P'ing*, scene 1, p. 4a, l. 8; and *Liu sheng mi Lien chi, chüan* 3, p. 17b, l. 12. It is quoted in the same form as in the novel in a fragment of a lost work entitled *Pao-yin chi-t'an* (Recorded sayings of an eremitic leopard), by Chou Tsun-tao (cs 1097), in *Sung shih-hua ch'üan-pien* (Complete compendium of Sung dynasty talks on poetry), ed. Wu Wen-chih, 10 vols. (Nanking: Chiang-su ku-chi ch'u-pan she, 1998), 10:10430, ll. 12–13; *Mu-lien chiu-mu ch'üan-shan hsi-wen, chüan* 2, p. 25b, l. 10, and *Ku-chin t'an-kai, chüan* 29, p. 917, l. 17.

9. See Roy, *The Plum in the Golden Vase*, vol. 1, chap. 20, n. 54.

10. The locus classicus for this four-character expression is a line in the *Lan-t'ing shih hsü* (Preface to the Orchid Pavilion poems), by Wang Hsi-chih (321–379), composed in the year 353. See *Chin-shu*, vol. 7, *chüan* 80, p. 2099, l. 4; and *An Anthology of Chinese Literature*, comp. Stephen Owen (New York: W. W. Norton, 1996), p. 283, l. 10. It occurs ubiquitously in later Chinese literature. See, e.g., a funeral eulogy by Yang Chiung (650–c. 694), *Ch'üan T'ang wen*, vol. 5, *chüan* 196, p. 21a, l. 9; a lyric by Li Kang (1083–1140), *Ch'üan Sung tz'u*, 2:906, upper register, ll. 8–9; a lyric by Lu Wen-kuei (1256–1340), *Ch'üan Chin Yüan tz'u*, 2:823, lower register, l. 11; a song by Hsü Tsai-ssu (14th century), *Ch'üan Yüan san-ch'ü*, 2:1032, l. 11; a song suite by

Hsia Wen-fan (16th century), *Ch'üan Ming san-ch'ü*, 1:828, l. 4; *Shui-hu ch'üan-chuan*, vol. 2, ch. 42, p. 677, l. 13; *Pai-chia kung-an, chüan* 4, ch. 40, p. 18b, l. 11; and *San-pao t'ai-chien Hsi-yang chi t'ung-su yen-i*, vol. 1, ch. 6, p. 73, l. 6.

11. This four-character expression, which is of Buddhist origin, occurs in *Ta-pan nieh-p'an ching* (The Mahāparinirvāṇasūtra), trans. Dharmakṣema (fl. 385–433), in *Taishō shinshū daizōkyō*, vol. 12, no. 374, *chüan* 13, p. 445, upper register, l. 26. It is ubiquitous in later Chinese literature, both Buddhist and secular. See, e.g., a speech attributed to the Buddhist monk Ta-t'ung (819–914), *Wu-teng hui-yüan*, vol. 1, *chüan* 5, p. 297, l. 11; a speech attributed to the Buddhist monk Wu-yin (884–960), *Tsu-t'ang chi, chüan* 12, p. 269, l. 20; the T'ang dynasty work *Mu-lien yüan-ch'i* (Story of Maudgalyāyana), in *Tun-huang pien-wen chi*, 2:703, l. 6; a remark attributed to Ts'ai Ching (1046–1126) in a work by his son Ts'ai T'ao (d. after 1147) entitled *T'ieh-wei shan ts'ung-t'an* (Collected remarks from the Iron Cordon Mountains) (Peking: Chung-hua shu-chü, 1997), *chüan* 4, p. 62, l. 2; *Yüan-ch'ü hsüan*, 2:743, l. 8; *Yüan-ch'ü hsüan wai-pian*, 1:138, l. 14; *Hsiu-ju chi*, scene 23, p. 65, l. 2; *Shui-hu ch'üan-chuan*, vol. 1, ch. 2, p. 24, l. 8; Chüeh-lien's (16th century) commentary to *[Hsiao-shih] Chin-kang k'o-i [hui-yao chu-chieh]*, *chüan* 9, p. 750, lower register, l. 2; *P'u-ming ju-lai wu-wei liao-i pao-chüan*, p. 524, l. 2; *[Hsiao-shih] Chen-k'ung sao-hsin pao-chüan*, 19:124, l. 3; the preface to *P'u-ching ju-lai yao-shih pao-chüan*, 5:39, l. 2; and a document by Li Chih (1527–1602), in *Hsü Fen-shu, chüan* 4, p. 98, l. 14.

12. This four-character expression occurs in a song by Wang Chiu-ssu (1468–1551), *Ch'üan Ming san-ch'ü*, 1:939, l. 9; and a song suite by Ch'en So-wen (d. c. 1604), ibid., 2:2562, l. 2.

13. This is an allusion to a story from a lost work entitled *Shu-chih* (Records of Shu), as quoted in *Yüan-chien lei-han*, vol. 2, *chüan* 58, p. 40b, ll. 3–5. The story reads as follows: "In olden times an emperor of the state of Shu sired a princess and engaged a wet nurse, née Ch'en, to nurture her. Ms. Ch'en took her infant son with her, and they resided with the princess in the palace for more than ten years. Later, because of palace regulations, they were required to move outside the palace for six years. Her son became extremely lovesick for the princess, as a result of which, when Ms. Ch'en went into the palace, she exhibited a sorrowful countenance. When the princess inquired into the reason for this, Ms. Ch'en secretly told her the truth. The princess, accordingly, arranged an assignation with Ms. Ch'en's son on the pretext of paying a formal visit to the Zoroastrian Temple. When the princess entered the temple, she found Ms. Ch'en's son fast asleep, at which she left a jade disk that they had played with as children on his breast and departed. When Ms. Ch'en's son awoke and saw the disk, he was so chagrined that his anger turned to flames and set the temple on fire."

14. This four-character onomatopoetic expression for the sound made by crackling flames occurs in *Yüan-ch'ü hsüan*, 2:695, l. 2; and 4:1651, l. 18. An orthographic variant of the same expression also occurs in *Shui-hu ch'üan-chuan*, vol. 1, ch. 6, p. 100, l. 12.

15. This four-character onomatopoetic expression describing the sound of beating wings occurs in *Yüan-ch'ü hsüan*, 1:60, l. 12; and a song suite by Wang T'ing-hsiu (13th century), *Ch'üan Yüan san-ch'ü*, 1:318, l. 4.

16. This four-character expression occurs in a song suite by Ch'ien Lin (14th century), *Ch'üan Yüan san-ch'ü*, 2:1030, ll. 8–9; *Ch'ing feng-nien Wu-kuei nao Chung*

K'uei, scene 1, p. 2b, l. 10; *Shui-hu ch'üan-chuan*, vol. 3, ch. 56, p. 940, ll. 8–9; and *Ta-T'ang Ch'in-wang tz'u-hua*, vol. 1, *chüan* 2, ch. 10, p. 18a, l. 3.

17. This line occurs in a song suite by Yang I-ch'ing (1454–1530), *Ch'üan Ming san-ch'ü*, 1:443, l. 12. It is an allusion to a famous poem on the irrevocable consequences of elopement by Po Chü-i (772–486), the first two lines of which read: "One may attempt to recover the silver vase that has fallen to the bottom of the well, / But though one may wish to pull it up, the silken cord is broken." See *Ch'üan T'ang shih*, vol. 7, *chüan* 427, p. 4707, l. 12.

18. This song is from scene 4 of a famous Yüan tsa-chü entitled *Ch'ien-nü li-hun* ([Chang] Ch'ien-nü's disembodied soul), by Cheng Kuang-tsu (fl. early 14th century). See *Yüan-ch'ü hsüan*, 2:717, l. 19–718, l. 1. The first line of the song in the extant version of the above drama, however, is completely different from that in the novel, whereas the entire text of the song as given in the novel is identical with the version in *T'ai-ho cheng-yin p'u*, p. 67, ll. 3–5, which is probably the proximate source. Variant versions of this song are also preserved in *Tz'u-lin chai-yen*, 2:1089, ll. 1–5; and *Yung-hsi yüeh-fu, ts'e* 1, p. 29a, ll. 4–8.

19. This idiomatic expression occurs in *Hsiu-ju chi*, scene 10, p. 26, l. 6.

20. This four-character expression occurs in *Yen-chih chi, chüan* 2, scene 40, p. 33b, l. 10; an excerpt from a lost ch'uan-ch'i dramatic version of *Chung-ch'ing li-chi* by Chao Yü-li (fl. late 16th century), entitled *Huang-ying chi* (The oriole), in *Ta ming-ch'un* (Great bright spring), comp. Ch'eng Wan-li (Chien-yang: Chin K'uei, n.d.), fac. repr. of Wan-li (1573–1620) ed., in *Shan-pen hsi-ch'ü ts'ung-k'an*, 6:109, upper register, l. 6; and *Shih-hou chi*, scene 20, p. 65, l. 2.

21. This four-character expression occurs in *Yüan-ch'ü hsüan*, 1:197, l. 21.

22. This four-character expression occurs in a poem by Hsiao I (508–54), Emperor Yüan (r. 552–54) of the Liang dynasty (502–57), *Hsien-Ch'in Han Wei Chin Nan-pei ch'ao shih*, 3:2059, l. 1; a funerary dirge by Ch'en Tzu-liang (d. 632), *Ch'üan T'ang wen*, vol. 3, *chüan* 134, p. 10a, l. 1; a lyric by Yen Shu (991–1055), *Ch'üan Sung tz'u*, 1:99, lower register, l. 4; a lyric by Ch'ang-ch'üan-tzu (13th century), *Ch'üan Chin Yüan tz'u*, 1:590, lower register, l. 8; a song suite by P'eng Shou-chih (13th century), *Ch'üan Yüan san-ch'ü*, 1:88, l. 7; a song by Pai P'u (1226–c. 1306), ibid., 1:199, l. 11; *Chang Hsieh chuang-yüan*, scene 6, p. 39, l. 2; and *Hsüan-ho i-shih*, p. 10, l. 8.

23. This four-character expression occurs in an anonymous Yüan dynasty song suite. See *Ch'üan Yüan san-ch'ü*, 2:1847, l. 7.

24. This four-character expression occurs in a lyric by Chang Hsien (990–1078), *Ch'üan Sung tz'u*, 1:72, lower register, l. 2; a lyric by Yen Chi-tao (c. 1031–c. 1106), ibid., 1:250, upper register, l. 15; *[Chi-p'ing chiao-chu] Hsi-hsiang chi*, play no. 5, scene 2, p. 183, l. 14; *Wang Wen-hsiu Wei-t'ang ch'i-yü chi*, scene 3, p. 5b, l. 2; and an anonymous set of songs published in 1471, *Ch'üan Ming san-ch'ü*, 4:4519, l. 13.

25. This formulaic four-character expression occurs ubiquitously in Chinese vernacular literature. See, e.g., a song suite by Kuan Yün-shih (1286–1324), *Ch'üan Yüan san-ch'ü*, 1:383, l. 13; a song by Ch'iao Chi (d. 1345), ibid., 1:625, l. 2; a song suite by Lü Chih-an (14th century), ibid., 2:1134, l. 9; a song suite by Sung Fang-hu (14th century), ibid., 2:1308, l. 7; a lyric by the poetess Chang Yü-niang (14th century), *Ch'üan Chin Yüan tz'u*, 2:871, upper register, ll. 6–7; *Chang Yü-hu su nü-chen kuan chi*, p. 15b, l. 7; *Yu-kuei chi*, scene 22, p. 65, l. 8; a song by Chu Yu-tun (1379–1439), *Ch'üan Ming san-ch'ü*, 1:323, l. 3; a song included in the front matter of the 1498

edition of *Hsi-hsiang chi*, p. 11a, ll. 9–10; *Yü-huan chi*, scene 5, p. 11, ll. 5–6; a lyric by Ku Hsün (1418–1505), *Ch'üan Ming tz'u*, 1:288, upper register, l. 10; *Ming-chu chi*, scene 10, p. 30, l. 4; a song by Yang Shen (1488–1559), *Ch'üan Ming san-ch'ü*, 2:1409, l. 9; *Ssu-hsi chi*, scene 14, p. 35, l. 11; and an abundance of other occurrences, too numerous to list.

26. These two songs are excerpted from a song suite by Kuan Han-ch'ing (13th century), *Ch'üan Yüan san-ch'ü*, 1:176, ll. 12–15. They occur by themselves verbatim in *T'ai-ho cheng-yin p'u*, p. 93, l. 7–p. 94, l. 2, which is probably the proximate source. Versions of the song suite in question, including these two songs, are also preserved in *Ch'ao-yeh hsin-sheng t'ai-ping yüeh-fu* (New songs from court and country: ballads from an era of great peace), comp. Yang Ch'ao-ying (14th century), preface dated 1351 (Peking: Chung-hua shu-chü, 1987), *chüan* 7, p. 288, ll. 7–10; *Yung-hsi yüeh-fu*, *ts'e* 15, p. 15a, l. 8–p. 15b, l. 3; and *Pei kung tz'u-chi* (Anthology of northern-style song lyrics), comp. Ch'en So-wen (d. c. 1604), in *Nan-pei kung tz'u-chi*, vol. 4, *chüan* 6, p. 634, ll. 1–4.

27. This line occurs in a song by Ch'iao Chi (d. 1345), *Ch'üan Yüan san-ch'ü*, 1:629, ll. 9–10; an anonymous Yüan dynasty song, ibid., 2:1770, l. 11; an anonymous Yüan dynasty song suite, ibid., 2:1838, l. 10; a song by Ch'en To (fl. early 16th century), *Ch'üan Ming san-ch'ü*, 1:503, l. 5; and a song suite by Ch'ang Lun (1493–1526), ibid., 2:1556, l. 5.

28. This line occurs in *Yüan-ch'ü hsüan wai-pien*, 3:780, ll. 19–20.

29. This line has been inadvertently omitted in the text as given in the novel.

30. This four-character expression occurs in a lyric by Wang Meng-tou (13th century), *Ch'üan Sung tz'u*, 5:3312, upper register, l. 10; a song suite by Teng Hsüeh-k'o (14th century), *Ch'üan Yüan san-ch'ü*, 1:697, l. 2; a song by Chang K'o-chiu (1270–1348), ibid., 1:852, l. 9; an anonymous Yüan dynasty song suite, ibid., 2:1658, l. 3; a lyric by Liu Ping (14th century), *Ch'üan Ming tz'u*, 1:134, lower register, ll. 14–15; and a lyric by Wang Yüeh (1423–98), ibid., 1:313, upper register, ll. 4–5.

31. The last word of this line has been inadvertently omitted in the text as given in the novel.

32. The proximate source of this song is probably *T'ai-ho cheng-yin p'u*, p. 98, ll. 6–8. The ultimate source is a lyric by Chao Ping-wen (1159–1233), *Ch'üan Chin Yüan tz'u*, 1:47, upper register, ll. 13–16.

33. This four-character expression occurs in a poem by Liu Yü-hsi (772–842), *Ch'üan T'ang shih*, vol. 6, *chüan* 360, p. 4072, l. 1; a poem by Po Chü-i (772–846), ibid., vol. 7, *chüan* 448, p. 5050, l. 1; and a lyric by Ch'en Chu (1214–97), *Ch'üan Sung tz'u*, 4:3034, upper register, l. 3.

34. This is an allusion to a famous passage in the *Lun-yü* (The analects of Confucius). See *Lun-yü yin-te*, Book 7, p. 12, l. 7; and *Confucian Analects*, trans. James Legge (Hong Kong: University of Hong Kong Press, 1960), p. 197, ll. 12–13. The same passage is quoted in *Ta-Sung chung-hsing yen-i*, *chüan* 2, p. 20a, l. 5.

35. The *Songs of Ch'u*, or *Ch'u-tz'u*, is an anthology of early Chinese poetry, associated with the state of Ch'u and with Ch'ü Yüan (c. 340–278 B.C.), a famous poet and official, who committed suicide in protest against the failure of his ruler to appreciate him at his true worth. His death by drowning in the area of the Hsiang River is commemorated by the Dragon Boat Festival on the fifth day of the fifth lunar month. The introduction of this song into the text of the novel is surely intended to reflect ironically

on Hsi-men Ch'ing, who never evinces the slightest interest in Confucian eremitism and, unlike Ch'ü Yüan, is happy to serve as a corrupt official under the aegis of an irresponsible emperor. This song is excerpted from a longer work by Chang Ming-shan (14th century), *Ch'üan Yüan san-ch'ü*, 2:1279, ll. 7–9. The proximate source is probably *T'ai-ho cheng-yin p'u*, p. 79, ll. 1–2, where this excerpt occurs in exactly the same form as in the novel. It is noteworthy that the above three songs in chapter 54, as well as the two songs in chapter 53, are all to be found in close proximity in pages 67–115 of *T'ai-ho cheng-yin p'u*, a source that is not drawn upon anywhere else in the novel. This is but one indication, among many others, that these chapters are by a different hand than the rest of the novel.

36. See Roy, *The Plum in the Golden Vase*, vol. 1, chap. 13, n. 8.

37. For the translation of this term, *san-chiao*, the history of the concept, and the terminological problems involved in rendering it, see Manfred Porkert, *The Theoretical Foundations of Chinese Medicine* (Cambridge: MIT Press, 1974), pp. 158–62.

38. These four diagnostic methods are discussed in the early Chinese medical text *Nan-ching* (The classic of difficult issues), probably compiled in the second century A.D. See *Nan-ching: The Classic of Difficult Issues*, trans. Paul U. Unschuld (Berkeley: University of California Press, 1986), issue no. 61, p. 539. References to these four diagnostic methods occur in *Yu-kuei chi*, scene 25, p. 71, l. 4; *Hsi-yu chi*, vol. 2, ch. 68, p. 781, l. 7; *Mu-tan t'ing*, scene 18, p. 90, l. 2: and recur in the *Chin P'ing Mei tz'u-hua*, vol. 4, ch. 61, p. 23a, l. 1.

39. Close variants of this proverbial saying occur in *Chin-ch'ai chi*, scene 15, p. 32, l. 1; and *Yü-tsan chi*, scene 25, p. 90, l. 5.

40. See Roy, *The Plum in the Golden Vase*, vol. 1, chap. 20, n. 16. A variant of this idiomatic expression occurs as the first line of an anonymous quatrain inspired by an examination scandal in 1495. See *Chih-shih yü-wen* (Recollections of a well-governed age), by Ch'en Hung-mo (1474–1555), originally completed in 1521 (Peking: Chung-hua shu-chü, 1985), *hsia-p'ien* (second section), *chüan* 2, p. 48, l. 13. It occurs in the same form as in the novel in *I-hsia chi*, scene 12, p. 30, l. 12.

41. On Hsi-shih, see Roy, *The Plum in the Golden Vase*, vol. 1, chap. 4, n. 2. Legend has it that this famous beauty looked just as captivating with knitted brows as she did when smiling.

42. The last five characters of each of these two lines, taken together, constitute a proverbial couplet that occurs in *Kuan-shih-yin p'u-sa pen-hsing ching*, p. 93a, ll. 5–6; *P'i-p'a chi*, scene 22, p. 134, l. 2; *Yu-kuei chi*, scene 25, p. 71, l. 8; *Ming-hsin pao-chien*, *chüan* 2, p. 4b, l. 1; *Nan Hsi-hsiang chi* (A southern version of the *Romance of the western chamber*), by Lu Ts'ai (1497–1537), in *Hsi-hsiang hui-pien* (Collected versions of the *Romance of the western chamber*), comp. Huo Sung-lin (Chi-nan: Shan-tung wen-i ch'u-pan she, 1987), *chüan* 1, scene 7, p. 342, ll. 16–17; *Liu-ch'ing jih-cha* (Daily jottings worthy of preservation), by T'ien I-heng (1524–c. 1574), pref. dated 1572, fac. repr. of 1609 ed. (Shanghai: Shang-hai ku-chi ch'u-pan she, 1985), *chüan* 27, p. 11b, l. 9; and recurs in the *Chin P'ing Mei tz'u-hua*, vol. 4, ch. 79, p. 15b, l. 8. A virtually synonymous version of this couplet occurs in *Mu-lien chiu-mu ch'üan-shan hsi-wen*, *chüan* 1, p. 75a, l. 9; and the tsa-chü drama entitled *Ko tai hsiao* (A song in place of a shriek), attributed to Hsü Wei (1521–93), in *Ssu-sheng yüan*, scene 2, p. 131, l. 10. The second line of this couplet, in the same form as it appears in the novel, also occurs independently in *Mu-lien chiu-mu ch'üan-shan hsi-wen*, *chüan* 1, p. 60b, l. 1.

CHAPTER 55

1. The six directions are Heaven, Earth, and the four cardinal directions. The five waterways are five river systems located in southwestern China.

2. The term "four barbarian tribes" refers to ethnically non-Han peoples to the north, south, east, and west of China. The three isles are the three Isles of the Blest in Taoist mythology.

3. Hsi-ho is the charioteer of the sun in Chinese mythology, who is responsible for propelling the sun and moon in their orbits. Note that the numbers eight through two in descending order occur in lines three through seven of this poem. This is a common type of Chinese wordplay.

4. The discontinuity and redundancy of the opening of this chapter are but two of several indications that this chapter was probably not by the same hand as the two preceding chapters.

5. The name Ch'in-t'ung has been inadvertently omitted at this point in the text. I have supplied it on the basis of the fact that the text specifically refers to four page boys but names only three, and its occurrence later in the chapter. See the Chin P'ing Mei tz'u-hua, vol. 3, ch. 55, p. 7b, l. 9.

6. This formulaic four-character expression occurs ubiquitously in Chinese literature. See, e.g., a lyric by Huang T'ing-chien (1045–1105), Ch'üan Sung tz'u, 1:402, upper register, l. 16; a lyric by Chao Yen-tuan (1121–75), ibid., 3:1441, lower register, ll. 9–10; a quotation from an anonymous prophetic poem in T'ing-shih, chüan 2, p. 13, ll. 5–6; a lyric by Yüan Hao-wen (1190–1257), Ch'üan Chin Yüan tz'u, 1:125, lower register, ll. 5–6; a lyric by Tuan K'o-chi (1196–1254), ibid., 1:143, upper register, l. 7; a lyric by Liu Ping-chung (1216–74), ibid., 2:611, upper register, ll. 1–2; [Chi-p'ing chiao-chu] Hsi-hsiang chi, play no. 5, scene 1, p. 173, l. 11; Yüan-ch'ü hsüan wai-pien, 2:416, l. 8; a song suite by Pu-hu-mu (d. 1300), Ch'üan Yüan san-ch'ü, 1:77, l. 10; Ching-ch'ai chi, scene 5, p. 10, l. 11; Cheng Chieh-shih li-kung shen-pi kung, p. 658, l. 9; the anonymous Yüan-Ming tsa-chü drama Meng-mu san-i (The mother of Mencius moves three times), in Ku-pen Yüan Ming tsa-chü, vol. 2, scene 4, p. 10b, l. 7; a song suite by Yang Wen-k'uei (14th century), Ch'üan Ming san-ch'ü, 1:213, l. 5; Chien-teng hsin-hua, chüan 2, p. 39, ll. 12–13; a lyric by Lan Mao (1397–1476), Ch'üan Ming tz'u, 1:258, lower register, ll. 6–7; Chung-ch'ing li-chi, vol. 2, chüan 6, p. 15a, l. 14; San-kuo chih t'ung-su yen-i, vol. 2, chüan 16, p. 740, l. 20; the middle-period vernacular story K'ung Shu-fang shuang-yü shan-chui chuan (The story of K'ung Shu-fang and the pair of fish-shaped fan pendants), in Hsiung Lung-feng ssu-chung hsiao-shuo, p. 63, l. 7; Shui-hu ch'üan-chuan, vol. 1, ch. 5, p. 81, l. 6; Lieh-kuo chih-chuan, vol. 1, chüan 2, p. 26a, l. 9; a song suite by Ku Ying-hsiang (1483–1565), Ch'üan Ming san-ch'ü, 2:1334, l. 10; Hai-fu shan-t'ang tz'u-kao, chüan 2b, p. 131, l. 1; and an abundance of other occurrences, too numerous to list.

7. This formulaic four-character expression occurs ubiquitously in Chinese vernacular literature. See, e.g., Hsi-hu san-t'a chi, p. 31, l. 5; Pai Niang-tzu yung-chen Lei-feng T'a, p. 424, l. 13; Yu-kuei chi, scene 24, p. 67, l. 3; Jen chin shu ku-erh hsün-mu, scene 1, p. 3b, l. 1; Shui-hu ch'üan-chuan, vol. 1, ch. 2, p. 21, l. 16; the tsa-chü drama Chung-shan lang yüan-pen (Yüan-pen on the wolf of Chung-shan), by Wang Chiu-ssu (1468–1551), in Ming-jen tsa-chü hsüan, p. 263, l. 12; T'ien-yüan ch'i-yü,

vol. 3, *chüan* 7, p. 23a, l. 1; *Ts'an-T'ang Wu-tai shih yen-i chuan*, ch. 49, p. 198, ll. 11–12; *Hsi-yu chi*, vol. 1, ch. 5, p. 56, l. 16; *Mu-lien chiu-mu ch'üan-shan hsi-wen*, *chüan* 1, p. 16a, l. 10; *Ch'üan-Han chih-chuan*, vol. 2, *chüan* 1, p. 6a, l. 4; *Ta-T'ang Ch'in-wang tz'u-hua*, vol. 1, *chüan* 2, ch. 14, p. 50b, l. 3; *Shuang-lieh chi*, scene 4, p. 11, l. 7; *Yü-ching t'ai*, scene 39, p. 104, l. 5; and an abundance of other occurrences, too numerous to list.

8. This formulaic four-character expression occurs in an anonymous Yüan dynasty song suite, *Ch'üan Yüan san-ch'ü*, 2:1798, l. 7; *Ch'ing feng-nien Wu-kuei nao Chung K'uei*, scene 4, p. 11a, l. 12; and *T'an-shih wu-wei pao-chüan*, p. 518, l. 3.

9. This formulaic four-character expression occurs ubiquitously in Chinese literature. See, e.g., *Yu hsien-k'u*, p. 17, l. 3; a biography by Su Shih (1037–1101), *Su Shih wen-chi*, vol. 2, *chüan* 13, p. 428, l. 7; a lyric by the Buddhist priest Fo-yin (1032–98), *Ch'üan Sung tz'u*, 1:369, upper register, l. 8; a lyric by Shih Hao (1106–94), ibid., 2:1251, upper register, l. 16; a speech attributed to the Buddhist monk Chih-yü (1185–1269), *Hsü-t'ang Ho-shang yü-lu*, *chüan* 1, p. 984, lower register, l. 25; *Yüan-ch'ü hsüan*, 2:714, l. 14; *Yüan-ch'ü hsüan wai-pien*, 2:576, l. 7; *Ch'in ping liu-kuo p'ing-hua*, p. 57, l. 2; *Lo-yang san-kuai chi*, p. 72, l. 11; *Yu-kuei chi*, scene 3, p. 3, l. 5; a set of songs by Wang Yüan-heng (14th century), *Ch'üan Yüan san-ch'ü*, 2:1384, l. 3; *San-kuo chih t'ung-su yen-i*, vol. 1, *chüan* 8, p. 354, ll. 13–14; *Sui-T'ang liang-ch'ao shih-chuan*, vol. 5, ch. 45, p. 28b, ll. 8–9; *Ts'an-T'ang Wu-tai shih yen-i chuan*, ch. 13, p. 44, l. 15; *Ku-Hang hung-mei chi*, *chüan* 8, p. 8a, l. 5; *Hsi-yu chi*, vol. 1, ch. 7, p. 75, l. 2; and *Chu-fa chi*, *chüan* 2, scene 17, p. 2a, l. 6.

10. This four-character expression occurs in Chu Hsi's (1130–1200) commentary to the *Lun-yü* (The analects of Confucius), *Ssu-shu chang-chü chi-chu*, p. 60, l. 3; *Yüan-ch'ü hsüan*, 3:1168, l. 7; *Yüan-ch'ü hsüan wai-pien*, 2:617, l. 18; *Ju-i chün chuan*, p. 21a, l. 10; *Huai-hsiang chi*, scene 37, p. 122, l. 6; a postface dated 1542 to *Tung-t'ien hsüan-chi*, p. 17a, l. 3; *Lieh-kuo chih-chuan*, vol. 3, *chüan* 8, p. 36b, l. 12; *Huan-sha chi*, scene 25, p. 87, ll. 10–11; *Ta-T'ang Ch'in-wang tz'u-hua*, vol. 1, *chüan* 1, ch. 3, p. 34a, l. 9; *Ko tai hsiao*, scene 1, p. 118, l. 3; and *San-pao t'ai-chien Hsi-yang chi t'ung-su yen-i*, vol. 1, ch. 18, p. 230, l. 13.

11. See Roy, *The Plum in the Golden Vase*, vol. 2, chap. 31, n. 9.

12. Ma-ku wine was a regional vintage, much esteemed in the mid-Ming period, that was said to be made with spring water from Ma-ku Mountain in Kiangsi province. The mountain in question is named for Ma-ku, a female transcendent in Taoist mythology, whose name is also associated with wine making. On the various legends about this figure, see Robert Ford Campany, *To Live as Long as Heaven and Earth: A Translation and Study of Ge Hong's Traditions of Divine Transcendents* (Berkeley: University of California Press, 2002), pp. 259–70.

13. This four-character expression occurs in two lyrics by Liu K'o-chuang (1187–1269), written in 1239 and 1264, *Ch'üan Sung tz'u*, 4:2620, lower register, l. 2; and 4:2607, upper register, l. 12; and a song suite by Chang Lien (cs 1544), *Ch'üan Ming san-ch'ü*, 2:1696, l. 12.

14. This formulaic four-character expression occurs ubiquitously in Chinese vernacular literature. See, e.g., *Chao Po-sheng ch'a-ssu yü Jen-tsung*, p. 173, l. 15; *K'an p'i-hsüeh tan-cheng Erh-lang Shen*, p. 244, l. 15; *Ching-ch'ai chi*, scene 6, p. 14, ll. 9–10; *P'o-yao chi*, *chüan* 2, scene 25, p. 27b, l. 8; *San-kuo chih t'ung-su yen-i*, vol. 1, *chüan* 1, p. 29, l. 24; *Huai-hsiang chi*, scene 32, p. 106, l. 12; *Tu Li-niang mu-se huan-*

hun, p. 536, l. 23; *Shui-hu ch'üan-chuan*, vol. 2, ch. 30, p. 459, l. 2; *T'ang-shu chih-chuan t'ung-su yen-i*, vol. 1, *chüan* 5, p. 36a, l. 11; *Nan Sung chih-chuan*, vol. 1, *chüan* 1, p. 18a, l. 6; *Pei Sung chih-chuan*, vol. 2, *chüan* 1, p. 6b, l. 9; *Lieh-kuo chih-chuan*, vol. 3, *chüan* 7, p. 77b, l. 9; *Ts'an-T'ang Wu-tai shih yen-i chuan*, ch. 47, p. 59, ll. 19–20; *Ssu-hsi chi*, scene 21, p. 56, l. 11; *Hsi-yu chi*, vol. 1, ch. 9, p. 99, l. 4; *Mu-lien chiu-mu ch'üan-shan hsi-wen*, *chüan* 2, p. 39b, l. 2; *Ch'üan-Han chih-chuan*, vol. 2, *chüan* 4, p. 28b, l. 6; *Huang-Ming k'ai-yün ying-wu chuan*, *chüan* 1, p. 18b, l. 2; *San-pao t'ai-chien Hsi-yang chi t'ung-su yen-i*, vol. 1, ch. 32, p. 423, l. 5; *Yang-chia fu shih-tai chung-yung yen-i chih-chuan*, vol. 1, *chüan* 4, p. 14a, l. 3; and *Ta-T'ang Ch'in-wang tz'u-hua*, vol. 1, *chüan* 1, ch. 6, p. 67a, l. 5.

15. This four-character expression occurs in *Yüan-ch'ü hsüan*, 4:1459, l. 7; *Yüan-ch'ü hsüan wai-pien*, 1:214, l. 10; and an anonymous Yüan dynasty song, *Ch'üan Yüan san-ch'ü*, 2:1763, l. 1.

16. This was the name of a famous villa constructed south of Lo-yang by the T'ang dynasty prime minister P'ei Tu (765–839) when he was living there in retirement near the end of his career. See his biography in *Chiu T'ang-shu*, vol. 14, *chüan* 170, p. 4432, ll. 6–10. This four-character expression occurs in a lyric by Liu Ping (14th century), *Ch'üan Ming tz'u*, 1:134, upper register, l. 2.

17. See Roy, *The Plum in the Golden Vase*, vol. 1, chap. 3, n. 11.

18. This formulaic four-character expression occurs in a lyric by Lu Yu (1125–1210), *Ch'üan Sung tz'u*, 3:1587, lower register, l. 8; *P'u-tung Ts'ui Chang chu-yü shih-chi*, p. 19a, l. 12; *Ch'ien-t'ang hu-yin Chi-tien Ch'an-shih yü-lu*, p. 50b, l. 2; *Hai-fu shan-t'ang tz'u-kao*, *chüan* 3, p. 146, l. 8; *Hsi-yu chi*, vol. 2, ch. 82, p. 940, l. 3; *Su Ying huang-hou ying-wu chi*, *chüan* 1, scene 11, p. 21a, l. 8; and *Ta-T'ang Ch'in-wang tz'u-hua*, vol. 2, *chüan* 5, ch. 39, p. 60a, l. 10.

19. This four-character expression occurs in *Shui-hu ch'üan-chuan*, vol. 1, ch. 21, p. 312, ll. 12–13.

20. *Hsing-chiu shih*, or "sobering stones," refers to a rare type of rock, alleged to help one recover from inebriation. They were utilized by the T'ang dynasty prime minister Li Te-yü (787–850) to enhance his villa near Lo-yang. See *Chiu Wu-tai shih*, vol. 3, *chüan* 60, p. 806, ll. 10–14.

21. It is alleged that Yang Kuo-chung (d. 756), another T'ang dynasty prime minister, was in the habit, in cold weather, of arraying the plumper of his maidservants and concubines around himself to keep out the wind and benefit from the warmth exuded by their bodies. He called these groupings "fleshly formations." See *K'ai-yüan T'ien-pao i-shih*, *chüan* 2, p. 95, l. 7. Later, a certain vice magistrate of Hang-chou named Tu Hsün, who engaged in the same practice, named these formations "fleshly screens." See *Ch'i-hsiu lei-kao* (Categorized notes under seven rubrics), by Lang Ying (1487–c. 1566), 2 vols. (Peking: Chung-hua shu-chü, 1961), vol. 2, *chüan* 44, p. 641, l. 6. This term also occurs in a song by Chia Chung-ming (1343–c. 1422), *Ch'üan Ming san-ch'ü*, 1:185, l. 5; and *Lien-huan chi*, scene 21, p. 55, l. 5.

22. Red-duster is the heroine of a T'ang dynasty literary tale, of uncertain authorship, entitled *Ch'iu-jan k'o chuan* (The curly-bearded guest). See *T'ang Sung ch'uan-ch'i chi*, *chüan* 4, pp. 165–71; and Wang, *Ladies of the Tang*, pp. 135–50.

23. It is said that the Lord of Ch'un-shen (d. 238 B.C.), the prime minister of the state of Ch'u, had three thousand retainers in his service, who once discountenanced an emissary from the state of Chao by showing up at an audience wearing pearl-studded

shoes. See his biography in *Shih-chi*, vol. 7, *chüan* 78, p. 2395, ll. 8–9. This four-character expression occurs ubiquitously in later Chinese literature. See, e.g., a poem by Li Po (701–62), *Ch'üan T'ang shih*, vol. 3, *chüan* 170, p. 1753, l. 15; a poem by Chang Chi (cs 753), ibid., vol. 4, *chüan* 242, p. 2724, l. 10; a poem by Wu Yüan-heng (758–815), ibid., vol. 5, *chüan* 317, p. 3571, l. 10; a poem by Tu Mu (803–52), ibid., vol. 8, *chüan* 521, p. 5958, l. 1; a poem by Li Ch'ün-yü (c. 813–c. 861), ibid., vol. 9, *chüan* 569, p. 6601, l. 14; a poem by Ch'en T'ao (c. 803–c. 879), ibid., vol. 11, *chüan* 746, p. 8492, l. 4; a poem by the Buddhist monk Kuan-hsiu (832–912), ibid., vol. 12, *chüan* 835, p. 9413, l. 2; a lyric by Liu Yung (cs 1034), *Ch'üan Sung tz'u*, 1:20, upper register, ll. 4–5; a lyric by Shih Hao (1106–94), ibid., 2:1282, upper register, l. 12; a lyric by Liu Ch'en-weng (1232–97), ibid., 5:3226, upper register, l. 11; *[Hsin-pien] Wu-tai shih p'ing-hua*, p. 115, l. 14; a set of songs by Wang Yüan-heng (14th century), *Ch'üan Yüan san-ch'ü*, 2:1380, l. 9; *P'o-yao chi*, *chüan* 1, scene 5, p. 14a, l. 3; *Chin-ch'ai chi*, scene 32, p. 59, l. 12; *Shuang-chu chi*, scene 38, p. 133, l. 4; *Lien-huan chi*, scene 3, p. 5, l. 8; *Huai-hsiang chi*, scene 39, p. 132, l. 7; a song by Wang Chiu-ssu (1468–1551), *Ch'üan Ming san-ch'ü*, 1:861, l. 12; *Huan-sha chi*, scene 4, p. 9, l. 11; *Pa-i chi*, scene 6, p. 10, l. 10; and *San-pao ta'i-chien Hsi-yang chi t'ung-su yen-i*, vol. 1, ch. 15, p. 195, l. 5.

24. It is said that Lord Meng-ch'ang, the title of T'ien Wen (d. 279 B.C.), a member of the ruling house of the state of Ch'i, had a retainer named Feng Hsüan who gained his attention by strumming on his sword and singing a song about the inadequacy of the treatment he was receiving. Later, he proved his worth by rendering invaluable assistance to his patron. See *Chan-kuo ts'e*, vol. 1, *chüan* 10, pp. 395–401; and *Chan-Kuo Ts'e*, trans. J. I. Crump (Oxford: Oxford University Press, 1970), pp. 189–92.

25. This four-character expression occurs in a poem by Lu Chao-lin (634–86), *Ch'üan T'ang shih*, vol. 1, *chüan* 42, p. 532, l. 5; a lyric by Su Shih (1037–1101), *Ch'üan Sung tz'u*, 1:277, upper register, ll. 12–13; a lyric by Ts'ao Hsün (1098–1174), ibid., 2:1212, lower register, l. 4; *Hsü-t'ang Ho-shang yü-lu*, p. 992, upper register, ll. 17–18, and *Mu-lien chiu-mu ch'üan-shan hsi-wen*, *chüan* 1, p. 3b, l. 10.

26. This four-character expression occurs in *Hsüan-ho i-shih*, p. 10, l. 9; *Chien-teng yü-hua*, *chüan* 1, p. 143, l. 6; *Shui-hu ch'üan-chuan*, vol. 1, ch. 9, p. 138, ll. 4–5; a set of songs by Liu Liang-ch'en (1482–1551), *Ch'üan Ming san-ch'ü*, 2:1319, l. 8; *Hsi-yu chi*, vol. 1, ch. 17, p. 196, l. 4; an anonymous song in *Kuo-se t'ien-hsiang*, vol. 1, *chüan* 2, p. 33a, upper register, l. 10; *San-pao t'ai-chien Hsi-yang chi t'ung-su yen-i*, vol. 1, ch. 47, p. 610, l. 5; *Ta-T'ang Ch'in-wang tz'u-hua*, vol. 2, *chüan* 5, ch. 39, p. 60b, l. 3; and a set of songs by Wang Hsi-chüeh (1534–1610), *Ch'üan Ming san-ch'ü*, 3:2908, l. 10.

27. Chin Mi-ti (134–86 B.C.) and Chang An-shih (d. 62 B.C.) were two high officials in the Han dynasty, whose descendants maintained superior status for successive generations. Their surnames became proverbial for the families of favored courtiers. The components of this four-character expression occur in reverse order in a poem by Meng Hao-jan (689–740), *Ch'üan T'ang shih*, vol. 3, *chüan* 160, p. 1661, l. 14.

28. Māra is the Buddhist equivalent of the Devil, who is believed to send his voluptuous daughters to Earth in order to tempt men to evil. For a description of this dance, of which Yüan Hui-tsung (r. 1333–68), the last emperor of the Yüan dynasty, is said to have been particularly fond, see W. L. Idema, *The Dramatic Oeuvre of Chu Yu-tun (1379–1439)* (Leiden: E. J. Brill, 1985), p. 74.

29. This is perhaps the most famous of all Chinese dances. It was performed at the court of Emperor Hsüan-tsung of the T'ang dynasty (r. 712–56) and is associated with the infatuation with music and dance, at the expense of affairs of state, that is believed to have contributed to his downfall.

30. The first two of these dances are attested as early as the T'ang dynasty, while the third is known to have been popular during the sixteenth century.

31. This four-character expression occurs in *Kuan-shih-yin p'u-sa pen-hsing ching*, *chüan* 2, p. 72b, ll. 9–10; and *Lieh-kuo chih-chuan*, vol. 1, *chüan* 3, p. 34a, l. 4.

32. This reduplicative four-character expression occurs in *San-pao-t'ai-chien Hsi-yang chi t'ung-su yen-i*, vol. 2, ch. 70, p. 906, l. 13; and *Chieh-hsia chi*, scene 12, p. 27, l. 9.

33. This four-character expression occurs in an inscription by Wang Hsien-chih (344–88), *Ch'üan Shang-ku San-tai Ch'in Han San-kuo Liu-ch'ao wen*, vol. 2, *Ch'üan Chin wen* (Complete prose of the Chin dynasty), *chüan* 27, p. 11b, l. 7; an essay written in the year 817 by Po Chü-i (772–846), *Ch'üan T'ang wen*, vol. 14, *chüan* 676, p. 2b, l. 5; an anecdote in *Ch'ing-po tsa-chih [chiao-chu]* (Miscellaneous notes by one who lives near the Ch'ing-po Gate [with collected commentary and critical annotation]), by Chou Hui (1127–c. 1198), author's pref. dated 1192, ed. and annot. Liu Yung-hsiang (Peking: Chung-hua shu-chü, 1997), *chüan* 8, p. 342, l. 11; the prose introduction to a lyric by Chang Yen (1248–1322), *Ch'üan Sung tz'u*, 5:3500, upper register, l. 10; *Chien-teng yü-hua*, *chüan* 5, p. 286, l. 1; *Wen-ching yüan-yang hui*, p. 161, l. 12; the literary tale *Liao-yang hai-shen chuan* (The sea goddess of Liao-yang), by Ts'ai Yü (d. 1541), in *Ku-tai wen-yen tuan-p'ien hsiao-shuo hsüan-chu, erh-chi*, p. 387, l. 10; *Shui-hu ch'üan-chuan*, vol. 4, ch. 90, p. 1472, l. 11; a literary tale in *Yüan-chu chih-yü: hsüeh-ch'uang t'an-i*, *chüan* 2, p. 44, l. 7; and *Chieh-hsia chi*, scene 11, p. 26, l. 5.

34. This type of folding armchair is traditionally associated with the name of Ch'in Kuei (1090–1155), perhaps the most universally vilified chief minister in Chinese history. For a description of this type of chair and an illustration of what it looked like, see Craig Clunas, *Chinese Furniture* (Chicago: Art Media Resources, 1997), pp. 24–28.

35. This four-character expression is derived from a proverbial couplet that reads:

> If one bothers to carry a goose feather a thousand li,
> Though the gift may be slight the feeling is profound.

The abbreviated expression occurs in the same form as in the novel in a poem by Huang T'ing-chien (1045–1105), *Ch'üan Sung shih*, 17:11522, l. 13.

36. See Roy, *The Plum in the Golden Vase*, vol. 1, chap. 10, n. 25.

37. An ancient Chinese name for Ceylon was the Lion Country, the natives of which were known as Lion Barbarians. Girdle plaques embellished with this motif were worn by officials during the Sung dynasty. See the treatise on official costumes in *Sung shih*, vol. 11, *chüan* 153, p. 3565, ll. 1–6, where they are described as coming in different grades, weighing anywhere between eighteen and twenty-five ounces.

38. This four-character expression occurs in *Ming-feng chi*, scene 18, p. 75, l. 10; and recurs in the *Chin P'ing Mei tz'u-hua*, vol. 4, ch. 66, p. 5b, l. 7.

39. This four-character expression occurs in a speech attributed to Wu Tzu-hsü (d. 484 B.C.) in *Wu Yüeh ch'un-ch'iu* (The annals of Wu and Yüeh), by Chao Yeh (1st

century A.D.). See *Wu Yüeh ch'un-ch'iu chu-tzu so-yin* (A concordance to the *Wu Yüeh ch'un-ch'iu*) (Hong Kong: Shang-wu yin-shu kuan, 1993), *chüan* 3, p. 5, l. 11; a memorial by Chai P'u (fl. early 2nd century), *Hou-Han shu*, vol. 6, *chüan* 48, p. 1602, l. 13; a letter written to Yü-wen Hu (514–72) in the year 564, *Chou shu*, vol. 1, *chüan* 11, p. 171, l. 5; and a document by Ch'en Liang (1143–94), *Ch'en Liang chi [tseng-ting pen]* (Collected works of Ch'en Liang [augmented and revised edition]), ed. Teng Kuang-ming, 2 vols. (Peking: Chung-hua shu-chü, 1987), vol. 2, *chüan* 26, p. 302, l. 14.

40. This four-character expression occurs in *San-pao t'ai-chien Hsi-yang chi t'ung-su yen-i*, vol. 1, ch. 48, p. 622, ll. 11–12.

41. Li Yen (d. 1126) is a historical figure. For his biography, see *Sung shih*, vol. 39, *chüan* 468, pp. 13664–65.

42. This formulaic four-character expression occurs in a rhapsody on physiognomy attributed to Kuan Lu (210–56), *Shen-hsiang ch'üan-pien*, *chüan* 639, p. 13a, l. 9. It appears ubiquitously in Chinese vernacular literature. See, e.g., *Yüan-ch'ü hsüan*, 2:422, l. 8; *Yüan-ch'ü hsüan wai-pien*, 1:203, l. 21; the early vernacular story *Wu-chieh Ch'an-shih ssu Hung-lien chi* (The Ch'an Master Wu-chieh defiles Hung-lien), in *Ch'ing-p'ing shan-t'ang hua-pen*, p. 137, l. 15; *Pai Niang-tzu yung-chen Lei-feng T'a*, p. 439, l. 11; *Meng-mu san-i*, scene 1, p. 4a, l. 12; *San-kuo chih t'ung-su yen-i*, vol. 1, *chüan* 2, p. 95, l. 22; the middle-period vernacular story *Li Yüan Wu-chiang chiu chu-she* (Li Yüan saves a red snake on the Wu River), in *Ch'ing-p'ing shan-t'ang hua-pen*, p. 327, l. 13; the middle-period vernacular story *P'ei Hsiu-niang yeh-yu Hsi-hu chi* (P'ei Hsiu-niang's night outing on the West Lake), in Hu Shih-ying, *Hua-pen hsiao-shuo kai-lun*, vol. 1, p. 344, l. 24; *Shui-hu ch'üan-chuan*, vol. 1, ch. 14, p. 205, l. 17; *Lieh-kuo chih-chuan*, vol. 1, *chüan* 1, p. 43a, l. 9; *Yen-chih chi*, *chüan* 1, scene 8, p. 10a, l. 3; *Hsi-yu chi*, vol. 1, ch. 27, p. 305, l. 16; *Pa-i chi*, scene 10, p. 24, l. 7; *Ts'an-T'ang Wu-tai shih yen-i chuan*, ch. 9, p. 25, l. 15; *San-pao t'ai-chien Hsi-yang chi t'ung-su yen-i*, vol. 1, ch. 10, p. 131, l. 10; *Sui-T'ang liang-ch'ao shih-chuan*, *chüan* 1, ch. 6, p. 33b, ll. 3–4; and *Ta-T'ang Ch'in-wang tz'u-hua*, vol. 2, *chüan* 5, ch. 36, p. 34a, l. 4. It also recurs in the *Chin P'ing Mei tz'u-hua*, vol. 5, ch. 93, p. 9a, l. 1; and ch. 100, p. 3b, l. 11.

43. This four-character expression is derived from a proverbial saying that means "The gentleman does not appropriate the source of another's pleasure." Variants of this saying occur in a speech attributed to the famous Ch'an monk Chao-chou Ts'ung-shen (778–897), *Ku tsun-su yü-lu*, *chüan* 13, p. 159b, upper register, l. 5; and *Ju-i chün chuan*, p. 16a, l. 6. It occurs in the same form as in the novel in *Yüan-ch'ü hsüan*, 4:1682, l. 6; *Yüan-ch'ü hsüan wai-pien*, 1:32, ll. 4–5; and, 2:623, l. 11; and an anonymous Yüan dynasty song suite, *Ch'üan Yüan san-ch'ü*, 2:1849, l. 10.

44. A variant of this four-character expression occurs in *Yü-huan chi*, scene 27, p. 99, l. 4; *San-kuo chih t'ung-su yen-i*, vol. 2, *chüan* 22, p. 1076, l. 18; and *Lieh-kuo chih-chuan*, vol. 1, *chüan* 3, p. 51a, l. 3. It occurs in the same form as in the novel in *Chung-ch'ing li-chi*, vol. 2, *chüan* 6, p. 34a, l. 13; *Mu-lien chiu-mu ch'üan-shan hsi-wen*, *chüan* 1, p. 81b, l. 9; and recurs in the *Chin P'ing Mei tz'u-hua*, vol. 3, ch. 55, p. 10b, l. 2.

45. This formulaic four-character expression occurs in a poem by Yin Yao-fan (cs 814), *Ch'üan T'ang shih*, vol. 8, *chüan* 492, p. 5569, l. 9. It appears ubiquitously in later vernacular literature. See, e.g., *Hsiao Sun-t'u*, scene 12, p. 303, l. 17; the anonymous early hsi-wen drama *Liu Wen-lung ling-hua ching* (Liu Wen-lung's caltrop-pat-

terned mirror), *Sung-Yüan hsi-wen chi-i*, p. 214, l. 18; *P'i-p'a chi*, scene 7, p. 49, l. 11; *Hsiang-nang chi*, scene 6, p. 18, l. 9; *Yüeh Fei p'o-lu tung-ch'uang chi*, chüan 1, scene 21, p. 33b, l. 4; *Pao-chien chi*, scene 19, p. 38, l. 2; a song suite by Liang Ch'en-yü (1519–91), written in 1571, *Ch'üan Ming san-ch'ü*, 2:2229, l. 14; *Mu-lien chiu-mu ch'üan-shan hsi-wen*, chüan 1, p. 54a, ll. 2–3; *Yen-chih chi*, chüan 2, scene 28, p. 12b, l. 3; *Hsi-yu chi*, vol. 1, ch. 36, p. 410, l. 4; *Shuang-lieh chi*, scene 7, p. 20, l. 2; and *Shih-hou chi*, scene 6, p. 16, l. 8.

46. This formulaic four-character expression occurs ubiquitously in Chinese vernacular literature. See, e.g., a lyric by Shih Hao (1106–94), *Ch'üan Sung tz'u*, 2:1284, lower register, l. 16; a lyric by Chao Shih-hsia (cs 1175), ibid., 3:2096, upper register, l. 16; *Kuan-shih-yin p'u-sa pen-hsing ching*, p. 32a, l. 7; a song by Chao Hsien-hung (14th century), *Ch'üan Yüan san-ch'ü*, 2:1178, l. 9; *Yüan-ch'ü hsüan*, 3:1089, l. 2; *Cheng Chieh-shih li-kung shen-pi kung*, p. 666, l. 3; *Chin-ming ch'ih Wu Ch'ing feng Ai-ai*, p. 468, l. 11; *Hsi-hu san-t'a chi*, p. 27, l. 8; *Hua-teng chiao Lien-nü ch'eng-Fo chi*, p. 200, l. 12; *Fo-yin shih ssu t'iao Ch'in-niang*, p. 236, l. 10; *Pai Niang-tzu yung-chen Lei-feng T'a*, p. 422, l. 11; *Shih-wu kuan hsi-yen ch'eng ch'iao-huo*, p. 691, l. 8; *Ching-ch'ai chi*, scene 3, p. 6, l. 8; the anonymous Yüan-Ming tsa-chü drama *Nü ku-ku shuo-fa sheng- t'ang chi* (The nun who took the pulpit to expound the dharma), in *Ku-pen Yüan Ming tsa-chü*, vol. 3, *hsieh-tzu* (wedge), p. 2b, l. 9; *Chin-ch'ai chi*, scene 40, p. 66, l. 3; *Ch'en Hsün-chien Mei-ling shih-ch'i chi*, p. 122, l. 5; *Yü-huan chi*, scene 8, p. 28, l. 4; *Chiang Shih yüeh-li chi*, chüan 4, scene 39, p. 17b, l. 5; *Hsiu-ju chi*, scene 4, p. 7, ll. 9–10; *Pao-chien chi*, scene 48, p. 87, l. 2; *Shuang-lieh chi*, scene 3, p. 7, l. 5; and *Shih-hou chi*, scene 10, p. 30, l. 6.

47. This four-character expression occurs in an anonymous poem from the T'ang dynasty, *Ch'üan T'ang shih*, vol. 11, chüan 796, p. 8965, l. 8. It is ubiquitous in later Chinese literature. See, e.g., a speech attributed to the Buddhist monk Fa-yen (d. 1104), *Ku tsun-su yü-lu*, chüan 21, p. 213b, lower register, l. 3; a lyric by Chu Shu-chen (fl. 1078–1138), *Ch'üan Sung tz'u*, 2:1405, upper register, l. 14; a lyric by Shih Hsiao-yu (cs 1166), ibid., 3:2053, lower register, ll. 4–5; a passage of poetic criticism by Wang Mao (1151–1213), *Sung shih-hua ch'üan-pien*, 7:7468, l. 7; *Ssu-shih hua-yüeh sai chiao-jung*, scene 1, p. 2b, l. 14; a song suite by T'ang Yin (1470–1524), *Ch'üan Ming san-ch'ü*, 1:1083, l. 10; *Chiang Shih yüeh-li chi*, chüan 1, scene 10, p. 16a, l. 10; *Shui-hu ch'üan-chuan*, vol. 1, ch. 1, p. 2, l. 15; *Pao-chien chi*, scene 52, p. 95, l. 23; *Pei Sung chih-chuan*, vol. 2, chüan 5, p. 10b, ll. 5–6; *Su Ying huang-hou ying-wu chi*, chüan 1, scene 8, p. 15b, l. 4; *Pai-chia kung-an*, chüan 1, p. 6a, l. 6; *Ch'eng-yün chuan*, chüan 4, p. 5a, l. 1; and *Ta-T'ang Ch'in-wang tz'u-hua*, vol. 1, chüan 3, ch. 24, p. 84b, l. 1.

48. No such event occurs in the version of the supplied chapters included in *Chin P'ing Mei tz'u-hua*, but there is such an incident in chapter 54 in the B edition of the novel. See *[Hsin-k'o hsiu-hsiang p'i-p'ing] Chin P'ing Mei* ([Newly cut illustrated commentarial edition] of the *Chin P'ing Mei*), 2 vols. (Chi-nan: Ch'i-Lu shu-she, 1989), vol. 2, ch. 54, p. 709, ll. 11–15.

49. This couplet is from a poem by Su Shih (1037–1101), written in 1073, in which he gently pokes fun at his friend and bureaucratic superior, the famous poet Chang Hsien (990–1078), who was still maintaining a bevy of concubines at the age of eighty-four. See *Su Shih shih-chi*, vol. 2, chüan 11, p. 523, ll. 7–9. Ying-ying is the inamorata of a young man named Chang in the literary tale *Ying-ying chuan* (Story of Ying-ying),

by Yüan Chen (775–831). See Roy, *The Plum in the Golden Vase*, vol. 1, preface, n. 11. Yen-yen is said to have been the name of a concubine of the poet Chang Hu (c. 792–c. 854). See *Su Shih shih-chi*, vol. 2, *chüan* 11, p. 523, l. 10. The first line of this couplet occurs independently in a song suite by Chu Yu-tun (1379–1439), *Ch'üan Ming san-ch'ü*, 1:355, l. 6; and in a song by Yang Shen (1488–1559), ibid., 2:1409, ll. 2–3.

50. This is the first couplet from a quatrain traditionally attributed, if somewhat doubtfully, to Wang Chu (cs 1100). See *Ch'üan Sung shih*, 22:14978, l. 10. That it was already current during the twelfth century is attested by the fact that it is quoted in *Jung-chai sui-pi* (Miscellaneous notes from the Tolerant Study), by Hung Mai (1123–1202), 2 vols. (Shanghai: Shang-hai ku-chi ch'u-pan she, 1978), vol. 2, collection no. 4, *chüan* 8, p. 701, l. 10. It occurs ubiquitously in later Chinese literature. See, e.g., *Pai-t'u chi*, scene 7, p. 21, l. 3; the anonymous Ming ch'uan-ch'i drama *Ku-ch'eng chi* (The reunion at Ku-ch'eng), in *Ku-pen hsi-ch'ü ts'ung-k'an*, *ch'u-chi*, item 25, *chüan* 2, scene 23, p. 15a, ll. 8–9; *Chin-ch'ai chi*, scene 22, p. 43, l. 12; *Jen hsiao-tzu lieh-hsing wei shen*, p. 572, l. 16; *Pao-chien chi*, scene 29, p. 56, l. 14; and *Hung-fu chi*, scene 10, p. 18, l. 12. It recurs in the *Chin P'ing Mei tz'u-hua*, vol. 5, ch. 97, p. 11a, l. 5. The first line of this couplet occurs independently in *Ching-ch'ai chi*, scene 26, p. 83, l. 9; *Shuang-chu chi*, scene 8, p. 23, l. 2; *Ssu-hsi chi*, scene 8, p. 21, l. 4; *Hsi-yu chi*, vol. 2, ch. 87, p. 997, l. 8; and *Hai-ling i-shih*, *chüan* 2, p. 114, l. 5. The second line occurs independently in *Yang Ssu-wen Yen-shan feng ku-jen*, p. 369, l. 16; *T'ao Yüan-ming tung-li shang-chü*, scene 3, p. 11a, l. 1; a song suite by P'eng Tse (cs 1490), *Ch'üan Ming san-ch'ü*, 1:840, l. 5; *Ssu-hsi chi*, scene 40, p. 102, l. 5; and *Mu-lien chiu-mu ch'üan-shan hsi-wen*, *chüan* 3, p. 8b, l. 4.

51. This four-character expression occurs in a song by Chu Yu-tun (1379–1439), *Ch'üan Ming san-ch'ü*, 1:274, l. 13; a song by Ch'en To (fl. early 16th century), ibid., 1:512, l. 14; *Huan-sha chi*, scene 16, p. 54, l. 7; *Pai-chia kung-an*, *chüan* 1, ch. 7, p. 26a, l. 13; and a song suite by Ch'en So-wen (d. c. 1604), *Ch'üan Ming san-ch'ü*, 2:2586, l. 13.

52. This four-character expression occurs in a remark attributed to Ch'eng Hao (1032–85), *Sung shih*, vol. 36, *chüan* 427, p. 12712, l. 15; a poem by Chu Hsi (1130–1200), *Ch'üan Sung shih*, 44:27592, l. 14; a lyric by Hsiao Chung-jui (13th century), *Ch'üan Sung tz'u*, 5:3541, lower register, l. 12; a song by Chang Yang-hao (1270–1329), *Ch'üan Yüan san-ch'ü*, 1:421, l. 5; a song by Chang K'o-chiu (1270–1348), ibid., 1:800. l. 11; a lyric by Hsieh Ying-fang (1296–1392), *Ch'üan Chin Yüan tz'u*, 2:1062, upper register, l. 10; a lyric by Ku Hsün (1418–1505), *Ch'üan Ming tz'u*, 1:301, lower register, l. 9; a song by K'ang Hai (1475–1541), *Ch'üan Ming san-ch'ü*, 1:1122, l. 11; a song by Chang Lien (cs 1544), ibid., 2:1673, l. 3; *Chin-lan ssu-yu chuan*, p. 1b, l. 9; *Hai-fu shan-t'ang tz'u-kao*, *chüan* 2b, p. 116, l. 11; a song suite by Ch'en So-wen (d. c. 1604), *Ch'üan Ming san-ch'ü*, 2:2566, l. 4; and *Shih-hou chi*, scene 26, p. 90, l. 3.

53. This four-character expression occurs in *Hsüan-ho i-shih*, p. 7, l. 4; and *Lieh-kuo chih-chuan*, vol. 1, *chüan* 1, p. 22a, l. 8.

54. See chap. 53, n. 33.

55. This four-character expression occurs in *Hsi-yu chi*, vol. 2, ch. 86, p. 976, l. 10.

56. These are the names of two ancient tunes that were regarded as being difficult to perform and possessing appeal only to cultivated as opposed to vulgar tastes. The

earliest reference to these tunes is in a statement attributed to Sung Yü (3rd century B.C.) in *Hsin-hsü* (New exordia), comp. Liu Hsiang (79–8 B.C.). See *Hsin-hsü chu-tzu so-yin* (A concordance to the *Hsin-hsü*) (Hong Kong: Shang-wu yin-shu kuan, 1992), section 1, p. 5, item no. 16, l. 3. The names of these two tunes occur together ubiquitously in later Chinese literature. See, e.g., a statement attributed to Wang Chih-huan (688–742) in the collection of literary anecdotes entitled *Chi-i chi* (Collected records of the unusual), by Hsüeh Yung-jo (fl. early 9th century), in *Ku-shih wen-fang hsiao-shuo* (Fiction from the library of Mr. Ku), comp. Ku Yüan-ch'ing (1487–1565), 10 *ts'e*, fac. repr. (Shanghai: Shang-wu yin-shu-kuan, 1934), *ts'e* 5, *chüan* 2, p. 4a, ll. 5–6; the title of a poem by Ou-yang Kun (cs 825), *Ch'üan T'ang shih*, vol. 8, *chüan* 512, p. 5854, l. 12; a poem by Shao Yung (1011–77), *Ch'üan Sung shih*, 7:4515, l. 9; a lyric by Chao Ting (1085–1147), *Ch'üan Sung tz'u*, 2:945, lower register, l. 4; a lyric by Chang Hsiao-hsiang (1132–69), ibid., 3:1691, upper register, l. 16; a lyric by Hsin Ch'i-chi (1140–1207), ibid., 3:1878, upper register, l. 12; *Tsui-weng t'an-lu, chia-chi* (first collection), *chüan* 1, p. 1, l. 4; a lyric by Chang Yeh (13th–14th centuries), *Ch'üan Chin Yüan tz'u*, 2:894, upper register, l. 12; a song suite by Chao Yen-hui (14th century), *Ch'üan Yüan san-ch'ü*, 2:1232, l. 12; *Yüan-ch'ü hsüan wai-pien*, 3:770, ll. 12–13; a song suite by Wang Chiu-ssu (1468–1551), *Ch'üan Ming san-ch'ü*, 1:963, l. 5; *Hsi-yu chi*, vol. 2, ch. 64, p. 736, l. 7; a song by Hsüeh Lun-tao (c. 1531–c. 1600), *Ch'üan Ming san-ch'ü*, 3:2722, l. 5; and the ch'uan-ch'i drama *Chin-lien chi* (The golden lotus [lamp]), by Ch'en Ju-yüan (fl. 1572–1629), *Liu-shih chung ch'ü* ed., scene 3, p. 8, l. 3.

57. This formulaic four-character expression occurs in a poem attributed to Lü Tung-pin (9th century), *Ch'üan T'ang shih*, vol. 12, *chüan* 857, p. 9688, l. 13. It appears ubiquitously in later Chinese literature. See, e.g., *Kuan-shih-yin p'u-sa pen-hsing ching*, p. 53b, l. 7; a song suite by Liu Shih-chung (14th century), *Ch'üan Yüan san-ch'ü*, 1:670, l. 15; a song suite by Lü Shih-chung (14th century), ibid., 2:1153, l. 7; *Yüan-ch'ü hsüan*, 1:417, l. 19; *Yüan-ch'ü hsüan wai-pien*, 2:588, l. 2; *Yü-huan chi*, scene 2, p. 4, l. 1; *Shih Chen-jen ssu-sheng so pai-yüan*, scene 1, p. 2b, l. 9; *Shuang-chu chi*, scene 7, p. 19, l. 3; *Huai-hsiang chi*, scene 37, p. 123, l. 1; *Wang Lan-ch'ing chen-lieh chuan*, scene 2, p. 4b, l. 13; a song by Hsia Yang (16th century), *Ch'üan Ming san-ch'ü*, 1:810, l. 4; a song suite by Lu Chih (1496–1576), ibid., 2:1732, l. 11; *Lieh-kuo chih-chuan*, vol. 2, *chüan* 5, p. 78a, ll. 7–8; *San-pao t'ai-chien Hsi-yang chi t'ung-su yen-i*, vol. 2, ch. 95, p. 1222, l. 12; *Tung-yu chi: shang-tung pa-hsien chuan*, *chüan* 1, p. 2a, ll. 6–7; and *Yü-ching t'ai*, scene 17, p. 44, ll. 6–7.

58. This formulaic four-character expression occurs ubiquitously in Chinese vernacular literature. See, e.g., *San-kuo chih p'ing-hua*, p. 61, l. 2; *Yüan-ch'ü hsüan*, 2:523, l. 16; *San-kuo chih t'ung-su yen-i*, vol. 1, *chüan* 1, p. 10, l. 8; *Shui-hu ch'üan-chuan*, vol. 1, ch. 5, p. 87, l. 10; *T'ang-shu chih-chuan t'ung-su yen-i*, vol. 1, *chüan* 3, p. 39a, l. 5; *Ts'an-T'ang Wu-tai shih yen-i chuan*, ch. 7, p. 19, l. 11; *Nan Sung chih-chuan*, vol. 1, *chüan* 5, p. 9a, l. 7; *Hsi-yu chi*, vol. 1, ch. 13, p. 152, l. 8; *Ch'üan-Han chih-chuan*, vol. 2, *chüan* 4, p. 30a, l. 5; *Sui-T'ang liang-ch'ao shih-chuan*, *chüan* 3, ch. 25, p. 28a, l. 9; *Yang-chia fu shih-tai chung-yung yen-i chih-chuan*, vol. 1, *chüan* 1, p. 34a, l. 6; and *Ta-T'ang Ch'in-wang tz'u-hua*, vol. 1, *chüan* 2, ch. 16, p. 71b, l. 3.

59. This couplet occurs in *Yu-kuei chi*, scene 22, p. 54, l. 8; *Hsiang-nang chi*, scene 7, p. 20, l. 3; *Mu-tan t'ing*, scene 49, p. 244, ll. 6–7; *Ch'ün-yin lei-hsüan*, 3:1838, l. 7; and *I-hsia chi*, scene 22, p. 56, ll. 8–9, where the two lines are quoted in reverse order

with another line in between. It also recurs in the *Chin P'ing Mei tz'u-hua*, vol. 5, ch. 98, p. 4b, l. 1. Variants of the couplet occur in *Yüan-ch'ü hsüan*, 3:1189, ll. 2–3; and *Shui-hu ch'üan-chuan*, vol. 1, ch. 9, p. 137, l. 5. The first line also occurs independently in *Wu Lun-ch'üan Pei*, *chüan* 1, scene 2, p. 4a, l. 6.

60. "Flying white" is the name of a style of calligraphy in which the brush is dragged over the writing surface so fast that the hairs of the brush do not consistently touch the surface, leaving irregular white streaks within the black strokes.

61. Variants of this idiomatic expression occur in *Shui-hu ch'üan-chuan*, vol. 2, ch. 45, p. 744, l. 13; and a song by Chin Luan (1494–1583), *Ch'üan Ming san-ch'ü*, 2:1586, l. 5.

62. This four-character expression occurs in *Yüan-ch'ü hsüan*, 2:458, l. 18; and *Hsi-yu chi*, vol. 2, ch. 57, p. 660, l. 17.

63. This four-character expression is listed as proverbial in the thirteenth-century encyclopedia *Shih-lin kuang-chi* (Expansive gleanings from the forest of affairs), fac. repr. of 14th-century ed. (Peking: Chung-hua shu-chü, 1963), *ch'ien-chi*, *chüan* 9, p. 9b, l. 10. It occurs ubiquitously in later Chinese literature. See, e.g., *Yüan-ch'ü hsüan*, 2:422, l. 19; *Yüan-ch'ü hsüan wai-pien*, 2:361, l. 2; *Yu-kuei chi*, scene 26, p. 77, l. 4; *San-yüan chi*, scene 10, p. 23, l. 12; *Hung-fu chi*, scene 28, p. 58, l. 9; *Hsi-yu chi*, vol. 1, ch. 36, p. 414, l. 1; and *Shuang-lieh chi*, scene 8, p. 22, l. 6.

64. This four-character expression occurs in a lyric by Ch'ang-ch'üan-tzu (13th century), *Ch'üan Chin Yüan tz'u*, 1:584, upper register, l. 2; *K'an p'i-hsüeh tan-cheng Erh-lang Shen*, p. 247, l. 2; and *Hsiu-ju chi*, scene 41, p. 109, l. 10.

65. This four-character expression occurs in a lyric by Ho Chu (1052–1125), *Ch'üan Sung tz'u*, 1:538, lower register, l. 16; *Wang Wen-hsiu Wei-t'ang ch'i-yü chi*, scene 3, p. 7b, l. 12; *Yen-chih chi*, *chüan* 2, scene 37, p. 27a, l. 3; and *San-pao t'ai-chien Hsi-yang chi t'ung-su yen-i*, vol. 2, ch. 88, p. 1131, ll. 12–13.

66. The story of the friendship between Fan Shih and Chang Shao, two figures of the Later Han dynasty (25–220), is recorded in the biography of Fan Shih in *Hou-Han shu*, vol. 8, *chüan* 81, pp. 2676–77. It is also the subject of the middle-period vernacular story *Ssu-sheng chiao Fan Chang chi-shu* (The chicken and millet life and death friendship between Fan Shih and Chang Shao), in *Ch'ing-p'ing shan-t'ang hua-pen*, pp. 280–83.

67. This four-character expression occurs in *Ta-Sung chung-hsing yen-i*, vol. 2, *chüan* 6, p. 43b, l. 1; and *Lieh-kuo chih-chuan*, vol. 3, *chüan* 7, p. 21a, l. 6.

68. This four-character expression occurs in *Yüan-ch'ü hsüan*, 4:1462, l. 12; *Sha-kou chi*, scene 7, p. 23, l. 12; *Hsi-yu chi*, vol. 2, ch. 54, p. 621, l. 7; *Mu-lien chiu-mu ch'üan-shan hsi-wen*, *chüan* 1, p. 10a, ll. 5–6; and *San-pao t'ai-chien Hsi-yang chi t'ung-su yen-i*, vol. 1, ch. 36, p. 468, l. 12.

69. This formulaic four-character expression occurs in a poem by Han Chü (1080–1135), *Ch'üan Sung shih*, 25:16582, l. 1; *Yüan-ch'ü hsüan wai-pien*, 1:207, l. 18; *Hua-teng chiao Lien-nü ch'eng-Fo chi*, p. 203, l. 2; *Shen-hsiang ch'üan-pien*, *chüan* 631, p. 9b, l. 6; *Lieh-kuo chih-chuan*, vol. 1, *chüan* 2, p. 60b, l. 12; *Ch'üan-Han chih-chuan*, vol. 2, *chüan* 1, p. 15a, l. 9; *Li Yün-ch'ing te-wu sheng-chen*, scene 3, p. 10b, l. 11; a legal document quoted in *Kuo-se t'ien-hsiang*, vol. 2, *chüan* 6, p. 3a, upper register, l. 16; *Ch'ün-yin lei-hsüan*, 3:1726, l. 3; *San-pao t'ai-chien Hsi-yang chi t'ung-su yen-i*, vol. 1, ch. 3, p. 38, l. 6; and *Mu-tan t'ing*, scene 55, p. 276, l. 3.

70. For the "Kao-t'ang fu," see Roy, *The Plum in the Golden Vase*, vol. 1, chap. 2, n. 47. This line is from a famous lyric by Su Shih (1037–1101), *Ch'üan Sung tz'u*, 1:278, lower register, l. 10. It also occurs in *Yüan-ch'ü hsüan*, 3:1162, l. 1; *Yüan-ch'ü hsüan wai-pien*, 2:358, l. 6; a song suite by Fan Chü-chung (fl. 1297–1307), *Ch'üan Yüan san-ch'ü*, 1:535, l. 1; an anonymous Yüan dynasty song suite, ibid., 2:1793, l. 11; *Ching-ch'ai chi*, scene 46, p. 133, l. 7; and verse 9 of a suite of one hundred songs to the tune "Hsiao-t'ao hung" that retells the story of the *Ying-ying chuan* by a Ming dynasty figure named Wang Yen-chen, *Yung-hsi yüeh-fu*, ts'e 19, p. 33b, ll. 7–8.

71. This four-character expression occurs in a lyric by Hsin Ch'i-chi (1140–1207), *Ch'üan Sung tz'u*, 3:1896, lower register, l. 8; a lyric by Kuo Ying-hsiang (b. 1158, cs 1181), ibid., 4:2232, upper register, l. 13; and a song by Hsüeh Kang (c. 1535–95), *Ch'üan Ming san-ch'ü*, 3:2967, l. 10.

72. The "Airs of Pin" is the name of a section, comprising songs no. 154–60, in the *Shih-ching* (Book of Songs), in which the pleasures of rural life are celebrated. See *Mao-shih yin-te*, pp. 31–33.

73. The song "Blue Waters" is quoted in *Mencius*. See *Meng-tzu yin-te*, p. 27, 4A.9. It is also found in the *Ch'u-tz'u* (Songs of Ch'u), comp. Wang I (d. 158), under the title *Yü-fu* (The fisherman), where it is provided with a prose setting that makes it more meaningful. See *Ch'u-tz'u pu-chu [fu so-yin]* (Songs of Ch'u with supplementary annotation [and a concordance]), comp. Hung Hsing-tsu (1090–1155) (Kyoto: Chū-bun shuppan-sha, 1972), *chüan* 7, pp. 1a-3a; and *The Songs of the South*, trans. David Hawkes (New York: Penguin Books, 1985), pp. 206–7.

74. This line occurs in a lyric by Yeh Ching-shan (11th century), *Ch'üan Sung tz'u pu-chi*, p. 22, upper register, l. 5.

75. The expression "mulberry and elm" stands for one's declining years, the metaphor being that when the setting sun illuminates the upper branches of the mulberry and the elm, the light will not last for long.

76. This set of four lyrics celebrating the idealized pleasures of the bucolic life throughout the cycle of the seasons, as well as the aesthetic satisfactions provided by poetry and painting, is surely intended to reflect ironically on Hsi-men Ch'ing, whose life-style is antithetical to that depicted in the lyrics.

77. This four-character expression occurs in a lyric by Wang Kuan (cs 1057), *Ch'üan Sung tz'u pu-chi*, p. 5, lower register, ll. 10–11; and a lyric by Shih Hao (1106–94), *Ch'üan Sung tz'u*, 2:1270, lower register, l. 16.

CHAPTER 56

1. The term *su-feng*, or "untitled nobility," is from a passage in *chüan* 129 of the *Shih-chi*, "The Biographies of the Money-Makers," which Burton Watson translates: "Now there are men who receive no ranks or emoluments from the government and who have no revenue from titles or fiefs, and yet they enjoy just as much ease as those who have all these; they may be called the 'untitled nobility.' " See *Shih-chi*, vol. 10, *chüan* 129, p. 3272, l. 1; and Watson, *Records of the Grand Historian of China*, 2:492, ll. 21–24.

2. This line alludes to a famous passage in *Chuang-tzu*, which Burton Watson translates as follows: "Once Chuang Chou dreamt he was a butterfly, a butterfly flitting and fluttering around, happy with himself and doing as he pleased. He didn't know

he was Chuang Chou. Suddenly he woke up and there he was, solid and unmistakable Chuang Chou. But he didn't know if he was Chuang Chou who had dreamt he was a butterfly, or a butterfly dreaming he was Chuang Chou." See *Chuang-tzu yin-te*, ch. 2, p. 7, ll. 11–13; and Watson, *The Complete Works of Chuang Tzu*, p. 49, ll. 15–21.

3. The Citadel at Mei was built as a fortified and luxuriously stocked rural retreat by Tung Cho (d. 192), a ruthless dictator who aspired to usurp the throne but was, instead, assassinated only a few years later. See his biography in *Hou-Han shu*, vol. 8, *chüan* 72, p. 2329, ll. 15–16; and *San-kuo chih t'ung-su yen-i*, vol. 1, *chüan* 2, p. 70, ll. 15–19.

4. Teng T'ung (2d century B.C.) was the male favorite of Emperor Wen (r. 180–157 B.C.) of the Han dynasty, who rewarded him by giving him the right to mine the Copper Mountains in Szechwan and mint his own coinage, so that his wealth became proverbial. But after Emperor Wen died, he was reduced to penury and came to an ignominious end. See Roy, *The Plum in the Golden Vase*, vol. 1, chap. 3, n. 4.

5. Pao Shu-ya (7th century B.C.) is chiefly remembered for his friendship with Kuan Chung (d. 645 B.C.), the chief minister who enabled Duke Huan of Ch'i (r. 685–643 B.C.) to establish himself as hegemon among the rulers of the feudal states in ancient China. In Kuan Chung's biography in the *Shih-chi* he is quoted as saying, "Once, when I was suffering from adversity, I engaged in trade with Pao Shu-ya and in dividing the proceeds took more than my share for myself, but Pao Shu-ya did not consider me greedy because he knew that I was impoverished." See *Shih-chi*, vol. 7, *chüan* 62, p. 2131, l. 13.

6. See chap. 51, n. 63.

7. This four-character expression occurs in *Wu Lun-ch'üan Pei*, *chüan* 3, scene 21, p. 34b, l. 2; and recurs in the *Chin P'ing Mei tz'u-hua*, vol. 4, ch. 76, p. 1a, l. 4.

8. This four-character expression occurs in a poem attributed to the Buddhist monk Chih-hsien (d. 898), *Tsu-t'ang chi*, *chüan* 19, p. 417, l. 11; *Yüan-ch'ü hsüan*, 3:1062, l. 14; *K'u-kung wu-tao chüan*, 1:90, ll. 2–3; *Cheng-hsin ch'u-i wu hsiu cheng tzu-tsai pao-chüan*, 3:126, l. 1; *Tung-t'ien hsüan-chi*, scene 2, p. 9b, l. 7; and the middle-period vernacular story *Chang Tzu-fang mu-tao chi* (The story of Chang Liang's pursuit of the Way), in *Ch'ing-p'ing shan-t'ang hua-pen*, p. 104, l. 14.

9. This four-character expression occurs in a poem attributed to Lü Tung-pin (9th century), *Ch'üan T'ang shih*, vol. 12, *chüan* 859, p. 9715, l. 13; a lyric by Chao Ch'ang-ch'ing (12th century), *Ch'üan Sung tz'u*, 3:1806, upper register, l. 12; a lyric by Yin Chih-p'ing (1169–1251), *Ch'üan Chin Yüan tz'u*, 2:1183, upper register, l. 3; a collection of moral observations entitled *Tung-ku so chien* (Observations of Tung-ku), by Li Chih-yen (13th century), author's pref. dated 1268, in *Shuo-fu san-chung*, 6:3428, p. 19a, l. 7; a song by Teng Yü-pin (13th century), *Ch'üan Yüan san-ch'ü*, 1:303, l. 6; a song suite by Ch'ien Lin (14th century), ibid., 2:1031, l. 2; *Yüan-ch'ü hsüan*, 4:1679, l. 11; a song by Wang Chiu-ssu (1468–1551), *Ch'üan Ming san-ch'ü*, 1:898, ll. 11–12; a set of songs by Liu Liang-ch'en (1482–1551), ibid., 2:1318, ll. 11–12; *[Hsiao-shih] Chen-k'ung pao-chüan*, 19:297, l. 5; and *I-hsia chi*, scene 26, p. 69, l. 4.

10. This formulaic four-character expression is ubiquitous in Chinese vernacular literature. See, e.g., *Ch'in ping liu-kuo p'ing-hua*, p. 55, ll. 6–7; *Ching-ch'ai chi*, scene 27, p. 86, l. 11; *Yu-kuei chi*, scene 4, p. 9, l. 10; *Pai-she chi*, *chüan* 2, scene 28, p. 30b, l. 8; *Chiang Shih yüeh-li chi*, *chüan* 2, scene 19, p. 8b, l. 1; *Lien-huan chi*, scene 3, p. 7, l. 4; *Lieh-kuo chih-chuan*, vol. 3, *chüan* 8, p. 83a, l. 11; *Mu-lien chiu-mu ch'üan-*

shan hsi-wen, chüan 2, p. 45b, l. 8; *Yü-ching t'ai*, scene 28, p. 76, l. 5; *Su Ying huang-hou ying-wu chi, chüan* 1, scene 11, p. 21a, l. 10; *Tung-yu chi: shang-tung pa-hsien chuan*, 1:192, ll. 1–2; and *San-pao t'ai-chien Hsi-yang chi t'ung-su yen-i*, vol. 1, ch. 12, p. 153, l. 14.

11. This four-character expression occurs in a poem by Li Po (701–62), *Ch'üan T'ang shih*, vol. 3, *chüan* 162, p. 1682, l. 15.

12. These two lines are derived, with some textual variation, from the final couplet of a quatrain by Ssu-k'ung Shu (c. 720–c. 790), the title of which indicates that it was written when he had to marry off a favorite singing girl to someone else because of his illness. See *Ch'üan T'ang shih*, vol. 5, *chüan* 292, p. 3324, l. 14. This poem has also been attributed to Han Huang (723–87), ibid., vol. 4, *chüan* 262, p. 2909, l. 8. Variants of the same couplet also occur in *Shuang-chung chi, chüan* 1, scene 14, p. 28a, ll. 3–4; and *Shuang-lieh chi*, scene 39, p. 109, l. 4.

13. This four-character expression occurs in a lyric by Hsieh Ying-fang (1296–1392), *Ch'üan Ming tz'u*, 1:9, lower register, l. 11; a lyric by Yang Chi (1326–78), ibid., 1:118, lower register, l. 15; and *Hung-fu chi*, scene 26, p. 53, l. 8.

14. This proverbial injunction is ubiquitous in Chinese vernacular literature. See, e.g., *Yüan-ch'ü hsüan*, 1:49, l. 11; *Sha-kou chi*, scene 3, p. 5, l. 7; *Ching-ch'ai chi*, scene 6, p. 14, l. 6; *P'i-p'a chi*, scene 5, p. 36, l. 12; *[Hsin-pien] Liu Chih-yüan huan-hsiang Pai-t'u chi*, p. 29b, l. 7; *Chao-shih ku-erh chi, chüan* 1, scene 14, p. 27a, l. 1; *Chin-yin chi, chüan* 1, scene 9, p. 18a, l. 7; *Chin-ch'ai chi*, scene 5, p. 11, l. 18; *Yüeh Fei p'o-lu tung-ch'uang chi, chüan* 1, scene 5, p. 6b. l. 8; *Huai-hsiang chi*, scene 18, p. 50, l. 8; *Hsün-ch'in chi*, scene 7, p. 23, l. 11; *Chiang Shih yüeh-li chi, chüan* 4, scene 34, p. 3b, l. 1; *Hsiu-ju chi*, scene 19, p. 51, ll. 6–7; *Yü-chüeh chi*, scene 16, p. 49, l. 1; *Yen-chih chi, chüan* 1, scene 3, p. 4a, l. 10; *Hung-fu chi*, scene 19, p. 38, l. 10; *Shuang-lieh chi*, scene 13, p. 37, l. 9; the anonymous Ming drama *Wei Feng-hsiang ku Yü-huan chi* (The old version of Wei Kao [746–806] and the story of the jade ring), in *Ku-pen hsi-ch'ü ts'ung-k'an, ch'u-chi*, item 22, *chüan* 1, scene 12, p. 25b, l. 6; *Yü-ching t'ai*, scene 6, p. 12, ll. 9–10; and *Yang-chia fu shih-tai chung-yung yen-i chih-chuan*, vol. 2, *chüan* 6, p. 27a, l. 1. It recurs in the *Chin P'ing Mei tz'u-hua*, vol. 5, ch. 82, p. 7b, ll. 4–5. Truncated variants also occur in *Hsing-t'ien Feng-yüeh t'ung-hsüan chi*, scene 5, p. 14b, l. 6; and *Hai-ling i-shih*, p. 81, ll. 3–4.

15. The two components of this four-character expression occur in reverse order in a poem by Tu Fu (712–70), *Ch'üan T'ang shih*, vol. 4, *chüan* 227, p. 2450, l. 8. In the form in which it appears in the novel it occurs ubiquitously in later Chinese literature. See, e.g., a lyric by Li Kang (1083–1140), *Ch'üan Sung tz'u*, 2:905, lower register, l. 16; a poem by Wang Chih (1135–89), *Ch'üan Sung shih*, 46:28850, l. 14; a lyric by Shih Hsiao-yu (cs 1166), *Ch'üan Sung tz'u*, 3:2036, lower register, l. 2; a lyric by Hsü Ching-sun (1192–1273), ibid., 4:2720, upper register, l. 12; *Chiao Hung chuan*, p. 280, l. 10; *Yüan-ch'ü hsüan*, 3:1187, l. 16; a song suite by Li Pang-chi (14th century), *Ch'üan Yüan san-ch'ü*, 2:1145, l. 6; a song by T'ang Shih (14th–15th centuries), ibid., 2:1578, l. 4; *Chin-ch'ai chi*, scene 28, p. 52, l. 13; a song by Li K'ai-hsien (1502–68) written in 1548, *Li K'ai-hsien chi*, 3:923, l. 5; a song suite by Yin Shih-tan (1522–82), *Ch'üan Ming san-ch'ü*, 2:2344, l. 14; and *Yü-chüeh chi*, scene 34, p. 106, l. 2. It also recurs in the *Chin P'ing Mei tz'u-hua*, vol. 5, ch. 81, p. 1a, l. 11.

16. A variant of this line occurs in *Shih-lin kuang-chi, ch'ien-chi, chüan* 9, p. 8b, l. 8; *Chang Hsieh chuang-yüan*, scene 19, p. 99, l. 13; *Yang Wen lan-lu hu chuan*, p.

173, l. 6; *Ming-hsin pao-chien, chüan* 1, p. 10b, ll. 10–11; *P'i-p'a chi*, scene 16, p. 97, l. 11; *Chin-yin chi, chüan* 2, scene 12, p. 6a, l. 5; *P'o-yao chi, chüan* 1, scene 11, p. 33b, l. 9; the middle-period vernacular story *Tung Yung yü-hsien chuan* (The story of Tung Yung's encounter with an immortal), in *Ch'ing-p'ing shan-t'ang hua-pen*, p. 236, l. 9; *Ch'ün-yin lei-hsüan*, 3:1729, l. 5; and the *Chin P'ing Mei tz'u-hua*, vol. 3, ch. 60, p. 9a, l. 8. It occurs in the same form as in the novel in *Hsün-ch'in chi*, scene 5, p. 11, l. 6.

17. This four-character reduplicative expression is ubiquitous in Chinese vernacular literature. See, e.g., a song suite by Chu T'ing-yü (14th century), *Ch'üan Ming san-ch'ü*, 2:1214, l. 3; *Chin-ming ch'ih Wu Ch'ing feng Ai-ai*, p. 464, l. 7; *Sha-kou chi*, scene 17, p. 64, l. 12; *P'o-yao chi, chüan* 2, scene 19, p. 9a, l. 2; *Yü-huan chi*, scene 17, p. 65, l. 10; *Ming-chu chi*, scene 22, p. 62, l. 12; *Chiang Shih yüeh-li chi, chüan* 2, scene 21, p. 11b, l. 9; a song by Wang Chiu-ssu (1468–1551), *Ch'üan Ming san-ch'ü*, 1:892, l. 12; a song by Han Pang-ch'i (1479–1555), ibid., 2:1252, ll. 11–12; *Hai-fu shan-t'ang tz'u-kao, chüan* 2a, p. 64, l. 1; *Mu-lien chiu-mu ch'üan-shan hsi-wen, chüan* 1, p. 43a, l. 4; *Yen-chih chi, chüan* 1, scene 16, p. 24b, l. 3; a set of songs by Liu Hsiao-tsu (1522–89), *Ch'üan Ming san-ch'ü*, 2:2316, l. 13; *Hsi-yu chi*, vol. 1, ch. 20, p. 224, l. 6; *San-pao t'ai-chien Hsi-yang chi t'ung-su yen-i*, vol. 1, ch. 23, p. 297, l. 8; *Ch'ün-yin lei-hsüan*, 3:1730, l. 1; *Yang-chia fu shih-tai chung-yung yen-i chih-chuan*, vol. 2, *chüan* 5, p. 33b, l. 4; and *Shih-hou chi*, scene 13, p. 44, l. 3.

18. This four-character expression occurs in the biography of Chu Chü (190–246), in *San-kuo chih*, vol. 5, *chüan* 57, p. 1340, ll. 6–7; the biography of Hsiao Hui (476–526), in *Liang shu* (History of the Liang dynasty [502–57]), comp. Yao Ch'a (533–606) and Yao Ssu-lien (d. 637), 3 vols. (Peking: Chung-hua shu-chü, 1973), vol. 2, *chüan* 22, p. 352, l. 1; a letter by Li Po (701–62), in *Ch'üan T'ang wen*, vol. 8, *chüan* 348, p. 13b, l. 7; and the biography of Chu Tz'u (742–84), in *Chiu T'ang shu*, vol. 16, *chüan* 200b, p. 5385, ll. 8–9.

19. This four-character expression, the meaning of which is to increase one's prestige, occurs in *Lieh-kuo chih-chuan*, vol. 3, *chüan* 7, p. 16a, ll. 8–9.

20. This four-character expression, the meaning of which is that what goes around comes around, occurs in a poem by Chu I (1097–1167), *Ch'üan Sung shih*, 33:20818, l. 15; *Yüan-shih shih-fan* (Mr. Yüan's precepts for social life), by Yüan Ts'ai (cs 1163), completed in 1178, ed. and annot. Ho Heng-chen and Yang Liu (Tientsin: T'ien-chin ku-chi ch'u-pan she, 1995), *chüan* 3, p. 163, l. 4; *[Hsin-pien] Wu-tai shih p'ing-hua*, p. 159, l. 12; *Hsiao-p'in chi*, p. 68, l. 5; *San-kuo chih t'ung-su yen-i*, vol. 1, *chüan* 11, p. 514, l. 12; *Shui-hu ch'üan-chuan*, vol. 3, ch. 68, p. 1152, l. 4; *Lieh-kuo chih-chuan*, vol. 2, *chüan* 6, p. 52a, l. 13; *Ming-feng chi*, scene 40, p. 170, l. 4; *Mi-teng yin-hua*, p. 322, l. 8; *Ta-T'ang Ch'in-wang tz'u-hua*, vol. 1, *chüan* 3, ch. 21, p. 51a, l. 7; and a song by Hsüeh Lun-tao (c. 1531–c. 1600), *Ch'üan Ming san-ch'ü*, 3:2769, l. 5.

21. This four-character expression occurs in *Ssu-tzu ching* (Four-character classic), by the T'ang dynasty Buddhist monk Te-hsing, in *Ts'ung-shu chi-ch'eng*, vol. 715, p. 30, l. 8; *San-shui hsiao-tu, chüan* 2, p. 20, l. 9; an anonymous Sung dynasty lyric, *Ch'üan Sung tz'u*, 5:3774, lower register, l. 14; *Kuan-shih-yin p'u-sa pen-hsing ching*, p. 11b, l. 1; a set of songs by Chang K'o-chiu (1270–1348), *Ch'üan Yüan san-ch'ü*, 1:850, l. 10; an anonymous Yüan dynasty lyric, *Ch'üan Chin Yüan tz'u*, 2:1287, lower register, l. 6; *Sha-kou chi*, scene 5, p. 10, l. 7; *Chin-ch'ai chi*, scene 3, p. 7, l. 6; *Shen-hsiang ch'üan-pien, chüan* 634, p. 17a, l. 1; a song suite by Ch'en To (fl. early 16th

century), *Ch'üan Ming san-ch'ü*, 1:590, l. 6; *San-kuo chih t'ung-su yen-i*, vol. 1, *chüan* 2, p. 89, l. 19; *Yen-chih chi*, *chüan* 1, scene 20, p. 30b, l. 8; and *Hsi-yu chi*, vol. 1, ch. 12, p. 129, l. 12.

22. This four-character expression occurs in a poem by Yin Yao-fan (cs 814), *Ch'üan T'ang shih*, vol. 8, *chüan* 492, p. 5570, l. 6; a quatrain by Wei Fu (cs 830), ibid., *chüan* 516, p. 5898, l. 15; a poem by Tu Mu (803–52), ibid., *chüan* 524, p. 5998, l. 2; a poem by Han Wo (844–923), ibid., vol. 10, *chüan* 683, p. 7836, l. 7; a lyric by Shen Tuan-chieh (12th century), *Ch'üan Sung tz'u*, 3:1683, lower register, l. 5; a lyric by Wang Yüan-liang (13th century), *Ch'üan Sung tz'u pu-chi*, p. 86, upper register, ll. 14–15; a set of songs by Chang Lien (cs 1544), *Ch'üan Ming san-ch'ü*, 2:1680, l. 3; *Hung-fu chi*, scene 3, p. 4, l. 7; *P'u-ching ju-lai yao-shih pao-chüan*, *chüan* 2, p. 68a, l. 7; *Yü-ching t'ai*, scene 22, p. 55, l. 11; and *Ta-T'ang Ch'in-wang tz'u-hua*, vol. 1, *chüan* 1, p. 1b. l. 1.

23. This four-character expression occurs in the tsa-chü drama *Chung-shan lang* (The wolf of Chung-shan), by K'ang Hai (1475–1541), in *Ming-jen tsa-chü hsüan*, scene 1, p. 238, ll. 7–8; *Hsin-ch'iao shih Han Wu mai ch'un-ch'ing*, p. 72, l. 14; *Ch'ien-t'ang hu-yin Chi-tien Ch'an-shih yü-lu*, p. 18b, l. 11; *Hsün-ch'in chi*, scene 29, p. 93, l. 4; and recurs in the *Chin P'ing Mei tz'u-hua*, vol. 5, ch. 98, p. 13a, l. 1.

24. Because traditional Chinese coins were round with a square hole in the middle, they were humorously referred to as "square-holed brothers," a euphemism that was also applied to money in any form.

25. This idiomatic expression occurs in *Huan-sha chi*, scene 17, p. 58, l. 9.

26. This four-character expression occurs in *Hsiu-ju chi*, scene 24, p. 67, l. 11; and *Ch'ün-yin lei-hsüan*, 4:2499, l. 3.

27. This four-character expression occurs in *Ssu-hsi chi*, scene 23, p. 82, l. 2; *Yü-chüeh chi*, scene 10, p. 30, l. 11; and *Mu-tan t'ing*, scene 30, p. 162, l. 5.

28. This four-character expression occurs in a speech attributed to the Buddhist monk Hsing-ch'ung (10th century), *Tsu-t'ang chi*, *chüan* 13, p. 302, l. 21; *Sha-kou chi*, scene 15, p. 55, l. 6; *Shen-hsiang ch'üan-pien*, *chüan* 638, p. 23b, l. 8; and *Shuang-chu chi*, scene 27, p. 87, l. 8.

29. This four-character expression occurs in *Chiang Shih yüeh-li chi*, *chüan* 4, scene 39, p. 18a, l. 7.

30. This four-character expression occurs in a lyric by Wang Yün (1228–1304), *Ch'üan Chin Yüan tz'u*, 2:666, lower register, l. 8; and a song by Wang K'o-tu (c. 1526–c. 1594), *Ch'üan Ming san-ch'ü*, 2:2459, l. 7.

31. The characters *she* and *kuan* combine to make the character *kuan*, which designates the post of a live-in tutor or secretary.

32. This statement alludes to the second line of an early poem by Tu Fu (712–70) in which he bemoans the fact that the possession of a scholar's cap often leads to false expectations. See *Ch'üan T'ang shih*, vol. 4, *chüan* 216, p. 2251, l. 14.

33. This is the first line of song no. 91 in the *Shih-ching* (Book of songs). See *Mao-shih yin-te*, song no. 91, p. 19. According to the traditional commentary, students in ancient China wore uniforms with blue collars.

34. This four-character expression occurs in a set of songs by Wang Chiu-ssu (1468–1551), *Ch'üan Ming san-ch'ü*, 1:907, l. 3; a set of songs by Liu Hsiao-tsu (1522–89), ibid., 2:2321, l. 4; a song by Hsüeh Lun-tao (c. 1531–c. 1600), ibid., 3:2805, l. 5; and *Ch'üan-Han chih-chuan*, vol. 3, *chüan* 2, p. 21b, l, 5.

35. This formulaic four-character expression occurs ubiquitously in Chinese vernacular literature. See, e.g., *Ch'in ping liu-kuo p'ing-hua*, p. 17, l. 13; *San-kuo chih p'ing-hua*, p. 67, l. 11; *Yüan-ch'ü hsüan*, 2:852, l. 19; *Yüan-ch'ü hsüan wai-pien*, 1:71, l. 17; *Hsüan-ho i-shih*, p. 71, l. 3; *Lü Tung-pin fei-chien chan Huang-lung*, p. 459, l. 6; *P'o-yao chi, chüan* 1, scene 13, p. 38a, l. 1; *Chiang Shih yüeh-li chi, chüan* 1, scene 2, p. 4a, l. 7; *Ssu-shih hua-yüeh sai chiao-jung*, scene 3, p. 7a, l. 9; *Tung-t'ien hsüan-chi*, scene 2, p. 9a, l. 1; *Lieh-kuo chih-chuan*, vol. 2, *chüan* 6, p. 59b, l. 9; *Hsi-yu chi*, vol. 1, ch. 33, p. 386, l. 8; *Mu-lien chiu-mu ch'üan-shan hsi-wen, chüan* 1, p. 36b, l. 6; and *Ch'eng-yün chuan, chüan* 2, p. 8b, l. 9. It also recurs in the *Chin P'ing Mei tz'u-hua*, vol. 5, ch. 89, p. 3a, l. 9.

36. This reduplicative four-character expression occurs in a lyric by Wang Ch'ien-ch'iu (12th century), *Ch'üan Sung tz'u*, 3:1471, upper register, l. 10; *Chu-tzu yü-lei*, vol. 2, *chüan* 18, p. 4b, l. 4; and *Hsi-yu chi*, vol. 1, ch. 32, p. 365, l. 1.

37. During the Ming dynasty biannual sacrifices to Confucius were held in Confucian temples and state schools on the first *ting* days of the second and eighth lunar months.

38. This four-character expression is said to have been uttered by Śākyamuni Buddha immediately after his birth. See, e.g., *Ta-T'ang hsi-yü chi [chiao-chu]* (Great T'ang record of the western regions [edited and annotated]), by Hsüan-tsang (602–64), ed. and annot. Chi Hsien-lin et al., originally completed in 646 (Peking: Chung-hua shu-chü, 1985), *chüan* 6, p. 523, l. 9; *Tsu-t'ang chi, chüan* 1, p. 6, l. 25; *T'ai-tzu ch'eng-tao ching* (Sutra on how the crown prince [Śākyamuni] attained the Way), in *Tun-huang pien-wen chi*, 1:289, l. 11; a commentary on the *Diamond sutra* by Wang Jih-hsiu (d. 1173), as quoted in *Chin-kang ching chi-chu*, p. 94b, col. 3; and *Wu-teng hui-yüan*, vol. 1, *chüan* 1, p. 4, l. 13. It also occurs in *Yüan-ch'ü hsüan*, 4:1545, l. 17; and *Yüan-ch'ü hsüan wai-pien*, 2:428, l. 13.

39. These four lines are derived, with some textual variation, from a passage in the biography of Ch'un-yü K'un (4th century B.C.) in *Shih-chi*, vol. 10, *chüan* 125, p. 3197, l. 10. The last line occurs independently in *Kuan-yüan chi*, scene 3, p. 5, l. 9.

40. This four-character expression, the literal meaning of which is "to escape the womb and change the bones," occurs in a lyric by Ko Ch'ang-keng (1134–1229), *Ch'üan Sung tz'u*, 4:2564, upper register, ll. 10–11; a passage of poetic criticism by Yü Yen (1258–1314), *Sung shih-hua ch'üan-pien*, 10:10416, ll. 13–14; a song by Ch'iao Chi (d. 1345), *Ch'üan Yüan san-ch'ü*, 1:600, l. 3; *K'an p'i-hsüeh tan-cheng Erh-lang Shen*, p. 251, l. 13; *Pei Sung chih-chuan*, vol. 3, *chüan* 7, p. 7a, l. 12; *Hsi-yu chi*, vol. 1, ch. 27, p. 304, l. 3; *Tung-yu chi: shang-tung pa-hsien chuan, chüan* 2, p. 5a, l. 1; and *San-pao t'ai-chien Hsi-yang chi t'ung-su yen-i*, vol. 2, ch. 98, p. 1265, l. 9.

41. This formulaic four-character expression occurs ubiquitously in Chinese vernacular literature. See, e.g., *Ching-ch'ai chi*, scene 28, p. 88, ll. 11–12; *Chin-ch'ai chi*, scene 8, p. 19, l. 15; *Lien-huan chi*, scene 2, p. 3, l. 15; *Ming-chu chi*, scene 12, p. 37, l. 9; *Chiang Shih yüeh-li chi, chüan* 2, scene 25, p. 24a, l. 4; *Yü-huan chi*, scene 8, p. 28, l. 6; *Shui-hu ch'üan-chuan*, vol. 4, ch. 90, p. 1473, l. 9; *Hung-fu chi*, scene 16, p. 30, l. 7; *Ssu-hsi chi*, scene 19, p. 49, l. 12; *Huan-sha chi*, scene 27, p. 97, l. 9; *Ming-feng chi*, scene 25, p. 107, l. 10; *Hsi-yu chi*, vol. 2, ch. 54, p. 630, ll. 5–6; *Mu-lien chiu-mu ch'üan-shan hsi-wen, chüan* 1, p. 83b, l. 7; *Ssu-sheng yüan*, play no. 1, p. 10, l. 11; *Shuang-lieh chi*, scene 2, p. 5, l. 8; *Yü-ching t'ai*, scene 27, p. 72, ll. 8–9; *Ta-T'ang*

Ch'in-wang tz'u-hua, vol. 2, *chüan* 8, ch. 61, p. 47a, l. 1; and *Chieh-hsia chi*, scene 9, p. 21, l. 3.

42. The above jeu d'esprit is included in the late Ming anthology of satirical pieces entitled *K'ai-chüan i-hsiao* (Open this volume and get a laugh), where it is attributed to T'u Lung (1542–1605). See *K'ai-chüan i-hsiao*, 3 vols., fac. repr. of late Ming edition, in *Ming-Ch'ing shan-pen hsiao-shuo ts'ung-k'an, ch'u-pien*, vol. 2, *chüan* 5, pp. 11a–12b. It is also included, without the opening poem and without attribution, in the late Ming miscellany entitled *Hsiu-ku ch'un-jung* (Spring vistas in a varicolored valley), 4 vols., fac. repr. of late Ming edition, in ibid., vol. 3, *chüan* 9, pp. 18b–19b. This fact has led some scholars to speculate that the *Chin P'ing Mei tz'u-hua* may have been written by T'u Lung, but, since this piece occurs in one of the five supplied chapters, it is irrelevant to the questions of the authorship and dating of the authentic part of the novel.

43. Pan Ku (32–92) and Yang Hsiung (53 B.C.–A.D. 18) are two of the most admired scholars of the Han dynasty.

44. This four-character expression occurs in an anonymous Yüan dynasty song. See *Ch'üan Yüan san-ch'ü*, 2:1677, l. 11.

CHAPTER 57

1. This four-character expression occurs in *Yüan-ch'ü hsüan*, 4:1342, l. 11; and *Hsi-yu chi*, vol. 1, ch. 13, p. 146, l. 12.

2. This four-character expression occurs in *Shen-hsiang ch'üan-pien*, *chüan* 644, p. 12b, l. 3; and *Hsi-yu chi*, vol. 2, ch. 78, p. 895, l. 12.

3. This poem occurs, with some textual variation, as the chapter-opening verse of chapter 35 of *Hsi-yu chi*, which is probably its proximate source. See ibid., vol. 1, ch. 35, p. 399, ll. 2–3.

4. This date would correspond to the year 521 in the Western calendar.

5. See chap. 53, n. 8.

6. Wan-hui (632–711) is the name of a Buddhist monk about whom many legends have accumulated. The dates given in this line of the novel do not fit with the information in the standard sources for his biography. Versions of the following legend about him are found in *Yu-yang tsa-tsu, ch'ien-chi* (first collection), *chüan* 3, p. 39, ll. 2–4; *T'ai-p'ing kuang-chi*, vol. 2, *chüan* 92, p. 606, l. 13–p. 607, l. 6; and *Sung Kao-seng chuan* (Biographies of eminent monks compiled during the Sung dynasty), comp. Tsan-ning (919–1001), preface dated 988, 2 vols. (Peking: Chung-hua shu-chü, 1987), vol. 2, *chüan* 18, p. 454.

7. This formulaic four-character expression occurs in *Yüan-ch'ü hsüan*, 3:1147, l. 10; *Yüan-ch'ü hsüan wai-pien*, 1:202, ll. 6–7; *Huang T'ing-tao yeh-tsou Liu-hsing ma*, scene 3, p. 105, l. 8; *Hsing-t'ien Feng-yüeh t'ung-hsüan chi*, scene 8, p. 21b, l. 6; *Ming-chu chi*, scene 14, p. 41, l. 6; *Sui-T'ang liang-ch'ao shih-chuan*, *chüan* 2, p. 25b, l. 3; and recurs in the *Chin P'ing Mei tz'u-hua*, vol. 5, ch. 85, p. 5b, l. 3; and p. 6a, l. 3.

8. This four-character expression occurs in *San-kuo chih p'ing-hua*, p. 52, l. 10.

9. This four-character expression occurs in a lyric by Lu Jui (d. 1266), *Ch'üan Sung tz'u*, 4:2861, upper register, l. 14; *Yüan-ch'ü hsüan*, 1:114, l. 13; *Shui-hu ch'üan-chuan*, vol. 1, ch. 7, p. 113, l. 12; *Hai-fu shan-t'ang tz'u-kao*, *chüan* 4, p. 194, l. 11; *[Hsiao-shih] Chen-k'ung sao-hsin pao-chüan*, 19:82, l. 2; *Ch'üan-Han chih-chuan*,

vol. 3, *chüan* 5, p. 23a, l. 8; *Ch'eng-yün chuan*, *chüan* 1, p. 7b, l. 6; and *I-hsia chi*, scene 23, p. 59, l. 6.

10. This formulaic four-character expression occurs in *Yüan-ch'ü hsüan*, 2:559, l. 17; *Yüan-ch'ü hsüan wai-pien*, 3:945, l. 10; *Jen hsiao-tzu lieh-hsing wei shen*, p. 575, l. 7; *Cheng Yüan-ho*, 4:1420, l. 8; *Ch'ün-yin lei-hsüan*, 4:2489, l. 4; and *Shih-hou chi*, scene 11, p. 35, l. 6.

11. This formulaic four-character expression occurs in *[Chi-p'ing chiao-chu] Hsi-hsiang chi*, play no. 3, scene 2, p. 114, ll. 2–3; *Ts'ui Ya-nei pai-yao chao-yao*, p. 266, l. 15; *Ch'en Hsün-chien Mei-ling shih-ch'i chi*, p. 130, l. 9; *Shui-hu ch'üan-chuan*, vol. 1, ch. 9, p. 140, l. 1; *Hsi-yu chi*, vol. 1, ch. 10, p. 107, l. 13; *Tung-yu chi: shang-tung pa-hsien chuan*, 1:72, l. 7; and *San-pao t'ai-chien Hsi-yang chi t'ung-su yen-i*, vol. 2, ch. 69, p. 894, l. 13.

12. This formulaic four-character expression occurs ubiquitously in Chinese vernacular literature. See, e.g., a poem by Tai Shu-lun (732–89), *Ch'üan T'ang shih*, vol. 5, *chüan* 273, p. 3070, l. 10; *Nü lun-yü* (The female analects), by Sung Jo-shen (d. c. 820), in *Lü-ch'uang nü-shih* (Female scribes of the green gauze windows), 7 vols., fac. repr. of late Ming edition, in *Ming-Ch'ing shan-pen hsiao-shuo ts'ung-k'an, ch'u-pien*, vol. 1, ch. 11, p. 8a, l. 1; a lyric by Wang Shen (1155–1227), *Ch'üan Sung tz'u*, 3:2199, lower register, l. 16; a lyric by Ching T'an (13th century), *Ch'üan Chin Yüan tz'u*, 1:53, upper register, l. 12; a lyric by Yüan Hao-wen (1190–1257), ibid., 1:87, upper register, l. 16; a lyric by Huang Chi (13th century), *Ch'üan Sung Tz'u*, 4:2530, upper register, l. 12; a song by Jen Yü (14th century), *Ch'üan Yüan san-ch'ü*, 1:1012, l. 3; *Yüan-ch'ü hsüan wai-pien*, 1:219, l. 11; *Sha-kou chi*, scene 12, p. 42, l. 1; *Pai Niang-tzu yung-chen Lei-feng T'a*, p. 440, l. 17; a set of poems by Ch'ü Yu (1341–1427), as quoted in *Hsi-hu yu-lan chih-yü*, *chüan* 20, p. 356, l. 10; a song suite by Ch'en To (fl. early 16th century), *Ch'üan Ming san-ch'ü*, 1:619, ll. 11–12; *Hai-fu shan-t'ang tz'u-kao*, *chüan* 1, p. 11, l. 12; and a set of songs by Hsüeh Lun-tao (c. 1531–c. 1600), *Ch'üan Ming san-ch'ü*, 3:2700, l. 11.

13. This four-character expression occurs in *Chu-tzu yü-lei*, vol. 2, *chüan* 18, p. 22a, l. 14; *Shui-hu ch'üan-chuan*, vol. 1, ch. 2, p. 26, l. 13; the middle-period vernacular story *Nü han-lin* (The female academician), in *Tsui yü-ch'ing*, 4:1472, upper register, l. 6; and *Ch'ien-t'ang hu-yin Chi-tien Ch'an-shih yü-lu*, p, 46b, l. 9.

14. This four-character expression occurs in a song suite by Su Tzu-wen (16th century), *Ch'ün-yin lei-hsüan*, 4:2038, l. 10; *P'u-ching ju-lai yao-shih pao-chüan*, preface, p. 4a, l. 3; and *Huang-Ming k'ai-yün ying-wu chuan*, *chüan* 7, p. 4b, l. 10.

15. This four-character expression occurs in *K'an p'i-hsüeh tan-cheng Erh-lang Shen*, p. 260, l. 2.

16. This formulaic four-character expression is ubiquitous in Chinese vernacular literature. See, e.g., *Ta-T'ang San-tsang ch'ü-ching shih-hua* (Prosimetric account of how the monk Tripitaka of the great T'ang [made a pilgrimage] to procure sutras), printed in the 13th century but probably older (Shanghai: Chung-kuo ku-tien wen-hsüeh ch'u-pan she, 1955), episode 11, p. 25, l. 9; *Ch'i-kuo ch'un-ch'iu p'ing-hua* (The p'ing-hua on the events of the seven states), originally published in 1321–23 (Shanghai: Ku-tien wen-hsüeh ch'u-pan she, 1955), p. 66, l. 9; *Yüan-ch'ü hsüan*, 2:590, l. 18; *Yüan-ch'ü hsüan wai-pien*, 2:657, l. 7; *Lü Tung-pin fei-chien chan Huang-lung*, p. 464, l. 2; *K'u-kung wu-tao chüan*, p. 163, l. 1; a song suite by Ch'en To (fl. early 16th century), *Ch'üan Ming san-ch'ü*, 1:610, l. 13; *Yao-shih pen-yüan kung-te pao-chüan*, p.

354, l. 5; *Shui-hu ch'üan-chuan*, vol. 2, ch. 31, p. 484, l. 10; *Ch'en Hsün-chien Mei-ling shih-ch'i chi*, p. 124, l. 16; *Tung-t'ien hsüan-chi*, p. 8a, l. 3; *P'u-ming ju-lai wu-wei liao-i pao-chüan*, p. 518, l. 1; *Hsi-yu chi*, vol. 1, ch. 4, p. 43, l. 3; *Mu-lien chiu-mu ch'üan-shan hsi-wen*, chüan 2, p. 58b, l. 3; *Shih Chen-jen ssu-sheng so pai-yüan*, p. 2a, l. 7; *Ch'ing feng-nien Wu-kuei nao Chung K'uei*, p. 2a, l. 3; *Pai-chia kung-an*, chüan 3, ch. 29, p. 30a, l. 10; *Tung-yu chi: shang-tung pa-hsien chuan*, chüan 2, p. 49b, l. 3; *San-pao t'ai-chien Hsi-yang chi t'ung-su yen-i*, vol. 1, ch. 6, p. 80, l. 15; *Yang-chia fu shih-tai chung-yung yen-i chih-chuan*, vol. 2, chüan 8, p. 44a, l. 3; and *[Hsiao-shih] Chen-k'ung pao-chüan*, p. 263, l. 11.

17. Shih Hu (295–349) was the name of Emperor Wu (r. 335–49) of the Later Chao dynasty (319–52).

18. This story is traditionally related about Kumārajīva (344–413), the famous translator of Buddhist literature into Chinese. See his biography in *Chin-shu*, vol. 8, chüan 95, p. 2502, ll. 3–4; and Werner, *A Dictionary of Chinese Mythology*, p. 90, ll. 27–30.

19. This four-character expression occurs in a lyric by Su Shih (1037–1101), *Ch'üan Sung tz'u*, 1:312, lower register, l. 7; and a song suite by Tu Tzu-hua (16th century), *Ch'üan Ming san-ch'ü*, 3:3022, l. 5.

20. This four-character expression occurs in a letter by Li K'o-yung (856–908) written in the year 907, *Chiu Wu-tai shih*, vol. 2, chüan 26, p. 361, l. 8; and a lyric by Chang Chung-fu (12th century), *Ch'üan Chin Yüan tz'u*, 1:57, lower register, l. 6.

21. The *Pai-chang ch'ing-kuei*, said to have been compiled by the Buddhist monk Pai-chang Huai-hai (749–814), is no longer extant in its original form but has come to be used as a generic term for monastic codes of conduct. For a recent study of this subject, see Yifa, *The Origins of Buddhist Monastic Codes in China* (Honolulu: University of Hawaii Press, 2002).

22. This four-character reduplicative compound occurs in *Hsi-yu chi*, vol. 1, ch. 6, p. 58, l. 3.

23. This line occurs in *Yüan-ch'ü hsüan*, 3:1019, l. 14.

24. This four-character expression occurs in *Ming-feng chi*, scene 34, p. 139, l. 7.

25. This four-character expression occurs in a lyric by Huang T'ing-chien (1045–1105), *Ch'üan Sung tz'u*, 1:397, lower register, l. 10; a sermon by the Buddhist monk Tao-k'ai (1043–1118), *Wu-teng hui-yüan*, vol. 3, chüan 14, p. 885, l. 11; a statement about Bodhidharma (fl. 470–528) in *Pi-yen lu*, 48:140, lower register, l. 5; a lyric by Wang Che (1112–70), *Ch'üan Chin Yüan tz'u*, 1:244, upper register, l. 12; *Ju-ju chü-shih yü-lu*, chia-chi, chüan 2, p. 7a, l. 14; and *Ssu-sheng yüan*, play no. 2, scene 1, p. 20, l. 13. It also recurs in the *Chin P'ing Mei tz'u-hua*, vol. 3, ch. 57, p. 6a, l. 5.

26. This formulaic four-character expression occurs ubiquitously in Chinese vernacular literature. See, e.g., a lyric by Ch'ao Tuan-li (1046–1113), *Ch'üan Sung tz'u*, 1:441, upper register, l. 16; a lyric by the Buddhist monk Chung-shu (fl. late 11th century), ibid., 1:545, lower register, l. 8; a lyric by Chou Pang-yen (1056–1121), ibid., 2:604, upper register, ll. 3–4; a lyric by Tseng Ti (1109–80), ibid., 2:1325, lower register, ll. 13–14; a lyric attributed to a concubine of Lu Yu (1125–1210), ibid., 3:1604, upper register, ll. 1–2; *Ta-T'ang San-tsang ch'ü-ching shih-hua*, episode 9, p. 18, l. 6; *Kuan-shih-yin p'u-sa pen-hsing ching*, p. 23a, l. 3; *Tung Chieh-yüan Hsi-hsiang chi*, chüan 3, p. 69, l. 14; *Sung Ssu-kung ta-nao Chin-hun Chang*, p. 547, l. 11; a song by Chang K'o-chiu (1270–1348), *Ch'üan Yüan san-ch'ü*, 1:867, ll. 6–7; *Chin-t'ung Yü-nü Chiao Hung chi*, p. 40, l. 1; *Shen-hsiang ch'üan-pien*, chüan 634, p. 29a, l. 1; *Hsi-yu*

chi, vol. 1, ch. 45, p. 517, l. 3; *P'u-ching ju-lai yao-shih pao-chüan*, *chüan* 2, p. 49b, l. 3; and a song by Hsüeh Lun-tao (c. 1531–c. 1600), *Ch'üan Ming san-ch'ü*, 3:2776, l. 5. It also recurs in the *Chin P'ing Mei tz'u-hua*, vol. 3, ch. 59, p. 4a, ll. 6–7.

27. This four-character expression is from the *T'eng-wang ko hsü* (Preface to the poem on the Prince of T'eng's Pavilion), by Wang Po (649–76), in *Ch'üan T'ang wen*, vol. 4, *chüan* 281, p. 18a, l. 9. It also occurs independently in the early vernacular story *Nao Fan-lou to-ch'ing Chou Sheng-hsien* (The disturbance in the Fan Tavern and the passionate Chou Sheng-hsien), in *Hsing-shih heng-yen*, vol. 1, *chüan* 14, p. 264, l. 3; and *San-kuo chih t'ung-su yen-i*, vol. 1, *chüan* 12, p. 574, l. 14. It has already been quoted earlier in the novel. See the *Chin P'ing Mei tz'u-hua*, vol. 2, ch. 31, p. 13b, l. 9; and Roy, *The Plum in the Golden Vase*, 2:236, l. 8.

28. This four-character expression occurs in *Hsi-yu chi*, vol. 1, ch. 40, p. 462, l. 9; and *Pai-chia kung-an*, *chüan* 10, ch. 87, p. 1a, l. 5.

29. This formulaic four-character expression refers to brush, ink cake, paper, and inkstone. It is ubiquitous in Chinese vernacular literature. See, e.g., a poem by Mei Yao-ch'en (1002–60) written in 1055, *Ch'üan Sung shih*, 5:3151, l. 12; the title of a poem by Shao Yung (1011–77), ibid., 7:4599, l. 9; *Tung Chieh-yüan Hsi-hsiang chi*, *chüan* 4, p. 87, l. 7; *[Chi-p'ing chiao-chu] Hsi-hsiang chi*, play no. 5, hsieh-tzu (wedge), p. 172, l. 6; *Ch'i-kuo ch'un-ch'iu p'ing-hua*, p. 16, l. 8; *Yüan-ch'ü hsüan*, 2:745, l. 18; *Yüan-ch'ü hsüan wai-pien*, 1:27. ll. 7–8; *Chien-t'ieh ho-shang*, p. 7, l. 9; *Shih Hung-chao lung-hu chün-ch'en hui*, p. 213, l. 7; *Yang Ssu-wen Yen-shan feng ku-jen*, p. 378, l. 10; *Ch'ien-t'ang meng*, p. 4b, l. 8; *Wu-chieh Ch'an-shih ssu Hung-lien chi*, p. 141, l. 14; *Chao Po-sheng ch'a-ssu yü Jen-tsung*, p. 167, l. 4; *Yü Chung-chü t'i-shih yü shang-huang*, p. 76, l. 3; *Fo-yin shih ssu t'iao Ch'in-niang*, p. 235, l. 15; *Lü Tung-pin fei-chien chan Huang-lung*, p. 465, l. 9; *Ching-ch'ai chi*, scene 7, p. 17, l. 2; *Chien-teng yü-hua*, *chüan* 3, p. 219, l. 1; *K'uei-kuan Yao Pien tiao Chu-ko*, p. 310, l. 11; the middle-period vernacular story *Mei Hsing cheng-ch'un* (The plum and the apricot compete for precedence among spring flowers), in *Ch'ing-p'ing shan-t'ang hua-pen*, p. 192, l. 1; *P'ei Hsiu-niang yeh-yu Hsi-hu chi*, p. 346, ll. 11–12; *Tu Li-niang mu-se huan-hun*, p. 534, l. 21; *Yüeh-ming Ho-shang tu Liu Ts'ui*, p. 439, l. 9; *San-kuo chih t'ung-su yen-i*, vol. 1, *chüan* 8, p. 364, l. 16; *Shui-hu ch'üan-chuan*, vol. 3, ch. 72, p. 1216, ll. 5–6; *Ming-chu chi*, scene 33, p. 105, l. 6; the Ming tsa-chü *Tu Tzu-mei ku-chiu yu-ch'un* (Tu Fu buys wine for a spring excursion), by Wang Chiu-ssu (1468–1551), in *Sheng-Ming tsa-chü*, *erh-chi*, scene 2, p. 9b, l. 7; *Yü-huan chi*, scene 32, p. 122, l. 11; *Ch'ien-t'ang hu-yin Chi-tien Ch'an-shih yü-lu*, p. 13b, l. 2; *Ming-feng chi*, scene 11, p. 48, l. 1; *Hsi-yu chi*, vol. 2, ch. 94, p. 1065, l. 9; *Mu-lien chiu-mu ch'üan-shan hsi-wen*, *chüan* 1, p. 31a, l. 8; *Hai-fu shan-t'ang tz'u-kao*, *chüan* 1, p. 25, l. 9; *Su Ying huang-hou ying-wu chi*, *chüan* 2, scene 30, p. 22b, l. 6; *Yen-chih chi*, *chüan* 2, scene 24, p. 7a, l. 9; *San-pao t'ai-chien Hsi-yang chi t'ung-su yen-i*, vol. 2, ch. 54, p. 699, ll. 7–8; *Mu-tan t'ing*, scene 7, p. 28, l. 2; and *Ta-T'ang Ch'in-wang tz'u-hua*, vol. 1, *chüan* 1, ch. 2, p. 16b, ll. 4–5. It also recurs in the *Chin P'ing Mei tz'u-hua*, vol. 4, ch. 73, p. 13a, l. 9.

30. This is said to have been the name of a type of ink cake favored by Emperor Hsüan-tsung (r. 712–56) of the T'ang dynasty. See *Yün-hsien san-lu* (Miscellaneous records of the Cloud Immortal), comp. Feng Chih (fl. early 10th century), preface dated 926, ed. Chang Li-wei (Peking: Chung-hua shu-chü, 1998), p. 2, l. 10. It is said to have been provided for imperial use during the eleventh century, and to have been praised by Su Shih (1037–1101). See *Fu-hsüan tsa-lu* (Random jottings while basking

in the sun), comp. Ku Wen-chien (13th century), in *Shuo-fu* (The frontiers of apocrypha), comp. T'ao Tsung-i (c. 1360–c. 1403), 2 vols. (Taipei: Hsin-hsing shu-chü, 1963), vol. 1, *chüan* 18, p. 20b, ll. 2–4. It is also mentioned in a song by Chang K'o-chiu (1270–1348), *Ch'üan Yüan san-ch'ü*, 1:764, l. 4.

31. This type of brush is mentioned in a work by Wang Hsi-chih (321–79), who alleges that it was favored by famous calligraphers as early as the second century. See *Pi-ching* (The brush classic), by Wang Hsi-chih, in *Shuo-fu san-chung*, 7:4520, p. 1b, ll. 3–4. It is also alleged in an essay by Ho Yen-chih (fl. early 8th century) that Wang Hsi-chih used this type of brush himself in writing his most famous work, the *Lan-t'ing shih hsü* (Preface to the Orchid Pavilion poems), composed in the year 353. See *Ch'üan T'ang wen*, vol. 7, *chüan* 301, p. 16b, ll. 8–9. Su Shih (1037–1101) refers to his use of this type of brush in an inscription on one of his own works written in the year 1096. See *Su Shih wen-chi*, vol. 5, *chüan* 69, p. 2202, l. 7.

32. This term refers to stationery of fine white silk or paper with vertical columns delineated by black lines. It is mentioned in the literary tale *Huo Hsiao-yü chuan* (The Story of Huo Hsiao-yü), by Chiang Fang (early 9th century), in *T'ang Sung ch'uan-ch'i chi*, p. 72, l. 2; *T'ang kuo-shih pu* (Supplement to the History of the T'ang), comp. Li Chao (early 9th century) (Shanghai: Ku-tien wen-hsüeh ch'u-pan she, 1957), *chüan* 3, p. 60, l. 9; a poem by Lu Yu (1125–1210), *Ch'üan Sung shih*, 39:24503, l. 11; and *Chien-teng hsin-hua*, p. 113, l. 13.

33. This four-character expression occurs in *Huai-hsiang chi*, scene 28, p. 91, l. 11.

34. This formulaic four-character expression occurs ubiquitously in Chinese vernacular literature. See, e.g., *[Chi-p'ing chiao-chu] Hsi-hsiang chi*, play no. 4, scene 4, p. 169, l. 2; *Yüan-ch'ü hsüan*, 2:436, l. 14; *Yüan-ch'ü hsüan wai-pien*, 1:91, l. 17; a song suite by Fan K'ang (14th century), *Ch'üan Yüan san-ch'ü*, 1:469, l. 2; *Sha-kou chi*, scene 30, p. 108, l. 8; *Ching-ch'ai chi*, scene 6, p. 13, l. 5; *Cheng Chieh-shih li-kung shen-pi kung*, p. 668, l. 16; *Yü Chung-chü t'i-shih yü shang-huang*, p. 67, l. 14; *Nü ku-ku shuo-fa sheng-t'ang chi*, second *hsieh-tzu* (wedge), p. 9a, l. 3; *Jen chin shu ku-erh hsün-mu*, scene 1, p. 4b, l. 7; *Ch'ing feng-nien Wu-kuei nao Chung K'uei*, *hsieh-tzu* (wedge), p. 1b, l. 11; *Yü-huan chi*, scene 17, p. 68, l. 6; *Ming-chu chi*, scene 22, p. 63, l. 12; *Wang Lan-ch'ing chen-lieh chuan*, scene 1, p. 1a, l. 12; *Ch'en Hsün-chien Mei-ling shih-ch'i chi*, p. 122, l. 6; *Hai-fu shan-t'ang tz'u-kao*, *chüan* 1, p. 22, l. 11; *Hsi-yu chi*, vol. 1, ch. 9, p. 89, l. 9; *Pai-chia kung-an*, *chüan* 7, ch. 59, p. 11a, l. 7; *San-pao t'ai-chien Hsi-yang chi t'ung-su yen-i*, vol. 2, ch. 52, p. 677, ll. 14–15; *Shuang-lieh chi*, scene 13, p. 39, l. 2; and *Ta-T'ang Ch'in-wang tz'u-hua*, vol. 1, *chüan* 3, ch. 21, p. 54a, l. 10.

35. These articles of clothing were symbols of rank that were bestowed upon ladies who had received patents of nobility. This four-character expression occurs frequently in Chinese vernacular literature. See, e.g., *Kuan-shih-yin p'u-sa pen-hsing ching*, p. 14a, l. 2; *Yüan-ch'ü hsüan*, 3:1171, l. 12; *P'o-yao chi*, *chüan* 1, scene 5, p. 16a, ll. 2–3; *Hsiu-ju chi*, scene 40, p. 109, l. 2; *Yü-chüeh chi*, scene 36, p. 114, l. 4; and *Mu-tan t'ing*, scene 55, p. 277, l. 1.

36. This four-character expression occurs in a poem by Po Chü-i (772–846), written in the year 834, *Ch'üan T'ang shih*, vol. 7, *chüan* 453, p. 5122, l. 5.

37. Variants of this idiomatic expression occur in *Tung Yung yü-hsien chuan*, p. 236, l. 2; *Shen Hsiao-kuan i-niao hai ch'i-ming*, p. 392, l. 7; and *Jen hsiao-tzu lieh-hsing wei shen*, p. 572, l. 14.

38. This formulaic four-character expression occurs in a lyric by Chao Shan-k'uo (12th century), *Ch'üan Sung tz'u*, 3:1986, upper register, l. 12; a lyric by Ch'en Li (1252–1334), *Ch'üan Chin Yüan tz'u*, 2:803, upper register, l. 5; a song suite by Wang Chiu-ssu (1468–1551), *Ch'üan Ming san-ch'ü*, 1:977, l. 5; a song suite by Chang Lien (cs 1544), ibid., 2:1697, l. 6; a song suite by Ch'en So-wen (d. c. 1604), ibid., 2:2532, l. 11; a set of songs by Shen Chu-hung (1535–1615), ibid., 3:2918, l. 11; and the ch'uan-ch'i drama *Tzu-hsiao chi* (The story of the purple flute), by T'ang Hsien-tsu (1550–1616), completed in 1580, in *T'ang Hsien-tsu chi* (Collected works of T'ang Hsien-tsu), ed. Hsü Shuo-fang and Ch'ien Nan-yang, 4 vols. (Peking: Chung-hua shu-chü, 1962), vol. 4, scene 15, p. 2505, l. 8.

39. This four-character expression occurs in *P'ei Hsiu-niang yeh-yu Hsi-hu chi*, p. 343, l. 20; and *Shui-hu ch'üan-chuan*, vol. 2, ch. 51, p. 844, l. 13.

40. This formulaic four-character expression occurs ubiquitously in Chinese popular literature. See, e.g., *Yeh-k'o ts'ung-shu*, chüan 27, p. 310, l. 8; *San-kuo chih p'ing-hua*, p. 15, l. 14; a song suite by Teng Yü-pin (13th century), *Ch'üan Yüan san-ch'ü*, 1:310, l. 13; *Yüan-ch'ü hsüan*, 2:441, ll. 1–2; *Yüan-ch'ü hsüan wai-pien*, 1:44, l. 7; *Cho Wen-chün ssu-pen Hsiang-ju*, scene 4, p. 134, l. 8; a set of songs by Chu Yu-tun (1379–1439), *Ch'üan Ming san-ch'ü*, 1:332, l. 6; *Yü-huan chi*, scene 12, p. 41, ll. 11–12; *Shui-hu ch'üan-chuan*, vol. 3, ch. 82, p. 1354, l. 1; *T'ao Yüan-ming tung-li shang-chü*, scene 4, p. 16a, l. 4; the anonymous Ming tsa-chü drama *Sung ta-chiang Yüeh Fei ching-chung* (The perfect loyalty of the Sung general-in-chief Yüeh Fei), in *Ku-pen Yüan Ming tsa-chü*, vol. 3, scene 4, p. 13b, l. 10; *Ch'ing feng-nien Wu-kuei nao Chung K'uei*, scene 2, p. 4b, l. 1; a song suite by Ho T'ang (1474–1543), *Ch'üan Ming san-ch'ü*, 1:1118, l. 8; *Hai-fu shan-t'ang tz'u-kao*, chüan 2a, p. 93, l. 1; *Mu-lien chiu-mu ch'üan-shan hsi-wen*, chüan 3, p. 61a, l. 10; *Ts'an-T'ang Wu-tai shih yen-i chuan*, ch. 36, p. 142, l. 11; and the ch'uan-ch'i drama *Han-tan meng chi* (The dream at Han-tan), by T'ang Hsien-tsu (1550–1616), author's pref. dated 1601, in *T'ang Hsien-tsu chi*, vol. 4, scene 14, p. 2345, l. 14.

41. This four-character expression occurs in a quatrain by Chang Chi (cs 753), *Ch'üan T'ang shih*, vol. 4, chüan 242, p. 2725, l. 10; and *Yüan-ch'ü hsüan wai-pien*, 2:691, l. 20.

42. According to a pious legend that is probably apocryphal, Buddhism was first introduced into China in the mid-first century A.D. when two foreign monks named Chu Fa-lan and Kāśyapa Matanga arrived in Lo-yang from central Asia with a selection of Buddhist sutras loaded on the back of a white horse. See Maspero, *Taoism and Chinese Religion*, pp. 402–3. They are said to have translated the *Ssu-shih erh chang ching* (The scripture in forty-two sections), the first Buddhist text to be rendered into Chinese. See Robert H. Sharf, "The Scripture in Forty-two Sections," in Donald S. Lopez, Jr., ed., *Religions of China in Practice* (Princeton: Princeton University Press, 1996), pp. 360–71.

43. This formulaic four-character expression occurs in *Yüan-ch'ü hsüan*, 1:295, l. 21; *Huang-chi chin-tan chiu-lien cheng-hsin kuei-chen huan-hsiang pao-chüan*, 8:5, l. 2; *Cheng-hsin ch'u-i wu hsiu cheng tzu-tsai pao-chüan*, 3:159, l. 3; *Yao-shih pen-yüan kung-te pao-chüan*, 14:195, l. 5; *P'u-ming ju-lai wu-wei liao-i pao-chüan*, 4:409, l. 4; and *[Hsiao-shih] Chen-k'ung sao-hsin pao-chüan*, 18:392, l. 3.

44. This four-character expression occurs in *Ch'üan-Han chih-chuan*, vol. 3, chüan 2, p. 14a, l. 11.

45. This four-character expression occurs in *P'i-p'a chi*, scene 33, p. 182, l. 3.

46. This four-character expression occurs in *[Chi-p'ing chiao-chu] Hsi-hsiang chi*, play no. 1, scene 1, p. 6, l. 12; and *Chien-teng yü-hua*, *chüan* 2, p. 179, l. 13.

47. The story of how Anâtapindika purchased the Jetavana Park in the city of Śrāvastī by paving the entire grounds with gold in order to provide a monastery, or vihara, for Śākyamuni Buddha is told in many different Buddhist sources. See, e.g., the lengthy prosimetric account in *Hsiang-mo pien-wen* (Transformation text on the subduing of demons), in *Tun-huang pien-wen chi*, 1:361–72; and *Tun-huang Popular Narratives*, trans. Victor H. Mair (Cambridge: Cambridge University Press, 1983), pp. 31–57.

48. A variant of this four-character expression occurs in a lyric by Yang Wu-chiu (1097–1171), *Ch'üan Sung tz'u*, 2:1204, lower register, l. 8. It occurs in the same form as in the novel in *Yüan-ch'ü hsüan wai-pien*, 2:689, l. 6; and *Cheng-hsin ch'u-i wu hsiu cheng tzu-tsai pao-chüan*, 3:194, ll. 1–2.

49. This four-character expression occurs in *Yüan-ch'ü hsüan*, 3:1101, l. 6; and a song suite by T'ang Shih (14th–15th centuries), *Ch'üan Yüan san-ch'ü*, 2:1495, l. 13.

50. This four-character expression occurs in a poem by Po Chü-i (772–846), *Ch'üan T'ang shih*, vol. 7, *chüan* 427, p. 4708, l. 12; a lyric by Hou Shan-yüan (12th century), *Ch'üan Chin Yüan tz'u*, 1:521, lower register, l. 1; a lyric by Kao Tao-k'uan (1196–1277), ibid., 2:1193, lower register, l. 11; *Yüan-ch'ü hsüan*, 3:1129, ll. 13–14; *Yüan-ch'ü hsüan wai-pien*, 2:435, l. 13; *Ts'ui Ya-nei pai-yao chao-yao*, p. 271, l. 16; and *Huang T'ing-tao yeh-tsou Liu-hsing ma*, scene 2, p. 95, l. 12.

51. This four-character expression occurs in a lyric by Ma Yü (1123–83), *Ch'üan Chin Yüan tz'u*, 1:278, lower register, l. 3; *Yüan-ch'ü hsüan wai-pien*, 3:721, l. 4; *Shen-hsiang ch'üan-pien*, *chüan* 642, p. 32a, l. 7; and *Tung-t'ien hsüan-chi*, scene 4, p. 12a, l. 14.

52. This formulaic four-character expression is ubiquitous in Chinese vernacular literature. See, e.g., *Hsü-t'ang Ho-shang yü-lu*, p. 995, middle register, l. 10; *Ming-hsin pao-chien*, *chüan* 2, p. 2a, l. 1; *Nan Hsi-hsiang chi* (Li Jih-hua), scene 27, p. 77, l. 7; *Shui-hu ch'üan-chuan*, vol. 1, ch. 26, p. 407, ll. 10–11; a song by Hsü Wen-chao (c. 1464–1553), *Ch'üan Ming san-ch'ü*, 1:819, l. 7; *Lieh-kuo chih-chuan*, vol. 3, *chüan* 8, p. 33b, l. 6; *Ming-feng chi*, scene 31, p. 130, l. 9; *Su Ying huang-hou ying-wu chi*, *chüan* 1, scene 17, p. 37b, l. 7; and *San-pao t'ai-chien Hsi-yang chi t'ung-su yen-i*, vol. 1, ch. 4, p. 51, l. 6.

53. This four-character expression occurs in *Ming-chu chi*, scene 38, p. 121, l. 7; and *Lieh-kuo chih-chuan*, vol. 2, *chüan* 5, p. 33a, l. 6.

54. The ultimate source of this four-character expression is the first line of song no. 237 in the *Shih-ching* (Book of songs), where the two components occur in reverse order. See *Mao-shih yin-te*, p. 59, no. 237, l. 1. It occurs in the same form as in the novel in an inscription by Ch'üan Te-yü (759–818), *Ch'üan T'ang wen*, vol. 11, *chüan* 495, p. 9b, l. 4; *Wu Lun-ch'üan Pei*, *chüan* 2, scene 12, p. 17b, ll. 7–8; a song suite by Wang Chiu-ssu (1468–1551), *Ch'üan Ming san-ch'ü*, 1:983, ll. 2–3; *Yen-chih chi*, *chüan* 2, scene 41, p. 35b, l. 5; and *Yü-huan chi*, scene 12, p. 42, l. 1.

55. Locust trees stand for the three dukes, the three highest offices in the imperial bureaucracy, and cassia trees stand for holders of the *chin-shih* degree. Thus this expression refers to a lineage group's outstanding success in the competition for bureaucratic office.

56. This four-character expression occurs in the Ming ch'uan-ch'i drama *Ching-chung chi* (A tale of perfect loyalty), *Liu-shih chung ch'ü* ed., scene 13, p. 35, l. 11.

57. This reduplicative four-character expression occurs in *Huan-sha chi*, scene 14, p. 48, l. 10.

58. For Tung Cho, see chap. 56, n. 3.

59. This four-character expression occurs in *Hai-ling i-shih*, p. 104, l. 6.

60. This four-character expression occurs in *Ch'ün-yin lei-hsüan*, 3:1729, l. 10.

61. A variant of this idiomatic expression occurs in *Ho-lin yü-lu* (Jade dew from Ho-lin), by Lo Ta-ching (cs 1226), originally completed in 1252 (Peking: Chung-hua shu-chü, 1983), *ping-pien* (third section), *chüan* 1, p. 239, l. 4.

62. This four-character expression occurs in *Mu-lien chiu-mu ch'üan-shan hsi-wen*, *chüan* 1, p. 6b, l. 1.

63. This four-character expression occurs in a description of the early character of Emperor Kao-tsu (r. 202–195 B.C.), the founder of the Han dynasty, *Han-shu*, vol. 1, *chüan* 1a, p. 24, ll. 14–15; a criticism of the misconduct of Taoist libationers, probably dating from the fourth century, in a work entitled *Lao-chün shuo i-pai pa-shih chieh* (The 180 precepts enunciated by Lord Lao), in *Yün-chi ch'i-ch'ien*, *chüan* 39, p. 217, left column, l. 12; *Ch'ao-yeh ch'ien-tsai* (Comprehensive record of affairs within and without the court), comp. Chang Cho (cs 675) (Peking: Chung-hua shu-chü, 1979), *chüan* 6, p. 139, l. 2; *Ch'ien-chin chi*, scene 12, p. 34, l. 9; *Shui-hu ch'üan-chuan*, vol. 2, ch. 32, p. 502, l. 13; *Huan-sha chi*, scene 43, p. 152, l. 4; *Pai-chia kung-an*, *chüan* 4, ch. 34, p. 8a, l. 6; and *Sui-T'ang liang-ch'ao shih-chuan*, *chüan* 11, p. 2a, l. 7.

64. This four-character expression occurs in *[Chi-p'ing chiao-chu] Hsi-hsiang chi*, play no. 2, scene 3, p. 72, l. 2; *Yüan-ch'ü hsüan wai-pien*, 2:423, ll. 16–17; *Chin-ch'ai chi*, scene 31, p. 58, l. 3; a song suite by K'ang Hai (1475–1541), *Ch'üan Ming san-ch'ü*, 1:1203, l. 11; *Chiang Shih yüeh-li chi*, *chüan* 4, scene 36, p. 6b, ll. 6–7; and *Yü-huan chi*, scene 6, p. 13, l. 4.

65. This four-character expression occurs in a set of songs by Kuan Yün-shih (1286–1324), *Ch'üan Yüan san-ch'ü*, 1:358, l. 2; and a song suite by Sun Chi-ch'ang (14th century), ibid., 2:1239, l. 6.

66. For a definitive study of this subject, see Stephen F. Teiser, *The Scripture on the Ten Kings and the Making of Purgatory in Medieval Chinese Buddhism* (Honolulu: University of Hawaii Press, 1994).

67. Hsü Fei-ch'iung is a mythological female musician in the entourage of the Queen Mother of the West.

68. This four-character expression occurs in *Sha-kou chi*, scene 16, p. 58, l. 6; *Ching-ch'ai chi*, scene 28, p. 87, l. 9; *Nan Hsi-hsiang chi* (Lu Ts'ai), *chüan* 1, scene 19, p. 371, l. 3; *Yü-tsan chi*, scene 17, p. 64, l. 15; *Hsi-yu chi*, vol. 2, ch. 74, p. 845, l. 1; *San-pao t'ai-chien Hsi-yang chi t'ung-su yen-i*, vol. 1, ch. 11, p. 141, l. 7; and a song by Hu Wen-huan (fl. 1592–1617), *Ch'üan Ming san-ch'ü*, 3:2927, l. 4.

69. This four-character expression occurs in the middle-period vernacular story entitled *K'uai-tsui Li Ts'ui-lien chi* (The story of the sharp-tongued Li Ts'ui-lien), in *Ch'ing-p'ing shan-t'ang hua-pen*, p. 55, l. 12.

70. This four-character expression occurs in a letter by Ch'en Liang (1143–94) written in the year 1185, *Ch'en Liang chi [tseng-ting pen]*, vol. 2, *chüan* 28, p. 342, l. 14; and *Hai-fu shan-t'ang tz'u-kao*, *chüan* 2a, p. 93, l. 10.

71. The three female professionals are Buddhist nuns, Taoist nuns, and female fortune tellers. The six dames are matchmakers, white slavers, procuresses, medicine women, mediums, and midwives. This four-character expression occurs in *Li-hsüeh chih-nan* (A guidebook to the subbureaucracy), by Hsü Yüan-jui (fl. early 14th century), author's pref. dated 1301 (N.p.: Che-chiang ku-chi ch'u-pan she, 1988), p. 146, l. 8; *Ch'o-keng lu*, *chüan* 10, p. 126, l. 7; and *Liu-ch'ing jih-cha*, vol. 2, *chüan* 21, p. 8b, l. 7.

72. This song also occurs in the anthology of scurrilous tales about the Buddhist clergy entitled *Seng-ni nieh-hai* (Monks and nuns in a sea of iniquity), originally published in the early 17th century, in *Ssu wu-hsieh hui-pao*, 24:303, ll. 4–7.

73. This song also occurs in *Seng-ni nieh-hai*, 24:303, ll. 2–3; and the collection of vernacular stories entitled *Huan-hsi yüan-chia* (Adversaries in delight), comp. Kao I-wei (17th century), pref. dated 1640, in *Ssu wu-hsieh hui-pao*, vol. 11, ch. 22, p. 737, ll. 4–5.

74. The locus classicus for this four-character expression is a statement by Huang-fu Mi (215–282) that King Wu (r. 1045–1043 B.C.), the founder of the Chou dynasty, had five sons and two daughters. It is quoted by K'ung Ying-ta (574–648) in his commentary on song no. 24 in the *Shih-ching* (Book of songs). See *Shih-san ching chu-shu* (The thirteen classics with their commentaries), comp. Juan Yüan (1764–1849), 2 vols. (Peking: Chung-hua shu-chü, 1982), 1:293, middle register, column 17. The expression came to stand for prolific offspring, regardless of the actual numbers. It occurs in *Tung-ching meng-hua lu* (A dream of past splendors in the Eastern Capital), comp. Meng Yüan-lao (12th century), pref. dated 1147, in *Tung-ching meng-hua lu [wai ssu-chung]* (A dream of past splendors in the Eastern Capital [plus four other works]), comp. Meng Yüan-lao (12th century) et al. (Shanghai: Shang-hai ku-chi wen-hsüeh ch'u-pan she, 1956), *chüan* 5, p. 32, l. 6; *Yüan-ch'ü hsüan*, 1:284, ll. 6–7; *San hsien-shen Pao Lung-t'u tuan-yüan*, p. 174, l. 12; and *Chiang Shih yüeh-li chi*, *chüan* 1, scene 6, p. 10a, l. 1.

75. This four-character expression occurs together with the preceding line in *Chiang Shih yüeh-li chi*, *chüan* 1, scene 6, p. 10a, l. 1.

76. This four-character expression occurs in the biography of the Buddhist monk Pen-chi (840–901), in *Tsu-t'ang chi*, *chüan* 8, p. 182, l. 20; and in the popular Taoist work *Hsüan-t'ien shang-ti ch'ui-chieh wen* (Admonitions of the Supreme Sovereign of the Mysterious Celestial Realm), in *Kuo-se t'ien-hsiang*, vol. 2, *chüan* 4, p. 53b, upper register, l. 5. It also recurs in the *Chin P'ing Mei tz'u-hua*, vol. 3, ch. 57, p. 12a, l. 7.

77. This four-character expression occurs in *T'ai-tzu ch'eng-tao ching*, 1:297, l. 2; *P'o-mo pien-wen* (Transformation text on destroying the demons), dated 944, in *Tun-huang pien-wen chi*, 1:346, l. 9; *Wu-teng hui-yüan*, vol. 1, *chüan* 1, p. 30, l. 2; and *Kuan-shih-yin p'u-sa pen-hsing ching*, p. 51b, l. 5.

78. A variant of this four-character expression occurs in the biography of Bodhidharma (fl. 470–528) in *Tsu-t'ang chi*, *chüan* 2, p. 46, l. 6.

79. Hui-k'o's dates are traditionally given as 487–593.

80. This four-character expression occurs in *Tsu-t'ang chi*, *chüan* 2, p. 46, ll. 6–7. Variants also occur in *Kuan-shih-yin p'u-sa pen-hsing ching*, p. 44b, ll. 3–4; a lyric by Ma Yü (1123–83), *Ch'üan Chin Yüan tz'u*, 1:283, lower register, l. 2; and *Shui-hu ch'üan-chuan*, vol. 2, ch. 46, p. 760, l. 6.

81. See note 47 above.

82. This four-character expression occurs in a set of songs by Li K'ai-hsien (1502–68), *Li K'ai-hsien chi*, 3:918, l. 5.

83. This four-character expression occurs in a lyric by Li Ch'ing-chao (1084–c. 1151), *Ch'üan Sung tz'u*, 2:931, lower register, l. 4; two anonymous Sung dynasty lyrics, ibid., 5:3739, lower register, l. 5; and 5:3842, upper register, l. 12; and *Pai-chia kung-an, chüan* 7, ch. 58, p. 1b, l. 3.

84. This four-character expression occurs in *Huang-chi chin-tan chiu-lien cheng-hsin kuei-chen huan-hsiang pao-chüan*, 8:259, l. 4; *Yao-shih pen-yüan kung-te pao-chüan*, 14:260, l. 3; and *[Hsiao-shih] Chen-k'ung sao-hsin pao-chüan*, 19:103, l. 3.

85. This four-character expression occurs in *Mu-lien chiu-mu ch'üan-shan hsi-wen*, *chüan* 3, p. 3b, l. 6.

86. The yojana is variously defined as eighty li, sixty li, forty li, or the distance that can be traversed by an army in a day's march. Nowhere is it defined as five hundred li. This exaggeration on the part of Nun Hsüeh is doubtless intended to convey to the informed reader the extent of her ignorance of Buddhism.

87. This four-character expression occurs in a stele inscription commemorating Hui-neng (638–713), the sixth Ch'an patriarch, by Wang Wei (699–761), *Ch'üan T'ang wen*, vol. 7, *chüan* 327, p. 3a, l. 4; *Yüan-ch'ü hsüan*, 3:1045, l. 2; and *P'o-yao chi*, *chüan* 2, scene 26, p. 32b, l. 4.

88. This four-character expression occurs in Chüeh-lien's commentary (pref. dated 1551) to the *Chin-kang k'o-i*. See *[Hsiao-shih] Chin-kang k'o-i [hui-yao chu-chieh]*, *chüan* 5, p. 706, middle register, ll. 14–15.

89. This four-character expression occurs ubiquitously in Chinese vernacular literature. See, e.g., a lyric by Kuan Chien (12th century), *Ch'üan Sung tz'u*, 3:1568, lower register, ll. 9–10; a lyric by Wei Liao-weng (1178–1237), ibid., 4:2367, upper register, ll. 7–8; a lyric by Tuan K'o-chi (1196–1254), *Ch'üan Chin Yüan tz'u*, 1:146, lower register, l. 7; a lyric by Ch'en Chu (1214–97), *Ch'üan Sung tz'u*, 4:3036, upper register, ll. 6–7; *Yüan-ch'ü hsüan*, 4:1345, l. 15; *Yüan-ch'ü hsüan wai-pien*, 1:194, l. 21; *Ch'ang-an ch'eng ssu-ma t'ou-T'ang*, scene 2, p. 7b, l. 12; *Chung-ch'ing li-chi*, vol. 2, *chüan* 6, p. 1b, l. 10; *Shuang-chu chi* scene 37, p. 129, l. 7; a song suite by Chin Luan (1494–1583), *Ch'üan Ming san-ch'ü*, 2:1618, l. 10; a song suite by Ch'en So-wen (d. c. 1604), ibid., 2:2532, l. 14; and a song by Hsüeh Lun-tao (c. 1531–c. 1600), ibid., 3:2862, l. 1.

90. This formulaic four-character expression occurs ubiquitously in Chinese literature. See, e.g., a letter by Ts'ao Chih (192–232), written in the year 215 or 216, *Ts'ao Chih chi chiao-chu, chüan* 1, p. 143, l. 1; a treatise on the art of war by Li Ching (571–649), *Li Ching ping-fa chi-pen chu-i* (A reconstituted, annotated, and translated edition of Li Ching's *Art of war*), ed. Teng Tse-tsung (Peking: Chieh-fang chün ch'u-pan she, 1990), *chüan* 1, p. 1, l. 10; a poem by Li Po (701–62), *Ch'üan T'ang shih*, vol. 3, *chüan* 168, p. 1739, l. 12; a lyric by Wang Chih (1135–89), *Ch'üan Sung tz'u*, 3:1645, upper register, l. 11; *Chiao Hung chuan*, p. 293, l. 14; a treatise on physiognomy by Yüan Kung (1335–1410), in *Shen-hsiang ch'üan-pien*, *chüan* 639, p. 21b, l. 6; *Lieh-kuo chih-chuan*, vol. 1, *chüan* 1, p. 7a, l. 7; *Ming-feng chi*, scene 13, p. 56, l. 5; an essay by Li Chih (1527–1602), in his *Fen-shu* (A book to be burned) (Peking: Chung-hua shu-chü, 1961), *chüan* 5, p. 227, l. 7; *Mi-teng yin-hua, chüan* 1, p. 326, l. 11; *Pai-chia kung-an, chüan* 10, ch. 89, p. 4b, l. 1; *Yang-chia fu shih-tai chung-yung yen-i chih-chuan*,

vol. 1, *chüan* 4, p. 43a, l. 3; and *Sui-T'ang liang-ch'ao shih-chuan, chüan* 9, ch. 84, p. 19a, l. 5.

91. This four-character expression, which is a component in a number of proverbial couplets, occurs ubiquitously in Chinese vernacular literature. See, e.g., a lyric by Wang Kuan (cs 1057), *Ch'üan Sung tz'u pu-chi*, p. 5, lower register, l. 15; a speech by the Buddhist monk Wen-chun (1061–1115), *Wu-teng hui-yüan*, vol. 3, *chüan* 17, p. 1151, l. 12; *Hsiao Sun-t'u*, scene 10, p. 297, l. 3; *Shih-lin kuang-chi, ch'ien-chi, chüan* 9, p. 8b, l. 2; a song by Ts'ao Te (14th century), *Ch'üan Yüan san-ch'ü*, 2:1080, l. 3; *[Hsin-pien] Wu-tai shih p'ing-hua*, p. 183, l. 12; *Sha-kou chi*, scene 4, p. 10, l. 4; *P'i-p'a chi*, scene 30, p. 172, l. 5; *Yüan-ch'ü hsüan wai-pien*, 2:682, l. 10; *Lien-huan chi*, scene 25, p. 65, l. 7; *Huai-hsiang chi*, scene 27, p. 87, l. 11; a set of songs by Li K'ai-hsien (1502–68), the author's pref. to which is dated 1544, *Li K'ai-hsien chi*, 3:872, l. 5; *Chiang Shih yüeh-li chi, chüan* 4, scene 34, p. 3b, l. 4; *Yen-chih chi, chüan* 2, scene 34, p. 20b, l. 11; *Huan-sha chi*, scene 28, p. 101, l. 8; *Ming-feng chi*, scene 6, p. 26, l. 8; *Tzu-ch'ai chi*, scene 14, p. 58, l. 8; *Liu sheng mi Lien chi, chüan* 3, p. 11a, l. 8; *Kuan-yüan chi*, scene 3, p. 5, ll. 10–11; and *I-hsia chi*, scene 35, p. 98, l. 4.

92. On this game, see Roy, *The Plum in the Golden Vase*, vol. 1, chap. 13, n. 8.

93. Ho Chih-chang (659–744) was a well-known T'ang poet and contemporary of Tu Fu (712–70).

94. This line probably refers to the first of the four short plays that constituted the lost Ming ch'uan-ch'i drama *Ssu-chieh chi* (The four seasons), by Shen Ts'ai (15th century). See the excerpt from this play in *Yüeh-fu hung-shan*, vol. 2, *chüan* 10, pp. 9a–13b.

95. This line probably refers to the third of the four short plays that constituted the lost Ming ch'uan-ch'i drama *Ssu-chieh chi*. See the excerpt from this play in ibid., pp. 27a–30b. Red Cliff was the site of a famous naval battle in which the forces of Ts'ao Ts'ao (155–220) were decisively defeated in the year 208. A visit with friends to the putative site of this battle in the year 1082 is celebrated in two famous rhapsodies by Su Shih (1037–1101). Huang T'ing-chien (1045–1105) was a close friend of Su Shih's but was not one of the participants in the above excursion.

96. This four-character expression is commonly paired with another that means "severally display their magic powers." According to legend, on one occasion, when the eight Taoist immortals crossed the sea, each of them demonstrated his or her super-natural powers. This story is related in the anonymous Ming tsa-chü drama entitled *Cheng yü-pan pa-hsien kuo ts'ang-hai* (Contending for the jade tablet the Eight Immortals cross the azure sea), in *Ku-pen Yüan Ming tsa-chü*, vol. 4; and in *Tung-yu chi: shang-tung pa-hsien chuan*, 1:194–230. It is alluded to in *Hsi-yu chi*, vol. 2, ch. 81, p. 925, ll. 10–11. The four-character expression occurs in a song suite by Ch'en To (fl. early 16th century), *Ch'üan Ming san-ch'ü*, 1:673, l. 13; *Yü-huan chi*, scene 2, p. 2, l. 12; and *San-pao t'ai-chien Hsi-yang chi t'ung-su yen-i*, vol. 1, ch. 38, p. 494, l. 4.

97. The first of these two combinations is illustrated in *Hsüan-ho p'ai-p'u* (A manual for Hsüan-ho [1119–25] dominoes), by Ch'ü Yu (1341–1427), in *Shuo-fu hsü* (The frontiers of apocrypha continued), comp. T'ao T'ing (cs 1610), fac. repr. of Ming ed. in *Shuo-fu san-chung*, vol. 10, *chüan* 38, p. 16b. They are both illustrated, together with two additional variations of the second combination in *P'ai-t'u* (Illustrated domino combinations), in *San-ts'ai t'u-hui* (Assembled illustrations from the three realms), comp. Wang Ch'i (c. 1535–c. 1614), pref. dated 1609, 6 vols., fac. repr. (Taipei:

Ch'eng-wen ch'u-pan she, 1970), vol. 4, *jen-shih* (Human affairs), *chüan* 8, pp. 50b and 51a; and *Hsüan-ho p'u ya-p'ai hui-chi* (A manual for Hsüan-ho [1119–25] dominoes with supplementary materials), original compiler's pref. dated 1757, redactor's pref. dated 1886 (N.p.: Hung-wen chai, 1888), *chüan* 1, p. 9a. They are mentioned together in *Nan Hsi-hsiang chi* (Li Jih-hua), scene 7, p. 21, l. 1; and *Ta-T'ang Ch'in-wang tz'u-hua*, vol. 2, *chüan* 6, ch. 47, p. 58b, l. 3; and the second combination is mentioned in *Hsi-yu chi*, vol. 2, ch. 80, p. 911, l. 3. In all of the last three sources these names occur in passages of poetry that play on the names of domino combinations.

98. This combination is illustrated in *Hsüan-ho p'ai-p'u*, p. 8b; *P'ai-t'u*, p. 45b; and *Hsüan-ho p'u ya-p'ai hui-chi*, *chüan* 1, p. 6b.

99. It was said of Chi K'ang (223–62) that when he was drunk he leaned crazily like a jade mountain about to collapse. See Mather, *Shih-shuo Hsin-yü*, p. 309, item 5. This four-character expression occurs in *Huai-ch'un ya-chi*, *chüan* 9, p. 18a, l. 16; *Mu-tan t'ing*, scene 12, p. 59, l. 3; *San-pao t'ai-chien Hsi-yang chi t'ung-su yen-i*, vol. 1, ch. 34, p. 447, l. 1; and *Shih-hou chi*, scene 15, p. 50, l. 4.

100. It was said of Shan Chien (253–312) that when he was drunk he would wear his egret cap askew. See Mather, *Shih-shuo Hsin-yü*, p. 378, l. 4. This allegation is alluded to in a poem by Po Chü-i (772–846), *Ch'üan T'ang shih*, vol. 7, *chüan* 452, p. 5117, l. 2.

101. A variant of this line occurs in a lyric by Chang Kang (1083–1166), *Ch'üan Sung tz'u*, 2:923 upper register, l. 7.

102. This formulaic four-character expression occurs ubiquitously in Chinese vernacular literature. See, e.g., a lyric by Hsin Ch'i-chi (1140–1207), *Ch'üan Sung tz'u*, 3:1885, upper register, l. 11; a lyric by Ch'en San-p'in (12th century) written in 1186, ibid., 3:2022, lower register, l. 9; a lyric by Liu Chih-yüan (13th century), *Ch'üan Chin Yüan tz'u*, 1:573, upper register, l. 11; a lyric by Ch'ang-ch'üan-tzu (13th century), ibid., 1:590, upper register, ll. 11–12; a lyric by Wang Yün (1228–1304), ibid., 2:659, lower register, l. 15; a song by Sun Chou-ch'ing (14th century), *Ch'üan Yüan san-ch'ü*, 2:1063, l. 4; an anonymous Yüan dynasty song suite, ibid., 2:1798, l. 9; *P'i-p'a chi*, scene 29, p. 165, l. 2; *Hsing-t'ien Feng-Yüeh t'ung-hsüan chi*, scene 6, p. 15a, l. 8; a set of songs by Yang T'ing-ho (1459–1529), *Ch'üan Ming san-ch'ü*, 1:749, ll. 5–6; *Hsiu-ju chi*, scene 13, p. 37, l. 12; a song suite by Wang Chiu-ssu (1468–1551), *Ch'üan Ming san-ch'ü*, 1:985, l. 10; *Ming-feng chi*, scene 1, p. 1, l. 3; a song suite by Chin Luan (1494–1583), *Ch'üan Ming san-ch'ü*, 2:1617, l. 2; and *Mu-lien chiu-mu ch'üan-shan hsi-wen*, *chüan* 1, p. 42b, l. 10.

103. The locus classicus for this four-character expression is the prose preface to a set of eight poems by Hsieh Ling-yün (385–433), *Wen-hsüan*, vol. 2, *chüan* 30, p. 27b, l. 5. It occurs ubiquitously in later Chinese literature. See, e.g., the prose preface to a poem by Po Chü-i (772–846), *Ch'üan T'ang shih*, vol. 7, *chüan* 456, p. 5178, l. 6; a lyric by Nieh Kuan-ch'ing (988–1042), *Ch'üan Sung tz'u*, 1:10, upper register, l. 3; a literary tale entitled *T'an I-ko*, by Ch'in Ch'un (11th century), in *Ch'ing-so kao-i* (Lofty sentiments from the green latticed windows), comp. Liu Fu (fl. 1040–1113) (Shanghai: Ku-tien wen-hsüeh ch'u-pan she, 1958), *pieh-chi* (supplementary collection), *chüan* 2, p. 197, l. 5; a poem by Wang An-shih (1021–86), *Ch'üan Sung shih*, 10:6630, l. 3; a lyric by Hsin Ch'i-chi (1140–1207), *Ch'üan Sung tz'u*, 3:1886, lower register, l. 8; a lyric by Yüan Hao-wen (1190–1257), *Ch'üan Chin Yüan tz'u*, 1:87, upper register, l. 12; a song suite by Chang K'o-chiu (1270–1348), *Ch'üan Yüan san-ch'ü*, 1:993, l. 10;

Hsiao Sun-t'u, scene 1, p. 257, l. 10; *Yüan-ch'ü hsüan*, 2:474, l. 16; *Yüan-ch'ü hsüan wai-pien*, 1:26, l. 8; *Nao Fan-lou to-ch'ing Chou Sheng-hsien*, p. 265, l. 3; *Chien-teng hsin-hua, chüan* 4, p. 87, l. 6; a set of songs by P'eng Tse (cs 1490), *Ch'üan Ming san-ch'ü*, 1:836, l. 7; *Yü-huan chi*, scene 10, p. 31, l. 12; *Hung-fu chi*, scene 1, p. 1, l. 5; *Liu sheng mi Lien chi, chüan* 2, p. 12b, l. 8; *Ming-feng chi*, scene 1, p. 1, l. 3; *Hai-fu shan-t'ang tz'u-kao, chüan* 1, p. 21, l. 11; *Mu-tan t'ing*, scene 10, p. 45, l. 12; and *Ta-T'ang Ch'in-wang tz'u-hua*, vol. 2, *chüan* 7, ch. 53, p. 39b, l. 2.

CHAPTER 58

1. See Roy, *The Plum in the Golden Vase*, vol. 2, chap. 38, n. 34.

2. See ibid., vol. 1, chap. 2, n. 1.

3. According to legend, the two daughters of the Emperor Yao (3rd millennium B.C.) became consorts of his successor, the Emperor Shun (3rd millennium B.C.), upon whose death they shed tears that speckled the bamboos growing along the Hsiang River. After their deaths by drowning they were apotheosized as the Nymphs of the Hsiang River. See *Po-wu chih* (A treatise on curiosities), comp. Chang Hua (232–300), ed. Fan Ning (Peking: Chung-hua shu-chü, 1980), *chüan* 8, p. 93, l. 6.

4. This four-character expression occurs in *Lü-shih ch'un-ch'iu* (The spring and autumn annals of Mr. Lü), comp. Lü Pu-wei (d. 235 B.C.), in *Chu-tzu chi-ch'eng*, vol. 6, *chüan* 1, p. 4, l. 5; *Yüan-ch'ü hsüan wai-pien*, 2:601, l. 6; and a song suite by Chi Tzu-an (14th century), *Ch'üan Yüan san-ch'ü*, 2:1459, l. 2.

5. This four-character expression occurs in a poem by Tu Fu (712–70), *Ch'üan T'ang shih*, vol. 4, *chüan* 216, p. 2268, l. 10. It has become ubiquitous in later Chinese literature. See, e.g., a lyric by Liao Kang (1070–1143), *Ch'üan Sung tz'u*, 2:701, lower register, l. 7; a lyric by Li Kang (1083–1140), ibid., 2:901, upper register, l. 9; a lyric by Yüan Ch'ü-hua (cs 1145), ibid., 3:1506, lower register, l. 2; the preface to a lyric by Wang Chi (cs 1151) written in 1184, *Ch'üan Chin Yüan tz'u*, 1:34, upper register, l. 3; a lyric by Hsin Ch'i-chi (1140–1207), *Ch'üan Sung tz'u*, 3:1926, lower register, l. 3; a song suite by Tseng Jui (c. 1260–c. 1330), *Ch'üan Yüan san-ch'ü*, 1:511, l. 6; a song suite by Ch'ien Lin (14th century), ibid., 2:1030, l. 12; a song by Li Ch'i-hsien (1287–1367), ibid., 2:1076, l. 10; a song suite by T'ang Shih (14th–15th centuries), ibid., 2:1491, l. 11; *K'an p'i-hsüeh tan-cheng Erh-lang Shen*, p. 245, l. 13; *K'uei-kuan Yao Pien tiao Chu-ko*, p. 308, l. 14; *Yü-huan chi*, scene 14, p. 50, l. 6; *Shui-hu ch'üan-chuan*, vol. 1, ch. 1, p. 6, l. 6; a set of songs by K'ang Hai (1475–1541), *Ch'üan Ming san-ch'ü*, 1:1122, ll. 9–10; *Liao-yang hai-shen chuan*, p. 381, l. 11; *Su Ying huang-hou ying-wu chi, chüan* 1, scene 13, p. 28b, l. 6; and *Ta-T'ang Ch'in-wang tz'u-hua*, vol. 2, *chüan* 5, ch. 34, p. 12b, l. 1. It also recurs in the *Chin P'ing Mei tz'u-hua*, vol. 5, ch. 84, p. 3a, l. 7.

6. This four-character expression occurs in the middle-period vernacular story *Liu Ch'i-ch'ing shih-chiu Wan-chiang Lou chi* (Liu Ch'i-ch'ing indulges in poetry and wine in the Riverside Pavilion), in *Ch'ing-p'ing shan-t'ang hua-pen*, p. 1, l. 10; and *Pai-chia kung-an, chüan* 10, ch. 93, p. 9a, l. 6.

7. The locus classicus for this four-character expression is *Hsin-yü* (New discourses), by Lu Chia (c. 228–c. 140 B.C.), in *Chu-tzu chi-ch'eng*, vol. 7, ch. 7, p. 12, l. 14. It also occurs in a letter by Ssu-ma Ch'ien (145–c. 90 B.C.), *Han-shu*, vol. 6, *chüan* 62, p.

2729, l. 3; and the prose preface to a rhapsody by Hsiang Hsiu (3rd century), *Wen-hsüan*, vol. 1, *chüan* 16, p. 12a, l. 3.

8. This formulaic four-character expression occurs in *Tung Chieh-yüan Hsi-hsiang chi*, *chüan* 1, p. 3, l. 12; *Yüan-ch'ü hsüan*, 4:1592, l. 14; *Yüan-ch'ü hsüan wai-pien*, 3:949, l. 10; *Huai-hsiang chi*, scene 4, p. 7, l. 12; *Yü-huan chi*, scene 10, p. 35, l. 4; and *I-hsia chi*, scene 2, p. 2, l. 7.

9. For the locus classicus of this four-character expression, see *Meng-tzu yin-te*, p. 11, 2A.2, l. 6. It also occurs in a lyric by Feng Jung (fl. early 13th century), *Ch'üan Sung tz'u*, 4:2471, upper register, l. 12; a song suite by Chang K'o-chiu (1270–1348), *Ch'üan Yüan san-ch'ü*, 1:989, l. 6; a set of songs by Wang Ai-shan (14th century), ibid., 2:1191, l. 1; a song suite by Li Chih-yüan (14th century), ibid., 2:1257, l. 9; *Wu Lun-ch'üan Pei*, *chüan* 3, scene 21, p. 34a, l. 3; *Yü-huan chi*, scene 6, p. 18, l. 9; and *Mu-tan t'ing*, scene 2, p. 3, l. 3.

10. The proximate source of these four lines, with one textual variant, is *Hsiu-ju chi*, scene 3, p. 5, ll. 2–3.

11. This four-character expression occurs in a self-eulogy by the Buddhist monk Miao-p'u (1071–1142), *Wu-teng hui-yüan*, vol. 3, *chüan* 18, p. 1179, ll. 4–5; a poem by Ma Yü (1123–83), *Ch'üan Chin shih*, 1:329, l. 11; a lyric by Li Ch'un-fu (1185–1231), *Ch'üan Chin Yüan tz'u*, 1:70, lower register, l. 6; a lyric by Li Tao-ch'un (fl. late 13th century), ibid., 2:1227, lower register, ll. 12–13; a lyric by Wang Chieh (fl. early 14th century), ibid., 2:1261, lower register, l. 3; and *Tung-t'ien hsüan-chi*, scene 1, p. 6a, l. 4.

12. The proximate source of these two lines, with some textual variation, is *Hsiu-ju chi*, scene 3, p. 5, l. 3.

13. Variants of this four-character expression occur in a lyric by Hou Shan-yüan (12th century), *Ch'üan Chin Yüan tz'u*, 1:526, upper register, l. 13; *Yüan-ch'ü hsüan*, 3:890, l. 8; a set of songs by Wang Yüan-heng (14th century), *Ch'üan Yüan san-ch'ü*, 2:1389, l. 4; and *Ming-feng chi*, scene 4, p. 12, l. 10. It occurs in the same form as in the novel in a speech by the Buddhist monk K'o-ch'in (1063–1135), in *Yüan-wu Fo-kuo ch'an-shih yü-lu* (Recorded sayings of Ch'an Master Yüan-wu Fo-Kuo), pref. dated 1134, in *Taishō shinshū daizōkyō*, vol. 47, no. 1997, *chüan* 4, p. 731, middle register, l. 28.

14. The locus classicus for this four-character expression is the biography of Ching K'o (d. 227 B.C.), in *Shih-chi*, vol. 8, *chüan* 86, p. 2528, l. 2. It is ubiquitous in later Chinese literature. See, e.g., the biography of Juan Chi (210–63), in *Ming-shih chuan* (Biographies of famous men), by Yüan Hung (328–76), as quoted in Liu Chün's (465–521) commentary to the *Shih-shuo hsin-yü*, *Shih-shuo hsin-yü chiao-chien* (A critical edition of the *Shih-shuo hsin-yü*), ed. Yang Yung (Hong Kong: Ta-chung shu-chü, 1969), ch. 23, item 11, p. 553, l. 13; the biography of Hsieh Shang (308–57), in *Chin-shu*, vol. 7, *chüan* 79, p. 2069, ll. 10–11; *Li-wa chuan*, p. 102, l. 13; the prose preface to a lyric by Chang Yüan-kan (1091–c. 1162) written in the year 1145, *Ch'üan Sung tz'u*, 2:1092, lower register, ll. 8–9; a lyric by Wang I (13th century), ibid., 5:3297, upper register, l. 9; *Yüan-ch'ü hsüan wai-pien*, 1:102, l. 9; [*Hsin-pien*] *Wu-tai shih p'ing-hua*, p. 35, l. 8; *Chien-teng hsin-hua*, *chüan* 1, p. 22, l. 6; *Chien-teng yü-hua*, *chüan* 3, p. 220, l. 5; *San-kuo chih t'ung-su yen-i*, vol. 1, *chüan* 1, p. 23, l. 13; *Shui-hu ch'üan-chuan*, vol. 3, ch. 75, p. 1256, ll. 8–9; the middle-period vernacular story *Yen P'ing-chung erh-t'ao sha san-shih* (Yen P'ing-chung kills three stalwarts with two peaches),

in *Ku-chin hsiao-shuo*, vol. 2, *chüan* 25, p. 386, l. 14; a set of songs by Li K'ai-hsien (1502–68) written in the year 1531, *Li K'ai-hsien chi*, 3:911, l. 15; *Nan Sung chih-chuan*, vol. 1, *chüan* 2, p. 28a, l. 10; *Pei Sung chih-chuan*, vol. 2, *chüan* 4, p. 6a, l. 6; *Ch'üan-Han chih-chuan*, vol. 3, *chüan* 4, p. 13a, l. 4; *Lieh-kuo chih-chuan*, vol. 3, *chüan* 7, p. 22b, l. 8; *Yang-chia fu shih-tai chung-yung yen-i chih-chuan*, vol. 1, *chüan* 2, p. 37a, l. 1; and *Sui-T'ang liang-ch'ao shih-chuan*, *chüan* 2, ch. 16, p. 31a, ll. 2–3.

15. This four-character expression occurs in *[Chi-p'ing chiao-chu] Hsi-hsiang chi*, play no. 2, scene 5, p. 92, l. 2.

16. This formulaic four-character expression occurs in *Tung Chieh-yüan Hsi-hsiang chi*, *chüan* 8, p. 157, l. 3; a song suite by Shen Hsi (14th century), *Ch'üan Yüan san-ch'ü*, 1:1002, l. 1; an anonymous set of songs on the subject of women's shoes from the Yüan dynasty, ibid., 2:1673, l. 8; a song by Ch'en To (fl. early 16th century), *Ch'üan Ming san-ch'ü*, 1:566, l. 7; and *Ta-T'ang Ch'in-wang tz'u-hua*, vol. 2, *chüan* 6, ch. 43, p. 22b, l. 9.

17. This formulaic four-character expression occurs ubiquitously in Chinese vernacular literature. See, e.g., a song suite by P'eng Shou-chih (13th century), *Ch'üan Yüan san-ch'ü*, 1:88, l. 11; a song suite by Kuan Han-ch'ing (13th century), ibid., 1:190, l. 1; an anonymous song suite from the Yüan dynasty, ibid., 2:1797, l. 4; *Liu Ch'i-ch'ing shih-chiu Wan-chiang Lou chi*, p. 1, l. 7; *Tung Yung yü-hsien chuan*, p. 237, l. 14; *Shui-hu ch'üan-chuan*, vol. 3, ch. 69, p. 1170, l. 14; a song suite by Chang Lien (cs 1544), *Ch'üan Ming san-ch'ü*, 2:1687, l. 11; *Lieh-kuo chih-chuan*, vol. 3, *chüan* 8, p. 52a, l. 13; *Ch'ien-t'ang hu-yin Chi-tien Ch'an-shih yü-lu*, p. 22b, l. 5; *Ch'üan-Han chih-chuan*, vol. 2, *chüan* 1, p. 15a, l. 10; a song suite by Chang Chia-yin (1527–88), *Ch'üan Ming san-ch'ü*, 3:2618, l. 10; *Pai-chia kung-an*, *chüan* 1, ch. 7, p. 27a, l. 13; and a song suite by Chang Feng-i (1527–1602), *Ch'üan Ming san-ch'ü*, 3:2608, l. 11.

18. This four-character expression occurs in a song by Chu Yu-tun (1379–1439), *Ch'üan Ming san-ch'ü*, 1:295, l. 3; and a set of songs by Huang O (1498–1569), ibid., 2:1751, l. 1.

19. This entire line occurs in *Shui-hu ch'üan-chuan*, vol. 3, ch. 81, p. 1336, l. 1.

20. This idiomatic four-character expression recurs in the *Chin P'ing Mei tz'u-hua*, vol. 5, ch. 91, p. 12b, l. 6.

21. This formulaic four-character expression occurs ubiquitously in Chinese vernacular literature. See, e.g., *Yüan-ch'ü hsüan wai-pien*, 2:450, l. 12; *K'an p'i-hsüeh tan-cheng Erh-lang Shen*, p. 251, l. 11; *Sha-kou chi*, scene 12, p. 41, l. 11; *Yu-kuei chi*, scene 26, p. 82, l. 6; *Ssu-shih hua-yüeh sai chiao-jung*, scene 1, p. 2a, l. 6; *Cho Wen-chün ssu-pen Hsiang-ju*, scene 3, p. 128, l. 14; *Wu Lun-ch'üan Pei*, *chüan* 4, scene 28, p. 29b, l. 7; *Yüeh Fei p'o-lu tung-ch'uang chi*, *chüan* 1, scene 20, p. 32a, l. 2; a song suite by Ch'en To (fl. early 16th century), *Ch'üan Ming san-ch'ü*, 1:628, l. 8; *Shui-hu ch'üan-chuan*, vol. 2, ch. 28, p. 438, l. 6; a set of songs in *Yung-hsi yüeh-fu*, ts'e 19, p. 39a, l. 8; *Yü-chüeh chi*, scene 17, p. 54, l. 12; *Lieh-kuo chih-chuan*, vol. 2, *chüan* 6, p. 60b, l. 3; *Hsi-yu chi*, vol. 1, ch. 41, p. 471, ll. 9–10; *Ssu-sheng yüan*, play no. 3, scene 2, p. 56, l. 9; *Su Ying huang-hou ying-wu chi*, *chüan* 1, scene 18, p. 40a, l. 9; a set of songs by Hsüeh Lun-tao (c. 1531–c. 1600), *Ch'üan Ming san-ch'ü*, 3:2763, l. 12; and *Yü-ching t'ai*, scene 37, p. 99, l. 3.

22. On this play, see Roy, *The Plum in the Golden Vase*, vol. 2, chap. 32, n. 8.

23. See ibid., chap. 36, p. 351, ll. 26–27.

24. This couplet is from a famous lyric by Yen Chi-tao (c. 1031–c. 1106), *Ch'üan Sung tz'u*, 1:225, lower register, ll. 8–9. It is also quoted, with occasional textual variations, in *Chang Hsieh chuang-yüan*, scene 51, p. 210, l. 6; *Yüan-ch'ü hsüan*, 3:1092, ll. 18–19; *Yüan-ch'ü hsüan wai-pien*, 2:698, ll. 2–3; *Wu Lun-ch'üan Pei, chüan* 1, scene 2, p. 4b, l. 4; a song suite by Chu Yün-ming (1460–1526), *Ch'üan Ming san-ch'ü*, 1:784, l. 14; *Feng-yüeh Nan-lao chi*, scene 1, p. 1b, l. 9; *Huan-sha chi*, scene 7, p. 19, ll. 10–11; *Ming-feng chi*, scene 13, p. 56, l. 7; *Shuang-lieh chi*, scene 19, p. 54, l. 10; and recurs in the *Chin P'ing Mei tz'u-hua*, vol. 5, ch. 98, p. 4b, l. 6. The first line also occurs independently in *Pao-chien chi*, scene 2, p. 7, l. 16; and the second line occurs independently in *Yüan-ch'ü hsüan*, 3:1094, l. 21; and a song by Ch'en So-wen (d. c. 1604), *Ch'üan Ming san-ch'ü*, 2:2491, ll. 8–9.

25. This idiomatic expression recurs in the *Chin P'ing Mei tz'u-hua*, vol. 4, ch. 75, p. 2a, ll. 6–7.

26. See Roy, *The Plum in the Golden Vase*, vol. 1, chap. 15, n. 11.

27. This formulaic four-character expression occurs ubiquitously in Chinese vernacular literature. See, e.g., a lyric attributed to Lü Tung-pin (9th century), *Ch'üan T'ang shih*, vol. 12, *chüan* 900, p. 10168, l. 14; a lyric by Hou Shan-yüan (12th century), *Ch'üan Chin Yüan tz'u*, 1:523, upper register, l. 16; *Yüan-ch'ü hsüan*, 2:483, l. 2; *Yüan-ch'ü hsüan wai-pien*, 2:390, l. 16; *Chang Yü-hu su nü-chen kuan chi*, p. 21a, ll. 11–12; *Ch'ien-chin chi*, scene 9, p. 21, l. 1; *Shui-hu ch'üan-chuan*, vol. 1, ch. 21, p. 307, l. 2; a song suite by Chang Lien (cs 1544), *Ch'üan Ming san-ch'ü*, 2:1720, ll. 13–14; *Yü-huan chi*, scene 5, p. 11, l. 11; *Hai-fu shan-t'ang tz'u-kao, chüan* 3, p. 163, l. 2; and a song suite by Shen Ching (1553–1610), *Ch'üan Ming san-ch'ü*, 3:3267, l. 6.

28. These two lines are the opening clauses of a famous song suite from *[Chi-p'ing chiao-chu] Hsi-hsiang chi*, play no. 4, scene 2, p. 148, l. 14. The final four-character expression is from chapter 7 of the *Tao-te ching* (Book of the Way and its power). See *Lao Tzu Tao Te Ching*, trans. D. C. Lau (New York: Penguin Books, 1963), p. 63, l. 1. It occurs ubiquitously in later Chinese literature.

29. This four-character expression is derived, with one variant, from the opening line of a famous lyric by Yen Chi-tao (c. 1031–c. 1106), *Ch'üan Sung tz'u*, 1:225, lower register, l. 8. It occurs in the same form as in the novel in a song by Yao Sui (1238–1313), *Ch'üan Yüan san-ch'ü*, 1:212, l. 8; a song by Chang Yang-hao (1270–1329), ibid., 1:405, l. 5; a song by Chang K'o-chiu (1270–1348), ibid., 1:766, l. 4; a song by Hsüeh Ang-fu (14th century), ibid., 1:714, l. 2; a song suite by Shen Hsi (14th century), ibid., 1:1002, ll. 2–3; a song by Ku Te-jun (14th century), ibid., 2:1071, l. 11; a song suite by T'ung-t'ung (14th century), ibid., 2:1262, l. 3; a song suite by Liu T'ing-hsin (14th century), ibid., 2:1444, l. 6; a song suite by T'ang Shih (14th–15th centuries), ibid., 2:1503, l. 13; *[Chi-p'ing chiao-chu] Hsi-hsiang chi*, play no. 2, scene 5, p. 91, l. 10; *Yüan-ch'ü hsüan*, 3:902, l. 4; *Yüan-ch'ü hsüan wai-pien*, 2:603, l. 3; the tsa-chü drama *Ch'ung-mo-tzu tu-pu Ta-lo T'ien* (Ch'ung-mo-tzu ascends to the Grand Veil Heaven), by Chu Ch'üan (1378–1448), in *Ku-pen Yüan Ming tsa-chü*, vol. 2, scene 3, p. 7b, ll. 2–3; a set of songs by Chu Yu-tun (1379–1439), *Ch'üan Ming san-ch'ü*, 1:286, l. 3; a set of songs by Ch'en To (fl. early 16th century), ibid., 1:502, l. 5; *Pao Chien chi*, scene 2, p. 7, l. 3; and a song suite by Wang Chih-teng (1535–1612), *Ch'üan Ming san-ch'ü*, 3:2914, l. 4.

30. This four-character expression, with one variant, is probably derived from a line in a song by Chang Yang-hao (1270–1329), in which the preceding four-character expression also occurs in the following line. See *Ch'üan Yüan san-ch'ü*, 1:405, l. 4.

31. This poem, with a few minor variants, has already appeared in the *Chin P'ing Mei tz'u-hua*, vol. 2, ch. 27, p. 13a, ll. 7–8; and recurs in ibid., vol. 5, ch. 97, p. 12a, ll. 3–4.

32. This four-character expression occurs in a quatrain by Hsüeh Neng (cs 846), *Ch'üan T'ang shih*, vol. 9, *chüan* 561, p. 6514, l. 13; a lyric by Tseng Ti (1109–80), *Ch'üan Sung tz'u*, 2:1312, upper register, ll. 3–4; and a song suite by Shen Ching (1553–1610), *Ch'üan Ming san-ch'ü*, 3:3285, l. 2.

33. The Weaving Maid and the Herd Boy, corresponding to the stars Vega and Altair, meet each other across the Milky Way once a year, on the night of the seventh day of the seventh month. See Roy, *The Plum in the Golden Vase*, vol. 1, chap. 2, n. 40. The legend that they crossed the Milky Way on a bridge of magpies is at least as old as the Han dynasty. See *Feng-su t'ung-i [chiao-chu]* (A comprehensive study of popular customs [edited and annotated]), comp. Ying Shao (fl. 167–195), ed. and annot. Wang Li-ch'i, 2 vols. (Peking: Chung-hua shu-chü, 1981), 2:600, l. 13.

34. It was a custom, ten days or so before the seventh day of the seventh month, to put the seeds of various leguminous plants in basins of water until they developed sprouts that could be tied together into bundles with colored cords, and displayed on the evening of the festival, no doubt as symbols of fertility. See, e.g., *Tung-ching meng-hua lu*, *chüan* 8, p. 49, ll. 3–4.

35. This song is attributed to Tu Jen-chieh (13th century). It is preserved in *Sheng-shih hsin-sheng*, p. 453, ll. 4–6; *Tz'u-lin chai-yen*, 2:893, ll. 6–9; *Yung-hsi yüeh-fu*, ts'e 14, p. 14a, ll. 6–9; and *Ch'üan Yüan san-ch'ü*, 1:34, ll. 8–9. The version in the novel is closest to that in *Yung-hsi yüeh-fu*.

36. These two formulaic four-character expressions occur together in *Yang Ssu-wen Yen-shan feng ku-jen*, p. 380, l. 3; *Cheng Chieh-shih li-kung shen-pi kung*, p. 667, l. 12; *San hsien-shen Pao Lung-t'u tuan-yüan*, p. 171, l. 15; *Hsi-hu san-t'a chi*, p. 29, l. 16; *Shui-hu ch'üan-chuan*, vol. 1, ch. 21, p. 316, l. 4; and recur in the *Chin P'ing Mei tz'u-hua*, vol. 5, ch. 94, p. 8b, l. 6.

37. This formulaic four-character expression occurs in *Shui-hu ch'üan-chuan*, vol. 2, ch. 49, p. 814, l. 4; *Hsi-yu chi*, vol. 1, ch. 23, p. 259, l. 15; and recurs in the *Chin P'ing Mei tz'u-hua*, vol. 4, ch. 72, p. 4b, l. 10; and vol. 5, ch. 95, p. 11a, l. 2.

38. See Roy, *The Plum in the Golden Vase*, vol. 2, chap. 25, n. 27.

39. This reduplicative four-character expression is ubiquitous in Chinese vernacular literature. See, e.g., *Sha-kou chi*, scene 30, p. 108, ll. 3–4; *Chang Sheng ts'ai-luan teng chuan*, p. 10, l. 6; *Cheng Yüan-ho*, 4:1441, l. 12; *Shui-hu ch'üan-chuan*, vol. 1, ch. 20, p. 291, l. 4; and *Pa-i chi*, scene 15, p. 34, l. 9.

40. This short text in three fascicles, the full title of which is *Fo-ting-hsin Kuan-shih-yin p'u-sa ta t'o-lo-ni ching* (Kuan-shih-yin Bodhisattva's great Dhāraṇī sutra of the Buddha's essence), is an indigenous apocryphal sutra, a handwritten copy of which, made in the early eleventh century, is among the documents brought back from Tun-huang by Paul Pelliot in 1907. See *Tun-huang pao-tsang* (Treasures from Tun-huang), comp. Huang Yung-wu, 140 vols. (Taipei: Hsin-wen-feng ch'u-pan kung-ssu, 1981–86), 132:65–71. Despite the fact that it is not included in any version of the Buddhist canon, it is known to have been popular during the Sung, Yüan, and Ming dynasties.

For a detailed description of this text, and a summary of its contents, see Chün-fang Yü, *Kuan-yin: The Chinese Transformation of Avalokiteśvara*, pp. 93–94 and 119–26.

41. This formulaic four-character expression occurs ubiquitously in Chinese literature. See, e.g., a lyric by Chang Yüan-kan (1091–c. 1162), *Ch'üan Sung tz'u*, 2:1073, lower register, l. 1; a lyric by Chang Hsiao-hsiang (1132–69), ibid., 3:1701, lower register, l. 9; a lyric by Hsin Ch'i-chi (1140–1207), ibid., 3:1885, lower register, l. 13; a lyric by Ch'en Te-wu (13th century), ibid., 5:3459, upper register, l. 3; a prefatory note to a lyric by Lu Chih (cs 1268), *Ch'üan Chin Yüan tz'u*, 2:727, lower register, l. 1; *Wu-wang fa Chou p'ing-hua*, p. 37, l. 13; *Ch'ien-Han shu p'ing-hua*, p. 27, l. 13; *Yüan-ch'ü hsüan*, 4:1466, l. 10; *Yüan-ch'ü hsüan wai-pien*, 2:588, l. 15; a set of songs by Chu Ch'üan (1378–1448), *Ch'üan Ming san-ch'ü*, 1:258, l. 9; *Ch'ien-chin chi*, scene 35, p. 116, l. 5; *P'u-tung Ts'ui Chang chu-yü shih-chi*, p. 19b, l. 10; *Wei-wei pu-tung T'ai-shan shen-ken chieh-kuo pao-chüan* (Precious volume of deeply rooted karmic fruits, majestic and unmoved like Mount T'ai), by Lo Ch'ing (1442–1527), originally published in 1509, in *Pao-chüan ch'u-chi*, 3:358, l. 4; *San-kuo chih t'ung-su yen-i*, vol. 2, *chüan* 17, p. 777, l. 10; *Chang Tzu-fang mu-tao chi*, p. 108, l. 4; *Hsi-yu chi*, vol. 1, ch. 21, p. 236, l. 7; *San-pao t'ai-chien Hsi-yang chi t'ung-su yen-i*, vol. 1, ch. 14, p. 183, l. 8; *Mu-tan t'ing*, scene 15, p. 74, l. 3; and *Ta-T'ang Ch'in-wang tz'u-hua*, vol. 2, *chüan* 5, ch. 34, p. 12b, l. 9.

42. This is a variant of a proverbial couplet, the more common form of which is given in *Ku-chin t'an-kai*, *chüan* 1, p. 30, l. 12. It is based on an anecdote recorded in *T'ieh-wei shan ts'ung-t'an*, *chüan* 4, p. 63, ll. 8–10; and *Lao-hsüeh An pi-chi* (Miscellaneous notes from an old scholar's retreat), by Lu Yu (1125–1210) (Peking: Chung-hua shu-chü, 1979), *chüan* 5, p. 61, ll. 4–5.

43. A variant of this proverbial couplet occurs in *Pai-t'u chi*, scene 10, p. 29, l. 9.

44. This four-character expression recurs in the *Chin P'ing Mei tz'u-hua*, vol. 4, ch. 62, p. 5b, ll. 7–8.

45. A variant of this proverbial observation occurs in ibid., vol. 3, ch. 60, p. 1a, ll. 9–10.

46. This four-character expression occurs in *San-pao t'ai-chien Hsi-yang chi t'ung-su yen-i*, vol. 2, ch. 96, p. 1237, l. 8.

47. This formulaic four-character expression occurs in *Sha-kou chi*, scene 12, p. 42, l. 6; *San-kuo chih t'ung-su yen-i*, vol. 1, *chüan* 12, p. 537, l. 12; *Hsiu-ju chi*, scene 11, p. 31, ll. 3–4; *Ming-feng chi*, scene 10, p. 40, l. 10; and *Hsi-yu chi*, vol. 1, ch. 34, p. 390, l. 15.

48. See Roy, *The Plum in the Golden Vase*, vol. 2, chap. 30, n. 50.

CHAPTER 59

1. See Roy, *The Plum in the Golden Vase*, vol. 1, chap. 2, n. 47.

2. The bridge over the Pa River, northeast of the T'ang dynasty capital Ch'ang-an, was a spot at which it was customary to see off one's departing relatives or friends, and to pluck a willow branch in commemoration of the occasion.

3. This poem is by Tu Mu (803–52). See *Ch'üan T'ang shih*, vol. 8, *chüan* 522, p. 5972, ll. 3–4.

4. A variant of this four-character expression occurs in *Hsi-yu chi*, vol. 1, ch. 46, p. 537, ll. 7–8.

5. Variants of this proverbial couplet occur in *Huan-men tzu-ti ts'o li-shen*, scene 11, p. 241, l. 13; *Nao Fan-lou to-ch'ing Chou Sheng-hsien*, p. 271, ll. 12–13; *Yu-kuei chi*, scene 22, p. 54, l. 10; *Pai-t'u chi*, scene 23, p. 64, l. 7; *Chin-yin chi*, chüan 1, scene 10, p. 24a, l. 5; *Chin-ch'ai chi*, scene 5, p. 12, ll. 19–20; *San-yüan chi*, scene 8, p. 19, ll. 9–10; *Hsiu-ju chi*, scene 7, p. 16, l. 11; *Yen-chih chi*, chüan 1, scene 3, p. 5a, l. 10; *Pa-i chi*, scene 3, p. 4, ll. 6–7; *Mu-lien chiu-mu ch'üan-shan hsi-wen*, chüan 3, p. 80b, l. 6; and *Ch'ün-yin lei-hsüan*, 3:1837, ll. 1–2.

6. This quatrain is probably derived, with considerable variation, from one in *Hsiu-ju chi*, scene 4, p. 9, ll. 1–2. Another version of this poem recurs in the *Chin P'ing Mei tz'u-hua*, vol. 5, ch. 97, p. 10a, ll. 1–2.

7. This formulaic four-character expression occurs ubiquitously in Chinese vernacular literature. See, e.g., *Nao Fan-lou to-ch'ing Chou Sheng-hsien*, p. 264, l. 7; *Ching-ch'ai chi*, scene 32, p. 100, l. 5; *P'i-p'a chi*, scene 12, p. 78, l. 10; *Chin-t'ung Yü-nü Chiao Hung chi*, p. 40, l. 7; *P'o-yao chi*, chüan 2, scene 21, p. 13b, l. 3; *Shuang-chu chi*, scene 8, p. 21, l. 11; a song suite by Ch'en To (fl. early sixteenth century), *Ch'üan Ming san-ch'ü*, 1:656, l. 4; *Ming-chu chi*, scene 10, p. 26, l. 11; a song suite by K'ang Hai (1475–1541), *Ch'üan Ming san-ch'ü*, 1:1222, l. 2; *Ssu-hsi chi*, scene 32, p. 79, l. 9; *Hai-fu shan-t'ang tz'u-kao*, chüan 3, p. 181, l. 12; *Mu-lien chiu-mu ch'üan-shan hsi-wen*, chüan 3, p. 22a, l. 9; *Ch'üan-Han chih-chuan*, vol. 2, chüan 3, p. 14a, l. 14; *Hsi-yu chi*, vol. 2, ch. 62, p. 714, l. 6; and *Chieh-hsia chi*, scene 13, p. 31, l. 10. It also recurs in the *Chin P'ing Mei tz'u-hua*, vol. 5, ch. 89, p. 5a, l. 10.

8. These Dutch doors, which divide horizontally so that the lower part can be shut while the upper remains open, were a distinctive feature of brothels in Ming times. No doubt they were designed to facilitate the semipublic display of the courtesans within.

9. This four-character expression recurs in the *Chin P'ing Mei tz'u-hua*, vol. 4, ch. 65, p. 16b, ll. 5–6.

10. The first two of these four pentasyllabic lines are of unknown authorship, but the second two are from a poem by Yü Liang-shih (fl. late 8th century), *Ch'üan T'ang shih*, vol. 5, chüan 275, p. 3118, l. 5. All four lines occur, both together and independently, in later Chinese literature and were frequently used as topics for poetic composition or pictorial representation. The first line occurs by itself in a lyric by Wu Ch'ien (1196–1262), *Ch'üan Sung tz'u*, 4:2759, upper register, l. 16; as the title of a song by Tseng Jui (c. 1260–c. 1330), *Ch'üan Yüan san-ch'ü*, 1:480, l. 11; as the subject of a painting on which a lyric was inscribed by Ch'ü Yu (1341–1427), *Ch'üan Ming tz'u*, 1:181, upper register, l. 14; and in *Hai-ling i-shih*, p. 51, l. 5. The second line occurs by itself as the title of a lyric by Ch'iu Yüan (1247–1326), *Ch'üan Sung tz'u*, 5:3401, upper register, l. 14; in a song by Lu Chih (cs 1268), *Ch'üan Yüan san-ch'ü*, 1:108, l. 7; in a song by Kuan Han-ch'ing (13th century), ibid., 1:167, l. 4; in a song by Ts'ao Te (14th century), ibid., 2:1077, l. 12; in an anonymous song suite from the Yüan dynasty, ibid., 2:1834, l. 13; and in *Yüan-ch'ü hsüan*, 4:1348. l. 2; and 4:1437, l. 10. The first two lines occur together as titles for two contiguous poems by Lin Hsi-i (cs 1235), *Ch'üan Sung shih*, 59:37345, ll. 10 and 13; as subjects for two contiguous anonymous lyrics from the Sung dynasty, *Ch'üan Sung tz'u*, 5:3829–30; in *Yüan-ch'ü hsüan*, 2:487, l. 9; 2:727, l. 8; and 3:1243, l. 10; and in an anonymous song suite from the Yüan dynasty, *Ch'üan Yüan san-ch'ü*, 2:1798, l. 14. The third line occurs by itself as the subject of a painting on which a lyric was inscribed by Ch'ü Yu (1341–1427),

Ch'üan Ming tz'u, 1:181, lower register, l. 3; and in *San-pao t'ai-chien Hsi-yang chi t'ung-su yen-i*, vol. 1, ch. 2, p. 26, l. 10. The last two lines occur together as a Zen Koan, in Isshū Miura and Ruth Fuller Sasaki, *The Zen Koan: Its History and Use in Rinzai Zen* (New York: Harcourt, Brace & World, 1965), p. 92, ll. 2–3; as titles for two contiguous poems by Chu Shu-chen (fl. 1078–1138), *Ch'üan Sung shih*, 28:17977, ll. 3 and 8; as titles for two contiguous poems by Lin Hsi-i (cs 1235), ibid., 59:37340, l. 17, and 59:37341, l. 3; and as titles for two contiguous song suites by Ma Chih-yüan (c. 1250–c. 1325), *Ch'üan Yüan san-ch'ü*, 1:255, l. 7, and 1:256, l. 1. And all four lines occur together as subjects for two sets of four consecutive lyrics by Ch'en Te-wu (13th century), *Ch'üan Sung tz'u*, 5:3453–54 and 5:3456–57; as inscriptions on four paintings of beautiful women in *Chien-teng yü-hua, chüan* 3, p. 225, ll. 1–2; as subjects for four consecutive song suites in *Yung-hsi yüeh-fu, ts'e* 9, pp. 6b–8b; as titles for four songs by Yang Shen (1488–1559) inscribed on paintings of beautiful women, in *Ch'üan Ming san-ch'ü*, 2:1442–43; and in *Mu-lien chiu-mu ch'üan-shan hsi-wen, chüan* 3, p. 23a, ll. 8–9.

11. See Roy, *The Plum in the Golden Vase*, vol. 2, chap. 34, n. 4.

12. For a detailed description of this type of varnish, see R. H. Van Gulik, *The Lore of the Chinese Lute* (Tokyo: Sophia University, 1940), pp. 176–79.

13. This four-character expression occurs in a lyric by Li Kuang (1078–1159), *Ch'üan Sung tz'u*, 2:786, lower register, l. 13.

14. This formulaic four-character expression occurs ubiquitously in Chinese vernacular literature. See, e.g., a song by K'ung Wen-sheng (13th century), *Ch'üan Yüan san-ch'ü*, 1:136, l. 10; a song by Chang K'o-chiu (1270–1348), ibid., 1:767, l. 10; a song by Cha Te-ch'ing (14th century), ibid., 2:1158, l. 6; a song suite by Chao Yen-hui (14th century), ibid., 2:1232, l. 10; a song suite by T'ang Shih (14th–15th centuries), ibid., 2:1547, l. 3; *Yüan-ch'ü hsüan wai-pien*, 1:39, l. 4; a song suite by Chang Lien (cs 1544), *Ch'üan Ming san-ch'ü*, 2:1690, ll. 6–7; a song suite by Ch'en So-wen (d. c. 1604), ibid., 2:2588, l. 9; and a set of songs by Hsüeh Kang (c. 1535–95), ibid., 3:2964, l. 12.

15. Wu Tao-tzu (d. 792) is the most renowned T'ang dynasty painter of religious scenes.

16. Mao Yen-shou (1st century B.C.) was a court painter who is famous for having depicted the members of the harem of Emperor Yüan (r. 49–33 B.C.) of the Han dynasty.

17. The proximate source of these four lines is *Huai-ch'un ya-chi, chüan* 10, p. 33b, l. 16–p. 34a, l. 1.

18. For an illustrated description of this type of incense burner that represents a miniature version of a mythological world, see Rolf A. Stein, *The World in Miniature: Container Gardens and Dwellings in Far Eastern Religious Thought*, trans. Phyllis Brooks (Stanford: Stanford University Press, 1990), pp. 41–48. For a color illustration of a famous example from the second century B.C., see Wen Fong, ed., *The Great Bronze Age of China: An Exhibition from the People's Republic of China* (New York: The Metropolitan Museum of Art and Alfred A. Knopf, 1980), p. 298.

19. The proximate source of this line is *Huai-ch'un ya-chi, chüan* 10, p. 33b, l. 8.

20. *Hsiang-ch'üan*, or "Tinkling Spring," is the name of a famous zither made by Li Mien (717–88) of the T'ang dynasty. See his biography in *Hsin T'ang shu* (New history of the T'ang dynasty), comp. Ou-yang Hsiu (1007–72) and Sung Ch'i (998–

1061), 20 vols. (Peking: Chung-hua shu-chü, 1975), vol. 14, *chüan* 131, p. 4507, l. 9; and *T'ang-yü lin* (Forest of T'ang anecdotes), comp. Wang Tang (fl. late 11th century) (Shanghai: Ku-tien wen-hsüeh ch'u-pan she, 1957), *chüan* 6, p. 214, ll. 4–5.

21. *Tzu-sun*, or "Purple Bamboo Shoot," is the name of a highly valued tea plant that is mentioned as early as the year 815 in a poem by Po Chü-i (772–846), *Ch'üan T'ang shih*, vol. 7, *chüan* 438, p. 4864, l. 9; and in a poem by Su Shih (1037–1101), *Su Shih shih-chi*, vol. 2, *chüan* 7, p. 344, l. 15. The proximate source of these two lines, which have been somewhat garbled, is *Huai-ch'un ya-chi*, *chüan* 10, p. 33b, ll. 9–10.

22. The proximate source of these two lines is ibid., *chüan* 10, p. 33b, ll. 8–9.

23. This four-character expression occurs in the biography of Hui-neng (638–713), in *Wu-teng hui-yüan*, vol. 1, *chüan* 1, p. 57, l. 2; the late ninth-century literary tale *Ling-ying chuan* (A story of miraculous responses), in *T'ai-p'ing kuang-chi*, vol. 10, *chüan* 492, p. 4037, l. 12; the prose preface to a lyric by Wang Yün (1228–1304), *Ch'üan Chin Yüan tz'u*, 2:669, upper register, l. 11; *Ch'ien-t'ang meng*, p. 3b, l. 10; *Hua-ying chi*, p. 906, l. 27; *Huan-sha chi*, scene 41, p. 145, l. 11; and *Mu-tan t'ing*, scene 35, p. 184, l. 2.

24. This four-character expression occurs in *Sui-T'ang liang-ch'ao shih-chuan*, *chüan* 8, ch. 79, p. 44b, l. 2.

25. This four-character expression occurs in a speech attributed to the Buddhist monk Ying-fu (11th century), *Wu-teng hui-yüan*, vol. 3, *chüan* 16, p. 1040, ll. 1–2; a lyric by Shih Hao (1106–94), *Ch'üan Sung tz'u*, 2:1271, upper register, l. 5; a lyric by Wu Ch'ien (1196–1262), ibid., 4:2748, upper register, l. 5; a lyric by Chiang Chieh (cs 1274), ibid., 5:3448, lower register, l. 16; *Hsi-hu san-t'a chi*, p. 26, l. 15; *Yu-kuei chi*, scene 29, p. 90, l. 9; *Chieh-chih-erh chi*, p. 250, l. 13; a song suite by Yang Hsün-chi (1458–1546), *Ch'üan Ming san-ch'ü*, 1:736, l. 9; a song by Wang Chiu-ssu (1468–1551), ibid., 1:855, l. 11; and *San-pao t'ai-chien Hsi-yang chi t'ung-su yen-i*, vol. 2, ch. 68, p. 882, l. 3.

26. The proximate source of these three lines is *Huai-ch'un ya-chi*, *chüan* 10, p. 34a, l. 3, where they occur verbatim.

27. See Roy, *The Plum in the Golden Vase*, vol. 1, chap. 18, n. 24.

28. For illustrations of this combination, which consists of a double two, a three-two, and another double two, see *Hsüan-ho p'ai-p'u*, p. 4b; *P'ai-p'u* (A manual for dominoes), by Ku Ying-hsiang (1483–1565), in *Hsin-shang hsü-pien* (A collectanea on connoiseurship continued), comp. Mao I-hsiang (16th century), Ming ed. in the Gest Collection of the Princeton University Library, *chüan* 9, p. 5a; *P'ai-t'u*, p. 43b; and *Hsüan-ho p'u ya-p'ai hui-chi*, *chüan* 1, p. 5b. It is also mentioned in *Nan Hsi-hsiang chi* (Li Jih-hua), scene 7, p. 21, l. 10.

29. For illustrations of this combination, which consists of two double ones, see *Hsüan-ho p'ai-p'u*, p. 2a; and *Hsüan-ho p'u ya-p'ai hui-chi*, *chüan* 1, p. 3b.

30. See Roy, *The Plum in the Golden Vase*, vol. 2, chap. 21, n. 64.

31. For illustrations of this combination, which consists of two double fours, see *Hsüan-ho p'ai-p'u*, p. 2b; and *Hsüan-ho p'u ya-p'ai hui-chi*, *chüan* 1, p. 3b.

32. See Roy, *The Plum in the Golden Vase*, vol. 2, chap. 21, n. 69.

33. This four-character expression occurs in a quatrain by Po Chü-i (772–846), *Ch'üan T'ang shih*, vol. 7, *chüan* 439, p. 4882, l. 10; *P'o-mo pien-wen*, p. 351, l. 10;

[Chi-p'ing chiao-chu] Hsi-hsiang chi, play no. 5, scene 2, p. 182, l. 5; *Yüan-ch'ü hsüan*, 4:1557, l. 17; and *Yüan-ch'ü hsüan wai-pien*, 2:444, l. 13.

34. This four-character expression occurs in *Yu hsien-k'u*, p. 4, l. 4; and *San-pao t'ai-chien Hsi-yang chi t'ung-su yen-i*, vol. 1, ch. 42, p. 547, l. 12.

35. This couplet has already occurred in the *Chin P'ing Mei tz'u-hua*, vol. 1, ch. 11, p. 8a, l. 11. See Roy, *The Plum in the Golden Vase*, vol. 1, chap. 11, p. 217, ll. 16–19.

36. The locus classicus for this line is *[Chi-p'ing chiao-chu]* Hsi-hsiang chi, play no. 4, scene 1, p. 142, l. 7. It also occurs independently in a song by Ch'ang Lun (1493– 1526), *Ch'üan Ming san-ch'ü*, 2:1540, l. 9; and *San-pao t'ai-chien Hsi-yang chi t'ung- su yen-i*, vol. 2, ch. 57, p. 735, l. 8. The song suite that opens with this line is by Ch'en To (fl. early 16th century), *Ch'üan Ming san-ch'ü*, 1:585–86. Versions of it may also be found in *[Hsin-pien] Nan chiu-kung tz'u*, chüan 3, pp. 5a–5b; *Nan-kung tz'u-chi*, vol. 1, *chüan* 1, pp. 32–33; *Ch'ün-yin lei-hsüan*, 4:2056–58; *Nan-tz'u yün-hsüan*, *chüan* 6, pp. 35–36; *Wu-yü ts'ui-ya*, 12:178–80; *Wu-sao ho-pien*, ts'e 2, chüan 2, pp. 19a–20a; and *Nan-yin san-lai*, ts'e 1, pp. 44a–44b.

37. This line occurs in *Lien-huan chi*, scene 20, p. 50, ll. 6–7.

38. This four-character expression recurs in the *Chin P'ing Mei tz'u-hua*, vol. 4, ch. 69, p. 8b, l. 2.

39. On Chinese dice only the one spots and four spots are colored red, while all the others are black. The name *Ch'iang-hung*, or "Competing for the Red," is used for various dice games, involving different numbers of dice, in which the winner is determined by the number of red spots thrown.

40. This idiomatic expression occurs in *Yüan-ch'ü hsüan*, 4:1718, l. 15; 4:1743, l. 4; and *Li K'ai-hsien chi*, 3:1013, l. 3. It also recurs three times in the *Chin P'ing Mei tz'u-hua*, vol. 4, ch. 69, p. 4a, l. 9; ch. 78, p. 12b, l. 6; and ch. 79, p. 12a, l. 11.

41. This formulaic four-character expression occurs ubiquitously in Chinese ver- nacular literature. See, e.g., *[Chi-p'ing chiao-chu] Hsi-hsiang chi*, play no. 1, scene 2, p. 20, l. 8; a song suite by Ch'iao Chi (d. 1345), *Ch'üan Yüan san-ch'ü*, 1:646, l. 6; a song suite by Hsiao Te-jun (14th century), ibid., 2:1414, l. 2; an anonymous Yüan dynasty song suite, ibid., 2:1861, ll. 7–8; *Yüan-ch'ü hsüan*, 2:531, ll. 13–14; *Chung- ch'ing li-chi*, vol. 2, chüan 6, p. 22b, l. 8; a set of songs by Ch'en To (fl. early 16th century), *Ch'üan Ming san-ch'ü*, 1:494, l. 13; *Hua-shen san-miao chuan*, p. 16a, l. 10; *Yen-chih chi*, chüan 2, scene 24, p. 7b, l. 8; a song suite by Cheng Jo-yung (16th century), *Ch'üan Ming san-ch'ü*, 2:1513, ll. 4–5; a song suite by Wang Ch'ung (1494– 1533), ibid., 2:1572, l. 8; a set of songs by Chin Luan (1494–1583), ibid., 2:1602, l. 11; a song suite by T'ang Shun-chih (1507–1560), ibid., 2:1883, l. 2; *Haifu shan-t'ang tz'u-kao*, chüan 3, p. 180, l. 6; *Hsi-yu chi*, vol. 2, ch. 55, p. 636, l. 5; a set of songs by Hsüeh Lun-tao (c. 1531–c. 1600), *Ch'üan Ming san-ch'ü*, 3:2871, l. 9; *Chin-chien chi*, scene 39, p. 119, l. 3; and a song by Chao Nan-hsing (1550–1627), *Ch'üan Ming san- ch'ü*, 3:3220, l. 14.

42. This formulaic four-character expression occurs ubiquitously in Chinese ver- nacular literature. See, e.g., a lyric by Cheng Chin (1047–1113), *Ch'üan Sung tz'u*, 1:444, lower register, l. 12; a lyric by Teng Yen (cs 1262), ibid., 5:3309, upper register, l. 14; *Chin-ch'ai chi*, scene 65, p. 117, l. 18; *Hua-shen san-miao chuan*, p. 16a, l. 8; a set of songs by Ch'ang Lun (1493–1526), *Ch'üan Ming san-ch'ü*, 2:1535, l. 5; a song suite by Wang Ch'ung (1494–1533), ibid., 2:1569, l. 2; a set of songs by Hsüeh Kang

(c. 1535–95), ibid., 3:2966, l. 14; and *Yang-chia fu shih-tai chung-yung yen-i chih-chuan*, vol. 2, *chüan* 6, p. 40b, l. 4.

43. This four-character expression recurs in the *Chin P'ing Mei tz'u-hua*, vol. 4, ch. 65, p. 10a, l. 2.

44. This couplet has already occurred in the *Chin P'ing Mei tz'u-hua*, vol. 1, ch. 10, p. 8b, l. 9. See Roy, *The Plum in the Golden Vase*, vol. 1, chap. 10, p. 204, ll. 4–7.

45. *Hsi-yüan*, or West Park, is the name of an imperial park to the west of Yeh, the capital city of the Wei dynasty (220–65).

46. Ho-yang was famous for its flowering peach and plum trees, which were said to have been planted by P'an Yüeh (247–300) when he was the district magistrate there.

47. Cheng-tzu, or Master Cheng, probably refers to Cheng Fa-shih (6th century), one of the most famous artists of the Sui dynasty (581–618). In a quotation from a lost work by Li Ssu-chen (d. 696), his painting is described as follows: "Flying towers and many storeyed buildings are set about with lofty groves and lovely trees; jade-green pools and silk-white rapids are covered with a profusion of various flowers and fragrant herbs, so that one cannot help but have vague thoughts of a terrace in spring—in this he is beyond all comparison." See *Some T'ang and Pre-T'ang Texts on Chinese Painting*, trans. William R. B. Acker, vol. 2, part 1 (Leiden: E. J. Brill, 1974), p. 197, ll. 20–25.

48. Wang Wei (699–761) was not only one of the best-known poets of his day, but also one of the most famous painters.

49. The source of this poem, the text of which as given in the novel has been somewhat garbled, is *Huai-ch'un ya-chi*, *chüan* 10, p. 38a, ll. 10–13. I have amended the text accordingly. Like many similar poetic works, this poem, while ostensibly depicting a flowering plant, simultaneously serves to suggest the salient features of a beautiful woman.

50. This four-character expression, the literal meaning of which is "to donate coal during snowy weather," i.e., to proffer aid when the need is greatest, occurs in *Ssu-tzu ching*, p. 3, l. 5; and *Chiang Shih yüeh-li chi*, *chüan* 4, scene 38, p. 13a, ll. 6–7. It also occurs in a variant form in a poem by Kao Teng (d. 1148), *Ch'üan Sung shih*, 31:20100, l. 6; and the title of a poem by Fan Ch'eng-ta (1126–93), ibid., 41:26008, l. 17. In view of the role played by the cat in the novel, this name is clearly intended to be ironic.

51. Variants of this couplet occur in the prose preface to a eulogy of Wang Su (1007–73) by Su Shih (1037–1101), *Su Shih wen-chi*, vol. 2, *chüan* 21, p. 604, ll. 9–10; and *San-pao t'ai-chien Hsi-yang chi t'ung-su yen-i*, vol. 2, ch. 98, p. 1266, l. 10.

52. This couplet has already occurred in the *Chin P'ing Mei tz'u-hua*, vol. 1, ch. 17, p. 6a, l. 2. See Roy, *The Plum in the Golden Vase*, vol. 1, chap. 17, p. 346, ll. 15–18.

53. A variant form of this idiomatic saying occurs in *Yü-ch'iao hsien-hua*, scene 3, p. 8b, l. 6.

54. A variant of this idiomatic expression occurs in the *Chin P'ing Mei tz'u-hua*, vol. 5, ch. 81, p. 7a, l. 9.

55. This couplet has already occurred in the *Chin P'ing Mei tz'u-hua*, vol. 3, ch. 47, p. 3a, l. 3. See chap. 47, n. 14.

56. This four-character expression recurs in the *Chin P'ing Mei tz'u-hua*, vol. 4, ch. 72, p. 14b, l. 2.

57. The military official T'u-an Ku (fl. late 7th century B.C.) and the grand councilor Chao Tun (fl. late 7th century B.C.) were rivals at the court of Duke Ling of the state of Chin (r. 620–606 B.C.). According to legend, T'u-an Ku made a straw effigy of Chao Tun, dressed it in his court costume, placed the entrails of a sheep in a cavity in its guts, and trained his dog, Shen-ao, to attack it and devour the entrails. When he loosed the dog at court, it went after Chao Tun and would have killed him, had he not been rescued by a man whom he had formerly befriended. The nucleus of this story is in the *Tso-chuan* under the year 607 B.C. See *The Tso chuan: Selections from China's Oldest Narrative History*, trans. Burton Watson (New York: Columbia University Press, 1989), p. 78; but it was made famous by its dramatic elaborations in the tsa-chü drama *Chao-shih ku-erh* (The orphan of Chao), by Chi Chün-hsiang (13th century), *Yüan-ch'ü hsüan*, 4:1476–98, see especially p. 1476; *Chao-shih ku-erh chi*; and *Pa-i chi*, scenes 14 and 19.

58. This four-character expression occurs in *Yüan-ch'ü hsüan*, 1:33, l. 9; 4:1510, l. 16; and 4:1587, l. 11; *Yü-ching t'ai*, scene 33, p. 91, l. 11; and *Ta-T'ang Ch'in-wang tz'u-hua*, vol. 2, *chüan* 8, ch. 61, p. 47a, l. 4.

59. This line occurs in *Yüan-ch'ü hsüan*, 2:561, l. 2; 2:781, l. 21; 4:1584, l. 13; and 4:1615, ll. 11–12; *Yüan-ch'ü hsüan wai-pien*, 2:408, l. 17; 2:563, l. 3; 3:861, l. 10; and 3:922, l. 8; *[Hsin-pien] Liu Chih-yüan huan-hsiang Pai-t'u chi*, p. 13b, ll. 8–9; *Yüeh Fei p'o-lu tung-ch'uang chi*, *chüan* 2, scene 31, p. 16b, ll. 6–7; *Ch'ien-chin chi*, scene 27, p. 95, ll. 2–3; a set of songs by Wang Chiu-ssu (1468–1551), *Ch'üan Ming san-ch'ü*, 1:926, ll. 6–7; and *Mu-lien chiu-mu ch'üan-shan hsi-wen*, *chüan* 1, p. 59b, l. 10.

60. These two lines occur together in *Yu-kuei chi*, scene 7, p. 16, l. 3; *Pai-t'u chi*, scene 33, p. 90, l. 3; *Jen-tsung jen-mu chuan* (The story of how Emperor Jen-tsung [r. 1022–63] reclaimed his mother), fac. repr. in *Ming Ch'eng-hua shuo-ch'ang tz'u-hua ts'ung-k'an*, ts'e 4, p. 19b, l. 4; and, with insignificant variants in the second line, *[Hsin-pien] Liu Chih-yüan huan-hsiang Pai-t'u chi*, p. 46b, l. 9; and *P'u-ching ju-lai yao-shih pao-chüan*, 5:185, l. 8.

61. This formulaic four-character expression occurs ubiquitously in Chinese literature. See, e.g., *Hsi-cheng fu* (Rhapsody on a westward journey), by P'an Yüeh (247–300), in *Wen-hsüan*, vol. 1, *chüan* 10, p. 1b, l. 6; a poem by Li Ch'i (cs 735), *Ch'üan T'ang shih*, vol. 2, *chüan* 133, p. 1348, l. 11; a poem by Tu Fu (712–70), ibid., vol. 4, *chüan* 222, p. 2356, l. 1; a poem by Po Chü-i (772–846), ibid., vol. 7, *chüan* 438, p. 4874, l. 12; a poem by Tu Mu (803–52), ibid., vol. 8, *chüan* 522, p. 5966, l. 5; a poem by the Buddhist monk Kuan-hsiu (832–912), ibid., vol. 12, *chüan* 827, p. 9319, l. 6; a lyric by Su Shih (1037–1101), *Ch'üan Sung tz'u*, 1:289, upper register, l. 4; and an abundance of other occurrences, too numerous to list.

62. This line occurs independently in *Liang-shan wu-hu ta chieh-lao*, scene 4, p. 7b, l. 14; *[Hsin-pien] Liu Chih-yüan huan-hsiang Pai-t'u chi*, p. 44b, l. 5; *Shen Hsiao-kuan i-niao hai ch'i-ming*, p. 399, l. 1; and *Pai-chia kung-an*, *chüan* 7, ch. 63, p. 23b, l. 12. The first, second, and fourth lines of this quatrain occur together verbatim, but with a variety of different third lines, in *Ming-hsin pao-chien*, *chüan* 1, p. 3a, ll. 10–12; *Pao Lung-t'u tuan wai-wu p'en chuan* (The story of how Academician Pao judged the case of the misshapen black pot), published in 1472, fac. repr. in *Ming Ch'eng-hua shuo-ch'ang tz'u-hua ts'ung-k'an*, ts'e 5, p. 31b, ll. 7–8; *Pao Lung-t'u tuan Ts'ao Kuo-chiu kung-an chuan* (The story of how Academician Pao judged the case of Imperial Brother-in-law Ts'ao), originally published in the 1470s, fac. repr. in ibid., ts'e 6,

p. 43b, ll. 7–8; *Shuang-chung chi, chüan* 2, scene 27, p. 17b, l. 10–p. 18a, l. 1; and *Shen Hsiao-kuan i-niao hai ch'i-ming*, p. 402, l. 5.

63. This four-character reduplicative expression occurs in *[Chi-p'ing chiao-chu] Hsi-hsiang chi*, play no. 4, scene 3, p. 158, l. 8; *Yüan-ch'ü hsüan*, 4:1506, l. 4; *K'ung Shu-fang shuang-yü shan-chui chuan*, p. 68, l. 1; *Huan-sha chi*, scene 17, p. 57, l. 10; *Yen-chih chi, chüan* 1, scene 16, p. 21a, l. 8; *Hai-fu shan-t'ang tz'u-kao, chüan* 3, p. 178, ll. 4–5; *Hsi-yu chi*, vol. 1, ch. 13, p. 146, l. 3; *San-pao t'ai-chien Hsi-yang chi t'ung-su yen-i*, vol. 1, ch. 26, p. 342, l. 7; a set of songs by Hsüeh Lun-tao (c. 1531–c. 1600), *Ch'üan Ming san-ch'ü*, 3:2837, l. 9; and *Shih-hou chi*, scene 21, p. 71, l. 10.

64. See Roy, *The Plum in the Golden Vase*, vol. 1, chap. 11, notes 13, 14, and 15.

65. A similar line occurs in *Ta-T'ang Ch'in-wang tz'u-hua*, vol. 1, *chüan* 4, ch. 25, p. 7b, l. 9.

66. A variant form of this couplet occurs in *Hsi-yu chi*, vol. 1, ch. 14, p. 156, ll. 5–6; and a similar couplet, with the order of its two components reversed, occurs in *San-pao t'ai-chien Hsi-yang chi t'ung-su yen-i*, vol. 1, ch. 37, p. 479, l. 12.

67. For a book-length study of the fox fairy as a motif in Chinese literature, see Rania Huntington, *Alien Kind: Foxes and Late Imperial Chinese Narrative* (Cambridge: Harvard University Press, 2003).

68. This four-character expression recurs twice in the *Chin P'ing Mei tz'u-hua*, vol. 4, ch. 62, p. 1a, l. 7; and ch. 79, p. 19b, l. 7. In the first of these two recurrences it presages the death of Li P'ing-erh, and in the second, the death of Hsi-men Ch'ing.

69. This four-character expression occurs in a memorial to the throne written in the year 1570 by Hai Jui (1514–87). See *Hai Jui chi* (The works of Hai Jui), by Hai Jui, ed. Ch'en I-chung, 2 vols. (Peking: Chung-hua shu-chü, 1981), vol. 1, p. 235, l. 1.

70. This four-character expression occurs in a passage on good generalship by Chu-ko Liang (181–234), *Chu-ko Liang chi* (The works of Chu-ko Liang), ed. Tuan Hsi-chung and Wen Hsü-ch'u (Peking: Chung-hua shu-chü, 1960), *chüan* 2, p. 41, l. 13; a passage about Yin Chung-k'an (d. c. 400) from *Chung-hsing shu* (The restoration [of the Chin dynasty]), by Ho Fa-sheng (5th century), as quoted in Liu Chün's (465–521) commentary to the *Shih-shuo hsin-yü*, *Shih-shuo hsin-yü chiao chien*, ch. 25, item 61, p. 618, l. 12; a passage about Emperor Tai-tsung of the T'ang dynasty (r. 761–79), *Chiu T'ang shu*, vol. 2, *chüan* 11, p. 268, l. 5; *Nü lun-yü*, ch. 5, p. 3b, l. 7; *Yüan-ch'ü hsüan wai-pien*, 2:427, l. 2; *San-kuo chih t'ung-su yen-i*, vol. 1, *chüan* 2, p. 77, l. 7; *Hua-ying chi*, p. 844, l. 26; *Wen-ching yüan-yang hui*, p. 163, l. 14; *Nan Sung chih-chuan*, vol. 1, *chüan* 6, p. 23b, l. 6; *Huai-ch'un ya-chi, chüan* 10, p. 20b, l. 9; and *Hsi-yu chi*, vol. 2, ch. 55, p. 637, l. 11.

71. This four-character expression recurs in the *Chin P'ing Mei tz'u-hua*, vol. 4, ch. 71, p. 9b, l. 3.

72. This four-character expression occurs in *T'ieh-wei shan ts'ung-t'an, chüan* 3, p. 60, l. 9; *Chang Hsieh chuang-yüan*, scene 32, p. 152, l. 13; *P'i-p'a chi*, scene 20, p. 119, l. 9; *San-kuo chih t'ung-su yen-i*, vol. 1, *chüan* 10, p. 470, ll. 19–20; *Nan Sung chih-chuan*, vol. 2, *chüan* 9, p. 29a, l. 1; *Pei Sung chih-chuan*, vol. 3, *chüan* 7, p. 22b, l. 5; *Lieh-kuo chih-chuan*, vol. 1, *chüan* 2, p. 81b, l. 4; *Ts'an-T'ang Wu-tai shih yen-i chuan*, ch. 30, p. 118, ll. 16–17; *[Hsiao-shih] Chen-k'ung sao-hsin pao-chüan*, 19:219, l. 3; *Ch'üan-Han chih-chuan*, vol. 3, *chüan* 4, p. 40a, l. 13; *Pai-chia kung-an, chüan* 4, ch. 42, p. 23b, l. 4; *San-pao t'ai-chien Hsi-yang chi t'ung-su yen-i*, vol. 2, ch. 69, p. 888,

l. 13; *Shih-hou chi*, scene 24, p. 83, l. 9; and *Sui-T'ang liang-ch'ao shih-chuan*, *chüan* 8, ch. 75, p. 21a, l. 8.

73. This four-character expression occurs in a lyric by Ts'ai Shen (1088–1156), *Ch'üan Sung tz'u*, 2:1028, upper register, l. 8; a lyric by Ko Ch'ang-keng (1134–1229), ibid., 4:2574, upper register, l. 11; *Tung Chieh-yüan Hsi-hsiang chi*, *chüan* 7, p. 143, l. 8; an anonymous Yüan dynasty song suite, *Ch'üan Yüan san-ch'ü*, 2:1862, l. 5; and *Yü-chüeh chi*, scene 36, p. 110, l. 10.

74. Variants of this line occur in a speech attributed to Ch'an Master Chüeh (12th century) in *Wu-teng hui-yüan*, vol. 3, *chüan* 19, p. 1297, l. 7; and *Nao Fan-lou to-ch'ing Chou Sheng-hsien*, p. 268, l. 8. It occurs in the same form as in the novel in *Shui-hu ch'üan-chuan*, vol. 2, ch. 37, p. 579, l. 3; and *Hsi-yu chi*, vol. 1, ch. 42, p. 485, l. 7.

75. This couplet, with a variant form of the second line, occurs in *Hsi-yu chi*, vol. 1, ch. 35, p. 405, l. 11.

76. This four-character expression occurs in a poem by Wen T'ing-yün (c. 812–c. 870), *Ch'üan T'ang shih*, vol. 9, *chüan* 575, p. 6694, l. 8; a lyric by Ch'ao Tuan-li (1046–1113), *Ch'üan Sung tz'u pu-chi*, p. 9, upper register, l. 14; *Ju-ju chü-shih yü-lu, i-chi* (second collection), *chüan* 3, p. 5b, l. 11; a lyric by Yao Shu-yao (cs 1154), *Ch'üan Sung tz'u*, 3:1551, upper register, l. 2; a lyric by Kuo Ying-hsiang (b. 1158, cs 1181) written in the year 1204, ibid., 4:2224, upper register, l. 8; a lyric by Ch'iu Ch'u-chi (1148–1227), *Ch'üan Chin Yüan tz'u*, 1:457, upper register, l. 14; a lyric by Yü Chi (1272–1348), ibid., 2:865, upper register, l. 2; a song suite by Hou K'o-chung (13th century), *Ch'üan Yüan san-ch'ü*, 1:279, l. 8; a song suite by Chu T'ing-yü (14th century), ibid., 2:1216, l. 9; *Ch'ien-Han shu p'ing-hua*, p. 15, l. 11; *Yüan-ch'ü hsüan*, 1:175, l. 16; *Yüan-ch'ü hsüan wai-pien*, 2:696, l. 19; *Yu-kuei chi*, scene 4, p. 5, l. 2; *Hsing-t'ien Feng-yüeh t'ung-hsüan chi*, scene 6, p. 16a, l. 2; *Ch'ien-t'ang meng*, p. 3a, l. 11; *San-kuo chih t'ung-su yen-i*, vol. 2, *chüan* 21, p. 1005, l. 10; a song suite by Yang T'ing-ho (1459–1529), *Ch'üan Ming san-ch'ü*, 1:767, l. 11; a song suite by Wang Chiu-ssu (1468–1551), ibid., 1:987, l. 9; a song by Chin Luan (1494–1583), ibid., 2:1588, l. 6; *Hai-fu shan-t'ang tz'u-kao*, *chüan* 3, p. 172, l. 8; *Hsi-yu chi*, vol. 2, ch. 81, p. 921, l. 13; and a set of songs by Hsüeh Lun-tao (c. 1531–c. 1600), *Ch'üan Ming san-ch'ü*, 3:2759, l. 1.

77. This four-character expression occurs in a lyric by Ch'in Kuan (1049–1100), *Ch'üan Sung tz'u*, 1:468, upper register, l. 11; a song suite by Chu Yu-tun (1379–1439), *Ch'üan Ming san-ch'ü*, 1:364, l. 1; and *Ssu-hsi chi*, scene 33, p. 83, l. 7.

78. The proximate source of this set piece of descriptive parallel prose, with the exception of the last two lines, which have been modified to fit the context in the novel, is *Shui-hu ch'üan-chuan*, vol. 1, ch. 21, p. 312, l. 17–p. 313, l. 3. A very similar passage, with some textual variation, also occurs in *San Sui p'ing-yao chuan*, *chüan* 4, ch. 19, p. 30b, l. 8–p. 31a, l. 4.

79. This four-character expression occurs in *Ta-T'ang Ch'in-wang tz'u-hua*, vol. 2, *chüan* 7, ch. 50, p. 18b, l. 4; and recurs in the *Chin P'ing Mei tz'u-hua*, vol. 3 ch. 60, p. 2a, l. 1; and vol. 5, ch. 88, p. 4a, l. 11.

80. This four-character expression recurs in the *Chin P'ing Mei tz'u-hua*, vol. 3, ch. 60, p. 2a, ll. 5–6; vol. 5, ch. 88, p. 5b, l. 4; and ch. 100, p. 15a, l. 1.

81. This four-character expression alludes to a famous literary tale entitled *Nan-k'o t'ai-shou chuan* (The story of the governor of the Southern Branch), by Li Kung-tso (c. 778–c. 848), in which the protagonist dreams of becoming the governor of a province named Southern Branch, only to discover on awakening that the events of his

dream had taken place in a nest of ants in a nearby locust tree. See *T'ang Sung ch'uan-ch'i chi*, pp. 81–92; and "An Account of the Governor of the Southern Branch," trans. William H. Nienhauser, Jr., in *The Columbia Anthology of Traditional Chinese Literature*, ed. Victor H. Mair (New York: Columbia University Press, 1994), pp. 861–71. It occurs ubiquitously in later Chinese literature. See, e.g., *San-shui hsiao-tu*, p. 20, l. 10; a poem by Huang T'ing-chien (1045–1105), *Ch'üan Sung shih*, 17:11421, l. 2; a poem by Fang Wei-shen (1040–1122), ibid., 15:10186, l. 5; a lyric by Tseng Ti (1109–80), *Ch'üan Sung tz'u*, 2:1319, upper register, l. 12; a lyric by Ch'en San-p'in (12th century), ibid., 3:2021, upper register, l. 1; a song suite by Ma Chih-yüan (c. 1250–c. 1325), *Ch'üan Yüan san-ch'ü*, 1:273, l. 4; and an abundance of other occurrences, too numerous to list.

82. This formulaic four-character expression occurs in *Ts'ui Ya-nei pai-yao chao-yao*, p. 268, l. 12; *Chung-shan lang*, scene 3, p. 250, l. 5; *Shui-hu ch'üan-chuan*, vol. 1, ch. 2, p. 15, l. 8; *Chang Sheng ts'ai-luan teng chuan*, p. 9, l. 6; and *Hsin-ch'iao shih Han Wu mai ch'un-ch'ing*, p. 75, l. 13.

83. A variant of these two lines occurs in *Shui-hu ch'üan-chuan*, vol. 1, ch. 3, p. 52, l. 1.

84. This four-character expression occurs in *Pao-chien chi*, scene 48, p. 87, l. 8; a song suite by Liu Hsiao-tsu (1522–89), *Ch'üan Ming san-ch'ü*, 2:2324, l. 12; and *Chin-chien chi*, scene 14, p. 44, l. 1.

85. Orthographic variants of this four-character expression occur in *Hsi-yu chi*, vol. 1. ch. 1, p. 5, l. 3; and *Ko tai hsiao*, scene 1, p. 121, l. 2. Other variants also occur in *Yüan-ch'ü hsüan*, 2:645, l. 16; and *Nü ku-ku shuo-fa sheng-t'ang chi*, scene 2, p. 7a, l. 13.

86. This idiomatic expression recurs in the *Chin P'ing Mei tz'u-hua*, vol. 4, ch. 62, p. 19a, l. 11, where, significantly, it is uttered by Hsi-men Ch'ing upon the death of Li P'ing-erh.

87. This idiomatic expression occurs in *Yüan-ch'ü hsüan*, 4:1371, l. 15.

88. This four-character expression occurs in a lyric by Yang Tzu-hsien (13th century), *Ch'üan Sung tz'u*, 4:2959, upper register, l. 11; *T'ien-pao i-shih chu-kung-tiao*, p. 199, l. 5; and a song suite by Kao An-tao (14th century), *Ch'üan Yüan san-ch'ü*, 2:1109, l. 7.

89. Variants of this idiomatic expression recur in the *Chin P'ing Mei tz'u-hua*, vol. 4, ch. 62, p. 19b, ll. 9–10; and p. 23b, l. 3.

90. A variant of this expression recurs in ibid., vol. 4, ch. 62, p. 23b, ll. 2–3.

91. This four-character expression occurs in a song suite by Chang Ming-shan (14th century), *Ch'üan Yüan san-ch'ü*, 2:1286, l. 13; *Shui-hu ch'üan-chuan*, vol. 2, ch. 31, p. 483, l. 7; *Shih Chen-jen ssu-sheng so pai-yüan*, scene 1, p. 4a, l. 1; and a set of songs by Chin Luan (1494–1583), *Ch'üan Ming san-ch'ü*, 2:1600, l. 9.

92. This four-character expression occurs in *Ju-ju chü-shih yü-lu, chia-chi* (first collection), *chüan* 1, p. 6a, l. 8; a lyric by Liang Tung (1242–1305), *Ch'üan Sung tz'u*, 5:3375, lower register, l. 1; *Yüan-ch'ü hsüan*, 2:463, l. 19; a set of songs by T'ang Fu (14th century), *Ch'üan Ming san-ch'ü*, 1:219, l. 6; and *Mu-lien chiu-mu ch'üan-shan hsi-wen*, *chüan* 1, p. 14b, l. 8.

93. An orthographic variant of this four-character expression recurs in the *Chin P'ing Mei tz'u-hua*, vol. 5, ch. 99, p. 11b, l. 4.

94. This four-character expression recurs in ibid., vol. 5, ch. 89, p. 5a, l. 4; and ch. 91, p. 4a, l. 2.

95. This expression occurs in a set of songs by Liu Hsiao-tsu (1522–89), *Ch'üan Ming san-ch'ü*, 2:2313, l. 5; and recurs in the *Chin P'ing Mei tz'u-hua*, vol. 5, ch. 91, p. 4a, l. 2. A variant form also occurs in *Hsi-yu chi*, vol. 2, ch. 64, p. 735, l. 6.

96. *Hei-shu*, or *Black Book*, is a generic term for the esoteric hemerological and divinatory texts used by yin-yang masters and diviners to ascertain information about the past and future lives of the deceased, based on the dates of their birth and death.

97. This is one of the names for the eleventh of the twelve palaces into which the Chinese traditionally divided the zodiac.

98. On this baleful deity, see Ching-lang Hou, "The Chinese Belief in Baleful Stars," in Holmes Welch and Anna Seidel, eds. *Facets of Taoism: Essays in Chinese Religion* (New Haven: Yale University Press, 1979), pp. 200–209.

99. This formulaic four-character expression occurs in *Tsu-t'ang chi*, *chüan* 2, p. 46, l. 27; a lyric by Wang Chieh (fl. early 14th century), *Ch'üan Chin Yüan tz'u*, 2:1262, upper register, ll. 15–16; *K'an p'i-hsüeh tan-cheng Erh-lang Shen*, p. 250, l. 9; *K'u-kung wu-tao chüan*, 1:109, l. 1; and *Shui-hu ch'üan-chuan*, vol. 2, ch. 48, p. 798, l. 5.

100. This sutra was allegedly translated into Chinese by Paramiti in the year 705, but no original exists, and some scholars consider it to be an indigenous apocryphal text. For a translation, see *The Śūraṅgama Sūtra (Leng Yen Ching)*, trans. Charles Luk (London: Rider & Company, 1966).

101. A variant of this couplet recurs in the *Chin P'ing Mei tz'u-hua*, vol. 5, ch. 100, p. 11b, l. 9.

102. This four-character expression occurs in *Fo-shuo Wu-liang shou ching (Sukhā-vatīvyūha)*, trans. Sanghavarman in the year 252, in *Taishō shinshū daizōkyō*, vol. 12, no. 360, *chüan* 2, p. 274, lower register, ll. 3–4; the tenth-century vernacular narrative entitled *Lu-shan Yüan-kung hua* (Story of Hui-yüan [334–416] of Mount Lu), in *Tun-huang pien-wen chi*, 1:179, l. 7; a lyric by Ma Yü (1123–83), *Ch'üan Chin Yüan tz'u*, 1:289, lower register, l. 1; *Yüan-ch'ü hsüan*, 3:1145, l. 10; and *Fo-shuo Huang-chi chieh-kuo pao-chüan*, 10:405, l. 2. It also recurs in the *Chin P'ing Mei tz'u-hua*, vol. 4, ch. 62, p. 15a, l. 8.

103. This four-character expression occurs ubiquitously in Chinese literature. See, e.g., *Lun-heng*, ch. 32, p. 111, l. 1; *Liang shu*, vol. 3, *chüan* 54, p. 790, l. 14; *Chang Hsieh chuang-yüan*, scene 21, p. 112, ll. 4–5; *Shui-hu ch'üan-chuan*, vol. 2, ch. 34, p. 537, l. 12; *Pei Sung chih-chuan*, vol. 2, *chüan* 3, p. 26a, l. 4; and *Lieh-kuo chih-chuan*, vol. 2, *chüan* 4, p. 96b, ll. 1–2.

104. This four-character expression occurs in *Kuan-shih-yin p'u-sa pen-hsing ching*, p. 19b, ll. 7–8. These two lines occur together in *Fo-ting-hsin Kuan-shih-yin p'u-sa ta t'o-lo-ni ching*, p. 66, upper register, l. 8.

105. See chap. 58, n. 40.

106. This four-character expression occurs ubiquitously in Chinese vernacular literature. See, e.g., a lyric by Hou Shan-yüan (12th century), *Ch'üan Chin Yüan tz'u*, 1:525. lower register, ll. 9–10; *Shui-hu ch'üan-chuan*, vol. 3, ch. 80, p. 1315, l. 3; the middle-period vernacular story entitled *Han Li Kuang shih-hao Fei Chiang-chün* (Li Kuang of the Han dynasty has for generations been called the Flying General), in

Ch'ing-p'ing shan-t'ang hua-pen, p. 298, l. 5; *Pa-i chi*, scene 13, p. 29, l. 6; and *[Hsiao-shih] Chen-k'ung sao-hsin pao-chüan*, 19:76, ll. 3–4.

107. This four-character expression occurs ubiquitously in Chinese vernacular literature. See, e.g., *Lu-shan Yüan-kung hua*, p. 179, l. 2; an anonymous Yüan dynasty lyric, *Ch'üan Chin Yüan tz'u*, 2:1295, upper register, ll. 9–10; *T'an-shih wu-wei pao-chüan*, 1:342, l. 3; *San-kuo chih t'ung-su yen-i*, vol. 1, *chüan* 7, p. 325, l. 24; *Tz'u-nüeh*, 3:275, l. 1; and *Hsüan-t'ien shang-ti sh'ui-chieh wen*, p. 52b, l. 10.

108. This formulaic four-character expression occurs ubiquitously in Chinese vernacular literature. See, e.g., *Kuan-shih-yin p'u-sa pen-hsing ching*, p. 80a, l. 1; a song suite by Shih Tzu-chang (13th century), *Ch'üan Yüan san-ch'ü*, 1:458, l. 1; *Ch'ien-Han shu p'ing-hua*, p. 20, l. 13; *Yüan-ch'ü hsüan*, 2:830, l. 4; *Yüan-ch'ü hsüan wai-pien*, 2:411, l. 14; *Cheng Chieh-shih li-kung shen-pi kung*, p. 667, l. 16; *Huai-hsiang chi*, scene 33, p. 110, l. 1; the middle-period vernacular story *Ts'o-jen shih* (The wrongly identified corpse), in *Ch'ing-p'ing shan-t'ang hua-pen*, p. 226, l. 15; *Tung Yung yü-hsien chuan*, p. 238, l. 2; *Yüeh-ming Ho-shang tu Liu Ts'ui*, p. 429, l. 13; the middle-period vernacular story *Ch'en K'o-ch'ang Tuan-yang hsien-hua* (Ch'en K'o-ch'ang is transfigured on the Dragon Boat Festival), in *Ching-shih t'ung-yen*, *chüan* 7, p. 85, l. 13; *Ta-Sung chung-hsing yen-i*, vol. 1, *chüan* 4, p. 50b, l. 4; a song suite by Huang O (1498–1569), *Ch'üan Ming san-ch'ü*, 2:1767, l. 6; *Hsi-yu chi*, vol. 2, ch. 59, p. 684, l. 17; *Yang-chia fu shih-tai chung-yung yen-i chih-chuan*, vol. 2, *chüan* 6, p. 14b, l. 7; and *Ta-T'ang Ch'in-wang tz'u-hua*, vol. 1, *chüan* 2, ch. 15, p. 61b, l. 1.

109. This entire passage, with a few insignificant variants, is quoted from *Fo-ting hsin Kuan-shih-yin p'u-sa ta t'o-lo-ni ching*, p. 69, lower register, l. 8–p. 70, lower register, l. 5.

110. This four-character expression occurs in a deathbed farewell to his wife by P'eng Ju-li (1042–95), as recorded in the anonymous miscellany *Tao-shan ch'ing-hua* (Pure anecdotes from the Tao-shan Hall), postface dated 1130, in *Pai-ch'uan hsüeh-hai* (A sea of knowledge fed by a hundred streams), comp. Tso Kuei (13th century), pref. dated 1273, fac. repr. of original edition (Peking: Chung-kuo shu-tien, 1990), *kuei-chi* (tenth collection), p. 14a, l. 8.

111. These artificial ornaments, made out of paper or silk, are mentioned together in *Tung-ching meng-hua lu*, *chüan* 6, p. 37, l. 12.

112. This is an abbreviated reference to an early text of the Ling-pao, or Numinous Treasure, school of Taoism, probably dating from the fifth century. See *Chiu-t'ien sheng-shen chang ching* (Scripture of the stanzas of the vitalizing spirits of the Nine Heavens), in *Cheng-t'ung Tao-tsang*, *ts'e* 165. An earlier version of this scripture is also included in *Yün-chi ch'i-ch'ien*, *chüan* 16, pp. 90–93.

113. This four-character expression occurs in a quatrain by Li Shan-fu (9th century), *Ch'üan T'ang shih*, vol. 10, *chüan* 643, p. 7374, l. 6; and *Ming-chu chi*, scene 43, p. 142, l. 1.

114. This formulaic four-character expression occurs ubiquitously in Chinese vernacular literature. See, e.g., *Fu-mu en chung ching chiang-ching wen* (Sutra lecture on the Sutra on the importance of parental kindness), dated 927, in *Tun-huang pien-wen chi*, 2:691, l. 15; a speech attributed to the Buddhist monk Chih-yü (1185–1269), in *Hsü-t'ang Ho-shang yü-lu*, *chüan* 1, p. 984, lower register, l. 5; a poem by Ch'iu Wan-ch'ing (cs 1187, d. 1219), *Ch'üan Sung shih*, 52:32281, l. 13; a lyric by Ch'ang-ch'üan-tzu (13th century), *Ch'üan Chin Yüan tz'u*, 1:591, lower register, l. 16; a song suite by

Yao Shou-chung (13th century), *Ch'üan Yüan san-ch'ü*, 1:320, l. 3; *Yüan-ch'ü hsüan*, 2:444, l. 2; *Yüan-ch'ü hsüan wai-pien*, 1:126, l. 6; *Ching-ch'ai chi*, scene 48, p. 142, l. 5; *P'i-p'a chi*, scene 10, p. 69, ll. 3–4; *Chin-ch'ai chi*, scene 32, p. 60, l. 3; *Huang-chi chin-tan chiu-lien cheng-hsin kuei-chen huan-hsiang pao-chüan*, 8:133, l. 4; *T'an-shih wu-wei pao-chüan*, 1:343, l. 1; *Ming-chu chi*, scene 14, p. 41, l. 10; *Chung-shan lang*, scene 3, p. 249, l. 3; *Shui-hu ch'üan-chuan*, vol. 2, ch. 43, p. 699, l. 1; *Pao-chien chi*, scene 8, p. 19, l. 3; *Hsi-yu chi*, vol. 1, ch. 27, p. 313, l. 9; *Pai-chia kung-an, chüan* 7, ch. 58, p. 6b, l. 2; *Ch'eng-yün chuan, chüan* 1, p. 5a, l. 5; and *I-hsia chi*, scene 20, p. 52, l. 2.

115. Variants of this four-character expression occur in *Fu-mu en chung ching chiang-ching wen*, 2:681, l. 6; *Yüan-ch'ü hsüan*, 1:110, l. 21; and *Yüan-ch'ü hsüan wai-pien*, 3:719, l. 18. It occurs in the same form as in the novel in *Yüan-ch'ü hsüan*, 2:444, l. 3; and *Nü ku-ku shuo-fa sheng-t'ang chi*, scene 3, p. 12a, l. 10.

116. Variants of this idiomatic expression occur in *Yüan-ch'ü hsüan*, 3:1017, l. 14; *Shuang-chu chi*, scene 45, p. 161, l. 10; *Shui-hu ch'üan-chuan*, vol. 1, ch. 2, p. 22, ll. 9–10; and vol. 2, ch. 37, p. 581, ll. 2–3; *Hsi-yu chi*, vol. 1, ch. 27, p. 304, l. 12; and the *Chin P'ing Mei tz'u-hua*, vol. 5, ch. 89, p. 5a, l. 5. It occurs in the same form as it does here in *Hei Hsüan-feng chang-i shu-ts'ai*, scene 1, p. 98, l. 14; *Ssu-sheng yüan*, play no. 2, scene 1, p. 22, l. 2; and *Ta-T'ang Ch'in-wang tz'u-hua*, vol. 1, *chüan* 2, ch. 16, p. 74b, ll. 4–5. It also recurs in the *Chin P'ing Mei tz'u-hua*, vol. 5, ch. 86, p. 13b, ll. 1–2.

117. This four-character expression occurs in *Chung-shan lang*, scene 4, p. 256, l. 10; and *Ta-T'ang Ch'in-wang tz'u-hua*, vol. 2, *chüan* 5, ch. 35, p. 25b, l. 8.

118. This four-character expression occurs in *Yüan-ch'ü hsüan wai-pien*, 3:890, l. 3; *Wang Wen-hsiu Wei-t'ang ch'i-yü chi*, scene 4, p. 9b, l. 6; *Su Ying huang-hou ying-wu chi, chüan* 2, scene 30, p. 25a, l. 3; and recurs in the *Chin P'ing Mei tz'u-hua*, vol. 4, ch. 61, p. 4b, l. 5.

119. A variant of this proverbial saying occurs in *Hsi-yu chi*, vol. 1, ch. 17, p. 190, ll. 3–4.

120. This formulaic four-character expression occurs in *Yüan-ch'ü hsüan*, 2:495, l. 21; *Yüan-ch'ü hsüan wai-pien*, 1:57, l. 10; *San-kuo chih t'ung-su yen-i*, vol. 2, *chüan* 24, p. 1153, l. 13; *Hai-fu shan-t'ang tz'u-kao, chüan* 2a, p. 102, l. 7; and *Pa-i chi*, scene 41, p. 96, l. 9.

121. This four-character expression occurs in *Yüan-ch'ü hsüan*, 4:1373, l. 18; a song suite by Chang Lien (cs 1544), *Ch'üan Ming san-ch'ü*, 2:1718, l. 8; and a song by Chao Nan-hsing (1550–1627), ibid., 3:3221, l. 5.

122. This four-character expression occurs in a poem by Liu Sun (9th century), *Ch'üan T'ang shih*, vol. 9, *chüan* 596, p. 6909, l. 14; *Ching-ch'ai chi*, scene 35, p. 108, l. 5; a song suite by Liu Tui (fl. early 15th century), *Ch'üan Ming san-ch'ü*, 1:7, l. 6; a song suite by Chu Yu-tun (1379–1439), ibid., 1:782, l. 8; *Shuang-chu chi*, scene 12, p. 33, l. 6; *Chung-ch'ing li-chi*, vol. 3, *chüan* 7, p. 8a, l. 4; *Chiang Shih yüeh-li chi, chüan* 3, scene 28, p. 12b, l. 5; *Shui-hu ch'üan-chuan*, vol. 4, ch. 110, p. 1650, l. 7; *Ming-feng chi*, scene 22, p. 92, l. 6; *Mu-lien chiu-mu ch'üan-shan hsi-wen, chüan* 3, p. 96a, l. 1; *Su Ying huang-hou ying-wu chi, chüan* 2, scene 30, p. 22a, l. 2; and *San-pao t'ai-chien Hsi-yang chi t'ung-su yen-i*, vol. 1, ch. 21, p. 279, ll. 5–6.

123. This four-character expression occurs in *Chuang-tzu*. See *Chuang-tzu yin-te*, ch. 14, p. 38, l. 6. It occurs ubiquitously in later Chinese literature. See, e.g., *Hsün-*

tzu yin-te (A concordance to *Hsün-tzu*) (Taipei: Chinese Materials and Research Aids Service Center, 1966), ch. 22, p. 85, l. 5; *Mo-tzu yin-te* (A concordance to *Mo-tzu*) (Peking: Yenching University Press, 1948), ch. 70, p. 107, l. 7; *Kuan-tzu chiao-cheng* (The *Kuan-tzu* collated and corrected), ed. and annot. Tai Wang (1837–73), in *Chu-tzu chi-ch'eng*, vol. 5, *chüan* 1, ch. 2, p. 5, l. 15; *Lü-shih ch'un-ch'iu*, *chüan* 14, p. 139, l. 8; a speech attributed to the Buddhist monk Tao-k'uang (10th century), *Wu-teng hui-yüan*, vol. 2, *chüan* 8, p. 458, l. 11; *Shih-wu kuan hsi-yen ch'eng ch'iao-huo*, p. 694, l. 3; *T'an-shih wu-wei pao-chüan*, 1:428, l. 3; *P'o-hsieh hsien-cheng yao-shih chüan*, 2:174, l. 1; *Cheng-hsin ch'u-i wu hsiu cheng tzu-tsai pao-chüan*, 3:115, l. 3; *Wei-wei pu-tung T'ai-shan shen-ken chieh-kuo pao-chüan*, 3:517, l. 1; *Shui-hu ch'üan-chuan*, vol. 3, ch. 75, p. 1254, l. 14; *P'u-ching ju-lai yao-shih pao-chüan*, 5:133, l. 9; *Chu-fa chi*, *chüan* 1, scene 9, p. 18a, l. 7; *Ch'üan-Han chih-chuan*, vol. 3, *chüan* 5, p. 34b, ll. 3–4; *Hsi-yu chi*, vol. 1, ch. 27, p. 309, l. 11; and *San-pao t'ai-chien Hsi-yang chi t'ung-su yen-i*, vol. 2, ch. 55, p. 706, l. 2.

124. This proverbial saying recurs in the *Chin P'ing Mei tz'u-hua*, vol. 4, ch. 67, p. 15b, l. 9.

125. This four-character expression occurs in *Jen hsiao-tzu lieh-hsing wei shen*, p. 581, l. 10; *Shui-hu ch'üan-chuan*, vol. 3, ch. 61, p. 1026, l. 2; and *Ch'üan-Han chih-chuan*, vol. 2, *chüan* 5, p. 24b, l. 6.

126. Variants of this proverbial couplet occur in *Kuan-shih-yin p'u-sa pen-hsing ching*, p. 57a, l. 10; *Hsiao Sun-t'u*, scene 14, p. 307, l. 3; *Yu-kuei chi*, scene 32, p. 98, l. 4; *P'i-p'a chi*, scene 5, p. 38, l. 6; *Chin-ch'ai chi*, scene 45, p. 81, ll. 7–8; *Hsiang-nang chi*, scene 19, p. 54, l. 10; and scene 33, p. 99, l. 2; *Huan-tai chi*, *chüan* 2, scene 27, p. 18a, l. 5; *Hsün-ch'in chi*, scene 29, p. 95, l. 12; *Chiang Shih yüeh-li chi*, *chüan* 4, scene 39, p. 16a, l. 2; *Tuan-fa chi*, *chüan* 2, scene 26, p. 13a, l. 2; *Pao-chien chi*, scene 39, p. 71, l. 1; *Yü-huan chi*, scene 28, p. 103, ll. 11–12; *Chu-fa chi*, *chüan* 2, scene 19, p. 9a, l. 1; and recur in the *Chin P'ing Mei tz'u-hua*, vol. 5, ch. 86, p. 11b, l. 6.

CHAPTER 60

1. See Roy, *The Plum in the Golden Vase*, vol. 1, chap. 2, n. 1.

2. This four-character expression occurs in a quatrain by Ssu-k'ung T'u (837–908), *Ch'üan T'ang shih*, vol. 10, *chüan* 634, p. 7277, l. 5.

3. Versions of this couplet, with the components in reverse order, occur in *Yüan-ch'ü hsüan*, 1:197, l. 19; and *Yüan-ch'ü hsüan wai-pien*, 1:74, l. 2; 1:101, l. 11; and 2:481, l. 16. Versions of the first line also occur independently in *Yüan-ch'ü hsüan*, 3:1258, l. 2; and 4:1431, l. 9; and the *Chin P'ing Mei tz'u-hua*, vol. 4, ch. 80, p. 792, l. 8.

4. This four-character expression occurs in *Tung Chieh-yüan Hsi-hsiang chi*, *chüan* 4, p. 85, l. 8; a lyric by the Taoist master Feng Tsun-shih (14th century), *Ch'üan Chin Yüan tz'u*, 2:1240, lower register, l. 6; an anonymous Yüan dynasty song suite, *Ch'üan Yüan san-ch'ü*, 2:1855, l. 5; *Shuang-chu chi*, scene 18, p. 56, l. 7; *Ming-chu chi*, scene 39, p. 123, l. 8; a song suite by Wen Cheng-ming (1470–1559), *Ch'üan Ming san-ch'ü*, 1:1024, l. 2; a song suite by Wu Kuo-pao (cs 1550), ibid., 2:2284, ll. 6–7; *Hsün-fang ya-chi*, vol. 2, *chüan* 4, p. 5b, l. 10; *Yüan-chu chih-yü: hsüeh-ch'uang t'an-i*, *chüan* 2,

p. 77, l. 2; *Shuang-lieh chi*, scene 25, p. 70, l. 6; and a song suite by Mei Ting-tso (1549–1615), *Ch'üan Ming san-ch'ü*, 3:3200, l. 12.

5. A version of this four-character expression occurs in a speech attributed to Li Kang (547–631) in the year 619 in his biography in *Chiu T'ang shu*, vol. 7, *chüan* 62, p. 2376, l. 12; and a letter by Ch'en Liang (1143–94), *Ch'en Liang chi [tseng-ting pen]*, vol. 2, *chüan* 29, p. 397, l. 9. It occurs in the same form as it does in the novel, and in a similar context, in *K'an p'i-hsüeh tan-cheng Erh-lang Shen*, p. 242, l. 13.

6. This four-character expression occurs in *Shuang-ch'ing pi-chi*, p. 29a, l. 10.

7. These two lines are taken, with some textual variation in the second line, from the final couplet of a quatrain by Chu Shu-chen (fl. 1078–1138), *Ch'üan Sung shih*, 28:17976, l. 2.

8. This formulaic four-character expression occurs ubiquitously in Chinese vernacular literature. See, e.g., two anonymous lyrics from the Sung dynasty, *Ch'üan Sung tz'u*, 5:3664, upper register, ll. 4–5; and 5:3666, upper register, l. 6; *Yang Ssu-wen Yenshan feng ku-jen*, p. 371, l. 7; *Yu-kuei chi*, scene 25, p. 69, l. 12; *Wu Lun-ch'üan Pei*, *chüan* 3, scene 19, p. 26b, l. 2; *Tu Li-niang mu-se huan-hun*, p. 534, l. 11; *Hsin-ch'iao shih Han Wu mai ch'un-ch'ing*, p. 75, l. 2; *Yüeh-ming Ho-shang tu Liu Ts'ui*, p. 438, l. 7; *Shui-hu ch'üan-chuan*, vol. 2, ch. 42, p. 674, l. 9; *Ta-Sung chung-hsing yen-i*, vol. 2, *chüan* 7, p. 40b, l. 7; *T'ang-shu chih-chuan t'ung-su yen-i*, vol. 1, *chüan* 3, p. 26b, l. 4; *Nan Sung chih-chuan*, vol. 1, *chüan* 4, p. 26a, l. 5; *Ts'an-T'ang Wu-tai shih yen-i chuan*, ch. 9, p. 27, ll. 20–21; *Mu-tan t'ing*, scene 10, p. 48, l. 10; and *San-pao t'ai-chien Hsi-yang chi t'ung-su yen-i*, vol. 1, ch. 12, p. 152, l. 3.

9. This quatrain is made up, with minor textual variation, of the first and last couplets of an eight-line poem by Chu Shu-chen (fl. 1078–1138), *Ch'üan Sung shih*, 28:17968, ll. 1–2.

10. This song suite by Ts'ao Meng-hsiu (15th century) consists entirely of a paean of praise for the peaceful and benevolent rule of the reigning Ming emperor. See *Ch'üan Ming san-ch'ü*, 2:2418–20. It may also be found in *Sheng-shih hsin-sheng*, pp. 280–82; *Tz'u-lin chai-yen*, 2:1028–32; and *Yung-hsi yüeh-fu*, ts'e 9, pp. 72a–74a.

11. A version of this anonymous song is preserved in *Pei-kung tz'u-chi wai-chi* (Supplementary collection to northern-style song lyrics), comp. Ch'en So-wen (d. c. 1604), in *Nan-pei kung tz'u-chi*, *chüan* 2, p. 34, l. 5; and *Ch'üan Yüan san-ch'ü*, 2:1744, ll. 9–10. A version identical to that in the novel may be found in *Tang-ch'i hui-ch'ang ch'ü* (Songs that agitate the spirits and rend the guts), comp. Wang Yu-jan (20th century), preface dated 1928 (Shanghai: Ta-chiang shu-p'u, 1933), *chüan* 2, p. 14b, l. 10–p. 15a, l. 1. No source is cited, however, and the song is erroneously described as an anonymous Ch'ing dynasty composition.

12. This anonymous song may be found in *Tang-ch'i hui-ch'ang ch'ü, wai-chi* (supplementary selection), p. 9b, ll. 3–4, but no source is cited, and it is erroneously identified as an anonymous Ch'ing dynasty composition.

13. See Roy, *The Plum in the Golden Vase*, vol. 1, chap. 8, n. 43.

14. This game, the name of which in Chinese is *ting-chen hsü-ma*, which is written with various orthographic variants, and for which "thimble-stitching" is only a rough translation, occurs in a song suite by Ch'iao Chi (d. 1345), *Ch'üan Yüan san-ch'ü*, 1:639, ll. 4–5; *Yüan-ch'ü hsüan*, 1:193, l. 7; *Yüan-ch'ü hsüan wai-pien*, 3:883, l. 18; a set of songs by Chu Yu-tun (1379–1439), *Ch'üan Ming san-ch'ü*, 1:274, ll. 1–2; *Shui-*

hu ch'üan-chuan, vol. 3, ch. 61, p. 1026, l. 14; and a set of songs by Li K'ai-hsien (1502–68), the preface to which is dated 1544, *Li K'ai-hsien chi*, 3:881, l. 15.

15. Each of these ten lines, numbered from one to ten, contains a riddle based on the practice of splitting Chinese characters up into their component parts. I have italicized the words that stand for the two key characters in each line, and if one subtracts the second of these from the first, one will get the characters for one to ten. Needless to say, this kind of wordplay is difficult if not impossible to translate. A version of these ten lines, with some textual variation, may be found in *[Hsin-k'o] Shih-shang hua-yen ch'ü-lo t'an-hsiao chiu-ling* ([Newly printed] Currently fashionable jokes and drinking games to be enjoyed at formal banquets), 4 *chüan* (Ming edition published by the Wen-te T'ang), *chüan* 3, p. 10a, l. 10–p. 10b, l. 3.

16. See Roy, *The Plum in the Golden Vase*, 1:456, n. 5.

17. This is the name of a variety of peony.

18. Although the source of this line has not been identified, it is not from the *Four Books*.

19. This is the first line of an aria from *P'i-p'a chi*, scene 21, p. 127, l. 2, which has already been quoted in chapter 27 of the novel. See the *Chin P'ing Mei tz'u-hua*, vol. 2, ch. 27, p. 7b, l. 3; and Roy, *The Plum in the Golden Vase*, vol. 2, chap. 27, p. 139, l. 30. This line is not from the *Four Books* and is also anomalous because, although the first word, *lien*, or "ripple," is homophonous with the word *lien* that means lotus, it has an entirely unrelated meaning.

20. This line is a misquotation of a famous line from a Music Bureau ballad that reads, "Under the plum tree one does not adjust one's hat." The point of the line is that one should avoid even the appearance of impropriety, because if one adjusts one's hat under a plum tree, an observer could suspect that one was engaged in stealing plums. The substitution of the word "willow" for the word "plum tree" makes nonsense out of the saying, since the willow does not produce fruit that anyone would want to steal. Like the two preceding examples, this is not a quotation from the *Four Books*. The ballad from which this line in its correct form is taken is sometimes attributed to Ts'ao Chih (192–232) but is more likely to be anonymous. See *Yüeh-fu shih-chi* (Collection of Music Bureau ballads), comp. Kuo Mao-ch'ien (12th century), 4 vols. (Peking: Chung-hua shu-chü, 1979), vol. 2, *chüan*, 32, p. 467, l. 7; and *Ts'ao Chih chi chiao-chu*, *chüan* 3, p. 535, l. 1. It has become proverbial and occurs ubiquitously in later Chinese literature. See, e.g., *T'ai-kung chia-chiao* (Family teachings of T'ai-kung), in Chou Feng-wu, *Tun-huang hsieh-pen T'ai-kung chia-chiao yen-chiu*, p. 21, l. 4; *[Chi-p'ing chiao-chu] Hsi-hsiang chi*, play no. 1, scene 2, p. 20, l. 15; *Yüan-ch'ü hsüan*, 1:207, l. 19; *Ts'ui Ya-nei pai-yao chao-yao*, p. 268, l. 9; *Hsiao fu-jen chin-ch'ien tseng nien-shao*, p. 228, l. 17; *Yu-kuei chi*, scene 22, p. 62, l. 10; and *Ming-hsin pao-chien*, *chüan* 1, p. 8a, l. 5.

21. This is the name of a variety of peony.

22. This is a quotation from Book 10 of the *Lun-yü* (The analects of Confucius). See *Lun-yü yin-te*, Book 10, p. 18, l. 8.

23. This line is from a famous poem by the T'ang poet Ts'en Shen (c. 715–c. 770), *Ch'üan T'ang shih*, vol. 3, *chüan* 201, p. 2096, ll. 4–5. It is quoted frequently in Chinese vernacular literature. See, e.g., *P'i-p'a chi*, scene 15, p. 88, ll. 2–3; *Shui-hu ch'üan-chuan*, vol. 2, ch. 54, p. 909, l. 6; and vol. 4, ch. 119, p. 1794, l. 4; *Tu Tzu-mei ku-chiu yu-ch'un*, scene 3, p. 12b, ll. 3–4; *Mu-lien chiu-mu ch'üan-shan hsi-wen*, *chüan* 1, p.

17b, l. 6; and *Ta-T'ang Ch'in-wang tz'u-hua*, vol. 1, *chüan* 2, ch. 12, p. 35b, l. 3. It also recurs in the *Chin P'ing Mei tz'u-hua*, vol. 4, ch. 71, p. 13a, l. 8. Needless to say, it is not a quotation from the *Four Books*.

24. This is the name of a variety of chrysanthemum.

25. This is a quotation from Mencius (c. 372–c. 289 B.C.). See *Meng-tzu yin-te*, p. 32, 4B.26. Only two out of the six quotations cited by Licentiate Wen are from the *Four Books*, and the second and third lines quoted involve a phonological error and a nonsensical lexical substitution. The author probably intends this to show that Licentiate Wen's erudition is mediocre at best, and the fact that none of his companions calls him on these obvious errors indicates that their knowledge of literature is no better than his.

26. A variant of this *hsieh-hou yü* occurs in a contemporary collection of slang terms and *hsieh-hou yü* entitled *Liu-yüan hui-hsüan chiang-hu fang-yü* (Slang expressions current in the demimonde selected from the six licensed brothels [of Chin-ling]), in *Han-shang huan wen-ts'un* (Literary remains of the Han-shang Studio), by Ch'ien Nan-yang (Shanghai: Shang-hai wen-i ch'u-pan she, 1980), p. 161, upper register, l. 3.

27. This four-character expression occurs in a quatrain by Lu T'ung (d. 835), *Ch'üan T'ang shih*, vol. 6, *chüan* 387, p. 4372, l. 5; *Chin-kang pan-jo-po-lo-mi ching chiang-ching wen* (Sutra lecture on the *Vajracchedikā prajñāpāramitā sutra*), dated 920, in *Tun-huang pien-wen chi*, 2:446, l. 4; a song suite attributed to Kuan Han-ch'ing (13th century), *Ch'üan Yüan san-ch'ü*, 1:172, l. 10; a lyric by Huang Shu (14th century), *Ch'üan Ming tz'u*, 1:127, upper register, l. 6; *Ssu-shih hua-yüeh sai chiao-jung*, scene 2, p. 5b, l. 5; *Hsiu-ju chi*, scene 10, p. 27, l. 5; and *Mu-lien chiu-mu ch'üan-shan hsi-wen*, *chüan* 1, p. 7a, l. 4.

28. This four-character expression occurs in a lyric by Mo-ch'i Yung (12th century), *Ch'üan Sung tz'u*, 2:812, lower register, l. 6; a lyric by Chao Wen (b. 1238), ibid., 5:3323, upper register, l. 15; a lyric by Ts'ao Po-ch'i (1255–1333), *Ch'üan Chin Yüan tz'u*, 2:819, upper register, l. 9; a song by Hsü Wen-chao (c. 1464–1553), *Ch'üan Ming san-ch'ü*, 1:819, l. 8; a song by K'ang Hai (1475–1541), ibid., 1:1176, l. 3; a song suite by Huang O (1498–1569), ibid., 2:1760, l. 14; a song suite by Chang Feng-i (1527–1613), ibid., 3:2602, l. 7; a song suite by Huang Tsu-ju (16th century), ibid., 3:3240, l. 13; and *Yü-ching t'ai*, scene 3, p. 4, ll. 4–5.

29. A version of these six lines, with some textual variation, may be found in *[Hsin-k'o] Shih-shang hua-yen ch'ü-lo t'an-hsiao chiu-ling*, *chüan* 3, p. 14b, l. 10–p. 15a, l. 1.

30. The following passage conflicts redundantly with information that has already been given earlier on page 493 of this chapter. The most likely explanation for this redundancy, of which there are a number of instances in the novel, is that the author had experimented with inserting this material in two different places and had not yet made up his mind which place to put it before he lost control of the manuscript.

31. This proverbial couplet occurs in *Shih-lin kuang-chi*, *ch'ien-chi*, *chüan* 9, p. 8b, l. 8; *Ming-hsin pao-chien*, *chüan* 1, p. 10b, ll. 10–11; *Chang Hsieh chuang-yüan*, scene 19, p. 99, l. 13; *Yang Wen lan-lu hu chuan*, p. 173, l. 6; *P'i-p'a chi*, scene 16, p. 97, l. 11; *Hsün-ch'in chi*, scene 5, p. 11, ll. 5–6; *Tung Yung yü-hsien chuan*, p. 236, l. 9; *Ch'ün-yin lei-hsüan*, 3:1729, l. 5; and *Chin-chien chi*, scene 35, p. 106, l. 9. The first line occurs by itself in *Ts'ai-lou chi*, scene 10, p. 33, l. 3; and *Mu-lien chiu-mu ch'üan-shan hsi-wen*, *chüan* 2, p. 84b, l. 10. The second line occurs independently in *Chin-yin chi*, *chüan* 2, scene 12, p. 6a, l. 5; and *P'o-yao chi*, *chüan* 1, scene 11, p. 33b, l. 9.

32. The last five characters of this line are taken from the penultimate line in the first quatrain from the *Shen-t'ung shih* (Poems by infant prodigies), a popular poetic primer of uplifting pentasyllabic quatrains, at least some of which are traditionally attributed to Wang Chu (cs 1100). Its contents would have been familiar to any literate person in sixteenth-century China. See ibid., in *Chung-kuo ku-tai meng-hsüeh shu ta-kuan* (A corpus of traditional Chinese primers), comp. Lu Yang-t'ao (Shanghai: T'ung-chi ta-hsüeh ch'u-pan she, 1995), p. 266, l. 17. The same line is also quoted in *Chang Hsieh chuang-yüan*, scene 1, p. 2, l. 5; *Yüan-ch'ü hsüan*, 4:1338, l. 10; *Yüan-ch'ü hsüan wai-pien*, 3:817, l. 8; *Ching-ch'ai chi*, scene 2, p. 4, l. 9; and *P'i-p'a chi*, scene 9, p. 61, l. 6.

33. This couplet has already occurred in the *Chin P'ing Mei tz'u-hua*, vol. 1, ch. 5, p. 9b, l. 6. See Roy, *The Plum in the Golden Vase*, vol. 1, chap. 5, p. 110, ll. 1–4.

BIBLIOGRAPHY TO VOLUME 3

PRIMARY SOURCES
(Arranged Alphabetically by Title)

The Analects. By Confucius. Translated by D. C. Lau. New York: Penguin Books, 1979.

An Anthology of Chinese Literature. Compiled by Stephen Owen. New York: W. W. Norton & Company, 1996.

Cha-ch'uan Hsiao Ch'en pien Pa-wang 雪川蕭琛貶霸王 (In Cha-ch'uan Hsiao Ch'en rebukes the Hegemon-King). In *Ch'ing-p'ing shan-t'ang hua-pen*, pp. 313–22.

Chan-kuo ts'e 戰國策 (Intrigues of the Warring States). Compiled by Liu Hsiang 劉向 (79–8 B.C.). 3 vols. Shanghai: Shang-hai ku-chi ch'u-pan she, 1985.

Chan-Kuo Ts'e. Translated by J. I. Crump. Oxford: Oxford University Press, 1970.

Chang Hsieh chuang-yüan 張協狀元 (Top graduate Chang Hsieh). In *Yung-lo ta-tien hsi-wen san-chung chiao-chu*, pp. 1–217.

Chang Ku-lao chung-kua ch'ü Wen-nü 張古老種瓜娶文女 (Chang Ku-lao plants melons and weds Wen-nü). In *Ku-chin hsiao-shuo*, vol. 2, *chüan* 33, pp. 487–502.

Chang Sheng ts'ai-luan teng chuan 張生彩鸞燈傳 (The story of Chang Sheng and the painted phoenix lanterns). In *Hsiung Lung-feng ssu-chung hsiao-shuo*, pp. 1–13.

Chang Tzu-fang mu-tao chi 張子房慕道記 (The story of Chang Liang's pursuit of the Way). In *Ch'ing-p'ing shan-t'ang hua-pen*, pp. 102–113.

Chang Yü-hu su nü-chen kuan chi 張于湖宿女貞觀記 (Chang Yü-hu spends the night in a Taoist nunnery). In *Yen-chü pi-chi*, vol. 2, *chüan* 6, pp. 6b–24b, lower register.

Ch'ang-an ch'eng ssu-ma t'ou-T'ang 長安城四馬投唐 (In Ch'ang-an city four horsemen surrender to the T'ang). In *Ku-pen Yüan Ming tsa-chü*, vol. 3.

Chao Fei-yen wai-chuan 趙飛燕外傳 (Unofficial biography of Chao Fei-yen). Attributed to Ling Hsüan 伶玄 (1st century), but probably dating from the Six Dynasties period (222–589). In *Ssu wu-hsieh hui-pao wai-pien*, vol. 1, pp. 59–67.

Chao Po-sheng ch'a-ssu yü Jen-tsung 趙伯昇茶肆遇仁宗 (Chao Po-sheng encounters Emperor Jen-tsung in a tea shop), in *Ku-chin hsiao-shuo*, vol. 1, *chüan* 11, pp. 165–74.

Chao-shih ku-erh 趙氏孤兒 (The orphan of Chao). By Chi Chün-hsiang 紀君祥 (13th century). In *Yüan-ch'ü hsüan*, 4:1476–98.

Chao-shih ku-erh chi 趙氏孤兒記 (The story of the orphan of Chao). In *Ku-pen hsi-ch'ü ts'ung-k'an, ch'u-chi*, item 16.

Ch'ao-yeh ch'ien-tsai 朝野僉載 (Comprehensive record of affairs within and without the court). Compiled by Chang Cho 張鷟 (cs 675). Peking: Chung-hua shu-chü, 1979.

Ch'ao-yeh hsin-sheng t'ai-ping yüeh-fu 朝野新聲太平樂府 (New songs from court and country: ballads from an era of great peace). Compiled by Yang Ch'ao-ying 楊朝英 (14th century). Preface dated 1351. Peking: Chung-hua shu-chü, 1987.

Chen-ch'uan hsien-sheng chi 震川先生集 (Collected works of Kuei Yu-kuang). By Kuei Yu-kuang 歸有光 (1507–71). 2 vols. Shanghai: Shang-hai ku-chi ch'u-pan she, 1981.

Chen-kao 真誥 (Declarations of the perfected). Compiled by T'ao Hung-ching 陶弘景 (452–536). In *Cheng-t'ung Tao-tsang*, ts'e 637–40.

Ch'en Hsün-chien Mei-ling shih-ch'i chi 陳巡檢梅嶺失妻記 (Police chief Ch'en loses his wife in crossing the Mei-ling Range). In *Ch'ing-p'ing shan-t'ang hua-pen*, pp. 121–36.

Ch'en K'o-ch'ang Tuan-yang hsien-hua 陳可常端陽仙化 (Ch'en K'o-ch'ang is transfigured on the Dragon Boat Festival). In *Ching-shih t'ung-yen*, chüan 7, pp. 80–87.

Ch'en Liang chi [tseng-ting pen] 陳亮集[增訂本] (Collected works of Ch'en Liang [augmented and revised edition]). Edited by Teng Kuang-ming 鄧廣銘. 2 vols. Peking: Chung-hua shu-chü, 1987.

Cheng Chieh-shih li-kung shen-pi kung 鄭節使立功神臂弓 (Commissioner Cheng wins merit with his magic bow). In *Hsing-shih heng-yen*, vol. 2, chüan 31, pp. 656–73.

Cheng-hsin ch'u-i wu hsiu cheng tzu-tsai pao-chüan 正信除疑無修證自在寶卷 (Precious volume of self-determination needing neither cultivation nor verification which rectifies belief and dispels doubt). By Lo Ch'ing 羅清 (1442–1527). Originally published in 1509. In *Pao-chüan ch'u-chi*, 3:1–339.

Cheng-t'ung Tao-tsang 正通道藏 (The Cheng-t'ung [1436–49] Taoist canon). Shanghai: Shang-wu yin-shu kuan, 1926.

Cheng yü-pan pa-hsien kuo ts'ang-hai 爭玉板八仙過滄海 (Contending for the jade tablet the Eight Immortals cross the azure sea). In *Ku-pen Yüan Ming tsa-chü*, vol. 4.

Cheng Yüan-ho 鄭元和. In *Tsui yü-ch'ing*, pp. 1411–50, upper register.

Ch'eng-yün chuan 承運傳 (The story of the assumption of the mandate [by the Yung-lo emperor]). In *Ku-pen hsiao-shuo ts'ung-k'an, ti-pa chi*, vol. 3.

Chi-i chi 集異記 (Collected records of the unusual). By Hsüeh Yung-jo 薛用弱 (fl. early 9th century). In *Ku-shih wen-fang hsiao-shuo, ts'e* 5.

[Chi-p'ing chiao-chu] Hsi-hsiang chi [集評校注] 西廂記 (The romance of the western chamber [with collected commentary and critical annotation]). Edited and annotated by Wang Chi-ssu 王季思. Shanghai: Shang-hai ku-chi ch'u-pan she, 1987.

Chi Ya-fan chin-man ch'an-huo 計押番金鰻產禍 (Duty Group Leader Chi's golden eel engenders catastrophe). In *Ching-shih t'ung-yen*, chüan 20, pp. 274–88.

Ch'i-hsiu lei-kao 七修類稿 (Categorized notes under seven rubrics). By Lang Ying 郎瑛 (1487–c. 1566). 2 vols. Peking: Chung-hua shu-chü, 1961.

Ch'i-kuo ch'un-ch'iu p'ing-hua 七國春秋平話 (The p'ing-hua on the events of the seven states). Originally published in 1321–23. Shanghai: Ku-tien wen-hsüeh ch'u-pan she, 1955.

Ch'i-tung yeh-yü 齊東野語 (Rustic words of a man from eastern Ch'i). By Chou Mi 周密 (1232–98). Preface dated 1291. Peking: Chung-hua shu-chü, 1983.

Chiang Shih yüeh-li chi 姜詩躍鯉記 (The story of Chiang Shih and the leaping carp). By Ch'en P'i-chai 陳羆齋 (fl. early 16th century). In *Ku-pen hsi-ch'ü ts'ung-k'an, ch'u-chi*, item 36.

Chiao Hung chuan 嬌紅傳 (The Story of Chiao-niang and Fei-hung). By Sung Yüan 宋遠 (14th century). In *Ku-tai wen-yen tuan-p'ien hsiao-shuo hsüan-chu, erh-chi*, pp. 280–323.

Chieh-chih-erh chi 戒指兒記 (The story of the ring). In *Ch'ing-p'ing shan-t'ang hua-pen*, pp. 241–71.

Chieh-hsia chi 節俠記 (The steadfast knight errant). By Hsü San-chieh 許三階 (fl. late 16th century). *Liu-shih chung ch'ü* edition. Taipei: K'ai-ming shu-tien, 1970.

Chien-teng hsin-hua 剪燈新話 (New wick-trimming tales). By Ch'ü Yu 瞿佑 (1341–1427). In *Chien-teng hsin-hua [wai erh-chung]*, pp. 1–119.

Chien-teng hsin-hua [wai erh-chung] 剪燈新話 [外二種] (New wick-trimming tales [plus two other works]). Edited and annotated by Chou I 周夷. Shanghai: Ku-tien wen-hsüeh ch'u-pan she, 1957.

Chien-teng yü-hua 剪燈餘話 (More wick-trimming tales). By Li Ch'ang-ch'i 李昌祺 (1376–1452). Author's preface dated 1420. In *Chien-teng hsin-hua [wai erh-chung]*, pp. 121–312.

Chien-t'ieh ho-shang 簡貼和尚 (The Monk's billet-doux). In *Ch'ing-p'ing shan-t'ang hua-pen*, pp. 6–21.

Ch'ien-chin chi 千金記 (The thousand pieces of gold). By Shen Ts'ai 沈采 (15th century). *Liu-shih chung ch'ü* edition. Taipei: K'ai-ming shu-tien, 1970.

Ch'ien-chin fang 千金方 (Prescriptions worth a thousand pieces of gold). Compiled by Sun Ssu-miao 孫思邈 (581–682). Edited by Liu Keng-sheng 劉更生 and Chang Jui-hsien 張瑞賢. Peking: Hua-hsia ch'u-pan she, 1996.

Ch'ien-chin yao-fang 千金要方 (Essential prescriptions worth a thousand pieces of gold). Compiled by Sun Ssu-miao 孫思邈 (581–682). In *Ch'ien-chin fang*, pp. 1–434.

Ch'ien-Han shu p'ing-hua 前漢書平話 (The p'ing-hua on the history of the Former Han dynasty). Originally published in 1321–23. Shanghai: Ku-tien wen-hsüeh ch'u-pan she, 1955.

Ch'ien-nü li-hun 倩女離魂 ([Chang] Ch'ien-nü's disembodied soul). By Cheng Kuang-tsu 鄭光祖 (fl. early 14th century). In *Yüan-ch'ü hsüan*, 2:705–19.

Ch'ien-t'ang hu-yin Chi-tien Ch'an-shih yü-lu 錢塘湖隱濟顛禪師語錄 (The recorded sayings of the lakeside recluse of Ch'ien-t'ang, the Ch'an master Crazy Chi [Tao-chi (1148–1209)]). Fac. repr. of 1569 edition. In *Ku-pen hsiao-shuo ts'ung-k'an, ti-pa chi*, vol. 1.

Ch'ien-t'ang meng 錢塘夢 (The dream in Ch'ien-t'ang). Included as part of the front matter in the 1498 edition of the *Hsi-hsiang chi*, pp. 1a–4b.

Chih-shih yü-wen 治世餘聞 (Recollections of a well-governed age). By Ch'en Hung-mo 陳洪謨 (1474–1555). Originally completed in 1521. Peking: Chung-hua shu-chü, 1985.

Chin-ch'ai chi 金釵記 (The gold hairpin). Manuscript dated 1431. Modern edition edited by Liu Nien-tzu 劉念茲. Canton: Kuang-tung jen-min ch'u-pan she, 1985.

Chin-chien chi 金箋記 (The brocade note). By Chou Lü-ching 周履靖 (1549–1640). *Liu-shih chung ch'ü* edition. Taipei: K'ai-ming shu-tien, 1970.

Chin-kang ching chi-chu 金剛經集注 (The *Vajracchedikā prajñāpāramitā sutra* with collected commentaries). Compiled by the Yung-lo 永樂 emperor of the Ming dynasty (r. 1402–24). Preface dated 1424. Fac. repr. of original edition. Shanghai: Shang-hai ku-chi ch'u-pan she, 1984.

Chin-kang pan-jo-po-lo-mi ching chiang-ching wen 金剛般若波羅密經講經文 (Sutra lecture on the *Vajracchedikā prajñāpāramitā sutra*). Dated 920. In *Tun-huang pien-wen chi*, 2:426–46.

Chin-kang pan-jo-po-lo-mi ching chu 金剛般若波羅密經注 (Commentary on the *Vajracchedikā prajñāpāramitā sutra*). By Tao-ch'uan 道川 (fl. 1127–63). Preface dated 1179. In *[Shinzan] Dai Nihon zokuzōkyō*, vol. 24, no. 461, pp. 535–65.

Chin-lan ssu-yu chuan 金蘭四友傳 (The story of the four ardent friends). In *Kuo-se t'ien-hsiang*, vol. 3, *chüan* 9, upper register, pp. 1a–26b.

Chin-lien chi 金蓮記 (The golden lotus [lamp]). By Ch'en Ju-yüan 陳汝元 (fl. 1572–1629). *Liu-shih chung ch'ü* edition. Taipei: K'ai-ming shu-tien, 1970.

Chin-ming ch'ih Wu Ch'ing feng Ai-ai 金明池吳清逢愛愛 (Wu Ch'ing meets Ai-ai at Chin-ming Pond). In *Ching-shih t'ung-yen, chüan* 30, pp. 459–71.

Chin P'ing Mei tz'u-hua 金瓶每詞話 (Story of the plum in the golden vase). Preface dated 1618. 5 vols. Fac. repr. Tokyo: Daian, 1963.

Chin shu 晉書 (History of the Chin dynasty [265–420]). Compiled by Fang Hsüan-ling 房玄齡 (578–648) et al. 10 vols. Peking: Chung-hua shu-chü, 1974.

Chin-t'ung Yü-nü Chiao Hung chi 金童玉女嬌紅記 (The Golden Lad and the Jade Maiden: The story of Chiao-niang and Fei-hung). Attributed to Liu Tui 劉兌 (fl. early 15th century). In *Ming-jen tsa-chü hsüan*, pp. 1–83.

Chin-yin chi 金印記 (The golden seal). By Su Fu-chih 蘇復之 (14th century). In *Ku-pen hsi-ch'ü ts'ung-k'an, ch'u-chi*, item 27.

Ch'in ping liu-kuo p'ing-hua 秦併六國平話 (The p'ing-hua on the annexation of the Six States by Ch'in). Originally published in 1321–23. Shanghai: Ku-tien wen-hsüeh ch'u-pan she, 1955.

Ching-ch'ai chi 荊釵記 (The thorn hairpin). *Liu-shih chung ch'ü* edition. Taipei: K'ai-ming shu-tien, 1970.

Ching-chung chi 精忠記 (A tale of perfect loyalty). *Liu-shih chung ch'ü* edition. Taipei: K'ai-ming shu-tien, 1970.

Ching-shih t'ung-yen 警世通言 (Common words to warn the world). Edited by Feng Meng-lung 馮夢龍 (1574–1646). First published 1624. Peking: Tso-chia ch'u-pan she, 1957.

Ch'ing feng-nien Wu-kuei nao Chung K'uei 慶豐年五鬼鬧鍾馗 (Celebrating a prosperous year, the Five Devils plague Chung K'uei). In *Ku-pen Yüan Ming tsa-chü*, vol. 4.

Ch'ing-lou chi 青樓集 (Green bower collection). By Hsia T'ing-chih 夏庭芝 (c. 1316–c. 1368). In *Chung-kuo ku-tien hsi-ch'ü lun-chu chi-ch'eng*, 2:1–84.

Ch'ing-p'ing shan-t'ang hua-pen 清平山堂話本 (Stories printed by the Ch'ing-p'ing Shan-t'ang). Edited by T'an Cheng-pi 譚正璧. Shanghai: Ku-tien wen-hsüeh ch'u-pan she, 1957.

Ch'ing-po tsa-chih [chiao-chu] 清波雜志 [校注] (Miscellaneous notes by one who lives near the Ch'ing-po Gate [with collected commentary and critical annotation]). By Chou Hui 周煇 (1127–c. 1198). Author's preface dated 1192. Edited and annotated by Liu Yung-hsiang 劉永翔. Peking: Chung-hua shu-chü, 1997.

Ch'ing-so kao-i 青瑣高議 (Lofty sentiments from the green latticed windows). Compiled by Liu Fu 劉斧 (fl. 1040–1113). Shanghai: Ku-tien wen-hsüeh ch'u-pan she, 1958.

Chiu-pien nan chiu-kung p'u 舊編南九宮譜 (Formulary for the old repertory of the nine southern musical modes). Compiled by Chiang Hsiao 蔣孝 (16th century). Preface dated 1549. Fac. repr. in *Shan-pen hsi-ch'ü ts'ung-k'an*, vol. 26.

Chiu T'ang shu 舊唐書 (Old history of the T'ang dynasty). Compiled by Liu Hsü 劉昫 (887–946) et al. 16 vols. Peking: Chung-hua shu-chü, 1975.

Chiu-t'ien sheng-shen chang ching 九天生神章經 (Scripture of the stanzas of the vitalizing spirits of the Nine Heavens). In *Cheng-t'ung Tao-tsang*, ts'e 165.

Chiu Wu-tai shih 舊五代史 (Old history of the Five Dynasties). Compiled by Hsüeh Chü-cheng 薛居正 (912–981) et al. 6 vols. Peking: Chung-hua shu-chü, 1976.

Ch'iu-jan k'o chuan 虬髯客傳 (The curly-bearded guest). In *T'ang Sung ch'uan-ch'i chi*, pp. 165–71.

Cho Wen-chün ssu-pen Hsiang-ju 卓文君私奔相如 (Cho Wen-chün elopes with [Ssuma] Hsiang-ju). By Chu Ch'üan 朱權 (1378–1448). In *Ming-jen tsa-chü hsüan*, pp. 113–39.

Ch'o-keng lu 輟耕錄 (Notes recorded during respites from the plough). By T'ao Tsung-i 陶宗儀 (c. 1316–c. 1403). Preface dated 1366. Peking: Chung-hua shu-chü, 1980.

Chou-i yin-te 周易引得 (A concordance to the *I-ching*). Taipei: Chinese Materials and Research Aids Service Center, 1966.

Chou shu 周書 (History of the Chou dynasty [557–81]). Compiled by Ling-hu Te-fen 令狐德棻 (583–666). 3 vols. Peking: Chung-hua shu-chü, 1971.

Chu-fa chi 祝髮記 (Taking the tonsure). By Chang Feng-i 張鳳翼 (1527–1613). Completed in 1586. In *Ku-pen hsi-ch'ü ts'ung-k'an, ch'u-chi*, item 61.

Chu-ko Liang chi 諸葛亮集 (The works of Chu-ko Liang). By Chu-ko Liang 諸葛亮 (181–234). Edited by Tuan Hsi-chung 段熙仲 and Wen Hsü-ch'u 聞旭初. Peking: Chung-hua shu-chü, 1960.

Chu-kung-tiao liang-chung 諸宮調兩種 (Two exemplars of the medley in various modes). Edited and annotated by Ling Ching-yen 凌景埏 and Hsieh Po-yang 謝伯陽. N.p.: Ch'i-Lu shu-she, 1988.

Chu-tzu chi-ch'eng 諸子集成 (A corpus of the philosophers). 8 vols. Hong Kong: Chung-hua shu-chü, 1978.

Chu-tzu yü-lei 朱子語類 (Classified sayings of Master Chu). Compiled by Li Ching-te 李靖德 (13th century). 8 vols. Taipei: Cheng-chung shu-chü, 1982.

Ch'u-tz'u pu-chu [fu so-yin] 楚辭補注 [附索引] (Songs of Ch'u with supplementary annotation [and a concordance]). Compiled by Hung Hsing-tsu 洪興祖 (1090–1155). Kyoto: Chūbun shuppan-sha, 1972.

Chuang-tzu yin-te 莊子引得 (A concordance to *Chuang-tzu*). Cambridge: Harvard University Press, 1956.

Ch'un-ch'iu fan-lu chu-tzu so-yin 春秋繁露逐字索引 (A concordance to the *Chun-ch'iu fan-lu*). Hong Kong: Shang-wu yin-shu kuan, 1994.

Chung-ch'ing li-chi 鍾情麗集 (A pleasing tale of passion). In *Yen-chü pi-chi*, vol. 2, *chüan* 6, pp. 1a–40b, and vol. 3, *chüan* 7, pp. 1a–30a, upper register.

Chung-hua tao-chiao ta tz'u-tien 中華道教大辭典 (Encyclopedia of the Chinese Taoist religion). Compiled by Hu Fu-ch'en 胡孚琛 et al. Peking: Chung-kuo she-hui k'o-hsüeh ch'u-pan she, 1995.

Chung-kuo chi-hsiang t'u-an 中國吉祥圖案 (Chinese auspicious art motifs). Compiled by Nozaki Seikin 野崎誠近. Taipei: Chung-wen t'u-shu ku-fen yu-hsien kung-ssu, 1979.

Chung-kuo fu-shih wu-ch'ien nien 中國服飾五千年 (Five thousand years of Chinese costume). Compiled by Chou Hsün 周汛 and Kao Ch'un-ming 高春明. Hong Kong: Shang-wu yin-shu kuan, 1984.

Chung-kuo i-kuan fu-shih ta tz'u-tien 中國衣冠服飾大辭典 (Comprehensive dictionary of Chinese costume and its decorative motifs). Compiled by Chou Hsün 周汛 and Kao Ch'un-ming 高春明. Shanghai: Shang-hai tz'u-shu ch'u-pan she, 1996.

Chung-kuo ku-tai meng-hsüeh shu ta-kuan 中國古代蒙學書大觀 (A corpus of traditional Chinese primers). Compiled by Lu Yang-t'ao 陸養濤. Shanghai: T'ung-chi ta-hsüeh ch'u-pan she, 1995.

Chung-kuo ku-tien hsi-ch'ü lun-chu chi-ch'eng 中國古典戲曲論著集成 (A corpus of critical works on classical Chinese drama). Compiled by Chung-kuo hsi-ch'ü yen-chiu yüan 中國戲曲研究院 (The Chinese Academy of Dramatic Arts). 10 vols. Peking: Chung-kuo hsi-chü ch'u-pan she, 1959.

Chung-shan lang 中山狼 (The wolf of Chung-shan). By K'ang Hai 康海 (1475–1541). In *Ming-jen tsa-chü hsüan*, pp. 237–59.

Chung-shan lang yüan-pen 中山狼院本 (Yüan-pen on the wolf of Chung-shan). By Wang Chiu-ssu 王九思 (1468–1551). In *Ming-jen tsa-chü hsüan*, pp. 261–68.

Ch'ung-mo-tzu tu-pu Ta-lo T'ien 沖漠子獨步大羅天 (Ch'ung-mo tzu ascends to the Grand Veil Heaven). By Chu Ch'üan 朱權 (1378–1448). In *Ku-pen Yüan Ming tsa-chü*, vol. 2.

Ch'ü-wei chiu-wen 曲洧舊聞 (Old stories heard in Ch'ü-wei). By Chu Pien 朱弁 (d. 1144). In *Pi-chi hsiao-shuo ta-kuan*, vol. 4, ts'e 8.

Ch'üan Chin shih 全金詩 (Complete poetry of the Chin dynasty [1115–1234]). Compiled by Hsüeh Jui-chao 薛瑞兆 and Kuo Ming-chih 郭明志. 4 vols. Tientsin: Nan-k'ai ta-hsüeh ch'u-pan she, 1995.

Ch'üan Chin Yüan tz'u 全金元詞 (Complete lyrics of the Chin and Yüan dynasties). Compiled by T'ang Kuei-chang 唐圭璋. 2 vols. Peking: Chung-hua shu-chü, 1979.

Ch'üan-Han chih-chuan 全漢志傳 (Chronicle of the entire Han dynasty). 12 *chüan*. Chien-yang: K'o-ch'in chai, 1588. Fac. repr. in *Ku-pen hsiao-shuo ts'ung-k'an, ti-wu chi*, vols. 2–3.

Ch'üan Ming san-ch'ü 全明散曲 (Complete nondramatic song lyrics of the Ming). Compiled by Hsieh Po-yang 謝伯陽. 5 vols. Chi-nan: Ch'i-Lu shu-she, 1994.

Ch'üan Ming tz'u 全明詞 (Complete *tz'u* lyrics of the Ming). Compiled by Jao Tsung-i 饒宗頤 and Chang Chang 張璋. 6 vols. Peking: Chung-hua shu-chü, 2004.

Ch'üan Shang-ku San-tai Ch'in Han San-kuo Liu-ch'ao wen 全上古三代秦漢三國六朝文 (Complete Prose from High Antiquity, the Three Dynasties, Ch'in, Han, the Three Kingdoms, and the Six Dynasties). Compiled by Yen K'o-chün 嚴可均 (1762–1843). 5 vols. Peking: Chung-hua shu-chü, 1965.

Ch'üan Sung shih 全宋詩 (Complete poetry of the Sung). Compiled by Fu Hsüan-ts'ung 傅璇琮 et al. 72 vols. Peking: Pei-ching ta-hsüeh ch'u-pan she, 1991–98.

Ch'üan Sung tz'u 全宋詞 (Complete *tz'u* lyrics of the Sung). Compiled by T'ang Kuei-chang 唐圭璋. 5 vols. Hong Kong: Chung-hua shu-chü, 1977.

Ch'üan Sung tz'u pu-chi 全宋詞補輯 (Supplement to Complete *tz'u* lyrics of the Sung). Compiled by K'ung Fan-li 孔凡禮. Peking: Chung-hua shu-chü, 1981.

Ch'üan T'ang shih 全唐詩 (Complete poetry of the T'ang). 12 vols. Peking: Chung-hua shu-chü, 1960.

Ch'üan T'ang wen 全唐文 (Complete prose of the T'ang). 20 vols. Kyoto: Chūbun shuppan-sha, 1976.

Ch'üan Yüan san-ch'ü 全元散曲 (Complete nondramatic song lyrics of the Yüan). Compiled by Sui Shu-sen 隋樹森. 2 vols. Peking: Chung-hua shu-chü, 1964.

Ch'ün-yin lei-hsüan 群音類選 (An anthology of songs categorized by musical type). Compiled by Hu Wen-huan 胡文煥 (fl. 1592–1617). 4 vols. Fac. repr. Peking: Chung-hua shu-chü, 1980.

The Columbia Anthology of Traditional Chinese Literature. Edited by Victor H. Mair. New York: Columbia University Press, 1994.

The Complete Works of Chuang Tzu. Translated by Burton Watson. New York: Columbia University Press, 1968.

Confucian Analects. Translated by James Legge. Hong Kong: University of Hong Kong Press, 1960.

A Feast of Mist and Flowers: The Gay Quarters of Nanking at the End of the Ming Dynasty. Translated by Howard S. Levy. Yokohama: Mimeographed private edition, 1966.

Fei-lung p'ien 飛龍篇 (The flying dragon). By Ts'ao Chih 曹植 (192–232). In *Ts'ao Chih chi chiao-chu*, *chüan* 3, pp. 397–98.

Fen-shu 焚書 (A book to be burned). By Li Chih 李贄 (1527–1602). Peking: Chung-hua shu-chü, 1961.

Feng Po-yü feng-yüeh hsiang-ssu hsiao-shuo 馮伯玉風月相思小説 (The story of Feng Po-yü: a tale of romantic longing). In *Hsiung Lung-feng ssu-chung hsiao-shuo*, pp. 31–49.

Feng-su t'ung-i [chiao-chu] 風俗通義 [校注] (A comprehensive study of popular customs [edited and annotated]). Compiled by Ying Shao 應劭 (fl. 167–195). Edited and annotated by Wang Li-ch'i 王利器. 2 vols. Peking: Chung-hua shu-chü, 1981.

Feng-yüeh hsiang-ssu 風月相思 (A tale of romantic longing). In *Ch'ing-p'ing shan-t'ang hua-pen*, pp. 79–94.

Feng-yüeh Jui-hsien T'ing 風月瑞仙亭 (The romance in the Jui-hsien Pavilion). In *Ch'ing-p'ing shan-t'ang hua-pen*, pp. 38–45.

Feng-yüeh Nan-lao chi 風月南牢記 (Romance in the South Prison). In *Ku-pen Yüan Ming tsa-chü*, vol. 4.

Fo-shuo Huang-chi chieh-kuo pao-chüan 佛説皇極結果寶卷 (Precious volume expounded by the Buddha on the karmic results of the era of the Imperial Ultimate). Originally published in 1430. In *Pao-chüan ch'u-chi*, 10:219–406.

Fo-shuo Wu-liang shou ching 佛說無量壽經 (*Sukhāvatīvyūha*). Translated by Sangha-varman in 252. In *Taishō shinshū daizōkyō*, vol. 12, no. 360, pp. 265–79.

Fo-ting-hsin Kuan-shih-yin p'u-sa ta t'o-lo-ni ching 佛頂心觀世音菩薩大陀羅尼經 (Kuan-shih-yin Bodhisattva's great Dhāranī sutra of the Buddha's essence). 3 fascicles. In *Tun-huang pao-tsang*, 132:65–71.

Fo-yin shih ssu t'iao Ch'in-niang 佛印師四調琴娘 (The priest Fo-yin teases Ch'in-niang four times). In *Hsing-shih heng-yen*, vol. 1, *chüan*, 12, pp. 232–40.

Fu-hsüan tsa-lu 負暄雜錄 (Random jottings while basking in the sun). Compiled by Ku Wen-chien 顧文薦 (13th century). In *Shuo-fu*, vol. 1, *chüan* 18, pp. 7a–20b.

Fu Lu Shou san-hsing tu-shih 福祿壽三星度世 (The three stellar deities of Fortune, Emolument, and Longevity visit the mundane world). In *Ching-shih t'ung-yen*, *chüan* 39, pp. 583–91.

Fu-mu en chung ching chiang-ching wen 父母恩重經講經文 (Sutra lecture on the Sutra on the importance of parental kindness). Dated 927. In *Tun-huang pien-wen chi*, 2:672–94.

Hai-fu shan-t'ang tz'u-kao 海浮山堂詞稿 (Draft lyrics from Hai-fu shan-t'ang). By Feng Wei-min 馮惟敏 (1511–80). Preface dated 1566. Shanghai: Shang-hai ku-chi ch'u-pan she, 1981.

Hai Jui chi 海瑞集 (The works of Hai Jui). By Hai Jui 海瑞 (1514–87). Edited by Ch'en I-chung 陳義鍾. 2 vols. Peking: Chung-hua shu-chü, 1981.

Hai-ling i-shih 海陵佚史 (The debauches of Emperor Hai-ling of the Chin dynasty [r. 1149–61]). In *Ssu wu-hsieh hui-pao*, vol. 1.

Han Ch'ang-li wen-chi chiao-chu 韓昌黎文集校注 (The prose works of Han Yü 韓愈 [768–824] with critical annotation). Edited by Ma T'ung-po 馬通伯. Shanghai: Ku-tien wen-hsüeh ch'u-pan she, 1957.

Han Li Kuang shih-hao Fei Chiang-chün 漢李廣世號飛將軍 (Li Kuang of the Han dynasty has for generations been called the Flying General). In *Ch'ing-p'ing shan-t'ang hua-pen*, pp. 298–304.

Han-shang huan wen-ts'un 漢上宦文存 (Literary remains of the Han-shang Studio). By Ch'ien Nan-yang 錢南揚. Shanghai: Shang-hai wen-i ch'u-pan she, 1980.

Han-shu 漢書 (History of the Former Han dynasty). Compiled by Pan Ku 班固 (32–92). 8 vols. Peking: Chung-hua shu-chü, 1962.

Han-tan meng chi 邯鄲夢記 (The dream at Han-tan). By T'ang Hsien-tsu 湯顯祖 (1550–1616). Author's preface dated 1601. In *T'ang Hsien-tsu chi*, 4:2277–2432.

Han Wu-ti nei-chuan 漢武帝內傳 (Esoteric traditions regarding Emperor Wu of the Han dynasty). Traditionally attributed to Pan Ku 班固 (32–92), but more probably dating from the fifth or sixth century. In *Ts'ung-shu chi-ch'eng*, 1st series, vol. 3436.

Hei Hsüan-feng chang-i shu-ts'ai 黑旋風仗義疏財 (The Black Whirlwind is chivalrous and openhanded). By Chu Yu-tun 朱有燉 (1379–1439). In *Shui-hu hsi-ch'ü chi, ti-i chi*, pp. 95–112.

Ho-lin yü-lu 鶴林玉露 (Jade dew from Ho-lin). By Lo Ta-ching 羅大經 (cs 1226). Originally completed in 1252. Peking: Chung-hua shu-chü, 1983.

Hou-Han shu 後漢書 (History of the Later Han dynasty). Compiled by Fan Yeh 范曄 (398–445). 12 vols. Peking: Chung-hua shu-chü, 1965.

Hou-ts'un Ch'ien-chia shih chiao-chu 後村千家詩校注 (Liu K'o-chuang's poems by a thousand authors edited and annotated). Compiled by Liu K'o-chuang 劉克莊 (1187–1269). Edited and annotated by Hu Wen-nung 胡問儂 and Wang Hao-sou 王皓叟. Kuei-yang: Kuei-chou jen-min ch'u-pan she, 1986.

Hsi-cheng fu 西征賦 (Rhapsody on a westward journey). By P'an Yüeh 潘岳 (247–300). In *Wen-hsüan*, vol. 1, chüan 10, pp. 1a–31b.

Hsi-hsiang chi 西廂記 (The romance of the western chamber). Fac. repr. of 1498 edition. Taipei: Shih-chieh shu-chü, 1963.

Hsi-hsiang hui-pien 西廂匯編 (Collected versions of the *Romance of the western chamber*) Compiled by Huo Sung-lin 霍松林. Chi-nan: Shan-tung wen-i ch'u-pan she, 1987.

Hsi-hu san-t'a chi 西湖三塔記 (The three pagodas at West Lake). In *Ch'ing-p'ing shan-t'ang hua-pen*, pp. 22–32.

Hsi-hu yu-lan chih-yü 西湖遊覽志餘 (Supplement to the Guide to the West Lake). Compiled by T'ien Ju-ch'eng 田汝成 (cs 1526). Peking: Chung-hua shu-chü, 1958.

Hsi-yu chi 西遊記 (The journey to the west). 2 vols. Peking: Tso-chia ch'u-pan she, 1954.

Hsiang-mo pien-wen 降魔變文 (Transformation text on the subduing of demons). In *Tun-huang pien-wen chi*, 1:361–89.

Hsiang-nang chi 香囊記 (The scent bag). By Shao Ts'an 邵璨 (15th century). *Liu-shih chung ch'ü* edition. Taipei: K'ai-ming shu-tien, 1970.

Hsiang-nang yüan 香囊怨 (The tragedy of the scent bag). By Chu Yu-tun 朱有燉 (1379–1439). Author's preface dated 1433. In *Sheng-Ming tsa-chü, erh-chi*.

Hsiao fu-jen chin-ch'ien tseng nien-shao 小夫人金錢贈年少 (The merchant's wife offers money to a young clerk). In *Ching-shih t'ung-yen*, chüan 16, pp. 222–33.

Hsiao-p'in chi 效顰集 (Emulative frowns collection). By Chao Pi 趙弼. Author's postface dated 1428. Shanghai: Ku-tien wen-hsüeh ch'u-pan she, 1957.

[Hsiao-shih] Chen-k'ung pao-chüan [銷釋] 真空寶卷 ([Clearly presented] Precious volume on [the teaching of the Patriarch] Chen-k'ung). In *Pao-chüan ch'u-chi*, 19:261–300.

[Hsiao-shih] Chen-k'ung sao-hsin pao-chüan [銷釋] 真空掃心寶卷 ([Clearly presented] Precious volume on [the Patriarch] Chen-k'ung's [instructions for] sweeping clear the mind). Published in 1584. In *Pao-chüan ch'u-chi*, 18:385–19:259.

[Hsiao-shih] Chin-kang k'o-i [hui-yao chu-chieh] [銷釋] 金剛科儀 [會要註解] ([Clearly presented] liturgical exposition of the Diamond sutra [with critical commentary]). Edited and annotated by Chüeh-lien 覺連. Preface dated 1551. In *[Shinzan] Dai Nihon zoku zōkyō*, 24:650–756.

Hsiao Sun-t'u 小孫屠 (Little Butcher Sun). In *Yung-lo ta-tien hsi-wen san-chung chiao-chu*, pp. 257–324.

Hsien-Ch'in Han Wei Chin Nan-pei ch'ao shih 先秦漢魏晉南北朝詩 (Complete poetry of the Pre-Ch'in, Han, Wei, Chin, and Northern and Southern dynasties). Compiled by Lu Ch'in-li 逯欽立. 3 vols. Peking: Chung-hua shu-chü, 1983.

Hsin-ch'iao shih Han Wu mai ch'un-ch'ing 新橋市韓五賣春情 (Han Wu-niang sells her charms at New Bridge Market). In *Ku-chin hsiao-shuo*, vol. 1, *chüan* 3, pp. 62–79.

Hsin-hsü chu-tzu so-yin 新序逐字索引 (A concordance to the *Hsin-hsü*). Hong Kong: Shang-wu yin-shu kuan, 1992.

[Hsin-k'o hsiu-hsiang p'i-p'ing] Chin P'ing Mei [新刻繡像批評] 金瓶梅 ([Newly cut illustrated commentarial edition] of the *Chin P'ing Mei*). 2 vols. Chi-nan: Ch'i-Lu shu-she, 1989.

[Hsin-k'o] Shih-shang hua-yen ch'ü-lo t'an-hsiao chiu-ling [新刻] 時尚華筵趣樂談笑酒令 ([Newly printed] Currently fashionable jokes and drinking games to be enjoyed at formal banquets). 4 *chüan*. Ming edition published by the Wen-te T'ang.

Hsin-lun (New Treatise) and Other Writings by Huan T'an. Translated by Timoteus Pokora. Ann Arbor: Center for Chinese Studies, University of Michigan, 1975.

[Hsin-pien] Liu Chih-yüan huan-hsiang Pai-t'u chi [新編] 劉知遠還鄉白兔記 ([Newly compiled] Liu Chih-yüan's return home: The white rabbit). In *Ming Ch'eng-hua shuo-ch'ang tz'u-hua ts'ung-k'an*, ts'e 12.

[Hsin-pien] Nan chiu-kung tz'u [新編] 南九宮詞 ([Newly compiled] Anthology of song lyrics in the nine southern modes). Fac. repr. of Wan-li (1573–1620) edition. Taipei: Shih-chieh shu-chü, 1961.

[Hsin-pien] Wu-tai shih p'ing-hua [新編] 五代史平話 ([Newly compiled] p'ing-hua on the history of the Five Dynasties). Originally published in the 14th century. Shanghai: Chung-kuo ku-tien wen-hsüeh ch'u-pan she, 1954.

Hsin-shang hsü-pien 欣賞續編 (A collectanea on connoiseurship continued). Compiled by Mao I-hsiang 茅一相 (16th century). Ming edition in the Gest Collection of the Princeton University Library.

Hsin T'ang shu 新唐書 (New history of the T'ang dynasty). Compiled by Ou-yang Hsiu 歐陽修 (1007–72) and Sung Ch'i 宋祁 (998–1061). 20 vols. Peking: Chung-hua shu-chü, 1975.

Hsin-yü 新語 (New discourses). By Lu Chia 陸賈 (c. 228–c. 140 B.C.). In *Chu-tzu chi-ch'eng*, 7:1–21.

Hsing-shih heng-yen 醒世恆言 (Constant words to awaken the world). Edited by Feng Meng-lung 馮夢龍 (1574–1646). First published in 1627. 2 vols. Hong Kong: Chung-hua shu-chü, 1958.

Hsing-t'ien Feng-yüeh t'ung-hsüan chi 性天風月通玄記 (The Master of Breeze and Moonlight utilizes his Heaven-bestowed nature to penetrate the mysteries). By Lan Mao 蘭茂 (1403–76). Preface dated 1454. In *Ku-pen hsi-ch'ü ts'ung-k'an, wu-chi*, item 1.

Hsiu-ju chi 繡襦記 (The embroidered jacket). By Hsü Lin 徐霖 (1462–1538). *Liu-shih chung ch'ü* edition. Taipei: K'ai-ming shu-tien, 1970.

Hsiu-ku ch'un-jung 繡谷春容 (Spring vistas in a varicolored valley). 4 vols. Fac. repr. of late Ming edition. In *Ming-Ch'ing shan-pen hsiao-shuo ts'ung-k'an, ch'u-pien*.

Hsiung Lung-feng ssu-chung hsiao-shuo 熊龍峯四種小說 (Four vernacular stories published by Hsiung Lung-feng 熊龍峯 [fl. c. 1590]). Edited by Wang Ku-lu 王古魯. Shanghai: Ku-tien wen-hsüeh ch'u-pan she, 1958.

Hsü Fen-shu 續焚書 (Supplement to A book to be burned). By Li Chih 李贄 (1527–1602). Peking: Chung-hua shu-chü, 1961.

Hsü Po-wu chih 續博物志 (Supplement to Record of the investigation of things). Compiled by Li Shih 李石 (1108–81). In *Pai-tzu ch'üan-shu*, vol. 7.

Hsü-t'ang Ho-shang yü-lu 虛堂和尚語錄 (Recorded sayings of the Monk Hsü-t'ang). In *Taishō shinshū daizōkyō*, vol. 47, no. 2000, pp. 984–1064.

Hsü Tsang-ching 續藏經 (Continuation of the Buddhist canon). 150 vols. Fac. repr. Hong Kong: Hsiang-kang ying-yin *Hsü Tsang-ching* wei-yüan hui, 1967.

Hsü Tzu-chih t'ung-chien 續資治通鑑 (A continuation of the Comprehensive mirror for aid in government). Compiled by Pi Yüan 畢沅 (1730–97). 4 vols. Peking: Ku-chi ch'u-pan she, 1958.

Hsüan-ho i-shih 宣和遺事 (Forgotten events of the Hsüan-ho reign period [1119–25]). Shanghai: Shang-hai ku-tien wen-hsüeh ch'u-pan she, 1955.

Hsüan-ho p'ai-p'u 宣和牌譜 (A manual for Hsüan-ho [1119–25] dominoes). By Ch'ü Yu 瞿佑 (1341–1427). In *Shuo-fu hsü*, vol. 10, *chüan* 38, pp. 1a–17a.

Hsüan-ho p'u ya-p'ai hui-chi 宣和普牙牌彙集 (A manual for Hsüan-ho [1119–25] dominoes with supplementary material). Original compiler's preface dated 1757, redactor's preface dated 1886. N.p.: Hung-wen chai, 1888.

Hsüan-t'ien shang-ti ch'ui-chieh wen 玄天上帝垂誡文 (Admonitions of the Supreme Sovereign of the Mysterious Celestial Realm). In *Kuo-se t'ien-hsiang*, vol. 2, *chüan* 4, upper register, pp. 51b–53b.

Hsün-ch'in chi 尋親記 (The quest for the father). *Liu-shih chung ch'ü* edition. Taipei: K'ai-ming shu-tien, 1970.

Hsün-fang ya-chi 尋芳雅集 (Elegant vignettes of fragrant pursuits). In *Kuo-se t'ien-hsiang*, vol. 2, *chüan* 4, pp. 1a–57a, lower register.

Hsün-tzu yin-te 荀子引得 (A concordance to *Hsün-tzu*). Taipei: Chinese Materials and Research Aids Service Center, 1966.

Hua-shen san-miao chuan 花神三妙傳 (The flower god and the three beauties). In *Kuo-se t'ien-hsiang*, vol. 2, *chüan* 6, lower register, pp. 1a–61a.

Hua-teng chiao Lien-nü ch'eng-Fo chi 花燈轎蓮女成佛記 (The girl Lien-nü attains Buddhahood in her bridal palanquin). In *Ch'ing-p'ing shan-t'ang hua-pen*, pp. 193–205.

Hua-ying chi 花影集 (Flower shadows collection). By T'ao Fu 陶輔 (1441–c. 1523).

Author's preface dated 1523. In *Ming-Ch'ing hsi-chien hsiao-shuo ts'ung-k'an*, pp. 831–940.

Huai-ch'un ya-chi 懷春雅集 (Elegant vignettes of spring yearning). In *Yen-chü pi-chi*, vol. 3, *chüan* 9, pp. 16b–32a, and *chüan* 10, pp. 1a–39b, upper register.

Huai-hsiang chi 懷香記 (The stolen perfume). By Lu Ts'ai 陸采 (1497–1537). *Liu-shih chung ch'ü* edition. Taipei: K'ai-ming shu-tien, 1970.

Huan-hsi yüan-chia 歡喜冤家 (Adversaries in delight). Compiled by Kao I-wei 高一葦 (17th century). Preface dated 1640. In *Ssu wu-hsieh hui-pao*, vols. 10–11.

Huan-men tzu-ti ts'o li-shen 宦門子弟錯立身 (The scion of an official's family opts for the wrong career). In *Yung-lo ta-tien hsi-wen san-chung chiao-chu*, pp. 219–55.

Huan-sha chi 浣紗記 (The girl washing silk). By Liang Ch'en-yü 梁辰魚 (1519–91). *Liu-shih chung ch'ü* edition. Taipei: K'ai-ming shu-tien, 1970.

Huan-tai chi 還帶記 (The return of the belts). By Shen Ts'ai 沈采 (15th century). In *Ku-pen hsi-ch'ü ts'ung-k'an, ch'u-chi*, item 32.

Huang-ch'ao pien-nien kang-mu pei-yao 皇朝編年綱目備要 (Chronological outline of the significant events of the imperial [Sung] dynasty). Compiled by Ch'en Chün 陳均 (c. 1165–c. 1236). Preface dated 1229. 2 vols. Fac. repr. Taipei: Ch'eng-wen ch'u-pan she, 1966.

Huang-chi chin-tan chiu-lien cheng-hsin kuei-chen huan-hsiang pao-chüan 皇極金丹 九蓮正信皈真還鄉寶卷 (Precious volume of the golden elixir and nine-petaled lotus of the Imperial Ultimate period that leads to rectifying belief, reverting to the real, and returning to our true home). Originally published in 1498. In *Pao-chüan ch'u-chi*, 8:1–482.

Huang hsiao-tzu 黃孝子 (The filial son Huang [Chüeh-ching] 黃覺經). In *Ku-pen hsi-ch'ü ts'ung-k'an, ch'u-chi*, item 23.

Huang-Ming k'ai-yün ying-wu chuan 皇明開運英武傳 (Chronicle of the heroic military exploits that initiated the reign of the imperial Ming dynasty). Nanking: Yang Ming-feng, 1591. Fac. repr. in *Ku-pen hsiao-shuo ts'ung-k'an, ti san-shih liu chi*, vol. 1.

Huang T'ing-tao yeh-tsou Liu-hsing ma 黃廷道夜走流星馬 (Huang T'ing-tao steals the horse Shooting Star by night). By Huang Yüan-chi 黃元吉 (14th century). In *Ming-jen tsa-chü hsüan*, pp. 85–111.

Hui-an hsien-sheng Chu Wen-kung wen-chi 晦庵先生朱文公文集 (The collected literary works of Chu Hsi 朱熹 [1130–1200]). *Ssu-pu pei-yao* edition. Shanghai: Chung-hua shu-chü, 1936.

Hung-fu chi 紅拂記 (The story of Red Duster). By Chang Feng-i 張鳳翼 (1527–1613). *Liu-shih chung ch'ü* edition. Taipei: K'ai-ming shu-tien, 1970.

Hung-hsiao mi-yüeh: Chang Sheng fu Li-shih niang 紅綃密約張生負李氏娘 (The secret tryst [arranged by means of] a red silk [handkerchief]: How Chang Sheng betrayed Ms. Li). In *Tsui-weng t'an-lu, jen-chi* (9th collection), *chüan* 1, pp. 96–103.

Huo-hsi lüeh 火戲略 (An outline of pyrotechnics). Compiled by Chao Hsüeh-min 趙 學敏 (c. 1719–c. 1805). Author's preface dated 1780. 2 vols. Fac. repr. N.p.: T'ien-chin Library, n.d..

Huo Hsiao-yü chuan 霍小玉傳 (The story of Huo Hsiao-yü). By Chiang Fang 蔣防 (early 9th century). In *T'ang Sung ch'uan-ch'i chi*, pp. 68–78.

I-chien chih 夷堅志 (Records of I-chien). Compiled by Hung Mai 洪邁 (1123–1202). 4 vols. Peking: Chung-hua shu-chü, 1981.

I-hsia chi 義俠記 (The righteous knight-errant). By Shen Ching 沈璟 (1553–1610). *Liu-shih chung ch'ü* edition. Taipei: K'ai-ming shu-tien, 1970.

Jen chin shu ku-erh hsün-mu 認金梳孤兒尋母 (Identifying the gold [hairpins] and the [jade] comb an orphan seeks his mother). In *Ku-pen Yüan-Ming tsa-chü*, vol. 3.

Jen hsiao-tzu lieh-hsing wei shen 任孝子烈性爲神 (The apotheosis of Jen the filial son). In *Ku-chin hsiao-shuo*, vol. 2, *chüan* 38, pp. 571–86.

Jen-tsung jen-mu chuan 仁宗認母傳 (The story of how Emperor Jen-tsung [r. 1022–63] reclaimed his mother). Fac. repr. in *Ming Ch'eng-hua shuo-ch'ang tz'u-hua ts'ung-k'an*, *ts'e* 4.

Ju-i chün chuan 如意君傳 (The tale of Lord As You Like It). Japanese movable type edition, colophon dated 1880.

Ju-ju chü-shih yü-lu 如如居士語錄 (The recorded sayings of layman Ju-ju). By Yen Ping 顏丙 (d. 1212). Preface dated 1194. Photocopy of manuscript in the Kyoto University Library.

Jung-chai sui-pi 容齋隨筆 (Miscellaneous notes from the Tolerant Study). By Hung Mai 洪邁 (1123–1202). 2 vols. Shanghai: Shang-hai ku-chi ch'u-pan she, 1978.

K'ai-chüan i-hsiao 開卷一笑 (Open this volume and get a laugh). 3 vols. Fac. repr. of late Ming edition. In *Ming-Ch'ing shan-pen hsiao-shuo ts'ung-k'an, ch'u-pien*.

K'ai-yüan T'ien-pao i-shih 開元天寶遺事 (Forgotten events of the K'ai-yüan [713–41] and T'ien-pao [742–56] reign periods). Compiled by Wang Jen-yü 王仁裕 (880–942). In *K'ai-yüan T'ien-pao i-shih shih-chung*, pp. 65–109.

K'ai-yüan T'ien-pao i-shih shih-chung 開元天寶遺事十種 (Ten works dealing with forgotten events of the K'ai-yüan [713–41] and T'ien-pao [742–56] reign periods). Edited by Ting Ju-ming 丁如明. Shanghai: Shang-hai ku-chi ch'u-pan she, 1985.

K'an p'i-hsüeh tan-cheng Erh-lang Shen 勘皮靴單證二郎神 (Investigation of a leather boot convicts Erh-lang Shen). In *Hsing-shih heng-yen*, vol. 1, *chüan* 13, pp. 241–63.

Ko tai hsiao 歌代嘯 (A song in place of a shriek). Attributed to Hsü Wei 徐渭 (1521–93). In *Ssu-sheng yüan*, pp. 107–68.

Ku-ch'eng chi 古城記 (The reunion at Ku-ch'eng). In *Ku-pen hsi-ch'ü ts'ung-k'an, ch'u-chi*, item 25.

Ku-chin hsiao-shuo 古今小説 (Stories old and new). Edited by Feng Meng-lung 馮夢龍 (1574–1646). 2 vols. Peking: Jen-min wen-hsüeh ch'u-pan she, 1958.

Ku-chin t'an-kai 古今譚概 (A representative selection of anecdotes ancient and modern). Compiled by Feng Meng-lung 馮夢龍 (1574–1646). Preface dated 1620. Fu-chou: Hai-hsia wen-i ch'u-pan she, 1985.

Ku-chin t'u-shu chi-ch'eng 古今圖書集成 (A comprehensive corpus of books and illustrations ancient and modern), presented to the emperor in 1725. Fac. repr. Taipei: Wen-hsing shu-tien, 1964.

Ku-Hang hung-mei chi 古杭紅梅記 (The story of the red plum of old Hang-chou). In *Kuo-se t'ien-hsiang*, vol. 3, *chüan* 8, upper register, pp. 1a–18b.

Ku hsiao-shuo kou-ch'en 古小説鉤沉 (Rescued fragments of early fiction). Compiled by Lu Hsün 魯迅. Peking: Jen-min wen-hsüeh ch'u-pan she, 1955.

Ku-pen hsi-ch'ü ts'ung-k'an, ch'u-chi 古本戲曲叢刊, 初集 (Collectanea of rare editions of traditional drama, first series). Shanghai: Shang-wu yin-shu kuan, 1954.

Ku-pen hsi-ch'ü ts'ung-k'an, ssu-chi 古本戲曲叢刊, 四集 (Collectanea of rare editions of traditional drama, fourth series). Shanghai: Shang-wu yin-shu kuan, 1958.

Ku-pen hsi-ch'ü ts'ung-k'an, wu-chi 古本戲曲叢刊, 五集 (Collectanea of rare editions of traditional drama, fifth series). Shanghai: Shang-hai ku-chi ch'u-pan she, 1986.

Ku-pen hsiao-shuo ts'ung-k'an, ti-erh chi 古本小説叢刊, 第二集 (Collectanea of rare editions of traditional fiction, second series). Peking: Chung-hua shu-chü, 1990.

Ku-pen hsiao-shuo ts'ung-k'an, ti erh-shih liu chi 古本小説叢刊, 第二十六集 (Collectanea of rare editions of traditional fiction, twenty-sixth series). Peking: Chung-hua shu-chü, 1991.

Ku-pen hsiao-shuo ts'ung-k'an, ti-liu chi 古本小説叢刊, 第六集 (Collectanea of rare editions of traditional fiction, sixth series). Peking: Chung-hua shu-chü, 1990.

Ku-pen hsiao-shuo ts'ung-k'an, ti-pa chi 古本小説叢刊, 第八集 (Collectanea of rare editions of traditional fiction, eighth series). Peking: Chung-hua shu-chü, 1990.

Ku-pen hsiao-shuo ts'ung-k'an, ti san-shih ch'i chi 古本小説叢刊, 第三十七集 (Collectanea of rare editions of traditional fiction, thirty-seventh series). Peking: Chung-hua shu-chü, 1991.

Ku-pen hsiao-shuo ts'ung-k'an, ti san-shih chiu chi 古本小説叢刊, 第三十九集 (Collectanea of rare editions of traditional fiction, thirty-ninth series). Peking: Chung-hua shu-chü, 1991.

Ku-pen hsiao-shuo ts'ung-k'an, ti san-shih liu chi 古本小説叢刊, 第三十六集 (Collectanea of rare editions of traditional fiction, thirty-sixth series). Peking: Chung-hua shu-chü, 1991.

Ku-pen hsiao-shuo ts'ung-k'an, ti san-shih ssu chi 古本小説叢刊, 第三十四集 (Collectanea of rare editions of traditional fiction, thirty-fourth series). Peking: Chung-hua shu-chü, 1991.

Ku-pen hsiao-shuo ts'ung-k'an, ti-ssu chi 古本小説叢刊, 第四集 (Collectanea of rare editions of traditional fiction, fourth series). Peking: Chung-hua shu-chü, 1990.

Ku-pen hsiao-shuo ts'ung-k'an, ti-wu chi 古本小説叢刊, 第五集 (Collectanea of rare editions of traditional fiction, fifth series). Peking: Chung-hua shu-chü, 1990.

Ku-pen Yüan Ming tsa-chü 孤本元明雜劇 (Unique editions of Yüan and Ming tsa-chü drama). Edited by Wang Chi-lieh 王季烈. 4 vols. Peking: Chung-kuo hsi-chü ch'u-pan she, 1958.

Ku-shih wen-fang hsiao-shuo 顧氏文房小説 (Fiction from the library of Mr. Ku). Compiled by Ku Yüan-ch'ing 顧元慶 (1487–1565). 10 *ts'e*. Fac. repr. Shanghai: Shang-wu yin-shu-kuan, 1934.

Ku-tai wen-yen tuan-p'ien hsiao-shuo hsüan-chu, erh-chi 古代文言短篇小説選注, 二集 (An annotated selection of classic literary tales, second collection). Edited by Ch'eng Po-ch'üan 成伯泉. Shanghai: Shang-hai ku-chi ch'u-pan she, 1984.

Ku tsun-su yü-lu 古尊宿語錄 (The recorded sayings of eminent monks of old). Compiled by Tse Tsang-chu 賾藏主 (13th century). In *Hsü Tsang-ching*, 118:79a–418a.

K'u-kung wu-tao chüan 苦功悟道卷 (Precious volume on awakening to the Way through bitter toil). By Lo Ch'ing 羅清 (1442–1527). Originally published in 1509. In *Pao-chüan ch'u-chi*, 1:1–293.

K'uai-tsui Li Ts'ui-lien chi 快嘴李翠蓮記 (The story of the sharp-tongued Li Ts'ui-lien). In *Ch'ing-p'ing shan-t'ang hua-pen*, pp. 52–67.

Kuan-shih-yin p'u-sa pen-hsing ching 觀世音菩薩本行經 (Sutra on the deeds of the bodhisattva Avalokiteśvara). Also known as *Hsiang-shan pao-chüan* 香山寶卷 (Precious scroll on Hsiang-shan). Attributed to P'u-ming 普明 (fl. early 12th century). N.p., n.d. (probably 19th century).

Kuan-tzu chiao-cheng 管子校正 (The *Kuan-tzu* collated and corrected). Edited and annotated by Tai Wang 戴望 (1837–73). In *Chu-tzu chi-ch'eng*, 5:1–427.

Kuan-yüan chi 灌園記 (The story of the gardener). By Chang Feng-i 張鳳翼(1527–1613). *Liu-shih chung ch'ü* edition. Taipei: K'ai-ming shu-tien, 1970.

Kuei-chien chiao-ch'ing 貴賤交情 (An intimate bond between the exalted and the humble). In *Tsui-yü ch'ing*, pp. 1524–64, upper register.

K'uei-kuan Yao Pien tiao Chu-ko 夔關姚卞弔諸葛 (At K'uei-kuan Yao Pien commemorates Chu-ko Liang). In *Ch'ing-p'ing shan-t'ang hua-pen*, pp. 304–12.

K'ung Shu-fang shuang-yü shan-chui chuan 孔淑芳雙魚扇墜傳 (The story of K'ung Shu-fang and the pair of fish-shaped fan pendants), in *Hsiung Lung-feng ssu-chung hsiao-shuo*, pp. 63–70.

Kuo-se t'ien-hsiang 國色天香 (Celestial fragrance of national beauties). Compiled by Wu Ching-so 吳敬所 (fl. late 16th century). Preface dated 1587. 3 vols. Fac. repr. in *Ming-Ch'ing shan-pen hsiao-shuo ts'ung-k'an, ti-erh chi*.

Ladies of the Tang. Translated by Elizabeth Te-chen Wang. Taipei: Heritage Press, 1961.

Lao-chün shuo i-pai pa-shih chieh 老君說一百八十戒 (The 180 precepts enunciated by Lord Lao), in *Yün-chi ch'i-ch'ien*, chüan 39, pp. 217–22.

Lao-hsüeh An pi-chi 老學菴筆記 (Miscellaneous notes from an Old Scholar's Retreat). By Lu Yu 陸游 (1125–1210). Peking: Chung-hua shu-chü, 1979.

Lao Tzu Tao Te Ching. Translated by D. C. Lau. New York: Penguin Books, 1963.

Li-chi 禮記 (The book of rites). In *Shih-san ching ching-wen*.

Li Chi: Book of Rites. Translated by James Legge. 2 vols. New Hyde Park, N.Y.: University Books, 1967.

Li Ching ping-fa chi-pen chu-i 李靖兵法輯本注譯 (A reconstituted, annotated, and translated edition of Li Ching's Art of war). Edited by Teng Tse-tsung 鄧澤宗. Peking: Chieh-fang chün ch'u-pan she, 1990.

Li-hsüeh chih-nan 吏學指南 (A guidebook to the subbureaucracy). By Hsü Yüan-jui 徐元瑞 (fl. early 14th century). Author's preface dated 1301. N.p.: Che-chiang ku-chi ch'u-pan she, 1988.

Li K'ai-hsien chi 李開先集 (The collected works of Li K'ai-hsien). By Li K'ai-hsien (1502–68). Edited by Lu Kung 路工. 3 vols. Peking: Chung-hua shu-chü, 1959.

Li-wa chuan 李娃傳 (The story of Li Wa). By Po Hsing-chien 白行簡 (776–826). In *T'ang Sung ch'uan-ch'i chi*, pp. 97–108.

Li Yüan Wu-chiang chiu chu-she 李元吳江救朱蛇 (Li Yüan saves a red snake on the Wu River). In *Ch'ing-p'ing shan-t'ang hua-pen*, pp. 324–34.

Li Yün-ch'ing te-wu sheng-chen 李雲卿得悟昇真 (Li Yün-ch'ing attains enlightenment and achieves transcendence). In *Ku-pen Yüan Ming tsa-chü*, vol. 4.

Liang-shan wu-hu ta chieh-lao 梁山五虎大劫牢 (The five tigers of Liang-shan carry out a great jailbreak). In *Ku-pen Yüan Ming tsa-chü*, vol. 3.

Liang-shih yin-yüan 兩世姻緣 (Two lives of love). By Ch'iao Chi 喬吉 (d. 1345). In *Yüan-ch'ü hsüan*, 3:971–86.

Liang shu 梁書 (History of the Liang dynasty [502–57]). Compiled by Yao Ch'a 姚察 (533–606) and Yao Ssu-lien 姚思廉 (d. 637). 3 vols. Peking: Chung-hua shu-chü, 1973.

Liao-yang hai-shen chuan 遼陽海神傳 (The sea goddess of Liao-yang). By Ts'ai Yü 蔡羽 (d. 1541). In *Ku-tai wen-yen tuan-p'ien hsiao-shuo hsüan-chu, erh-chi*, pp. 381–89.

Le Lie-sien Tchouan. Translated by Max Kaltenmark. Peking: Université de Paris, Publications du Centre d'études sinologiques de Pékin, 1953.

Lieh-kuo chih-chuan 列國志傳 (Chronicle of the feudal states). By Yü Shao-yü 余邵
魚 (fl. mid 16th century). 8 *chüan*. Chien-yang: San-t'ai kuan, 1606. Fac. repr. in
Ku-pen hsiao-shuo ts'ung-k'an, ti-liu chi, vols. 1–3.

Lien-huan chi 連環記 (A stratagem of interlocking rings). By Wang Chi 王濟 (1474–
1540). Peking: Chung-hua shu-chü, 1988.

Lin Ling-su chuan 林靈素傳 (The story of Lin Ling-su). By Keng Yen-hsi 耿延禧 (fl.
early 12th century). In *Pin-t'ui lu, chüan* 1, pp. 5a–8a.

Liu Ch'i-ch'ing shih-chiu Wan-chiang Lou chi 柳耆卿詩酒翫江樓記 (Liu Ch'i-ch'ing
indulges in poetry and wine in the Riverside Pavilion). In *Ch'ing-p'ing shan-t'ang
hua-pen*, pp. 1–5.

Liu Chih-yüan chu-kung-tiao [chiao-chu] 劉知遠諸宮調 [校注] (Medley in various
modes on Liu Chih-yüan [collated and annotated]). Edited by Lan Li-ming 藍立
蓂. Ch'eng-tu: Pa-Shu shu-she, 1989.

Liu-ch'ing jih-cha 留青日札 (Daily jottings worthy of preservation). By T'ien I-heng
田藝蘅 (1524–c. 1574). Preface dated 1572. Fac. repr. of 1609 edition. Shanghai:
Shang-hai ku-chi ch'u-pan she, 1985.

Liu sheng mi Lien chi 劉生覓蓮記 (The story of Liu I-ch'un's 劉一春 quest of Sun
Pi-lien 孫碧蓮). In *Kuo-se t'ien-hsiang*, vol. 1, *chüan* 2, pp. 1a–40b, and *chüan* 3,
pp. 1a–41b, lower register.

Liu-shih chung ch'ü 六十種曲 (Sixty ch'uan-ch'i dramas). Compiled by Mao Chin 毛
晉 (1599–1659). 60 vols. Taipei: K'ai-ming shu-tien, 1970.

Liu-tsu ta-shih fa-pao t'an-ching 六祖大師法寶壇經 (The Dharma treasure of the
platform sutra of the Sixth Patriarch). Edited by Tsung-pao 宗寶 (13th century). In
Taishō shinshū daizōkyō, vol. 48, no. 2008, pp. 345–65.

Liu Wen-lung ling-hua ching 劉文龍菱花鏡 (Liu Wen-lung's caltrop-patterned mirror).
In *Sung-Yüan hsi-wen chi-i*, pp. 214–18.

Liu-yüan hui-hsüan chiang-hu fang-yü 六院彙選江湖方語 (Slang expressions current
in the demimonde selected from the six licensed brothels [of Chin-ling]). In *Han-
shang huan wen-ts'un*, pp. 158–65.

Lo-shen fu 洛神賦 (Rhapsody on the Goddess of the Lo River). By Ts'ao Chih 曹植
(192–232). In *Wen-hsüan*, vol. 1, *chüan* 19, pp. 11b–16a.

Lo-yang mu-tan chi 洛陽牡丹記 (A record of the peonies of Lo-yang). By Ou-yang Hsiu
歐陽修 (1007–72). Written in 1034. In *Ou-yang Yung-shu chi*, vol. 2, *ts'e* 9, *chü-shih
wai-chi* (additional works), *chüan* 22, pp. 2–10.

Lo-yang san-kuai chi 洛陽三怪記 (The three monsters of Lo-yang). In *Ch'ing-p'ing
shan-t'ang hua-pen*, pp. 67–78.

Lu-shan Yüan-kung hua 廬山遠公話 (Story of Hui-yüan 慧遠 [334–416] of Mount
Lu). In *Tun-huang pien-wen chi*, 1:167–193.

Lun-heng 論衡 (Discourses weighed in the balance). By Wang Ch'ung 王充 (27–
c. 97). In *Chu-tzu chi-ch'eng*, vol. 7.

Lun-Heng: Philosophical Essays of Wang Ch'ung. Translated by Alfred Forke. 2 vols.
New York: Paragon Book Gallery, 1962.

Lun-yü yin-te 論語引得 (A concordance to the *Analects*). Taipei: Chinese Materials
and Research Aids Service Center, 1966.

Lü-ch'uang nü-shih 綠窗女史 (Female scribes of the green gauze windows). 7 vols.
Fac. repr. of late Ming edition. In *Ming-Ch'ing shan-pen hsiao-shuo ts'ung-k'an,
ch'u-pien*.

Lü-shih ch'un-ch'iu 呂氏春秋 (The spring and autumn annals of Mr. Lü). Compiled by Lü Pu-wei 呂不韋 (d. 235 B.C.). In *Chu-tzu chi-ch'eng*, 6:1–346.

Lü Tung-pin fei-chien chan Huang-lung 呂洞賓飛劍斬黃龍 (Lü Tung-pin beheads Huang-lung with his flying sword). In *Hsing-shih heng-yen*, vol. 2, *chüan* 21, pp. 453–66.

Mai-wang kuan ch'ao-chiao pen ku-chin tsa-chü 脈望館鈔校本古今雜劇 (Ancient and modern tsa-chü: manuscripts and collated editions of Mai-wang hall). 84 *ts'e*. Fac. repr. in *Ku-pen hsi-ch'ü ts'ung-k'an, ssu-chi.*

Mao-shih yin-te 毛詩引得 (Concordance to the Mao version of the *Book of Songs*). Tokyo: Japan Council for East Asian Studies, 1962.

Mao Ying chuan 毛穎傳 (The biography of Mao Ying). By Han Yü 韓愈 (768–824). In *Han Ch'ang-li wen-chi chiao-chu, chüan* 8, pp. 325–27.

Mei Hsing cheng-ch'un 梅杏爭春 (The plum and the apricot compete for precedence among spring flowers), in *Ch'ing-p'ing shan-t'ang hua-pen*, pp. 190–92.

Mencius. Translated by D. C. Lau. Baltimore: Penguin Books, 1970.

Meng-mu san-i 孟母三移 (The mother of Mencius moves three times). In *Ku-pen Yüan Ming tsa-chü*, vol. 2.

Meng-tzu yin-te 孟子引得 (A Concordance to *Meng-tzu*). Taipei: Chinese Materials and Research Aids Service Center, 1966.

Mi-teng yin-hua 覓燈因話 (Tales told while searching for a lamp). By Shao Ching-chan 邵景詹 (16th century). Author's preface dated 1592. In *Chien-teng hsin-hua [wai erh-chung]*, pp. 313–51.

Ming Ch'eng-hua shuo-ch'ang tz'u-hua ts'ung-k'an 明成化說唱詞話叢刊 (Corpus of prosimetric tz'u-hua narratives published in the Ch'eng-hua reign period [1465–87] of the Ming dynasty). 12 *ts'e*. Shanghai: Shanghai Museum, 1973.

Ming-Ch'ing hsi-chien hsiao-shuo ts'ung-k'an 明清稀見小說叢刊 (Collectanea of rare works of fiction from the Ming-Ch'ing period). Chi-nan: Ch'i-Lu shu-she, 1996.

Ming-Ch'ing shan-pen hsiao-shuo ts'ung-k'an, ch'u-pien 明清善本小說叢刊, 初編 (Collectanea of rare editions of Ming-Ch'ing fiction, first series). Taipei: T'ien-i ch'u-pan she, 1985.

Ming-Ch'ing shan-pen hsiao-shuo ts'ung-k'an, ti-erh chi 明清善本小說叢刊, 第二輯 (Collectanea of rare editions of Ming-Ch'ing fiction, second series). Taipei: T'ien-i ch'u-pan she, 1985.

Ming-chu chi 明珠記 (The luminous pearl). By Lu Ts'ai 陸采 (1497–1537). *Liu-shih chung ch'ü* edition. Taipei: K'ai-ming shu-tien, 1970.

Ming-feng chi 鳴鳳記 (The singing phoenix). *Liu-shih chung ch'ü* edition. Taipei: K'ai-ming shu-tien, 1970.

Ming-hsiang chi 冥祥記 (Signs from the unseen realm). Compiled by Wang Yen 王琰 (fl. late 5th-early 6th centuries). In *Ku hsiao-shuo kou-ch'en*, pp. 375–458.

Ming-hsin pao-chien 明心寶鑑 (A precious mirror to illuminate the mind). Microfilm copy of a Ming edition in the East Asian Library, University of Chicago.

Ming-jen tsa-chü hsüan 明人雜劇選 (An anthology of Ming tsa-chü drama). Compiled by Chou I-pai 周貽白. Peking: Jen-min wen-hsüeh ch'u-pan she, 1958.

Ming shih 明史 (History of the Ming dynasty). Compiled by Chang T'ing-yü 張廷玉 (1672–1755) et al. 28 vols. Peking: Chung-hua shu-chü, 1974.

Ming-tai lü-li hui-pien 明代律例彙編 (Comprehensive edition of the Ming penal code and judicial regulations). Compiled by Huang Chang-chien 黃彰健. 2 vols. Taipei: Academia Sinica, 1979.

Mo-tzu yin-te 墨子引得 (A concordance to *Mo-tzu*). Peking: Yenching University Press, 1948.

The Moon and the Zither: The Story of the Western Wing. By Wang Shifu. Translated by Stephen H. West and Wilt L. Idema. Berkeley: University of California Press, 1991.

Mu-lien chiu-mu ch'üan-shan hsi-wen 目連救母勸善戲文 (An exhortatory drama on how Maudgalyāyana rescued his mother from the underworld). By Cheng Chih-chen 鄭之珍 (1518–95). Author's preface dated 1582. In *Ku-pen hsi-ch'ü ts'ung-k'an, ch'u-chi*, item 67.

Mu-lien yüan-ch'i 目連緣起 (Story of Maudgalyāyana). In *Tun-huang pien-wen chi*, 2:701–13.

Mu-tan t'ing 牡丹亭 (The peony pavilion). By T'ang Hsien-tsu 湯顯祖 (1550–1616). Edited and annotated by Hsü Shuo-fang 徐朔方 and Yang Hsiao-mei 楊笑梅. Peking: Chung-hua shu-chü, 1959.

Nan-ching: The Classic of Difficult Issues. Translated by Paul U. Unschuld. Berkeley: University of California Press, 1986.

Nan Hsi-hsiang chi 南西廂記 (A southern version of the *Romance of the western chamber*). Usually attributed to Li Jih-hua 李日華 (fl. early 16th century). *Liu-shih chung ch'ü* edition. Taipei: K'ai-ming shu-tien, 1970).

Nan Hsi-hsiang chi 南西廂記 (A southern version of the *Romance of the western chamber*). By Lu Ts'ai 陸采 (1497–1537). In *Hsi-hsiang hui-pien*, pp. 323–416.

Nan-k'o t'ai-shou chuan 南柯太守傳 (The story of the governor of the Southern Branch). By Li Kung-tso 李公佐 (c. 778–c. 848). In *T'ang Sung ch'uan-ch'i chi*, pp. 81–92.

Nan-kung tz'u-chi 南宮詞紀 (Anthology of southern-style lyrics). Compiled by Ch'en So-wen 陳所聞 (d. c. 1604). In *Nan-pei kung tz'u-chi*, vols. 1–2.

Nan-pei kung tz'u-chi 南北宮詞紀 (Anthology of southern- and northern-style song lyrics). Compiled by Ch'en So-wen 陳所聞 (d. c. 1604). Edited by Chao Ching-shen 趙景深. 4 vols. Peking: Chung-hua shu-chü, 1959.

Nan-pei kung tz'u-chi chiao-pu 南北宮詞紀校補 (Collation notes and supplements to *Nan-pei kung tz'u-chi*). Compiled by Wu Hsiao-ling 吳曉鈴. Peking: Chung-hua shu-chü,1961.

Nan shih 南史 (History of the Southern dynasties). Compiled by Li Yen-shou 李延壽 (7th century). Completed in 659. 6 vols. Peking: Chung-hua shu-chü, 1975.

Nan Sung chih-chuan 南宋志傳 (Chronicle of the Sung conquest of the south). Attributed to Hsiung Ta-mu 熊大木 (mid-16th century). 10 *chüan*. Nanking: Shih-te t'ang, 1593. Fac. repr. in *Ku-pen hsiao-shuo ts'ung-k'an, ti san-shih ssu chi*, vols. 1–2.

Nan-tz'u hsü-lu 南詞敘錄 (A preliminary account of southern-style drama). By Hsü Wei 徐渭 (1521–93). In *Chung-kuo ku-tien hsi-ch'ü lun-chu chi-ch'eng*, 3:233–56.

Nan-tz'u yün-hsüan 南詞韻選 (An anthology of southern-style song lyrics arranged by rhyme). Compiled by Shen Ching 沈璟 (1553–1610). Edited by Cheng Ch'ien 鄭騫. Taipei: Pei-hai ch'u-pan kung-ssu, 1971.

Nan-yin san-lai 南音三籟 (Three kinds of southern sound). Compiled by Ling Meng-ch'u 凌濛初 (1580–1644). 4 *ts'e*. Fac. repr. of late Ming edition. Shanghai: Shang-hai ku-chi shu-tien, 1963.

Nao Fan-lou to-ch'ing Chou Sheng-hsien 鬧樊樓多情周勝仙 (The disturbance in the Fan Tavern and the passionate Chou Sheng-hsien). In *Hsing-shih heng-yen*, vol. 1, *chüan* 14, pp. 264–76.

Nü han-lin 女翰林 (The female academician). In *Tsui yü-ch'ing*, pp. 1450–1503, upper register.

Nü hsiang-ssu fu 女相思賦 (Rhapsody on female lovesickness). In *Kuo-se t'ien-hsiang*, vol. 1, *chüan* 3, upper register, pp. 2a–3a.

Nü ku-ku shuo-fa sheng-t'ang chi 女姑姑說法陞堂記 (The nun who took the pulpit to expound the dharma). In *Ku-pen Yüan Ming tsa-chü*, vol. 3.

Nü lun-yü 女論語 (The female analects). By Sung Jo-shen 宋若莘 (d. c. 820). In *Lü-ch'uang nü-shih*, 1:1a–8b.

Ou-yang Yung-shu chi 歐陽永叔集 (The collected works of Ou-yang Hsiu 歐陽修 [1007–72]). 3 vols. Shanghai: Shang-wu yin-shu kuan, 1958.

Pa-hsiang pien 八相變 (Pien-wen on the eight aspects [of Śākyamuni Buddha's life]. In *Tun-huang pien-wen chi*, 1:329–42.

Pa-i chi 八義記 (The story of the eight righteous heroes). *Liu-shih chung ch'ü* edition. Taipei: K'ai-ming shu-tien, 1970.

Pai-chia kung-an 百家公案 (A hundred court cases). 1594 edition. Fac. repr. in *Ku-pen hsiao-shuo ts'ung-k'an, ti-erh chi*, vol. 4.

Pai-ch'uan hsüeh-hai 百川學海 (A sea of knowledge fed by a hundred streams). Compiled by Tso Kuei 左圭 (13th century). Preface dated 1273. Fac. repr. of original edition. Peking: Chung-kuo shu-tien, 1990.

Pai-i Ta-pei wu yin-hsin t'o-lo-ni ching 白衣大悲五印心陀羅尼經 (Dhāranī sutra of five mudrās of the Great Compassionate White-Robed Kuan-yin), a stele inscription reproduced in Chün-fang Yü, *Kuan-yin: The Chinese Transformation of Avalokiteśvara*, p. 128.

Pai Niang-tzu yung-chen Lei-feng T'a 白娘子永鎮雷峰塔 (The White Maiden is eternally imprisoned under Thunder Peak Pagoda). In *Ching-shih t'ung-yen*, *chüan* 28, pp. 420–48.

Pai-she chi 白蛇記 (The story of the white snake). By Cheng Kuo-hsüan 鄭國軒 (14th century). In *Ku-pen hsi-ch'ü ts'ung-k'an, ch'u-chi*, item 43.

Pai-t'u chi 白兔記 (The white rabbit). *Liu-shih chung ch'ü* edition. Taipei: K'ai-ming shu-tien, 1970.

Pai-tzu ch'üan-shu 百子全書 (Complete works of the hundred philosophers). Fac. repr. 8 vols. Hang-chou: Che-chiang jen-min ch'u-pan she, 1984.

Pai-yüeh t'ing chi 拜月亭記 (Moon prayer pavilion). In *Ku-pen hsi-ch'ü ts'ung-k'an, ch'u-chi*, item 9.

P'ai-p'u 牌譜 (A manual for dominoes). By Ku Ying-hsiang 顧應祥 (1483–1565). In *Hsin-shang hsü-pien*, *chüan* 9, pp. 1a–31b.

P'ai-t'u 牌圖 (Illustrated domino combinations). In *San-ts'ai t'u-hui*, vol. 4, *jen-shih* (Human affairs), *chüan* 8, pp. 43a–51b.

P'ang Chü-shih wu-fang lai-sheng chai 龐居士誤放來生債 (Layman P'ang mistakenly incurs debts in a future life). By Liu Chün-hsi 劉君錫 (14th century). In *Yüan-ch'ü hsüan*, 1:294–314.

Pao-chien chi 寶劍記 (The story of the precious sword). By Li K'ai-hsien 李開先 (1502–68). In *Shui-hu hsi-ch'ü chi, ti-erh chi*, pp. 1–98.

Pao-chüan ch'u-chi 寶卷初集 (Precious volumes, first collection). Compiled by

Chang Hsi-shun 張希舜 et al. 40 vols. T'ai-yüan: Shan-hsi jen-min ch'u-pan she, 1994.

Pao Lung-t'u tuan Ts'ao Kuo-chiu kung-an chuan 包龍圖斷曹國舅公案傳 (The story of how Academician Pao judged the case of Imperial Brother-in-law Ts'ao). Originally published in the 1470s. Fac. repr. in *Ming Ch'eng-hua shuo-ch'ang tz'u-hua ts'ung-k'an, ts'e* 6.

Pao Lung-t'u tuan wai-wu p'en chuan 包龍圖斷歪烏盆傳 (The story of how Academician Pao judged the case of the misshapen black pot). Published in 1472. Fac. repr. in *Ming Ch'eng-hua shuo-ch'ang tz'u-hua ts'ung-k'an, ts'e* 5.

Pao-p'u tzu 抱朴子 (The master who embraces simplicity). By Ko Hung 葛洪 (283–343). In *Chu-tzu chi-ch'eng,* 8:1–234.

The Peach Blossom Fan. Translated by Chen Shih-hsiang and Harold Acton with the collaboration of Cyril Birch. Berkeley: University of California Press, 1976.

Pei kung tz'u-chi 北宮詞紀 (Anthology of northern-style song lyrics). Compiled by Ch'en So-wen 陳所聞 (d. c. 1604). In *Nan-pei kung tz'u-chi,* vols. 3–4.

Pei-kung tz'u-chi wai-chi 北宮詞紀外集 (Supplementary collection to northern-style song lyrics). Compiled by Ch'en So-wen 陳所聞 (d. c. 1604). 3 *chüan.* In *Nan-pei kung tz'u-chi chiao-pu,* pp. 1–89.

Pei Sung chih-chuan 北宋志傳 (Chronicle of the Sung conquest of the north). Attributed to Hsiung Ta-mu 熊大木 (mid-16th century). 10 *chüan.* Nanking: Shih-te t'ang, 1593. Fac. repr. in *Ku-pen hsiao-shuo ts'ung-k'an, ti san-shih ssu chi,* vols. 2–3.

P'ei Hang 裴航. By P'ei Hsing 裴鉶 (825–80). In *P'ei Hsing Ch'uan-ch'i,* pp. 54–57.

P'ei Hsing Ch'uan-ch'i 裴鉶傳奇 (P'ei Hsing's [825–80] Tales of the marvelous). Edited and annotated by Chou Leng-ch'ieh 周楞伽. Shanghai: Shang-hai ku-chi ch'u-pan she, 1980).

P'ei Hsiu-niang yeh-yu Hsi-hu chi 裴秀娘夜游西湖記 (P'ei Hsiu-niang's night outing on the West Lake). In Hu Shih-ying, *Hua-pen hsiao-shuo kai-lun,* 1:343–49.

Pen-ts'ao kang-mu 本草綱目 (Materia medica arranged by categories and topics). By Li Shih-chen 李時珍 (1518–93). 6 vols. Hong Kong: Shang-wu yin-shu kuan, 1974.

P'eng-lai hsien-sheng chuan 蓬萊先生傳 (The story of Mr. P'eng-lai). In *Hsiao-p'in chi,* pp. 69–76.

Pi-chi hsiao-shuo ta-kuan 筆記小說大觀 (Great collectanea of note-form literature). 17 vols. Yang-chou: Chiang-su Kuang-ling ku-chi k'o-yin she, 1984.

Pi-ching 筆經 (The brush classic). By Wang Hsi-chih 王羲之 (321–79). In *Shuo-fu san-chung,* 7:4520.

Pi-yen lu 碧巖錄 (Blue cliff record). Compiled by Yüan-wu 圜悟 (1063–1135). First published in 1128. In *Taishō shinshū daizōkyō,* 48:139–225.

P'i-p'a chi 琵琶記 (The lute). By Kao Ming 高明 (d. 1359). Edited by Ch'ien Nan-yang 錢南揚. Peking: Chung-hua shu-chü, 1961.

Pin-t'ui lu 賓退錄 (Records written after my guests have left). By Chao Yü-shih 趙與時 (1175–1231). Taipei: Kuang-wen shu-chü, 1970.

The Plum in the Golden Vase or, Chin P'ing Mei. Volume One: *The Gathering.* Translated by David Tod Roy. Princeton: Princeton University Press, 1993.

The Plum in the Golden Vase or, Chin P'ing Mei. Volume Two: *The Rivals.* Translated by David Tod Roy. Princeton: Princeton University Press, 2001.

Po-wu chih 博物志 (A treatise on curiosities). Compiled by Chang Hua 張華 (232–300). Edited by Fan Ning 范寧. Peking: Chung-hua shu-chü, 1980.

P'o-hsieh hsien-cheng yao-shih chüan 破邪顯正鑰匙卷 (Precious volume on the key to refuting heresy and presenting evidence [for correct doctrine]). By Lo Ch'ing 羅清 (1442–1527). Originally published in 1509. In *Pao-chüan ch'u-chi*, 2:1–508

P'o-mo pien-wen 破魔變文 (Transformation text on destroying the demons). Dated 944. In *Tun-huang pien-wen chi*, 1:344–55.

P'o-yao chi 破窯記 (The dilapidated kiln). In *Ku-pen hsi-ch'ü ts'ung-k'an, ch'u-chi*, item 19.

P'u-ching ju-lai yao-shih pao-chüan 普靜如來鑰匙寶卷 (Precious volume of the Tathāgatha P'u-ching: the Buddha of the Key [to salvation]). By P'u-ching 普靜 (d. 1586). In *Pao-chüan ch'u-chi*, 5:21–186.

P'u-ming ju-lai wu-wei liao-i pao-chüan 普明如來無為了義寶卷 (Precious volume of the Tathāgatha P'u-ming who thoroughly comprehends the meaning of Nonactivism). By P'u-ming 普明 (d. 1562). Completed in 1558. In *Pao-chüan ch'u-chi*, 4:373–605.

P'u-tung Ts'ui Chang chu-yü shih-chi 浦東崔張珠玉詩集 (Collection of poetic gems about [the affair of] Ts'ui [Ying-ying] and Chang [Chün-jui] in P'u-tung). Included as part of the front matter in the 1498 edition of *Hsi-hsiang chi*, pp. 13a–21a.

The Recorded Sayings of Layman P'ang: A Ninth-century Zen Classic. Translated by Ruth Fuller Sasaki, Yoshitaka Iriya, and Dana R. Fraser. New York: Weatherhill, 1971.

Records of the Grand Historian of China. Translated by Burton Watson. 2 vols. New York: Columbia University Press, 1961.

Records of the Grand Historian: Qin Dynasty. Translated by Burton Watson. New York: Columbia University Press, 1993.

Records of the Historian. Translated by Yang Hsien-yi and Gladys Yang. Hong Kong: Commercial Press, 1974.

San-chiao yüan-liu sou-shen ta-ch'üan 三教源流搜神大全 (Complete compendium on the pantheons of the three religions). Preface dated 1593. Fac. repr. Taipei: Lien-ching ch'u-pan shih-yeh kung-ssu, 1980.

San hsien-shen Pao Lung-t'u tuan-yüan 三現身包龍圖斷冤 (After three ghostly manifestations Academician Pao rights an injustice). In *Ching-shih t'ung-yen, chüan* 13, pp. 169–84.

San-kuo chih 三國志 (History of the Three Kingdoms). Compiled by Ch'en Shou 陳壽 (233–97). 5 vols. Peking: Chung-hua shu-chü, 1973.

San-kuo chih p'ing-hua 三國志平話 (The p'ing-hua on the history of the Three Kingdoms). Originally published in 1321–23. Shanghai: Ku-tien wen-hsüeh ch'u-pan she, 1955.

San-kuo chih t'ung-su yen-i 三國志通俗演義 (The romance of the Three Kingdoms). Attributed to Lo Kuan-chung 羅貫中 (14th century). Preface dated 1522. 2 vols. Shanghai: Shang-hai ku-chi ch'u-pan she, 1980.

San-ming t'ung-hui 三命通會 (Comprehensive compendium on the three fates). Compiled by Wan Min-ying 萬民英 (cs 1550). In *[Ying-yin Wen-yüan ko] Ssu-k'u ch'üan-shu*, 810:1–691.

San-pao t'ai-chien Hsi-yang chi t'ung-su yen-i 三寶太監西洋記通俗演義 (The romance of Eunuch Cheng Ho's expedition to the Western Ocean). By Lo Mao-teng 羅懋登. Author's preface dated 1597. 2 vols. Shanghai: Shang-hai ku-chi ch'u-pan she, 1985.

San-shui hsiao-tu 三水小牘 (Short pieces by the man from San-shui). By Huang-fu Mei 皇甫枚 (10th century). Completed in 910. Peking: Chung-hua shu-chü, 1960.

San Sui p'ing-yao chuan 三遂平妖傳 (The three Sui quash the demons' revolt). Fac. repr. Tokyo: Tenri daigaku shuppan-bu, 1981.

San-ts'ai t'u-hui 三才圖會 (Assembled illustrations from the three realms). Compiled by Wang Ch'i 王圻 (c. 1535–c. 1614). Preface dated 1609. 6 vols. Fac. repr. Taipei: Ch'eng-wen ch'u-pan she, 1970.

San-yüan chi 三元記 (Feng Ching 馮京 [1021–94] wins first place in three examinations). By Shen Shou-hsien 沈受先 (15th century). *Liu-shih chung ch'ü* edition. Taipei: K'ai-ming shu-tien, 1970.

Seng-ni kung-fan 僧尼共犯 (A monk and a nun violate their vows). By Feng Wei-min 馮惟敏 (1511–80). In *Ming-jen tsa-chü hsüan*, pp. 333–50.

Seng-ni nieh-hai 僧尼孽海 (Monks and nuns in a sea of iniquity). Originally published in the early 17th century. In *Ssu wu-hsieh hui-pao*, 24:151–339.

Sha-kou chi 殺狗記 (The stratagem of killing a dog). *Liu-shih chung ch'ü* edition. Taipei: K'ai-ming shu-tien, 1970.

Shan-chü hsin-hua 山居新話 (New tales recorded while dwelling in the mountains). Compiled by Yang Yü 楊瑀 (1285–1361). In *Pi-chi hsiao-shuo ta-kuan*, vol. 5, ts'e 11.

Shan-pen hsi-ch'ü ts'ung-k'an 善本戲曲叢刊 (Collectanea of rare editions of works on dramatic prosody). Taipei: Hsüeh-sheng shu-chü, 1984–87.

Shen-hsiang ch'üan-pien 神相全編 (Complete compendium on effective physiognomy). Compiled by Yüan Chung-ch'e 袁忠徹 (1376–1458). In *Ku-chin t'u-shu chi-ch'eng*, section 17, *i-shu tien*, *chüan* 631–44.

Shen Hsiao-kuan i-niao hai ch'i-ming 沈小官一鳥害七命 (Master Shen's bird destroys seven lives). In *Ku-chin hsiao-shuo*, vol. 2, *chüan* 26, pp. 391–403.

Shen-t'ung shih 神童詩 (Poems by infant prodigies). Traditionally attributed to Wang Chu 汪洙 (cs 1100). In *Chung-kuo ku-tai meng-hsüeh shu ta-kuan*, pp. 263–80.

Sheng-Ming tsa-chü, erh-chi 盛明雜劇, 二集 (Tsa-chü dramas of the glorious Ming dynasty, second collection). Compiled by Shen T'ai 沈泰 (17th century). Fac. repr. of 1641 edition. Peking: Chung-kuo hsi-chü ch'u-pan she, 1958.

Sheng-shih hsin-sheng 盛世新聲 (New songs of a surpassing age). Preface dated 1517. Fac. repr. Peking: Wen-hsüeh ku-chi k'an-hsing she, 1955.

Shih Chen-jen ssu-sheng so pai-yüan 時真人四聖鎖白猿 (Perfected Man Shih and the four generals subdue the white gibbon). In *Ku-pen Yüan Ming tsa-chü*, vol. 4.

Shih-chi 史記 (Records of the historian). By Ssu-ma Ch'ien 司馬遷 (145–c. 90 B.C.). 10 vols. Peking: Chung-hua shu-chü, 1972.

Shih-hou chi 獅吼記 (The lion's roar). By Wang T'ing-no 汪廷訥 (fl. 1593–1611). *Liu-shih chung ch'ü* edition. Taipei: K'ai-ming shu-tien, 1970.

Shih Hung-chao lung-hu chün-ch'en hui 史弘肇龍虎君臣會 (Shih Hung-chao: The meeting of dragon and tiger, ruler and minister). In *Ku-chin hsiao-shuo*, vol. 1, *chüan* 15, pp. 212–38.

Shih-lin kuang-chi 事林廣記 (Expansive gleanings from the forest of affairs). Fac. repr. of 14th-century edition. Peking: Chung-hua shu-chü, 1963.

Shih-san ching ching-wen 十三經經文 (The texts of the thirteen classics). Taipei: K'ai-ming shu-tien, 1955.

Shih-san ching chu-shu 十三經注疏 (The thirteen classics with their commentaries). Compiled by Juan Yüan 阮元 (1764–1849). 2 vols. Peking: Chung-hua shu-chü, 1982.

Shih-shuo Hsin-yü: A New Account of Tales of the World. By Liu I-ch'ing; translated by Richard B. Mather. Minneapolis: University of Minnesota Press, 1976.

Shih-shuo hsin-yü chiao-chien 世說新語校箋 (A critical edition of the *Shih-shuo hsin-yü*). Edited by Yang Yung 楊勇. Hong Kong: Ta-chung shu-chü, 1969.

Shih-t'ien hsien-sheng chi 石田先生集 (The collected literary works of Shen Chou). By Shen Chou 沈周 (1427–1509). 2 vols. Fac. repr. of Wan-li edition. Preface dated 1615. Taipei: Kuo-li Chung-yang t'u-shu kuan, 1968.

Shih-wu kuan hsi-yen ch'eng ch'iao-huo 十五貫戲言成巧禍 (Fifteen strings of cash: a casual jest leads to uncanny disaster). In *Hsing-shih heng-yen*, vol. 2, *chüan* 33, pp. 691–706.

[Shinzan] Dai Nihon zokuzōkyō [新纂] 大日本續藏經 ([Newly compiled] great Japanese continuation of the Buddhist canon). 100 vols. Tokyo: Kokusho kankōkai, 1977.

The Shoo King or The Book of Historical Documents. Translated by James Legge. Hong Kong: University of Hong Kong Press, 1960.

Shou-t'ing hou nu chan Kuan P'ing 壽亭侯怒斬關平 (The Marquis of Shou-t'ing angrily executes Kuan P'ing). In *Ku-pen Yüan Ming tsa-chü*, vol. 3.

Shuang-ch'ing pi-chi 雙卿筆記 (A record of the two Ch'ing [Chang Cheng-ch'ing 張正卿 and Chang Shun-ch'ing 張順卿]). In *Kuo-se t'ien-hsiang*, vol. 2, *chüan* 5, lower register, pp. 1a–31b.

Shuang-chu chi 雙珠記 (The pair of pearls). By Shen Ch'ing 沈鯖 (15th century). *Liu-shih chung ch'ü* edition. Taipei: K'ai-ming shu-tien, 1970.

Shuang-chung chi 雙忠記 (The loyal pair). By Yao Mao-liang 姚茂良 (15th century). In *Ku-pen hsi-ch'ü ts'ung-k'an, ch'u-chi*, item 33.

Shuang-lieh chi 雙烈記 (The heroic couple). By Chang Ssu-wei 張四維 (late 16th century). *Liu-shih chung ch'ü* edition. Taipei: K'ai-ming shu-tien, 1970.

Shui-hu ch'üan-chuan 水滸全傳 (Variorum edition of the *Outlaws of the Marsh*). Edited by Cheng Chen-to 鄭振鐸 et al. 4 vols. Hong Kong: Chung-hua shu-chü, 1958.

Shui-hu hsi-ch'ü chi, ti-erh chi 水滸戲曲集, 第二集 (Corpus of drama dealing with the *Shui-hu* cycle, second series). Edited by Fu Hsi-hua 傅惜華. Shanghai: Ku-tien wen-hsüeh ch'u-pan she, 1958.

Shui-hu hsi-ch'ü chi, ti-i chi 水滸戲曲集, 第一集 (Corpus of drama dealing with the *Shui-hu* cycle, first series). Edited by Fu Hsi-hua 傅惜華 and Tu Ying-t'ao 杜穎陶. Shanghai: Ku-tien wen-hsüeh ch'u-pan she, 1957.

Shui-tung jih-chi 水東日記 (Daily jottings east of the river). By Yeh Sheng 葉盛 (1420–74). Peking: Chung-hua shu-chü, 1980.

Shuo-fu 說郛 (The frontiers of apocrypha). Compiled by T'ao Tsung-i 陶宗儀 (c. 1360–c. 1403). 2 vols. Taipei: Hsin-hsing shu-chü, 1963.

Shuo-fu hsü 說郛續 (*The frontiers of apocrypha* continued). Compiled by T'ao T'ing 陶珽 (cs 1610). Fac. repr. of Ming ed. In *Shuo-fu san-chung*, vols. 9–10.

Shuo-fu san-chung 說郛三種 (*The frontiers of apocrypha*: Three recensions). 10 vols. Shanghai: Shang-hai ku-chi ch'u-pan she, 1988.

Some T'ang and Pre-T'ang Texts on Chinese Painting. Translated by William R. B. Acker. Vol. 2, part 1. Leiden: E. J. Brill, 1974.

The Songs of the South. Translated by David Hawkes. New York: Penguin Books, 1985.

Ssu-hsi chi 四喜記 (The four occasions for delight). By Hsieh Tang 謝讜 (1512–69). *Liu-shih chung ch'ü* edition. Taipei: K'ai-ming shu-tien, 1970.

Ssu-pu pei-yao 四部備要 (Collectanea of works from the four treasuries). Shanghai: Chung-hua shu-chü, 1936.

Ssu-sheng chiao Fan Chang chi-shu 死生交范張鷄黍 (The chicken and millet life and death friendship between Fan Shih 范式 and Chang Shao 張劭). In *Ch'ing-p'ing shan-t'ang hua-pen*, pp. 280–83.

Ssu-sheng yüan 四聲猿 (Four cries of a gibbon). By Hsü Wei 徐渭 (1521–93). Originally published in 1588. Edited and annotated by Chou Chung-ming 周中明. Shanghai: Shang-hai ku-chi ch'u-pan she, 1984.

Ssu-shih hua-yüeh sai chiao-jung 四時花月賽嬌容 (The flowers and moonlight of the four seasons compete in loveliness). By Chu Yu-tun 朱有燉 (1379–1439). In *Ku-pen Yüan Ming tsa-chü*, vol. 2.

Ssu-shu chang-chü chi-chu 四書章句集注 (Collected commentary on the paragraphed and punctuated text of the Four books). By Chu Hsi 朱熹 (1130–1200). Peking: Chung-hua shu-chü, 1983.

Ssu-tzu ching 四字經 (Four character classic). Attributed to the Buddhist monk Te-hsing 德行 (T'ang dynasty). In *Ts'ung-shu chi-ch'eng*, 715:1–36.

Ssu wu-hsieh hui-pao 思無邪匯寶 (No depraved thoughts collectanea). Compiled by Ch'en Ch'ing-hao 陳慶浩 and Wang Ch'iu-kuei 王秋桂. 45 vols. Taipei: Encyclopedia Britannica, 1995–97.

Ssu wu-hsieh hui-pao wai-pien 四無邪匯寶外編 (Supplement to No depraved thoughts collectanea). Compiled by Ch'en Ch'ing-hao 陳慶浩 and Wang Ch'iu-kuei 王秋桂. 2 vols. Taipei: Encyclopedia Britannica, 1997.

Stories Old and New: A Ming Dynasty Collection. Compiled by Feng Menglong (1574–1646). Translated by Shuhui Yang and Yunqin Yang. Seattle: University of Washington Press, 2000.

Su-hsiang T'ing Chang Hao yü Ying-ying 宿香亭張浩遇鶯鶯 (In Su-hsiang T'ing Chang Hao meets [Li] Ying-ying). In *Ching-shih t'ung-yen*, chüan 29, pp. 449–57.

Su Shih shih-chi 蘇軾詩集 (Collected poetry of Su Shih). By Su Shih 蘇軾 (1037–1101). 8 vols. Peking: Chung-hua shu-chü, 1982.

Su Shih wen-chi 蘇軾文集 (Collected prose of Su Shih). By Su Shih 蘇軾 (1037–1101). 6 vols. Peking: Chung-hua shu-chü, 1986.

Su Wu mu-yang chi 蘇武牧羊記 (Su Wu herds sheep). In *Ku-pen hsi-ch'ü ts'ung-k'an, ch'u-chi*, item 20.

Su Ying huang-hou ying-wu chi 蘇英皇后鸚鵡記 (The story of Empress Su Ying's parrot). In *Ku-pen hsi-ch'ü ts'ung-k'an, ch'u-chi*, item 45.

Sui-T'ang liang-ch'ao shih-chuan 隋唐兩朝史傳 (Historical chronicle of the Sui and T'ang dynasties). 12 chüan. Su-chou: Kung Shao-shan, 1619. Microfilm of unique copy in Sonkeikaku Bunko, Tokyo.

Sung Kao-seng chuan 宋高僧傳 (Biographies of eminent monks compiled during the Sung dynasty). Compiled by Tsan-ning 贊寧 (919–1001). Preface dated 988. 2 vols. Peking: Chung-hua shu-chü, 1987.

Sung shih 宋史 (History of the Sung dynasty). Compiled by T'o-t'o 脫脫 (1313–55) et al. 40 vols. Peking: Chung-hua shu-chü, 1977.

Sung shih-hua ch'üan-pien 宋詩話全編 (Complete compendium of Sung dynasty talks on poetry). Edited by Wu Wen-chih 吳文治. 10 vols. Nanking: Chiang-su ku-chi ch'u-pan she, 1998.

Sung Ssu-kung ta-nao Chin-hun Chang 宋四公大鬧禁魂張 (Sung the Fourth raises hell with Tightwad Chang). In *Ku-chin hsiao-shuo*, vol. 2, *chüan* 36, pp. 525–50.

Sung ta-chiang Yüeh Fei ching-chung 宋大將岳飛精忠 (The perfect loyalty of the Sung general-in-chief Yüeh Fei). In *Ku-pen Yüan Ming tsa-chü*, vol. 3.

Sung tsai-fu pien-nien lu [chiao-pu] 宋宰輔編年錄 [校補] ([Collated and supplemented recension of] A chronological record of the rescripts appointing and demoting the chief ministers of the Sung dynasty). Compiled by Hsü Tzu-ming 徐自明 (fl. early 13th century). Edited by Wang Jui-lai 王瑞來. 4 vols. Peking: Chung-hua shu-chü, 1986.

Sung-Yüan hsi-wen chi-i 宋元戲文輯佚 (Collected fragments of Sung and Yüan hsi-wen drama). Compiled by Ch'ien Nan-yang 錢南揚. Shanghai: Shang-hai ku-tien wen-hsüeh ch'u-pan she, 1956.

The Śūraṅgama Sūtra (Leng Yen Ching). Translated by Charles Luk. London: Rider & Company, 1966.

Ta ming-ch'un 大明春 (Great bright spring). Compiled by Ch'eng Wan-li 程萬里. Chien-yang: Chin K'uei, n.d. Fac. repr. of Wan-li (1573–1620) edition. In *Shan-pen hsi-ch'ü ts'ung-k'an*, vol. 6.

Ta-pan nieh-p'an ching 大般涅槃經 (The Mahāparinirvāṇasūtra). Translated by Dharmakṣema (fl. 385–433). In *Taishō shinshū daizōkyō*, vol. 12, no. 374, pp. 365–603.

Ta-Sung chung-hsing yen-i 大宋中興演義 (The romance of the restoration of the great Sung dynasty). By Hsiung Ta-mu 熊大木 (mid-16th century). 8 *chüan*. Chien-yang: Ch'ing-pai t'ang, 1552. Fac. repr. in *Ku-pen hsiao-shuo ts'ung-k'an, ti san-shih ch'i chi*, vols. 1–3.

Ta-T'ang Ch'in-wang tz'u-hua 大唐秦王詞話 (Prosimetric story of the Prince of Ch'in of the Great T'ang). 2 vols. Fac. repr. of early 17th-century edition. Peking: Wen-hsüeh ku-chi k'an-hsing she, 1956.

Ta-T'ang hsi-yü chi [chiao-chu] 大唐西域記 [校注] (Great T'ang record of the western regions [edited and annotated]). By Hsüan-tsang 玄奘 (602–64). Edited and annotated by Chi Hsien-lin 季羨林 et al. Originally completed in 646. Peking: Chung-hua shu-chü, 1985.

Ta-T'ang San-tsang ch'ü-ching shih-hua 大唐三藏取經詩話 (Prosimetric account of how the monk Tripitaka of the great T'ang [made a pilgrimage] to procure sutras). Printed in the 13th century but probably older. Shanghai: Chung-kuo ku-tien wen-hsüeh ch'u-pan she, 1955.

Taishō shinshū daizōkyō 大正新修大藏經 (The newly edited great Buddhist canon compiled in the Taishō reign period [1912–26]). 85 vols. Tokyo: Taishō issaikyō kankōkai, 1922–32.

T'ai-ho cheng-yin p'u 太和正音譜 (Formulary for the correct sounds of great harmony). Compiled by Chu Ch'üan 朱權 (1378–1448). In *Chung-kuo ku-tien hsi-ch'ü lun-chu chi-ch'eng*, 3:1–231.

T'ai-kung chia-chiao 太公家教 (Family teachings of T'ai-kung). In Chou Feng-wu, *Tun-huang hsieh-pen T'ai-kung chia-chiao yen-chiu*, pp. 9–28.

T'ai-p'ing ching ho-chiao 太平經合校 (A collated text of the Scripture on great peace). Edited by Wang Ming 王明. Peking: Chung-hua shu-chü, 1985.

T'ai-p'ing kuang-chi 太平廣記 (Extensive gleanings from the reign of Great Tranquility). Compiled by Li Fang 李昉 (925–96) et al. First printed in 981. 10 vols. Peking: Chung-hua shu-chü, 1961.

T'ai-shang chu-kuo chiu-min tsung-chen pi-yao 太上助國救民總真祕要 (Secret essentials of the assembled perfected of the Most High for the relief of the state and the deliverance of the people). Compiled by Yüan Miao-tsung 元妙宗 (fl. 1086–1116). Preface dated 1116. In *Cheng-t'ung Tao-tsang, ts'e* 986–87.

T'ai-tzu ch'eng-tao ching 太子成道經 (Sutra on how the crown prince [Śākyamuni] attained the Way). In *Tun-huang pien-wen chi*, 1:285–300.

T'an-shih wu-wei pao-chüan 嘆世無爲寶卷 (Precious volume on Nonactivism in lamentation for the world). By Lo Ch'ing 羅清 (1442–1527). Originally published in 1509. In *Pao-chüan ch'u-chi*, 1:295–572.

Tang-ch'i hui-ch'ang ch'ü 盪氣迴腸曲 (Songs that agitate the spirits and rend the guts). Compiled by Wang Yu-jan 王悠然 (20th century). Preface dated 1928. Shanghai: Ta-chiang shu-p'u, 1933.

T'ang chih-yen 唐摭言 (A gleaning of T'ang anecdotes). By Wang Ting-pao 王定保 (870–c. 954). Shanghai: Ku-tien wen-hsüeh ch'u-pan she, 1957.

T'ang Hsien-tsu chi 湯顯祖集 (Collected works of T'ang Hsien-tsu [1550–1616]). Edited by Hsü Shuo-fang 徐朔方 and Ch'ien Nan-yang 錢南揚. 4 vols. Peking: Chung-hua shu-chü, 1962.

T'ang kuo-shih pu 唐國史補 (Supplement to the History of the T'ang). Compiled by Li Chao 李肇 (early 9th century). Shanghai: Ku-tien wen-hsüeh ch'u-pan she, 1957.

T'ang-lü shu-i 唐律疏議 (The T'ang code with subcommentary). Compiled by Chang-sun Wu-chi 長孫無忌 (d. 659). Taipei: Shang-wu yin-shu kuan, 1973.

T'ang-shu chih-chuan t'ung-su yen-i 唐書志傳通俗演義 (The romance of the chronicles of the T'ang dynasty). By Hsiung Ta-mu 熊大木 (mid-16th century). 8 *chüan*. Chien-yang: Ch'ing-chiang t'ang, 1553. Fac. repr. in *Ku-pen hsiao-shuo ts'ung-k'an, ti-ssu chi*, vols. 1–2.

T'ang Sung ch'uan-ch'i chi 唐宋傳奇集 (An anthology of literary tales from the T'ang and Sung dynasties). Edited by Lu Hsün 魯迅. Peking: Wen-hsüeh ku-chi k'an-hsing she, 1958.

T'ang-yü lin 唐語林 (Forest of T'ang anecdotes). Compiled by Wang Tang 王讜 (fl. late 11th century). Shanghai: Ku-tien wen-hsüeh ch'u-pan she, 1957.

Tao-men t'ung-chiao pi-yung chi 道門通教必用集 (Anthology of essentials on the comprehensive teachings of the Taoist sect). Compiled by Lü T'ai-ku 呂太古 (fl. late 12th-early 13th century). Introduction dated 1201. In *Cheng-t'ung Tao-tsang, ts'e* 984–85.

Tao-shan ch'ing-hua 道山清話 (Pure anecdotes from the Tao-shan Hall). Postface dated 1130. In *Pai-ch'uan hsüeh-hai, kuei-chi* (tenth collection), pp. 1a–35b.

T'ao-hua shan 桃花扇 (The peach blossom fan). By K'ung Shang-jen 孔尚任 (1648–1718). Edited by Wang Chi-ssu 王季思 and Su Huan-chung 蘇寰中. Peking: Jen-min wen-hsüeh ch'u-pan she, 1958.

T'ao Yüan-ming tung-li shang-chü 陶淵明東籬賞菊 (T'ao Yüan-ming enjoys the chrysanthemums by the eastern hedge). In *Ku-pen Yüan Ming tsa-chü*, vol. 3.

T'eng-wang ko hsü 滕王閣序 (Preface to the poem on the Prince of T'eng's Pavilion). By Wang Po 王勃 (649–76). In *Ch'üan T'ang wen*, vol. 4, *chüan* 281, pp. 18a–20a.

Ti-ching sui-shih chi-sheng 帝京歲時紀勝 (Record of the outstanding seasonal observances in the imperial capital). By P'an Jung-pi 潘榮陛 (18th century). Author's preface dated 1758. Peking: Pei-ching ku-chi ch'u-pan she, 1981.

T'ieh-wei shan ts'ung-t'an 鐵圍山叢談 (Collected remarks from the Iron Cordon Mountains). By Ts'ai T'ao 蔡絛 (d. after 1147). Peking: Chung-hua shu-chü, 1997.

T'ien-kung k'ai-wu 天工開物 (The exploitation of the works of nature). By Sung Ying-hsing 宋應星 (1587–c. 1666). Hong Kong: Chung-hua shu-chü, 1978.

T'ien-kung k'ai-wu: Chinese Technology in the Seventeenth Century. Translated by E-tu Zen Sun and Shiou-chuan Sun. University Park: Pennsylvania State University Press, 1966.

T'ien-pao i-shih chu-kung-tiao 天寶遺事諸宮調 (Medley in various modes on the forgotten events of the T'ien-pao [742–56] reign period). By Wang Po-ch'eng 王伯成 (fl. late 13th century). In *Chu-kung-tiao liang-chung*, pp. 88–256.

T'ien-yüan ch'i-yü 天緣奇遇 (Celestial destinies remarkably fulfilled). In *Kuo-se t'ien-hsiang*, vol. 3, *chüan* 7, pp. 1a–29b; and *chüan* 8, pp. 1a–30b, lower register.

T'ing-shih 桯史 (Tabletop notes). By Yüeh K'o 岳珂 (1183–c. 1240). Peking: Chung-hua shu-chü, 1981.

Ts'ai-lou chi 彩樓記 (The gaily colored tower). Edited by Huang Shang 黃裳. Shanghai: Shang-hai ku-tien wen-hsüeh ch'u-pan she, 1956.

Ts'ai-pi ch'ing-tz'u 彩筆情詞 (Emotive lyrics from variegated brushes). Compiled by Chang Hsü 張栩. Preface dated 1624. Fac. repr. In *Shan-pen hsi-ch'ü ts'ung-k'an*, vols. 75–76.

Ts'an-T'ang Wu-tai shih yen-i chuan 殘唐五代史演義傳 (Romance of the late T'ang and Five Dynasties). Peking: Pao-wen t'ang shu-tien, 1983.

Tsao-chiao Lin Ta-wang chia-hsing 皂角林大王假形 (A feat of impersonation by the King of Tsao-chiao Wood), in *Ching-shih t'ung-yen*, *chüan* 36, pp. 546–55.

Ts'ao Chih chi chiao-chu 曹植集校注 (Ts'ao Chih's collected works collated and annotated). Edited by Chao Yu-wen 趙幼文. Peking: Jen-min wen-hsüeh ch'u-pan she, 1984.

Ts'ao Po-ming ts'o-k'an tsang chi 曹伯明錯勘贓記 (The story of Ts'ao Po-ming and the mistaken identification of the booty). In *Ch'ing-p'ing shan-t'ang hua-pen*, pp. 206–11.

The Tso chuan: Selections from China's Oldest Narrative History. Translated by Burton Watson. New York: Columbia University Press, 1989.

Ts'o-jen shih 錯認屍 (The wrongly identified corpse). In *Ch'ing-p'ing shan-t'ang hua-pen*, pp. 212–35.

Tsu-t'ang chi 祖堂集 (Patriarchal hall collection). Edited by Wu Fu-hsiang 吳福祥 and Ku Chih-ch'uan 顧之川. Originally published in 952. Ch'ang-sha: Yüeh-lu shu-she, 1996.

Tsui-weng t'an-lu 醉翁談錄 (The old drunkard's selection of tales). Compiled by Lo Yeh 羅燁 (13th century). Taipei: Shih-chieh shu-chü, 1972.

Tsui yü-ch'ing 最娛情 (Superlative delights). Preface dated 1647. Fac. repr. In *Ku-pen hsiao-shuo ts'ung-k'an, ti erh-shih liu chi*, 4:1411–1566.

Ts'ui Ya-nei pai-yao chao-yao 崔衙内白鷴招妖 (The white falcon of Minister Ts'ui's son embroils him with demons). In *Ching-shih t'ung-yen*, *chüan* 19, pp. 261–73.

Tsung-ching lu 宗鏡錄 (The mirror of the source). Compiled by Yen-shou 延壽 (904–75). In *Taishō shinshū daizōkyō*, vol. 48, no. 2016, pp. 415–957.

Ts'ung-shu chi-ch'eng 叢書集成 (A corpus of works from collectanea). 1st series. Shanghai: Shang-wu yin-shu kuan, 1935–37.

Tu Li-niang mu-se huan-hun 杜麗娘慕色還魂 (Tu Li-niang yearns for love and returns to life). In Hu Shih-ying, *Hua-pen hsiao-shuo kai-lun*, 2:533–37.

Tu Tzu-mei ku-chiu yu-ch'un 杜子美沽酒遊春 (Tu Fu buys wine for a spring excursion). By Wang Chiu-ssu 王九思 (1468–1551). In *Sheng-Ming tsa-chü, erh-chi*.

Tuan-fa chi 斷髮記 (The severed tresses). By Li K'ai-hsien 李開先 (1502–68). In *Ku-pen hsi-ch'ü ts'ung-k'an, wu-chi*, item 2.

Tun-huang pao-tsang 敦煌寶藏 (Treasures from Tun-huang). Compiled by Huang Yung-wu 黃永武. 140 vols. Taipei: Hsin-wen-feng ch'u-pan kung-ssu, 1981–86.

Tun-huang pien-wen chi 敦煌變文集 (Collection of pien-wen from Tun-huang). Edited by Wang Chung-min 王重民 et al. 2 vols. Peking: Jen-min wen-hsüeh ch'u-pan she, 1984.

Tun-huang Popular Narratives. Translated by Victor H. Mair. Cambridge: Cambridge University Press, 1983.

Tung Chieh-yüan Hsi-hsiang chi 董解元西廂記 (Master Tung's Western chamber romance). Edited and annotated by Ling Ching-yen 凌景埏. Peking: Jen-min wen-hsüeh ch'u-pan she, 1962.

Tung-ching meng-hua lu 東京夢華錄 (A dream of past splendors in the Eastern Capital). Compiled by Meng Yüan-lao 孟元老 (12th century). Preface dated 1147. In *Tung-ching meng-hua lu [wai ssu-chung]*, pp. 1–87.

Tung-ching meng-hua lu [wai ssu-chung] 東京夢話錄 [外四種] (A dream of past splendors in the Eastern Capital [plus four other works]). Compiled by Meng Yüan-lao 孟元老 (12th century) et al. Shanghai: Shang-hai ku-chi wen-hsüeh ch'u-pan she, 1956.

Tung-ku so chien 東谷所見 (Observations of Tung-ku). By Li Chih-yen 李之彥 (13th century). Author's preface dated 1268. In *Shuo-fu san-chung*, 6:3419–29.

Tung-t'ien hsüan-chi 洞天玄記 (Mysterious record of the grotto heaven). Attributed to Yang Shen 楊慎 (1488–1559). In *Ku-pen Yüan Ming tsa-chü*, vol. 2.

Tung-yu chi: shang-tung pa-hsien chuan 東遊記: 上洞八仙傳 (Journey to the east: the story of the eight immortals of the upper realm). Compiled by Wu Yüan-t'ai 吳元泰 (16th century). Appendix dated 1596. Fac. repr. of Chien-yang edition published by Yü Hsiang-tou 余象斗 (c. 1550–1637). In *Ku-pen Hsiao-shuo ts'ung-k'an, ti san-shih chiu chi*, 1:1–260.

Tung Yung yü-hsien chuan 董永遇仙傳 (The story of Tung Yung's encounter with an immortal). In *Ch'ing-p'ing shan-t'ang hua-pen*, pp. 235–44.

T'ung-lo Yüan Yen Ch'ing po-yü 同樂院燕青博魚 (In T'ung-lo Tavern Yen Ch'ing gambles for fish), in *Shui-hu hsi-ch'ü chi, ti-i chi*, pp. 16–30.

Tzu-ch'ai chi 紫釵記 (The story of the purple hairpin). By T'ang Hsien-tsu 湯顯祖 (1550–1616); edited and annotated by Hu Shih-ying 胡士瑩. Peking: Jen-min wen-hsüeh ch'u-pan she, 1982.

Tzu-chih t'ung-chien 資治通鑑 (Comprehensive mirror for aid in government). Compiled by Ssu-ma Kuang 司馬光 (1019–86). 4 vols. Peking: Ku-chi ch'u-pan she, 1957.

Tzu-hsiao chi 紫簫記 (The story of the purple flute). By T'ang Hsien-tsu 湯顯祖 (1550–1616). Completed in 1580. In *T'ang Hsien-tsu chi*, 4:2433–2587.

Tz'u-lin chai-yen 詞林摘艶 (Select flowers from the forest of song). Compiled by Chang Lu 張祿. Preface dated 1525. 2 vols. Fac. repr. Peking: Wen-hsüeh ku-chi k'an-hsing she, 1955.

Tz'u-lin i-hsiang 詞林逸響 (Lingering notes from the forest of song). Compiled by Hsü Yü 許宇 (fl. early 17th century). Preface dated 1623. Fac. repr. in *Shan-pen hsi-ch'ü ts'ung-k'an*, vols. 17–18.

Tz'u-nüeh 詞謔 (Pleasantries on lyrical verse). By Li K'ai-hsien 李開先 (1502–68). In *Chung-kuo ku-tien hsi-ch'ü lun-chu chi-ch'eng*, 3:257–418.

Wan Hsiu-niang ch'ou-pao shan-t'ing-erh 萬秀娘仇報山亭兒 (Wan Hsiu-niang gets her revenge with a toy pavilion). In *Ching-shih t'ung-yen, chüan* 37, pp. 556–71.

Wan-shu tsa-chi 宛署雜記 (Miscellaneous records concerning the magistracy of Wan-p'ing). By Shen Pang 沈榜. Preface dated 1592. Peking: Pei-ching ku-chi ch'u-pan-she, 1980.

Wang Chao-chün pien-wen 王昭君變文 (The pien-wen on Wang Chao-chün). In *Tun-huang pien-wen chi*, 1:98–107.

Wang Chih-ku wei hu chao-hsü 王知古為狐招壻 (Wang Chih-ku is selected as a son-in-law by a lair of foxes). By Huang-fu Mei 皇甫枚 (10th century). In *San-shui hsiao-tu, chüan* 1, pp. 12–17.

Wang Ching-wen kung shih Li Pi chu 王荊文公詩李壁注 (The poetry of Wang An-shih 王安石 [1021–86] with commenatary by Li Pi 李壁 [1159–1222]). 2 vols. Fac. repr. of Korean movable type edition. Shanghai: Shang-hai ku-chi ch'u-pan she, 1993.

Wang K'uei 王魁 (The story of Wang K'uei). In *Tsui yü-ch'ing*, pp. 1503–21, upper register.

Wang Lan-ch'ing chen-lieh chuan 王蘭卿貞烈傳 (The story of Wang Lan-ch'ing's heroic refusal to remarry). By K'ang Hai 康海 (1475–1541). In *Ku-pen Yüan Ming tsa-chü*, vol. 2.

Wang Wen-hsiu Wei-t'ang ch'i-yü chi 王文秀渭塘奇遇記 (The story of Wang Wen-hsiu's remarkable encounter in Wei-t'ang). In *Ku-pen Yüan Ming tsa-chü*, vol. 4.

Wang Yüeh-ying yüan-yeh liu-hsieh chi 王月英元夜留鞋記 (Wang Yüeh-ying leaves her shoe behind on the Lantern Festival). In *Yüan-ch'ü hsüan*, 3:1265–79.

Wei Chuang chi chiao-chu 韋莊集校注 (A collated and annotated edition of the works of Wei Chuang [836–910]). Edited by Li I 李誼. Ch'eng-tu: Ssu-ch'uan sheng she-hui k'o-hsüeh yüan ch'u-pan she, 1986.

Wei Feng-hsiang ku Yü-huan chi 韋鳳翔古玉環記 (The old version of Wei Kao 韋皋 [746–806] and the story of the jade ring). In *Ku-pen hsi-ch'ü ts'ung-k'an, ch'u-chi*, item 22.

Wei-wei pu-tung T'ai-shan shen-ken chieh-kuo pao-chüan 巍巍不動太山深根結果寶卷 (Precious volume of deeply rooted karmic fruits, majestic and unmoved like Mount T'ai). By Lo Ch'ing 羅清 (1442–1527). Originally published in 1509. In *Pao-chüan ch'u-chi*, 3:341–647.

Wen-ching yüan-yang hui 刎頸鴛鴦會 (The fatal rendezvous). In *Ch'ing-p'ing shan-t'ang hua-pen*, pp. 154–69.

Wen-hsüan 文選 (Selections of refined literature). Compiled by Hsiao T'ung 蕭統 (501–31). 3 vols. Fac. repr. Peking: Chung-hua shu-chü, 1981.

Wen-shih chuan 文士傳 (Biographies of literary figures). Compiled by Chang Yin 張隱 (4th century). In *Shuo-fu san-chung*, 5:2694–95.

Wen xuan or Selections of Refined Literature. Translated and annotated by David R. Knechtges. 3 vols. Princeton: Princeton University Press, 1982–96.

Wu-chieh Ch'an-shih ssu Hung-lien chi 五戒禪師私紅蓮記 (The Ch'an Master Wu-chieh defiles Hung-lien). In *Ch'ing-p'ing shan-t'ang hua-pen*, pp. 136–54.

Wu Lun-ch'üan Pei 伍倫全備 (Wu Lun-ch'üan 伍倫全 and Wu Lun-pei 伍倫備, or the five cardinal human relationships completely exemplified). By Ch'iu Chün 邱濬(1421–95). In *Ku-pen hsi-ch'ü ts'ung-k'an, ch'u-chi*, item 37.

Wu-sao ho-pien 吳騷合編 (Combined anthology of the songs of Wu). Compiled by Chang Ch'i 張琦 (fl. early 17th century) and Chang Hsü-ch'u 張旭初 (fl. early 17th century). Preface dated 1637. 4 *ts'e*. Fac. repr. Shanghai: Shang-wu yin-shu kuan, 1934.

Wu-teng hui-yüan 五燈會元 (The essentials of the five lamps). Compiled by P'u-chi 普濟 (1179–1253). 3 vols. Peking: Chung-hua shu-chü, 1984.

Wu-wang fa Chou p'ing-hua 武王伐紂平話 (The p'ing-hua on King Wu's conquest of King Chou). Originally published in 1321–23. Shanghai: Chung-kuo ku-tien wen-hsüeh ch'u-pan she, 1955.

Wu-yü ts'ui-ya 吳歙萃雅 (A florilegium of song lyrics from Wu). Compiled by Chou Chih-piao 周之標 (fl. early 17th cent.). Preface dated 1616. Fac. repr. in *Shan-pen hsi-ch'ü ts'ung-k'an*, vols. 12–13.

Wu Yüeh ch'un-ch'iu chu-tzu so-yin 吳越春秋逐字索引 (A concordance to the *Wu Yüeh ch'un-ch'iu*). Hong Kong: Shang-wu yin-shu kuan, 1993.

Yang-chia fu shih-tai chung-yung yen-i chih-chuan 楊家府世代忠勇演義志傳 (Popular chronicle of the generations of loyal and brave exploits of the Yang household). Preface dated 1606. 2 vols. Fac. repr. Taipei: Kuo-li chung-yang t'u-shu kuan, 1971.

Yang Ssu-wen Yen-shan feng ku-jen 楊思溫燕山逢故人 (Yang Ssu-wen encounters an old acquaintance in Yen-shan). In *Ku-chin hsiao-shuo*, vol. 2, *chüan* 24, pp. 366–81.

Yang Wen lan-lu hu chuan 楊溫攔路虎傳 (The story of Yang Wen, the road-blocking tiger). In *Ch'ing-p'ing shan-t'ang hua-pen*, pp. 169–86.

Yao-ch'ih hui Pa-hsien ch'ing-shou 瑤池會八仙慶壽 (Meeting at the Jasper Pool the Eight Immortals celebrate longevity). By Chu Yu-tun 朱有燉 (1379–1439). Preface dated 1432. In *Mai-wang kuan ch'ao-chiao pen ku-chin tsa-chü, ts'e* 40.

Yao-shih pen-yüan kung-te pao-chüan 藥師本願功德寶卷 (Precious volume on the original vows and merit of the Healing Buddha). Published in 1544. In *Pao-chüan ch'u-chi*, 14:189–385.

Yeh Chia chuan 葉嘉傳 (Biography of Yeh Chia). By Su Shih 蘇軾 (1037–1101). In *Su Shih wen-chi*, vol. 2, *chüan* 13, pp. 429–31.

Yeh-k'o ts'ung-shu 野客叢書 (Collected writings of a rustic sojourner). By Wang Mao 王楙 (1151–1213). Peking: Chung-hua shu-chü, 1987.

Yen-chih chi 胭脂記 (The story of the rouge). By T'ung Yang-chung 童養中 (16th century). In *Ku-pen hsi-ch'ü ts'ung-k'an, ch'u-chi*, item 49.

Yen-chü pi-chi 燕居筆記 (A miscellany for leisured hours). Edited by Lin Chin-yang 林近陽 (fl. early 17th century). 3 vols. Fac. repr. of Ming edition. In *Ming-Ch'ing shan-pen hsiao-shuo ts'ung-k'an, ch'u-pien*.

Yen P'ing-chung erh-t'ao sha san-shih 晏平仲二桃殺三士 (Yen P'ing-chung kills three stalwarts with two peaches). In *Ku-chin hsiao-shuo*, vol. 2, *chüan* 25, pp. 384–90.

Yen-shih chia-hsün [chi-chieh] 顏氏家訓 [集解] (Family instructions for the Yen clan [with collected commentaries]). By Yen Chih-t'ui 顏之推 (531–91). Edited by Wang Li-ch'i 王利器. Shanghai: Shang-hai ku-chi ch'u-pan she, 1980.

Yin-chih chi-shan 陰隲積善 (A secret good deed accumulates merit). In *Ch'ing-p'ing shan-t'ang hua-pen*, pp. 115–19.

Ying-wu fu 鸚鵡賦 (Rhapsody on the parrot). By Mi Heng 禰衡 (173–98). In *Wen-hsüan*, vol. 1, *chüan* 13, pp. 20b–23b.

[Ying-yin Wen-yüan ko] Ssu-k'u ch'üan-shu [景印文淵閣] 四庫全書 ([Facsimile reprint of the Wen-yüan ko Imperial Library copy of the] Complete library of the four treasuries). 1500 vols. Taipei: T'ai-wan Shang-wu yin-shu kuan, 1986.

Ying-ying chuan 鶯鶯傳 (Story of Ying-ying). By Yüan Chen 元稹 (775–831). In *T'ang Sung ch'uan-ch'i chi*, pp. 127–36.

Yu hsien-k'u 游仙窟 (Excursion to the dwelling of the goddesses). By Chang Cho 張鷟 (cs 675). Shanghai: Chung-kuo ku-tien wen-hsüeh ch'u-pan she, 1955.

Yu-kuei chi 幽閨記 (Tale of the secluded chambers). *Liu-shih chung ch'ü* edition. Taipei: K'ai-ming shu-tien, 1970.

Yu-yang tsa-tsu 酉陽雜俎 (Assorted notes from Yu-yang). Compiled by Tuan Ch'eng-shih 段成式 (803–63). Peking: Chung-hua shu-chü, 1981.

Yung-hsi yüeh-fu 雍熙樂府 (Songs of a harmonious era). Preface dated 1566. 20 *ts'e*. Fac. repr. Shanghai: Shang-wu yin-shu kuan, 1934.

Yung-lo ta-tien hsi-wen san-chung chiao-chu 永樂大典戲文三種校注 (An annotated recension of the three hsi-wen preserved in the *Yung-lo ta-tien*). Edited and annotated by Ch'ien Nan-yang 錢南揚. Peking: Chung-hua shu-chü, 1979.

Yü-ch'iao hsien-hua 漁樵閑話 (A casual dialogue between a fisherman and a wood-cutter). In *Ku-pen yüan Ming tsa-chü*, vol. 4.

Yü-chien 寓簡 (Meaningful notes). By Shen Tso-che 沈作喆 (cs 1135). Author's preface dated 1174. In *Ts'ung-shu chi-ch'eng*, 1st series, vol. 296.

Yü-ching t'ai 玉鏡臺 (The jade mirror stand). By Chu Ting 朱鼎 (16th century). *Liu-shih chung ch'ü* edition. Taipei: K'ai-ming shu-tien, 1970.

Yü Chung-chü t'i-shih yü shang-huang 俞仲舉題詩遇上皇 (Yü Chung-chü composes a poem and meets the retired emperor, Sung Kao-tsung [r. 1127–62]). In *Ching-shih t'ung-yen*, *chüan* 6, pp. 63–76.

Yü-chüeh chi 玉玦記 (The jade thumb-ring). By Cheng Jo-yung 鄭若庸 (16th century). *Liu-shih chung ch'ü* edition. Taipei: K'ai-ming shu-tien, 1970.

Yü-hu ch'ing-hua 玉壺清話 (Elegant anecdotes from Yü-hu). By Wen-ying 文瑩 (11th century). In *Pi-chi hsiao-shuo ta-kuan*, vol. 1, *ts'e* 2, pp. 17–46.

Yü-huan chi 玉環記 (The story of the jade ring). *Liu-shih chung ch'ü* edition. Taipei: K'ai-ming shu-tien, 1970.

Yü-tsan chi 玉簪記 (The story of the jade hairpin). By Kao Lien 高濂 (1527–c. 1603). Probably written in 1570. Edited and annotated by Huang Shang 黃裳. Shanghai: Shang-hai ku-tien wen-hsüeh ch'u-pan she, 1956.

Yüan-chien lei-han 淵鑑類函 (A comprehensive encyclopedia arranged by categories). Compiled under the aegis of the K'ang-hsi emperor (r. 1661–1722) by Chang Ying 張英 (1638–1708) et al. 7 vols. Fac. repr. of the Palace edition of 1710. Taipei: Hsin-hsing shu-chü, 1967.

Yüan-chu chih-yü: hsüeh-ch'uang t'an-i 鴛渚誌餘: 雪窗談異 (Supplementary guide to Mandarin Duck Island: tales of the unusual from the snowy window). Peking: Chung-hua shu-chü, 1997.

Yüan-ch'ü hsüan 元曲選 (An anthology of Yüan tsa-chü drama). Compiled by Tsang Mao-hsün 臧懋循 (1550–1620). 4 vols. Peking: Chung-hua shu-chü, 1979.

Yüan-ch'ü hsüan wai-pien 元曲選外編 (A supplementary anthology of Yüan tsa-chü drama). Compiled by Sui Shu-sen 隋樹森. 3 vols. Peking: Chung-hua shu-chü, 1961.

Yüan shih hsüan, ch'u-chi 元詩選, 初集 (An anthology of Yüan poetry, first collection). Compiled by Ku Ssu-li 顧嗣立 (1665–1722). 3 vols. Peking: Chung-hua shu-chü, 1987.

Yüan-shih shih-fan 袁氏世范 (Mr. Yüan's precepts for social life). By Yüan Ts'ai 袁采 (cs 1163). Completed in 1178. Edited and annotated by Ho Heng-chen 賀恒禎 and Yang Liu 楊柳. Tientsin: T'ien-chin ku-chi ch'u-pan she, 1995.

Yüan tien-chang 元典章 (Institutions of the Yüan). Fac. repr. of 1303 edition. Peking: Chung-kuo shu-tien, 1990.

Yüan-wu Fo-kuo ch'an-shih yü-lu 圓悟佛果禪師語錄 (Recorded sayings of Ch'an Master Yüan-wu Fo-Kuo). Preface dated 1134. In *Taishō shinshū daizōkyō*, vol. 47, no. 1997, pp. 713–810.

Yüeh Fei p'o-lu tung-ch'uang chi 岳飛破虜東窗記 (Yüeh Fei defeats the barbarians: the plot at the eastern window). By Chou Li 周禮(15th century). In *Ku-pen hsi-ch'ü ts'ung-k'an, ch'u-chi*, item no. 21.

Yüeh-fu ch'ün-chu 樂府群珠 (A string of lyric pearls). Modern edition edited by Lu Ch'ien 盧前. Shanghai: Shang-wu yin-shu kuan, 1957.

Yüeh-fu hung-shan 樂府紅冊 (The red coral anthology of dramatic excerpts). Compiled by Chi Chen-lun 紀振倫 (fl. early 17th century). Preface dated 1602. Fac. repr. in *Shan-pen hsi-ch'ü ts'ung-k'an*, vols. 10–11.

Yüeh-fu shih-chi 樂府詩集 (Collection of Music Bureau ballads). Compiled by Kuo Mao-ch'ien 郭茂倩 (12th century). 4 vols. Peking: Chung-hua shu-chü, 1979.

Yüeh-ming Ho-shang tu Liu Ts'ui 月明和尚度柳翠 (The monk Yüeh-ming converts Liu Ts'ui). In *Ku-chin hsiao-shuo*, vol. 2, *chüan* 29, pp. 428–41.

Yün-chi ch'i ch'ien 雲笈七簽 (Seven lots from the bookbag of the clouds). Compiled by Chang Chün-fang 張君房 (c. 965–c. 1045). Edited and annotated by Chiang Li-sheng 蔣力生 et al. Peking: Hua-hsia ch'u-pan she, 1996.

Yün-chien chü-mu ch'ao 雲間據目抄 (Jottings on matters eyewitnessed in Yün-chien). By Fan Lien 范濂 (b. 1540). Preface dated 1593. In *Pi-chi hsiao-shuo ta-kuan*, vol. 6, *ts'e* 13.

Yün-hsien san-lu 雲仙散錄 (Miscellaneous records of the Cloud Immortal). Compiled by Feng Chih 馮贄 (fl. early 10th century). Preface dated 926. Edited by Chang Li-wei 張李偉. Peking: Chung-hua shu-chü, 1998.

Yün-t'ai Men chü erh-shih pa chiang 雲臺門聚二十八將 (The twenty-eight generals gather at Yün-t'ai Gate), in *Ku-pen Yüan Ming tsa-chü*, vol. 2.

SECONDARY SOURCES

(Arranged Alphabetically by Author)

Bickford, Maggie, et al. *Bones of Jade, Soul of Ice: The Flowering Plum in Chinese Art.* New Haven: Yale University Art Gallery, 1985.

Bol, Peter K. *"This Culture of Ours": Intellectual Transitions in T'ang and Sung China.* Stanford: Stanford University Press, 1992.

Campany, Robert Ford. *To Live as Long as Heaven and Earth: A Translation and Study of Ge Hong's Traditions of Divine Transcendents.* Berkeley: University of California Press, 2002.

Carlitz, Katherine. *The Rhetoric of Chin p'ing mei*. Bloomington: Indiana University Press, 1986.

Chou Feng-wu 周鳳五. *Tun-huang hsieh-pen T'ai-kung chia-chiao yen-chiu* 敦煌寫本 太公家教研究 (A study of the Tun-huang manuscripts of the *T'ai-kung chia-chiao*). Taipei: Ming-wen shu-chü, 1986.

Clunas, Craig. *Chinese Furniture*. Chicago: Art Media Resources, 1997.

Despeux, Catherine. "Gymnastics: the Ancient Tradition." In Livia Kohn, ed. *Taoist Meditation and Longevity Techniques*, pp. 225–61.

Dudbridge, Glen. *The Legend of Miao-shan*. London: Ithaca Press, 1978.

Fong, Wen, ed. *The Great Bronze Age of China: An Exhibition from the People's Republic of China*. New York: The Metropolitan Museum of Art and Alfred A. Knopf, 1980.

Fontein, Jan, and Money L. Hickman. *Zen Painting and Calligraphy*. Boston: Museum of Fine Arts, 1970.

Goodrich, Anne S. *Peking Paper Gods: A Look at Home Worship*. Nettetal: Steyler Verlag, 1991.

Hanan, Patrick. "Sources of the *Chin P'ing Mei*." *Asia Major*, n.s. 10, 1 (1963): 23–67.

———. "The Text of the *Chin P'ing Mei*." *Asia Major*, n.s. 9, 1 (1962): 1–57.

Hightower, James R. "Han Yü as Humorist." *Harvard Journal of Asiatic Studies* 44, 1 (June 1984), 5–27.

Hou, Ching-lang. "The Chinese Belief in Baleful Stars." In Holmes Welch and Anna Seidel, eds. *Facets of Taoism: Essays in Chinese Religion*, pp. 193–228.

Hu Shih-ying 胡士瑩. *Hua-pen hsiao-shuo kai-lun* 話本小説概論 (A comprehensive study of promptbook fiction). 2 vols. Peking: Chung-hua shu-chü, 1980.

Huang, Ray. *Taxation and Governmental Finance in Sixteenth-Century Ming China*. Cambridge: Cambridge University Press, 1974.

Hucker, Charles O. *A Dictionary of Official Titles in Imperial China*. Stanford: Stanford University Press, 1985.

Huntington, Rania. *Alien Kind: Foxes and Late Imperial Chinese Narrative*. Cambridge: Harvard University Press, 2003.

Idema, W. L. *The Dramatic Oeuvre of Chu Yu-tun (1379–1439)*. Leiden: E. J. Brill, 1985.

Jackson, Beverley, and David Hugus. *Ladder to the Clouds: Intrigue and Tradition in Chinese Rank*. Berkeley: Ten Speed Press, 1999.

Johnson, Dale R. *Yuarn Music Dramas: Studies in Prosody and Structure and a Complete Catalogue of Northern Arias in the Dramatic Style*. Ann Arbor: Center for Chinese Studies, University of Michigan, 1980.

Kohn, Livia, ed. *Taoist Meditation and Longevity Techniques*. Ann Arbor: Center for Chinese Studies, University of Michigan, 1989.

Lessa, William A. *Chinese Body Divination: Its Forms, Affinities, and Functions*. Los Angeles: United World, 1968.

Leung, K. C. *Hsü Wei as Drama Critic: An Annotated Translation of the Nan-tz'u Hsü-lu*. N.p.: University of Oregon Asian Studies Program, 1988.

Liu Chung-kuang 劉中光. "*Chin P'ing Mei* jen-wu k'ao-lun" 金瓶梅人物考論 (A study of the historical figures in the *Chin P'ing Mei*). In Yeh Kuei-t'ung et al., eds. *Chin P'ing Mei tso-che chih mi*, pp. 105–224.

Lopez, Donald S., Jr., ed. *Religions of China in Practice*. Princeton: Princeton University Press, 1996.

Lowe, H. Y. *The Adventures of Wu: The Life Cycle of a Peking Man.* 2 vols. Princeton: Princeton University Press, 1983.

Lu Ko 魯歌 and Ma Cheng 馬征. *Chin P'ing Mei jen-wu ta-ch'üan* 金瓶梅人物大全 (Great compendium of the characters in the *Chin P'ing Mei*). Ch'ang-ch'un: Chi-lin wen-shih ch'u-pan she, 1991.

Maspero, Henri. *Taoism and Chinese Religion.* Translated by Frank A. Kierman, Jr. Amherst: University of Massachusetts Press, 1981.

Miura, Isshū, and Ruth Fuller Sasaki. *The Zen Koan: Its History and Use in Rinzai Zen.* New York: Harcourt, Brace & World, 1965.

Needham, Joseph, and Lu Gwei-djen. *Science and Civilisation in China.* Volume 5, part 5: *Spagyrical Discovery and Invention: Physiological Alchemy.* Cambridge: Cambridge University Press, 1983.

Needham, Joseph et al. *Science and Civilisation in China.* Volume 5, part 7: *Military Technology: The Gunpowder Epic.* Cambridge: Cambridge University Press, 1986.

Palmer, Martin. *T'ung Shu: The Ancient Chinese Almanac.* Boston: Shambhala, 1986.

Peng Xinwei. *A Monetary History of China.* Translated by Edward H. Kaplan. 2 vols. Bellingham: Center for East Asian Studies, Western Washington University, 1993.

Pian, Rulan Chao. *Sonq Dynasty Musical Sources and Their Interpretation.* Cambridge: Harvard University Press, 1967.

Porkert, Manfred. *The Theoretical Foundations of Chinese Medicine.* Cambridge: MIT Press, 1974.

Pu Chien 卜鍵. *Chin P'ing Mei tso-che Li K'ai-hsien k'ao* 金瓶梅作者李開先考 (An inquiry into Li K'ai-hsien's authorship of the *Chin P'ing Mei*). Lan-chou: Kan-su jen-min ch'u-pan she, 1988.

Satyendra, Indira. "Toward a Poetics of the Chinese Novel: A Study of the Prefatory Poems in the *Chin P'ing Mei tz'u-hua*." Ph.D. dissertation, University of Chicago, 1989.

Schipper, Kristofer M. *Le Fen-teng: rituel taoiste.* Paris: École Française D'Extrême-Orient, 1975.

Scott, A. C. *The Classical Theatre of China.* New York: Macmillan, 1957.

Shahar, Meir. *Crazy Ji: Chinese Religion and Popular Literature.* Cambridge: Harvard University Press, 1998.

Sharf, Robert H. "The Scripture in Forty-two Sections." In Donald S. Lopez, Jr., ed. *Religions of China in Practice*, pp. 360–71.

Shen Ts'ung-wen 沈從文. *Chung-kuo ku-tai fu-shih yen-chiu* 中國古代服飾研究 (A study of traditional Chinese costume). Hong Kong: Shang-wu yin-shu kuan, 1981.

Smith, Richard J. *Fortune-tellers and Philosophers: Divination in Traditional Chinese Society.* Boulder: Westview Press, 1991.

Sponberg, Alan, and Helen Hardacre, eds. *Maitreya, the Future Buddha.* Cambridge: Cambridge University Press, 1988.

Stein, Rolf A. *The World in Miniature: Container Gardens and Dwellings in Far Eastern Religious Thought.* Translated by Phyllis Brooks. Stanford: Stanford University Press, 1990.

Stone, Charles R. *The Fountainhead of Chinese Erotica: The Lord of Perfect Satisfaction (Ruyijun zhuan).* Honolulu: University of Hawai'i Press, 2003.

Tai I-hsüan 戴裔煊. *Sung-tai ch'ao-yen chih-tu yen-chiu* 宋代鈔鹽制度研究 (A study of the salt voucher system of the Sung dynasty). Shanghai: Shang-wu yin-shu kuan, 1957.

Teiser, Stephen F. *The Scripture on the Ten Kings and the Making of Purgatory in Medieval Chinese Buddhism*. Honolulu: University of Hawaii Press, 1994.

Van Gulik, R. H. *The Lore of the Chinese Lute*. Tokyo: Sophia University, 1940.

Weidner, Marsha, ed. *Latter Days of the Law: Images of Chinese Buddhism 850–1850*. Lawrence, KS: Spencer Museum of Art, 1994.

Welch, Holmes, and Anna Seidel, eds. *Facets of Taoism: Essays in Chinese Religion*. New Haven: Yale University Press, 1979.

Werner, E.T.C. *A Dictionary of Chinese Mythology*. New York: The Julian Press, 1961.

Williams, C.A.S. *Encyclopedia of Chinese Symbolism and Art Motives*. New York: The Julian Press, 1960.

Williamson, H. R. *Wang An Shih: A Chinese Statesman and Educationalist of the Sung Dynasty*. 2 vols. London: Arthur Probstain, 1935–37.

Yeh Kuei-t'ung 葉桂桐 et al., eds. *Chin P'ing Mei tso-che chih mi* 金瓶梅作者之謎 (The riddle of the authorship of the *Chin P'ing Mei*). N.p.: Ning-hsia jen-min ch'u-pan she, 1988.

Yifa. *The Origins of Buddhist Monastic Codes in China*. Honolulu: University of Hawaii Press, 2002.

Yü, Chün-fang. *Kuan-yin: The Chinese Transformation of Avalokiteśvara*. New York: Columbia University Press, 2001.

INDEX

CPSIA information can be obtained at www.ICGtesting.com
Printed in the USA
LVOW13*0911060214

372604LV00002B/8/P